THE HERITAGE of SHANNARA

By Terry Brooks

SHANNARA
First King of Shannara
The Sword of Shannara
The Elfstones of Shannara
The Wishsong of Shannara

The Sword of Shannara Trilogy

THE HERITAGE OF SHANNARA
The Scions of Shannara
The Druid of Shannara
The Elf Queen of Shannara
The Talismans of Shannara

The Heritage of Shannara (Omnibus)

THE MAGIC KINGDOM OF LANDOVER
Magic Kingdom for Sale—Sold!
The Black Unicorn
Wizard at Large
The Tangle Box
Witches' Brew

THE WORD AND THE VOID
Running with the Demon
Knight of the World
Angel Fire East

The Word and the Void (Omnibus)

THE HERITAGE of SHANNARA

TERRY BROOKS

www.orbitbooks.co.uk

ORBIT

First published in Great Britain in 2005 by Orbit
Reprinted 2006

This omnibus was originally published by Orbit
in separate volumes under the titles:

The Scions of Shannara, copyright © 1990 by Terry Brooks
The Druid of Shannara, copyright © 1991 by Terry Brooks
The Elf Queen of Shannara, copyright © 1992 by Terry Brooks
The Talismans of Shannara, copyright © 1993 by Terry Brooks

Maps on pages vi, vii, 632 by Shelley Shapiro.
Copyright © 1990 by Random House, Inc.

A CIP catalogue record of this book
is available from the British Library.

ISBN 1 84149 355 4

Typeset in Bembo
Printed and bound in Great Britain by
William Clowes Ltd, Beccles, Suffolk

Orbit
An imprint of
Little, Brown Book Group
Brettenham House
Lancaster Place
London WC2E 7EN

A Member of the Hachette Livre Group of Companies

www.littlebrown.co.uk

CONTENTS

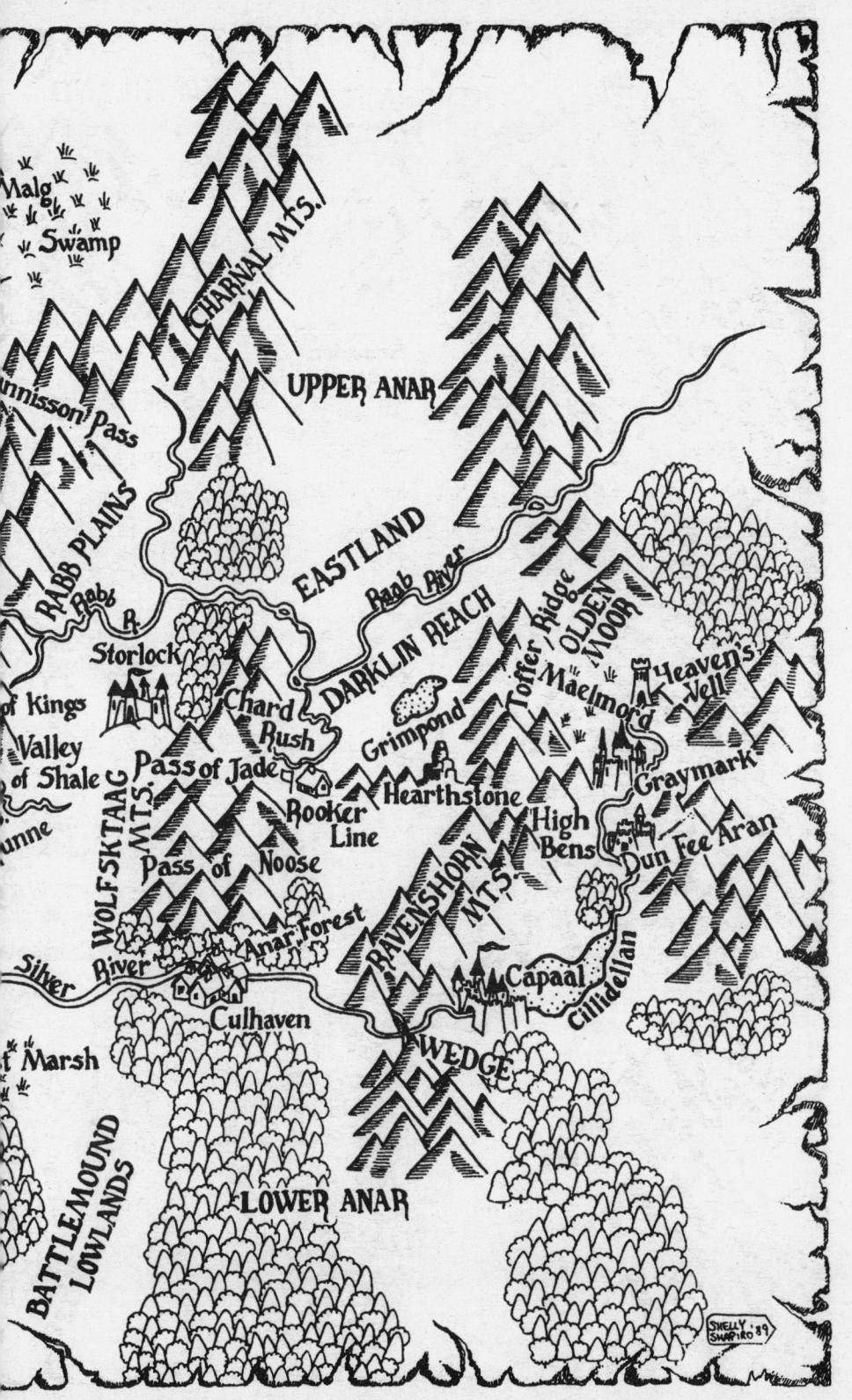

THE SCIONS of SHANNARA

For Judine,
who makes all the magic possible

T he old man sat alone in the shadow of the Dragon's Teeth and
watched the coming darkness chase the daylight west. The day had
been cool, unusually so for midsummer, and the night promised to
be chill. Scattered clouds masked the sky, casting their silhouettes upon the
earth, drifting in the manner of aimless beasts between moon and stars. A
hush filled the emptiness left by the fading light like a voice waiting to
speak.

It was a hush that whispered of magic, the old man thought.

A fire burned before him, small still, just the beginning of what was
needed. After all, he would be gone for several hours. He studied the fire
with a mixture of expectation and uneasiness before reaching down to add
the larger chunks of deadwood that brought the flames up quickly. He
poked at it with a stick, then stepped away, driven back by the heat. He
stood at the edge of the light, caught between the fire and the growing
dark, a creature who might have belonged to neither or both.

His eyes glittered as he looked off into the distance. The peaks of the
Dragon's Teeth jutted skyward like bones the earth could not contain. There
was a hush to the mountains, a secrecy that clung like mist on a frosty
morning and hid all the dreams of the ages.

The fire sparked sharply and the old man brushed at a stray bit of glowing ash that threatened to settle on him. He was just a bundle of sticks,
loosely tied together, that might crumble into dust if a strong wind were to
blow. Gray robes and a forest cloak hung on him as they would have on a
scarecrow. His skin was leathery and brown and had shrunken close against
his bones. White hair and beard wreathed his head, thin and fine, like wisps
of gauze against the firelight. He was so wrinkled and hunched down that
he looked to be a hundred years old.

He was, in fact, almost a thousand.

Strange, he thought suddenly, remembering his years. Paranor, the Councils of the Races, even the Druids—gone. Strange that he should have out-
lasted them all.

He shook his head. It was so long ago, so far back in time that it was a
part of his life he only barely recognized. He had thought that part finished, gone forever. He had thought himself free. But he had never been
that, he guessed. It wasn't possible to be free of something that, at the very
least, was responsible for the fact that he was still alive.

How else, after all, save for the Druid Sleep, could he still be standing
there?

He shivered against the descending night, darkness all about him now as the last of the sunlight slipped below the horizon. It was time. The dreams had told him it must be now, and he believed the dreams because he understood them. That, too, was a part of his old life that would not let him go—dreams, visions of worlds beyond worlds, of warnings and truths, of things that could and sometimes must be.

He stepped away from the fire and started up the narrow pathway into the rocks. Shadows closed about him, their touch chill. He walked for a long time, winding through narrow defiles, scrambling past massive boulders, angling along craggy drops and jagged splits in the rock. When he emerged again into the light, he stood within a shallow, rock-strewn valley dominated by a lake whose glassy surface reflected back at him with a harsh, greenish cast.

The lake was the resting place for the shades of Druids come and gone. It was to the Hadeshorn that he had been summoned.

"Might as well get on with it," he growled softly.

He walked slowly, cautiously downward into the valley, his steps uneasy, his heart pounding in his ears. He had been away a long time. The waters before him did not stir; the shades lay sleeping. It was best that way, he thought. It was best that they not be disturbed.

He reached the lake's edge and stopped. All was silent. He took a deep breath, the air rattling from his chest as he exhaled like dry leaves blown across stone. He fumbled at his waist for a pouch and loosened its drawstrings. Carefully he reached within and drew out a handful of black powder laced with silver sparkle. He hesitated, then threw it into the air over the lake.

The powder exploded skyward with a strange light that brightened the air about him as if it were day again. There was no heat, only light. It shimmered and danced against the nighttime like a living thing. The old man watched, robes and forest cloak pulled close, eyes bright with the reflected glow. He rocked back and forth slightly and for a moment felt young again.

Then a shadow appeared suddenly in the light, lifting out of it like a wraith, a black form that might have been something strayed from the darkness beyond. But the old man knew better. This was nothing strayed; this was something called. The shadow tightened and took shape. It was the shade of a man cloaked all in black, a tall and forbidding apparition that anyone who had ever seen before would have recognized at once.

"So, Allanon," the old man whispered.

The hooded face tilted back so that the light revealed the dark, harsh features clearly—the angular bearded face, the long thin nose and mouth, the fierce brow that might have been cast of iron, the eyes beneath that seemed to look directly into the soul. The eyes found the old man and held him fast.

—I need you—

The voice was a whisper in the old man's mind, a hiss of dissatisfaction and urgency. The shade communicated by using thoughts alone. The old man shrank back momentarily, wishing that the thing he had called would instead be gone. Then he recovered himself and stood firm before his fears.

"I am no longer one of you!" he snapped, his own eyes narrowing dangerously, forgetting that it was not necessary to speak aloud. "You cannot command me!"

—I do not command. I request. Listen to me. You are all that is left, the last that may be until my successor is found. Do you understand—

The old man laughed nervously. "Understand? Ha! Who understands better than me?"

—A part of you will always be what once you would not have questioned. The magic stays within you. Always. Help me. I send the dreams and the Shannara children do not respond. Someone must go to them. Someone must make them see. You—

"Not me! I have lived apart from the races for years now. I wish nothing more to do with their troubles!" The old man straightened his stick form and frowned. "I shed myself of such nonsense long ago."

The shade seemed to rise and broaden suddenly before him, and he felt himself lifted free of the earth. He soared skyward, far into the night. He did not struggle, but held himself firm, though he could feel the other's anger rushing through him like a black river. The shade's voice was the sound of bones grating.

—Watch—

The Four Lands appeared, spread out before him, a panorama of grasslands, mountains, hills, lakes, forests, and rivers, bright swatches of earth colored by sunlight. He caught his breath to see it so clearly and from so far up in the sky, even knowing that it was only a vision. But the sunlight began to fade almost at once, the color to wash. Darkness closed about, filled with dull gray mist and sulfurous ash that rose from burned-out craters. The land lost its character and became barren and lifeless. He felt himself drift closer, repulsed as he descended by the sights and smells of it. Humans wandered the devastation in packs, more animals than men. They rent and tore at each other; they howled and shrieked. Dark shapes flitted among them, shadows that lacked substance yet had eyes of fire. The shadows moved through the humans, joining with them, becoming them, leaving them again. They moved in a dance that was macabre, yet purposeful. The shadows were devouring the humans, he saw. The shadows were feeding on them.

—Watch—

The vision shifted. He saw himself then, a skeletal, ragged beggar facing a cauldron of strange white fire that bubbled and swirled and whispered his name. Vapors lifted from the cauldron and snaked their way down to where he stood, wrapping about him, caressing him as if he were their child. Shadows flitted all about, passing by at first, then entering him as if he were a hollow casing in which they might play as they chose. He could feel their touch; he wanted to scream.

—Watch—

The vision shifted once more. There was a huge forest and in the middle of the forest a great mountain. Atop the mountain sat a castle, old and weathered, towers and parapets rising up against the dark of the land. Paranor, he thought! It was Paranor come again! He felt something bright and hopeful well up within him, and he wanted to shout his elation. But the vapors were already coiling about the castle. The shadows were already flitting close. The ancient fortress began to crack and crumble, stone and mortar giving way as if caught in a vise. The earth shuddered and screams lifted from the humans become animals. Fire erupted out of the earth, splitting apart the mountain on which Paranor sat and then the castle itself. Wailing filled the air, the sound of one bereft of the only hope that had remained to him. The old man recognized the wailing as his own.

Then the images were gone. He stood again before the Hadeshorn, in the shadow of the Dragon's Teeth, alone with the shade of Allanon. In spite of his resolve, he was shaking.

The shade pointed at him.

—It will be as I have shown you if the dreams are ignored. It will be so if you fail to act. You must help. Go to them—the boy, the girl, and the Dark Uncle. Tell them the dreams are real. Tell them to come to me here on the first night of the new moon when the present cycle is complete. I will speak with them then—

The old man frowned and muttered and worried his lower lip. His fingers once more drew tight the drawstrings to the pouch, and he shoved it back into his belt. "I will do so because there is no one else!" he said finally, spitting out the words in distaste. "But do not expect . . . !"

—Only go to them. Nothing more is required. Nothing more will be asked. Go—

The shade of Allanon shimmered brightly and disappeared. The light faded, and the valley was empty again. The old man stood looking out over the still waters of the lake for a moment, then turned away.

The fire he had left behind still burned on his return, but it was small now and frail-looking against the night. The old man stared absently at the flames, then hunkered down before them. He stirred at the ashes already forming and listened to the silence of his thoughts.

The boy, the girl, and the Dark Uncle—he knew them. They were the Shannara children, the ones who could save them all, the ones who could bring back the magic. He shook his grizzled head. How was he to convince them? If they would not heed Allanon, what chance that they would heed him?

He saw again in his mind the frightening visions. He had best find a way to make them listen, he thought. Because, as he was fond of reminding himself, he knew something of visions, and there was a truth to these that even one such as he, one who had foresworn the Druids and their magic, could recognize.

If the Shannara children failed to listen, these visions would come to pass.

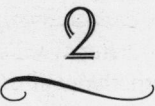

2

Par Ohmsford stood in the rear doorway of the Blue Whisker Ale House and stared down the darkened tunnel of the narrow street that ran between the adjoining buildings into the glimmer of Varfleet's lights. The Blue Whisker was a ramshackle, sprawling old building with weathered board walls and a wood shingle roof and looked for all the world as if once it had been someone's barn. It had sleeping rooms upstairs over the serving hall and storerooms in the back. It sat at the base of a block of buildings that formed a somewhat lopsided U, situated on a hill at the western edge of the city.

Par breathed deeply the night air, savoring its flavors. City smells, smells of life, stews with meats and vegetables laced with spice, sharp-flavored liquors and pungent ales, perfumes that scented rooms and bodies, leather harness, iron from forges still red with coals kept perpetually bright, the sweat of animals and men in close quarters, the taste of stone and wood and dust, mingling and mixing, each occasionally breaking free—they were all there. Down the alleyway, beyond the slat-boarded, graffiti-marked backs of the shops and businesses, the hill dropped away to where the central part of the city lay east. An ugly, colorless gathering of buildings in daylight, a maze of stone walls and streets, wooden siding and pitch-sealed roofs, the city took on a different look at night. The buildings faded into the darkness and the lights appeared, thousands of them, stretching away as far as the eye could see like a swarm of fireflies. They dotted the masked landscape, flickering in the black, trailing lines of gold across the liquid skin of the Mermidon as it passed south. Varfleet was beautiful now, the scrubwoman become a fairy queen, transformed as if by magic.

Par liked the idea of the city being magic. He liked the city in any case, liked its sprawl and its meld of people and things, its rich mix of life. It was far different from his home of Shady Vale, nothing like the forested hamlet that he had grown up in. It lacked the purity of the trees and streams, the solitude, the sense of timeless ease that graced life in the Vale. It knew nothing of that life and couldn't have cared less. But that didn't matter to Par. He liked the city anyway. There was nothing to say that he had to choose between the two, after all. There wasn't any reason he couldn't appreciate both.

Coll, of course, didn't agree. Coll saw it quite differently. He saw Varfleet as nothing more than an outlaw city at the edge of Federation rule, a den of miscreants, a place where one could get away with anything. In all of Callahorn, in all of the entire Southland for that matter, there was no place worse. Coll hated the city.

Voices and the clink of glasses drifted out of the darkness behind him, the sounds of the ale house breaking free of the front room momentarily as a door was opened, then disappearing again as it was closed. Par turned. His brother moved carefully down the hallway, nearly faceless in the gloom.

"It's almost time," Coll said when he reached his brother.

Par nodded. He looked small and slender next to Coll, who was a big, strong youth with blunt features and mud-colored hair. A stranger would not have thought them brothers. Coll looked a typical Valeman, tanned and rough, with enormous hands and feet. The feet were an ongoing joke. Par was fond of comparing them to a duck's. Par was slight and fair, his own features unmistakably Elven from the sharply pointed ears and brows to the high, narrow bones of his face. There was a time when the Elven blood had been all but bred out of the line, the result of generations of Ohms-fords living in the Vale. But four generations back (so his father had told him) his great-great-grandfather had returned to the Westland and the Elves, married an Elven girl, and produced a son and a daughter. The son had married another Elven girl, and for reasons never made clear the young couple who would become Par's great-grandparents had returned to the Vale, thereby infusing a fresh supply of Elven blood back into the Ohms-ford line. Even then, many members of the family showed nothing of their mixed heritage; Coll and his parents Jaralan and Mirianna were examples. Par's bloodlines, on the other hand, were immediately evident.

Being recognizable in this way, unfortunately, was not necessarily desir-able. While in Varfleet, Par disguised his features, plucking his brows, wear-ing his hair long to hide his ears, shading his face with darkener. He didn't have much choice. It wasn't wise to draw attention to one's Elven lineage these days.

"She has her gown nicely in place tonight, doesn't she?" Coll said, glancing off down the alleyway to the city beyond. "Black velvet and sparkles, not a thread left hanging. Clever girl, this city. Even the sky is her friend."

Par smiled. My brother, the poet. The sky was clear and filled with the brightness of a tiny crescent moon and stars. "You might come to like her if you gave her half a chance."

"Me?" Coll snorted. "Not likely. I'm here because you're here. I wouldn't stay another minute if I didn't have to."

"You could go if you wanted."

Coll bristled. "Let's not start again, Par. We've been all through that. You were the one who thought we ought to come north to the cities. I didn't like the idea then, and I don't like it any better now. But that doesn't change the fact that we agreed to do this together, you and me. A fine brother I'd be if I left you here and went back to the Vale now! In any case, I don't think you could manage without me."

"All right, all right, I was just . . ." Par tried to interrupt.

"Attempting to have a little fun at my expense!" Coll finished heatedly. "You have done that on more than one occasion of late. You seem to take some delight in it."

"That is not so."

Coll ignored him, gazing off into the dark.

"I would never pick on anyone with duck feet."

Coll grinned in spite of himself. "Fine talk from a little fellow with pointed ears. You should be grateful I choose to stay and look after you!"

Par shoved him playfully, and they both laughed. Then they went quiet, staring at each other in the dark, listening to the sounds of the ale house and the streets beyond. Par sighed. It was a warm, lazy midsummer night that made the cool, sharp days of the past few weeks seem a distant memory. It was the kind of night when troubles scatter and dreams come out to play.

"There are rumors of Seekers in the city," Coll informed him suddenly, spoiling his contentment.

"There are always rumors," he replied.

"And the rumors are often true. Talk has it that they plan to snatch up all the magic-makers, put them out of business and close down the ale houses." Coll was staring intently at him. "Seekers, Par. Not simple soldiers. Seekers."

Par knew what they were. Seekers—Federation secret police, the enforcement arm of the Coalition Council's Lawmakers. He knew.

They had arrived in Varfleet two weeks earlier, Coll and he. They journeyed north from Shady Vale, left the security and familiarity and protective confines of their family home and came into the Borderlands of Callahorn. They did so because Par had decided they must, that it was time for them to tell their stories elsewhere, that it was necessary to see to it that others besides the Vale people knew. They came to Varfleet because Varfleet was an open city, free of Federation rule, a haven for outlaws and refugees but also for ideas, a place where people still listened with open minds, a place where magic was still tolerated—even courted. He had the magic and, with Coll in tow, he took it to Varfleet to share its wonder. There was already magic aplenty being practiced by others, but his was of a far different sort. His was real.

They found the Blue Whisker the first day they arrived, one of the biggest and best known ale houses in the city. Par persuaded the owner to hire them in the first sitting. He had expected as much. After all, he could persuade anyone to do just about anything with the wishsong.

Real magic. He mouthed the words without speaking them.

There wasn't much real magic left in the Four Lands, not outside the remote wilderness areas where Federation rule did not yet extend. The wishsong was the last of the Ohmsford magic. It had been passed down through ten generations to reach him, the gift skipping some members of his family altogether, picking and choosing on a whim. Coll didn't have it. His parents didn't. In fact, no one in the Ohmsford family had had it since his great-grandparents had returned from the Westland. But the magic of the wishsong had been his from the time he was born, the same magic that had come into existence almost three hundred years ago with his ancestor Jair. The stories told him this, the legends. Wish for it, sing for it. He could create images so lifelike in the minds of his listeners that they appeared to be real. He could create substance out of air.

That was what had brought him to Varfleet. For three centuries the Ohmsford family had handed down stories of the Elven house of Shannara. The practice had begun with Jair. In truth, it had begun long before that, when the stories were not of the magic because it had not yet been discovered but of the old world before its destruction in the Great Wars and the tellers were the few who had survived that frightening holocaust. But Jair was the first to have use of the wishsong to aid in the telling, to give substance to the images created from his words, to make his tales come alive in the minds of those who heard them. The tales were of the old days: of the legends of the Elven house of Shannara; of the Druids and their Keep at Paranor; of Elves and Dwarves; and of the magic that ruled their lives. The tales were of Shea Ohmsford and his brother Flick and their search to find the Sword of Shannara; of Wil Ohmsford and the beautiful, tragic Elven girl Amberle and their struggle to banish the Demon hordes back into the Forbidding; of Jair Ohmsford and his sister Brin and their journey into the fortress of Graymark and confrontation with the Mord Wraiths and the Ildatch; of the Druids Allanon and Bremen; of the Elven King Eventine Elessedil; of warriors such as Balinor Buckhannah and Stee Jans; of heroes many and varied. Those who had command of the wishsong made use of its magic. Those who did not relied on simple words. Ohmsfords had come and gone, many carrying the stories with them to distant lands. Yet for three generations now, no member of the family had told the stories outside the Vale. No one had wanted to risk being caught.

It was a considerable risk. The practice of magic in any form was outlawed in the Four Lands—or at least anywhere the Federation governed, which was practically the same thing. It had been so for the past hundred years. In all that time no Ohmsford had left the Vale. Par was the first. He had grown tired of telling the same stories to the same few listeners over and over. Others needed to hear the stories as well, to know the truth about the Druids and the magic, about the struggle that preceded the age in which they now lived. His fear of being caught was outweighed by the calling he felt. He made his decision despite the objections of his parents and Coll. Coll, ultimately, decided to come with him—just as he always did whenever he thought Par needed looking after. Varfleet was to be the beginning, a city where magic was still practiced in minor forms, an open secret defying intervention by the Federation. Such magic as was found in Varfleet was small stuff really and scarcely worth the trouble. Callahorn was only a protectorate of the Federation, and Varfleet so distant as to be almost into the free territories. It was not yet army occupied. The Federation so far had disdained to bother with it.

But Seekers? Par shook his head. Seekers were another matter altogether. Seekers only appeared when there was a serious intent on the part of the Federation to stamp out a practice of magic. No one wanted any part of them.

"It grows too dangerous for us here," Coll said, as if reading Par's mind. "We will be discovered."

Par shook his head. "We are but one of a hundred practicing the art," he replied. "Just one in a city of many."

Coll looked at him. "One in a hundred, yes. But the only one using real magic."

Par looked back. It was good money the ale house paid them, the best they had ever seen. They needed it to help with the taxes the Federation demanded. They needed it for their family and the Vale. He hated to give up because of a rumor.

His jaw tightened. He hated to give up even more because it meant the stories must be returned to the Vale and kept hidden there, untold to those who needed to hear. It meant that the repression of ideas and practices that clamped down about the Four Lands like a vise had tightened one turn more.

"We have to go," Coll said, interrupting his thoughts.

Par felt a sudden rush of anger before realizing his brother was not saying they must go from the city, but from the doorway of the ale house to the performing stage inside. The crowd would be waiting. He let his anger slip away and felt a sadness take its place.

"I wish we lived in another age," he said softly. He paused, watching the way Coll tensed. "I wish there were Elves and Druids again. And heroes. I wish there could be heroes again—even one."

He trailed off, thinking suddenly of something else.

Coll shoved away from the doorjamb, clapped one big hand to his brother's shoulder, turned him about and started him back down the darkened hallway. "If you keep singing about it, who knows? Maybe there will be."

Par let himself be led away like a child. He was no longer thinking about heroes though, or Elves or Druids, or even about Seekers.

He was thinking about the dreams.

They told the story of the Elven stand at Halys Cut, how Eventine Elessedil and the Elves and Stee Jans and the Legion Free Corps fought to hold the Breakline against the onslaught of the Demon hordes. It was one of Par's favorite stories, the first of the great Elven battles in that terrible Westland war. They stood on a low platform at one end of the main serving room, Par in the forefront, Coll a step back and aside, the lights dimmed against a sea of tightly packed bodies and watchful eyes. While Coll narrated the story, Par sang to provide the accompanying images, and the ale house came alive with the magic of his voice. He invoked in the hundred or more gathered the feelings of fear, anger, and determination that had infused the defenders of the Cut. He let them see the fury of the Demons; he let them hear their battle cries. He drew them in and would not let them go. They stood in the pathway of the Demon assault. They saw the wounding of Eventine and the emergence of his son Ander as leader of the Elves. They watched the Druid Allanon stand virtually alone against the Demon magic and turn it aside. They experienced life and death with an intimacy that was almost terrifying.

When Coll and he were finished, there was stunned silence, then a wild thumping of ale glasses and cheers and shouts of elation unmatched in any performance that had gone before. It seemed for a moment that those gathered might bring the rafters of the ale house down about their ears, so vehement were they in their appreciation. Par was damp with his own sweat, aware for the first time how much he had given to the telling. Yet his mind was curiously detached as they left the platform for the brief rest they were permitted between tellings, thinking still of the dreams.

Coll stopped for a glass of ale by an open storage room and Par continued down the hallway a short distance before coming to an empty barrel turned upright by the cellar doors. He slumped down wearily, his thoughts tight.

He had been having the dreams for almost a month now, and he still didn't know why.

The dreams occurred with a frequency that was unsettling. They always began with a black-cloaked figure that rose from a lake, a figure that might be Allanon, a lake that might be the Hadeshorn. There was a shimmering of images in his dreams, an ethereal quality to the visions that made them difficult to decipher. The figure always spoke to him, always with the same words. "Come to me; you are needed. The Four Lands are in gravest danger; the magic is almost lost. Come now, Shannara child."

There was more, although the rest varied. Sometimes there were images of a world born of some unspeakable nightmare. Sometimes there were images of the lost talismans—the Sword of Shannara and the Elfstones. Sometimes there was a call for Wren as well, little Wren, and sometimes a call for his uncle Walker Boh. They were to come as well. They were needed, too.

He had decided quite deliberately after the first night that the dreams were a side effect of his prolonged use of the wishsong. He sang the old stories of the Warlock Lord and the Skull Bearers, of Demons and Mord Wraiths, of Allanon and a world threatened by evil, and it was natural that something of those stories and their images would carry over into his sleep. He had tried to combat the effect by using the wishsong on lighter tellings, but it hadn't helped. The dreams persisted. He had refrained from telling Coll, who would have simply used that as a new excuse to advise him to stop invoking the magic of the wishsong and return to the Vale.

Then, three nights ago, the dreams had stopped coming as suddenly as they had started. Now he was wondering why. He was wondering if perhaps he had mistaken their origin. He was considering the possibility that instead of being self-induced, they might have been sent.

But who would have sent them?

Allanon? Truly Allanon, who was three hundred years dead?

Someone else?

Some*thing* else? Something that had a reason of its own and meant him no good?

He shivered at the prospect, brushed the matter from his mind, and went quickly back up the hallway to find Coll.

The crowd was even larger for the second telling, the walls lined with standing men who could not find chairs or benches to sit upon. The Blue Whisker was a large house, the front serving room over a hundred feet across and open to the rafters above a stringing of oil lamps and fish netting that lent a sort of veiled appearance that was apparently designed to suggest intimacy. Par couldn't have tolerated much more intimacy, so close were the patrons of the ale house as they pressed up against the platform, some actually sitting on it now as they drank. This was a different group than earlier, although the Valeman was hard-pressed to say why. It had a different feel to it, as if there was something foreign in its makeup. Coll must have felt it, too. He glanced over at Par several times as they prepared to perform, and there was uneasiness mirrored in his dark eyes.

A tall, black-bearded man wrapped in a dun-colored forest cloak waded through the crowd to the platform's edge and eased himself down between two other men. The two looked up as if they intended to say something, then caught a close glimpse of the other's face and apparently thought better of it. Par watched momentarily and looked away. Everything felt wrong.

Coll leaned over as a rhythmic clapping began. The crowd was growing restless. "Par, I don't like this. There's something . . ."

He didn't finish. The owner of the ale house came up and told them in no uncertain terms to begin before the crowd got out of hand and started breaking things. Coll stepped away wordlessly. The lights dimmed, and Par started to sing. The story was the one about Allanon and the battle with the Jachyra. Coll began to speak, setting the stage, telling those gathered what sort of day it was, what the glen was like into which the Druid came with Brin Ohmsford and Rone Leah, how everything suddenly grew hushed. Par created the images in the minds of his listeners, instilling in them a sense of anxiety and expectation, trying unsuccessfully not to experience the same feelings himself.

At the rear of the room, men were moving to block the doors and windows, men suddenly shed of cloaks and dressed all in black. Weapons glittered. There were patches of white on sleeves and breasts, insignia of some sort. Par squinted, Elven vision sharp.

A wolf's head.

The men in black were Seekers.

Par's voice faltered and the images shimmered and lost their hold. Men began to grumble and look about. Coll stopped his narration. There was movement everywhere. There was someone in the darkness behind them. There was someone all about.

Coll edged closer protectively.

Then the lights rose again, and a wedge of the black-garbed Seekers pushed forward from the front door. There were shouts and groans of protest, but the men making them were quick to move out of the way. The owner of the Blue Whisker tried to intervene, but was shoved aside.

The wedge of men came to a stop directly in front of the platform. Another group blocked the exits. They wore black from head to toe, their faces covered above their mouths, their wolf-head insignia gleaming. They were armed with short swords, daggers, and truncheons, and their weapons were held ready. They were a mixed bunch, big and small, stiff and bent, but there was a feral look to all of them, as much in the way they held themselves as in their eyes.

Their leader was a huge, rangy man with tremendously long arms and a powerful frame. There was a craggy cast to his face where the mask ended, and a half-beard of coarse reddish hair covered his chin. His left arm was gloved to the elbow.

"Your names?" he asked. His voice was soft, almost a whisper.

Par hesitated. "What is it that we have done?"

"Is your name Ohmsford?" The speaker was studying him intently.

Par nodded. "Yes. But we haven't . . ."

"You are under arrest for violating Federation Supreme Law," the soft voice announced. There was a grumbling sound from the patrons. "You have used magic in defiance of . . ."

"They was just telling stories!" a man called out from a few feet away. One of the Seekers lashed out swiftly with his truncheon and the man collapsed in a heap.

"You have used magic in defiance of Federation dictates and thereby endangered the public." The speaker did not even bother to glance at the fallen man. "You will be taken . . ."

He never finished. An oil lamp dropped suddenly from the center of the ceiling to the crowded ale house floor and exploded in a shower of flames. Men sprang to their feet, howling. The speaker and his companions turned in surprise. At the same moment the tall, bearded man who had taken a seat on the platform's edge earlier came to his feet with a lunge, vaulted several other astonished patrons, and slammed into the knot of Seekers, spilling them to the floor. The tall man leaped onto the stage in front of Par and Coll and threw off his shabby cloak to reveal a fully armed hunter dressed in forest green. One arm lifted, the hand clenched in a fist.

"Free-born!" he shouted into the confusion.

It seemed that everything happened at once after that. The decorative netting, somehow loosened, followed the oil lamp to the floor, and practically everyone gathered at the Blue Whisker was suddenly entangled. Yells and curses rose from those trapped. At the doors, green-clad men pounced on the bewildered Seekers and hammered them to the floor. Oil lamps were smashed, and the room was plunged into darkness.

The tall man moved past Par and Coll with a quickness they would not have believed possible. He caught the first of the Seekers blocking the back entrance with a sweep of one boot, snapping the man's head back. A short sword and dagger appeared, and the remaining two went down as well.

"This way, quick now!" he called back to Par and Coll.

They came at once. A dark shape clawed at them as they rushed past, but Coll knocked the man from his feet into the mass of struggling bodies. He reached back to be certain he had not lost his brother, his big hand closing on Par's slender shoulder. Par yelled in spite of himself. Coll always forgot how strong he was.

They cleared the stage and reached the back hallway, the tall stranger several paces ahead. Someone tried to stop them, but the stranger ran right over him. The din from the room behind them was deafening, and flames were scattered everywhere now, licking hungrily at the flooring and walls. The stranger led them quickly down the hall and through the rear door into the alleyway. Two more of the green-clad men waited. Wordlessly, they surrounded the brothers and rushed them clear of the ale house. Par glanced back. The flames were already leaping from the windows and crawling up toward the roof. The Blue Whisker had seen its last night.

They slipped down the alleyway past startled faces and wide eyes, turned into a passageway Par would have sworn he had never seen before despite his many excursions out that way, passed through a scattering of doors and anterooms and finally emerged into a new street entirely. No one spoke. When at last they were beyond the sound of the shouting and the glow of the fire, the stranger slowed, motioned his two companions to take up watch and pulled Par and Coll into a shadowed alcove.

All were breathing heavily from the run. The stranger looked at them in turn, grinning. "A little exercise is good for the digestion, they say. What do you think? Are you all right?"

The brothers both nodded. "Who are you?" asked Par.

The grin broadened. "Why, practically one of the family, lad. Don't you recognize me? Ah, you don't, do you? But, then, why should you? After all, you and I have never met. But the songs should remind you." He closed his left hand into a fist, then thrust a single finger sharply at Par's nose. "Remember now?"

Mystified, Par looked at Coll, but his brother appeared as confused as he was. "I don't think . . ." he started.

"Well, well, it doesn't matter just at the moment. All in good time." He bent close. "This is no longer safe country for you, lad. Certainly not here in Varfleet and probably not in all of Callahorn. Maybe not anywhere. Do you know who that was back there? The ugly one with the whisper?"

Par tried to place the rangy speaker with the soft voice. He couldn't. He shook his head slowly.

"Rimmer Dall," the stranger said, the smile gone now. "First Seeker, the high mucky-muck himself. Sits on the Coalition Council when he's not out swatting flies. But you, he's taken a special interest if he's come all the way to Varfleet to arrest you. That's not part of his ordinary fly-swatting.

That's hunting bear. He thinks you are dangerous, lad—very dangerous, indeed, or he wouldn't have bothered coming all the way here. Good thing I was looking out for you. I was, you know. Heard Rimmer Dall was going to come for you and came to make sure he didn't get the job done. Mind now, he won't give up. You slipped his grasp this time, but that will make him just that much more determined. He'll keep coming for you."

He paused, gauging the effect of what he was saying. Par was staring at him speechlessly, so he went on. "That magic of yours, the singing, that's real magic, isn't it? I've seen enough of the other kind to know. You could put that magic to good use, lad, if you had a mind to. It's wasted in these ale houses and backstreets."

"What do you mean?" Coll asked, suddenly suspicious.

The stranger smiled, charming and guileless. "The Movement has need of such magic," he said softly.

Coll snorted. "You're one of the outlaws!"

The stranger executed a quick bow. "Yes, lad, I am proud to say I am. More important, I am free-born and I do not accept Federation rule. No right-thinking man does." He bent close. "You don't accept it yourself now, do you? Admit it."

"Hardly," Coll answered defensively. "But I question whether the outlaws are any better."

"Harsh words, lad!" the other exclaimed. "A good thing for you I do not take offense easily." He grinned roguishly.

"What is it you want?" Par interrupted quickly, his mind clear again. He had been thinking of Rimmer Dall. He knew the man's reputation and he was frightened of the prospect of being hunted by him. "You want us to join you, is that it?"

The stranger nodded. "You would find it worth your time, I think."

But Par shook his head. It was one thing to accept the stranger's help in fleeing the Seekers. It was another to join the Movement. The matter needed a great deal more thought. "I think we had better decline for now," he said evenly. "That is, if we're being given a choice."

"Of course you are being given a choice!" The stranger seemed offended.

"Then we have to say no. But we thank you for the offer and especially for your help back there."

The stranger studied him a moment, solemn again. "You are quite welcome, believe me. I wish only the best for you, Par Ohmsford. Here, take this." He removed from one hand a ring that was cast in silver and bore the insigne of a hawk. "My friends know me by this. If you need a favor—or if you change your mind—take this to Kiltan Forge at Reaver's End at the north edge of the city and ask for the Archer. Can you remember that?"

Par hesitated, then took the ring, nodding. "But why . . . ?"

"Because there is much between us, lad," the other said softly, anticipating his question. One hand reached out to rest on his shoulder. The eyes took in Coll as well. "There is history that binds us, a bond of such strength that it requires I be there for you if I can. More, it requires that we stand together against what is threatening this land. Remember that, too. One day, we will do so, I think—if we all manage to stay alive until then."

He grinned at the brothers and they stared back silently. The stranger's hand dropped away. "Time to go now. Quickly, too. The street runs east to the river. You can go where you wish from there. But watch yourselves. Keep your backs well guarded. This matter isn't finished."

"I know," Par said and extended his hand. "Are you certain you will not tell us your name?"

The stranger hesitated. "Another day," he said.

He gripped Par's hand tightly, then Coll's, then whistled his companions to him. He waved once, then melted into the shadows and was gone.

Par stared down momentarily at the ring, then glanced questioningly at Coll. Somewhere close at hand, the sound of shouting started up.

"I think the questions will have to wait," said Coll.

Par jammed the ring into his pocket. Wordlessly, they disappeared into the night.

3

It was nearing midnight by the time Par and Coll reached the waterfront section of Varfleet, and it was there that they first realized how ill-prepared they were to make their escape from Rimmer Dall and his Federation Seekers. Neither had expected that flight would prove necessary, so neither had brought anything that a lengthy journey might require. They had no food, no blankets, no weapons save for the standard long knives all Valemen wore, no camping gear or foul-weather equipment, and worst of all, no money. The ale house keeper hadn't paid them in a month. What money they had managed to save from the month before had been lost in the fire along with everything else they owned. They had only the clothes on their backs and a growing fear that perhaps they should have stuck with the nameless stranger a bit longer.

The waterfront was a ramshackle mass of boathouses, piers, mending shops, and storage sheds. Lights burned along its length, and dockworkers and fishermen drank and joked in the light of oil lamps and pipes. Smoke rose out of tin stoves and barrels, and the smell of fish hung over everything.

"Maybe they've given up on us for the night," Par suggested at one point. "The Seekers, I mean. Maybe they won't bother looking anymore until morning—or maybe not at all."

Coll glanced at him and arched one eyebrow meaningfully. "Maybe cows can fly too." He looked away. "We should have insisted we be paid more promptly for our work. Then we wouldn't be in this fix."

Par shrugged. "It wouldn't have made any difference."

"It wouldn't? We'd at least have some money!"

"Only if we'd thought to carry it with us to the performance. How likely is that?"

Coll hunched his shoulders and screwed up his face. "That ale house keeper owes us."

They walked all the way to the south end of the docks without speaking further, stopped finally as the lighted waterfront gave way to darkness, and stood looking at each other. The night was cooler now and their clothes were too thin to protect them. They were shivering, their hands jammed down in their pockets, their arms clamped tightly against their sides. Insects buzzed about them annoyingly.

Coll sighed. "Do you have any idea where we're going, Par? Do you have some kind of plan in mind?"

Par took out his hands and rubbed them briskly. "I do. But it requires a boat to get there."

"South, then—down the Mermidon?"

"All the way."

Coll smiled, misunderstanding. He thought they were headed back to Shady Vale. Par decided it was best to leave him with that impression.

"Wait here," Coll said suddenly and disappeared before Par could object.

Par stood alone in the dark at the end of the docks for what seemed like an hour, but was probably closer to half that. He walked over to a bench by a fishing shack and sat down, hunched up against the night air. He was feeling a mix of things. He was angry, mostly—at the stranger for spiriting them away and then abandoning them—all right, so Par had asked to have it that way, that didn't make him feel any better—at the Federation for chasing them out from the city like common thieves, and at himself for being stupid enough to think he could get away with using real magic when it was absolutely forbidden to do so. It was one thing to play around with the magics of sleight of hand and quick change; it was another altogether to employ the magic of the wishsong. It was too obviously the real thing, and he should have known that sooner or later word of its use would get back to the authorities.

He put his legs out in front of him and crossed his boots. Well, there was nothing to be done about it now. Coll and he would simply have to start over again. It never occurred to him to quit. The stories were too important for that; it was his responsibility to see to it that they were not forgotten. He was convinced that the magic was a gift he had received expressly for that purpose. It didn't matter what the Federation said—that magic was outlawed and that it was a source of great harm to the land and its people. What did the Federation know of magic? Those on the Coalition Council lacked any practical experience. They had simply decided that something needed to be done to address the concerns of those who claimed parts of the Four Lands were sickening and men were being turned into something like the dark creatures of Jair Ohmsford's time, creatures from some nether existence that defied understanding, beings that drew their power from the night and from magics lost since the time of the Druids.

They even had names, these creatures. They were called Shadowen.

Suddenly, unpleasantly, Par thought again of the dreams and of the dark thing within them that had summoned him.

He was aware then that the night had gone still; the voices of the fishermen and dockworkers, the buzz of the insects, and even the rustle of the night wind had disappeared. He could hear the sound of his own pulse in his ears, and a whisper of something else . . .

Then a splash of water brought him to his feet with a start. Coll appeared, clambering out of the Mermidon at the river's edge a dozen feet away, shedding water as he came. He was naked. Par recovered his composure and stared at him in disbelief.

"Shades, you frightened me! What were you doing?"

"What does it look like I was doing?" Coll grinned. "I was out swimming!"

What he was really doing, Par discovered after applying a bit more pressure, was appropriating a fishing skiff owned by the keeper of the Blue Whisker. The keeper had mentioned it to Coll once or twice when bragging about his fishing skills. Coll had remembered it when Par had mentioned needing a boat, remembered as well the description of the boat shed where the man said it was kept, and gone off to find it. He'd simply swum up to where it was stored, snapped the lock on the shed, slipped the mooring lines and towed it away.

"It's the least he owes us after the kind of business we brought in," he said defensively as he brushed himself dry and dressed.

Par didn't argue the point. They needed a boat worse than the ale house keeper, and this was probably their only chance to find one. Assuming the Seekers were still scouring the city for them, their only other alternative was to strike out on foot into the Runne Mountains—an undertaking that would require more than a week. A ride down the Mermidon was a journey of only a few days. It wasn't as if they were stealing the boat, after all. He caught himself. Well, maybe it was. But they would return it or provide proper compensation when they could.

The skiff was only a dozen feet in length, but it was equipped with oars, fishing gear, some cooking and camping equipment, a pair of blankets, and a canvas tarp. They boarded and pushed off into the night, letting the current carry them out from the shore and sweep them away.

They rode the river south for the remainder of the night, using the oars to keep it in mid-channel, listening to the night sounds, watching the shoreline, and trying to stay awake. As they traveled, Coll offered his theory on what they should do next. It was impossible, of course, to go back into Callahorn any time in the immediate future. The Federation would be looking for them. It would be dangerous, in fact, to travel to any of the major Southland cities because the Federation authorities stationed there would be alerted as well. It was best that they simply return to the Vale.

They could still tell the stories—not right away perhaps, but in a month or so after the Federation had stopped looking for them. Then, later, they could travel to some of the smaller hamlets, the more isolated communities, places the Federation seldom visited. It would all work out fine.

Par let him ramble. He was willing to bet that Coll didn't believe a word of it; and even if he did, there was no point in arguing about it now.

They pulled into shore at sunrise and made camp in a grove of shade trees at the base of a windswept bluff, sleeping until noon, then rising to catch and eat fish. They were back on the river by early afternoon and continued on until well after sunset. Again they pulled into shore and made camp. It was starting to rain, and they put up the canvas to provide shelter. They made a small fire, pulled the blankets close, and sat silently facing the river, watching the raindrops swell its flow and form intricate patterns on its shimmering surface.

They spoke then for a while about how things had changed in the Four Lands since the time of Jair Ohmsford.

Three hundred years ago, the Federation governed only the deep South-land cities, adopting a strict policy of isolationism. The Coalition Council provided its leadership even then, a body of men selected by the cities as representatives to its government. But it was the Federation armies that gradually came to dominate the Council, and in time the policy of isolationism gave way to one of expansion. It was time to extend its sphere of influence, the Federation determined—to push back its frontiers and offer a choice of leadership to the remainder of the Southland. It was logical that the Southland should be united under a single government, and who better to do that than the Federation?

That was the way it started. The Federation began a push north, gobbling up bits and pieces of the Southland as it went. A hundred years after the death of Jair Ohmsford, everything south of Callahorn was Federation governed. The other races, the Elves, the Trolls, the Dwarves, and even the Gnomes cast nervous glances south. Before long, Callahorn agreed to become a protectorate, its Kings long dead, its cities feuding and divided, and the last buffer between the Federation and the other lands disappeared.

It was about this same time that the rumors of the Shadowen began to surface. It was said that the magic of the old days was at fault, magic that had taken seed in the earth and nurtured there for decades and was now coming to life. The magic took many forms, sometimes as nothing more than a cold wind, sometimes as something vaguely human. It was labeled, in any case, as Shadowen. The Shadowen sickened the land and its life, turning pockets of it into quagmires of decay and lifelessness. They attacked mortal creatures, man or beast, and, when they were sufficiently weakened, took them over completely, stealing into their bodies and residing there, hidden wraiths. They needed the life of others for their own sustenance. That was how they survived.

The Federation lent credibility to those rumors by proclaiming that such creatures might indeed exist and only it was strong enough to protect against them.

No one argued that the magic might not be at fault or that the Shadowen or whatever it was that was causing the problem had nothing to do with magic at all. It was easier simply to accept the explanation offered. After all, there hadn't been any magic in the land since the passing of the Druids. The Ohmsfords told their stories, of course, but only a few heard and fewer still believed. Most thought the Druids just a legend. When Callahorn agreed to become a protectorate and the city of Tyrsis was occupied, the Sword of Shannara disappeared. No one thought much of it. No one knew how it happened, and no one much cared. The Sword hadn't even been seen for over two hundred years. There was only the vault that was said to contain it, the blade set in a block of Tre-Stone, there in the center of the People's Park—and then one day that was gone as well.

The Elfstones disappeared not long after. There was no record of what became of them. Not even the Ohmsfords knew.

Then the Elves began to disappear as well, entire communities, whole cities at a time, until even Arborlon was gone. Finally, there were no more Elves at all; it was as if they had never been. The Westland was deserted, save for a few hunters and trappers from the other lands and the wandering bands of Rovers. The Rovers, unwelcome anyplace else, had always been there, but even the Rovers claimed to know nothing of what had become of the Elves. The Federation quickly took advantage of the situation. The Westland, it declared, was the seeding ground for the magic that was at the root of the problems in the Four Lands. It was the Elves, after all, who introduced magic into the Lands years earlier. It was the Elves who first practiced it. The magic had consumed them—an object lesson on what would happen to all those who tried to do likewise.

The Federation emphasized the point by forbidding the practice of magic in any form. The Westland was made a protectorate, albeit an unoccupied one since the Federation lacked enough soldiers to patrol so vast a territory unaided, but one that would be cleansed eventually, it was promised, of the ill effects of any lingering magic.

Shortly after that, the Federation declared war on the Dwarves. It did so ostensibly because the Dwarves had provoked it, although it was never made clear in what way. The result was practically a forgone conclusion. The Federation had the largest, most thoroughly equipped and best trained army in the Four Lands by this time, and the Dwarves had no standing army at all. The Dwarves no longer had the Elves as allies, as they had all those years previous, and the Gnomes and Trolls had never been friends. Nevertheless, the war lasted nearly five years. The Dwarves knew the mountainous Eastland far better than the Federation, and even though Culhaven fell almost immediately, the Dwarves continued to fight in the high country until eventually they were starved into submission. They were brought down out of the mountains and sent south to the Federation mines. Most died there. After seeing what happened to the Dwarves, the Gnome tribes fell quickly into line. The Federation declared the Eastland a protectorate as well.

There remained a few pockets of isolated resistance. There were still a handful of Dwarves and a scattering of Gnome tribes that refused to recognize Federation rule and continued to fight from the deep wilderness areas north and east. But they were too few to make any difference.

To mark its unification of the greater portion of the Four Lands and to honor those who had worked to achieve it, the Federation constructed a monument at the north edge of the Rainbow Lake where the Mermidon poured through the Runne. The monument was constructed entirely of black granite, broad and square at its base, curved inward as it rose over two hundred feet above the cliffs, a monolithic tower that could be seen for miles in all directions. The tower was called Southwatch.

That was almost a hundred years ago, and now only the Trolls remained a free people, still entrenched deep within the mountains of the Northland, the Charnals, and the Kershalt. That was dangerous, hostile country, a natural fortress, and no one from the Federation wanted much to do with it. The decision was made to leave it alone as long as the Trolls did not interfere with the other lands. The Trolls, very much a reclusive people for the whole of their history, were happy to oblige.

"It's all so different now," Par concluded wistfully as they continued to sit within their shelter and watch the rain fall into the Mermidon. "No more Druids, no Paranor, no magic—except the fake kind and the little we know. No Elves. Whatever happened to them, do you think?" He paused, but Coll didn't have anything to say. "No monarchies, no Leah, no Buckhannahs, no Legion Free Corps, no Callahorn for all intents and purposes."

"No freedom," Coll finished darkly.

"No freedom," Par echoed.

He rocked back, drawing his legs tight against his chest. "I wish I knew how the Elfstones disappeared. And the Sword. What happened to the Sword of Shannara?"

Coll shrugged. "Same thing that happens to everything eventually. It got lost."

"What do you mean? How could they let it get lost?"

"No one was taking care of it."

Par thought about that. It made sense. No one bothered much with the magic after Allanon died, after the Druids were gone. The magic was simply ignored, a relic from another time, a thing feared and misunderstood for the most part. It was easier to forget about it, and so they did. They all did. He had to include the Ohmsfords as well—otherwise they would still have the Elfstones. All that was left of their magic was the wishsong.

"We know the stories, the tales of what it was like; we have all that history, and we still don't know anything," he said softly.

"We know the Federation doesn't want us talking about it," Coll offered archly. "We know that."

"There are times that I wonder what difference it makes anyway." Par's face twisted into a grimace. "After all, people come to hear us and the day after, who remembers? Anyone besides us? And what if they do? It's all ancient history—not even that to some. To some, it's legend and myth, a lot of nonsense."

"Not to everyone," Coll said quietly.

"What's the use of having the wishsong, if the telling of the stories isn't going to make any difference? Maybe the stranger was right. Maybe there are better uses for the magic."

"Like aiding the outlaws in their fight against the Federation? Like getting yourself killed?" Coll shook his head. "That's as pointless as not using it at all."

There was a sudden splash from somewhere out in the river, and the brothers turned as one to seek out its source. But there was only the churning of rain-swollen waters and nothing else.

"Everything seems pointless." Par kicked at the earth in front of him. "What are we doing, Coll? Chased out of Varfleet as much as if we were outlaws ourselves, forced to take that boat like thieves, made to run for home like dogs with our tails between our legs." He paused, looking over at his brother. "Why do you think we still have use of the magic?"

Coll's blocky face shifted slightly toward Par's. "What do you mean?"

"Why do we have it? Why hasn't it disappeared along with everything else? Do you think there's a reason?"

There was a long silence. "I don't know," Coll said finally. He hesitated. "I don't know what it's like to have the magic."

Par stared at him, realizing suddenly what he had asked and ashamed he had done so.

"Not that I'd want it, you understand," Coll added hastily, aware of his brother's discomfort. "One of us with the magic is enough." He grinned.

Par grinned back. "I expect so." He looked at Coll appreciatively for a moment, then yawned. "You want to go to sleep?"

Coll shook his head and eased his big frame back into the shadows a bit. "No, I want to talk some more. It's a good night for talking."

Nevertheless, he was silent then, as if he had nothing to say after all. Par studied him for a few moments, then they both looked back out over the Mermidon, watching as a massive tree limb washed past, apparently knocked down by the storm. The wind, which had blown hard at first, was quiet now, and the rain was falling straight down, a steady, gentle sound as it passed through the trees.

Par found himself thinking about the stranger who had rescued them from the Federation Seekers. He had puzzled over the man's identity for the better part of the day, and he still hadn't a clue as to who he was. There was something familiar about him, though—something in the way he talked, an assurance, a confidence. It reminded him of someone from one of the stories he told, but he couldn't decide who. There were so many tales and many of them were about men like that one, heroes in the days of magic and Druids, heroes Par had thought were missing from this age. Maybe he had been wrong. The stranger at the Blue Whisker had been impressive in his rescue of them. He seemed prepared to stand up to the Federation. Perhaps there was hope for the Four Lands yet.

He leaned forward and fed another few sticks of deadwood into the little fire, watching the smoke curl out from beneath the canvas shelter into the night. Lightning flashed suddenly farther east, and a long peal of thunder followed.

"Some dry clothes would be good right now," he muttered. "Mine are damp just from the air."

Coll nodded. "Some hot stew and bread, too."

"A bath and a warm bed."

"Maybe the smell of fresh spices."

"And rose water."

Coll sighed. "At this point, I'd just settle for an end to this confounded rain." He glanced out into the dark. "I could almost believe in Shadowen on a night like this, I think."

Par decided suddenly to tell Coll about the dreams. He wanted to talk about them, and there no longer seemed to be any reason not to. He debated only a moment, then said, "I haven't said anything before, but I've been having these dreams, the same dream actually, over and over." Quickly he described it, focusing on his confusion about the dark-robed figure who spoke to him. "I don't see him clearly enough to be certain who he is," he explained carefully. "But he might be Allanon."

Coll shrugged. "He might be anybody. It's a dream, Par. Dreams are always murky."

"But I've had this same dream a dozen, maybe two dozen times. I thought at first it was just the magic working on me, but . . ." He stopped, biting his lip. "What if . . . ?" He stopped again.

"What if what?"

"What if it isn't just the magic? What if it's an attempt by Allanon—or someone—to send me a message of some sort?"

"A message to do what? To go traipsing off to the Hadeshorn or somewhere equally dangerous?" Coll shook his head. "I wouldn't worry about it if I were you. And I certainly wouldn't consider going." He frowned. "You aren't, are you? Considering going?"

"No," Par answered at once. *Not until I think about it, at least,* he amended silently, surprised at the admission.

"That's a relief. We have enough problems as it is without going off in search of dead Druids." Coll obviously considered the matter settled.

Par didn't reply, choosing instead to poke at the fire with a stray stick, nudging the embers this way and that. He was indeed thinking about going, he realized. He hadn't considered it seriously before, but all of a sudden he had a need to know what the dreams meant. It didn't matter if they came from Allanon or not. Some small voice inside him, some tiny bit of recognition, hinted that finding the source of the dreams might allow him to discover something about himself and his use of the magic. It bothered him that he was thinking like this, that he was suddenly contemplating doing exactly what he had told himself he must not do right from the time the dreams had first come to him. But that was no longer enough to deter him. There was a history of dreams in the Ohmsford family and almost always the dreams had a message.

"I just wish I was sure," he murmured.

Coll was stretched out on his back now, eyes closed against the firelight. "Sure about what?"

"The dreams," he hedged. "About whether or not they were sent."

Coll snorted. "I'm sure enough for the both of us. There aren't any Druids. There aren't any Shadowen either. There aren't any dark wraiths trying to send you messages in your sleep. There's just you, overworked and under-rested, dreaming bits and pieces of the stories you sing about."

Par lay back as well, pulling his blanket up about him. "I suppose so," he agreed, inwardly not agreeing at all.

Coll rolled over on his side, yawning. "Tonight, you'll probably dream about floods and fishes, damp as it is."

Par said nothing. He listened for a time to the sound of the rain, staring up at the dark expanse of the canvas, catching the flicker of the firelight against its damp surface.

"Maybe I'll choose my own dream," he said softly.

Then he was asleep.

He did dream that night, the first time in almost two weeks. It was the dream he wanted, the dream of the dark-robed figure, and it was as if he were able to reach out and bring it to him. It seemed to come at once, to slip from the depths of his subconscious the moment sleep came. He was shocked at its suddenness, but didn't wake. He saw the dark figure rise from the lake, watched it come for him, vague yet faceless, so menacing that he would have fled if he could. But the dream was master now and would not let him. He heard himself asking why the dream had been absent for so long, but there was no answer given. The dark figure simply approached in silence, not speaking, not giving any indication of its purpose.

Then it came to a stop directly before him, a being that could have been anything or anyone, good or evil, life or death.

Speak to me, he thought, frightened.

But the figure merely stood there, draped in shadow, silent and immobile. It seemed to be waiting.

Then Par stepped forward and pushed back the cowl that hid the other, emboldened by some inner strength he did not know he possessed. He drew the cowl free and the face beneath was as sharp as if etched in bright sunlight. He knew it instantly. He had sung of it a thousand times. It was as familiar to him as his own.

The face was Allanon's.

When he came awake the next morning, Par decided not to say anything to Coll about his dream. In the first place, he didn't know what to say. He couldn't be sure if the dream had occurred on its own or because he had been thinking so hard about having it—and even then he had no way of knowing if it was the real thing. In the second place, telling Coll would just start him off again on how foolish it was for Par to keep thinking about something he obviously wasn't going to do anything about. Was he? Then, if Par was honest with him, they would fight about the advisability of going off into the Dragon's Teeth in search of the Hadeshorn and a three-hundred-year-dead Druid. Better just to let the matter rest.

They ate a cold breakfast of wild berries and some stream water, lucky to have that. The rains had stopped, but the sky was overcast, and the day was gray and threatening. The wind had returned, rather strong out of the northwest, and tree limbs bent and leaves rustled wildly against its thrust. They packed up their gear, boarded the skiff, and pushed off onto the river.

The Mermidon was heavily swollen, and the skiff tossed and twisted roughly as it carried them south. Debris choked the waters, and they kept the oars at hand to push off any large pieces that threatened damage to the boat. The cliffs of the Runne loomed darkly on either side, wrapped in trailers of mist and low-hanging clouds. It was cold in their shadow, and the brothers felt their hands and feet grow quickly numb.

They pulled into shore and rested when they could, but it accomplished little. There was nothing to eat and no way to get warm without taking time to build a fire. By early afternoon, it was raining again. It grew quickly colder in the rainfall, the wind picked up, and it became dangerous to continue on the river. When they found a small cove in the shelter of a stand of old pine, they quickly maneuvered the skiff ashore and set camp for the night.

They managed a fire, ate the fish Coll caught and tried their best to dry out beneath the canvas with rain blowing in from every side. They slept poorly, cold and uncomfortable, the wind blowing down the canyon of the mountains and the river churning against its banks. That night, Par didn't dream at all.

Morning brought a much-needed change in the weather. The storm moved east, the skies cleared and filled with bright sunlight, and the air warmed once more. The brothers dried out their clothing as their craft bore them south, and by midday it was balmy enough to strip off tunics and boots and enjoy the feel of the sun on their skin.

"As the saying goes, things always get better after a storm," Coll declared in satisfaction. "There'll be good weather now, Par—you watch. Another three days and we'll be home."

Par smiled and said nothing.

The day wore on, turning lazy, and the summer smells of trees and flowers began to fill the air again.

They sailed beneath Southwatch, its black granite bulk jutting skyward out of the mountain rock at the edge of the river, silent and inscrutable. Even from as far away as it was, the tower looked forbidding, its stone grainy and opaque, so dark that it seemed to absorb the light. There were all sorts of rumors about Southwatch. Some said it was alive, that it fed upon the earth in order to live. Some said it could move. Almost everyone agreed that it seemed to keep getting bigger through some form of ongoing construction. It appeared to be deserted. It always appeared that way. An elite unit of Federation soldiers were supposed to be in service to the tower, but no one ever saw them. Just as well, Par thought as they drifted past undisturbed.

By late afternoon, they reached the mouth of the river where it opened into the Rainbow Lake. The lake spread away before them, a broad expanse of silver-tipped blue water turned golden at its western edge by the sun as it slipped toward the horizon. The rainbow from which it took its name arched overhead, faint now in the blaze of sunlight, the blues and purples almost invisible, the reds and yellows washed of their color. Cranes glided silently in the distance, long graceful bodies extended against the light.

The Ohmsfords pulled their boat to the shore's edge and beached it where a stand of shade trees fronted a low bluff. They set their camp, hanging the canvas in the event of a change back in the weather, and Coll fished while Par went off to gather wood for an evening fire.

Par wandered the shoreline east for a ways, enjoying the bright glaze of the lake's waters and the colors in the air. After a time, he moved back up into the woods and began picking up pieces of dry wood. He had gone only a short distance when the woods turned dank and filled with a decaying smell. He noticed that many of the trees seemed to be dying here, leaves wilted and brown, limbs broken off, bark peeling. The ground cover looked unwell, too. He poked and scraped at it with his boot and looked about curiously. There didn't appear to be anything living here; there were no small animals scurrying about and no birds calling from the trees. The forest was deserted.

He decided to give up looking for firewood in this direction and was working his way back toward the shoreline when he caught sight of the house. It was a cottage, really, and scarcely that. It was badly overgrown with weeds, vines, and scrub. Boards hung loosely from its walls, shutters lay on the ground, and the roof was caving in. The glass in the windows was broken out, and the front door stood open. It sat at the edge of a cove that ran far back into the trees from the lake, and the water of the cove was still and greenish with stagnation. The smell that it gave off was sickening.

Par would have thought it deserted if not for the tiny column of smoke that curled up from the crumbling chimney.

He hesitated, wondering why anyone would live in such surroundings. He wondered if there really was someone there or if the smoke was merely a residue. Then he wondered if whoever was there needed help.

He almost went over to see, but there was something so odious about the cottage and its surroundings that he could not make himself do so. Instead, he called out, asking if anyone was home. He waited a moment, then called out again. When there was no reply, he turned away almost gratefully and continued on his way.

Coll was waiting with the fish by the time he returned, so they hastily built a fire and cooked dinner. They were both a little tired of fish, but it was better than nothing and they were more hungry than either would have imagined. When the dinner was consumed, they sat watching as the sun dipped into the horizon and the Rainbow Lake turned to silver. The skies darkened and filled with stars, and the sounds of the night rose out of dusk's stillness. Shadows from the forest trees lengthened and joined and became dark pools that enveloped the last of the daylight.

Par was in the process of trying to figure out a way to tell Coll that he didn't think they should return to Shady Vale when the woodswoman appeared.

She came out of the trees behind them, shambling from the dark as if one of its shadows, all bent over and hunched down against the fire's faint light. She was clothed in rags, layers of them, all of which appeared to have been wrapped about her at some time in the distant past and left there. Her head was bare, and her rough, hard face peered out through long wisps of dense, colorless hair. She might have been any age, Par thought; she was so gnarled it was impossible to tell.

She edged out of the forest cautiously and stopped just beyond the circle of the fire's yellow light, leaning heavily on a walking stick worn with sweat and handling. One rough arm raised as she pointed at Par. "You the one called me?" she asked, her voice cracking like brittle wood.

Par stared at her in spite of himself. She looked like something brought out of the earth, something that had no right to be alive and walking about. There was dirt and debris hanging from her as if it had settled and taken root while she slept.

"Was it?" she pressed.

He finally figured out what she was talking about. "At the cottage? Yes, that was me."

The woodswoman smiled, her face twisting with the effort, her mouth nearly empty of teeth. "You ought to have come in, not just stood out there," she whined. "Door was open."

"I didn't want . . ."

"Keep it that way to be certain no one goes past without a welcome. Fire's always on."

"I saw your smoke, but . . ."

"Gathering wood, were you? Come down out of Callahorn?" Her eyes shifted as she glanced past them to where the boat sat beached. "Come a long way, have you?" The eyes shifted back. "Running from something, maybe?"

Par went instantly still. He exchanged a quick look with Coll.

The woman approached, the walking stick probing the ground in front of her. "Lots run this way. All sorts. Come down out of the outlaw country looking for something or other." She stopped. "That you? Oh, there's those who'd have no part of you, but I'm not one. No, not me!"

"We're not running," Coll spoke up suddenly.

"No? That why you're so well fitted out?" She swept the air with the walking stick. "What's your names?"

"What do you want?" Par asked abruptly. He was liking this less and less.

The woodswoman edged forward another step. There was something wrong with her, something that Par hadn't seen before. She didn't seem to be quite solid, shimmering a bit as if she were walking through smoke or out of a mass of heated air. Her body didn't move right either, and it was more than her age. It was as if she were fastened together like one of the marionettes they used in shows at the fairs, pinned at the joints and pulled by strings.

The smell of the cove and the crumbling cottage clung to the woodswoman even here. She sniffed the air suddenly as if aware of it. "What's that?" She fixed her eyes on Par. "Do I smell magic?"

Par went suddenly cold. Whoever this woman was, she was no one they wanted anything to do with.

"Magic! Yes! Clean and pure and strong with life!" The woodswoman's tongue licked out at the night air experimentally. "Sweet as blood to wolves!"

That was enough for Coll. "You had better find your way back to wherever you came from," he told her, not bothering to disguise his antagonism. "You have no business here. Move along."

But the woodswoman stayed where she was. Her mouth curled into a snarl and her eyes suddenly turned as red as the fire's coals.

"Come over here to me!" she whispered with a hiss. "You, boy!" She pointed at Par. "Come over to me!"

She reached out with one hand. Par and Coll both moved back guardedly, away from the fire. The woman came forward several steps more, edging past the light, backing them further toward the dark.

"Sweet boy!" she muttered, half to herself. "Let me taste you, boy!"

The brothers held their ground against her now, refusing to move any further from the light. The woodswoman saw the determination in their eyes, and her smile was wicked. She came forward, one step, another step . . .

Coll launched himself at her while she was watching Par, trying to grasp her and pin her arms. But she was much quicker than he, the walking stick slashing at him and catching him alongside the head with a vicious whack that sent him sprawling to the earth. Instantly, she was after him, howling like a maddened beast. But Par was quicker. He used the wish-song, almost without thinking, sending forth a string of terrifying images. She fell back, surprised, trying to fend the images off with her hands and the stick. Par used the opportunity to reach Coll and haul him to his feet. Hastily he pulled his brother back from where his attacker clawed at the air.

The woodswoman stopped suddenly, letting the images play about her, turning toward Par with a smile that froze his blood. Par sent an image of a Demon wraith to frighten her, but this time the woman reached out for the image, opened her mouth and sucked in the air about her. The image evaporated. The woman licked her lips and whined.

Par sent an armored warrior. The woodswoman devoured it greedily. She was edging closer again, no longer slowed by the images, actually anxious that he send more. She seemed to relish the taste of the magic; she seemed eager to consume it. Par tried to steady Coll, but his brother was sagging in his arms, still stunned. "Coll, wake up!" he whispered urgently.

"Come, boy," the woodswoman repeated softly. She beckoned and moved closer. "Come feed me!"

Then the fire exploded in a flash of light, and the clearing was turned as bright as day. The woodswoman shrank away from the brightness, and her sudden cry ended in a snarl of rage. Par blinked and peered through the glow.

An old man emerged from the trees, white-haired and gray-robed, with skin as brown as seasoned wood. He stepped from the darkness into the light like a ghost come into being. There was a fierce smile on his mouth and a strange brightness in his eyes. Par wheeled about guardedly, fumbling for the long knife at his belt. Two of them, he thought desperately, and again he shook Coll in an effort to rouse him.

But the old man paid him no notice. He concentrated instead on the woodswoman. "I know you," he said softly. "You frighten no one. Begone from here or you shall deal with me!"

The woodswoman hissed at him like a snake and crouched as if to spring. But she saw something in the old man's face that kept her from attacking. Slowly, she began to edge back around the fire.

"Go back into the dark," whispered the old man.

The woodswoman hissed a final time, then turned and disappeared into the trees without a sound. Her smell lingered on a moment longer, then faded. The old man waved almost absently at the fire, and it returned to normal. The night filled again with comforting sounds, and everything was as before.

The old man snorted and came forward into the firelight. "Bah. One of nighttime's little horrors come out to play," he muttered in disgust. He looked at Par quizzically. "You all right, young Ohmsford? And this one? Coll, is it? That was a nasty blow he took."

Par eased Coll to the ground, nodding. "Yes, thanks. Could you hand me that cloth and a little water?"

The old man did as he was asked, and Par wiped the side of Coll's head where an ugly bruise was already beginning to form. Coll winced, sat forward, and put his head down between his legs, waiting for the throbbing to ease off. Par looked up. It dawned on him suddenly that the old man had used Coll's name.

"How do you know who we are?" he asked, his tone guarded.

The old man kept his gaze steady. "Well, now. I know who you are because I've come looking for you. But I'm not your enemy, if that's what you're thinking."

Par shook his head. "Not really. Not after helping us the way you did. Thank you."

"No need for thanks."

Par nodded again. "That woman, or whatever she was—she seemed frightened of you." He didn't make it a question, he made it a statement of fact.

The old man shrugged. "Perhaps."

"Do you know her?"

"I know of her."

Par hesitated, uncertain whether to press the matter or not. He decided to let it drop. "So. Why are you looking for us?"

"Oh, that's rather a long story, I'm afraid," the old man answered, sounding very much as if the effort required to tell it was entirely beyond him. "I don't suppose we might sit down while we talk about it? The fire's warmth provides some relief for these aging bones. And you wouldn't happen to have a touch of ale, would you? No? Pity. Well, I suppose there was no chance to procure such amenities, the way you were hustled out of Varfleet. Lucky to escape with your skins under the circumstances."

He ambled in close and lowered himself gingerly to the grass, folding his legs before him, draping his gray robes carefully about. "Thought I'd catch up with you there, you know. But then that disruption by the Federation occurred, and you were on your way south before I could stop you."

He reached for a cup and dipped it into the water bucket, drinking deeply. Coll was sitting up now, watching, the damp cloth still held to the side of his head. Par sat down next to him.

The old man finished his water and wiped his mouth on his sleeve. "Allanon sent me," he declared perfunctorily.

There was a long silence as the Ohmsford brothers stared first at him, then at each other, then back again at him.

"Allanon?" Par repeated.

"Allanon has been dead for three hundred years," Coll interjected bluntly.

The old man nodded. "Indeed. I misspoke: It was actually Allanon's ghost, his shade—but Allanon, still, for all intents and purposes."

"Allanon's shade?" Coll took the cloth from the side of his head, his injury forgotten. He did not bother to hide his disbelief.

The old man rubbed his bearded chin. "Now, now, you will have to be patient for a moment or two until I've had a chance to explain. Much of what I am going to tell you will be hard for you to accept, but you must try. Believe me when I tell you that it is very important."

He rubbed his hands briskly in the direction of the fire. "Think of me as a messenger for the moment, will you? Think of me as a messenger sent by Allanon, for that's all I am to you just now. You, Par. Why have you been ignoring the dreams?"

Par stiffened. "You know about that?"

"The dreams were sent by Allanon to bring you to him. Don't you understand? That was his voice speaking to you, his shade come to address you. He summons you to the Hadeshorn—you, your cousin Wren, and . . ."

"Wren?" Coll interrupted, incredulous.

The old man looked perturbed. "That's what I said, didn't I? Am I going to have to repeat everything? Your cousin, Wren Ohmsford. And Walker Boh as well."

"Uncle Walker," Par said softly. "I remember."

Coll glanced at his brother, then shook his head in disgust. "This is ridiculous. No one knows where either of them is!" he snapped. "Wren lives somewhere in the Westland with the Rovers. She lives out of the back of a wagon! And Walker Boh hasn't been seen by anyone for almost ten years. He might be dead, for all we know!"

"He might, but he isn't," the old man said testily. He gave Coll a meaningful stare, then returned his gaze to Par. "All of you are to come to the Hadeshorn by the close of the present moon's cycle. On the first night of the new moon, Allanon will speak with you there."

Par felt a chill go through him. "About magic?"

Coll seized his brother's shoulders. "About Shadowen?" he mimicked, widening his eyes.

The old man bent forward suddenly, his face gone hard. "About what he chooses! Yes, about magic! And about Shadowen! About creatures like the one that knocked you aside just now as if you were a baby! But mostly, I think, young Coll, about this!"

He threw a dash of dark powder into the fire with a suddenness that caused Par and Coll to jerk back sharply. The fire flared as it had when the old man had first appeared, but this time the light was drawn out of the air and everything went dark.

Then an image formed in the blackness, growing in size until it seemed to be all around them. It was an image of the Four Lands, the countryside barren and empty, stripped of life and left ruined. Darkness and a haze of ash-filled smoke hung over everything. Rivers were filled with debris, the waters poisoned. Trees were bent and blasted, shorn of life. Nothing but scrub grew anywhere. Men crept about like animals, and animals fled at their coming. There were shadows with strange red eyes circling everywhere, dipping and playing within those humans who crept, twisting and turning them until they lost their shape and became unrecognizable.

It was a nightmare of such fury and terror that it seemed to Par and Coll Ohmsford as if it were happening to them, and that the screams emanating from the mouths of the tortured humans were their own.

Then the image was gone, and they were back again about the fire, the old man sitting there, watching them with hawk's eyes.

"That was a part of my dream," Par whispered.

"That was the future," the old man said.

"Or a trick," a shaken Coll muttered, stiffening against his own fear.

The old man glared. "The future is an ever-shifting maze of possibilities until it becomes the present. The future I have shown you tonight is not yet fixed. But it is more likely to become so with the passing of every day because nothing is being done to turn it aside. If you would change it, do as I have told you. Go to Allanon! Listen to what he will say!"

Coll said nothing, his dark eyes uneasy with doubt.

"Tell us who you are," Par said softly.

The old man turned to him, studied him for a moment, then looked away from them both, staring out into the darkness as if there were worlds and lives hidden there that only he could see. Finally, he looked back again, nodding.

"Very well, though I can't see what difference it makes. I have a name, a name you should both recognize quickly enough. My name is Cogline."

For an instant, neither Par nor Coll said anything. Then both began speaking at once.

"Cogline, the same Cogline who lived in the Eastland with . . . ?"

"You mean the same man Kimber Boh . . . ?"

He cut them short irritably. "Yes, yes! How many Coglines can there possibly be!" He frowned as he saw the looks on their faces. "You don't believe me, do you?"

Par took a deep breath. "Cogline was an old man in the time of Brin Ohmsford. That was three hundred years ago."

Unexpectedly, the other laughed. "An old man! Ha! And what do you know of old men, Par Ohmsford? Fact is, you don't know a whisker's worth!" He laughed, then shook his head helplessly. "Listen. Allanon was alive five hundred years before he died! You don't question that, do you? I think not, since you tell the story so readily! Is it so astonishing then that I have been alive for a mere three hundred years?" He paused, and there was a surprisingly mischievous look in his eye. "Goodness, what would you have said if I had told you I had been alive longer even than that?"

Then he waved his hand dismissively. "No, no, don't bother to answer. Answer me this instead. What do you know about me? About the Cogline of your stories? Tell me."

Par shook his head, confused. "That he was a hermit, living off in the Wilderun with his granddaughter, Kimber Boh. That my ancestor, Brin Ohmsford, and her companion, Rone Leah, found him there when they . . ."

"Yes, yes, but what about the *man*? Think now of what you've seen of me!"

Par shrugged. "That he . . ." He stopped. "That he used powders that exploded. That he knew something of the old sciences, that he'd studied them somewhere." He was remembering the specifics of the tales of Cogline now, and in remembering found himself thinking that maybe this old man's claim wasn't so farfetched. "He employed different forms of power, the sorts that the Druids had discarded in their rebuilding of the old world. Shades! If you are Cogline, you must still have such power. Do you? Is it magic like my own?"

Coll looked suddenly worried. "Par!"

"Like your own?" the old man asked quickly. "Magic like the wishsong? Hah! Never! Never so unpredictable as that! That was always the trouble with the Druids and their Elven magics—too unpredictable! The power I wield is grounded in sciences proven and tested through the years by reliable study! It doesn't act of its own accord; it doesn't evolve like something alive!" He stopped, a fierce smile creasing his aged face. "But then, too, Par Ohmsford, my power doesn't sing either!"

"Are you really Cogline?" Par asked softly, his amazement at it being possible apparent in his voice.

"Yes," the old man whispered back. "Yes, Par." He swung quickly then to face Coll, who was about to interrupt, placing a narrow, bony finger to his lips. "Shhhh, young Ohmsford, I know you still disbelieve, and your brother as well, but just listen for a moment. You are children of the Elven house of Shannara. There have not been many and always much has been expected of them. It will be so with you as well, I think. More so, perhaps. I am not permitted to see. I am just a messenger, as I have told you—a poor messenger at best. An unwilling messenger, truth is. But I am all that Allanon has."

"But why you?" Par managed to interject, his lean face troubled now and intense.

The old man paused, his gnarled, wrinkled face tightening even further as if the question demanded too much of him. When he spoke finally, it was in a stillness that was palpable.

"Because I was a Druid once, so long ago I can scarcely remember what it felt like. I studied the ways of the magic and the ways of the discarded sciences and chose the latter, forsaking thereby any claim to the former and the right to continue with the others. Allanon knew me, or if you prefer, he knew about me, and he remembered what I was. But, wait. I embellish a bit by claiming I actually was a Druid. I wasn't; I was simply a student of the ways. But Allanon remembered in any case. When he came to me, it was as one Druid to another, though he did not say as much. He lacks anyone but myself to do what is needed now, to come after you and the others, to advise them of the legitimacy of their dreams. All have had them by now, you understand—Wren and Walker Boh as well as you. All have been given a vision of the danger the future holds. No one responds. So he sends me."

The sharp eyes blinked away the memory. "I was a Druid once, in spirit if not in practice, and I practice still many of the Druid ways. No one knew. Not my grandchild Kimber, not your ancestors, no one. I have lived many different lives, you see. When I went with Brin Ohmsford into the country of the Maelmord, it was as Cogline the hermit, half-crazed, half-able, carrying magic powders filled with strange notions. That was who I was then. That was the person I had become. It took me years afterward, long after Kimber had gone, to recover myself, to act and talk like myself again."

He sighed. "It was the Druid Sleep that kept me alive for so long. I knew its secret; I had carried it with me when I left them. I thought many times not to bother, to give myself over to death and not cling so. But something kept me from giving way, and I think now that perhaps it was Allanon, reaching back from his death to assure that the Druids might have at least one spokesman after he was gone."

He saw the beginning of the question in Par's eyes, anticipated its wording, and quickly shook his head. "No, no, not me! I am not the spokesman he needs! I barely have time enough left me to carry the message I have been given. Allanon knows that. He knew better than to come to me to ask that I accept a life I once rejected. He must ask that of someone else."

"Me?" asked Par at once.

The old man paused. "Perhaps. Why don't you ask him yourself?"

No one said anything, hunched forward toward the firelight as the darkness pressed close all about. The cries of the night birds echoed faintly across the waters of the Rainbow Lake, a haunting sound that somehow seemed to measure the depth of the uncertainty Par felt.

"I want to ask him," he said finally. "I need to, I think."

The old man pursed his thin lips. "Then you must."

Coll started to say something, then thought better of it. "This whole business needs some careful thought," he said finally.

"There is little time for that," the old man grumbled.

"Then we shouldn't squander what we have," Coll replied simply. He was no longer abrasive as he spoke, merely insistent.

Par looked at his brother a moment, then nodded. "Coll is right. I will have to think about this."

The old man shrugged as if to indicate that he realized there was nothing more he could do and came to his feet. "I have given you the message I was sent to give, so I must be on my way. There are others to be visited."

Par and Coll rose with him, surprised. "You're leaving now, tonight?" Par asked quickly. Somehow he had expected the old man to stay on, to keep trying to persuade him of the purpose of the dreams.

"Seems best. The quicker I get on with my journey, the quicker it ends. I told you, I came first to you."

"But how will you find Wren or Walker?" Coll wanted to know.

"Same way I found you." The old man snapped his fingers and there was a brief flash of silver light. He grinned, his face skeletal in the firelight. "Magic!"

He reached out his bony hand. Par took it first and found the old man's grip like iron. Coll found the same. They glanced at each other.

"Let me offer you some advice," the old man said abruptly. "Not that you'll necessarily take it, of course—but maybe. You tell these stories, these tales of Druids and magic and your ancestors, all of it a kind of litany of what's been and gone. That's fine, but you don't want to lose sight of the fact that what's happening here and now is what counts. All the telling in the world won't mean a whisker if that vision I showed you comes to pass. You have to live in this world—not in some other. Magic serves a lot of purposes, but you don't use it any way but one. You have to see what else it can do. And you can't do that until you understand it. I suggest you don't understand it at all, either one of you."

He studied them a moment, then turned and shambled off into the dark. "Don't forget, first night of the new moon!" He stopped when he was just a shadow and glanced back. "Something else you'd better remember and that's to watch yourselves." His voice had a new edge to it. "The Shadowen aren't just rumors and old wives' tales. They're as real as you and I. You may not have thought so before tonight, but now you know different. They'll be out there, everywhere you're likely to go. That woman, she was one of them. She came sniffing around because she could sense you have the magic. Others will do the same."

He started moving away again. "Lots of things are going to be hunting you," he warned softly.

He mumbled something further to himself that neither of them could hear as he disappeared slowly into the darkness.

Then he was gone.

5

Par and Coll Ohmsford did not get much sleep that night. They stayed awake long after the old man was gone, talking and sometimes arguing, worrying without always saying as much, eyes constantly scanning the darkness against the promise that *things*, Shadowen or otherwise, were likely to be hunting them. Even after that, when there was nothing left to say, when they had rolled themselves wearily into their blankets and closed their eyes against their fears, they did not sleep well. They rolled and tossed in their slumber, waking themselves and each other with distressing regularity until dawn.

They rose then, dragged themselves from the warmth of their coverings, washed in the chilling waters of the lake, and promptly began talking and arguing all over again. They continued through breakfast, which was just as well because once again there wasn't much to eat and it took their minds off their stomachs. The talk, and more often now the arguments, centered around the old man who claimed to be Cogline and the dreams that might or might not have been sent and if sent might or might not have been sent by Allanon, but included such peripheral topics as Shadowen, Federation Seekers, the stranger who had rescued them in Varfleet, and whether there was sense to the world anymore or not. They had established their positions on these subjects fairly well by this time, positions that, for the most part, weren't within a week's walk of each other. That being the case, they were reduced to communicating with each other across vast stretches of intractability.

Before their day was even an hour old, they were already thoroughly fed up with each other.

"You cannot deny that the possibility exists that the old man really is Cogline!" Par insisted for what must have been the hundredth time as they carried the canvas tarp down to the skiff for stowing.

Coll managed a quick shrug. "I'm not denying it."

"And if he really is Cogline, then you cannot deny the possibility that everything he told us is the truth!"

"I'm not denying that either."

"What about the woodswoman? What was she if not a Shadowen, a night thing with magic stronger than our own?"

"Your own."

Par fumed. "Sorry. My own. The point is, she *was* a Shadowen! She had to be! That makes at least part of what the old man told us the truth, no matter how you view it!"

"Wait a minute." Coll dropped his end of the tarp and stood there with his hands on his hips, regarding his brother with studied dismay. "You do this all the time when we argue. You make these ridiculous leaps in logic and act as if they make perfect sense. How does it follow that, if that woman was a Shadowen, the old man was telling the truth?"

"Well, because, if . . ."

"I won't even question your assumption that she *was* a Shadowen," Coll interrupted pointedly. "Even though we haven't the faintest idea what a Shadowen is. Even though she might just as easily have been something else altogether."

"Something else? What sort of . . . ?"

"Like a companion to the old man, for instance. Like a decoy to give his tale validity."

Par was incensed. "That's ridiculous! What would be the purpose of that?"

Coll pursed his lips thoughtfully. "To persuade you to go with him to the Hadeshorn, naturally. To bring you back into Callahorn. Think about it. Maybe the old man is interested in the magic, too—just like the Federation."

Par shook his head vehemently. "I don't believe it."

"That's because you never like to believe anything that you haven't thought of first," Coll declared pointedly, picking up his end of the tarp again. "You decide something and that's the end of it. Well, this time you had better not make your decision too quickly. There are other possibilities to consider, and I've just given you one of them."

They walked down to the shoreline in silence and deposited the tarp in the bottom of the skiff. The sun was barely above the eastern horizon, and already the day was beginning to feel warm. The Rainbow Lake was smooth, the air windless and filled with the scent of wildflowers and long grass.

Coll turned. "You know, it's not that I mind you being decisive about things. It's just that you then assume I ought simply to agree. I shouldn't argue, I should acquiesce. Well, I am not going to do that. If you want to strike out for the Hadeshorn and the Dragon's Teeth—fine, you go right ahead. But quit acting as if I ought to jump at the chance to go along."

Par didn't say anything back right away. Instead, he thought about what it had been like for them growing up. Par was the older by two years and while physically smaller than Coll, he had always been the leader. He had the magic, after all, and that had always set him apart. It was true, he was decisive; it had been necessary to be decisive when faced with the temptation to use the magic to solve every situation. He had not been as even-tempered as he should have; he wasn't any better now. Coll had always been the more controlled of the two—slower to anger, thoughtful and deliberate, a born peacemaker in the neighborhood fights and squabbles because no one else had the physical and emotional presence. Or was as well liked, he added—because Coll was always that, the sort of fellow that everyone takes to instantly. He spent his time looking after everyone, smoothing over hard feelings, restoring injured pride. Par was always charging around, oblivious to such things, busy searching for new places to explore, new challenges to engage, new ideas to develop. He was visionary, but he lacked Coll's sensitivity. He foresaw so clearly life's possibilities, but Coll was the one who understood best its sacrifices.

There had been a good many times when they had covered for each other's mistakes. But Par had the magic to fall back on and covering up for Coll had seldom cost him anything. It hadn't been like that for Coll. Covering up for Par had sometimes cost him a great deal. Yet Par was his brother, whom he loved, and he never complained. Sometimes, thinking back on those days, Par was ashamed of how much he had let his brother do for him.

He brushed the memories aside. Coll was looking at him, waiting for his response. Par shifted his feet impatiently and thought about what that response ought to be. Then he said simply, "All right. What do you think we should do?"

"Shades, I don't know what we should do!" Coll said at once. "I just know that there are a lot of unanswered questions, and I don't think we should commit ourselves to anything until we've had a chance to answer some of them!"

Par nodded stoically. "Before the time of the new moon, you mean."

"That's better than three weeks away and you know it!"

Par's jaw tightened. "That's not as much time as you make it seem! How are we supposed to answer all the questions we have before then?"

Coll stared at him. "You are impossible, you know that?"

He turned and walked back from the shoreline to where the blankets and cooking gear were stacked and began carrying them down to the skiff. He didn't look at Par. Par stood where he was and watched his brother in silence. He was remembering how Coll had pulled him half-drowned from the Rappahalladran when he had fallen in the rapids on a camping trip. He had gone under and Coll had been forced to dive down for him. He became sick afterward and Coll had carried him home on his back, shaking with fever and half-delirious. Coll was always looking out for him, it seemed. Why was that, he wondered suddenly, when he was the one with the magic?

Coll finished packing the skiff, and Par walked over to him. "I'm sorry," he said and waited.

Coll looked down at him solemnly a moment, then grinned. "No, you're not. You're just saying that."

Par grinned back in spite of himself. "I am not!"

"Yes, you are. You just want to put me off my guard so you can start in again with your confounded decision-making once we're out in the middle of that lake where I can't walk away from you!" His brother was laughing openly now.

Par did his best to look mortified. "Okay, it's true. I'm not sorry."

"I knew it!" Coll was triumphant.

"But you're wrong about the reason for the apology. It has nothing to do with getting you out in the middle of the lake. I'm just trying to shed the burden of guilt I've always felt at being the older brother."

"Don't worry!" Coll was doubled over. "You've always been a terrible older brother!"

Par shoved him, Coll shoved back, and for the moment their differences were forgotten. They laughed, took a final look about the campsite, and pushed the skiff out onto the lake, clambering aboard as it reached deeper water. Coll took up the oars without asking and began to row.

They followed the shoreline west, listening contentedly as the distant sounds of birds rose out of the trees and rushes, letting the day grow pleasantly warm about them. They didn't talk for a while, satisfied with the renewed feeling of closeness they had found on setting out, anxious to avoid arguing again right away.

Nevertheless, Par found himself rehashing matters in his mind—much the same as he was certain Coll was doing. His brother was right about one thing—there were a lot of unanswered questions. Reflecting on the events of the previous evening, Par found himself wishing he had thought to ask the old man for a bit more information. Did the old man know, for instance, who the stranger was who had rescued them in Varfleet? The old man had known about their trouble there and must have had some idea how they escaped. The old man had managed to track them, first to Varfleet, then down the Mermidon, and he had frightened off the woodswoman—Shadowen or whatever—without much effort. He had some form of power at his command, possibly Druid magic, possibly old world science—but he had never said what it was or what it did. Exactly what was his relationship with Allanon? Or was that simply a claim without any basis in fact? And why was it that he had given up on Par so easily when Par had said he must think over the matter of going off to the Hadeshorn for a meeting with Allanon? Shouldn't he have worked harder at persuading Par to go?

But the most disturbing question was one that Par could not bring himself to discuss with Coll at all—because it concerned Coll himself. The dreams had told Par that he was needed and that his cousin Wren and his uncle Walker Boh were needed as well. The old man had said the same— that Par, Wren, and Walker had been called.

Why was there no mention of Coll?

It was a question for which he had no answer at all. He had thought at first that it was because he had the magic and Coll didn't, that the summons had something to do with the wishsong. But then why was Wren needed? Wren had no magic either. Walker Boh was different, of course, since it had always been rumored that he knew something of magic that none of the others did. But not Wren. And not Coll. Yet Wren had been specifically named and Coll hadn't.

It was this more than anything that made him question what he should do. He wanted to know the reason for the dreams; if the old man was right about Allanon, Par wanted to know what the Druid had to say. But he did not want to know any of it if it meant separating from Coll. Coll was more than his brother; he was his closest friend, his most trusted companion, practically his other self. Par did not intend to become involved in something where both were not wanted. He simply wasn't going to do it.

Yet the old man had not forbidden Coll to come. Nor had the dreams. Neither had warned against it.

They had simply ignored him.

Why would that be?

The morning lengthened, and a wind came up. The brothers rigged a sail and mast using the canvas tarp and one of the oars, and soon they were speeding across the Rainbow Lake, the waters slapping and foaming about them. Several times they almost went over, but they stayed alert to sudden shifts in the wind and used their body weight to avoid capsizing. They set a southwest course and by early afternoon had reached the mouth of the Rappahalladran.

There they beached the skiff in a small cove, covered it with rushes and boughs, left everything within but the blankets and cooking gear, and began hiking upriver toward the Duln forests. It soon became expedient to cut across country to save time, and they left the river, moving up into the Highlands of Leah. They hadn't spoken about where they were going since the previous evening, when the tacit understanding had been that they would debate the matter later. They hadn't, of course. Neither had brought the subject up again, Coll because they were moving in the direction he wanted to go anyway, and Par because he had decided that Coll was right that some thinking needed to be done before any trip back north into Callahorn was undertaken. Shady Vale was as good a place as any to complete that thinking.

Oddly enough, though they hadn't talked about the dreams or the old man or any of the rest of it since early that morning, they had begun separately to rethink their respective positions and to move closer together— each inwardly conceding that maybe the other made some sense after all.

By the time they began discussing matters again, they were no longer arguing. It was midafternoon, the summer day hot and sticky now, the sun a blinding white sphere before them as they walked, forcing them to shield their eyes protectively. The country was a mass of rolling hills, a carpet of grasses and wildflowers dotted with stands of broad-leafed trees and patches of scrub and rock. The mists that blanketed the Highlands year-round had retreated to the higher elevations in the face of the sun's brightness and clung to the tips of the ridgelines and bluffs like scattered strips of linen.

"I think that woodswoman was genuinely afraid of the old man," Par was saying as they climbed a long, gradual slope into a stand of ash. "I don't think she was pretending. No one's that good an actor."

Coll nodded. "I think you're right. I just said all that earlier about the two of them being in league to make you think. I can't help wondering, though, if the old man is telling us everything he knows. What I mostly remember about Allanon in the stories is that he was decidedly circumspect in his dealings with the Ohmsfords."

"He never told them everything, that's true."

"So maybe the old man is the same way."

They crested the hill, moved into the shade of the ash trees, dropped their rolled-up blankets wearily and stood looking out at the Highlands. Both were sweating freely, their tunics damp against their backs.

"We won't make Shady Vale tonight," Par said, settling to the ground against one of the trees.

"No, it doesn't look like it." Coll joined him, stretching until his bones cracked.

"I was thinking."

"Good for you."

"I was thinking about where we might spend the night. It would be nice to sleep in a bed for a change."

Coll laughed. "You won't get any argument out of me. Got any idea where we can find a bed out here in the middle of nowhere?"

Par turned slowly and looked at him. "Matter-of-fact, I do. Morgan's hunting lodge is just a few miles south. I bet we could borrow it for the night."

Coll frowned thoughtfully. "Yes, I bet we could."

Morgan Leah was the eldest son in a family whose ancestors had once been Kings of Leah. But the monarchy had been overthrown almost two hundred years ago when the Federation had expanded northward and simply consumed the Highlands in a single bite. There had been no Leah kings since, and the family had survived as gentlemen farmers and craftsmen over the years. The current head of the family, Kyle Leah, was a landholder living south of the city who bred beef cattle. Morgan, his oldest son, Par and Coll's closest friend, bred mostly mischief.

"You don't think Morgan will be around, do you?" Coll asked, grinning at the possibility.

Par grinned back. The hunting lodge was really a family possession, but Morgan was the one who used it the most. The last time the Ohmsford brothers had come into the Highlands they had stayed for a week at the lodge as Morgan's guests. They had camped, hunted and fished, but mostly they had spent their time recounting tales of Morgan's ongoing efforts to cause distress to the members of the Federation government-in-residence at Leah. Morgan Leah had the quickest mind and the fastest pair of hands in the Southland, and he harbored an abiding dislike for the army that occupied his land. Unlike Shady Vale, Leah was a major city and required watching. The Federation, after abolishing the monarchy, had installed the provisional governor and cabinet and stationed a garrison of soldiers to insure order. Morgan regarded that as a personal challenge. He took every opportunity that presented itself, and a few that didn't, to make life miserable for the officials that now lodged comfortably and without regard for proper right of ownership in his ancestral home. It was never a contest. Morgan was a positive genius at disruption and much too sharp to allow the Federation officials to suspect he was the thorn in their collective sides that they could not even find, let alone remove. On the last go-around, Morgan had trapped the governor and vice-governor in a private bathing court with a herd of carefully muddied pigs and jammed all the locks on the doors. It was a very small court and a whole lot of pigs. It took two hours to free them all, and Morgan insisted solemnly that by then it was hard to tell who was who.

The brothers regained their feet, hoisted their packs in place, and set off once more. The afternoon slipped away as the sun followed its path westward, but the air stayed quiet and the heat grew even more oppressive. The land at this elevation at midsummer was so dry that the grass crackled where they walked, the once-green blades dried to a brownish gray crust. Dust curled up in small puffs beneath their boots, and their mouths grew dry.

It was nearing sunset by the time they caught sight of the hunting lodge, a stone and timber building set back in a grouping of pines on a rise that overlooked the country west. Hot and sweating, they dumped their gear by the front door and went directly to the bathing springs nestled in the trees a hundred yards back. When they reached the springs, a cluster of clear blue pools that filled from beneath and emptied out into a sluggish little stream, they began stripping off their clothes immediately, heedless of anything but their by now overwhelming need to sink down into the inviting water.

Which was why they didn't see the mud creature until it was almost on top of them.

It rose up from the bushes next to them, vaguely manlike, encrusted in mud and roaring with a ferocity that shattered the stillness like glass. Coll gave a howl, sprang backward, lost his balance and tumbled headfirst into the springs. Par jerked away, tripped and rolled, and the creature was on top of him.

"Ahhhh! A tasty Valeman!" the creature rasped in a voice that was suddenly very familiar.

"Shades, Morgan!" Par twisted and turned and shoved the other away. "You scared me to death, confound it!"

Coll pulled himself out of the springs, still wearing boots and pants halfway off, and said calmly, "I thought it was only the Federation you intended to drive out of Leah, not your friends." He heaved himself up and brushed the water from his eyes.

Morgan Leah was laughing merrily from within his mud cocoon. "I apologize, I really do. But it was an opportunity no man could resist. Surely you can understand that!"

Par tried to wipe the mud from his clothes and finally gave up, stripping bare and carrying everything into the springs with him. He gave a sigh of relief, then glanced back at Morgan. "What in the world are you doing anyway?"

"Oh, the mud? Good for your skin." Morgan walked to the springs and lowered himself into the water gingerly. "There are mud baths about a mile back. I found them the other day quite by accident. Never knew they were here. I can tell you honestly that there is nothing like mud on your body on a hot day to cool you down. Better even than the springs. So I rolled about quite piglike, then hiked back here to wash off. That was when I heard you coming and decided to give you a proper Highlands greeting."

He ducked down beneath the water; when he surfaced, the mud monster had been replaced by a lean, sinewy youth approximately their own age with skin so sun-browned it was almost the color of chocolate, shoulder-length reddish hair, and clear gray eyes that looked out of a face that was at once both clever and guileless. "Behold!" he exclaimed and grinned.

"Marvelous," Par replied tonelessly.

"Oh, come now! Not every trick can be earth-shattering. Which reminds me." Morgan bent forward questioningly. He spent much of his time wearing an expression that suggested he was secretly amused about something, and he showed it to them now. "Aren't you two supposed to be up in Callahorn somewhere dazzling the natives? Wasn't that the last I heard of your plans? What are you doing here?"

"What are *you* doing here?" Coll shot back.

"Me? Oh, just another little misunderstanding involving the governor— or more accurately, I'm afraid, the governor's wife. They don't suspect me, of course—they never do. Still, it seemed a good time for a vacation." Morgan's grin widened. "But come on now, I asked you first. What's going on?"

He was not to be put off and there had never been any unshared secrets among the three in any case, so Par, with considerable help from Coll, told him what had happened to them since that night in Varfleet when Rimmer Dall and the Federation Seekers had come looking for them. He told him of the dreams that might have been sent by Allanon, of their encounter with the frightening woodswoman who might have been one of the Shadowen, and of the old man who had saved them and might have been Cogline.

"There are a good number of 'might have beens' in that story," the Highlander observed archly when they were finished. "Are you certain you're not making this all up? It would be a fine joke at my expense."

"I just wish we were," Coll replied ruefully.

"Anyway, we thought we'd spend the night here in a bed, then go on to the Vale tomorrow," Par explained.

Morgan trailed one finger through the water in front of him and shook his head. "I don't think I'd do that if I were you."

Par and Coll looked at each other.

"If the Federation wanted you badly enough to send Rimmer Dall all the way to Varfleet," Morgan continued, his eyes coming up suddenly to meet their own, "then don't you think it likely they might send him to Shady Vale as well?"

There was a long silence before Par finally said, "I admit, I hadn't thought of that."

Morgan stroked over to the edge of the springs, heaved himself out, and began wiping the water from his body. "Well, thinking has never been your strong point, my boy. Good thing you've got me for a friend. Let's walk back up to the lodge and I'll fix you something to eat—something besides fish for a change—and we'll talk about it."

They dried, washed out their clothes and returned to the lodge where Morgan set about preparing dinner. He cooked a wonderful stew filled with meat, carrots, potatoes, onions, and broth, and served it with hot bread and cold ale. They sat out under the pines at a table and benches and consumed the better part of their food and drink, the day finally beginning to cool as night approached and an evening breeze rustled down out of the hills. Morgan brought out pears and cheese for dessert, and they nibbled contentedly as the sky turned red, then deep purple, and finally darkened and filled with stars.

"I love the Highlands," Morgan said after they had been silent for a time. They were seated on the stone steps of the lodge now. "I could learn to love the city as well I expect, but not while it belongs to the Federation. I sometimes find myself wondering what it would have been like to live in the old home, before they took it from us. That was a long time ago, of course—six generations ago. No one remembers what it was like anymore. My father won't even talk about it. But here—well, this is still ours, this land. The Federation hasn't been able to take that away yet. There's just too much of it. Maybe that's why I love it so much—because it's the last thing my family has left from the old days."

"Besides the sword," Par reminded.

"Do you still carry that battered old relic?" Coll asked. "I keep thinking you will discard it in favor of something newer and better made."

Morgan glanced over. "Do you remember the stories that said the Sword of Leah was once magic?"

"Allanon himself was supposed to have made it so," Par confirmed.

"Yes, in the time of Rone Leah." Morgan furrowed his brow. "Sometimes I think it still is magic. Not as it once was, not as a weapon that could withstand Mord Wraiths and such, but in a different way. The scabbard has been replaced half-a-dozen times over the years, the hilt once or twice at least, and both are worn again. But the blade—ah, that blade! It is still as sharp and true as ever, almost as if it cannot age. Doesn't that require magic of a sort?"

The brothers nodded solemnly. "Magic sometimes changes in the way it works," Par said. "It grows and evolves. Perhaps that has happened with the Sword of Leah." He was thinking as he said it how the old man had told him he did not understand the magic at all and wondering if that were true.

"Well, truth is, no one wants the weapon in any case, not anymore." Morgan stretched like a cat and sighed. "No one wants anything that belongs to the old days, it seems. The reminders are too painful, I think. My father didn't say a word when I asked for the blade. He just gave it to me."

Coll reached over and gave the other a friendly shove. "Well, your father ought to be more careful to whom he hands out his weapons."

Morgan managed to look put upon. "Am I the one being asked to join the Movement?" he demanded. They laughed. "By the way. You mentioned the stranger gave you a ring. Mind if I take a look?"

Par reached into his tunic, fished out the ring with the hawk insigne and passed it over. Morgan took it and examined it carefully, then shrugged and handed it back. "I don't recognize it. But that doesn't necessarily mean anything. I hear there are a dozen outlaw bands within the Movement and they all change their markings regularly to confuse the Federation."

He took a long drink from his ale glass and leaned back again. "Sometimes I think I ought to go north and join them—quit wasting time here playing games with those fools who live in my house and govern my land and don't even know the history." He shook his head sadly and for a moment looked old.

Then he brightened. "But now about you." He swung his legs around and sat forward. "You can't risk going back until you're certain it's safe. So you'll stay here for a day or so and let me go ahead. I'll make certain the Federation hasn't gotten there before you. Fair enough?"

"More than fair," Par said at once. "Thanks, Morgan. But you have to promise to be careful."

"Careful? Of those Federation fools? Ha!" The Highlander grinned ear to ear. "I could step up and spit in their collective eye and it would still take them days to work it out! I haven't anything to fear from them!"

Par wasn't laughing. "Not in Leah, perhaps. But there may be Seekers in Shady Vale."

Morgan quit grinning. "Your point is well-taken. I'll be careful."

He drained the last of his ale and stood up. "Time for bed. I'll want to leave early."

Par and Coll stood up with him. Coll said, "What was it exactly that you did to the governor's wife?"

Morgan shrugged. "Oh, that? Nothing much. Someone said she didn't care for the Highlands air, that it made her queasy. So I sent her a perfume to sweeten her sense of smell. It was contained in a small vial of very delicate glass. I had it placed in her bed, a surprise for her. She accidently broke it when she lay on it."

His eyes twinkled. "Unfortunately, I somehow got the perfume mixed up with skunk oil."

The three of them looked at each other in the darkness and grinned like fools.

The Ohmsfords slept well that night, wrapped in the comfort and warmth of real beds with clean blankets and pillows. They could easily have slept until noon, but Morgan had them awake at dawn as he prepared to set out for Shady Vale. He brought out the Sword of Leah and showed it to them, its hilt and scabbard badly worn, but its blade as bright and new as the Highlander had claimed. Grinning in satisfaction at the looks on their faces, he strapped the weapon across one shoulder, stuck a long knife in the top of one boot, a hunting knife in his belt, and strapped an ash bow to his back.

He winked. "Never hurts to be prepared."

They saw him out the door and down the hill west for a short distance where he bade them goodbye. They were still sleepy-eyed and their own goodbyes were mixed with yawns.

"Go on back to bed," Morgan advised. "Sleep as long as you like. Relax and don't worry. I'll be back in a couple of days." He waved as he moved off, a tall, lean figure silhouetted against the still-dark horizon, brimming with his usual self-confidence.

"Be careful!" Par called after him.

Morgan laughed. "Be careful yourself!"

The brothers took the Highlander's advice and went back to bed, slept until afternoon, then wasted the remainder of the day just lying about. They did better the second day, rising early, bathing in the springs, exploring the countryside in a futile effort to find the mud baths, cleaning out the hunting lodge, and preparing and eating a dinner of wild fowl and rice. They talked a long time that night about the old man and the dreams, the magic and the Seekers, and what they should do with their immediate future. They did not argue, but they did not reach any decisions either.

The third day turned cloudy and by nightfall it was raining. They sat before the fire they had built in the great stone hearth and practiced the storytelling for a long time, working on some of the more obscure tales, trying to make the images of Par's song and the words of Coll's story mesh. There was no sign of Morgan Leah. In spite of their unspoken mutual resolve not to do so, they began to worry.

On the fourth day, Morgan returned. It was late afternoon when he appeared, and the brothers were seated on the floor in front of the fire repairing the bindings on one of the dinner table chairs when the door opened suddenly and he was there. It had been raining steadily all day, and the Highlander was soaked through, dripping water everywhere as he lowered his backpack and weapons to the floor and shoved the door closed behind him.

"Bad news," he said at once. His rust-colored hair was plastered against his head, and the bones of his chiseled features glistened with rainwater. He seemed heedless of his condition as he crossed the room to confront them.

Par and Coll rose slowly from where they had been working. "You

can't go back to the Vale," Morgan said quietly. "There are Federation soldiers everywhere. I can't be certain if there are Seekers as well, but I
wouldn't be surprised. The village is under 'Federation Protection'—that's
the euphemism they use for armed occupation. They're definitely waiting
for you. I asked a few questions and found out right away; no one's making
any secret of it. Your parents are under house arrest. I think they're okay,
but I couldn't risk trying to talk to them. I'm sorry. There would have been
too many questions."

He took a deep breath. "Someone wants you very badly, my friends."

Par and Coll looked at each other, and there was no attempt by either
to disguise the fear. "What are we going to do?" Par asked softly.

"I've been thinking about that the whole way back," Morgan said. He
reached over and put a hand on his friend's slim shoulder. "So I'll tell you
what we're going to do—and I do mean 'we' because I figure I'm in this
thing with you now."

His hand tightened. "We're going east to look for Walker Boh."

Morgan Leah could be very persuasive when he chose, and he
proved it that night in the rain-shrouded Highlands to Par and
Coll.

He obviously had given the matter a great deal of thought, just as he
claimed he had, and his reasoning was quite thorough. Simply stated, it was
all a matter of choices. He took just enough time to strip away his wet
clothing and dry off before seating the brothers cross-legged before the
warmth of the fireplace with glasses of ale and hot bread in hand to hear his
explanation.

He started with what they knew. They knew they could not go back to
Shady Vale—not now and maybe not for a long time. They could not go
back to Callahorn either. Matter of fact, they could not go much of anywhere they might be expected to go because, if the Federation had expended this much time and effort to find them so far, they were hardly
likely to stop now. Rimmer Dall was known to be a tenacious enforcer. He
had personally involved himself in this hunt, and he would not give it up
easily. The Seekers would be looking for the brothers everywhere Federation rule extended—and that was a long, long way. Par and Coll could consider themselves, for all intents and purposes, to be outlaws.

So what were they to do? Since they could not go anyplace where they
were expected, they must go someplace they were not expected. The trick,

of course, was not to go just anywhere, but to go where they might accomplish something useful.

"After all, you could stay here if you chose, and you might not be discovered for who-knows-how-long because the Federation wouldn't know enough to look for you in the Highlands." He shrugged. "It might even be fun for a while. But what would it accomplish? Two months, four months, whatever, you would still be outlaws, you would still be unable to go home, and nothing would have changed. Doesn't make sense, does it? What you need to do is to take control of things. Don't wait for events to catch up with you; go out and meet them head-on!"

What he meant was that they should attempt to solve the riddle of the dreams. There was nothing they could do about the fact that the Federation was hunting them, that soldiers occupied Shady Vale, or that they were perceived to be outlaws. One day, all that might change—but not in the immediate future. The dreams, on the other hand, were something with which they might be able to come to grips. If the dreams were the real thing, they were worth knowing more about. The old man had told them to come to the Hadeshorn on the first night of the new moon. They hadn't wanted to do that before for two very sound reasons. First, they didn't know enough about the dreams to be certain they were real, and second, there were only the two of them and they might be placing themselves in real danger by going.

"So why not do something that might ease those concerns," the Highlander finished. "Why not go east and find Walker Boh. You said the old man told you the dreams had been sent to Walker as well. Doesn't it make sense to find out what he thinks about all this? Is he planning on going? The old man was going to talk to him, too. Whether that's happened or not, Walker is certain to have an opinion on whether the dreams are real or not. I always thought your uncle was a strange bird, I'll admit, but I never thought he was stupid. And we all know the stories about him. If he has the use of any part of the Shannara magic, now might be a good time to find out."

He took a long drink and leaned forward, jabbing his finger at them. "If Walker believes in the dreams and decides to go to the Hadeshorn, then you might be more inclined to go as well. There would be four of us then. Anything out there that might cause trouble would have to think twice."

He shrugged. "Even if you decide not to go, you'll have satisfied yourselves better than you would have by just hiding out here or somewhere like here. Shades, the Federation won't think to look for you in the Anar! That's just about the last place they'll think to look for you!"

He took another drink, bit off a piece of fresh bread and sat back, eyes questioning. He had that look on his face again, that expression that suggested he knew something they didn't and it amused him no end. "Well?" he said finally.

The brothers were silent. Par was thinking about his uncle, remembering the whispered stories about Walker Boh. His uncle was a self-professed student of life who claimed he had visions; he insisted he could see and feel things others could not. There were rumors that he practiced magic of a sort different from any known. Eventually, he had gone away from them, leaving the Vale for the Eastland. That had been almost ten years ago. Par and Coll had been very young, but Par still remembered.

Coll cleared his throat suddenly, eased himself forward and shook his head. Par was certain his brother was going to tell Morgan how ridiculous his idea was, but instead he asked, "How do we go about finding Walker?"

Par looked at Morgan and Morgan looked at Par, and there was an instant of shared astonishment. Both had anticipated that Coll would prove intractable, that he would set himself squarely in the path of such an outrageous plan, and that he would dismiss it as foolhardy. Neither had expected this.

Coll caught the look that passed between them and said, "I wouldn't say what I was thinking, if I were you. Neither of you knows me as well as he thinks. Now how about an answer to my question?"

Morgan quickly masked the flicker of guilt that passed across his eyes. "We'll go first to Culhaven. I have a friend there who will know where Walker is."

"Culhaven?" Coll frowned. "Culhaven is Federation-occupied."

"But safe enough for us," Morgan insisted. "The Federation won't be looking for you there, and we need only stay a day or two. Anyway, we won't be out in the open much."

"And our families? Won't they wonder what's happened to us?"

"Not mine. My father is used to not seeing me for weeks at a time. He's already made up his mind that I'm undependable. And Jaralan and Mirianna are better off not knowing what you're about. They're undoubtedly worried enough as it is."

"What about Wren?" Par asked.

Morgan shook his head. "I don't know how to find Wren. If she's still with the Rovers, she could be anywhere." He paused. "Besides, I don't know how much help Wren would be to us. She was only a girl when she left the Vale, Par. We don't have time to find both. Walker Boh seems a better bet."

Par nodded slowly. He looked uncertainly at Coll and Coll looked back. "What do you think?" he asked.

Coll sighed. "I think we should have stayed in Shady Vale in the first place. I think we should have stayed in bed."

"Oh, come now, Coll Ohmsford!" Morgan exclaimed cheerfully. "Think of the adventure! I'll look out for you, I promise!"

Coll glanced at Par. "Should I feel comforted by that?"

Par took a deep breath. "I say we go."

Coll studied him intently, then nodded. "I say what have we got to lose?"

So the issue was decided. Thinking it over later, Par guessed he was not surprised. After all, it was indeed a matter of choices, and any way you looked at it the other choices available had little to recommend them.

They slept that night at the lodge and spent the following morning outfitting themselves with foodstuffs stored in the cold lockers and provisions from the closets. There were weapons, blankets, travel cloaks, and extra clothing (some of it not a bad fit) for the brothers. There were cured meats, vegetables and fruits, and cheese and nuts. There were cooking implements, water pouches, and medications. They took what they needed, since the lodge was well-stocked, and by noon they were ready to set out.

The day was gray and clouded when they stepped through the front door and secured it behind them; the rain had turned to drizzle, the ground beneath their feet no longer hard and dusty, but as damp and yielding as a sponge. They made their way north again toward the Rainbow Lake, intent on reaching its shores by nightfall. Morgan's plan for making the first leg of their journey was simple. They would retrieve the skiff the brothers had concealed earlier at the mouth of the Rappahalladran and this time follow the southern shoreline, staying well clear of the Lowlands of Clete, the Black Oaks, and the Mist Marsh, all of which were filled with dangers best avoided. When they reached the far shore, they would locate the Silver River and follow it east to Culhaven.

It was a good plan, but not without its problems. Morgan would have preferred to navigate the Rainbow Lake at night when they would be less conspicuous, using the moon and stars to guide them. But it quickly became apparent as the day drew to a close and the lake came in sight that there would be no moon or stars that night and as a result no light at all to show them the way. If they tried to cross in this weather, there was a very real possibility of them drifting too far south and becoming entangled in the dangers they had hoped to avoid.

So, after relocating the skiff and assuring themselves that she was still seaworthy, they spent their first night out in a chill, sodden campsite set close back against the shoreline of the lake, dreaming of warmer, more agreeable times. Morning brought a slight change in the weather. It stopped raining entirely and grew warm, but the clouds lingered, mixing with a mist that shrouded everything from one end of the lake to the other.

Par and Coll studied the morass dubiously.

"It will burn off," Morgan assured them, anxious to be off.

They shoved the skiff out onto the water, rowed until they found a breeze, and hoisted their makeshift sail. The clouds lifted a few feet and the skies brightened a shade, but the mist continued to cling to the surface of the lake like sheep's wool and blanketed everything in an impenetrable haze. Noon came and went with little change, and finally even Morgan admitted he had no idea where they were.

By nightfall, they were still on the lake and the light was gone completely. The wind died and they sat unmoving in the stillness. They ate a little food, mostly because it was necessary and not so much because anyone was particularly hungry, then they took turns trying to sleep.

"Remember the stories about Shea Ohmsford and a thing that lived in the Mist Marsh?" Coll whispered to Par at one point. "I fully expect to discover firsthand whether or not they were true!"

The night crept by, filled with silence, blackness, and a sense of impending doom. But morning arrived without incident, the mist lifted, the skies brightened, and the friends found that they were safely in the middle of the lake pointing north. Relaxed now, they joked about their own and the others' fears, turned the boat east again, and took turns rowing while they waited for a breeze to come up. After a time, the mist burned away altogether, the clouds broke up, and they caught sight of the south shore. A northeasterly breeze sprang up around noon, and they stowed the oars and set sail.

Time drifted, and the skiff sped east. Daylight was disappearing into nightfall when they finally reached the far shore and beached their craft in a wooded cove close to the mouth of the Silver River. They shoved the skiff into a reed-choked inlet, carefully secured it with stays, and began their walk inland. It was nearing sunset by now, and the skies turned a peculiar pinkish color as the fading light reflected off a new mix of low-hanging clouds and trailers of mist. It was still quiet in the forest, the night sounds waiting expectantly for the day to end before beginning their symphony. The river churned beside them sluggishly as they walked, choked with rainwater and debris. Shadows reached out to them, the trees seemed to draw closer together and the light faded. Before long, they were enveloped in darkness.

They talked briefly of the King of the Silver River.

"Gone like all the rest of the magic," Par declared, picking his way carefully along the rain-slicked trail. They could see better this night, though not as well as they might have liked; the moon and stars were playing hide-and-seek with the clouds. "Gone like the Druids, the Elves— everything but the stories."

"Maybe, maybe not," Morgan philosophized. "Travelers still claim they see him from time to time, an old man with a lantern, lending guidance and protection. They admit his reach is not what it was, though. He claims only the river and a small part of the land about it. The rest belongs to us."

"The rest belongs to the Federation, like everything else!" Coll snorted.

Morgan kicked at a piece of deadwood and sent it spinning into the dark. "I know a man who claims to have spoken to the King of the Silver River—a drummer who sells fancy goods between the Highlands and the Anar. He comes through this country all the time, and he said that once he lost his way in the Battlemound and this old man appeared with his lantern and took him clear." Morgan shook his head. "I never knew whether to believe the man or not. Drummers make better storytellers than truth-sayers."

"I think he's gone," Par said, filled with a sense of sadness at his own certainty. "The magic doesn't last when it isn't practiced or believed in. The King of the Silver River hasn't had the benefit of either. He's just a story now, just another legend that no one but you and I and Coll and maybe a handful of others believe was ever real."

"We Ohmsfords always believe," Coll finished softly.

They walked on in silence, listening to the night sounds, following the trail as it wound eastward. They would not reach Culhaven that night, but they were not yet ready to stop either, so they simply kept on without bothering to discuss it. The woods thickened as they moved farther inland, deeper into the lower Anar, and the pathway narrowed as scrub began to inch closer from the darkness. The river turned angry as it passed through a series of rapids, and the land grew rough, a maze of gullies and hillocks peppered with stray boulders and stumps.

"The road to Culhaven isn't what it once was," Morgan muttered at one point. Par and Coll had no idea if that was so or not since neither had ever been to the Anar. They glanced at each other, but gave no reply.

Then the trail ended abruptly, blocked by a series of fallen trees. A secondary pathway swung away from the river and ran off into the deep woods. Morgan hesitated, then took it. The trees closed about overhead, their branches shutting out all but a trickle of moonlight, and the three friends were forced to grope their way ahead. Morgan was muttering again, inaudibly this time, although the tone of his voice was unmistakable. Vines and overhanging brush were slapping at them as they passed, and they were forced to duck their heads. The woods began to smell oddly fetid, as if the undergrowth was decaying. Par tried to hold his breath against the stench, irritated by its pervasiveness. He wanted to move faster, but Morgan was in the lead and already moving as fast as he could.

"It's as if something died in here," Coll whispered from behind him.

Something triggered in Par's memory. He remembered the smell that had emanated from the cottage of the woodswoman the old man had warned them was a Shadowen. The smell here was exactly the same.

In the next instant, they emerged from the tangle of the forest into a clearing that was ringed by the lifeless husks of trees and carpeted with mulch, deadwood, and scattered bones. A single stagnant pool of water bubbled at its center in the fashion of a cauldron heated by fire. Gimlet-eyed scavengers peered out at them from the shadows.

The companions came to an uncertain halt. "Morgan, this is just like it was . . ." Par began and then stopped.

The Shadowen stepped noiselessly from the trees and faced them. Par never questioned what it was; he knew instinctively. Skepticism and disbelief were erased in an instant's time, the discarded trappings of years of certainty that Shadowen were what practical men said they were—rumors and fireside tales. Perhaps it was the old man's warning whispering in his ear that triggered his conversion. Perhaps it was simply the look of the thing. Whatever it was, the truth that was left him was chilling and unforgettable.

This Shadowen was entirely different than the last. It was a huge, shambling thing, manlike but twice the size of a normal man, its body covered in coarse, shaggy hair, its massive limbs ending in paws that were splayed and clawed, its body hunched over at the shoulders like a gorilla. There was a face amid all that hair, but it could scarcely be called human. It was wrinkled and twisted about a mouth from which teeth protruded like stunted bones, and it hid within leathery folds eyes that peered out with insistent dislike and burned like fire. It stood looking at them, studying them in the manner of a slow-witted brute.

"Oh-oh," Morgan said softly.

The Shadowen came forward a step, a hitching movement that suggested a stalking cat. "Why are you here?" it rasped from some deep, empty well within.

"We took a wrong . . ." Morgan began.

"You trespass on what is mine!" the other cut him short, teeth snapping wickedly. "You cause me to be angered!"

Morgan glanced back at Par and the Valeman quickly mouthed the word "Shadowen" and glanced in turn at Coll. Coll was pale and tense. Like Par, he was no longer questioning.

"I will have one of you in payment!" the Shadowen growled. "Give me one of you! Give me!"

The three friends looked at each other once more. They knew there was only one way out of this. There was no old man to come to their aid this time. There was no one but themselves.

Morgan reached back and slid the Sword of Leah from its scabbard. The blade reflected brightly in the eyes of the monster. "Either you let us pass safely . . ." he began.

He never finished. The Shadowen launched itself at him with a shriek, bounding across the little clearing with frightening swiftness. He was on top of Morgan almost at once, claws ripping. Even so, the Highlander managed to bring the flat of the blade about in time to deflect the blow and knock the creature off-balance, driving it sideways so that its attack missed. Coll slashed at it with the short sword he was carrying as he leaped past toward the pool, and Par struck at it with the magic of the wishsong, clouding its vision with a swarm of buzzing insects.

The Shadowen surged back to its feet with a roar of anger, flailed madly at the air, then rushed them once more. It caught Morgan a stinging blow as the Highlander jumped aside and knocked him sprawling. The Shadowen turned, and Coll struck it so hard with the short sword that he severed one arm above the elbow. The Shadowen reeled away, then darted back, snatched up its severed limb and retreated again. Carefully, it placed its arm back against its shoulder. There was sudden movement, an entwining of sinew and muscle and bone, like snakes moving. The limb had reattached itself.

The Shadowen hissed in delight.

Then it came at them. Par tried to slow it with images of wolves, but the Shadowen barely saw them. It slammed into Morgan, shoving past the blade of his sword, throwing the Highlander back. He might have been lost then if not for the Ohmsfords, who flung themselves on the beast and bore it to the ground. They held it there for only an instant. It heaved upward, freed itself, and sent them flying. One great arm caught Par across the face, snapping his head back, causing flashes to cloud his vision as he tumbled away. He could hear the thing coming for him, and he threw out every image he could muster, rolling and crawling to regain his feet. He could hear Coll's cry of warning and a series of grunts. He pushed himself upright, forcing his vision to clear.

The Shadowen was right in front of him, clawed forelimbs spread wide to embrace him. Coll lay slumped against a tree a dozen paces to his left. There was no sign of Morgan. Par backed away slowly, searching for an escape. There was no time for the magic now. The creature was too close. He felt the rough bark of a tree trunk jammed against his back.

Then Morgan was there, launching himself from the darkness, crying out "Leah, Leah" as he hammered into the Shadowen. There was blood on his face and clothing, and his eyes were bright with anger and determination. Down came the Sword of Leah, an arc of glittering metal—and something wondrous happened. The sword struck the Shadowen full on and burst into fire.

Par flinched and threw one arm across his face protectively. No, he thought in amazement, it wasn't fire he was seeing, it was magic!

The magic happened all at once, without warning, and it seemed to freeze the combatants in the circle of its light. The Shadowen stiffened and screamed, a shriek of agony and disbelief. The magic spread from the Sword of Leah into the creature's body, ripping through it like a razor through cloth. The Shadowen shuddered, seemed to sag inward against itself, lost definition, and began to disintegrate. Quickly Par dropped under the thing and rolled free. He saw it heave upward desperately, then flare as brightly as the weapon that was killing it and disappear into ash.

The Sword of Leah winked instantly into darkness. The air was a blanket of sudden silence. Smoke floated in a cloud across the little clearing, its smell thick and pungent. The stagnant pool bubbled once and went still.

Morgan Leah dropped to one knee, the sword falling to the ground before him, striking the little mound of ash and flaring once. He flinched and then shuddered. "Shades!" he whispered, his voice choked with astonishment. "The power I felt, it was . . . I never thought it possible . . ."

Par came to him at once, knelt beside him and saw the other's face, cut and bruised and drained of blood. He took the Highlander in his arms and held him.

"It still has the magic, Morgan!" he whispered, excited that such a thing could be. "All these years, and no one has known it, but it still has the magic!" Morgan looked at him uncomprehendingly. "Don't you see? The magic has been sleeping since the time of Allanon! There's been no need for it! It took another magic to bring it awake! It took a creature like the Shadowen! That's why nothing happened until the magics touched . . ."

He trailed off as Coll stumbled over to them and dropped down as well. One arm hung limply. "Think I broke it," he muttered.

He hadn't, but he had bruised it severely enough that Par felt it wise to bind it against his body in a cradle for a day or so. They used their drinking water to wash themselves, bandaged their cuts and scrapes, picked up their weapons, and stood looking at each other. "The old man said there would be lots of things hunting us," Par whispered.

"I don't know if that thing was hunting us or if we were just unlucky enough to stumble on it." Coll's voice was ragged. "I do know I don't want to run across any more like it."

"But if we do," Morgan Leah said quietly and stopped. "If we do, we have the means now to deal with them." And he fingered the blade of the Sword of Leah as he might have the soft curve of a woman's face.

Par would never forget what he felt at that moment. The memory of it would overshadow even that of their battle with the Shadowen, a tiny piece of time preserved in perfect still life. What he felt was jealousy. Before, he had been the one who had possessed real magic. Now it was Morgan Leah. He still had the wishsong, of course, but its magic paled in comparison to that of the Highlander's sword. It was the sword that had destroyed the Shadowen. Par's best images had proven to be little more than an irritation.

It made him wonder if the wishsong had any real use at all.

7

Par remembered something later that night that forced him to come to grips with what he was feeling toward Morgan. They had continued on to Culhaven, anxious to complete their journey, willing to walk all night and another day if need be rather than attempt one moment's sleep in those woods. They had worked their way back to the main pathway where it ran parallel to the Silver River and pushed eastward. As they trudged on, nudged forward by apprehension one step, dragged backward by weariness the next, buffeted and tossed, their thoughts strayed like grazing cattle to sweeter pastures, and Par Ohmsford found himself thinking of the songs.

That was when he remembered that the legends had it that the power of the Sword of Leah was literally two-edged. The sword had been made magic by Allanon in the time of Brin Ohmsford while the Druid was journeying east with the Valegirl and her would-be protector, Morgan's ancestor, Rone Leah. The Druid had dipped the sword's blade into the forbidden waters of the Hadeshorn and changed forever its character. It became more than a simple blade; it became a talisman that could withstand even the Mord Wraiths. But the magic was like all the magics of old; it was both blessing and curse. Its power was addictive, causing the user to become increasingly dependent. Brin Ohmsford had recognized the danger, but her warnings to Rone Leah had gone unheeded. In their final confrontation with the dark magic, it was her own power and Jair's that had saved them and put an end to further need for the magic of the sword. There was no record of what had become of the weapon after—only that it was not required and therefore not used again.

Until now. And now it seemed it might be Par's obligation to warn Morgan of the danger of further use of the sword's magic. But how was he to do that? Shades, Morgan Leah was his best friend next to Coll, and this newfound magic Par envied so had just saved their lives! He was knotted up with guilt and frustration at the jealousy he was feeling. How was he supposed to tell Morgan that he shouldn't use it? It didn't matter that there might be good reason to do so; it still sounded impossibly grudging. Besides, they would need the magic of the Sword of Leah if they encountered any further Shadowen. And there was every reason to expect that they might.

He struggled with his dilemma only briefly. He simply could not ignore his discomfort and the vivid memory of that creature breathing over him. He decided to keep quiet. Perhaps there would be no need to speak out. If there was, he would do so then. He put the matter aside.

They talked little that night, and when they did it was mostly about the Shadowen. There was no longer any doubt in their minds that these beings were real. Even Coll did not equivocate when speaking of what it was that had attacked them. But acceptance did not bring enlightenment. The Shadowen remained a mystery to them. They did not know where they had come from or why. They did not even know what they were. They had no idea as to the source of their power, though it seemed it must derive from some form of magic. If these creatures were hunting them, they did not know what they could do about it. They knew only that the old man had been right when he had warned them to be careful.

It was just after dawn when they reached Culhaven, emerging aching and sleepy-eyed from the fading night shadows of the forest into the half-light of the new day. Clouds hung across the Eastland skies, scraping the treetops as they eased past, lending the Dwarf village beneath a gray and wintry cast. The companions stumbled to a halt, stretched, yawned, and looked about. The trees had thinned before them and there was a gathering of cottages with smoke curling out of stone chimneys, sheds filled with tools and wagons, and small yards with animals staked and penned. Vegetable gardens the size of thumbprints fought to control tiny patches of earth as weeds attacked from everywhere. Everything seemed crammed together, the cottages and sheds, the animals, the gardens and the forest, each on top of the other. Nothing looked cared for; paint was peeling and chipped, mortar and stone were cracked, fences broken and sagging, animals shaggy and unkempt, and gardens and the weeds grown so much into each other as to be almost indistinguishable.

Women drifted through doors and past windows, old mostly, some with laundry to hang, some with cooking to tend, all with the same ragged, disheveled look. Children played in the yards, on the pathways, and in the roads, as shabby and wild as mountain sheep.

Morgan caught Par and Coll staring and said, "I forgot—the Culhaven you're familiar with is the one you tell about in your stories. Well, all that's in the past. I know you're tired, but, now that you're here, there are things you need to see."

He took them down a pathway that led into the village. The housing grew quickly worse, the cottages replaced by shacks, the gardens and animals disappearing entirely. The path became a roadway, rutted and pocked from lack of repair, filled with refuse and stones. There were more children here, playing as the others had, and there were more women working at household chores, exchanging a few words now and then with each other and the children, but withdrawn mostly into themselves. They watched guardedly as the three strangers walked past, suspicion and fear mirrored in their eyes.

"Culhaven, the most beautiful city in the Eastland, the heart and soul of the Dwarf nation," Morgan mused quietly. He didn't look at them. "I know the stories. It was a sanctuary, an oasis, a haven of gentle souls, a monument to what pride and hard work could accomplish." He shook his head. "Well, this is the way it is now."

A few of the children came up to them and begged for coins. Morgan shook his head gently, patted one or two, and moved past.

They turned off into a lane that led down to a stream clogged with trash and sewage. Children walked the banks, poking idly at what floated past. A walkway took them across to the far bank. The air was fetid with the smell of rotting things.

"Where are all the men?" Par asked.

Morgan looked over. "The lucky ones are dead. The rest are in the mines or in work camps. That's why everything looks the way it does. There's no one left in this city but children, old people, and a few women." He stopped walking. "That's how it has been for fifty years. That's how the Federation wants it. Come this way."

He led them down a narrow pathway behind a series of cottages that seemed better tended. These homes were freshly painted, the stone scrubbed, the mortar intact, the gardens and lawns immaculate. Dwarves worked the yards and rooms here as well, younger women mostly, the tasks the same, but the results as different from before as night is to day. Everything here was bright and new and clean.

Morgan took them up a rise to a small park, easing carefully into a stand of fir. "See those?" he pointed to the well-tended cottages. Par and Coll nodded. "That's where the Federation soldiers and officials garrisoned here live. The younger, stronger Dwarf women are forced to work for them. Most are forced to live with them as well." He glanced at them meaningfully.

They walked from the park down a hillside that led toward the center of the community. Shops and businesses replaced homes, and the foot traffic grew thick. The Dwarves they saw here were engaged in selling and buying, but again they were mostly old and few in number. The streets were clogged with outlanders come to trade. Federation soldiers patrolled everywhere.

Morgan steered the brothers down byways where they wouldn't be noticed, pointing out this, indicating that, his voice at once both bitter and ironic. "Over there. That's the silver exchange. The Dwarves are forced to extract the silver from the mines, kept underground most of the time—you know what that means—then compelled to sell it at Federation prices and turn the better part of the proceeds over to their keepers in the form of taxes. And the animals belong to the Federation as well—on loan, supposedly. The Dwarves are strictly rationed. Down there, that's the market. All the vegetables and fruits are grown and sold by the Dwarves, and the profits of sale disposed of in the same manner as everything else. That's what it's like here now. That's what being a 'protectorate' means for these people."

He stopped them at the far end of the street, well back from a ring of onlookers crowded about a platform on which young Dwarf men and women chained and bound were being offered for sale. They stood looking for a moment and Morgan said, "They sell off the ones they don't need to do the work."

He took them from the business district to a hillside that rose above the city in a broad sweep. The hillside was blackened and stripped of life, a vast smudge against a treeless skyline. It had been terraced once, and what was left of the buttressing poked out of the earth like gravestones.

"Do you know what this is?" he asked them softly. They shook their heads. "This is what is left of the Meade Gardens. You know the story. The Dwarves built the Gardens with special earth hauled in from the farmlands, earth as black as coal. Every flower known to the races was planted and tended. My father said it was the most beautiful thing he had ever seen. He was here once, when he was a boy."

Morgan was quiet a moment as they surveyed the ruin, then said, "The Federation burned the Gardens when the city fell. They burn them anew every year so that nothing will ever grow again."

As they walked away, veering back toward the outskirts of the village, Par asked, "How do you know all this, Morgan? Your father?"

Morgan shook his head. "My father hasn't been back since that first visit. I think he prefers not to see what it looks like now, but to remember it as it was. No, I have friends here who tell me what life for the Dwarves is like—that part of life I can't see for myself whenever I come over. I haven't told you much about that, have I? Well, it's only been recently, the last half year or so. I'll tell you about it later."

They retraced their steps to the poorer section of the village, following a new roadway that was nevertheless as worn and rutted as the others. After a short walk, they turned into a walkway that led up to a rambling stone and wood structure that looked as if once it might have been an inn of some sort. It rose three stories and was wrapped by a covered porch filled

with swings and rockers. The yard was bare, but clear of debris and filled
with children playing.

"A school?" Par guessed aloud.

Morgan shook his head. "An orphanage."

He led them through the groups of children, onto the porch and
around to a side door settled well back in the shadows of an alcove. He
knocked on the door and waited. When the door opened a crack, he said,
"Can you spare a poor man some food?"

"Morgan!" The door flew open. An elderly Dwarf woman stood in
the opening, gray-haired and aproned, her face bluff and squarish, her
smile working its way past lines of weariness and disappointment. "Morgan
Leah, what a pleasant surprise! How are you, youngster?"

"I am my father's pride and joy, as always," Morgan replied with a grin.
"May we come in?"

"Of course. Since when have you needed to ask?" The woman stepped
aside and ushered them past, hugging Morgan and beaming at Par and Coll,
who smiled back uncertainly. She shut the door behind them and said, "So
you would like something to eat, would you?"

"We would gladly give our lives for the opportunity," Morgan declared
with a laugh. "Granny Elise, these are my friends, Par and Coll Ohmsford
of Shady Vale. They are temporarily . . . homeless," he finished.

"Aren't we all," Granny Elise replied gruffly. She extended a callused
hand to the brothers, who each gripped it in his own. She examined them
critically. "Been wrestling with bears, have you, Morgan?"

Morgan touched his face experimentally, tracing the cuts and scrapes.
"Something worse than that, I'm afraid. The road to Culhaven is not what
it once was."

"Nor is Culhaven. Have a seat, child—you and your friends. I'll bring
you a plate of muffins and fruit."

There were several long tables with benches in the center of the rather
considerable kitchen and the three friends chose the nearest and sat. The
kitchen was large but rather dark, and the furnishings were poor. Granny
Elise bustled about industriously, providing the promised breakfast and
glasses of some sort of extracted juice. "I'd offer you milk, but I have to ration what I have for the children," she apologized.

They were eating hungrily when a second woman appeared, a Dwarf
as well and older still, small and wizened, with a sharp face and quick, birdlike movements that never seemed to cease. She crossed the room matter-
of-factly on seeing Morgan, who rose at once and gave her a small peck on
the cheek.

"Auntie Jilt," Morgan introduced her.

"Most pleased," she announced in a way that suggested they might
need convincing. She seated herself next to Granny Elise and immediately
began work on some needlepoint she had brought with her into the room,
fingers flying.

"These ladies are mothers to the world," Morgan explained as he returned to his meal. "Me included, though I'm not an orphan like their other charges. They adopted me because I'm irresistibly charming."

"You begged like the rest of them the first time we saw you, Morgan Leah!" Auntie Jilt snapped, never looking up from her work. "That is the only reason we took you in—the only reason we take any of them in."

"Sisters, though you'd never know it," Morgan quickly went on. "Granny Elise is like a goose-down comforter, all soft and warm. But Auntie Jilt— well, Auntie Jilt is more like a stone pallet!"

Auntie Jilt sniffed. "Stone lasts a good deal longer than goose down in these times. And both longer still than Highland syrup!"

Morgan and Granny Elise laughed, Auntie Jilt joined in after a moment, and Par and Coll found themselves smiling as well. It seemed odd to do so, their thoughts still filled with images of the village and its people, the sounds of the orphaned children playing outside a pointed reminder of how things really stood. But there was something indomitable about these old women, something that transcended the misery and poverty, something that whispered of promise and hope.

When breakfast was finished, Granny Elise busied herself at the sink and Auntie Jilt departed to check on the children. Morgan whispered, "These ladies have been operating the orphanage for almost thirty years. The Federation lets them alone because they help keep the children out from underfoot. Nice, huh? There are hundreds of children with no parents, so the orphanage is always full. When the children are old enough, they are smuggled out. If they are allowed to stay too long, the Federation sends them to the work camps or sells them. Every so often, the ladies guess wrong." He shook his head. "I don't know how they stand it. I would have gone mad long ago."

Granny Elise came back and sat with them. "Has Morgan told you how we met?" she asked the Ohmsfords. "Oh, well, it was quite something. He brought us food and clothes for the children, he gave us money to buy what we could, and he helped guide a dozen children north to be placed with families in the free territories."

"Oh, for goodness sake, Granny!" Morgan interjected, embarrassed.

"Exactly! And he works around the house now and then when he visits, too," she added, ignoring him. "We have become his own private little charity, haven't we, Morgan?"

"That reminds me—here." Morgan reached into his tunic and extracted a small pouch. The contents jingled as he passed it over. "I won a wager a week or so back about some perfume." He winked at the Valemen.

"Bless you, Morgan." Granny Elise rose and came around to kiss him on the cheek. "You seem quite exhausted—all of you. There are spare beds in the back and plenty of blankets. You can sleep until dinnertime."

She ushered them from the kitchen to a small room at the rear of the big house where there were several beds, a wash basin, blankets, and towels.

Par glanced around, noticing at once that the windows were shuttered and the curtains carefully drawn.

Granny Elise noticed the look that the Valeman exchanged with his brother. "Sometimes, my guests don't wish to draw attention to themselves," she said quietly. Her eyes were sharp. "Isn't that the case with you?"

Morgan went over and kissed her gently. "Perceptive as always, old mother. We'll need a meeting with Steff. Can you take care of it?"

Granny Elise looked at him a moment, then nodded wordlessly, kissed him back and slipped from the room.

It was twilight when they woke, the shuttered room filled with shadows and silence. Granny Elise appeared, her bluff face gentle and reassuring, slipping through the room on cat's feet as she touched each and whispered that it was time, before disappearing back the way she had come. Morgan Leah and the Ohmsfords rose to find their clothes clean and fresh-smelling again. Granny Elise had been busy while they slept.

While they were dressing, Morgan said, "We'll meet with Steff tonight. He's part of the Dwarf Resistance, and the Resistance has eyes and ears everywhere. If Walker Boh still lives in the Eastland, even in the deepest part of the Anar, Steff will know."

He finished pulling on his boots and stood up. "Steff was one of the orphans Granny took in. He's like a son to her. Other than Auntie Jilt, he's the only family she has left."

They went out from the sleeping room and down the hall to the kitchen. The children had already finished dinner and retired to their rooms on the upper two stories, save for a handful of tiny ones that Auntie Jilt was in the process of feeding, patiently spooning soup to first one mouth, then the next and so on until it was time to begin the cycle all over again. She looked up as they entered and nodded wordlessly.

Granny Elise sat them down at one of the long tables and brought them plates of food and glasses of harsh ale. From overhead came the sounds of thumping and yelling as the children played. "It is hard to supervise so many when there is only the two of us," she apologized, serving Coll a second helping of meat stew. "But the women we hire to help out never seem to stay very long."

"Were you able to get a message to Steff?" Morgan asked quietly.

Granny Elise nodded, her smile suddenly sad. "I wish I could see more of that child, Morgan. I worry so about him."

They finished their meal and sat quietly in the evening shadows as Granny Elise and Auntie Jilt finished with the children and saw them all off to bed. A pair of candles burned on the table where the three sat, but the remainder of the room was left dark. The voices upstairs faded away one by one, and the silence deepened.

Auntie Jilt came back into the kitchen after a time and sat with them. She didn't speak, her sharp face lowered as she concentrated on her needlepoint, her head bobbing slightly. Outside, somewhere, a bell rang three times and went still. Auntie Jilt looked up briefly. "Federation curfew," she muttered. "No one is allowed out after it sounds."

The room went silent again. Granny Elise appeared and worked quietly at the sink. One of the children upstairs began to cry and she went out again. The Ohmsfords and Morgan Leah looked at each other and the room and waited.

Then, suddenly, there was a soft tapping at the kitchen door. Three taps. Auntie Jilt looked up, her fingers stilled, and waited. The seconds slipped away. Then the tapping came again, three times, a pause, three times again.

Auntie Jilt rose quickly, walked to the door, unlatched it and peeked out. Then she opened the door wide for an instant and a shadowy figure slipped into the room. Auntie Jilt pushed the door closed again. Granny Elise appeared at the same instant from the hall, motioned Morgan and the Ohmsford brothers to their feet, and led them over to where the stranger stood.

"This is Teel," said Granny Elise. "She will take you to Steff."

It was hard to tell much of anything about Teel. She was a Dwarf, but smaller than most, rather slight, clothed in dark, nondescript forest clothing including a short cloak and hood. Her features were hidden by a strange leather mask that wrapped the whole of her face, save for her right jaw and her mouth. A glimmer of dusky blond hair was visible within the covering of the hood.

Granny Elise reached up and hugged Morgan. "Be careful, youngster," she cautioned. She smiled, patted Par and Coll gently on the shoulder, and hastened to the door. She peeked through the curtains for a moment, then nodded. Teel went out through the door without a word. The Ohmsfords and Morgan Leah went with her.

Outside, they slipped silently along the side of the old house and through a back fence onto a narrow pathway. They followed the pathway to an empty road, then turned right. The mix of cottages and shacks that lined the roadway were dark, their silhouettes ragged and broken against the sky. Teel moved them down the road quickly and into a patch of fir. She stopped then and dropped into a crouch, motioning them down with her. Moments later, a Federation patrol of five appeared. They joked and talked among themselves as they passed, unconcerned with any who might hear them. Then their voices faded and they were gone. Teel stood up, and they were off again.

They stayed on the road for another hundred yards, then turned into the forest. They were on the very edge of the village now, almost due north, and the sounds of insects began to break through the stillness. They slipped along silently through the trees, Teel pausing now and then to listen before continuing on. The smell of wildflowers filled the air, sweet and strong against the reek of garbage.

Then Teel stopped at a line of thick brush, pushed the branches aside, reached down to grip a hidden iron ring and pulled. A trapdoor lifted clear of the earth to reveal a stairway. They felt their way along its walls until they were completely inside and crouched there in the dark. Teel secured the trapdoor behind them, lit a candle and took the lead once more. The company started down.

It was a short descent. The stairs ended after two dozen steps and became a tunnel, the walls and ceiling shored by thick wooden beams and pinned by iron bolts. Teel offered no explanation for the tunnel, but simply moved ahead into it. Twice the tunnel branched in several directions, and each time she made her choice without hesitating. It occurred to Par that if they had to find their way out again without Teel, they probably couldn't do it.

The tunnel ended minutes later at an iron door. Teel struck the door sharply with the hilt of her dagger, paused, then struck it twice more. The locks on the other side snapped free and the door swung open.

The Dwarf who stood there was no older than they, a stout, muscular fellow with a shading of beard and long hair the color of cinnamon, a face that was scarred all over, and the biggest mace Par had ever seen strapped across his back. He had the top half of one ear missing and a gold ring dangling from the remainder.

"Morgan!" he greeted and embraced the Highlander warmly. His smile brightened his fierce countenance as he pulled the other inside and looked past him to where Par and Coll stood nervously waiting. "Friends?"

"The best," Morgan answered at once. "Steff, this is Par and Coll Ohmsford from Shady Vale."

The Dwarf nodded. "You are welcome here, Valemen." He broke away from Morgan and reached out to grip their hands. "Come take a seat, tell me what brought you."

They were in an underground room filled with stores, boxed, crated and wrapped, that surrounded a long table with benches. Steff motioned them onto the benches, then poured each a cup of ale and joined them. Teel took up a position by the door, settling carefully onto a small stool.

"Is this where you live now?" Morgan asked, glancing about. "It needs work."

Steff's smile wrinkled his rough face. "I live a lot of places, Morgan, and they all need work. This one is better than most. Underground, though, like the others. We Dwarves all live underground these days, either here or in the mines or in our graves. Sad."

He hoisted his mug. "Good health to us and misfortune to our enemies," he toasted. They all drank but Teel, who sat watching. Steff placed his mug back on the table. "Is your father well?" he asked Morgan.

The Highlander nodded. "I brought Granny Elise a little something to buy bread with. She worries about you. How long since you've been to see her?"

The Dwarf's smile dropped away. "It's too dangerous to go just now. See my face?" He pointed, tracing the scars with his finger. "The Federation caught me three months back." He glanced at Par and Coll conspiratorially. "Morgan wouldn't know, you see. He hasn't been to see me of late.

When he comes to Culhaven, he prefers the company of old ladies and children."

Morgan ignored him. "What happened, Steff?"

The Dwarf shrugged. "I got away—parts of me, at least." He held up his left hand. The last two fingers were missing, sheared off. "Enough of that, Highlander. Leave off. Instead, tell me what brings you east."

Morgan started to speak, then took a long look at Teel and stopped. Steff saw the direction his gaze had taken, glanced briefly over his shoulder and said, "Oh, yes. Teel. Guess I'll have to talk about it after all."

He looked back at Morgan. "I was taken by the Federation while raiding their weapons stores in the main compound in Culhaven. They put me in their prisons to discover what I could tell them. That was where they did this." He touched his face. "Teel was a prisoner in the cell next to mine. What they did to me is nothing compared to what they did to her. They destroyed most of her face and much of her back punishing her for killing the favorite dog of one of the members of the provisional government quartered in Culhaven. She killed the dog for food. We talked through the walls and came to know each other. One night, less than two weeks after I was taken, when it became apparent that the Federation had no further interest in me and I was to be killed, Teel managed to lure the jailor on watch into her cell. She killed him, stole his keys, freed me, and we escaped. We have been together ever since."

He paused, his eyes as hard as flint. "Highlander, I think much of you, and you must make your own decision in this matter. But Teel and I share everything."

There was a long silence. Morgan glanced briefly at Par and Coll. Par had been watching Teel closely during Steff's narration. She never moved. There was no expression on her face, nothing mirrored in her eyes. She might have been made of stone.

"I think we must rely on Steff's judgment in this matter," Par said quietly, looking to Coll for approval. Coll nodded wordlessly.

Morgan stretched his legs beneath the table, reached for his ale mug and took a long drink. He was clearly making up his own mind. "Very well," he said finally. "But nothing I say must leave this room."

"You haven't said anything as yet worth taking out," Steff declared pointedly and waited.

Morgan smiled, then placed the ale mug carefully back on the table. "Steff, we need you to help us find someone, a man we think is living somewhere in the deep Anar. His name is Walker Boh."

Steff blinked. "Walker Boh," he repeated quietly, and the way he spoke the name indicated he recognized it.

"My friends, Par and Coll, are his nephews."

Steff looked at the Valemen as if he were seeing them for the first time. "Well, now. Tell me the rest of it."

Quickly, Morgan related the story of the journey that had brought them to Culhaven, beginning with the Ohmsford brothers' flight from

Varfleet and ending with their battle with the Shadowen at the edge of the Anar. He told of the old man and his warnings, of the dreams that had come to Par that summoned him to the Hadeshorn, and of his own discovery of the dormant magic of the Sword of Leah. Steff listened to it all without comment. He sat unmoving, his ale forgotten, his face an expressionless mask.

When Morgan was finished, Steff grunted and shook his head. "Druids and magic and creatures of the night. Highlander, you constantly surprise me." He rose, walked around the table, and stood looking at Teel momentarily, his rough face creased in thought. Then he said, "I know of Walker Boh." He shook his head.

"And?" Morgan pressed.

He wheeled back slowly. "And the man scares me." He looked at Par and Coll. "Your uncle, is he? And how long since you've seen him—ten years? Well, listen close to me, then. The Walker Boh I know may not be the uncle you remember. This Walker Boh is more whispered rumor than truth, and very real all the same—someone that even the things that live out in the darker parts of the land and prey on travelers, wayfarers, strays, and such are said to avoid."

He sat down again, took up the ale mug and drank. Morgan Leah and the Ohmsfords looked at one another in silence. At last, Par said, "I think we are decided on the matter. Whoever or whatever Walker Boh is now, we share a common bond beyond our kinship—our dreams of Allanon. I have to know what my uncle intends to do. Will you help us find him?"

Steff smiled faintly, unexpectedly. "Direct. I like that." He looked at Morgan. "I assume he speaks for his brother. Does he speak for you as well?" Morgan nodded. "I see." He studied them for long moments, lost in thought. "Then I will help," he said finally. He paused, judging their reaction. "I will take you to Walker Boh—if he can be found. But I will do so for some reasons of my own, and you'd best know what they are."

His face lowered momentarily into shadow, and the scars seemed like strands of iron mesh pressed against his skin. "The Federation has taken your homes from you, from all of you, taken them and made them their own. Well, the Federation has taken more than that from me. It has taken everything—my home, my family, my past, even my present. The Federation has destroyed everything that was and is and left me only what might be. It is the enemy of my life, and I would do anything to see it destroyed. Nothing I do here will accomplish that end in my lifetime. What I do here merely serves to keep me alive and to give me some small reason to stay that way. I have had enough of that. I want something more."

His face lifted, and his eyes were fierce. "If there is magic that can be freed from time's chains, if there are Druids yet, ghosts or otherwise, able to wield it, then perhaps there are ways of freeing my homeland and my people—ways that have been kept from us all. If we discover those ways, if the knowledge of them passes into our hands, they must be used to help my people and my homeland." He paused. "I'll want your promise on this."

There was a long moment of silence as his listeners looked at one another.

Then Par said softly, "I am ashamed for the Southland when I see what has happened here. I don't begin to understand it. There is nothing that could justify it. If we discover anything that will give the Dwarves back their freedom, we will put it to use."

"We will," Coll echoed, and Morgan Leah nodded his agreement as well.

Steff took a deep breath. "The possibility of being free—just the possibility—is more than the Dwarves dare hope for in these times." He placed his thick hands firmly on the table. "Then we have a bargain. I will take you to find Walker Boh—Teel and I, for she goes where I go." He glanced at each of them quickly for any sign of disapproval and found none. "It will take a day or so to gather up what we need and to make an inquiry or two. I need not remind you, but I will anyway, how difficult and dangerous this journey is likely to be. Go back to Granny's and rest. Teel will take you. When all is in place, I will send word."

They rose, and the Dwarf embraced Morgan, then smiled unexpectedly and slapped him on the back. "You and I, Highlander—let the worst that's out there be wary!" He laughed and the room rang with the sound of it.

Teel stood apart from them and watched with eyes like chips of ice.

Two days passed, and they did not hear from Steff. Par and Coll Ohmsford and Morgan Leah passed the time at the orphanage completing some much-needed repairs on the old home and helping Granny Elise and Auntie Jilt with the children. The days were warm, lazy ones, filled with the sounds of small voices at play. It was a different world within the confines of the rambling house and the shaded grounds, a world quite apart from the one that crouched begging a dozen yards in any direction beyond the enclosing fence. There was food here, warm beds, comfort and love. There was a sense of security and future. There wasn't a lot of anything, but there was some of everything. The remainder of the city faded into a series of unpleasant memories—the shacks, the broken old people, the ragged children, the missing mothers and fathers, the grime and the wear, the desperate and defeated looks, and the sense that there was no hope. Several times, Par thought to leave the orphanage and walk again through the city of Culhaven, unwilling to leave without seeing once more sights he felt he should never forget. But the old ladies discouraged it. It was dangerous for him to walk about. He might unwittingly draw attention to himself. Better to stay where he was, let the world outside stay where it was, and the both of them get on the best they could.

"There is nothing to be done for the misery of the Dwarves," Auntie Jilt declared bitterly. "It's a misery that's put down deep roots."

Par did as he was told, feeling at once both unhappy and relieved. The ambiguity bothered him. He couldn't pretend he didn't know what was happening to the people of the city—didn't want to, in fact—but at the same time it was a difficult knowledge to face. He could do as the old ladies said and let the world without get along as best as it could, but he couldn't forget that it was there, pressed up against the gate like some starving beast waiting for food.

On the third day of waiting, the beast snapped at them. It was early morning, and a squad of Federation soldiers marched up the roadway and into the yard. A Seeker was leading them. Granny Elise sent the Valemen and the Highlander to the attic and with Auntie Jilt in tow went out to confront their visitors. From the attic, the three in hiding watched what happened next. The children were forced to line up in front of the porch. They were all too small to be of any use, but three were selected anyway. The old women argued, but there was nothing they could do. In the end, they were forced to stand there helplessly while the three were led away.

Everyone was subdued after that, even the most active among the children. Auntie Jilt retired to a windowseat overlooking the front yard where she could sit and watch the children and work on her needlepoint, and she didn't say a word to anyone. Granny Elise spent most of her time in the kitchen baking. Her words were few, and she hardly smiled at all. The Ohmsfords and Morgan went about their work as unobtrusively as they could, feeling as if they should be somewhere else, secretly wishing that they were.

Late that afternoon, Par could stand his discomfort no longer and went down to the kitchen to talk to Granny Elise. He found her sitting at one of the long tables, sipping absently at a cup of amber tea, and he asked her quite directly why it was that the Dwarves were being treated so badly, why it was that soldiers of the Federation—Southlanders like himself, after all—could be a part of such cruelty.

Granny Elise smiled sadly, took his hand and pulled him down next to her. "Par," she said, speaking his name softly. She had begun using his name the past day or so, a clear indication that she now considered him another of her children. "Par, there are some things that cannot ever be explained—not properly, not so as we might understand them the way we need to. I think sometimes that there must be a reason for what's happening and other times that there cannot be because it lacks any semblance of logic. It has been so long since it all started, you see. The war was fought over a hundred years ago. I don't know that anyone can remember the beginning of it anymore, and if you cannot remember how it began, how can you determine *why* it began?"

She shook her squarish head and hugged him impulsively. "I'm sorry, Par, but I don't have any better answer to give you. I suppose I gave up trying to find one a long time ago. All my energy these days is given over to caring for the children. I guess I don't believe questions are important anymore, so I don't look for answers. Someone else will have to do that. All that matters to me is saving the life of one more child, and one more after that, and another, and another, until the need to save them doesn't exist anymore."

Par nodded silently and hugged her back, but the answer didn't satisfy him. There was a reason for everything that happened, even if the reason wasn't immediately apparent. The Dwarves had lost the war to the Federation; they were a threat to no one. Why, then, were they being systematically ground down? It would have made better sense to heal the wounds that the war had opened than to throw salt into them. It almost seemed as if the Dwarves were being intentionally provoked, as if a cause for them to resist was being provided. Why would that be?

"Perhaps the Federation wants an excuse to exterminate them altogether," Coll suggested blackly when Par asked his opinion that night after dinner.

"You mean you think the Federation believes the Dwarves are of no further use, even in the mines?" Par was incredulous. "Or that they're too much trouble to supervise or too dangerous, so they ought to simply be done away with? The entire nation?"

Coll's blocky face was impassive. "I mean, I know what I've seen here— what we've both seen. It seems pretty clear to me what's happening!"

Par wasn't so sure. He let the matter drop because for the moment he didn't have any better answer. But he promised himself that one day he would.

He slept poorly that night and was already awake when Granny Elise slipped into the sleeping room before dawn to whisper that Teel had come for them. He rose quickly and dragged the covers from Coll and Morgan. They dressed, strapped on their weapons and went down the hall to the kitchen where Teel was waiting, a shadow by the door, masked and wrapped in a drab forest cloak that gave her the look of a beggar. Granny Elise gave them hot tea and cakes and kissed each of them, Auntie Jilt warned them sternly to keep safe from whatever dangers might lie in wait for them, and Teel led them out into the night.

It was dark still, the dawn not yet even a small glimmer in the distant trees, and they slipped silently through the sleeping village, four ghosts in search of a haunt. The morning air was chill, and they could see their breath cloud the air before them in small puffs. Teel took them down back pathways and through dense groves of trees and gatherings of brush, keeping to the shadows, staying away from the roads and lights. They moved north out of the village without seeing anyone. When they reached the Silver

River, Teel took them downstream to a shallows, avoiding the bridges. They crossed water like ice as it lapped at their legs. They were barely into the trees again when Steff appeared out of the shadows to join them. He wore a brace of long knives at his waist, and the giant mace was slung across his back. He said nothing, taking the lead from Teel and guiding them ahead. A few faint streaks of daylight appeared in the east, and the sky began to brighten. The stars winked out and the moon disappeared. Frost glimmered on leaves and grasses like scattered bits of crystal.

A bit farther on, they reached a clearing dominated by a massive old willow, and Steff brought them to a halt. Backpacks, rolled blankets, foul-weather gear, cooking implements, water bags, and forest cloaks for each of them were concealed in an old hollow tree trunk that had fallen into the brush. They strapped everything in place without speaking and were off again.

They walked the remainder of the day at a leisurely pace, bearing directly north. There was little discussion, none whatsoever as to where they were going. Steff offered no explanation, and neither the Valemen nor the Highlander were inclined to ask. When the Dwarf was ready to tell them, he would. The day passed quickly and by midafternoon they had reached the foothills south of the Wolfsktaag. They continued on for what was perhaps another hour, following the forestline upward to where it began to thin before the wall of the mountains, then Steff called a halt in a pine-sheltered clearing close to a small stream that trickled down out of the rocks. He led them over to a fallen log and seated himself comfortably, facing them.

"If the rumors are to be believed—and in this case, rumors are all we have—Walker Boh will be found in Darklin Reach. To get there, we will travel north through the Wolfsktaag—in through the Pass of Noose, out through the Pass of Jade, and from there east into the Reach."

He paused, considering what he saw in their faces. "There are other ways, of course—safer ways, some might argue—but I disagree. We could skirt the Wolfsktaag to the east or west, but either way we risk an almost certain encounter with Federation soldiers or Gnomes. There will be neither in the Wolfsktaag. Too many spirits and things of old magic live in the mountains; the Gnomes are superstitious about such and stay away. The Federation used to send patrols in, but most of them never came out. Truth is, most of them just got lost up there because they didn't know the way. I do."

His listeners remained silent. Finally Coll said, "I seem to remember that a couple of our ancestors got into a good bit of trouble when they took this same route some years back."

Steff shrugged. "I wouldn't know about that. I do know that I have been through these mountains dozens of times and know what to look for. The trick is to stay on the ridgelines and out of the deep forests. What lives in the Wolfsktaag prefers the dark. And there's nothing magic about most of it."

Coll shook his head and looked at Par. "I don't like it."

"Well, the choice is between the devil we know and the one we suspect," Steff declared bluntly. "Federation soldiers and their Gnome allies, which we know are out there, or spirits and wraiths, which we don't."

"Shadowen," Par said softly.

There was a moment of silence. Steff smiled grimly. "Haven't you heard, Valeman—there aren't any Shadowen. That's all a rumor. Besides, you have the magic to protect us, don't you? You and the Highlander here? What would dare challenge that?"

He looked about, sharp eyes darting from one face to the next. "Come now. No one ever suggested that this journey would be a safe one. Let us have a decision. But you have heard my warning about the choices left us if we forgo the mountains. Pay heed."

There wasn't much any of them could say after that, and they left it to the Dwarf's best judgment. This was his country after all, not theirs, and he was the one who knew it. They were relying on him to find Walker Boh, and it seemed foolish to second-guess the way he thought best to go about it.

They spent the night in the clearing of pines, smelling needles and wildflowers and the crispness of air, sleeping undisturbed and dreamless in a silence that stretched far beyond where they could see. At dawn, Steff took them up into the Wolfsktaag. They slipped into the Pass of Noose, where Gnomes had once tried to trap Shea and Flick Ohmsford, crossed the rope walkway that bridged the chasm at its center, wound their way steadily upward through the ragged, blunted peaks of slab-sided stone and forested slopes, and watched the sun work its way across the cloudless summer sky. Morning passed into afternoon, and they reached the ridgelines running north and began following their twists and bends. Travel was easy, the sun warm and reassuring, and the fears and doubts of the night before began to fade. They watched for movement in the shadows of rock and wood, but saw nothing. Birds sang in the trees, small animals scampered through the brush, and the forests here seemed very much the same as forests everywhere in the Four Lands. The Valemen and the Highlander found themselves smiling at one another; Steff hummed tonelessly to himself, and only Teel showed nothing of what she was feeling.

When nightfall approached, they made camp in a small meadow nestled between two ridgelines cropped with fir and cedar. There was little wind, and the day's warmth lingered in the sheltered valley long after the sun was gone. Stars glimmered faintly in the darkening skies, and the moon hung full against the western horizon. Par recalled again the old man's admonition to them—that they were to be at the Hadeshorn on the first day of the new moon. Time was slipping past.

But it wasn't of the old man or Allanon that Par found himself thinking that night as the little company gathered around the fire Steff had permitted them and washed down their dinner with long draughts of spring water. It was of Walker Boh. Par hadn't seen his uncle in almost ten years, but what he remembered of him was strangely clear. He had been just a boy then, and his uncle had seemed rather mysterious—a tall, lean man with dark features and eyes that could see right through you. The eyes— that was what Par remembered most, though he remembered them more for how remarkable they had seemed than for any discomfort they might have caused him. In fact, his uncle had been very kind to him, but always rather introspective or perhaps just withdrawn, sort of there but at the same time somewhere else.

There were stories about Walker Boh even then, but Par could recall few of them. It was said he used magic, although it was never made clear exactly what sort of magic. He was a direct descendent of Brin Ohmsford, but he had not had use of the wishsong. No one on his side of the family had, not in ten generations. The magic had died with Brin. It had worked differently for her than for her brother Jair, of course. Where Jair had only been able to use the wishsong to create images, his sister had been able to use it to create reality. Her magic had been by far the stronger of the two. Nevertheless, hers had disappeared with her passing, and only Jair's had survived.

Yet there had always been stories of Walker Boh and the magic. Par remembered how sometimes his uncle could tell him things that were happening at other places, things he could not possibly have known yet somehow did. There were times when his uncle could make things move by looking at them, even people. Sometimes he could tell what you were thinking, too. He would look at you and tell you not to worry, that this or that would happen, and it would turn out that it was exactly what you were thinking about.

Of course, it was possible that his uncle had simply been astute enough to reason out what he was thinking, and that it had simply appeared that the older man could read his thoughts.

But there was the way he could turn aside trouble, too—make it disappear almost as fast as it came. Anything threatening always seemed to give way when it encountered him. That seemed a sort of magic.

And he was always encouraging to Par when he saw the boy attempting to use the wishsong. He had warned Par to learn to control the images, to be cautious about their use, to be selective in the ways in which he exposed the magic to others. Walker Boh had been one of the few people in his life who had not been afraid of its power.

So as he sat there with the others in the silence of the mountain night, the memories of his uncle skipping through his mind, his curiosity to know more was piqued anew, and finally he gave in to it and asked Steff what tales the other had heard of Walker Boh.

Steff looked thoughtful. "Most of them come from woodsmen, hunters, trackers and such—a few from Dwarves who fight in the Resistance like myself and who pass far enough north to hear of the man. They say the Gnome tribes are scared to death of him. They say they think of Walker Boh in the same way they think of spirits. Some of them believe that he's been alive for hundreds of years, that he's the same as the Druids of legend." He winked. "Guess that's just talk, though, if he's your uncle."

Par nodded. "I don't remember anyone ever suggesting he hadn't lived the same number of years as any normal man."

"One fellow swore to me that your uncle talked with animals and that the animals understood. He said he saw it happen, that he watched your uncle walk right up to a moor cat the size of a plains bull and speak with it the same way I'm speaking with you."

"It was said that Cogline could do that," Coll interjected, suddenly interested. "He had a cat called Whisper that followed him. The cat protected his niece, Kimber. Her name was Boh as well, wasn't it, Par?"

Par nodded, remembering that his uncle had taken the name Boh from his mother's side of the family. Strange, now that he thought about it, but he could never remember his uncle using the Ohmsford name.

"There was one story," Steff said, pausing then to mull the details over in his mind. "I heard it from a tracker who knew the deep Anar better than most and, I think, knew Walker Boh as well, though he'd never admit to it. He told me that something born in the days of the old magic wandered down out of Ravenshorn into Darklin Reach two years back and started living off the life it found there. Walker Boh went out to find it, confronted it, and the creature turned around and went back to wherever it had come from—just like that." Steff shook his head and rubbed his chin slowly. "It makes you think, doesn't it?"

He stretched his hands toward the fire. "That's why he scares me—because there doesn't appear to be much of anything that scares him. He comes and goes like a ghost, they say—here one minute, gone the next, just a shadow out of night. I wonder if even the Shadowen frighten him. I'd guess not."

"Maybe we should ask him," Coll offered with a sly grin.

Steff brightened. "Well, now, maybe we should," he agreed. "I suggest you be the one to do it!" He laughed. "That reminds me, has the Highlander told you yet how we happened on each other that first time?"

The Ohmsford brothers shook their heads no, and despite some loud grumbling from Morgan, Steff proceeded to tell the tale. Morgan was fishing the eastern end of the Rainbow Lake at the mouth of the Silver River some ten months earlier when a squall capsized his craft, washed away his gear, and left him to make his way ashore as best he could. He was drenched and freezing and trying without success to start a fire when Steff came across him and dried him out.

"He would have died of exposure, I expect, if I hadn't taken pity on him," Steff finished. "We talked, exchanged information. Before you know it, he was on his way to Culhaven to see whether life in the homeland of the Dwarves was as grim as I had described it." Steff cast an amused look at the chagrined Highlander. "He kept coming back after that—each time with a little something to help out Granny and Auntie and the Resistance as well. His conscience won't allow him to stay away, I suppose."

"Oh, for goodness sake!" Morgan huffed, embarrassed.

Steff laughed, his voice booming out through the stillness, filling up the night. "Enough, then, proud Highland Prince! We will talk of someone else!" He shifted his weight and looked at Par. "That stranger, the one who gave you the ring—let's talk about him. I know something of the outlaw bands that serve in the Movement. A rather worthless bunch, for the most part; they lack leadership and discipline. The Dwarves have offered to work with them, but the offer hasn't been accepted as yet. The problem is that the whole Movement has been too fragmented. In any case, that ring you were given—does it bear the emblem of a hawk?"

Par sat bolt upright. "It does, Steff. Do you know whose it is?"

Steff smiled. "I do and I don't, Valeman. As I said, the Southland outlaws have been a fragmented bunch in the past—but that may be changing. There are rumors of one among them who seems to be taking control, uniting the bands together, giving them the leadership they have been lacking. He doesn't use his name to identify himself; he uses the symbol of a hawk."

"It must be the same man," Par declared firmly. "He was reluctant to give his name to us as well."

Steff shrugged. "Names are often kept secret in these times. But the way in which he managed your escape from the Seekers—well, that sounds like the man I have been hearing about. They say he would dare anything where the Federation is concerned."

"He was certainly bold enough that night," Par agreed, smiling.

They talked a bit longer of the stranger, the outlaw bands in both Southland and Eastland, and the way in which the Four Lands festered like an open sore under Federation rule. They never did get back to the subject of Walker Boh, but Par was content with where they had left it. He had his mind made up where his uncle was concerned. It did not matter how frightening Walker Boh appeared to others, to Steff or anyone else; he would remain for Par the same man he had been when the Valeman was a boy until something happened to change his mind—and he had a curious feeling that nothing would.

Their talk dwindled finally, interrupted by frequent yawns and distracted looks, and one by one they began to roll into their blankets. Par offered to build the fire up one final time before they went to sleep and walked to the edge of the trees in search of deadwood. He was in the process of gathering some pieces of an old cedar that had been blown down by the winds last winter when he suddenly found himself face-to-face with Teel. She seemed to materialize right in front of him, her masked face intent, her eyes quite steady as she looked at him.

"Can you make the magic for me?" she asked quietly.

Par stared. He had never heard her speak, not once, not a single time since he had encountered her that first night in Granny Elise's kitchen. As far as he had been able to determine, she couldn't. She had traveled with them as if she were Steff's faithful dog, obedient to him, watchful of them, unquestioning and aloof. She had sat there all evening listening and not speaking, keeping what she knew and what she thought carefully to herself. Now, this.

"Can you make the images?" she pressed. Her voice was low and rough. "Just one or two, so I can see them? I would like it very much if you could."

He saw her eyes then, where he hadn't seen them before. They were a curious azure, the way the sky had been that day so high up in the mountains, clear and depthless. He was startled by how bright they were, and he remembered suddenly that her hair was a honey color beneath the covering hood, behind the concealing mask. She had seemed rather unpleasant before in the way in which she chose to distance herself from them, but now, standing here amid the silence and shadows, she just seemed small.

"What images would you like to see?" he asked her.

She thought for a moment. "I would like to see what Culhaven was like in the days of Allanon."

He started to tell her he wasn't sure what Culhaven had been like that long ago, then caught himself and nodded. "I can try," he said.

He sang softly to her, alone in the trees, reaching out with the magic of the wishsong to fill her mind with images of the village as it might have looked three hundred years ago. He sang of the Silver River, of the Meade Gardens, of the cottages and homes all carefully tended and kept, of life in the home city of the Dwarves before the war with the Federation. When he was finished, she studied him expressionlessly for a moment, then turned without a word and disappeared back into the night.

Par stared after her in confusion for a moment, then shrugged, finished picking up the deadwood and went off to sleep.

They struck out again at dawn, working their way along the upper stretches of the Wolfsktaag where the forests thinned and the sky hovered close. It was another warm, bright day filled with good smells and a sense of endless possibilities. Breezes blew gently against their faces, the woods and rocks were filled with tiny creatures that darted and flew, and the mountains were at peace.

Despite all of that, Par was uneasy. He hadn't felt that way the previous two days, but he did so on this one. He tried to dispel the uneasiness, telling himself it lacked any discernible cause, that it was probably the result of needing something to worry about when it appeared that Steff had been right about this being the safest way after all. He tried studying the faces of the others to see if they were experiencing any discomfort, but the others seemed quite content. Even Teel, who seldom showed anything, walked with an air of total unconcern.

The morning slipped away into afternoon, and the uneasiness grew into a certainty that something was following them. Par found himself glancing back on any number of occasions, not knowing what it was he was looking for, but knowing nevertheless that it was back there. He hunted through the distant trees and across the rocks and there was nothing to be seen. Above, to their right, the ridgeline rose into the cliffs and defiles where the rock was too barren and dangerous to traverse. Below, to their left, the forest was thick with shadows that gathered in pools amid a tangle of heavy brush and close-set black trunks.

Several times, the trail branched downward into the murk. Steff, who was in the lead with Teel, motioned that way once and said, "That is what might have happened to those missing Federation parties. You don't want to wander into the dark places in these mountains."

It was Par's hope that this was the source of his discomfort. Identifying the source should allow him to dismiss it, he told himself. But just as he was prepared to believe that the matter had resolved itself, he glanced over his shoulder one final time and saw something move in the rocks.

He stopped where he was. The others walked on a few steps, then turned and looked at him. "What is it?" Steff asked at once.

"There's something back there," Par said quietly, not shifting his eyes from where he had last seen the movement.

Steff walked back to him. "There, in the rocks," Par said and pointed.

They stood together and looked for a long time and saw nothing. The afternoon was waning, and the shadows were lengthening in the mountains as the sun dropped low against the western horizon, so it was difficult to discern much of anything in the mix of half-light. Par shook his head finally, frustrated. "Maybe I was mistaken," he admitted.

"Maybe you weren't," Steff said.

Ignoring the surprised look Par gave him, he started them walking again with Teel in the lead and himself trailing with Par. Once or twice, he told Par to glance back, and once or twice he did so himself. Par never saw anything, although he still had a sense of something being back there. They crossed a ridgeline that ran from east to west and started down. The far side was cloaked in shadow, the sun's fading light blocked away entirely, and the trail below wound its way through a maze of rocks and scrub that were clustered on the mountainside like huddled sheep. The wind was at their backs now, and the sound of Steff's voice, when he spoke, carried ahead to them.

"Whatever's back there is tracking us, waiting for dark or at least twilight before showing itself. I don't know what it is, but it's big. We have to find a place where we can defend ourselves."

No one said anything. Par experienced a sudden chill. Coll glanced at him, then at Morgan. Teel never turned.

They were through the maze of rocks and brush and back on an open trail leading up again when the thing finally emerged from the shadows and let them see what it was. Steff saw it first, called out sharply and brought them all about. The creature was still more than a hundred yards back, crouched on a flat rock where a narrow shaft of sunlight sliced across its blunted face like a lance. It looked like some sort of monstrous dog or wolf with a massive chest and neck thick with fur and a face that was all misshapen. It had oddly fat legs, a barrel body, small ears and tail, and the look of something that had no friends. Its jaws parted once, the biggest jaws Par had ever seen on anything, and spittle drooled out. The jaws snapped shut, and it started toward them in a slow amble.

"Keep moving," Steff said quietly, and they did. They walked ahead steadily, following the weave of the trail, trying not to look back.

"What is it?" Morgan asked, his voice low.

"They call it a Gnawl," Steff answered calmly. "It lives east in the deepest part of the Anar, beyond the Ravenshorn. Very dangerous." He paused. "I never heard of one being seen in the central Anar, though—let alone in the Wolfsktaag."

"Until now, you mean," muttered Coll.

They made their way through a broad split in the mountains where the trail began to dip sharply downward into a hollows. The sun was gone, and gray twilight hung over everything like a shroud. It was getting hard to see. The thing behind them appeared and disappeared in fits and starts, causing Par to wonder what would happen when they lost sight of it altogether.

"I never heard of one stalking men either," Steff declared suddenly from just behind him.

The strange hunt continued, the Gnawl trailing them at a distance of about a hundred yards, apparently content to wait for darkness to descend completely. Steff urged them on, searching for a spot where they could make a stand.

"Why don't you simply let me go after it!" Morgan snapped back at him at one point.

"Because you would be dead quicker than I could say your name, Highlander," the Dwarf answered, his voice cold. "Don't be fooled. This creature is more than a match for the five of us if it catches us unprepared. All the magic in the world won't make a difference if that happens!"

Par froze, wondering suddenly if the magic in Morgan's sword was of any use against this beast. Wasn't the sword's magic triggered only by an encounter with similar magic? Wasn't it simply a common sword when otherwise employed? Wasn't that what Allanon had intended when he had given the blade its power? He struggled to remember the particulars of the story and failed. But the other magics, those of the Sword of Shannara and of the Elfstones, had been effective only against things of magic—he remembered that well enough. It was very likely the same with . . .

"Ahead, down by that hollows," Steff said abruptly, ending his speculation. "That's where we will . . ."

He never finished. The Gnawl came at them, hurtling through the darkness, a huge, black shape bounding across the broken rock and scrub with a speed that was astonishing. "Go!" Steff shouted at them, pointed hurriedly down the trail and turned to face the beast.

They went without thinking, all but Morgan who wrenched free the Sword of Leah and rushed to stand with his friend. Teel, Coll, and Par dashed ahead, glancing back just as the Gnawl reached their companions. The creature lunged at Steff, but the Dwarf was waiting, the huge mace held ready. He caught the beast full against the side of its head with a blow that would have dropped anything else. But the Gnawl shrugged the blow aside and came at the Dwarf again. Steff hammered it a second time, then broke past it, pulling the Highlander after him. They came down the trail in a spring, quickly catching the fleeing Valemen and Teel.

"Down the slope!" Steff yelled, literally shoving them off the trail. They rushed into the scrub and rocks, skidding and sliding. Par went down, tumbled head-over-heels, and came back to his feet all in the same motion. He was disoriented, and there was blood in his eyes. Steff jerked him about and dragged him forward, down the slide, the sound of labored breathing and shouting all about him.

Then he was aware of the Gnawl. He heard it before he saw it, its heavy body churning up the ground behind them, scattering rocks and dirt as it came, its cry an ugly whine of hunger. The magic, Par thought, distracted— I have to use the magic. The wishsong will work, confuse it, at least . . .

Steff pulled him onto a flat rock, and he felt the others bunch around him. "Stay together!" the Dwarf ordered. "Don't leave the rock!"

He stepped out to meet the Gnawl's rush.

Par would never forget what happened next. Steff took the Gnawl's charge on the slope just to the left of the rock. He let the creature come right up against him, then suddenly fell back, mace jamming upward into the Gnawl's throat, booted feet thrusting against its massive chest. Steff went down, and the Gnawl went right over him, the momentum of its lunge carrying it past. The Gnawl could not catch itself. It tumbled past Steff, rolled wildly down the slope into the hollows below, right up against the fringe of the trees. It came to its feet instantly, growling and snarling. But then something huge shot out of the trees, snapped up the Gnawl in a single bite and pulled back again into the murk. There was a sharp cry, a crunching of bones, and silence.

Steff came to his feet, put a finger to his lips, and beckoned them to follow. Silently, or as nearly so as they could keep it, they climbed back up to the trail and stood looking downward into the impenetrable dark.

"In the Wolfsktaag, you have to learn what to look out for," Steff whispered with a grim smile. "Even if you're a Gnawl."

They brushed themselves off and straightened their packs. Their cuts and bruises were slight. The Pass of Jade, which would take them clear of the mountains, was no more than another hour or two ahead, Steff advised.

They decided to keep walking.

I t took longer than Steff had estimated to reach the Pass of Jade, and it
was almost midnight when the little company finally broke clear of the
Wolfsktaag. They slept in a narrow canyon screened by a tangle of fir and
ancient spruce, so exhausted that they did not bother with either food or
fire, but simply rolled into their blankets and dropped off to sleep. Par
dreamed that night, but not about Allanon or the Hadeshorn. He dreamed
instead of the Gnawl. It tracked him relentlessly through the landscape of
his mind, chasing him from one dark corner to the next, a vaguely distinguishable shadow whose identity was nevertheless as certain as his own. It
came for him and he ran from it, and the terror he felt was palpable. Finally
it cornered him, backing him into a shallow niche of rock and forest, and
just as he was about to attempt to spring past it, something monstrous
lunged from the dark behind him and took him into its maw, dragging him
from sight as he screamed for the help that wouldn't come.

He came awake with a start.

It was dark, though the sky was beginning to lighten in the east, and his
companions still slept. The scream was only in his mind, it seemed. There
was sweat on his face and body, and his breathing was quick and ragged. He
lay back quietly, but did not sleep again.

They walked east that morning into the central Anar, winding through
a maze of forested hills and ravines, five pairs of eyes searching the shadows
and dark places about them as they went. There was little talking, the encounter of the previous day having left them uneasy and watchful. The day
was clouded and gray, and the forests about them seemed more secretive
somehow. By noon, they came upon the falls of the Chard Rush, and they
followed the river in until nightfall.

It rained the next day, and the land was washed in mist and damp.
Travel slowed, and the warmth and brightness of the previous few days
faded into memory. They passed the Rooker Line Trading Center, a tiny
waystation for hunters and traders in the days of Jair Ohmsford that had
built itself into a thriving fur exchange until the war between the Dwarves
and the Federation disrupted and finally put an end altogether to Eastland
commerce north of Culhaven. Now it stood empty, its doors and windows
gone, its roof rotted and sagging, its shadows filled with ghosts from another time.

At lunch, huddled beneath the canopy of a massive old willow that
overhung the banks of the river, Steff talked uneasily of the Gnawl, insisting again that one had never before been seen west of the Ravenshorn.

Where did this one come from? How did it happen to be here? Why had it chosen to track them? There were answers to his questions, of course, but none that any of them cared to explore. Chance, they all agreed outwardly, and inwardly thought just the opposite.

The rain slowed with the approach of nightfall, but continued in a steady drizzle until morning, when it changed to a heavy mist. The company pushed on, following the Chard Rush as it wound its way down into Darklin Reach. Travel grew increasingly difficult, the forests thick with brush and fallen timber, the pathways almost nonexistent. When they left the river at midday, the terrain transformed itself into a series of gullies and ravines, and it became almost impossible to determine their direction. They slogged through the mud and debris, Steff in the lead, grunting and huffing rhythmically. The Dwarf was like a tireless machine when he traveled, tough and seemingly inexhaustible. Only Teel was his equal, smaller than Steff but more agile, never slowing or complaining, always keeping pace. It was the Valemen and the Highlander who grew tired, their muscles stiffened, their wind spent. They welcomed every chance to rest that the Dwarf offered them, and when it was time to start up again it was all they could do to comply. The dreariness of their travel was beginning to affect them as well, especially the Valemen. Par and Coll had been running either from or toward something for weeks now, had spent much of that time in hiding, and had endured three very frightening encounters with creatures best left to one's imagination. They were tired of keeping constant watch, and the darkness, mist, and damp just served to exhaust them further. Neither said anything to the other, and neither would have admitted it if the other had asked, but both were starting to wonder if they really knew what they were doing.

It was late afternoon when the rain finally stopped, and the clouds suddenly broke apart to let through a smattering of sunlight. They crested a ridge and came upon a shallow, forested valley dominated by a strange rock formation shaped like a chimney. It rose out of the trees as if a sentinel set at watch, black and still against the distant skyline. Steff brought the others to a halt and pointed down.

"There," he said quietly. "If Walker Boh's to be found, this is the place he's said to be."

Par shoved aside his exhaustion and despondency, staring in disbelief. "I know this place!" he exclaimed. "This is Hearthstone! I recognize it from the stories! This is Cogline's home!"

"Was," Coll corrected wearily.

"Was, is, what's the difference?" Par was animated as he confronted them. "The point is, what is Walker Boh doing here? I mean, it makes sense that he would be here because this was once the home of the Bohs, but it was Cogline's home as well. If Walker lives here, then why didn't the old man tell us? Unless maybe the old man isn't Cogline after all or unless for some reason he doesn't know Walker is here, or unless Walker . . ." He stopped suddenly, confused to the point of distraction. "Are you sure this is where my uncle is supposed to live?" he demanded of Steff.

The Dwarf had been watching him during all this the same way he might have watched a three-headed dog. Now he simply shrugged. "Valeman, I am sure of very little and admit to less. I was told this was where the man makes his home. So if you're all done talking about it, why don't we simply go down there and see?"

Par shut his mouth, and they began their descent. When they reached the valley floor, they found the forest surprisingly clear of scrub and deadwood. The trees opened into clearings that were crisscrossed with streams and laced with tiny wildflowers colored white, blue, and deep violet. The day grew still, the wind calmed, and the lengthening shadows that draped the way forward seemed soft and unthreatening. Par forgot about the dangers and hardships of his journey, put aside his weariness and discomfort, and concentrated instead on thinking further about the man he had come to find. He was admittedly confused, but at least he understood the reason. When Brin Ohmsford had come into Darklin Reach three hundred years earlier, Hearthstone had been the home of Cogline and the child he claimed as his granddaughter, Kimber Boh. The old man and the little girl had guided Brin into the Maelmord where she had confronted the Ildatch. They had remained friends afterward, and that friendship had endured for ten generations. Walker Boh's father had been an Ohmsford and his mother a Boh. He could trace his father's side of the family directly back to Brin and his mother's side to Kimber. It was logical that he would choose to come back here—yet illogical that the old man, the man who claimed to be Cogline, the very same Cogline of three hundred years earlier, would know nothing about it.

Or say nothing, if in fact he knew.

Par frowned. What *had* the old man said about Walker Boh when they had talked with him? His frown deepened. Only that he knew Walker was alive, he answered himself. That and nothing else.

But was there more between them than what the old man had revealed? Par was certain of it. And he meant to discover what it was.

The brief flurry of late sunlight faded and twilight cloaked the valley in darkening shades of gray. The sky remained clear and began to fill with stars, and the three-quarter moon, waning now toward the end of its cycle, bathed the forest in milky light. The little company walked cautiously ahead, working its way steadily in the direction of the chimney-shaped rock formation, crossing the dozens of little streams and weaving through the maze of clearings. The forest was still, but its silence did not feel ominous. Coll nudged Par at one point when he caught sight of a gray squirrel sitting up on its hind legs and regarding them solemnly. There were night sounds, but they seemed distant and far removed from the valley.

"It feels sort of . . . protected here, don't you think?" Par asked his brother quietly, and Coll nodded.

They continued on for almost an hour without encountering anyone. They had reached the approximate center of the valley when a sudden glimmer of light winked at them through the forest trees. Steff slowed, signaled for caution, then led them forward. The light drew closer, flickering brightly through the dark, changing from a single pinprick of brightness to a cluster. *Lamps,* Par thought. He pushed ahead to reach Steff, his sharp Elven senses picking out the source. "It's a cottage," he whispered to the Dwarf.

They broke clear of the trees and stepped into a broad, grassy clearing. There was indeed a cottage. It stood before them, precisely at the center of the clearing, a well-kept stone and timber structure with front and rear porches, stone walkways, gardens, and flowering shrubs. Spruce and pine clustered about it like miniature watchtowers. Light streamed forth from its windows and mingled with moonglow to brighten the clearing as if it were midday.

The front door stood open.

Par started forward at once, but Steff quickly yanked him back. "A little caution might be in order, Valeman," he lectured.

He said something to Teel, then left them all to go on alone, sprinting across the open spaces between the spruce and pine, keeping carefully to the shadows between, eyes fixed on the open door. The others watched him make his way forward, crouched down now at Teel's insistence at the edge of the forest. Steff reached the porch, hunkered down close to it for a long time, then darted up the steps and through the front door. There was a moment of silence, then he reappeared and waved them forward.

When they reached him, he said, "No one is here. But it appears we are expected."

They discovered his meaning when they went inside. A pair of chimneys bracketed the central room, one for a seating area in which chairs and benches were drawn up, the other for a cooking grill and oven. Fires burned brightly in both. A kettle of stew simmered over the grill and hot bread cooled on a cutting board. A long trestle table was carefully set with plates and cups for five. Par stepped forward for a closer look. Cold ale had been poured into all five cups.

The members of the little company looked at each other silently for a moment, then glanced once more about the room. The wood of the walls and beams was polished and waxed. Silver, crystal, carved wooden pieces, and clothwork hangings gleamed in the light of oil lamps and hearth flames. There was a vase of fresh flowers on the trestle table, others in the sitting area. A hall led back into the sleeping rooms. The cottage was bright and cheerful and very empty.

"Is this Walker's?" Morgan asked doubtfully of Par. Somehow it didn't fit the image he had formed of the man.

Par shook his head. "I don't know. There isn't anything here I recognize."

Morgan moved silently to the back hall, disappeared from sight for a moment and returned. "Nothing," he reported, sounding disappointed.

Coll walked over to stand with Par, sniffed the stew experimentally, and shrugged. "Well, obviously our coming here isn't such a surprise after all. I don't know about the rest of you, but that stew smells awfully good. Since someone has gone to the trouble of making it—Walker Boh or whoever—I think the least we can do is sit down and eat it."

Par and Morgan quickly agreed, and even Teel seemed interested. Steff was again inclined to be cautious, but since it was apparent Coll was probably right in his analysis of the situation he quickly gave in. Nevertheless, he insisted on checking first to make certain neither food nor drink was tainted in any way. When he had pronounced the meal fit, they seated themselves and eagerly consumed it.

When dinner was over, they cleared and washed the dishes and put them carefully away in a cabinet built to contain them. Then they searched the cottage a second time, the grounds around it, and finally everything for a quarter-mile in every direction. They found nothing.

They sat around the fire after that until midnight, waiting. No one came. There were two small bedrooms in back with two beds in each. The beds were turned down and the linens and blankets fresh. They took turns sleeping, one keeping watch for the others. They slept the night undisturbed, the forest and the valley at peace about them. Dawn brought them awake feeling much refreshed. Still no one came.

That day, they searched the entire valley from one end to the other, from the cottage to the odd, chimney-shaped rock, from north wall to south, from east to west. The day was warm and bright, filled with sunshine and gentle breezes and the smell of growing things. They took their time, wandering along the streams, following the pathways, exploring the few dens that burrowed the valley slopes like pockets. They found scattered prints, all of them made by animals, and nothing else. Birds flew overhead, sudden flashes of color in the trees, tiny woods creatures watched with darting eyes, and insects buzzed and hummed. Once a badger lumbered into view as Par and Coll hunted the west wall by the rock tower, refusing to give way to them. Other than that, none of them saw anything.

They had to fix their own meal that night, but there was fresh meat and cheese in a cold locker, day-old bread from the previous evening, and vegetables in the garden. The Valemen helped themselves, forcing the others to partake as well despite Steff's continued misgivings, convinced that this was what was expected of them. The day faded into a warm and pleasant night, and they began to grow comfortable with their surroundings. Steff sat with Teel before the gathering fire and smoked a long-stemmed pipe, Par worked in the kitchen with Coll cleaning the dishes, and Morgan took up watch on the front steps.

"Someone has put a lot of effort into keeping up this cottage," Par observed to his brother as they finished their task. "It doesn't seem reasonable that they would just go off and leave it."

"Especially after taking time to make us that stew," Coll added. His broad face furrowed. "Do you think it belongs to Walker?"

"I don't know. I wish I did."

"None of this really seems like him though, does it? Not like the Walker I remember. Certainly not like the one Steff tells us about."

Par wiped the last few droplets of dishwater from a dinner plate and carefully put it away. "Maybe that's how he wants it to appear," he said softly.

It was several hours after midnight when he took the watch from Teel, yawning and stretching as he came out onto the front porch to look for her. The Dwarf was nowhere to be seen at first, and it wasn't until he had come thoroughly awake that she appeared from behind a spruce some several dozen yards out. She slipped noiselessly through the shadows to reach him and disappeared into the cottage without a word. Par glanced after her curiously, then sat down on the front steps, propped his chin in his hands, and stared off into the dark.

He had been sitting there for almost an hour when he heard the sound.

It was a strange sound, a sort of buzzing like a swarm of bees might make, but deep and rough. It was there and then just as quickly gone again. He thought at first he must have made it up, that he had heard it only in his mind. But then it came again, for just an instant, before disappearing once more.

He stood up, looked around tentatively, then walked out onto the pathway. The night was brilliantly clear and the sky filled with stars and bright. The woods about him were empty. He felt reassured and walked slowly around the house and out back. There was an old willow tree there, far back in the shadows, and beneath it a pair of worn benches. Par walked over to them and stopped, listening once again for the noise and hearing nothing. He sat down on the nearest bench. The bench had been carved to the shape of his body, and he felt cradled by it. He sat there for a time, staring out through the veil of the willow's drooping branches, daydreaming in the darkness, listening to the night's silence. He wondered about his parents—if they were well, if they worried for him. Shady Vale was a distant memory.

He closed his eyes momentarily to rest them against the weariness he was feeling. When he opened them again, the moor cat was standing there.

Par's shock was so great that at first he couldn't move. The cat was right in front of him, its whiskered face level with his own, its eyes a luminous gold in the night. It was the biggest animal that Par had ever seen, bigger even than the Gnawl. It was solid black from head to tail except for the eyes, which stared at him unblinkingly.

Then the cat began to purr, and he recognized it as the sound he had heard earlier. The cat turned and walked away a few paces and looked back, waiting. When Par continued to stare at it, it returned momentarily, started away again, stopped and waited.

It wanted him to follow, Par realized.

He rose mechanically, unable to make his body respond in the way he wanted it to, trying to decide if he should do as the cat expected or attempt to break away. He discarded any thought of the latter almost immediately. This was no time to be trying anything foolish. Besides, if the cat wanted to harm him, it could have done so earlier.

He took a few steps forward, and the cat turned away again, moving off into the trees.

They wound through the darkened forest for long minutes, moving silently, steadily into the night. Moonlight flooded the open spaces, and Par had little trouble following. He watched the cat move effortlessly ahead of him, barely disturbing the forest about him, a creature that seemed to have the substance of a shadow. His shock was fading now, replaced by curiosity. Someone had sent the cat to him, and he thought he knew who.

Finally, they reached a clearing in which several streams emptied through a series of tiny rapids into a wide, moonlit pool. The trees here were very old and broad, and their limbs cast an intricate pattern of shadows over everything. The cat walked over to the pool, drank deeply for a moment, then sat back and looked at him. Par came forward a few steps and stopped.

"Hello, Par," someone greeted.

The Valeman searched the clearing for a moment before finding the speaker, who sat well back in the dark on a burled stump, barely distinguishable from the shadows about him. When Par hesitated, he rose and stepped into the light.

"Hello, Walker," Par replied softly.

His uncle was very much as he remembered him—and at the same time completely different. He was still tall and slight, his Elven features apparent though not as pronounced as Par's, his skin a shocking white hue that provided a marked contrast to the shoulder-length black hair and close-cropped beard. His eyes hadn't changed either; they still looked right through you, even when shadowed as they were now. What was different was more difficult to define. It was mostly in the way Walker Boh carried himself and the way he made Par feel when he spoke, even though he had said almost nothing. It was as if there were an invisible wall about him that nothing could penetrate.

Walker Boh came forward and took Par's hands in his own. He was dressed in loose-fitting forest clothing—pants, tunic, a short cloak, and soft boots, all colored like the earth and trees. "Have you been comfortable at the cottage?" he asked.

Par seemed to remember himself then. "Walker, I don't understand. What are you doing out here? Why didn't you meet us when we arrived? Obviously, you knew we were coming."

His uncle released his hands and stepped away. "Come sit with me, Par," he invited, and moved back again into the shadows without waiting for his nephew's response. Par followed, and the two seated themselves on the stump from which Walker had first risen.

Walker looked him over carefully. "I will only be speaking with you," he said quietly. "And only this once."

Par waited, saying nothing. "There have been many changes in my life," his uncle went on after a moment. "I expect you remember little of me from your childhood, and most of what you remember no longer has much to do with who I am now in any case. I gave up my Vale life, any claim to being a Southlander, and came here to begin again. I left behind me the madness of men whose lives are governed by the baser instincts. I separated myself from men of all races, from their greed and their preju- dice, their wars and their politics, and their monstrous conception of bet- terment. I came here, Par, so that I could live alone. I was always alone, of course; I was made to feel alone. The difference now is that I am alone, not because others choose it for me, but because I choose it for myself. I am free to be exactly what I am—and not to feel strange because of it."

He smiled faintly. "It is the time we live in and who we are that make it difficult for both of us, you know. Do you understand me, Par? You have the magic, too—a very tangible magic in your case. It will not win you friends; it will set you apart. We are not permitted to be Ohmsfords these days because Ohmsfords have the magic of their Elven forebears and nei- ther magic nor Elves are appreciated or understood. I grew tired of finding it so, of being set apart, of being constantly looked at with suspicion and mistrust. I grew tired of being thought different. It will happen to you as well, if it hasn't done so already. It is the nature of things."

"I don't let it bother me," Par said defensively. "The magic is a gift."

"Oh? Is it now? How so? A gift is not something you hide as you would a loathsome disease. It is not something of which you are ashamed or cautious or even frightened. It is not something that might kill you."

The words were spoken with such bitterness that Par felt chilled. Then his uncle's mood seemed to change instantly; he grew calm again, quiet. He shook his head in self-reproach. "I forget myself sometimes when speak- ing of the past. I apologize. I brought you here to talk with you of other things. But only with you, Par. I leave the cottage for your companions to use during their stay. But I will not come there to be with them. I am only interested in you."

"But what about Coll?" Par asked, confused. "Why speak with me and not with him?"

His uncle's smile was ironic. "Think, Par. I was never close with him the way I was with you."

Par stared at him silently. That was true, he supposed. It was the magic that had drawn Walker to him, and Coll had never been able to share in that. The time he had spent with his uncle, the time that had made him feel close to the man, had always been time away from Coll.

"Besides," the other continued softly, "what we need to talk about concerns only us."

Par understood then. "The dreams." His uncle nodded. "Then you have experienced them as well—the figure in black, the one who appears to be Allanon, standing before the Hadeshorn, warning us, telling us to come?" Par was breathless. "What about the old man? Has he come to you also?" Again, his uncle nodded. "Then you do know him, don't you? Is it true, Walker? Is he really Cogline?"

Walker Boh's face emptied of expression. "Yes, Par, he is."

Par flushed with excitement, and rubbed his hands together briskly. "I cannot believe it! How old is he? Hundreds of years, I suppose—just as he claimed. And once a Druid. I knew I was right! Does he live here still, Walker—with you?"

"He visits, sometimes. And sometimes stays a bit. The cat was his before he gave it to me. You remember that there was always a moor cat. The one before was called Whisper. That was in the time of Brin Ohmsford. This one is called Rumor. The old man named it. He said it was a good name for a cat—especially one who would belong to me."

He stopped, and something Par couldn't read crossed his face briefly and was gone. The Valeman glanced over to where the cat had been resting, but it had disappeared.

"Rumor comes and goes in the manner of all moor cats," Walker Boh said as if reading his thoughts.

Par nodded absently, then looked back at him. "What are you going to do, Walker?"

"About the dreams?" The strange eyes went flat. "Nothing."

Par hesitated. "But the old man must have . . ."

"Listen to me," the other said, cutting him short. "I am decided on this. I know what the dreams have asked of me; I know who sent them. The old man has come to me, and we have talked. He left not a week past. None of that matters. I am no longer an Ohmsford; I am a Boh. If I could strip away my past, with all its legacy of magic and all its glorious Elven history, I would do so in an instant. I want none of it. I came into the Eastland to find this valley, to live as my ancestors once lived, to be just once where everything is fresh and clean and untroubled by the presence of others. I have learned to keep my life in perfect order and to order the life around me. You have seen this valley; my mother's people made it that way and I have learned to keep it. I have Rumor for company and occasionally the old man. Once in a while, I even visit with those from the outside. Darklin Reach has become a haven for me and Hearthstone my home."

He bent forward, his face intense. "I have the magic, Par—different from yours, but real nevertheless. I can tell what others are thinking sometimes, even when they are far away. I can communicate with life in ways that others cannot. All forms of life. I can disappear sometimes, just like the moor cat. I can even summon power!" He snapped his fingers suddenly, and a brief spurt of blue fire appeared on his fingers. He snuffed it out. "I lack the magic of the wishsong, but apparently some of its power has taken root inside me. Some of what I know is innate; some is self-taught; some was taught to me by others. But I have all I need, and I wish no more. I am comfortable here and will never leave. Let the world get on as best it can without me. It always did so before."

Par struggled to respond. "But what if the dream is right, Walker?" he asked finally.

Walker Boh laughed derisively. "Par! The dreams are never right! Have you not paid heed to your own stories? Whether they manifest themselves as they have this time or as they did when Allanon was alive, one fact remains unchanged—the Ohmsfords are never told everything, only what the Druids deem necessary!"

"You think that we are being used." Par made it a statement of fact.

"I think I would be a fool to believe anything else! I do not trust what I am being told." The other's eyes were as hard as stone. "The magic you insist on regarding as a gift has always been little more than a useful tool to the Druids. I do not intend to let myself be put to whatever new task they have discovered. If the world needs saving as these dreams suggest, let Allanon or the old man go out and save it!"

There was a long moment of silence as the two measured each other. Par shook his head slowly. "You surprise me, Walker. I don't remember the bitterness or the anger from before."

Walker Boh smiled sadly. "It was there, Par. It was always there. You just didn't bother to look for it."

"Shouldn't it be gone by now?"

His uncle kept silent.

"So you are decided on this matter, are you?"

"Yes, Par. I am."

Par took a deep breath. "What will you do, Walker, if the things in the dream come to pass? What will become of your home then? What will happen if the evil the dream showed us decides to come looking for you?"

His uncle said nothing, but the steady gaze never wavered. Par nodded slowly. "I have a different view of matters from yours, Walker," he said softly. "I have always believed that the magic was a gift, and that it was given to me for a reason. It appeared for a long time that it was meant to be used to tell the stories, to keep them from being forgotten completely. I have changed my mind about that. I think now that the magic is meant for something more."

He shifted, straightening himself because he was feeling suddenly small in the presence of the other. "Coll and I cannot go back to the Vale because the Federation has found out about the magic and is hunting for us. The old man, Cogline, says there may be other things hunting us as well— perhaps even Shadowen. Have you seen the Shadowen? I have. Coll and I are scared to death, Walker, though we don't talk about it much. The funny thing is, I think the things hunting us are scared, too. It's the magic that scares them." He paused. "I don't know why that is, but I mean to find out."

There was a flicker of surprise in Walker Boh's eyes. Par nodded. "Yes, Walker, I have decided to do as the dreams have asked. I believe they were sent by Allanon, and I believe they should be heeded. I will go to the Hadeshorn. I think I made the decision just now; I think listening to you helped me decide. I haven't told Coll. I don't really know what he will do. Maybe I will end up going alone. But I will go. If for no other reason, I will go because I think Allanon can tell me what the magic is intended to do."

He shook his head sadly. "I can't be like you, Walker. I can't live apart from the rest of the world. I want to be able to go back to Shady Vale. I don't want to go away and start life over. I came this way through Culhaven. The Dwarves who brought us are from there. All of the prejudice and greed, the politics and wars, all of the madness you speak about is very much in evidence there. But unlike you I don't want to escape it; I want to find a way to end it! How can that happen if I simply pretend it doesn't exist!"

His hands tightened into fists. "You see, I keep thinking, what if Allanon knows something that can change the way things are? What if he can tell me something that will put an end to the madness?"

They faced each other in the dark for a long time without speaking, and Par thought he saw things in his uncle's dark eyes that he hadn't seen since his childhood—things that whispered of caring and need and sacrifice. Then the eyes were flat again, expressionless, empty. Walker Boh came to his feet.

"Will you reconsider?" Par asked him quietly.

Walker regarded him silently, then walked to the pool at the center of the clearing and stood looking down. When his fingers snapped, Rumor materialized from out of nowhere and came over to him.

He turned momentarily and looked back. "Good luck, Par," was all he said.

Then he turned, the cat beside him, and disappeared into the night.

P ar waited until morning to tell the others of his meeting with Walker Boh. There did not seem to be any reason to hurry it. Walker had made clear his intentions, and there was nothing any of them could do about it in any case. So Par made his way back to the cottage, surprising himself at how easily he was able to retrace his steps, resumed his watch without disturbing the others, lost himself in his thoughts, and waited for dawn.

Reactions were mixed when he finally related his story. There was some initial doubt as to whether he was mistaken about what happened, but that dissipated almost at once. They made him tell the story twice more after that, interjecting comments and questions in equal measure as he went.

Morgan was outraged that Walker should treat them like this, declaring that they deserved at the very least the courtesy of a direct confrontation. He insisted that they search the valley again, convinced that the man must be close by and should be found and made to face them all. Steff was more pragmatic. He was of the opinion that Walker Boh was no different from most, preferring to stay out of trouble when he could, avoiding situations in which trouble would most probably result.

"It seems to me that his behavior, however irritating you might find it, is certainly not out of character," the Dwarf declared with a shrug. "After all, you said yourselves that he came here to escape involvement with the Races. By refusing to go to the Hadeshorn, he is simply doing what he said he would do."

Teel, as usual, had nothing to say. Coll only said, "I wish I could have spoken with him," and dropped the matter.

There was no reason now to stay longer at Hearthstone, but they decided to postpone leaving for at least another day. The moon was still more than half full, and they had at least another ten days left to them before they were required to be at the Hadeshorn—if, indeed, they were going at all. The subject of what was to happen next was being carefully avoided. Par had made up his own mind, but had not yet told the others. They, of course, were waiting to hear from him. While they played at this game of cat-and-mouse, they finished breakfast and decided to go along with Morgan's suggestion and scout the valley one more time. It gave them something to do while they considered the implications of Walker Boh's decision. Tomorrow morning would be time enough to make any decisions of their own.

So they went back to the clearing where Par had met with Walker and the moor cat the previous night and began a second search, agreeing to meet back at the cottage by late afternoon. Steff and Teel formed one group, Par and Coll a second, and Morgan went alone. The day was warm and filled with sunshine, and a light breeze blew down out of the distant mountains. Steff scoured the clearing for signs of any sort and found nothing—not even the tracks of the cat. Par had a feeling that it was going to be a long day.

He walked east with Coll after parting from the others, his mind crowding with thoughts of what he should say to his brother. A mix of emotions worked their way through him, and he found it difficult to sort them out. He ambled along halfheartedly, conscious of Coll watching him from time to time, but avoiding his gaze. After they had wandered through several dozen clearings and forded half that many streams without coming on even a trace of Walker Boh, Par called a halt.

"This is a waste of time," he announced, a hint of exasperation creeping into his voice. "We're not going to find anything."

"I don't imagine we are," Coll replied.

Par turned to him, and they faced each other silently for a moment. "I have decided to go on to the Hadeshorn, Coll. It doesn't matter what Walker does; it only matters what I do. I have to go."

Coll nodded. "I know." Then he smiled. "Par, I haven't been your brother all these years without learning something about the way you think. The moment you told me that Walker had said he would have nothing to do with the matter, I knew you'd decided you would. That's the way it is with you. You're like a dog with a bone in its teeth—you can't let go."

"I suppose that's the way it seems sometimes, doesn't it?" Par shook his head wearily and moved over to a patch of shade beneath an old hickory. He turned his back to the trunk and slid to the ground. Coll joined him. They sat staring out at the empty woodlands. "I admit that I made the decision pretty much the way you describe it. I just couldn't accept Walker's position. Truth is, Coll, I couldn't even understand it. I was so upset, I didn't even think to ask him whether he believed the dreams were real or not."

"Not consciously, perhaps—but you thought about it. And you decided at some point it wasn't necessary. Walker said that he'd had the same dreams as you. He told you the old man had come to him just as he did to us. He admitted the old man was Cogline. He didn't dispute any of it. He simply said he didn't want to become involved. The implication is that he believes the dreams are real—otherwise, there wouldn't be anything to get involved with."

Par's jaw tightened. "I don't understand it, Coll. That was Walker I spoke with last night; I know it was. But he didn't talk like Walker. All that business about not becoming involved, about his decision to separate himself from the Races, and to live out here like a hermit. Something's not right; I can feel it! He wasn't telling me everything. He kept talking about how the Druids kept secrets from the Ohmsfords, but he was doing the same thing with me! He was hiding something!"

Coll looked unconvinced. "Why would he do that?"

Par shook his head. "I don't know. I just sense it." He looked at his brother sharply. "Walker never backed down from anything in his entire life; we both know that. He was never afraid to stand up and be counted when he was needed. Now he talks as if he can scarcely bear the thought of getting up in the morning! He talks as if the only important thing in life is to look out for himself!" The Valeman leaned back wearily against the hickory trunk. "He made me feel embarrassed for him. He made me feel ashamed!"

"I think you might be reading too much into this." Coll scuffed the ground with the heel of his boot. "It may be just the way he says it is. He's lived alone out here for a long time, Par. Maybe he simply isn't comfortable with people anymore."

"Even you?" Par was incensed. "For goodness sake, Coll—he wouldn't even speak with you!"

Coll shook his head and held his gaze steady. "The truth is, Par, we never spoke much as it was. You were the one he cared about, because you were the one with the magic."

Par looked at him and said nothing. Walker's exact words, he thought. He was just fooling himself when he tried to equate Coll's relationship with their uncle to his own. It had never been the same.

He frowned. "There is still the matter of the dreams. Why doesn't he share my curiosity about them? Doesn't he want to know what Allanon has to say?"

Coll shrugged. "Maybe he already knows. He seems to know what everyone is thinking most of the time."

Par hesitated. He hadn't considered that. Was it possible his uncle had already determined what the Druid would tell them at the Hadeshorn? Could he read the mind of a shade, a man three hundred years dead?

He shook his head. "No, I don't think so. He would have said something more than he did about the reason for the dreams. He spent all of his time dismissing the matter as one more instance when the Ohmsfords would be used by the Druids; he didn't care what the reason was."

"Then perhaps he is relying on you to tell him."

Par nodded slowly. "That makes better sense. I told him I was going; maybe he thinks that one of us going is enough."

Coll stretched his big frame full length on the ground and stared up into the trees. "But you don't believe that either, do you?"

His brother smiled faintly. "No."

"You still think that it's something else."

"Yes."

They didn't speak for a time, staring off into the woods, thinking their separate thoughts. Slender streams of sunlight played along their bodies through chinks in the limbs canopied overhead, and the songs of birds filtered through the stillness. "I like it here," Par said finally.

Coll had his eyes closed. "Where do you think he's hiding?"

"Walker? I don't know. Under a rock, I suppose."

"You're too quick to judge him, Par. You don't have the right to do that."

Par bit off what he was going to say next and contented himself with watching a ray of sunlight work its way across Coll's face until it was in his eyes, causing him to blink and shift his body. Coll sat up, his squarish face a mask of contentment. Not much of anything ruffled him; he always managed to keep his sense of balance. Par admired him for that. Coll always understood the relative importance of events in the greater scheme of things.

Par was aware suddenly of how much he loved his brother.

"Are you coming with me, Coll?" he asked then. "To the Hadeshorn?"

Coll looked at him and blinked. "Isn't it odd," he replied, "that you and Walker and even Wren have the dreams and I don't, that all of you are mentioned in them, but never me, and that all of you are called, but not me?" There was no rancor in his voice, only puzzlement. "Why do you think that is? We've never talked about it, you and I, have we? Not once. I think we have both been very careful to avoid talking about it."

Par stared at him and didn't know what to say. Coll saw his discomfort and smiled. "Awkward, isn't it? Don't look so miserable, Par. It isn't as if the matter is any fault of yours." He leaned close. "Maybe it has something to do with the magic—something none of us knows yet. Maybe that's it."

Par shook his head and sighed. "I'd be lying if I said that the whole business of me having dreams and you not having them doesn't make me very uncomfortable. I don't know what to say. I keep expecting you to involve yourself in something that doesn't really concern you. I shouldn't even ask—but I guess I can't help it. You're my brother, and I want you with me."

Coll reached out and put a hand on Par's shoulder. His smile was warm. "Now and then, Par, you do manage to say the right thing." He tightened his grip. "I go where you go. That's the way it is with us. I'm not saying I always agree with the way you reason things out, but that doesn't change how I feel about you. So if you believe you must go to the Hadeshorn to resolve this matter of the dreams, then I am going with you."

Par put his arms around his brother and hugged him, thinking of all the times Coll had stood by him when he was asked, warmed by the feeling it gave him to know that Coll would be with him again now. "I knew I could depend on you," was all he said.

It was late afternoon by the time they started back. They had intended to return earlier, but had become preoccupied with talking about the dreams and Allanon and had wandered all the way to the east wall of the valley before realizing how late it had become. Now, with the sun already inching toward the rim of the western horizon, they began to retrace their steps.

"It looks as if we might get our feet wet," Coll announced as they worked their way back through the trees.

Par glanced skyward. A mass of heavy rain clouds had appeared at the northern edge of the valley, darkening the whole of the skyline. The sun was already beginning to disappear, enveloped in the growing darkness. The air was warm and sticky, and the forest was hushed.

They made their way more quickly now, anxious to avoid a drenching. A stiff breeze sprang up, heralding the approach of the storm, whipping the leafy branches of the trees about them in frantic dances. The temperature began to drop, and the forest grew dark and shadowed.

Par muttered to himself as he felt a flurry of scattered raindrops strike his face. It was bad enough that they were out there looking for someone who wasn't about to be found in the first place. Now they were going to get soaked for their efforts.

Then he saw something move in the trees.

He blinked and looked again. This time he didn't see anything. He slowed without realizing it, and Coll, who was trailing a step or so behind, asked what was wrong. Par shook his head and picked up the pace again.

The wind whipped into his face, forcing him to lower his head against its sting. He glanced right, then left. There were flashes of movement to either side.

Something was tracking them.

Par felt the hair on the back of his neck prickle, but he forced himself to keep moving. Whatever was out there didn't have the look or the movement of either Walker Boh or the cat. Too quick, too agile. He tried to gather his thoughts. How far were they from the cottage—a mile, maybe less? He kept his head up as he walked, trying to follow the movement out of the corner of his eye. Movements, he corrected himself. There was clearly more than one of them.

"Par!" Coll said as they brushed close passing through a narrow winding of trees. "There's something . . ."

"I know!" Par cut him short. "Keep moving!"

They made their way through a broad stand of fir, and the rain began to fall in earnest. The sun, the walls of the valley, even the dark pinnacle of Hearthstone had disappeared. Par felt his breathing quicken. Their pursuers were all around them now, shadows that had taken on vaguely human form as they flitted through the trees.

They're closing in on us, Par thought frantically. How much farther was the cottage?

Coll cried out suddenly as they pushed through a stand of red maple into a small, empty clearing. "Par, run for it! They're too close . . . !"

He grunted sharply and pitched forward. Par wheeled instinctively and caught him. There was blood on Coll's forehead, and he was unconscious.

Par never had time to figure out what had happened. He looked up, and the shadows were on top of him. They broke from the concealment of the trees all around him, bounding into view in a flurry of motion. Par caught a brief glimpse of bent, crooked forms covered with coarse, black hair and of glinting, ferret eyes, and then they were all over him. He flung them away as he struggled to escape, feeling tough, wiry limbs grapple at him. For a moment, he kept his feet. He cried out frantically, summoning the magic of the wishsong, sending forth a scattering of frightful images in an effort to protect himself. There were howls of fear, and his attackers shrank from him.

This time, he got a good look at them. He saw the strange, insectlike forms with their vaguely human faces, all twisted and hairy.

Spider Gnomes, he thought in disbelief!

Then they were on him once more, bearing him down by the sheer weight of their numbers. He was enveloped in a mass of sinew and hair and thrown to the ground. He could no longer summon the magic. His arms were being forced back, and he was being choked. He struggled desperately, but there were too many.

He had only a moment more to try to call out for help, and then everything went dark.

11

When he came awake again, Par Ohmsford found himself in the middle of a nightmare. He was bound hand and foot and hanging from a pole. He was being carried through a forest thick with mist and shadows, the dark crease of a deep ravine visible to his left, the jagged edge of a ridgeline sharp against the night sky to his right. Scrub and the dense tangle of grasses and weeds slapped at his back and head as he swung helplessly from the pole, and the air was thick, humid, and still.

There were Spider Gnomes all around him, creeping soundlessly through the half-light on crooked legs.

Par closed his eyes momentarily to shut out the images, then opened them again. The skies were dark and overcast, but a scattering of stars shone through creases in the clouds and there was a faint hint of brightness beyond the drop of the ravine. Night had come and gone, he realized. It was almost morning.

He remembered then what had happened to him, how the Spider Gnomes had chased him, seized him, and taken him away. Coll! What had happened to Coll? He craned his neck in an effort to see if his brother had been brought as well, but there was no sign of him. He clenched his jaw in rage, remembering Coll falling, then sprawled on the ground with blood on his face . . .

He wiped the image quickly from his mind. It was useless to dwell on it. He must find a way to get free and return for his brother. He worked momentarily against the ropes that bound him, testing their strength, but there was no give. Hanging as he was, he could not find the leverage necessary to loosen them. He would have to wait. He wondered then where he was being taken—why he had been taken in the first place, for that matter. What did the Spider Gnomes want of him?

Insects buzzed in his face, flying at his eyes and mouth. He buried his face into his arms and left it there.

When he brought it out again, he tried to determine where he was. The light was to his left, the beginnings of the new day. East, then, he decided—the Spider Gnomes were traveling north. That made sense. The Spider Gnomes had made their home on Toffer Ridge in Brin Ohmsford's time. That was probably where he was. He swallowed against the dryness in his mouth and throat. Thirst and fear, he thought. He tried to recall what he could of Spider Gnomes from the stories of the old days, but he was unable to focus his thoughts. Brin had encountered them when she, Rone

Leah, Cogline, Kimber Boh, and the moor cat Whisper had gone after the missing Sword of Leah. There was something else, something about a wasteland and the terrifying creatures that lived within it . . .

Then he remembered. *Werebeasts.* The name whispered in his mind like a curse.

The Spider Gnomes turned down a narrow defile, filling it with their hairy forms like a dark stain, chittering now in what appeared to be anticipation. The brightness in the east disappeared, and shadows and mist closed about them like a wall. His wrists and ankles ached, and his body felt stretched beyond help. The Gnomes were small and carried him close to the ground so that he bumped and scraped himself at every turn. He watched from his upside down position as the defile broadened into a shelf that opened out over a vast, mist-shrouded stretch of emptiness that seemed to run on forever. The shelf became a corridor through a series of boulders that dotted the side of Toffer Ridge like knots on the back of a boar. Firelight flickered in the distance, pinpricks of brightness playing hide-and-seek among the rocks. A handful of Spider Gnomes bounded ahead, skittering effortlessly over the rocks.

Par took a deep breath. Wherever it was they were going, they were almost there.

A moment later, they emerged from the rocks and came to a halt on a low bluff that ran back to a series of burrows and caves tunneled into the side of the ridge. Fires burned all about, and hundreds of Spider Gnomes hoved into view. Par was dumped unceremoniously, the bonds that secured him cut and the pole removed. He lay there on his back for a moment, rubbing his wrists and ankles, finding creases so deep that he bled, conscious all the time of the eyes watching him. Then he was hauled to his feet and dragged toward the caves and burrows. They bypassed the latter in favor of the former, the gnarled hands of the Gnomes fastened on him at every conceivable point, the stink of their bodies filling his nostrils. They chittered at each other in their own language, their talk incessant now and meaningless to him. He did not resist; he could barely stand upright. They took him through the largest of the cave openings, propelled him past a small fire that burned at its mouth and stopped. There was some discussion, a few moments' worth at best, and then he was thrust forward. He saw they were in a smallish cave that ran back only twenty yards or so and was no more than eight feet at its highest point. A pair of iron rings had been hammered into the rock wall at the cave's deepest point, and the Spider Gnomes lashed him to those. Then they left him, all but two who remained behind to take up watch by the fire at the cave entrance.

Par let his mind clear, listening to the silence, waiting to see what would happen next. When nothing did, he took a careful look about. He had been left spread-eagle against the rock wall, one arm secured to each of the iron rings. He was forced to remain standing because the rings were fastened too high up on the rock to allow him to sit. He tested his bonds.

They were leather and secured so tightly that his wrists could not slip within them even the smallest amount.

He sagged back momentarily in despair, forcing down the panic that threatened to overwhelm him. The others would be looking for him by now—Morgan, Steff, Teel. They would already have found Coll. They would track the Spider Gnomes and come for him. They would find him and rescue him.

He shook his head. He was just kidding himself, he knew. It was almost dark when the Gnomes had taken him and the rain had been a hard one. There would have been no time for a search and no real chance of finding a trail. The best he could hope for was that Coll had been found or revived himself and gone to the others to tell them what had happened.

He swallowed again against the dryness. He was so thirsty!

Time slipped away, turning seconds to minutes, minutes to hours. The darkness outside brightened minimally, bringing a barely penetrable daylight, choked with heat and mist. The faint sounds of the Spider Gnomes disappeared altogether, and he would have thought them gone completely if not for the two who sat hunkered down by the cave's entrance. The fire went out, smoking for a time, then turning to ash. The day slipped away. Once, one of the guards rose and brought him a cup of water. He drank it greedily from the hands that held it up to his mouth, spilling most of it, soaking his shirt front. He grew hungry as well, but no food was offered.

When the day began to fade to darkness again, the guards rebuilt the fire at the mouth of the cave, then disappeared.

Par waited expectantly, forgetting for the first time the ache of his body, the hunger and the fear. Something was going to happen now. He could feel it.

What happened was altogether unexpected. He was working again at his bonds, his sweat loosening them now, mingling with traces of his blood from the cuts the ties had made, when a figure appeared from the shadows. It came past the fire and into the light and stopped.

It was a child.

Par blinked. The child was a girl, perhaps a dozen years of age, rather tall and skinny with dark, lank hair and deepset eyes. She was not a Gnome, but of the Race of Man, a Southlander, with a tattered dress, worn boots, and a small silver locket about her neck. She looked at him curiously, studied him as she might a stray dog or cat, then came slowly forward. She stopped when she reached him, then lifted one hand to brush back his hair and touch his ear.

"Elf," she said quietly, fingering the ear's tip.

Par stared. What was a child doing out here among the Spider Gnomes? He wet his lips. "Untie me," he begged.

She looked at him some more, saying nothing. "Untie me!" Par said again, more insistent this time. He waited, but the child just looked at him.

He felt the beginnings of doubt creep through him. Something was not right.

"Hug you," the child said suddenly.

She came to him almost anxiously, wrapping her arms about him, fastening herself to him like a leech. She clung to him, burying herself in his body, murmuring over and over again something he could not understand. What was the matter with this child, he wondered in dismay? She seemed lost, frightened perhaps, needing to hold him as much as he . . .

The thought died away as he felt her stirring against him, moving within her clothes, against his clothes, then against his skin. Her fingers had tightened into him, and he could feel her pressing, pressing. Shock flooded through him. She was right against him, against his skin, as if they wore no clothes at all, as if all their garments had been shed. She was burrowing, coming against him, then coming into him, merging somehow with him, making herself a part of him.

Shades! What was happening?

Repulsion filled him with a suddenness that was terrifying. He screamed, shook himself in horror, kicked out desperately and at last flung her away. She fell in a crouch, her child's face transformed into something hideous, smiling like a beast at feeding, eyes sharp and glinting with pinpricks of red light.

"Give me the magic, boy!" she rasped in a voice that sounded nothing of a child's.

Then he knew. "Oh, no, oh, no," he whispered over and over, bracing himself as she came slowly back to her feet.

This child was a Shadowen!

"Give it to me!" she repeated, her voice demanding. "Let me come into you and taste it!"

She came toward him, a spindly little thing, a bit of nothing, if her face had not betrayed her. She reached for him and he kicked out at her desperately. She smiled wickedly and stepped back.

"You are mine," she said softly. "The Gnomes have given you to me. I will have your magic, boy. Give yourself to me. See what I can feel like!"

She came at him like a cat at its prey, avoiding his kick, fastening herself to him with a howl. He could feel her moving almost immediately—not the child herself, but something within the child. He forced himself to look down and could see the faintest whisper of a dark outline shimmering within the child's body, trying to move into his own. He could feel its presence, like a chill on a summer's day, like fly's feet against his skin. The Shadowen was touching, seeking. He threw back his head, clenched his jaw, made his body as rigid as iron, and fought it. The thing, the Shadowen, was trying to come into him. It was trying to merge with him. Oh, Shades! He must not let it! He must not!

Then, unexpectedly, he cried out, releasing the magic of the wishsong in a howl of mingled rage and anguish. It took no form, for he had already determined that even his most frightening images were of no use against these creatures. It came of its own volition, breaking free from some dark corner of his being to take on a shape he did not recognize. It was a dark, unrecognizable thing, and it whipped about him like webbing from a spider about its prey. The Shadowen hissed and tore itself away, spitting and clawing at the air. It dropped again into a crouch, the child's body contorted and shivering from something unseen. Par's cry died into silence at the sight of it, and he sagged back weakly against the cave wall.

"Stay back from me!" he warned, gasping for breath. "Don't touch me again!"

He didn't know what he had done or how he had done it, but the Shadowen hunched down against the firelight and glared at him in defeat. The hint of the being within the child's body shimmered briefly and was gone. The glint of red in the eyes disappeared. The child rose slowly and straightened, a child in truth once more, frail and lost. Dark eyes studied him for long moments and she said faintly once more, "Hug me."

Then she called into the gathering darkness without, and the Spider Gnomes reappeared, several dozen strong, bowing and scraping to the child as they entered. She spoke to them in their own language while they knelt before her, and Par remembered how superstitious these creatures were, believing in gods and spirits of all sorts. And now they were in the thrall of a Shadowen. He wanted to scream.

The Spider Gnomes came for him, loosened the bonds that secured him, seized his arms and legs, and pulled him forward. The child blocked their way. "Hug me?" She looked almost forlorn.

He shook his head, trying to break free of the dozens of hands that held him. He was dragged outside in the twilight haze where the smoke of the fires and the mist of the lowlands mingled and swirled like dreams in sleep. He was stopped at the bluff's edge, staring down into a pit of emptiness.

The child was beside him, her voice soft, insidious. "Olden Moor," she whispered. "Werebeasts live there. Do you know Werebeasts, Elf-boy?" He stiffened. "They shall have you now if you do not hug me. Feed on you despite your magic."

He broke free then, flinging his captors from him. The Shadowen hissed and shrank away, and the Spider Gnomes scattered. He lunged, trying to break through, but they blocked his way and bore him back. He whirled, buffeted first this way, then that. Hands reached for him, gnarled and hairy and grasping. He lost himself in a whirl of coarse bodies and chittering voices, hearing only his own voice screaming from somewhere inside not to be taken again, not to be held.

He was suddenly at the edge of the bluff. He summoned the magic of the wishsong, striking out with images at the Spider Gnomes who beset him, desperately trying to force a path through their midst. The Shadowen had disappeared, lost somewhere in the smoke and shadows.

Then he felt his feet go out from under him, the edge of the bluff giving way beneath the weight of his attackers. He grappled for them, for a handhold anywhere, and found nothing. He toppled clear of the bluff, falling into the abyss, tumbling into the swirl of mist. The Shadowen, the Spider Gnomes, the fires, caves, and burrows all disappeared behind him. Down he fell, head-over-heels, tumbling through scrub brush and grasses, across slides and between boulders. Miraculously, he missed the rocks that might have killed or crippled him, falling clear finally in a long, agonizing drop that ended in jarring blackness.

He was unconscious for a time; he didn't know how long. When he came awake again, he found himself in a crushed bed of damp marsh grasses. The grasses, he realized, must have broken his fall and probably saved his life. He lay there, the breath knocked from his body, listening to the sound of his heart pumping in his breast. When his strength returned and his vision cleared, he climbed gingerly to his feet and checked himself. His entire body was a mass of cuts and bruises, but there appeared to be nothing broken. He stood without moving then and listened. From somewhere far above, he could hear the voices of the Spider Gnomes.

They would be coming for him, he knew. He had to get out of there.

He looked about. Mist and shadows chased each other through a twilight world of gathering darkness, night descending quickly now. Small, almost invisible things skipped and jumped through the tall grasses. Ooze sucked and bubbled all about, hidden quagmires surrounding islands of solid earth. Stunted trees and brush defined the landscape, frozen in grotesque poses. Sounds were distant and directionless. Everything seemed and looked the same, a maze without end.

Par took a deep breath to steady himself. He could guess where he was. He had been on Toffer Ridge. His fall had taken him down off the ridge and right into Olden Moor. In his efforts to escape his fate, he had only managed to find it sooner. He had put himself exactly where the Shadowen had threatened to send him—into the domain of the Werebeasts.

He set his jaw and started moving. He was only at the edge of the moor, he told himself—not fully into it yet, not lost. He still had the ridge behind him to serve as a guide. If he could follow it far enough south, he could escape. But he had to be quick.

He could almost feel the Werebeasts watching him.

The stories of the Werebeasts came back to him now, jarred free by the realization of where he was and sharpened by his fear. They were an old magic, monsters who preyed off strayed and lost creatures who wandered into the moor or were sent there, stealing away their strength and spirit and feeding on their lives. The Spider Gnomes were their principal food; the Spider Gnomes believed the Werebeasts were spirits that required appeasement, and they sacrificed themselves accordingly. Par went cold at the thought. That was what the Shadowen had intended for him.

Fatigue slowed him and made him unsteady. He stumbled several times, and once he stepped hip-deep into a quagmire before quickly pulling free. His vision was blurred, and sweat ran down his back. The moor's heat was stultifying, even at night. He glanced skyward and realized that the last of the light was fading. Soon it would be completely black.

Then he would not be able to see at all.

A massive pool of sludge barred his passage, the wall of the ridge eaten away so that it was impossible to climb past. His only choice was to go around, deeper into the moor. He moved quickly, following the line of the swamp, listening for sounds of pursuit. There were none. The moor was still and empty. He swung back toward the bluff, encountered a maze of gullies with masses of things moving through them, and swung wide again. Steadily, he went on, exhausted, but unable to rest. The darkness deepened. He found the end of the maze and started back again toward the bluff. He walked a long way, circling quagmires and sinkholes, peering expectantly through the gloom.

He could not find Toffer Ridge.

He walked more quickly now, anxious, fighting down the fear that threatened to overwhelm him. He was lost, he realized—but he refused to accept it. He kept searching, unable to believe that he could have mistaken his direction so completely. The base of the ridge had been right there! How could he have become so turned about?

At last he stopped, unable to continue with the charade. There was no point in going on, because the truth of the matter was he had no idea where he was going. He would simply continue to wander about endlessly until either the swamp or the Werebeasts claimed him. It was better that he stand and fight.

It was an odd decision, one brought about less by sound reasoning than by fatigue. After all, what hope was there for him if he didn't escape the moor and how could he escape the moor if he stopped moving? But he was tired and he didn't like the idea of running about blindly. And he kept thinking of that child, that Shadowen—shrinking from him, driven back by some shading of his magic that he hadn't even known existed. He still didn't understand what it was, but if he could somehow summon it again and master it in even the smallest way, then he had a chance against the Werebeasts and anything else the swamp might send against him.

He glanced about momentarily, then walked to a broad hillock with quagmire on two sides, jutting rocks on a third, and only one way in. Only one way out, as well, he reminded himself as he ascended the rise, but then he wasn't going anywhere, was he? He found a flat rock and seated himself, facing out into the mist and night. Until it grew light again, this was where he would make his stand.

The minutes slipped away. Night descended, the mist thickened, but there was still light, a sort of curious phosphorescence given off by the sparse vegetation. Its glow was faint and deceptive, but it gave Par the means to distinguish what lay about him and the belief that he could catch sight of anything sneaking up.

Nevertheless, he didn't see the Shadowen until it was almost on top of him. It was the child again, tall, thin, wasted. She appeared seemingly out of nowhere, no more than a few yards in front of him, and he started with the suddenness of her coming.

"Get back from me!" he warned, coming quickly to his feet. "If you try to touch me . . ."

The Shadowen shimmered into mist and disappeared.

Par took a deep breath. It hadn't been a Shadowen after all, he thought, but a Werebeast—and not so tough, if he could send it packing with just a threat!

He wanted to laugh. He was near exhaustion, both physically and emotionally, and he knew he was no longer entirely rational. He hadn't chased anything away. That Werebeast had simply come in for a look. They were toying with him, the way they did with their prey—taking on familiar forms, waiting for the right opportunity, for fatigue or fright or foolishness to give them an opening. He thought again about the stories, about the inevitability of the stalking, then pushed it all from his mind.

Somewhere in the distance, far from where he sat, something cried out once, a quick shriek of dismay. Then everything was still again.

He stared into the mist, watching. He found himself thinking of the circumstances that had brought him here—of his flight from the Federation, of his dreams, his meeting with the old man, and his search for Walker Boh. He had come a long way because of those circumstances and he still wasn't anywhere. He felt a pang of disappointment that he hadn't accomplished more, that he hadn't learned anything useful. He thought again of his conversation with Walker. Walker had told him the wishsong's magic was not a gift, despite his insistence that it was, and that there wasn't anything worthwhile to discover about its use. He shook his head. Well, perhaps there wasn't. Perhaps he had just been kidding himself all along.

But something about it had frightened that Shadowen. Something.

Yet only that child, not any of the others that he had encountered.

What had been different?

There was movement again at the edge of the mists, and a figure detached itself and moved toward him. It was the second Shadowen, the great, shambling creature they had encountered at the edge of the Anar. It slouched toward him, grunting, carrying a monstrous club. For a moment, he forgot what he was facing. He panicked, remembering that the wishsong had been ineffective against this Shadowen, that he had been helpless. He started to back away, then caught himself, thrust away his confusion and shook clear his mind. Impulsively, he used the wishsong, its magic creating an identical image of the creature facing him, an image that he used to cloak himself. Shadowen faced Shadowen. Then the Werebeast shimmered and faded back into the mist.

Par went still and let the image concealing him dissolve. He sat down again. How long could he keep this up?

He wondered if Coll was all right. He saw his brother stretched upon the earth bleeding and he remembered how helpless he had felt at that moment. He thought about how much he depended on his brother.

Coll.

His mind wandered, shifted. There was a use for his magic, he told himself sternly. It was not as Walker had said. There was a purpose in his having it; it was indeed a gift. He would find the answers at the Hadeshorn. He would find them when he spoke to Allanon. He must simply get free of this moor and . . .

A gathering of shadowy forms emerged from the mists before him, dark and forbidding bits of ethereal motion in the night. The Werebeasts had decided to wait no longer. He jerked to his feet, facing them. They eased gradually closer, first one, then another, none with any discernible shape, all shifting and changing as rapidly as the mists.

Then he saw Coll, pulled from the darkness behind the shadows, gripped in substanceless hands, his face ashen and bloodied. Par went cold. *Help me,* he heard his brother call out, though the sound of the voice was only in his mind. *Help me, Par.*

Par screamed something with the magic of the wishsong, but it dissipated into the dank air of Olden Moor in a scattering of broken sounds. Par shook as if chilled. Shades! That really was Coll! His brother struggled, fighting to break free, calling out repeatedly, *Par, Par!*

He went to his brother's aid almost without thinking. He attacked the Werebeasts with a fury that was entirely unexpected. He cried out, the wishsong's magic thrusting at the creatures, hammering them back. He reached Coll and seized him, pulling him free. Hands groped for him, touching. He felt pain, freezing and burning both at once. Coll gripped him, and the pain intensified. Poison flooded into him, bitter and harsh. His strength almost gave out, but he managed to keep his feet, hauling his brother clear of the shadows, pulling him onto the rise.

Below, the shadows clustered and shifted watchfully. Par howled down at them, knowing he was infected, feeling the poison work its way through his body. Coll stood next to him, not speaking. Par's thoughts scattered, and his sense of what he was about drifted away.

The Werebeasts began to close.

Then there was fresh movement on the rocks to his right, and something huge appeared. Par tried to move away, but the effort brought him to his knees. Great, luminous yellow eyes blinked into the night, and a massive black shadow bounded to his side.

"Rumor!" he whispered in disbelief.

The moor cat edged carefully past him to face Coll. The huge cat growled, a low, dangerous warning cough that seemed to break through the mist and fill the darkness with shards of sound. "Coll?" Par called out to his brother and started forward, but the moor cat quickly blocked his way, shoving him back. The shadows were moving closer, taking on form now, becoming lumbering things, bodies covered with scales and hair, faces that showed demon eyes and jaws split wide in hunger. Rumor spat at them and lunged, bringing them up short to hiss back at him.

Then he whirled with claws and teeth bared and tore Coll to pieces.

Coll—what had appeared to be Coll—turned into a thing of indescribable horror, bloodied and shredded, then shimmered and disappeared— another deception. Par cried out in anguish and fury. Tricked! Ignoring the pain and the sudden nausea, he sent the magic of the wishsong hurtling at the Werebeasts, daggers and arrows of fury, images of things that could rend and tear. The Werebeasts shimmered and the magic passed harmlessly by.

Re-forming, the Werebeasts attacked.

Rumor caught the closest a dozen paces off, hammering it away with a single breathtaking swipe of one great paw. Another lunged, but the cat caught it as well and sent it spinning. Others were appearing now from the shadows and mist behind those already creeping forward. Too many, thought Par frantically! He was too weak to stand, the poison from the Werebeasts' touch seeping through him rapidly now, threatening to drop him into that familiar black abyss that had begun to open within.

Then he felt a hand on his shoulder, firm and instantly comforting, re-assuring him and at the same time holding him in place, and he heard a voice call sharply, "Rumor!"

The moor cat edged back, never turning to look, responding to the sound of the voice alone. Par lifted his face. Walker Boh was beside him, wrapped in black robes and mist, his narrow, chiseled face set in a look that turned Par cold, his skin so white it might have been drawn in chalk.

"Keep still, Par," he said.

He moved forward to face the Werebeasts. There were more than a dozen now, crouched down at the edge of the rise, drifting in and out of the mist and night. They hesitated at Walker Boh's approach, almost as if they knew him. Par's uncle came directly down to them, stopping when he was less than a dozen yards from the nearest.

"Leave," he said simply and pointed off into the night. The Werebeasts held their ground. Walker came forward another step, and this time his voice was so hard that it seemed to shiver the air. "Leave!"

One of them lunged at him, a monstrous thing, jaws snapping as it reached for the black-robed figure. Walker Boh's hand shot out, dust scattering into the beast. Fire erupted into the night with an explosion that rocked the bottomland, and the Werebeast simply disappeared.

Walker's extended hand swept the circle of those that remained, threatening. An instant later, the Werebeasts had faded back into the night and were gone.

Walker turned and came back up the rise, kneeling next to Par. "This is my fault," he said quietly.

Par struggled to speak and felt his strength give out. He was sick. Consciousness slipped away. For the third time in less than two days, he tumbled into the abyss. He remembered thinking as he fell that this time he was not sure he would be able to climb out again.

12

Par Ohmsford drifted through a landscape of dreams.

He was both within himself and without as he journeyed, a participant and a viewer. There was constant motion, sometimes as charged as a voyage across a stormy sea, sometimes as gentle as the summer wind through the trees. He spoke to himself alternately in the dark silence of his mind and from within a mirrored self-image. His voice was a disembodied whisper and a thunderous shout. Colors appeared and faded to black and white. Sounds came and departed. He was all things on his journey, and he was none.

The dreams were his reality.

He dreamed in the beginning that he was falling, tumbling downward into a pit as black as night and as endless as the cycle of the seasons. There were pain and fear in him; he could not find himself. Sometimes there were voices, calling to him in warning, in comfort, or in horror. He convulsed within himself. He knew somehow that if he did not stop falling, he would be forever lost.

He did stop finally. He slowed and leveled, and his convulsions ceased. He was in a field of wildflowers as wondrous as a rainbow. Birds and butterflies scattered at his approach, filling the air with new brightness, and the smells of the field were soft and fragrant. There was no sound. He tried to speak so that there might be, but found himself voiceless. Nor did he have touch. He could feel nothing of himself, nothing of the world about him. There was warmth, soothing and extended, but that was all.

He drifted and a voice somewhere deep within him whispered that he was dead.

The voice, he thought, belonged to Walker Boh.

Then the world of sweet smells and sights disappeared, and he was in a world of darkness and stench. Fire erupted from the earth and spat at an angry, smudge-colored sky. Shadowen flitted and leaped, red eyes glinting as they whipped about him, hovering one moment, ducking away the next. Clouds rolled overhead, filled with lightning, borne on a wind that howled in fury. He felt himself buffeted and tossed, thrown like a dried leaf across the earth, and he sensed it was the end of all things. Touch and voice returned, and he felt his pain once more and cried out with it.

"Par?"

The voice came once and was gone again—Coll's voice. But he saw Coll in his dream then, stretched against a gathering of rocks, lifeless and bloodied, eyes open in accusation. "You left me. You abandoned me." He screamed and the magic of the wishsong threw images everywhere. But the images turned into monsters that wheeled back to devour him. He could feel their teeth and claws. He could feel their touch . . .

He came awake.

Rain fell into his face, and his eyes opened. There was darkness all about, the sense of others close at hand, a feeling of motion, and the coppery taste of blood. There was shouting, voices that called to one another against the fury of a storm. He rose up, choking, spitting. Hands bore him back again, slipping against his body and face.

". . . awake again, hold him . . ."

". . . too strong, like he's ten instead of . . ."

"Walker! Hurry!"

Trees thrashed in the background, long-limbed giants lifting into the roiling black, the wind howling all about them. They threw shadows against cliffs that blocked their passage and threatened to pen them up. Par heard himself scream.

Lightning crashed and thunder rolled, filling the dark with echoes of madness. A wash of red screened his vision.

Then Allanon was there—Allanon! He came from nowhere, all in black robes, a figure out of legend and time. He bent close to Par, his voice a whisper that somehow managed to rise above the chaos. Sleep, Par, he soothed. One weathered hand reached out and touched the Valeman, and the chaos dissipated and was replaced by a profound sense of peace.

Par drifted away again, far down into himself, fighting now because he sensed that he would live if he could just will it to be so. Some part of him remembered what had happened—that the Werebeasts had seized him, that their touch had poisoned him, that the poison had made him sick, and that the sickness had dropped him into that black abyss. Walker had come for him, found him somehow, and saved him from those creatures. He saw Rumor's yellow lamp eyes, blinking in warning, lidding and going out. He saw Coll and Morgan. He saw Steff, his smile sardonic, and Teel, enigmatic and silent.

He saw the Shadowen girl-child, begging again to be hugged, trying to enter his body. He felt himself resist, saw her thrown back, watched as she disappeared. Shades! She had tried to enter him, to come into him, to put herself within his skin and become him! That was what they were, he thought in a burst of understanding—shadows that lacked substance of their own and took the bodies of men. And women. And children.

But can shadows have life?

His thoughts jumbled around unanswerable questions, and he slipped from reason to confusion. His mind slept, and his journey through the land of dreams wore on. He climbed mountains filled with creatures like the Gnawl, crossed rivers and lakes of mist and hidden dangers, traversed forests where daylight never penetrated, and swept on into moors where mist stirred in an airless, empty cauldron of silence.

Help me, he begged. But there was no one to hear.

Time suspended then. The journey ended and the dreams faded into nothingness. There was a moment's pause at their end, and then waking. He knew he had slept, but not for how long. He knew only that there had been a passage of time when the dreams had ended and dreamless sleep had begun.

More important, he knew that he was alive.

He stirred gingerly, barely more than a twitch, feeling the softness of sheets and a bed beneath him, aware that he was stretched out full-length and that he was warm and snug. He did not want to move yet, frightened that he might still be dreaming. He let the feel of the sheets soak through him. He listened to the sound of his own breathing in his ears. He tasted the dryness of the air.

Then he let his eyes slip open. He was in a small, sparsely furnished room lit by a single lamp set on a table at his bedside. The walls of the room were bare, the ceiling beams uncovered. A comforter wrapped him and pillows cradled his head. A break in the curtains that covered the windows opposite where he lay told him it was night.

Morgan Leah dozed in a chair just inside the circle of light given off by the lamp, his chin resting on his chest, his arms folded loosely. "Morgan?" he called, his voice sounding fuzzy.

The Highlander's eyes snapped open, his hawk face instantly alert. He blinked, then jumped to his feet. "Par! Par, are you awake? Good heavens, we've been worried sick!" He rushed over as if to hug his friend, then thought better of it. He ran the fingers of one hand through his rust-colored hair distractedly. "How do you feel? Are you all right?"

Par grinned weakly. "I don't know yet. I'm still waking up. What happened?"

"What *didn't* happen is more like it!" the other replied heatedly. "You almost died, do you realize that?"

Par nodded. "I guessed it. What about Coll, Morgan?"

"Sleeping, waiting for you to come around. I packed him off several hours ago when he fell out of his chair. You know Coll. Wait here, I'll get him." He grinned. "Wait here, I tell you—as if you were going anywhere. Pretty funny."

Par had a dozen things he wanted to say, questions he wanted to ask, but the Highlander was already out the door and gone. It didn't matter, he guessed. He lay back quietly, flooded with relief. All that mattered was that Coll was all right.

Morgan returned almost immediately, Coll beside him, and Coll, unlike Morgan, did not hesitate as he reached down and practically squeezed the life out of Par in his enthusiasm at finding him awake. Par hugged him back, albeit weakly, and the three laughed as if they had just enjoyed the biggest joke of their lives.

"Shades, we thought we'd lost you!" Coll exclaimed softly. He wore a bandage taped to his forehead, and his face seemed pale. "You were very sick, Par."

Par smiled and nodded. He'd heard enough of that. "Will someone tell me what happened?" His eyes shifted from one face to the other. "Where are we anyway?"

"Storlock," Morgan announced. One eyebrow arched. "Walker Boh brought you here."

"Walker?"

Morgan grinned with satisfaction. "Thought you'd be surprised to learn that—Walker Boh coming out of the Wilderun, Walker Boh appearing in the first place for that matter." He sighed. "Well, it's a long story, so I guess we'd better start at the beginning."

He did, telling the story with considerable help from Coll, the two of them stepping on each other's words in their eagerness to make certain that nothing was overlooked. Par listened in growing surprise as the tale unfolded.

Coll, it seemed, had been felled by a Gnome sling when the Spider Gnomes attacked them in that clearing at the eastern end of the valley at Hearthstone. He had only been stunned, but, by the time he had recovered consciousness, Par and their attackers were gone. It was raining buckets by then, the trail disappearing back into the earth as quickly as it was made, and Coll was too weak to give chase in any case. So he stumbled back to the cottage where he found the others and told them what had occurred. It was already dark by then and still raining, but Coll demanded they go back out anyway and search for his brother. They did, Morgan, Steff, Teel, and himself, groping about blindly for hours and finding nothing. When it became impossible to see anything, Steff insisted they give it up for the night, get some rest and start out again fresh in the morning. That was what they did, and that was how Coll encountered Walker Boh.

"We split up, trying to cover as much ground as possible, working the north valley, because I knew from the stories of Brin and Jair Ohmsford that the Spider Gnomes made their homes on Toffer Ridge and it was likely they had come from there. At least, I hoped so, because that was all we had to go on. We agreed that if we didn't find you right away we would just keep on going until we reached the Ridge." He shook his head. "We were pretty desperate."

"We were," Morgan agreed.

"Anyway, I was all the way to the northeast edge of the valley when, all of a sudden, there was Walker and that giant cat, big as a house! He said that he'd sensed something. He asked me what had happened, what was wrong. I was so surprised to see him that I didn't even think to ask what he was doing there or why he had decided to appear after hiding all that time. I just told him what he wanted to know."

"Do you know what he said then?" Morgan interrupted, gray eyes finding Par's, a hint of the mischievousness in them.

"He said," Coll took control again of the conversation, " 'Wait here, this is no task for you; I will bring him back'—as if we were children playing at a grown-up's game!"

"But he was as good as his word," Morgan noted.

Coll sighed. "Well, true enough," he admitted grudgingly.

Walker Boh was gone a full day and night, but when he returned to Hearthstone, where Coll and his companions were indeed waiting, he had Par with him. Par had been infected by the touch of the Werebeasts and was near death. The only hope for him, Walker insisted, lay at Storlock, the community of Gnome healers. The Stors had experience in dealing with afflictions of the mind and spirit and could combat the Werebeasts' poison.

They set out at once, the six of them less the cat, who had been left behind. They pushed west out of Hearthstone and the Wilderun, following the Chard Rush upriver to the Wolfsktaag, crossing through the Pass of Jade, and finally reaching the village of the Stors. It had taken them two days, traveling almost constantly. Par would have died if not for Walker, who had used an odd sort of magic that none of them had understood to prevent the poison from spreading and to keep Par sleeping and calm. At times, Par had thrashed and cried out, waking feverish and spitting blood— once in the middle of a ferocious storm they had encountered in the Pass of Jade—but Walker had been there to soothe him, to touch him, to say something that let him sleep once more.

"Even so, we've been in Storlock for almost three days and this is the first time you've been awake," Coll finished. He paused, eyes lowering. "It was very close, Par."

Par nodded, saying nothing. Even without being able to remember anything clearly, he had a definite sense of just how close it had been. "Where is Walker?" he asked finally.

"We don't know," Morgan answered with a shrug. "We haven't seen him since we arrived. He just disappeared."

"Gone back to the Wilderun, I suppose," Coll added, a touch of bitterness in his voice.

"Now, Coll," Morgan soothed.

Coll held up his hands. "I know, Morgan—I shouldn't judge. He was there to help when we needed him. He saved Par's life. I'm grateful for that."

"Besides, I think he's still around," Morgan said quietly. When the other two looked inquiringly at him, he simply shrugged.

Par told them what had befallen him after his capture by the Spider Gnomes. He was still reasoning out a good part of it, so he hesitated from time to time in his telling. He was convinced that the Spider Gnomes had been sent specifically to find him, otherwise they would have taken Coll as well. The Shadowen had sent them, that girl-child. Yet how had it known who he was or where he could be found?

The little room was silent as they thought. "The magic," Morgan suggested finally. "They all seem interested in the magic. This one must have sensed it as well."

"All the way from Toffer Ridge?" Par shook his head doubtfully.

"And why not go after Morgan as well?" Coll asked suddenly. "After all, he commands the magic of the Sword of Leah."

"No, no, that's not the sort of magic they care about," Morgan replied quickly. "It's Par's sort of magic that interests them, draws them—magic that's part of the body or spirit."

"Or maybe it's simply Par," Coll finished darkly.

They let the thought hang a moment in the silence. "The Shadowen tried to come into me," Par said finally, then explained it to them in more detail. "It wanted to merge with me, to be a part of me. It kept saying, 'hug me, hug me'—as if it were a lost child or something."

"Hardly that," Coll disputed quickly.

"More leech than lost child," Morgan agreed.

"But what are they?" Par pressed, bits and pieces of his dreams coming back to him, flashes of insight that lacked meaning. "Where is it that they come from and what is it that they want?"

"Us," Morgan said quietly.

"You," Coll said.

They talked a bit longer, mulling over what little they knew of Shadowen and their interest in magic, then Coll and Morgan rose. Time for Par to rest again, they insisted. He was still sick, still weak, and he needed to get his strength back.

The Hadeshorn, Par remembered suddenly! How much time did they have before the new moon?

Coll sighed. "Four days—if you still insist on going."

Morgan grinned from behind him. "We'll be close by if you need us. Good to see you well again, Par."

He slipped out the door. "It is good," Coll agreed and gripped his brother's hand tightly.

When they were gone, Par lay with his eyes open for a time, letting his thoughts nudge and push one another. Questions whispered at him, asking for answers he didn't have. He had been chased and harried from Varfleet to the Rainbow Lake, from Culhaven to Hearthstone, by the Federation and the Shadowen, by things that he had only heard about and some he hadn't even known existed. He was tired and confused; he had almost lost his life. Everything centered on his magic, and yet his magic had been virtually useless to him. He was constantly running from one thing and toward another without really understanding much of either. He felt helpless.

And despite the presence of his brother and his friends, he felt oddly alone.

His last thought before he fell asleep was that, in a way he didn't yet comprehend, he was.

He slept fitfully, but without dreaming, waking often amid stirrings of dissatisfaction and wariness that darted through the corridors of his mind like harried rats. Each time he came awake it was still night, until the last time when it was almost dawn, the sky beyond the curtained window brightening faintly, the room in which he lay still and gauzy. A white-robed Stor passed briefly through the room, appearing from out of the shadows like a ghost to pause at his bedside and touch his wrist and forehead with hands that were surprisingly warm before turning and disappearing back the way he had come. Par slept soundly after that, drifting far down within himself and floating undisturbed in a sea of black warmth.

When he woke again, it was raining. His eyes blinked open and he stared fixedly into the grayness of his room. He could hear the sound of the raindrops beating on the windows and roof, a steady drip and splash in the stillness. There was daylight yet; he could see it through the part in the curtains. Thunder rolled in the distance, echoing in long, uneven peals.

Gingerly, he hoisted himself up on one elbow. He saw a fire burning in a small stove that he hadn't even noticed the previous night, tucked back in the shadows. It gave a solid warmth to the room that wrapped and cradled him and made him feel secure. There was tea by his bedside and tiny cakes. He pushed himself up the rest of the way, propping himself against the headboard of his bed with his pillows and pulling the cakes and tea to him. He was famished, and he devoured the cakes in seconds. Then he drank a small portion of the tea, which had gone cold in the sitting, but was wonderful in any case.

He was midway through his third cup when the door opened soundlessly and Walker Boh appeared. His uncle paused momentarily on seeing him awake, then closed the door softly and came over to stand at his bedside. He was dressed in forest green—tunic and pants belted tight, soft leather boots unlaced and muddied, long travel cloak spotted with rain. There was rain on his bearded face as well, and his dark hair was damp against his skin.

He pushed the travel cloak back across his shoulders. "Feeling better?" he asked quietly.

Par nodded. "Much." He set his cup aside. "I understand I have you to thank for that. You saved me from the Werebeasts. You brought me back to Hearthstone. It was your idea to bring me to Storlock. Coll and Morgan tell me that you even used magic to see to it that I stayed alive long enough to complete the journey."

"Magic." Walker repeated the word softly, his voice distracted. "Words and touching in combination, a sort of variation on the workings of the wishsong. My legacy from Brin Ohmsford. I haven't the curse of the fullness of her powers—only the annoyance of its shadings. Still, now and again, it does become the gift you insist it must be. I can interact with another living thing, feel its life force, sometimes find a way to strengthen it." He paused. "I don't know if I would call it magic, though."

"And what you did to the Werebeasts in Olden Moor when you stood up for me—was that not magic?"

His uncle's eyes shifted away from him. "I was taught that," he said finally.

Par waited a moment, but when nothing more was forthcoming he said, "I'm grateful for all of it in any case. Thank you."

The other man shook his head slowly. "I don't deserve your thanks. It was my fault that it happened in the first place."

Par readjusted himself carefully against his pillows. "I seem to remember you saying that before."

Walker moved to the far end of the bed and sat down on its edge. "If I had watched over you the way I should have, the Spider Gnomes would never have even gotten into the valley. Because I chose to distance myself from you, they did. You risked a fair amount in coming to find me in the first place; the least I could have done was to make certain that once you reached me, you would be safe. I failed to do that."

"I don't blame you for what happened," Par said quickly.

"But I do." Walker rose, as restless as a cat, stalking to the windows and peering out into the rain. "I live apart because I choose to. Other men in other times made me decide that it was best. But I forget sometimes that there is a difference between disassociating and hiding. There are limits to the distances we can place between ourselves and others—because the dictates of our world don't allow for absolutes." He looked back, his skin pale against the grayness of the day. "I was hiding myself when you came to find me. That was why you went unprotected."

Par did not fully understand what Walker was trying to say, but he chose not to interrupt, anxious to hear more. Walker turned from the window after a moment and came back. "I haven't been to see you since you were brought here," he said, coming to a stop at Par's bedside. "Did you know that?"

Par nodded, again keeping silent. "It wasn't that I was ignoring you. But I knew you were safe, that you would be well, and I wanted time to think. I went out into the woodlands by myself. I returned for the first time this morning. The Stors told me that you were awake, that the poison was dispelled, and I decided to come to see you."

He broke off, his gaze shifting. When he spoke again, he chose his words carefully. "I have been thinking about the dreams."

There was another brief silence. Par shifted uncomfortably in the bed, already beginning to feel tired. His strength would be awhile returning. Walker seemed to recognize the problem and said, "I won't be staying much longer."

He sat down again slowly. "I anticipated that you might come to me after the dreams began. You were always impulsive. I thought about the possibility, about what I would say to you." He paused. "We are close in ways you do not entirely understand, Par. We share the legacy of the magic; but more than that, we share a preordained future that may preclude our right to any meaningful form of self-determination." He paused again, smiling faintly. "What I mean, Par, is that we are the children of Brin and Jair

Ohmsford, heirs to the magic of the Elven house of Shannara, keepers of a trust. Remember now? It was Allanon who gave us that trust, who said to Brin when he lay dying that the Ohmsfords would safeguard the magic for generations to come until it was again needed."

Par nodded slowly, beginning to understand now. "You believe we might be the ones for whom the trust was intended."

"I believe it—and I am frightened by the possibility as I have never been frightened of anything in my life!" Walker's voice was a low hiss. "I am terrified of it! I want no part of the Druids and their mysteries! I want nothing to do with the Elven magic, with its demands and its treacheries! I wish only to be left alone, to live out my life in a way I believe useful and fulfilling—and that is all I wish!"

Par let his eyes drop protectively against the fury of the other man's words. Then he smiled sadly. "Sometimes the choice isn't ours, Walker."

Walker Boh's reply was unexpected. "That was what I decided." His lean face was hard as Par looked up again. "While I waited for you to wake, while I kept myself apart from the others, out there in the forests beyond Storlock, that was what I decided." He shook his head. "Events and circumstances sometimes conspire against us; if we insist on inflexibility for the purpose of maintaining our beliefs, we end up compromising ourselves nevertheless. We salvage one set of principles only to forsake another. My staying hidden within the Wilderun almost cost you your life once. It could do so again. And what would that, in turn, cost me?"

Par shook his head. "You cannot hold yourself responsible for the risks I choose to take, Walker. No man can hold himself up to that standard of responsibility."

"Oh, but he can, Par. And he must when he has the means to do so. Don't you see? If I have the means, I have the responsibility to employ them." He shook his head sadly. "I might wish it otherwise, but it doesn't change the fact of its being."

He straightened. "Well, I came to tell you something, and I still haven't done so. Best that I get it over with so you can rest." He rose, pulling the damp forest cloak about him as if to ward off a chill. "I am going with you," he said simply.

Par stiffened in surprise. "To the Hadeshorn?"

Walker Boh nodded. "To meet with Allanon's shade—if indeed it is Allanon's shade who summons us—and to hear what it will say. I make no promises beyond that, Par. Nor do I make any further concessions to your view of matters—other than to say that I think you were right in one respect. We cannot pretend that the world begins and ends at the boundaries we might make for it. Sometimes, we must acknowledge that it extends itself into our lives in ways we might prefer it wouldn't, and we must face up to the challenges it offers."

His face was lined with emotions Par could only begin to imagine. "I, too, would like to know something of what is intended for me," he whispered.

He reached down, his pale, lean hand fastening briefly on one of Par's. "Rest now. We have another journey ahead and only a day or two to prepare for it. Let that preparation be my responsibility. I will tell the others and come for you all when it is time to depart."

He started away, then hesitated and smiled. "Try to think better of me after this."

Then he was out the door and gone, and the smile belonged now to Par.

Walker Boh proved as good as his word. Two days later he was back, appearing shortly after sunrise with horses and provisions. Par had been out of bed and walking about for the past day and a half now, and he was much recovered from his experience in Olden Moor. He was dressed and waiting on the porch of his compound with Steff and Teel when his uncle walked out of the forest shadows with his pack train in tow into a morning clouded by fog and half-light.

"There's a strange one," Steff murmured. "Haven't seen him for more than five minutes for the entire time we've been here. Now, back he comes, just like that. More ghost than man." His smile was rueful and his eyes sharp.

"Walker Boh is real enough," Par replied without looking at the Dwarf. "And haunted by ghosts of his own."

"Brave ghosts, I am inclined to think."

Par glanced over now. "He still frightens you, doesn't he?"

"Frightens me?" Steff's voice was gruff as he laughed. "Hear him, Teel? He probes my armor for chinks!" He turned his scarred face briefly. "No, Valeman, he doesn't frighten me anymore. He only makes me wonder."

Coll and Morgan appeared, and the little company prepared to depart. Stors came out to see them off, ghosts of another sort, dressed in white robes and cloaked in self-imposed silence, a perpetually anxious look on their pale faces. They gathered in groups, watchful, curious, a few coming forward to help as the members of the company mounted. Walker spoke with one or two of them, his words so quiet they could be heard by no one else. Then he was aboard with the others and facing briefly back to them.

"Good fortune to us, my friends," he said and turned his horse west toward the plains.

Good fortune, indeed, Par Ohmsford prayed silently.

13

Sunlight sprayed the still surface of the Myrian Lake through breaks in the distant trees, coloring the water a brilliant red-gold and causing Wren Ohmsford to squint against its glare. Farther west, the Irrybis Mountains were a jagged black tear across the horizon that separated earth and sky and cast the first of night's shadows across the vast sprawl of the Tirfing.

Another hour, maybe a bit more, and it would be dark, she thought.

She paused at the edge of the lake and, for just a moment, let the solitude of the approaching dusk settle through her. All about, the Westland stretched away into the shimmering heat of the dying summer's day with the lazy complacency of a sleeping cat, endlessly patient as it waited for the coming of night and the cool it would bring.

She was running out of time.

She cast about momentarily for the signs she had lost some hundred yards back and found nothing. He might as well have vanished into thin air. He was working hard at this cat-and-mouse game, she decided. Perhaps she was the cause.

The thought buoyed her as she pressed ahead, slipping silently through the trees along the lake front, scanning the foliage and the earth with renewed determination. She was small and slight of build, but wiry and strong. Her skin was nut-brown from weather and sun, and her ash-blond hair was almost boyish, cut short and tightly curled against her head. Her features were Elven, sharply so, the eyebrows full and deeply slanted, the ears small and pointed, the bones of her face lending it a narrow and high-cheeked look. She had hazel eyes, and they shifted restlessly as she moved, hunting.

She found his first mistake a hundred feet or so farther on, a tiny bit of broken scrub, and his second, a boot indentation against a gathering of stones, just after. She smiled in spite of herself, her confidence growing, and she hefted the smooth quarterstaff she carried in anticipation. She would have him yet, she promised.

The lake cut into the trees ahead forming a deep cove, and she was forced to swing back to her left through a thick stand of pine. She slowed, moving more cautiously. Her eyes darted. The pines gave way to a mass of thick brush that grew close against a grove of cedar. She skirted the brush, catching sight of a fresh scrape against a tree root. He's getting careless, she thought—or wants me to think so.

She found the snare at the last moment, just as she was about to put her foot into it. Its lines ran from a carefully concealed noose back into a mass of brush and from there to a stout sapling, bent and tied. Had she not seen it, she would have been yanked from her feet and left dangling.

She found the second snare immediately after, better concealed and designed to catch her avoiding the first. She avoided that one, too, and now became even more cautious.

Even so, she almost missed seeing him in time when he swung down out of the maple not more than fifty yards farther on. Tired of trying to lose her in the woods, he had decided to finish matters in a quicker manner. He dropped silently as she slipped beneath the old shade tree, and it was only her instincts that saved her. She sprang aside as he landed, bringing the quarterstaff about and catching him alongside his great shoulders with an audible thwack. Her attacker shrugged off the blow, coming to his feet with a grunt. He was huge, a man of formidable size who appeared massive in the confines of the tiny forest clearing. He leaped at Wren, and she used the quarterstaff to vault quickly away from him. She slipped on landing, and he was on top of her with a swiftness that was astonishing. She rolled, using the staff to block him, came up underneath with the makeshift dagger and jammed the flat of its blade against his belly.

The sun-browned, bearded face shifted to find her own, and the deepset eyes glanced downward. "You're dead, Garth," she told him, smiling. Then her fingers came up to make the signs.

The giant Rover collapsed in mock submission before rolling over and climbing to his feet. Then he smiled, too. They brushed themselves off and stood grinning at each other in the fading light. "I'm getting better, aren't I?" Wren asked, signing with her hands as she spoke the words.

Garth replied soundlessly, his fingers moving rapidly in the language he had taught her. "Better, but not yet good enough," she translated. Her smile broadened as she reached out to clasp his arm. "Never good enough for you, I suspect. Otherwise, you would be out of a job!"

She picked up the quarterstaff and made a mock feint that caused the other to jump back in alarm. They fenced for a moment, then broke it off and started back toward the lakeshore. There was a small clearing just beyond the cove, not more than half an hour away, that offered an ideal campsite for the night. Wren had noticed it during the hunt and made for it now.

"I'm tired and I ache and I have never felt better," the girl said cheerfully as they walked, enjoying the last of the day's sunlight on her back, breathing in the smells of the forest, feeling alive and at peace. She sang a bit, humming some songs of the Rovers and the free life, of the ways that were and the ways that would be. Garth trailed along, a silent shadow at her back.

They found the campsite, built a fire, prepared and ate their dinner, and began trading drinks from a large leather aleskin. The night was warm and comforting, and Wren Ohmsford's thoughts wandered contentedly. They had another five days allotted to them before they were expected back. She enjoyed her outings with Garth; they were exciting and challenging. The big Rover was the best of teachers—one who let his students learn from experience. No one knew more than he did about tracking, concealment, snares, traps, and tricks of all sorts in the fine art of staying alive. He had been her mentor from the first. She had never questioned why he chose her; she had simply felt grateful that he had.

She listened momentarily to the sounds of the forest, trying to visualize out of habit what she heard moving in the dark. It was a strenuous, demanding life she led, but she could no longer imagine leading any other. She had been born a Rover girl and lived with them for all but the very early years of her youth when she had resided in the Southland hamlet of Shady Vale with her cousins, the Ohmsfords. She had been back in the Westland for years now, traveling with Garth and the others, the ones who had claimed her after her parents died, taught her their ways, and showed her their life. All of the Westland belonged to the Rovers, from the Kershalt to the Irrybis, from the Valley of Rhenn to the Blue Divide. Once, it had belonged to the Elves as well. But the Elves were all gone now, disappeared. They had passed back into legend, the Rovers said. They had lost interest in the world of mortal beings and gone back into faerie.

Some disputed it. Some said that the Elves were still there, hidden. She didn't know about the truth of that. She only knew that what they had abandoned was a wilderness paradise.

Garth passed her the aleskin and she drank deeply, then handed it back again. She was growing sleepy. Normally, she drank little. But she was feeling especially proud of herself tonight. It wasn't often that she got the best of Garth.

She studied him momentarily, thinking of how much he had come to mean to her. Her time in Shady Vale seemed long ago and far away, although she remembered it well enough. And the Ohmsfords, especially Par and Coll—she still thought about them. They had been her only family once. But it felt as if all that might have happened in another life. Garth was her family now, her father, mother, and brother all rolled into one, the only real family she knew anymore. She was tied to him in ways she had never been tied to anyone else. She loved him fiercely.

Nevertheless, she admitted, she sometimes felt detached from everyone, even him—orphaned and homeless, a stray shunted from one family to the next without belonging to anyone, having no idea at all who she really was. It bothered her that she didn't know more about herself and that no one else seemed to know either. She had asked often enough, but the explanations were always vague. Her father had been an Ohmsford. Her mother had been a Rover. It was unclear how they had died. It was uncertain what had become of any other members of her immediate family. It was unknown who her ancestors had been.

She possessed, in fact, but one item that offered any clue at all as to who she was. It was a small leather bag she wore tied about her neck that contained three perfectly formed stones. Elfstones, one might have thought—until one looked more closely and saw that they were just common rocks painted blue. But they had been found on her as a baby and they were all she had to suggest the heritage that might be hers.

Garth knew something about the matter, she suspected. He had told her that he didn't when she had asked once, but there was something in the way he had made his disavowal that convinced her he was hedging. Garth kept secrets better than most, but she knew him too well to be fooled completely. Sometimes, when she thought about it, she wanted to shake an answer out of him, angry and frustrated at his refusal to be as open with her in this as he was in everything else. But she kept her anger and her frustration to herself. You didn't push Garth. When he was ready to tell her, he would.

She shrugged as she always ended up doing whenever she considered the matter of her family history. What difference did it make? She was who she was, whatever her lineage. She was a Rover girl with a life that most would envy, if they bothered to be honest about it. The whole world belonged to her, because she was tied to no part of it. She could go where she wanted and do what she pleased, and that was more than most could say. Besides, many of her fellow Rovers were of dubious parentage, and you never heard them complain. They reveled in their freedom, in their ability to lay claim to anything and anyone that caught their fancy. Wasn't that good enough for her as well?

She stirred the dirt in front of her with her boot. Of course, none of them were Elven, were they? None of them had the Ohmsford-Shannara blood, with its history of Elven magic. None of them were plagued by the dreams . . .

Her hazel eyes shifted abruptly as she became aware of Garth looking at her. She signed some innocuous response, thinking as she did so that none of the other Rovers had been as thoroughly trained to survive as she had and wondering why.

They drank a little more of the ale, built the fire up again, and rolled into their blankets. Wren lay awake longer than she wished to, caught up in the unanswered questions and unresolved puzzles that marked her life. When she did sleep, she tossed restlessly beneath her blankets, teased by fragments of dreams that slipped from her like raindrops through her fingers in a summer storm and were forgotten as quickly.

It was dawn when she came awake, and the old man was sitting across from her, poking idly at the ashes of the fire with a long stick. "It's about time," he snorted.

She blinked in disbelief, then started sharply out of her blankets. Garth was still sleeping, but awoke with the suddenness of her movement. She reached for the quarterstaff at her side, her thoughts scattering into questions. Where had this old man come from? How had he managed to get so close without waking them?

The old man lifted one sticklike arm reassuringly, saying, "Don't be getting yourself all upset. Just be grateful I let you sleep."

Garth was on his feet as well now, crouched, but to Wren's astonishment the old man began speaking to the Rover in his own language, signing, telling him what he had already told Wren, and adding that he meant no harm. Garth hesitated, obviously surprised, then sat back watchfully.

"How did you know to do that?" Wren demanded. She had never seen anyone outside the Rover camp master Garth's language.

"Oh, I know a thing or two about communication," the old man replied gruffly, a self-satisfied smile appearing. His skin was weather-browned and seamed, his white hair and beard wispy, his lank frame scarecrow-thin. A gathering of dusty gray robes hung loosely about him. "For instance," he said, "I know that messages may be sent by writing on paper, by word of mouth, by use of hands . . ." He paused. "Even by dreams."

Wren caught her breath sharply. "Who are you?"

"Well, now," the old man said, "that seems to be everyone's favorite question. My name doesn't matter. What matters is that I have been sent to tell you that you can no longer afford to ignore your dreams. Those dreams, Rover girl, come from Allanon."

As he spoke he signed to Garth, repeating his words with the language of his fingers, as dexterous at the skill as if he had known it all his life. Wren was aware of the big Rover looking at her, but she couldn't take her eyes off the old man. "How do you know of the dreams?" she asked him softly.

He told her who he was then, that he was Cogline, a former Druid pressed back into service because the real Druids were gone from the Four Lands and there was no other who could go to the members of the Ohmsford family and warn them that the dreams were real. He told her that Allanon's ghost had sent him to convince her of the purpose of the dreams, to persuade her that they spoke the truth, that the Four Lands were in gravest danger, that the magic was almost lost, that only the Ohmsfords could restore it, and that they must come to him on the first night of the new moon to discover what must be done. He finished by saying that he had gone first to Par Ohmsford, then to Walker Boh—recipients of the dreams as well—and now finally he had come to her.

When he was done, she sat thinking for a moment before speaking. "The dreams have troubled me for some time now," she confessed. "I thought them dreams like any other and nothing more. The Ohmsford magic has never been a part of my life . . ."

"And you question whether or not you are an Ohmsford at all," the old man interrupted. "You are not certain, are you? If you are not an Ohmsford, then the magic has no part in your life—which might be just as well as far as you're concerned, mightn't it?"

Wren stared at him. "How do you know all this, Cogline?" She didn't question that he was who he claimed; she accepted it because she believed that it didn't really matter one way or the other. "How do you know so much about me?" She leaned forward, suddenly anxious. "Do you know the truth of who I really am?"

The old man shrugged. "It is not nearly so important to know who you are as who you might be," he answered enigmatically. "If you wish to learn something of that, then do as the dreams have asked. Come to the Hadeshorn and speak to Allanon."

She eased away slowly, glancing momentarily at Garth before looking back. "You're playing with me," she told the old man.

"Perhaps."

"Why?"

"Oh, quite simple, really. If you are intrigued enough by what I say, you might agree to do as I ask and come with me. I chose to chastise and berate the other members of your family. I thought I might try a new approach with you. Time grows short, and I am just an old man. The new moon is only six days distant now. Even on horseback, it will require at least four days to reach the Hadeshorn—five, if I am to make the journey."

He was signing everything he said, and now Garth made a quick response. The old man laughed. "Will I choose to make the journey? Yes, by golly, I think I will. I have gone about a shades's business for some weeks now. I believe I am entitled to know what the culmination of that business might be." He paused, thoughtful. "Besides, I am not altogether sure I have been given a choice . . ." He trailed off.

Wren glanced eastward to where the sun was a pale white ball of fire resting atop the horizon, screened by clouds and haze, its warmth still distant. Gulls swooped across the mirrored waters of the Myrian, fishing. The stillness of the early morning let her thoughts whisper undisturbed within her.

"What did my cousin . . . ?" she began, then caught herself. The word didn't sound right when she spoke it. It distanced her from him in a way she didn't care for. "What did Par say that he was going to do?" she finished.

"He said he was going to think the matter over," the old man replied. "He and his brother. They were together when I found them."

"And my uncle?"

The other shrugged. "The same."

But there was something in his eyes that said otherwise. Wren shook her head. "You are playing with me again. What did they say?"

The old man's eyes narrowed. "Rover girl, you try my patience. I haven't the energy to sit about and repeat entire conversations just so you can use that as an excuse for making your decision in this matter. Haven't you a mind of your own? If they go, they will do so for their own reasons and not for any you might provide. Shouldn't you do likewise?"

Wren Ohmsford was a rock. "What did they say?" she repeated once again, measuring each word carefully before she spoke it.

"What they chose!" the other snapped, his fingers flicking his responses angrily now at Garth, though his eyes never left Wren's. "Am I a parrot to repeat the phrases of others for your amusement?"

He glared at her a moment, then threw up his hands. "Very well! Here is the whole of it, then! Young Par, his brother with him, has been chased from Varfleet by the Federation for making use of the magic to tell stories of their family history and the Druids. He thought to go home when I last saw him, to think about the dreams a bit. He will have discovered by now that he cannot do so, that his home is in Federation hands and his parents—your own of sorts, once upon a time—are prisoners!"

Wren started in surprise, but the old man ignored her. "Walker Boh is another matter. He thinks himself severed from the Ohmsford family. He lives alone and prefers it that way. He wants nothing to do with his family and the world at large and Druids in particular. He thinks that only he knows the proper uses of magic, that the rest of us who possess some small skill are incapable of reason! He forgets who taught him what! He . . ."

"You," Wren interjected.

". . . charges about on some self-proclaimed mission of . . ." He stopped short. "What? What did you say?"

"You," she repeated, her eyes locking on his. "You were his teacher once, weren't you?"

There was a moment of silence as the sharp old eyes studied her appraisingly. "Yes, girl. I was. Are you satisfied now? Is that the revelation you sought? Or do you require something more?"

He had forgotten to sign what he was saying, but Garth seemed to have read his lips in any case. He caught Wren's attention, nodding in approval. Always try to learn something of your adversary that he doesn't want you to know, he had taught her. It gives you an edge.

"So he isn't going then, is he?" she pressed. "Walker, I mean."

"Ha!" the old man exclaimed in satisfaction. "Just when I conclude what a smart girl you are, you prove me wrong!" He cocked an eyebrow on his seamed face. "Walker Boh says he isn't going, and he thinks he isn't going. But he is! The young one, too—Par. That's the way it will be. Things work out the way we least expect them to sometimes. Or maybe that's just the Druid magic at work, twisting those promises and oaths we so recklessly take, steering us where we didn't think we could ever be made to go." He shook his head in amusement. "Always was a baffling trick."

He drew his robes about him and bent forward. "Now what is it to be with you, little Wren? Brave bird or timid flyaway—which will you be?"

She smiled in spite of herself. "Why not both, depending on what is needed?" she asked.

He grunted impatiently. "Because the situation calls for one or the other. Choose."

Wren let her eyes shift briefly to Garth, then off into the woods, slipping deep into the shadows where the still-distant sunlight had not yet penetrated. Her thoughts and questions of the previous night came back to her, darting through her mind with harrying insistence. Well, she could go if she chose, she knew. The Rovers wouldn't stop her, not even Garth—though he would insist on going as well. She could confront the shade of Allanon. She could speak with the shade of a legend, a man many said never existed at all. She could ask the questions of him she had carried about with her for so many years now, perhaps learn some of the answers, possibly come to an understanding about herself that she had lacked before. A rather ambitious task, she thought. An intriguing one.

She felt sunlight slipping across the bridge of her nose, tickling her. It would mean a reunion with Par and Coll and Walker Boh—her other family that maybe wasn't really family at all. She pursed her lips thoughtfully. She might enjoy that.

But it would also mean confronting the reality of her dreams—or at least a shade's version of that reality. And that could mean a change in the course of her life, a life with which she was perfectly content. It could mean disruption of that life, an involvement in matters that she might better avoid.

Her mind raced. She could feel the presence of the little bag with the painted stones pressing against her breast as if to remind her of what might be. She knew the stories of the Ohmsfords and the Druids, too, and she was wary.

Then, unexpectedly, she found herself smiling. Since when had being wary ever stopped her from doing anything? Shades! This was an unlocked door that begged to be opened! How could she live with herself if she passed it up?

The old man interrupted her thoughts. "Rover girl, I grow weary. These aging bones require movement to keep from locking up. Let me have your decision. Or do you, like the others in your family, require untold amounts of time to puzzle this matter through?"

Wren glanced over at Garth, cocking one eyebrow. The giant Rover's nod was barely perceptible.

She looked back at Cogline. "You are so testy, old grandfather!" she chided. "Where is your patience?"

"Gone with my youth, child," he said, his voice unexpectedly soft. His hands folded before him. "Now what's it to be?"

She smiled. "The Hadeshorn and Allanon," she answered. "What did you expect?"

But the old man did not reply.

14

Five days later, with the sun exploding streamers of violet and red fire all across the western horizon in the kind of day's-end fireworks display that only summer provides, Wren, Garth, and the old man who said he was Cogline reached the base of the Dragon's Teeth and the beginning of the winding, narrow rock trail that led into the Valley of Shale and the Hadeshorn.

Par Ohmsford was the first to see them. He had gone up the trail a few hundred yards to a rock shelf where he could sit and look out over the sweep of Callahorn south and be by himself. He had arrived with Coll, Morgan, Walker, Steff, and Teel one day earlier, and his patience at waiting for the arrival of the first night of the new moon had begun to wear a little thin. He was immersed mostly in his admiration for the majesty of the sunset when he caught sight of the odd trio as they rode their horses out of the westward glare from a screen of poplar trees and started toward him. He came to his feet slowly, refusing to trust his eyes at first. Then, having determined that he was not mistaken, he leaped from his perch and charged back down the trail to alert the others of his little company who were camped immediately below.

Wren got there almost before he did. Her sharp Elven eyes caught sight of him at about the same time he saw her. Acting on impulse and leaving her companions to follow as best they could, she spurred her horse ahead recklessly, came charging into camp, vaulted from the saddle before her mount was fully checked, rushed up to Par with a wild yell, and hugged him with such enthusiasm that he was almost knocked from his feet. When she was done with him, she gave the same reception to an astonished, but delighted Coll. Walker got a more reserved kiss on the cheek and Morgan, whom she barely remembered from her childhood, a handshake and a nod.

While the three Ohmsford siblings—for they seemed such, despite the fact that Wren wasn't a true sister—traded hugs and words of greeting, those with them stood around uncomfortably and sized up one another with wary glances. Most of the sizing up was reserved for Garth, who was twice as big as any of the rest of them. He was dressed in the brightly colored clothing common to the Rovers, and the garishness of his garb made him seem larger still. He met the stares of the others without discomfort, his gaze steady and implacable. Wren remembered him after a moment and began the required series of introductions. Par followed with Steff and Teel. Cogline hung back from the others; since everyone seemed to know who he was, in any case, no formal introduction was attempted. There were nods and handshakes all around, courtesies observed as expected, but the wariness in the faces of most did not subside. When they all moved over to the fire that formed the center of the little campsite to partake of the dinner that the Dwarves had been in the process of preparing when Wren and her companions had appeared, the newly formed company of nine quickly fragmented into groups. Steff and Teel turned their attention to the completion of the meal, mute as they hovered over the pots and cooking fire, Walker withdrew to a patch of shade under a scrawny pine, and Cogline disappeared into the rocks without a word to anyone. He was so quiet about it that he was gone almost before they realized it. But Cogline was not really considered a part of the company, so no one much bothered about it. Par, Coll, Wren, and Morgan clustered together by the horses, unsaddling them and rubbing them down, and talked about old times, old friends, the places they had been, the things they had seen, and the vicissitudes of life.

"You are much grown, Wren," Coll marveled. "Not at all the broomstick little girl I remember when you left us."

"A rider of horses, wild as the wind! No boundaries for you!" Par laughed, throwing up his hands in a gesture meant to encompass the whole of the land.

Wren grinned back. "I live a better life than the lot of you, resting on your backsides, singing old tales and rousting tired dogs. The Westland's a good country for free-spirited things, you know." Then her grin faded. "The old man, Cogline, told me of what's happened in the Vale. Jaralan and Mirianna were my parents for a time, too, and I care for them still. Prisoners, he said. Have you heard anything of them?"

Par shook his head. "We have been running ever since Varfleet."

"I am sorry, Par." There was genuine discomfort in her eyes. "The Federation does its best to make all of our lives miserable. Even the Westland has its share of soldiers and administrative lackeys, though it's country they mostly ignore. The Rovers know how to avoid them in any case. If need be, you would be welcome to join us."

Par gave her another quick hug. "Best that we see how this business of the dreams turns out first," he whispered.

They ate a dinner of fried meats, fresh-baked hard bread, stewed vegetables, cheese, and nuts, and washed it all down with ale and water while they watched the sun disappear beneath the horizon. The food was good, and everyone said so, much to Steff's pleasure, for he had prepared the better part of it. Cogline remained absent, but the others began talking a bit more freely among themselves, all but Teel, who never seemed to want to speak. As far as Par knew, he was the only one besides Steff to whom the Dwarf girl had ever said anything.

When the dinner was complete, Steff and Teel took charge of cleaning the dishes, and the others drifted away in ones and twos as the dusk settled slowly into the night. While Coll and Morgan went down to a spring a quarter-mile off to draw fresh water, Par found himself ambling back up the trail that led into the mountains and the Valley of Shale in the company of Wren and the giant Garth.

"Have you been back there yet?" Wren asked as they walked, nodding in the direction of the Hadeshorn.

Par shook his head. "It's several hours in and no one's much wanted to hurry matters along. Even Walker has refused to go there before the scheduled time." He glanced skyward where clusters of stars dotted the heavens in intricate patterns and a small, almost invisible crescent moon hung low against the horizon north. "Tomorrow night," he said.

Wren didn't reply. They walked on in silence until they reached the shelf of rock that Par had occupied earlier that day. There they stopped, looking back over the country south.

"You've had the dreams, too?" Wren asked him then and went on to describe her own. When he nodded, she said, "What do you think?"

Par eased himself down on the rock, the other two sitting with him. "I think that ten generations of Ohmsfords have lived their lives since the time of Brin and Jair, waiting for this to happen. I think that the magic of the Elven house of Shannara, Ohmsford magic now, is something more than we realize. I think Allanon—or his shade, at least—will tell us what that something is." He paused. "I think it may turn out to be something wondrous—and something terrible."

He was aware of her staring at him with those intense hazel eyes, and he shrugged apologetically. "I don't mean to be overdramatic. That's just the sense I have of things."

She translated his comments automatically for Garth, who gave no indication of what he thought. "You and Walker have some use of the magic," she said quietly. "I have none. What of that?"

He shook his head. "I'm not sure. Morgan's magic is stronger than mine these days and he wasn't called." He went on to tell her about their confrontation with the Shadowen and the Highlander's discovery of the magic that had lain dormant in the Sword of Leah. "I find myself wondering why the dreams didn't command him to appear instead of me, for all the use the wishsong has been."

"But you don't know for certain how strong your magic is, Par," she said quietly. "You should remember from the stories that none of the Ohmsfords, from Shea on down, fully understood when they began their quests the uses of the Elven magic. Might it not be the same with you?"

It might, he realized with a shiver. He cocked his head. "Or you, Wren. What of you?"

"No, no, Par Ohmsford. I am a simple Rover girl with none of the blood that carries the magic from generation to generation in me." She laughed. "I'm afraid I must make do with a bag filled with make-believe Elfstones!"

He laughed as well, remembering the little leather bag with the painted rocks that she had guarded so carefully as a child. They traded life stories for a time, telling each other what they had been doing, where they had been, and whom they had encountered on their journeys. They were relaxed, much as if their separation had been but a few weeks rather than years. Wren was responsible for that, Par decided. She had put him immediately at ease. He was struck by the inordinate amount of confidence that she exhibited in herself, such a wild, free girl, obviously content with her Rover life, seemingly unshackled by demands or constraints that might hold her back. She was strong both inwardly and outwardly, and he admired her greatly for it. He found himself wishing that he could display but a fraction of her pluck.

"How do you find Walker?" she asked him after a time.

"Distant," he said at once. "Still haunted by demons that I cannot begin to understand. He talks about his mistrust of the Elven magic and the Druids, yet seems to have magic of his own that he uses freely enough. I don't really understand him."

Wren relayed his comments to Garth, and the giant Rover responded with a brief signing. Wren looked at him sharply, then said to Par, "Garth says that Walker is frightened."

Par looked surprised. "How does he know that?"

"He just does. Because he is deaf, he works harder at using his other senses. He detects other people's feelings more quickly than you or I would—even those that are kept hidden."

Par nodded. "Well, he happens to be exactly right in this instance. Walker is frightened. He told me so himself. He says he's frightened of what this business with Allanon might mean. Odd, isn't it? I have trouble imagining anything frightening Walker Boh."

Wren signed to Garth, but the giant merely shrugged. They sat back in silence for a time, thinking separate thoughts. Then Wren said, "Did you know that the old man, Cogline, was once Walker's teacher?"

Par looked at her sharply. "Did he tell you that?"

"I tricked it from him, mostly."

"Teacher of what, Wren? Of the magic?"

"Of something." Her dark features turned introspective momentarily, her gaze distant. "There is much between those two that, like Walker's fear, is kept hidden, I think."

Par, though he didn't say so, was inclined to agree.

The members of the little company slept undisturbed that night in the shadow of the Dragon's Teeth, but by dawn they were awake again and restless. Tonight was the first night of the new moon, the night they were to meet with the shade of Allanon. Impatiently, they went about their business. They ate their meals without tasting them. They spoke little to one another, moving about uneasily, finding small tasks that would distract them from thinking further on what lay ahead. It was a clear, cloudless day filled with warm summer smells and lazy sunshine, the kind of day that, under other circumstances, might have been enjoyed, but which on this occasion simply seemed endless.

Cogline reappeared about midday, wandering down out of the mountains like some tattered prophet of doom. He looked dusty and unkempt as he came up to them, his hair wild, his eyes shadowed from lack of sleep. He told them that all was in readiness—whatever that meant—and that he would come for them after nightfall. Be ready, he advised. He refused to say anything more, though pressed by the Ohmsfords to do so, and disappeared back the way he had come.

"What do you suppose he is doing up there?" Coll muttered to the others as the ragged figure dwindled into a tiny black speck in the distance and then into nothing at all.

The sun worked its way westward as if dragging chains in its wake, and the members of the little company retreated further into themselves. The enormity of what was about to happen began to emerge in their unspoken thoughts, a specter of such size that it was frightening to contemplate. Even Walker Boh, who might have been assumed to be more at home with the prospect of encountering shades and spirits, withdrew into himself like a badger into its hole and became unapproachable.

Nevertheless, when it was nearing midafternoon, Par happened on his uncle while wandering the cooler stretches of the hills surrounding the springs. They slowed on coming together, then stopped and stood looking at each other awkwardly.

"Do you think he will really come?" Par asked finally.

Walker's pale features were shadowed beneath the protective hood of his cloak, making his face difficult to read. "He will come," his uncle said.

Par thought a moment, then said, "I don't know what to expect."

Walker shook his head. "It doesn't matter, Par. Whatever you choose to expect, it won't be enough. This meeting won't be like anything you might envision, I promise you. The Druids have always been very good at surprises."

"You suspect the worst, don't you?"

"I suspect . . ." He trailed off without finishing.

"Magic," said Par.

The other frowned.

"Druid magic—that's what you think we will see tonight, don't you? I hope you are right. I hope that it sweeps and resounds and that it opens all the doors that have been closed to us and lets us see what magic can really do!"

Walker Boh's smile, when it finally overcame his astonishment, was ironic. "Some doors are better left closed," he said softly. "You would do well to remember that."

He put his hand on his nephew's arm for a moment, then continued silently on his way.

The afternoon crawled toward evening. When the sun at last completed its long journey west and began to slip beneath the horizon, the members of the little company filtered back to the campsite for the evening meal. Morgan was garrulous, an obvious sign of nerves with him, and talked incessantly of magic and swords and all sorts of wild happenings that Par hoped would never be. The others were mostly silent, eating without comment and casting watchful glances northward toward the mountains. Teel wouldn't eat at all, sitting off by herself in a gathering of shadows, the mask that covered her face like a wall that separated her from everyone. Even Steff let her alone.

Darkness descended and the stars began to flicker into view, a scattering here and there at first, and then the sky was filled with them. No moon showed itself; it was the promised time when the sun's pale sister wore black. Daylight's sounds faded and night's remained hushed. The cooking fire crackled and snapped in the silence as conversation lagged. One or two smoked, and the air was filled with the pungent smell. Morgan took out the bright length of the Sword of Leah and began to polish it absently. Wren and Garth fed and curried the horses. Walker moved up the trail a short distance and stood staring into the mountains. Others sat lost in thought.

Everyone waited.

It was midnight when Cogline returned for them. The old man appeared out of the shadows like a ghost, materializing so suddenly that they all started. No one, not even Walker, had seen him coming.

"It is time," he announced.

They came to their feet voicelessly and followed him. He took them up the trail from their campsite into the gradually thickening shadows of the Dragon's Teeth. Although the stars shone brightly overhead when they started out, the mountains soon began to close about, leaving the little company shrouded in blackness. Cogline did not slow; he seemed to possess cat's eyes. His charges struggled to keep pace. Par, Coll, and Morgan were closest to the old man, Wren and Garth came next, Steff and Teel behind them, and Walker Boh brought up the rear. The trail steepened quickly after they reached the beginning peaks, and they moved through a narrow defile that opened like a pocket into the mountains. It was silent here, so still that they could hear one another breathe as they labored upward.

The minutes slipped away. Boulders and cliff walls hindered their passage, and the trail wound about like a snake. Loose rock carpeted the whole of the mountains, and the climbers had to scramble over it. Still Cogline pressed on. Par stumbled and scraped his knees, finding the loose rock as sharp as glass. Much of it was a strange, mirrorlike black that reminded him of coal. He scooped up a small piece out of curiosity and stuck it in his pocket.

Then abruptly the mountains split apart before them, and they stepped out onto the rim of the Valley of Shale. It was little more than a broad, shallow depression strewn with crushed stone that glistened with the same mirrored blackness as the rock Par had pocketed. Nothing grew in the valley; it was stripped of life. There was a lake at its center, its greenish black waters moving in sluggish swirls in the windless expanse.

Cogline stopped momentarily and looked back at them. "The Hadeshorn," he whispered. "Home for the spirits of the ages, for the Druids of the past." His weathered old face had an almost reverent look to it. Then he turned away and started them down into the valley.

Except for the huff of their breathing and the rasp of their boots on the loose rock, the valley, too, was wrapped in silence. Echoes of their movements played in the stillness like children in the slow heat of a midsummer's day. Eyes darted watchfully, seeking ghosts where there were none to find, imagining life in every shadow. It was strangely warm here, the heat of the day captured and held in the airless bowl through the cool of the night. Par felt a trickle of sweat begin to run down his back.

Then they were on the valley floor, closely bunched as they made their way toward the lake. They could see the movement of the waters more clearly now, the way the swirls worked against each other, haphazard, unbidden. They could hear the rippling of tiny waves as they lapped. There was the pungent scent of things aging and decayed.

They were still several dozen yards from the water's edge when Cogline brought them to a halt, both hands lifting in caution. "Stand fast, now. Come no closer. The waters of the Hadeshorn are death to mortals, poison to the touch!" He crouched down and put a finger to his lips as if hushing a child.

They did as they were bidden, children indeed before the power they sensed sleeping there. They could feel it, all of them, a palpable thing that hung in the air like wood smoke from a fire. They remained where they were, alert, anxious, filled with a mix of wonder and hesitancy. No one spoke. The star-filled sky stretched away endlessly overhead, canopied from horizon to horizon, and it seemed as if the whole of the heavens was focused on the valley, that lake, and the nine of them who kept watch.

At last Cogline lifted from his crouch and came back to them, beckoning with birdlike movements of his hands to draw them close about him. When they were gathered in a knot that locked them shoulder to shoulder, he spoke.

"Allanon will come just before dawn." The sharp old eyes regarded them solemnly. "He wishes me to speak with you first. He is no longer what he was in life. He is just a shade now. His purchase in this world is but the blink of an eye. Each time he crosses over from the spirit world, it requires tremendous effort. He can stay only a little while. What time he is allotted he must use wisely. He will use that time to tell you of the need he has of you. He has left it to me to explain to you why that need exists. I am to tell you of the Shadowen."

"You've spoken to him?" asked Walker Boh quickly.

Cogline said nothing.

"Why wait until now to tell us about the Shadowen?" Par was suddenly irritated. "Why now, Cogline, when you could have done so before?"

The old man shook his head, his face both reproving and sympathetic. "It was not permitted, youngster. Not until all of you had been brought together."

"Games!" Walker muttered and shook his head in disgust.

The old man ignored him. "Think what you like, only listen. This is what Allanon would have me tell you of the Shadowen. They are an evil beyond all imagining. They are not the rumors or the tall tales that men would have them be, but creatures as real as you and I. They are born of a circumstance that Allanon in all his wisdom and planning did not foresee.

When he passed from the world of mortal men, Allanon believed the age of magic at an end and a new age begun. The Warlock Lord was no more. The Demons of the old world of faerie were again imprisoned within the Forbidding. The Ildatch was destroyed. Paranor was gone into history and the last of the Druids were about to go with it. It seemed the need for magic was past."

"The need is never past," Walker said quietly.

Again, the old man ignored him. "The Shadowen are an aberration. They are a magic that grew out of the use of other magics, a residue of what has gone before. They began as a seeding that lay dormant within the Four Lands, undetected during the time of Allanon, a seeding that came to life only after the Druids and their protective powers were gone. No one could have known they were there, not even Allanon. They were the leavings of magic come and gone, and they were as invisible as dust on a pathway."

"Wait a minute!" Par interjected. "What are you saying, Cogline? That the Shadowen are just bits and pieces of some stray magic?"

Cogline took a deep breath, his hands locking before him. "Valeman, I told you once before that for all the use you have of magic, you still know little about it. Magic is as much a force of nature as the fire at the earth's core, the tidal waves that sweep out of the ocean, the winds that flatten forests or the famine that starves nations. It does not happen and then disappear without effect! Think! What of Wil Ohmsford and his use of the Elfstones when his Elven blood no longer permitted such use? It left as its residue the wishsong that found life in your ancestors! Was that an inconsequential magic? All uses of the magic have effects beyond the immediate. And all are significant."

"Which magic was it that created the Shadowen?" asked Coll, his blocky face impassive.

The old man shook his wispy head. "Allanon does not know. There is no way of being certain. It could have happened at any time during the lives of Shea Ohmsford and his descendents. There was always magic in use in those times, much of it evil. The Shadowen could have been born of any part of it."

He paused. "The Shadowen were nothing at first. They were the debris of magic spent. Somehow they survived, their presence unknown. It was not until Allanon and Paranor were gone that they emerged into the Four Lands and began to gain strength. There was a vacuum in the order of things by then. A void must be filled in all events, and the Shadowen were quick to fill this one."

"I don't understand," Par said quickly. "What sort of vacuum do you mean?"

"And why didn't Allanon foresee it happening?" added Wren.

The old man held up his fingers and began crooking them downward one by one as he spoke. "Life has always been cyclical. Power comes and goes; it takes different forms. Once, it was science that gave mankind power. Of late, it has been magic. Allanon foresaw the return of science as a means to progress—especially with the passing of the Druids and Paranor. That was the age that would be. But the development of science failed to materialize quickly enough to fill the vacuum. Partly this was because of the Federation. The Federation kept the old ways intact; it proscribed the use of any form of power but its own—and its own was primitive and military. It expanded its influence throughout the Four Lands until all were subject to its dictates. The Elves had an effect on matters as well; for reasons we still don't know they disappeared. They were a balancing force, the last people of the faerie world of old. Their presence was necessary, if the transition from magic to science was to be made faultlessly."

He shook his head. "Yet even had the Elves remained in the world of men and the Federation been less a presence, the Shadowen might have come alive. The vacuum was there the moment the Druids passed away. There was no help for it." He sighed. "Allanon did not foresee as he should have. He did not anticipate an aberration on the order of the Shadowen. He did what he could to keep the Four Lands safe while he was alive—and he kept himself alive for as long as was possible."

"Too little of each, it seems," Walker said pointedly.

Cogline looked at him, and the anger in his voice was palpable. "Well, Walker Boh. Perhaps one day you will have an opportunity to demonstrate that you can do it better."

There was a strained moment of silence as the two faced each other in the blackness. Then Cogline looked away. "You need to understand what the Shadowen are. The Shadowen are parasites. They live off mortal creatures. They are a magic that feeds on living things. They enter them, absorb them, become them. But for some reason the results are not always the same. Young Par, think of the woodswoman that you and Coll encountered at the time of our first meeting. She was a Shadowen of the more obvious sort, a once-mortal creature infected, a ravaged thing that could no more help herself than an animal made mad. But the little girl on Toffer Ridge, do you remember her?"

His fingers brushed Par's cheek lightly. Instantly, the Valeman was filled with the memory of that monster to whom the Spider Gnomes had given him. He could feel her stealing against him, begging him, "hug me, hug me," desperate to make him embrace her. He flinched, shaken by the impact of the memory.

Cogline's hand closed firmly about his arm. "That, too, was a Shadowen, but one that could not be so easily detected. They appear to varying extents as we do, hidden within human form. Some become grotesque in appearance and behavior; those you can readily identify. Others are more difficult to recognize."

"But why are there some of one kind and some of the other?" Par asked uncertainly.

Cogline's brow furrowed. "Once again, Allanon does not know. The Shadowen have kept their secret even from him."

The old man looked away for a long moment, then back again. His face was a mask of despair. "This is like a plague. The sickness is spread until the number infected multiplies impossibly. Any of the Shadowen can transmit the disease. Their magic gives them the means to overcome almost any defense. The more of them there are, the stronger they become. What would you do to stop a plague where the source was unknown, the symptoms undetectable until after they had taken root, and the cure a mystery?"

The members of the little company glanced at one another uneasily in the silence that followed.

Finally, Wren said, "Do they have a purpose in what they do, Cogline? A purpose beyond simply infecting living things? Do they think as you and I or are they . . . mindless?"

Par stared at the girl in undisguised admiration. It was the best question any of them had asked. He should have been the one to ask it.

Cogline was rubbing his hands together slowly. "They think as you and I, Rover girl, and they most certainly do have a purpose in what they do. But that purpose remains unclear."

"They would subvert us," Morgan offered sharply. "Surely that's purpose enough."

But Cogline shook his head. "They would do more still, I think."

And abruptly Par found himself recalling the dreams that Allanon had sent, the visions of a nightmarish world in which everything was blackened and withered and life was reduced to something barely recognizable. Reddened eyes blinked like bits of fire, and shadow forms flitted through a haze of ash and smoke.

This is what the Shadowen would do, he realized.

But how could they bring such a vision to pass?

He glanced without thinking at Wren and found his question mirrored in her eyes. He recognized what she was thinking instinctively. He saw it reflected in Walker Boh's eyes as well. They had shared the dreams and those dreams bound them, so much so that for an instant their thinking was the same.

Cogline's face lifted slightly, pulling free of the darkness that shaded it. "Something guides the Shadowen," he whispered. "There is power here that transcends anything we have ever known . . ."

He let the sentence trail off, ragged and unfinished, as if unable to give voice to any ending. His listeners looked at one another.

"What are we to do?" Wren asked finally.

The old man rose wearily. "Why, what we came here to do, Rover girl—listen to what Allanon would tell us."

He moved stiffly away, and no one called after him.

15

They moved apart from each other after that, drifting away one by one, finding patches of solitude in which to think their separate thoughts. Eyes wandered restlessly across the valley's glistening carpet of black rock, always returning to the Hadeshorn, carefully searching the sluggishly churning waters for signs of some new movement.

There was none.

Perhaps nothing is going to happen, Par thought. Perhaps it was all a lie after all.

He felt his chest constrict with mixed feelings of disappointment and relief and he forced his thoughts elsewhere. Coll was less than a dozen paces away, but he refused to look at him. He wanted to be alone. There were things that needed thinking through, and Coll would only distract him.

Funny how much effort he had put into distancing himself from his brother since this journey had begun, he thought suddenly. Perhaps it was because he was afraid for him . . .

Once again, this time angrily, he forced his thoughts elsewhere. Cogline. Now there was an enigma of no small size. Who was this old man who seemed to know so much about everything? A failed Druid, he claimed. Allanon's messenger, he said. But those brief descriptions didn't seem nearly complete enough. Par was certain that there was more to him than what he claimed. There was a history of events behind his relationships with Allanon and Walker Boh that was hidden from the rest of them. Allanon would not have gone to a failed Druid for assistance, not even in the most desperate of circumstances. There was a reason for Cogline's involvement with this gathering beyond what any of them knew.

He glanced warily at the old man who stood an uncomfortable number of feet closer than the rest of them to the waters of the Hadeshorn. He knew all about the Shadowen, somehow. He had spoken more than once with Allanon, somehow again. He was the only living human being to have done so since the Druid's death three hundred years ago. Par thought a moment about the stories of Cogline in the time of Brin Ohmsford—a half-crazed old man then, wielding magic against the Mord Wraiths like some sort of broom against dust—that's the picture the tales conjured up. Well, he wasn't like that now. He was controlled. Cranky and eccentric, yes—but mostly controlled. He knew what he was about—enough so that he didn't seem particularly pleased with any of it. He hadn't said that, of course. But Par wasn't blind.

There was a flash of light from somewhere far off in the night skies, a momentary brightness that winked away instantly and was gone. A life ended, a new life begun, his mother used to say. He sighed. He hadn't thought of his parents much since the flight out of Varfleet. He felt a twinge of guilt. He wondered if they were all right. He wondered if he would see them again.

His jaw tightened with determination. Of course he would see them again! Things would work out. Allanon would have answers to give him—about the uses of the magic of the wishsong, the reasons for the dreams, what to do about the Shadowen and the Federation . . . all of it.

Allanon would know.

Time slipped away, minutes into hours, the night steadily working its way toward dawn. Par moved over to talk with Coll, needing now to be close to his brother. The others shifted, stretched, and moved about uneasily. Eyes grew heavy and senses dulled.

Far east, the first twinges of the coming dawn appeared against the dark line of the horizon.

He's not coming, Par thought dismally.

And as if in answer the waters of the Hadeshorn heaved upward, and the valley shuddered as if something beneath it had come awake. Rock shifted and grated with the movement, and the members of the little company went into a protective crouch. The lake began to boil, the waters to thrash, and spray shot skyward with a sharp hiss. Voices cried out, inhuman and filled with longing. They rose out of the earth, straining against bonds that were invisible to the nine gathered in the valley, but which they could all too readily imagine. Walker's arms flung wide against the sound, scattering bits of silver dust that flared in a protective curtain. The others cupped their ears protectively, but nothing could shut the sound away.

Then the earth began to rumble, thunder that rolled out of its depth and eclipsed even the cries. Cogline's stick-thin arm lifted, pointing rigidly to the lake. The Hadeshorn exploded into a whirlpool, waters churning madly, and from out of the depths rose . . .

"Allanon!" Par cried out excitedly against the fury of sounds.

It was the Druid. They knew him instantly, all of them. They remembered him from the tales of three centuries gone; they recognized him in their heart of hearts, that secret innermost whisper of certainty. He rose into the night air, light flaring about him, released somehow from the waters of the Hadeshorn. He lifted free of the lake to stand upon its surface, a shade from some netherworld, cast in transparent gray, shimmering faintly against the dark. He was cloaked and cowled from head to foot, a tall and powerful image of the man that once was, his long, sharp-featured, bearded face turned toward them, his penetrating eyes sweeping clear their defenses, laying bare their lives for examination and judgment.

Par Ohmsford shivered.

The churning of the waters subsided, the rumbling ceased, the wails died into a hush that hung suspended across the expanse of the valley. The shade moved toward them, seemingly without haste, as if to discredit Cogline's word that it could stay only briefly in the world of men. Its eyes never left their own. Par had never been so frightened. He wanted to run. He wanted to flee for his life, but he stood rooted to the spot on which he stood, unable to move.

The shade came to the water's edge and stopped. From somewhere deep within their minds, the members of the little company heard it speak.

—I am Allanon that was—

A murmur of voices filled the air, voices of things no longer living, echoing the shade's words.

—I have called you to me in your dreams—Par, Wren, and Walker. Children of Shannara, you have been summoned to me. The wheel of time comes around again—for rebirthing of the magic, for honoring the trust that was given you, for beginning and ending many things—

The voice, deep and sonorous within them, grew rough with feelings that scraped the bone.

—The Shadowen come. They come with a promise of destruction, sweeping over the Four Lands with the certainty of day after night—

There was a pause as the shade's lean hands wove a vision of his words through the fabric of the night air, a tapestry that hung momentarily in brilliant colors against the misted black. The dreams he had sent them came alive, sketches of nightmarish madness. Then they faded and were gone. The voice whispered soundlessly.

—It shall be so, if you do not heed—

Par felt the words reverberate through his body like a rumble from the earth. He wanted to look at the others, wanted to see what was on their faces, but the voice of the shade held him spellbound.

Not so Walker Boh. His uncle's voice was as chilling as the shade's. "Tell us what you would, Allanon! Be done with it!"

Allanon's flat gaze shifted to the dark figure and settled on him. Walker Boh staggered back a step in spite of himself. The shade pointed.

—Destroy the Shadowen! They subvert the people of the Races, creeping into their bodies, taking their forms as they choose, becoming them, using them, turning them into the misshapen giant and maddened woodswoman you have already encountered—and into things worse still. No one prevents it. No one will, if not you—

"But what are we supposed to do?" Par asked at once, almost without thinking.

The shade had been substantial when it had first appeared, a ghost that had taken on again the fullness of life. But already the lines and shadings were beginning to pale, and he who was once Allanon shimmered with the translucent and ephemeral inconsistency of smoke.

—Shannara child. There are balances to be restored if the Shadowen are to be destroyed—not for a time, not in this age only, but forever. Magic is needed. Magic to put an end to the misuse of life. Magic to restore the fabric of man's existence in the mortal world. That magic is your heritage— yours, Wren's, and Walker's. You must acknowledge it and embrace it—

The Hadeshorn was beginning to roil again, and the members of the little company fell back before its hiss and spray—all but Cogline who stood rock-still before the others, his head bowed upon his frail chest.

The shade of Allanon seemed to swell suddenly against the night, rising up before them. The robes spread wide. The shade's eyes fixed on Par, and the Valeman felt the stab of an invisible finger penetrate his breast.

—Par Ohmsford, bearer of the wishsong's promise, I charge you with recovering the Sword of Shannara. Only through the Sword can truth be revealed and only through truth shall the Shadowen be overcome. Take up the Sword, Par; wield it according to the dictates of your heart—the truth of the Shadowen shall be yours to discover—

The eyes shifted.

—Wren, child of hidden, forgotten lives, yours is a charge of equal importance. There can be no healing of the Lands or of their people without the Elves of faerie. Find them and return them to the world of men. Find them, Rover girl. Only then can the sickness end—

The Hadeshorn erupted with a booming cough.

—And Walker Boh, you of no belief, seek that belief—and the understanding necessary to sustain it. Search out the last of the curatives that is needed to give life back to the Lands. Search out disappeared Paranor and restore the Druids—

There was astonishment mirrored in the faces of all, and for an instant it smothered the shouts of disbelief that struggled to surface. Then everyone was yelling at once, the words tumbling over one another as each sought to make himself heard above the tumult. But the cries disappeared instantly as the shade's arms came up in a sweep that caused the earth to rumble anew.

—Cease—

The waters of the Hadeshorn spit and hissed behind him as he faced them. It was growing lighter now in the east; dawn was threatening to break.

The shade's voice was again a whisper.

—You would know more. I wish that it could be so. But I have told you what I can. I cannot tell you more. I lack the power in death that I possessed in life. I am permitted to see only bits and pieces of the world that was or the future that will be. I cannot find what is hidden from you for I am sealed away in a world where substance has small meaning. Each day, the memory of it slips further from me. I sense what is and what is possible; that must suffice. Therefore, pay heed to me. I cannot come with you. I cannot guide you. I cannot answer the questions you bring with you—not of magic or family or self-worth. All that you must do for yourselves. My time in the Four Lands is gone, children of Shannara. As it once was for Bremen, so it is now for me. I am not chained by shackles of failure as was he, but I am chained nevertheless. Death limits both time and being. I am the past. The future of the Four Lands belongs to you and to you alone—

"But you ask impossible things of us!" Wren snapped desperately.

"Worse! You ask things that should never be!" Walker raged. "Druids come again? Paranor restored?"

The shade's reply came softly.

—I ask for what must be. You have the skills, the heart, the right, and the need to do what I have asked. Believe what I have told you. Do as I have said. Then will the Shadowen be destroyed—

Par felt his throat tighten in desperation. Allanon was beginning to fade.

"Where shall we look?" he cried out frantically. "Where do we begin our search? Allanon, you have to tell us!"

There was no answer. The shade withdrew further.

"No! You cannot go!" Walker Boh howled suddenly.

The shade began to sink into the waters of the Hadeshorn.

"Druid, I forbid it!" Walker screamed in fury, throwing off sparks of his own magic as he flung his arms out as if to hold the other back.

The whole of the valley seemed to explode in response, the earth shaking until rocks bounced and rattled ferociously, the air filling with a wind that whipped down out of the mountains as if summoned, the Hadeshorn churning in a maelstrom of rage, the dead crying out—and the shade of Allanon bursting into flame. The members of the little company were thrown flat as the forces about them collided, and everything was caught up in a whirlwind of light and sound.

At last it was still and dark again. They lifted their heads cautiously and looked about. The valley was empty of shades and spirits and all that accompanied them. The earth was at rest once more and the Hadeshorn a silent, placid stretch of luminescence that reflected the sun's brilliant image from where it lifted out of the darkness in the east.

Par Ohmsford climbed slowly to his feet. He felt that he might have awakened from a dream.

When they recovered their composure, the members of the little company discovered that Cogline was missing. At first they thought such a thing impossible, certain that they must be mistaken, and they cast about for him expectantly, searching the lingering nighttime shadows. But the valley offered few places to hide, and the old man was nowhere to be found.

"Perhaps Allanon's shade whisked him away," Morgan suggested in an attempt to make a joke of it.

Nobody laughed. Nobody even smiled. They were already sufficiently distressed by everything else that had happened that night, and the strange disappearance of the old man only served to unsettle them further. It was one thing for the shades of Druids dead and gone to appear and vanish without warning; it was something else again when it was a flesh-and-blood person. Besides, Cogline had been their last link to the meaning behind the dreams and the reason for their journey here. With the apparent severing of that link, they were all too painfully aware that they were now on their own.

They stood around uncertainly a moment or two longer. Then Walker muttered something about wasting his time. He started back the way he had come, the others of the little company trailing after him. The sun was above the horizon now, golden in a sky that was cloudless and blue, and the warmth of the day was already settling over the barren peaks of the Dragon's Teeth. Par glanced over his shoulder as they reached the valley rim. The Hadeshorn stared back at him, sullen and unresponsive.

The walk back was a silent one. They were all thinking about what the Druid had said, sifting and measuring the revelations and charges, and none of them were ready yet to talk. Certainly Par wasn't. He was so confounded by what he had been told that he was having trouble accepting that he had actually heard it. He trailed the others with Coll, watching their backs as they wound single file through the breaks in the rocks, following the pathway that led down through the cliff pocket to the foothills and their campsite, thinking mostly that Walker had been right after all, that whatever he might have imagined this meeting with the shade of Allanon would be like, he would have imagined wrong. Coll asked him at one point if he were all right and he nodded without replying, wondering inwardly if indeed he would ever be all right again.

Recover the Sword of Shannara, the shade had commanded him. Sticks and stones, how in the world was he supposed to do that?

The seeming impossibility of the task was daunting. He had no idea where to begin. No one, to the best of his knowledge, had even seen the Sword since the occupation of Tyrsis by the Federation—well over a hundred years ago. And it might have disappeared before that. Certainly no one had seen it since. Like most things connected with the time of the Druids and the magic, the Sword was part of a legend that was all but forgotten. There weren't any Druids, there weren't any Elves, and there wasn't any magic—not anymore, not in the world of men. How often had he heard that?

His jaw tightened. Just exactly what was he supposed to do? What were any of them supposed to do? Allanon had given them nothing to work with beyond the bare charging of their respective quests and his assurance that what he asked of them was both possible and necessary.

He felt a hot streak race through him. There had been no mention of his own magic, of the uses of the wishsong that he believed were hidden from him. Nothing had been said about the ways in which it might be employed. He hadn't even been given a chance to ask questions. He didn't know one thing more about the magic than he had before.

Par was angry and disappointed and a dozen other things too confusing to sort out. Recover the Sword of Shannara, indeed! And then what? What was he supposed to do with it? Challenge the Shadowen to some sort of combat? Go charging around the countryside searching them out and destroying them one by one?

His face flushed. Shades! Why should he even *think* about doing such a thing?

He caught himself. Well, that was really the crux of things, wasn't it? Should he even consider doing what Allanon had asked—not so much the hunting of the Shadowen with the Sword of Shannara, but the hunting of the Sword of Shannara in the first place?

That was what needed deciding.

He tried pushing the matter from his mind for a moment, losing himself in the cool of the shadows where the cliffs still warded the pathway; but, like a frightened child clinging to its mother, it refused to release its grip. He saw Steff ahead of him saying something to Teel, then to Morgan and shaking his head vehemently as he did so. He saw the stiff set of Walker Boh's back. He saw Wren striding after her uncle as if she might walk right over him. All of them were as angry and frustrated as he was; there was no mistaking the look. They felt cheated by what they had been told—or not told. They had expected something more substantial, something definitive, something that would give them answers to the questions they had brought with them.

Anything besides the impossible charges they had been given!

Yet Allanon had said the charges were not impossible, that they could be accomplished, and that the three charged had the skills, the heart, and the right to accomplish them.

Par sighed. Should he believe that?

And again he was back to wondering whether or not he should even consider doing what he had been asked.

But he was already considering exactly that, wasn't he? What else was he doing by debating the matter, if not that?

He passed out of the cliff shadows onto the pebble-strewn trail leading downward to the campsite. As he did so, he made a determined effort to put aside his anger and frustration and to think clearly. What did he know that he could rely upon? The dreams had indeed been a summons from Allanon—that much appeared certain now. The Druid had come to them as he had come to Ohmsfords in the past, asking their help against dark magic that threatened the Four Lands. The only difference, of course, was that this time he had been forced to come as a shade. Cogline, a former Druid, had been his messenger in the flesh to assure that the summons was heeded. Cogline had Allanon's trust.

Par took a moment to consider whether or not he really believed that last statement and decided he did.

The Shadowen were real, he went on. They were dangerous, they were evil, they were certainly a threat of some sort to the Races and the Four Lands. They were magic.

He paused again. If the Shadowen were indeed magic, it would probably take magic to defeat them. And if he accepted that, it made much of what Allanon and Cogline had told them more convincing. It made possible the tale of the origin and growth of the Shadowen. It made probable the claim that the balance of things was out of whack. Whether you accepted the premise that the Shadowen were to blame or not, there was clearly much wrong in the Four Lands. Most of the blame for what was bad had been attributed by the Federation to the magic of the Elves and Druids—magic that the old stories claimed was good. But Par thought the truth lay somewhere in between. Magic in and of itself—if you believed in it as Par did—was never bad or good; it was simply power. That was the lesson of the wishsong. It was all in how the magic was used.

Par frowned. That being so, what if the Shadowen were using magic to cause problems among the Races in ways that none of them could see? What if the only way to combat such magic was to turn it against the user, to cause it to revert to the uses for which it was intended? What if Druids and Elves and talismans like the Sword of Shannara were indeed needed to accomplish that end?

There was sense in the idea, he admitted reluctantly.

But was there enough sense?

The campsite appeared ahead, undisturbed since their leave-taking the previous night, streaked by early sunlight and fading shadows. The horses nickered at their approach, still tied to the picket line. Par saw that Cogline's horse was among them. Apparently the old man had not returned here.

He found himself thinking of the way Cogline had come to them before, appearing unexpectedly to each, to Walker, Wren, and himself, saying what he had to say, then departing as abruptly as he had come. It had been that way each time. He had warned each of them what was required, then let them decide what they would do. Perhaps, he thought suddenly, that was what he had done this time as well—simply left them to decide on their own.

They reached the camp, still without having spoken more than a few brief words to one another, and came to an uneasy halt. There was some suggestion of eating or sleeping first, but everyone quickly decided against it. No one really wanted to eat or sleep; they were neither hungry nor tired. They were ready now to talk about what had happened. They wanted to put the matter to discussion and give voice to the thoughts and emotions that had been building and churning inside them during the walk back.

"Very well," Walker Boh said curtly, after a moment's strained silence. "Since no one else cares to say it, I will. This whole business is madness. Paranor is gone. The Druids are gone. There haven't been any Elves in the Four Lands in over a hundred years. The Sword of Shannara hasn't been seen for at least that long. We haven't, any of us, the vaguest idea of how to go about recovering any of them—if, indeed, recovery is possible. I suspect it isn't. I think this is just one more instance of the Druids playing games with the Ohmsfords. And I resent it very much!"

He was flushed, his face sharply drawn. Par remembered again how angry he had been back in the valley, almost uncontrolled. This was not the Walker Boh he remembered.

"I am not sure we can dismiss what happened back there as simple game-playing," Par began, but then Walker was all over him.

"No, of course not, Par—you see all this as a chance to satisfy your misguided curiosity about the uses of magic! I warned you before that magic was not the gift you envisioned, but a curse! Why is it that you persist in seeing it as something else?"

"Suppose the shade spoke the truth?" Coll's voice was quiet and firm, and it turned Walker's attention immediately from Par.

"The truth isn't in those cowled tricksters! When has the truth ever been in them? They tell us bits and pieces, but never the whole! They use us! They have always used us!"

"But not unwisely, not without consideration for what must be done— that's not what the stories tell us." Coll held his ground. "I am not necessarily advocating that we do as the shade suggested, Walker. I am only saying that it is unreasonable to dismiss the matter out of hand because of one possibility in a rather broad range."

"The bits and pieces you speak of—those were always true in and of themselves," Par added to Coll's surprisingly eloquent defense. "What you mean is that Allanon never told the whole truth in the beginning. He always held something back."

Walker looked at them as if they were children, shaking his head. "A half-truth can be as devastating as a lie," he said quietly. The anger was fading now, replaced by a tone of resignation. "You ought to know that much."

"I know that there is danger in either."

"Then why persist in this? Let it go!"

"Uncle," Par said, the reprimand in his voice astonishing even to himself, "I haven't taken it up yet."

Walker looked at him for a long time, a tall, pale-skinned figure against the dawn, his face unreadable in its mix of emotions. "Haven't you?" he replied softly.

Then he turned, gathered up his blankets and gear and rolled them up. "I will put it to you another way, then. Were everything the shade told us true, it would make no difference. I have decided on my course of action. I will do nothing to restore Paranor and the Druids to the Four Lands. I can think of nothing I wish less. The time of the Druids and Paranor saw more madness than this age could ever hope to witness. Bring back those old men with their magics and their conjuring, their playing with the lives of men as if they were toys?"

He rose and faced them, his pale face as hard as granite. "I would sooner cut off my hand than see the Druids come again!"

The others glanced at one another in consternation as he turned away to finish putting together his pack.

"Will you simply hide out in your valley?" Par shot back, angry now himself.

Walker didn't look at him. "If you will."

"What happens if the shade spoke the truth, Walker? What happens if all it has foreseen comes to pass, and the Shadowen reach extends even into Hearthstone? Then what will you do?"

"What I must."

"With your own magic?" Par spat. "With magic taught to you by Cogline?"

His uncle's pale face lifted sharply. "How did you learn of that?"

Par shook his head stubbornly. "What difference is there between your magic and that of the Druids, Walker? Isn't it all the same?"

The other's smile was hard and unfriendly. "Sometimes, Par, you are a fool," he said and dismissed him.

When he rose a moment later, he was calm. "I have done my part in this. I came as I was bidden and I listened to what I was supposed to hear. I have no further obligation. The rest of you must decide for yourselves what you will do. As for me, I am finished with this business."

He strode through them without pausing, moving down to where the horses were tethered. He strapped his pack in place, mounted, and rode out. He never once looked back.

The remaining members of the little company watched in silence. That was a quick decision, Par thought—one that Walker Boh seemed altogether too anxious to make. He wondered why.

When his uncle was gone, he looked at Wren. "What of you?"

The Rover girl shook her head slowly. "I haven't Walker's prejudices and predispositions to contend with, but I do have his doubts." She walked over to a gathering of rocks and seated herself.

Par followed. "Do you think the shade spoke the truth?"

Wren shrugged. "I am still trying to decide if the shade was even who it claimed, Par. I sensed it was, felt it in my heart, and yet . . ." She trailed off. "I know nothing of Allanon beyond the stories, and I know the stories but poorly. You know them better than I. What do you think?"

Par did not hesitate. "It was Allanon."

"And do you think he spoke the truth?"

Par was conscious of the others moving over to join them, silent, watchful. "I think there is reason to believe that he did, yes." He outlined his thoughts as far as he had developed them during the walk back from the valley. He was surprised at how convincing he sounded. He was no longer floundering; he was beginning to gain a measure of conviction in his arguments. "I haven't thought it through as much as I would like," he finished. "But what reason would the shade have for bringing us here and for telling us what it did if not to reveal the truth? Why would it tell us a lie? Walker seems convinced there is a deception at work in this, but I cannot find what form it takes or what purpose it could possibly serve.

"Besides," he added, "Walker is frightened of this business—of the Druids, of the magic, of whatever. He keeps something from us. I can sense it. He plays the same game he accuses Allanon of playing."

Wren nodded. "But he also understands the Druids." When Par looked confused, she smiled sadly. "They do hide things, Par. They hide whatever they do not wish revealed. That is their way. There are things being hidden here as well. What we were told was too incomplete, too circumscribed. However you choose to view it, we are being treated no differently from our ancestors before us."

There was a long silence. "Maybe we should go back into the valley tonight and see if the shade won't come to us again," Morgan suggested in a tone of voice that whispered of doubt.

"Perhaps we should give Cogline a chance to reappear," Coll added.

Par shook his head. "I don't think we will be seeing any more of either for now. I expect whatever decisions we make will have to be made without their help."

"I agree." Wren stood up again. "I am supposed to find the Elves and—how did he put it?—return them to the world of men. A very deliberate choice of words, but I don't understand them. I haven't any idea where the Elves are or even where to begin to look for them. I have lived in the Westland for almost ten years now, Garth for many more than that, and between us we have been everywhere there is to go. I can tell you for a fact that there are no Elves to be found there. Where else am I to look?"

She came over to Par and faced him. "I am going home. There is nothing more for me to do here. I will have to think on this, but even thinking may be of no use. If the dreams come again and tell me something of where to begin this search, then perhaps I will give it a try. But for now . . ."

She shrugged. "Well. Goodbye, Par."

She hugged and kissed him, then did the same for Coll and even Morgan this time. She nodded to the Dwarves and began gathering up her things. Garth joined her silently.

"I wish you would stay a bit longer, Wren," Par tried, quiet desperation welling up like a knot in his stomach at the thought of being left alone to wrestle with this matter.

"Why not come with me instead?" she answered. "You would probably be better off in the Westland."

Par looked at Coll, who frowned. Morgan looked away. Par sighed and shook his head reluctantly. "No, I have to make my own decision first. I have to do that before I can know where I should be."

She nodded, seeming to understand. She had her things together, and she walked up to him. "I might think differently if I had the magic for protection like you and Walker. But I don't. I don't have the wishsong or Cogline's teachings to rely on. I have only a bag of painted stones." She kissed him again. "If you need me, you can find me in the Tirfing. Be careful, Par."

She rode out of the camp with Garth trailing. The others watched them go, the curly haired Rover girl and her giant companion in his bright patchwork clothes. Minutes later, they were specks against the western horizon, their horses almost out of sight.

Par kept looking after them even when they had disappeared. Then he glanced east again after Walker Boh. He felt as if parts of himself were being stolen away.

Coll insisted they have something to eat then, all of them, because it had been better than twelve hours since their last meal and there was no point in trying to think something through on an empty stomach. Par was grateful for the respite, unwilling to confront his own decision-making in the face of the disappointment he felt at the departure of Walker and Wren. He ate the broth that Steff prepared along with some hard bread and fruit, drank several cupfuls of ale, and walked down to the spring to wash. When he returned, he agreed to his brother's suggestion that he lie down for a few minutes and after doing so promptly fell asleep.

It was midday when he woke, his head throbbing, his body aching, his throat hot and dry. He had dreamed snatches of things he would have been just as happy not dreaming at all—of Rimmer Dall and his Federation Seekers hunting him through empty, burned-out city buildings; of Dwarves that watched, starving and helpless in the face of an occupation they could do nothing to ease; of Shadowen lying in wait behind every dark corner he passed in his flight; of Allanon's shade calling out in warning with each new hazard, but laughing as well at his plight. His stomach felt unsettled, but he forced the feeling aside. He washed again, drank some more ale, seated himself in the shade of an old poplar tree, and waited for the sickness to pass. It did, rather more quickly than he would have expected, and soon he was working on a second bowl of the broth.

Coll joined him as he ate. "Feeling better? You didn't look well when you first woke up."

Par finished eating and put the bowl aside. "I wasn't. But I'm all right now." He smiled to prove it.

Coll eased down next to him against the roughened tree trunk, settling his solid frame in place, staring out from the comfort of the shade into the midday heat. "I've been thinking," he said, the blocky features crinkling thoughtfully. He seemed reluctant to continue. "I've been thinking about what I would do if you decided to go looking for the Sword."

Par turned to him at once. "Coll, I haven't even . . ."

"No, Par. Let me finish." Coll was insistent. "If there's one thing I've learned about being your brother, it's to try to get the jump on you when it comes to making decisions. Otherwise, you make them first and once they're made, they might as well be cast in stone!"

He glanced over. "You may recall that we've had this discussion before?

I keep telling you I know you better than you know yourself. Remember that time a few years back when you fell into the Rappahalladran and almost drowned while we were off in the Duln hunting that silver fox? There wasn't supposed to be one like it left in the Southland, but that old trapper said he'd seen one and that was enough for you. The Rappahalladran was cresting, it was late spring, and Dad told us not to try a crossing—made us promise not to try. I knew the minute you made that promise that you would break it if you had to. The very minute you made it!"

Par frowned. "Well, I wouldn't say . . ."

Coll cut him short. "The point is, I can usually tell when you've made up your mind about something. And I think Walker was right. I think you've made up your mind about going after the Sword of Shannara. You have, haven't you?"

Par stared at him, surprised.

"Your eyes say you're going after it, Par," Coll continued calmly, actually smiling. "Whether it's out there or not, you're going after it. I know you. You're going because you still think you can learn something about your own magic by doing so, because you want to do something fine and noble with it, because you have this little voice inside you whispering that the magic is meant for something. No, no, hold on, now—hear me out." He held up his hands at Par's attempt to dispute him. "I don't think there is anything wrong with that. I understand it. But I don't know if you do or whether you can admit to it. And you have to be able to admit to it because otherwise you won't ever be at peace with yourself about why you are going. I know I don't have any magic of my own, but the fact is that in some ways I do understand the problem better than you."

He paused, somber. "You always look for the challenges no one else wants. That's part of what's happening here. You see Walker and Wren walk away from this and right away you want to do just the opposite. That's the way you are. You couldn't give it up now if you had to."

He cocked his head reflectively. "Believe it or not, I have always admired that in you."

Then he sighed. "I know there are other considerations as well. There's the matter of the folks, still under confinement back in the Vale, and us with no home, no real place to go, outlaws of a sort. If we abandon this search, this quest Allanon's shade has given us, where do we go? What possible thing can we do that will change matters more thoroughly than finding the Sword of Shannara? I know there's that. And I know . . ."

Par interrupted. "You said 'we.' "

Coll stopped. "What?"

Par was studying him critically. "Just then. You said 'we.' Several times. You said, what if 'we' abandon this search and where do 'we' go?"

Coll shook his head ruefully. "So I did. I start talking about you and almost before I know it I'm talking about me as well. But that's exactly the problem, I guess. We're so close that I sometimes think of us as if we were the same—and we're not. We're very different and no more so than in this

instance. You have the magic and the chance to learn about it and I don't.
You have the quest and I haven't. So what should I do if you go, Par?"

Par waited a moment, then said, "Well?"

"Well. After all is said and done, after all the arguments for and against
have been laid on the table, I keep coming back to a couple of things." He
shifted so he was facing Par. "First, I'm your brother and I love you. That
means I don't abandon you, even when I'm not sure if I agree with what
you're doing. I've told you that before. Second, if you go . . ." He paused.
"You are going, aren't you?"

There was a long moment of silence. Par did not reply.

"Very well. If you go, it will be a dangerous journey, and you will need
someone to watch your back. And that's what brothers are supposed to do
for each other. That's second."

He cleared his throat. "Last, I've thought it all out from the point of
view of what I would do if I were you, go or not go, measuring what I
perceive to be the right and wrong of the matter." He paused. "If it were
up to me, if I were you, I think I'd go."

He leaned back against the poplar trunk and waited. Par took a deep
breath. "To be honest, Coll, I think that's just about the last thing I ever expected to hear from you."

Coll smiled. "That's probably why I said it. I don't like to be predictable."

"So you would go, would you? If you were me?" Par studied his
brother silently for a moment, letting the possibility play itself out in his
mind. "I don't know if I believe you."

Coll let the smile broaden. "Of course you do."

They were still staring at each other as Morgan wandered up and sat
down across from them, faintly puzzled as he saw the same look registered
on both faces. Steff and Teel came over as well. All three glanced at one another. "What's going on?" Morgan asked finally.

Par stared at him momentarily without seeing him. He saw instead
the land beyond, the hills dotted with sparse groves, running south out of
the barren stretches of the Dragon's Teeth, fading into a heat that made the
earth shimmer. Dust blew in small eddies where sudden breezes scooped at
the roadway leading down. It was still beneath the tree, and Par was thinking about the past, remembering the times that Coll and he had shared.
The memories were an intimacy that comforted him; they were sharp and
clear, most of them, and they made him ache in a sweet, welcome way.

"Well?" Morgan persisted.

Par blinked. "Coll tells me he thinks I ought to do what the shade said.
He thinks I ought to try to find the Sword of Shannara." He paused.
"What do you think, Morgan?"

Morgan didn't hesitate. "I think I'm going with you. It gets tiresome
spending all of my time tweaking the noses of those Federation dunder-
heads who try to govern Leah. There's better uses for a man like me." He
lunged to his feet. "Besides, I have a blade that needs testing against things
of dark magic!" He reached back in a mock feint for his sword. "And as all

here can bear witness, there's no better way to do so than to keep company with Par Ohmsford!"

Par shook his head despairingly. "Morgan, you shouldn't joke . . ."

"Joke! But that's just the point! All I've been doing for months now is playing jokes! And what good has it done?" Morgan's lean features were hard. "Here is a chance for me to do something that has real purpose, something far more important than causing Leah's enemies to suffer meaningless irritations and indignities. Come, now! You have to see it as I do, Par. You cannot dispute what I say." His eyes shifted abruptly. "Steff, how about you? What do you intend? And Teel?"

Steff laughed, his rough features wrinkling. "Well now, Teel and I share pretty much the same point of view on the matter. We have already reached our decision. We came with you in the first place because we were hoping to get our hands on something, magic or whatever, that could help our people break free of the Federation. We haven't found that something yet, but we might be getting closer. What the shade said about the Shadowen spreading the dark magic, living inside men and women and children to do so, might explain a good part of the madness that consumes the Lands. It might even have something to do with why the Federation seems so bent on breaking the backs of the Dwarves! You've seen it for yourself—that's surely what the Federation is about. There's dark magic at work there. Dwarves can sense it better than most because the deeper stretches of the Eastland have always provided a hiding place for it. The only difference in this instance is that, instead of hiding, it's out in the open like a crazed animal, threatening us all. So maybe finding the Sword of Shannara as the shade says will be a step toward penning that animal up again!"

"There, now!" Morgan cried triumphantly. "What better company for you, Par Ohmsford, than that?"

Par shook his head in bewilderment. "None, Morgan, but . . ."

"Then say you'll do it! Forget Walker and Wren and their excuses! This has meaning! Think of what we might be able to accomplish!" He gave his friend a plaintive look. "Confound it, Par, how can we lose by trying when by trying we have everything to gain?"

Steff reached over and poked him. "Don't push so hard, Highlander. Give the Valeman room to breathe!"

Par stared at them each in turn, at the bluff-faced Steff, the enigmatic Teel, the fervently eager Morgan Leah, and finally Coll. He remembered suddenly that his brother had never finished revealing his own decision. He had only said that if he were Par, he would go.

"Coll . . ." he began.

But Coll seemed to read his thoughts. "If you're going, I'm going." His brother's features might have been carved from stone. "From here to wherever this all ends."

There was a long moment of silence as they faced each other, and the anticipation mirrored in their eyes was a whisper that rustled the leaves of their thoughts as if it were the wind.

Par Ohmsford took a deep breath. "Then I guess the matter's settled," he said. "Now where do we start?"

As usual, Morgan Leah had a plan.

"If we expect to have any luck at all locating the Sword, we're going to need help. The five of us are simply too few. After all these years, finding the Sword of Shannara is likely to be like finding the proverbial needle in the haystack—and we don't begin to know enough about the haystack. Steff, you and Teel may be familiar with the Eastland, but Callahorn and the Borderlands are foreign ground. It's the same with the Valemen and myself—we simply don't know enough about the country. And let's not forget that the Federation will be prowling about every place we're likely to go. Dwarves and fugitives from the law aren't welcome in the Southland, the last I heard. We'll have to be on the lookout for Shadowen as well. Truth is, they seem drawn to the magic like wolves to the scent of blood, and we can't assume we've seen the last of them. It will be all we can to do watch our backs, let alone figure out what's happened to the Sword. We can't do it alone. We need someone to help us, someone who has a working knowledge of the Four Lands, someone who can supply us with men and weapons."

He shifted his gaze from the others to Par and smiled that familiar smile that was filled with secretive amusement. "We need your friend from the Movement."

Par groaned. He was none too keen to reassociate with the outlaws; it seemed an open invitation to trouble. But Steff and Teel and even Coll liked the idea, and after arguing about it for a time he was forced to admit that the Highlander's proposal made sense. The outlaws possessed the resources they lacked and were familiar with the Borderlands and the free territories surrounding them. They would know where to look and what pitfalls to avoid while doing so. Moreover, Par's rescuer seemed a man you could depend upon.

"He told you that if you ever needed help, you could come to him," Morgan pointed out. "It seems to me that you could use a little now."

There was no denying that, so the matter was decided. They spent what remained of the day at the campsite below the foothills leading to the Valley of Shale and the Hadeshorn, sleeping restlessly through the second night of the new moon at the base of the Dragon's Teeth. When morning came, they packed up their gear, mounted their horses and set out. The plan was simple. They would travel to Varfleet, search out Kiltan Forge at

Reaver's End in the north city, and ask for the Archer—all as Par's mysterious rescuer had instructed. Then they would see what was what.

They rode south through the scrub country that bordered the Rabb Plains until they crossed the east branch of the Mermidon, then turned west. They followed the river through midday and into early afternoon, the sun baking the land out of a cloudless sky, the air dry and filled with dust. No one said much of anything as they traveled, locked away in the silence of their own thoughts. There had been no further talk of Allanon since setting out. There had been no mention of Walker or Wren. Par fingered the ring with the hawk insigne from time to time and wondered anew about the identity of the man who had given it to him.

It was late afternoon when they passed down through the river valley of the Runne Mountains north of Varfleet and approached the outskirts of the city. It sprawled below them across a series of hills, dusty and sweltering against the glare of the westward fading sun. Shacks and hovels ringed the city's perimeter, squalid shelters for men and women who lacked even the barest of means. They called out to the travelers as they passed, pressing up against them for money and food, and Par and Coll handed down what little they had. Morgan glanced back reprovingly, somewhat as a parent might at a naive child, but made no comment.

A little farther on, Par found himself wishing belatedly that he had thought to disguise his Elven features. It had been weeks since he had done so, and he had simply gotten out of the habit. He could take some consolation from the fact that his hair had grown long and covered his ears. But he would have to be careful nevertheless. He glanced over at the Dwarves. They had their travel cloaks pulled close, the hoods wrapping their faces in shadow. They were in more danger than he of discovery. Everyone knew that Dwarves were not permitted to travel in the Southland. Even in Varfleet, it was risky.

When they reached the city proper and the beginnings of streets that bore names and shops with signs, the traffic increased markedly. Soon, it was all but impossible to move ahead. They dismounted and led their horses afoot until they found a stable where they could board them. Morgan made the transaction while the others stood back unobtrusively against the walls of the buildings across the way and watched the people of the city press against one another in a sluggish flow. Beggars came up to them and asked for coins. Par watched a fire-eater display his art to a wondering crowd of boys and men at a fruit mart. The low mutter of voices filled the air with a ragged sound.

"Sometimes you get lucky," Morgan informed them quietly as he returned. "We're standing in Reaver's End. This whole section of the city is Reaver's End. Kiltan Forge is just a few streets over."

He beckoned them on, and they slipped past the steady throng of bodies, working their way into a side street that was less crowded, if more ill-smelling, and soon they were hurrying along a shadowed alley that twisted and turned past a rutted sewage way. Par wrinkled his nose in distaste. This was the city as Coll saw it. He risked a quick glance back at his brother, but his brother was busy watching where he was stepping.

They crossed several more streets before emerging onto one that seemed to satisfy Morgan, who promptly turned right and led them through the crowds to a broad, two-story barn with a sign that bore the name Kiltan Forge seared on a plaque of wood. The sign and the building were old and splintering, but the furnaces within burned red-hot, spitting and flaming as metals were fed in and removed by tenders. Machines ground, and hammers pounded and shaped. The din rose above the noise of the street and echoed off the walls of the surrounding buildings, to disappear finally into the suffocating embrace of the lingering afternoon heat.

Morgan edged his way along the fringes of the crowd, the others trailing silently after, and finally managed to work his way up to the Forge entrance. A handful of men worked the furnaces under the direction of a large fellow with drooping mustaches and a balding pate colored soot-black. The fellow ignored them until they had come all the way inside, then turned and asked, "Something I can help you with?"

Morgan said, "We're looking for the Archer."

The fellow with the mustaches ambled over. "Who did you say, now?"

"The Archer," Morgan repeated.

"And who's that supposed to be?" The other man was broad-shouldered and caked with sweat.

"I don't know," Morgan admitted. "We were just told to ask for him."

"Who by?"

"Look . . ."

"Who by? Don't you know, man?"

It was hot in the shadow of Kiltan Forge, and it was clear that Morgan was going to have trouble with this man if things kept going the way they were. Heads were already starting to turn. Par pushed forward impulsively, anxious to keep from drawing attention to themselves and said, "By a man who wears a ring that bears the insigne of a hawk."

The fellow's sharp eyes narrowed, studying the Valeman's face with its Elven features.

"This ring," Par finished and held it out.

The other flinched as if he had been stung. "Don't be showing that about, you young fool!" he snapped and shoved it away from him as if it were poison.

"Then tell us where we can find the Archer!" Morgan interjected, his irritation beginning to show through.

There was sudden activity in the street that caused them all to turn hurriedly. A squad of Federation soldiers was approaching, pushing through the crowd, making directly for the Forge. "Get out of sight!" the fellow with the mustaches snapped urgently and stepped away.

The soldiers came into the Forge, glancing about the fire-lit darkness. The man with the mustaches came forward to greet them. Morgan and the Valemen gathered up the Dwarves, but the soldiers were between them and the doorway leading to the street. Morgan edged them all toward the deep shadows.

"Weapons order, Hirehone," the squad leader announced to the man with the mustaches, thrusting out a paper. "Need it by week's end. And don't argue the matter."

Hirehone muttered something unintelligible, but nodded. The squad leader talked to him some more, sounding weary and hot. The soldiers were casting about restlessly. One moved toward the little company. Morgan tried to stand in front of his companions, tried to make the soldier speak with him. The soldier hesitated, a big fellow with a reddish beard. Then he noticed something and pushed past the Highlander. "You there!" he snapped at Teel. "What's wrong with you?" One hand reached out, pulling aside the hood. "Dwarves! Captain, there's . . . !"

He never finished. Teel killed him with a single thrust of her long knife, jamming the blade through his throat. He was still trying to talk as he died. The other soldiers reached for their weapons, but Morgan was already among them, his own sword thrusting, forcing them back. He cried out to the others, and the Dwarves and Valemen broke for the doorway. They reached the street, Morgan on their heels, the Federation soldiers a step behind. The crowd screamed and split apart as the battle careened into them. There were a dozen soldiers in pursuit, but two were wounded and the rest were tripping over one another in their haste to reach the Highlander. Morgan cut down the foremost, howling like a madman. Ahead, Steff reached a barred door to a warehouse, brought up the suddenly revealed mace, and hammered the troublesome barrier into splinters with a single blow. They rushed through the darkened interior and out a back door, turned left down an alley and came up against a fence. Desperately, they wheeled about and started back.

The pursuing Federation soldiers burst through the warehouse door and came at them.

Par used the wishsong and filled the disappearing gap between them with a swarm of buzzing hornets. The soldiers howled and dove for cover. In the confusion, Steff smashed enough boards of the fence to allow them all to slip through. They ran down a second alley, through a maze of storage sheds, turned right and pushed past a hinged metal gate.

They found themselves in a yard of scrap metal behind the Forge. Ahead, a door to the back of the Forge swung open. "In here!" someone called.

They ran without questioning, hearing the sound of shouting and blare of horns all about. They shoved through the opening into a small storage room and heard the door slam shut behind them.

Hirehone faced them, hands on hips. "I hope you turn out to be worth all the trouble you've caused!" he told them.

He hid them in a crawlspace beneath the floor of the storage room, leaving them there for what seemed like hours. It was hot and close, there was no

light, and the sounds of booted feet tramped overhead twice in the course
of their stay, each time leaving them taut and breathless. When Hirehone
finally let them out again, it was night, the skies overcast and inky, the lights
of the city fragmented pinpricks through the gaps in the boards of the
Forge walls. He took them out of the storage room to a small kitchen that
was adjacent, sat them down about a spindly table, and fed them.

"Had to wait until the soldiers finished their search, satisfied themselves
you weren't coming back or hiding in the metal," he explained. "They
were angry, I'll tell you—especially about the killing."

Teel showed nothing of what she was thinking, and no one else spoke.
Hirehone shrugged. "Means nothing to me either."

They chewed in silence for a time, then Morgan asked, "What about
the Archer? Can we see him now?"

Hirehone grinned. "Don't think that'll be possible. There isn't any such
person."

Morgan's jaw dropped. "Then why . . . ?"

"It's a code," Hirehone interrupted. "It's just a way of letting me know
what's expected of me. I was testing you. Sometimes the code gets broken.
I had to make sure you weren't spying for the Federation."

"You're an outlaw," Par said.

"And you're Par Ohmsford," the other replied. "Now finish up eating,
and I'll take you to the man you came to see."

They did as they were told, cleaned off their plates in an old sink, and
followed Hirehone back into the bowels of Kiltan Forge. The Forge was
empty now, save for a single tender on night watch who minded the fire-
breathing furnaces that were never allowed to go cold. He paid them no attention. They passed through the cavernous stillness on cat's feet, smelling
ash and metal in a sulfurous mix, watching the shadows dance to the fire's
cadence.

When they slipped through a side door into the darkness, Morgan
whispered to Hirehone, "We left our horses stabled several streets over."

"Don't worry about it," the other whispered back. "You won't need
horses where you're going."

They passed quietly and unobtrusively down the byways of Varfleet,
through its bordering cluster of shacks and hovels and finally out of the city
altogether. They traveled north then along the Mermidon, following the
river upstream where it wound below the foothills fronting the Dragon's
Teeth. They walked for the remainder of the night, crossing the river just
above its north-south juncture where it passed through a series of rapids
that scattered its flow into smaller streams. The river was down at this time
of the year or the crossing would never have been possible without a boat.
As it was, the water reached nearly to the chins of the Dwarves at several
points, and all of them were forced to walk with their backpacks and weapons hoisted over their heads.

Once across the river, they came up against a heavily forested series of defiles and ravines that stretched on for miles into the rock of the Dragon's Teeth.

"This is the Parma Key," Hirehone volunteered at one point. "Pretty tricky country if you don't know your way."

That was a gross understatement, Par quickly discovered. The Parma Key was a mass of ridges and ravines that rose and fell without warning amid a suffocating blanket of trees and scrub. The new moon gave no light, the stars were masked by the canopy of trees and the shadow of the mountains, and the company found itself in almost complete blackness. After a brief penetration of the woods, Hirehone sat them down to wait for daybreak.

Even in daylight, any passage seemed impossible. It was perpetually shadowed and misted within the mountain forests of the Parma Key, and the ravines and ridges crisscrossed the whole of the land. There was a trail, invisible to anyone who hadn't known it before, a twisting path that Hirehone followed without effort but that left the members of the little company uncertain of the direction in which they were moving. Morning slipped toward midday, and the sun filtered down through the densely packed trees in narrow streamers of brightness that did little to chase the lingering fog and seemed to have strayed somehow from the outer world into the midst of the heavy shadows.

When they stopped for a quick lunch, Par asked their guide if he would tell them how much farther it was to where they were going.

"Not far," Hirehone answered. "There." He pointed to a massive outcropping of rock that rose above the Parma Key where the forest flattened against the wall of the Dragon's Teeth. "That, Ohmsford, is called the Jut. The Jut is the stronghold of the Movement."

Par looked, considering. "Does the Federation know it's there?" he asked.

"They know it's in here somewhere," Hirehone replied. "What they don't know is exactly where and, more to the point, how to reach it."

"And Par's mysterious rescuer, your still-nameless outlaw chief—isn't he worried about having visitors like us carrying back word of how to do just that?" Steff asked skeptically.

Hirehone smiled. "Dwarf, in order for you to find your way in again, you first have to find your way out. Think you could manage that without me?"

Steff smirked grudgingly, seeing the truth of the matter. A man could wander forever in this maze without finding his way clear.

It was late afternoon when they reached the outcropping they had been pointing toward all day, the shadows falling in thick layers across the wilderness, casting the whole of the forest in twilight. Hirehone had whistled ahead several times during the last hour, each time waiting for an answering whistle before proceeding farther. At the base of the cliffs, a gated lift waited, settled in a clearing, its ropes disappearing skyward into the rocks overhead. The lift was large enough to hold all of them, and they stepped into it, grasping the railing for support as it hoisted them up, slowly, steadily, until at last they were above the trees. They drew even with a narrow ledge and were pulled in by a handful of men working a massive winch. A second lift waited and they climbed aboard. Again they were hoisted up along the face of the rock wall, dangling out precariously over the earth. Par looked down once and quickly regretted it. He caught a glimpse of Steff's face, bloodless beneath its sun-browned exterior. Hirehone seemed unconcerned and whistled idly as they rose.

There was a third lift as well, this one much shorter, and when they finally stepped off they found themselves on a broad, grassy bluff about midway up the cliff that ran back several hundred yards into a series of caves. Fortifications lined the edge of the bluff and ringed the caves, and there were pockets of defense built into the cliff wall overhead where it was riddled with craggy splits. There was a narrow waterfall spilling down off the mountain into a pool, and several clusters of broad-leaf trees and fir scattered about the bluff. Men scurried everywhere, hauling tools and weapons and crates of stores, crying out instructions, or answering back.

Out of the midst of this organized confusion strode Par's rescuer, his tall form clothed in startling scarlet and black. He was clean-shaven now, his tanned face weather-seamed and sharp-boned in the sunlight, a collection of planes and angles. It was a face that defied age. His brown hair was swept back and slightly receding. He was lean and fit and moved like a cat. He swept toward them with a deep-voiced shout of welcome, one arm extending first to hug Hirehone, then to gather in Par.

"So, lad, you've had a change of heart, have you? Welcome, then, and your companions as well. Your brother, a Highlander, and a brace of Dwarves, is it? Strange company, now. Have you come to join up?"

He was as guileless as Morgan had ever thought to be, and Par felt himself blush. "Not exactly. We have a problem."

"Another problem?" The outlaw chief seemed amused. "Trouble just follows after you, doesn't it? I'll have my ring back now."

Par removed the ring from his pocket and handed it over. The other man slipped it back on his finger, admiring it. "The hawk. Good symbol for a free-born, don't you think?"

"Who are you?" Par asked him bluntly.

"Who am I?" The other laughed merrily. "Haven't you figured that out yet, my friend? No? Then I'll tell you." The outlaw chief leaned forward. "Look at my hand." He held up the closed fist with the finger pointed at Par's nose. "A missing hand with a pike. Who am I?"

His eyes were sea-green and awash with mischief. There was a moment of calculated silence as the Valeman stared at him in confusion.

"My name, Par Ohmsford, is Padishar Creel," the outlaw chief said finally. "But you would know me better as the great, great, great, and then some, grandson of Panamon Creel."

And finally Par understood.

That evening, over dinner, seated at a table that had been moved purposefully away from those of the other occupants of the Jut, Par and his companions listened in rapt astonishment while Padishar Creel related his story.

"We have a rule up here that everyone's past life is his own business," he advised them conspiratorially. "It might make the others feel awkward hearing me talk about mine."

He cleared his throat. "I was a landowner," he began, "a grower of crops and livestock, the overseer of a dozen small farms and countless acres of forestland reserved for hunting. I inherited the better part of it from my father and he from his father and so on back some years further than I care to consider. But it apparently all began with Panamon Creel. I am told, though I cannot confirm it of course, that after helping Shea Ohmsford recover the Sword of Shannara, he returned north to the Borderlands where he became quite successful at his chosen profession and accumulated a rather considerable fortune. This, upon retiring, he wisely invested in what would eventually become the lands of the Creel family."

Par almost smiled. Padishar Creel was relating his tale with a straight face, but he knew as well as the Valemen and Morgan that Panamon Creel had been a thief when Shea Ohmsford and he had stumbled on each other.

"Baron Creel, he called himself," the other went on, oblivious. "All of the heads of family since have been called the same way. Baron Creel." He paused, savoring the sound of it. Then he sighed. "But the Federation seized the lands from my father when I was a boy, stole them without a thought of recompense, and in the end dispossessed us. My father died when he tried to get them back. My mother as well. Rather mysteriously."

He smiled. "So I joined the Movement."

"Just like that?" Morgan asked, looking skeptical.

The outlaw chief skewered a piece of beef on his knife. "My parents went to the governor of the province, a Federation underling who had moved into our home, and my father demanded the return of what was rightfully his, suggesting that if something wasn't done to resolve the matter, the governor would regret it. My father never was given to caution. He was denied his request, and he and my mother were summarily dismissed. On their way back from whence they had come, they disappeared. They were found later hanging from a tree in the forests nearby, gutted and flayed."

He said it without rancor, matter-of-factly, all with a calm that was frightening. "I grew up fast after that, you might say," he finished.

There was a long silence. Padishar Creel shrugged. "It was a long time ago. I learned how to fight, how to stay alive. I drifted into the Movement, and after seeing how poorly it was managed, formed my own company." He chewed. "A few of the other leaders didn't like the idea. They tried to give me over to the Federation. That was their mistake. After I disposed of them, most of the remaining bands came over to join me. Eventually, they all will."

No one said anything. Padishar Creel glanced up. "Isn't anyone hungry? There's a good measure of food left. Let's not waste it."

They finished the meal quickly, the outlaw chief continuing to provide further details of his violent life in the same disinterested tone. Par wondered what sort of man he had gotten himself mixed up with. He had thought before that his rescuer might prove to be the champion the Four Lands had lacked since the time of Allanon, his standard the rallying point for all of the oppressed Races. Rumor had it that this man was the charismatic leader for which the freedom Movement had been waiting. But he seemed as much a cutthroat as anything. However dangerous Panamon Creel might have been in his time, Par found himself convinced that Padishar Creel was more dangerous still.

"So, that is my story and the whole of it," Padishar Creel announced, shoving back his plate. His eyes glittered. "Any part of it that you'd care to question me about?"

Silence. Then Steff growled suddenly, shockingly, "How much of it is the truth?"

Everyone froze. But Padisher Creel laughed, genuinely amused. There was a measure of respect in his eyes for the Dwarf that was unmistakable as he said, "Some of it, my Eastland friend, some of it." He winked. "The story improves with every telling."

He picked up his ale glass and poured a full measure from a pitcher. Par stared at Steff with newfound admiration. No one else would have dared ask that question.

"Come, now," the outlaw chief interjected, leaning forward. "Enough of history past. Time to hear what brought you to me. Speak, Par Ohmsford." His eyes were fixed on Par. "It has something to do with the magic, hasn't it? There wouldn't be anything else that would bring you here. Tell me."

Par hesitated. "Does your offer to help still stand?" he asked instead.

The other looked offended. "My word is my bond, lad! I said I would help and I will!"

He waited. Par glanced at the others, then said, "I need to find the Sword of Shannara."

He told Padishar Creel of his meeting with the ghost of Allanon and the task that had been given him by the Druid. He told of the journey that had brought the five of them gathered to this meeting, of the encounters with Federation soldiers and Seekers and the monsters called Shadowen. He held nothing back, despite his reservations about the man. He decided it was better neither to lie nor to attempt half-truths, better that it was all laid out for him to judge, to accept or dismiss as he chose. After all, they would be no worse off than they were now, whether he decided to help them or not.

When he had finished, the outlaw chief sat back slowly and drained the remainder of the ale from the glass he had been nursing and smiled conspiratorially at Steff. "It would seem appropriate for me to now ask how much of *this* tale is true!"

Par started to protest, but the other raised his hand quickly to cut him off. "No, lad, save your breath. I do not question what you've told me. You tell it the way you believe it, that's clear enough. It's only my way."

"You have the men, the weapons, the supplies and the network of spies to help us find what we seek," Morgan interjected quietly. "That's why we're here."

"You have the spirit for this kind of madness as well, I'd guess," Steff added with a chuckle.

Padishar Creel rubbed his chin roughly. "I have more than these, my friends," he said, smiling like a wolf. "I have a sense of fate!"

He rose wordlessly and took them from the table to the edge of the bluff, there to stand looking out across the Parma Key, a mass of treetops and ridgelines bathed in the last of the day's sunlight as it faded west across the horizon.

His arm swept the whole of it. "These are my lands now, the lands of Baron Creel, if you will. But I'll hold them no longer than the ones before them if I do not find a way to unsettle the Federation!" He paused. "Fate, I told you. That's what I believe in. Fate made me what I am and it will unmake me as easily, if I do not take a hand in its game. The hand I must take, I think, is the one you offer. It is not chance, Par Ohmsford, that you have come to me. It is what was meant to be. I know that to be true, now especially—now, after hearing what you seek. Do you see the way of it? My ancestor and yours, Panamon Creel and Shea Ohmsford, went in search of the Sword of Shannara more than three hundred years ago. Now it is our turn, yours and mine. A Creel and an Ohmsford once again, the start of change in the land, a new beginning. I can feel it!"

He studied them, his sharp face intense. "Friendship brought you all together; a need for change in your lives brought you to me. Young Par, there are indeed ties that bind us, just as I said when first we met. There is a history that needs repeating. There are adventures to be shared and battles to be won. That is what fate has decreed for you and me!"

Par was a bit confused in the face of all this rhetoric as he asked, "Then you'll help us?"

"Indeed, I will." The outlaw chief arched one eyebrow. "I hold the Parma Key, but the Southland is lost to me—my home, my lands, my heritage. I want them back. Magic is the answer now as it was those many years past, the catalyst for change, the prod that will turn back the Federation beast and send it scurrying for its cave!"

"You've said that several times," Par interjected. "Said it several different ways—that the magic can in some way undermine the Federation. But it's the Shadowen that Allanon fears, the Shadowen that the Sword is meant to confront. So why . . . ?"

"Ah, ah, lad," the other interrupted hurriedly. "You strike to the heart of the matter once again. The answer to your question is this—I perceive threads of cause and effect in everything. Evils such as the Federation and the Shadowen do not stand apart in the scheme of things. They are connected in some way, joined perhaps as Ohmsfords and Creels are joined, and if we can find a way to destroy one, we will find a way to destroy the other!"

The look he gave them was one of such fierce determination that for a long moment no one said anything further. The last of the sunlight was fading away below the horizon, and the gray of twilight cloaked the Parma Key and the lands south and west in a mantle of gauze. The men behind them were stirring from their eating tables and beginning to retire to sleeping areas that lay scattered about the bluff. Even at this high elevation, the summer night was warm and windless. Stars and the beginnings of the first quarter's moon were slipping into view.

"All right," Par said quietly. "True or not, what can you do to help us?"

Padishar Creel smoothed back the wrinkles in the scarlet sleeves of his tunic and breathed deeply the smells of the mountain air. "I can do, lad, what you asked me to do. I can help you find the Sword of Shannara."

He glanced over with a quick grin and matter-of-factly added, "You see, I think I know where it is."

18

For the next two days, Padishar Creel had nothing more to say about the Sword of Shannara. Whenever Par or one of the others of the little company tried to engage him in conversation on the matter, he would simply say that time would tell or that patience was a virtue or offer up some similar platitude that just served to irritate them. He was unfailingly cheerful about it, though, so they kept their feelings to themselves.

Besides, for all the show the outlaw chief made of treating them as his guests, they were prisoners of a sort, nevertheless. They were permitted the run of the Jut, but forbidden to leave it. Not that they necessarily could have left in any event. The winches that raised and lowered the baskets from the heights into the Parma Key were always heavily guarded and no one was allowed near them without reason. Without the lifts to carry them down, there was no way off the bluff from its front. The cliffs were sheer and had been carefully stripped of handholds, and what small ledges and clefts had once existed in the rock had been meticulously chipped away or filled. The cliffs behind were sheer as well for some distance up and warded by the pocket battlements that dotted the high rock.

That left the caves. Par and his friends ventured into the central cavern on the first day, curious to discover what was housed there. They found that the mammoth, cathedral-like central chamber opened off into dozens of smaller chambers where the outlaws stored supplies and weapons of all sorts, made their living quarters when the weather outside grew forbidding, and established training and meeting rooms. There were tunnels leading back into the mountain, but they were cordoned off and watched. When Par asked Hirehone, who had stayed on a few extra days, where the tunnels led, the master of Kiltan Forge smiled sardonically and told him that, like the trails in the Parma Key, the tunnels of the Jut led into oblivion.

The two days passed quickly despite the frustration of being put off on the subject of the Sword. All five visitors spent their time exploring the outlaw fortress. As long as they stayed away from the lifts and the tunnels they were permitted to go just about anywhere they wished. Not once did Padishar Creel question Par about his companions. He seemed unconcerned about who they were and whether they could be trusted, almost as if it didn't matter. Perhaps it didn't, Par decided after thinking it over. After all, the outlaw lair seemed impregnable.

Par, Coll, and Morgan stayed together most of the time. Steff went with them on occasion, but Teel kept away completely, as aloof and uncommunicative as ever. The Valemen and the Highlander became a familiar sight to the outlaws as they wandered the bluff, the fortifications, and the caverns, studying what man and nature had combined to form, talking with the men who lived and worked there when they could do so without bothering them, fascinated by everything they encountered.

But there was nothing and no one more fascinating than Padishar Creel. The outlaw chief was a paradox. Dressed in flaming scarlet, he was immediately recognizable from anywhere on the bluff. He talked constantly, telling stories, shouting orders, commenting on whatever came to mind. He was unremittingly cheerful, as if smiling was the only expression he had ever bothered to put on. Yet beneath that bright and ingratiating exterior was a core as hard as granite. When he ordered that something be done, it was done. No one ever questioned him. His face could be wreathed in a smile as warm as the summer sun while his voice could take on a frosty edge that chilled to the bone.

He ran the outlaw camp with organization and discipline. This was no ragtag band of misfits at work here. Everything was precise and thorough. The camp was neat and clean and kept that way scrupulously. Stores were separated and cataloged and anything could be found at a moment's notice. There were tasks assigned to everyone, and everyone made certain those tasks were carried out. There were a little more than three hundred men living on the Jut, and not one of them seemed to have the slightest doubt about what he was doing or whom he would answer to, if he were to let down.

On the second day of their stay, two of the outlaws were brought before Padishar Creel on a charge of stealing. The outlaw chief listened to the evidence against them, his face mild, then offered to let them speak in their own defense. One admitted his guilt outright, the other denied it—rather unconvincingly. Padishar Creel had the first flogged and sent back to work and the second thrown over the cliff. No one seemed to give the matter another thought afterward.

Later that same day, Padishar came over to Par when the Valeman was alone and asked if he was disturbed by what had happened. Barely waiting for Par's response, he went on to explain how discipline in a camp such as his was essential, and justice in the event of a breakdown must be swift and sure.

"Appearances often count for more than equities, you see," he offered rather enigmatically. "We are a close band here, and we must be able to rely on one another. If a man proves unreliable in camp, he most likely will prove unreliable in the field. And there's more than just his own life at stake there!"

He switched subjects abruptly then, admitting rather apologetically that he hadn't been entirely forthcoming about his background that first night and the truth of the matter was that his parents, rather than being landowners who had been strung up in the woods, had been silk merchants and had died in a Federation prison after they had refused to pay their taxes. He said the other simply made a better story.

When Par encountered Hirehone a short time later, he asked him—Padishar Creel's tale being still fresh in his mind at that point—whether he had known the outlaw chief's parents, and Hirehone said, "No, the fever took them before I came on board."

"In prison, you mean?" Par followed up, confused.

"Prison? Hardly. They died while on a caravan south out of Wayford. They were traders in precious metals. Padishar told me so himself."

Par related both conversations to Coll that night after dinner. They had secluded themselves at the edge of the bluff in a redoubt, where the sounds of the camp were comfortably distant and they could watch the twilight slowly unveil the nighttime sky's increasingly intricate pattern of stars. Coll laughed when Par was finished and shook his head. "The truth isn't in that fellow when it comes to telling anything about himself. He's more like Panamon Creel than Panamon probably ever thought of being!"

Par grimaced. "True enough."

"Dresses the same, talks the same—just as outrageous and quixotic." Coll sighed. "So why am I laughing? What are we doing here with this madman?"

Par ignored him. "What do you suppose he's hiding, Coll?"

"Everything."

"No, not everything. He's not that sort." Coll started to protest, but Par put out his hands quickly to calm him. "Think about it a moment. This whole business of who and what he is has been carefully staged. He spins out these wild tales deliberately, not out of whimsy. Padishar Creel has something else in common with Panamon, if we can believe the stories. He has re-created himself in the minds of everyone around him—drawn a picture of himself that doesn't square from one telling to the next, but is nevertheless bigger than life." He bent close. "And you can bet that he's done it for a reason."

Further speculation about the matter of Padishar Creel's background ended a few minutes later when they were summoned to a meeting. Hirehone collected them with a gruff command to follow and led them across the bluff and into the caves to a meeting chamber where the outlaw chief was waiting. Oil lamps on black chains hung from the chamber ceiling like spiders, their glimmer barely reaching into the shadows that darkened the corners and crevices. Morgan and the Dwarves were there, seated at a table along with several outlaws Par had seen before in the camp. Chandos was a truly ferocious-looking giant with a great black beard, one eye and one ear on the same side of his face missing, and scars everywhere. Ciba Blue was a young, smooth-faced fellow with lank blond hair and an odd cobalt birthmark on his left cheek that resembled a half-moon. Stasas and Drutt were lean, hard, older men with close-cropped dark beards, faces that were seamed and brown, and eyes that shifted watchfully. Hirehone ushered in the Valemen, closed the chamber door, and stood purposefully in front of it.

For just a moment Par felt the hair on the back of his neck prickle in warning.

Then Padishar Creel was greeting them, cheerful and reassuring. "Ah, young Par and his brother." He beckoned them onto benches with the others, made quick introductions, and said, "We are going after the Sword tomorrow at dawn."

"Where is it?" Par wanted to know at once.

The outlaw chief's smile broadened. "Where it won't get away from us."

Par glanced at Coll.

"The less said about where we're going, the better the chance of keeping it a secret." The big man winked.

"Is there some reason we need to keep it a secret?" Morgan Leah asked quietly.

The outlaw chief shrugged. "No reason out of the ordinary. But I am always cautious when I make plans to leave the Jut." His eyes were hard. "Humor me, Highlander."

Morgan held his gaze and said nothing. "Seven of us will go," the other continued smoothly. "Stasas, Drutt, Blue, and myself from the camp, the Valemen and the Highlander from without." Protests were already starting from the mouths of the others and he moved quickly to squelch them. "Chandos, you'll be in charge of the Jut in my absence. I want to leave someone behind I can depend upon. Hirehone, your place is back in Varfleet, keeping an eye on things there. Besides, you'd have trouble explaining yourself if you were spotted where we're going.

"As for you, my Eastland friends," he spoke now to Steff and Teel, "I would take you if I could. But Dwarves outside the Eastland are bound to draw attention, and we can't be having that. It's risky enough allowing the Valemen to come along with the Seekers still looking for them, but it's their quest."

"Ours as well now, Padishar," Steff pointed out darkly. "We have come a long way to be part of this. We don't relish being left behind. Perhaps a disguise?"

"A disguise would be seen through, particularly where we are going," the outlaw chief answered, shaking his head. "You are a resourceful fellow, Steff—but we can take no chances on this outing."

"There's a city and people involved, I take it?"

"There is."

The Dwarf studied him hard. "I would be most upset if there were games being played here at our expense."

There was a growl of warning from the outlaws, but Padishar Creel silenced it instantly. "So would I," he replied, and his gaze locked on the Dwarf.

Steff held that gaze for a long moment. Then he glanced briefly at Teel and nodded. "Very well. We'll wait."

The outlaw chief's eyes swept the table. "We'll leave at first light and be gone about a week. If we're gone longer than that, chances are we won't be coming back. Are there any questions?"

No one spoke. Padishar Creel gave them a dazzling smile. "A drink, then? Outside with the others, so they can give us a toast and a wish for success! Up, lads, and strength to us who go to brave the lion in his den!"

He went out into the night, the others following. Morgan and the Valemen trailed, shuffling along thoughtfully.

"The lion in his den, eh?" Morgan muttered half to himself. "I wonder what he means by that?"

Par and Coll glanced at each other. Neither was certain that they wanted to know.

Par spent a restless night, plagued by dreams and anxieties that fragmented his sleep and left him bleary-eyed with the coming of dawn. He rose with Coll and Morgan to find Padishar Creel and his companions already awake and in the midst of their breakfast. The outlaw chief had shed his scarlet clothing in favor of the less conspicuous green and brown woodsmen's garb worn by his men. The Valemen and the Highlander hurried to dress and eat, shivering a bit from the night's lingering chill. Steff and Teel joined them, wordless shadows hunkered down next to the cooking fire. When the meal was consumed, the seven strapped on their backpacks and walked to the edge of the bluff. The sun was creeping into view above the eastern horizon, its early light a mix of gold and silver against the fading dark. Steff muttered for them to take care and, with Teel in tow, disappeared back into the dark. Morgan was rubbing his hands briskly and breathing the air as if he might never have another chance. They boarded the first lift and began their descent, passing wordlessly to the second and third, the winches creak-

ing eerily in the silence as they were lowered. When they reached the floor
of the Parma Key, they struck out into the misty forests, Padishar Creel leading with Blue, the Valemen and the Highlander in the middle, and the
remaining two outlaws, Stasas and Drutt, trailing. Within seconds, the rock
wall of the Jut had disappeared from view.

They traveled south for the better part of the day, turning west around
midafternoon when they encountered the Mermidon. They followed the
river until sunset, staying on its north shore, and camped that night just below the south end of the Kennon Pass in the shadow of the Dragon's
Teeth. They found a cove sheltered by cypress where a stream fed down out
of the rocks and provided them with drinking water. They built a fire, ate
their dinner, and sat back to watch the stars come out.

After a time, Stasas and Drutt went off to take the first watch, one upstream, one down. Ciba Blue rolled into his blankets and was asleep in moments, his youthful face looking even younger in sleep. Padishar Creel sat
with the Valemen and the Highlander, poking at the fire with a stick while
he sipped at a flask of ale.

Par had been puzzling over their eventual destination all day, and now
he said abruptly to the outlaw chief, "We're going to Tyrsis, aren't we?"

Padishar glanced over in surprise, then nodded. "No reason you
shouldn't know now."

"But why look for the Sword of Shannara in Tyrsis? It disappeared
from there over a hundred years ago when the Federation annexed Callahorn. Why would it be back there now?"

The other smiled secretively. "Perhaps because it never left."

Par and his companions stared at the outlaw chief in astonishment.

"You see, the fact that the Sword of Shannara disappeared doesn't necessarily mean that it went anywhere. Sometimes a thing can disappear and
still be in plain sight. It can disappear simply because it doesn't look like
what it used to. We see it, but we don't recognize it."

"What are you saying?" Par asked slowly.

Padishar Creel's smile broadened perceptibly. "I am saying that the
Sword of Shannara may very well be exactly where it was three hundred
years ago."

"Locked away in a vault in the middle of the People's Park in Tyrsis all
these years and no one's figured it out?" Morgan Leah was aghast. "How
can that possibly be?"

Padishar sipped speculatively at his flask and said, "We'll be there by tomorrow. Why don't we wait and see?"

Par Ohmsford was tired from the day's march and last night's lack of
sleep, but he was awake a long time, nevertheless, after the others were already snoring. He couldn't stop thinking about what Padishar Creel had
said. More than three hundred years ago, after Shea Ohmsford had used it
to destroy the Warlock Lord, the Sword of Shannara had been embedded
in a block of red marble and entombed in a vault in the People's Park in the
Southland city of Tyrsis. There it had remained until the coming of the

Federation into Callahorn. It was common knowledge that it had disappeared after that. If it hadn't, why did so many people believe it had? If it was right where it had been three hundred years ago, how come no one recognized it now?

He considered. It was true that much of what had happened during the time of Allanon had lost credibility; many of the tales had taken on the trappings of legend and folklore. By the time the Sword of Shannara disappeared, perhaps no one believed in it anymore. Perhaps no one even understood what it could do. But they at least knew it was *there*! It was a national monument, for goodness sake! So how could they say it was gone if it wasn't? It didn't make sense!

Yet Padishar Creel seemed so positive.

Par fell asleep with the matter still unresolved.

They rose again at sunrise, crossed the Mermidon at a shallows less than a mile upstream and turned south for Tyrsis. The day was hot and still, and the dust of the grasslands filled their nostrils and throats. They kept to the shade when they could, but the country south grew more open as the forests gave way to grasslands. They used their water sparingly and paced themselves as they walked, but the sun climbed steadily in the cloudless summer sky and the travelers soon were sweating freely. By midday, as they approached the walls of the city, their clothing lay damp against their skin.

Tyrsis was the home city of Callahorn, its oldest city, and the most impregnable fortress in the entire Southland. Situated on a broad plateau, it was warded by towering cliffs to the south, and a pair of monstrous battle walls to the north. The Outer Wall rose nearly a hundred feet above the summit of the plateau, a massive armament that had been breached only once in the city's history when the armies of the Warlock Lord had attacked in the time of Shea Ohmsford. A second wall sat back and within the first, a redoubt for the city's defenders. Once the Border Legion, the Southland's most formidable army, had defended the city. But the Legion was gone now, disbanded when the Federation moved in, and now only Federation soldiers patrolled the walls and byways, occupiers of lands that, until a hundred years ago, had never been occupied. The Federation soldiers were quartered in the Legion barracks within the first wall, and the citizens of the city still lived and worked within the second, housed in the city proper from where it ran back along the plateau to the base of the cliffs south.

Par, Coll, and Morgan had never been to Tyrsis. What they knew of the city, they knew from the stories they had heard of the days of their ancestors. As they approached it now, they realized how impossible it was for words alone to describe what they were seeing. The city rose up against the skyline like a great, hulking giant, a construction of stone blocks and mortar that dwarfed anything they had ever encountered. Even in the bright sunlight of midday, it had a black cast to it—as if the sunlight were being absorbed somehow in the rock. The city shimmered slightly, a side effect of the heat, and assumed a miragelike quality. A massive rampway led up from the plains to the base of the plateau, twisting like a snake through gates and causeways. Traffic was heavy, wagons and animals traveling in both directions in a steady stream, crawling through the heat and the dust.

The company of seven worked their way steadily closer. As they reached the lower end of the rampway, Padishar Creel turned back to the others and said, "Careful now, lads. Nothing to call attention to ourselves. Remember that it is as hard to get out of this city as it is to get in."

They blended into the stream of traffic that climbed toward the plateau's summit. Wheels thudded, traces jingled and creaked, animals brayed, and men whistled and shouted. Federation soldiers manned the checkpoints leading up, but made no effort to interfere with the flow. It was the same at the gates—massive portals that loomed so high overhead that Par was aghast to think that any army had managed to breach them—the soldiers seeming to take no notice of who went in or out. It was an occupied city, Par decided, that was working hard at pretending to be free.

They passed beneath the gates, the shadow of the gatehouse overhead falling over them like a pall. The second wall rose ahead, smaller, but no less imposing. They moved toward it, keeping in the thick of the traffic. The grounds between the walls were clear of everyone but soldiers and their animals and equipment. There were plenty of each, a fair-sized army housed and waiting. Par studied the rows of drilling men out of the corner of one eye, keeping his head lowered in the shadow of his hooded cloak.

Once through the second set of gates, Padishar pulled them from the Tyrsian Way, the main thoroughfare of homes and businesses that wound through the center of the city to the cliff walls and what was once the palace of its rulers, and steered them into a maze of side streets. There were shops and residences here as well, but fewer soldiers and more beggars. The buildings grew dilapidated as they walked and eventually they entered a district of ale houses and brothels. Padishar did not seem to notice. He kept them moving, ignoring the pleas of the beggars and street vendors, working his way deeper into the city.

At last they emerged into a bright, open district containing markets and small parks. A sprinkling of residences with yards separated the markets, and there were carriages with silks and ribbons on the horses. Vendors sold banners and sweets to laughing children and their mothers. Street shows were being performed on every corner—actors, clowns, magicians, musicians, and animal trainers. Broad, colorful canopies shaded the markets and the park pavilions where families spread their picnic lunches, and the air was filled with shouts, laughter, and applause.

Padishar Creel slowed, casting about for something. He took them through several of the stalls, along tree-shaded blocks where small gatherings were drawn by a multitude of delights, then stopped finally at a cart selling apples. He bought a small sackful for them all to share, took one for himself, and leaned back idly against a lamp pole to eat it. It took Par several moments to realize that he was waiting for something. The Valeman ate his apple with the others and looked about watchfully. Fruits of all sorts were on display in the stalls of a market behind him, there were ices being sold across the way, a juggler, a mime, a girl doing sleight of hand, a pair of dancing monkeys with their trainer, and a scattering of children and adults watching it all. He found his eyes returning to the girl. She had flaming red hair that seemed redder still against the black silk of her clothing and cape. She was drawing coins out of astonished children's ears, then making them disappear again. Once she brought fire out of the air and sent it spinning away. He had never seen that done before. The girl was very good.

He was so intent on watching her, in fact, that he almost missed seeing Padishar Creel hand something to a dark-skinned boy who had come up to him. The boy took what he was given without a word and disappeared. Par looked to see where he had gone, but it was as if the earth had swallowed him up.

They stayed where they were a few minutes longer, and then the outlaw chief said, "Time to go," and led them away. Par took a final look at the red-haired girl and saw that she was causing a ring to float in midair before her audience, while a tiny, blond-headed boy leaped and squealed after it.

The Valeman smiled at the child's delight.

On their way back through the gathering of market stalls, Morgan Leah caught sight of Hirehone. The master of Kiltan Forge was at the edge of a crowd applauding a juggler, his large frame wrapped in a great cloak. There was only a momentary glimpse of the bald pate and drooping mustaches, then he was gone. Morgan blinked, deciding almost immediately that he had been mistaken. What would Hirehone be doing in Tyrsis?

By the time they reached the next block, he had dismissed the matter from his mind.

They spent the next several hours in the basement of a storage house annexed to the shop of a weapons-maker, a man clearly in the service of the outlaws, since Padishar Creel knew exactly where in a crevice by the frame to find a key that would open the door. He took them inside without hesitating. They found food and drink waiting, along with pallets and blankets for sleeping and water to wash up with. It was cool and dry in the basement, and the heat of the day quickly left them. They rested for a time, eating and talking idly among themselves, waiting for whatever was to come next. Only the outlaw chief seemed to know and, as usual, he wasn't saying. Instead, he went to sleep.

It was several hours before he awoke. He stood up, stretched, took time to wash his face, and walked over to Par. "We're going out," he said. He turned to the others. "Everyone else stay put until we get back. We won't be long and we won't be doing anything dangerous."

Both Coll and Morgan started to protest, then thought better of it. Par followed Padishar up the basement stairs, and the trapdoor closed behind them. Padishar took a moment at the outer door, then beckoned Par after him, and they stepped out into the street.

The street was still crowded, filled with tradesmen and artisans, buyers, and beggars. The outlaw chief took Par south toward the cliffs, striding rapidly as the shadows of late afternoon began to spread across the city. They did not return along any of the avenues that had brought them in, but followed a different series of small, rutted backstreets. The faces they passed were masks of studied disinterest, but the eyes were feral. Padishar ignored them, and Par kept himself close to the big man. Bodies pressed up against him, but he carried nothing of value, so he worried less than he might have otherwise.

As they approached the cliffs, they turned onto the Tyrsian Way. Ahead, the Bridge of Sendic lifted over the People's Park, a carefully trimmed stretch of lawn with broad-leaf trees that spread away toward a low wall and a cluster of buildings where the bridge ended. Beyond, a forest grew out of a wide ravine, and beyond that the spires and walls of what had once been the palace of the rulers of Tyrsis rose up against the fading light.

Par studied the park, the bridge, and the palace as they approached. Something about their configuration did not seem quite right. Wasn't the Bridge of Sendic supposed to have ended at the gates of the palace?

Padishar dropped back momentarily. "So, lad. Hard to believe that the Sword of Shannara could be hidden anywhere so open, eh?"

Par nodded, frowning. "Where is it?"

"Patience now. You'll have your answer soon enough." He put one arm about the Valeman and bent close. "Whatever happens next, do not act surprised."

Par nodded. The outlaw chief slowed, moved over to a flower cart and stopped. He studied the flowers, apparently trying to select a batch. He had done so when Par felt an arm go about his waist and turned to find the red-haired girl who practiced sleight of hand pressing up against him.

"Hello, Elf-boy," she whispered, her cool fingers brushing at his ear as she kissed him on the cheek.

Then two small children were beside them, a girl and a boy, the first reaching up to grasp Padishar's rough hand, the second reaching up to grasp Par's. Padishar smiled, lifted the little girl so that she squealed, kissed her, and gave half of the flowers to her and half to the boy. Whistling, he started the five of them moving into the park. Par had recovered sufficiently to notice that the red-haired girl was carrying a basket covered with a bright cloth. When they were close to the wall that separated the park from the ravine, Padishar chose a maple tree for them to sit under, the red-haired girl spread the cloth, and all of them began unpacking the basket which contained cold chicken, eggs, hard bread and jam, cakes, and tea.

Padishar glanced over at Par as they worked. "Par Ohmsford, meet Damson Rhee, your betrothed for purposes of this little outing."

Damson Rhee's green eyes laughed. "Love is fleeting, Par Ohmsford. Let's make the most of it." She fed him an egg.

"You are my son," Padishar added. "These other two children are your siblings, though their names escape me at the moment. Damson, remind me later. We're just a typical family, out for a late afternoon picnic, should anyone ask."

No one did. The men ate their meal in silence, listening to the children as they chattered on and acted as if what was happening was perfectly normal. Damson Rhee looked after them, laughing right along with them, her smile warm and infectious. She was pretty to begin with, but when she smiled, Par found her beautiful. When they were finished eating, she did the coin trick with each child, then sent them off to play.

"Let's take a walk," Padishar suggested, rising.

The three of them strolled through the shade trees, moving without seeming purpose toward the wall that blocked away the ravine. Damson clung lovingly to Par's waist. He found he didn't mind. "Things have changed somewhat in Tyrsis since the old days," the outlaw chief said to Par as they walked. "When the Buckhannah line died out, the monarchy came to an end. Tyrsis, Varfleet, and Kern ruled Callahorn by forming the Council of the Cities. When the Federation made Callahorn a protectorate, the Council was disbanded. The palace had served as an assembly for the Council. Now the Federation uses it—except that no one knows exactly what they use it for."

They reached the wall and stopped. The wall was built of stone block to a height of about three feet. Spikes were embedded in its top. "Have a look," the outlaw chief invited.

Par did. The ravine beyond dropped away sharply into a mass of trees and scrub that had grown so thick it seemed to be choking on itself. Mist curled through the wilderness with an insistence that was unsettling, clinging to even the uppermost reaches of the trees. The ravine stretched away for perhaps a mile to either side and a quarter of that distance to where the palace stood, its doors and windows shuttered and dark, its gates barred. The stone of the palace was scarred and dirty, and the whole of it had the look of something that had not seen use for decades. A narrow catwalk ran from the buildings in the foreground to its sagging gates.

He looked back at Padishar. The outlaw chief was facing toward the city. "This wall forms the dividing line between past and present," he said quietly. "The ground we stand upon is called the People's Park. But the true People's Park, the one from the time of our ancestors—" He paused and turned back to the ravine. "—is down there." He took a moment to let that sink in. "Look. Below the Federation Gatehouse that wards the catwalk." Par followed his gaze and caught sight of a scattering of huge stone blocks barely poking up out of the forest. "That," the outlaw chief continued somberly, "is what remains of the real Bridge of Sendic. It was badly cracked, I am told, during the assault on Tyrsis by the Warlock Lord during the time of Panamon Creel. Some years later, it collapsed altogether. This other bridge," he waved indifferently, "is merely for show."

He glanced sideways at Par. "Now do you see?"

Par did. His mind was working rapidly now, fitting the pieces into place. "And the Sword of Shannara?" He caught a glimpse of Damson Rhee's startled look out of the corner of his eye.

"Down there somewhere, unless I miss my guess," Padishar replied smoothly. "Right where it's always been. You have something to say, Damson?"

The red-haired girl took Par's arm and steered him away from the wall. "This is what you have come for, Padishar?" She sounded angry.

"Forbear, lovely Damson. Don't let's be judgmental."

The girl's grip tightened on Par's arm. "This is dangerous business, Padishar. I have sent men into the Pit before, as you well know, and not one of them has returned."

Padishar smiled indulgently. "The Pit—that's what Tyrsians call the ravine these days. Fitting, I suppose."

"You take too many risks!" the girl pressed.

"Damson is my eyes and ears and strong right arm inside Tyrsis," the other continued smoothly. He smiled at her. "Tell the Valeman what you know of the Sword, Damson."

She gave him a dangerous look, then swung her face away. "The collapse of the Bridge of Sendic occurred at the same time the Federation annexed Callahorn and began occupation of Tyrsis. The forest that now blankets the old People's Park, where the Sword of Shannara was housed, grew up virtually overnight. The new park and bridge came about just as quickly. I asked the old ones of the city some years ago what they remembered, and this is what I learned. The Sword didn't actually disappear from its vault; it was the vault that disappeared into the forest. People forget, especially when they're being told something else. Almost everyone believes there was only one People's Park and one Bridge of Sendic—the ones they see. The Sword of Shannara, if it ever existed, simply disappeared."

Par was looking at her in disbelief. "The forest, the bridge, and the park changed overnight?"

She nodded. "Just so."

"But . . . ?"

"Magic, lad," Padishar Creel whispered in answer to his unfinished question.

They walked on a bit, nearing the brightly colored cloth that contained the remains of their picnic. The children were back, nibbling contentedly at the cakes.

"The Federation doesn't use magic," Par argued, still confused. "They have outlawed it."

"Outlawed its use by others, yes," the big man acknowledged. "Perhaps the better to use it themselves? Or to allow someone else to use it? Or some*thing*?" He emphasized the last syllable.

Par looked over sharply. "Shadowen, you mean?"

Neither Padishar nor Damson said anything. Par's mind spun. The

Federation and the Shadowen in league somehow, joined for purposes none of them understood—was that possible?

"I have wondered about the fate of the Sword of Shannara for a long time," Padishar mused, stopping just out of earshot of the waiting children. "It is a part of the history of my family as well. It always seemed strange to me that it should have vanished so completely. It was embedded in marble and locked in a vault for two hundred years. How could it simply disappear? What happened to the vault that contained it? Was it all somehow spirited away?" He glanced at Par. "Damson spent a long time finding out the answer. Only a few remembered the truth of how the disappearance came about. They're all dead now—but they left their story to me."

His smile was wolfish. "Now I have an excuse to discover whether that story is true. Is the Sword of Shannara down there in that ravine? You and I shall discover the answer. Resurrection of the magic of the Elven house of Shannara, young Ohmsford—the key, perhaps, to the freedom of the Four Lands. We must know."

Damson Rhee shook her titian head. "You are far too eager, Padishar, to throw your life away. And the lives of others like this boy. I will never understand."

She moved away from them to gather up the children. Par didn't care much for being called a boy by a girl who looked younger still.

"Watch out for that one, Par Ohmsford," the outlaw chief murmured.

"She doesn't have much faith in our chances," Par observed.

"Ah, she worries without cause! We have the strength of seven of us to withstand whatever might guard the Pit. And if there's magic as well, we have your wishsong and the Highlander's blade. Enough said."

He studied the sky. "It will be dark soon, lad." He put his arm about the Valeman companionably and moved them forward to join Damson Rhee and the children. "When it is," he whispered, "we'll have a look for ourselves at what's become of the Sword of Shannara."

As Padishar Creel's makeshift family reached the edge of the park and prepared to step out onto the Tyrsian Way, Damson Rhee turned to the outlaw chief and said, "The sentries who patrol the wall make a change at midnight in front of the Federation Gatehouse. I can arrange for a small disturbance that will distract them long enough for you to slip into the Pit—if you are determined on this. Be certain you go in at the west end."

Then she reached up and plucked a silver coin from behind Par's ear and gave it to him. The coin bore her likeness. "For luck, Par Ohmsford," she said. "You will be needing it if you continue to follow *him*."

She gave Padishar a hard look, took the children by the hand, and strode off into the crowds without looking back, her red hair shining. The outlaw chief and the Valeman watched her go.

"Who is she, Padishar?" Par asked when she was no longer in view.

Padishar shrugged. "Whoever she chooses to be. There are as many stories about her origins as there are about my own. Come now. Time for us to be going as well."

He took Par back through the city, keeping to the lesser streets and by-ways. The crowds were still heavy, everyone pushing and shoving, their faces dust-streaked and their tempers short. Twilight had chased the sunlight west, lengthening the shadows into evening, but the heat of midday remained trapped by the city's walls, rising out of the stone of the streets and buildings to hang in the still summer air. It was like being in a furnace. Par glanced skyward. Already the quarter-moon was visible northward, a sprinkling of stars east. He tried to think about what he had learned of the disappearance of the Sword of Shannara, but found himself thinking instead of Damson Rhee.

Padishar had him safely back down in the basement of the storage house behind the weapons shop before dark, where Coll and Morgan waited impatiently to receive them. Cutting short a flurry of questions, the outlaw chief smiled cheerfully and announced that everything was arranged. At midnight the Valemen, the Highlander, Ciba Blue, and he would make a brief foray into the ravine that fronted what had once been the palace of the city's rulers. They would descend using a rope ladder. Stasas and Drutt would remain behind. They would haul the ladder up when their companions were safely down and hide until summoned. Any sentries would be dispatched, the ladder would be lowered again, and they would all disappear back the way they had come.

He was succinct and matter-of-fact. He made no mention of why they were doing all this and none of his own men bothered to ask. They simply let him finish, then turned immediately back to whatever they had been doing before. Coll and Morgan, on the other hand, could barely contain themselves, and Par was forced to take them aside and tell them in detail everything that had happened. The three of them huddled in one corner of the basement, seated on sacks of scrubbing powder. Oil lamps lit the darkness, and the city above them began to go still.

When Par concluded, Morgan shook his head doubtfully.

"It is hard to believe that an entire city has forgotten there was more than one People's Park and Bridge of Sendic," he declared softly.

"Not hard at all when you remember that they have had more than a hundred years to work on it," Coll disagreed quickly. "Think about it, Morgan. How much more than a park and a bridge has been forgotten in that time? The Federation has saddled the Four Lands with three hundred years of revisionist history."

"Coll's right," Par said. "We lost our only true historian when Allanon passed from the Lands. The Druid Histories were the only written compilations the Races had, and we don't know what's become of those. All we have left are the storytellers, with their word-of-mouth recitations, most of them imperfect."

"Everything about the old world has been called a lie," Coll said, his dark eyes hard. "We know it to be the truth, but we are virtually alone in that belief. The Federation has changed everything to suit its own purposes. After a hundred years, it is little wonder that no one in Tyrsis remembers that the People's Park and the Bridge of Sendic are not the same as they once were. The fact of the matter is, who even cares anymore?"

Morgan frowned. "Perhaps so. But something's still not right about this." His frown deepened. "It bothers me that the Sword of Shannara, vault and all, has been down in this ravine all these years and no one's seen it. It bothers me that no one who's gone down to have a look has come back out again."

"That troubles me, too," Coll agreed.

Par glanced briefly at the outlaws, who were paying no attention to them. "None of us thought for a minute that it wouldn't be dangerous trying to recover the Sword," he whispered, a hint of exasperation in his voice. "Surely you didn't expect to just walk up and take it? Of course no one's seen it! It wouldn't be missing if they had, would it? And you can bet that the Federation has made certain no one who got down into the Pit got back out again! That's the reason for the guards and the Gatehouse! Besides, the fact that the Federation has gone to so much trouble to hide the old bridge and park suggests to me that the Sword is down there!"

Coll looked at his brother steadily. "It also suggests that that's where it's meant to stay."

The conversation broke off and the three of them drifted away to separate corners of the basement. Evening passed quickly into nightfall and the heat of the day finally faded. The little company ate an uneventful dinner amid long stretches of silence. Only Padishar had much of anything to say, ebullient as always, tossing off stories and jokes as if this night were the same as any other, seemingly heedless of the fact that his audience remained unresponsive. Par was too excited to eat or talk and spent the time wondering if Padishar were as unaffected as he appeared. Nothing seemed to alter the mood of the outlaw chief. Padishar Creel was either very brave or very foolish, and it bothered the Valeman that he wasn't sure which it was.

Dinner ended and they sat around talking in hushed voices and staring at the walls. Padishar came over to Par at one point and crouched down beside him. "Are you anxious to be about our business, lad?" he asked softly.

No one else was close enough to hear. Par nodded.

"Ah, well, it won't be long now." The outlaw patted his knee. The hard eyes held his own. "Just remember what we're about. A quick look and out again. If the Sword is there for the taking, fine. If not, no delays."

His smile was wolfish. "Caution in all things." He slipped away, leaving Par to stare after him.

The minutes lengthened with the wearing slowness of shadows at midday. Par and Coll sat side by side without speaking. Par could almost hear his brother's thoughts in the silence. The oil lamps flickered and spat. A giant swamp fly buzzed about the ceiling until Ciba Blue killed it. The basement room began to smell close.

Then finally Padishar stood up and said it was time. They came to their feet eagerly, anticipation flickering in their eyes. Weapons were strapped down and cloaks pulled close. They went up the basement stairs through the trapdoor and out into the night.

The city streets were empty and still. Voices drifted out of ale houses and sleeping rooms, punctuated by raucous laughter and occasional shouts. The lamps were mostly broken or unlit on the back streets that Padishar took them down, and there was only moonlight to guide them through the shadows. They did not move furtively, only cautiously, not wishing to draw attention to themselves. They ducked back into alleyways several times to avoid knots of swaying, singing revellers who were making their way homeward. Drunks and beggars who saw them pass barely glanced up from the doorways and alcoves in which they lay. They saw no Federation soldiers. The Federation left the back streets and the poor of Tyrsis to manage for themselves.

When they reached the People's Park and the Bridge of Sendic, Padishar sent them across the broad expanse of the Tyrsian Way in twos and threes into the shadows of the park, dispatching them in different directions to regroup later, carefully watching the well-lighted Way for any approach of the Federation patrols he knew would be found there. Only one patrol passed, and it saw nothing of the company. A watch was posted before the Gatehouse at the center of the wall that warded the Pit, but the soldiers had lamplight reflecting all about them and could not see outside its glow to the figures lost in the dark beyond. Padishar took the company swiftly through the deserted park, west to where the ravine approached its juncture with the cliffs. There, he settled them in to wait.

Par crouched motionlessly in the dark and listened to the sound of his heart pumping in his ears. The silence about him was filled with the hum of insects. Locusts buzzed in raucous cadence in the black. The seven men were concealed in a mass of thicket, invisible to anyone without. But anyone beyond their concealment was invisible to them as well. Par was uneasy with their placement and wondered at its choice. He glanced at Padishar Creel, but the outlaw chief was busy overseeing the untangling of the rope ladder that would lower them into the ravine . . .

Par hesitated. The Pit. Lower them into the Pit. He forced himself to say the word.

He took a deep breath, trying to steady himself. He wondered if Damson Rhee was anywhere close.

A patrol of four Federation soldiers materialized out of the dark almost directly in front of them, walking the perimeter of the wall. Though the sound of their boots warned of their coming, it was chilling when they appeared, nevertheless. Par and the others flattened themselves in the scratchy tangle of their concealment. The soldiers paused, spoke quietly among themselves for a moment, then turned back the way they had come, and were gone.

Par exhaled slowly. He risked a quick glance over at the dark bowl of the ravine. It was a soundless, depthless well of ink.

Padishar and the other outlaws were fixing the rope ladder in place, preparing for the descent. Par came to his feet, eager to relieve the muscles that were beginning to cramp, anxious to be done with this whole business. He should have felt confident. He did not. He was growing steadily more uneasy and he couldn't say why. Something was tugging at him frantically, warning him, some sixth sense that he couldn't identify.

He thought he heard something—not ahead in the ravine, but behind in the park. He started to turn, his sharp Elf eyes searching.

Then abruptly there was a flurry of shouts from the direction of the Gatehouse, and cries of alarm pierced the night.

"Now!" Padishar Creel urged, and they bolted their cover for the wall.

The ladder was already knotted in place, tied down to a pair of the wall spikes. Quickly, they lowered it into the black. Ciba Blue went over first, the cobalt birthmark on his cheek a dark, hollow place in the moonlight. He tested the ladder first with his weight, then disappeared from view.

"Remember, listen for my signal," Padishar was saying hurriedly to Stasas and Drutt, his voice a rough whisper above the distant shouts.

He was turning to start Par down the ladder after Ciba Blue when a swarm of Federation soldiers appeared out of the dark behind them, armed with spears and crossbows, silent figures that seemed to come from nowhere. Everyone froze. Par felt his stomach lurch with shock. He found himself thinking, "I should have known, I should have sensed them," and thinking in the next breath that indeed he had.

"Lay down your weapons," a voice commanded.

For just an instant, Par was afraid that Padishar Creel would choose to fight rather than surrender. The outlaw chief's eyes darted left and right, his tall form rigid. But the odds were overwhelming. His face relaxed, he gave a barely perceptible smile, and dropped his sword and long knife in front of him wordlessly. The others of the little company did the same, and the Federation soldiers closed about. Weapons were scooped up and arms bound behind backs.

"There's another of them down in the Pit," a soldier advised the leader of their captors, a smallish man with short-cropped hair and commander's bars on his dark tunic.

The commander glanced over. "Cut the ropes, let him drop."

The rope ladder was cut through in a moment. It fell soundlessly into the black. Par waited for a cry, but there was none. Perhaps Ciba Blue had already completed his descent. He glanced at Coll, who just shook his head helplessly.

The Federation commander stepped up to Padishar. "You should know, Padishar Creel," he said quietly, his tone measured, "that you were betrayed by one of your own."

He waited momentarily for a response, but there was none. Padishar's face was expressionless. Only his eyes revealed the rage that he was some-how managing to contain.

Then the silence was shattered by a terrifying scream that rose out of the depths of the Pit. It lifted into the night like a stricken bird, hovering against the cliff rock until at last, mercifully, it dropped away.

The scream had been Ciba Blue's, Par thought in horror.

The Federation commander gave the ravine a perfunctory glance and ordered his prisoners led away.

They were taken through the park along the ravine wall toward the Gate-house, kept in single file and apart from each other by the soldiers guarding them. Par trudged along with the others in stunned silence, the sound of Ciba Blue's scream still echoing in his mind. What had happened to the outlaw down there alone in the Pit? He swallowed against the sick feel-ing in his stomach and forced himself to think of something else. Betrayed, the Federation commander had said. But by whom? None of them there, obviously—so someone who wasn't. One of Padishar's own . . .

He tripped over a tree root, righted himself and stumbled on. His mind whirled with a scattering of thoughts. They were being taken to the Federa-tion prisons, he concluded. Once there, the grand adventure was over. There would be no more searching for the missing Sword of Shannara. There would be no further consideration of the charge given him by Allanon. No one ever came out of the Federation prisons.

He had to escape.

The thought came instinctively, clearing his mind as nothing else could. He had to escape. If he didn't, they would all be locked away and forgotten. Only Damson Rhee knew where they were, and it occurred suddenly to Par that Damson Rhee had been in the best position to betray them.

It was an unpleasant possibility. It was also unavoidable.

His breathing slowed. This was the best opportunity to break free that he would get. Once within the prisons, it would be much more difficult to manage. Perhaps Padishar would come up with a plan by then, but Par didn't care to chance it. Uncharitably, perhaps, he was thinking that Padishar was the one who had gotten them into this mess.

He watched the lights of the Gatehouse flicker ahead through the trees of the park. He only had a few minutes more. He thought he could manage it, but he would have to go alone. He would have to leave Coll and Morgan. There wasn't any choice.

Voices sounded from ahead, other soldiers waiting for their return. The line began to string out and some of the guards were straying a bit. Par took a deep breath. He waited until they were passing along a cluster of scrub birch, then used the wishsong. He sang softly, his voice blending into the sounds of the night, a whisper of breeze, a bird's gentle call, a cricket's brief chirp. He let the wishsong's magic reach out and fill the minds of the guards immediately next to him, distracting them, turning their eyes away from him, letting them forget that he was there . . .

And then he simply stepped into the birch and shadows and disappeared.

The line of prisoners passed on without him. No one had noticed that he was gone. If Coll or Morgan or any of the others had seen anything, they were keeping still about it. The Federation soldiers and their prisoners continued moving toward the lights ahead, leaving him alone.

When they were gone, he moved soundlessly off into the night.

He managed to free himself almost immediately of the ropes that held his hands. He found a spike with a jagged edge on the ravine wall a hundred yards from where he had slipped away and, boosting himself up on the wall, sawed through the ropes in only minutes. No alarm had gone up yet from the watch; apparently he hadn't been missed. Maybe they hadn't bothered to count the original number of their prisoners, he reasoned. After all, it had been dark, and the capture had taken place in a matter of seconds.

At any rate, he was free. So what was he going to do now?

He worked his way back through the park toward the Tyrsian Way, keeping to the shadows, stopping every few seconds to listen for the sounds of the pursuit that never came. He was sweating freely, his tunic sticking to his back, his face streaked with dust. He was exhilarated by his escape and devastated by the realization that he didn't know how to take advantage of it. There was no help for him in Tyrsis and no help for him without. He didn't know who to contact within the city; there was no one he could afford to trust. And he had no idea how to get back into the Parma Key. Steff would help if he knew his companions were in trouble. But how would the Dwarf find out before it was too late to matter?

The lights of the Way came into view through the trees. Par stumbled to the edge of the park, close to its western boundaries, and collapsed in despair against the trunk of an old maple. He had to do something; he couldn't just wander about. He brushed at his face with his sleeve and let his head sink back against the rough bark. He was suddenly sick and it took every ounce of willpower he could muster to prevent himself from retching.

He had to get back to Coll and Morgan. He had to find a way to free them.

Use the wishsong, he thought.

But how?

A Federation patrol came down the Way, boots clumping in the still-ness. Par shrank back into the shadows and waited until they were out of sight. Then he moved from his cover along the edge of the park toward a fountain bordering the walk. Once there, he leaned over and hurriedly splashed water on his hands and face. The water ran along his skin like liquid silver.

He paused, letting his head sink against his chest. He was suddenly very tired.

The arm that yanked him around was strong and unyielding, snapping his head back violently. He found himself face-to-face with Damson Rhee.

"What happened?" she demanded, her voice low.

Frantically, Par reached for his long knife. But his weapons were gone, taken by the Federation. He shoved at the girl, trying to rip free of her grip, but she sidestepped the blow without effort and kicked him so hard in the stomach that he doubled over.

"What are you doing, you idiot?" she whispered angrily.

Without waiting for an answer, she hauled him back into the concealing shadows of the park and threw him to the ground. "If you try something like that again with me, I will break both your arms!" she snapped.

Par pulled himself up to a sitting position, still looking for a way to escape. But she shoved him back against the ground and crouched close. "Why don't we try again, my beloved Elf-boy? Where are the others? What has happened to them?"

Par swallowed against his rage. "The Federation has them! They were waiting for us, Damson! As if you didn't know!"

The anger in her eyes was replaced by surprise. "What do you mean, 'as if I didn't know'?"

"They were waiting for us. We never got past the wall. We were betrayed! The Federation commander told us so! He said it was one of our own—an outlaw, Damson!" Par was shaking.

Damson Rhee's gaze was steady. "And you have decided that it was me, have you, Par Ohmsford?"

Par forced himself up on his elbows. "Who better than you? You were the only one who knew what we were about—the only one not taken! No one else knew! If not you, then who could it possibly have been?"

There was a long silence as they stared at each other in the dark. The sound of voices nearby grew slowly distinct. Someone was approaching.

Damson Rhee suddenly bent close. "I don't know. But it wasn't me! Now lie still until they pass!"

She pushed him into a gathering of bushes, then backed in herself and lay down beside him. Par could feel the warmth of her body. He could smell the sweet scent of her. He closed his eyes and waited. A pair of Federation soldiers worked their way out of the park, paused momentarily, then started back again and were gone.

Damson Rhee put her lips close against Par's ear. "Do they know you are missing yet?"

Par hesitated. "I can't be certain," he whispered back.

She took his chin with her smooth hand and turned his face until it was level with her own. "I didn't betray you. It may seem as if I must have, but I didn't. If I intended to betray you to the Federation, Par, I would have simply turned you over to that pair of soldiers and been done with it."

The green eyes glittered faintly with moonlight that had penetrated the branches of their concealment. Par stared at those eyes and found no hint of deception mirrored there. Still, he hesitated.

"You have to decide here and now whether you believe me," she said quietly.

He shook his head warily. "It isn't that easy!"

"It has to be! Look at me, Par. I have betrayed no one—not you or Padishar or the others, not now, not ever! Why would I do something like that? I hate the Federation as much as anyone!" She paused, exasperated. "I told you that this was a dangerous undertaking. I warned you that the Pit was a black hole that swallowed men whole. Padishar was the one who insisted you go!"

"That doesn't make him responsible for what happened."

"Nor me! What about the distraction I promised? Did it come about as I said it would?"

Par nodded.

"You see! I fulfilled my part of the bargain! Why would I bother if I intended your betrayal?"

Par said nothing.

Damson's nostrils flared. "You will admit to nothing, will you?" She shook back her auburn hair in a flash of color. "Will you at least tell me what happened?"

Par took a deep breath. Briefly, he related the events that surrounded their capture, including the frightening disappearance of the outlaw Ciba Blue. He kept deliberately vague the circumstances of his own escape. The magic was his business. Its secret belonged to him.

But Damson was not about to be put off. "So the fact of the matter is, you might as easily be the betrayer as I," she said. "How else is it that you managed to escape when the others could not?"

Par flushed, resentful of the accusation, irritated by her persistence. "Why would I do such a thing to my friends?"

"My own argument exactly," she replied.

They studied each other wordlessly, each measuring the strength of the other. Damson was right, Par knew. There was as much reason to believe that he had been the betrayer as she. But that didn't change the fact that he knew he wasn't while he didn't know the same of her.

"Decide, Par," she urged quietly. "Do you believe me or not?"

Her features were smooth and guileless in the scattering of light, her skin dappled with shadows from the tiny leaves of the bushes. He found himself drawn to her in a way he had not believed possible. There was something special about this girl, something that made him push aside his misgivings and cast out his doubts. The green eyes held him, insinuating and persuasive. He saw only truth in them.

"Okay, I believe you," he said finally.

"Then tell me how it is that you escaped when the others did not," she demanded. "No, don't argue the matter. I must have proof of your own innocence if we are to be of any use to each other or to our friends."

Par's resolve to keep to himself the secret of the wishsong slipped slowly away. Again, she was right. She was asking only what he would have asked in her place. "I used magic," he told her.

She inched closer, as if to judge better the truth of what he was saying. "Magic? What sort?"

He hesitated yet.

"Sleight of hand? Cloud spells?" she pressed. "Some sort of vanishing act?"

"Yes," he replied. She was waiting. "I have the ability to make myself invisible when I wish."

There was a long silence. He read the curiosity in her eyes. "You command real magic, don't you?" she said finally. "Not the pretend kind that I use, where coins appear and disappear and fire dances on the air. You have the sort that is forbidden. That is why Padishar is so interested in you." She paused. "Who are you, Par Ohmsford? Tell me."

It was still within the park now, the voices of the watch passed from hearing, the night gone deep and silent once more. There might have been no one else in all the world but the two of them. Par weighed the advisability of his reply. He was stepping on stones that floated in quicksand.

"You can see who I am for yourself," he said finally, hedging. "I am part Elf and that part of me carries the magic of my forebears. I have their magic to command—or some small part of it, at least."

She looked at him for a long time then, thinking. At last she seemed to have made up her mind. She crawled from the concealment of the bushes, pulling him out with her. They stood together in the shadows, brushing themselves off, breathing deeply the cool night air. The park was deserted.

She came up to him and stood close. "I was born in Tyrsis, the child of a forger of weapons and his wife. I had one brother and one sister, both older. When I was eight, the Federation discovered my father was supplying arms to the Movement. Someone—a friend, an acquaintance, I never knew who—betrayed him. Seekers came to our house in the middle of the night, fired it and burned it to the ground. My family was locked inside and burned with it. I escaped only because I was visiting my aunt. Within a year she was dead as well, and I was forced to live in the streets. That is where I grew up. My family was all gone. I had no friends. A street magician took me as his apprentice and taught me my trade. That has been my life." She paused. "You deserve to know why it is that I would never betray anyone to the Federation."

She reached up with her hand and her fingers brushed his cheek for just a moment. Then her hand trailed down to his arm and fastened there.

"Par, we must do whatever it is we are going to do tonight or it will be too late. The Federation knows who they have. Padishar Creel. They will send for Rimmer Dall and his Seekers to question Padishar. Once that happens, rescue will be pointless." She paused, making certain that he took her meaning. "We have to help them now."

Par went cold at the thought of Coll and Morgan in the hands of Rimmer Dall—let alone Padishar. What would the First Seeker do to the leader of the Movement?

"Tonight," she continued, her voice soft, but insistent. "While they are not expecting it. They will still have Padishar and the others in the cells at the Gatehouse. They won't have moved them yet. They will be tired, sleepy with the coming of morning. We won't get a better chance."

He stared at her incredulously. "You and I?"

"If you agree to come with me."

"But what can the two of us do?"

She pulled him close. Her red hair shimmered darkly in the moonlight. "Tell me about your magic. What can you do with it, Par Ohmsford?"

There was no hesitation now. "Make myself invisible," he said. "Make myself to appear to be different than I am. Make others think they are seeing things that aren't there." He was growing excited. "Just about anything that I want if it's not for too long and not too extended. It's just illusion, you understand."

She walked away from him, paced into the trees close by and stopped. She stood there in the shadows, lost in thought. Par waited where he was, feeling the cool night air brush his skin in a sudden breath of wind, listening to the silence that spread across the city like the waters of an ocean across its floor. He could almost swim through that silence, drifting away to better times and places. There was fear in him that he could not suppress— fear at the thought of returning for his friends, fear at the thought of failing in the attempt. But to attempt nothing at all was unthinkable.

Still, what could they do—just this slip of a girl and himself?

As if reading his mind she came back to him then, green eyes intense, seized his arms tightly, and whispered, "I think I know a way, Par."

He smiled in spite of himself.

"Tell me about it," he said.

20

Walker Boh journeyed directly back to Hearthstone after taking leave of the company at the Hadeshorn. He rode his horse east across the Rabb, bypassed Storlock and its Healers, climbed the Wolfsktaag through the Pass of Jade, and worked his way upriver along the Chard Rush until he entered Darklin Reach. Three days later he was home again. He talked with no one on the way, keeping entirely to himself as he traveled, pausing only long enough to eat and sleep. He was not fit company for other men and he knew it. He was obsessed with thoughts of his encounter with the shade of Allanon. He was haunted by them.

The Anar was enveloped by a particularly violent midsummer storm within twenty-four hours of his return, and Walker secluded himself truculently in his cottage home while winds lashed its shaved-board walls and rains beat down upon its shingled roof. The forested valley was deluged, wracked by the crack and flash of lightning, shaken by the long, ominous peals of thunder, pelted and washed. The cadence of the rains obliterated every other sound, and Walker sat amid their constant thrum in brooding silence, wrapped in blankets and a blackness of spirit he would not have thought possible.

He found himself despairing.

It was the inevitability of things that he feared. Walker Boh, whatever name he chose to bear, was nevertheless an Ohmsford by blood, and he knew that Ohmsfords, despite their misgivings, had always been made to take up the Druid cause. It had been so with Shea and Flick, with Wil, and with Brin and Jair before him. Now it was to be his turn. His and Wren's and Par's. Par embraced the cause willingly, of course. Par was an incurable romantic, a self-appointed champion of the downtrodden and the abused. Par was a fool.

Or a realist, depending on how you viewed the matter. Because, if history proved an accurate indicator, Par was merely accepting without argument what Walker, too, would be forced to embrace—Allanon's will, the cause of a dead man. The shade had come to them like some scolding patriarch out of death's embrace—chiding them for their lack of diligence, scolding them for their misgivings, charging them with missions of madness and self-destruction. Bring back the Druids! Bring back Paranor! Do these things because I say they must be done, because I say they are necessary, because I—a thing of no flesh and dead mind—demand it!

Walker's mood darkened further as the weight of the matter continued to settle steadily over him, a pall mirroring the oppressiveness of the storms without. Change the whole of the face of the world—that was what the shade was asking of them, of Par, Wren, and himself. Take three hundred years of evolution in the Four Lands and dispense with it in an instant's time. What else was the shade asking, if not that? A return of the magic, a return of the wielders of that magic, of its shapers, of all the things ended by this same shade those three hundred years past. Madness! They would be playing with lives in the manner of creators—and they were not entitled!

Through the gray haze of his anger and his fear, he could conjure in his mind the features of the shade. Allanon. The last of the Druids, the keeper of the Histories of the Four Lands, the protector of the Races, the dispenser of magic and secrets. His dark form rose up against the years like a cloud against the sun, blocking away the warmth and the light. Everything that had taken place while he lived bore his touch. And before that, it was Bremen, and before that the Druids of the First Council of the Races. Wars of magic, struggles for survival, the battles between light and dark— or grays perhaps—had all been the result of the Druids.

And now he was being asked to bring all that back.

It could be argued that it was necessary. It had always been argued so. It could be said that the Druids merely worked to preserve and protect, never to shape. But had there ever been one without the other? And necessity was always in the eye of the beholder. Warlock Lords, Demons, and Mord Wraiths past—they had been exchanged for Shadowen. But what were these Shadowen that men should require the aid of Druids and magic? Could not men take it upon themselves to deal with the ills of the world rather than defer to power they scarcely understood? Magic carried grief as well as joy, its dark side as apt to influence and change as its light. Bring it back again, should he, only to give it to men who had repeatedly demonstrated that they were incapable of mastering its truths?

How could he?

Yet without it, the world might become the vision Allanon's shade had shown them—a nightmare of fire and darkness in which only creatures such as the Shadowen belonged. Perhaps it was true after all that magic was the only means of keeping the Races safe against such beings.

Perhaps.

The truth of the matter was that he simply didn't want to be part of what was to happen. He was not a child of the Races of the Four Lands, not in body or in spirit, and never had been. He had no empathy with their men and women. He had no place among them. He had been cursed with magic of his own, and it had stripped him of his humanity and his place among humans and isolated him from every other living thing. Ironic, because he alone had no fear of the Shadowen. Perhaps he could even protect against them, were he asked to do so. But he would not be asked. He was as much feared as they. He was the Dark Uncle, the descendent of Brin Ohmsford, the bearer of her seed and her trust, keeper of some nameless charge from Allanon . . .

Except, of course, that the charge was nameless no more. The charge was revealed. He was to bring back Paranor and the Druids, out of the void of yesteryear, out of the nothingness.

That was what the shade had demanded of him, and the demand tracked relentlessly through the landscape of his mind, hurdling arguments, circumventing reason, whispering that it was and therefore must be.

So he worried the matter as a dog would its bone, and the days dragged by. The storms passed and the sun returned to bake the plains dry but leave the forestlands weltering in the heat and damp. He went out after a time, walking the valley floor with only Rumor for company, the giant moor cat having wandered down out of the rain forests east with the changing of the weather, luminous eyes as depthless as the despair the Dark Uncle felt. The cat gave him companionship, but offered no solution to his dilemma and no relief from his brooding. They walked and sat together as the days and nights passed, and time hung suspended against a backdrop of events taking place beyond their refuge that neither could know nor see.

Until, on the same night that Par Ohmsford and his companions were betrayed in their attempt to lay hands upon the Sword of Shannara, Cogline returned to the valley of Hearthstone and the illusion of separateness that Walker had worked so hard to maintain was shattered. It was late evening, the sun had gone west, the skies were washed with moonlight and filled with stars, and the summer air was sweet and clean with the smell of new growth. Walker was coming back from a visit to the pinnacle, a refuge he found particularly soothing, the massive stone a source from which it seemed he could draw strength. The cottage door was open and the rooms within lighted as always, but Walker sensed the difference, even before Rumor's purr stilled and his neck ruff bristled.

Cautiously, he moved onto the porch and into the doorway.

Cogline sat at the old wooden dining table, skeletal face bent against the glare of the oil lamps, his gray robes a weathered covering for goods long since past repair. A large, squarish package bound in oilcloth and tied with cord rested close beside him. He was eating cold food, a glass of ale almost untouched at his elbow.

"I have been waiting for you, Walker," he told the other while he was still in the darkness beyond the entry.

Walker moved into the light. "You might have saved yourself the trouble."

"Trouble?" The old man extended a sticklike hand, and Rumor padded forward to nuzzle it familiarly. "It was time I saw my home again."

"Is this your home?" Walker asked. "I would have thought you more comfortable amid the relics of the Druid past." He waited for a response, but there was none. "If you have come to persuade me to take up the charge given me by the shade, then you should know at once that I will never do so."

"Oh, my, Walker. Never is such an impossible amount of time. Besides, I have no intention of trying to persuade you to do anything. A sufficient amount of persuading has already been done, I suspect."

Walker was still standing in the doorway. He felt awkward and exposed and moved over to the table to sit across from Cogline. The old man took a long sip of the ale.

"Perhaps you thought me gone for good after my disappearance at the Hadeshorn," he said softly. His voice was distant and filled with emotions that the other could not begin to sort out. "Perhaps you even wished it."

Walker said nothing.

"I have been out into the world, Walker. I have traveled into the Four Lands, walked among the Races, passed through cities and countrysides; I have felt the pulse of life and found that it ebbs. A farmer speaks to me on the grasslands below the Streleheim, a man worn and broken by the futility of what he has encountered. 'Nothing grows,' he whispers. 'The earth sickens as if stricken by some disease.' The disease infects him as well. A merchant of wooden carvings and toys journeys from a small village beyond Varfleet, directionless. 'I leave,' he says, 'because there is no need for me. The people cease to have interest in my work. They do nothing but brood and waste away.' Bits and pieces of life in the Four Lands, Walker— they wither and fade like a spotting that spreads across the flesh. Pockets here and pockets there—as if the will to go on were missing. Trees and shrubs and growing things fail; animals and men alike sicken and die. All become dust, and a haze of that dust rises up and fills the air and leaves the whole of the ravaged land a still life in miniature of the vision shown us by Allanon."

The sharp, old eyes squinted up at the other. "It begins, Walker. It begins."

Walker Boh shook his head. "The land and her people have always suffered failings, Cogline. You see the shade's vision because you want to see it."

"No, not I, Walker." The old man shook his head firmly. "I want no part of Druid visions, neither in their being nor in their fulfillment. I am as much a pawn of what has happened as yourself. Believe what you will, I do not wish involvement. I have chosen my life in the same manner that you have chosen yours. You don't accept that, do you?"

Walker smiled unkindly. "You took up the magic because you wished to. Once-Druid, you had a choice in your life. You dabbled in a mixture of old sciences and magics because they interested you. Not so myself. I was born with a legacy I would have been better born without. The magic was forced upon me without my consent. I use it because I have no choice. It is a millstone that would drag me down. I do not deceive myself. It has made my life a ruin." The dark eyes were bitter. "Do not attempt to compare us, Cogline."

The other's thin frame shifted. "Harsh words, Walker Boh. You were eager enough to accept my teaching in the use of that magic once upon a time. You felt comfortable enough with it then to learn its secrets."

"A matter of survival and nothing more. I was a child trapped in a

Druid's monstrous casting. I used you to keep myself alive. You were all I had." The white skin of his lean face was taut with bitterness. "Do not look to me for thanks, Cogline. I haven't the grace for it."

Cogline stood up suddenly, a whiplash movement that belied his fragile appearance. He towered above the dark-robed figure seated across from him, and there was a forbidding look to his weathered face. "Poor Walker," he whispered. "You still deny who you are. You deny your very existence. How long can you keep up this pretense?"

There was a strained silence between them that seemed endless. Rumor, curled on a rug before the fire at the far end of the room, looked up expectantly. An ember from the hearth spat and snapped, filling the air with a shower of sparks.

"Why have you come, old man?" Walker Boh said finally, the words a barely contained thrust of rage. There was a coppery taste in his mouth that he knew came not from anger, but from fear.

"To try to help you," Cogline said. There was no irony in his voice. "To give you direction in your brooding."

"I am content without your interference."

"Content?" The other shook his head. "No, Walker. You will never be content until you learn to quit fighting yourself. You work so hard at it. I thought that the lessons you received from me on the uses of the magic might have weaned you away from such childishness—but it appears I was wrong. You face hard lessons, Walker. Maybe you won't survive them."

He shoved the heavy parcel across the table at the other man. "Open it."

Walker hesitated, his eyes locked on the offering. Then he reached out, snapped apart the binding with a flick of his fingers and pulled back the oilcloth.

He found himself looking at a massive, leatherbound book elaborately engraved in gold. He reached out and touched it experimentally, lifted the cover, peered momentarily inside, then flinched away from it as if his fingers had been burned.

"Yes, Walker. It is one of the missing Druid Histories, a single volume only." The wrinkled old face was intense.

"Where did you get it?" Walker demanded harshly.

Cogline bent close. The air seemed filled with the sound of his breathing. "Out of lost Paranor."

Walker Boh came slowly to his feet. "You lie."

"Do I? Look into my eyes and tell me what you see."

Walker flinched away. He was shaking. "I don't care where you got it— or what fantasies you have concocted to make me believe what I know in my heart cannot possibly be so! Take it back to where you got it or let it sink into the bogs! I'll have no part of it!"

Cogline shook his wispy head. "No, Walker, I'll not take it back. I carried it out of a realm of yesterdays filled with gray haze and death to give to you. I am not your tormentor—never that! I am the closest thing to a friend you will ever know, even if you cannot yet accept it!" The weathered face softened. "I said before that I came to help you. It is so. Read the book, Walker. There are truths in there that need learning."

"I will not!" the other cried furiously.

Cogline stared at the younger man for long minutes, then sighed. "As you will. But the book remains. Read it or not, the choice is yours. Destroy it even, if you wish." He drained off the remainder of his ale, set the glass carefully on the table, and looked down at his gnarled hands. "I am finished here."

He came around the table and stood before the other. "Goodbye, Walker. I would stay if it would help. I would give you whatever it is within my power to give you if you would take it. But you are not yet ready. Another day, perhaps."

He turned then and disappeared into the night. He did not look back as he went. He did not deviate from his course. Walker Boh watched him fade away, a shadow gone back into the darkness that had made him.

The cottage, as if by his going, turned empty and still.

"It will be dangerous, Par," Damson Rhee whispered. "If there were a safer way, I should snatch it up in an instant."

Par Ohmsford said nothing. They were deep within the People's Park once more, crouched in the shadows of a grove of cedar just beyond the broad splash of light cast by the lamps of the Gatehouse. It was midway toward dawn, the deepest, fullest hours of sleep, when everything slowed to a crawl amid dreams and rememberings. The Gatehouse rose up against the moonlit darkness like massive blocks stacked one upon the other by a careless child. Barred windows and bolted doors were shallow indentations in a skin made rough and coarse by weather and time. The walls warding the ravine ran off to either side and the crossing bridge stretched away behind, a spider web connecting to the tumbledown ruin of the old palace. A watch had been stationed before the main entry where a pair of matched iron portals stood closed behind a hinged grate of bars. The watch dozed on its feet, barely awake in the enveloping stillness. No sound or movement from the Gatehouse disturbed their rest.

"Can you remember enough of him to conjure up a likeness?" Damson asked, her words a brush of softness against his ear. Par nodded. It was not likely he would ever forget the face of Rimmer Dall.

She was quiet a moment. "If we are stopped, keep their attention focused on yourself. I will deal with any threats."

He nodded once more. They waited, motionless within their concealment, listening to the stillness, thinking their separate thoughts. Par was frightened and filled with doubts, but he was mostly determined. Damson and he were the only real chance Coll and the others had. They would succeed in this risky business because they must.

The Gate watch came awake as those patrolling the west wall of the park appeared out of the night. The guards greeted each other casually, spoke for a time, and then the watch from the east wall appeared as well. A flask was passed around, pipes were smoked, and then the guards dispersed. The patrols disappeared east and west. The Gate watch resumed their station.

"Not yet," Damson whispered as Par shifted expectantly.

The minutes dragged by. The solitude that had shrouded the Gatehouse earlier returned anew. The guards yawned and shifted. One leaned wearily on the haft of his poleaxe.

"Now," Damson Rhee said. She caught the Valeman by the shoulder and leaned into him. Her lips brushed his cheek. "Luck to us, Par Ohmsford."

Then they were up and moving. They crossed into the circle of light boldly, striding out of the shadows as if they were at home in them, coming toward the Gatehouse from the direction of the city. Par was already singing, weaving the wishsong's spell through the night's stillness, filling the minds of the watch with the images he wished them to see.

What they saw were two Seekers cloaked in forbidding black, the taller of the two First Seeker Rimmer Dall.

They snapped to attention immediately, eyes forward, barely looking at the two who approached. Par kept his voice even, the magic weaving a constant spell of disguise in the minds of the willing men.

"Open!" Damson Rhee snapped perfunctorily as they reached the Gatehouse entry.

The guards could not comply quickly enough. They pulled back the hinged grate, released the outer locks, and hammered anxiously on the doors to alert the guards within. A tiny door opened and Par shifted the focus of his concentration slightly. Bleary eyes peered out in grouchy curiosity, widened, and the locks released. The doors swung back, and Par and Damson pushed inside.

They stood in a wardroom filled with weapons stacked in wall racks and stunned Federation soldiers. The soldiers had been playing cards and drinking, clearly convinced the night's excitement was over. They were caught off guard by the appearance of the Seekers and it showed. Par filled the room with the faint hum of the wishsong, blanketing it momentarily with his magic. It took everything he had.

Damson understood how tenuous was his hold. "Everyone out!" she ordered, her voice flinty with anger.

The room emptied instantly. The entire squad dispersed through adjoining doors and disappeared as if formed of smoke. One guard remained, apparently the senior watch officer. He stood uncertainly, stiffly, eyes averted, wishing he were anywhere else but where he was, yet unable to go.

"Take us to the prisoners," Damson said softly, standing at the man's left shoulder.

The soldier cleared his throat after trying futilely to speak. "I'll need my commander's permission," he ventured. Some small sense of responsibility for his assigned duty yet remained to him.

Damson kept her eyes fixed on the man's ear, forcing him thereby to look elsewhere. "Where is your commander?" she asked.

"Sleeping below," the man answered. "I'll wake him."

"No." Damson stayed his effort to depart. "We'll wake him together."

They went through a heavily bolted door directly across the room and started down a stairwell dimly lit by oil lamps. Par kept the wishsong's music lingering in the frightened guard's ears, teasing him with it, letting him see them as much bigger than life and much more threatening. It was all going as planned, the charade working exactly as Damson and he had hoped. Down the empty stairs they went, circling from landing to landing, the thudding of their boots the only sound in the hollow silence. At the bottom of the well there were two doors. The one on the left was open and led into a lighted corridor. The guard took them through that door to another, stopped and knocked. When there was no response, he knocked again, sharply.

"What is it, drat you?" a voice snapped.

"Open up at once, Commander!" Damson replied in a voice so cold it made even Par shiver.

There was a fumbling about and the door opened. The Federation commander with the short-cropped hair and the unpleasant eyes stood there, his tunic half buttoned. Shock registered on his face instantly as the wishsong's magic took hold. He saw the Seekers. Worse, he saw Rimmer Dall.

He gave up trying to button his clothing and came quickly into the hall. "I didn't expect anyone this soon. I'm sorry. Is there a problem?"

"We'll discuss it later, Commander," Damson said severely. "For now, take us to the prisoners."

For just an instant there was a flicker of doubt in the other man's eyes, a shading of worry that perhaps everything was not quite right. Par tightened the hold of the magic on the man's mind, giving him a glimpse of the terror that awaited him should he question the order. That glimpse was enough. The commander hastened back down the corridor to the stairwell, produced a key from a ring at his waist, and opened the second door.

They stepped into a passageway lit by a single lamp hung next to the door. The commander took the lamp in hand and led the way forward. Damson followed. Par motioned the watch officer ahead of him and brought up the rear. His voice was beginning to grow weary from the effort of maintaining the charade. It was more difficult to project to several different points. He should have sent the second man away.

The passageway was constructed of stone block and smelled of mold and decay. Par realized that they were underground, apparently beneath the ravine. Things of considerable size darted from the light, and there were streaks of phosphorescence and dampness in the stone.

They had only gone a short distance when they came to the cells, a collection of low-ceilinged cages, not high enough for a man to stand in, dusty and cobwebbed, the doors constructed of rusted iron bars. The entire company was crammed into the first of these, crouched or sitting on a stone slab floor. Eyes blinked in disbelief, widened as the lie of the magic played hide-and-seek with the truth. Coll knew what was going on. He was already on his feet, pushing to the door, motioning the others up with him. Even Padishar obeyed the gesture, realizing what was about to happen.

"Open the door," Damson ordered.

Again, the eyes of the Federation commander registered his misgivings.

"Open the door, Commander," Damson repeated impatiently. "Now!"

The commander fumbled for a second key within the cluster at his belt, inserted it into the lock and turned. The cell door swung open. Instantly, Padishar Creel had the astonished man's neck in his hands, tightening his grip until the other could scarcely breathe. The watch officer stumbled back, turned, tried unsuccessfully to run over Par, was caught from behind by Morgan, and hammered into unconsciousness.

The prisoners crowded into the narrow passageway, greeting Par and Damson with handclasps and smiles. Padishar paid them no heed. His attention was focused entirely on the hapless Federation commander.

"Who betrayed us?" he said with an impatient hiss.

The commander struggled to free himself, his face turning bright red from the pressure on his throat.

"It was one of us, you said! Who?"

The commander choked. "Don't . . . know. Never saw . . ."

Padishar shook him. "Don't lie to me!"

"Never . . . Just a . . . message."

"Who was it?" Padishar insisted, the cords on the back of his hands gone white and hard.

The terrified man kicked out violently, and Padishar slammed his head sharply against the stone wall. The commander went limp, sagging like a rag doll.

Damson pulled Padishar about. "Enough of this," she said evenly, ignoring the fury that still burned in the other's eyes. "We're wasting time. He clearly doesn't know. Let's get out of here. There's been enough risk-taking for one day."

The outlaw chief studied her wordlessly for a moment, then let the unconscious man drop. "I'll find out anyway, I promise you," he swore.

Par had never seen anyone so angry. But Damson ignored it. She turned and motioned for Par to get moving. The Valeman led the way back up the stairwell, the others trailing behind him in a staggered line. They had devised no plan for getting out again when they had made the decision to come after their friends. They had decided that it would be best simply to take what opportunity offered and make do.

Opportunity gave them everything they needed this night. The wardroom was empty when they reached it, and they moved swiftly to pass through. Only Morgan paused, rummaging through the weapons racks until he had located the confiscated Sword of Leah. Smiling grimly, he strapped it across his back and went after the others.

Their luck held. The guards outside were overpowered before they knew what was happening. All about, the night was silent, the park empty, the patrols still completing their rounds, the city asleep. The members of the little band melted into the shadows and vanished.

As they hurried away, Damson swung Par around and gave him a brilliant smile and a kiss full on the mouth. The kiss was hungry and filled with promise.

Later, when there was time to reflect, Par Ohmsford savored that moment. Yet it was not Damson's kiss that he remembered most from the events of that night. It was the fact that the magic of the wishsong had proved useful at last.

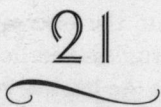

The Druid History became for Walker Boh a challenge that he was determined to win.

For three days after Cogline's departure, Walker ignored the book. He left it on the dining table, still settled amid its oilcloth wrappings and broken binding cord, its burnished leather cover collecting motes of dust and gleaming faintly in sunshine and lamplight. He disdained it, going about his business as if it weren't there, pretending it was a part of his surroundings that he could not remove, testing himself against its temptation. He had thought at first to rid himself of it immediately, then decided against it. That would be too easy and too quickly second-guessed later on. If he could withstand its lure for a time, if he could live in its presence without giving in to his understandable desire to uncover its secrets, then he could dispose of it with a clean conscience. Cogline expected him either to open it or dispose of it at once. He would do neither. The old man would get no satisfaction in his efforts to manipulate Walker Boh.

The only one who paid any attention to the parcel was Rumor, who sniffed at it from time to time but otherwise ignored it. The three days passed and the book sat unopened.

But then something odd happened. On the fourth day of this strange contest, Walker began to question his reasoning. Did it really make any better sense to dispose of the book after a week or even a month than it did to dispose of it immediately? Would it matter either way? What did it demonstrate other than a sort of perverse hardheadedness on his part? What sort of game was he playing and for whose benefit was he playing it?

Walker mulled the matter over as the daylight hours waned and darkness closed about, then sat staring at the book from across the room while the fire in the hearth burned slowly to ash and the midnight hour neared.

"I am not being strong," he whispered to himself. "I am being frightened."

He considered the possibility in the silence of his thoughts. Finally he stood up, crossed the room to the dining table and stopped. For a moment, he hesitated. Then he reached down and picked up the Druid History. He hefted it experimentally.

Better to know the Demon that pursues you than to continue to imagine him.

He crossed back to his reading chair and seated himself once more, the book settled on his lap. Rumor lifted his massive head from where he slept in front of the fire, and his luminous eyes fixed on Walker. Walker stared back. The cat blinked and went back to sleep.

Walker Boh opened the book.

He read it slowly, working his way through its thick parchment pages with deliberate pacing, letting his eyes linger on the gold edges and ornate calligraphy, determined that now that the book was opened nothing should be missed. The silence after midnight deepened, broken only by an occasional throaty sound from the sleeping moor cat and the snapping of embers in the fire. Only once he thought to wonder how Cogline had really come by the book—surely not out of Paranor!—and then the matter was forgotten as the recorded history caught him up and swept him away as surely as if he were a leaf upon a windswept ocean.

The time chronicled was that of Bremen when he was among the last of the Druids, when the Warlock Lord and his minions had destroyed nearly all of the members of the Council. There were stories of the dark magic that had changed the rebel Druids into the horrors they had become. There were accounts of its varied uses, conjurings, and incantations that Bremen had uncovered but had been smart enough to fear. All of the frightening secrets of what the magic could do were touched upon, interspersed with the cautions that so many who tried to master the power would ignore. It was a time of upheaval and frightening change in the Four Lands, and Bremen alone had understood what was at stake.

Walker paged ahead, growing anxious now. Cogline had meant for him to read something particular within this history. Whatever it was, he had not yet come upon it.

The Skull Bearers had seized Paranor for themselves, the chronicles related. Paranor, they had thought, would now be their home. But the Warlock Lord had felt threatened there, wary of latent magic within the stones of the Keep, within the depths of the earth where the furnaces beneath the castle fortress burned. So he had called the Skull Bearers to him and gone north . . .

Walker frowned. He had forgotten that part. For a time Paranor had been abandoned completely when it could have belonged to the rebels. After all, the Second War of the Races had dragged on for years.

He paged ahead once more, skimming the words, searching without knowing exactly what it was he was searching for. He had forgotten his resolve of earlier, his promise to himself that he was not to be caught up in Cogline's snare. His curiosity and intellect were too demanding to be stayed by caution. There were secrets here that no man had set eyes upon for hundreds of years, knowledge that only the Druids had enjoyed, dispensing it to the Races as they perceived necessary and never otherwise. Such power! How long had it been hidden from everyone but Allanon, and before him Bremen, and before him Galaphile and the first Druids, and before them . . . ?

He stopped reading, aware suddenly that the flow of the narrative had changed. The script had turned smaller, more precise. There were odd markings amid the words, runes that symbolized gestures.

Walker Boh went cold to his bones. The silence that enveloped the room became enormous, an unending, suffocating ocean.

Shades! he whispered in the darkest corner of his mind. *It is the invocation for the magic that sealed away Paranor!*

His breathing sounded harsh in his own ears as he forced his eyes away from the book. His pale face was taut. This was what Cogline had meant for him to find—why, he didn't know—but this was it. Now that he had found it, he wondered if he might not be better off closing the book at once.

But that was the fear whispering in his ear again, he knew.

He lowered his eyes once more and began to read. The spell was there, the invocation of magic that Allanon had used three hundred years ago to close away Paranor from the world of men. He found to his surprise that he understood it. His training with Cogline was more complete than he would have imagined. He finished the narrative of the spell and turned the page.

There was a single paragraph. It read:

Once removed, Paranor shall remain lost to the world of men for the whole of time, sealed away and invisible within its casting. One magic alone has the power to return it—that singular Elfstone that is colored Black and was conceived by the faerie people of the old world in the manner and form of all Elfstones, combining nevertheless in one stone alone the necessary properties of heart, mind, and body. Whosoever shall have cause and right shall wield it to its proper end.

That was all it said. Walker read on, found that the subject matter abruptly changed and skipped back. He read the paragraph again, slowly, searching for anything he might have missed. There was no question in his mind that this was what Cogline had meant for him to find. A Black Elfstone. A magic that could retrieve lost Paranor. The means to the end of the charge that the shade of Allanon had given him.

Bring back Paranor and restore the Druids. He could hear again the words of the charge in his mind.

Of course, there were no longer any Druids. But maybe Allanon intended that Cogline should take up the cause, once Paranor was restored. It seemed logical despite the old man's protestations that his time was past—

but Walker was astute enough to recognize that where Druids and their magics were concerned logic often traveled a tortuous path.

He was two-thirds of the way through the history. He spent another hour finishing it, found nothing further that he believed was intended for him, and turned back again to the paragraph on the Black Elfstone. Dawn was creeping out of the east, a faint golden light in the dark horizon. Walker rubbed his eyes, and tried to think. Why was there so little digression on the purpose and properties of this magic? What did it look like and what could it do? It was a single stone instead of three—why? How was it that no one had ever heard of it before?

The questions buzzed around inside his head like trapped flies, annoying and at the same time intriguing him. He read the paragraph several times more—read it, in fact, until he could recite it from memory—and closed the book. Rumor stretched and yawned on the floor in front of him, lifted his head and blinked.

Talk to me, cat, Walker thought. *There are always secrets that only a cat knows. Maybe this is one of them.*

But Rumor only got up and went outside, disappearing into the fading shadows.

Walker fell asleep then and did not come awake again until midday. He rose, bathed and dressed anew, ate a slow meal with the closed book in front of him, and went out for a long walk. He passed south through the valley to a favorite glade where a stream rippled noisily over a meandering rock bed and emptied into a pool that contained tiny fish colored brilliant red and blue. He lingered there for a time, thinking, then returned again to the cottage. He sat on the porch and watched the sun creep westward in a haze of purple and scarlet.

"I should never have opened the book," he chided himself softly, for its mystery had proven irresistible after all. "I should have bound it back up and dropped it into the deepest hole I could find."

But it was too late for that. He had read it and knowledge acquired could not be readily forgotten. A sense of futility mingled with anger. He had thought it impossible that Paranor could be restored. Now he knew that there was a magic that could do exactly that. Once again, there was that sense of the inevitability of things prophesied by the Druids.

Still, his life was his own, wasn't it? He needn't accept the charge of Allanon's shade, whatever its viability.

But his curiosity was relentless. He found himself thinking of the Black Elfstone, even when he tried not to. The Black Elfstone was out there, somewhere, a forgotten magic. Where? Where was it?

That and all the other questions pressed in about him as the evening passed. He ate his dinner, walked again for a time, read from the few precious books of his own library, wrote a bit in his journal, and mostly thought of that single, beguiling paragraph on the magic that would bring back Paranor.

He thought about it as he prepared for bed.

He was still thinking about it as midnight approached.

Teasingly, insinuatingly, it wormed about restlessly inside his mind, suggesting this possibility and that, opening doors just a crack into unlighted rooms, hinting at understandings and insights that would bring him the knowledge he could not help but crave.

And with it, perhaps, peace of mind.

His sleep was troubled and restless. The mystery of the Black Elfstone was an irritation that would not be dispelled.

By morning, he had decided that he must do something about it.

Par Ohmsford came awake that morning with a decision of his own to make. It had been five days since Damson and he had rescued Coll, Morgan, Padishar Creel, and the other two outlaws from the cells of the Federation Gatehouse, and the bunch of them had been on the run ever since. They had not attempted to leave the city, certain that the gates would be closely watched and the risk of discovery too great. They had not returned to the basement of the weapons-maker's shop either, feeling that it might have been compromised by their mysterious betrayer. Instead, they had skipped from one shelter to the next, never remaining more than one night, posting guards throughout their brief stay at each, jumping at every sound they heard and every shadow they saw.

Well, enough was enough. Par had decided that he was through running.

He rose from the makeshift bed he occupied in the attic of the grain house and glanced over at Coll next to him, who was still asleep. The others were already up and presumably downstairs in the main warehouse, which was closed until the beginning of the work week. Gingerly he crossed to the tiny, shuttered window that let in what small amount of light the room enjoyed and peered out. The street below was empty except for a stray dog sniffing at a refuse bin and a beggar sleeping in the door of the tin factory across the way. Clouds hung low and gray across the skies, threatening rain before the close of the day.

When he crossed back to pull on his boots, he found Coll awake and looking at him. His brother's coarse hair was ruffled and his eyes were clouded with sleep and disgruntlement.

"Ho-hum, another day," Coll muttered and then yawned hugely. "What fascinating storage room will we be visiting today, do you suppose?"

"None, as far as I'm concerned." Par dropped down beside him.

Coll's eyebrows arched. "That so? Have you told Padishar?"

"I'm on my way."

"I suppose you have an alternative in mind—to hiding out, that is." Coll pushed himself up on one elbow. "Because I don't think Padishar Creel is going to give you the time of day if you don't. He hasn't been in the best of moods since he found out he might not be as well-loved among his men as he thought he was."

Par doubted that Padishar Creel ever had allowed himself to become
deluded enough to believe that he was well-loved by his men, but Coll was
certainly right enough about the outlaw chief's present temperament. His
betrayal at the hands of one of his own men had left him taciturn and bitter. He had retreated somewhere deep inside himself these several days past,
still clearly in command as he led them through the network of Federation
patrols and checkpoints that had been thrown out across the city, still able
to find them refuge when it seemed there could be none, but at the same
time had become uncharacteristically withdrawn from everyone about him.
Damson Rhee had come with them, whether by choice or not Par still
wasn't sure, but even she could not penetrate the defenses the outlaw chief
had thrown up around himself. Except for exercising his authority as leader,
Padishar had removed himself from them as surely as if he were no longer
physically present.

Par shook his head. "Well, we have to do something besides simply hop
about from place to place for the rest of our lives." He was feeling rather
sullen about matters himself. "If there's a need for a plan, Padishar should
come up with one. Nothing's being accomplished the way things stand
now."

Coll sat up and began dressing. "You probably don't want to hear this,
Par, but it may be time to rethink this whole business of allying ourselves
with the Movement. We might be better off on our own again."

Par said nothing. They finished dressing and went downstairs to find
the others. There was cold bread, jam, and fruit for breakfast, and they ate
it hungrily. Par could not understand how he could be so famished after
doing so little. He listened as he ate to Stasas and Drutt compare notes on
hunting in the forests of their respective homes somewhere below Varfleet.
Morgan was keeping watch by the doors leading into the warehouse and
Coll went to join him. Damson Rhee sat on an empty packing crate
nearby, carving something. He had seen little of her during the past several
days; she was often out with Padishar, scouting the city while the rest of
them hid.

Padishar was nowhere to be seen.

After eating, Par went back upstairs to gather his things together, anticipating that, whatever the result of his confrontation with Padishar, it
would likely involve a move.

Damson followed him up. "You grow restless," she observed when they
were alone. She seated herself on the edge of his pallet, shaking back her
reddish mane. "An outlaw's life is not what you had in mind, is it?"

He smiled faintly. "Sitting about in warehouses and basements isn't
what I had in mind. What is Padishar waiting around for?"

She shrugged. "What we all wait around for from time to time—that
little voice buried somewhere deep inside that tells us what to do next. It
might be intuition or it might be common sense or then again it might be
the advent of circumstances beyond our control." She gave him a wicked
smile. "Is it speaking now to you?"

"Something certainly is." He sat down next to her. "Why are you still here, Damson? Does Padishar keep you?"

She laughed. "Hardly. I come and go as I please. He knows I was not the one who betrayed him. Or you, I think."

"Then why stay?"

She considered him thoughtfully for a moment. "Maybe I stay because you interest me," she said at last. She paused as if she wanted to say more, but thought better of it. She smiled. "I have never met anyone who uses real magic. Just the pretend kind, like me."

She reached up and deftly plucked a coin from behind his ear. It was carved from cherry wood. She handed it to him. It bore her likeness on one side and his on the other. He looked up at her in surprise. "That's very good."

"Thank you." He thought she colored slightly. "You may keep it with the other for good luck."

He tucked the coin into his pocket. They sat silent for a time, exchanging uncertain glances. "There isn't much difference, you know, between your kind of magic and mine," he said finally. "They both rely on illusion."

She shook her head. "No, Par. You are wrong. One is an acquired skill, the other innate. Mine is learned and, once learned, has become all it can. Yours is constantly growing, and its lessons are limitless. Don't you see? My magic is a trade, a way to make a living. Your magic is much more; it is a gift around which you must build your life."

She smiled, but there was a hint of sadness in it. She stood up. "I have work to do. Finish your packing." She moved past him and disappeared down the ladder.

The morning hours crawled past and still Padishar did not return. Par busied himself doing nothing, growing anxious for something—anything—to happen. Coll and Morgan drifted over from time to time, and he spoke to them of his intention to confront the outlaw chief. Neither seemed very optimistic about his chances.

The skies grew more threatening, the wind picking up until it made a rather mournful howl about the loose-fitting jambs and shutters of the old building they were housed in, but still it didn't rain. Card games were played to pass the time and topics of conversation exhausted.

It was nearing midafternoon when Padishar returned. He slipped in through the front doors without a word, crossed the room to Par, and motioned him to follow. He took the Valeman into a small office situated at the back of the main floor and shut the door behind them.

When they were alone, he seemed at a loss for words.

"I have been thinking rather carefully about what we should do," he said finally. "Or, if you prefer, what we should not do. Any mistake we make now could be our last."

He pulled Par over to a bench that had been shoved back against the wall and sat them both down. "There's the problem of this traitor," he said quietly. His eyes were bright and hard with something Par couldn't read. "I was certain at first that it must be one of us. But it isn't me or Damson. Damson is above suspicion. It isn't you. It might be your brother; but it isn't him either, is it?"

He made it a statement of fact rather than a question. Par shook his head in agreement.

"Or the Highlander."

Par shook his head a second time.

"That leaves Ciba Blue, Stasas, and Drutt. Blue is likely dead; that means that if he's the one, he was stupid enough to let himself get killed in the bargain. Doesn't sound like Blue. And the other two have been with me almost from the first. It is inconceivable that either of them would betray me—whatever the price offered or the reason supplied. Their hatred of the Federation is nearly a match for my own."

The muscles in his jaw tightened. "So perhaps it isn't any of us after all. But who else could have discovered our plan? Do you see what I mean? Your friend the Highlander mentioned this morning something he had almost forgotten. When we first came into the city and went down to the market stalls, he thought he saw Hirehone. He thought then he was mistaken; now he wonders. Forgetting momentarily the fact that Hirehone held my life in his hands any number of times before this and did not betray me, how would he have gone about doing so now? No one, outside of Damson and those I brought with me, knew the where, when, how, or why of what we were about. Yet those Federation soldiers were waiting for us. They knew."

Par had forgotten momentarily his plan to tell Padishar he was fed up with matters. "Then who was it?" he asked eagerly. "Who could it have been?"

Padishar's smile was forced. "The question plagues me like flies a sweating horse. I don't know yet. You may rest assured that sooner or later I will. For the moment, it doesn't matter. We have bigger fish to fry."

He leaned forward. "I spent the morning with a man I know, a man who has access to what happens within the higher circles of Federation authority in Tyrsis. He is a man I am certain of, one I can trust. Even Damson doesn't know of him. He told me some interesting things. It seems that you and Damson came to my rescue just in time. Rimmer Dall arrived early the next morning to see personally to my questioning and ultimate disposal." The outlaw chief's voice emitted a sigh of satisfaction. "He was very disappointed to find I had left early."

Padishar shifted his weight and brought his head close to Par's. "I know you are impatient for something to happen, Par. I can read the signs of it in you as if you were a notice posted on the wall by my bed. But haste results in an early demise in this line of work, so caution is always necessary." He smiled again. "But you and I, lad—we're a force to be reckoned with in this business of the Federation and their game-playing. Fate brought you to me, and she has something definite in mind for the two of us, something that will shake the Federation and their Coalition Council and their Seekers and all the rest right to the foundation of their being!"

One hand clenched before Par's face, and the Valeman flinched back in spite of himself. "So much effort has been put into hiding all traces of the old People's Park—the Bridge of Sendic destroyed and rebuilt, the old park walled away, guards running all about it like ants at a picnic dinner! Why? Because there's something down there that they don't want anyone to know about! I can feel it, lad! I am as convinced of it now as I was when we went in five nights ago!"

"The Sword of Shannara?" Par whispered.

Padishar's smile was genuine this time. "I'd stake ten years of my life on it! But there's still only one way to find out, isn't there?"

He brought his hands up to grip Par's shoulders. The weathered, sharp-boned face was a mask of cunning and ruthless determination. The man who had led them for the past five days had disappeared; this was the old Padishar Creel speaking.

"The man I spoke to, the one who has ears in the Federation chambers, tells me that Rimmer Dall believes we've fled. He thinks us back within the Parma Key. Whatever we came here for we've given up on, he's decided. He lingers in the city only because he has not decided what needs doing next. I suggest we give him some direction, young Par."

Par's eyes widened. "What . . . ?"

"What he least expects, of course!" Padishar anticipated his question and pounced on it. "The last thing he and his black-cloaked wolves will look for—that's what!" His eyes narrowed. "We'll go back down into the Pit!"

Par quit breathing.

"We'll go back down before they have a chance to figure out where we are or what we intend, back down into that most carefully guarded hidey-hole, and if the Sword of Shannara is there, why, we'll snatch it away from under their very noses!"

He brought an astonished Par to his feet with a jerk. "And we'll do it tonight!"

22

It was nearing twilight by the time Walker Boh reached his destination. He had been journeying northward from Hearthstone since midmorning, traveling at a comfortable pace, not hurrying, allowing himself adequate time to think through what he was about to do. The skies had been

clear and filled with sunshine when he had set out, but as the day lengthened toward evening clouds began to drift in from the west and the air
turned dense and gray. The land through which he traveled was rugged, a
series of twisting ridges and drops that broke apart the symmetry of the
forests and left the trees leaning and bent like spikes driven randomly into
the earth. Deadwood and outcroppings of rock blocked the trail repeatedly
and mist hung shroudlike in the trees, trapped there it seemed, unmoving.

Walker stopped. He stared downward between two massive, jagged
ridgelines into a narrow valley that cradled a tiny lake. The lake was barely
visible, screened away by pine trees and a thick concentration of mist that
clung tenaciously above its surface, swirling sluggishly, listlessly, haphazardly
in the nearly windless expanse.

The lake was the home of the Grimpond.

Walker did not pause long, starting down into the valley almost immediately. The mist closed quickly about him as he went, filling his mouth
with its metallic taste, clouding his vision of what lay ahead. He ignored the
sensations that attacked him—the pressing closeness, the imagined whispers, the discomfiting deadness—and kept his concentration focused on
putting one foot in front of the other. The air grew quickly cool, a damp
layer against his skin that smelled of things decayed. The pines rose up
about him, their numbers increasing until there was nowhere they did not
stand watch. Silence cloaked the valley and there was only the soft scrape of
his boots against the stone.

He could feel the eyes of the Grimpond watching.

It had been a long time.

Cogline had warned him early about the Grimpond. The Grimpond
was the shade that lived in the lake below, a shade older than the world of
the Four Lands itself. It claimed to predate the Great Wars. It boasted that it
had been alive in the age of faerie. As with all shades, it had the ability to
divine secrets hidden from the living. There was magic at its command. But
it was a bitter and spiteful creature, trapped in this world for all eternity for
reasons no one knew. It could not die and it hated the substanceless, empty
existence it was forced to endure. It vented itself on the humans who came
to speak with it, teasing them with riddles of the truths they sought to uncover, taunting them with their mortality, showing them more of what
they would keep hidden than what they would reveal.

Brin Ohmsford had come to the Grimpond three hundred years earlier
to find a way into the Maelmord so that she might confront the Ildatch.
The shade toyed with her until she used the wishsong to ensnare it by trickery, forcing it to reveal what she wished to discover. The shade had never
forgotten that; it was the only time a human had bested it. Walker had heard
the story any number of times while growing up. It was only after he came
north to Hearthstone to live, forsaking the Ohmsford name and legacy, that
he discovered that the Grimpond was waiting for him. Brin Ohmsford
might be dead and gone, but the Grimpond was alive forever and it had determined that someone must be made to pay for its humiliation. If not the

one directly responsible, why, then another of that one's bloodline would do nicely.

Cogline advised him to stay clear. The Grimpond would see him destroyed if it was given the opportunity. His parents had been given the same advice and had heeded it. But Walker Boh had reached a point in his life when he was through making excuses for who and what he was. He had come to the Wilderun to escape his legacy; he did not intend to spend the rest of his life wondering if there was something out there that could undo him. Best to deal with the shade at once. He went looking for the Grimpond. Because the shade never appeared to more than one person at a time, Cogline was forced to remain behind. When the confrontation came, it was memorable. It lasted for almost six hours. During that time, the Grimpond assailed Walker Boh with every imaginable trick and ploy at its disposal, divulging real and imagined secrets of his present and his future, showering him with rhetoric designed to drive him into madness, revealing to him visions of himself and those he loved that were venomous and destructive. Walker Boh withstood it all. When the shade exhausted itself, it cursed Walker and disappeared back into the mist.

Walker returned to Hearthstone, feeling that the matter of the past was settled. He let the Grimpond alone and the Grimpond—though it could be argued that he had no choice since he was bound to the waters of the lake— did the same to him.

Until today, Walker Boh had not been back.

He sighed. It would be more difficult this time, since this time he wanted something from the shade. He could pretend otherwise. He could keep to himself the truth of why he had come—to learn from the Grimpond the whereabouts of the mysterious Black Elfstone. He could talk about this and that, or assume some role that would confuse the creature, since it loved games and the playing of them. But it was unlikely to make any difference. Somehow the Grimpond always divined the reason you were there.

Walker Boh felt the mist brush against him with the softness of tiny fingers, clinging insistently. This was not going to be pleasant.

He continued ahead as daylight failed and darkness closed about. Shadows, where they could find purchase in the graying haze, lengthened in shimmering parody of their makers. Walker wrapped his cloak closer to his body, thinking through the words he would say to the Grimpond, the arguments he would put forth, the games he would play if forced to do so. He recounted in his mind the events of his life that the shade was likely to play upon—most of them drawn from his youth when he was discomfited by his differences and beset by his insecurities.

"Dark Uncle" they had called him even then—the playmates of Par and Coll, their parents, and even people of the village of Shady Vale that didn't know him. Dark for the color of his life and being, this pale, withdrawn young man who could sometimes read minds, who could divine things that would happen and even cause them to be so, who could understand so much of what was hidden from others. Par and Coll's strange uncle, without parents of his own, without a family that was really his, without a history that he cared to share. Even the Ohmsford name didn't seem to fit him. He was always the "Dark Uncle," somehow older than everyone else, not in years but in knowledge. It wasn't knowledge he had learned; it was knowledge he had been born with. His father had tried to explain. It was the legacy of the wishsong's magic that caused it. It manifested itself this way. But it wouldn't last; it never did. It was just a stage he must pass through because of who he was. But Par and Coll did not have to pass through it, Walker would argue in reply. No, only you and I, only the children of Brin Ohmsford, because we hold the trust, his father would whisper. We are the chosen of Allanon . . .

He swept the memories from his mind angrily, the bitterness welling up anew. The "chosen of Allanon" had his father said? The "cursed of Allanon" was more like it.

The trees gave way before him abruptly, startling him with the suddenness of their disappearance. He stood at the edge of the lake, its rocky shores wending into the mist on either side, its waters lapping gently, endlessly in the silence. Walker Boh straightened. His mind tightened and closed down upon itself as if made of iron, his concentration focused, his thoughts cleared.

A solitary statue, he waited.

There was movement in the fog, but it emanated from more than one place. Walker tried to fix on it, but it was gone as quickly as it had come. From somewhere far away, above the haze that hung across the lake, beyond the rock walls of the ridgelines enfolding the narrow valley, a voice whispered in some empty heaven.

Dark Uncle.

Walker heard the words, tauntingly close and at the same time nowhere he would ever be, not from inside his head or from any other place discernible, but there nevertheless. He did not respond to them. He continued to wait.

Then the scattered movements that had disturbed the mist moments earlier focused themselves on a single point, coming together in a colorless outline that stood upon the water and began to advance. It took surer form as it came, growing in size, becoming larger than the human shape it purported to represent, rising up as if it might crush anything that stood in its way. Walker did not move. The ethereal shape became a shadow, and the shadow became a person . . .

Walker Boh watched expressionlessly as the Grimpond stood before him, suspended in the vapor, its face lifting out of shadow to reveal who it had chosen to become.

"Have you come to accept my charge, Walker Boh?" it asked.

Walker was startled in spite of his resolve. The dark, brooding countenance of Allanon stared down at him.

The warehouse was hushed, its cavernous enclosure blanketed by stillness from floor to ceiling as six pairs of eyes fastened intently on Padishar Creel.

He had just announced that they were going back down into the Pit.

"We'll be doing it differently this time," he told them, his raw-boned face fierce with determination, as if that alone might persuade them to his cause. "No sneaking about through the park with rope ladders this go-around. There's an entry into the Pit from the lower levels of the Gate-house. That's how we'll do it. We'll go right into the Gatehouse, down into the Pit and back out again—and no one the wiser."

Par risked a quick glance at the others. Coll, Morgan, Damson, the outlaws Stasas and Drutt—there was a mix of disbelief and awe etched on their faces. What the outlaw chief was proposing was outrageous; that he might succeed, even more so. No one tried to interrupt. They wanted to hear how he was going to do it.

"The Gatehouse watch changes shifts twice each day—once at sun-rise, once at sunset. Two shifts, six men each. A relief comes in for each shift once a week, but on different days. Today is one of those days. A relief for the day shift comes in just after sunset. I know; I made it a point to find out."

His features creased with the familiar wolfish smile. "Today a special detail will arrive a couple of hours before the shift change because there's to be an inspection of the Gatehouse quarters this evening at the change, and the commander of the Gatehouse wants everything spotless. The day watch will be happy enough to let the detail past to do its work, figuring it's no skin off their noses." He paused. "That detail, of course, will be us."

He leaned forward, his eyes intense. "Once inside, we'll dispatch the night watch. If we're quiet enough about it, the day watch won't even know what's happening. They'll continue with their rounds, doing part of our job for us—keeping everyone outside. We'll bolt the door from within as a precaution in any case. Then we'll go down through the Gatehouse stairs to the lower levels and out into the Pit. It should still be light enough to find what we're looking for fairly quickly. Once we have it, we'll go back up the stairs and out the same way we came in."

For a moment, no one said anything. Then Drutt said, his voice grav-elly, "We'll be recognized, Padishar. Bound to be some of the same soldiers there as when we were taken."

Padishar shook his head. "There was a shift change three days ago. That was the shift that was on duty when we were seized."

"What about that commander?"

"Gone until the beginning of the work week. Just a duty officer."

"We'd need Federation uniforms."

"We have them. I brought them in yesterday."

Drutt and Stasas exchanged glances. "Been thinking about this for a time, have you?" the latter asked.

The outlaw chief laughed softly. "Since the moment we walked out of those cells."

Morgan, who had been seated on a bench next to Par, stood up. "If anything goes wrong and they discover what we're about, they'll be all over the Gatehouse. We'll be trapped, Padishar."

The big man shook his head. "No, we won't. We'll carry in grappling hooks and ropes with our cleaning equipment. If we can't go back the way we came, we'll climb out of the Pit using those. The Federation will be concentrating on getting at us through the Gatehouse entry. It won't even occur to them that we don't intend to come back that way."

The questions died away. There was a long silence as the six sifted through their doubts and fears and waited for something inside to reassure them that the plan would work. Par found himself thinking that there were an awful lot of things that could go wrong.

"Well, what's it to be?" Padishar's patience gave out. "Time's something we don't have to spare. We all know that there's risks involved, but that's the nature of the business. I want a decision. Do we try it or not? Who says we do? Who's with me?"

Par listened to the silence lengthen. Coll and Morgan were statues on the bench to either side of him. Stasas and Drutt, who it had seemed might speak first, now had their eyes fixed firmly on the floor. Damson was looking at Padishar, who in turn was looking at her. Par realized all at once that no one was going to say anything, that they were all waiting on him.

He surprised himself. He didn't even have to think about it. He simply said, "I'll go."

"Have you lost your mind?" Coll whispered urgently in his ear. Stasas and Drutt had Padishar's momentary attention, declaring that they, too, would go. "Par, this was our chance to get out!"

Par leaned close to him. "He's doing this for me, don't you see? I'm the one who wants to find the Sword! I can't let Padishar take all the risks! I have to go!"

Coll shook his head helplessly. Morgan, with a wink at Par over Coll's shoulder, cast his vote in favor of going as well. Coll just raised his hand wordlessly and nodded.

That left Damson. Padishar had his sharp gaze fixed on her, waiting. It suddenly occurred to Par that Padishar needn't have asked who wanted to go with him; he simply could have ordered it. Perhaps in asking he was also testing. There was still a traitor loose. Padishar had told him earlier that he didn't believe it was any of them—but he might have it in his mind to make sure.

"I will wait for you in the park," Damson Rhee said, and everyone stared at her. She did not seem to notice. "I would have to disguise myself as a man in order to go in with you. That is one more risk you would be taking—and to what end? There is nothing I can offer by being with you. If there is trouble, I will be of better use to you on the outside."

Padishar's smile was immediately disarming. "Your thinking is correct as usual, Damson. You will wait in the park."

It seemed to Par that he was a little too quick to agree.

Geysers exploded and died from the flat, gray surface of the lake, and the spray felt like bits of ice where it landed on Walker Boh's skin.

"Tell me why you come here, Dark Uncle?" Allanon's shade whispered.

Walker felt the chill burn away as his determination caught fire. "I need tell you nothing," he replied. "You are not Allanon. You are only the Grimpond."

Allanon's visage shimmered and faded in the half-light, replaced by Walker's own. The Grimpond emitted a hollow laugh. "I am you, Walker Boh. Nothing more and nothing less. Do you recognize yourself?"

His face went through a flurry of transformations—Walker as a child, as a boy, as a youth, as a man. The images came and went so quickly that Walker could barely register them. It was somehow terrifying to watch the phases of his life pass by so quickly. He forced himself to remain calm.

"Will you speak with me, Grimpond?" he asked.

"Will you speak with yourself?" came the reply.

Walker took a deep breath. "I will. But for what purpose should I do so? There is nothing to talk about with myself. I already know all that I have to say."

"Ah, as do I, Walker. As do I."

The Grimpond shrank until it was the same size as Walker. It kept his face, taunting him with it, letting it reveal flashes of the age that would one day claim it, giving it a beaten cast as if to demonstrate the futility of his life.

"I know why you have come to me," the Grimpond said suddenly. "I know the private-most thoughts of your mind, the little secrets you would keep even from yourself. There need be no games between us, Walker Boh. You are surely my equal in the playing of them, and I have no wish to do battle with you again. You have come to ask where you must go to find the Black Elfstone. Fair enough. I will tell you."

Immediately, Walker mistrusted the shade. The Grimpond never volunteered anything without twisting it. He nodded in response, but said nothing.

"How sad you seem, Walker," soothed the shade. "No jubilation at my submission, no elation that you will have what you want? Is it so difficult then to admit that you have dispensed with pride and self-resolution, that you have forsaken your lofty principles, that you have been won over after all to the Druid cause?"

Walker stiffened in spite of himself. "You misread matters, Grimpond. Nothing has been decided."

"Oh, yes, Dark Uncle! Everything has been decided! Make no mistake. Your life weaves out before my eyes as a thread straight and undeviating, the years a finite number, their course determined. You are caught in the snare of the Druid's words. His legacy to Brin Ohmsford becomes your own, whether you would have it so or not. You have been shaped!"

"Tell me, then, of the Black Elfstone," Walker tried.

"All in good time. Patience, now."

The words died away into stillness, the Grimpond shifting within its covering of mist. Daylight had faded into darkness, the gray turned black, the moon and stars shut away by the valley's thick haze. Yet there was light where Walker stood, a phosphorescence given off by the waters beneath the air on which the Grimpond floated, a dull and shallow glow that played wickedly through the night.

"So much effort given over to escaping the Druids," the Grimpond said softly. "What foolishness." Walker's face dissipated and was replaced by his father's. His father spoke. "Remember, Walker, that we are the bearers of Allanon's trust. He gave it to Brin Ohmsford as he lay dying, to be passed from one generation to the next, to be handed down until it was needed, sometime far, far in the distant future . . ."

His father's visage leered at him. "Perhaps now?"

Images flared to life above him, borne on the air as if tapestries threaded on a frame, woven in the fabric of the mist. One after another they appeared, brilliant with color, filled with the texture and depth of real life.

Walker took a step back, startled. He saw himself in the images, anger and defiance in his face, his feet positioned on clouds above the cringing forms of Par and Wren and the others of the little company who had gathered at the Hadeshorn to meet with the shade of Allanon. Thunder rolled out of a darkness that welled away into the skies overhead, and lightning flared in jagged streaks. Walker's voice was a hiss amid the rumble and the flash, the words his own, spoken as if out of his memory. *I would sooner cut off my hand than see the Druids come again!* And then he lifted his arm to reveal that his hand, indeed, was gone.

The vision faded, then sharpened anew. He saw himself again, this time on a high, empty ridgeline that looked out across forever. The whole world spread away below him, the nations and their Races, the creatures of land and water, the lives of everyone and everything that were. Wind whipped at his black robes and whistled ferociously in his ears. There was a girl with him. She was woman and child both, a magical being, a creature of impossible beauty. She stunned him with the intensity of her gaze, depthless black eyes from which he could not turn away. Her long, silver hair flowed from her head in a shimmering mass. She reached for him, needing his balance to keep her footing on the treacherous rock—and he thrust her violently away. She fell, tumbling into the abyss below, soundless as she shrank from sight, silver hair fading into a ribbon of brightness and then into nothing at all.

Again, the vision faded, then returned. He saw himself a third time, now in a castle fortress that was empty of life and gray with disuse. Death stalked him relentlessly, creeping through walls and along corridors, cold fingers probing for signs of his life. He felt the need to run from it, knew that he must if he were to survive—and yet he couldn't. He stood immobile, letting Death approach him, reach for him, close about him. As his life ended, the cold filled him, and he saw that a dark, robed shape stood behind him, holding him fast, preventing him from fleeing. The shape bore the face of Allanon.

The visions disappeared, the colors faded, and the grayness returned, shifting sluggishly in the lake's phosphorescent glow. The Grimpond brought its robed arms downward slowly, and the lake hissed and spit with dissatisfaction. Walker Boh flinched from the spray that cascaded down upon him.

"What say you, Dark Uncle?" the Grimpond whispered. It bore Walker's pale face once more.

"That you play games still," Walker said quietly. "That you show lies and half-truths designed to taunt me. That you have shown me nothing of the Black Elfstone."

"Have I not?" The Grimpond shimmered darkly. "Is it all a game, do you think? Lies and half-truths only?" The laugh was mirthless. "You must think what you will, Walker Boh. But I see a future that is hidden from you, and it would be foolish to believe I would show you none of it. Remember, Walker. I am you, the telling of who and what you are—just as I am for all who come to speak with me."

Walker shook his head. "No, Grimpond, you can never be me. You can never be anyone but who you are—a shade without identity, without being, exiled to this patch of water for all eternity. Nothing you do, no game you play, can ever change that."

The Grimpond sent spray hissing skyward, anger in its voice. "Then go from me, Dark Uncle! Take with you what you came for and go!" The visage of Walker disappeared and was replaced by a death's head. "You think my fate has nothing to do with you? Beware! There is more of me in you than you would care to know!"

Robes flared wide, throwing shards of dull light into the mist. "Hear me, Walker! Hear me! You wish to know of the Black Elfstone? Then listen! Darkness hides it, a black that light can never penetrate, where eyes turn a man to stone and voices turn him mad! Beyond, where only the dead lie, is a pocket carved with runes, the signs of time's passing. Within that pocket lies the Stone!"

The death's head disappeared into nothingness, and only the robes remained, hanging empty against the fog. "I have given you what you wish, Dark Uncle," the shade whispered, its voice filled with loathing. "I have done so because the gift will destroy you. Die, and you will end your cursed line, the last of it! How I long to see that happen! Go, now! Leave me! I bid you swift journey to your doom!"

The Grimpond faded into the mist and was gone. The light it had brought with it dissipated as well. Darkness cloaked the whole of the lake and the shore surrounding it, and Walker was left momentarily sightless. He stood where he was, waiting for his vision to clear, feeling the chill touch of the mist as it brushed against his skin. The Grimpond's laughter echoed in the silence of his mind.

Dark Uncle came the harsh whisper.

He cast himself in stone against it. He sheathed himself in iron.

When his vision returned, and he could make out the vague shape of the trees behind him, he turned from the lake with his cloak wrapped close about him and walked away.

23

Afternoon slid toward evening. A slow, easy rain fell on the city of Tyrsis, washing its dusty streets, leaving them slick and glistening in the fading light. Storm clouds brushed low against the trees of the People's Park, trailing downward in ragged streamers to curl about the roughened trunks. The park was empty, silent save for the steady patter of the rain.

Then footsteps broke the silence, a heavy thudding of boots, and a Federation squad of six materialized out of the gray, cloaked and hooded, equipment packs rattling. A pair of blackbirds perched on a peeling birch glanced over alertly. A dog rummaging amid the garbage slunk quickly away. From a still-dry doorway, a homeless child huddled against the chill and peered out, caution mirrored in its eyes. No other notice was taken. The streets were deserted, the city hunkered down and unseeing in the damp, unpleasant gloom.

Padishar Creel took his little band across the circle of the Tyrsian Way and into the park. Wrapped against the weather, they were indistinguishable one from the other, one from anyone else. They had come all the way from their warehouse lair without challenge. They had barely seen another living thing. Everything was going exactly as planned.

Par Ohmsford watched the faint, dark outline of the Gatehouse appear through the trees and felt his mind fold in upon itself. He hunched his shoulders against the chill of the rain and the heat of the sweat that ran beneath his clothing. He was trapped within himself and yet at the same time able to watch from without as if disembodied. The way forward was far darker than the day's light made it seem. He had stumbled into a tunnel, its walls round and twisting and so smooth he could not find a grip. He was falling, his momentum carrying him relentlessly toward the terror he sensed waiting ahead.

He was in danger of losing control of himself, he knew. He had been afraid before, yes—when Coll and he fled Varfleet, when the woodswoman appeared to confront them below the Runne, when Cogline told them what they must do, when they crossed the Rainbow Lake in night and fog with Morgan, when they fought the giant in the forests of the Anar, when they ran from the Gnawl in the Wolfsktaag, and when the Spider Gnomes and the girl-child who was a Shadowen seized him. He had been afraid when Allanon had come. But his fear then and since was nothing compared to what it was now. He was terrified.

He swallowed against the dryness he felt building in his throat and tried to tell himself he was all right. The feeling had come over him quite suddenly, as if it were a creature that had lain in wait along the rain-soaked streets of the city, its tentacles lashing out to snare him. Now he was caught up in a grip that bound him like iron and there was no way to break free. It was pointless to say anything to the others of what he was experiencing. After all, what could he say that would have any meaning—that he was frightened, even terrified? And what, did he suppose, were they?

A gust of wind shook the water-laden trees and showered him with droplets. He licked the water from his lips, the moisture cool and welcome. Coll was a bulky shape immediately ahead, Morgan another one behind. Shadows danced and played about him, nipping at his fading courage. This was a mistake, he heard himself whispering from somewhere deep inside. His skin prickled with the certainty of it.

He had a sense of his own mortality that had been missing before, locked away in some forgotten storeroom of his mind, kept there, he supposed, because it was so frightening to look upon. It seemed to him in retrospect as if he had treated everything that had gone before as some sort of game. That was ridiculous, he knew; yet some part of it was true. He had gone charging about the countryside, a self-declared hero in the mold of those in the stories he sang about, determined to confront the reality of his dreams, decided that he would know the truth of who and what he was. He had thought himself in control of his destiny; he realized now that he was not.

Visions of what had been swept through his mind in swift disarray, chasing one another with vicious purpose. He had caromed from one mishap to the next, he saw—always wrongly believing that his meddling was somehow useful. In truth, what had he accomplished? He was an outlaw running for his life. His parents were prisoners in their own home. Walker believed him a fool. Wren had abandoned him. Coll and Morgan stayed with him only because they felt he needed looking after. Padishar Creel believed him something he could never be. Worst of all, as a direct result of his misguided decision to accept the charge of a man three hundred years dead, five men were about to offer up their lives.

"Watch yourself," he had cautioned Coll in a vain attempt at humor as they departed their warehouse concealment. "Wouldn't want you tripping over those feet, duck's weather or no."

Coll had sniffed. "Just keep your ears pricked. Shouldn't be hard for someone like you."

Teasing, playing at being brave. Fooling no one.

Allanon! He breathed the Druid's name like a prayer in the silence of his mind. *Why don't you help me?*

But a shade, he knew, could help no one. Help could come only from the living.

There was no more time to think, to agonize over decisions past making, or to lament those already made. The trees broke apart, and the Gatehouse was before them. A pair of Federation guards standing watch stiffened as the patrol approached. Padishar never hesitated. He went directly to them, informed them of the patrol's purpose, joked about the weather, and had the doors open within moments. In a knot of lowered heads and tightened cloaks, the little band hastened inside.

The men of the night watch were gathered about a wooden table playing cards, six of them, heads barely lifting at the arrival of the newcomers. The watch commander was nowhere to be seen.

Padishar glanced over his shoulder, nodded faintly to Morgan, Stasas, and Drutt, and motioned them to spread out about the table. As they did so, one of the players glanced up suspiciously.

"Who're you?" he demanded.

"Clean-up detail," Padishar answered. He moved around behind the speaker and bent over to read his cards. "That's a losing hand, friend."

"Back off, you're dripping on me," the other complained.

Padishar hit him on the temple with his fist, and the man dropped like a stone. A second followed almost as fast. The guards surged to their feet, shouting, but the outlaws and Morgan felled them all in seconds. Par and Coll began pulling ropes and strips of cloth from their packs.

"Drag them into the sleeping quarters, tie and gag them," Padishar whispered. "Make sure they can't escape."

There was a quick knock at the door. Padishar waited until the guards were dispatched, then cracked the peep window. Everything was fine, he assured the guards without, who thought they might have heard something. The card game was breaking up; everyone thought it would be best to start getting things in order.

He closed the window with a reassuring smile.

After the men of the night watch were secured in the sleeping quarters, Padishar closed the door and bolted it. He hesitated, then ordered the locks to the entry doors thrown as well. No point in taking any chances, he declared. They couldn't afford to leave any of their company behind to make certain they were not disturbed.

With oil lamps to guide them, they descended through the gloom of the stairwell to the lower levels of the Gatehouse, the sound of the rain lost behind the heavy stone. The dampness penetrated, though, so chill that Par found himself shivering. He followed after the others in a daze, prepared to do whatever was necessary, his mind focused on putting one foot in front of the other until they were out of there. There was no reason to be frightened, he kept telling himself. It would all be over quick enough.

At the lower level, they found the watch commander sleeping—a new man, different from the one that had been waiting for them when they had tried to slip over the ravine wall. This one fared no better. They subdued him without effort, bound and gagged him, and locked him in his room.

"Leave the lamps," Padishar ordered.

They bypassed the watch commander's chambers and went down to the end of the hall. A single, ironbound door stood closed before them, twice as high as their tallest, the angular Drutt. A massive handle, emblazoned with the wolf's head insigne of the Seekers, jutted out. Padishar reached down with both hands and twisted. The latch gave, the door slid open. Murk and darkness filled the gap, and the stench of decay and mold slithered in.

"Stay close, now," Padishar whispered over his shoulder, his eyes dangerous, and stepped out into the gloom.

Coll turned long enough to reach back and squeeze Par's shoulder, then followed.

They stood in a forest of jumbled tree trunks, matted brush, vines, brambles, and impenetrable mist. The thick, sodden canopy of the treetops overhead all but shut out the little daylight that remained. Mud oozed and sucked in tiny bogs all about them. Creatures flew in ragged jumps through the jungle—birds or something less pleasant, they couldn't tell which. Smells assailed them—the decay and the mold, but something more as well, something even less tolerable. Sounds rose out of the murk, distant, indistinguishable, threatening. The Pit was a well of endless gloom.

Every nerve ending on Par Ohmsford's body screamed at him to get out of there.

Padishar motioned them ahead. Drutt followed, then Coll, Par, Morgan, and Stasas, a line of rain-soaked forms. They picked their way forward slowly, following the edge of the ravine, moving in the direction of the rubble from the old Bridge of Sendic. Par and Coll carried the grappling hooks and ropes, the others drawn weapons. Par glanced over his shoulder momentarily and saw the light from the open door leading back into the Gatehouse disappear into the fog. He saw the Sword of Leah glint dully in Morgan's hand, the rain trickling off its polished metal.

The earth they walked upon was soft and yielding, but it held them as they pushed steadily into the gloom. The Pit had the feel of a giant maw, open and waiting, smelling of things already eaten, its breath the mist that closed them away. Things wriggled and crawled through the pools of stagnant water, oozed down decaying logs, and flashed through bits of scrub like quicksilver. The silence was deafening; even the earlier sounds had disappeared at their approach. There was only the rain, slow and steady, seeping downward through the murk.

They walked for what seemed to Par a very long time. The minutes stretched away in an endless parade until there was no longer either beginning or end to them. How far could it be to the fallen bridge, he wondered? Surely they should be there by now. He felt trapped within the Pit, the wall of the ravine on his left, the trees and mist to his right, gloom and rain overhead and all about. The black cloaks of his companions gave them the look of mourners at a funeral, buriers of the dead.

Then Padishar Creel stopped, listening. Par had heard it, too—a sort of hissing sound from somewhere deep within the murk, like steam escaping from a fissure. The others craned their necks and peered unsuccessfully about. The hissing stopped, the silence filling again with the sound of their breathing and the rain.

Padishar's broadsword glimmered as he motioned them ahead once more. He took them more quickly now, as if sensing that all was not right, that speed might have to take precedence over caution. Scores of massive, glistening trunks came and went, silent sentinels in the gloom. The light was fading rapidly, turned from gray to cobalt.

Par sensed suddenly that something was watching them. The hair on the back of his neck stiffened with the feel of its gaze, and he glanced about hurriedly. Nothing moved in the mist; nothing showed.

"What is it?" Morgan whispered in his ear, but he could only shake his head.

Then the stone blocks of the shattered Bridge of Sendic came into view, bulky and misshapen as they jutted like massive teeth from the tangled forest. Padishar hurried forward, the others following. They moved away from the ravine wall and deeper into the trees. The Pit seemed to swallow them in its mist and dark. Bridge sections lay scattered amid the stone rubble beneath the covering of the forest, moss-grown and worn, spectral in the failing light.

Par took a deep breath. The Sword of Shannara had been embedded blade downward in a block of red marble and placed in a vault beneath the protective span of the Bridge of Sendic, the old legends told.

It had to be here, somewhere close.

He hesitated. The Sword was embedded in red marble; could he free it? Could he even enter the vault?

His eyes searched the mist. What if it was buried beneath the rubble of the bridge? How would they reach it then?

So many unanswered questions, he thought, feeling suddenly desperate. Why hadn't he asked them before? Why hadn't he considered the possibilities?

The cliffs loomed faintly through the murky haze. He could see the west corner of the crumbling palace of the Kings of Callahorn, a dark shadow through a break in the trees. He felt his throat tighten. They were almost to the far wall of the ravine. They were almost out of places to look.

I won't leave without the Sword, he swore wordlessly. *No matter what it takes, I won't!* The fire of his conviction burned through him as if to seal the covenant.

Then the hissing sounded again, much closer now. It seemed to be coming from more than one direction. Padishar slowed and stopped, turning guardedly. With Drutt and Stasas on either side, he stepped out a few paces to act as a screen for the Valemen and the Highlander, then began inching cautiously along the fringe of the broken stone.

The hissing grew louder, more distinct. It was no longer hissing. It was breathing.

Par's eyes searched the darkness frantically. Something was coming for them, the same something that had devoured Ciba Blue and all those before him who had gone down into the Pit and not come out again. His certainty of it was terrifying. Yet it wasn't for their stalker that he searched. It was for the vault that held the Sword of Shannara. He was desperate now to find it. He could see it suddenly in his mind, as clear as if it were a picture drawn and mounted for his private viewing. He groped for it uncertainly, within his mind, then without in the mist and the dark.

Something strange began to happen to him.

He felt a tightening within that seemed grounded in the magic of the wishsong. It was a pulling, a tugging that wrenched against shackles he could neither see nor understand. He felt a pressure building within himself that he had never experienced before.

Coll saw his face and went pale. "Par?" he whispered anxiously and shook him.

Red pinpricks of light appeared in the mist all about them, burning like tiny fires in the damp. They shifted and winked and drew closer. Faces materialized, no longer human, the flesh decaying and half-eaten, the features twisted and fouled. Bodies shambled out of the night, some massive, some gnarled, all misshapen beyond belief. It was as if they had been stretched and wrenched about to see what could be made of them. Most walked bent over; some crawled on all fours.

They closed about the little company in seconds. They were things out of some loathsome nightmare, the fragments and shards of sleep's horror come into the world of waking. Dark, substanceless wraiths flitted in and out of their bodies, through mouths and eyes, from the pores of skin and the bristles of hair.

Shadowen!

The pressure inside Par Ohmsford grew unbearable. He felt something drop away in the pit of his stomach. He was seeing the vision in his dreams come alive, the dark world of animal-like humans and Shadowen masters. It was seeing Allanon's promise come to pass.

The pressure broke free. He screamed, freezing his companions with the sharpness of his cry. The sound took form and became words. He sang, the wishsong ripping through the air as if a flame, the magic lighting up the darkness. The Shadowen jerked away, their faces horrible in the unexpected glare, the lesions and cuts on their bodies vivid streaks of scarlet. Par stiffened, flooded with a power he had never known the wishsong to possess. He was aware of a vision within his mind—a vision of the Sword of Shannara.

The light from the magic, only an illusion at first, was suddenly real. It brightened, lancing the darkness in a way Par found strangely familiar, flaring with intensity as it probed the gloom. It twisted and turned like a captured thing trying to escape, winding past the stone wreckage of the fallen Bridge of Sendic, leaping across the carcasses of fallen trees, burning through the ragged brush to where a singular stone chamber sat alone amid a tangle of vines and grasses not a hundred yards from where he stood.

He felt a surge of elation race through him.

There!

The word hissed in the white silence of his mind, cocooned away from the magic and the chaos. He saw weathered black stone, the light of his magic burning into its pocked surface, scouring its cracks and crevices, picking out the scrolled words carved into its facing:

> *Herein lies the heart and soul of the nations.*
> *Their right to be free men,*
> *Their desire to live in peace,*
> *Their courage . . .*

His strength gave out suddenly before he could complete his reading, and the magic flared sharply and died into blackness, gone as quickly as it had come. He staggered backward with a cry, and Coll caught him in his arms. Par couldn't hear him. He couldn't hear anything but the strange ringing that was the wishsong's residue, the leavings of a magic he now realized he had not yet begun to understand.

And in his mind the vision lingered, a shimmering image at the forefront of his thoughts—all that remained of what moments earlier the magic had uncovered in the mist and dark.

The weathered stone vault. The familiar words in scroll.

The Sword of Shannara.

Then the ringing stopped, the vision disappeared, and he was back in the Pit, drowning in weakness. The Shadowen were closing, shambling forward from all directions to trap them against the stone of the bridge. Padishar stepped forward, tall and forbidding, to confront the nearest, a huge bearish thing with talons for hands. It reached for him and he cut at it with the broadsword—once, twice, a third time—the strokes so rapid Par could barely register them. The creature sagged back, limbs drooping—but it did not fall. It barely seemed aware of what had been done to it, its eyes fixed, its features twisting with some inner torment.

Par watched the Shadowen through glazed eyes. Its limbs reconnected in the manner of the giant they had fought in the Anar.

"Padishar, the Sword . . ." he started to say, but the outlaw chief was already shouting, directing them back the way they had come, retreating along the wall of stone. "No!" Par shrieked in dismay. He could not put into words the certainty he felt. They had to reach the Sword. He lurched up, trying to break free of Coll, but his brother held him fast, dragging him along with the others.

The Shadowen attacked in a shambling rush. Stasas went down, dragged beyond the reach of his companions. His throat was ripped out and then something dark entered his body while he was still alive, gasping. It jerked him upright, brought him about to face them, and he became another attacker. The company retreated, swords slashing. Ciba Blue appeared—or what was left of him. Impossibly strong, he blocked Drutt's sword, caught hold of his arms, and wrapped himself about his former comrade like a leech. The outlaw shrieked in pain as first one arm and then the other was ripped from his body. His head went last. He was left behind, Ciba Blue's remains still fastened to him, feeding.

Padishar was alone then, besieged on all sides. He would have been dead if he were not so quick and so strong. He feinted and slashed, dodging the fingers that grappled for him, twisting to stay free. Hopelessly outnumbered, he began to give ground quickly.

It was Morgan Leah who saved him. Abandoning his role as defender of Par and Coll, the Highlander rushed to the aid of the outlaw chief. His red hair flying, he charged into the midst of the Shadowen. The Sword of Leah arced downward, catching fire as it struck. Magic surged through the blade and into the dark things, burning them to ash. Two fell, three, then more. Padishar fought relentlessly beside him, and together they began cutting a path through the gathering of eyes, calling wildly for Par and Coll to follow. The Valemen stumbled after them, avoiding the grasp of Shadowen who had slipped behind. Par abandoned all hope of reaching the Sword. Two of their number were already dead; the rest of them would be killed as well if they didn't get out of there at once.

Back toward the wall of the ravine they staggered, warding off the Shadowen as they went, the magic of the Sword of Leah keeping the creatures at bay. They seemed to be everywhere, as if the Pit were a nest in which they bred. Like the woodswoman and the giant, they seemed impervious to any damage done to them by conventional weapons. Only Morgan could hurt them; his was magic that they could not withstand.

The retreat was agonizingly slow. Morgan grew weary, and as his own strength drained away so did the power of the Sword of Leah. They ran when they could, but more and more frequently the Shadowen blocked their way. Par attempted in vain to invoke the magic of the wishsong; it simply would not come. He tried not to think of what that meant, still struggling to make sense of what had occurred, to understand how the magic had broken free. Even in flight, his mind wrestled with the memory. How could he have lost control like that? How could the magic have provided him with that strange light, a thing that was real and not illusion. Had he simply willed it to be? What was it that had happened to him?

Somehow they reached the wall of the ravine and sagged wearily against it. Shouts sounded from the park above and torches flared. Their battle with the Shadowen had alerted the Federation watch. In moments, the Gatehouse would be under siege.

"The grappling hooks!" Padishar gasped.

Par had lost his, but Coll's was still slung across his shoulder. The Vale-man stepped back, uncoiled the rope, and heaved the heavy iron skyward. It flew out of sight and caught. Coll tested it with his weight and it held.

Padishar braced Par against the wall, and their eyes met. Behind him, the forests of the Pit were momentarily empty. "Climb," he ordered roughly. His breath came in short gasps. He pulled Coll to him as well. "Both of you. Climb until you are safely out, then flee into the park. Damson will find you and take you back to the Jut."

"Damson," Par repeated dumbly.

"Forget your suspicions and mine as well," the outlaw whispered harshly. There was a glint of something sad in his hard eyes. "Trust her, lad—she is the better part of me!"

The Shadowen materialized once more out of the murk, their breath-ing a slow hiss in the night air. Morgan had already pushed out from the wall to face them. "Get out of here, Par," he called back over his shoulder.

"Climb!" Padishar Creel snapped. "Now!"

"But you . . ." Par began.

"Shades!" the other exploded. "I remain with the Highlander to see that you escape! Don't waste the gesture!" He caught Par roughly by the shoulders. "Whatever happens to any of the rest of us, you must live! The Shannara magic is what will win this fight one day, and you are the one who must wield it! Now go!"

Coll took charge then, half-pushing and half-lifting Par onto the rope. It was knotted, and the Valeman found an easy grip. He began to climb, tears of frustration filling his eyes. Coll followed him up, urging him on, his blocky face taut beneath its sheen of sweat.

Par paused only once to glance downward. Shadowen ringed Padishar Creel and Morgan Leah as they stood protectively before the ravine wall.

Too many Shadowen.

The Valeman looked away again. Biting back against his rage, he con-tinued to climb into black.

Morgan Leah did not turn around as the scraping of boots on the ravine wall faded away; his eyes remained fixed on the encircling Shadowen. He was aware of Padishar standing at his left shoulder. The Shadowen were no longer advancing on them; they were hanging back guardedly at the edge of the mist's thick curtain, keeping their distance. They had learned what Morgan's weapon could do, and they had grown cautious.

Mindless things, the Highlander thought bitterly. *I could have come to a better end than this, you'd think!*

He feinted at the nearest of them, and they backed away.

Morgan's weariness dragged at him like chains. It was the work of the magic, he knew. Its power had gone all through him, a sort of inner fire drawn from the sword, an exhilarating rush at first, then after a time simply a wearing down. And there was something more. There was an insidious binding of the magic to his body that made him crave it in a way he could not explain, as if to give it up now, even to rest, would somehow take away from who and what he was.

He was suddenly afraid that he might not be able to relinquish it until he was too weak to do otherwise.

Or too dead.

He could no longer hear Par and Coll climbing. The Pit was again encased in silence save for the hissing of the Shadowen.

Padishar leaned close to him. "Move, Highlander!" he rasped softly.

They began to ease their way down the ravine wall, slowly at first, and then, when the Shadowen did not come at them right away, more quickly. Soon they were running, stumbling really, for they no longer had the strength to do anything more. Mist swirled about them, gray tendrils against the night. The trees shimmered in the haze of falling rain and seemed to move. Morgan felt himself ease into a world of unfeeling half-sleep that stole away time and place.

Twice more the Shadowen attacked as they fled, brief forays each time, and twice they were driven back by the magic of the Sword of Leah. Grotesque bodies launched themselves like slow rolling boulders down a mountainside and were turned to ash. Fire burned in the night, quick and certain, and Morgan felt a bit of himself fall away with each burst.

He began to wonder if in some strange way he was killing himself.

Above, where the park lay hidden behind the wall of the ravine, the shouts continued to grow, reaching out to them like a false lifeline of hope. There were no friends to be found there, Morgan knew. He stumbled, and it required an incredible amount of effort to right himself.

And then, at last, the Gatehouse came into view, a shadowy, massive tower lifting out of the trees and mist.

Morgan was dimly aware that something was wrong.

"Get through the door!" Padishar Creel cried frantically, shoving at him so hard he almost fell.

Together they sprinted for the door—or where the door should have been, for it was unexplainably missing. No light seeped through the opening they had left; the stone wall was black and faceless. Morgan felt a surge of fear and disbelief well up in the pit of his stomach.

Someone—or something—had sealed off their escape!

With Padishar a step behind, he came up against the Gatehouse wall, against the massive portal that had admitted them into the Pit, now closed and barred against their re-entry. They heaved against it in desperation, but it was fastened securely. Morgan's fingers searched its edges, probing, finding to his horror small markings all about, markings they had somehow overlooked before, runes of magic that glowed faintly in the graying mist and prevented their escape more certainly than any lock and key ever could.

Behind him, he could hear the Shadowen massing. He wheeled away, rushed the night things in a frenzy and caused them to scatter. Padishar was hammering at the invisible lock, not yet aware that it was magic and not iron that kept them out.

Morgan turned back, his lean face a mask of fury. "Stand away, Padishar!" he shouted.

He went at the door as if it were one of the Shadowen, the Sword of Leah raised, its blade a brilliant silver streak against the dark. Down came the weapon like a hammer—once, twice, then again and again. The runes carved into the door's iron surface glowed a deep, wicked green. Sparks flew with each blow, shards of flame that screamed in protest. Morgan howled as if gone mad, and the power of the sword's magic drew the last of his strength from him in a rush.

Then everything exploded into white fire, and Morgan was consumed by darkness.

Par lifted himself out of the Pit's murky blackness to the edge of the ravine wall and pulled himself over its spikes. Cuts and scrapes burned his arms and legs. Sweat stung his eyes, and his breath came in short gasps. For a moment, his vision blurred, the night about him an impenetrable mask dotted with weaving bits of light.

Torches, he realized, clustered about the entry to the Gatehouse. There were shouts as well and a hammering of heavy wood. The watch and whoever else had been summoned were trying to break down the bolted door.

Coll came over the wall behind him, grunting with the effort as he dropped wearily to the cool, sodden earth. Rain matted his dark hair where the hood of his cloak had fallen away, and his eyes glittered with something Par couldn't read.

"Can you walk?" his brother whispered anxiously.

Par nodded without knowing if he could or not. They came to their feet slowly, their muscles aching, their breathing labored. They stumbled from the wall into the shadow of the trees and paused in the blackness, waiting to discover if they had been seen, listening to the commotion that surrounded the Gatehouse.

Coll bent his head close. "We have to get out of here, Par." Par's eyes lifted accusingly. "I know! But we can't help them anymore. Not now, at least. We have to save ourselves." He shook his head helplessly. "Please!"

Par clasped him momentarily and nodded into his shoulder, and they stumbled ahead. They made their way slowly, keeping to the darkest shadows, staying clear of the paths leading toward the Gatehouse. The rain had stopped without their realizing it, and the great trees shed their surface water in sudden showers as the wind gusted in intermittent bursts. Par's mind spun with the memory of what had happened to them, whispering anew the warning it had given him earlier, teasing him with self-satisfied, purposeless glee. Why hadn't he listened, it whispered? Why had he been so stubborn?

The lights of the Tyrsian Way burned through the darkness ahead, and moments later they stumbled to the edge of the street. There were people clustered there, dim shapes in the night, faceless shadows that stood mute witness to the chaos beyond. Most were farther down near the park's entry and saw nothing of the two ragged figures who emerged. Those who did see quickly looked away when they recognized the Federation uniforms.

"Where do we go now?" Par whispered, leaning against Coll for support. He was barely able to stand.

Coll shook his head wordlessly and pulled his brother toward the street, away from the lights. They had barely reached its cobblestones when a lithe figure materialized out of the shadows some fifty feet away and moved to intercept them. *Damson,* Par thought. He whispered her name to Coll, and they slowed expectantly as she hurried up.

"Keep moving," she said quietly, boosting Par's free arm about her shoulders to help Coll support him. "Where are the others?"

Par's eyes lifted to meet hers. He shook his head slowly and saw the stricken look that crossed her face.

Behind them, deep within the park, there was a brilliant explosion of fire that rocketed skyward into the night. Gasps of dismay rose out of those gathered on the streets.

The silence that followed was deafening.

"Don't look back," Damson whispered, tight-lipped.

The Valemen didn't need to.

Morgan Leah lay sprawled upon the scorched earth of the Pit, steam rising from his clothing, the acrid stench of smoke in his mouth and nostrils. Somehow he was still alive, he sensed—barely. Something was terribly wrong with him. He felt broken, as if everything had been smashed to bits within his skin, leaving him an empty, scoured shell. There was pain, but it wasn't physical. It was worse somehow, a sort of emotional agony that wracked not only his body but his mind as well.

"Highlander!"

Padishar's rough voice cut through the layers of hurt and brought his eyes open. Flames licked the ground inches away.

"Get up—quickly!" Padishar was pulling at him, hauling him forcibly to his feet, and he heard himself scream. A muddled sea of trees and stone blocks swam in the mist and darkness, slowly steadied and at last took shape.

Then he saw. He was still gripping the hilt of the Sword of Leah, but its blade was shattered. No more than a foot remained, a jagged, blackened shard.

Morgan began to shake. He could not stop himself. "What have I done?" he whispered.

"You saved our lives, my friend!" Padishar snapped, dragging him forward. "That's what you did!" Light poured through a massive hole in the wall of the Gatehouse. The door that had been sealed against their return had disappeared. Padishar's voice was labored. "Your weapon did that. Your magic. Shattered that door into smoke! Gives us the chance we need, if we're quick enough. Hurry, now! Lean on me. Another minute or two . . ."

Padishar shoved him through the opening. He was dimly aware of the corridor they stumbled down, the stairs they climbed. The pain continued to rip through his body, leaving him incoherent when he tried to speak. He could not take his eyes from the broken sword. His sword—his magic— himself. He could not differentiate among them.

Shouts and a heavy thudding broke into his thoughts, causing him to flinch. "Easy, now," Padishar cautioned, the outlaw's voice a buzzing in his ears that seemed to come from very far away.

They reached the ward room with its weapons and debris. There was a frantic pounding on the entry doors. Their iron shielding was buckled and staved.

"Lie here," Padishar ordered, leaning him back against the wall to one side. "Say nothing when they enter, just keep still. With luck, they'll think us victims of what's happened here and nothing more. Here, give me that." He reached down and pried the broken Sword of Leah from Morgan's nerveless fingers. "Back in its case with this, lad. We'll see to its fixing later."

He shoved the weapon into its shoulder scabbard, patted Morgan's cheek, and moved to open the entry doors.

Black-garbed Federation soldiers poured into the room, shouting and yelling and filling the chamber with a din that was suffocating. A disguised Padishar Creel shouted and yelled back, directing them down the stairwell, into the sleeping quarters, over this way and out that. There was mass confusion. Morgan watched it all without really understanding or even caring. The sense of indifference he felt was outweighed only by his sense of loss. It was as if his life no longer had a purpose, as if any reason for it had evaporated as suddenly and thoroughly as the blade of the Sword of Leah.

No more magic, he thought over and over. I have lost it. I have lost everything.

Then Padishar was back, hauling him to his feet again, steering him through the chaos of the Gatehouse to the entry doors and from there into the park. Bodies surged past, but no one challenged them. "It's a fine madness we've let loose with this night's work," Padishar muttered darkly. "I just hope it doesn't come back to haunt us."

He took Morgan swiftly from the circle of the Gatehouse lights into the concealing shadows beyond.

Moments later, they were lost from sight.

24

I t was just after dawn when Par Ohmsford came awake the first time. He lay motionless on his pallet of woven mats, collecting his scattered thoughts in the silence of his mind. It took him awhile to remember where he was. He was in a storage shed behind a gardening shop somewhere in the center of Tyrsis. Damson had brought them there last night to hide after . . .

The memory returned to him in an unpleasant rush, images that swept through his mind with horrific clarity.

He forced his eyes open and the images disappeared. A faint wash of gray, hazy light seeped through cracks in the shuttered windows of the shed, lending vague definition to the scores of gardening tools stacked upright like soldiers at watch. The smell of dirt and sod filled the air, rich and pungent. It was silent beyond the walls of their concealment, the city still sleeping.

He lifted his head cautiously and glanced about. Coll was asleep beside him, his breathing deep and even. Damson was nowhere to be seen.

He lay back again for a time, listening to the silence, letting himself come fully awake. Then he rose, gingerly easing himself from beneath his blankets and onto his feet. He was stiff and cramped, and there was an aching in his joints that caused him to wince. But his strength was back; he could move about again unaided.

Coll stirred fitfully, turning over once before settling down again. Par watched his brother momentarily, studying the shadowed line of his blunt features, then stepped over to the nearest window. He was still wearing his clothing; only his boots had been removed. The chill of early morning seeped up from the plank flooring into his stockinged feet, but he ignored it. He put his eye to a crack in the shutters and looked out. It had stopped raining, but the skies were clouded and the world had a damp, empty look. Nothing moved within the range of his vision. A jumbled collection of walls, roofs, streets, and shadowed niches stared back at him from out of the mist.

The door behind him opened, and Damson stepped noiselessly into the shed. Her clothing was beaded with moisture and her red hair hung limp.

"Here, what are you doing?" she whispered, her forehead creasing with annoyance. She crossed the room quickly and took hold of him as if he were about to topple over. "You're not to be out of bed yet! You're far too weak! Back you go at once!"

She steered him to his pallet and forced him to lie down again. He made a brief attempt to resist and discovered that he had less strength than he first believed.

"Damson, listen . . ." he began, but she quickly put a hand over his mouth.

"No, you listen, Elf-boy." She paused, staring down at him as she might a curious discovery. "What is the matter with you, Par Ohmsford? Haven't you an ounce of common sense to call your own? You barely escaped with your life last night and already you are looking to risk it again. Haven't you the least regard for yourself?"

She took a deep breath, and he found himself thinking suddenly of how warm her hand felt against his face. She seemed to read his thoughts and lifted it away. Her fingers trailed across his cheek.

He caught her hand in his and held it. "I'm sorry. I couldn't sleep anymore. I was drifting in and out of nightmares about last night." Her hand felt small and light in his own. "I can't stop thinking about Morgan and Padishar . . ."

He trailed off, not wanting to say more. It was too frightening, even now. Next to him, Coll's eyes blinked open and fixed on him. "What's going on?" he asked sleepily.

Damson's fingers tightened on Par's. "Your brother cannot seem to sleep for worrying about everyone but himself."

Par stared up at her wordlessly for a moment, then said, "Is there any news, Damson?"

She smiled faintly. "I will make a bargain with you. If you promise me that you will try to go back to sleep for a time—or at least not leave this bed—I promise you that I will try to learn the answer to your question. Fair enough?"

The Valeman nodded. He found himself pondering anew Padishar's final admonition to him: *Trust her. She is the better part of me!*

Damson glanced over at Coll. "I depend on you to make certain that he keeps his word." Her hand slipped from Par's and she stood up. "I will bring back something to eat as well. Stay quiet, now. No one will disturb you here."

She paused momentarily, as if reluctant even then to leave, then turned and disappeared out the door.

Silence filled the shadowed room. The brothers looked at each other without speaking for a moment, and then Coll said quietly, "She's in love with you."

Par flushed, then quickly shook his head. "No. She's just being protective, nothing more."

Coll lay back, sighed and closed his eyes. "Oh, is that it?" He let his breathing slow. Par thought he was sleeping again when he suddenly said, "What happened to you last night, Par?"

Par hesitated. "You mean the wishsong?"

Coll's eyes slipped open. "Of course I mean the wishsong." He glanced over sharply. "I know how the magic works better than anyone other than yourself, and I've never seen it do that. That wasn't an illusion you created; that was the real thing! I didn't think you could do that."

"I didn't either."

"Well?"

Par shook his head. What had happened indeed? He closed his eyes momentarily and then opened them again. "I have a theory," he admitted finally. "I came up with it between sleep and bad dreams, you might say. Remember how the magic of the wishsong came about in the first place? Wil Ohmsford used the Elfstones in his battle with the Reaper. He had to in order to save the Elf-girl Amberle. Shades, we've told that story often enough, haven't we? It was dangerous for him to do so because he hadn't enough true Elf blood to allow it. It changed him in a way he couldn't determine at first. It wasn't until after his children were born, until after Brin and Jair, that he discovered what had been done. Some part of the Elf magic of the Stones had gone into him. That part was passed to Brin and Jair in the form of the wishsong."

He raised himself up on one elbow; Coll did likewise. The light was sufficient now to let them see each other's faces clearly. "Cogline told us that first night that we didn't understand the magic. He said that it works in different ways—something like that—but that until we understood it, we could only use it in one. Then, later, at the Hadeshorn, he told us how the magic changes, leaving wakes in its passing like the water of a lake disturbed. He made specific reference to Wil Ohmsford's legacy of magic, the magic that became the wishsong."

He paused. The room was very still. When he spoke again, his voice sounded strange in his ears. "Now suppose for a moment that he was right, that the magic is changing all the time, evolving in some way. After all, that's what happened when the magic of the Elfstones passed from Wil Ohmsford to his children. So what if it has changed again, this time in me?"

Coll stared. "What do you mean?" he asked finally. "How do you think it could change?"

"Suppose that the magic has worked its way back to what it was in the beginning. The blue Elfstones that Allanon gave to Shea Ohmsford when they went in search of the Sword of Shannara all those years ago had the power to seek out that which was hidden from the holder."

"Par!" Coll breathed his name softly, the astonishment apparent in his voice.

"No, wait. Let me finish. Last night, the magic released itself in a way it has never done before. I could barely control it. You're right, Coll; there was no illusion in what it did. But it did respond in a recognizable way. It sought out what was hidden from me, and I think it did so because subconsciously I willed it." His voice was fierce. "Coll. Suppose that the power that once was inherent in the magic of the Elfstones is now inherent in the magic within me!"

There was a long silence between them. They were close now, their faces not two feet apart, their eyes locked. Coll's rough features were knotted in concentration, the enormity of what Par was suggesting weighing down on him like a massive stone block. Doubt mirrored in his eyes, then acceptance, and suddenly fear.

His face went taut. His rough voice was very soft. "The Elfstones possessed another property as well. They could defend the holder against danger. They could be a weapon of tremendous power."

Par waited, saying nothing, already knowing what was coming.

"Do you think that the magic of the wishsong can now do the same for you?"

Par's response was barely audible. "Yes, Coll. I think maybe it can."

By midday, the haze of early morning had burned away and the clouds had moved on. Sunshine shone down on Tyrsis, blanketing the city in heat. Puddles and streams evaporated as the temperature rose, the stone and clay of the streets dried, and the air grew humid and sticky.

Traffic at the gates of the Outer Wall was heavy and slowmoving. The Federation guards on duty, double the usual number as a result of the previous night's disturbance, were already sweating and irritable when the bearded gravedigger approached from out of the backstreets beyond the inner wall. Travelers and merchants alike moved aside at his approach. He was ragged and stooped, and he smelled to the watch as if he had been living in a sewer. He was wheeling a heavy cart in front of him, the wood rotted and splintered. There was a body in the cart, wrapped in sheets and bound with leather ties.

The guards glanced at one another as the gravedigger trudged up to them, his charge wheeled negligently before him, rolling and bouncing.

"Hot one for work, isn't it, sirs?" the gravedigger wheezed, and the guards flinched in spite of themselves from the stench of him.

"Papers," said one perfunctorily.

"Sure, sure." One ragged hand passed over a document that looked as if it had been used to wipe up mud. The gravedigger gestured at the body. "Got to get this one in the ground quick, don't you know. Won't last long on a day such as this."

One of the guards stepped close enough to prod the corpse with the point of his sword. "Easy now," the gravedigger advised. "Even the dead deserve some respect."

The soldier looked at him suspiciously, then shoved the sword deep into the body and pulled it out again. The gravedigger cackled. "You might want to be cleaning your sword there, sir—seeing as how this one died of the spotted fever."

The soldier stepped back quickly, pale now. The others retreated as well. The one holding the gravedigger's papers handed them hastily back and motioned him on.

The gravedigger shrugged, picked up the handles of the cart and wheeled his body down the long ramp toward the plain below, whistling tunelessly as he went.

What a collection of fools, Padishar Creel thought disdainfully to himself.

When he reached the first screening of trees north, the city of Tyrsis a distant grayish outline against the swelter, Padishar eased the handles of the cart down, shoved the body he had been hauling aside, took out an iron bar and began prying loose the boards of the cart's false bottom. Gingerly, he helped Morgan extricate himself from his place of hiding. Morgan's face was pale and drawn, as much from the heat and discomfort of his concealment as from the lingering effects of last night's battle.

"Take a little of this." The outlaw chief offered him an aleskin, trying unsuccessfully not to look askance. Morgan accepted the offering wordlessly. He knew what the other was thinking—that the Highlander hadn't been right since their escape from the Pit.

Abandoning the cart and its body, they walked a mile further on to a river where they could wash. They bathed, dressed in clean clothes that Padishar had hidden with Morgan in the cart's false bottom, and sat down to have something to eat.

The meal was a silent one until Padishar, unable to stand it any longer, growled, "We can see about fixing the blade, Highlander. It may be the magic isn't lost after all."

Morgan just shook his head. "This isn't something anyone can fix," he said tonelessly.

"No? Tell me why. Tell me how the sword works, then. You explain it to me." Padishar wasn't about to let the matter alone.

Morgan did as the other asked, not because he particularly wanted to, but because it was the easiest way to get Padishar to stop talking about it. He told the story of how the Sword of Leah was made magic, how Allanon dipped its blade in the waters of the Hadeshorn so that Rone Leah would have a weapon with which to protect Brin Ohmsford. "The magic was in the blade, Padishar," he finished. He was having trouble being patient by now. "Once broken, it cannot be repaired. The magic is lost."

Padishar frowned doubtfully, then shrugged. "Well, it was lost for a good cause, Highlander. After all, it saved our lives. A good trade any day of the week."

Morgan looked up at him, his eyes haunted. "You don't understand. There was some sort of bond between us, the sword and me. When the sword broke, it was as if it was happening to me! It doesn't make any sense, I know—but it's there anyway. When the magic was lost, some part of me was lost as well."

"But that's just your sense of it now, lad. Who's to say that won't change?" Padishar gave him an encouraging smile. "Give yourself a little time. Let the wound heal, as they say."

Morgan put down his food, uninterested in eating, and hunched his knees close against his chest. He remained quiet, ignoring the fact that the outlaw chief was waiting for a response, contemplating instead the nagging recognition that nothing had gone right since their decision to go down into the Pit after the missing Sword of Shannara.

Padishar's brow furrowed irritably. "We have to go," he announced abruptly and stood up. When Morgan didn't move right away, he said, "Now, listen to me, Highlander. We're alive and that's the way we're going to stay, sword or no sword, and I'll not allow you to continue acting like some half-dead puppy . . ."

Morgan came to his feet with a bound. "Enough, Padishar! I don't need you worrying about me!" His voice sounded harsher than he had meant it to, but he could not disguise the anger he was feeling. That anger quickly found a focus. "Why don't you try worrying about the Valemen? Do you have any idea at all what's happened to them? Why have we left them behind like this?"

"Ah." The other spoke the word softly. "So that's what's really eating at you, is it? Well, Highlander, the Valemen are likely better off than we are. We were seen getting out of that Gatehouse, remember? The Federation isn't so stupid that it will overlook the report of what happened and the fact that two so-called guards are somehow missing. They'll have our description. If we hadn't gotten out of the city right away, we likely wouldn't have gotten out at all!"

He jabbed his finger at the Highlander. "Now the Valemen, on the other hand—no one saw them. No one will recognize their faces. Besides, Damson will have them in hand by now. She knows to bring them to the Jut. She'll get them out of Tyrsis easily enough when she has the chance."

Morgan shook his head stubbornly. "Maybe. Maybe not. You were confident as well about our chances of retrieving the Sword of Shannara and look what happened."

Padishar flushed angrily. "The risks involved in that were hardly a secret to any of us!"

"Tell that to Stasas and Drutt and Ciba Blue!"

The big man snatched hold of Morgan's tunic and yanked him forward violently. His eyes were hard with anger. "Those were my friends that died back there, Highlander—not yours. Don't be throwing it up in my face! What I did, I did for all of us. We need the Sword of Shannara! Sooner or later we're going to have to go back for it—Shadowen or not! You know that as well as I! As for the Valemen, I don't like leaving them any better than you do! But we had precious little choice in the matter!"

Morgan tried unsuccessfully to jerk free. "You might have gone looking for them, at least!"

"Where? Where would I look? Do you think they would be hidden in any place we could find? Damson's no fool! She has them tucked away in the deepest hole in Tyrsis! Shades, Highlander! Don't you realize what's happening back there? We uncovered a secret last night that the Federation has gone to great pains to conceal! I'm not sure either of us understands what it all means yet, but it's enough that the Federation thinks we might! They'll want us dead for that!"

His voice was a snarl. "I caught a glimpse of what's to come when I passed you through the gates. The Federation authorities no longer concern themselves merely with doubling guards and increasing watch patrols. They have mobilized the entire garrison! Unless I am badly mistaken, young Morgan Leah, they have decided to eliminate us once and for all—you and me and any other members of the Movement they can run to earth. We are a real threat to them now, because, for the first time, we begin to understand what they are about—and that's something they will not abide!"

His grip tightened, fingers of stone. "They'll come hunting us, and we had best not be anywhere we can be found!"

He released the Highlander with a shove. He took a deep breath and straightened. "In any case, I don't choose to argue the matter with you. I am leader here. You fought well back there in the Pit, and perhaps it cost you something. But that doesn't give you the right to question my orders. I understand the business of staying alive better than you, and you had best remember it."

Morgan was white with rage, but he kept himself in check. He knew there was nothing to be gained by arguing the matter further; the big man was not about to change his mind. He knew as well, deep down inside where he could admit it to himself, that what Padishar was saying about staying around in an effort to find Par and Coll was the truth.

He stepped away from Padishar and smoothed his rumpled clothing carefully. "I just want to be certain that we are agreed that the Valemen will not be forgotten."

Padishar Creel's smile was quick and hard. "Not for a moment. Not by me, at least. You are free to do as you choose in the matter."

He wheeled away, moving off into the trees. After a moment's hesitation, Morgan swallowed his anger and pride and followed.

Par came awake for the second time that day toward midafternoon. Coll was shaking him and the smell of hot soup filled the close confines of their shelter. He blinked and sat up slowly. Damson stood at a pruning bench, spooning broth into bowls, the steam rising thickly as she worked. She glanced over at the Valeman and smiled. Her flaming hair shimmered brightly in the shards of sunlight that filtered through the cracks in the shuttered windows, and Par experienced an almost irresistible need to reach out and stroke it.

Damson served the Valemen the soup together with fresh fruit, bread, and milk, and Par thought it was the most wonderful meal he had ever tasted. He ate everything he was given, Coll with him, both ravenous beyond what they would have thought possible. Par was surprised that he had been able to go back to sleep, but he was unquestionably the better for it, his body rested now and shed of most of its aches and pains. There was little talk during the meal, and that left him free to think. His mind had begun working almost immediately on waking, skipping quickly from the memory of last night's horrors to the prospect of what lay ahead—to sift through the information he had gathered, to consider carefully what he suspected, to make plans for what he now believed must be.

The process made him shudder inwardly with excitement and foreboding. Already, he discovered, he was beginning to relish the prospect of attempting the unthinkable.

When the Valemen had finished eating, they washed in a basin of fresh water. Then Damson sat them down again and told them what had become of Padishar and Morgan.

"They escaped," she began without preamble. Her green eyes reflected amusement and awe. "I don't know how they managed it, but they did. It took me awhile to verify that they had indeed gotten free, but I wanted to make certain of what I was being told."

Par grinned at his brother in relief. Coll stifled his own grin and instead simply shrugged. "Knowing those two, they probably talked their way out," he responded gruffly.

"Where are they now?" Par asked. He felt as if years had been added back onto his life. Padishar and Morgan had escaped—it was the best news he could have been given.

"That I don't know," Damson replied. "They seem to have disappeared. Either they have gone to ground in the city or—more likely—they have left it altogether and are on their way back to the Jut. The latter seems the better guess because the entire Federation garrison is mobilizing and there's only one reason they would do that. They mean to go after Padishar and his men in the Parma Key. Apparently, whatever he—and you—did last night made them very angry. There are all sorts of rumors afloat. Some say dozens of Federation soldiers were killed at the Gatehouse by monsters. Some say the monsters are loose in the city. Whatever the case, Padishar will have read the signs as easily as I. He'll have slipped out by now and gone north."

"You're certain the Federation hasn't found him instead?" Par was still anxious.

Damson shook her head. "I would have heard." She was propped against the leg of the pruning bench as they sat on the pallets that had served as their beds the night before. She let her head tilt back against the roughened wood so that the soft curve of her face caught the light. "It is your turn now. Tell me what happened, Par. What did you find in the Pit?"

With help from Coll, Par related what had befallen them, deciding as he did that he would do as Padishar had urged, that he would trust Damson in the same way that he had trusted the outlaw chief. Thus he told her not only of their encounter with the Shadowen, but of the strange behavior of the wishsong, of the unexpected way its magic had performed, even of his suspicions of the influence of the Elfstones.

When he had finished, the three of them sat staring wordlessly at one another for a moment, of different minds as they reflected on what the foray into the Pit had uncovered and what it all meant.

Coll spoke first. "It seems to me that we have more questions to answer now than we did when we went in."

"But we know some things, too, Coll," Par argued. He bent forward, eager to speak. "We know that there is some sort of connection between the Federation and the Shadowen. The Federation has to know what it has down there; it can't be ignorant of the truth. Maybe it even helped create those monsters. For all we know they might be Federation prisoners thrown into the Pit like Ciba Blue and changed into what we found. And why are they still down there if the Federation isn't keeping them so? Wouldn't they have escaped long ago if they could?"

"As I said, there are more questions than answers," Coll declared. He shifted his heavy frame to a more comfortable position.

Damson shook her head. "Something seems wrong here. Why would the Federation have any dealings with the Shadowen? The Shadowen represent everything the Federation is against—magic, the old ways, the subversion of the Southland and its people. How would the Federation even go about making such an arrangement? It has no defense against the Shadowen magic. How would it protect itself?"

"Maybe it doesn't have to," Coll said suddenly. They looked at him. "Maybe the Federation has given the Shadowen someone else to feed on besides itself, someone the Federation has no use for in any case. Perhaps that's what became of the Elves." He paused. "Perhaps that's what's happening now to the Dwarves."

They were silent as they considered the possibility. Par hadn't thought about the Dwarves for a time, the horrors of Culhaven and its people shoved to the back of his mind these past few weeks. He remembered what he had seen there—the poverty, the misery, the oppression. The Dwarves were being exterminated for reasons that had never been clear. Could Coll be right? Could the Federation be feeding the Dwarves to the Shadowen as a part of some unspeakable bargain between them?

His face tightened in dismay. "But what would the Federation get in return?"

"Power," Damson Rhee said immediately. Her face was still and white.

"Power over the Races, over the Four Lands," Coll agreed, nodding. "It makes sense, Par."

Par shook his head slowly. "But what happens when there is no one left but the Federation? Surely someone must have thought of that. What keeps the Shadowen from feeding on them as well?"

No one answered. "We're still missing something," Par said softly. "Something important."

He rose, walked to the other side of the room, stood looking into space for a long moment, shook his head finally, turned, and came back. His lean face was stubborn with determination as he reseated himself.

"Let's get back to the matter of the Shadowen in the Pit," he declared quietly, "since that, at least, is a mystery that we might be able to solve." He folded his legs in front of him and eased forward. He looked at each of them in turn, then said, "I think that the reason they are down there is to keep anyone from getting to the Sword of Shannara."

"Par!" Coll tried to object, but his brother cut him off with a quick shake of his head.

"Think about it a moment, Coll. Padishar was right. Why would the Federation go to all the trouble of remaking the People's Park and the Bridge of Sendic? Why would they hide what remains of the old park and bridge in that ravine? Why, if not to conceal the Sword? And we've seen the vault, Coll! We've seen it!"

"The vault, yes—but not the Sword," Damson pointed out quietly, her green eyes intense as they met those of the Valemen.

"But if the Sword isn't down in the Pit as well, why are the Shadowen there?" Par asked at once. "Surely not to protect an empty vault! No, the Sword is still there, just as it has been for three hundred years. That's why Allanon sent me after it—he knew it was there, waiting to be found."

"He could have saved us a lot of time and trouble by telling us as much," said Coll pointedly.

Par shook his head. "No, Coll. That isn't the way he would do it. Think about the history of the Sword. Bremen gave it to Jerle Shannara some thousand years ago to destroy the Warlock Lord and the Elf King couldn't master it because he wasn't prepared to accept what it demanded of him. When Allanon chose Shea Ohmsford to finish the job five hundred years later, he decided that the Valeman must first prove himself. If he was not strong enough to wield it, if he did not want it badly enough, if he were not willing to give enough of himself to the task that finding it entailed, then the power of the Sword would prove too much for him as well. And he knew if that happened, the Warlock Lord would escape again."

"And he believes it will be the same now with you," Damson finished. She was looking at Par as if she were seeing him for the first time. "If you are not strong enough, if you are not willing to give enough, the Sword of Shannara will be useless to you. The Shadowen will prevail."

Par's answering nod was barely discernible.

"But why would the Shadowen—or the Federation, for that matter—leave the Sword in the Pit all these years?" Coll demanded, irritated that they were even talking about the matter after what had happened to them last night. "Why not simply remove it—or better yet, why not destroy it?"

Par's face was intense. "I don't think either the Federation or the Shadowen can destroy it—not a talisman of such power. I doubt that the Shadowen can even touch it. The Warlock Lord couldn't. What I can't figure out is why the Federation hasn't taken it out and hidden it."

He clasped his hands tightly before him. "In any case, it doesn't matter. The fact remains the Sword is still there, still in its vault." He paused, eyes level. "Waiting for us."

Coll gaped at him, realizing for the first time what he was suggesting. For a moment, he couldn't speak at all. "You can't be serious, Par," he managed finally, the disbelief in his voice undisguised. "After what happened last night? After seeing . . ." He forced himself to stop, then snapped, "You wouldn't last two minutes."

"Yes, I would," Par replied. His eyes were bright with determination. "I know I would. Allanon told me as much."

Coll was aghast. "Allanon! What are you talking about?"

"He said we had the skills needed to accomplish what was asked— Walker, Wren, and myself. Remember? In my case, I think he was talking about the wishsong. I think he meant that the magic of the wishsong would protect me."

"Well, it's done a rather poor job of it up to now!" Coll snapped, lashing out furiously.

"I didn't understand what it could do then. I think I do now."

"You think? You think? Shades, Par!"

Par remained calm. "What else are we to do? Run back to the Jut? Run home? Spend the rest of our days sneaking about?" Par's hands were shaking. "Coll, I haven't any choice. I have to try."

Coll's strong face closed in upon itself in dismay, his mouth tightening against whatever outburst threatened to break free. He wheeled on Damson, but the girl had her eyes locked on Par and would not look away.

The Valeman turned back, gritting his teeth. "So you would go back down into the Pit on the strength of an unproven and untested belief. You would risk your life on the chance that the wishsong—a magic that has failed to protect you three times already against the Shadowen—will somehow protect you now. And all because of what you perceive as your newfound insight into a dead man's words!" He drew his breath in slowly. "I cannot believe you would do anything so . . . stupid! If I could think of anything worse to call it, I would!"

"Coll . . ."

"No, don't say another word to me! I have gone with you everywhere, followed after you, supported you, done everything I could to keep you safe—and now you plan to throw yourself away! Just waste your life! Do you understand what you are doing, Par? You are sacrificing yourself! You still think you have some special ability to decide what's right! You are obsessed! You can't ever let go, even when common sense tells you you should!"

Coll clenched his fists before him. His face was rigid and furrowed, and it was all he could do to keep his voice level. Par had never seen him so angry. "Anyone else would back away, think it through, and decide to go for help. But you're not planning on any of that, are you? I can see it in your eyes. You haven't the time or the patience. You've made up your mind. Forget Padishar or Morgan or anyone else but yourself. You mean to have that Sword! You'd even give up your life to have it, wouldn't you?"

"I am not so blind . . ."

"Damson, you talk to him!" Coll interrupted, desperate now. "I know you care for him; tell him what a fool he is!"

But Damson Rhee shook her head. "No. I won't do that." Coll stared at her, stunned. "I haven't the right," she finished softly.

Coll went silent then, his rough features sagging in defeat. No one spoke immediately, letting the momentary stillness settle across the room. Daylight had shifted with the sun's movement west, gone now to the far side of the little storage shed, the shadows beginning to lengthen slightly in its wake. A scattering of voices sounded from somewhere in the streets beyond and faded away. Par felt an aching deep within himself at the look he saw on his brother's face, at the sense of betrayal he knew Coll was feeling. But there was no help for it. There was but one thing Par could say that would change matters, and he was not about to say it.

"I have a plan," he tried instead. He waited until Coll's eyes lifted. "I know what you think, but I don't propose to take any more chances than I have to." Coll gave him an incredulous look, but kept still. "The vault sits close to the base of the cliffs, just beneath the walls of the old palace. If I could get into the ravine from the other side, I would have only a short distance to cover. Once I had the Sword in my hands, I would be safe from the Shadowen."

There were several huge assumptions involved in that last statement, but neither Coll nor Damson chose to raise them. Par felt the sweat bead on his forehead. The difficulty of what he was about to suggest was terrifying.

He swallowed. "That catwalk from the Gatehouse to the old palace would give me a way across."

Coll threw up his hands. "You plan to go back into the Gatehouse yet a third time?" he exclaimed, exasperated beyond reason.

"All I need is a ruse, a way to distract . . ."

"Have you lost your mind completely? Another ruse won't do the trick! They'll be looking for you this go-around! They'll spy you out within two seconds of the time you . . ."

"Coll!" Par's own temper slipped.

"He is right," Damson Rhee said quietly.

Par wheeled on her, then caught himself. He jerked back toward his brother. Coll dared him to speak, red-faced, but silent. Par shook his head. "Then I'll have to come up with another way."

Coll looked suddenly weary. "The truth of the matter is, there isn't any other way."

"There might be one." It was Damson who spoke, her low voice compelling. "When the armies of the Warlock Lord besieged Tyrsis in the time of Balinor Buckhannah, the city was betrayed twice over from within— once by the front gates, the second time by passageways that ran beneath the city and the cliffs backing the old palace to the cellars beneath. Those passageways might still exist, giving us access to the ravine from the palace side."

Coll looked away wordlessly, disgust registering on his blocky features. Clearly, he had hoped for better than this from Damson.

Par hesitated, then said carefully, "That all happened more than four hundred years ago. I had forgotten about those passageways completely—even telling the stories as often as I do." He hesitated again. "Do you know anything about them—where they are, how to get into them, whether they can be traversed anymore?"

Damson shook her head slowly, ignoring the deliberate lift of Coll's eyebrows. She said, "But I know someone who might. If he will talk to us." Then she met Coll's gaze and held it. There was a sudden softness in her face that surprised Par. "We all have a right to make our own choices," she said quietly.

Coll's eyes seemed haunted. Par studied his brother momentarily, debating whether to say anything to him, then turned abruptly to Damson. "Will you take me to this person—tonight?"

She stood up then, and both Valemen rose with her. She looked small between them, almost delicate; but Par knew the perception was a false one. She seemed to deliberate before saying, "That depends. You must first promise me something. When you go back into the Pit, however you manage it, you will take Coll and me with you."

There was a stunned silence. It was hard to tell which of the Valemen was more astonished. Damson gave them a moment to recover, then said to Par, "I'm not giving you any choice in the matter, I'm afraid. I cannot. You would feel compelled to do the right thing and leave us both behind to keep us safe—which would be exactly the wrong thing. You need us with you."

The she turned to Coll. "And we need to be there, Coll. Don't you see? This won't end, any of it, not Federation oppression or Shadowen evil or the sickness that infects all the Lands, until someone makes it end. Par may have a chance to do that. But we cannot let him try it alone. We have to do whatever we can to help because this is our fight, too. We cannot just sit back and wait for someone else to come along and help us. No one will. If I've learned anything in this life, it's that."

She waited, looking from one to the other. Coll looked confused, as if he thought there ought to be an obvious alternative to his choices but couldn't for the life of him recognize what it was. He glanced briefly at Par and away again. Par had gone blank, his gaze focused on the floor, his face devoid of expression.

"It is bad enough that I must go," he said finally.

"Worse than bad," Coll muttered.

Par ignored him, looking instead at Damson. "What if it turns out that only I can go in?"

Damson came up to him, took his hands in her own and squeezed them. "That won't happen. You know it won't." She leaned up and kissed him softly. "Are we agreed?"

Par took a deep breath, and a frightening sense of inevitability welled up inside him. Coll and Damson Rhee—he was risking both their lives by going after the Sword. He was being stubborn beyond reason, intractable to the point of foolhardiness; he was letting himself be caught up in his own self-perceived needs and ambitions. There was every reason to believe that his insistence would kill them all.

Then give it up, he whispered fiercely to himself. *Just walk away.*

But even as he thought it, he knew he wouldn't.

"Agreed," he said.

There was a brief silence. Coll looked up and shrugged. "Agreed," he echoed quietly.

Damson reached up to touch Par's face, then stepped over to Coll and hugged him. Par was more than a little surprised when his brother hugged her back.

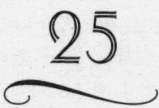

It was dusk on the following day when Padishar Creel and Morgan Leah finally reached the Jut. Both were exhausted.

They had traveled hard since leaving Tyrsis, stopping only for meals. They had slept less than six hours the previous night. Nevertheless, they would have arrived even sooner and in better condition if not for Padishar's insistence on doing everything possible to disguise their trail. Once they entered the Parma Key, he backtracked continuously, taking them down ravines, through riverbeds, and over rocky outcroppings, all the while watching the land behind him like a hawk.

Morgan had thought the outlaw chief overcautious and, after growing impatient enough, had told him so. "Shades, Padishar—we're wasting time! What do you think is back there anyway?"

"Nothing we can see, lad," had been the other's enigmatic reply.

It was a sultry evening, the air heavy and still, and the skies hazy where the red ball of the sun settled into the horizon. As they rose in the basket lift toward the summit of the Jut, they could see night's shadows begin to fill the few wells of daylight that still remained in the forests below, turning them to pools of ink. Insects buzzed annoyingly about them, drawn by their body sweat. The swelter of the day lay across the land in a suffocating blanket. Padishar still had his gaze turned south toward Tyrsis, as if he might spy whatever it was he suspected had followed them. Morgan looked with him, but as before saw nothing. The big man shook his head. "I can't see it," he whispered. "But I can feel it coming."

He didn't explain what he meant by that and the Highlander didn't ask. Morgan was tired and hungry, and he knew that nothing either Padishar or he did was likely to change the plans of whatever might be out there. Their journey was completed, they had done everything humanly possible to disguise their passing, and there wasn't anything to be gained by worrying now. Morgan felt his stomach rumble and thought of the dinner that would be waiting. Lunch that day had been a sparse affair—a few roots, stale bread, hard cheese, and some water.

"I realize that outlaws are supposed to be able to subsist on next to nothing, but surely you could have done better than this!" he had complained. "This is pathetic!"

"Oh, surely, lad!" the outlaw chief had replied. "And next time you be the gravedigger and I'll be the body!"

Their differences had been put aside by then—not forgotten perhaps, but at least placed in proper perspective. Padishar had dismissed their confrontation five minutes after it ended, and Morgan had concluded by the end of the day that things were back to normal. He bore a grudging respect for the man—for his brash and decisive manner, because it reminded the Highlander of his own, for the confidence he so readily displayed in himself, and for the way he drew other men to him. Padishar Creel wore the trappings of leadership as if they were his birthright, and somehow that seemed fitting. There was undeniable strength in Padishar Creel; it made you want to follow him. But Padishar understood that a leader must give something back to his followers. Acutely aware of Morgan's role in bringing the Valemen north, he had made a point of acknowledging the legitimacy of the Highlander's concern for their safety. Several times after their argument he had gone out of his way to reassure Morgan that Par and Coll Ohmsford would never be abandoned, that he would make certain that they were safe. He was a complex, charismatic fellow, and Morgan liked him despite a nagging suspicion that Padishar Creel would never in the world be able to deliver everything he promised.

Outlaws clasped Padishar's hand in greeting at each station of their ascent. If they believe so strongly in him, Morgan asked himself, shouldn't I?

But he knew that belief was as ephemeral as magic. He thought momentarily of the broken sword he carried. Belief and magic forged as one, layered into iron, then shattered. He took a deep breath. The pain of his loss was still there, deep and insidious despite his resolve to put it behind him, to do as Padishar had suggested and to give himself time to heal. There was nothing he could do to change what had happened, he had told himself; he must get on with his life. He had lived for years without the use of the sword's magic—without even knowing it existed. He was no worse off now than he had been then. He was the same man.

And yet the pain lingered. It was an emptiness that scraped the bones of his body from within, leaving him fragmented and in search of the parts that would make him whole again. He could argue that he was unchanged, but what he had experienced through wielding of the magic had left its stamp upon him as surely as if he had been branded by a hot iron. The memories remained, the images of his battles, the impressions made by the power he had been able to call upon, the strength he had enjoyed. It was lost to him now. Like the loss of a parent or a sibling or a child, it could never be completely forgotten.

He looked out across the Parma Key and felt himself shrinking away to nothing.

When they reached the Jut, Chandos was waiting. Padishar's one-eyed second-in-command looked larger and blacker than Morgan remembered, his bearded, disfigured face furrowed and lined, his body wrapped in a great cloak that seemed to lend his massive body added size. He seized Padishar's hand and gripped it hard. "Good hunting?"

"Dangerous would be a better word for it," the big man replied shortly.

Chandos glanced at Morgan. "The others?"

"They've fought their last, save for the Valemen. Where's Hirehone? Somewhere about or gone back to Varfleet?"

Morgan glanced quickly at him. So Padishar was still looking to discover who had betrayed them, he thought. There had been no mention of the master of Kiltan Forge since Morgan had reported seeing him in Tyrsis.

"Hirehone?" Chandos looked puzzled. "He left after you did, same day. Went back to Varfleet like you told him, I expect. He's not here." He paused. "You have visitors, though."

Padishar yawned. "Visitors?"

"Trolls, Padishar."

The outlaw chief came awake at once. "You don't say? Trolls? Well, well. And how do they come to be here?"

They started across the bluff toward the fires, Padishar and Chandos shoulder to shoulder, Morgan trailing. "They won't say," Chandos said. "Came out of the woods three days back, easy as you please, as if finding us here wasn't any trouble at all for them. Came in without a guide, found us like we were camped in the middle of a field with our pennants flying." He grunted. "Twenty of them, big fellows, down out of the north country, the Charnals. Kelktic Rock, they call themselves. Just hung about until I went down to talk to them, then asked to speak with you. When I said you were gone, they said they'd wait."

"No, is that so? Determined, are they?"

"Like falling rock looking to reach level ground. I brought them up when they agreed to give over their arms. Didn't seem right leaving them sitting down in the Parma Key when they'd come all that way to find you—and done such a good job of it in the bargain." He smirked within his beard. "Besides, I figured three hundred of us ought to be able to stop a handful of Trolls."

Padishar laughed softly. "Doesn't hurt to be cautious, old friend. Takes more than a shove to bring down a Troll. Where are they?"

"Over there, the fire on the left."

Morgan and Padishar peered through the gloom. A cluster of faceless shadows were already on their feet, watching their approach. They looked huge. Unconsciously, Morgan reached back to finger the handle of his sword, remembering belatedly that a handle was just about all he had.

"The leader's name is Axhind," Chandos finished, his voice deliberately low now. "He's the Maturen."

Padishar strode up to the Trolls, his weariness shed somewhere back, his tall form commanding. One of the Trolls stepped forward to meet him.

Morgan Leah had never seen a Troll. He had heard stories about them, of course; everyone told stories about the Trolls. Once, long before Morgan was born, Trolls had come down out of the Northland, their traditional home, to trade with the members of the other Races. For a time, some of them had even lived among the men of Callahorn. But all that ended with the coming of the Federation and its crusade for Southland domination. Trolls were no longer welcome below the Streleheim, and the few who had come south quickly went north again. Reclusive by nature, it took very little to send them back to their mountain strongholds. Now, they never came out—or at least no one Morgan knew had ever heard of them coming out. To find a band this far south was very unusual.

Morgan tried not to stare at the visitors, but it was hard. The Trolls were heavily muscled, almost grotesque, their bodies tall and wide, their skin nut-brown and rough like bark. Their faces were flat and nearly featureless. Morgan couldn't find any ears at all. They wore leather and heavy armor, and great cloaks lay scattered about their fire like discarded shadows.

"I'm Baron Creel, Leader of the Movement." Padishar's voice boomed out.

The Troll facing him rumbled something incomprehensible. Morgan caught only the name Axhind. The two gripped hands briefly, then Axhind beckoned Padishar to sit with him at their fire. The Trolls stepped aside as the outlaw chief and his companions moved into the light to seat themselves. Morgan glanced about uneasily as the massive creatures closed about. He had never felt so unprotected. Chandos seemed unconcerned, positioning himself behind Padishar and a few feet back. Morgan eased down next to him.

The talk began in earnest then, but the Highlander didn't understand any of it. It was all done in the guttural language of the Trolls, a language of which Morgan knew nothing. Padishar seemed comfortable with it, however, pausing only infrequently to consider what he was saying. There was a great deal of what sounded like grunting, some heavy slurs, and much of what was said was emphasized by sharp gestures.

"How does Padishar speak their language?" Morgan whispered early on to Chandos.

The other never even glanced at him. "We see a bit more of life in Callahorn than you Highlanders," he said.

Morgan's hunger was threatening to consume him, but he forced it from his mind, holding himself erect against encroaching weariness, keep-

ing himself deliberately still. The talk went on. Padishar seemed pleased
with its direction.

"They want to join us," Chandos whispered after a time, apparently deciding that Morgan should be rewarded for his patience. He listened some
more. "Not just these few—an entire twenty-one tribes!" He grew excited.
"Five thousand men! They want to make an alliance!"

Morgan grew excited himself. "With us? Why?"

Chandos didn't answer right away, motioning for Morgan to wait.
Then he said, "The Movement has approached them before, asked them to
help. But they always believed it too divided, too undependable. They've
changed their minds of late." He glanced over briefly. "They say Padishar
has pulled the separate factions together sufficiently to reconsider. They're
looking for a way to slow the Federation advance on their homelands." His
rough voice was filled with satisfaction. "Shades, what a stroke of good fortune this might turn out to be!"

Axhind was passing out cups now and filling them with something
from a great jar. Morgan took the cup he was offered and glanced down.
The liquid it contained was as black as pitch. He waited until both the Troll
leader and Padishar saluted, then drank. It was all he could do to keep from
retching. Whatever he had been given tasted like bile.

Chandos caught the look on his face. "Troll milk," he said and smiled.

They drained the offering, even Morgan who found that it curbed his
appetite instantly. Then they rose, Axhind and Padishar shook hands once
more, and the Southlanders moved away.

"Did you hear?" Padishar asked quietly as they disappeared into the
shadows. Stars were beginning to wink into view overhead, and the last of
the daylight had faded away. "Did you hear it all, the whole of it?"

"Every last word," Chandos replied, and Morgan nodded wordlessly.

"Five thousand men! Shades! We could challenge the best that the Federation had to offer if we had a force like that!" Padishar was ecstatic.
"There might be two thousand and some that the Movement could call
upon, and more than that from the Dwarves! Shades!"

He slammed his fist into his open palm, then reached over and clapped
both Chandos and Morgan heartily on the back. "It's about time something
went our way, wouldn't you agree, lads?"

Morgan had dinner after that, sitting alone at a table near the cooking
fire, his appetite restored by the smells that emanated from the stew kettles.
Padishar and Chandos had gone off to confer on what had been happening
during the former's absence, and Morgan saw no need to be part of that.
He looked about for Steff and Teel, but there was no sign of either, and it
wasn't until he was almost finished eating that Steff appeared out of the
darkness and slumped down beside him.

"How did it go?" the Dwarf asked perfunctorily, forgoing any greeting, his gnarled hands clutched about a tankard of ale he had carried over.
He looked surprisingly worn.

Briefly, Morgan related the events of the past week. When he was finished, Steff rubbed at his cinnamon beard and said, "You're lucky to be alive—any of you." His scarred face was haggard-looking; the mix of half-light and shadows seemed to etch more deeply its lines. "There's been some strange happenings taking place while you were away."

Morgan pushed back his plate and looked over, waiting.

The Dwarf cleared his throat, glancing about before he spoke. "Teel took sick the same day you left. They found her collapsed by the bluff about noon. She was breathing, but I couldn't bring her awake. I took her inside and wrapped her in blankets and sat with her for most of a week. I couldn't do anything for her. She just lay there, barely alive." He took a deep breath. "I thought she'd been poisoned."

His mouth twisted. "Could of been, it seemed to me. Lots in the Movement have no use for the Dwarves. But then she woke finally, retching and so weak she could barely move. I fed her broth to give her back her strength, and she came around finally. She doesn't know what happened to her. She said the last thing she remembered was wondering something about Hirehone . . ."

Morgan's sharp intake of breath stopped him. "That mean something to you, Morgan?"

Morgan nodded faintly. "It might. I thought I saw Hirehone in Tyrsis after we arrived there. He shouldn't have been, and I decided then I must have been mistaken. I'm not so certain now. Someone gave us over to the Federation. It could have been Hirehone."

Steff shook his head. "Doesn't sound right. Why Hirehone, of all people? He could have turned us in that first time in Varfleet. Why wait until now?" The stocky form shifted. "Besides, Padishar trusts him completely."

"Maybe," Morgan muttered, sipping at his ale. "But Padishar was quick enough to ask about him when we got back here."

Steff considered that a moment, then dismissed the matter. "There's more. They found a handful of guards at the cliff edge two days back, night watch, the ones on the lifts, all dead, their throats torn out. No sign of who did it." He looked away momentarily, then back again. Shadows darkened his eyes. "The baskets were all up, Morgan."

They stared at each other. Morgan frowned. "So it was someone already here who did it?"

"Don't know. Seems like. But what was the reason for it, then? And if it was someone from the outside, how did they get up and then back down again with the baskets in place?"

Morgan looked off into the shadows and thought about it, but no answers would come. Steff rose. "I thought you should know. Padishar will hear on his own, I expect." He drained his tankard. "I've got to get back to Teel; I don't like leaving her alone after what's happened. She's still awfully weak." He rubbed his forehead and grimaced. "I don't feel so well myself."

"Off you go, then," Morgan said, rising with him. "I'll come see you both in the morning. Right now, though, I'm in desperate need of about two days' sleep." He paused. "You know about the Trolls?"

"Know about them?" Steff gave him a wry smile. "I've spoken with them already. Axhind and I go back a ways."

"Well, well. Another mystery. Tell me about it tomorrow, will you?"

Steff began moving away. "Tomorrow, it is." He was almost out of sight when he said, "Better watch your back, Highlander."

Morgan Leah had already decided as much.

He slept well that night and woke rested. The midmorning sun had crested the treeline and begun to heat up the day. There was activity in the outlaw camp, more so than usual, and Morgan was immediately anxious to find out what was happening. He thought momentarily that the Valemen might have returned, but then discarded the possibility, deciding that he would have been awakened if they had. He pulled on his clothing and boots, rolled up his blankets, washed, ate, and went down to the bluff edge. He caught sight of Padishar immediately, dressed once more in his crimson garb, shouting orders and directing men this way and that.

The outlaw chief glanced over as the Highlander approached and grunted. "I trust the noise didn't wake you." He turned to yell instructions to a group of men by the lifts before continuing in a normal tone of voice, "I would hate to think you were disturbed."

Morgan muttered something under his breath, but stopped when he caught a glimpse of the other's mocking grin. "Ah, ah. Just teasing you a bit, Highlander," the other soothed. "Let's not begin the day on the wrong foot—there's too much that needs doing. I've sent scouts to sweep the Parma Key to reassure myself that my neck hairs mislead me about what's out there, and I've sent south for Hirehone. We will see what we will see. Meanwhile, the Trolls await, Axhind and his brood. Close kin, the bunch of them, I'm told. Yesterday was merely an overture. Today we talk about the how and the wherefore of it all. You want to come along?"

Morgan did. Buckling on the scabbard that held the remains of the Sword of Leah, which he was carrying now mostly out of habit, he followed Padishar along the bluff face and then back toward the campsite where the Trolls were already gathering. As they walked, he asked if there was any news of Par and Coll. There wasn't. He looked about expectantly for Steff and Teel, but there was no sign of either. He promised himself that he would seek them out later.

When they reached the Trolls, Axhind embraced the outlaw chief, then greeted the Highlander with a solemn nod and a handclasp like iron, and beckoned them both to take seats. Moments later, Chandos appeared with several companions, men Morgan didn't know, and the meeting got under way.

It lasted the remainder of the morning and the better part of the afternoon. Once again, Morgan was unable to follow what was being said, and this time Chandos was too preoccupied with his own participation to worry about him. Morgan listened attentively nevertheless, studying the gestures and movements of the bearish Trolls, trying to read something of what they were thinking behind their expressionless faces. He was mostly unsuccessful. They looked like great tree stumps brought to life and given the rudiments of human form to allow them to move about. Few did much of anything besides watch. The ones who spoke did so sparingly, even Axhind. There was an economy of effort behind everything they did. Morgan wondered briefly what they were like in a fight and decided that he probably already knew.

The sun moved across the sky, changing the light from dim to bright and back again, erasing and then lengthening shadows, filling the day with heat and then letting it linger in a suffocating swelter that left everyone shifting uncomfortably in a futile search for relief. There was a short break for lunch, an exchange of ales and wines, and even a brief allusion to the Highlander that had something to do with the extent of the support that the Movement enjoyed. Morgan stayed wisely silent during that exchange. He knew he had been brought there for support, not to contradict.

The afternoon was waning when the runner appeared, winded and frightened-looking. Padishar caught sight of him, frowned in annoyance at the interruption, and excused himself. He listened intently to what the runner had to say, hesitated, then glanced at the Highlander and beckoned. Morgan came to his feet in a hurry. He did not care for what he saw in Padishar Creel's face.

Padishar dismissed the runner when Morgan reached them. "They found Hirehone," he said softly, evenly. "Out along the west edge of the Parma Key, close to the path we followed on our return. He's dead." His eyes shifted uncomfortably. "The patrol that found him said he looked as if he had been turned inside out."

Morgan felt his throat tighten at the image. "What's going on, Padishar?" he asked quietly.

"Be sure you let me know when you figure it out, Highlander. Meantime, there's worse news still. My neck hairs never lie. There's a Federation army not two miles off—the garrison at Tyrsis or I'm not my mother's favorite son." The hard face creased with lines of irony. "They're coming right for us, lad. Not a whit of deviation in their approach. Somehow they've discovered where we are—and I guess we both know how that might have happened, don't we?"

Morgan was stunned. "Who?" He barely breathed the word.

Padishar shrugged and laughed softly. "Does it really matter now?" He glanced over his shoulder. "Time to finish up here. I don't relish telling Axhind and his clan what's happened, but it wouldn't do to play games with them. If I were them, I'd disappear out of here faster than a hare gone to ground."

The Trolls were of a different mind, however. When the meeting broke up, Axhind and his companions showed no inclination to leave. Instead,

they requested their weapons back—an
and broadswords—and on receiving them s.
fashion to sharpen the blades. It seemed as if ι.

Morgan went off to find the Dwarves. They
secluded grove of fir at the far end of the cliff base
of rock formed a natural shelter from the weather. Steff
out much enthusiasm. Teel was sitting up, her strange, mas.
ing nothing of her thoughts, though her eyes glittered wa
looked stronger, her dusky hair brushed out, her hands steady as
cepted Morgan's own. He spoke with her briefly, but she said almost no ɹing
in return. Morgan gave them the news of Hirehone and the approaching
Federation army. Steff nodded soberly; Teel didn't even do that. He left
them feeling vaguely dissatisfied with the entire visit.

The Federation army arrived with the coming of nightfall, spread out
in the forestlands directly below the cliffs of the Jut, and began clearing the
land for its use, working with the industrious determination of ants. They
streamed out of the trees, several thousand strong, their pennants flying, their
weapons gleaming. Standards were raised before each company—banners of
solid black with one red and one white stripe where there were regular
Federation soldiers and a grinning white wolf's head where there were
Seekers. Tents went up, weapons racks were assembled, supplies were positioned to the rear, and fires sparked to life. Almost immediately teams of
men began building siege weapons, and the sounds of saws felling trees and
axes hewing limbs filled the air.

The outlaws watched from the heights, their own fortifications already
in place. Morgan watched with them. They seemed relaxed and easy. There
were only three hundred of them, but the Jut was a natural fortification that
could resist an army five times the size of this one. The lifts had already
been drawn to the bluff, and now there was no way up or down except by
scaling the walls. That would require climbing by hand, ladder, or grappling
hook. Even a handful of men could put a stop to that.

It was fully dark by the time Morgan was able to speak again with
Padishar. They stood by the lifts, now under heavy guard, and looked out
over the broad scattering of watch fires below. The men of the Federation
continued to work, the sound of their building rising out of the darkened
forests into the still night air.

"I don't mind telling you that all this effort bothers me," the outlaw
chief muttered, his brow furrowing.

Morgan frowned with him. "Even with siege equipment, how can they
possibly hope to reach us?"

Padishar shook his head. "They can't. That's what bothers me."

They watched a bit longer, then Padishar steered Morgan to a secluded
part of the bluff, keeping him close as he whispered. "I needn't remind you
that we've been betrayed twice now. Whoever's responsible is still out
there—probably still among us. If the Jut's to be taken, that's my guess as to
how it's to be done."

...ed to Morgan, his strong, weathered face close. "I'll do my part ...e that the Jut's kept secure. But you keep your eyes open as well, Highlander. You might see things differently from me, being fresh here. Maybe you'll see something I'd otherwise miss. Watch us all, and it's a big favor I'll owe you if you turn up something."

Morgan nodded wordlessly. It gave him a purpose for being there, something he was beginning to suspect he lacked. He was consumed by the feeling of emptiness he had experienced on shattering his sword. He was distressed that he had been forced to leave Par and Coll Ohmsford behind. This charge, if nothing else, would give him something to concentrate on. He was grateful to Padishar for that.

When they finished, he went to the armorer and asked to be given a broadsword. He picked one that suited him, withdrew his own broken sword and replaced it with the new one. Then he hunted about for a discarded scabbard until he found one the Sword of Leah would fit, cut the scabbard to the sword's shortened length, bound the severed end, and strapped the makeshift sheath carefully to his belt.

He felt better about himself for the first time in days.

He slept well that night, too—even though the Federation continued to assemble its siege weapons until dawn. When the sun appeared, the building ceased. He woke then, the sudden stillness disconcerting, pulled on his clothes, strapped on his weapons, and hurried down to the bluff edge. The outlaws were settling into place, arms at the ready. Padishar was there, with Steff, Teel, and the contingent of Trolls. All watched silently what was taking place below.

The Federation army was forming up, squads into companies. They were well drilled, and there was no confusion as they marched into place. They encircled the base of the Jut, stretching from one end of the cliffs to the other, their lines just out of range of long bow and sling. Scaling ladders and ropes with grappling hooks were piled next to them. Siege towers stood ready, though the towers were crude and scarcely a third of the height of the cliffs leading up. Commanders barked orders crisply, and the gaps between companies slowly began to fill.

Morgan touched Steff briefly on the shoulder. The Dwarf glanced about uncertainly, nodded without saying anything, and looked away again.

Morgan frowned. Steff wasn't carrying any weapons.

Trumpets sounded, and the Federation lines straightened. Everything went still once more. Sunlight glinted off armor and weapons as the skies in the east brightened. Dew glistened off leaves and grasses, the birdsongs lifted cheerfully, the sound of water running came from somewhere distant, and it seemed to Morgan Leah that it might have been any of a thousand mornings he had greeted when he still roamed and hunted the hills of his homeland.

Then from back in the trees, behind the long lines of soldiers, something moved. There was a jerking of limbs and trunks and a rasping of scraped bark. The Federation ranks suddenly split in two, opening a hole that was better than a hundred feet across. The outlaws and their allies stiffened expectantly, frowns creasing their faces as the forest continued to shake with the approach of whatever was hidden there.

Shades, Morgan whispered to himself.

The thing emerged from out of the fading shadows. It was huge, a creature of impossible size, an apparition comprised of the worst bits and pieces of things scavengers might have left. It was formed of hair and sinew and bone, but at the same time of metal plates and bars. There were jagged ends and shiny surfaces, iron grafted onto flesh, flesh grown into iron. It had the look of a monstrous, misshapen crustacean or worm, but was neither. It shambled forward, its glittering eyes rolling upward to find the edge of the bluff. Pinchers clicked like knives and claws scraped heedlessly the roughened stone.

For an instant, Morgan thought it was a machine. Then, a heartbeat later, he realized it was alive.

"Demon's blood!" Steff cried in recognition, his gruff voice angry and frightened. "They've brought a Creeper!"

Hunching its way slowly through the ranks of the Federation army, the Creeper came for them.

M organ Leah remembered the stories then.

It seemed as if there had always been stories of the Creepers, tales that had been handed down from grandfather to father, from father to son, from generation to generation. They were told in the Highlands and in most parts of the Southland he had visited. Men whispered of the Creepers over glasses of ale around late night fires and sent shivers of excitement and horror down the spines of boys like Morgan, who listened at the circle's edge. No one put much stock in the stories, though; after all, they were told in the same breath as those wild imaginings of Skull Bearers and Mord Wraiths and other monsters out of a time that was all but forgotten. Yet no one was quite ready to dismiss them out-of-hand, either. Because whatever the men of the Southland might believe, there were Dwarves in the Eastland who swore by them.

Steff was one of those Dwarves. He had repeated the stories to Morgan—long after Morgan had already heard them—not as legend but as truth. They had happened, he insisted. They were real.

It was the Federation, he told Morgan, who made the Creepers. A hundred years ago, when the war against the Dwarves had bogged down deep in the wilderness of the Anar, when the armies of the Southland were thwarted by the jungle and the mountains and by the tangle of brush and the walls of rock that prevented them from engaging and trapping their elusive quarry, the Federation had called the Creepers to life. The Dwarves had taken the offensive away from the Federation by then, a sizeable resistance force that was determined to avoid capture and to harass the invaders until they were driven from their homeland. From their fortress lairs within the maze of canyons and defiles of the Ravenshorn and the cavelike hollows of the surrounding forests, the Dwarves counterattacked the heavier and more cumbersome Federation armies almost at will and slipped away with the ease of night's shadows. The months dragged on as the Federation effort stalled, and it was then that the Creepers appeared.

No one knew for certain where they came from. There were some who claimed they were simply machines constructed by the Federation builders, juggernauts without capacity to think, whose only function was to bring down the Dwarf fortifications and the Dwarves with them. There were others who said that no machine could have done what the Creepers did, that such things possessed cunning and instinct. A few whispered that they were formed of magic. Whatever their origin, the Creepers materialized within the wilderness of the central Anar and began to hunt. They were unstoppable. They tracked the Dwarves relentlessly and, when they caught up to them, destroyed them all. The war ended in a little more than a month, the Dwarf armies annihilated, the backbone of the resistance shattered.

After that, the Creepers vanished as mysteriously as they had appeared, as if the earth had swallowed them whole. Only the stories remained, growing more lurid and at the same time less accurate with each telling, losing the force of truth as time passed, until only the Dwarves themselves remained certain of what had happened.

Morgan Leah stared downward for a moment longer as the stories of his childhood came to life, then wrenched his eyes away from the drop, away from the nightmare below, and looked frantically at Steff. The Dwarf was staring back at him, half-turned as if to bolt from the fortifications, his scarred face stricken.

"A Creeper, Morgan. A Creeper—after all these years. Do you know what that means?"

Morgan didn't have time to speculate. Padishar Creel was suddenly beside them, having heard the Dwarf speak. His hands gripped Steff's shoulders and he pulled the other about to face him. "Tell me now, quickly! What do you know of this thing?"

"It's a Creeper," Steff repeated, his voice stiff and unnatural, as if naming it said everything.

"Yes, yes, fine and well!" Padishar snapped impatiently. "I don't care what it is! I want to know how to stop it!"

Steff shook his head slowly, as if trying to clear it, as if dazed and unable to think. "You can't stop it. There isn't any way to stop it. No one has ever found a way."

There were mutterings from the men closest to them as they heard the Dwarf's words, and a sense of restless misgiving began to ripple through the lines of defenders. Morgan was stunned; he had never heard Steff sound so defeated. He glanced quickly at Teel. She had moved Steff away from Padishar protectively, her eyes bits of hard, glistening rock within her mask.

Padishar ignored them, turning instead to face his own men. "Stand where you are!" he roared angrily at those who had begun to whisper and move back. The whispers and the movement stopped immediately. "I'll skin the first rabbit who does otherwise!"

He gave Steff a withering glance. "No way, is there? Not for you, perhaps—though I would have thought it otherwise and you a better man, Steff." His voice was low, controlled. "No way? There's always a way!"

There was a scraping sound from below, and they all pushed back to the breastworks. The Creeper had reached the base of the cliff wall and was beginning to work its way up, securing a grip in cracks and crevices where human hands and feet could not hope to find purchase. Sunlight glinted off patches of armor-plating and bits of iron rod, and the muscles of its worm-like body rippled. The marching drums of the Federation had begun to sound, pounding a steady cadence to mark the monster's approach.

Padishar leaped recklessly atop the defenses. "Chandos! A dozen archers to me—now!"

The archers appeared immediately and as rapidly as they could manage sent a rain of arrows into the Creeper. It never slowed. The arrows bounced off its armor or buried themselves in its thick hide without effect. Even its eyes, those hideous black orbs that shifted and turned lazily with the movement of its body, seemed impervious.

Padishar withdrew the archers. A cheer went up from the ranks of the Federation army and a chanting began, matching the throb of the drums. The outlaw chief called for spearmen, but even the heavy wooden shafts and iron heads could not slow the monster's approach. They broke off or shattered on the rocks, and the Creeper came on.

Massive boulders were brought forward and sent rolling over the cliff edge. Several crashed into the Creeper. They grazed it or struck it full on, and the result was the same. It kept coming. The mutterings resumed, born of fear and frustration. Padishar shouted angrily to quiet them, but the task was growing harder. He called for brush to be brought forward, had it fired and sent tumbling into the Creeper—to no effect. Furious, he had a cask of cooking oil brought up, broken open and spilled down the cliff wall, then ignited. It burned ferociously against the barren rock, engulfing the approaching Creeper in a haze of black smoke and flames. Cries rose from the ranks of the Federation and the drums went still. Heat lifted into the morning air in waves so suffocating that the defenders were forced back. Morgan retreated with the rest, Steff and Teel next to him. Steff's face was drawn and pale, and he seemed strangely disoriented. Morgan helped him step away, unable to fathom what had happened to his friend.

"Are you sick?" he asked, whispering to the other as he eased him to a sitting position. "Steff, what's wrong?"

But the other didn't appear to have an answer. He simply shook his head. Then with an effort he said, "Fire won't stop it. It's been tried, Morgan. It doesn't work."

He was right. When the flames and the heat died away enough to permit the defenders to return to the walls, the Creeper was still there, working its way steadily upward, almost halfway up by now, as scorched and blackened as the rock to which it clung but otherwise unchanged. The drumming and the chanting from the Federation soldiers below resumed, an eager, confident swell of sound that engulfed the whole of the Jut.

The outlaws were dismayed. Arguments began to spring up, and it was clear that by now no one believed that the Creeper could be stopped. What would they do when it reached them? Seemingly invulnerable to spears and arrows, could it be stopped by swords? The frantic outlaws could make a pretty good guess.

Only Axhind and his Rock Trolls seemed unperturbed by what was happening. They stood at the far end of the outlaw defenses, protecting a shelf that slanted down from the main bluff to the cliff wall, weapons held ready, a small island of calm amid the tumult. They were not talking. They did not appear nervous. They were watching Padishar Creel, apparently waiting to see what he would do next.

Padishar was quick to show them. He had noticed something that everyone else had missed, and it gave him a glimmer of hope for the besieged outlaws.

"Chandos!" he called out, shoving and pushing his men back into place as he walked down the breastworks. His burly, black-bearded lieutenant appeared. "Bring up whatever oil we've got—cooking, cleaning, anything! Don't waste time asking questions, just do it!"

Chandos closed his mouth and hurried off. Padishar wheeled and came back down the line toward Morgan and the Dwarves. "Ready one of the lifts!" he called past them. Then unexpectedly he stopped. "Steff. How are these things on slick surfaces, these Creepers? How do they grip?"

Steff looked at him blankly, as if the question were too perplexing for him to consider. "I don't know."

"But they have to grip to climb, don't they?" the other demanded. "What happens if they can't?"

He turned away without waiting for an answer. The morning had grown hot, and he was sweating heavily now. He stripped off his tunic, throwing it aside irritably. Snatching a set of cross belts from another outlaw, he buckled them on, picked up a short-handled axe, shoved it through one of the belt loops, and moved ahead to the lifts. Morgan followed, beginning to see now what the outlaw planned to do. Chandos hurried up from the caves, followed by a knot of men carrying casks of varying sizes and weights.

"Load them," Padishar ordered, motioning. When the loading was begun, he put his hands on his lieutenant's broad shoulders. "I'm going over in the lift, down where the beast climbs, and dump the oil on it."

"Padishar!" Chandos was horrified.

"No, listen now. The Creeper can't get up here if it can't climb, and it can't climb if it can't grip. The oil will make everything so slick the slug won't be able to move. It might even fall." He grinned fiercely. "Wouldn't that put a nice finish to things?"

Chandos shook his woolly head, a frantic look in his eyes. The Trolls had drifted over and were listening. "You think the Federation will let you get that far? Their bowmen will cut you to pieces!"

"Not if you keep them back, they won't." The grin vanished. "Besides, old friend—what other choice do we have?"

He sprang into the lift, crouching within the shelter of its railing to present the smallest target possible. "Just don't let me drop," he shouted and gripped the axe tightly.

The lift went over the side, Chandos letting it down quickly, bringing the boom close above where the Creeper worked its way upward, now high on the wall, a large black smudge that oozed across the rock. A howl went up from the Federation army as they saw what was happening, and lines of bowmen surged forward. The outlaws were waiting. Shooting unobstructed from their defenses far above, they broke the assault in moments. Immediately more lines rushed forward, and arrows began to shatter against the cliff face all about the dropping lift. The outlaws returned the Federation fire. Again, the assault broke apart and fell back.

But by now catapults had been brought forward, and massive rocks began to hurtle into the cliff face, smashing all about the fragile lift as Federation marksmen sought to find the range. One barrage of loose rock hammered into the lift and sent it careening into the wall. Wood splintered and cracked. From directly below, the Creeper looked up.

Morgan Leah stood at the edge of the bluff and watched in horror, Steff and Teel beside him. The lift with Padishar Creel twisted and spun as if caught in a fierce wind.

"Hold him!" Chandos screamed to the men on the ropes, turning back in dismay. "Hold him steady!"

But they were losing him. The rope slipped, and the effort to retrieve it dragged its handlers toward the cliff edge where they frantically struggled to brace themselves. Federation arrows raked the bluff, and two of the handlers dropped. No one took their place, uncertain what to do in the chaos of the attack. Chandos looked back over his shoulder, eyes wide. The rope slipped further.

They can't hold it, Morgan realized in horror.

He darted forward, shouting frantically. But Axhind was quicker. With a speed that belied his size, the Maturen of the Kelktic Rock bounded through the onlookers and seized the rope in his massive hands. The other holders fell back in confusion. Alone, the giant Troll held the lift and Padishar Creel. Then another Troll appeared and then two more. Bracing themselves, they hauled back on the rope as Chandos shouted instructions from the edge.

Morgan peered out over the bluff again. The Parma Key stretched away in a sea of deep green that disappeared into a midmorning sky that was cloudless and blue, filled with sweet smells and a sense of timelessness. The Jut was an island of chaos in its midst. At the base of the cliffs, Federation soldiers lay dying in heaps. The orderly lines were ragged now, their neat formations scattered in the rush to attack. Catapults launched their missiles and arrows flew from everywhere. The lift still dangled from its rope, a tiny bit of bait that was seemingly only inches above the black monstrosity that hunched its way steadily closer.

Then suddenly, almost unexpectedly, Padishar Creel was lifted into view, short-handled axe splintering the first of the oil casks and spilling its contents down the cliff side and over the Creeper. The head and upper body of the creature were saturated in the glistening liquid, and the Creeper stopped moving. The contents of a second cask followed the first, and then the contents of a third. The Creeper and the cliff wall were saturated. Arrows from the Federation bows pinged all about Padishar as he stood exposed. Then he was struck, once, twice, and he went down.

"Haul him up!" Chandos screamed.

The Trolls jerked on the line in response, the watching outlaws howling in fury and shooting down into the ranks of the Federation archers.

But then somehow Padishar was back on his feet, and the last two remaining casks were splintered and their contents dumped down the rock wall onto the Creeper. The beast hung there, no longer moving, letting the oil run down into it, under it, over it, streams of glistening oil and grease spreading down the cliff face in the harsh glare of the morning sun.

A catapult struck the lift squarely then and shattered it to pieces. The outlaws on the bluff cried out as the lift fell apart. But Padishar did not fall; he caught hold of the rope and dangled there, arrows and stones flying all about him, a perfect target. There was blood on his chest and arms, and the muscles of his body were corded with the effort it required for him to hang on.

Swiftly the rope came up, Padishar Creel was hauled to the edge of the bluff, and his men reached out to pull him to safety. For a moment the battle was forgotten. Chandos shouted in vain for everyone to get back, but the outlaws ignored him as they crowded around their fallen leader. Then Padishar was on his feet, blood streaming down his body from his wounds, arrows protruding from deep within his right shoulder and through the fleshy part of his left side, his face pale and drawn with pain. Reaching down, he snapped the arrow in his side in two and with a grimace pulled the shaft clear.

"Get back to the wall!" he roared. "Now!"

The outlaws scattered. Padishar pushed past Chandos and staggered to the breastworks, peering down at the Creeper.

The Creeper was still hanging there, still not moving, as if glued to the rock. The Federation archers and catapults were continuing their barrage on the outlaw defenses, but the effort had become a halfhearted one as they, too, waited to see what would happen.

"Fall, drat you!" Padishar cried furiously.

The Creeper stirred, shifting slightly, edging right, trying to maneuver away from the glistening sheet of oil. Claws rasped as it hunched and squirmed to keep its hold. But the oil had done its job. The creature's grip began to loosen, slowly at first, then more rapidly as one after another of its appendages slipped free. A howl of dismay went up from the Federation ranks, a cheer from the outlaws. The Creeper was sliding down more quickly now, skidding on a track of oil that followed after it relentlessly, coating its tubular body. Its grip gave way altogether and down it went, tumbling, rolling, falling with a crunch of metal and bone. When it struck the earth at last, dust rose in a massive cloud, and the whole of the cliff face shook with the impact.

The Creeper lay motionless at the base of the cliffs, its oiled bulk shuddering.

"That's more like it!" Padishar Creel sighed and slid down the breastworks into a sitting position, his eyes closing wearily.

"You've finished him sure enough!" Chandos exclaimed, dropping into a crouch beside him. His smile was ferocious. Morgan, standing close at hand, found himself grinning as well.

But Padishar simply shook his head. "This doesn't finish anything. That was today's horror. Tomorrow will surely bring another. And what do we do for oil then, with the last of it spilled out today?" The dark eyes opened. "Cut this other arrow out of me so I can get some sleep."

The Federation did not attack again that day. It withdrew its army to the edge of the forest, there to tend to the dead and wounded. Only the catapults were left in place, sending their loads skyward periodically, though most fell short and the assault proved more annoying than effective.

The Creeper, unfortunately, was not dead. After a time, it seemed to recover, and it rolled over sluggishly and crawled off into the shelter of the Parma Key. It was impossible to guess how badly it had been damaged, but no one was ready to predict that they had seen the last of it.

Padishar Creel was treated for his wounds, bound up, and put to bed. He was weak from loss of blood and in no small amount of pain, but his injuries would not leave him disabled. Even as Chandos was seeing to his care, Padishar was giving instructions for continuing the defense of the Jut. A special weapon was to be built. Morgan heard Chandos speak of it as he gathered a select group of men and sent them off into the largest of the caves to construct it. Work began almost immediately, but when Morgan asked what it was that was being assembled, Chandos was unwilling to talk about it.

"You'll see it when it's completed, Highlander," he responded gruffly. "Leave it at that."

Morgan did, but only because he hadn't any other choice. At something of a loss as to what to do with himself, he drifted over to where Steff had been taken by Teel and found his friend wrapped in blankets and feverish. Teel watched suspiciously as the Highlander felt Steff's forehead, a watchdog that no longer trusted anyone. Morgan could hardly blame her. He spoke quietly with Steff for a few moments, but the Dwarf was barely conscious. It seemed better to let him sleep. The Highlander stood up, glanced a final time at the unresponsive Teel, and walked away.

He spent the remainder of the day passing back and forth between the fortifications and the caves, checking on the Federation army and the secret weapon and on Padishar Creel and Steff. He didn't accomplish much, and the hours of the late morning and then the afternoon passed slowly. Morgan found himself wondering once again what good he was doing anyone, trapped at the Jut with these outlaws, resistance fighters or no, far from Par and Coll and what really mattered. How would he ever find the Valemen again, now that they had been separated? Certainly they would not attempt to come into the Parma Key, not while a Federation army had them under siege. Damson Rhee would never permit it.

Or would she? It suddenly occurred to Morgan that she might, if she thought there was a safe way to do so. That made him think. What if there was more than one way into the Jut? Didn't there have to be, he asked himself? Even with the defenses as strong as they were, Padishar Creel would never take the chance that they might somehow be breached, leaving the outlaws trapped against the rocks. He would have an escape route, another way out. Or in.

He decided to find out. It was almost dusk, however, before he got his chance. Padishar was awake again by then, and Morgan found him sitting on the edge of his bed, heavily bandaged, streaks of blood showing vividly against his weathered skin, studying a set of crudely sketched drawings with Chandos. Another man would still be sleeping, trying to regain his strength; Padishar looked ready to fight. The men glanced up as he approached, and Padishar tucked the drawings out of sight. Morgan hesitated.

"Highlander," the other greeted. "Come sit with me."

Surprised, Morgan came over, taking a seat on a packing crate filled with metal fittings. Chandos nodded, got up without a word, and walked out.

"And how is our friend the Dwarf?" Padishar asked, rather too casually. "Better, now?"

Morgan studied the other man. "No. Something is very wrong with him, but I don't know what it is." He paused. "You don't trust anyone, do you? Not even me."

"Especially not you." Padishar waited a moment, grinned disarmingly, and then made the smile disappear in the quickness of an eye's blink. "I can't afford to trust anyone anymore. Too much has happened to suggest that I shouldn't." He shifted his weight and grimaced with the pain it caused. "So tell me. What brings you to visit? Have you seen something you think I should know about?"

The truth was that with the excitement of the events of that morning, Morgan had forgotten about the charge that Padishar had given him to try to find out who it was that had betrayed them. He didn't say so, however; he simply shook his head.

"I have a question," he said. "About Par and Coll Ohmsford. Do you think that Damson Rhee might still try to bring them here? Is there another way into the Jut that she might use?"

The look that Padishar Creel gave him was at once indecipherable and filled with meaning. There was a long silence, and Morgan felt himself grow suddenly cold as he realized how it must look for him to be asking such a question.

He took a deep breath. "I'm not asking where it is, only if . . ."

"I understand what you're asking and why," the other said, cutting short his protestation. The hard face furrowed about the eyes and mouth. Padishar said nothing for a moment, studying the Highlander intently. "As a matter of fact, there is another way," he said finally. "You must have figured that out on your own, though. You understand enough of tactics to know that there must always be more than one way in or out of a refuge."

Morgan nodded wordlessly.

"Well, then, Highlander, I can only add that Damson would not put the Valemen at risk by trying to bring them here while the Jut was under siege. She would keep them safe in Tyrsis or elsewhere, whatever the situation might require."

He paused, eyes hard with hidden thoughts. Then he said, "No one but Damson, Chandos, and I know the other way—now that Hirehone is dead. Better that we keep it so until the identity of our traitor is discovered, don't you think? I wouldn't want the Federation walking in through the back door while we were busy holding shut the front."

Morgan hadn't considered the possibility of such a thing happening until now. It was a chilling thought. "Is the back way secure?" he asked hesitantly.

Padishar pursed his lips. "Very. Now take yourself off to dinner, Highlander. And remember to keep your eyes open."

He turned back to his drawings. Morgan hesitated a moment, thinking to say something more, then turned abruptly and left.

That night, as daylight faded into evening and stars began to appear, Morgan sat alone at the far end of the bluff where a grove of aspen trees sheltered a small grassy clearing, looked out across the valley of the Parma Key to where the moon, half-full again, lifted slowly out of the horizon into the darkening skies, and marshalled his powers of reason. The camp was quiet now except for the muffled sounds of work being done back in the caves on Padishar's secret weapon. The catapults and bows were stilled, the men of both the Federation army and the Movement sleeping or lost in their own private contemplations. Padishar was meeting with the Trolls and Chandos, a meeting to which Morgan had not been invited. Steff was resting, his fever seemingly no worse, but his strength sapped and his general health no better. There was nothing to be done, nothing to occupy the time but to sleep or think, and Morgan Leah had chosen the latter.

For as long as he could remember, he had been clever. It was a gift, admittedly, one that could be traced to his ancestors, to men such as Menion and Rone Leah—real Princes in those days, heroes—but an ability, too, that Morgan had worked long and hard to perfect. The Federation had supplied him with both a purpose and a direction for his skill. He had spent almost the whole of his youth concentrating on finding ways to outwit the Federation officials who occupied and governed his homeland, to irritate them at every opportunity so that they might never feel secure, to make them experience a futility and a frustration that would one day drive them from Leah forever. He was very good at it; perhaps he was the best there was. He knew all the tricks, had conceived most of them himself. He could outthink and outsmart almost anyone, if he were given time and opportunity to do so.

He smiled ruefully. At least, that was what he had always told himself. Now it was time to prove that it was so. It was time to figure out how the Federation had known so often what they were about, how it was that they had been betrayed—the outlaws, the Valemen, the little company from Culhaven, everyone connected with this misadventure—and most important of all, who was responsible.

It was something he could reason out.

He let his lean frame drape itself against the grassy base of a twisted, old trunk, drew his knees partway up to his chest, and considered what he knew.

The list of betrayals was a long one. Someone had informed the Federation when Padishar had taken them into Tyrsis to recover the Sword of Shannara. Someone had found out what they were going to do and gotten word to the Federation watch commander ahead of their arrival. One of your own, the watch commander had told Padishar. Then someone had revealed the location of the Jut to the army that now besieged it—again, someone who knew where it could be found and how to find it.

He frowned. The betrayals had actually begun before that, though. If you accepted the premise—and he was now prepared to—that someone had sent the Gnawl to track them in the Wolfsktaag and had gotten word to the Shadowen on Toffer Ridge where the Spider Gnomes could snatch Par, why then, the betrayals went all the way back to Culhaven.

So had someone been tracking them all the way from Culhaven?

He discarded the possibility immediately. No one could have managed such a feat.

But there was more to the puzzle. There was the sighting of Hirehone in Tyrsis and his subsequent murder in the Parma Key. And there was the killing of the lift watch with the lifts still drawn up. What did those events have to do with anything?

He let all the pieces sift through his mind for a few minutes, waiting to see if he would discover something he had missed. Night birds called out from below in the darkness of the Parma Key, and the wind blew gently across his face, warm and fragrant. When nothing further occurred, he took each piece in turn and tried to fit it to the puzzle, working to see if a recognizable picture would emerge. The minutes paraded past him silently. The pieces refused to fit.

He was missing something.

He rubbed his hands together briskly. He would try it another way. He would eliminate what didn't work and see what was left. He took a steadying breath and relaxed.

No one could have followed them—not for all that time. So it must be someone among them. One of them. But if that someone were responsible for the Gnawl and the Shadowen as well as everything that had happened since their arrival at the outlaw camp, then didn't it have to be one of the members of the original company? Par, Coll, Steff, Teel, or himself? He went back to Teel momentarily, for he knew less of her than of any of them. He could not bring himself to believe it was either of the Valemen or Steff. But why was Teel any better as a candidate? Hadn't she suffered at least as much as Steff?

Besides, what did Hirehone have to do with any of this? Why were the men of the lift watch killed?

He caught himself. They were killed so that someone could either get in or get out of the outlaw camp undetected. It made sense. But the lifts were drawn up. They had to have been killed after bringing someone into the camp—killed perhaps to hide that someone's identity.

He wrestled with the possibilities. It all kept coming back to Hirehone. Hirehone was the key. What if it had been Hirehone he had seen in Tyrsis? What if Hirehone had indeed betrayed them to the Federation? But Hirehone had never returned to the Jut after leaving. So how could he have killed the watch? And why would he be killed after doing so in any case? And by whom? Could there be more than one traitor involved—Hirehone and someone else?

Something clicked into place.

Morgan Leah jerked forward in recognition. Who was the enemy here—the real enemy? Not the Federation. The real enemy was the Shadowen. Wasn't that what Allanon's shade had told them? Wasn't that what they had been warned against? And the Shadowen could take the form and body and speech of anyone. Some of them could, at least—the most dangerous. Cogline had said so.

Morgan felt his pulse quicken and his face flush with excitement. They weren't dealing with a human being in this matter. They were dealing with a Shadowen! The pieces of the puzzle suddenly began to fit together. A

Shadowen could have hidden among them and they would not have known. A Shadowen could have summoned a Gnawl, sent word to Toffer Ridge to another of its kind, have gotten to Tyrsis ahead of Padishar's company, have spied out its purpose, and slipped away again before its return. A Shadowen could get close enough. And it could disguise itself as Hirehone. No, not disguise—it could *be* Hirehone! And it could have killed him when he had served his purpose, and killed the lift watch because they would have reported seeing it, no matter whose face it had worn. It had revealed the location of the Jut to the Federation army—even mapped a path for them to follow!

Who? All that remained was to determine . . .

Morgan sagged back slowly against the trunk of the aspen behind him, the puzzle suddenly complete. He knew who. Steff or Teel. It had to be one or the other. They were the only ones, besides himself, who had been with the company from the very beginning, from Culhaven to the Jut, to Tyrsis and back. Teel had been unconscious practically the entire time Padishar's band was in Tyrsis. That would have given either of the Dwarves, or more specifically the Shadowen within, the opportunity to slip away and then back again. They were alone much of the time in any case—just the two of them.

He stiffened against the weight of his suspicions as they bore down on him. For an instant, he thought he was crazy, that he should discard his reasoning entirely and start over again. But he couldn't do that. He knew he was right.

The wind brushed at him, and he pulled his cloak closer in spite of the evening's warmth. He sat without moving in the protective shadow of his haven and examined carefully the conclusions he had reached, the reasonings he had devised, the speculations that had slowly assumed the trappings of truth. It was silent now in the outlaw camp, and he could imagine himself to be the only human being living in all the vast, dark expanse of the Parma Key.

Shades.

Steff or Teel.

His instincts told him it was Teel.

27

It was three days after they had made their decision to go back down into the Pit to recover the Sword of Shannara that Damson at last took the Valemen from their garden shed hideaway into the streets of Tyrsis. By then Par was beside himself with impatience. He had wanted to go immediately; time was everything, he had argued. But Damson had flatly refused. It was too dangerous, she insisted. Too many Federation patrols were still combing the city. They had to wait. Par had been left with no choice but to do so.

Even now, when she finally judged the margin of risk small enough to permit them to venture forth, it was on a night when reasonable men would think twice about doing so, a night that was bone-cold, the city wrapped in a blanket of mist and rain that prevented even friends of long standing from recognizing each other from a distance of more than a few feet and sent the few citizens who had worked past their normal quitting time scurrying down the glistening, empty streets for the warmth and comfort of their homes.

Damson had provided the little company with foul-weather cloaks, hooded and caped, and they wore them now pulled close as they made their way through the damp and the silence. Their boots thudded softly on the stone roadway as they walked, echoing in the stillness, filling up the night with a strange, rushed cacophony. Water dripped from eaves and trickled down mortared grooves, and the mist settled on their skin with a chill, possessive adherence that was faintly distasteful. They followed the backstreets as always, avoiding the Tyrsian Way and the other main thoroughfares where Federation patrols still kept watch, steering into the narrow avenues that burrowed like tunnels through the colorless, semi-abandoned blocks of the city's poor and homeless.

They were on their way to find the Mole.

"That is how he is known," Damson told them just before they went out. "All of the street people call him that because that is what he chooses to call himself. If he ever had a real name, I doubt that he remembers it. His past is a closely kept secret. He lives in the sewers and catacombs beneath Tyrsis, a recluse. He almost never comes out into the light. His whole world is the underbelly of the city, and no one knows more about it than he does."

"And if there are still passageways that run beneath the palace of the Kings of Tyrsis, the Mole will know about them?" Par pressed.

"He will know."

"Can we trust him?"

"The problem is not whether we can trust him, but whether he will decide to trust us. As I said, he is very reclusive. He may not even choose to talk with us."

And Par said simply, "He must."

Coll said nothing. He had said little the entire day, barely a word since they had decided to go back into the Pit. He had swallowed the news of what they were going to do as if he had ingested a medicine that would either cure or kill him and he was waiting to see which it would be. He seemed to have decided that it was pointless to debate the matter further or to argue what he perceived as the folly of their course of action, so he had taken a fatalistic stance, bowing to the inevitability of Par's determination and the fortune or misfortune that would befall them because of it, and he had gone into a shell as hard and impenetrable as iron.

He trailed now as they made their way through the murk of the Tyrsian evening, tracking Par as closely as his own shadow, intruding with his mute presence in a way that distressed rather than comforted. Par didn't like feeling that way about his brother, but there was no help for it. Coll had determined his own role. He would neither accept what Par was doing nor cut himself free of it. He would simply stick it out, for better or worse, until a resolution was reached.

Damson steered them to the top of a narrow flight of stone steps that cut through a low wall connecting two vacant, unlighted buildings and wound its way downward into the dark. Par could hear water running, a low gurgle that splashed and chugged through some obstruction. They made a cautious descent of the slick stone, finding a loose, rusted railing that offered an uncertain handhold. When they reached the end of the stairs, they found themselves on a narrow walkway that ran parallel to a sewer trench. It was down the trench that the water ran, spilling from a debris-choked passageway that opened from underneath the streets above.

Damson took the Valemen into the tunnel.

It was black inside and filled with harsh, pungent smells. The rain disappeared behind them. Damson paused, fumbled about in the dark for a moment, then produced a torch coated with pitch on one end, which she managed to light with the aid of a piece of flint. The firelight brightened the gloom enough to permit them to see their way a few steps at a time, and so they proceeded. Unseen things scurried away in the darkness ahead, soundless but for the scratching of tiny claws. Water dripped from the ceiling, ran down the walls, and churned steadily through the trench. The air was chill and empty of life.

They reached a second set of stairs descending further into the earth and took them. They passed through several levels this time, and the sound of the water faded. The scratchings remained, however, and the chill clung to them with irritating persistence. The Valemen pulled their cloaks tighter. The stairs ended and a new passageway began, this one narrower than the other. They were forced to crouch in order to proceed, and the dampness gave way to dust. They moved ahead steadily, and the minutes slipped past. They were deep beneath the city by now, well within the core of rock and earth that formed the plateau on which Tyrsis rested. The Valemen had lost all sense of direction.

When they reached the bottom of a dry well with an iron ladder that led up, Damson paused. "It is not far now," she said quietly. "Just another several hundred yards when we reach the top of this ladder. We should find him then—or he us. He brought me here once long ago when I showed him a bit of kindness." She hesitated. "He is very gentle, but peculiar as well. Be careful how you treat him."

She took them up the ladder to a landing that opened into a series of passageways. It was warmer there, less dusty, the air stale but not malodorous. "These tunnels were bolt holes once for the city's defenders; at some points they lead all the way down to the plains." Her red hair shimmered as she brushed it back from her face. "Stay close to me."

They entered one of the corridors and started down. The pitch coating on the torch head sizzled and steamed. The tunnel twisted about, criss-crossed other tunnels, wound through rooms shored up with timbers and fastening bolts, and left the Valemen more confused than ever as to where they were. But Damson never hesitated, certain of her way, either reading signs that were hidden from them or calling to memory a map that she kept within her head.

At last they entered a room that was the first of several, all intercon-nected, large chambers with wooden beams, stone block floors, walls from which hangings and tapestries dangled, and a storehouse of bizarre treasures. Piled floor to ceiling, wall to wall, there were trunks of old clothing, piles of furniture crammed and laden with clasps, fittings, writings gone almost to dust, feathers, cheap jewelry, and toy animals of all sorts, shapes, and sizes. The animals were all carefully arranged, some seated in groups, some lined up on shelves and on divans, some placed at watch atop bureaus and at door-ways. There were a few rusted weapons scattered about and an armful of baskets woven from cane and rush.

There were lights as well—oil lamps fastened to the beams overhead and the wall beneath, filling the rooms with a vague brightness, the residual smoke venting through airholes that disappeared at the corners of the room into the rock above.

The Valemen looked about expectantly. There was no one there.

Damson did not seem surprised. She led them into a room, dominated by a trestle table and eight highback chairs of carved oak, and motioned for them to sit. There were animals occupying all the chairs, and the Valemen looked inquiringly at the girl.

"Choose your place, pick up the animal that's seated there, and hold it," she advised and proceeded to show them what she meant. She selected a chair with a worn, stuffed velvet rabbit resting on it, lifted the tattered crea-ture, and placed it comfortably on her lap as she sat down.

Coll did the same, his face empty as he fixed his gaze on a spot on the far wall, as if convinced that what was happening was no stranger than what he had expected. Par hesitated, then sat down as well, his companion some-thing that might have been either a cat or a dog—it was impossible to tell which. He felt slightly ridiculous.

They sat there then and waited, not speaking, barely looking at each other. Damson began stroking the worn fur backing on her rabbit. Coll was a statue. Par's patience began to slip as the minutes passed and nothing happened.

Then one after another, the lights went out. Par started to his feet, but Damson said quickly, "Sit still."

All of the lights but one disappeared. The one that remained was at the opening of the first room they had entered. Its glow was distant and barely reached to where they sat. Par waited for his eyes to adjust to the near darkness; when they did, he found himself staring at a roundish, bearded face that had popped up across from him two seats down from Damson. Blank, dilated ferret eyes peered at him, shifted to find Coll, blinked, and stared some more.

"Good evening to you, Mole," Damson Rhee said.

The Mole lifted his head a shade; his neck and shoulders came into view, and his hands and arms lifted onto the table. He was covered with hair, a dark, furry coat. It grew on every patch of skin showing, save for where his nose and cheeks and a swatch of forehead glimmered like ivory in the faint light. His rounded head swiveled slowly, and his child's fingers locked together in a pose of contentment.

"Good evening to you, lovely Damson," he said.

He spoke in a child's voice, but it sounded queer somehow, as if he were speaking from out of a barrel or through a screen of water. His eyes moved from Par to Coll, from Coll to Par.

"I heard you coming and put on the lights for you," he said. "But I don't much like the lights, so now that you are here, I have put them out again. Is that all right?"

Damson nodded. "Perfectly."

"Whom have you brought with you on your visit?"

"Valemen."

"Valemen?"

"Brothers, from a village south of here, a long way away. Par Ohmsford. Coll Ohmsford."

She pointed to each and the eyes shifted. "Welcome to my home. Shall we have tea?"

He disappeared without waiting for an answer, moving so quietly that, try as he might, even in the almost utter silence, Par could not hear him. He could smell the tea as it was brought, yet failed to see it materialize until the cups were placed before him. There were two of them, one regular size and one quite tiny. They were old, and the paint that decorated them was faded and worn.

Par watched doubtfully while Damson offered a sip from the smaller cup to the toy rabbit she held. "Are all the children fine?" she asked conversationally.

"Quite well," the Mole replied, seated again now where he had first appeared. He was holding a large bear, to whom he offered his own cup. Coll and Par followed the ritual without speaking. "Chalt, you know, has been bad again, sneaking his tea and cookies when he wishes, disrupting things rather thoroughly. When I go up to hear the news through the street grates and wall passages, he seems to believe he has license to reorganize things to his own satisfaction. Very annoying." He gave the bear a cross look. "Lida had a very bad fever, but is recovered now. And Westra cut her paw."

Par glanced at Coll, and this time his brother glanced back.

"Anyone new to the family?" Damson asked.

"Everlind," the Mole said. He stared at her for a moment, then pointed to the rabbit she was holding. "She came to live with us just two nights ago. She likes it much better here than on the streets."

Par hardly knew what to think. The Mole apparently collected junk discarded by the people of the city above and brought it down into his lair like a pack rat. To him, the animals were real—or at least that was the game he played. Par wondered uneasily if he knew the difference.

The Mole was looking at him. "The city whispers of something that has upset the Federation—disruptions, intruders, a threat to its rule. The street patrols are increased and the gate watches challenge everyone. There is a tightening of the chains." He paused, then turned to Damson. He said, almost eagerly, "It is better to be here, lovely Damson—here, underground."

Damson put down her cup. "The disruption is part of the reason we have come, Mole."

The Mole didn't seem to hear. "Yes, better to be underground, safe within the earth, beneath the streets and the towers, where the Federation never comes."

Damson shook her head firmly. "We are not here for sanctuary."

The Mole blinked, disappointment registering in his eyes. He set his own cup aside and the animal he held with it, and he cocked his rounded head. "I found Everlind at the back of the home of a man who provides counting services for the Federation tax collectors. He is quick with numbers and tallies far more accurately than others of his skill. Once, he was an advisor to the people of the city, but the people couldn't pay him as well as the Federation, so he took his services there. All day long, he works in the building where the taxes are held, then goes home to his family, his wife and his daughter, to whom Everlind once belonged. Last week, the man bought his daughter a new toy kitten, silky white fur and green button eyes. He bought it with money the Federation gave him from what they had collected. So his daughter discarded Everlind. She found the new kitten far prettier to look upon."

He looked at them. "Neither the father nor the daughter understands what they have given up. Each sees only what is on the surface and nothing of what lies beneath. That is the danger of living above ground."

"It is," Damson agreed softly. "But that is something we must change, those of us who wish to continue to live there."

The Mole rubbed his hands again, looking down at them as he did so, lost in some contemplation of his own. The room was a still life in which the Mole and his visitors sat among the discards and rejects of other lives and listened to what might have been the whisper of their own.

The Mole looked up again, his eyes fixing on Damson. "Beautiful Damson, what is it that you wish?"

Damson's willowy form straightened, and she brushed back the stray locks of her fiery hair. "There were once tunnels beneath the palace of the Kings of Tyrsis. If they are still there, we need to go into them."

The Mole stiffened. "Beneath the palace?"

"Beneath the palace and into the Pit."

There was a long silence as the Mole stared at her unblinking. Almost unconsciously, his hands went out to retrieve the animal he had been holding. He patted it gently. "There are things out of darkest night and mind in the Pit," he said softly.

"Shadowen," Damson said.

"Shadowen? Yes, that name suits them. Shadowen."

"Have you seen them, Mole?"

"I have seen everything that lives in the city. I am the earth's own eyes."

"Are there tunnels that lead into the Pit? Can you take us through them?"

The Mole's face lost all expression, then pulled away from the table's edge and dropped back into shadow. For an instant, Par thought he was gone. But he was merely hiding, returned to the comfort of the dark to consider what he was being asked. The toy animal went with him, and the girl and the Valemen were left alone as surely as if the little fellow had truly disappeared. They waited patiently, not speaking.

"Tell them how we met," the Mole spoke suddenly from his concealment. "Tell them how it was."

Damson turned obediently to the Valemen. "I was walking in one of the parks at night, just as the dusk was ending, the stars brightening in the sky. It was summer, the air warm and filled with the smell of flowers and new grass. I rested on a bench for a moment, and Mole appeared beside me. He had seen me perform my magic on the streets, hidden somewhere beneath them as he watched, and he asked me if I would do a trick especially for him. I did several. He asked me to come back the next night, and I did. I came back each night for a week, and then he took me underground and showed me his home and his family. We became friends."

"Good friends, lovely Damson. The best of friends." The Mole's face slipped back into view, easing from the shadows. The eyes were solemn. "I cannot refuse anything you ask of me. But I wish you would not ask this."

"It is important, Mole."

"You are more important," the Mole replied shyly. "I am afraid for you."

She reached over slowly and touched the back of his hand. "It will be all right."

The Mole waited until she took her hand away, then quickly tucked his own under the table. He spoke reluctantly. "There are tunnels all through the rock beneath the palace of the Kings of Tyrsis. They connect with cellars and dungeons that lie forgotten. Some, one or two perhaps, open into the Pit."

Damson nodded. "We need you to take us there."

The Mole shivered. "Dark things—Shadowen—will be there. What if they find us? What will we do?"

Damson's eyes locked on Par. "This Valeman has use of magic as well, Mole. But it is not magic like mine that plays tricks and entertains, it is real magic. He is not afraid of the Shadowen. He will protect us."

Par felt his stomach tighten at the words—words that made promises he knew deep down inside he might not be able to keep.

The Mole was studying him once more. His dark eyes blinked. "Very well. Tomorrow I will go into the tunnels and make certain they can still be traversed. Come back when it is night again, and if the way is open I will take you."

"Thank you, Mole," Damson said.

"Finish your tea," the Mole said quietly, not looking at her.

They sat in silence in the company of the toy animals and did so.

It was still raining when they left the maze of underground tunnels and sewer channels and slipped back through the empty streets of the city. Damson led the way, surefooted in the mist and damp, a cat that didn't mind the wet. She returned the Valemen to the storage shed behind the gardening shop and left them there to get some sleep. She said she would return for them after midday. There were things that she needed to do first.

But Par and Coll didn't sleep. They kept watch instead, sitting at the windows and looking out into a curtain of fog that was filled with the movement of things that weren't there and thick with the reflected light of the coming day. It was almost morning by then, and the sky was brightening in the east. It was cold in the shed, and the brothers huddled in blankets and tried to put aside their discomfort and the disquieting thought of what lay ahead.

For a long time neither of them spoke. Finally Par, his impatience used up, said to his brother, "What are you thinking about?"

Coll took a moment to consider, then simply shook his head.

"Are you thinking about the Mole?"

Coll sighed. "Some." He hunched himself within his blanket. "I should be worried about placing my life in the hands of a fellow who lives underground with the relics of other people's lives for possessions and toy animals for companions, but I'm not. I don't really know why that is. I guess it is because he doesn't seem any stranger than anyone else connected with what's happened since we left Varfleet. Certainly, he doesn't seem any crazier."

Par didn't respond to that. There wasn't anything he could say that hadn't already been said. He knew his brother's feelings. He pulled his own blanket tight and let his eyes close against the movement of the fog. He wished the waiting was over and that it was time to get started. He hated the waiting.

"Why don't you go to sleep?" he heard Coll say.

"I can't," he replied. His eyes slipped open again. "Why don't you?"

Coll shrugged. The movement seemed an effort. Coll was lost within himself, struggling to maintain direction while mired in a steadily tightening morass of circumstances and events from which he knew he should extricate himself but could not.

"Coll, why don't you let me do this alone," Par said suddenly, impulsively. His brother looked over. "I know we've already had this discussion; don't bother reminding me. But why don't you? There isn't any reason for you to go. I know what you think about what I'm doing. Maybe you're right. So stay here and wait for me."

"No."

"But why not? I can look out for myself."

Coll stared. "As a matter of fact, you can't," he said quietly. His rough features crinkled with disbelief. "I think that might be the most ridiculous thing I've ever heard you say."

Par flushed angrily. "Just because . . ."

"There hasn't been a single moment during this entire expedition or trek or whatever you want to call it that you haven't needed help from someone." The dark eyes narrowed. "Don't misunderstand me. I'm not saying you were the only one. We've all needed help, needed each other—even Padishar Creel. That's the way life works." One strong hand lifted and a finger jabbed Par roughly. "The thing is, everyone but you realizes and accepts it. But you keep trying to do everything on your own, trying to be the one who knows best, who has all the answers, recognizes all the options, and has some special insight the rest of us lack that allows you to decide what's best. You blind yourself to the truth. Do you know what, Par? The Mole, with his family of toy animals and his underground hideout—you're just like him. You're exactly the same. You create your own reality—it doesn't matter what the truth is or what anyone else thinks."

He slipped his hand back into his blanket and pulled the covering tight again. "That's why I'm going. Because you need me to go. You need me to tell you the difference between the toy animals and the real ones."

He turned away again, directing his gaze back out the rain-streaked window to where the night's fading shadows continued to play games in the mist.

Par's mouth tightened. His brother's face was infuriatingly calm. "I know the difference, Coll!" he snapped.

Coll shook his head. "No you don't. It's all the same to you. You decide whatever you want to decide and that's the end of the matter. That's the way it was with Allanon's ghost. That's the way it was with the charge he gave you to find the Sword of Shannara. That's the way it is now. Toy animals or real ones, the fact of what they are doesn't matter. What matters is how you perceive it."

"That's not true!" Par was incensed.

"Isn't it? Then tell me this. What happens tomorrow if you're mistaken? About anything. What if the Sword of Shannara isn't there? What if the Shadowen are waiting for us? What if the wishsong doesn't work the way you think it will? Tell me, Par. What if you're just plain wrong?"

Par gripped the edges of his blanket until his knuckles were white.

"What happens if the toy animals turn out to be real ones? What do you plan to do then?" He waited a moment, then said, "That's why I'm going, too."

"If it turns out that I'm wrong, what difference will it make if you do go?" Par shouted furiously.

Coll didn't respond right away. Then slowly he looked over once again. He gave Par a small, ironic smile. "Don't you know?"

He turned away again. Par bit his lip in frustration. The rain picked up momentarily, the drops beating on the shed's wooden roof with fresh determination. Par felt suddenly small and frightened, knowing that his brother was right, that he was being foolish and impulsive, that his insistence in going back into the Pit was risking all their lives, but knowing too that it didn't make any difference; he must go. Coll was right about that as well; the decision had been made and he would not change it. He remained rigid and upright next to his brother, refusing to give way to his fears, but within he curled tight and tried to hide from the faces they showed him.

Then Coll said quietly, "I love you, Par. And I suppose when you get right down to it, that's why I'm going most of all."

Par let the words hang in the silence that followed, unwilling to disturb them. He felt himself uncurl and straighten, and a flush of warmth spread through him. When he tried to speak, he could not. He let his breath out in a long, slow, inaudible sigh.

"I need you with me, Coll," he managed finally. "I really do."

Coll nodded. Neither of them said anything after that.

28

Walker Boh returned to Hearthstone following his confrontation with the Grimpond and for the better part of a week did nothing more than consider what he had been told. The weather was pleasant, the days warm and sunny, the air filled with fragrant smells from the woodland trees and flowers and streams. He felt sheltered by the valley; he was content to remain in seclusion there. Rumor provided all the company he required. The big moor cat trailed after him on the long walks he took to while away his days, padding silently down the solitary trails, along the moss-covered stream banks, through the ancient massive trees, a soundless and reassuring presence. At night, the two sat upon the cottage porch, the cat dozing, the man staring skyward at the canopy of moon and stars.

He was always thinking. He could not stop thinking. The memory of the Grimpond's words haunted him even at Hearthstone, at his home, where nothing should have been able to threaten him. The words played unpleasant games within his mind, forcing him to confront them, to try to reason through how much of what they whispered was truth and how much a lie. He had known it would be like this before he had gone to see the Grimpond—that the words would be vague and distressing and that they would speak riddles and half-truths and leave him with a tangled knot of threads leading to the answers he sought, a knot that only a clairvoyant could manage to sort out. He had known and still he was not prepared for how taxing it would be.

He was able to determine the location of the Black Elfstone almost immediately. There was only one place where eyes could turn a man to stone and voices drive him mad, one place where the dead lay in utter blackness—the Hall of Kings, deep in the Dragon's Teeth. It was said that the Hall of Kings had been fashioned even before the time of the Druids, a vast and impenetrable cavern labyrinth in which the dead monarchs of the Four Lands were interred, a massive crypt in which the living were not permitted, protected by darkness, by statues called Sphinxes that were half-man, half-beast and could turn the living to stone, and by formless beings called Banshees who occupied a section of the caverns called the Corridor of Winds and whose wail could drive men mad instantly.

And the Tomb itself, where the pocket carved with runes hid the Black Elfstone, was watched over by the serpent Valg.

At least it was if the serpent was still alive. There had been a terrible battle fought between the serpent and the company under Allanon's leadership, who had gone in search of the Sword of Shannara in the time of Shea Ohmsford. The company had encountered the serpent unexpectedly and been forced to battle its way clear. But no one had ever determined if the serpent had survived that battle. As far as Walker knew, no one had ever gone back to see.

Allanon might have returned once upon a time, of course. But Allanon had never said.

The difficulty in any event was not in determining the mystery of the Elfstone's whereabouts, but in deciding whether or not to go after it. The Hall of Kings was a dangerous place, even for someone like Walker who had less to fear than ordinary men. Magic, even the magic of a Druid, might not be protection enough—and Walker's magic was far less than Allanon's had ever been. Walker was concerned as well with what the Grimpond hadn't told him. There was certain to be more to this than what had been revealed; the Grimpond never gave out everything it knew. It was holding something back, and that was probably something that could kill Walker.

There was also the matter of the visions. There had been three of them, each more disturbing than the one before. In the first, Walker had stood on clouds above the others in the little company who had come to the Hadeshorn and the shade of Allanon, one hand missing, mocked by his own claim that he would lose that hand before he would allow the Druids to come again. In the second, he had pushed to her death a woman with silver hair, a magical creature of extraordinary beauty. In the third, Allanon had held him fast while death reached to claim him.

There was some measure of truth in each of these visions, Walker knew—enough truth so that he must pay heed to them and not simply dismiss them as the Grimpond's tauntings. The visions meant something; the Grimpond had left it to him to try to figure out what.

So Walker Boh debated. But the days passed and still the answers he needed would not come. All that was certain was the location of the Black Elfstone—and its claim upon the Dark Uncle grew stronger, a lure that drew him like a moth to flame, though the moth understood the promise of death that waited and flew to it nevertheless.

And fly to it Walker did as well in the end. Despite his resolve to wait until he had puzzled out the Grimpond's riddles, his hunger to reclaim the missing Elfstone finally overcame him. He had thought the conversation through until he was sick of repeating it in his mind. He became convinced that he had learned all from it that he was going to learn. There was no other course of action left to him but to go in search of the Black Elfstone and to discover by doing what he could discover in no other way. It would be dangerous; but he had survived dangerous situations before. He resolved not to be afraid, only to be careful.

He left the valley at the close of the week, departing with the sunrise, traveling afoot, wearing a long forest cloak for protection against the weather and carrying only a rucksack full of provisions. Most of what he would need he would find on the way. He walked west into Darklin Reach and did not look back until Hearthstone was lost from view. Rumor remained behind. It was difficult to leave the big cat; Walker would have felt better having him along. Few things living would challenge a full-grown moor cat. But it would be dangerous for Rumor as well outside the protective confines of the Eastland, where he could not conceal himself as easily and where his natural protection would be stripped from him. Besides, this was Walker's quest and his alone.

The irony of his choosing to make the quest at all did not escape him. He was the one who had vowed never to have anything to do with the Druids and their machinations. He had gone grudgingly with Par on his journey to the Hadeshorn. He had left the meeting with the shade of Allanon convinced that the Druid was playing games with the Ohmsfords, using them to serve his own hidden purposes. He had practically thrown Cogline from his own home, insisting that the other's efforts to teach the secrets of the magic had retarded his growth rather than enhanced it. He had threatened to take the Druid History that the old man had brought him and throw it into the deepest bog.

But then he had read about the Black Elfstone, and somehow everything had changed. He still wasn't sure why. His curiosity was partly to blame, his insatiable need to know. Was there such a thing as the Black Elfstone? Could it bring back disappeared Paranor as the history promised?

Questions to be answered—he could never resist the lure of their secrets. Such secrets had to be solved, their mysteries revealed. There was knowledge waiting to be discovered. It was the purpose to which he had dedicated his life.

He wanted to believe that his sense of fairness and compassion made him go as well. Despite what he believed about the Druids, there might be something in Paranor itself—if, indeed, the Druid's Keep could be brought back—that would help the Four Lands against the Shadowen. He was uneasy with the possibility that in not going he was condemning the Races to a future like that which the Druid shade had described.

He promised himself as he departed that he would do no more than he must and certainly no more than he believed reasonable. He would remain, first and always, his own master rather than the plaything that Allanon's shade would have him be.

The days were still and sultry, the summer's heat building as he traversed the forest wilderness. Clouds were massed in the west, somewhere below the Dragon's Teeth. There would be storms waiting in the mountains.

He passed along the Chard Rush, then climbed into the Wolfsktaag and out again. It took him three days of easy travel to reach Storlock. There he reprovisioned with the help of the Stors and on the morning of the fourth day set out to cross the Rabb Plains. The storms had reached him by then, and rain began to fall in a slow, steady drizzle that turned the landscape gray. Patrols of Federation soldiers on horseback and caravans of traders appeared and faded like wraiths without seeing him. Thunder rumbled in the distance, muted and sluggish in the oppressive heat, a growl of dissatisfaction echoing across the emptiness.

Walker camped that night on the Rabb Plains, taking shelter in a cottonwood grove. There was no dry wood for a fire and Walker was already drenched through, so he slept wrapped in his cloak, shivering with the damp and cold.

Morning brought a lessening of the rains, the clouds thinning and letting the sun's brightness shine through in a screen of gray light. Walker roused himself stoically, ate a cold meal of fruit and cheese, and struck out once more. The Dragon's Teeth rose up before him, sullen and dark. He reached the pass that led upward into the Valley of Shale and the Hadeshorn and, beyond, the Hall of Kings.

That was as far as he went that day. He made camp beneath an outcropping of rock where the earth was still dry. He found wood, built a fire, dried his clothes, and warmed himself. He would be ready now when tomorrow came and it was time to enter the caverns. He ate a hot meal and watched the darkness descend in a black pall of clouds, mist, and night across the empty reaches about him. He thought for a time about his boyhood and wondered what he might have done to make it different. It began to rain again, and the world beyond his small fire disappeared.

He slept well. There were no dreams, no nervous awakenings. When he woke, he felt rested and prepared to face whatever fate awaited him. He was confident, though not carelessly so. The rain had stopped again. He listened for a time to the sounds of the morning waking around him, searching for hidden warnings. There were none.

He wrapped himself in his forest cloak, shouldered his rucksack, and started up.

The morning slipped away as he climbed. He was more cautious now, his eyes searching across the barren rock, defiles, and crevices for movement that meant danger, his ears sorting through the small noises and scrapes for those that truly menaced. He moved quietly, deliberately, studying the landscape ahead before proceeding into it, choosing his path with care. The mountains about him were vast, empty, and still—sleeping giants rooted so utterly by time to the earth beneath that even if they somehow managed to wake they would find they could no longer move.

He passed into the Valley of Shale. Black rock glistened damply within its bowl, and the waters of the Hadeshorn stirred like a thick, greenish soup. He circled it warily and left it behind.

Beyond, the slope steepened and the climb grew more difficult. The wind began to pick up, blowing the mist away until the air was sharp and clear and there was only the gray ceiling of the clouds between Walker and the earth. The temperature dropped, slowly at first, then rapidly until it was below freezing. Ice began to appear on the rock, and snow flurries swirled past his face in small gusts. He wrapped his cloak about him more tightly and pressed on.

His progress slowed then, and for a very long time it seemed to Walker as if he were not moving at all. The pathway was uneven and littered with loose stone, twisting and winding its way through the larger rocks. The wind blew into him remorselessly, biting at his face and hands, buffeting him so that it threatened to knock him backward. The mountainside remained unchanging, and it was impossible to tell at any given point how far he had come. He quit trying to hear or see anything beyond what lay immediately in front of him and limited his concentration to putting one foot in front of the other, drawing into himself as far as he could to block away the cold.

He found himself thinking of the Black Elfstone, of how it would look and feel, of what form its magic might take. He played with the vision in the silence of his mind, shutting out the world he traveled through and the discomfort he was feeling. He held the image before him like a beacon and used it to brighten the way.

It was noon when he entered a canyon, a broad split between the massive peaks with their canopy of clouds that opened into a valley and beyond the valley into a narrow, twisting passageway that disappeared into the rock. Walker traversed the canyon floor to the defile and started in. The wind died away to a whisper, an echo that breathed softly in the suddenly enfolding stillness. Moisture trapped by the peaks collected in pools. Walker felt the chill lose its bite. He came out of himself again, newly alert, tense as he searched the dark rifts and corners of the corridor he followed.

Then the walls fell away and his journey was finished.

The entrance to the Hall of Kings stood before him, carved into the wall of the mountain, a towering black maw, bracketed by huge stone sentries fashioned in the shape of armor-clad warriors, the blades of their swords jammed downward into the earth. The sentries faced out from the cavern mouth, faces scarred by wind and time, eyes fastened on Walker as if they might somehow really see.

Walker slowed, then stopped. The way forward was wrapped in darkness and silence. The wind, its echo still ringing in his ears, had faded away completely. The mist was gone. Even the cold had mutated into a sort of numbing, empty chill.

What Walker felt at that moment was unmistakable. The feeling wrapped about him like a second skin, permeated his body, and reached down into his bones. It was the feeling of death.

He listened to the silence. He searched the blackness. He waited. He let his mind reach out into the world. He could discover nothing.

The minutes faded away.

Finally Walker Boh straightened purposefully, hitched up the rucksack, and started forward once again.

It was midafternoon in the Westland where the Tirfing stretched from the sun-baked banks of the Mermidon south along the broad, empty stretches of the Shroudslip. The summer had been a dry one, and the grasses were withered from the heat, even where there had been a measure of shade to protect them. Where there had been no shade at all, the land was burned bare.

Wren Ohmsford sat with her back against the trunk of a spreading oak, close to where the horses nosed into a muddy pool of water, and watched the sun's fire turn red against the west sky, edging toward the horizon and the day's close. The glare blinded her to anything approaching from that direction, and she shaded her eyes watchfully. It was one thing to be caught napping by Garth; it was something else again to let her guard down against whoever it was that was tracking them.

She pursed her lips thoughtfully. It had been more than two days now since they had first discovered they were being followed—sensed it, really, since their shadow had remained carefully hidden from them. He or she or it—they still didn't know. Garth had backtracked that morning to find out, stripping off his brightly colored clothing and donning mud-streaked plains garb, shading his face, hands, and hair, disappearing into the heat like a wraith.

Whoever was tracking them was in for an unpleasant surprise.

Still, it was nearing day's end and the giant Rover hadn't returned. Their shadow might be more clever than they imagined.

"What does it want?" she mused.

She had asked Garth the same question that morning, and he had drawn his finger slowly across his throat. She tried to argue against it, but she lacked the necessary conviction. It could be an assassin following them as easily as anyone else.

Her gaze wandered to the expanse of the plains east. It was disturbing enough to be tracked like this. It was even more disturbing to realize that it probably had something to do with her inquiries about the Elves.

She sighed fitfully, vaguely irritated with the way things were working out. She had come back from her meeting with the shade of Allanon in an unsettled state, dissatisfied with what she had heard, uncertain as to what she should do. Common sense told her that what the shade had asked of her was impossible. But something inside, that sixth sense she relied upon so heavily, whispered that maybe it wasn't, that Druids had always known more than humans, that their warnings and chargings to the people of the Races had always had merit. Par believed. He was probably already in search of the missing Sword of Shannara. And while Walker had departed from them in a rage, vowing never to have anything to do with the Druids, his anger had been momentary. He was too rational, too controlled to dismiss the matter so easily. Like her, he would be having second thoughts.

She shook her head ruefully. She had believed her own decision irrevocable for a time. She had persuaded herself that common sense must necessarily govern her course of action, and she had returned with Garth to her people, putting the business of Allanon and the missing Elves behind her. But the doubts had persisted, a nagging sense of something being not quite right about her determination to drop the matter. So, almost reluctantly, she had begun to ask questions about the Elves. It was easy enough to do; the Rovers were a migrating people and traveled the Westland from end to end during the course of a year's time, trading for what they needed, bartering with what they had. Villages and communities came and went, and there were always new people to talk to. What harm could it do them to inquire about the Elves?

Sometimes she had asked her questions directly, sometimes almost jokingly. But the answers she had received were all the same. The Elves were gone, had been since before anyone could remember, since before the time of their grandfathers and grandmothers. No one had ever seen an Elf. Most weren't sure there had ever really been any to see.

Wren had begun to feel foolish even asking, had begun to consider giving up asking at all. She broke away from her people to hunt with Garth, anxious to be alone to think, hoping to gain some insight into the dilemma through solitary consideration of it.

And then their shadow had appeared, stalking them. Now she was wondering if there wasn't something to be found out after all.

She saw movement out of the corner of her eye, a vague blur in the swelter of the plains, and she came cautiously to her feet. She stood without moving in the shadow of the oak as the shape took form and became Garth. The giant Rover trotted up to her, sweat coating his heavily muscled frame. He seemed barely winded, a tireless machine that even the intense midsummer heat could not affect. He signed briefly, shaking his head. Whoever was out there had eluded him.

Wren held his gaze a moment, then reached down to hand him the waterskin. As he drank, she draped her lanky frame against the roughened bark of the oak and stared out into the empty plains. One hand came up in an unconscious movement to touch the small leather bag about her neck. She rolled the contents thoughtfully between her fingers. Make-believe Elfstones. Her good luck charm. What sort of luck were they providing her now?

She brushed aside her uneasiness, her sun-browned face a mask of determination. It didn't matter. Enough was enough. She didn't like being followed, and she was going to put an end to it. They would change the direction of their travel, disguise their trail, backtrack once or twice, ride all night if need be, and lose their shadow once and for all.

She took her hand away from the bag and her eyes were fierce.

Sometimes you had to make your own luck.

Walker Boh entered the Hall of Kings on cat's feet, passing noiselessly between the massive stone sentinels, stepping through the cavern mouth into the blackness beyond. He paused there, letting his eyes adjust. There was light, a faint greenish phosphorescence given off by the rock. He would not need to light a torch to find the way.

A picture of the caverns flashed momentarily in his mind, a reconstruction of what he expected to find. Cogline had drawn it for him on paper once, long ago. The old man had never been into the caverns himself, but others of the Druids had, Allanon among them, and Cogline had studied the maps that they had devised and revealed their secrets to his pupil. Walker felt confident that he could find the way.

He started ahead.

The passageway was broad and level, its walls and floors free from sharp projections and crevices. The near-dark was wrapped in silence, deep and hushed, and there was only the faint echo of his boots as he walked. The air was bone-chilling, a cold that had settled into the mountain rock over the centuries and could not be dislodged. It seeped into Walker despite his clothing and made him shiver. A prickling of unpleasant feelings crept through him—loneliness, insignificance, futility. The caverns dwarfed him; they reduced him to nothing, a tiny creature whose very presence in such an ancient, forbidden place was an affront. He fought back against the feelings, recognizing what they would do to him, and after a brief struggle they faded back into the cold and the silence.

He reached the cave of the Sphinxes shortly after. He paused again, this time to steady his mind, to take himself deep down inside where the stone spirits couldn't reach him. When he was there, wrapped in whispers of caution and warning, blanketed in words of power, he went forward. He kept his eyes fixed on the dusty floor, watching the stone pass away, looking only at the next few feet he must cover.

In his mind, he saw the Sphinxes looming over him, massive stone monoliths fashioned by the same hands that had made the sentinels. The Sphinxes were said to have human faces carved on the bodies of beasts—creatures of another age that no living man had ever seen. They were old, so incredibly ancient that their lives could be measured by hundreds of generations of mortal men. So many monarchs had passed beneath their gaze, carried from life to endless rest within their mountain tombs. So many, never to return.

Look at us, they whispered! *See how wondrous we are!*

He could sense their eyes on him, hear the whisper of their voices in his mind, feel them tearing and ripping at the layers of protection he had fashioned for himself, begging him to look up. He moved more quickly now, fighting to banish the whispers, resisting the urge to obey them. The stone monsters seemed to howl at him, harsh and insistent.

Walker Boh! Look at us! You must!

He struggled forward, his mind swarming with their voices, his resolve crumbling. Sweat beaded on his face despite the cold, and his muscles knotted until they hurt. He gritted his teeth against his weakness, chiding himself, thinking suddenly of Allanon in a bitter, desperate reminder that the Druid had come this way before him with seven men under his protection and had not given in.

In the end, neither did he. Just as he thought he would, that he must, he reached the far end of the cavern and stepped into the passageway beyond. The whispers faded and were gone. The Sphinxes were left behind. He looked up again, carefully resisted the urge to glance back, then moved ahead once more.

The passageway narrowed and began to wind downward. Walker slowed, uncertain as to what might lurk around the darkened corners. The greenish light could be found only in small patches here, and the corridor was thick with shadows. He dropped into a crouch, certain that something waited to attack him, feeling its presence grow nearer with every step he took. He considered momentarily using his magic to light the passageway so that he might better see what hid from him, but he quickly discarded the idea. If he invoked the magic, he would alert whatever might be there that he possessed special powers. Better to keep the magic secret, he thought. It was a weapon that would serve him best if its use was unexpected.

Yet nothing appeared. He shrugged his uneasiness aside and pressed on until the passageway straightened and began to widen out again.

Then the sound began.

He knew it was coming, that it would strike all at once, and still he was not prepared when it came. It lashed out at him, wrapping about with the strength of iron chains, dragging him ahead. It was the scream of winds through a canyon, the howl and rip of storms across a plain, the pounding of seas against shoreline cliffs. And beneath, just under the skin of it, was the horrifying shriek of souls in unimaginable pain, scraping their bones against the rock of the cavern walls.

Frantically, Walker Boh brought his defenses to bear. He was in the Corridor of Winds, and the Banshees were upon him. He blocked everything away in an instant, closing off the terrifying sound with a strength of will that rocked him, focusing his thoughts on a single picture within his mind—an image of himself. He constructed the image with lines and shadings, coloring in the gaps, giving himself life and strength and determination. He began to walk forward. He muffled the sound of the Banshees until they were no more than a strange buzzing that whipped and tore about him, trying to break through. He watched the Corridor of Winds pass away about him, a bleak and empty cavern in which everything was invisible but the wailing, a whirl of color that flashed like maddened lightning through the black.

Nothing Walker did would lessen it. The shrieks and howls hammered into him, buffeting his body as if they were living things. He could feel his strength ebbing as it had before the onslaught of the Sphinxes, his defenses giving way. The fury of the attack was frightening. He fought back against it, a hint of desperation creeping through him as he watched the image he had drawn of himself begin to shimmer and disappear. He was losing control. In another minute, maybe two, his protection would crumble completely.

And then, once again, he broke clear just when it seemed he must give way. He stumbled from the Corridor of Winds into a small cave that lay beyond. The screams of the Banshees vanished. Walker collapsed against the closest wall, sliding down the smooth rock into a sitting position, his entire body shaking. He breathed in and out slowly, steadily, coming back to himself in bits and pieces. Time slowed, and for a moment he allowed his eyes to close.

When he opened them again, he was looking at a pair of massive stone doors fastened to the rock by iron hinges. Runes were carved into the doors, the ancient markings as red as fire.

He had reached the Assembly, the Tomb where the Kings of the Four Lands were interred.

He climbed to his feet, hitched up the rucksack, and walked to the doors. He studied the markings a moment, then placed one hand carefully upon them and shoved. The door swung open and Walker Boh stepped through.

He stood in a giant, circular cavern streaked by greenish light and shadow. Sealed vaults lined the walls, the dead within closed away by mortar and stone. Statues stood guarding their entombed rulers, solemn and ageless. Before each was piled the wealth of the master in casks and trunks— jewels, furs, weapons, treasures of all sorts. They were so covered with dust that they were barely recognizable. The walls of the chamber loomed upward until they disappeared, the ceiling an impenetrable canopy of black.

The chamber appeared empty of life.

At its far end, a second pair of doors stood closed. It was beyond that the serpent Valg had lived. The Pyre of the Dead was there, an altar on which the deceased rulers of the Four Lands lay in state for a requisite number of days before their interment. A set of stone stairs led down from the altar to a pool of water in which Valg hid. Supposedly, the serpent kept watch over the dead. Walker wouldn't have been surprised to learn that he just fed on them.

He listened for long moments for the sound of anything moving, anything breathing. He heard nothing. He studied the Tomb. The Black Elfstone was hidden here—not in the cavern beyond. If he were quick and if he were careful, he might avoid having to discover whether or not the serpent Valg was still alive.

He began moving slowly, noiselessly past the crypts of the dead, their statues and their wealth. He ignored the treasures; he knew from Cogline that they were coated with a poison instantly fatal to anyone who touched them. He picked his way forward, skirting each bastion of death, studying the rock walls and the rune markings that decorated them. He circled the chamber and found himself back where he had started.

Nothing.

His brow furrowed in thought. Where was the pocket that contained the Black Elfstone?

He studied the cavern a second time, letting his eyes drift through the haze of greenish light, skipping from one pocket of shadows to the next. He must have missed something. What was it?

He closed his eyes momentarily and let his thoughts reach out, searching the blackness. He could feel something, a very small presence that seemed to whisper his name. His eyes snapped open again. His lean, ghostlike face went taut. The presence was not in the wall; it was in the floor!

He began moving again, this time directly across the chamber, letting himself be guided by what he sensed was waiting there. It was the Black Elfstone, he concluded. An Elfstone would have life of its own, a presence that it could summon if called upon. He strode away from the statues and their treasures, away from the vaults, no longer even seeing them, his eyes fastening on a point almost at the center of the cavern.

When he reached that point, he found a rectangular slab of rock resting evenly on the floor. Runes were carved in its surface, markings so faded that he could not make them out. He hesitated, uneasy that the writing was so obscured. But if the runes were Elven script, they might be thousands of years old; he could not expect to be able to read them now.

He knelt down, a solitary figure in the center of the cavern, isolated even from the dead. He brushed at the stone markings and tried a moment longer to decipher them. Then, his patience exhausted, he gave up. Using both hands, he pushed at the stone. It gave easily, moving aside without a sound.

He felt a momentary rush of excitement.

The hole beneath was dark, so cloaked in shadow that he could make nothing out. Yet there was something . . .

Casting aside momentarily the caution that had served him so well, Walker Boh reached down into the opening.

Instantly, something wrapped about his hand, seizing him. There was a moment of excruciating pain and then numbness. He tried to jerk free, but he could not move. Panic flooded through him. He still could not see what was down there.

Desperate now, he used the magic, his free hand summoning light and sending it swiftly down into the hole.

What he saw caused him to go cold. There was no Elfstone. Instead, a snake was fastened to his hand, coiled tightly about it. But this was no ordinary snake. This was something far more deadly, and he recognized it instantly. It was an Asphinx, a creature out of the old legends, conceived at the same time as its massive counterparts in the caves without, the Sphinxes. But the Asphinx was a creature of flesh and blood until it struck. Only then did it turn to stone.

And whatever it struck turned to stone as well.

Walker's teeth clenched against what he saw happening. His hand was already turning gray, the Asphinx still wrapped firmly about it, dead now and hardened, cemented against the floor of the compartment in a tight spiral from which it could not be broken loose.

Walker Boh pulled violently against the creature's grasp. But there was no escape. He was embedded in stone, fastened to the Asphinx and the cavern floor as surely as if by chains.

Fear ripped through him, tearing at him as a knife edge might his flesh. He was poisoned. Just as his hand was turning to stone, so would the rest of him. Slowly. Inexorably.

Until he was a statue.

Dawn at the Jut brought a change in the weather as the leading edge of the storm that was passing through Tyrsis drifted north into the Parma Key. It was still dark when the first cloud banks began to blanket the skies, blotting out the moon and stars and turning the whole of the night an impenetrable black. Then the wind died, its whisper fading away almost before anyone still awake in the outlaw camp noticed it was gone, and the air became still and sullen. A few drops fell, splashing on the upturned faces of the watch, spattering onto the dry, dusty rock of the bluff in widening stains. Everything grew hushed as the drops came quicker. Steam rose off the floor of the forestland below, lifting above the treetops to mix with the clouds until there was nothing left to see, even with the sharpest eyes. When dawn finally broke, it came as a line of brightness along the eastern horizon so faint that it went almost unnoticed. By then, the rain was falling steadily, a heavy drizzle that sent everyone scurrying for shelter, including the watch.

Which was why no one saw the Creeper.

It must have come out of the forest under cover of darkness and begun working its way up the cliffside when the clouds took away the only light that would have revealed its presence. There were sounds of scraping as it climbed, the rasp of its claws and armor-plating as it dragged itself upward, but the sounds were lost in the rumble of distant thunder, the splatter of the rain, and the movement of men and animals in the camps. Besides, the outlaws on watch were tired and irritable and convinced that nothing was going to happen before dawn.

The Creeper was almost on top of them before they realized their mistake and began to scream.

The cries brought Morgan Leah awake with a start. He had fallen asleep in the grove of aspen at the far end of the bluff, still mulling over what to do about his suspicions as to the identity of the traitor. He was curled in a ball under the canopy of the largest tree, his hunting cloak wrapped about him for warmth. His muscles were so sore and cramped that at first he could not bring himself to stand. But the cries grew quickly more frantic, filled with terror. Ignoring his own discomfort, he forced himself to his feet, pulled free the broadsword he had strapped to his back, and stumbled out into the rain.

The bluff was in pandemonium. Men were charging back and forth everywhere, weapons drawn, dark shadows in a world of grayness and damp. A few torches appeared, bright beacons against the black, but their flames were extinguished almost immediately by the downpour. Morgan hurried ahead, following the tide, searching the gloom for the source of the madness.

And then the saw it. The Creeper was atop the bluff, rearing out of the chasm, looming over the outlaw fortifications and the men who threatened it, its claws digging into the rock to hold it fast. A dead man dangled from one of its massive pinchers, cut nearly in half—one of the watch who had realized what was happening.

The outlaws surged forward recklessly, seizing poles and spears, jamming them into the Creeper's massive body, trying desperately to force the monster back over the edge. But the Creeper was huge; it towered above them like a wall. Morgan slowed in dismay. They might as well have been trying to turn a river from its course. Nothing that large could be dislodged by human strength alone.

The Creeper lunged forward, throwing itself into its attackers. Poles and spears snapped and splintered as it hurtled down. The men caught beneath died instantly, and several more were quickly snatched up by the pinchers. An entire section of the Jut's fortifications collapsed under the creature's weight. The outlaws fell back as it hunched its way into them, smashing weapons, stores, and campsites, catching up anything that moved. Blows from swords and knives rained down on its body, but the Creeper seemed unaffected. It advanced relentlessly, stalking the men who retreated from it, destroying everything in its path.

"Free-born!" the cry rang out suddenly. "To me!"

Padishar Creel materialized from out of nowhere, a bright scarlet figure in the rain and mist, rallying his men. They cried out in answer and rushed to stand beside him. He formed them quickly into squads; half counterattacked the Creeper with massive posts to fend off the pinchers while the balance hacked at the monster's sides and back. The Creeper writhed and twisted, but came on.

"Free-born, free-born!" The cries sounded from everywhere, lifting into the dawn, filling the grayness with their fury.

Then Axhind and his Rock Trolls appeared, their massive bodies armored head to foot, wielding their huge battleaxes. They attacked the Creeper head-on, striking for the pinchers. Three died almost instantly, torn apart so fast that they disappeared in a blur of limbs and blood. But the others cut and hacked with such determination that they shattered the left pincher, leaving it broken and useless. Moments later, they cut it off entirely.

The Creeper slowed. A trail of bodies littered the ground behind it. Morgan still stood between the monster and the caves, undecided as to what he should do and unable to understand why. It was as if he had become mired in quicksand. He saw the beast lift itself clear of the earth. Its head and pincher came up, and it hung suspended like a snake about to strike, braced on the back half of its body, prepared to throw itself on its attackers and smash them. The Trolls and the outlaws fell back in a rush, shouting to one another in warning.

Morgan looked for Padishar, but the outlaw chief had disappeared. The Highlander could not find him anywhere. For an instant, he thought Padishar must have fallen. Rain trickled down his face into his eyes, and he blinked it away impatiently. His hand tightened on the handle of his broadsword, but still he hung back.

The Creeper was inching forward, casting right and left to protect against flanking attacks. A twitch of its tail sent several men flying. Spears and arrows flew into it and bounced away. Steadily it came on, forcing the defenders ever closer to the caves. Soon, there would be nowhere left for them to go.

Morgan Leah was shaking. *Do something!* his mind screamed.

In that same instant Padishar reappeared at the mouth of the largest of the Jut's caves, calling out to his men to fall back. Something huge lumbered into view behind him, creaking and rumbling as it came. Morgan squinted through the gloom and mist. Lines of men appeared, hauling on ropes, and the thing began to take shape. Morgan could see it now as it cleared the cavern entrance and crawled into the light.

It was a great, wooden crossbow.

Padishar had its handlers wheel it into position facing the Creeper. Atop its base, Chandos used a heavy winch to crank back the bowstring. A massive, sharpened bolt was fitted in place.

The Creeper hesitated, as if to measure the potential danger of this new weapon. Then, lowering itself slightly, it advanced, its remaining pincher clicking in anticipation.

Padishar ordered the first bolt fired when the creature was still fifty feet away. The shot flew wide. The Creeper picked up speed as Chandos hurriedly rewound the bowstring. The crossbow fired again, but the bolt glanced off a section of armor-plating and caromed away. The Creeper was knocked sideways, slowed momentarily by the force of the blow, and then it straightened itself and came on.

Morgan saw at once that there would be no time for a third shot. The Creeper was too close. Yet Chandos stayed atop the crossbow, desperately cranking back the bowstring a third time. The Creeper was only yards away. Outlaws and Trolls harassed it from all sides, axes and swords hammering against it, but it refused to be deterred. It recognized the crossbow as the only thing it really had to fear and moved swiftly to destroy it.

Chandos shoved the third bolt into place and reached for the trigger.

He was too late. The Creeper lunged and came down atop the crossbow, smashing into its works. Wood splintered, and the wheels supporting the weapon gave way. Chandos was thrown into the night. Men scattered everywhere, crying out. The Creeper shifted atop the wreckage, then lifted free. It drew itself up deliberately, sensing its victory, knowing it needed only one further lunge to finish the job.

But Padishar Creel was quicker. While the other outlaws fled, Chandos lay unconscious in the darkness, and Morgan struggled with his indecision, Padishar attacked. Little more than a scarlet blur in the mist and half-light of the rain-soaked dawn, the outlaw chief seized one of the crossbow bolts that had been spilled from its rack, darted beneath the Creeper, and braced the bolt upright against the earth. The Creeper never saw him, so intent was it on destroying the crossbow. The monster hammered down, smashing through the already crippled weapon onto the iron-tipped bolt. The force of its lunge sent the bolt through iron and flesh, in one side of its body and out the other.

Padishar barely managed to roll clear as the Creeper struck the earth.

Back the monster reared, shuddering with pain and surprise, transfixed on the bolt. It lost its balance and toppled over, writhing madly in an effort to dislodge the killing shaft. It crashed to the ground, belly up, coiling into a ball. "Free-born!" Padishar Creel cried out, and the outlaws and Trolls were upon it. Bits and pieces of the creature flew apart as swords and axes hacked. The second pincher was sheared off. Padishar shouted encouragement to his men, attacking with them, swinging his broadsword with every ounce of strength he possessed.

The battle was ferocious. Though badly injured, the Creeper was still dangerous. Men were pinned beneath it and crushed, sent flying as it thrashed, and ripped by its claws. All efforts to put an end to it were stymied until finally another of the scattered crossbow bolts was brought forward and rammed through the monster's eye and into its brain. The Creeper convulsed one last time and went still.

Morgan Leah watched it all as if from a great distance, too far removed from what was happening to be of any use. He was still shaking when it ended. He was bathed in sweat. He had not lifted a finger to help.

There was a change in the outlaw camp after that, a shift in attitude that reflected the growing belief that the Jut was no longer invulnerable. It was apparent almost immediately. Padishar slipped into the blackest of moods, railing at everyone, furious at the Federation for using a Creeper, at the dead monster for the damage it had inflicted, at the watch for not being more alert, and at himself especially for not being better prepared. His men went about their tasks grudgingly, a dispirited bunch that slogged through the rain and murk and mumbled darkly to themselves. If the Federation had sent one Creeper, they said, what was to prevent it from sending another? If another was sent, what would they do to stop this one? And what would they do if the Federation sent something worse?

Eighteen men died in the attack and twice that number were injured, some of whom would be dead before the day was out. Padishar had the casualties buried at the far end of the bluff and the injured moved into the largest cave, which was converted into a temporary hospital. There were medicines and some few men with experience in treating battle wounds to administer them, but the outlaws did not have the services of a genuine Healer. The cries of the injured and dying lingered in the early morning stillness.

The Creeper was dragged to the edge of the bluff and thrown over. It was a difficult, exhausting task, but Padishar would not tolerate the creature's presence on the bluff a second longer than was necessary. Ropes and pulleys were used, one end of the lines fastened to the monster's dead bulk, the other end passed through the hands of dozens of men who pulled and strained as the Creeper was hauled inch by inch through the wreckage of the camp. It took the outlaws all morning. Morgan worked with them, not speaking to anyone, trying hard to remain inconspicuous, still struggling to understand what had happened to him.

He figured it out finally. He was still immersed in the effort to drag the Creeper to the bluff edge, his body aching and weary, but his mind grown unexpectedly sharp. It was the Sword of Leah that was responsible, he realized—or more accurately, the magic it contained, or had once contained. It was the loss of the magic that had crippled him and had caused him to be so indecisive, so frightened. When he had discovered the magic of the Sword, he had thought himself inivincible. The feeling of power was like nothing he had ever experienced or would have believed possible. With that sort of power at his command, he could do anything. He could still remember what it had felt like to stand virtually alone against the Shadowen in the Pit. Wondrous. Exhilarating.

But draining, as well. Each time he invoked the power, it seemed to take something away from him.

When he had broken the Sword of Leah and lost all use of the magic, he had begun to understand just how much it was that had been taken from him. He sensed the change in himself almost immediately. Padishar had insisted he was mistaken, had told him he would forget his loss, that he would heal, and that time would see him back to the way he had been. He knew now that it wasn't so. He would never heal—not completely. Having once used the magic, he was changed irrevocably. He couldn't give it up; he wasn't the same man without it. Though he had possessed it only briefly, the effect of having had it for even that long was permanent. He hungered to have it back again. He needed to have it back. He was lost without it; he was confused and afraid. That was the reason he had failed to act during the battle with the Creeper. It was not that he lacked a sense of what he should do or how he should do it. It was that he no longer could invoke the magic to aid him.

Admitting this cost him something he couldn't begin to define. He continued to work, a machine without feelings, numbed by the idea that loss of the magic could paralyze him so. He hid himself in his thoughts, in the rain and the gray, hoping that no one—especially Padishar Creel—had noticed his failure, agonizing over what he would do if it happened again.

After a time, he found himself thinking about Par. He had never considered before what it must be like for the Valeman to have to continually struggle with his own magic. Forced to confront what the magic of the Sword of Leah meant to him, Morgan thought he understood how difficult it must be for Par. How had his friend learned to live with the uncertainty of the wishsong's power? What did he feel when it failed him, as it had so many times on their journey to find Allanon? How had he managed to accept his weakness? It gave Morgan a measure of renewed strength to know that the Valeman had somehow found a way.

By midday, the Creeper was gone and the damage it had caused to the camp was mostly repaired. The rain ceased finally as the storms drifted east, scraping along the rim of the Dragon's Teeth. The clouds broke apart, and sunlight appeared through the breaks in long, narrow streamers that played across the dark green spread of the Parma Key. The mist burned off, and all that remained was a sheen of dampness that blanketed everything with a lustrous silver coating.

The Federation immediately hauled forward its catapults and siege towers and renewed its assault on the Jut. The catapults flung their stones and the siege towers were lined with archers who kept a steady fire on the outlaw camp. No effort was made to scale the heights; the attack was limited to a constant barrage against the bluff and its occupants, a barrage that lasted through the afternoon and went on into the night, a steady, constant, ceaseless harassment. There was nothing that the outlaws could do to stop it; their attackers were too far away and too well-protected. There was nowhere outside of the caves where it was safe to walk. It seemed clear that the loss of the Creeper hadn't discouraged the Federation. The siege would not be lifted. It would go on until the defenders were sufficiently weakened to be overcome by a frontal assault. If it were to take days or weeks or months, the end would be the same. The Federation army was content to wait.

On the heights, the defenders dodged and darted through the rain of missiles, yelled defiantly down at their attackers, and went about their work as best they could. But in the privacy of their shelters they grumbled and muttered their suspicions with renewed conviction. No matter what they had once believed, the Jut could not be held.

Morgan Leah was faced with worries of his own. The Highlander had deliberately gone off by himself and was secluded once more within the shelter of the aspen grove at the far end of the bluff, away from the major defensive positions of the camp where most of the Federation attack was being concentrated. Having managed to put aside for the moment the matter of his inability to accept losing the magic of the Sword of Leah, he was now forced to confront the equally troubling dilemma of his suspicions as to the identity of the traitor.

It was difficult to know what to do. Surely he should tell someone. He *had* to tell someone. But who?

Padishar Creel? If he told Padishar, the outlaw chief might or might not believe him, but in either case he was unlikely to leave the matter to chance. Padishar didn't care a fig for either Steff or Teel at this point; he would simply do away with them—both of them. After all, there was no way of knowing which one it was—or even if it was either. And Padishar was in no mood to wait around for the answer.

Morgan shook his head. He couldn't tell Padishar.

Steff? If he chose to do that, he was deciding, in effect, that Teel was the traitor. That was what he wanted to believe, but was that the truth of the matter? Even if it was, he knew what Steff's reaction would be. His friend was in love with Teel. Teel had saved his life. He would hardly be willing to accept what Morgan was telling him without some sort of proof to back it up. And Morgan didn't have any proof—at least, nothing you could hold in your hand and point to. Speculation was all he had, well-reasoned or not.

He eliminated Steff.

Someone else? There wasn't anyone else. He would have told Par or Coll if they were there, or Wren, or even Walker Boh. But the members of the Ohmsford family were scattered to the four winds, and he was alone. There was no one he could trust.

He sat within the trees and listened to the distant shouts and cries of the defenders, to the sound of catapults and bows, the creaking of iron and wood, the hum of missiles sent flying, and the ping and crash and thud of their impact. He was isolated, an island within the heart of a battle that had somehow caught him up, lost in a sea of indecision and doubt. He had to do something—but the direction he should take refused to reveal itself. He had wanted so badly to be a part of the fight against the Federation, to come north to join the outlaws, to undertake the search for the Sword of Shannara, to see the Shadowen destroyed. Such aspirations he had harbored when he had set out—such bold plans! He was to be shed of his claustrophobic existence in the Highlands, his meaningless tweaking of the noses of the bureaucrats the Federation had sent to govern, finished at last with conducting meaningless experiments in aggravation against men who could change nothing, even if they wished to do so. He was to do something grand, something wonderful . . .

Something that would make a difference.

Well, now he had his chance. He could make the difference no one else could. And there he sat, paralyzed.

Afternoon drifted into evening, the siege continued unabated, and Morgan's dilemma remained unresolved. He left the grove once to check on Steff and Teel—or more accurately, perhaps, to spy on them, to see if they might give anything away. But the Dwarves seemed no different from before. Steff was still weak and able to converse for only a few minutes before dropping off to sleep; Teel was taciturn, guarded. He studied them both as surreptitiously as he could, working at seeing something that would give him a clue as to whether his suspicions had any basis in fact—any possibility of truth at all—and he left as empty-handed as he had come.

It was almost dark when Padishar Creel found him. He was lost in thought, still trying to puzzle through what course of action he should take, and he didn't hear the big man approach. It wasn't until Padishar spoke that he realized anyone was there.

"Keeping to yourself quite a bit, aren't you?"

Morgan jumped. "What? Oh, Padishar. Sorry."

The big man sat down across from him. His face was tired and streaked with dust and sweat. If he noticed Morgan's uneasiness, he didn't let on. He stretched his legs and leaned back, supporting himself on his elbows, wincing from the pain of his wounds. "This has been a foul day, Highlander," he said. It came out in a long sigh of aggravation. "Twenty-two men dead now, another two likely to be gone by morning, and here we cower like foxes brought to bay."

Morgan nodded without responding. He was trying desperately to decide what he should say.

"Truth is, I don't much care for the way this is turning out." The hard face was impossible to read. "The Federation will lay siege to this place until we've all forgotten why it was that we came here in the first place, and that doesn't do much to advance my plans or the hopes of the free-born.

Bottled up like we are, we're not much use to anyone. There's other havens, and there'll be other times to square matters with those cowards who would send things conceived of dark magic to do their work rather than face us themselves." He paused. "So I've decided that it's time to think about getting out."

Morgan sat forward now. "Escape?"

"Out that back door we talked about. I thought you should know. I'll be needing your help."

Morgan stared. "My help?"

Padishar straightened slowly to a sitting position. "I want someone to carry a message to Tyrsis—to Damson and the Valemen. They need to know what's happened. I'd go myself, but I have to stay to see the men safely out. So I thought you might be interested."

Morgan agreed at once. "I am. I'll do it."

The other's hand lifted in warning. "Not so fast. We won't be leaving the Jut right away, probably not for another three days or so. The injured shouldn't be moved just yet. But I'll want you to leave sooner. Tomorrow, in fact. Damson's a smart girl with a good head on her shoulders, but she's wilful. I've been thinking matters over a bit since you asked me whether she might attempt to bring the Valemen here. I could be wrong; she might try to do just that. You have to make certain she doesn't."

"I will."

"Out the back door, then—as I've said. And you go alone."

Morgan's brow furrowed.

"Alone, lad. Your friends stay with me. First, you can't be wandering about Callahorn with a pair of Dwarves in tow—even if they were up to it, which at least the one isn't. The Federation would have you in irons in two minutes. And second, we can't be taking any chances after all the treachery that's been done. No one is to know your plans."

The Highlander considered a moment. Padishar was right. There was no point in taking needless risks. He would be better off going by himself and telling no one what he was about—especially Steff and Teel. He almost gave voice to what he was thinking, then thought better of it. Instead, he simply nodded.

"Good. The matter is settled. Except for one thing." Padishar climbed back to his feet. "Come with me."

He took Morgan through the camp and into the largest of the caves that opened on the cliffs backing the bluff, led him past the bay in which the wounded were being cared for and into the chambers beyond. The tunnels began there, a dozen or more, opening off each other, disappearing back into the darkness. Padishar had picked up a torch on their way in; now he touched it to one that burned from an iron bracket hammered into the cave wall, glanced about for a moment to reassure himself that no one was paying any special attention, then beckoned Morgan ahead. Ignoring the tunnels, he guided the Highlander through the piles of stores to the very deepest part of the caves, several hundred feet back into the cliff rock to a wall where crates were stacked twenty feet high. It was quiet there, the noise left behind. Again he glanced back, scanning the darkness.

Then, handing his torch to Morgan, he reached up with both hands, fitted his fingers into the seams of the crates and pulled. An entire section swung free, a false front on hidden hinges that opened into a tunnel beyond.

"Did you see how I did that, lad?" he asked softly. Morgan nodded.

Padishar took back his torch and poked it inside. Morgan leaned forward. The walls of the secret tunnel twisted and wound downward into the rock until they were lost from view.

"It goes all the way through the mountain," Padishar said. "Follow it to its end and you come out above the Parma Key just south of the Dragon's Teeth, east of the Kennon Pass." He looked at Morgan pointedly. "If you were to attempt to find your way through the other passageways—the ones I keep a guard on for show—we might never see you again. Understand?"

He shoved the secret door closed again and stepped back. "I'm showing you all this now because, when you're ready to go, I won't be with you. I'll be out there, keeping a close watch on your backside." He gave Morgan a small, hard smile. "Be certain you get clear quickly."

They went back through the storage chambers and out through the main cavern to the bluff. It was dark now, the last of the daylight faded into dusk. The outlaw chief stopped, stretched, and took a deep breath of evening air.

"Listen to me, lad," he said quietly. "There's one thing more. You have to stop brooding about what happened to that sword you carry. You can't haul that burden around with you and expect to stay clearheaded; it's much too heavy a load, even for a determined fellow like you. Lay it down. Leave it behind you. You've got enough heart in you to manage without it."

He knows about this morning, Morgan realized at once. He knows and he's telling me that it's all right.

Padishar sighed. "Every bone in my body aches, but none of them aches nearly so bad as my heart. I hate what's happened here. I hate what's been done to us." He looked squarely at Morgan. "That's what I mean about useless baggage. You think about it."

He turned and strode off into the dark. Morgan almost called him back. He even took a step after him, thinking that now he would tell him his suspicions about the traitor. It would have been easy to do so. It would have freed him of the frustration he felt at having to keep the matter to himself. It would have absolved him of the responsibility of being the only one who knew.

He wrestled with his indecision as he had wrestled with it all that day.

But once again he lost.

He slept after that, wrapping himself in his cloak and curling up on the ground within the shadow of the aspen. The earth had dried after the morning rain; the night was warm, and the air was filled with the smells of the forest. His sleep was dreamless and complete. Worries and indecisions slipped away like water shed from his skin. Banished were the wraiths of his lost magic and of the traitor, driven from his mind by the weariness that wrapped protectively about him and gave him peace. He drifted, suspended in the passing of time.

And then he came awake.

A hand clutched his shoulder, tightening. It happened so abruptly, so shockingly, that for a moment he thought he was being attacked. He thrashed himself clear of his cloak and bounded to his feet, wheeling about frantically in the dark.

He found himself face-to-face with Steff.

The Dwarf was crouched before him, wrapped in his blankets, his hair stiff and spikey, his scarred face pale and drawn and sweating despite the night's comfortable feel. His dark eyes burned with fever, and there was something frightened and desperate in their look.

"Teel's gone," he whispered harshly.

Morgan took a deep, steadying breath. "Gone where?" he managed, one hand still fastened tightly about the handle of the dagger at his waist.

Steff shook his head, his breathing ragged in the night's silence. "I don't know. She left about an hour ago. I saw her. She thought I was sleeping, but . . ." He trailed off. "Something's wrong, Morgan. Something." He could barely speak. "Where is she? Where's Teel?"

And instantly, Morgan Leah knew.

30

It was on that same night that Par Ohmsford went down into the Pit after the Sword of Shannara for the final time.

Darkness had descended on the city of Tyrsis, a cloak of impenetrable black. The rain and mist had turned into fog so thick that the roofs and walls of buildings, the carts and stalls of the markets, even the stones of the streets disappeared into it as if they had melted away. Neither moon nor stars could be seen, and the lights of the city flickered like candles that might be snuffed out at any instant.

Damson Rhee led the Valemen from the garden shed into the haze, cloaked and hooded once more. The fog was suffocating; it was damp and heavy and it clung to clothing and skin alike in a fine sheen. The day had ended early, shoved into nightfall by the appearance of the fog as it rose out of the grasslands below the bluff and built upon itself like a tidal wave until it simply rolled over Tyrsis' walls and buried her. The chill of the previous night had been replaced by an equally unpleasant warmth that smelled of must and rot. All day the people of the city muttered in ill-disguised concern over the strangeness of the weather; when the last of the day's thin, gray light began to fade, they barricaded themselves in their homes as if they were under siege.

Damson and the Valemen found themselves virtually alone in the silent, shrouded streets. When travelers passed by, once or twice only, their presence was but momentary, as if ghosts that had ventured forth from the netherworld only to be swallowed back up again. There were sounds, but they lacked both a source and a direction. Footsteps, the soft thudding of boots, rose into the silence from out of nowhere and disappeared the same way. Things moved about them, shapes and forms without definition that floated rather than walked and that came and went with the blink of an eye.

It was a night for imagining things that weren't there.

Par did his best to avoid that, but he was only partially successful. He harbored within him ghosts of his own making, and they seemed to find their identity in the shadows that played in the mist. There, left of the pinprick of light that was a streetlamp, rose the promise Par had made to keep Coll and Damson safe this night when they went down into the Pit—a small, frightened wisp of nothing. There, just behind it, was his belief that he possessed in the magic of the wishsong sufficient power to keep that promise, that he could somehow use the wishsong as the Elfstones had once been used—not as a maker of images and deceptions, but as a weapon of strength and power. His belief chased after his promise, smaller and frailer yet. Across the way, crawling along the barely visible wall of a shop front, hunching itself across the stone blocks as if mired in quicksand, was the guilt he felt at heeding no one but himself as he sought to vindicate both promise and belief—a guilt that threatened to rise up and choke him.

And hanging over all of them like a giant bird of prey—over promise, belief, and guilt, at home within the faceless night, blind and reckless and cast in stone—was his determination to heed the charge of the shade of Allanon and retrieve from the Pit and its Shadowen the missing Sword of Shannara.

It was down there in its vault, he reassured himself in the privacy of his thoughts. The Sword of Shannara. It was waiting for him.

But the ghosts would not be banished, and the whisper of their doubts swarmed about his paper-thin self-assurances like scavengers, insistent in their purpose, taunting him for his pride and his foolish certainty, teasing him with vivid images of the fate that awaited them all if he was wrong. He walled himself away from the ghosts, just as he had walled himself away all along. But he could not ignore their presence. He could not pretend they weren't there. He fled down inside himself as the three companions worked their way slowly, blindly through the empty city streets, the fog, and the damp and found refuge in the hard core of his resolve. He was risking everything on being right. But what if he wasn't? Who, besides Coll and Damson, would suffer for his mistake?

He thought for a time about those from whom he had become separated on his odyssey—those who had faded away into the events that had brought him to this night. His parents were Federation prisoners, under house arrest at their home in the village of Shady Vale—kind, gentle folk who had never hurt anyone and knew nothing of what this business was about. What, he wondered, would happen to them if he failed? What of Morgan Leah, the sturdy Dwarf Steff, and the enigmatic Teel? He supposed that even now they were hatching plans against the Federation, hidden away at the Jut, deep within the protective confines of the Parma Key. Would his failure exact a price from them as well? And what of the others who had come to the Hadeshorn? Walker Boh had returned to Hearthstone. Wren had gone back into the Westland. Cogline had disappeared.

And Allanon. What of the Druid shade? What of Allanon, who might never even have existed?

But this wasn't a mistake and he wasn't wrong. He knew it. He was certain of it.

Damson slowed. They had reached the narrow stone steps that wound downward to the sewers. She glanced back at Par and Coll momentarily, her green eyes hard. Then, beckoning them after, she began her descent. The Valemen followed. Par's ghosts went with him, closing tightly about, their breath as real as his own as it brushed against his face. Damson led the way; Coll brought up the rear. No one spoke. Par was not certain he could speak if he tried. His mouth and throat felt as if they were lined with cotton.

He was afraid.

Once again, Damson produced a torch to light the way, a flare of brightness in the dark, and they moved noiselessly ahead. Par glanced at Damson and Coll in turn. Their faces were pale and taut. Each met his gaze briefly and looked away.

It took them less than an hour to reach the Mole. He was waiting for them when they climbed out of the dry well, hunched down in the shadows, a bristling cluster of hair from which two glittering eyes peeked out.

"Mole?" Damson called softly to him.

For a moment, there was no response. The Mole was crouched within a cleft in the rock wall of the chamber, almost invisible in the dark. If it hadn't been for the torch Damson bore, they would have missed him completely. He stared out at them without speaking, as if measuring the truth of who they appeared to be. Finally, he shuffled forward a foot or two and stopped.

"Good evening, lovely Damson," he whispered. He glanced briefly at the Valemen but said nothing to them.

"Good evening, Mole," Damson replied. She cocked her head. "Why were you hiding?"

The Mole blinked like an owl. "I was thinking."

Damson hesitated, her brow furrowing. She stuck the torch into a crack in the rock wall behind her where the light would not disturb her strange friend. Then she crouched down in front of him. The Valemen remained standing.

"What have you discovered, Mole?" Damson asked quietly.

The Mole shifted. He was wearing some sort of leather pants and tunic, but they were almost completely enveloped in the fur of his body. His feet were covered with hair as well. He wore no shoes.

"There is a way into the palace of the Kings of Tyrsis and from there into the Pit," the Mole said. He hunched lower. "There are also Shadowen."

Damson nodded. "Can we get past them?"

The Mole rubbed his nose with his hand. Then he studied her expectantly for a very long time, as if discovering something in her face that before this had somehow escaped his notice. "Perhaps," he said finally. "Shall we try?"

Damson smiled briefly and nodded again. The Mole stood up. He was tiny, a ball of hair with arms and legs that looked as if they might have been stuck on as an afterthought. What was he, Par wondered? A Dwarf? A Gnome? What?

"This way," the Mole said, and beckoned them after him into a darkened passageway. "Bring the torch if you wish. We may use it for a while." He glanced pointedly at the Valemen. "But there must be no talking."

So it began. He took them down into the bowels of the city, its deepest sewers, the catacombs that tunneled its basements and sublevels, passageways that no one had used for hundreds of years. Dust lay upon the rock and earthen floors in thick layers that showed no signs of having ever been disturbed. It was warmer here; the damp and fog did not penetrate. The corridors burrowed into the cliffs, rising and falling through rooms and chambers that had once been used as bolt holes for the defenders of the city, to store foodstuffs and weapons, and on occasion to hide the entire population—men, women, and children—of Tyrsis. There were doors now and then, all rusted and falling off their hinges, bolts broken and shattered, wooden timbers rotting. Rats stirred from time to time in the darkness, but fled at the approach of the humans and the light.

Time slipped away. Par lost all track of how long they navigated the underground channels, working their way steadily forward behind the squat form of the Mole. He let them rest now and again, though he himself did not appear to need to. The Valemen and the girl carried water and some small food to keep their strength up, but the Mole carried nothing. He didn't even appear to have a weapon. When they stopped, those few brief times, they sat about in a circle in the near-dark, four solitary beings buried under hundreds of feet of rock, three sipping water and nibbling food, the fourth watching like a cat, all of them silent participants in some strange ritual.

They walked until Par's legs began to ache. Dozens of corridors lay behind them, and the Valeman had no idea where they were or what direction they were going. The torch they had started out with had burned away and been replaced twice. Their clothing and boots were coated with dust, their faces streaked with it. Par's throat was so parched he could barely swallow.

Then the Mole stopped. They were in a dry well through which a scattering of tunnels ran. Against the far wall, a heavy iron ladder had been bolted into the rock. It rose into the dark and disappeared.

The Mole turned, pointed up and held one scruffy finger to his mouth. No one needed to be told what that meant.

They climbed the ladder in silence, one foot after the other, listening to the rungs creak and groan beneath their weight. The torchlight cast their shadows on the walls of the well in strange, barely recognizable shapes. The corridors beneath faded into the black.

At the top of the ladder there was a hatchway. The Mole braced himself on the ladder and lifted. The hatchway rose an inch or two, and the Mole peeked out. Satisfied, he pushed the hatchway open, and it fell over with a hollow thud. The Mole scrambled out, Damson and the Valemen on his heels.

They stood in a huge empty cellar, a stone-block dungeon with enormous casks banded by strips of iron, shackles and chains scattered about, cell doors fashioned of iron bars, and countless corridors that disappeared at every turn into black holes. A single broad stairway at the far end of the cellar lifted into shadow. The silence was immense, as if become so much a part of the stone that it echoed with a voice of its own. Darkness hung over everything, chased only marginally by the smoking light of the single torch the company bore.

The Mole edged close against Damson and whispered something. Damson nodded. She turned to the Valemen, pointed to where the stairs rose into the black and mouthed the word "Shadowen."

The Mole took them quickly through the cellar to a tiny door set into the wall on their right, unlatching it soundlessly, ushering them through, then closing it tightly behind them. They were in a short corridor that ended at another door. The Mole took them through this door as well and into the room beyond.

The room was empty, with nothing in it but some pieces of wood that might have come from packing crates, some loose pieces of metal shielding, and a rat that scurried hastily into a crack in the wall's stone blocks.

The Mole tugged at Damson's sleeve and she bent down to listen. When he had finished, she faced the Valemen.

"We have come under the city, through the cliffs at the west end of the People's Park and into the palace. We are in its lower levels, down where the prisons used to be. It was here that the armies of the Warlock Lord attempted a breakthrough in the time of Balinor Buckhannah, the last King of Tyrsis."

The Mole said something else. Damson frowned. "The Mole says that there may be Shadowen in the chambers above us—not Shadowen from the Pit, but others. He says he can sense them, even if he cannot see them."

"What does that mean?" Par asked at once.

"It means that sensing them is as close as he cares to get." Damson's face tilted away from the torchlight as she scanned the ceiling of the room. "It means that if he gets close enough to see them, they can undoubtedly see him as well."

Par followed her gaze uneasily. They had been talking in whispers, but was it safe to do even that? "Can they hear us?" he asked, lowering his voice further, pressing his mouth close to her ear.

She shook her head. "Not here, apparently. But we won't be able to talk much after this." She looked over at Coll. He was motionless in the dark. "Are you all right?" Coll nodded, white-faced nevertheless, and she looked back at Par. "We are some distance from the Pit still. We have to use the catacombs under the palace to reach the cliff hatch that will let us in. Mole knows the way. But we have to be very careful. There were no Shadowen in the tunnels yesterday when he explored, but that may have changed."

Par glanced at the Mole. He was squatting down against one wall, barely visible at the edge of the torchlight, eyes gleaming as he watched them. One hand stroked the fur of his arm steadily.

The Valeman felt a twinge of uneasiness. He shifted his feet until he had placed Damson between the Mole and himself. Then he said, so that he believed only she could hear, "Are you sure we can trust him?"

Damson's pale face did not change expression, but her eyes seemed to look somewhere far, far away. "As sure as I can be." She paused. "Do you think we have a choice?"

Par shook his head slowly.

Damson's smile was faint and ironic. "Then I guess there is no point worrying about it, is there?"

She was right, of course. There was no help for his suspicions unless he agreed to turn back, and Par Ohmsford had already decided that he would never do that. He wished that he could test the magic of the wishsong, that he had thought to do so earlier—just to see if it could do what he thought it could. That would provide some reassurance. Yet he knew, even as he completed the thought, that there was no way to test the magic, at least not in the way that he needed to—that it would not reveal itself. He could make images, yes. But he could not summon the wishsong's real power, not until there was something to use it against. And maybe not even then.

But the power was there, he insisted once again, a desperate reassurance against the whisperings of his ghosts. It had to be.

"We won't be needing this anymore," Damson said, gesturing with the torch. She handed it to Par, then fished through her pockets and produced a pair of strange white stones streaked with silver. She kept one and handed him the other. "Put out the torch," she instructed him. "Then place your hands tightly about the stone to warm it. When you feel its heat, open them."

Par doused the torch in the dust, smothering the flame. The room went completely black. He put the strange stone between his hands and held it there. After a few seconds, he could feel it grow warm. When he took one hand away, the stone gave off a meager silver light. As his eyes adjusted, he saw that the light was strong enough to reveal the faces of his companions and an area beyond of several feet.

"If the light begins to dim, warm the stone again with your hands."

She closed her hand over his, tight about the stone, held it there, then lifted it away. The silver light radiated even more brightly. Par smiled in spite of himself, the amazement in his eyes undisguised. "That's a nice trick, Damson," he breathed.

"A bit of my own magic, Valeman," she said softly, and her eyes fixed on him. "Street magic from a street girl. Not so wonderful as the real thing, but reliable. No smoke, no smell, easily tucked away. Better than torchlight, if we want to stay hidden."

"Better," he agreed.

The Mole took them from the room then, guiding them into the black without the benefit of any light at all, apparently needing none. Damson followed, carrying one stone, Par came after carrying the other, and Coll once again brought up the rear. They went out through a second door into a passageway that twisted about and ran past other doors and rooms. They moved soundlessly, their boots scraping softly on the stone, their breathing a shallow hiss, their voices stilled.

Par found himself wondering again about the Mole. Could the Mole be trusted? Was the little fellow what he claimed to be or something else? The Shadowen could appear as anyone. What if the Mole was a Shadowen? So many questions again, and no answers to be found. There was no one he could trust, he thought bleakly—no one but Coll. And Damson. He trusted Damson.

Didn't he?

He beat back the sudden cloud of doubt that threatened to envelop him. He could not afford to be asking such questions now. It was too late to make any difference, if the answers were the wrong ones. He was risking everything on his judgment of Damson, and he must believe that his judgment was correct.

Thinking again of the Shadowen enigma, the mystery of who and what they were and how they could be so many things, he was led to wonder suddenly if there were Shadowen in the outlaw camp, if the enemy they were so desperately seeking to remain hidden from was in fact already among them. The traitor that Padishar Creel sought could be a Shadowen, one that only looked human, that only seemed to be one of them. How were they to know? Was magic the only test that would reveal them? Was that to be the purpose of the Sword of Shannara, to reveal the true identity of the enemy they sought? It was what he had wondered from the moment Allanon had sent him in search of the Sword. But how impossible it seemed that the talisman could be meant for such endless, exhausting work. It would take forever to test it against everyone who might be a Shadowen.

He heard in his mind the whisper of Allanon's voice.

Only through the Sword can truth be revealed and only through truth shall the Shadowen be overcome.

Truth. The Sword of Shannara was a talisman that revealed truth, destroyed lies, and laid bare what was real against the pretense of what only seemed so. That was the use to which Shea Ohmsford had put it when the little Valeman had defeated the Warlock Lord. It must be the use for which the talisman was meant this time as well.

They climbed a long, spiral staircase to a landing. A door in the wall before them stood closed and bolted. The wall behind and the ceiling above were lost in shadow. The drop below seemed endless. They crowded together on the landing while the Mole worked the bolts, first one, then another, then a third. One by one, the metal grating softly, they slid free. The Mole twisted the handle slowly. Par could hear the sound of his own breathing, of his pulse, and of his heartbeat, all working in response to the fear that coursed through him. He could feel Shadowen watching, hidden in the dark. He could sense their presence. It was irrational, imagined—but there nevertheless.

Then the Mole had the door open, and they slipped quickly through.

They found themselves in a tiny, windowless room with a stairwell in the exact center that spiraled down into utter blackness and a door to the left that opened into an empty corridor. Light filtered through slits in the walls of the corridor, faint and wispy. At the corridor's far end, maybe a hundred feet away, a second door stood closed.

The Mole motioned them into the corridor and shut the first door behind them. Par edged over to one of the slits in the wall and peered out. They were somewhere in the palace, aboveground again. Cliffs rose up before him, their slopes a tangle of pine trees. Above the trees, clouds hung thick across the skyline, their underbellies flat and hard and sullen.

Par drew back. Darkness was beginning to give way to daylight. It was almost morning. They had been walking all night.

"Lovely Damson," the Mole was saying softly as Par joined them. "There is a catwalk ahead that crosses the palace court. Using it will save us considerable time. If you and your friends will keep watch, I will make certain the shadow things are nowhere about."

Damson nodded. "Where do you want us?"

Where he wanted them was at each end of the corridor, listening for the sound of anything that might approach. It was agreed that Coll would remain where he was. Par and Damson went on with the Mole to the corridor's far end. There, after a reassuring nod, the Mole slipped past them through the door and was gone.

The Valeman and the girl sat across from each other, close against the door. Par glanced back down the dimly lighted corridor to make certain that Coll was in sight. His brother's rough face lifted briefly, and Par gave a cursory wave. Coll waved back.

They sat in silence then, waiting. The minutes passed and the Mole did not return.

Par grew uneasy. He edged closer to Damson. "Do you think he is all right?" he asked in a whisper.

She nodded without speaking.

Par sat back again, took a deep breath, and let it out slowly. "I hate waiting like this."

She made no response. Her head tilted back against the wall and her eyes closed. She remained like that for a long time. Par thought she might be sleeping. He looked down the corridor again at Coll, found him exactly as he had left him, and turned back to Damson. Her eyes were open, and she was looking at him.

"Would you like me to tell you something about myself that no one else knows?" she asked quietly.

He studied her face wordlessly—her fine, even features, so intense now, her emerald eyes and pale skin shadowed under the sweep of her red hair. He found her beautiful and enigmatic, and he wanted to know everything about her.

"Yes," he replied.

She moved over until their shoulders were touching. She glanced at him briefly, then looked away. He waited.

"When you tell someone a secret about yourself, it is like giving a part of yourself away," she said. "It is a gift, but it is worth much more than something you buy. I don't tell many people things about myself. I think it is because I have never had much besides myself, and I don't want to give what little I have away."

She looked down and her hair spilled forward, veiling her face so that he couldn't see it clearly. "But I want to give something to you. I feel close to you. I have from the very beginning, from that first day in the park. Maybe it is because we have the magic in common—we share that. Maybe that is what makes me feel we're alike. Your magic is different from mine, but that doesn't matter. What matters is that using the magic is how we live. It is what we are. Magic gives us our identity."

She paused, and he thought she might be waiting for a response, so he nodded. He could not tell if she saw the nod or not.

She sighed. "Well, I like you, Elf-boy. You are stubborn and determined, and sometimes you don't take notice of anything or anyone around you—only of yourself. But I am like that, too. Maybe that is how we keep ourselves from becoming exactly like everyone else. Maybe it is how we survive."

She paused, then faced him. "I was thinking that if I were to die, I would want to leave something of myself with you, something that only you would have. Something special."

Par started to protest, but she put her fingers quickly against his mouth. "Just let me finish. I am not saying that I think I will die, but it is surely possible. So perhaps telling you this secret will protect me against it, like a talisman, and keep me safe from harm. Do you see?"

His mouth tightened and she took her fingers away. "Do you remember when I first told you about myself, that night you escaped from the Federation watch after the others were captured? I was trying to convince you that I was not your betrayer. We told ourselves some things about each other. You told me about the magic, about how it worked. Do you remember?"

He nodded. "You told me that you were orphaned when you were eight, that the Federation was responsible."

She drew her knees up like a child. "I told you that my family died in a fire set by Federation Seekers after it was discovered that my father was supplying weapons to the Movement. I told you a street magician took me in shortly after and that is how I learned my trade."

She took a deep breath and shook her head slowly. "What I told you was not entirely true. My father didn't die in the fire. He escaped. With me. It was my father who raised me, not an aunt, not a street magician. I grew up with street magicians and that is how I learned my trade, but it was my father who looked after me. It is my father who looks after me still."

Her voice shook. "My father is Padishar Creel."

Par stared in wonderment. "Padishar Creel is your father?"

Her eyes never left him. "No one knows but you. It is safer that way. If the Federation found out who I was, they would use me to get to him. Par, what you needed to know that night when I told you about my childhood was that I could never betray anyone after the way my family was betrayed to the Federation. That much was true. That is why my father, Padishar Creel, is so furious that there might be a traitor among his own men. He can never forget what happened to my mother, brother, and sister. The possibility of losing anyone close to him again because of someone's treachery terrifies him."

She paused, studying him intently. "I promised never to tell anyone who I really was, but I am breaking that promise for you. I want you to know. It is something I can give you that will belong only to you."

She smiled then, and some of the tension drained out of him. "Damson," he said, and he found himself smiling back at her. "Nothing had better happen to you. If it does, it will be my fault for talking you into bringing me down here. How will I face Padishar, then?" His voice was a soft whisper of laughter. "I wouldn't be able to go within a hundred miles of him!"

She started laughing as well, shaking soundlessly at the thought, and she shoved him as if they were children at play. Then she reached over and hugged herself against him. He let her hold him without responding for a moment, his eyes straying to where Coll sat, a vague shadow at the other end of the hall. But his brother wasn't looking. There had been friends and traitors mixed up in this enterprise from the beginning, and it had been all but impossible to tell which was which. Except for Coll. And now Damson.

He put his arms around her and hugged her back.

Moments later, the Mole returned. He came upon them so quietly that they didn't even know he was there until the door began to open against them. Par released Damson and jumped to his feet, the blade of his long knife flashing free. The Mole peeked through the door and then ducked hurriedly out of sight again. Damson grabbed Par's arm. "Mole!" she whispered. "It's all right!"

The Mole's roundish face eased back into view. Upon seeing that the weapon had been put away, he came all the way through. Coll was already hastening down the corridor. When he joined them, the Mole said, calm again, "The catwalk is clear and will stay that way if we hurry. But be very quiet, now."

They slipped from the corridor and found themselves on a balcony that encircled a vast, empty rotunda. They moved quickly along it, passing scores of closed, latched doors and shadowed alcoves. Halfway around, the Mole led them into a hall and down its length to a set of iron-barred doors that opened out over the main courtyard of the palace. A catwalk ran across the drop to a massive wall. The courtyard had once been a maze of gardens and winding pathways; now there were only crumbling flagstones and bare earth. Beyond the wall lay the dark smudge of the Pit.

The Mole beckoned anxiously. They stepped onto the catwalk, feeling it sway slightly beneath their combined weight, hearing it creak in protest. The wind blew in quick gusts, and the sound it made as it rushed over the bare stone walls and across the empty courtyard was a low, sad moan. Weeds whipped and shuddered below them and debris scattered about the court, careening from wall to wall. There was no sign of life, no movement in the shadows and murk, no Shadowen in sight.

They crossed the catwalk quickly, once they were upon it, ignoring the creak and groan of its iron stays. They kept their feet moving, their hands on the railing, and their eyes focused carefully ahead, watching the palace wall draw closer. When the crossing was completed they stepped hurriedly onto the battlement, each reaching back to help the next person, grateful to be done.

The Mole took them into a stairwell where they found a fresh set of steps winding downward into blackness. Using the light of the stones Damson had supplied, they descended silently. They were close now; the stone of the wall was all that separated them from the Pit. Par's excitement sent the blood pumping through him, a pounding in his ears, and his nerve endings tightened.

Just a few more minutes . . .

At the bottom of the stairwell, there was a passageway that ended at a weathered, ironbound wooden door. The Mole walked to the door and stopped. When he turned back to face them, Par knew at once what lay beyond.

"Thank you, Mole," he said softly.

"Yes, thank you," echoed Damson.

The Mole blinked shyly. Then he said, "You can look through here."

He reached up and carefully pulled back a tiny shutter that revealed a slit in the wood. Par stepped forward and peered out.

The floor of the Pit stretched away before him, a vast, fog-bound wilderness of trees and rock, a bottomland that was strewn with decaying logs and tangled brush, a darkness in which shadows moved and shapes formed and faded again like wraiths. The wreckage of the Bridge of Sendic lay just to the right and disappeared into the gray haze.

Par squinted into the murk a moment longer. There was no sign of the vault that held the Sword of Shannara.

But he had seen it, right there, just beyond the wall of the palace. The magic of the wishsong revealed it. It was out there. He could feel its presence like a living thing.

He let Damson take a look, then Coll. When Coll stepped back, the three of them stood facing one another.

Par slipped out of his cloak. "Wait for me here. Keep watch for the Shadowen."

"Keep watch for them yourself," Coll said bluntly, shrugging off his own cloak. "I'm going with you."

"I'm going, too," said Damson.

But Coll blocked her way instantly. "No, you're not. Only one of us can go besides Par. Look about you, Damson. Look at where we are. We're in a box, a trap. There is no way out of the Pit except through this door and no way out of the palace except back up the stairs and across the catwalk. The Mole can watch the catwalk, but he can't watch this door at the same time. You have to do that."

Damson started to object, but Coll cut her short. "Don't argue, Damson. You know I'm right. I've listened to you when I should; this time you listen to me."

"It doesn't matter who listens to whom. I don't want either of you going," insisted Par sharply.

Coll ignored him, shifting his short sword in his belt until it was in front of him. "You don't have any choice."

"Why shouldn't I be the one to go?" Damson demanded angrily.

"Because he's my brother!" Coll's voice cracked like a whip, and his rough features were hard. But when he spoke next, his voice was strangely soft. "It has to be me; it's why I came in the first place. It's why I'm here at all."

Damson went still, frozen and voiceless. Her gaze shifted. "All right," she agreed, but her mouth was tight and angry as she said it. She turned away. "Mole, watch the catwalk."

The little fellow was glancing at each of them in turn, a mix of uncertainty and bewilderment in his bright eyes. "Yes, lovely Damson," he murmured and disappeared up the stairs.

Par started to say something more, but Coll took him by the shoulders and pushed him back up against the weathered door. Their eyes met and locked.

"Let's not waste any more time arguing about this, huh?" Coll said. "Let's just get it over with. You and me."

Par tried to twist free, but Coll's big hands were like iron clamps. He sagged back, frustrated. Coll released him. "Par," he said, and the words were almost a plea. "I spoke the truth. I have to go."

They faced each other in silence. Par found himself thinking of what they had come through to reach this point, of the hardships they had endured. He wanted to tell Coll that it all meant something, that he loved him, that he was frightened for him now. He wanted to remind his brother about his duck feet, to warn him that duck feet were too big to sneak around in. He thought he might scream.

But, instead, he said simply, "I know."

Then he moved to the heavy, weathered door, released its fastenings, and pulled on its worn handle. The door swung open, and the half-light and fog, the rancid smells and cloying chill, the hiss of swamp sounds, and the high, distant call of a solitary bird rushed in.

Par looked back at Damson Rhee. She nodded. That she would wait? That she understood? He didn't know.

With Coll beside him, he stepped out into the Pit.

Where was Teel?

Morgan Leah knelt hurriedly beside Steff, touched his face, and felt the chill of his friend's skin through his fingers. Impulsively, he put his hands on Steff's shoulders and gripped him, but Steff did not seem to feel it. Morgan took his hands away and rocked back on his heels. His eyes scanned the darkness about him, and shivered with something more than the cold. The question repeated itself in his mind, racing from corner to corner as if trying to hide, a dark whisper.

Where was Teel?

The possibilities paraded before him in his mind. Gone to get Steff a drink of water, something hot to eat, another blanket perhaps? Gone to look around, spooked from her sleep by one of those instincts or sixth-senses that kept you alive when you were constantly being hunted? Close by, about to return?

The possibilities shattered into broken pieces and disappeared. No. He knew the answer. She had gone into the secret tunnel. She had gone there to lead the soldiers of the Federation into the Jut from the rear. She was about to betray them one final time.

No one but Damson, Chandos, and I know the other way—now that Hire-hone is dead.

That was what Padishar Creel had told him, speaking of the hidden way out, the tunnel—something Morgan had all but forgotten until now. He shivered at the clarity of the memory. If his reasoning was correct and the traitor was a Shadowen who had taken Hirehone's identity to follow them to Tyrsis, then that meant the Shadowen had possession of Hirehone's memories and knew of the tunnel as well.

And if the Shadowen was now Teel . . .

Morgan felt the hairs on the back of his neck prickle. It would take the Federation months to take the Jut by siege. But what if the siege was nothing more than a decoy? What if the Creeper itself had been, even in failing, just a decoy? What if the Federation's intent from the beginning, was to take the Jut from within, by betrayal once again, through the tunnel that was to have been the outlaws' escape?

I have to do something!

Morgan Leah felt leaden. He must leave Steff and get to Padishar Creel at once. If his suspicions about Teel were correct, she had to be found and stopped.

If.

The horror of what he was thinking knotted in his throat—that Teel could be the very worst of the enemies that had hunted them all since Culhaven, that she could have deceived them so completely, especially Steff, who believed that he owed her his life and who was in love with her. The knot tightened. He knew that the horror he felt didn't come from the possibility of betrayal—it came from the certainty of it.

Steff saw something of that horror mirrored in his eyes and grappled angrily with him. "Where is she, Morgan? You know! I can see it!"

Morgan did not try to break away. Instead, he faced his friend and said, "I think I know. But you have to wait here, Steff. You have to let me go after her."

"No." Steff shook his head adamantly, his scarred face knotting. "I'm going with you."

"You can't. You're too sick . . ."

"I'm going, Morgan! Now where is she?"

The Dwarf was shaking with fever, but Morgan knew that he was not going to be able to free himself unless he did so by force. "All right," he agreed, taking a slow breath. "This way."

He put his arm under his friend to support him and started into the dark. He could not leave Steff behind, even knowing how difficult it would make things having his friend along. He would simply do what he must in spite of him. He stumbled suddenly and fought his way back to his feet, hauling Steff up with him, not having seen the coil of rope that lay on the ground in his path. He forced himself to slow, realizing as he did so that he hadn't even taken time yet to think through what he had surmised. Teel was the traitor. He must accept that. Steff could not, but he must. Teel was the one . . .

He stopped himself.

*No. Not Teel. Don't call that thing Teel. Teel is dead. Or close enough to being
dead that there is no distinction to be made. So, not Teel. The Shadowen that hid
in Teel.*

His breathing grew rapid as he hastened through the night, Steff clinging to him. The Shadowen must have left her body and taken Hirehone's in
order to follow Padishar's little company to Tyrsis and betray it to the Federation. Then it had abandoned Hirehone's body, returned to the camp,
killed the watch because it could not ascend the Jut unseen, and reinhabited
Teel. Steff had never realized what was happening. He had believed Teel
poisoned. The Shadowen had let him think as much. It had even managed
to cast suspicion on Hirehone with that tale of following him to the bluff
before falling into unconsciousness. He wondered how long Teel had been
a Shadowen. A long time, he decided. He pictured her in his mind, nothing more than a shell, a hollow skin, and his teeth ground at the image. He
remembered Par's description of what it had been like when the Shadowen
on Toffer Ridge, the one who had taken the body of the little girl, had
tried to come into him. He remembered the horror and revulsion the Valeman had expressed. That was what it must have been like for Teel.

There was no further time to consider the matter. They were approaching the main cave. The entrance was ablaze with torchlight. Padishar Creel
stood there. The outlaw chief was awake, just as Morgan had hoped he
would be, brilliant in his scarlet clothing, talking with the men who cared
for the sick and injured, his broadsword and long knives strapped in place.

"What are you doing?" Steff cried angrily. "This is between you and
me, Morgan! Not him!"

But Morgan ignored his protestations, dragging him into the light.
Padishar Creel turned as the two men staggered up to him and caught hold
of them by the shoulders.

"Whoa, now, lads—slow down! What's the reason for charging about
in the dark like this?" The other man's grip tightened as Steff tried to break
free, and the rough voice lowered. "Careful, now. Your eyes say something's
frightened you. Let's keep it to ourselves. What's happened?"

Steff was rigid with anger, and his eyes were hard. Morgan hesitated.
The others in Padishar's company were looking at them curiously, and they
were close enough to hear what he might say. He smiled disarmingly.
"I think I've found the person you've been looking for," he said to the
big man.

Padishar's face went taut momentarily, then quickly relaxed. "Ah, that's
all, is it?" He spoke as much to his men as to them, his voice almost joking.
"Well, well, come on outside a minute and tell me about it." He put his
arm about their shoulders as if all was well, waved to those listening, and
steered the Highlander and the Dwarf outside.

There he backed them into the shadows. "What is it you've found?" he
demanded.

Morgan glanced at Steff, then shook his head. He was sweating now
beneath his clothes, and his face was flushed. "Padishar," he said. "Teel's

missing. Steff doesn't know what's happened to her. I think she might have gone down into the tunnel."

He waited, his gaze locked on the big man's, silently pleading with him not to demand more, not to make him explain. He still wasn't certain, not absolutely, and Steff would never believe him in any case.

Padishar understood. "Let's have a look. You and I, Highlander."

Steff seized him by the arm. "I'm coming too." His face was bathed in sweat, and his eyes were glazed, but there was no mistaking his determination in the matter.

"You haven't the strength for it, lad."

"That's my concern!"

Padishar's face turned sharply into the light. It was crisscrossed with welts and cuts from last night's battle, tiny lines that seemed to reflect the deeper scars the Dwarf bore. "And none of mine," he said quietly. "So long as you understand."

They went into the sick bay, where Padishar took one of the other outlaws aside and spoke softly to him. Morgan could just make out what was being said.

"Rouse Chandos," Padishar ordered. "Tell him I want the camp mobilized. Check the watch, be certain it's awake and alive. Make ready to move everyone out. Then he's to come after me into the hidden tunnel, the bolt hole. With help. Tell him I said that we're all done with secrecy, so it doesn't matter now who knows what he's about. Now get to it!"

The man scurried off, and Padishar beckoned wordlessly to Morgan and Steff. He led them through the main cavern into the deep recesses where the stores were kept. He lit three torches, kept one for himself and gave one each to the Highlander and the Dwarf. Then he took them into the very back of the farthest chamber where the cases were stacked against the rock wall, handed his torch to Morgan, grabbed the cases in both hands and pulled. The false front opened into the tunnel beyond. They slipped through the opening, and Padishar pulled the packing crates back into place.

"Stay close," he warned.

They hurried into the dark, the torches smoking above them, casting their weak yellow light against the shadows. The tunnel was wide, but it twisted and turned. Rock outcroppings made the passage hazardous; there were stalactites and stalagmites both, wicked stone icicles. Water dripped from the ceiling and pooled in the rock, the only sound in the silence other than their footsteps. It was cold in the caves, and the chill quickly worked its way through Morgan's clothes. He shivered as he trailed after Padishar. Steff trailed them both, walking haltingly on his own, his breathing ragged and quick.

Morgan wondered suddenly what they were going to do when they found Teel.

He made a mental check of his weapons. He had the newly acquired broadsword strapped across his back, a dagger in his belt, and another in his boot. At his waist, he wore the shortened scabbard and the remains of the Sword of Leah.

Not much help against a Shadowen, he thought worriedly. And how much use would Steff be, even after he discovered the truth? What would he do?

If only I still had the magic . . .

He forced that thought away from him, knowing what it would lead to, determined that he would not allow his indecision to bind him again.

The seconds ticked by, and the echo of their passing reverberated in the sound of the men's hurried footsteps. The walls of the tunnel narrowed down sharply, then broadened out again, a constant change of size and shape. They passed through a series of underground caverns where the torchlight could not even begin to penetrate the shadows that cloaked the hollow, vaulted roofs. A little farther on, a series of crevices opened before them, several almost twenty feet across. Bridges had been built to span them, wooden slats connected by heavy ropes, the ropes anchored in the rock by iron pins. The bridges swayed and shook as they crossed, but held firm.

All the while they walked, they kept watch for Teel. But there was no sign of her.

Steff was beginning to have trouble keeping up. He was enormously strong and fit when well, but whatever sickness had attacked him—if indeed it was a sickness and he had not been poisoned as Morgan was beginning to surmise—had left him badly worn. He fell repeatedly and had to drag himself up again each time. Padishar never slowed. The big man had meant what he said—Steff was on his own. The Dwarf had gotten this far on sheer determination, and Morgan did not see how he could maintain the pace the outlaw chief was setting much longer. The Highlander glanced back at his friend, but Steff didn't seem to see him, his haunted eyes searching the shadows, sweeping the curtain of black beyond the light.

They were more than a mile into the mountain when a glimmer of light appeared ahead, a pinprick that quickly became a glow. Padishar did not slow or bother to disguise his coming. The tunnel broadened, and the opening ahead brightened with the flicker of torches. Morgan felt his heartbeat quicken.

They entered a massive underground cavern ablaze with light. Torches were jammed into cracks in the walls and floors, filling the air with smoke and the smell of charred wood and burning pitch. At the center of the cavern a huge crevice split the chamber floor end to end, a twisted maw that widened and narrowed as it worked its way from wall to wall. Another bridge had been built to span the crevice at its narrowest juncture, this one a massive iron structure. Machinery had been installed on the near side of the crevice to raise and lower it. The bridge was down at the moment, linking the halves of the cavern floor. Beyond, the flat rock stretched away to where the tunnel disappeared once more into darkness.

Teel stood next to the bridge machinery, hammering.

Padishar Creel stopped, and Morgan and Steff quickly came up beside him. Teel hadn't heard or seen them yet, their torchlight enveloped by the cavern's own brightness.

Padishar laid down his torch. "She's jammed the machinery. The bridge can't be raised again." His eyes found Steff's. "If we let her, she will bring the Federation right to us."

Steff stared wildly. "No," he gasped in disbelief.

Padishar ignored him. He unsheathed his broadsword and started forward.

Steff lunged after him, tripping, falling, then crying out frantically, "Teel!"

Teel whirled about. She held an iron bar in her hands, the smooth surface bright with nicks from where she had been smashing the bridge works. Morgan could see the damage clearly now, winches split apart, pulleys forced loose, gears stripped. Teel's hair glittered in the light, flashing with traces of gold. She faced them, her mask revealing nothing of what she was thinking, an expressionless piece of leather strapped about her head, the eyeholes dark and shadowed.

Padishar closed both big hands about the broadsword, lifting its blade into the light. "End of the line for you, girl," he snapped.

The echo filled the cavern, and Steff came to his feet, lurching ahead. "Padishar, wait!" he howled.

Morgan jumped to intercept him, caught hold of his arm, and jerked him about. "No, Steff, that isn't Teel! Not anymore!" Steff's eyes were bright with anger and fear. Morgan lowered his voice, speaking quickly, calmly. "Listen to me. That's a Shadowen, Steff. How long since you've seen the face beneath that mask? Have you looked at it? It isn't Teel under there anymore. Teel's been gone a long time."

The anger and fear turned to horror. "Morgan, no! I would know! I could tell if it wasn't her!"

"Steff, listen . . ."

"Morgan, he's going to kill her! Let me go!"

Steff jerked free and Morgan grabbed him again. "Steff, look at what she's done! She's betrayed us!"

"No!" the Dwarf screamed and struck him.

Morgan went down in a heap, the force of the blow leaving him stunned. His first reaction was surprise; he hadn't thought it possible that Steff could still possess such strength. He pushed himself to his knees, watching as the Dwarf raced after Padishar, screaming something the Highlander couldn't understand.

Steff caught up with the big man when they were just a few steps from Teel. The Dwarf threw himself on Padishar from behind, seizing his sword arm, forcing it down. Padishar shouted in fury, tried to break free and failed. Steff was all over him, wrapped about him like a second skin.

In the confusion, Teel struck. She was on them like a cat, the iron bar lifted. The blows hammered down, quick and unchallenged, and in a matter of seconds both Padishar and Steff lay bleeding on the cavern floor.

Morgan staggered to his feet alone to face her.

She came for him unhurriedly, and as she did so there was a moment in which all of his memories of her came together at once. He saw her as the small, waiflike girl that he had met at Culhaven in the darkened kitchen of Granny Elise and Auntie Jilt, her honey-colored hair just visible beneath the folds of her hooded cloak, her face concealed by the strange leather mask. He saw her listening at the edges of the campfire's light to the conversation shared by the members of the little company who had journeyed through the Wolfsktaag. He saw her crowded close to Steff at the base of the Dragon's Teeth before they went to meet with the shade of Allanon, suspicious, withdrawn, fiercely protective.

He forced the images away, seeing her only as she was now, striking down Padishar and Steff, too swift and strong to be what she pretended. Even so, it was hard to believe that she was a Shadowen, harder still to accept that they had all been fooled so completely.

He pulled free the broadsword and waited. He would have to be quick. Maybe he would have to be more than quick. He remembered the creatures in the Pit. Iron alone hadn't been enough to kill them.

Teel went into a crouch as she reached him, her eyes dark pools within the mask, the look that was reflected there hard and certain. Morgan gave a quick feint, then cut viciously at the girl's legs. She sidestepped the blow easily. He cut again—once, twice. She parried, and the shock of the sword blade striking the iron bar washed through him. Back and forth they lunged, each waiting for the other to provide an opening.

Then a series of blows brought the flat of the broadsword against the iron bar and the blade shattered. Morgan ripped at the bar with what was left, the handle catching it and twisting it free. Both sword and bar skittered away into the dark.

Instantly Teel threw herself on Morgan, her hands closing about his throat. She was incredibly strong. He had only a moment to act as he fell backward. His hand closed on the dagger at his waist, and he shoved it into her stomach. She drew back, surprised. He kicked at her, thrusting her back, drew the dagger in his boot and jammed it into her side, ripping upward.

She backhanded him so hard that he was knocked off his feet. He landed with a grunt, jarred so that the breath was knocked from his body. Spots danced before his eyes, but he gasped air into his lungs and scrambled up.

Teel was standing where he had left her, the daggers still embedded in her body. She reached down and calmly pulled them free, tossing them away.

She knows I can't hurt her, he thought in despair. *She knows I haven't anything that can stop her.*

She seemed unhurt as she advanced on him. There was blood on her clothing, but not much. There was no expression to be seen behind the mask, nothing in her eyes or on her mouth, just an emptiness that was as chilling as ice. Morgan edged away from her, searching the cavern floor for any kind of weapon at all. He caught sight of the iron bar and desperately snatched it up.

Teel seemed unworried. There was a shimmer of movement all about her body, a darkness that seemed to lift slightly and settle back again—as if the thing that lived within her was readying itself.

Morgan backed away, maneuvering toward the crevice. Could he somehow manage to lure this thing close enough to the drop to shove it over? Would that kill it? He didn't know. He knew only that he was the only one left to stop it, to prevent it from betraying the entire Jut, all those men, to the Federation. If he failed, they would die.

But I'm not strong enough—not without the magic!

He was only a few feet from the crevice edge. Teel closed the gap that separated them, moving swiftly. He swung at her with the iron bar, but she caught the bar in her hand, broke his grip on it, and flung it away.

Then she was on him, her hands at his throat, choking off his air, strangling him. He couldn't breathe. He fought to break free, but she was far too strong. His eyes squeezed shut against the pain, and there was a coppery taste in his mouth.

A huge weight dropped across him.

"Teel, don't!" he heard someone cry—a disembodied voice choked with pain and fatigue.

Steff!

The hands loosened marginally, and his eyes cleared enough so that he could see Steff atop Teel, arms locked about her, hauling back. There was blood streaking his face. A gaping wound had been opened at the top of his head.

Morgan's right hand groped at his belt and found the handle of the Sword of Leah.

Teel ripped free of Steff, turned and pulled him about. There was a fury in her eyes, in the way the cords of her throat went taut, that even the mask could not conceal. Yanking Steff's dagger from its sheath, she buried it deep in his chest. Steff toppled backward, gasping.

Teel turned back then to finish Morgan, half-raised over him, and he thrust the broken blade of his sword into her stomach.

Back she reared, screaming so that Morgan arched away from her in spite of himself. But he kept his hands fastened on the handle of the sword. Then something strange began to happen. The Sword of Leah grew warm and flared with light. He could feel it stir and come to life.

The magic! Oh, Shades—it was the magic!

Power surged through the blade, linking them together, flowing into Teel. Crimson fire exploded through her. Her hands tore at the blade, at her body, at her face, and the mask came free. Morgan Leah would never forget what lay beneath, a countenance born of the blackest pits of the netherworld, ravaged and twisted and alive with demons that he had only imagined might exist. Teel seemed to disappear entirely, and there was only the Shadowen behind the face, a thing of blackness and no substance, an emptiness that blocked and swallowed the light.

Invisible hands fought to thrust Morgan away, to strip him of his weapon and of his soul.

"Leah! Leah!" He sounded the battle cry of his ancestors, of the Kings and Princes of his land for a thousand years, and that single word became the talisman to which he clung.

The Shadowen's scream became a shriek. Then it collapsed, the darkness that sustained it crumbling and fading away. Teel returned, a frail, limp bundle, empty of life and being. She fell forward atop him, dead.

It took several minutes for Morgan to find the strength to push Teel away. He lay there in the wetness of his own sweat and blood, listening to the sudden silence, exhausted, pinned to the cavern floor by the dead girl's weight. His only thought was that he had survived.

Then slowly his pulse quickened. It was the magic that had saved him. It was the magic of the Sword of Leah. Shades, it wasn't gone after all! At least some part of it still lived, and if part of it lived then there was a chance that it could be completely restored, that the blade could be made whole again, the magic preserved, the power . . .

His ruminations scattered uncontrollably in their frantic passing and disappeared. He gulped air into his lungs, mustered his strength, and pushed Teel's body aside. She was surprisingly light. He looked down at her as he rolled onto his hands and knees. She was all shrunken in, as if something had dissolved her bones. Her face was still twisted and scarred, but the demons he had seen there were gone.

Then he heard Steff gasp. Unable to rise, he crawled to his friend. Steff lay on his back, the dagger still protruding from his chest. Morgan started to remove it, then slowly drew back. He knew at a glance that it was too late to make any difference. Gently, he touched his friend's shoulder.

Steff's eyes blinked open and shifted to find him. "Teel?" he asked softly.

"She's dead," Morgan whispered back.

The Dwarf's scarred face tightened with pain, then relaxed. He coughed blood. "I'm sorry, Morgan. Sorry . . . I was blind, so this had to happen."

"It wasn't only you."

"I should have seen . . . the truth. Should have recognized it. I just . . . didn't want to, I guess."

"Steff, you saved our lives. If you hadn't awakened me . . ."

"Listen to me. Listen, Highlander. You are my closest friend. I want you . . . to do something." He coughed again, then tried to steady his voice. "I want you to go back to Culhaven and make certain . . . that Granny Elise and Auntie Jilt are all right." His eyes squeezed shut and opened again. "You understand me, Morgan? They will be in danger because Teel . . ."

"I understand," Morgan cut him short.

"They are all I have left," Steff whispered, reaching out to fasten his hand on Morgan's arm. "Promise me."

Morgan nodded wordlessly, then said, "I promise."

Steff sighed, and the words he spoke were little more than a whisper. "I loved her, Morgan."

Then his hand slid away, and he died.

Everything that happened after that was something of a blur to Morgan Leah. He stayed at Steff's side for a time, so dazed that he could think of doing nothing else. Then he remembered Padishar Creel. He forced himself to his feet and went over to check on the big man. Padishar was still alive, but unconscious, his left arm broken from warding off the blows struck by the iron bar, his head bleeding from a deep gash. Morgan wrapped the head injury to stop the blood loss, but left the arm alone. There was no time to set it now.

The machinery that operated the bridge was smashed and there was no way that he could repair it. If the Federation was sending an attack force into the tunnels tonight—and Morgan had to assume they were—then the bridge could not be raised to prevent their advance. It was only a few hours until dawn. That meant that Federation soldiers were probably already on their way. Even without Teel to guide them, they would have little trouble following the tunnel to the Jut.

He found himself wondering what had become of Chandos and the men he was supposed to bring with him. They should have arrived by now.

He decided he couldn't risk waiting for them. He had to get out of there. He would have to carry Padishar since his efforts to waken him had failed. Steff would have to be left behind.

It took several minutes to decide what was needed. First he salvaged the Sword of Leah, slipping it carefully back into its makeshift sheath. Then he carried Teel and afterward Steff to the edge of the crevice and dropped them over. He wasn't sure it was something he could do until after it was done. It left him feeling sick and empty inside.

He was incredibly tired by then, so weak that he did not think he could make it back through the tunnels by himself, let alone carrying Padishar. But somehow he managed to get the other across his shoulders and, with one of the torches to guide him, he started out.

He walked for what seemed like hours, seeing nothing, hearing only the sound of his own boots as they scraped across the stone. Where was Chandos, he asked himself over and over again. Why hadn't he come? He stumbled and fell so many times that he lost count, tripped up by the tunnel's rock and by his own weariness. His knees and hands were torn and bloodied, and his body began to grow numb. He found himself thinking of curious things, of his boyhood and his family, of the adventures he had shared growing up with Par and Coll, of the steady, reliable Steff and the Dwarves of Culhaven. He cried some of the time, thinking of what had become of them all, of how much of the past had been lost. He talked to Padishar when he felt himself on the verge of collapse, but Padishar slept on.

He walked, it seemed, forever.

Yet when Chandos finally did appear, accompanied by a swarm of outlaws and Axhind and his Trolls, Morgan was no longer walking at all. He had collapsed in the tunnel, exhausted.

He was carried with Padishar the rest of the way, and he tried to explain what had happened. He was never certain exactly what he said. He knew that he rambled, sometimes incoherently. He remembered Chandos saying something about a new Federation assault, that the assault had prevented him coming as quickly as he had wanted. He remembered the strength of the other's gnarled hand as it held his own.

It was still dark when they regained the bluff, and the Jut was indeed under attack. Another diversion, perhaps, to draw attention away from the soldiers sneaking through the tunnels, but one that required dealing with nevertheless. Arrows and spears flew from below, and the siege towers had been hauled forward. Numerous attempts at scaling the heights had already been repelled. Preparations for making an escape, however, were complete. The wounded were set to move out, those that could walk risen to their feet, those that couldn't placed on litters. Morgan went with the latter group as they were carried back into the caves to where the tunnels began. Chandos appeared, his fierce, black-bearded face hovering close to Morgan as he spoke.

"All is well, Highlander," Morgan would remember the other man saying, his voice a faint buzz. "There's Federation soldiers in the hidden tunnel already, but the rope bridges have been cut. That will slow them a bit—long enough for us to be safely away. We'll be going into these other tunnels. There's a way out through them as well, you see, one that only Padishar knows. It's rougher going, a good number of twists and turns and a few tricky choices to be made. But Padishar knows what to do. Never leaves anything to chance. He's awake again, bringing the rest of them down, making sure everyone's out. He's a tough one, old Padishar. But no tougher than you. You saved his life, you did. You got him out of there just in time. Rest now, while you can. You won't have long."

Morgan closed his eyes and drifted off to sleep. He slept poorly, brought awake time and again by the jostling of the litter on which he lay and by the sounds of the men who were crowded about him, whispering and crying out in pain. Darkness cloaked the tunnels, a hazy black that even torchlight could not cut through entirely. Faces and bodies passed in and out of view, but his lasting impression was of impenetrable night.

Once or twice, he thought he heard fighting, the clash of weapons, the grunts of men. But there was no sense of urgency in those about him, no indication that anything threatened, and he decided after a time that he must be dreaming.

He forced himself awake finally, not wishing to sleep any longer, afraid to sleep when he was not certain what was happening. Nothing around him appeared to have changed. It seemed that he could not have been asleep for more than a few moments.

He tried lifting his head, and pain stabbed down the back of his neck. He lay back again, thinking suddenly of Steff and Teel and of the thinness of the line that separated life and death.

Padishar Creel came up beside him. He was heavily bandaged about the head, and his arm was splinted and strapped to his side. "So, lad," he greeted quietly.

Morgan nodded, closed his eyes and opened them again.

"We're getting out now," the other said. "All of us, thanks to you. And to Steff. Chandos told me the story. He had great courage, that one." The rough face looked away. "Well, the Jut's lost but that's a small price to pay for our lives."

Morgan found that he didn't want to talk about the price of lives. "Help me up, Padishar," he said quietly. "I want to walk out of here."

The outlaw chief smiled. "Don't we all, lad," he whispered.

He reached out his good hand and pulled Morgan to his feet.

32

It was a nightmarish world where Par and Coll Ohmsford walked. The silence was intense and endless, a cloak of emptiness that stretched further than time itself. There were no sounds, no cries of birds or buzzings of insects, no small skitterings or scrapes, not even the rustle of the wind through the trees to give evidence of life. The trees rose skyward like statues of stone carved by some ancient civilization and left in mute testament to the futility of man's works. They had a gray and wintry look to them, and even the leaves that should have softened and colored their bones bore the look of a scarecrow's rags. Scrub brush and saw grass rubbed up against their trunks like stray children, and bramble bushes twisted together in a desperate effort to protect against life's sorrows.

The mist was there as well, of course. The mist was there first, last, and always, a deep and pervasive sea of gray that shut everything vibrant away. It hung limp in the air, unmoving as it smothered trees and brush, rocks and earth, and life of any kind or sort, a screen that blocked away the sun's light and warmth. There was an inconsistency to it, for in some places it was thin and watery and merely gave a fuzzy appearance to what it sought to cloak, while in others it was as impenetrable as ink. It brushed at the skin with a cold, damp insistence that whispered of dead things.

Par and Coll moved slowly, cautiously through their waking dream, fighting back against the feeling that they had become disembodied. Their eyes darted from shadow to shadow, searching for movement, finding only stillness. The world they had entered seemed lifeless, as if the Shadowen they knew to be hidden there were not in fact there at all but were simply a lie of the dream that their senses could not reveal.

They moved quickly to the rubble of the Bridge of Sendic so that they could follow its broken trail to the vault. Their footsteps were soundless in the tall grasses and the damp, yielding earth. At times their boots disappeared entirely in the carpet of mist. Par glanced back to the door they had come through. It was nowhere to be seen.

In seconds, the cliff face itself, the whole of what remained of the palace of the Kings of Tyrsis, had vanished as well.

As if it had never been, Par thought darkly.

He felt cold and empty inside, but hot where sweat made the skin beneath his clothing feel prickly and damp. The emotions that churned inside would not be sorted out or dispersed; they screamed with voices that were garbled and confused, each desperate to be heard, each mindless. He could feel his heart pounding within his chest, his pulse racing in response, and he sensed the imminency of his own death with every step he took. He wished again that he could summon for just a moment the magic, even in its most rudimentary form, so that he could be reassured that he possessed some measure of power to defend himself. But use of the magic would alert whatever lived within the Pit, and he wanted to believe that as yet that had not happened.

Coll brushed his arm, pointing to where the earth had opened before them in a wicked-looking crack that disappeared into blackness. They would have to go around. Par nodded, leading the way. Coll's presence was reassuring to him, as if the simple fact of his being there might somehow deter the evil that threatened. Coll—his large, blocky form like a rock at Par's back, his rough face so determined that it seemed his strength of will alone would see them through. Par was glad beyond anything words could express that his brother had come. It was a selfish reaction, he knew, but an honest one. Coll's courage in this business was to a large extent the source of his own.

They skirted the pitfall and worked their way back to the tumbled remains of the bridge. Everything about them was unchanged, silent and unmoving, empty of life.

But then something shimmered darkly in the mists ahead, a squarish shape that lifted out of the rubble.

Par took a deep steadying breath. It was the vault.

They moved toward it hurriedly, Par in the lead, Coll just a step behind. Stone-block walls came sharply into focus, losing the surreal haziness in which the mists had cloaked them. Brush grew up against its sides, vines looped over its sloped roof, and moss colored its foundation in shadings of rust and dark green. The vault was larger than Par had imagined, a good fifty feet across and as much as twenty feet high at its peak. It had the look and feel of a crypt.

The Valemen reached its nearest wall and edged their way cautiously around the corner to the front. They found writing carved there in the pitted stone, an ancient scroll ravaged by time and weather, many of its words nearly erased. They stopped, breathless, and read:

> *Herein lies the heart and soul of the nations.*
> *Their right to be free men,*
> *Their desire to live in peace,*
> *Their courage to seek out truth.*
> *Herein lies the Sword of Shannara.*

Just beyond, a massive stone door stood ajar. The brothers glanced at each other wordlessly, then started forward. When they reached the door, they peered inside. There was a wall that formed a corridor leading left; the corridor disappeared into darkness.

Par frowned. He hadn't expected the vault to be a complex structure; he had thought it would be nothing more than a single chamber with the Sword of Shannara at its center. This suggested something else.

He looked at Coll. His brother was clearly upset, peering about anxiously, studying first the entry, then the dark tangle of the forest surrounding them. Coll reached out and pulled on the door. It moved easily at his touch.

He bent close. "This looks like a trap," he whispered so softly that Par could barely hear him.

Par was thinking the same thing. A door to a vault that was three hundred years old and had been subjected to the climate of the Pit should not give way so readily. It would be a simple matter for someone to shut it again once he was inside.

And yet he knew he would go in anyway. He had already made up his mind to do so. He had come through too much to turn back now. He raised his eyebrows and gave Coll a questioning look. What was Coll suggesting, the look asked?

Coll's mouth tightened, knowing that Par was determined to continue, that the risks no longer made any difference. It took a supreme effort for him to speak the words. "All right. You go after the Sword; I'll stand guard out here." One big hand grasped Par's shoulder. "But hurry!"

Par nodded, smiled triumphantly, and clutched his brother back.

Then he was through the door, moving swiftly down the passageway into the dark. He went as far as he could with the faint light of the outside world to guide him, but it soon faded. He felt along the walls for the corridor's end, but couldn't find it. He remembered then that he still carried the stone Damson had given him. He reached into his pocket, took it out, clasped it momentarily between his hands to warm it, and held it out before him. Silver light flooded the darkness. His smile grew fierce. Again, he started forward, listening to the silence, watching the shadows.

He wound along the passageway, descended a set of stairs, and entered a second corridor. He traveled much further than he would have thought possible, and for the first time he began to grow uneasy. He was no longer in the vault, but somewhere deep underground. How could that be?

Then the passageway ended. He stepped into a room with a vaulted ceiling and walls carved with images and runes, and he caught his breath with a suddenness that hurt.

There, at the very center of the room, blade downward in a block of red marble, was the Sword of Shannara.

He blinked to make certain that he was not mistaking what he saw, then moved forward until he stood before it. The blade was smooth and unmarked, a flawless piece of workmanship. The handle was carved with the image of a hand thrusting a torch skyward. The talisman glistened like new metal in the soft light, faintly blue in color.

Par felt his throat tighten. It was indeed the Sword.

A sharp rush of elation surged through him. He could hardly keep himself from calling out to Coll, from shouting aloud to him what he was feeling. A wave of relief swept over him. He had gambled everything on what had amounted to little more than a hunch—and his hunch had been right. Shades, it had been right all along! The Sword of Shannara had indeed been down in the Pit, concealed by its tangle of trees and brush, by the mist and night, by the Shadowen . . . !

He shoved aside his elation abruptly. Thinking of the Shadowen reminded him in no uncertain terms how precarious his position was. There would be time to congratulate himself later, when Coll and he were safely out of this rat hole.

There were stairs cut in a stone base on which rested the block of marble and the Sword embedded in it, and he started for them. But he had taken only a single step when something detached itself from the darkness of the wall beyond. Instantly, he froze, terror welling up in his throat.

A single word screamed out in his mind.

Shadowen!

But he saw at once that he was mistaken. It wasn't a Shadowen. It was a man dressed all in black, cloaked and hooded, the insigne of a wolf's head sewn on his chest.

Par's fear did not lessen when he realized who the other was. The man approaching him was Rimmer Dall.

At the entrance to the vault, Coll waited impatiently. He stood with his back against the stone, just to one side of the opening, his eyes searching the mist. Nothing moved. No sound reached him. He was alone, it seemed; yet he did not feel that way. The dawn's light filtered down through the canopy of the trees, washing him in its cold, gray haze.

Par had been gone too long already, he thought. It shouldn't be taking him this much time.

He glanced quickly over his shoulder at the vault's black opening. He would wait another five minutes; then he was going in himself.

Rimmer Dall came to a stop a dozen feet away from Par, reached up casually and pulled back the hood of his cloak. His craggy face was unmasked, yet in the half-light of the vault it was so streaked with shadows as to be practically unrecognizable. It made no difference. Par would have known him anywhere. Their one and only meeting that night so many weeks ago at the Blue Whisker was not something he would ever forget. He had hoped it would never be repeated; yet here they were, face to face once more. Rimmer Dall, First Seeker of the Federation, the man who had tracked him across the length and breadth of Callahorn and nearly had him so many times, had caught up with him at last.

The door through which Par had entered remained open behind him, a haven that beckoned. The Valeman poised to flee.

"Wait, Par Ohmsford," the other said, almost as if reading his thoughts. "Are you so quick to run? Do you frighten so easily?"

Par hesitated. Rimmer Dall was a huge, rangy man; his red-bearded face might have been chiseled out of stone, so hard and menacing did it appear. Yet his voice—and Par had not forgotten it either—was soft and compelling.

"Shouldn't you hear what I have to say to you first?" the big man continued. "What harm can it do? I have been waiting here to talk to you for a very long time."

Par stared. "Waiting?"

"Certainly. This is where you had to come sooner or later once you made up your mind about the Sword of Shannara. You have come for the Sword, haven't you? Of course you have. Well, then, I was right to wait, wasn't I? We have much to discuss."

"I wouldn't think so." Par's mind raced. "You tried to arrest Coll and me in Varfleet. You imprisoned my parents in Shady Vale and occupied the village. You have been chasing after me and those with me for weeks."

Rimmer Dall folded his arms. Par noticed again how the left was gloved to the elbow. "Suppose I stand here and you stand there," the big man offered. "That way you can leave any time you choose. I won't do anything to prevent it."

Par took a deep breath and stepped back. "I don't trust you."

The big man shrugged. "Why should you? However, do you want the Sword of Shannara or don't you? If you want it, you must first listen to me. After you've done so, you can take it with you if you wish. Fair enough?"

Par felt the hairs on the back of his neck prickle in warning. "Why should you make a bargain like that after all you've done to keep me from getting the Sword?"

"Keep you from getting the Sword?" The other laughed, a low, pleasant chuckle. "Par Ohmsford. Did you once think to ask for the Sword? Did you ever consider the possibility that I might simply give it to you? Wouldn't that have been easier than sneaking about the city and trying to steal it like a common thief?" Rimmer Dall shook his head slowly. "There is so much that you don't know. Why not let me tell it to you?"

Par glanced about uncertainly, not willing to believe that this wasn't some sort of trick to put him off his guard. The vault was a maze of shadows that whispered of other things lurking there, hidden and waiting. Par rubbed briskly the stone that Damson had given him to brighten its light.

"Ah, you think I have others concealed in the darkness with me, is that it?" Rimmer Dall whispered, the words coming from somewhere deep down inside his chest to rumble through the silence. "Well, here then!"

He raised his gloved hand, made a quick motion with it, and the room was flooded with light. Par gasped in surprise and took another step back.

"Do you think, Par Ohmsford, that you are the only one who has use of magic?" Rimmer Dall asked quietly. "Well, you aren't. As a matter of fact, I have magic at my command that is much greater than yours, greater perhaps than that of the Druids of old. There are others like me, too. There are many in the Four Lands who possess the magic of the old world, of the world before the Four Lands and the Great Wars and man himself."

Par stared at him wordlessly.

"Would you listen to me now, Valeman? While you still can?"

Par shook his head, not in response to the question he had been asked, but in disbelief. "You are a Seeker," he said finally. "You hunt those who use magic. Any use—even by you—is forbidden!"

Rimmer Dall smiled. "So the Federation has decreed. But has that stopped you from using your magic, Par? Or your uncle Walker Boh? Or anyone who possesses it? It is, in fact, a foolish decree, one that could never be enforced except against those who don't care about it in the first place. The Federation dreams of conquest and empire-building, of uniting the lands and the Races under its rule. The Coalition Council schemes and plans, a remnant of a world that has already destroyed itself once in the wars of power. It thinks itself chosen to govern because the Councils of the Races are no more and the Druids gone. It sees the disappearance of the Elves as a blessing. It seizes the provinces of the Southland, threatens Callahorn until it submits, and destroys the wilful Dwarves simply because it can. It sees all this as evidence of its mandate to rule. It believes itself omniscient! In a final gesture of arrogance it outlaws magic! It doesn't once bother asking what purpose magic serves in the scheme of things—it simply denies it!"

The dark figure hunched forward, the arms unfolding. "The fact of the matter is that the Federation is a collection of fools that understands nothing of what the magic means, Valeman. It was magic that brought our world to pass, the world in which we live, in which the Federation believes itself supreme. Magic creates everything, makes everything possible. And the Federation would dismiss such power as if it were meaningless?"

Rimmer Dall straightened, looming up against the strange light he had created, a dark form that seemed only vaguely human.

"Look at me, Par Ohmsford," he whispered.

His body began to shimmer, then to separate. Par watched in horror as a dark shape rose up against the shadows and half-light, its eyes flaring with crimson fire.

"Do you see, Valeman?" Rimmer Dall's disembodied voice whispered with a hiss of satisfaction. "I am the very thing the Federation would destroy, and they haven't the faintest idea of it!"

The irony of the idea was wasted on Par, who saw nothing beyond the fact that he had placed himself in the worst possible danger. He shrank from the man who called himself Rimmer Dall, the creature who wasn't in fact a man at all, but was a Shadowen. He edged backward, determined to flee. Then he remembered the Sword of Shannara, and abruptly, recklessly, changed his mind. If he could get to the Sword, he thought fiercely, he would have a weapon with which to destroy Rimmer Dall.

But the Shadowen seemed unconcerned. Slowly the dark shape settled back into Rimmer Dall's body and the big man's voice returned. "You have been lied to, Valeman. Repeatedly. You have been told that the Shadowen are evil things, that they are parasites who invade the bodies of men to subvert them to their cause. No, don't bother to deny it or to ask how I know," he said quickly, cutting short Par's exclamation of surprise. "I know everything about you, about your journey to Culhaven, the Wilderun, the Hadeshorn, and beyond. I know of your meeting with the shade of Allanon. I know of the lies he told you. Lies, Par Ohmsford—and they begin with the Druids! They tell you what you must do if the Shadowen are to be destroyed, if the world is to be made safe again! You are to seek the Sword, Wren the Elves, and Walker Boh vanished Paranor— I know!"

The craggy face twisted in anger. "But listen now to what you were not told! The Shadowen are not an aberration that has come to pass in the absence of the Druids! We are their successors! We are what evolved out of the magic with their passing! And we are not monsters invading men, Valeman—we are men ourselves!"

Par shook his head to deny what he was hearing, but Rimmer Dall brought up his gloved hand quickly, pointing to the Valeman. "There is magic in men now as there was once magic in the creatures of faerie. In the Elves, before they took themselves away. In the Druids later." His voice had gone soft and insistent. "I am a man like any other except that I possess the magic. Like you, Par. Somehow I inherited it over the generations of my family that lived before me in a world in which use of magic was commonplace. The magic scattered and seeded itself—not within the ground, but within the bodies of the men and women of the Races. It took hold and grew in some of us, and now we have the power that was once the province of the Druids alone."

He nodded slowly, his eyes fixed on Par. "You have such power. You cannot deny it. Now you must understand the truth of what having that power means."

He paused, waiting for Par to respond. But Par had gone cold to the bone as he sensed what was coming, and he could only howl silently in denial.

"I can see in your eyes that you understand," Rimmer Dall said, his voice softer still. "It means, Par Ohmsford, that you are a Shadowen, too."

Coll counted the seconds in his mind, stretching the process out for as long as he could, thinking as he numbered each that Par must surely appear. But there was no sign of his brother.

The Valeman shook his head in despair. He paced away from the craggy wall of the vault and back again. Five minutes was up. He couldn't wait any longer. He had to go in. It frightened him that in doing so he would be leaving their backs unprotected, but he had no choice. He had to discover what had happened to Par.

He took a deep breath to steady himself as he prepared to enter.

That was when the hands seized him from behind and dragged him down.

"You're lying!" Par shouted at Rimmer Dall, forgetting his fear, taking a step forward threateningly.

"There is nothing wrong with being a Shadowen," the other answered sharply. "It is only a word that others have used to label something they don't fully understand. If you can forget the lies you have been told and think of the possibilities, you will be better able to understand what I am telling you. Suppose for a moment that I am right. If the Shadowen are simply men who are meant to be successors to the Druids, then wielding the magic is not only their right, it is their responsibility. The magic is a trust—wasn't that what Allanon told Brin Ohmsford when he died and marked her with his blood? The magic is a tool that must be used for the betterment of the Races and the Four Lands. What is so difficult to accept about that? The problem is not with myself or with you or with the others like us. The problem is with fools like those who govern the Federation and think that anything they cannot control must be suppressed! They see anyone different than themselves as an enemy!"

The strong face tightened. "But who is it that seeks domination over the Four Lands and its people? Who drives the Elves from the Westland, enslaves the Dwarves in the East, besieges the Trolls in the North, and claims all of the Four Lands as its own? Why is it, do you think, that the Four Lands begin to wither and die? Who causes that? You have seen the poor creatures who live in the Pit. Shadowen, you think them, don't you? Well, they are—but their condition is brought about by their keepers. They are men like you and me. The Federation locks them away because they show evidence of possessing magic and are thought dangerous. They become what they are thought to be. They are starved of the life the magic could feed them and they grow mad! That child on Toffer Ridge—what happened to her that caused her to become what she is? She was starved of the magic she needed, of the use of it, and of everything that would have kept her sane. She was driven into exile. Valeman, it is the Federation that causes disruption in the Four Lands with its foolish, blind decrees and its crushing rule! It is the Shadowen who have a chance to set things right!

"As for Allanon, he is first and always a Druid with a Druid's mind and ways. What he seeks is known only to him and likely to remain that way. But you are well advised to be cautious of accepting too readily what he tells you."

He spoke with such conviction that for the first time Par Ohmsford began to doubt. What if indeed the shade of Allanon had lied? Wasn't it true that the Druids had always played games with those from whom they wanted something? Walker had warned him that this was so, that it was a mistake to accept what Allanon was telling them. Something in what Rimmer Dall was saying seemed to whisper that it was true in this instance as well. It was possible, he thought in despair, that he had been misled completely.

The tall, cloaked form before him straightened. "You belong with us, Par Ohmsford," he said quietly.

Par shook his head quickly. "No."

"You are one of us, Valeman. You can deny it as long and as loudly as you like, but the fact remains. We are the same, you and I—possessors of the magic, successors to the Druids, keepers of the trust." He paused, considering. "You still fear me, don't you? A Shadowen. Even the name frightens you. It is the unavoidable result of having accepted as truth the lies you have been told. You think of me as an enemy rather than as kindred."

Par said nothing.

"Let us see who lies and who tells the truth. There." He pointed suddenly to the Sword. "Remove it from its stone, Valeman. It belongs to you; it is your bloodright as heir to the Elven house of Shannara. Pick it up. Touch me with it. If I am the black creature you have been warned against, then the Sword will destroy me. If I am an evil that hides within a lie, the Sword will reveal it. Take it in your hands, then. Use it."

Par remained motionless for a long moment, then bounded up the steps to the block of red marble, seized the Sword of Shannara in both hands, and pulled it forth. It slid free unhindered, gleaming and smooth. He turned quickly and faced Rimmer Dall.

"Come close, Par," the other whispered. "Touch me."

Memories whirled madly in Par's mind, bits and pieces of the songs he had sung, of the stories he had told. What he held now was the Sword of Shannara, the Elven talisman of truth against which no lie could stand.

He came down off the steps, the carved hilt with its burning torch pressed into his palm, the blade held cautiously before him. Rimmer Dall stood waiting. When Par was within striking distance, he stretched out the blade of the talisman and laid it firmly against the other's body.

Nothing happened.

Keeping his eyes riveted on the other, he held the blade steady and willed that the truth be revealed. Still nothing happened. Par waited for as long as he could stand it, then lowered the blade in despair and stepped away.

"Now you know. There is no lie about me," Rimmer Dall said. "The lie is in what you have been told."

Par found that he was shaking. "But why would Allanon lie? What purpose could that possibly serve?"

"Think for a moment on what you have been asked to do." The big man was relaxed, his voice calm and reassuring. "You have been asked to bring back the Druids, to restore to them their talismans, to seek our destruction. The Druids want to regain what was lost to them, the power of life and magic. Is that any different, Par, than what the Warlock Lord sought to do ten centuries ago?"

"But you hunted us!"

"To talk to you, to explain."

"You imprisoned my parents!"

"I kept them safe from harm. The Federation knew of you and would have used them to find you, if I hadn't gone to them first."

Par caught his breath, his arguments momentarily exhausted. Was what he was being told true? Shades, was everything the lie that Rimmer Dall claimed it to be? He could not believe it, yet he could not bring himself to disbelieve it either. His confusion wrapped him like a blanket and left him feeling small and vulnerable.

"I have to think," he said wearily.

"Then come with me and do so," Rimmer Dall responded at once. "Come with me and we shall talk more of this. You have many questions that require answers, and I can give them to you. There is much you need to know about how the magic can be used. Come, Valeman. Put aside your fears and misgivings. No harm shall come to you—never to one whose magic is so promising."

He spoke reassuringly, compellingly, and for an instant Par was almost persuaded. It would have been so easy to agree. He was tired, and he wanted this odyssey to end. It would be comforting to have someone to talk to about the frustrations of possessing the magic. Rimmer Dall would surely know, having experienced them himself. As much as he hated to admit it, he no longer felt threatened by the man. There seemed to be no reason to deny what he was asking.

But he did nevertheless. He did without really understanding why. "No," he said quietly.

"Think of what we can share if you come with me," the other persisted. "We have so much in common! Surely you have longed to talk of your magic, the magic you have been forced to conceal. There has never been anyone for you to do that with before me. I can feel the need in you; I can sense it! Come with me! Valeman, you have . . ."

"No."

Par stepped away. Something ugly whispered suddenly in his mind, some memory that did not yet have a face, but whose voice he clearly recognized.

Rimmer Dall watched him, his craggy features gone suddenly hard. "This is foolish, Valeman."

"I am leaving," Par said quietly, tense now, back on his guard. What was it that bothered him so? "And I am taking the Sword."

The black-cloaked form became another shadow in the half-light. "Stay, Valeman. There are dark secrets kept from you, things that would be better learned from me. Stay and hear them."

Par edged toward the passageway that had brought him in.

"The door is directly behind you," Rimmer Dall said suddenly, his voice sharp. "There are no passageways, no stairs. That was all illusion, my magic invoked to closet you long enough so that we might talk. But if you leave now, something precious will be destroyed. Truth waits for you, Valeman—and there is horror in its face. You cannot withstand it. Stay, and listen to me! You need me!"

Par shook his head. "You sounded for a moment, Rimmer Dall, like those others, those Shadowen who look nothing like you outwardly, yet speak with your need. Like them, you would possess me."

Rimmer Dall stood silently before him, not moving, simply watching as he backed away. The light the First Seeker had produced faded, and the chamber slid rapidly into darkness.

Par Ohmsford grasped the Sword of Shannara in both hands and bolted for freedom.

Rimmer Dall had been right about the passageways and stairs. There were none. It was all illusion, a magic Par should have recognized at once. He burst from the blackness of the vault directly into the gray half-light of the Pit. The damp and mist closed about him instantly. He blinked and whirled about, searching.

Coll.

Where was Coll?

He stripped the cloak from his back and wrapped it hurriedly about the Sword of Shannara. Allanon had said he would need it—if Allanon was still to be believed. At the moment, he didn't know. But the Sword should be cared for; it must have purpose. Unless it had lost its magic. Could it have lost its magic?

"Par."

The Valeman jumped, startled by the voice. It was right behind him, so close that it might have been a whisper in his ear if not for the harshness of its sound. He turned.

And there was Coll.

Or what had once been Coll.

His brother's face was barely recognizable, ravaged by some inner torment that he could only begin to imagine, a twisting that had distorted the familiar features and left them slack and lifeless. His body was misshapen as well, all pulled out of joint and hunched over, as if the bones had been re-arranged. There were marks on his skin, tears and lesions, and the eyes burned with a fever he recognized immediately.

"They took me," Coll whispered despairingly. "They made me. Please, Par, I need you. Hug me? Please?"

Par cried out, howling as if he would never stop, willing the thing before him to go away, to disappear from his sight and mind. Chills shook him, and the emptiness that opened inside threatened to collapse him completely.

"Coll!" he sobbed.

His brother stumbled and jerked toward him, arms outstretched. Rimmer Dall's warning whispered in Par's ear—the truth, the truth, the horror of it! Coll was a Shadowen, had somehow become one, a creature like the others in the Pit that Rimmer Dall claimed the Federation had destroyed! How? Par had been gone only minutes, it seemed. What had been done to his brother?

He stood there, stunned and shaking, as the thing before him caught hold of him with its fingers, then with its arms, enfolding him, whispering all the time, "hug me, hug me," as if it were a litany that would set it free. Par wished he were dead, that he had never been born, that he could somehow disappear from the earth and leave all that was happening behind. He wished a million impossible things—anything that could save him. The Sword of Shannara dropped from his nerveless fingers, and he felt as if everything he had known and believed in had in a single instant been betrayed.

Coll's hands began to rip at him.

"Coll, no!" he screamed.

Then something happened deep inside, something that he struggled against for only an instant's time before it overpowered him. A burning surged within his chest and spread outward through his body like a fire out of control. It was the magic—not the magic of the wishsong, the magic of harmless images and pretended things, but the other. It was the magic that had belonged once to the Elfstones, the magic that Allanon had given to Shea Ohmsford all those years ago, that had seeded itself in Wil Ohmsford and passed through generations of his family to him, changing, evolving, a constant mystery. It was alive in him, a magic greater than the wishsong, hard and unyielding.

It rushed through him and exploded forth. He screamed to Coll to let go of him, to get away, but his brother did not seem to hear. Coll, a ruined creature, a caricature of the blood and flesh human Par had loved, was con-sumed with his own inner madness, the Shadowen that he had become needing only to feed. The magic took him, enveloped him, and in an in-stant turned him to ash.

Par watched in horror as his brother disintegrated before his eyes.

Stunned, speechless, he collapsed to his knees, feeling his own life disappear with Coll's.

Then other hands were reaching for him, grappling with him, pulling him down. A whirl of twisted, ravaged faces and bodies pressed into him. The Shadowen of the Pit had come for him as well. There were scores of them, their hands grasping for him, their fingers ripping and tearing as if to shred him. He felt himself coming apart, breaking beneath the weight of their bodies.

And then the magic returned, exploding forth once more, and they were flung away like deadwood.

The magic took form this time, an unbidden thought brought to life. It coalesced in his hands, a jagged shard of blue fire, the flames as cool and hard as iron. He did not understand it yet, did not comprehend its source or being—yet he understood instinctively its purpose. Power radiated through him. Crying out in fury he swung his newfound weapon in a deadly arc, cutting through the creatures about him as if they were made of paper. They collapsed instantly, their voices unintelligible and remote as they died. He lost himself in the haze of his killing, striking out like a madman, giving sweet release to the fury and despair that had been born with the death of his brother.

The death he had caused!

The Shadowen fell back from him, those he did not destroy, staggering and shambling like stringed puppets. Bellowing at them still, gripping the shard of magic fire in one hand, Par reached down and snatched up the fallen Sword of Shannara.

He felt it burn him, searing his hand, the pain harsh and shocking.

Instantly his own magic flared and died. He jerked back in surprise, tried to invoke it anew and found he could not. The Shadowen started for him at once. He hesitated, then ran. Down the line of bridge rubble he raced, tripping and sliding on the dampened earth, gasping in rage and frustration. He could not tell how close the creatures of the Pit were to him. He ran without looking back, desperate to escape, fleeing as much from the horror of what had befallen him as the Shadowen in pursuit.

He was almost to the wall of the cliff when he heard Damson call. He ran for her, his mind shriveled so that he could think of nothing but the need to get free. The Sword of Shannara was clutched tightly to his chest, the burning gone now, just a simple blade wrapped within his muddied cloak. He went down, sprawling on his face, sobbing. He heard Damson again, calling out, and he shouted back in answer.

Then she had him in her arms, hauling him back to his feet, pulling him away, asking, "Par, Par, what's wrong with you? Par, what's happened?"

And he, replying in gasps and sobs, "He's dead, Damson! Coll's dead! I've killed him!"

The door into the cliff wall stood open ahead, a black aperture with a small, furry, wide-eyed creature framed in the opening. With Damson supporting him, he stumbled through and heard the door slam shut behind him.

Then everything and everyone disappeared in the white sound of his scream.

33

It was raining in the Dragon's Teeth, a cold, gray, insistent drizzle that masked the skyline from horizon to horizon. Morgan Leah stood at the edge of a trailside precipice and stared out from beneath the hood of his cloak. South, the foothills appeared as low, rolling shadows against the haze. The Mermidon could not be seen at all. The world beyond where he stood was a vague and distant place, and he had an unpleasant sense of not being able to fit back into it again.

He blinked away the flurry of drops that blew into his eyes, shielding himself with his hands. His reddish hair was plastered against his forehead, and his face was cold. Beneath his sodden clothing, his body was scraped and sore. He shivered, listening to the sounds around him. The wind whipped across the cliffs and down through the trees, its howl rising momentarily above the thunder that rumbled far to the north. Flood streams cascaded through the rocks behind him, rushing and splashing, the water building on itself as it tumbled downward into mist.

It was a day for rethinking one's life, Morgan decided grimly. It was a day for beginning anew.

Padishar Creel came up behind him, a cloaked, bulky form. Rain streaked his hard face, and his clothing, like Morgan's, was soaked through.

"Time to be going?" he asked quietly.

Morgan nodded.

"Are you ready, lad?"

"Yes."

Padishar looked away into the rain and sighed. "It's not turned out as we expected, has it?" he said quietly. "Not a bit of it."

Morgan thought a minute, then replied, "I don't know, Padishar. Maybe it has."

Under Padishar's guidance, the outlaws had emerged from the tunnels below the Jut early that morning and made their way east and north into the mountains. The trails they followed were narrow and steep and made dangerously slick by the rain, but Padishar felt it was safer to travel them than to try to slip through the Kennon Pass, which would surely be watched. The weather, bad as it was, was more help than hindrance. The rain washed away their footprints, erasing any trace of where they had been or where they were going. They had seen nothing of the Federation army since their flight began. Any pursuit was either bogged down or confused. The Jut might be lost, but the outlaws had escaped to fight another day.

It was now midafternoon, and the ragtag band had worked its way to a point somewhere above the juncture of the Mermidon where it branched south to the Rainbow Lake and east to the Rabb Plains. On a bluff where the mountain trails diverged in all directions, they had paused to rest before parting company. The Trolls would turn north for the Charnals and home. The outlaws would regroup at Firerim Reach, another of their redoubts. Padishar would return to Tyrsis in search of Damson and the missing Valemen. Morgan would go east to Culhaven and keep his promise to Steff. In four weeks' time, they would all meet again at Jannisson Pass. Hopefully by then the Troll army would be fully mobilized and the Movement would have consolidated its splintered groups. It would be time to begin mapping out a specific strategy for use in the continuing struggle against the Federation.

If any of them were still alive to do the mapping, Morgan thought dismally. He wasn't convinced any longer that they would be. What had happened with Teel had left him angry and doubting. He knew now how easy it was for the Shadowen—and therefore their Federation allies—to infiltrate those who stood against them. Anyone could be the enemy; there was no way to tell. Betrayal could come from any quarter and likely would. What were they to do to protect themselves when they could never be certain whom to trust?

It was bothering Padishar as well, Morgan knew—though the outlaw chief would be the last to admit it. Morgan had been watching him closely since their escape, and the big man was seeing ghosts at every turn.

But, then, so was he.

He felt a dark resignation chill him as if seeking to turn him to ice. It might be best for both of them to be alone for a while.

"Will it be safe for you to try going back to Tyrsis so soon?" he asked abruptly, wanting to make some sort of conversation, to hear the other's voice, but unable to think of anything better to say.

Padishar shrugged. "As safe as it ever is for me. I'll be disguised in any case." He looked over, dipping his head briefly against a gust of wind and rain. "Don't be worrying, Highlander. The Valemen will be all right. I'll make certain of it."

"It bothers me that I'm not going with you." Morgan could not keep the bitterness from his voice. "I was the one who talked Par and Coll into coming here in the first place—or at least I had a lot to do with it. I abandoned them once already in Tyrsis, and here I am abandoning them again." He shook his head wearily. "But I don't know what else I can do. I have to do what Steff asked of me. I can't just ignore . . ."

What he was going to say caught sharply in his throat as the memory of his dying friend flashed through his mind and the pain of his loss returned, sharp and poignant. He thought momentarily that there might be tears, but there weren't. Perhaps he had cried them all out.

Padishar reached out and put a hand on his shoulder. "Highlander, you must keep your promise. You owe him that. When it's finished, come back. The Valemen and I will be waiting, and we'll all begin again."

Morgan nodded, still unable to speak. He tasted the rain on his lips and licked it away.

Padishar's strong face bent close, blocking out everything else for just an instant. "We do what we must in this struggle, Morgan Leah. All of us. We are free-born as the rally cry says—Men, Dwarves, Trolls, all of us. There is no separate war to fight; it's a war that we all share. So you go to Culhaven and help those who need it there, and I'll go to Tyrsis and do the same. But we won't forget about each other, will we?"

Morgan shook his head. "No, we won't, Padishar."

The big man stepped back. "Well, then. Take this." He handed Morgan his ring with the hawk emblem. "When you need to find me again, show this to Matty Roh at the Whistledown in Varfleet. I'll see to it that she knows the way to where I'll be. Don't worry. It served the purpose once; it will serve it twice. Now, be on your way. And good luck to you."

He extended his hand and Morgan took it with a firm grasp. "Luck to you as well, Padishar."

Padishar Creel laughed. "Always, lad. Always."

He walked back across the bluff to a grove of towering fir where the outlaws and Trolls waited. Everyone who could came to their feet. Words of parting were spoken, distant and faint through the rain. Chandos was hugging Padishar, others were clapping him on the back, a few from their stretchers lifted their hands for him to take.

Even after all that's happened, he's still the only leader they want, Morgan thought in admiration.

He watched the Trolls begin to move north into the rocks, the huge, lumbering figures quickly becoming indistinguishable from the landscape through which they passed.

Padishar was looking at him now. He lifted his arm and waved in farewell.

He turned east into the foothills. The rain lashed at him, and he kept his head bent low to protect his face. His eyes focused on the path before him. When he thought to look back again, to see those he had fought beside and traveled with one final time, they had disappeared.

It occurred to him then that he said nothing to Padishar about the magic that still lingered in the broken Sword of Leah, the magic that had saved both their lives. He had never told the other how he had defeated Teel, how it was that he had managed to overcome the Shadowen. There had been no time to talk of it. He supposed that there had been no real reason. It was something he didn't yet fully understand. Why there was still magic in the blade, he didn't know. Why he had been able to summon it, he wasn't certain. He had thought it all used up before. Was it all used up now? Or was there enough left to save him one more time if the need should arise?

He found himself wondering how long it would be before he had to find out.

Moving cautiously down the mountainside, he faded away into the rain.

Par Ohmsford drifted.

He did not sleep, for in sleeping he would dream and his dreams haunted him. Nor did he wake, for in waking he would find the reality that he was so desperate to escape.

He simply drifted, half in and half out of any recognizable existence, tucked somewhere back in the gray in-between of what is and what isn't, where his mind could not focus and his memories remained scattered, where he was warm and secure from the past and future both, curled up deep inside. There was a madness upon him, he knew. But the madness was welcome, and he let it claim him without a struggle. It made him disoriented and distorted his perceptions and his thoughts. It gave him shelter. It cloaked him in a shroud of nonbeing that kept everything walled away—and that was what he needed.

Yet even walls have chinks and cracks that let through the light, and so it was with his madness. He sensed things—whispers of life from the world he was trying so hard to hide from. He felt the blankets that wrapped him and the bed on which he lay. He saw candles burning softly through a liquid haze, pinpricks of yellow brightness like islands on a dark sea. Strange beasts looked down at him from cabinets, shelves, boxes, and dressers, and their faces were formed of cloth and fur with button eyes and sewn noses, with ears that drooped and tipped, and with studied, watchful poses that never changed. He listened as words were spoken, floating through the air as motes of dust on streamers from the sun.

"He's very sick, lovely Damson," he heard one voice say.

And the other replied, "He's protecting himself, Mole."

Damson and Mole. He knew who they were, although he couldn't quite place them. He knew as well that they were talking about him. He didn't mind. What they were saying didn't make any difference.

Sometimes he saw their faces through the chinks and cracks.

The Mole was a creature with round, furry features and large, questioning eyes who stood above him, looking thoughtful. Sometimes he brought the strange beasts to sit close by. He looked very much the same as the beasts, Par thought. He called them by name. He spoke with them. But the beasts never answered back.

The girl fed him sometimes. Damson. She spooned soup into his mouth and made him drink, and he did so without argument. There was something perplexing about her, something that fascinated him, and he tried talking to her once or twice before giving up. Whatever it was he wished to say refused to show itself. The words ran away and hid. His thoughts faded. He watched her face fade with them.

She kept coming back, though. She sat beside him and held his hand. He could feel it from where he hid inside himself. She spoke softly, touched his face with her fingers, let him feel her presence even when she was doing nothing. It was her presence more than anything that kept him from drifting away altogether. He would have liked it better if she had let him go. He thought that it would happen that way eventually, that he would drift far enough that everything would disappear. But she prevented that, and, while it frustrated and even angered him at times, it also interested him. Why was she doing this? Was she anxious to keep him with her, or did she simply want to be taken along?

He began to listen more intently when she spoke. Her words seemed to grow clearer.

"It wasn't your fault," was what she told him most often. She told him that over and over, and for the longest time he didn't know why.

"That creature was no longer Coll." She told him that, too. "You had to destroy it."

She said these things, and once in a while he thought he almost understood. But fierce, dark shadows cloaked his understanding, and he was quick to hide from them.

But one day she spoke the words and he understood immediately. The drifting stopped, the walls broke apart, and everything rushed in with the cold fury of a winter ice storm. He began screaming, and he could not seem to stop. The memories returned, sweeping aside everything he had so carefully constructed to keep them out, and his rage and anguish were boundless. He screamed, and the Mole shrank from him, the strange beasts tumbled from his bedside, he could see the candles flickering through the tears he cried, and the shadows danced with glee.

It was the girl who saved him. She fought past the rage and anguish, ignored the screams, and held him to her. She held him as if the drifting might begin anew, as if he were in danger of being swept away completely, and she refused to let go. When his screams finally stopped, he found that he was holding her back.

He slept then, a deep and dreamless sleep that submerged him completely and let him rest. The madness was gone when he awoke, the drifting ended, and the gray half-sleep washed away. He knew himself again; he knew his surroundings and the faces of Damson Rhee and the Mole as they passed beside him. They bathed him and gave him fresh clothes, fed him and let him sleep some more. They did not speak to him. Perhaps they understood that he could not yet respond.

When he woke this time, the memories from which he had hidden surfaced in the forefront of his mind like creatures seeking air. They were no longer so loathsome to look upon, though they made him sad and confused and left him feeling empty. He faced them one by one, and allowed them to speak. When they had done so, he took their words and framed them in windows of light that revealed them clearly.

What they meant, he decided, was that the world had been turned upside down.

The Sword of Shannara lay on the bed beside him. He wasn't sure if it had been there all along or if Damson had placed it there after he had come back to himself. What he did know was that it was useless. It was supposed to provide a means to destroy the Shadowen, and it had been totally ineffective against Rimmer Dall. He had risked everything to gain the Sword, and it appeared that the risk had been pointless. He still did not possess the talisman he had been promised.

Of lies and truth there were more than enough and no way to separate one from the other. Rimmer Dall was lying surely—he could sense that much. But he had also spoken the truth. Allanon had spoken the truth—but he had been lying as well. Neither of them was entirely what he pretended to be. Nothing was completely as either portrayed it. Even he might be something other than what he believed, his magic the two-edged sword about which his uncle Walker had always warned him.

But the harshest and most bitter of the memories he faced was of poor, dead Coll. His brother had been changed into a Shadowen while trying to protect him, made a creature of the Pit, and Par had killed him for it. He hadn't meant to, certainly hadn't wanted to, but the magic had come forth unbidden and destroyed him. Probably there hadn't been anything he could have done to stop it, but such rationalization offered little in the way of solace or forgiveness. Coll's death was his fault. His brother had come on this journey because of him. He had gone down into the Pit because of him. Everything he had done had been because of Par.

Because Coll loved him.

He thought suddenly of their meeting with the shade of Allanon where so much had been entrusted to all of the Ohmsfords but Coll. Had Allanon known then that Coll was going to die? Was that why no mention had been made of him, why no charge had been given to him?

The possibility enraged Par.

His brother's face hovered in the air before him, changing, running through the gamut of moods he remembered so well. He could hear Coll's voice, the nuances of its rough intensity, the mix of its tones. He replayed in his mind all the adventures they had shared while growing up, the times they had gone against their parents' wishes, the places they had traveled to and seen, the people they had met and of whom they had talked. He retraced the events of the past few weeks, beginning with their flight from Varfleet. Much of it was tinged with his own sense of guilt, his need to assign himself blame. But most of it was free of everything but the wish to remember what his brother Coll had been like.

Coll, who was dead.

He lay for hours thinking of it, holding up the fact of it to the light of his understanding, in the silence of his thoughts, trying to find a way to make it real. It wasn't real, though—not yet. It was too awful to be real, and the pain and despair were too intense to be given release. Some part of him refused to admit that Coll was gone. He knew it was so, and yet he could not banish entirely that small, hopelessly absurd denial. In the end, he gave up trying.

His world compressed. He ate and he rested. He spoke sparingly with Damson. He lay in the Mole's dark underground lair amid the refuse of the upper world, himself a discard, only a little more alive than the toy animals that kept watch over him.

Yet all the while his mind was at work. Eventually he would grow strong again, he promised himself. When he did, someone would answer for what had been done to Coll.

The prisoner came awake, easing out of the drug-induced sleep that had kept him paralyzed almost from the moment he was taken. He lay on a sleeping mat in a darkened room. The ropes that had bound his hands and feet had been removed, and the cloths with which he had been gagged and blindfolded were gone. He was free to move about.

He sat up slowly, fighting to overcome a sudden rush of dizziness. His eyes adjusted to the dark, and he was able to make out the shape and dimensions of his jail. The room was large, more than twenty feet square. There was the mat, a wooden bench, a small table, and two chairs pushed into it. There was a window with metal shutters and a metal door. Both were closed.

He reached out experimentally and touched the wall. It was constructed of stone blocks and mortar. It would take a lot of digging to get through.

The dizziness passed finally, and he rose to his feet. There was a tray with bread and water on the table, and he sat down and ate the bread and drank the water. There was no reason not to; if they had wanted him dead, he would be so by now. He retained faint impressions of the journey that had brought him there—the sounds of the wagon in which he rode and the horses that pulled it, the low voices of the men, the rough grasp of the hands that held him when he was being fed and bedded, and the ache that he felt whenever he was awake long enough to feel anything.

He could still taste the bitterness of the drugs they had forced down his throat, the mix of crushed herbs and medicines that had burned through him and left him unconscious, drifting in a world of dreams that lacked any semblance to reality.

He finished his meal and came back to his feet. Where had they brought him, he wondered?

Taking his time, for he was still very weak, he made his way over to the shuttered window. The shutters did not fit tightly, and there were cracks in the fittings. Cautiously, he peered out.

He was a long way up. The summer sunlight brightened a countryside of forests and grassy knolls that stretched away to the edge of a huge lake that shimmered like liquid silver. Birds flew across the lake, soaring and diving, their calls ringing out in the stillness. High overhead, the faint traces of a vast, brightly colored rainbow canopied the lake from shoreline to shoreline.

The prisoner caught his breath in surprise. It was the Rainbow Lake.

He shifted his gaze hurriedly to the outer walls of his prison. He could just catch a glimpse of them as the window well opened up and dropped away.

They were formed of black granite.

This time his revelation stunned him. For a moment, he could not believe it. He was inside Southwatch.

Inside.

But who were his jailors—the Federation, the Shadowen, or someone else altogether? And why Southwatch? Why was he here? Why was he even still alive for that matter?

His frustration overcame him for a moment, and he lowered his head against the window ledge and closed his eyes. So many questions once again. It seemed that the questions would never end.

What had become of Par?

Coll Ohmsford straightened, and his eyes slipped open. He pressed his face back against the shutters, peered into the distant countryside, and wondered what fate his captors had planned for him.

That night Cogline dreamed. He lay in the shelter of the forest trees that ringed the barren heights on which ancient Paranor had once stood, tossing beneath the thin covering of his robes, beset by visions that chilled him more surely than any night wind. When he came awake, it was with a start. He was shaking with fear.

He had dreamed that the Shannara children were all dead.

For a moment he was convinced that it must be so. Then fear gave way to nervous irritation and that in turn to anger. He realized that what he had experienced was more probably a premonition of what might be than a vision of what was.

Steadying himself, he built a small fire, let it burn awhile to warm him, then took a pinch of silver powder from a pouch at his waist and dropped it into the flames. Smoke rose, filling the air before him with images that shimmered with iridescent light. He waited, letting them play themselves out, watching them closely until they had faded away.

Then he grunted in satisfaction, kicked out the fire, rolled himself back into his robes, and lay down again. The images told him only a little, but a little was all he needed to know. He was reassured. The dream was only a dream. The Shannara children lived. There were dangers that threatened them, of course—just as there had been from the beginning. He had sensed them in the images, monstrous and frightening, dark wraiths of possibility.

But that was as it must be.

The old man closed his eyes and his breathing slowed. There was nothing to be done about it this night.

Everything, he repeated, was as it must be.

Then he slept.

THE DRUID of SHANNARA

To Laurie and Peter,
for their love, support, and encouragement
in all things

1

The King of the Silver River stood at the edge of the Gardens that had been his domain since the dawn of the age of faerie and looked out over the world of mortal men. What he saw left him sad and discouraged. Everywhere the land sickened and died, rich black earth turning to dust, grassy plains withering, forests becoming huge stands of deadwood, and lakes and rivers either stagnating or drying away. Everywhere the creatures who lived upon the land sickened and died as well, unable to sustain themselves as the nourishment they relied upon grew poisoned. Even the air had begun to turn foul.

And all the while, the King of the Silver River thought, *the Shadowen grow stronger.*

His fingers reached out to brush the crimson petals of the cyclamen that grew thick about his feet. Forsythia clustered just beyond, dogwood and cherry farther back, fuchsia and hibiscus, rhododendrons and dahlias, beds of iris, azaleas, daffodils, roses, and a hundred other varieties of flowers and flowering plants that were always in bloom, a profusion of colors that stretched away into the distance until lost from sight. There were animals to be seen as well, both large and small, creatures whose evolution could be traced back to that distant time when all things lived in harmony and peace.

In the present world, the world of the Four Lands and the Races that had evolved out of the chaos and destruction of the Great Wars, that time was all but forgotten. The King of the Silver River was its sole remnant. He had been alive when the world was new and its first creatures were just being born. He had been young then, and there had been many like him. Now he was old and he was the last of his kind. Everything that had been, save for the Gardens in which he lived, had passed away. The Gardens alone survived, changeless, sustained by the magic of faerie. The Word had given the Gardens to the King of the Silver River and told him to tend them, to keep them as a reminder of what had once been and what might one day be again. The world without would evolve as it must, but the Gardens would remain forever the same.

Even so, they were shrinking. It was not so much physical as spiritual. The boundaries of the Gardens were fixed and unalterable, for the Gardens existed in a plane of being unaffected by changes in the world of mortal men. The Gardens were a presence rather than a place. Yet that presence was diminished by the sickening of the world to which it was tied, for the work of the Gardens and their tender was to keep that world strong. As the Four Lands grew poisoned, the work became harder, the effects of that work grew shorter, and the boundaries of human belief and trust in its existence—always somewhat marginal—began to fail altogether.

The King of the Silver River grieved that this should be. He did not grieve for himself; he was beyond that. He grieved for the people of the Four Lands, the mortal men and women for whom the magic of faerie was in danger of being lost forever. The Gardens had been their haven in the land of the Silver River for centuries, and he had been the spirit friend who protected its people. He had watched over them, had given them a sense of peace and well-being that transcended physical boundaries, and gave promise that benevolence and goodwill were still accessible in some corners of the world to all. Now that was ended. Now he could protect no one. The evil of the Shadowen, the poison they had inflicted upon the Four Lands, had eroded his own strength until he was virtually sealed within his Gardens, powerless to go to the aid of those he had worked so long to protect.

He stared out into the ruin of the world for a time as his despair worked its relentless will on him. Memories played hide-and-seek in his mind. The Druids had protected the Four Lands once. But the Druids were gone. A handful of descendents of the Elven house of Shannara had been champions of the Races for generations, wielding the remnants of the magic of faerie. But they were all dead.

He forced his despair away, replacing it with hope. The Druids could come again. And there were new generations of the old house of Shannara. The King of the Silver River knew most of what was happening in the Four Lands even if he could not go out into them. Allanon's shade had summoned a scattering of Shannara children to recover the lost magic, and perhaps they yet would if they could survive long enough to find a means to do so. But all of them had been placed in extreme peril. All were in danger of dying, threatened in the east, south, and west by the Shadowen and in the north by Uhl Belk, the Stone King.

The old eyes closed momentarily. He knew what was needed to save the Shannara children—an act of magic, one so powerful and intricate that nothing could prevent it from succeeding, one that would transcend the barriers that their enemies had created, that would break past the screen of deceit and lies that hid everything from the four on whom so much depended.

Yes, *four*, not three. Even Allanon did not understand the whole of what was meant to be.

He turned and made his way back toward the center of his refuge. He let the songs of the birds, the fragrances of the flowers, and the warmth of the air soothe him as he walked and he drew in through his senses the color and taste and feel of all that lay about him. There was virtually nothing that he could not do within his Gardens. Yet his magic was needed without. He knew what was required. In preparation he took the form of the old man that showed himself occasionally to the world beyond. His gait became an unsteady shamble, his breathing wheezed, his eyes dimmed, and his body ached with the feelings of life fading. The birdsong stopped, and the small animals that had crowded close edged quickly away. He forced himself to separate from everything he had evolved into, receding into what he might have been, needing momentarily to feel human mortality in order to know better how to give that part of himself that was needed.

When he reached the heart of his domain, he stopped. There was a pond of clearest water fed by a small stream. A unicorn drank from it. The earth that cradled the pond was dark and rich. Tiny, delicate flowers that had no name grew at the water's edge; they were the color of new snow. A small, intricately formed tree lifted out of a scattering of violet grasses at the pond's far end, its delicate green leaves laced with red. From a pair of massive rocks, streaks of colored ore shimmered brightly in the sunshine.

The King of the Silver River stood without moving in the presence of the life that surrounded him and willed himself to become one with it. When he had done so, when everything had threaded itself through the human form he had taken as if joined by bits and pieces of invisible lacing, he reached out to gather it all in. His hands, wrinkled human skin and brittle bones, lifted and summoned his magic, and the feelings of age and time that were the reminders of mortal existence disappeared.

The little tree came to him first, uprooted, transported, and set down before him, the framework of bones on which he would build. Slowly it bent to take the shape he desired, leaves folding close against the branches, wrapping and sealing away. The earth came next, handfuls lifted by invisible scoops to place against the tree, padding and defining. Then came the ores for muscle, the waters for fluids, and the petals of the tiny flowers for skin. He gathered silk from the unicorn's mane for hair and black pearls for eyes. The magic twisted and wove, and slowly his creation took form.

When he was finished, the girl who stood before him was perfect in every way but one. She was not yet alive.

He cast about momentarily, then selected the dove. He took it out of the air and placed it still living inside the girl's breast where it became her heart. Quickly he moved forward to embrace her and breathed his own life into her. Then he stepped back to wait.

The girl's breast rose and fell, and her limbs twitched. Her eyes fluttered open, coal black as they peered out from her delicate white features. She was small boned and finely wrought like a piece of paper art smoothed and shaped so that the edges and corners were replaced by curves. Her hair was so white it seemed silver; there was a glitter to it that suggested the presence of that precious metal.

"Who am I?" she asked in a soft, lilting voice that whispered of tiny streams and small night sounds.

"You are my daughter," the King of the Silver River answered, discovering within himself the stirring of feelings he had thought long since lost.

He did not bother telling her that she was an elemental, an earth child created of his magic. She could sense what she was from the instincts with which he had endowed her. No other explanation was needed.

She took a tentative step forward, then another. Finding that she could walk, she began to move more quickly, testing her abilities in various ways as she circled her father, glancing cautiously, shyly at the old man as she went. She looked around curiously, taking in the sights, smells, sounds, and tastes of the Gardens, discovering in them a kinship that she could not immediately explain.

"Are these Gardens my mother?" she asked suddenly, and he told her they were. "Am I a part of you both?" she asked, and he told her yes.

"Come with me," he said gently.

Together, they walked through the Gardens, exploring in the manner of a parent and child, looking into flowers, watching for the quick movement of birds and animals, studying the vast, intricate designs of the tangled undergrowth, the complex layers of rock and earth, and the patterns woven by the threads of the Gardens' existence. She was bright and quick, interested in everything, respectful of life, caring. He was pleased with what he saw; he found that he had made her well.

After a time, he began to show her something of the magic. He demonstrated his own first, only the smallest bits and pieces of it so as not to overwhelm her. Then he let her test her own against it. She was surprised to learn that she possessed it, even more surprised to discover what it could do. But she was not hesitant about using it. She was eager.

"You have a name," he told her. "Would you like to know what it is?"

"Yes," she answered, and stood looking at him alertly.

"Your name is Quickening." He paused. "Do you understand why?"

She thought a moment. "Yes," she answered again.

He led her to an ancient hickory whose bark peeled back in great, shaggy strips from its trunk. The breezes cooled there, smelling of jasmine and begonia, and the grass was soft as they sat together. A griffin wandered over through the tall grasses and nuzzled the girl's hand.

"Quickening," the King of the Silver River said. "There is something you must do."

Slowly, carefully he explained to her that she must leave the Gardens and go out into the world of men. He told her where it was that she must go and what it was that she must do. He talked of the Dark Uncle, the Highlander, and the nameless other, of the Shadowen, of Uhl Belk and Eldwist, and of the Black Elfstone. As he spoke to her, revealing the truth behind who and what she was, he experienced an aching within his breast that was decidedly human, part of himself that had been submerged for many centuries. The ache brought a sadness that threatened to cause his voice to break and his eyes to tear. He stopped once in surprise to fight back against it. It required some effort to resume speaking. The girl watched him without comment—intense, introspective, expectant. She did not argue with what he told her and she did not question it. She simply listened and accepted.

When he was done, she stood up. "I understand what is expected of me. I am ready."

But the King of the Silver River shook his head. "No, child, you are not. You will discover that when you leave here. Despite who you are and what you can do, you are vulnerable nevertheless to things against which I cannot protect you. Be careful then to protect yourself. Be on guard against what you do not understand."

"I will," she replied.

He walked with her to the edge of the Gardens, to where the world of men began, and together they stared out at the encroaching ruin. They stood without speaking for a very long time before she said, "I can tell that I am needed there."

He nodded bleakly, feeling the loss of her already though she had not yet departed. *She is only an elemental,* he thought and knew immediately that he was wrong. She was a great deal more. As much as if he had given birth to her, she was a part of him.

"Goodbye, Father," she said suddenly and left his side.

She walked out of the Gardens and disappeared into the world beyond. She did not kiss him or touch him in parting. She simply left, because that was all she knew to do.

The King of the Silver River turned away. His efforts had wearied him, had drained him of his magic. He needed time to rest. Quickly he shed his human image, stripping away the false covering of skin and bones, washing himself clean of its memories and sensations, and reverting to the faerie creature he was.

Even so, what he felt for Quickening, his daughter, the child of his making, stayed with him.

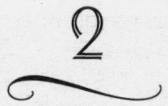

Walker Boh came awake with a shudder.

Dark Uncle.

The whisper of a voice in his mind jerked him back from the edge of the black pool into which he was sliding, pulled him from the inky dark into the gray fringes of the light, and he started so violently that the muscles of his legs cramped. His head snapped up from the pillow of his arm, his eyes slipped open, and he stared blankly ahead. There was pain all through his body, endless waves of it. The pain wracked him as if he had been touched by a hot iron, and he curled tightly into himself in a futile effort to ease it. Only his right arm remained outstretched, a heavy and cumbersome thing that no longer belonged to him, fastened forever to the floor of the cavern on which he lay, turned to stone to the elbow.

The source of the pain was there.

He closed his eyes against it, willing it to disperse, to disappear. But he lacked the strength to command it, his magic almost gone, dissipated by his struggle to resist the advancing poison of the Asphinx. It was seven days now since he had come into the Hall of Kings in search of the Black Elfstone, seven days since he had found instead the deadly creature that had been placed there to snare him.

Oh, yes, he thought feverishly. Definitely to snare him.

But by whom? By the Shadowen or by someone else? Who now had possession of the Black Elfstone?

He recalled in despair the events that had brought him to this end. There had been the summons from the shade of Allanon, dead three hundred years, to the heirs of the Shannara magic: his nephew Par Ohmsford, his cousin Wren Ohmsford, and himself. They had received the summons and a visit from the once-Druid Cogline urging them to heed it. They had done so, assembling at the Hadeshorn, ancient resting place of the Druids, where Allanon had appeared to them and charged them with separate undertakings that were meant to combat the dark work of the Shadowen who were using magic of their own to steal away the life of the Four Lands. Walker had been charged with recovering Paranor, the disappeared home of the Druids, and with bringing back the Druids themselves. He had resisted this charge until Cogline had come to him again, this time bearing a volume of the Druid Histories which told of a Black Elfstone which had the power to retrieve Paranor. That in turn had led him to the Grimpond, seer of the earth's and mortal men's secrets.

He searched the gloom of the cavern about him, the doors to the tombs of the Kings of the Four Lands dead all these centuries, the wealth piled before the crypts in which they lay, and the stone sentinels that kept watch over their remains. Stone eyes stared out of blank faces, unseeing, unheeding. He was alone with their ghosts.

He was dying.

Tears filled his eyes, blinding him as he fought to hold them back. He was such a fool!

Dark Uncle. The words echoed soundlessly, a memory that taunted and teased. The voice was the Grimpond's, that wretched, insidious spirit responsible for what had befallen him. It was the Grimpond's riddles that had led him to the Hall of Kings in search of the Black Elfstone. The Grimpond must have known what awaited him, that there would be no Elfstone but the Asphinx instead, a deadly trap that would destroy him.

And why had he thought it would be otherwise? Walker asked himself bleakly. Didn't the Grimpond hate him above all others? Hadn't it boasted to Walker that it was sending him to his doom by giving him what he asked for? Walker had simply gone out of his way to accommodate the spirit, anxiously rushing off to greet the death that he had been promised, blithely believing that he could protect himself against whatever evil he might encounter. Remember? he chided himself. Remember how confident you were?

He convulsed as the poison burned into him. Well and good. But where was his confidence now?

He forced himself to his knees and bent down over the opening in the cavern floor where his hand was pinned to the stone. He could just make out the remains of the Asphinx, the snake's stone body coiled about his own stone arm, the two of them forever joined, fastened to the rock of the mountain. He tightened his mouth and pulled up the sleeve of his cloak. His arm was hard and unyielding, gray to the elbow, and streaks of gray worked their way upward toward his shoulder. The process was slow, but steady. His entire body was turning to stone.

Not that it mattered if it did, he thought, because he would starve to death long before that happened. Or die of thirst. Or of the poison.

He let the sleeve fall back into place, covering the horror of what he had become. Seven days gone. What little food he'd brought with him had been consumed almost immediately, and he'd drunk the last of his water two days ago. His strength was failing rapidly now. He was feverish most of the time, his lucid periods growing shorter. He had struggled against what was happening at first, trying to use his magic to banish the poison from his body, to restore his hand and arm to flesh and blood. But his magic had failed him completely. He had worked at freeing his arm from the stone flooring, thinking that it might be pried loose in some way. But he was held fast, a condemned man with no hope of release. Eventually his exhaustion had forced him to sleep, and as the days passed he had slept more often, slipping further and further away from wanting to come awake.

Now, as he knelt in a huddle of darkness and pain, salvaged momentarily from the wreckage of his dying by the voice of the Grimpond, he realized with terrifying certainty that if he went to sleep again it would be for good. He breathed in and out rapidly, choking back his fear. He must not let that happen. He must not give up.

He forced himself to think. As long as he could think, he reasoned, he would not fall asleep. He retraced in his mind his conversation with the Grimpond, hearing again the spirit's words, trying anew to decipher their meaning. The Grimpond had not named the Hall of Kings in describing where the Black Elfstone could be found. Had Walker simply jumped to the wrong conclusion? Had he been deliberately misled? Was there any truth in what he had been told?

Walker's thoughts scattered in confusion, and his mind refused to respond to the demands he placed on it. He closed his eyes in despair, and it was with great difficulty that he forced them open again. His clothes were chill and damp with his own sweat, and his body shivered within them. His breathing was ragged, his vision blurred, and it was growing increasingly difficult to swallow. So many distractions—how could he think? He wanted simply to lie down and . . .

He panicked, feeling the urgency of his need threaten to swallow him up. He shifted his body, forcing his knees to scrape against the stone until they bled. A little more pain might help keep me awake, he thought. Yet he could barely feel it.

He forced his thoughts back to the Grimpond. He envisioned the wraith laughing at his plight, taking pleasure at it. He heard the taunting voice calling out to him. Anger gave him a measure of strength. There was something that he needed to recall, he thought desperately. There was something that the Grimpond had told him that he must remember.

Please, don't let me fall asleep!

The Hall of Kings did not respond to the urgency of his plea; the statues remained silent, disinterested, and oblivious. The mountain waited.

I have to break free! he howled wordlessly.

And then he remembered the visions, or more specifically the first of the three that the Grimpond had shown him, the one in which he had stood on a cloud above the others of the little company that had gathered at the Hadeshorn in answer to the summons of the shade of Allanon, the one in which he had said that he would sooner cut off his hand than bring back the Druids and then lifted his arm to show that he had done exactly that.

He remembered the vision and recognized its truth.

He banished the reaction it provoked in horrified disbelief and let his head droop until it was resting on the cavern stone. He cried, feeling the tears run down his cheeks, the sides of his face, stinging his eyes as they mingled with his sweat. His body twisted with the agony of his choices.

No! No, he would not!

Yet he knew he must.

His crying turned to laughter, chilling in its madness as it rolled out of him into the emptiness of the tomb. He waited until it expended itself, the echoes fading into silence, then looked up again. His possibilities had exhausted themselves; his fate was sealed. If he did not break free now, he knew he never would.

And there was only one way to do so.

He hardened himself to the fact of it, walling himself away from his emotions, drawing from some final reserve the last of his strength. He cast about the cavern floor until he found what he needed. It was a rock that was approximately the size and shape of an axe-blade, jagged on one side, hard enough to have survived intact its fall from the chamber ceiling where it had been loosened by the battle four centuries earlier between Allanon and the serpent Valg. The rock lay twenty feet away, clearly beyond reach of any ordinary man. But not him. He summoned a fragment of the magic that remained to him, forcing himself to remain steady during its use. The rock inched forward, scraping as it moved, a slow scratching in the cavern's silence. Walker grew light-headed from the strain, the fever burning through him, leaving him nauseated. Yet he kept the rock moving closer.

At last it was within reach of his free hand. He let the magic slip away, taking long moments to gather himself. Then he stretched out his arm to the rock, and his fingers closed tightly about it. Slowly he gathered it in, finding it impossibly heavy, so heavy in fact that he was not certain he could manage to lift it let alone . . .

He could not finish the thought. He could not dwell on what he was about to do. He dragged the rock over until it was next to him, braced himself firmly with his knees, took a deep breath, raised the rock overhead, hesitated for just an instant, then in a rush of fear and anguish brought it down. It smashed into the stone of his arm between elbow and wrist, hammering it with such force that it jarred his entire body. The resulting pain was so agonizing that it threatened to render him unconscious. He screamed as waves of it washed through him; he felt as if he were being torn apart from the inside out. He fell forward, gasping for breath, and the axe-blade rock dropped from his nerveless fingers.

Then he realized that something had changed.

He pushed himself upright and looked down at his arm. The blow had shattered the stone limb at the point of impact. His wrist and hand remained fastened to the Asphinx in the gloom of the hidden compartment of the cavern floor. But the rest of him was free.

He knelt in stunned disbelief for a long time, staring down at the ruin of his arm, at the gray-streaked flesh above the elbow and the jagged stone capping below. His arm felt leaden and stiff. The poison already within it continued to work its damage. There were jolts of pain all through him.

But he was free! Shades, he was free!

Suddenly there was a stirring in the chamber beyond, a faint and distant rustling like something had come awake. Walker Boh went cold in the pit of his stomach as he realized what had happened. His scream had given him away. The chamber beyond was the Assembly, and it was in the Assembly that the serpent Valg, guardian of the dead, had once lived.

And might live still.

Walker came to his feet, sudden dizziness washing through him. He ignored it, ignored the pain and weariness as well, and stumbled toward the heavy, ironbound entry doors that had brought him in. He shut away the sounds of everything about him, everything within, concentrating the whole of his effort on making his way across the cavern floor to the passageway that lay beyond. If the serpent was alive and found him now, he knew he was finished.

Luck was with him. The serpent did not emerge. Nothing appeared. Walker reached the doors leading from the tomb and pushed his way through into the darkness beyond.

What happened then was never clear afterward in his mind. Somehow he managed to work his way back through the Hall of Kings, past the Banshees whose howl could drive men mad, and past the Sphinxes whose gaze could turn men to stone. He heard the Banshees wail, felt the gaze of the Sphinxes burning down, and experienced the terror of the mountain's ancient magic as it sought to trap him, to make him another of its victims. Yet he escaped, some final shield of determination preserving him as he made his way clear, an iron will combining with weariness and pain and near madness to encase and preserve him. Perhaps his magic came to aid him as well; he thought it possible. The magic, after all, was unpredictable, a constant mystery. He pushed and trudged through near darkness and phantasmagoric images, past walls of rock that threatened to close about him, down tunnels of sight and sound in which he could neither see nor hear, and finally he was free.

He emerged into the outside world at daybreak, the sun's light chill and faint as it shone out of a sky thick with clouds and rain that lingered from the previous night's storm. With his arm tucked beneath his cloak like a wounded child, he made his way down the mountain trail toward the plains south. He never looked back. He could just manage to look ahead. He was on his feet only because he refused to give in. He could barely feel himself anymore, even the pain of his poisoning. He walked as if jerked along by strings attached to his limbs. His black hair blew wildly in the wind, whipping about his pale face, lashing it until his eyes blurred with tears. He was a scarecrow figure of madness as he wandered out of the mist and gray.

Dark Uncle, the Grimpond's voice whispered in his mind and laughed in glee.

He lost track of time completely. The sun's weak light failed to disperse the stormclouds and the day remained washed of color and friendless. Trails came and went, an endless procession of rocks, defiles, canyons, and drops. Walker remained oblivious to all of it. He knew only that he was descending, working his way downward out of the rock, back toward the world he had so foolishly left behind. He knew that he was trying to save his life.

It was midday when he emerged at last from the high peaks into the Valley of Shale, a tattered and aimless bit of human wreckage so badly fevered and weakened that he stumbled halfway across the crushed, glistening black rock of the valley floor before realizing where he was. When he finally saw, his strength gave out. He collapsed in the tangle of his cloak, feeling the sharp edges of the rock cutting into the skin of his hands and face, heedless of its sting as he lay facedown in exhaustion. After a time, he began to crawl toward the placid waters of the lake, inching his way painfully ahead, dragging his stone-tipped arm beneath him. It seemed logical to him in his delirium that if he could reach the Hadeshorn's edge he might submerge his ruined arm and the lethal waters would counteract the poison that was killing him. It was nonsensical, but for Walker Boh madness had become the measure of his life.

He failed even in this small endeavor. Too weak to go more than a few yards, he lapsed into unconsciousness. The last thing he remembered was how dark it was in the middle of the day, the world a place of shadows.

He slept, and in his sleep he dreamed that the shade of Allanon came to him. The shade rose out of the churning, boiling waters of the Hadeshorn, dark and mystical as it materialized from the netherworld of afterlife to which it had been consigned. It reached out to Walker, lifted him to his feet, flooded him with new strength, and gave clarity once more to his thoughts and vision. Spectral, translucent, it hung above the dark, greenish waters—yet its touch felt curiously human.

—Dark Uncle—

When the shade spoke the words, they were not taunting and hateful as they had been when spoken by the Grimpond. They were simply a designation of who and what Walker was.

—Why will you not accept the charge I have given you—

Walker struggled angrily to reply but could not seem to find the words.

—The need for you is great, Walker. Not my need, but the need of the Lands and their people, the Races of the new world. If you do not accept my charge, there is no hope for them—

Walker's rage was boundless. Bring back the Druids, who were no more, and disappeared Paranor? Surely, thought Walker in response. Surely, shade of Allanon. I shall take my ruined body in search of what you seek, my poisoned limb, though I be dying and cannot hope to help anyone, still I . . .

—Accept, Walker. You do not accept. Acknowledge the truth of yourself and your own destiny—

Walker didn't understand.

—Kinship with those who have gone before you, those who understood the meaning of acceptance. That is what you lack—

Walker shuddered, disrupting the vision of his dream. His strength left him. He collapsed at the Hadeshorn's edge, blanketed in confusion and fear, feeling so lost that it seemed to him impossible that he could ever again be found.

Help me, Allanon, he begged in despair.

The shade hung motionless in the air before him, ethereal against a backdrop of wintry skies and barren peaks, rising up like death's specter come to retrieve a fresh victim. It seemed suddenly to Walker that dying was all that was left to him.

Do you wish me to die? he asked in disbelief. *Is this what you demand of me?*

The shade said nothing.

Did you know that this would happen to me? He held forth his arm, jagged stone stump, poison-streaked flesh.

The shade remained silent.

Why won't you help me? Walker howled.

—Why won't you help me—

The words echoed sharply in his mind, urgent and filled with a sense of dark purpose. But he did not speak them. Allanon did.

Then abruptly the shade shimmered in the air before him and faded away. The waters of the Hadeshorn steamed and hissed, roiled in fury, and went still once more. All about the air was misted and dark, filled with ghosts and wild imaginings, a place where life and death met at a crossroads of unanswered questions and unresolved puzzles.

Walker Boh saw them for only a moment, aware that he was seeing them not in sleep but in waking, realizing suddenly that his vision might not have been a dream at all.

Then everything was gone, and he fell away into blackness.

When he came awake again there was someone bending over him. Walker saw the other through a haze of fever and pain, a thin, sticklike figure in gray robes with a narrow face, a wispy beard and hair, and a hawk nose, crouched close like something that meant to suck away what life remained to him.

"Walker?" the figure whispered gently.

It was Cogline. Walker swallowed against the dryness in his throat and struggled to raise himself. The weight of his arm dragged against him, pulling him back, forcing him down. The old man's hands groped beneath the concealing cloak and found the leaden stump. Walker heard the sharp intake of his breath.

"How did you . . . find me?" he managed.

"Allanon," Cogline answered. His voice was rough and laced with anger.

Walker sighed. "How long have I . . . ?"

"Three days. I don't know why you're still alive. You haven't any right to be."

"None," Walker agreed and reached out impulsively to hug the other man close. The familiar feel and smell of the old man's body brought tears to his eyes. "I don't think . . . I'm meant to die . . . just yet."

Cogline hugged Walker back. He said, "No, Walker. Not yet."

Then the old man was lifting him to his feet, hauling him up with strength Walker hadn't known he possessed, holding him upright as he pointed them both toward the south end of the valley. It was dawn again, the sunrise unclouded and brilliant gold against the eastern horizon, the air still and expectant with the promise of its coming.

"Hold on to me," Cogline urged, walking him along the crushed black rock. "There are horses waiting and help to be had. Hold tight, Walker."

Walker Boh held on for dear life.

<h1 style="text-align:center">3</h1>

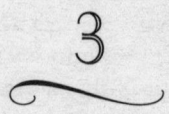

Cogline took Walker Boh to Storlock. Even on horseback with Walker lashed in place, it took until nightfall to complete the journey. They came down out of the Dragon's Teeth into a day filled with sunshine and warmth, turned east across the Rabb Plains, and made their way into the Eastland forests of the Central Anar to the legendary village of the Stors. Wracked with pain and consumed with thoughts of dying, Walker remained awake almost the entire time. Yet he was never certain where he was or what was happening about him, conscious only of the swaying of his horse and Cogline's constant reassurance that all would be well.

He did not believe that Cogline was telling him the truth.

Storlock was silent, cool and dry in the shadow of the trees, a haven from the swelter and dust of the plains. Hands reached up to take Walker from the saddle, from the smell of sweat and the rocking motion, and from the feeling that he must at any moment give in to the death that was waiting to claim him. He did not know why he was alive. He could give himself no reason. White-robed figures gathered all around, supporting him, easing him down—Stors, the Gnome Healers of the Village. Everyone knew of the Stors. Theirs was the most advanced source of healing in the Four Lands. Wil Ohmsford had studied with them once and become a healer, the only Southlander ever to do so. Shea Ohmsford had been healed after an attack in the Wolfsktaag. Earlier, Par had been brought to them as well, infected by the poison of the Werebeasts in Olden Moor. Walker had brought him. Now it was Walker's turn to be saved. But Walker did not think that would happen.

A cup was raised to his lips, and a strange liquid trickled down his throat. Almost immediately the pain eased, and he felt himself grow drowsy. Sleep would be good for him, he decided suddenly, surprisingly. Sleep would be welcome. He was carried into the Center House, the main care lodge, and placed in a bed in one of the back rooms where the forest could be seen through the weave of the curtains, a wall of dark trunks set at watch. He was stripped of his clothes, wrapped in blankets, given something further to drink, a bitter, hot liquid, and left to fall asleep.

He did so almost at once.

As he slept, the fever dissipated, and the weariness faded away. The pain lingered, but it was distant somehow and not a part of him. He sank down into the warmth and comfort of his bedding, and even dreams could not penetrate the shield of his rest. There were no visions to distress him, no dark thoughts to bring him awake. Allanon and Cogline were forgotten. His anguish at the loss of his limb, his struggle to escape the Asphinx and the Hall of Kings, and his terrifying sense of no longer being in command of his own destiny—all were forgotten. He was at peace.

He did not know how long he slept, for he was not conscious of time passing, of the sweep of the sun across the sky, or of the change from night to day and back again. When he began to come awake once more, floating out of the darkness of his rest through a world of half-sleep, memories of his boyhood stirred unexpectedly, small snatches of his life in the days when he was first learning to cope with the frustration and wonder of discovering who and what he was.

The memories were sharp and clear.

He was still a child when he first learned he had magic. He didn't call it magic then; he didn't call it anything. He believed such power common; he thought that he was like everyone else. He lived then with his father Kenner and mother Risse at Hearthstone in Darklin Reach, and there were no other children to whom he might compare himself. That came later. It was his mother who told him that what he could do was unusual, that it made him different from other children. He could still see her face as she tried to explain, her small features intense, her white skin striking against coal black hair that was always braided and laced with flowers. He could still hear her low and compelling voice. Risse. He had loved his mother deeply. She had not had magic of her own; she was a Boh and the magic came from his father's side, from the Ohmsfords. She told him that, sitting him down before her on a brilliant autumn day when the smell of dying leaves and burning wood filled the air, smiling and reassuring as she spoke, trying unsuccessfully to hide from him the uneasiness she felt.

That was one of the things the magic let him do. It let him see sometimes what others were feeling—not with everyone, but almost always with his mother.

"Walker, the magic makes you special," she said. "It is a gift that you must care for and cherish. I know that someday you are going to do something wonderful with it."

She died a year later after falling ill to a fever for which even her formidable healing skills could not find a cure.

He lived alone with his father then, and the "gift" with which she had believed him blessed developed rapidly. The magic was an enabler; it gave him insight. He discovered that frequently he could sense things in people without being told—changes in their mood and character, emotions they thought to keep secret, their opinions and ideas, their needs and hopes, even the reasons behind what they did. There were always visitors at Hearthstone—travelers passing through, peddlers, tradesmen, woodsmen, hunters, trappers, even Trackers—and Walker would know all about them without their having to say a word. He would tell them so. He would reveal what he knew. It was a game that he loved to play. It frightened some of them, and his father ordered him to stop. Walker did as he was asked. By then he had discovered a new and more interesting ability. He discovered that he could communicate with the animals of the forest, with birds and fish, even with plants. He could sense what they were thinking and feeling just as he could with humans, even though their thoughts and feelings were more rudimentary and limited. He would disappear for hours on excursions of learning, on make-believe adventures, on journeys of testing and seeking out. He designated himself early as an explorer of life.

As time passed, it became apparent that Walker's special insight was to help him with his schooling as well. He began reading from his father's library almost as soon as he learned how the letters of the alphabet formed words on the fraying pages of his father's books. He mastered mathematics effortlessly. He understood sciences intuitively. Barely anything had to be explained. Somehow he just seemed to understand how it all worked. History became his special passion; his memory of things, of places and events and people, was prodigious. He began to keep notes of his own, to write down everything he learned, to compile teachings that he would someday impart to others.

The older he grew, the more his father's attitude toward him seemed to change. He dismissed his suspicions at first, certain that he was mistaken. But the feeling persisted. Finally he asked his father about it, and Kenner—a tall, lean, quick-moving man with wide, intelligent eyes, a stammer he had worked hard to overcome, and a gift for crafting—admitted it was true. Kenner did not have magic of his own. He had evidenced traces of it when he was young, but it had disappeared shortly after he had passed out of boyhood. It had been like that with his father and his father's father before that and every Ohmsford he knew about all the way back to Brin. But it did not appear to be that way with Walker. Walker's magic just seemed to grow stronger. Kenner told him that he was afraid that his son's abilities would eventually overwhelm him, that they would develop to a point where he could no longer anticipate or control their effects. But he said as well, just as Risse had said, that they should not be suppressed, that magic was a gift that always had some special purpose in being.

Shortly after, he told Walker of the history behind the Ohmsford magic, of the Druid Allanon and the Valegirl Brin, and of the mysterious trust that the former in dying had bequeathed to the latter. Walker had been twelve when he heard the tale. He had wanted to know what the trust was supposed to be. His father hadn't been able to tell him. He had only been able to relate the history of its passage through the Ohmsford bloodline.

"It manifests itself in you, Walker," he said. "You in turn will pass it on to your children, and they to theirs, until one day there is need for it. That is the legacy you have inherited."

"But what good is a legacy that serves no purpose?" Walker had demanded.

And Kenner had repeated, "There is always purpose in magic—even when we don't understand what it is."

Barely a year later, as Walker was entering his youth and leaving his childhood behind, the magic revealed that it possessed another, darker side. Walker found out that it could be destructive. Sometimes, most often when he was angry, his emotions transformed themselves into energy. When that happened, he could move things away and break them apart without touching them. Sometimes he could summon a form of fire. It wasn't ordinary fire; it didn't burn like ordinary fire and it was different in color, a sort of cobalt. It wouldn't do much of what he tried to make it do; it did pretty much what it wished. It took him weeks to learn to control it. He tried to keep his discovery a secret from his father, but his father learned of it anyway, just as he eventually learned of everything about his son. Though he said little, Walker felt the distance between them widen.

Walker was nearing manhood when his father made the decision to take him out of Hearthstone. Kenner Ohmsford's health had been failing steadily for several years, his once strong body afflicted by a wasting sickness. Closing down the cottage that had been Walker's home since birth, he took the boy to Shady Vale to live with another family of Ohmsfords, Jaralan and Mirianna and their sons Par and Coll.

The move became for Walker Boh the worst thing that had ever happened to him. Shady Vale, though little more than a hamlet community, nevertheless seemed constricting after Hearthstone. Freedom there had been boundless; here, there were boundaries that he could not escape. Walker was not used to being around so many people and he could not seem to make himself fit in. He was required to attend school, but there was nothing for him to learn. His master and the other children disliked and mistrusted him; he was an outsider, he behaved differently than they, he knew entirely too much, and they quickly decided that they wanted nothing to do with him. His magic became a snare he could not escape. It manifested itself in everything he did, and by the time he realized he should have hidden it away it was too late to do so. He was beaten a number of times because he wouldn't defend himself. He was terrified of what would happen if he let the fire escape.

He was in the village less than a year when his father died. Walker had wished that he could die, too.

He continued to live with Jaralan and Mirianna Ohmsford, who were good to him and who sympathized with the difficulties he was encountering because their own son Par was just beginning to exhibit signs of having magic of his own. Par was a descendent of Jair Ohmsford, Brin's brother. Both sides of the family had passed the magic of their ancestors down through the bloodline in the years since Allanon's death, so the appearance of Par's magic was not entirely unexpected. Par's was a less unpredictable and complicated form of magic, manifesting itself principally in the boy's ability to create lifelike images with his voice. Par was still little then, just five or six, and he barely understood what was happening to him. Coll was not yet strong enough to protect his brother, so Walker ended up taking the boy under his wing. It seemed natural enough to do so. After all, only Walker understood what Par was experiencing.

His relationship with Par changed everything. It gave him something to focus on, a purpose beyond worrying about his own survival. He spent time with Par helping him adjust to the presence of the magic in his body. He counseled him in its use, advised him in the cautions that were necessary, the protective devices he must learn to employ. He tried to teach him how to deal with the fear and dislike of people who would choose not to understand. He became Par's mentor.

The people of Shady Vale began calling him "Dark Uncle." It began with the children. He wasn't Par's uncle, of course; he wasn't anybody's uncle. But he hadn't a firm blood tie in the eyes of the villagers; no one really understood the relationship he bore to Jaralan and Mirianna, so there were no constrictions on how they might refer to him. "Dark Uncle" became the appellation that stuck. Walker was tall by then, pale skinned and black haired like his mother, apparently immune to the browning effect of the sun. He looked ghostly. It seemed to the Vale children as if he were a night thing that never saw the light of day, and his relationship toward the boy Par appeared mysterious to them. Thus he became "Dark Uncle," the counselor of magic, the strange, awkward, withdrawn young man whose insights and comprehensions set him apart from everyone.

Nevertheless, the name "Dark Uncle" notwithstanding, Walker's attitude improved. He began to learn how to deal with the suspicion and mistrust. He was no longer attacked. He found that he could turn aside these assaults with not much more than a glance or even the set of his body. He could use the magic to shield himself. He found he could project wariness and caution into others and prevent them from following through on their violent intentions. He even became rather good at stopping fights among others. Unfortunately, all this did was distance him further. The adults and older youths left him alone altogether; only the younger children turned cautiously friendly.

Walker was never happy in Shady Vale. The mistrust and the fear remained, concealed just beneath the forced smiles, the perfunctory nods, and the civilities of the villagers that allowed him to exist among them but never gain acceptance. Walker knew that the magic was the cause of his problem. His mother and father might have thought of it as a gift, but he didn't. And he never would again. It was a curse that he felt certain would haunt him to the grave.

By the time he reached manhood, Walker had resolved to return to Hearthstone, to the home he remembered so fondly, away from the people of the Vale, from their mistrust and suspicion, from the strangeness they caused him to feel. The boy Par had adjusted well enough that Walker no longer felt concerned about him. To begin with, Par was a native of the Vale and accepted in a way that Walker never could be. Moreover, his attitude toward using magic was far different than Walker's. Par was never hesitant; he wanted to know everything the magic could do. What others thought did not concern him. He could get away with that; Walker never could. The two had begun to grow apart as they grew older. Walker knew it was inevitable. It was time for him to go. Jaralan and Mirianna urged him to stay, but understood at the same time that he could not.

Seven years after his arrival, Walker Boh departed Shady Vale. He had taken his mother's name by then, disdaining further use of Ohmsford because it linked him so closely with the legacy of magic he now despised. He went back into Darklin Reach, back to Hearthstone, feeling as if he were a caged wild animal that had been set free. He severed his ties with the life he had left behind him. He resolved that he would never again use the magic. He promised himself that he would keep apart from the world of men for the rest of his life.

For almost a year he did exactly as he said he would do. And then Cogline appeared and everything changed . . .

Half-sleep turned abruptly to waking, and Walker's memories faded away. He stirred in the warmth of his bed, and his eyes blinked open. For a moment he could not decide where he was. The room in which he lay was bright with daylight despite the brooding presence of a cluster of forest trees directly outside his curtained window. The room was small, clean, almost bare of furniture. There were a sitting chair and a small table next to his bed, the bed, and nothing else. A vase of flowers, a basin of water, and some cloths sat on the table. The single door leading into the room stood closed.

Storlock. That was where he was, where Cogline had brought him.

He remembered then what had happened to bring him here.

Cautiously, he brought his ruined arm out from beneath the bedding. There was little pain now, but the heaviness of the stone persisted and there was no feeling. He bit his lip in anger and frustration as his arm worked free. Nothing had changed beyond the lessening of the pain. The stone tip where the lower arm had shattered was still there. The streaks of gray where the poison worked its way upward toward his shoulder were there as well.

He slipped his arm from view again. The Stors had been unable to cure him. Whatever the nature of the poison that the Asphinx had injected into him, the Stors could not treat it. And if the Stors could not treat it—the Stors, who were the best of the Four Lands' Healers . . .

He could not finish the thought. He shoved it away, closed his eyes, tried to go back to sleep, and failed. All he could see was his arm shattering under the impact of the stone wedge.

Despair washed over him and he wept.

An hour had passed when the door opened and Cogline entered the room, an intrusive presence that made the silence seem even more uncomfortable.

"Walker," he greeted quietly.

"They cannot save me, can they?" Walker asked bluntly, the despair pushing everything else aside.

The old man became a statue at his bedside. "You're alive, aren't you?" he replied.

"Don't play word games with me. Whatever's been done, it hasn't driven out the poison. I can feel it. I may be alive, but only for the moment. Tell me if I'm wrong."

Cogline paused. "You're not wrong. The poison is still in you. Even the Stors haven't the means to remove it or to stop its spread. But they have slowed the process, lessened the pain, and given you time. That is more than I would have expected given the nature and extent of the injury. How do you feel?"

Walker's smile was slow and bitter. "Like I am dying, naturally. But in a comfortable fashion."

They regarded each other without speaking for a moment. Then Cogline moved over to the sitting chair and eased himself into it, a bundle of old bones and aching joints, of wrinkled brown skin. "Tell me what happened to you, Walker," he said.

Walker did. He told of reading the ancient, leatherbound Druid History that Cogline had brought to him and learning of the Black Elfstone, of deciding to seek the counsel of the Grimpond, of hearing its riddles and witnessing its visions, of determining that he must go to the Hall of Kings, of finding the secret compartment marked with runes in the floor of the Tomb, and finally of being bitten and poisoned by the Asphinx left there to snare him.

"To snare someone at least, perhaps anyone," Cogline observed.

Walker looked at him sharply, anger and mistrust flaring in his dark eyes. "What do you know of this, Cogline? Do you play the same games as the Druids now? And what of Allanon? Did Allanon know . . ."

"Allanon knew nothing," Cogline interrupted, brushing aside the accusation before it could be completed. The old eyes glittered beneath narrowed brows. "You undertook to solve the Grimpond's riddles on your own—a foolish decision on your part. I warned you repeatedly that the wraith would find a way to undo you. How could Allanon know of your predicament? You attribute far too much to a man three hundred years dead. Even if he were still alive, his magic could never penetrate that which shrouds the Hall of Kings. Once you were within, you were lost to him. And to me. It wasn't until you emerged again and collapsed at the Hadeshorn that he was able to discover what happened and summon me to help you. I came as quickly as I could and even so it took me three days."

One hand lifted, a sticklike finger jabbing. "Have you bothered to question why it is that you aren't dead? It is because Allanon found a way to keep you alive, first until I arrived and second until the Stors could treat you! Think on that a bit before you start casting blame about so freely!"

He glared, and Walker glared back at him. It was Walker who looked away first, too sick at heart to continue the confrontation. "I have trouble believing anyone just at the moment," he offered lamely.

"You have trouble believing anyone at any time," Cogline snapped, unappeased. "You cast your heart in iron long ago, Walker. You stopped believing in anything. I remember when that wasn't so."

He trailed off, and the room went silent. Walker found himself thinking momentarily of the time the old man referred to, the time when he had first come to Walker and offered to show him the ways in which the magic could be used. Cogline was right. He hadn't been so bitter then; he'd been full of hope.

He almost laughed. That was such a long time ago.

"Perhaps I can use my own magic to dispel the poison from my body," he ventured quietly. "Once I return to Hearthstone, once I'm fully rested. Brin Ohmsford had such power once."

Cogline dropped his eyes and looked thoughtful. His gnarled hands clasped loosely in the folds of his robe. It appeared as if he were trying to decide something.

Walker waited a moment, then asked, "What has become of the others—of Par and Coll and Wren?"

Cogline kept his gaze lowered. "Par has gone in search of the Sword, young Coll with him. The Rover girl seeks the Elves. They've accepted the charges Allanon gave to them." He looked up again. "Have you, Walker?"

Walker stared at him, finding the question both absurd and troubling, torn between conflicting feelings of disbelief and uncertainty. Once he would not have hesitated to give his answer. He thought again of what Allanon had asked him to do: Bring back disappeared Paranor and restore the Druids. A ridiculous, impossible undertaking, he had thought at the time. Game playing, he had decried. He would not be a part of such foolishness, he had announced to Par, Coll, Wren, and the others of the little company that had come with him to the Valley of Shale. He despised the Druids for their manipulation of the Ohmsfords. He would not be made their puppet. So bold he had been, so certain. He would sooner cut off his hand than see the Druids come again, he had declared.

And the loss of his hand was the price that had been exacted, it seemed.

Yet had that loss truly put an end to any possibility of the return of Paranor and the Druids? More to the point, was that what he now intended?

He was conscious of Cogline watching him, impatient as he waited for Walker Boh's answer to his question. Walker kept his eyes fixed on the old man without seeing him. He was thinking suddenly of the Druid History and its tale of the Black Elfstone. If he had not gone in search of the Elfstone, he would not have lost his arm. Why had he gone? Curiosity, he had thought. But that was a simplistic answer and he knew it was given too easily. In any case, didn't the very fact of his going indicate that despite any protestations to the contrary he indeed had accepted Allanon's charge?

If not, what was it that he was doing?

He focused again on the old man. "Tell me something, Cogline. Where did you get that book of the Druid Histories? How did you find it? You said when you brought it to me that you got it out of Paranor. Surely not."

Cogline's smile was faint and ironic. "Why 'surely not,' Walker?"

"Because Paranor was sent out of the world of men by Allanon three hundred years ago. It doesn't exist anymore."

Cogline's face crinkled like crushed parchment. "Doesn't exist? Oh, but it does, Walker. And you're wrong. Anyone can reach it if they have the right magic to help them. Even you."

Walker hesitated, suddenly uncertain.

"Allanon sent Paranor out of the world of the men, but it still exists," Cogline said softly. "It needs only the magic of the Black Elfstone to summon it back again. Until then, it remains lost to the Four Lands. But it can still be entered by those who have the means to do so and the courage to try. It does require courage, Walker. Shall I tell you why? Would you like to hear the story behind my journey into Paranor?"

Walker hesitated again, wondering if he wanted to hear anything ever again about the Druids and their magic. Then he nodded slowly. "Yes."

"But you are prepared to disbelieve what I am going to tell you, aren't you?"

"Yes."

The old man leaned forward. "Tell you what. I'll let you judge for yourself."

He paused, gathering his thoughts. Daylight framed him in brightness, exposing the flaws of old age that etched his thin frame in lines and hollows, that left his hair and beard wispy and thin, and that gave his hands a tremulous appearance as he clasped them tightly before him.

"It was after your meeting with Allanon. He sensed, and I as well, that you would not accept the charge you had been given, that you would resist any sort of involvement without further evidence of the possibility that you might succeed. And that there was reason to want to. You differ in your attitude from the others—you doubt everything that you are told. You came to Allanon already planning to reject what you would hear."

Walker started to protest, but Cogline held up his hands quickly and shook his head. "No, Walker. Don't argue. I know you better than you know yourself. Just listen to me for now. I went north on Allanon's summons, seeming to disappear, leaving you to debate among yourselves what course of action you would follow. Your decision in the matter was a foregone conclusion. You would not do as you had been asked. Since that was so, I resolved to try to change your mind. You see, Walker, I believe in the dreams; I see the truth in them that you as yet do not. I would not be a messenger for Allanon if there were any way to avoid it. My time as a Druid passed away long ago, and I do not seek to return to what was. But I am all there is and since that is so I will do what I think necessary. Dissuading you from refusing to involve yourself in the matter at hand is something I deem vital."

He was shaking with the conviction of his words and the look he extended Walker was one that sought to convey truths that the old man could not speak.

"I went north, Walker, as I said. I traveled out of the Valley of Shale and across the Dragon's Teeth to the valley of the Druid's Keep. Nothing remains of Paranor but a few crumbling outbuildings on a barren height. The forests still surround the spot on which it once stood, but nothing will grow upon the earth, not even the smallest blade of grass. The wall of thorns that once protected the Keep is gone. Everything has disappeared— as if some giant reached down and snatched it all away.

"I stood there, near twilight, looking at the emptiness, envisioning what had once been. I could sense the presence of the Keep. I could almost see it looming out of the shadows, rising up against the darkening eastern skies. I could almost define the shape of its stone towers and parapets. I waited, for Allanon knew what was needed and would tell me when it was time."

The old eyes gazed off into space. "I slept when I grew tired, and Allanon came to me in my dreams as he now does with all of us. He told me that Paranor was indeed still there, cast away by magic into a different place and time, yet there nevertheless. He asked me if I would enter and bring out from it a certain volume of the Druid Histories which would describe the means by which Paranor could be restored to the Four Lands. He asked if I would take that book to you." He hesitated, poised to reveal something more, then simply said, "I agreed.

"He reached out to me then and took my hand. He lifted me away from myself, my spirit out of my body. He cloaked me in his magic. I became momentarily something other than the man I am—but I don't know even now what that something was. He told me what I must do. I walked alone then to where the walls of the Keep had once stood, closed my eyes so that they would not deceive me, and reached out into worlds that lie beyond our own for the shape of what had once been. I found that I could do that. Imagine my astonishment when Paranor's walls materialized suddenly beneath my fingers. I risked taking a quick look at them, but when I did so there was nothing to see. I was forced to begin again. Even as a spirit I could not penetrate the magic if I violated its rules. I kept my eyes closed tightly this time, searched out the walls anew, discovered the hidden trapdoor concealed in the base of the Keep, pushed the catch that would release the locks, and entered."

Cogline's mouth tightened. "I was allowed to open my eyes then and look around. Walker, it was the Paranor of old, a great sprawling castle with towers that rose into clouds of ancient brume and battlements that stretched away forever. It seemed endless to me as I climbed its stairs and wandered its halls; I was like a rat in a maze. The castle was filled with the smell and taste of death. The air had a strange greenish cast; everything was swathed in it. Had I attempted to enter in my flesh-and-blood body, I would have been destroyed instantly; I could sense the magic still at work, scouring the rock corridors for any signs of life. The furnaces that had once been fueled by the fire at the earth's core were still, and Paranor was cold and lifeless. When I gained the upper halls I found piles of bones, grotesque and misshapen, the remains of the Mord Wraiths and Gnomes that Allanon had trapped there when he had summoned the magic to destroy Paranor. Nothing was alive in the Druid's Keep save myself."

He was silent for a moment as if remembering. "I sought out the vault in which the Druid Histories were concealed. I had a sense of where it was, quickened in part by the days in which I studied at Paranor, in part by Allanon's magic. I searched out the library through which the vault could be

entered, finding as I did so that I could touch things as if I were still a creature of substance and not of spirit. I felt along the dusty, worn edges of the
bookshelves until I found the catches that released the doors leading in.
They swung wide, and the magic gave way before me. I entered, discovered
the Druid Histories revealed, and took from its resting place the one that
was needed."

Cogline's eyes strayed off across the sunlit room, seeking visions that
were hidden from Walker. "I left then. I went back the same way as I had
come, a ghost out of the past as much as those who had died there, feeling
the chill of their deaths and the immediacy of my own. I passed down the
stairwells and corridors in a half-sleep that let me feel as well as see the
horror of what now held sway in the castle of the Druids. Such power,
Walker! The magic that Allanon summoned was frightening even yet. I fled
from it as I departed—not on foot, you understand, but in my mind. I was
terrified!"

The eyes swung back. "So I escaped. And when I woke, I had in my
possession the book that I had been sent to recover and I took it then
to you."

He went silent, waiting patiently as Walker considered his story.
Walker's eyes were distant. "It can be done then? Paranor can be entered
even though it no longer exists in the Four Lands?"

Cogline shook his head slowly. "Not by ordinary men." His brow furrowed. "Perhaps by you, though. With the magic of the Black Elfstone to
help you."

"Perhaps," Walker agreed dully. "What magic does the Elfstone possess?"

"I know nothing more of it than you," Cogline answered quietly.

"Not even where it can be found? Or who has it?"

Cogline shook his head. "Nothing."

"Nothing." Walker's voice was edged with bitterness. He let his eyes
close momentarily against what he was feeling. When they opened, they
were resigned. "This is my perception of things. You expect me to accept
Allanon's charge to recover disappeared Paranor and restore the Druids. I
can only do this by first recovering the Black Elfstone. But neither you nor
I know where the Elfstone is or who has it. And I am infected with the
poison of the Asphinx; I am being turned slowly to stone. I am dying!
Even if I were persuaded to . . ." His voice caught, and he shook his head.
"Don't you see? There isn't enough time!"

Cogline looked out the window, hunching down into his robes. "And
if there were?"

Walker's laugh was hollow, his voice weary. "Cogline, I don't know."

The old man rose. He looked down at Walker for a long time without
speaking. Then he said, "Yes, you do." His hands clasped tightly before
him. "Walker, you persist in your refusal to accept the truth of what is
meant to be. You recognize that truth deep in your heart, but you will not
heed it. Why is that?"

Walker stared back at him wordlessly.

Cogline shrugged. "I have nothing more to say. Rest, Walker. You will be well enough in a day or two to leave. The Stors have done all they can; your healing, if it is to be, must come from another source. I will take you back to Hearthstone."

"I will heal myself," Walker whispered. His voice was suddenly urgent, rife with both desperation and anger.

Cogline did not respond. He simply gathered up his robes and walked from the room. The door closed quietly behind him.

"I will," Walker Boh swore.

It took Morgan Leah the better part of three days after parting with Padishar Creel and the survivors of the Movement to travel south from the empty stretches of the Dragon's Teeth to the forest-sheltered Dwarf community of Culhaven. Storms swept the mountains during the first day, washing the ridgelines and slopes with torrents of rain, leaving the trailways sodden and slick with the damp, and wrapping the whole of the land in gray clouds and mist. By the second day the storms had passed away, and sunshine had begun to break through the clouds and the earth to dry out again. The third day brought a return of summer, the air warm and fragrant with the smell of flowers and grasses, the countryside bright with colors beneath a clear, windswept sky, the slow, lazy sounds of the wild things rising up from the pockets of shelter where they made their home.

Morgan's mood improved with the weather. He had been disheartened when he had set out. Steff was dead, killed in the catacombs of the Jut, and Morgan was burdened with a lingering sense of guilt rooted in his unfounded but persistent belief that he could have done something to prevent it. He didn't know what, of course. It was Teel who had killed Steff, who had almost killed him as well. Neither Steff nor he had known until the very last that Teel was something other than what she appeared, that she was not the girl the Dwarf had fallen in love with but a Shadowen whose sole purpose in coming with them into the mountains was to see them destroyed. Morgan had suspected what she was, yet lacked any real proof that his suspicions were correct until the moment she had revealed herself and by then it was too late. His friends the Valemen, Par and Coll Ohmsford, had disappeared after escaping the horrors of the Pit in Tyrsis and not been seen since. The Jut, the stronghold of the members of the Movement, had fallen to the armies of the Federation, and Padishar Creel and his outlaws had been chased north into the mountains. The Sword of Shannara, which was what all of them had come looking for in the first place, was still missing. Weeks of seeking out the talisman, of scrambling to unlock the puzzle of its hiding place, of hair-raising confrontations with and escapes from the Federation and the Shadowen, and of repeated frustration and disappointment, had come to nothing.

But Morgan Leah was resilient and after a day or so of brooding about what was past and could not be changed his spirits began to lift once more. After all, he was something of a veteran now in the struggle against the oppressors of his homeland. Before, he had been little more than an irritant to that handful of Federation officials who governed the affairs of the Highlands, and in truth he had never done anything that affected the outcome of larger events in the Four Lands. His risk had been minimal and the results of his endeavors equally so. But that had all changed. In the past few weeks he had journeyed to the Hadeshorn to meet with the shade of Allanon, he had joined in the quest for the missing Sword of Shannara, he had battled both Shadowen and Federation, and he had saved the lives of Padishar Creel and his outlaws by warning them of Teel before she could betray them one final time. He knew he had done something at last that had value and meaning.

And he was about to do something more.

He had made Steff a promise. As his friend lay dying, Morgan had sworn that he would go to Culhaven to the orphanage where Steff had been raised and warn Granny Elise and Auntie Jilt that they were in danger. Granny Elise and Auntie Jilt—the only parents Steff had ever known, the only kindred he was leaving—were not to be abandoned. If Teel had betrayed Steff, she would have betrayed them as well. Morgan was to help them get safely away.

It gave the Highlander a renewed sense of purpose, and that as much as anything helped bring him out of his depression. He had begun his journey disenchanted. He had lagged in his travel, bogged down by the weather and his mood. By the third day he had shaken the effects of both. His resolution buoyed him. He would spirit Granny Elise and Auntie Jilt out of Culhaven to somewhere safe. He would return to Tyrsis and find the Valemen. He would continue to search for the missing Sword of Shannara. He would find a way to rid Leah and the whole of the Four Lands of both Shadowen and Federation. He was alive and everything was possible. He whistled and hummed as he walked, let the sun's rays warm his face, and banished self-doubt and discouragement. It was time to get on with things.

Now and again as he walked his thoughts strayed to the lost magic of the Sword of Leah. He still wore the remains of the shattered blade strapped to his waist, cradled in the makeshift sheath he had constructed for it. He thought of the power it had given him and the way the absence of that power made him feel—as if he could never be whole again without it. Yet some small part of the magic still lingered in the weapon; he had managed to call it to life in the catacombs of the Jut when he destroyed Teel. There had been just enough left to save his life.

Deep inside, where he could hide it and not be forced to admit the implausibility of it, he harbored a belief that one day the magic of the Sword of Leah would be his again.

It was late afternoon on that third day of travel when he emerged from the forests of the Anar into Culhaven. The Dwarf village was shabby and worn where he walked, the refuge of those now too old and as yet too young who had not been taken by the Federation authorities to the mines or sold as slaves in the market. Once among the most meticulously maintained of communities, Culhaven was now a dilapidated collection of buildings and people that evidenced little of care or love. The forest grew right up against the outermost buildings, weeds intruding into yards and gardens, roadways rutted and choked with scrub. Wooden walls warped under peeling paint, tiles and shingles cracked and splintered, and trim about doorways and windows drooped away. Eyes peered out through the shadows, following after the Highlander as he made his way in; he could sense the people staring from behind windows and doors. The few Dwarves he encountered would not meet his gaze, turning quickly away. He walked on without slowing, his anger rekindled anew at the thought of what had been done to these people. Everything had been taken from them but their lives, and their lives had been brought to nothing.

He pondered anew, as Par Ohmsford had done when last they were there, at the purpose of it.

He kept clear of the main roads, staying on the side paths, not anxious to draw attention to himself. He was a Southlander and therefore free to come and go in the Eastland as he pleased, but he did not identify in any way with its Federation occupiers and preferred to stay clear of them altogether. Even if none of what had happened to the Dwarves was his doing, what he saw of Culhaven made him ashamed all over again of who and what he was. A Federation patrol passed him and the soldiers nodded cordially. It was all he could do to make himself nod back.

As he drew nearer to the orphanage, his anticipation of what he would find heightened perceptibly. Anxiety warred with confidence. What if he were too late? He brushed the possibility away. There was no reason to think that he was. Teel would not have risked jeopardizing her disguise by acting precipitately. She would have waited until she was certain it would not have mattered.

Shadows began to lengthen as the sun disappeared into the trees west. The air cooled and the sweat on Morgan's back dried beneath his tunic. The day's sounds began to fade away into an expectant hush. Morgan looked down at his hands, fixing his gaze on the irregular patchwork of white scars that crisscrossed the brown skin. Battle wounds were all over his body since Tyrsis and the Jut. He tightened the muscles of his jaw. Small things, he thought. The ones inside him were deeper.

He caught sight of a Dwarf child looking at him from behind a low stone wall with intense black eyes. He couldn't tell if it was a girl or a boy. The child was very thin and ragged. The eyes followed him a moment, then disappeared.

Morgan moved ahead hurriedly, anxious once more. He caught sight of the roof of the orphanage, the first of its walls, a window high up, a gable. He rounded a bend in the roadway and slowed. He knew instantly that something was wrong. The yard of the orphanage was empty. The grass was untended. There were no toys, no children. He fought back against the panic that rose suddenly within him. The windows of the old building were dark. There was no sign of anyone.

He came up to the gate at the front of the yard and paused. Everything was still.

He had assumed wrong. He was too late after all.

He started forward, then stopped. His eyes swept the darkness of the old house, wondering if he might be walking into some sort of trap. He stood there a long time, watching. But there was no sign of anyone. And no reason for anyone to be waiting here for him, he decided.

He pushed through the gate, walked up on the porch, and pushed open the front door. It was dark inside, and he took a moment to let his eyes adjust. When they had done so, he entered. He passed slowly through the building, searched each of its rooms in turn, and came back out again. There was dust on everything. It had been some time since anyone had lived there. Certainly no one was living there now.

So what had become of the two old Dwarf ladies?

He sat down on the porch steps and let his tall form slump back against the railing. The Federation had them. There wasn't any other explanation. Granny Elise and Auntie Jilt would never leave their home unless they were forced to. And they would never abandon the children they cared for. Besides, all of their clothes were still in the chests and closets, the children's toys, the bedding, everything. He had seen it in his search. The house wasn't closed up properly. Too much was in disarray. Nothing was as it would have been if the old ladies had been given a choice.

Bitterness flooded through him. Steff had depended on him; he couldn't quit now. He had to find Granny and Auntie. But where? And who in Culhaven would tell him what he needed to know? No one who knew anything, he suspected. The Dwarves surely wouldn't trust him—not a Southlander. He could ask until the sun rose in the west and set in the east.

He sat there thinking a long time, the daylight fading into dusk. After a while, he became aware of a small child looking at him through the front gate—the same child who had been watching him up the road. A boy, he decided this time. He let the boy watch him until they were comfortable with each other, then said, "Can you tell me what happened to the ladies who lived here?"

The boy disappeared instantly. He was gone so fast that it seemed as if the earth must have swallowed him up. Morgan sighed. He should have expected as much. He straightened his legs. He would have to devise a way to extract the information he needed from the Federation authorities. That would be dangerous, especially if Teel had told them about him as well as Granny and Auntie—and there was no reason now to believe that she

hadn't. She must have given the old ladies up even before the company began its journey north to Darklin Reach. The Federation must have come
for Granny and Auntie the moment Teel was safely beyond the village. Teel
hadn't worried that Steff or Morgan or the Valemen would find out; after
all, they would all be dead before it mattered.

Morgan wanted to hit something or someone. Teel had betrayed them
all. Par and Coll were lost. Steff was dead. And now these two old ladies
who had never hurt anyone . . .

"Hey, mister," a voice called.

He looked up sharply. The boy was back at the gate. An older boy
stood next to him. It was the second boy who spoke, a hefty fellow with a
shock of spiked red hair. "Federation soldiers took the old ladies away to
the workhouses several weeks ago. No one lives here now."

Then they were gone, disappeared as completely as before. Morgan
stared after them. Was the boy telling him the truth? The Highlander decided he was. Well and good. Now he had a little something to work with.
He had a place to start looking.

He came to his feet, went back down the pathway, and out the gate.
He followed the rutted road as it wound through the twilight toward the
center of the village. Houses began to give way to shops and markets, and
the road broadened and split in several directions. Morgan skirted the hub
of the business district, watching as the light faded from the sky and the
stars appeared. Torchlight brightened the main thoroughfare but was absent
from the roads and paths he followed. Voices whispered in the stillness,
vague sounds that lacked meaning and definition, hushed as if the speakers
feared being understood. The houses changed character, becoming well
tended and neat, the yards trimmed and nourished. Federation houses,
Morgan thought—stolen from Dwarves—tended by the victims. He kept
his bitterness at bay, concentrating on the task ahead. He knew where the
workhouses were and what they were intended to accomplish. The women
sent there were too old to be sold as personal slaves, yet strong enough to
do menial work such as washing and sewing and the like. The women were
assigned to the Federation barracks at large and made to serve the needs of
the garrison. If that boy had been telling the truth, that was what Granny
Elise and Auntie Jilt would be doing.

Morgan reached the workhouses several minutes later. There were five
of them, a series of long, low buildings that ran parallel to each other with
windows on both sides and doors at both ends. The women who worked
them lived in them as well. Pallets, blankets, washbasins, and chamber pots
were provided and pulled out from under the workbenches at night. Steff
had taken Morgan up to a window once to let him peer inside. Once had
been quite enough.

Morgan stood in the shadows of a storage shed across the way for long
moments, thinking through what he would do. Guards stood at all the
entrances and patroled the roadways and lanes. The women in the workhouses were prisoners. They were not permitted to leave their buildings for

any reason short of sickness or death or some more benevolent form of release—and the latter almost never occurred. They were permitted visitors infrequently and then closely watched. Morgan couldn't remember when it was that visits were permitted. Besides, it didn't matter. It infuriated him to think of Granny Elise and Auntie Jilt being kept in such a place. Steff would not have waited to free them, and neither would he.

But how was he going to get in? And how was he going to get Granny and Auntie out once he did?

The problem defeated him. There was no way to approach the workhouses without being seen and no way to know in which of the five workhouses the old ladies were being kept in any case. He needed to know a great deal more than he did now before he could even think of attempting any rescue. Not for the first time since he had left the Dragon's Teeth, he wished Steff were there to advise him.

At last he gave it up. He walked down into the center of the village, took a room at one of the inns that catered to Southland traders and businessmen, took a bath to wash off the grime, washed his clothes as well, and went off to bed. He lay awake thinking about Granny Elise and Auntie Jilt until sleep finally overcame him.

When he awoke the following morning he knew what he needed to do to rescue them.

He dressed, ate breakfast in the inn dining room, and set out. What he was planning was risky, but there was no help for it. After making a few inquiries, he discovered the names of the taverns most frequented by Federation soldiers. There were three of them, and all were situated on the same street close to the city markets. He walked until he found them, picked the most likely—a dimly lit hall called the High Boot—entered, found a table close to the serving bar, ordered a glass of ale, and waited. Although the day was still young there were soldiers drifting in already, men from the night shift not yet ready for bed. They were quick to talk about garrison life and not much concerned with who might be listening. Morgan listened closely. From time to time he looked up long enough to ask a friendly question. Occasionally he commented. Once in a while he bought a glass for someone. Mostly he waited.

Much of the talk revolved around a girl who was rumored to be the daughter of the King of the Silver River. She had appeared rather mysteriously out of the Silver River country south and west below the Rainbow Lake and was making her way east. Wherever she went, in whatever villages and towns she passed through, she performed miracles. There had never been such magic, it was said. She was on her way now to Culhaven.

The balance of the tavern's chatter revolved around complaints about the way the Federation army was run by its officers. Since it was the common soldiers who were doing the complaining, the nature of the talk was hardly surprising. This was the part that Morgan was interested in hearing. The day passed away in lazy fashion, sultry and still within the confines of the hall with only the cold glasses of ale and the talk to relieve the heat and boredom. Federation soldiers came and went, but Morgan remained where he was, an almost invisible presence as he sipped and watched. He had thought earlier to circulate from one tavern to the next, but it quickly became apparent that he would learn everything he needed to know by remaining at the first.

By midafternoon he had the information he needed. It was time to act on it. He roused himself from his seat and walked across the roadway to the second of the taverns, the Frog Pond, an aptly named establishment if ever there was one. Seating himself near the back at a green cloth table that sat amid the shadows like a lily pad in a dark pool, he began looking for his victim. He found him almost immediately, a man close to his own size, a common soldier of no significant rank, drinking alone, lost in some private musing that carried his head so far downward it was almost touching the serving bar. An hour passed, then two. Morgan waited patiently as the soldier finished his final glass, straightened, pushed away from the bar, lurched out through the entry doors. Then he followed.

The day was mostly gone, the sun already slipping into the trees of the surrounding forests, the daylight turning gray with the approach of evening. The soldier shuffled unsteadily down the road through knots of fellow soldiers and visiting tradesmen, making his way back to the barracks. Morgan knew where he was going and slipped ahead to cut him off. He intercepted him as he came around a corner by a blacksmith's shop, seeming to bump into him by accident but in fact striking him so hard that the man was unconscious before he touched the ground. Morgan let him fall, muttered in mock exasperation, then picked the fellow up, hoisting him over one shoulder. The blacksmith and his workers glanced over together with a few passersby, and Morgan announced rather irritably that he supposed he would have to carry the fellow back to his quarters. Then off he marched in mock disgust.

He carried the unconscious soldier to a feed barn a few doors down and slipped inside. No one saw them enter. There, in near darkness, he stripped the man of his uniform, tied and gagged him securely, and shoved him back behind a pile of oat sacks. He donned the discarded uniform, brushed it out and straightened its creases, stuffed his own clothes in a sack he had brought, strapped on his weapons, and emerged once more into the light.

He moved quickly after that. Timing was everything in his plan; he had to reach the administration center of the workhouses just after the shift change came on at dusk. His day at the taverns had told him everything he needed to know about people, places, and procedures; he need only put the information to use. Already the twilight shadows were spreading across the forestland, swallowing up the few remaining pools of sunlight. The streets were starting to empty as soldier, trader, and citizen alike made their way homeward for the evening meal. Morgan kept to himself, careful to acknowledge senior officers in passing, doing what he could to avoid drawing attention to himself. He assumed a deliberate look and stance designed to keep others at bay. He became a rather hard-looking Federation soldier about his business—no one to approach without a reason, certainly no one to anger. It seemed to work; he was left alone.

The workhouses were lighted when he reached them, the day's activities grinding to a close. Dinner in the form of soup and bread was being carried in by the guards. The food smells wafted through the air, somewhat less than appetizing. Morgan crossed the roadway to the storage sheds and pretended to be checking on something. The minutes slipped past, and darkness approached.

At precisely sunset the shift change occurred. New guards replaced the old on the streets and at the doors of the workhouses. Morgan kept his eyes fixed on the administration center. The officer of the day relinquished his duty to his nighttime counterpart. An aide took up a position at a reception desk. Two men on duty—that was all. Morgan gave everyone a few minutes to settle in, then took a deep breath and strode out from the shadows.

He went straight to the center, pushed through the doors, and confronted the aide at the reception desk. "I'm back," he announced.

The aide looked at him blankly.

"For the old ladies," Morgan added, allowing a hint of irritation to creep into his voice. He paused. "Weren't you told?"

The aide shook his head. "I just came on . . ."

"Yes, but there should be a requisition order still on your desk from no more than an hour ago," Morgan snapped. "Isn't it there?"

"Well, I don't . . ." The aide cast about the desktop in confusion, moving stacks of papers aside.

"Signed by Major Assomal."

The aide froze. He knew who Major Assomal was. There wasn't a Federation soldier garrisoned at Culhaven who didn't. Morgan had found out about the major in the tavern. Assomal was the most feared and disliked Federation officer in the occupying army. No one wanted anything to do with him if they could help it.

The aide rose quickly. "Let me get the watch captain," he muttered.

He disappeared into the back office and emerged moments later with his superior in tow. The captain was clearly agitated. Morgan saluted the senior officer with just the right touch of disdain.

"What's this all about?" the captain demanded, but the question came out sounding more like a plea than a demand.

Morgan clasped his hands behind his back and straightened. His heart was pounding. "Major Assomal requires the services of two of the Dwarf women presently confined to the workhouses. I selected them personally earlier in the day at his request. I left so that the paperwork could be completed and now I am back. It seems, however, that the paperwork was never done."

The watch captain was a sallow-skinned, round-faced man who appeared to have seen most of his service behind a desk. "I don't know anything about that," he snapped peevishly.

Morgan shrugged. "Very well. Shall I take that message back to Major Assomal, Captain?"

The other man went pale. "No, no, I didn't mean that. It's just that I don't . . ." He exhaled sharply. "This is very annoying."

"Especially since Major Assomal will be expecting me back momentarily." Morgan paused. "With the Dwarves."

The watch captain threw up his hands. "All right! What difference does it make! I'll sign them out to you myself! Let's have them brought up and be done with it!"

He opened the registry of names and with Morgan looking on determined that Granny Elise and Auntie Jilt were housed in building four. Hurriedly he scribbled out a release order for the workhouse guards. When he tried to dispatch the aide to collect the old ladies, Morgan insisted that he go as well.

"Just to make certain there are no further mix-ups, Captain," he explained. "After all, I have to answer to Major Assomal as well."

The watch captain didn't argue, obviously anxious to be shed of the matter as quickly as possible, and Morgan went out the door with the aide. The night was still and pleasantly warm. Morgan felt almost jaunty. His plan, risky or not, was going to work. They crossed the compound to building four, presented the release order to the guards stationed at the front doors, and waited while they perused it. Then the guards unfastened the locks and beckoned for them to proceed. Morgan and the aide pushed through the heavy wooden doors and stepped inside.

The workhouse was crammed with workbenches and bodies and smelled of stale air and sweat. Dust lay over everything, and the lamplight shone dully against walls that were dingy and unwashed. The Dwarf women were huddled on the floor with cups of soup and plates of bread in hand, finishing their dinner. Heads and eyes turned hurriedly as the two Federation soldiers entered, then turned just as quickly away again. Morgan caught the unmistakable look of fear and loathing.

"Call their names," he ordered the aide.

The aide did so, his voice echoing in the cavernous room and near the back two hunched forms came slowly to their feet.

"Now wait outside for me," Morgan said.

The aide hesitated, then disappeared back through the doors.

Morgan waited anxiously as Granny Elise and Auntie Jilt made their way gingerly through the clutter of bodies, benches, and pallets to where he stood. He barely recognized them. Their clothes were in tatters. Granny Elise's fine gray hair was unkempt, as if it were fraying all around the edges; Auntie Jilt's sharp, birdlike face was pinched and harsh. They were bent over with more than age, moving so slowly that it appeared it hurt them even to walk.

They came up to him with their eyes downcast and stopped.

"Granny," he said softly. "Auntie Jilt."

They looked up slowly and their eyes widened. Auntie Jilt caught her breath. "Morgan!" Granny Elise whispered in wonder. "Child, it's really you!"

He bent down quickly then and took them in his arms, hugging them close. They collapsed into him, rag dolls lacking strength of their own, and he could hear them both begin to cry. Behind them, the other Dwarf women were staring in confusion.

Morgan eased the two old ladies gently away. "Listen now," he said softly. "We haven't much time. I've tricked the watch captain into releasing you into my custody, but he's liable to catch on if we give him the chance so we have to hurry. Do you have somewhere that you can go to hide, someplace you won't be found?"

Auntie Jilt nodded, her narrow face a mask of determination. "The Resistance will hide us. We still have friends."

"Morgan, where's Steff?" Granny Elise interrupted.

The Highlander forced himself to meet her urgent gaze. "I'm sorry, Granny. Steff is dead. He was killed fighting against the Federation in the Dragon's Teeth." He saw the pain that filled her eyes. "Teel is dead, too. She was the one who killed Steff. She wasn't what any of us thought, I'm afraid. She was a creature called a Shadowen, a thing of dark magic linked to the Federation. She betrayed you as well."

"Oh, Steff," Granny Elise whispered absently. She was crying again.

"The soldiers came for us right after you left," Auntie Jilt said angrily. "They took the children away and put us in this cage. I knew something had gone wrong. I thought you might have been taken as well. Drat it, Morgan, that girl was like our own!"

"I know, Auntie," he answered, remembering how it had been. "It has become difficult to know who to trust. What about the Dwarves you plan to hide with? Can they be trusted? Are you sure you will be safe?"

"Safe enough," Auntie replied. "Stop your crying, Elise," she said and patted the other woman's hand gently. "We have to do as Morgan says and get out of here while we have the chance."

Granny Elise nodded, brushing away her tears. Morgan stood up again. He stroked each gray head in turn. "Remember, you don't know me, you're just my charges until we get clear of this place. And if something goes wrong, if we get separated, go where you'll be safe. I made a promise to Steff that I would see to it that you did. So you make certain I don't break that promise, all right?"

"All right, Morgan," Granny Elise said.

They went out the door then, Morgan leading, the two old ladies shuffling along behind with their heads bowed. The aide was standing rigidly to one side by himself; the guards looked bored. With the Dwarf ladies in tow, Morgan and the aide returned to the administration center. The watch captain was waiting impatiently, the promised release papers clutched in his hand. He passed them across the reception desk to Morgan for his signature, then shoved them at the aide and stalked back into his office. The aide looked at Morgan uncomfortably.

Inwardly congratulating himself on his success, Morgan said, "Major Assomal will be waiting."

He turned and was in the process of ushering Granny Elise and Auntie Jilt outside when the door opened in front of them and a new Federation officer appeared, this one bearing the crossed bars of a divisional commander.

"Commander Soldt!" The aide leaped to his feet and saluted smartly.

Morgan froze. Commander Soldt was the officer in charge of supervising the confinement of the Dwarves, the ranking officer off the field for the entire garrison. What he was doing at the center at this hour was anybody's guess, but it was certainly not going to do anything to help further Morgan's plans.

The Highlander saluted.

"What's this all about?" Soldt asked, glancing at Granny Elise and Auntie Jilt. "What are they doing out of their quarters?"

"Just a requisition, Commander," replied the aide. "From Major Assomal."

"Assomal?" Soldt frowned. "He's in the field. What would he want with Dwarves . . ." He glanced again at Morgan. "I don't know you, soldier. Let me see your papers."

Morgan hit him as hard as he could. Soldt fell to the floor and lay unmoving. Instantly Morgan went after the aide, who backed away shrieking in terror. Morgan caught him and slammed his head against the desk. The watch captain emerged just in time to catch several quick blows to the face. He staggered back into his office and went down.

"Out the door!" Morgan whispered to Granny Elise and Auntie Jilt.

They rushed from the administration center into the night. Morgan glanced about hurriedly and breathed out sharply in relief. The sentries were still at their posts. No one had heard the struggle. He guided the old ladies quickly along the street, away from the workhouses. A patrol appeared ahead. Morgan slowed, moving ahead of his charges, assuming a posture of command. The patrol turned off before it reached them, disappearing into the dark.

Then someone behind them was shouting, calling for help. Morgan pulled the old ladies into an alleyway and hastened them toward its far end. The shouts were multiplying now, and there was the sound of running feet. Whistles blew and an assembly horn blared.

"They'll be all over us now," Morgan muttered to himself.

They reached the next street over and turned onto it. The shouts were all around them. He pulled the ladies into a shadowed doorway and waited. Soldiers appeared at both ends of the street, searching. Morgan's rescue plans were collapsing about him. His hands tightened into fists. Whatever happened, he couldn't allow the Federation to recapture Granny and Auntie.

He bent to them. "I'll have to draw them away," he whispered urgently. "Stay here until they come after me, then run. Once you're hidden, stay that way—no matter what."

"Morgan, what about you?" Granny Elise seized his arm.

"Don't worry about me. Just do as I say. Don't come looking for me.

I'll find you when this whole business is over. Goodbye, Granny. Goodbye, Auntie Jilt."

Ignoring their pleas to remain, he kissed and hugged them hurriedly, and darted into the street. He ran until he caught sight of the first band of searchers and yelled to them, "They're over here!"

The soldiers came running as he turned down an alleyway, leading them away from Granny Elise and Auntie Jilt. He wrenched the broadsword he wore strapped to his back from its scabbard. Breaking free of the alleyway, he caught sight of another band and called them after him as well, gesturing vaguely ahead. To them he was just another soldier—for the moment, at least. If he could just maneuver them ahead of him, he might be able to escape as well.

"That barn, ahead of us," he shouted as the first bunch caught up with him. "They're in there!"

The soldiers charged past, one knot, then the second. Morgan turned and darted off in the opposite direction. As he came around the corner of a feed building, he ran right up against a third unit.

"They've gone into . . ."

He stopped short. The watch captain stood before him, howling in recognition.

Morgan tried to break free, but the soldiers were on him in an instant. He fought back valiantly, but there was no room to maneuver. His attackers closed and forced him to the ground. Blows rained down on him.

This isn't working out the way I expected, he thought bleakly and then everything went black.

5

Three days later she who was said to be the daughter of the King of the Silver River arrived in Culhaven. The news of her coming preceded her by half a day and by the time she reached the outskirts of the village the roadway leading in was lined with people for more than a mile. They had come from everywhere—from the village itself, from the surrounding communities of both the Southland and the Eastland, from the farms and cottages of the plains and deep forests, even the mountains north. There were Dwarves and Men and a handful of Gnomes of both sexes and all ages. They were ragged and poor and until now without hope. They jammed the roadside expectantly, some come simply out of a sense of curiosity, most come out of their need to find something to believe in again.

The stories of the girl were wondrous. She had appeared in the heart of the Silver River country close by the Rainbow Lake, a magical being sprung full-blown from the earth. She stopped at each village and town, farm and cottage, and performed miracles. It was said that she healed the land. She turned blackened, withered stalks to fresh, green shoots. She brought flowers to bloom, fruit to bear, and crops to harvest with the smallest of touches. She gave life back to the earth out of death. Even where the sickness was most severe, she prevailed. She bore some special affinity to the land, a kinship that sprang directly from her father's hands, from the legendary stewardship of the King of the Silver River. For years it had been believed that the spirit lord had died with the passing of the age of magic. Now it was known he had not; as proof he had sent his daughter to them. The people of the Silver River country were to be given back their old life. So the stories proclaimed.

No one was more anxious to discover the truth of the matter than Pe Ell.

It was midday, and he had been waiting for the girl within the shade of the towering old shagbark hickory on a rise at the very edge of town since just after sunrise when word had reached him that today was the day she would appear. He was very good at waiting, very patient, and so the time had gone quickly for him as he stood with the others of the growing crowd and watched the sun lift slowly into the summer sky and felt the heat of the day settle in. Conversation around him had been plentiful and unguarded, and he listened attentively. There were stories of what the girl had done and what it was believed she would do. There were speculations and judgments. The Dwarves were the most vehement in their beliefs—or lack thereof. Some said she was the savior of their people; some said she was nothing more than a Southland puppet. Voices raised in shouts, quarreled, and died away. Arguments wafted through the still, humid air like small explosions of steam out of a fiery earth. Tempers flared and cooled. Pe Ell listened and said nothing.

"She comes to drive out the Federation soldiers and restore our land to us, land that the King of the Silver River treasures! She comes to set us free!"

"Bah, old woman, you speak nonsense! There is nothing to say she is who she claims to be. What do you know of what she can or cannot do?"

"I know what I know. I sense what will be."

"Ha! That's the ache of your joints you feel, nothing more! You believe what you want to believe, not what is. The truth is that we have no more sense of who this girl is than we do of what tomorrow will bring. It is pointless to get our hopes up!"

"It is more pointless to keep them down!"

And so on, back and forth, an endless succession of arguments and counterarguments that accomplished nothing except to help pass the time. Pe Ell had sighed inwardly. He seldom argued. He seldom had cause to.

When at last she was said to approach, the arguments and conversation faded to mutterings and whispers. When she actually appeared, even the mutterings and whispers died away. A strange hush settled over those who lined the roadway suggesting that either the girl was not at all what they had expected or, perhaps, that she was something more.

She came up the center of the roadway surrounded by the would-be followers who had flocked to her during her journey east, a mostly bedraggled lot with tattered clothes and exhilarated faces. Her own garb was rough and poorly sewn, yet she evinced a radiance that was palpable. She was small and slight, but so exquisitely shaped as to seem not quite real. Her hair was long and silver, shining as water would when it shimmered in the moonlight. Her features were perfectly formed. She walked alone in a rush of bodies that crowded and stumbled about her yet could not bear to approach. She seemed to float among them. Voices called out anxiously to her, but she seemed unaware that anyone was there.

And then she passed by Pe Ell and turned deliberately to look at him. Pe Ell shuddered in surprise. The weight of that look—or perhaps simply the experience of it—was enough to stagger him. Almost immediately her strange black eyes shifted away again, and she was moving on, a sliver of brilliant sunlight that had momentarily left him blind. Pe Ell stared after her, not knowing what she had done to him, what it was that had occurred in that brief moment when their eyes met. It was as if she had looked into his heart and mind and read them quite clearly. It was as if with that single glance she had discovered everything there was to know about him.

He found her to be the most beautiful creature he had ever seen in his life.

She turned down the roadway into the village proper, the crowd trailing after, and Pe Ell followed. He was a tall, lean man, so thin that he appeared gaunt. His bones were prominent, and the muscles and skin of his body were molded tightly against them so as to suggest he might easily break. Nothing could have been further from the truth. He was as hard as iron. He had a long, narrow face with a hawk nose and a wide forehead with eyebrows set high above hazel eyes that were disarmingly frank to look upon. When he smiled, which was often, his mouth had a slightly lopsided appearance to it. His hair was brown and cropped close, rather spiky and uncontrolled. He slouched a bit when he walked and might have been either a gangly boy or a stalking cat. His hands were slim and delicate. He wore common forest clothing made of rough cloth dyed various shades of green and taupe, boots of worn leather laced back and across, and a short cloak with pockets.

He carried no visible weapon. The Stiehl was strapped to his thigh just below his right hip. The knife rode beneath his loose-fitting pants where it could not be seen but where it could be reached easily through a slit cut into a deep forward pocket.

He could feel the blade's magic warm him.

As he moved to keep up with the girl, people stepped aside—whether from what they saw in his face or the way he moved or the intangible wall they sensed surrounded him. He did not like to be touched, and everyone seemed instinctively to know it. As always, they shied away. He passed through them as a shadow chasing after the light, keeping the girl in sight as he did so, wondering. She had looked at him for a reason, and that intrigued him. He hadn't been certain what she would be like, how she would make him feel when he saw her for the first time—but he hadn't thought it would be anything like this. It surprised him, pleased him, and at the same time left him vaguely worried. He didn't like things that he couldn't control and he suspected that it would be difficult for anyone to exercise control over her.

Of course, he wasn't just anyone.

The crowd was singing now, an old song that told of the earth being reborn with the harvesting of new crops, the bearing of food from the fields to the tables of the people who had worked to gather it. There was praise for the seasons, for rain and sun, for the giving of life. Chants rose for the King of the Silver River; the voices grew steadily louder and more insistent. The girl seemed not to hear. She walked through the singing and the cries without responding, making her way first past the houses that lay at the edge of the village, then the larger shops that formed the core of the business center. Federation soldiers began to appear and tried to police the traffic as it surged ahead. They were too few and too ill-prepared, thought Pe Ell. Apparently they had misjudged badly the extent of the community's response to the coming of the girl.

The Dwarves were feverish in their adoration. It was as if they had been given back the lives that had been stolen from them. A broken, subjugated people for so many years, there had been little enough to happen to give them hope. But this girl seemed to be what they had been waiting for. It was more than the stories, more than the claims of who she was and what she could do. It was the look and feel of her. Pe Ell could sense it as readily as the people who rallied about her. He could feel something of it in himself. She was different from anyone he had ever seen. She had come here for a reason. She was going to *do* something.

Business ground to a halt in Culhaven as the whole of the village, oppressed and oppressors alike, turned out to discover what was happening and became a part of it. Pe Ell had the sense of a wave gathering force out in the ocean, growing in size until it dwarfed the vast body of water that had given life to it. It was so with this girl. There was a sense of all other events beyond this one ceasing to exist. Everything but what she was faded away and lost meaning. Pe Ell smiled. It was the most wonderful feeling.

The wave swept on through the village, past the shops and businesses, the slave markets, the workhouses, the compounds and soldiers' quarters, the shabby homes of the Dwarves and the well-kept houses of the Federation officials, down the main thoroughfare, and out again. No one seemed able to guess where it was going. No one but the girl, for she led even at the center of the maelstrom of bodies, guiding somehow the edges of the

wave, directing it as she wished. The cries and singing and chants continued unabated, exhilarated, rapturous. Pe Ell marveled.

And then the girl stopped. The crowd slowed, swirled about her, and
grew still. She stood at the foot of the blackened slopes that had once been
the Meade Gardens. She lifted her face to the stark line of the hill's barren
crest much as if she might have been looking beyond it to a place that no
one else could see. Few in the crowd looked where she was looking; they
simply stared at her. There were hundreds of them now, and all of them
waited to see what she would do.

Then slowly, deliberately she moved onto the slope. The crowd did not
follow, sensing perhaps that it was not meant to, divining from some small
movement or look that it was meant to wait. It parted for her, a sea of faces
rapt with expectation. A few hands stretched out in an attempt to touch
her, but none succeeded.

Pe Ell eased his way through the crowd until he stood at its foremost
edge less than ten yards from the girl. Although he was purposeful in his
advance, he did not yet know what he meant to do.

A knot of soldiers intercepted the girl, led by an officer bearing the
crossed shoulder bars of a Federation commander. The girl waited for them.
An unpleasant murmur rose from the crowd.

"You are not allowed here," announced the commander, his voice
steady and clear. "No one is. You must go back down."

The girl looked at him, waiting.

"This is forbidden ground, young lady," the other continued, an officer
addressing an inferior in a manner intended to demonstrate authority. "No
one is permitted to walk upon this earth. A proclamation of the Coalition
Council of the Federation government, which I have the honor to serve,
forbids it. Do you understand?"

The girl did not answer.

"If you do not turn around and leave willingly, I shall be forced to escort you."

A scattering of angry cries sounded.

The girl came forward a step.

"If you do not leave *at once*, I shall have to . . ."

The girl gestured and instantly the man's legs were entwined in ground
roots an inch thick. The soldiers who had accompanied him fell back with
gasps of dismay as the pikes they were holding turned to gnarled staffs of
deadwood that crumbled in their hands. The girl walked past them, unseeing. The blustering voice of the commander turned to a whisper of fear
and then disappeared in the shocked murmur of the crowd.

Pe Ell smiled fiercely. Magic! The girl possessed real magic! The stories
were true. It was more than he could have hoped for. Was she really the
daughter of the King of the Silver River? he wondered.

The soldiers kept away from her now, unwilling to challenge the kind
of power she obviously wielded. There were a few attempts at issuing orders

by lesser officers, but no one was sure what to do after what had happened to the commander. Pe Ell glanced swiftly about. Apparently there were no Seekers in the village. In the absence of Seekers, no one would act.

The girl proceeded up the empty, burned surface of the slope toward its summit, and her passing barely stirred the dry earth on which she walked. The sun beat down fiercely out of the midday sky, turning the empty stretch of ground into a furnace. The girl seemed not to notice, her face calm as she passed through the swelter.

As he stared at her, Pe Ell felt himself drawn to the rim of a vast chasm, knowing that beyond was something so impossible that he could not imagine it.

What will she do?

She came to the summit of the slope and stopped, a slim, ethereal form outlined against the sky. She paused for a moment, as if searching for something in the air around her, an invisible presence that would speak to her. Then she knelt. She dropped down to the charred earth of the hillside and buried her hands within it. Her head lowered and her hair fell about her in a veil of silver light.

The world about her went absolutely still.

Then the earth beneath began to tremble and shake, and a rumbling sound rose out of its depths. The crowd gasped and fell back. Men steadied themselves, women snatched up children, and cries and shouts began to sound. Pe Ell came forward a step, his hazel eyes intense. He was not frightened. This was what he had been waiting for, and nothing could have chased him away.

Light seemed to flare from the hillside then, a glow that dwarfed even the sunlight's brilliance. Geysers exploded from the earth, small eruptions that burst skyward, showering Pe Ell and the foremost members of the crowd with dirt and silt. There was a heaving as if some giant buried beneath was rising from his sleep, and huge boulders began to jut from the ground like the bones of the giant's hunched shoulders. The burned surface of the hillside began to turn itself over and disappear. Fresh earth rose up to cover it, rich and glistening, filling the air with a pungent smell. Massive roots lifted out like snakes, twisting and writhing in response to the rumblings. Green shoots began to unfold.

In the midst of it all, the girl knelt. Her body was rigid beneath the loose covering of her clothes, and her arms were buried in the earth up to her elbows. Her face was hidden.

Many in the crowd were kneeling now, some praying to the forces of magic once believed to have controlled the destiny of men, some simply steadying themselves against tremors which had grown so violent that even the most sturdy trees were being shaken. Excitement rushed through Pe Ell and left him flushed. He wanted to run to the girl, to embrace her, to feel what was happening within her, and to share in the power.

Boulders grated and boomed as they rearranged themselves, changing the shape of the hillside. Terraced walls formed out of the rock. Moss and ivy filled the gaps. Trails wound down from one level to the next in gentle descent. Trees appeared, roots become small saplings, the saplings in turn thickening and branching out, compressing dozens of seasons of growth into scant minutes. Leaves budded and spread as if desperate to reach the sunlight. Grasses and brush spread out across the empty earth, turning the blackened surface a vibrant green. And flowers! Pe Ell cried out in the silence of his mind. There were flowers everywhere, springing forth in a profusion of bright colors that threatened to blind him. Blues, reds, yellows, violets—the rainbow's vast spectrum of shades and tones blanketed the earth.

Then the rumbling ceased and the silence that followed was broken by the singing of birds. Pe Ell glanced at the crowd behind him. Most were on their knees still, their eyes wide, their faces rapt with wonder. Many were crying.

He turned back to the girl. In a span of no more than a few minutes she had transformed the entire hillside. She had erased a hundred years of devastation and neglect, of deliberate razing, of purposeful burning off and leveling out, and restored to the Dwarves of Culhaven the symbol of who and what they were. She had given them back the Meade Gardens.

She was still on her knees, her head lowered. When she came back to her feet she could barely stand. All of her strength had been expended in her effort to restore the Gardens; she seemed to have nothing left to give. She swayed weakly, her arms hanging limply at her sides, her beautiful, perfect face drawn and lined, her silver hair damp and tangled. Pe Ell felt her eyes fix upon him once more and this time he did not hesitate. He went up the hillside swiftly, bounding over rocks and brush, skipping past the trails as if they were hindrances. He felt the crowd surging after him, heard their voices crying out, but they were nothing to him and he did not look back. He reached the girl as she was falling and caught her in his arms. Gently he cradled her, holding her as he might a captured wild creature, protectively and possessively at once.

Her eyes stared into his, he saw the intensity and brilliance of them, the depth of feeling they held, and in that moment he was bound to her in a way that he could not describe. "Take me to where I can rest," she whispered to him.

The crowd was all about them now, their anxious voices a babble he could not lock out. A sea of faces pressed close. He said something to those closest to reassure them that she was only tired and heard his words pass from mouth to mouth. He caught a glimpse of Federation soldiers at the fringes of the crowd, but they were wisely choosing to keep their distance. He began moving away, carrying the girl, amazed at how little she weighed. There was nothing to her, he thought. And everything.

A handful of Dwarves intercepted him, asking him to follow them, to bring the daughter of the King of the Silver River to their home, to let her rest with them. Pe Ell let himself be guided by them. One home was as good as another for now. The eyes of the crowd followed after, but already it was dispersing at its fringes, straying off into the paradise of the Gardens, discovering for themselves the beauty that it held. There was singing again, softer now, songs of praise and thanksgiving for the girl, lyrical and sweet.

Pe Ell descended the hillside and passed out of the Meade Gardens and back into the village of Culhaven with the girl asleep in his arms. She had given herself into his keeping. She had placed herself under his protection. He found it ironic.

After all, he had been sent there to kill her.

Pe Ell carried the daughter of the King of the Silver River to the home of the Dwarves who had offered to keep her, a family that consisted of a man, his wife, their widowed daughter, and two small grandchildren. Their home was a stone cottage at the east end of the village sheltered by white oak and red elm and set back against the wall of the forest close by the channel of the river. It was quiet there, isolated from the village proper, and by the time they reached it most of the following crowd had turned back. A handful chose to stay and set up camp at the edge of the property, most of them those who had followed the girl up from the country south, zealots who were determined that she would be their savior.

But she wasn't for them, Pe Ell knew. She belonged now to him.

With the help of the family he placed the girl in a bed in a tiny back room where the man and woman slept. The husband and his wife and widowed daughter went out again to prepare something to eat for those who had chosen to keep vigil over the girl, but Pe Ell remained. He sat in a chair next to the bed and watched her sleep. For a time the children remained, curious to see what would happen, but eventually they lost interest, and he was left alone. The daylight faded into darkness and still he sat, waiting patiently for her to wake. He studied the line of her body as she lay sleeping, the curve of her hip and shoulder, the soft rounding of her back. She was such a tiny thing, just a little bit of flesh and bone beneath the coverings, the smallest spark of life. He marveled at the texture of her skin, at the coloring, at the absence of flaws. She might have been molded by some great artist whose reflection and skill had created a once-and-only masterpiece.

Fires were lit without, and the sound of voices drifted in through the curtained window. The sounds of night filled the silence between exchanges, the songs of birds and the buzzing of insects rising up against the faint rush of the river's waters. Pe Ell was not tired and had no need to sleep.

Instead, he used the time to think.

A week earlier he had been summoned to Southwatch and a meeting with Rimmer Dall. He had gone because it pleased him and not because it was necessary. He was bored and he was hopeful that the First Seeker would give him something interesting to do, that he would provide him with a challenge. To Pe Ell's way of thinking, that was all that mattered about Rimmer Dall. The rest of what the First Seeker did with his life and the lives of others was of no interest to him. He had no illusions, of course. He knew what Rimmer Dall was. He simply didn't care.

It took him two days to make the journey. He traveled north on horseback out of the rugged hill country below the Battlemound where he made his home and arrived at Southwatch at sunset on the second day. He dismounted while still out of sight of the sentries and made his approach by foot. He need not have bothered; he could have come all the way in and gained immediate admittance. But he liked the idea of being able to come and go as he chose. He liked demonstrating his talent.

Especially to the Shadowen.

Pe Ell was as they were as he came into the black monolith, seemingly through the creases in the stone, a wraith out of darkness. He went past the sentries unseen and unheard, as invisible to them as the air they breathed. Southwatch was silent and dark, its walls polished and smooth, its corridors empty. It had the feel and look of a well-preserved crypt. Only the dead belonged here, or those who trafficked in death. He worked his way through its catacombs, feeling the pulse of the magic imprisoned in the earth beneath, hearing the whisper of it as it sought to break free. A sleeping giant that Rimmer Dall and his Shadowen thought they would tame, Pe Ell knew. They kept their secret well, but there was no secret that could be kept from him.

When he was almost to the high tower where Rimmer Dall waited, he killed one of those who kept watch, a Shadowen, but it made no difference. He did so because he could and because he felt like it. He melted into the black stone wall and waited until the creature came past him, drawn by a faint noise that he had caused, then drew the Stiehl from its sheath within his pants and cut the life out of his victim with a single, soundless twist. The sentry died in his arms, its shade rising up before him like black smoke, the body crumbling into ash. Pe Ell watched the astonished eyes go flat. He left the empty uniform where it could be found.

He smiled as he floated through the shadows. He had been killing for a long time now and he was very good at it. He had discovered his talent early in life, his ability to seek out and destroy even the most guarded of victims, his sense of how their protection could be broken down. Death

frightened most people, but not Pe Ell. Pe Ell was drawn to it. Death was
the twin brother of life and the more interesting of the two. It was secretive, unknown, mysterious. It was inevitable and forever when it came. It
was a dark, infinitely chambered fortress waiting to be explored. Most entered only once and then only because they had no choice. Pe Ell wanted
to enter at every opportunity and the chance to do so was offered through
those he killed. Each time he watched someone die he would discover another room, glimpse another part of the secret. He would be reborn.

High within the tower, he encountered a pair of sentries posted before
a locked door. They failed to see him as he eased close. Pe Ell listened. He
could hear nothing, but he could sense that someone was imprisoned
within the room beyond. He debated momentarily whether he should discover who it was. But that would mean asking, which he would never do,
or killing the sentries, which he did not care to do. He passed on.

Pe Ell ascended a darkened flight of stairs to the apex of Southwatch
and entered a room of irregular chambers that connected together like corridors in a maze. There were no doors, only entryways. There were no sentries. Pe Ell slipped inside, a soundless bit of night. It was dark without
now, the blackness complete as clouds blanketed the skies and turned the
world beneath opaque. Pe Ell moved through several of the chambers, listening, waiting.

Then abruptly he stopped, straightened, and turned.

Rimmer Dall stepped out of the blackness of which he was a part. Pe
Ell smiled. Rimmer Dall was good at making himself invisible, too.

"How many did you kill?" the First Seeker asked in his hushed, whispery voice.

"One," Pe Ell said. His smile tugged at the corners of his mouth. "Perhaps I will kill another on the way out."

Dall's eyes shone a peculiar red. "One day you will play this game too
often. One day you will brush up against death by mistake and she will
snatch *you* up instead of your victim."

Pe Ell shrugged. His own dying did not trouble him. He knew it
would come. When it did, it would be a familiar face, one he had seen all
his life. For most, there was the past, the present, and the future. Not for Pe
Ell. The past was nothing more than memories, and memories were stale
reminders of what had been lost. The future was a vague promise—dreams
and puffs of smoke. He had no use for either. Only the present mattered,
because the present was the here and now of what you were, the happening
of life, the immediacy of death, and it could be controlled as neither past
nor future could. Pe Ell believed in control. The present was an ever-evolving
chain of moments that living and dying forged, and you were always there
to see it come.

A window opened on the night across a table and two chairs, and Pe
Ell moved to seat himself. Rimmer Dall joined him. They sat in silence for
a time, each looking at the other, but seeing something more. They had
known each other for more than twenty years. Their meeting had been an

accident. Rimmer Dall was a junior member of a policing committee of the Coalition Council, already deeply enmeshed in the poisonous politics of the Federation. He was ruthless and determined, barely out of boyhood, and already someone to be feared. He was a Shadowen, of course, but few knew it. Pe Ell, almost the same age, was an assassin with more than twenty kills behind him. They had met in the sleeping quarters of a man Rimmer Dall had come to dispatch, a man whose position in the Southland government he coveted and whose interference he had tolerated long enough. Pe Ell had gotten there first, sent by another of the man's enemies. They had faced each other in silence across the man's lifeless body, the night's shadows cloaking them both in the same blackness that mirrored their lives, and they had sensed a kinship. Both had use of the magic. Neither was what he seemed. Both were relentlessly amoral. Neither was afraid of the other. Without, the Southland city of Wayford buzzed and clanked and hissed with the intrigues of men whose ambitions were as great as their own but whose abilities were far less. They looked into each other's eyes and saw the possibilities.

They formed an irrevocable partnership. Pe Ell became the weapon, Rimmer Dall the hand that wielded it. Each served the other at his own pleasure; there were no constraints, no bonds. Each took what was needed and gave back what was required—yet neither really identified with nor understood what the other was about. Rimmer Dall was the Shadowen leader whose plans were an inviolate secret. Pe Ell was the killer whose occupation remained his peculiar passion. Rimmer Dall invited Pe Ell to eliminate those he believed particularly dangerous. Pe Ell accepted the invitation when the challenge was sufficiently intriguing. They nourished themselves comfortably on the deaths of others.

"Who is it that you keep imprisoned in the room below?" Pe Ell asked suddenly, breaking the silence, ending the flow of recollections.

Rimmer Dall's head inclined slightly, a mask of bones that gave his face the look of a fleshless skull. "A Southlander, a Valeman. One of two brothers named Ohmsford. The other brother believes he has killed this one. I arranged for him to think so. I planned it that way." The big man seemed pleased with himself. "When it is time, I will let them find each other again."

"A game of your own, it seems."

"A game with very high stakes, stakes that involve magic of unimaginable proportions—magic greater than either yours or mine or anyone else's. Unbounded power."

Pe Ell did not respond. He felt the weight of the Stiehl against his thigh, the warmth of its magic. It was difficult for him to imagine a magic more powerful—impossible to envision one more useful. The Stiehl was the perfect weapon, a blade that could cut through anything. Nothing could withstand it. Iron, stone, the most impenetrable of defenses—all were useless against it. No one was safe. Even the Shadowen were vulnerable; even they could be destroyed. He had discovered as much some years back when one had tried to kill him, sneaking into his bedchamber like a stalking cat. It had thought to catch him sleeping; but Pe Ell was always awake. He had killed the black thing easily.

Afterward it had occurred to him that the Shadowen might have been sent by Rimmer Dall to test him. He hadn't chosen to dwell on the possibility. It didn't matter. The Stiehl made him invincible.

Fate had given him the weapon, he believed. He did not know who had made the Stiehl, but it had been intended for him. He was twelve years old when he found it, traveling with a man who claimed to be his uncle—a harsh, embittered drunkard with a penchant for beating anything smaller and weaker than himself—on a journey north through the Battlemound to yet another in an endless succession of towns and villages they frequented so that the uncle might sell his stolen goods. They were camped in a ravine in a desolate, empty stretch of scrub country at the edge of the Black Oaks, fence-sitting between the Sirens and the forest wolves, and the uncle had beaten him again for some imagined wrong and fallen asleep with his bottle tucked close. Pe Ell didn't mind the beatings anymore; he had been receiving them since he was orphaned at four and his uncle had taken him in. He hardly remembered what it was like not to be abused. What he minded was the way his uncle went about it these days—as if each beating was being undertaken to discover the limits of what the boy could stand. Pe Ell was beginning to suspect he had reached those limits.

He went off into the failing light to be alone, winding down the empty ravines, trudging over the desolate rises, scuffing his booted feet, and waiting for the pain of his cuts and bruises to ease. The hollow was close, no more than several hundred yards away, and the cave at its bottom drew him as a magnet might iron. He sensed its presence in a way he could not explain, even afterward. Hidden by the scrub, half-buried in loose rock, it was a dark and ominous maw opening down into the earth. Pe Ell entered without hesitation. Few things frightened him even then. His eyesight had always been extraordinary, and even the faintest light was enough to let him find his way.

He followed the cave back to where the bones were gathered—human bones, centuries old, scattered about randomly as if kicked apart. The Stiehl lay among them, the blade gleaming silver in the dark, pulsing with life, its name carved on its handle. Pe Ell picked it up and felt its warmth. A talisman from another age, a weapon of great power—he knew at once that it was magic and that nothing could withstand it.

He did not hesitate. He departed the cave, returned to the camp, and cut his uncle's throat. He woke the man first to make certain that he knew who had done it. His uncle was the first man he killed.

It had all happened a long time ago.

"There is a girl," Rimmer Dall said suddenly and paused.

Pe Ell's gaze shifted back to the other's raw-boned face, silhouetted against the night. He could see the crimson eyes glitter.

The First Seeker's breath hissed from between his lips. "They say that she possesses magic, that she can change the character of the land simply by touching it, and that she can dispatch blight and disease and cause flowers to spring full grown from the foulest soil. They say that she is the daughter of the King of the Silver River."

Pe Ell smiled. "Is she?"

Rimmer Dall nodded. "Yes. She is who and what the stories claim. I do not know what she has been sent to do. She travels east toward Culhaven and the Dwarves. It appears that she has something specific in mind. I want you to find out what it is and then kill her."

Pe Ell stretched comfortably, his response unhurried. "Kill her yourself, why don't you?"

Rimmer Dall shook his head. "No. The daughter of the King of the Silver River is anathema to us. Besides, she would recognize a Shadowen instantly. Faerie creatures share a kinship that prohibits disguise. It must be someone other than one of us, someone who can get close enough, someone she will not suspect."

"Someone." Pe Ell's crooked smile tightened. "There are lots of someones, Rimmer. Send another. You have entire armies of blindly loyal cutthroats who will be more than happy to dispatch a girl foolish enough to reveal that she possesses magic. This business doesn't interest me."

"Are you certain, Pe Ell?"

Pe Ell sighed wearily. Now the bargaining begins, he thought. He stood up, his lean frame whiplike as he bent across the table so that he could see clearly the other's face. "I have listened to you tell me often enough how like the Shadowen you perceive me to be. We are much the same, you tell me. We wield magic against which there is no defense. We possess insight into the purpose of life which others lack. We share common instincts and skills. We smell, taste, sound, and feel the same. We are two sides of one coin. You go on and on. Well then, Rimmer Dall, unless you are lying I would be discovered by this girl as quickly as you, wouldn't I? Therefore, there is no point in sending me."

"It must be you."

"Must it, now?"

"Your magic is not innate. It is separate and apart from who and what you are. Even if the girl senses it, she will still not know who you are. She will not be warned of the danger you pose to her. You will be able to do what is needed."

Pe Ell shrugged. "As I said, this business doesn't interest me."

"Because you think there is no challenge in it?"

Pe Ell paused, then slowly sat down again. "Yes. Because there is no challenge."

Rimmer Dall leaned back in his chair and his face disappeared into shadow. "This girl is no simple flesh-and-blood creature; she will not be easily overcome. She has great magic, and her magic will protect her. It will take stronger magic still to kill her. Ordinary men with ordinary weapons haven't a chance. My legions of cutthroats, as you so disdainfully describe them, are worthless. Federation soldiers can get close to her, but cannot harm her. Shadowen cannot even get close. Even if they could, I am not certain it would make any difference. Do you understand me, Pe Ell?"

Pe Ell did not respond. He closed his eyes. He could feel Rimmer Dall watching him.

"This girl is dangerous, Pe Ell, the more so because she has obviously been sent to accomplish something of importance and I do not know what that something is. I have to find out and I have to put a stop to it. It will not be easy to do either. It may be too much even for you."

Pe Ell cocked his head thoughtfully. "Is that what you think?"

"Possibly."

Pe Ell was out of his chair with the swiftness of thought, the Stiehl snatched from its sheath and in his hand. The tip of the blade swept upward and stopped not an inch from Rimmer Dall's nose. Pe Ell's smile was frightening. "Really?"

Rimmer Dall did not flinch, did not even blink. "Do as I ask, Pe Ell. Go to Culhaven. Meet this girl. Find out what she plans to do. Then kill her."

Pe Ell was wondering if he should kill Rimmer Dall. He had thought about it before, contemplated it quite seriously. Lately the idea had begun to take on a certain fascination for him. He felt no loyalty to the man, cared nothing for him one way or the other beyond a vague appreciation of the opportunities he offered and even those were no longer as rewarding as they had once been. He was tired of the other's constant attempts to manipulate him. He no longer felt comfortable with their arrangement. Why not put an end to him?

The Stiehl wavered. The trouble was, of course, that there was no real point to it. Killing Rimmer Dall accomplished nothing, unless, of course, he was ready to discover what secrets might reveal themselves at the moment of the First Seeker's dying. That could prove interesting. On the other hand, why rush things? It was better to savor the prospect for a time. It was better to wait.

He sheathed the Stiehl with a quicksilver movement and backed away from Rimmer Dall. For just an instant he had a sense of missed opportunity, as if such a chance might never come again. But that was foolish. Rimmer Dall could not keep him away. The First Seeker's life was his to take when he chose.

He looked at Rimmer Dall for a moment, then spread his hands agreeably. "I'll do it."

He wheeled and started away. Rimmer Dall called after him. "Be warned, Pe Ell. This girl is more than a match for you. Do not play games with her. Once you have discovered her purpose, kill her quickly."

Pe Ell did not respond. He slipped from the room and melted back into the shadows of the keep, uninterested in anything Rimmer Dall thought or wished. It was enough that he had agreed to do what the Shadowen had asked. How he accomplished it was his own business.

He departed Southwatch for Culhaven. He did not kill any of the sentries on his way out. He decided it wasn't worth the effort.

Midnight approached. He grew tired of thinking and dozed in his chair as the hours slipped away. It was only several hours from dawn when the girl awoke. The cottage was silent, the Dwarf family asleep. The fires of those camped without had burned to coals and ash, and the last whispers of conversation had died away. Pe Ell came awake instantly as the girl stirred. Her eyes blinked open and fixed on him. She stared at him without speaking for a very long time and then slowly sat up.

"I am called Quickening," she said.

"I am Pe Ell," he replied.

She reached for his hand and took it in her own. Her fingers were as light as feathers as they traced his skin. Then she shivered and drew back.

"I am the daughter of the King of the Silver River," she said. She swung her legs off the bed and faced him. She smoothed back her tangled silver hair. Pe Ell was transfixed by her beauty, but she seemed completely unaware of it. "I need your help," she said. "I have come out of the Gardens of my father and into the world of men in search of a talisman. Will you journey with me to find it?"

The plea was so unexpected that for a moment Pe Ell did not respond but simply continued staring at the girl. "Why do you choose me?" he asked finally, confused.

And she said at once, "Because you are special."

It was exactly the right answer, and Pe Ell was astonished that she should know enough to give it, that she could sense what he wanted to hear. Then he remembered Rimmer Dall's warning and hardened himself. "What sort of talisman is it that we search for?"

She kept her eyes fastened on him. "One of magic, one with power enough to withstand even that of the Shadowen."

Pe Ell blinked. Quickening was so beautiful, but her beauty was a mask that distracted and confused. He felt suddenly stripped of his defenses, bared to his deepest corners, the light thrown on all his secrets. She knew him for what he was, he sensed. She could see everything.

In that instant, he almost killed her. What stopped him was how truly vulnerable she was. Despite her magic, formidable indeed, magic that could transform a barren, empty stretch of hillside back into what was surely no more than a memory in the minds of even the most elderly of the Dwarves, she lacked any form of defense against a killing weapon like the Stiehl. He could sense that it was so. She was helpless should he choose to kill her.

Knowing that, he decided not to. Not yet.

"Shadowen," he echoed softly.

"Are you frightened of them?" she asked him.

"No."

"Of magic?"

Pe Ell breathed in slowly. His narrow features twisted in upon themselves as he bent toward her. "What do you know of me?" he asked, his eyes searching her own.

She did not look away. "I know that I need you. That you will not be afraid to do what is necessary."

It seemed to Pe Ell that her words held more than one meaning, but he was unable to decide.

"Will you come?" she asked again.

Kill her quickly, Rimmer Dall had said. Find out her purpose and kill her. Pe Ell looked away, staring out the cottage window into the night, listening to the rushing sound of the river and the wind, soft and distant. He had never much bothered with the advice of others. Most of it was self-serving, useless to a man whose life depended on his ability to exercise his own judgment. Besides, there was a great deal more to this business than what Rimmer Dall had revealed. There were secrets waiting to be discovered. It might be that the talisman the girl searched for was something that even the First Seeker feared. Pe Ell smiled. What if the talisman happened to fall into his hands? Wouldn't that be interesting?

He looked back at her again. He could kill her anytime.

"I will come with you," he said.

She stood suddenly, reaching out her hands to take his own, drawing him up with her. They might have been lovers. "There are two more that must come with us, two like yourself who are needed," she said. "One of them is here in Culhaven. I want you to bring him to me."

Pe Ell frowned. He had already resolved to separate her from those fools camped without, misguided believers in miracles and fate who would only get in his way. Quickening belonged to him alone. He shook his head. "No."

She stepped close, her coal black eyes strangely empty. "Without them, we cannot succeed. Without them, the talisman is beyond our reach. No others need come, but they must."

She spoke with such determination that he found it impossible to argue with her. She seemed convinced that what she was saying was true. Perhaps it was, he decided; she knew more of what she was about at this point than he.

"Just two?" he asked. "No others? None of those without?"

She nodded wordlessly.

"All right," he agreed. No two men would be enough to cause him problems, to interfere with his plans. The girl would still be his to kill when he chose. "One man is here in the village, you say. Where am I to find him?"

For the first time since she had come awake, she turned away so that he could not see her.

"In the Federation prisons," she said.

7

Morgan Leah.

That was the name of the man that Pe Ell was supposed to find and bring to the daughter of the King of the Silver River.

The streets of Culhaven were deserted save for the homeless huddled in the crooks and crannies of the shops, shapeless bundles of rags waiting out the night. Pe Ell ignored them as he made his way toward the center of town and the Federation prisons. Dawn was the better part of two hours away; he had more than sufficient time to do what was needed. He might have postponed this rescue business another night, but he saw no reason to do so. The quicker this fellow was found, the quicker they would all be on their way. He hadn't asked the girl yet where it was that they were going. It didn't matter.

He kept to the shadows as he moved ahead, mulling over in his mind the ambivalent effect she had on him. He was both exhilarated and appalled. She made him feel as if he were a man in the process of rediscovering himself and at the same time as if he were a fool. Rimmer Dall would certainly claim he was the latter, that he was playing the most dangerous of games, that he was being led about by the nose and deluding himself into thinking he was in command. But Rimmer Dall had no heart, no soul, no sense of the poetry of life and death. He cared nothing for anything or anyone—only for the power he wielded or sought to secure. He was a Shadowen, and the Shadowen were empty things. However Rimmer Dall saw it, Pe Ell was less like him than the First Seeker thought. Pe Ell understood the harsh realities of existence, the practical necessities of staying alive, and of making oneself secure; but he also could feel the beauty of things, particularly in the prospect of death. Death possessed great beauty. Rimmer Dall saw it as extinction. But when Pe Ell killed, he did so to discover anew the grace and symmetry that made it the most wondrous of life's events.

He was certain that there would be incredible beauty in the death of Quickening. It would be unlike any other killing he had ever done.

So he would not rush it, not hurry the irrevocable fact of it; he would take time to anticipate it. The feelings she invoked in him would not alter or adversely effect the course of action he had set for himself. He would not disparage himself for experiencing them; they were part of his makeup, a reaffirmation of his humanity. Rimmer Dall and his Shadowen could know nothing of such feelings; they were as unfeeling as stone. But not Pe Ell. Not ever.

He slipped past the workhouses, avoiding the lights of the compound and the Federation soldiers on watch. The surrounding forest was hushed and sleeping, a black void in which sounds were disembodied and somehow frightening. Pe Ell became a part of that void, comfortable within its cloaking as he moved soundlessly ahead. He could see and hear what no one else could; it had always been that way. He could feel what lived within the dark even though it hid from him. The Shadowen were like that; but even they could not assimilate as he could.

He paused at a lighted crossway and waited to be certain it was clear. There were patrols everywhere.

He pictured Quickening's image in the aura cast by a solitary streetlamp. A child, a woman, a magical being—she was all of these and much more. She was the embodiment of the land's most beautiful things—a sunlit woodland glen, a towering falls, a blue sky at midday, a rainbow's kaleidoscope of color, an endless sweep of stars at night viewed from an empty plain. She was a creature of flesh and blood, of human life, and yet she was a part of the earth as well, of fresh-turned soil, of mountain streams, of great old rocks that would not yield to anything but time. It baffled him, but he could sense things in her that were at once incongruous and compatible. How could that be? What was she, beyond what she claimed?

He moved swiftly through the light and melted back into the shadows. He did not know, but he was determined to find out.

The squarish dark bulk of the prisons loomed ahead. Pe Ell took a moment to consider his options. He knew the design of the Federation prisons at Culhaven; he had even been in them once or twice, though no one knew about it but Rimmer Dall. Even in prison, there were men who needed to be killed. But that was not to be the case tonight. Admittedly, he had considered killing this man he had been sent to rescue, this Morgan Leah. That would be one way to prevent the girl from insisting that he accompany them in their search for the missing talisman. Kill this one now, the other one later, and that would be the end of the matter. He could lie about how it happened. But the girl might guess the truth, might even divine it. She trusted him; why take a chance on changing that? Besides, perhaps she was right about needing these men to reclaim the talisman. He did not know enough yet of what they were about. It was better to wait and see.

He let his lean frame disappear into the stone of the wall against which he rested, thinking. He could enter the prisons directly, confront the commanding officer with his Shadowen insignia, and secure the release of the man without further fuss. But that would mean revealing himself, and he preferred not to do that. No one knew about him now besides Rimmer Dall. He was the First Seeker's private assassin. None of the other Shadowen even suspected that he existed; none had ever seen him. Those who had encountered him, Shadowen or otherwise, were all dead. He was a secret to everyone and he preferred to keep it that way. It would be better to take the man out in the usual way, in silence and stealth, alone.

Pe Ell smiled his lopsided smile. Save the man now so that he could kill him later. It was a strange world.

He eased himself out from the wall and snaked his way through the darkness toward the prisons.

Morgan Leah was not asleep. He lay wrapped in a blanket in his cell on a pallet of straw, thinking. He had been awake for most of the night, too restless to sleep, plagued by worries and regrets and a nagging sense of futility that he could not seem to banish. The cell was claustrophobic, barely a dozen feet square while more than twenty feet from floor to ceiling with an iron door several inches thick and a single barred window so high up he could not manage to reach it to look out even by jumping. The cell had not been cleaned since he had been thrown into it, so consequently it stank. His food, such as it was, was brought to him twice a day and shoved through a slot at the base of the door. He was given water to drink in the same way, but none with which to wash. He had been imprisoned now for almost a week and no one had come to see him. He was beginning to think that no one would.

It was an odd prospect. When they had caught him he had been certain they would be quick to use whatever means they had at their disposal to find out why he had gone to so much trouble to free two old Dwarf ladies. He wondered even now if Granny Elise and Auntie Jilt had escaped, if they remained free; he had no way of knowing. He had struck a Federation commander, perhaps killed him. He had stolen a Federation uniform to impersonate a Federation soldier, used a Federation major's name to secure entry to the workhouses, deceived the Federation officer on duty, and made the Federation army in general appear like a bunch of incompetents. All for the purpose of freeing two old ladies. A maligned and misused Federation command had to want to know why. They had to be anxious to repay him for the humiliation and hurt he had caused them. Yet they had left him alone.

He played mind games with the possibilities. It seemed unlikely he was going to be ignored indefinitely, that he was to be left in that cell until he was simply forgotten. Major Assomal, as he had discovered, was in the field; perhaps they were waiting for him to return to begin the questioning. But would Commander Soldt be patient enough to wait after what had been done to him? Or was he dead; had Morgan killed him after all? Or were they all waiting for someone else?

Morgan sighed. Someone else. He always came back to the same inescapable conclusion. They were waiting for Rimmer Dall.

He knew that had to be it. Teel had betrayed Granny and Auntie to the Federation, but more particularly to the Shadowen. Rimmer Dall had to know of their connection to Par and Coll Ohmsford and all those who had gone in search of the Sword of Shannara. If someone tried to rescue them, surely he would be notified—and would come to see who it was that had been caught.

Morgan eased himself gingerly over on one side facing out from the wall into the blackness. He didn't hurt as much as he had the first few days;

the aches and pains of his beating were beginning to heal. He was lucky nothing had been broken—lucky, in fact, that he was still alive.

Or not so lucky, he amended his assessment, depending on how you looked at it. His luck, it appeared, had run out. He thought momentarily of Par and Coll and regretted that he would not be able to go to them, to look after them as he had promised he would. What would become of them without him? What had happened to them in his absence? He wondered if Damson Rhee had hidden them after their escape from the Pit of Tyrsis. He wondered if Padishar Creel had found out where they were.

He wondered a thousand things, and there were no answers to be found for any of them.

Mostly he wondered how much longer he would be kept alive.

He rolled onto his back again, thinking of how different things might have been for him. In another age he would have been a Prince of Leah and one day ruled his homeland. But the Federation had put an end to the monarchy more than two hundred years ago, and today his family ruled nothing. He closed his eyes, trying to dispel any thoughts of might-have-beens and would-have-beens, finding no comfort there. He remained hopeful, his spirit intact despite all that had happened, the resiliency that had seen him through so much still in evidence. He did not intend to give up. There was always a way.

He just wished he could discover what it was.

He dozed for a bit, lost in a flow of imaginings that jumbled together in a wash of faces and voices, teasing him with their disjointed, false connectings, lies of things that never were and could never be.

He drifted into sleep.

Then a hand came down over his mouth, cutting off his exclamation of surprise. A second hand pinned him to the floor. He struggled, but the grip that held him was unbreakable.

"Quiet, now," a voice whispered in his ear. "Hush."

Morgan went still. A hawk-faced man in a Federation uniform was bent over him, peering into his eyes intently. The hands released, and the man sat back. A smile tugged at the corners of his mouth, and laugh lines wreathed his narrow face.

"Who are you?" Morgan asked softly.

"Someone who can get you free of this place if you're smart enough to do as I say, Morgan Leah."

"You know my name?"

The laugh lines deepened. "A lucky guess. Actually, I stumbled in here by chance. Can you show me the way out again?"

Morgan stared at him, a tall, gaunt fellow who had the look of a man who knew what he was about. The smile he wore seemed wired in place and there was nothing friendly about it. Morgan shoved his blanket aside and came to his feet, noticing the way the other backed off as he did so, always keeping the same amount of space between them. Cautious, thought Morgan, like a cat.

"Are you with the Movement?" he asked the man.

"I'm with myself. Put this on."

He tossed Morgan some clothing. When the Highlander examined it, he found he was holding a Federation uniform. The stranger disappeared back into the dark for a moment, then reemerged carrying something bulky over one shoulder. He deposited his burden on the pallet with a grunt. Morgan started as he realized it was a body. The stranger picked up the discarded blanket and draped it over the dead man to make it look as if he were sleeping.

"It will take them longer this way to discover you're missing," he whispered with that unnerving smile.

Morgan turned away and dressed as quickly as he could. The other man beckoned impatiently when he was finished and together they slipped out through the open cell door.

The corridor without was narrow and empty. Lamplight brightened the darkness only marginally. Morgan had seen nothing of the prisons when they brought him in, still unconscious from his beating, and he was immediately lost. He trailed after the stranger watchfully, following the passageway as it burrowed through the stone block walls past rows of cell doors identical to his own, all locked and barred. They encountered no one.

When they reached the first watch station, it was deserted as well. There appeared to be no one on duty. The stranger moved quickly to the corridor beyond, but Morgan caught a glint of metal blades through a half-open door to one side. He slowed, peering in. Racks of weapons lined the walls of a small room. He suddenly remembered the Sword of Leah. He did not want to leave without it.

"Wait a minute!" he whispered to the man ahead.

The stranger turned. Quickly Morgan pushed at the door. It gave reluctantly, dragging against something. Morgan shoved until there was enough space to get through. Inside, wedged against the back of the door, was another dead man. Morgan swallowed against what he was feeling and forced himself to search the racks for the Sword of Leah.

He found it almost immediately, still in its makeshift sheath, hung on a nail behind a brace of pikes. He strapped the weapon on hurriedly, grabbed a broadsword as well, and went out again.

The stranger was waiting. "No more delays," he said pointedly. "The shift change comes just after sunrise. It's almost that now."

Morgan nodded. They went down a second corridor, a back set of stairs supported by timbers that creaked and groaned as they descended, and out through a courtyard. The stranger knew exactly where he was going. There were no guards until they reached a post just inside the walls and even then they were not challenged. They passed through the gates and out of the prison just as the first faint tinges of light began to appear on the horizon.

The stranger took Morgan down the roadway a short distance, then into a barn through a backdoor where the shadows were so thick the

Highlander had to feel his way. Inside, the stranger lit a lamp. Digging under a pile of empty feed sacks, he produced a change of clothing for each
of them, woods garb, indistinguishable from what most Eastland laborers
wore. They changed wordlessly, then stuffed the discarded Federation uniforms back beneath the sacks.

The stranger motioned Morgan after him and they went out again into
the first light of the new day.

"A Highlander, are you?" the stranger asked abruptly as they walked
eastward through the waking village.

Morgan nodded.

"Morgan Leah. Last name the same as the country. Your family ruled
the Highlands once, didn't they?"

"Yes," Morgan answered. His companion seemed more relaxed now,
his long strides slow and easy, though his eyes never stopped moving. "But
the monarchy hasn't existed for many years."

They took a narrow bridge across a sewage-fouled tributary of the Silver River. An old woman passed them carrying a small child. Both looked
hungry. Morgan glanced over at them. The stranger did not.

"My name is Pe Ell," he said. He did not offer his hand.

"Where are we going?" Morgan asked him.

The corners of the other's mouth tugged upward slightly. "You'll see."
Then he added, "To meet the lady who sent me to rescue you."

Morgan thought at once of Granny Elise and Auntie Jilt. But how
would they know someone like Pe Ell? The man had already said he was
not a part of the Free-born Movement; it seemed unlikely that he was al-
lied with the Dwarf Resistance either. Pe Ell, Morgan thought, was with
exactly who he had said he was with—himself.

But who then was the lady on whose behalf he had come?

They passed down lanes that wound through the Dwarf cottages and
shacks at the edge of Culhaven, crumbling stone and wood slat structures
falling down around the heads of those who lived within. Morgan could
hear the sluggish flow of the Silver River grow nearer. The houses separated as the trees thickened and soon there were few to be seen. Dwarves at
work in their yards and gardens looked up at them suspiciously. If Pe Ell
noticed, he gave no sign.

Sunlight was breaking through the trees ahead in widening streamers
by the time they reached their destination, a small, well-kept cottage surrounded by a ragged band of men who had settled in at the edge of the
yard and were in the process of completing breakfast and rolling up their
sleeping gear. The men whispered among themselves and looked long and
hard at Pe Ell as he approached. Pe Ell went past them without speaking,
Morgan in tow. They went up the steps to the front door of the cottage
and inside. A Dwarf family seated at a small table greeted them with nods
and brief words of welcome. Pe Ell barely acknowledged them. He took
Morgan to the back of the cottage and into a small bedroom and shut the
door carefully behind them.

A girl sat on the edge of the bed.

"Thank you, Pe Ell," she said quietly and rose.

Morgan Leah stared. The girl was stunningly beautiful with small, perfect features dominated by the blackest eyes the Highlander had ever seen. She had long, silver hair that shimmered like captured light, and a softness to her that invited protection. She wore simple clothes—a tunic, pants cinched at the waist with a wide leather belt, and boots—but the clothes could not begin to disguise the sensuality and grace of the body beneath.

"Morgan Leah," the girl whispered.

Morgan blinked, suddenly aware that he was staring. He flushed.

"I am called Quickening," the girl said. "My father is the King of the Silver River. He has sent me from his Gardens into the world of Men to find a talisman. I require your help to do so."

Morgan started to respond and stopped, not knowing what to say. He glanced at Pe Ell, but the other's eyes were on the girl. Pe Ell was as mesmerized as he.

Quickening came up to him, and the flush in his face and neck traveled down his body in a warm rush. She reached out her hands and placed her fingers gently on the sides of his face. He had never felt a touch like hers. He thought he might give anything to experience it again.

"Close your eyes, Morgan Leah," she whispered.

He did not question her; he simply did as she asked. He was immediately at peace. He could hear voices conversing somewhere without, the flow of the waters of the nearby river, the whisper of the wind, the singing of birds, and the scrape of a garden hoe. Then Quickening's fingers tightened marginally against his skin and everything disappeared in a wash of color.

Morgan Leah floated as if swept away in a dream. Hazy brightness surrounded him, but there was no focus to it. Then the brightness cleared and the images began. He saw Quickening enter Culhaven along a roadway lined with men, women, and children who cheered and called out to her as she passed, then followed anxiously after. He watched as she walked through growing crowds of Dwarves, Southlanders, and Gnomes to the barren stretch of hillside where the Meade Gardens had once flourished. It seemed that he became a part of the crowd, standing with those who had come to see what this girl would do, experiencing himself their sense of expectancy and hope. Then she ascended the hillside, buried her hands in the charred earth, and worked her wondrous magic. The earth was transformed before his eyes; the Meade Gardens were restored. The colors, smells, and tastes of her miracle filled the air, and Morgan felt an aching in his chest that was impossibly sweet. He began to cry.

The images faded. He found himself back in the cottage. He felt her fingers drop away and he brushed roughly at his eyes with the back of his hand as he opened them. She was staring at him.

"Was that real?" he asked, his voice catching in spite of his resolve to keep it firm. "Did that actually happen? It did, didn't it?"

"Yes," she answered.

"You brought back the Gardens. Why?"

Her smile was faint and sweet. "Because the Dwarves need to have something to believe in again. Because they are dying."

Morgan took a deep breath. "Can you save them, Quickening?"

"No, Morgan Leah," she answered, disappointing him, "I cannot." She turned momentarily into the room's shadows. "You can, perhaps, one day. But for now you must come with me."

The Highlander hesitated, unsure. "Where?"

She lifted her exquisite face back into the light. "North, Morgan Leah. To Darklin Reach. To find Walker Boh."

Pe Ell stood to one side in the little cottage bedroom, momentarily forgotten. He didn't like what he was seeing. He didn't like the way the girl touched the Highlander or the way the Highlander responded to it. She hadn't touched him like that. It bothered him, too, that she knew the Highlander's name. She knew the other man's name as well, this Walker Boh. She hadn't known his.

She turned to him then, drawing him back into the conversation with Morgan Leah, telling them both they must travel north to find the third man. After they found him they would leave in search of the talisman she had been sent to find. She did not tell them what that talisman was, and neither of them asked. It was a result of the peculiar effect she had on them, Pe Ell decided, that they did not question what she told them, that they simply accepted it. They believed. Pe Ell had never done that. But he knew instinctively that this girl, this child of the King of the Silver River, this creature of wondrous magic, did not lie. He did not believe she was capable of it.

"I need you to come with me," she said again to the Highlander.

He glanced at Pe Ell. "Are you coming?"

The way he asked the question pleased Pe Ell. There was a measure of wariness in the Highlander's tone of voice. Perhaps even fear. He smiled enigmatically and nodded. Of course, Highlander, but only to kill you both when it pleases me, he thought.

The Highlander turned back to the girl and began explaining something about two old Dwarf ladies he had rescued from the workhouses and how he needed to know that they were safe because of some promise he had made to a friend. He kept staring at the girl as if the sight of her gave him life. Pe Ell shook his head. This one was certainly no threat to him. He could not imagine why the girl thought he was necessary to their recovery of the mysterious talisman.

Quickening told the Highlander that among those who had come with her to the cottage was one who would be able to discover what had become of the Dwarf ladies. He would make certain that they were well. She would ask him to do so immediately.

"Then if you truly need me, I will come with you," Morgan Leah promised her.

Pe Ell turned away. The Highlander was coming because he had no choice, because the girl had captured him. He could see it in the youth's eyes; he would do anything for her. Pe Ell understood that feeling. He shared something of it as well. The only difference between them was what they intended to do about it.

Pe Ell wondered again what it would feel like when he finally killed the girl. He wondered what he would discover in her eyes.

Quickening guided Morgan toward her bed so that he could rest. Pe Ell departed the room in silence and walked out of the cottage into the light. He stood there with his eyes closed and let the sun's warmth bathe his face.

Coll Ohmsford was a prisoner at Southwatch for eight days before he discovered who had locked him away. His cell was the whole of his world, a room twenty feet square, high within the black granite tower, a stone-and-mortar box with a single metal door that never opened, a window closed off by metal shutters, a sleeping mat, a wooden bench, and a small table with two chairs. Light filtered through the shutters in thin, gray shafts when it was daytime and disappeared when it was night. He could peer through the cracks in the shutters and see the blue waters of the Rainbow Lake and the green canopy of the trees. He could catch glimpses of birds flying, cranes and terns and gulls, and he could hear their solitary cries.

Sometimes he could hear the howl of the wind blowing down out of the Runne through the canyons that channeled the Mermidon. Once or twice he could hear the howling of wolves.

Cooking smells reached him now and then, but they never seemed to emanate from the food that he was fed. His food came on a tray shoved through a hinged flap at the bottom of the iron door, a furtive delivery that lacked any discernible source. The food was consumed, and the trays remained where he stacked them by the door. There was a constant humming sound from deep beneath the castle, a sort of vibration that at first suggested huge machinery, then later something more akin to an earth tremor. It carried through the stone of the tower, and when Coll placed his hands against the walls he could feel the stone shiver. Everything was warm, the walls and floor, the door and window, the stone and mortar and metal. He didn't know how that could be with the nights sometimes chill enough to cause the air to bite, but it was. Sometimes he thought he could hear footsteps beyond his door—not when the food was delivered, but at other times when everything was still and the only other sound was the buzz of insects in the distant trees. The footsteps did not approach, but passed on without slowing. Nor did they seem to have an identifiable source; they might as easily come from below or above as without.

He could feel himself being watched, not often, but enough so that he was aware. He could feel someone's eyes fixed on him, studying him, waiting perhaps. He could not determine from where the eyes watched; it felt as if they watched from everywhere. He could hear breathing sometimes, but when he tried to listen for it he could hear only his own.

He spent most of his time thinking, for there was little else to do. He could eat and sleep; he could pace his cell and look through the cracks in the shutters. He could listen; he could smell and taste the air. But thinking was best, he found, an exercise that kept his mind sharp and free. His thoughts, at least, were not prisoners. The isolation he experienced threatened to overwhelm him, for he was closed away from everything and everyone he knew, without reason or purpose that he could discern, and by captors that kept themselves carefully hidden. He worried for Par so greatly that at times he nearly wept. He felt as if the rest of the world had forgotten him, had passed him by. Events were happening without him; perhaps everything he once knew had changed. Time stretched away in a slow, endless succession of seconds and minutes and hours and, after a while, days as well. He was lost in shadows and half-light and near-silence, his existence empty of meaning.

Thinking kept him together.

He thought constantly of how he might escape. The door and window were solidly seated in the stone of the fortress tower, and the walls and floor were thick and impenetrable. He lacked even the smallest digging tool in any event. He tried listening for those who patroled without, but the effort proved futile. He tried catching sight of those who delivered his meals, but they never revealed themselves. Escape seemed impossible.

He thought as well about what he might do to let someone know he was there. He could force a bit of cloth or a scrap of paper with a message scrawled on it through the cracks in the shutters of the window, but to what end? The wind would likely carry it away to the lake or the mountains and no one would ever find it. Or at least not in time to make any difference. He thought he might yell, but he knew he was so far up and away from any travelers that they would never hear him. He peered at the countryside unfailingly when it was light and never saw a single person. He felt himself to be completely alone.

He turned his thoughts finally to envisioning what was taking place beyond his door. He tried using his senses and when that failed, his imagination. His captors assumed multiple identities and behavioral patterns. Plots and conspiracies sprang to life, fleshed out with the details of their involvement of him. Par and Morgan, Padishar Creel and Damson Rhee, Dwarves,

Elves, and Southlanders alike came to the black tower to free him. Brave rescue parties sallied forth. But all efforts failed. No one could reach him. Eventually, everyone gave up trying. Beyond the walls of Southwatch, life went on, uncaring.

After a week of this solitary existence, Coll Ohmsford began to despair.

Then, on the eighth day of his captivity, Rimmer Dall appeared.

It was late afternoon, gray and rainy, stormclouds low and heavy across the skies, lightning a wicked spider's web flashing through the creases, thunder rolling out of the darkness in long, booming peals. The summer air was thick with smells brought alive by the damp, and it felt chill within Coll's cell. He stood close against the shuttered window, peering out through the cracks in the fittings, listening to the sound of the Mermidon as it churned through the canyon rocks below.

When he heard the lock on the door to his room release he did not turn at first, certain that he must be mistaken. Then he saw the door begin to open, caught sight of the movement out of the corner of his eye, and wheeled about instantly.

A cloaked form appeared, tall and dark and forbidding, lacking face or limbs, seemingly a wraith come out of the night. Coll's first thought was of the Shadowen, and he dropped into a protective crouch, frantically searching his suddenly diminished cell for a weapon with which to defend himself.

"Don't be frightened, Valeman," the wraith soothed in an oddly familiar, whispery voice. "You are in no danger here."

The wraith closed the door behind it and stepped into the room's faint light. Coll saw by turns the black clothing marked with a white wolf's head, the left hand gloved to the elbow, and the rawboned, narrow face with its distinctive reddish beard.

Rimmer Dall.

Instantly Coll thought of the circumstances of his capture. He had gone with Par, Damson, and the Mole through the tunnels beneath Tyrsis into the abandoned palace of the old city's kings, and from there the Ohmsford brothers had gone on alone into the Pit in search of the missing Sword of Shannara. He had stood guard outside the entry to the vault that was supposed to contain the Sword, keeping watch while his brother went inside. It was the last time he had seen Par. He had been seized from behind, rendered unconscious, and spirited away. Until now he had not known who was responsible. It made sense that it should be Rimmer Dall, the man who had come for them weeks ago in Varfleet and hunted them ever since across the length and breadth of the Four Lands.

The First Seeker moved to within a few feet of Coll and stopped. His craggy face was calm and reassuring. "Are you rested?"

"That's a stupid question," Coll answered before he could think better of it. "Where's my brother?"

Rimmer Dall shrugged. "I don't know. When I last saw him he was carrying the Sword of Shannara from its vault."

Coll stared. "You were there—inside?"

"I was."

"And you let Par take the Sword of Shannara? You just let him walk away with it?"

"Why not? It belongs to him."

"You want me to believe," Coll said carefully, "that you don't care if he has possession of the Sword, that it doesn't matter to you?"

"Not in the way you think."

Coll paused. "So you let Par go, but you took me prisoner. Is that right?"

"It is."

Coll shook his head. "Why?"

"To protect you."

Coll laughed. "From what? Freedom of choice?"

"From your brother."

"From Par? You must think me the biggest fool who ever lived!"

The big man folded his arms across his chest comfortably. "To be honest with you, there is more to it than just offering you protection. You are a prisoner for another reason as well. Sooner or later, your brother will come looking for you. When he does, I want another chance to talk with him. Keeping you here assures me that I will have that chance."

"What really happened," Coll snapped angrily, "is that you caught me, but Par escaped! He found the Sword of Shannara and slipped past you somehow and now you're using me as bait to trap him. Well, it won't work. Par's smarter than that."

Rimmer Dall shook his head. "If I was able to capture you at the entrance to the vault, how is it that your brother managed to escape? Answer me that?" He waited a moment, then moved over to the table with its wooden chairs and seated himself. "I'll tell you the truth of things, Coll Ohmsford, if you'll give me a chance. Will you?"

Coll studied the other's face wordlessly for a moment, then shrugged. What did he have to lose? He stayed where he was, standing, deliberately measuring the distance between them.

Rimmer Dall nodded. "Let's begin with the Shadowen. The Shadowen are not what you have been led to believe. They are not monsters, not wraiths whose only purpose is to destroy the Races, whose very presence has sickened the Four Lands. They are victims, for the most part. They are men, women, and children who possess some measure of the faerie magic. They are the result of man's evolution through generations in which the magic was used. The Federation hunts them like animals. You saw the poor creatures trapped within the Pit. Do you know what they are? They are Shadowen whom the Federation has imprisoned and starved into madness, changing them so that they have become worse than animals. You saw as well the woodswoman and the giant on your journey to Culhaven. What they are is not their fault."

The gloved hand lifted quickly as Coll started to speak. "Valeman, hear

me out. You wonder how it is that I know so much about you. I will explain if you will just be patient."

The hand came down again. "I became First Seeker in order to hunt
the Shadowen—not to harm or imprison them, but to warn them, to get
them to safety. That was why I came to you in Varfleet—to see that you and
your brother were protected. I did not have the chance to do so. I have
been searching for you ever since to explain what I know. I thought that
you might return to the Vale and so placed your parents under my protection. I believed that if I could reach you first, before the Federation found
you in some other way, you would be safe."

"I don't believe any of this," Coll interjected coldly.

Rimmer Dall ignored him. "Valeman, you have been lied to from the
beginning. That old man, the one who calls himself Cogline, told you
the Shadowen were the enemy. The shade of Allanon warned you at the
Hadeshorn in the Valley of Shale that the Shadowen must be destroyed.
Retrieve the lost magics of the old world, you were advised. Find the
Sword of Shannara. Find the missing Elfstones. Find lost Paranor and bring
back the Druids. But were you told what any of this would accomplish? Of
course not. Because the truth of the matter is that you are not supposed to
know. If you did, you would abandon this business at once. The Druids
care nothing for you and your kin and never have. They are interested only
in regaining the power they lost when Allanon died. Bring them back, restore their magics, and they will again control the destiny of the Races.
This is what they work for, Coll Ohmsford. The Federation, unwittingly,
ignorantly, helps them. The Shadowen provide the perfect victim for both
to prey upon. Your uncle recognized the truth of things. He saw that Allanon sought to manipulate him, to induce him to undertake a quest that
would benefit no one. He warned you all; he refused to be part of the
Druid madness. He was right. The danger is far greater than you realize."

He leaned forward. "I told all of this to your brother when he came
into the vault after the Sword of Shannara. I was waiting there for him—
had been waiting in fact for several days. I knew he would come back for
the Sword. He had to; he couldn't help himself. That's what having the
magic does to you. I know. I have the magic, too."

He stood up suddenly, and Coll shrank back in alarm. The black-clad
body began to shimmer in the gloom as if translucent. Then it seemed to
come apart, and Coll heard himself gasp. The dark form of a Shadowen
lifted slowly out of Rimmer Dall's body, red eyes glinting, hung suspended
in the air for a moment, and settled back again.

The First Seeker smiled coldly. "I am a Shadowen, you see. All of the
Seekers are Shadowen. Ironic, isn't it? The Federation doesn't know. They
believe us ordinary men, nothing more, men who serve their twisted interests, who seek as they do to rid the land of magic. They are fools. Magic
isn't the enemy of the people. They are. And the Druids. And any who
would keep men and women from being who and what they must."

One finger pointed at Coll like a dagger. "I told this to your brother,

and I told him one thing more. I told him that he, too, is a Shadowen.
Ah, you still don't believe me, do you? But listen, now. Par Ohmsford is
in truth a Shadowen, whether either of you cares to admit it or not. So
is Walker Boh. So is anyone who possesses real magic. That's what we are,
all of us—Shadowen. We are sane, rational, and for the most part ordinary
men, women, and children until we become hunted and imprisoned and
driven mad by fools like the Federation. Then the magic overwhelms us
and we become animals, like the woodswoman and the giant, like the
things in the Pit."

Coll was shaking his head steadily. "No. This is all a lie."

"How is it that I know so much about you, do you think?" Rimmer
Dall persisted, his voice maddeningly calm, even now. "I know all about
your flight south down the Mermidon, your encounters with the woodswoman and the old man, how you met with that Highlander and persuaded
him to join you, how you journeyed to Culhaven, then to Hearthstone,
and finally to the Hadeshorn. I know of the Dwarves and Walker Boh. I
know of your cousin Wren Ohmsford. I know of the outlaws and Padishar
Creel and the girl and all the rest. I knew when you were going down into
the Pit and tried to have you stopped. I knew that you would return and
waited there for you. How, Valeman? Tell me."

"A spy in the outlaw camp," Coll answered, suddenly unsure.

"Who?"

Coll hesitated. "I don't know."

"Then I will tell you. The spy was your brother."

Coll stared.

"Your brother, though he didn't realize it. Par is a Shadowen, and I
sometimes know what other Shadowen think. When they use their magic,
my own responds. It reveals to me their thoughts. When your brother used
the wishsong, it let me know what he was thinking. That was how I found
you. But Par's use of his magic alerted others as well. Enemies. That was
why the Gnawl tracked you in the Wolfsktaag and the Spider Gnomes at
Hearthstone.

"Think, Valeman! All that has befallen you has been the result of your
own doing. I did not seek to harm you in Tyrsis. It was Par's decision to go
down into the Pit that brought you to grief. I did not withhold the Sword
of Shannara. Yes, I kept it hidden—but only to force Par to come to me so
that I might save him."

Coll stiffened. "What do you mean?"

Rimmer Dall's pale eyes were intense. "I told you that the reason I
brought you here was to protect you from your brother. I spoke the truth.
The magic of a Shadowen is as two-edged as any sword. You have surely
thought the same thing many times. It can be either salvation or curse. It
can work to help or to hurt. But it is more complicated than that. A Shadowen can be affected by the stresses that use of the magic demands, particularly when he is threatened or hunted. The magic can grow frayed; it can
escape. Remember the creatures in the Pit? Remember those you encoun-

tered on your travels? What do you think happened to them? Your brother
has the wishsong as his magic. But the wishsong is only a thin shell covering the magic that lies beneath—a magic more powerful than your brother
imagines. It begins to grow stronger as he runs and hides and tries to keep
himself safe. If I don't reach him in time, if he continues to ignore my
warnings, that magic will consume him."

A long silence followed. Coll reflected silently. He remembered Par
telling him that he believed the magic of the wishsong was capable of doing much more than creating images, that he could feel it seeking a release.
He remembered the way it had responded during their first venture into
the Pit, casting a light through the gloom, illuminating the scroll of the
vault. He thought of the creatures trapped there, become monsters and
demons.

He wondered, just for an instant, if Rimmer Dall might not be telling
him the truth.

The First Seeker came forward a single step and stopped. "Think about
it, Coll Ohmsford," he suggested softly. He was big and dark against the
gloom and frightening to look at. But his voice was reassuring. "Reason it
through. You will have time enough to do so. I intend that you remain here
until your brother comes looking for you or he uses his magic. One way or
the other, I have to find him and warn him. I have to protect you both and
those with whom you will eventually come in contact. Help me. We must
find a way to reach your brother. We must try. I know you don't believe me
now, but that will change."

Coll shook his head. "I don't think so."

Outside, distant and low, thunder rumbled and faded into the hissing of
the rain. "So many lies have been told to you by others," Rimmer Dall said.
"In time, you will see."

He moved back toward the cell door and stopped. "You have been kept
in this room long enough. You may leave during the day. Just knock on the
door when you wish to go out. Go down to the exercise yard and practice
with the weapons. Someone will be there to help you. You should have
some training. You need to learn better how to protect yourself. Make no
mistake, though. You cannot leave. At night you will be locked in again. I
wish it could be otherwise, but it cannot. Too much is at stake."

He paused. "I have a short visit to make, a journey of several days. Another requires my attention. When I return, we will talk again."

He seemed to consider Coll for a long moment, as if measuring him
for something, then turned, and went out the way he had come. Coll
watched him go, then walked back to the shuttered window and stood
looking out again into the rain.

He slept poorly that night, plagued by dreams of dark things that bore his
brother's face, haunted when he came awake by what he had been told.
Nonsense, was his first thought. *Lies.* But his instincts told him that some
part of it, at least, was true—and that, in turn, suggested the unpleasant

possibility that it might all be. Par a Shadowen. The magic a weapon that could destroy him. Both of them threatened by dark forces beyond their understanding or control.

He no longer knew what to believe.

When he woke, he rapped on the door. A black-cloaked Seeker released him and walked him down to the exercise yard. Another, a gruff fellow with a shaven head and knots and scars all over him, offered to spar with him. Using padded cudgels, they trained through the morning. Coll sweated and strained. It felt good to make use of his body again.

Later, alone in his cell, the afternoon clearing as the clouds thinned and sunshine broke through to the distant south, he evaluated his new situation. He was a prisoner still, but not so much so. He was no longer confined to a single room. He had been offered the means to stay fit and strong. He did not feel as threatened.

Whether or not Rimmer Dall was playing mind games with him remained to be seen, of course. In any case, the First Seeker had made a mistake. He had given Coll Ohmsford the opportunity to explore Southwatch.

And the further opportunity to find a way to escape.

9

Walker Boh languished at Hearthstone in a prison far more forbidding than the one that had secured Morgan Leah. He had returned from Storlock filled with a fiery determination to cure the sickness that attacked him, to drive from his body the poison that the Asphinx had injected into it, and to heal himself as even the Stors could not. Within a week he had changed completely, grown dispirited and bitter, frightened that his hopes had been in vain, that he could not save himself after all. His days were long, heat-filled stretches of time in which he wandered the valley lost in thought, desperately trying to reason out what form of magic it would take to stem the poison's flow. His nights were empty and brooding, the dark hours expended in a silent, futile effort to implement his ideas.

Nothing worked.

He tried a little of everything. He began with a series of mind sets, inward delvings of his own magic that were designed to dissolve, break apart, turn back, or at least slow the poison's advance. None of these occurred. He used channeling of the magic in the form of an assault, the equivalent of an inner summoning of the fire that he sometimes used to protect and defend. The channeling could not seem to find a ready source; it scattered and lost its potency. He attempted spells and conjurings from the lore he had accumulated over the years, both that which was innate and that he had been taught. All failed. He resorted finally to the chemicals and powders that Cogline relied upon, the sciences of the old world brought into the new. He attacked the stone ruin of his arm and tried to burn it to the flesh so that cauterization might take place. He tried healing potions that were absorbed through the skin and permeated the stone. He used magnetic and electric fields. He used antitoxins. These, too, failed. The poison was too strong. It could not be overcome. It continued to work its way through his system, slowly killing him.

Rumor stayed at his side almost constantly, trailing silently after him on his long daytime walks, stretching out next to him in the darkness of his room as he struggled in vain to employ the magic in a way that would allow him to survive. The giant moor cat seemed to sense what was happening to Walker; it watched him as if fearful he might disappear at any moment, as if by watching closely it might somehow protect against this unseen thing that threatened. The luminous yellow eyes were always there, regarding him with intelligence and concern, and Walker found himself staring into them hopefully, searching for the answers he could find nowhere else.

Cogline, too, did what he could to help Walker in his struggle. Like the moor cat, he kept watch, albeit at a somewhat greater distance, afraid that Walker would not tolerate it if he came too close or stayed too long. There was still an antagonism between the two that would not be dispelled. It was difficult for them to remain in each other's presence for more than a few minutes at a time. Cogline offered what advice he could, mixing powders and potions at Walker's request, administering salves and healing medicines, suggesting forms of magic he thought might help. Mostly he provided what little reassurance he could that an antidote would be found.

Walker, though he would not admit it to the other, was grateful for that reassurance. For the first time in many years, he did not want to be alone. He had never given much thought to his own death, always convinced it was still far away and he would be prepared for it in any case when it arrived. He discovered now that he had been wrong on both counts. He was angry and frightened and confused; his emotions careened about inside him like stones tossed in a wagon bed, the debris of some emptied load. He fought to maintain his sense of balance, a belief in himself, some small measure of hope, but without the steadying presence of Cogline he would have been lost. The old man's face and voice, his movements, his idiosyncrasies, all so familiar, were handholds on the cliff to which Walker Boh clung, and they kept him from dropping away completely. He had known Cogline a long time; in the absence of Par and Coll, and to a lesser extent Wren, Cogline was his only link with the past—a past that he had in turn scorned, reviled, and finally cast away entirely, a past he was now desperate to regain as it was his link to the use of the magic that could save him. Had he not been so quick to disparage it, so anxious to be rid of its influence, had he taken more time to understand it, to learn from it, to master it and make it serve his needs, he might not be struggling so hard now to stay alive.

But the past is always irretrievable, and so Walker Boh found it here. Yet there was some comfort to be taken from the continued presence of the old man who had given him what understanding of the magic he had. With his future become so shockingly uncertain, he discovered a strange and compelling need to reach out to those things that remained his from the past. The most immediate of those was Cogline.

Cogline had come to him during the second year of his solitary life at Hearthstone. Risse had been dead fifteen years, Kenner five. He had been on his own ever since despite the efforts of Jaralan and Mirianna Ohmsford to make him a part of their family, an outcast from everyone because his magic would not let him be otherwise. While it had disappeared with the coming of age of all the Ohmsfords since Brin, it did not do so in him. Rather, it grew stronger, more insistent, more uncontrollable. It was bad enough when he lived in Shady Vale; it became intolerable at Hearthstone. It began to manifest itself in new ways—unwanted perceptions, strange foresights, harsh sensory recognition, and frightening exhibitions of raw power that threatened to shatter him. He could not seem to master them. He didn't understand them to begin with and therefore could not find a way to decipher their workings. It was best that he was alone; no one would have been safe around him. He found his sanity slipping away.

Cogline changed everything. He came out of the trees one afternoon, materializing from the mist that spilled down off the Wolfsktaag at autumn's close, a little old man with robes that hung precariously on his stick frame, wild unkempt hair, and sharp knowing eyes. Rumor was with him, a massive, immutable black presence that seemed to foreshadow the change that was to come into the Dark Uncle's life. Cogline related to Walker the history of his life from the days of Bremen and the Druid Council to the present, a thousand years of time. It was a straightforward telling that did not beg for acceptance but demanded it. Strangely enough, Walker complied. He sensed that this wild and improbable tale was the truth. He knew the stories of Cogline from the time of Brin Ohmsford, and this old man was exactly who and what the stories had described.

"I was sleeping the Druid sleep," Cogline explained at one point, "or I would have come sooner. I had not thought it was time yet, but the magic that resides within you, brought to life with your arrival at manhood, tells me that it is. Allanon planned it so when he gave the blood trust to Brin; there would come a time when the magic would be needed again and one among the Ohmsfords would be required to wield it. I think that perhaps you are meant to be that one, Walker. If so, you will need my help in understanding how the magic works."

Walker was filled with misgivings, but recognized that the old man might be able to show him how to bring the magic under control. He needed that control desperately. He was willing to take a chance that Cogline could give it to him.

Cogline stayed with him for the better part of three years. He revealed to Walker as a teacher to a student the lore of the Druids, the keys that would unlock the doors of understanding. He taught the ways of Bremen and Allanon, of going within to harness the magic's raw power, of working mind sets so that the power could be channeled and not loosed haphazardly. Walker had some knowledge to begin with; he had lived with the magic for many years and learned something of the self-denial and restraint that was necessary to survive its demands. Cogline expanded on that knowledge, advancing it into areas that Walker had not thought to go, instructing on methods he had not believed possible. Slowly, gradually, Walker began to find that the magic no longer governed his life; unpredictability gave way to self-control. Walker began to master himself.

Cogline instructed on the sciences of the old world as well, the chemicals and potions that he had developed and utilized over the years, the powders that burned through metal and exploded like fire, and the solutions that changed the form of both liquids and solids. Another set of doors opened for Walker; he discovered an entirely different form of power. His curiosity was such that he began to explore a combining of the two—old world and new world, a blending of magic and science that no one had ever successfully tried. He proceeded slowly, cautiously, determined that he would not become another of the victims that the power had claimed over the years, from the men of the old world who had brought about the Great Wars to the rebel Druid Brona, his Skull Bearers, and the Mord Wraiths who had sparked the Wars of the Races.

Then for some reason his thinking changed. Perhaps it was the exhilaration he felt when wielding the magic. Perhaps it was the insatiable need to know more. Whatever it was, he came to believe that complete mastery over the magic was not possible, that no matter how diligently he went about protecting himself against its adverse effects, the power would eventually claim him. His attitude toward using it reversed itself overnight. He tried to back away from it, to thrust it from him. His dilemma was enormous; he sought to distance himself from the magic yet could not do so successfully because it was an integral part of him. Cogline saw what was happening and tried to reason with him. Walker refused to listen, wondering all of a sudden why it was that Cogline had come to him in the first place, no longer believing it was simply to help. An effort was being made to manipulate him, a Druidic conspiracy that could be traced all the way back to the time of Shea Ohmsford. He would not be a part of it. He quarreled with Cogline, then fought. In the end, Cogline went away.

He came back, of course, over the years. But Walker would no longer accept instruction on use of the magic, fearing that further knowledge would result in an erosion of the control he had worked so hard to gain, that enhancement would lead to usurpation. Better simply to rely on what understanding he had, limited but manageable, and keep apart from the Races as he had planned from the first. Cogline could come and go, they could maintain their uneasy alliance, but he would not give himself over to the ways of Druids or once-Druids or anyone else. He would be his own person until the end.

And now that end had come, and he was no longer so sure of the path he had chosen to take. Death had arrived to claim him, and had he not distanced himself so from the magic he might have delayed its arrival a bit longer. Admission of the possibility required swallowing a bitter dose of pride. It was harsh to second-guess himself so, but it could not be avoided. Walker Boh had never in his life shied away from the truth; he refused to begin doing so now.

On the second week of his return from Storlock, sitting before the fire in the early evening hours, the pain of his sickness a constant reminder of things left undone, he said to Cogline, who was somewhere in the shadows behind rummaging through the books he kept at the cottage for his own use, "Come sit with me, old man."

He said it kindly, wearily, and Cogline came without argument, seating himself at Walker's elbow. Together they stared into the fire's bright glow.

"I am dying," Walker said after a time. "I have tried everything to dispel the poison, and nothing has worked. Even my magic has failed. And your science. We have to accept what that means. I intend to keep working to prevent it, but it seems that I will not survive." He shifted his arm uncomfortably against his side, a stone weight that worked relentlessly to pull him down, to make an end of him. "There are things I need to say to you before I die."

Cogline turned toward him and started to speak, but Walker shook his head. "I have embittered myself against you without reasonable cause. I have been unkind to you when you have been more than kind to me. I am sorry for that."

He looked at the old man. "I was afraid of what the magic would do to me if I continued to give myself over to it; I am still afraid. I have not changed my thinking completely. I still believe that the Druids use the Ohmsfords for their own purposes, that they tell us what they wish and direct us as they choose. It is a hard thing for me to accept, that I should be made their cat's-paw. But I was wrong to judge you one of them. Your purpose has not been theirs. It has been your own."

"As much as any purpose is mine and not one of circumstance and fate," Cogline said, and his face was sad. "We use so many words to describe what happens to us, and it all amounts to the same thing. We live out our lives as we are meant to live them—with some choice, with some chance, but mostly as a result of the persons we are." He shook his head. "Who is to say that I am any freer of the Druids and their manipulations than you, Walker? Allanon came to me in the same way as he did to you, young Par and Wren, and made me his. I cannot claim otherwise."

Walker nodded. "Nevertheless, I have been harsh with you and I wish I had not been. I wanted you to be the enemy because you were a flesh-and-blood person, not a Druid dead and gone or an unseen magic, and I could strike out at you. I wanted you to be the source of the fear I felt. It made things easier for me if I thought of you that way."

Cogline shrugged. "Do not apologize. The magic is a difficult burden for any to bear, but more so for you." He paused. "I don't believe you will ever be free of it."

"Except in death," Walker said.

"If death comes as swiftly as you think it will." The old eyes blinked. "Would Allanon establish a trust that could be thwarted so easily? Would he risk a complete undoing of his work on the chance that you might die too soon?"

Walker hesitated. "Even Druids can be wrong in their judgments."

"In this judgment?"

"Perhaps the timing was wrong. Another besides myself was meant to possess the magic beyond youth. I am the mistaken recipient. Cogline, what can possibly save me now? What is there left to try?"

The old man shook his head. "I do not know, Walker. But I sense that there is something."

They were silent then. Rumor, stretched out comfortably before the fire, lifted his head to check on Walker, and then let it drop again. The wood in the fireplace snapped loudly, and a whiff of smoke tinged the air of the room.

"So you think the Druids are not finished with me yet?" Walker said finally. "You think they will not let me give up my life?"

Cogline did not reply at once. Then he said, "I think you will determine what is to become of you, Walker. I have always thought that. What you lack is the ability to recognize what you are meant to do. Or at least an acceptance of it."

Walker felt a chill run through him. The old man's words echoed Allanon's. He knew what they meant. That he was to acknowledge that Brin Ohmsford's trust was meant for him, that he was to don the magic's armor and go forth into battle—like some invincible warrior brought forth out of time. That he was to destroy the Shadowen.

A dying man?

How?

The silence returned, and this time he did not break it.

Three days later Walker's condition took a turn for the worse. The medicines of the Stors and the ministerings of Cogline suddenly gave way before the onslaught of the poison. Walker woke feverish and sick, barely able to rise. He ate breakfast, walked out onto the porch to enjoy the warmth of the sun, and collapsed.

He remembered only snatches of what happened for several days after that. Cogline put him back to bed and bathed him with cold cloths while the poison's fever raged within him, an unquenchable fire. He drank liquids but could not eat. He dreamed constantly. An endless mirage of vile, frightening creatures paraded themselves before him, threatening him as he stood helpless, stripping him of his sanity. He fought back against them as best he could, but he lacked the necessary weapons. Whatever he brought to bear the monsters withstood. In the end, he simply gave himself over to them and drifted in black sleep.

From time to time he came awake and when he did so Cogline was always there. It was the old man's reassuring presence that saved him once again, a lifeline to which he clung, pulling him back from the oblivion into which he might otherwise have been swept. The gnarled hands reached out to him, sometimes gripping as if to hold him fast, sometimes stroking as if he were a child in need of comfort. The familiar voice soothed him, speaking words without meaning but filled with warmth. He could feel the other beside him, always near, waiting for him to wake.

"You are not meant to die, Walker Boh," he thought he heard more than once, though he could not be certain.

Sometimes he saw the old man's face bending close, leathery skin wrinkled and seamed, wispy hair and beard gray and disheveled, eyes bright and filled with understanding. He could smell the other, a forest tree with ancient limbs and trunk, but leaves as fresh and new as spring. When the sickness threatened to overwhelm him, Cogline was there to lift him free. It was because of the old man that he did not give up, that he fought back against the effects of the poison and willed himself to recover.

On the fourth day he awoke at midday and took some soup. The poison had been arrested temporarily, the medicines and ministerings and Walker's own will to survive taking command once more. Walker forced himself to explore the devastation of his shattered arm. The poison had progressed. His arm was turned to stone almost to the shoulder.

He wept that night in rage and frustration. Before he fell asleep he was aware of Cogline standing over him, a fragile presence against the vast, inexorable dark, telling him quietly that all would be well.

He awoke again in the slow, aimless hours between midnight and dawn when time seems to have lost its way. It was instinct that woke him, a sense that something was impossibly wrong. He struggled up on one elbow, weak and disoriented, unable to pinpoint the source of his trepidation. An odd, unidentifiable sound rose out of the night's stillness, a buzz of activity from somewhere without that sleep and sickness rendered indistinct. His breathing was ragged as he pushed himself into a sitting position, shivering beneath his bedclothes against the chill of the air.

Light flared sharply, suddenly visible through the breaks in his curtained window.

He heard voices. No, he thought anxiously. Not voices. Guttural, inhuman sounds.

It took what strength he had to crawl from the bedside to the window, working his way slowly and painfully through fatigue and fever. He kept still, aware of a need for caution, sensing that he should not reveal himself. Without, the sounds had risen, and an overpowering smell of decay had descended over everything.

Groping, he found the windowsill before him and pulled himself level with its edge.

What he saw through the part in the curtains turned his stomach to ice.

Cogline awoke when Rumor nudged him with his face, a rough, urgent shove that brought the old man upright instantly. He had not gone to bed until well after midnight, buried in his books of old-world science, fighting to discover some means by which Walker Boh's life could be saved. Eventually he had fallen asleep in his chair before the fire, the book he was perusing still open in his lap, and it was there that Rumor found him.

"Confound it, cat," he muttered.

His first thought was that something had happened to Walker. Then he heard the sounds, faint still, but growing louder. Growls and snarls and hisses. Animal sounds. And no effort being made to disguise their coming.

He pushed himself to his feet, taking a moment to wipe the sleep from his eyes. A single lamp burned at the dining table; the fire in the hearth had gone out. Cogline drew his robes close and shuffled toward the front door, uneasy, anxious to discover what was happening. Rumor went with him, moving ahead. The fur along the ridge of his back bristled, and his muzzle was drawn back to expose his teeth. Whatever was out there, the moor cat didn't like it.

Cogline opened the door and stepped out onto the covered porch that fronted the cottage. The sky was clear and depthless. Moonlight flooded down through the trees, bathing the valley in white luminescence. The air was cool and brought Cogline fully awake. He stopped at the edge of the porch and stared. Dozens of pairs of tiny red lights blinked at him from out of the shadows of the forest, a vast scattering of delicate scarlet blossoms that shone in the black. They were everywhere, it seemed, ringing the cottage and its clearing.

Cogline squinted to better make them out. Then he realized that they were eyes.

He jumped as something moved amid the eyes. It was a man dressed in a black uniform with the silver insignia of a wolf's head sewn on his breast. Cogline saw him clearly as he stepped into the moonlight, big and rawboned with a face that was hollowed and pitted and eyes that were empty of life.

Rimmer Dall, he thought at once and experienced a terrible sinking feeling.

"Old man," the other said, and his voice was a grating whisper.

Cogline did not respond, staring fixedly at the other, forcing himself to keep from looking to his right, to where the window to Walker's bedroom stood open, to where Walker slept. Fear and anger raced through him, and a voice within screamed at him to run, to flee for his life. Quickly, it warned. Wake Walker. Help him escape!

But he knew it was already too late for that.

He had known for some time now that it would be.

"We are here for you, old man," whispered Rimmer Dall, "my friends and I." He motioned, and the creatures with him began to edge into the light, one after another, horrors all, Shadowen. Some were misshapen creatures like the woodswoman he had chased from the camp of Par and Coll Ohmsford weeks ago; some had the look of dogs or wolves, bent down on all fours, covered with hair, their faces twisted into animal muzzles, teeth and claws showing. The sounds they made suggested that they were anxious to feed.

"Failures," their leader said. "Men who could not rise above their weaknesses. They serve a better purpose now." He came forward a step. "You are the last, old man—the last who stands against me. All the Shannara children are gone, swept from the earth. You are all that remains, a poor once-Druid with no one to save him."

The lines that etched Cogline's face deepened. "Is that so?" he said. "Killed them all, did you?" Rimmer Dall stared at him. Not half a chance of it, Cogline decided instantly. The truth is he hasn't killed a one, just wants me to think he has. "And you came all this way to tell me about it, did you?" he said.

"I came to put an end to you," Rimmer Dall replied.

Well, there you have it, the old man thought. Whatever the First Seeker had managed to do about the Shannara children, it wasn't enough; so now he had come after Cogline as well, easier prey, perhaps. The old man almost smiled. To think it had all come down to this. Well, it wasn't as if he hadn't known. Allanon had warned him weeks ago, warned him in fact when he'd summoned him to retrieve the Druid History from Paranor. Oh, he hadn't told Walker, of course. He had thought about it, but hadn't done it. There just didn't seem to be any point. *Know this, Cogline,* the shade had intoned, deep-voiced, prophetic. *I have read the netherworld signs; your time in this world is nearly finished. Death stalks you and she is an implacable huntress. When next you see the face of Rimmer Dall, she will have found you. Remember, then. When that time comes, take back the Druid History from Walker Boh and hold it to you as if it were your life. Do not release it. Do not give it up. Remember, Cogline.*

Remember.

Cogline collected his thoughts. The Druid History rested within a niche in the stone fireplace inside the cottage, right where Walker had hidden it.

Remember.

He sighed wearily, resignedly. He'd asked questions, of course, but the shade had given no answers. Very like Allanon. It was enough that Cogline knew what was coming, it seemed. It wasn't necessary that he know the particulars.

Rumor snarled, his fur standing on end all over. He was crouched protectively before the old man, and Cogline knew there was no way to save the big cat. Rumor would never leave him. He shook his head. Well. An odd sense of calm settled over him. His thoughts were quite clear. The Shadowen had come for him; they knew nothing at all about Walker Boh being there. That was the way he intended to keep it.

His brow furrowed. Would the Druid History, if he could reach it, aid him in this?

His eyes found Rimmer Dall's. This time he did smile. "I don't think there's enough of you to do the job," he said.

His arm swept up and silver dust flew at the First Seeker, bursting into flame as it struck him. Rimmer Dall screamed in fury and staggered away, and the creatures with him attacked. They came at Cogline from everywhere, but Rumor met them with a lunge, stopped them short of the porch and tore the foremost to pieces. Cogline flung handfuls of the silver dust at his would-be destroyers and whole lines of them were set ablaze. The Shadowen screeched and howled, blundering into one another as they sought first to attack, then to escape. Bodies lurched wildly through the moonlight, filling the clearing with burning limbs. They began attacking each other. They died by the dozens. *Easy prey, do they think!* Cogline experienced a wild, perverse elation as he flung back his robes and sent the night exploding into white brilliance.

For an impossible moment, he thought he might actually survive.

But then Rimmer Dall reappeared, too powerful to be overcome by Cogline's small magic, and lashed out with fire of his own at the creatures he commanded, at his dogs and wolves and half-humans, at his near-mindless brutes. The Shadowen-kind, terrified of him, attacked in a renewed frenzy of hate and anger. This time they would not be driven off. Rumor savaged the first wave, quick and huge amid their smaller forms, and then they were all over him, a maelstrom of teeth and claws. Cogline could do nothing to help the gallant cat; even with the silver dust exploding all through them, the Shadowen came on. Rumor slowly began to give ground.

Despairing, Cogline used the last of his powder, dashing handfuls to the earth, igniting a wall of flame that for just an instant brought a halt to the beasts' advance. Swiftly he darted inside and snatched the Druid History from its hiding place.

Now we'll see.

He barely made the front door again before the Shadowen-kind were through the wall of fire and on him. He heard Rimmer Dall screaming at them. He felt Rumor press back against him protectively. There was nowhere to run and no point in trying, so he simply stood his ground, clutching the book to his chest, a scarecrow in tattered robes before a whirlwind.

His attackers came on. When they had their hands on him, as his body was about to be ripped apart, he felt the rune markings on the book flare to life. Brilliant white fire burst forth, and everything within fifty feet was consumed.

It remains now for you, Walker, was Cogline's last thought.

He disappeared in the flames.

The final explosion threw Walker clear of the curtained window an instant before it was engulfed in flame. Even so, his face and hair were singed and his clothes were left steaming. He lay in a heap as the fire licked its way across the ceiling of his room. He ignored it, no longer caring what happened. He had been helpless to aid Cogline and Rumor, too weak to summon the magic, too weak even to rise and stand with them against the Shadowen, too weak to do anything but hang there on that window ledge and watch.

Useless! He screamed the word silently in his mind, rage and grief washing through him.

He lurched to his knees in desperation and peered out through the flames. Cogline and Rumor were gone. Rimmer Dall and what remained of the Shadowen-kind were melting back into the forest. He stared after them momentarily, and then his strength left him and he collapsed again.

Useless!

The fire's heat intensified about him. Timbers crashed down, fiery brands splintering off and searing his skin. His body jerked in pain, his stone arm an anchor that dragged against the wooden floor. His fate was assured, he realized. Another minute or two and he would be consumed. No one would come for him. No one even knew he was here. The old man and the giant moor cat had concealed his presence from the Shadowen; they had given up their lives to do so. . . .

He shuddered as an image of Rimmer Dall's face appeared in his mind, the dead eyes looking at him appraisingly.

He decided he did not want to die.

Almost without realizing what he was doing, he began to crawl.

10

Quickening found him two days later. Pe Ell and Morgan Leah were with her, drawn on by the mystery of who and what she was, by her promise that they were needed to recover the talisman that she insisted she had been sent to find, by curiosity, by passion, and by a dozen other things that neither could begin to define. They had made the journey north out of Culhaven in three days' time, traveling openly and on foot along the Rabb where it bordered on the Anar, safely west of the Wolfsktaag and the dark things that lived there. Secrecy seemed the least of Quickening's concerns. She had chosen to depart in daylight rather than under cover of darkness, having told her band of would-be followers that they must remain behind and continue her work to help restore the health of the land, and she had kept to the open plains the entire way up the forestline. While Morgan Leah had been relieved that he would not have to venture into the Wolfsktaag again, he had been certain that Federation patrols along the Rabb would attempt to detain them. Curiously, that did not happen. They were seen more than once and approached, but each time the patrols got close they suddenly veered away. It was almost as if they had decided they were mistaken—as if they had decided that they hadn't seen anything after all.

It was nearing dusk when the three finally arrived at Hearthstone, the men footsore, sweaty, and vaguely disgruntled by the quick pace the girl had set and the fact that she could maintain it seemingly without effort. They had bypassed Storlock, crossed through the Pass of Jade and come down the Chard Rush into Darklin Reach. The sun was behind them, dropping quickly toward the rim of the mountains, and the skies ahead were sharply etched by the light. A column of thick black smoke rose before them like a snake. They could see the smoke long before they were able to determine its source. They watched it lift into the darkening eastern skies and dissipate, and Morgan Leah began to worry. Quickening said nothing, but it seemed to the Highlander that her face grew more intense. By the time they reached the rim of the valley and there was no longer any doubt, the girl's face looked stricken.

They followed the smoke to the ruins of the cottage. Charred rubble was all that remained; the fire that had consumed it was so hot that it was still burning in spots, wood and ash glowing red, sending the black smoke curling skyward. The clearing about it was seared and lifeless, and huge knots of earth had been exploded away. It looked as if two great armies had fought a war in the space of a hundred yards. There was nothing left that was recognizable. Bits and pieces were scattered about of what once might have been something human, but it was impossible to tell. Even Pe Ell, who was usually so careful not to reveal anything of what he was thinking, stared.

"The Shadowen were here," Quickening said, and that brought both men about to search the shadows of the forest behind them, until she added, "But they are gone now and will not return."

At the girl's direction, they searched the clearing for Walker Boh. Morgan's heart sank. He had been hoping that Walker was not there, that the Shadowen attack had been for some other reason. Nothing could have survived this, he thought. He watched Pe Ell kick halfheartedly at piles of rubble, clearly of the same mind. Morgan did not like the man. He didn't trust him; he didn't understand him. Despite the fact that Pe Ell had saved him from the Federation prisons, Morgan couldn't bring himself to feel any friendship toward the other. Pe Ell had rescued him at Quickening's request; he wouldn't have lifted a finger if the girl hadn't asked. He had already told Morgan as much; he had made a point of telling him. Who he was remained a mystery, but the Highlander didn't think anything good would come of his being there. Even now, picking his way across the blackened clearing, he had the look of a cat in search of something to play with.

Quickening found Walker Boh moments later, calling out urgently to the other two when she did. How she determined where he was hiding was anyone's guess. He was unconscious and buried several feet beneath the earth. Pe Ell and Morgan dug him free, discovering when they did that he had apparently been trapped in an underground passageway that led from the cottage to the edge of the forest. Although the passageway had collapsed, probably during the Shadowen attack, sufficient air had been able to reach him to allow him to survive. They pulled him into the failing light, and Morgan saw the remains of his arm, the lower part gone entirely, a stone stub protruding from the shoulder. Walker's breathing was faint and shallow, his skin drawn and white. At first, the Highlander didn't think he was even alive.

They laid him carefully on the ground, brushed the dirt from his face, and Quickening knelt next to him. Her two hands reached out to take his one. She held it a moment, and his eyes flickered open. Morgan drew back. He had never seen Walker's eyes like this; they were terrifying to look into, filled with dark madness.

"Don't let me die," the Dark Uncle whispered harshly.

The girl touched his face and he was instantly asleep. Morgan took a deep breath and let it out again slowly. Walker Boh wasn't asking for help out of fear; he was asking out of rage.

They made camp beside the ruins of the cottage that night, backed into the shelter of the trees as the light gave way to darkness. Quickening had a fire built close to where Walker Boh lay sleeping and she took up a position at his side and did not move. Sometimes she held his hand; sometimes she stroked him. Morgan and Pe Ell were forgotten. She did not seem to have need of them or wish that they intrude, so the Highlander built a second fire some distance away and prepared dinner from the supplies they carried—bread, some dried meat, cheese, and fruit. He offered some to the girl, but she shook her head and he moved away. He ate alone. Pe Ell took his food off into the dark.

After a time Quickening lay down next to Walker Boh and went to sleep, her body pressed close against his. Morgan watched stone-faced, a surge of jealousy sweeping through him at the thought that the Dark Uncle should be so close to her. He studied her face in the firelight, the curve of her body, the softness of her. She was so beautiful. He could not explain the effect she had on him; he did not think he could refuse her anything. It wasn't that he had a reasonable hope that she felt for him as he did for her—or even that she felt anything for him. It was the need she roused in

him. He should not have come with her once he had escaped the prisons
and made certain that Granny Elise and Auntie Jilt were safe. He should
have gone after the Valemen, after Par and Coll Ohmsford. He had promised himself more than once while lying in the darkness and filth of that
Federation cell that if he ever got free, he would. Yet here he was, chasing
off into the deep Anar after this girl, searching out a talisman she said existed but hadn't once described, caught up with the enigmatic Pe Ell and
now Walker Boh. It baffled him, but he didn't question it. He was there because he wanted to be there. He was there because the moment he had met
Quickening he had fallen hopelessly in love with her.

He watched her until it hurt, then forced himself to look away. He was
surprised when he saw Pe Ell standing back in the shadows at the edge of
the trees watching too.

He was surprised again moments later when the other man came over
to sit next to him by the fire. Pe Ell made it seem the most natural thing in
the world, as if there had been no distance kept between them before, as if
they were companions and not strangers. Hatchet-faced, as lean as a wire's
shadow, he was not much more than a gathering of lines and angles that
threatened to disappear in the dark. He sat cross-legged, his thin frame relaxed, hunched down, his mouth breaking into a faint smile as he saw Morgan frown. "You don't trust me," he said. "You shouldn't."

Morgan said, "Why not?"

"Because you don't know me and you never trust anyone you don't
know. You don't trust most of those you do either. That's just the way it is.
Tell me, Highlander. Why do you think I'm here?"

"I don't know."

"I don't know either. I would be willing to bet that it is the same with
you. We're here, you and I, because the girl tells us she needs us, but we
really don't know what she means. It's just that we can't bring ourselves to
tell her no." Pe Ell seemed to be explaining things as much to himself as to
Morgan. He glanced Quickening's way briefly, nodding. "She's beautiful,
isn't she? How can you say no to someone who looks like that? But it's
more, because she has something inside as well, something special even in
this world. She has magic, the strongest kind of magic. She brings dead
things back to life—like the Gardens, like that one over there."

He looked back at Morgan. "We all want to touch that magic, to feel it
through her. That's what I think. Maybe we can, if we're lucky. But if the
Shadowen are involved in this, if there are things as bad as that to be dealt
with, why then we're going to have to look out for one another. So you
don't have to trust me or me you—maybe we shouldn't—but we have to
watch each other's backs. Do you agree?"

Morgan wasn't sure whether he did or not, but he nodded anyway.
What he thought was that Pe Ell didn't seem the kind who relied on anyone to watch his back. Or who watched anyone else's back either, for that
matter.

"Do you know what I am?" Pe Ell asked softly, looking down into the fire. "I am a craftsman. I get myself in and out of places without anyone knowing. I move things aside that don't want to be moved. I make people disappear." He looked up. "I have a little magic of my own. You do, too, don't you?"

Morgan shook his head, cautious. "There's the man with the magic," he offered, indicating Walker Boh.

Pe Ell smiled doubtfully. "Doesn't seem to have done him much good against the Shadowen."

"It might have kept him alive."

"Barely, it appears. And what use is he to us with that arm?" Pe Ell folded his hands carefully. "Tell me. What can he do with his magic?"

Morgan didn't like the question. "He can do a lot of what you do. Ask him yourself when he's better."

"If he gets better." Pe Ell stood up smoothly, an effortless motion that caught Morgan by surprise. Quick, the Highlander thought. Much quicker than me. The other was looking at him. "I sense the magic in you, Highlander. I want you to tell me about it sometime. Later, when we've traveled together a bit longer, when we know each other a little better. When you trust me."

He moved away into the shadows at the fire's edge, spread his blanket on the ground, and rolled into it. He was asleep almost at once.

Morgan sat staring at him for a moment, thinking it would be a long time before he trusted that one. Pe Ell smiled easily enough, but it seemed that only his mouth wanted to participate in the act. Morgan thought about what the man had said about himself, trying to make sense of it. Get in and out of places without being seen? Move things that don't want to be moved? Make people disappear? What sort of double-talk was that?

The fire burned low and everyone around him slept. Morgan thought about the past for a moment, about his friends who were dead or disappeared, about the inexorable flow of events that was dragging him along in its wake. Mostly he thought about the girl who said she was the daughter of the King of the Silver River. Quickening. He wondered about her.

What was she going to ask of him?

What was he going to be able to give?

Walker Boh came awake at sunrise, rising up from the black pit of his unconsciousness. His eyes blinked open to find the girl peering down at him. Her hands were on his face, her fingers cool and soft against his skin, and it seemed that she drew him up with no more effort than it would require to lift a feather.

"Walker Boh." She spoke his name gently.

She seemed strangely familiar to him although he was certain they had never met. He tried to speak and found he couldn't. Something forbade it, a sense of wonder at the exquisite beauty of her, at the feelings she invoked within him. He found her like the earth, filled with strange magic that was simple and complex at once, a vessel of elements, of soil, air, and water, a part of everything that gave life. He saw her differently than Morgan Leah and Pe Ell, though he couldn't know that yet. He was not drawn to her as a lover or a protector; he had no wish to possess her. Rather, there was an affinity between them that transcended passion and need. There were bonds of immediate understanding that united them as emotions never could. Walker recognized the existence of those bonds even without being able to define them. This girl was something of what he had struggled all his life to be. This girl was a reflection of his dreams.

"Look at me," she said.

His eyes locked on her. She took her fingers from his face and moved them to the shattered remnants of his arm, to the stone stump that hung inert and lifeless from his shoulder. Her fingers reached within his clothing, stroking his skin, working their way to where the skin hardened into stone. He flinched at her touch, not wanting her to feel the sickness in him, or to discover the corruption of his flesh. But her fingers persisted; her eyes did not look away.

Then he gasped as everything disappeared in a white-hot flash of pain. For an instant he saw the Hall of Kings again, the crypts of the dead, the stone slab with its rune markings, the black hole beneath, and the flash of movement as the Asphinx struck. After that he was floating, and there were only her eyes, black and depthless, folding him in a wave of sweet relief. The pain disappeared, drawing out of him in a red mist that dissipated into the air. He felt a weight lift away from him and he was at peace.

He might have slept for a time then; he was not certain. When he opened his eyes again, the girl was there beside him, looking down at him, and the dawn's light was faint and distant through the tips of the trees. He swallowed against the dryness in his mouth and throat, and she gave him water to drink from a skin. He was aware of Morgan Leah staring open-mouthed at him from one side, his lean brown face a mask of disbelief. There was another man next to him, one he didn't know, hard-faced and cunning. They had both been there when the girl found him, he remembered. What were they seeing now that so astonished them?

Then he realized that something was different. His arm felt lighter, freer. There was no pain. He used what little strength he had to raise his head and look down at himself. His clothes had been pulled away from his shoulder, revealing pink, healed flesh where the stone wreckage of his sickness had been removed.

His arm was gone.

So, too, was the poison of the Asphinx.

What did he feel? His emotions jumbled together within him. He stared at the girl and tried unsuccessfully to speak.

She looked down at him, serene and perfect. "I am Quickening," she said. "I am the daughter of the King of the Silver River. Look into my eyes and discover me."

He did as he was told, and she touched him. Instantly he saw what Morgan Leah had seen before him, what Pe Ell had witnessed—the coming of Quickening into Culhaven and the resurrection of the Meade Gardens out of ash and dust. He felt the wonder of the miracle and he knew instinctively that she was who she claimed. She possessed magic that defied belief, magic that could salvage the most pitiful of life's wreckage. When the images were gone, he was struck again by the unexplainable sense of kinship he felt for her.

"You are well again, Walker Boh," she told him. "The sickness will trouble you no more. Sleep now, for I have great need of you."

She touched him once and he drifted away.

He awoke again at midday, ravenous with hunger, dry with thirst. Quickening was there to give him food and water and to help him sit up. He felt stronger now, more the man he had been before his encounter with the Asphinx, able to think clearly again for the first time in weeks. His relief at being free of the poison of the Asphinx, at simply being alive for that matter, warred with his rage at what Rimmer Dall and the Shadowen had done to Cogline and Rumor. Just an old man and a bothersome cat, he had called them. He looked out across the clearing at the devastation. The girl did not ask him what had happened; she merely touched him and knew. All the images of that night's tragic events returned in a flood of memories that left him shaking and close to tears. She touched him again, to comfort and reassure, but he did not cry. He would not let himself. He kept his grief inside, walled away behind his determination to find and destroy those responsible.

Quickening said to him, away from Morgan Leah and the one she named Pe Ell, "You cannot give way to what you feel, Walker Boh. If you pursue the Shadowen now, they will destroy you. You lack the wisdom and the strength to overcome them. You will find both only through me."

Then, before he could respond, she called the other two over, seated them before her, and said, "I will tell you now of the need I have of you." She looked at them in turn and then seemed to look beyond. "A long time ago, in an age before Mankind, before the faerie wars, before everything you know, there were many like my father. They were the first of the faerie creatures, given life by the Word, given dominion over the land. Theirs was a trust to preserve and protect, and while they could, they did. But the world changed with the fading of the faerie creatures and the rise of Man. The evolution of the world took away almost everything that had existed in the beginning including those like my father. One by one, they died away, lost in the passing of the years and the changes of the world. The Great Wars destroyed many of them. The Wars of the Races destroyed more. Finally, there was only my father, a legend by now, the faerie Lord they called the King of the Silver River."

Her face lifted. "Except that my father was not alone as he believed.

There was another. Even my father did not know of him at first, believing that all his kindred had died out long ago, that he alone had survived. My father was wrong. Another like himself still lived, changed so markedly as to now be all but unrecognizable. All of the first faeries drew their magic from the elements of the land. My father's strength derived from the rivers and lakes, from the waters that fed the earth. He built his Gardens to nourish them, to give them life, and draw life back again. His brother, the one he did not know had survived along with him, took his magic from the earth's stone. Where my father found strength in fluidity and change, his brother found strength in constancy and immutability."

She paused. "His name is Uhl Belk. He is the Stone King. He had no name in the old days; none of my father's kindred did. There was no need for names. My father was given his name by the people of the land; he did not ask for it. Uhl Belk took his name out of fear. He took it because he felt that only in having a name could he be certain of surviving. A name implied permanency, he believed. Permanency became everything for him. All around him, the world was changing, the old dying out, giving way to the new. He could not accept that he must change, for like the stone from which he drew his strength, he was unyielding. To survive, he embedded himself deeper in the ways that had sustained him for so long, burrowing into the earth on which he relied. He hid while the Great Wars destroyed almost everything. He hid again when the wars of magic, the Wars of the Races, threatened to do the same. He took his name and wrapped himself in stone. Like my father, his world was reduced to almost nothing, to a tiny bit of existence that was all his magic could protect. He clung to it desperately while the wars of Mankind raged through the centuries and he waited for a measure of sanity to return.

"But, unlike my father, Uhl Belk put aside the trust that the Word had given him. He lost sight of his purpose in his struggle to survive; he became convinced that simply to exist at whatever cost was all that mattered. His pledge to preserve and protect the land was forgotten; his promise to care for the land's life lost meaning. He hoarded and built upon his magic with one thought in mind—that when he grew strong enough he would make certain that his existence would never be threatened by anything or anyone again."

Quickening's eyes glanced down and lifted again, filled with wonder. "Uhl Belk is master of Eldwist, a finger of land far north and east above the Charnal Mountains where the Eastland ends at the Tiderace. After centuries of hiding, he has come forth to claim the world of Men for his own. He does this through his magic, which grows in strength as he applies it. He applies it indiscriminately to the land—the soil, the waters, the trees, the creatures that take nourishment from them. He turns everything to stone and takes back such magic as will make him stronger still. The whole of Eldwist is stone and the land about begins to turn as well. The Tiderace holds him captive for now because it is huge, and even Uhl Belk's magic is not yet sufficient to overcome an ocean. But Eldwist connects to the Eastland at its tip, and nothing prevents the magic's poison from spreading south. Except my father."

"And the Shadowen," Morgan Leah added.

"No, Morgan," she said, and it did not escape any of them that she called him by his first name alone. "The Shadowen are not Uhl Belk's enemy. My father alone seeks to preserve the Four Lands. The Shadowen, like the Stone King, would see the Lands made over in a way that would leave them unrecognizable—barren and stripped of life. The Shadowen and Uhl Belk leave each other alone because neither has anything to fear from the other. One day that may change, but by then it will no longer matter to any of us."

She looked at Walker. "Think of your arm, Walker Boh. The poison that claimed it is Uhl Belk's. The Asphinx belonged to him. Whatever living thing the Stone King or his creatures touch becomes as your arm did— hard and lifeless. That is the source of Uhl Belk's power, that constancy, that changelessness."

"Why did he choose to poison me?" Walker asked.

Her silver hair caught a ray of sunlight and shimmered in momentary brilliance. She shook the light away. "He stole a Druid talisman from the Hall of Kings, and he wanted to be certain that whoever discovered the theft would die before he could do anything about it. You were simply unlucky enough to be that one. The Druids, when they lived, were strong enough to challenge Uhl Belk. He waited until they were all gone to come forth again. His only enemy now is my father."

Her dark eyes shifted to Pe Ell. "Uhl Belk seeks to consume the land and to do so he must destroy my father. My father sends me forth to prevent that. I cannot do so without your help. I need you to come north with me into Eldwist. Once there, we must find and recover from the Stone King the talisman he stole from the Hall of Kings, from the Druids. That talisman is called the Black Elfstone. As long as he possesses it, Uhl Belk is invincible. We must take it away from him."

Pe Ell's long, narrow face remained expressionless. "How are we supposed to do that?" he asked.

"You will find a way," the girl said, looking at each of them in turn. "My father said you would, that you possess the means. But it will take all three of you to succeed. Each of you has the magic that is required; we have not spoken of it, but it is so. All three magics are needed. All three of you must go."

"All three." Pe Ell glanced doubtfully at Walker and Morgan. "What is it that this Black Elfstone does? What sort of magic does it possess?"

Walker leaned forward to hear her answer, and Quickening's black eyes fixed on him. "It steals away the power of other magics. It swallows them up and makes them its own."

There was stunned silence. Walker had never heard of such magic. Even in the old Druid legends, there was no mention of it. He thought about the words contained in the Druid History that Cogline had brought to him, the words that described how Paranor could be restored:

Once removed, Paranor shall remain lost to the world of men for the whole of time, sealed away and invincible within its casting. One magic alone has the power to return it—that singular Elfstone which is colored Black and was conceived by the faerie people of the old world in the manner and form of all Elfstones, combining nevertheless in one stone alone the necessary properties of heart, mind, and body. Whosoever shall have cause and right shall wield it to its proper end.

He had memorized the words before hiding the book in a crevice in the fireplace of the cottage before departing for the Hall of Kings. The words explained something of how the Black Elfstone could be used to bring back Paranor. If Druid magic had sealed it away, the Black Elfstone would negate the magic and restore the Keep. Walker frowned. That seemed awfully easy. Worse, the power of such a magic suggested that once employed, nothing could defeat it. Why would the Druids take the chance that something so powerful would fall into the hands of an enemy like Uhl Belk?

On the other hand, they had done what they could to protect it, he supposed. Almost no one could have retrieved it from the Hall of Kings. Or even known it was there. How had the Stone King discovered it? he wondered.

"If the Black Elfstone can take away other magics," Pe Ell said suddenly, putting an end to Walker's musings, "how can anything overcome it? Our own magic, any magic, will be useless against it."

"Especially mine, since I don't have any," Morgan spoke up suddenly, causing all of them to glance sharply at him. "At least, not enough to bother about."

"Is there something you can do to help us against the Stone King?" Walker asked. "Can you make use of your own magic in some way?"

"No," the girl said, and they went silent, staring at her. "My magic is useless until you have regained possession of the Black Elfstone from Uhl Belk. Nor must he be allowed to discover who I am. If he should, he would make a quick end of me. I will go with you and advise you when I can. I will help if possible. But I cannot use my magic—not the smallest amount, not for even the shortest time."

"But you think that we can?" Pe Ell demanded incredulously.

"The Stone King will find your magic of no consequence; he will not feel threatened by you."

Pe Ell's face assumed such a black look that Walker was momentarily distracted from wondering what it was that Quickening was hiding from them. He was certain now that she was hiding something. Not lying to them, he didn't think that. But there was definitely something she wasn't telling them. The problem was, he hadn't the faintest idea what.

She said then, "There is another reason that you should help me." Her eyes held them. "All things are possible if you come with me. Walker Boh. I have driven the poison from your body and made you well. I have healed your arm, but I cannot make you whole again. Come with me in search of the Black Elfstone and you will find a way to do so. Morgan Leah. You would restore the magic of your shattered Sword. Come with me. Pe Ell. You would seek out magic greater than that of the Shadowen. Come with me. My father tells me that together you possess the keys that will unlock all of these secrets. My father knows what is possible. He would not lie."

Her face lifted toward them. "The Four Lands and her people are threatened by the Shadowen; but no more so than by Uhl Belk. The means of ending one threat shall be found through ending the other. The Black Elfstone is the talisman that shall enable the ending of both. I know you cannot yet understand that; I know I cannot explain it to you. I do not know how you shall fare in this quest. But I shall go with you, live or die with you, succeed or fail with you. We shall be bound forever by what happens."

As we are somehow bound already, Walker thought to himself and wondered anew why the feeling persisted.

Silence crystallized about them. No one wanted to break its shell. There were questions yet unasked and answers yet ungiven; there were doubts and misgivings and fears to be conquered. A future that had been settled for them all not a week gone now stretched ahead, a dark and uncertain pathway that would take them where it chose. Uhl Belk, the Stone King, waited at the end of that path, and they were going to seek him out. It was already decided. Without anyone having said so, it was resolved. Such was the strength of Quickening's magic, the magic she exercised over the lives of others, a magic that not only restored life to what was believed dead and gone but also liberated hopes and dreams in the living.

It was like that now.

Morgan Leah was thinking what it would be like to have the Sword of Leah restored to him. He was remembering how it felt when its magic was his to command. Pe Ell was thinking what it would be like to have possession of a weapon that no one could stand against. He was remembering how it felt when he used the Stiehl. He was wondering if this would be the same.

But Walker Boh was thinking not so much of himself as of the Black Elfstone. It remained the key to all the locked doors. Could Paranor be restored; could the Druids be brought back again? Allanon's charge to him, part of what must be done if the Shadowen were to be destroyed. And now, for the first time since the dreams had come to him, he wanted them destroyed. More, he wanted to be the one to do it.

He looked into Quickening's black eyes, and it seemed as if she could read his thoughts. A Druid trick. A faerie gift.

And suddenly, shockingly, he remembered where he had seen her before.

———

He went to her later that night to tell her. It took him a long time to decide to do so. It would have been easier to say nothing because in speaking he risked jeopardizing both his newfound friendship with her and his participation in the journey to Eldwist. But keeping silent would have been the same as lying, and he could not bring himself to do that. So he waited until Morgan and Pe Ell were slumbering, until the night was cloaked in blackness and time's passage slowed to a crawl, and he rose soundlessly from beneath his blankets, still aching and stiff from his ordeal, and crossed the fire-lit clearing to where she waited.

As he passed the ruins of the cottage, he glanced over. Earlier, while it was still light, he had searched the smoldering ashes for the missing Druid History. He had found nothing.

Quickening was not asleep; he knew she wouldn't be. She was sitting in the shadow of a massive fir where the trees that ringed the clearing were farthest from the sleepers. He was still weak and could not go far, but he did not wish to speak to her where the other two might hear. She seemed to sense this; she rose as he approached and went with him wordlessly into the forest. When they were a safe distance away, she slowed and faced him.

"What would you tell me, Walker Boh?" she asked and pulled him down with her onto the cool matting of the woodland floor.

It took him a moment to speak. He felt that odd kinship to her without yet understanding why, and it almost changed his mind, making him frightened of the words he had come to say and of the reaction they would cause.

"Quickening," he said finally, and the sound of her name coming from his lips stopped him anew. He tightened his resolve. "I was given a book of the Druid Histories by Cogline before he died. The book was destroyed in the fire. There was a passage in the book that said that the Black Elfstone is a Druid magic and possesses the power to bring back disappeared Paranor. That is the charge I was given by the shade of Allanon when I went to speak with him at the Hadeshorn some weeks ago—to restore Paranor and the Druids to the Four Lands. It was a charge that Cogline urged me to accept. He brought the Druid History to me to convince me it could be done."

"I know this," she said softly.

Her black eyes threatened to swallow him up, and he forced himself to look away. "I doubted him," he continued, the words coming harder now. "I questioned his purpose in telling me, accused him of serving the interests of the Druids. I wanted nothing to do with any of them. But my curiosity about the Black Elfstone persuaded me to pursue the matter anyway, even after he was gone. I decided to try to find out where the Elfstone was hidden. I went to see the Grimpond."

He looked up at her again and kept his gaze steady. "I was shown three visions. All three were of me. In the first I stood before the others in the company that had journeyed to the Hadeshorn to meet with the shade of Allanon and declared that I would sooner cut off my hand than help bring back the Druids. The vision mocked what I had said and showed me with my hand already gone. And now it is gone indeed. My hand and my arm both."

His voice was shaking. "The third vision is of no importance here. But in the second vision I stood at the crest of a ridgeline that looked out over the world. A girl was with me. She lost her balance and reached for me. When she did, I thrust her away, and she fell. That girl, Quickening, was you."

He waited for her response, the silence filling the space between them until it seemed to Walker as if nothing separated them. Quickening did not speak. She kept her eyes fixed on him, her features swept clean of expression.

"Surely you know of the Grimpond!" he exclaimed to her finally in exasperation.

Then he saw her blink and realized that she had been thinking of something else entirely. "It is an exiled spirit," she said.

"One that riddles and lies, but speaks a measure of truth as well, hiding it in devious ways. It did so with the first vision. My arm is gone. I would not have the same thing happen with your life!"

She smiled faintly then, just a trace of movement at the corners of her mouth. "You will not hurt me, Walker Boh. Are you worried that you must?"

"The vision," he repeated.

"The vision is that and nothing more," she interrupted gently. "Visions are as much illusion as truth. Visions tell us of possibilities and do not speak in absolutes. We are not bound by them; they do not govern what is to be. Especially those of a creature like the Grimpond. It teases with falsehoods; it deceives. Do you fear it, Walker Boh? No, not you. Nor I. My father tells me what is to be and that is enough. You will bring no harm to me."

Walker's face felt pinched and tight. "He might be mistaken in what he says; he might not see everything that is to be."

Quickening shook her head, reached out her slim hand, and touched his own. "You will be my protector on this journey, Walker Boh—all three of you, for as long as is necessary. Do not worry. I will be safe with you."

Walker shook his head. "I could remain behind . . ."

Her hand lifted quickly to his mouth and touched it as if to wipe away some new poison. "No." The word was sheathed in iron. "I will be safe if you are with me; I will be in danger only if you are not. You must come."

He stared at her doubtfully. "Can you tell me anything of what I am expected to do?"

She shook her head.

"Or of the means by which I am to claim the Black Elfstone from Uhl Belk?"

Again, no, firmly.

"Or even how I am to protect you when I have but one arm and . . . ?"

"No."

He let his body sag; he was suddenly very weary. The darkness was a cloak of doubt and indecision that hung about him in suffocating folds. "I am half a man," he whispered. "I have lost faith in who and what I am, in the promises I made to myself, in the tasks I set myself. I have been dragged about by Druid dreams and charges in which I do not believe. I have been stripped of my two closest friends, my home, and my sense of worth. I was the strongest of those who went to meet with Allanon, the one the others relied upon; now I am the weakest, barely able to stand on my own two feet. I cannot be as quick as you to dismiss the Grimpond's visions. I have been wrongly confident too many times. Now I must question everything."

"Walker Boh," she said.

He stared at her wonderingly as she reached out for him and brought him to his feet. "You will be strong again—but only if you believe."

She was so close he could feel the heat of her reaching out to him through the cool night air. "You are like me," she said quietly. "You have sensed as much already, though you fail to understand why it is so. It is because we are, before all other things, creatures of the magic we wield. The magic defines us, shapes us, and makes us who we are. For both of us, it is a birthright we cannot escape. You would protect me by telling me of this vision, by taking away the danger that your presence poses if the vision should be true. But, Walker Boh, we are bound in such a way that despite any vision's telling we cannot separate ourselves and survive. Do you not feel it? We must pick up the thread of this trail that leads to Eldwist and Uhl Belk and the Black Elfstone and follow it to its end. Visions of what might be cannot be allowed to deter us. Fears of our future cannot be permitted to intrude."

She paused. "Magic, Walker Boh. Magic governs my life's purpose, the magic given to me by my father. Can you say that it is any different for you?"

It wasn't a question she put to him; it was a statement of fact, of indisputable truth. He took a deep breath. "No," he acknowledged. "I cannot."

"We can neither deny it nor run from it, can we?"

"No."

"We have this in common—this, and separate charges to find the Black Elfstone and preserve the Four Lands, yours from the shade of Allanon, mine from my father. Beyond that, nothing matters. All paths lead to the Druid talisman." She lifted her face into the faint trailers of light that seeped downward through the trees from the starlit skies. "We must go in search of it together, Walker Boh."

She was so positive in her statement, so certain of what she said. Walker met her gaze, still filled with the doubts and fears she had urged him to cast aside, but comforted now in her sense of purpose and her strength of will. Once he had possessed both in equal measure. It made him ashamed and angry that he no longer did. He remembered Par Ohmsford's determination to do what was right, to find a use for his gift of magic. He thought of his own unspoken promise to the ghosts of Cogline and Rumor. He was still wary of the Grimpond's vision, but Quickening was right. He could not let it dissuade him from his quest.

He looked at her and nodded. A measure of determination returned. "We will not speak of the Grimpond's vision again," he promised.

"Not until there is need," she replied.

She took him by the arm and led him back through the darkened forest to sleep.

Par Ohmsford's strength returned to him slowly. Two weeks passed while he lay bedded in the Mole's underground lair, a gaunt and motionless skeleton draped in old linen, dappled by a mingling of shadows and candlelight, and surrounded by the strange, changeless faces of the Mole's adopted children. Time had no meaning at first, for he was lost to anything remotely connected with the real world. Then the madness faded, and he began to come back to himself. The days and nights took on definition. Damson Rhee and the Mole became recognizable. The blur of darkness and light sharpened to reveal the shapes and forms of the subterranean rooms in which he rested. The stuffed castoffs grew familiar once more, button noses and eyes, thread-sewn mouths, worn cloth limbs and bodies. He was able to give them names. Words assumed meaning out of idle talk. There was nourishment and there was sleep.

Mostly, though, there were the memories. They tracked him through sleep and waking alike, wraiths that hovered at the edge of his thoughts, anxious to sting and bite. There were memories of the Pit, the Shadowen, Rimmer Dall, and the Sword of Shannara, but mostly of Coll.

He could not forgive himself. Coll was dead because of him—not simply because he had struck the fatal blow, the killing stroke of his wishsong's magic, not because he had failed to adequately protect his brother from the packs of Shadowen that roamed the Pit while he was engaged with Rimmer Dall, not for any of this, but because he had from the first, from the moment they had fled Varfleet and the Seekers, thought only of himself. His need to know the truth about the wishsong, the Sword of Shannara, the charges of Allanon, the purpose of the magic—this was what had mattered. He had sacrificed everything to discover that truth, and in the end that sacrifice had included his brother.

Damson Rhee strove mightily to persuade him otherwise, seeing his torment and instinctively recognizing its cause.

"He wanted to be there with you, Par," she would tell him, over and over, her face bent close, her red hair tumbling down about her slender shoulders, her voice soft and gentle. "It was his choice. He loved you enough that it could not have been otherwise. You did your best to keep him from coming, to keep him safe. But there was that in Coll that would not be compromised. A sense of what's right, what's necessary. He was determined to protect you from the dangers you both knew waited. He gave his life to keep you safe, don't you see? Don't be so quick to steal away what that sacrifice meant by insisting it was your fault. There were choices and he made them. He was strong-willed, and you could not have changed his mind even had you tried harder than you did. He understood, Par. He recognized the purpose and need in what you do. You believed that was true before; you must believe it now. Coll did. Don't let his death have been for nothing."

But Coll's death might have been for exactly that, he feared, and the fear chased after him in his darkest thoughts. Exactly what had his brother's death accomplished? What did he have to show for it? The Sword of Shannara? Yes, he had gained possession of the legendary blade of his Elven-blooded ancestors, the talisman the shade of Allanon had sent him to find. And what use was it? It had failed utterly as a weapon against Rimmer Dall, even after the First Seeker had revealed himself as a Shadowen. If the Sword was a necessary magic as Allanon had claimed, why hadn't it destroyed his greatest enemy? Worse, if Dall were to be believed, the Sword of Shannara could have been his simply for the asking. There was no need for their agonizing, destructive descent into the Pit—no need, then, for the death of Coll.

And no purpose to it either if Rimmer Dall was right about one thing more—that Par Ohmsford, like himself, was a Shadowen. For if Par were the very thing they were fighting to protect the Four Lands against . . .

If Coll had died to save a Shadowen . . .

Unthinkable? He was no longer sure.

So the memories plagued him, bitter and terrible, and he was awash in a slew of anguish and disbelief and anger. He fought through that morass, struggled to keep himself afloat, to breathe, to survive. The fever disappeared, the starkness of his emotions softened, the edges dulled, and the aching of his heart and body scarred and healed.

He rose at the end of the two weeks' time, determined to lie about no longer, and began to walk short distances within the Mole's dark quarters. He washed at the basin, dressed, and took his meals at the table. He navigated the lair end to end, doorway to doorway, testing himself, feeling his way through his weakness. He pushed back the memories; he kept them carefully at bay. He did so mostly through simple motion. Doing something, anything, helped to keep him from dwelling so much on what was over and done. He made note of the smells and tastes that hung upon the trapped air. He studied the texture of the ruined furniture, of the various discards of the upper world, and of the walls and floors themselves. His resolution stiffened. He was alive and there was a reason for it. He shifted in and out of the candlelight and shadows, a ghost impelled by an inner vision.

Even when he was too tired to move about further he was reluctant to rest. He spent hours seated on the edge of his bed examining the Sword of Shannara, pondering its mystery.

Why had it failed to respond to him when he had touched its blade to Rimmer Dall?

"Is it possible," Damson asked him at one point, her voice cautious, "that you have been deceived in some way and that this is not the Sword of Shannara?"

He thought carefully before he answered. "When I saw it in the vault, Damson, and then when I touched it, I knew it was the Sword. I was certain of it. I have sung the story of it so many times, pictured it so often. There was no doubt in my mind." He shook his head slowly. "I still feel it to be so."

She nodded. She was seated next to him on the bed, legs folded beneath her, green eyes intense. "But your anticipation of finding it might have colored your judgment, Par. You might have wanted it so badly that you allowed yourself to be fooled."

"It might have happened like that, yes," he agreed. "Then. But now, as well? Look at the blade. See here. The handle is worn, aged—yet the blade shines like new. Like Morgan's sword—magic protects it. And see the carving of the torch with its flame . . ."

His enthusiasm trailed off with a sigh. He saw the doubt mirrored in her eyes. "Yet it doesn't work, it's true. It doesn't do a thing. I hold it, and it seems right, what it should be—and it doesn't do anything, give back anything, or let me feel even the slightest hint of its magic. So how can it be the Sword?"

"Counter-magic," the Mole said solemnly. He was crouched in a corner of the room close to them, almost invisible in the shadows. "A mask that hides." He stretched his face with his hands to change its shape.

Par looked at him and nodded. "A concealment of some kind. Yes, Mole. It might be. I have considered the possibility. But what magic exists that is strong enough to suppress that of the Sword of Shannara? How could the Shadowen produce such a magic? And if they could, why not simply use it to destroy the blade? And shouldn't I be able to break past any counter-magic if I am the rightful bearer of the Sword?"

The Mole regarded him solemnly, voiceless. Damson gave no reply.

"I don't understand," he whispered softly. "I don't understand what's wrong."

He wondered, too, at how willingly Rimmer Dall had let him depart with the Sword. If it were truly the weapon it was supposed to be, the weapon that could destroy the Shadowen, Dall would surely not have let Par Ohmsford have it. Yet he had given it to the Valeman without argument, almost with encouragement in fact, telling him instead that what he had been told of the Shadowen and the Sword was a lie.

And then virtually proved it by demonstrating that the touch of the Sword would not harm him.

Par wandered the Mole's quarters with the blade in hand, hefting it, balancing it, working to invoke the magic that lay within. Yet the secret of the Sword of Shannara continued to elude him.

Periodically Damson left their underground concealment and went up into the streets of Tyrsis. It was odd to think of an entire city existing just overhead, just beyond sight and sound, with people and buildings, sunlight and fresh air. Par longed to go with her, but she wisely counseled against it. He lacked strength yet for such an undertaking, and the Federation was still searching.

A week after Par had left his sickbed and begun moving about on his own, Damson returned with disquieting news.

"Some weeks ago," she advised, "the Federation discovered the location of the Jut. A spy in the outlaw camp apparently betrayed it. An army was dispatched from Tyrsis to penetrate the Parma Key and lay siege. The siege was successful. The Jut fell. It was taken close to the time, Par, when you escaped the Pit." She paused. "Everyone found there was killed."

Par caught his breath. "Everyone?"

"So the Federation claims. The Movement, it says, is finished."

There was momentary silence. They sat at the Mole's long table surrounded by his voiceless, unseeing children, saucers and cups set before them. It had become a midafternoon ritual.

"More tea, lovely Damson?" the Mole asked softly, his furry face poking up from the table's edge. She nodded without taking her eyes from Par.

Par frowned. "You don't seem distressed by this," he responded finally.

"I think it odd that it took weeks for word of this victory to reach the city."

"So it isn't true, then?"

She bit into one of the crackers that the Mole had provided for them and chewed. "It may be true that the Jut was taken. But I know Padishar Creel. It doesn't seem likely that he would let himself be trapped in his own lair. He's much too clever for that. More to the point, friends of the Movement here in the city with whom I spoke tell me that line soldiers with the army claim they killed almost no one, several dozen at most, and those were already dead when the Jut's summit was breached. What happened, then, to the others? There were three hundred men in that camp. Besides, if the Federation really had Padishar Creel, they'd spike his head atop the city gates to prove it."

"But there's no message from Padishar?"

She shook her head.

"And no word of Morgan or Steff or any of the others?"

She shook her head again. "They've vanished."

"So." He let the word hang.

She smiled ruefully. They finished their tea without speaking.

The following day, his body stronger, his mind determined, Par again announced that he wanted to go up into Tyrsis. He had been shut away long enough; he needed to see something of his own world again. He needed to feel sunlight on his skin and breathe fresh air. Besides, as long as he remained hidden away, nothing was being accomplished. It was time for him to *do* something.

Damson objected strongly, pointing out that he was not yet fully recovered and that it was extremely dangerous for him to go anywhere. The Federation knew who he was now; his description was everywhere. After his escape from the Pit, Seekers had begun searching the lower levels of the old palace and discovered the tunnels leading in. Now they were searching the tunnels as well. There were miles of tunnel and sewer to search, but the risk of discovery remained. For now, it was best to lie low.

In the end, they compromised. Par would be allowed to go into the tunnels close at hand as long as he was in the company of Damson or the Mole. He would not go aboveground, even for a moment. He would go where he was told and do what he was advised. But at least he would be out of his sickrooms. Par agreed.

He began his exploration eagerly, studying the lay of the tunnels as he trailed after Damson and the Mole, mapping it all out carefully in his mind. He tired quickly the first day and had to return early. He was stronger the second and continued to improve. He began to grow comfortable with his understanding of how the tunnels and sewers wove together—enough so that he believed he could find his way to the surface on his own should the need arise. The Mole advised him cautiously, watched him with intense, glittery eyes, and nodded in satisfaction. Damson stayed close, her hands constantly touching him, as if to shield against danger. He smiled inwardly at their protectiveness.

A week passed away. He was much better now, almost completely recovered. More than a month had elapsed since he had been carried beneath the city of Tyrsis and placed in hiding. He thought constantly of leaving, of picking up again the threads of his life.

At the same time he found himself wondering where he would begin.

In the end the decision was made for him.

It was late afternoon ten days after he had begun his exploration of the tunnels surrounding the Mole's lair. He was seated on the edge of his bed, once again examining the Sword of Shannara. Damson had gone up to the city to see what news she could learn of Padishar and the Federation. The Mole was a furtive shadow as he passed from room to room, straightening, arranging, and fussing with his possessions. Teatime had come and gone without the girl, and the Mole was unsettled. Par might have been if he had allowed himself to dwell on the matter, but as it was he was consumed with something else. His memory of the events surrounding the discovery of the Sword of Shannara and the death of Coll was still incomplete, the fragments piecing themselves back in place only intermittently as he recovered to form a complete picture. Now and then a new piece would re-call itself. One did so now.

It had to do with the wishsong, actually. He remembered all too clearly how his magic had gathered within him, summoned on its own almost, when Coll—the thing that had been Coll—threatened him. Then, after Coll was gone and the others of the Shadowen in the Pit came for him, the wishsong had given him a flaming sword, a weapon unlike anything the magic had ever produced. It had destroyed the Shadowen effortlessly. For a few moments he had been possessed, infused with fury and madness, driven beyond any semblance of reason. He remembered how that had felt. But there was something more, something he had forgotten completely until now. When the Shadowen were destroyed and he had reached down to re-trieve the Sword of Shannara from where it had fallen, the Sword had burned him—had seared his hand like fire. And instantly his own magic had died, and he had been unable to summon it again.

Why had the Sword of Shannara done that? What had happened to produce such a reaction?

He was pondering this, trying to make it fit with what little he knew of the mystery of the Sword, when Damson burst through the entry to the Mole's subterranean refuge, long hair disheveled, her breathing quick and frightened.

"Federation soldiers!" she announced, rushing up to Par, pulling him to his feet. "Dozens of them, hunting through the sewers, making a thor-ough sweep! Not at the palace, but here. I barely slipped in ahead of them. I don't know if someone betrayed us or if I was simply seen. But they have found the entry down and they're coming!" She paused, steadying herself. "If we stay, they will find us. We have to get out right away."

Par slung the Sword of Shannara over his shoulder and began shoving his few possessions into a sling pack. His thoughts scattered. He had been anxious to leave, but not like this.

"Mole!" Damson called out, and the furry fellow skittered quickly up to her. "You have to come with us. They will find you as well."

But the Mole shook his head solemnly, and his voice was calm. "No, beautiful Damson. This is my home. I will stay."

Damson knelt hurriedly. "You can't do that, Mole. You will be in great danger. These men will hurt you."

Par hurried over. "Come with us, Mole. Please. It is our fault that you are threatened."

The Mole regarded him quizzically. "I chose to bring you here. I chose to care for you. I did it for Damson—but for myself as well. I like you. I like how you make . . . lovely Damson feel."

Par saw Damson flush out of the corner of his eye and kept his gaze focused on the Mole. "None of that matters now. What matters is that we are your friends, and friends look out for one another. You have to come with us."

"I will not go back into the world above," the Mole insisted quietly. "This is my home. I must look out for it. What of my children? What of Chalt and little Lida and Westra and Everlind? Would you have me leave them?"

"Bring them, if you must!" Par was growing desperate.

"We will help you find a new home," Damson added quickly.

But the Mole shook his head stubbornly. "The world up there wants nothing to do with any of us. We do not belong there, lovely Damson. We belong down here. Do not worry for us. We know these tunnels. There are places to hide where we will never be found. We will go to them if we must." He paused. "You could come with us, both of you. You would be safe."

Damson rose, her brow furrowed. "It will be enough if you are safe, Mole. We have brought too much danger already into your life. Just promise me that you will go to one of these hiding places now. Take your children and stay there until this hunt is finished and the tunnels are safe again. Promise me."

The Mole nodded. "I promise, sweet Damson."

Damson flew to gather her own possessions, then joined Par at the entryway. The Mole stood looking at them from out of the shadows, little more than a pair of glittering eyes lost in the jumble of discarded goods and faint candlelight.

Damson shouldered her pack. "Goodbye, Mole," she called softly, then lowered her pack, walked to where he waited, and reached down to embrace him. When she returned to Par, she was crying.

"I owe you my life, Mole," Par told him. "Thank you for everything you have done for me."

One small hand lifted in a faint wave.

"Remember your promise!" Damson warned almost angrily. "Hide yourself!"

Then they were through the entry and into the tunnel beyond, slipping soundlessly ahead. Damson carried no torch, but instead produced one of the strange stones that glowed when warmed by her hand. She used its small, sure light to guide them, opening her fingers to provide direction, closing them again to protect against discovery. They moved swiftly away from the Mole's lair, down one tunnel and into another, then up a metal ladder and into a pit.

From somewhere distant, they heard the sound of boots scraping.

Damson led Par away from the sound, along a tunnel that was dank and slick with moisture. Already the temperature was rising and the air filling with sewer smells. Rats skittered about in the dark recesses, and water trickled along the crevices of the rock. They wound their way steadily through the maze. Voices reached them once, unfocused, indistinct. Damson ignored them.

They arrived at a joining of several sewer ways, a ringed pit with water collecting in a deep, shadowed well. A central convergence, Par thought. He was breathing heavily, his strength failing already in the face of this sudden activity. The muscles of his legs and back ached, and he stretched himself gingerly to relieve them.

Damson glanced back at him, concern mirrored in her eyes. She hesitated, then guided him forward.

The voices rose again, closer now, coming from more than one direction. Torchlight flared behind them. Damson took Par up another ladder and into a tunnel that was so narrow they were forced to crawl to get through. Dampness and filth soaked into Par's clothing and clung to his skin. He forced himself to breathe through his mouth and then only when he could hold his breath no longer.

They emerged at the beginning of a wider tunnel, this one trenched down its middle so that there were stone walkways to either side of where the sewer water flowed. A pair of smaller tunnels intersected. There was a flicker of torchlight in each. Damson hurried on. They rounded a bend and found torchlight waiting ahead as well. Damson stopped, shoving Par back against the rock wall.

When she faced him, there was a hint of desperation in her eyes. "The only way out," she whispered, her mouth close to his ear, "lies ahead. If we go back, we'll be trapped."

She stepped back so that she could see his response. He glanced past her to the lights, approaching rapidly now, and heard the thudding of boots and the first hint of voices. Fear welled within and threatened to drown him. It felt as if the Federation had been hunting him forever; it seemed that the hunting would never stop. So many times he had escaped capture. It could not go on. Sooner or later his luck was going to run out. He had barely survived the Pit and the Shadowen. He was worn and sick at heart and he just wanted to be left alone. But the Federation would never leave him alone; the cycle was endless.

For an instant despair claimed him completely. Then abruptly he thought of Coll. He remembered his vow that someone would pay for what had become of his brother. Anger replaced the despair instantly. No, he would not be taken prisoner, he swore silently. He would not be given over to Rimmer Dall.

He thought momentarily to summon the magic that had aided him in the Pit, to call forth that fiery sword that would cut his enemies to pieces. He brushed the impulse aside. It was too much power to face again so soon and still with so little understanding. Cunning, not brute force, was needed here. He remembered suddenly how he had escaped from the Federation that night in the People's Park. Pulling Damson after him, he hastened to a shadowed niche in the tunnel wall formed by the bracing. Crouched in the darkness with the girl, he put a finger to his lips and signaled for her to remain still.

The Federation soldiers approached, five strong, torches lifted to provide sufficient light for their search, the metal of their weapons glinting. Par took a deep breath and slipped down within himself. He would have only one chance. Just one.

He waited until they were almost upon them, then used the wishsong. He kept it tightly in check, taking no chances with what it might do, carefully controlling its release. He cast a net about the soldiers of whispered warnings, a hint of something that disturbed the waters of the sewer farther ahead, a shadowy movement. He infused them with a need to hurry if they were to catch it.

Almost as one, the soldiers broke into a run and hastened past without looking. The Valeman and the girl pressed back against the tunnel rock, breathless. In moments the soldiers were gone.

Slowly Damson and Par came back to their feet. Then Damson reached out impulsively and hugged the Valeman. "You are well again, Par Ohmsford," she whispered, and kissed him. "This way, now. We're almost free."

They hurried down the passageway, crossed a confluent, and entered a dry well. The torches and boots and voices had receded into silence. There was a ladder leading up. Damson went first, pausing at the top to push up against a trapdoor. Twilight seeped through the crack. She listened, peered about, then climbed through. Par followed.

They stood within a shed, slat-walled and closed away. A single door led out. Damson moved to it, opened it cautiously and with Par in tow stepped out.

The city of Tyrsis rose around them, fortress walls, spiraled towers, jumbled buildings of stone and wood. The air was thick with smells and sounds. It was early evening, the day gone west, the city's people turned homeward. Life was slow and weary in the stillness of the summer heat. Overhead the sky was turning to black velvet, and stars were beginning to spread like scattered bits of crystal. A wondrously bright full moon beamed cold white light across the world.

Par Ohmsford smiled, the aches forgotten, his fears momentarily behind him. He adjusted the weight of the Sword of Shannara across his shoulders. It felt good to be alive.

Damson reached over and took his hand, squeezing it gently.

Together they turned down the street and disappeared into the night.

Quickening kept her little company at Hearthstone for several days to allow Walker Boh to regain his strength. It returned quickly, the healing process augmented as much by the girl's small touches and sudden smiles, by the very fact of her presence, as by nature's hand. There was magic all about her, an invisible aura that surrounded her, that reached out to everything with which she came in contact, and that restored and renewed with a thoroughness and rapidity that was astounding. Walker grew strong again almost overnight, the effects of his poisoning gone into memory, to some small extent at least joined by the pain of losing Cogline and Rumor. The haunted look disappeared from his eyes, and he was able to put away his anger and his fear, to lock them in a small dark corner of his mind where they would not disturb him and yet not be forgotten when the time came to remember. His determination returned, his confidence, his sense of purpose and resolve, and he became more like the Dark Uncle of old. His magic aided him in his recovery, but it was Quickening who provided the impetus, moment by moment, a warmth that outshone the sun.

She did more. The clearing where the cottage had stood became cleansed of its scars and burns, and the signs of the battle with the Shadowen slowly disappeared. Grasses and flowers blossomed and filled the emptiness, swatches of color and patches of fragrance that soothed and comforted. Even the ruins of the cottage settled into dust and at last faded from view completely. It seemed that whenever she chose she could make the world over again.

Morgan Leah began to talk to Walker when Pe Ell was not around, the Highlander still uneasy, admitting to Walker that he was not certain yet who the other really was or why Quickening had brought him along. Morgan had grown since Walker had seen him last. Brash and full of himself when he had first come to Hearthstone, he seemed subdued now, more controlled, a cautious man without lacking courage, a well-reasoned man. Walker liked him better for it and thought that the events that had conspired to separate him from the Ohmsfords and bring him to Culhaven had done much to mature him. The Highlander told Walker what had befallen Par and Coll, of their joining Padishar Creel and the Movement, their journey to Tyrsis and attempts to recover the Sword of Shannara from the Pit, their battles with the Shadowen, and their separation and separate escapes. He told Walker of the Federation assault on the Jut, Teel's betrayal, her death and Steff's, and the outlaw's flight north.

"She gave us all away, Walker," Morgan declared when he had finished his narrative. "She gave up Granny and Auntie in Culhaven, the Dwarves working with the Resistance that she knew about, everyone. She must have given Cogline up as well."

But Walker did not believe so. The Shadowen had known of Cogline and Hearthstone since Par had been kidnapped from the valley by Spider Gnomes some months earlier. The Shadowen could have come for Cogline at any time, and they had not chosen to do so until now. Rimmer Dall had told Cogline before he killed him that the old man was the last who stood against the Shadowen, and that meant that he believed Cogline had become a threat. More worrisome to him than how Rimmer Dall had found them was the First Seeker's claim that the children of Shannara were all dead. Obviously he was mistaken about Walker, but what of Par and Wren, the others of the Shannara line dispatched by the shade of Allanon in search of those things lost and disappeared that would supposedly save the Four

Lands? Was Rimmer Dall mistaken about them as well or had they, too, gone the way of Cogline? He hadn't the means to discover the truth and he kept what he was thinking to himself. There was no point in saying anything to Morgan Leah, who was already struggling with the imagined consequences of his decision to follow after Quickening.

"I know I should not be here," he told Walker in confidence one afternoon. They were sitting within the shade of an aged white oak, listening to and watching the songbirds that darted overhead. "I kept my word to Steff and saw to the safety of Granny Elise and Auntie Jilt. But this! What of my promise to Par and Coll that I would protect them? I shouldn't be here; I should be back in Tyrsis looking for them!"

But Walker said, "No, Highlander, you should not. What good could you do even if you found them? How much help would you be against the Shadowen? You have a chance here to do something far more important— indeed, a need, if Quickening is right in what she says. Perhaps, too, you may find a way to restore the magic to your Sword, just as I may find a way to restore my arm. Slim hopes for those of us with pragmatic minds, yet hopes nevertheless. We feel her need, Highlander, and we respond to it; we are her children, aren't we? I think we cannot dismiss such stirrings so easily. For now at least, we belong with her."

He had come to believe that, swayed by his midnight talk with Quickening when he had told her of the Grimpond's vision and his fear that it would come to pass, won over by her insistence and determination that it would not. Morgan Leah was no less thoroughly bound, mesmerized by her beauty, chained by his longings, drawn to her in ways he could not begin to understand but could not deny. For each of the three, the attraction to Quickening was different. Morgan's was physical, a fascination with the look and movement of her, with the exquisite line and curve of her face and body, and with a loveliness that transcended anything he had ever known or even imagined. Walker's was more ethereal, a sense of kinship with her born of their common birthright of magic, an understanding of the ways in which she was compelled to think and act because of it, a binding together through a common chain of links where each link was a shared experience of reasoning grown out of the magic's lure.

Pe Ell's purpose in coming was the most difficult to discern. He called himself an artist, at various times of sleight-of-hand and escape, but he was clearly something more. That he was extremely dangerous was no mystery to anyone, yet he kept any truths about himself carefully concealed. He seldom spoke to any of them, even to Quickening, though he was as attracted to her as either Walker or Morgan and looked after her as carefully as they. But Pe Ell's attraction was more that of a man for his possessions than a man for his lover or a kindred spirit. He seemed drawn to Quickening in the way of a craftsman to something he has created and offers up as evidence of his skill. It was an attitude that Walker found difficult to understand, for Pe Ell had been brought along in the same way as the rest of them and had done nothing to make Quickening who or what she was. Yet the feeling persisted in him that Pe Ell viewed the girl as his own and when the time was right he would attempt to possess her.

The days of the week played themselves out until finally Quickening decided Walker was well enough to travel, and the company of four departed Hearthstone. Traveling afoot, for the country would permit nothing better, they journeyed north through Darklin Reach and the forests of the Anar along the western edge of Toffer Ridge to the Rabb, crossed where the waters narrowed, and proceeded on toward the Charnals. Progress was slow because the country was heavily wooded, choked with scrub and slashed by ravines and ridges, and they were forced constantly to alter their direction of travel away from their intended course to find passable terrain. The weather was good, however, warm days of sunshine and soft breezes, the summer's close, a slow, lazy winding down of hours that made every day seem welcome and endless. There was sickness even this far north, wilting and poisoning of the earth and its life, yet not as advanced as in the middle sections of the Four Lands, and the smells and tastes, the sights and sounds, were mostly fresh and new and unfouled. Streams were clear and forests green, and the life within both seemed unaffected by the gathering darkness with which the Shadowen threatened to blanket everything.

Nights were spent camped in wooded clearings by ponds or streams that provided fresh water and often fish for a meal, and there was talk now and then between the men, even by Pe Ell. It was Quickening who remained reticent, who kept herself apart when the day's travel was completed, who secluded herself back in the shadows, away from the firelight and the presence of the other three. It wasn't that she disdained them or hid from them; it was more that she needed the solitude. The wall went up early in their travels, an invisible distancing that she established the first night out and did not relinquish after. The three she had brought with her did not question, but instead watched her and each other surreptitiously and waited to see what would transpire. When nothing did, thrown together by her forced separation from them, they began to loosen up in each other's presence and to speak. Morgan would have talked in any case, an open and relaxed youth who enjoyed stories and the company of others. It was different with Walker and Pe Ell, both of whom were by nature and practice guarded and cautious. Conversations frequently became small battlegrounds between the two with each attempting to discover what secrets the other hid and neither willing to reveal anything about himself. They used their talk as a screen, careful to keep the conversation away from anything that really mattered.

They all speculated now and again on where they were going and what they were going to do when they got there. Those conversations ended quickly every time. No one would discuss what sort of magic he possessed, though Walker and Morgan already had some idea of each other's strengths, and no one would advance any plan of action for retrieving the talisman. They fenced with each other like swordsmen, probing for strengths and weaknesses, feinting with their questions and their suggestions, and trying to discover what sort of iron fortified the others. Walker and Pe Ell made little progress with each other, and while it became clear enough that Morgan was there because of the magic contained in the Sword of Leah it was impossible to learn anything substantive with the weapon shattered. Pe Ell, particularly, asked questions over and over again about what it was the Sword of Leah could do, what sort of materials it could penetrate, and how much power it contained. Morgan used all of his considerable talents to be both charming and confusing with his answers and to give the impression that the magic could do either anything or nothing. Eventually, Pe Ell left him alone.

The close of the first week of travel brought them north above the Anar to the foothills leading into the Charnals where for days thereafter they journeyed, always in the shadow of the mountains as they wound their way northeast toward the Tiderace. By now, they were beyond the lands any of them knew. Neither Morgan nor Pe Ell had ever been north of the Upper Anar, and Walker had not gone farther than the lower regions of the Charnals. In any case, it was Quickening who led them, seemingly un-perturbed by the fact that she knew less of the country than any of them, responding to some inner voice that none of them could hear, to instincts that none of them could feel. She admitted that she did not know exactly where she was going, that she could sense enough to lead them for now, but that eventually they would have to cross the Charnals, and then she would be lost as the mountains would prove unfathomable to her. Eldwist lay beyond the Charnals, and they would have to have help in finding it.

"Have you the magic for that, Walker?" Pe Ell teased when she finished, but Walker only smiled and wondered the same thing.

Rain caught up with them as the second week ended and followed them relentlessly into the third, dampening their trail, their packs and clothing, and their spirits. Clouds massed overhead along the line of the peaks and refused to budge, dark and persistent. Thunder boomed and lightning flashed against the wall of the mountains as if giants were playing shadow games with their hands. There were not many travelers this far north; most of those they encountered were Trolls. Few spoke and fewer still had anything useful to tell. There were several passes that led through the mountains a day or two ahead, all of them beginning at a town high in the foothills called Rampling Steep. Yes, some of the passes led all the way east to the Tiderace. No, they had never heard of Eldwist.

"Makes you wonder if it really exists," Pe Ell muttered, persisting in his role as agitator, a smile creasing his narrow face, cold and empty and devoid of humor. "Makes you think."

That night, two days short of the completion of their third week of travel, he broached the subject in a manner that left no one in doubt as to his feelings. The rains were still falling, a gray haze that chilled and numbed the senses, and tempers had grown short.

"This town, Rampling Steep," he began, an edge to his voice that brought them all around in the stillness of the twilight, "that's where we lose any idea of where we're going, isn't it?" He asked the question of Quickening, who made no response. "We're lost after that, and I don't like being lost. Maybe it's time we talked a bit more about this whole business."

"What would you know, Pe Ell?" the girl asked quietly, unperturbed.

"You haven't told us enough about what lies ahead," he said. "I think you should. Now."

She shook her head. "You ask for answers I do not have to give. I have to discover them as well."

"I don't believe that," he said, shaking his head for emphasis, his voice low and hard. Morgan Leah was looking at him with undisguised irritation and Walker Boh was on his feet. "I know something about people, even ones who have the magic like yourself and I know when they're telling me everything they know and when they're not. You're not. You better do so."

"Or you might turn around and go back?" Morgan challenged sharply.

Pe Ell looked at him expressionlessly.

"Why don't you do that, Pe Ell? Why don't you?"

Pe Ell rose, his eyes flat and seemingly disinterested. Morgan stood up with him. But Quickening stepped forward, coming swiftly between them, moving to separate them without seeming to mean to do so, but as if she sought only to face Pe Ell. She stood before him, small and vulnerable, silver hair swept back as she tilted her face to his. He frowned and for a moment looked as if he felt threatened and might lash out. Whip-thin and sinewy, he curled back like a snake. But she did not move, either toward him or away, and the tension slowly went out of him.

"You must trust me," she told him softly, speaking to him as if he were the only other person alive in all the world, holding him spellbound by the force of her voice, the intensity of her black eyes, and the closeness of her body. "What there is to know of Uhl Belk and Eldwist, I have told you. What there is to know of the Black Elfstone, I have told you. As much, at least, as I am given to know. Yes, there are things I keep from you just as you keep things from me. That is the way of all living creatures, Pe Ell. You cannot begrudge me my secrets when you have your own. I keep nothing back that will harm you. That is the best I can do."

The lean man stared down at her without speaking, everything closed away behind his eyes where his thoughts were at work.

"When we reach Rampling Steep, we will seek help in finding our way," she continued, her voice still barely above a whisper, yet bell-clear and certain. "Eldwist will be known and someone will point the way."

And to the surprise of both Walker and Morgan Leah, Pe Ell simply nodded and stepped away. He did not speak again that night to any of them. He seemed to have forgotten they existed.

The following day they reached a broad roadway leading west into the foothills and turned onto it. The roadway wound ahead snakelike into the light and then into shadow when the sun dropped behind the peaks of the Charnals. Night descended and they camped beneath the stars, the first clear sky in many days. They talked quietly as the evening meal was consumed, a sense of balance restored with the passing of the rains. No mention was made of the previous night's events. Pe Ell seemed satisfied with what Quickening had told him, although she had told him almost nothing. It was the way in which she had spoken to him, Walker thought on reflection. It was the way she employed her magic to turn aside his suspicion and anger.

They set out again early the following morning, traveling northeast once more, the sunrise bright and warming. By late afternoon they had climbed high into the foothills, close against the base of the mountains. By sunset they had arrived at the town of Rampling Steep.

The light was nearly gone by then, a dim glow from behind the mountains west that colored the skyline in shades of gold and silver. Rampling Steep was hunkered down in a deep pool of shadows, cupped in a shallow basin at the foot of the peaks where the forest trees began to thin and scatter into isolated clumps between the ridges of mountain rock. The buildings of the town were a sorry bunch, ramshackle structures built of stone foundations and wooden walls and roofs with windows and doors all shuttered and barred and closed away like the eyes of frightened children. There was a single street that wound between them as if looking for a way out. The buildings of the town crouched down on either side save for a handful of shacks and cottages that were settled back on the high ground like careless sentries. Everything was desperately in need of repair. Boards from walls were broken and hung loose, roofing shingles had slipped away, and porch fronts sagged and buckled. Slivers of light crept through cracks and crevices. There were teams of horses hitched to wagons pulled up close against the buildings, each looking a little more ruined than the one before, and shadowed figures on two legs moved between them like wraiths.

As the company drew nearer Walker saw that the figures were mostly Trolls, great, hulking figures in the twilight, their barklike faces impossible to read. A few glanced at the four as they passed down the roadway, but none bothered to speak or to give a second look. The sound of voices reached out to them now, disembodied grunts and mutterings and laughter that the dilapidated walls could not keep in. But despite the talk and the laughter and the movement of men, Rampling Steep had an empty feel to it, as if it had long ago been abandoned by the living.

Quickening took them up the roadway without pausing, glancing neither left nor right, as sure of herself now as she had been from the start. Morgan followed no more than a step behind, staying close, keeping watch, being protective although there was probably no need for him to do so. Pe Ell had drifted out to the right, distancing himself. Walker trailed.

There was a series of ale houses at the center of Rampling Steep, and it appeared that everyone had gathered there. Music came from some, and men lurched and swaggered through the doors, passing in and out of the light in faceless anonymity. A few women passed as well, worn and hard looking. Rampling Steep appeared to be a place of ending rather than beginning.

Quickening took them into the first of the ale houses and asked the keeper if he knew of someone who could guide them through the mountains to Eldwist. She asked the question as if there were nothing unusual about it. She was oblivious to the stir her presence caused, to the stares that were directed at her from every quarter, and to the dark hunger that lay behind a good many of the eyes that fixed upon her, or at least she seemed to be. Perhaps, Walker thought, as he watched her, it was all simply of no consequence to her. He saw that no one tried to approach and no one threatened. Morgan stood protectively at her back, facing that unfriendly, rapacious gathering—as if one man could make a difference if they should decide to do something—but it was not the Highlander that deterred them or Walker or even the forbidding Pe Ell. It was the girl, a creature so stunning that like a thing out of some wild imagining it could not be disturbed for fear it would prove false. The men gathered in the ale house watched, that crowd of wild-eyed men, not quite believing but not willing to prove themselves wrong.

There was nothing to be learned at the first ale house, so they moved on to the next. No one followed. The scenario of the first ale house was repeated at the second, this one smaller and closer inside, the smoke of pipes and the smell of bodies thicker and more pungent. There were Trolls, Gnomes, Dwarves, and Men in Rampling Steep, all drinking and talking together as if it were the natural order of things, as if what was happening in the rest of the Four Lands was of no importance here. Walker studied their faces dispassionately, their eyes when their faces told him nothing, and found them secretive and scared, the faces and eyes of men who lived with hardship and disappointment yet ignored both because to do otherwise would mean they could not survive. Some seemed dangerous, a few even desperate. But there was an order to life in Rampling Steep as there was in most places, and not much happened to disturb that order. Strangers came and went, even ones as striking as Quickening, and life went on nevertheless. Quickening was something like a falling star—it happened a few times and you were lucky if you saw it but you didn't do anything to change your life because of it.

They moved on to a third ale house and then a fourth. At each ale house, the answers to Quickening's questions were the same. No one knew anything of Eldwist and Uhl Belk and no one wanted to. There were maybe eight drinking houses in all along the roadway, most offering beds upstairs and supplies from storerooms out back, a few doubling as trading stations or exchanges. Because Rampling Steep was the only town for days in either direction that fronted the lower side of the Charnals and because it was situated where the trails leading down out of the mountains converged, a lot of traffic passed through, trappers and traders mostly, but others as well. Every ale house was filled and most gathered were temporary or sometime residents on their way to or from somewhere else. There was talk of all sorts, of business and politics, of roads traveled and wonders seen, of the people and places that made up the Four Lands. Walker listened without appearing to and thought that Pe Ell was doing the same.

At the fifth ale house they visited—Walker never even noticed the name—they finally got the response they were looking for. The keeper was a big, ruddy-complexioned fellow with a scarred face and a ready smile. He sized up Quickening in a way that made even Walker uncomfortable. Then he suggested that the girl should take a room with him for a few days, just to see if maybe she might like the town enough to stay. That brought Morgan Leah about with fire in his eyes, but Quickening screened him away with a slight shifting of her body, met the keeper's bold stare, and replied that she wasn't interested. The keeper did not press the suggestion. Instead, to everyone's amazement in the face of the rejection he had just been handed, he told her that the man she was seeking was down the street at the Skinned Cat. His name, he said, was Horner Dees.

They went back out into the night, leaving the keeper looking as if he wasn't at all sure what he had just done. The look was telling. Quickening had that gift; it was the essence of her magic. She could turn you around before you realized it. She could make you reveal yourself in ways you had never intended. She could make you want to please her. It was the kind of thing a beautiful woman could make a man do, but with Quickening it was something far more than her beauty that disarmed you. It was the creature within, the elemental that seemed human but was far more, an embodiment of magic that Walker thought reflected the father who had made her. He knew the stories of the King of the Silver River. When you met him, you told him what he wished to know and you did not dissemble. His presence alone was enough to make you *want* to tell him. Walker had seen how Morgan and Pe Ell and the men in the ale houses responded to her. And he as well. She was most certainly her father's child.

They found the Skinned Cat at the far end of the town, tucked back within the shadow of several massive, ancient shagbarks. It was a large, rambling structure that creaked and groaned simply from the movement of the men and women inside and seemed to hang together mostly out of stubbornness. It was as crowded as the others, but there was more space to fill and it had been divided along its walls into nooks and partitions to make it feel less barnlike. Lights were scattered about like distant friends reaching out through the gloom, and the patrons were gathered in knots at the serving bar and about long tables and benches. Heads turned at their entrance as they had turned at the other ale houses, and eyes watched. Quickening moved to find the keeper, who listened and pointed to the back of the room. There was a man sitting at a table there, alone in a shadowed nook, hunched over and faceless, pushed away from the light and the crowd.

The four walked over to stand before him.

"Horner Dees," Quickening said in that silken voice.

Massive hands brought an ale mug slowly away from a bearded mouth and back to the tabletop, and a large, shaggy head lifted. The man was huge, a great old bear of a fellow with the better part of his years behind him. There was hair all over him, on his forearms and the backs of his hands, at his throat and on his chest, and on his head and face, grown over him so completely that except for his eyes and nose his features were obscured almost entirely. It was impossible to guess how old he was, but the hair was silver gray, the skin beneath it wrinkled and browned and mottled, and the fingers gnarled like old roots.

"I might be," he rumbled truculently from out of some giant's cave. His eyes were riveted on the girl.

"My name is Quickening," she said. "These are my companions. We search for a place called Eldwist and a man named Uhl Belk. We are told you know of both."

"You were told wrong."

"Can you take us there?" she asked, ignoring his response.

"I just said . . ."

"Can you take us there?" she repeated.

The big man stared at her without speaking, without moving, with no hint of what he was thinking. He was like a huge, settled rock that had survived ages of weathering and erosion and found them to be little more than a passing breeze. "Who are you?" he asked finally. "Who, other than your name?"

Quickening did not hesitate. "I am the daughter of the King of the Silver River. Do you know of him, Horner Dees?"

The other nodded slowly. "Yes, I know him. And maybe you are who you say. And maybe I am who you think. Maybe I even know about Eldwist and Uhl Belk. Maybe I'm the only one who knows—the only one who's still alive to tell about it. Maybe I can even do what you ask and take you there. But I don't see the point. Sit."

He gestured at a scattering of empty chairs, and the four seated themselves across the table from him. He looked at the men in turn, then his eyes returned to the girl. "You don't look as if you're someone who doesn't know what they're doing. Why would you want to find Uhl Belk?"

Quickening's black eyes were fathomless, intense. "Uhl Belk stole something that doesn't belong to him. It must be returned."

Horner Dees snorted derisively. "You plan to steal it back, do you? Or just ask him to return it? Do you know anything about Belk? I do."

"He stole a talisman from the Druids."

Dees hesitated. His bearded face twitched as he chewed on something imaginary. "Girl, nobody who goes into Eldwist ever comes out again. Nobody except me, and I was just plain lucky. There's things there that nothing can stand against. Belk, he's an old thing, come out of some other age, full of dark magic and evil. You won't ever take anything away from him, and he won't ever give anything back."

"Those who are with me are stronger than Uhl Belk," Quickening said. "They have magic as well, and theirs will overcome his. My father says it will be so. These three," and she named them each in turn, "will prevail."

As she spoke their names, Horner Dees let his eyes shift to identify each, passing over their faces quickly, pausing only once—so briefly that Walker wasn't sure at first that there had been a pause at all—on Pe Ell.

Then he said, "These are men. Uhl Belk is something more. You can't kill him like an ordinary man. You probably can't even find him. He'll find you and by then it will be too late." He snapped his fingers and sat back.

Quickening eyed him momentarily across the table, then reached out impulsively and touched the table's wooden surface. Instantly a splinter curled up, a slender stem forming, leafing out and finally flowering with tiny bluebells. Quickening's smile was as magical as her touch. "Show us the way into Eldwist, Horner Dees," she said.

The old man wet his lips. "It will take more than flowers to do in Belk," he said.

"Perhaps not," she whispered, and Walker had the feeling that for a moment she had gone somewhere else entirely. "Wouldn't you like to come with us and see?"

Dees shook his head. "I didn't get old being stupid," he said. He thought a moment, then sat forward again. "It was ten years ago when I went into Eldwist. I'd found it some time before that, but I knew it was dangerous and I wasn't about to go in there alone. I kept thinking about it though, wondering what was in there, because finding out about things is what I do. I've been a Tracker, a soldier, a hunter, everything there is to be, and it all comes down to finding out what's what. So I kept wondering about Eldwist, about what was in there, all those old buildings, all that stone, everywhere you looked. I went back finally because I couldn't stand not knowing anymore. I took a dozen men with me, lucky thirteen of us. We thought we'd find something of value in there, a place as secret and old as that. We knew what it was called; there's been legends about it for years in the high country, over on the other side of the mountains where some of us had been. The Trolls know it. It's a peninsula—just a narrow strip of land, all rock, jutting out into the middle of the Tiderace. We went out there one morning, the thirteen of us. Full of life. By dawn of the next day, the other twelve were dead, and I was running like a scared deer!"

He hunched his shoulders. "You don't want to go there," he said. "You don't want anything to do with Eldwist and Uhl Belk."

He picked up his mug, drained it, and slammed it down purposefully. The sound brought the keeper immediately, a fresh drink in hand, and away again just as quickly. Dees never looked at him, his eyes still fixed on Quickening. The evening was wearing on toward midnight by now, but few among the alehouse customers had drifted away. They clustered as they had since sunset, since long before in some cases, their talk more liquid and disjointed than earlier and their posture more relaxed. Time had lost its hold on them momentarily, victims of all forms of strife and misadventure, refugees huddled within the shelter of their intoxication and their loose companionship. Dees was not one of them; Walker Boh doubted that he ever would be.

Quickening stirred. "Horner Dees," she said, saying his name as if she were examining it, a young girl trying on an old man's identity. "If you do nothing, Uhl Belk will come for you."

For the first time, Dees looked startled.

"In time, he will come," Quickening continued, her voice both gentle and sad. "He advances his kingdom beyond what it was and it grows more swiftly with the passing of time. If he is not stopped, if his power is not lessened, sooner or later he will reach you."

"I'll be long dead," the old man said, but he didn't sound sure.

Quickening smiled, magical once again, something perfect and wondrous. "There are mysteries that you will never solve because you will not have the chance," she said. "That is not the case with Uhl Belk. You are a man who has spent his life finding out about things. Would you stop doing so now? How will you know which of us is right about Uhl Belk if you do not come with us? Do so, Horner Dees. Show us the way into Eldwist. Make this journey."

Dees was silent for a long time, thinking it through. Then he said, "I would like to believe that monster could be undone by something . . ." He shook his head. "I don't know."

"Do you need to?" the girl asked softly.

Dees frowned, then smiled, a great, gap-toothed grin that wreathed his broad face in weathered lines. "Never have," he said and laughed. The grin disappeared. "This is a hard walk we're talking about, not some stroll across the street. The passes are tough going any time of the year and once we're over and beyond, we'll be on our own. No help over there. Nothing but Trolls, and they don't care spit about outsiders. Nothing to help us but us. Truth is, none of you look strong enough to make it."

"We might be stronger than you think," Morgan Leah said quietly.

Dees eyed him critically. "You'll have to be," he said. "A lot stronger." Then he sighed. "Well, well. Come to this, has it? Me, an old man, about to go out into the far reaches one more time." He chuckled softly and looked back at Quickening. "You have a way about you, I'll say that. Talk a nut right out of its shell. Even a hard old nut like me. Well, well."

He shoved his chair back from the table and came to his feet. He was even bigger standing than he had been sitting, like some pitted wall that refused to fall down even after years of enduring adverse weather. He stood before them, hunched over and hoary looking, his big arms hanging loose, and his eyes squinting as if he had just come into the light.

"All right, I'll take you," he announced, leaning forward to emphasize his decision, keeping his voice low and even. "I'll take you because it's true that I haven't seen everything or found all the answers and what's life for if not to keep trying—even when I don't believe that trying will be enough.

You meet me back here at sunrise, and I'll give you a list of what you need and where to find it. You do the gathering, I'll do the organizing. We'll give it a try. Who knows? Maybe some of us will even make it back."

He paused and looked at them as if seeing them for the first time. There was a hint of laughter around the edges of his voice as he said, "Won't it be a good joke on Belk if you really do have the stronger magic?"

Then he eased his way out from behind the table, shambled across the room and out the door, and disappeared into the night.

Horner Dees was as good as his word, meeting them early the next morning to direct preparations for the journey that would take them across the Charnals and into Eldwist. He met them at the door of the rooming house on which they had finally settled for their night's lodgings, a creaky two-storied rambler that in former times had been first a residence then later a store, and without bothering to explain how he had found them provided a list of supplies they would need and directions on where to obtain them. He was even more rumpled and bearish seeming than he had been the previous night, wider than the door he stood before and hunched over like some sodden jungle shrub. He muttered and grumbled, and his instructions were delivered as if he were suffering from too much drink. Pe Ell thought him a worthless sot, and Morgan Leah found him just plain unpleasant. Because they could see that Quickening expected it, they accepted their instructions wordlessly. A little of Horner Dees went a long way. But Walker Boh saw something different. To begin with, he had worried enough the previous night about Dees to take Quickening aside after the old man's departure and suggest to her that maybe this wasn't the man they were looking for. After all, what did they know about Dees beyond what he had told them? Even if he actually had gone into Eldwist, that was ten years ago. What if he had since forgotten the way? What if he remembered just enough to get them hopelessly lost? But Quickening had assured him in that way she had of dispelling all doubt that Horner Dees was the man they needed. Now, as he listened to the old Tracker, he was inclined to agree. Walker had made a good many journeys in his time and he understood the kinds of preparations that were required. It was clear that Dees understood as well. For all of his gruff talk and his grizzled look, Horner Dees knew what he was doing.

The preparation time passed quickly. Walker, Morgan, and Pe Ell gathered together the foodstuffs, bedding, canvases, ropes, climbing tools, cooking implements, clothing, and survival gear that Dees had sent them to find. Dees himself arranged for pack animals, shaggy mules that could carry the heavy loads they would need and weather the mountain storms. They brought everything to an old stable situated at the north end of Rampling Steep, a building that seemed to serve Dees as both workshop and home. He lived in the tack room and when he wasn't issuing orders or checking on their efforts to carry them out he kept himself there.

Quickening was even more reclusive. When she wasn't with them, which was most of the time, they had no idea where she was. She seemed to drift in the manner of an errant cloud, more shadow than substance. She might have walked the woodlands away from the town, for she would have been more comfortable there. She might have simply hidden away. Wherever she went, she disappeared with the completeness of the sun at day's end, and they missed her as much. Only when she returned did they feel warmed again. She spoke to them each day, always singly, never together. She gave them a measure of herself, some small reassurance that they could not quite define but not mistake either. Had she been someone else, they would have suspected her of game playing. But she was Quickening, the daughter of the King of the Silver River, and there was no time or wish or even need for games in her life. She transcended such behavior, and while they did not fully understand her and sensed that perhaps they never would, they were convinced that deception and betrayal were beyond her. Her presence alone kept them together, bound them to her so that they would not turn away. She was incandescent, a creature of overpowering brilliance, so magical that they were as captivated by her as they would have been by a rainbow's arc. She caused them to look for her everywhere. They watched for her to appear and when she did found themselves beguiled anew. They waited for her to speak to them, to touch them, for even the briefest look. She spun them in the vortex of her being, and even as they found themselves spellbound they yearned for it to go on. They watched each other like hawks, uncertain of their roles in her plans, of their uses, and of their needs. They fought to learn something of her that would belong only to them and they measured the time they spent with her as if it were gold dust.

Yet they were not entirely without doubts or misgivings. In the secrecy of their most private thoughts they still worried—about her wisdom in selecting them, about her foresight in the quest they had agreed to undertake, and about whether wanting to be near her was sufficient reason for them to go on.

Pe Ell's ruminations were the most intense. He had come on this journey in the first place because the girl intrigued him, because she was different from the others he had been sent to kill, because he wanted to learn as much about her as he could before he used the Stiehl, and because he wanted to discover, too, if this talisman of which she spoke, this Black Elfstone, was as powerful as she believed and if so whether he could make it his own. It had annoyed him when she had insisted on bringing along the brash Highlander and the tall, pale one-armed man. He would have preferred that they go alone, because in truth he believed that he was all she would need. Yet he had held his tongue and remained patient, convinced that the other two would cause him no problem.

But now there was Horner Dees to contend with as well, and there was something about this old man that bothered Pe Ell. It was odd that Dees should trouble him like this; he seemed a worthless old coot. The source of his discomfort, he supposed, was the fact that he was beginning to feel crowded. How many more did the girl intend to add to their little company? Soon, he would be stumbling over cripples and misfits at every turn, none of them worth even the small effort it would eventually require to eliminate them. Pe Ell was a loner; he did not like groups. Yet the girl persisted in swelling their number and all for a rather vague purpose. Her magic seemed almost limitless; she could do things no one else could, not even him. He was convinced that despite her protestations to the contrary her magic was sufficient to guide them into Eldwist. Once there, she had no need of anyone but him. What was the purpose then of including the others?

Two nights earlier, just before the rains had ended, Pe Ell had confronted her out of frustration and discontent, intending to force from her the truth of the matter. Quickening had turned him aside somehow, calmed him, stripping him of his determination to unmask her. The experience had left him perplexed at the ease with which she had manipulated him, and for a time afterward he had thought simply to kill her and be done with it. He had discovered her purpose, hadn't he? Why not do as Rimmer Dall had advised and be finished with this business, forget the Black Elfstone, and leave these fools to chase after it without him? He had decided to wait. Now he was glad he had. For as he considered the irritating presence of Dees and the others, he began to think that he understood their purpose. Quickening had brought them to serve as a diversion, nothing more. After all, what other service could they provide? One's strength was contained in a broken sword, the other's in a broken body. What were such paltry magics compared to that of the Stiehl? Wasn't he the assassin, the master killer, the one whose magic could bring down anything? That was most certainly why she had brought him. She had never said as much, but he knew it was so. Rimmer Dall had been wrong to think she would not recognize what he was. Quickening, with her formidable insight and intuition, would not have missed such an obvious truth. Which was why she had brought him, of course—why she had come to him before any of the others. She needed him to kill Belk; he was the only one who could. She needed the magic of the Stiehl. The others, Dees included, were so much kindling to be thrown into the fire. In the end, she would have to depend on him.

Morgan Leah, if Pe Ell had bothered to ask him, might have agreed. He was the youngest and despite his brash attitude the most insecure. He was still closer to being a boy than a grown man, a fact he was forced to admit to himself if to no one else. He had traveled fewer places and done fewer things. He knew less about practically everything. Almost the whole of his life had been spent in the Highlands of Leah, and although he had found ways to make occupation of his homeland unpleasant for the Federation officials who sought to govern, he had done little else of note. He was hopelessly in love with Quickening and he had nothing to offer her. The Sword of Leah was the weapon she needed in her quest for the Black Elfstone, the talisman whose magic could defeat Uhl Belk. Yet the Sword had lost the better part of its magic when it had shattered against the rune-marked doors leading from the Pit, and what remained was insufficient and, worse, unpredictable. Without it, he did not see how he would be of much use in this business. Perhaps Quickening was right when she said he might regain the Sword's magic if he went with her. But what would happen if she were threatened before then? Who among them would protect her? He had only a shattered Sword. Walker Boh, without his arm, seemed less formidable than he had before, a man in search of himself. Horner Dees was old and gray. Only Pe Ell, with his still secret magic and enigmatic ways, seemed capable of defending the daughter of the King of the Silver River.

Nevertheless Morgan was determined to continue the quest. He was not entirely certain why. Perhaps it was pride, perhaps a stubborn refusal to give up on himself. Whatever it was, it kept alive a dim hope that somehow he would prove useful to this strange and wondrous girl he had fallen in love with, that he would somehow be able to protect her against whatever threatened, and that with time and patience he would discover a way to restore the magic to the Sword of Leah. He worked diligently at the tasks Horner Dees gave him to aid in outfitting the little company for its journey north, trying a little harder most times than the others. He thought of Quickening constantly, playing with images of her in his mind. She was a gift, he knew. She was the possibility of everything he had always hoped might one day be. It was more than the fact that she was beautiful, or the look or feel or way of her, or that she had rescued him from the Federation prisons or restored the Meade Gardens to the Dwarves of Culhaven. It was what he sensed lay between them, an intangible bond different than that linking her to the others. It was there when she spoke to him, when she called him by his first name as she did not do with the others. It was there in the way she looked at him. It was something incredibly precious.

He made up his mind that he would not let it go, whatever it was, whatever it might turn out to be. It became, to his surprise and even his joy, the most important thing in his life.

Walker Boh had hold of something as well, but it was not as easily identifiable. As with Morgan's determination to love and Pe Ell's to kill, there was a bond that linked him to Quickening. There was that strange kinship between them, that sharing of magics that gave them insights into each other no one else possessed. Like the Highlander and the assassin, he believed his relationship with her different than that of the others, more personal and important, more lasting. He did not feel love for her as Morgan did and he had no wish to possess her like Pe Ell. What he needed was to understand her magic because in doing so he was convinced he would come to understand his own.

The dilemma lay in determining whether or not this was a good idea. It was not enough that his need was compelling; the deaths of Cogline and Rumor had made it that. He knew that he needed to understand the magic if he were to destroy the Shadowen. But he was frightened still of the consequences of such knowledge. With the magic, there was always a price. He had been intrigued with it since he had discovered he possessed it—and frightened of it as well. Fear and curiosity had pulled him in two directions all his life. It had been so when his father had told him of his legacy, when he had struggled unsuccessfully to make his home with the people of Shady Vale, when Cogline had come to him and offered to teach him how the magic worked, and when he had learned of the existence of the Black Elfstone from the pages of the Druid History and known that the charge given him by the shade of Allanon might be fulfilled. It was always the same. It was so now.

He had worried for a time that he had lost the magic entirely, that it had been destroyed by the poison of the Asphinx. But with the healing of his arm, his sense of himself had returned and with it an awareness that the magic had survived. He had tested it on this journey in little ways. He knew it was there, for example, when something within him reacted to Quickening's presence, to the way she used her own magic to bind Morgan and Pe Ell and himself to her, and to the effect she had on others. It was there, too, in the way he sensed things. He had caught the hesitation in the look Horner Dees gave Pe Ell—just a hint of recognition. He could feel the interaction between the members of the company and Quickening, a sense of the feelings that lay just beneath the surface of the looks and words they exchanged. He had insight, intuition, and foreknowledge in some cases. There was no doubt. The magic was still there.

Yet it was weakened and no longer the formidable weapon it had once been. That gave Walker pause. Here was an opportunity to move away from its influence, from the shadow it cast upon his life, from the legacy of Brin Ohmsford and the Druids, and from everything that had made him the Dark Uncle. If he did not probe, there would be no hurt. The magic would lie dormant, he believed, if it were not stirred. If left alone, it might let him break free.

But without it the Shadowen would be left free as well. And what purpose would it serve to make this journey into Eldwist and confront Uhl Belk if he did not intend to employ the magic? What use would he ever make of the Black Elfstone?

So they prowled within cages of their own making, Walker Boh and Morgan Leah and Pe Ell, suspicious cats with sharp eyes and hungry looks, their minds made up as to what they would do in the days that lay ahead and at the same time still quizzing themselves to make certain. They kept each other's company without ever getting close. Supplies were gathered and packs assembled, and the time passed quickly. Horner Dees seemed satisfied, but he was the only one. The other three chafed against the constraints of their uncertainty, impatience, and doubt despite their resolve to do otherwise, and nothing they could do or think would relieve them. There was a darkness that lay ahead, building upon itself like a stormcloud, and they could not see what waited beyond. They could see it rising up before them like a wall, a coming together of event and circumstance, an explosion of magic and raw strength, a revelation of need and purpose. Black and impenetrable, it would seek to devour them.

When it did, they sensed, not everyone would survive.

Three days later they departed Rampling Steep. They went out at sunrise, the skies thick with clouds that scraped against the mountains and shut away the light. The smell of rain was in the air, and the wind was sharp and chill as it swept down off the peaks. The town slept as they climbed away from it, hunkered down against the dark like a frightened animal, closed and still. A few forgotten oil lamps burned on porches and through the cracks of windows, but the people did not stir. As Walker Boh passed into the rocks he looked back momentarily at the cluster of colorless buildings and was reminded of locust shells, hollow and abandoned and fascinatingly ugly.

The rain began at midday and continued for a week without stopping. At times it slowed to a drizzle but never quit completely. The clouds remained locked in place overhead, thunder rumbled all about, and lightning flashed in the distance. They were cold and wet, and there was nothing they could do to relieve their discomfort. The foothills were forested lower down, but bare at the higher elevations. The wind swept over them unhindered and without the sun's warmth remained frost-edged and chill. Horner Dees set a steady pace, but the company could not travel rapidly while afoot and with mules in tow, and progress was slow. At night they slept beneath canvas shelters that kept the rain off and were able to strip away their wet clothing and wrap themselves in blankets. But there was no wood for a fire and the dampness persisted. They woke cramped and cold each morning, ate because it was necessary, and pressed ahead.

The foothills gave way to mountains after several days, and the path became less certain. The trail they had been following, broad and clear before, disappeared completely. Dees took them into a maze of ridges and defiles, along the rims of broad slides, and around massive boulders that would have dwarfed the buildings of Rampling Steep. The slope steepened dangerously, and they were forced to watch their footing at every turn. The clouds swept downward, filling the air with clinging moisture that sought to envelop them, that twisted about the rocks like some huge, substanceless worm, its skin a damp ooze. Thunder crashed, and it seemed as if they were at its center. Rain descended in torrents. They lost sight of everything that lay behind, and they could not discern what waited ahead.

Without Dees to guide them, they would have been lost. The Charnals swallowed them as an ocean would a stone. Everything looked the same. Cliffs were impassable walls through the mist and rain, canyons dropped into vast chasms of black emptiness, and the mountains spread away in a seemingly endless huddle of snowcapped peaks. It was so cold their skin grew numb. At times the rain turned to sleet and even to snow. They wrapped themselves in great cloaks and heavy boots and trudged on. Through it all Horner Dees remained steady and certain, a great shaggy presence they quickly learned to rely upon. He was at home in the mountains, comfortable despite the forbidding climate and terrain, at peace with himself. He hummed as he went, lost in private reveries of other times and places. He paused now and then to point something out that they would not have otherwise seen, determined that nothing should be missed. That he understood the Charnals was clear from the beginning; that he loved them soon became apparent. He spoke freely of that love, of the mix of wildness and serenity he found there, and of their vastness and permanency. His deep voice rumbled and shook as if filled with the tremors of the storms and the wind. He told stories of what life was like in the Charnals and he gave them a part of himself in the telling.

He gained no converts, however—except, perhaps, for Quickening, who as usual gave no indication of what she was thinking. The other three simply grumbled now and again, kept a studied silence the rest of the time, and fought a hopeless battle to ignore their discomfort. The mountains would never be their home; the mountains were simply a barrier they needed to get past. They labored stoically and waited for the journey to come to an end.

It did not do so. Instead it went on rather as if it were a lost dog searching for its master, the scent firmly in mind, yet distracted by other smells. The rains diminished and finally passed, but the air stayed frosty, the wind continued to buffet them, and the mountains stretched on. The men, the girl, and the animals trudged forward, shoved and pushed by the weather and the land. Midway through the second week Dees said they were starting down, but there was no way of knowing if that were true; nothing in the rocks and scrub about them indicated it was so. Wherever they looked, the Charnals were still there.

Twelve days out they were caught in a snowstorm high in a mountain pass and nearly died. The storm came on them so quickly that even Dees was caught by surprise. He quickly roped them together and because there was no shelter to be found in the pass he was forced to take them through. The air became a sheet of impenetrable white and everything about them disappeared. Their feet and hands began to freeze. The mules broke away in terror when part of the slope slid away, braying and stumbling past the frantic men until they tumbled over the mountainside and were lost. Only one was saved, and it carried no food.

They found shelter, survived the storm, and pushed on. Even Dees, who had shown himself to be the most durable among them, was beginning to tire. The remaining mule had to be destroyed the next day when it stepped in a snow-covered crevice and broke its leg. The heavy weather gear had been lost, and they were reduced to backpacks which contained a meager portion of food and water, some rope, and not much else.

That night the temperature plummeted. They would have frozen if Dees had not managed to find wood for a fire. They sat huddled together all night, pushed close to the flames, rubbing their hands and feet, talking to stay awake, afraid if they didn't they would die in their sleep. It was an odd tableau, the five of them settled back within the rocks, crouched close together about the tiny blaze, still wary of one another, protective of themselves, and forced to share space and time and circumstance. Yet the words they spoke revealed them, not so much for what was said as for how and when and why. It drew them together in a strange sort of way, bonding them as not much else could, and while the closeness that developed was more physical than emotional and decidedly limited in any case, it at least left them with a sense of fellowship that had been missing before.

The weather improved after that, the clouds breaking up and drifting on, the sun returning to warm the air, and the snow and rain disappearing at last. The Charnals began to thin ahead of them, and there was no mistaking the fact that they had begun their descent. Trees returned, a scattering at first, then whole groves, and finally forests for as far as the eye could see, spilling down into distant valleys. They were able to fish and hunt game for food, to sleep in warm arbors, and to wake dry and rested. Spirits improved.

Then, fifteen days out of Rampling Steep, they arrived at the Spikes.

They stood for a long time on a ridgeline and looked down onto the valley. It was nearing midday, the sun bright, the air warm and sweet smelling. The valley was broad and deep and shadowed by mountains that rose about it on either side. It was shaped like a funnel, wide mouth at the south end and narrow at the north where it disappeared into a line of distant hills. Trees grew thick upon its floor, but down its middle a jagged ridgeline rose, and the trees there had suffered a blight that had left them stripped of their foliage, bare trunks and branches jutting upward like the hackles on the back of a cornered animal.

Like spikes, Morgan Leah thought.

He glanced at Horner Dees. "What's down there?" he asked. His attitude toward the old Tracker had changed during the past two weeks. He no longer thought of him as an unpleasant old man. It had taken him longer than Walker Boh, but he had come to recognize that Dees was a thorough professional, better at what he did than anyone the Highlander had ever encountered. Morgan would have liked to be just half as good. He had begun paying attention to what the old man said and did.

Dees shrugged. "I don't know. It's been ten years since I passed this way." Dees, for his part, liked Morgan's enthusiasm and willingness to work.

He liked the fact that Morgan wasn't afraid to learn. He narrowed his brows thoughtfully as he returned the other's glance. "I'm just being careful, Highlander."

They studied the valley some more.

"Something is down there," Pe Ell said quietly.

No one disputed him. Pe Ell had remained the most secretive among them, yet they knew enough of him by now to trust his instincts.

"We have to pass this way," Dees said finally, "or skirt the mountains on one side or the other. If we do that, we'll lose a week's time."

They continued their vigil for long moments without speaking, thinking the matter through separately, until finally Horner Dees said, "Let's get on with it."

They worked their way downward, discovering a pathway that led directly toward the center of the valley and the barren ridge. They moved quietly, Dees leading, Quickening behind him, Morgan, Walker, and Pe Ell bringing up the rear. They passed out of sunlight into shadow, and the air turned cool. The valley rose up to meet them and for a time swallowed them up. Then the trail lifted onto the ridgeline, and they found themselves in the midst of the blighted trees. Morgan studied the lifeless skeletons for a time, the blackening of the bark, the wilting of leaves and buds where there were any to be seen at all, and turned instinctively to look at Walker. The Dark Uncle's pale, drawn face lifted, and the hard eyes stared back at him. They were both thinking the same thing. The Spikes had been sickened in the same way as the rest of the land. The Shadowen were at work here, too.

They crossed a band of sunlight that had slipped through a break in the peaks and then dipped downward into a hollow. It was abnormally still there, a pool of silence that magnified the sound of their footsteps as they worked their way ahead. Morgan had grown increasingly edgy, reminded of his encounter with the Shadowen on the journey to Culhaven with the Ohmsfords. His nose tested the air for the rank smell that would warn of the other's presence, and his ears strained to catch even the smallest sound. Dees moved ahead purposefully, Quickening's long hair a slender bit of silver trailing after. Neither exhibited any sign of hesitation. Yet there was tension in all of them; Morgan could feel it.

They passed out of the hollow and back onto the open ridge. For a time they were high enough above the trees that Morgan could see the valley from end to end. They were more than halfway through now, approaching the narrow end of the funnel where the mountains split apart and the trees thinned with the beginning of the hills beyond. Morgan's edginess began to dissipate and he found himself thinking of home, of the Highlands of Leah, and of the countryside he had grown up in. He missed the Highlands, he realized—much more than he would have expected. It was one thing to say that his home no longer belonged to him because the Federation occupied it; it was another to make himself believe it. Like Par Ohmsford, he lived with the hope that things might one day change.

The trail dipped downward again and another hollow appeared, this

one shaggy with brush and scrub that had filled the gaps left with the passing of the trees. They moved into it, shoving their way past brambles and
stickers, angling for the open spaces where the trail wound ahead. Shadows
lay thick across the hollow as the light began to creep westward. The forests
about them formed a wall of dark silence.

They had just entered a clearing at the center of the hollow when
Quickening suddenly slowed. "Stand still," she said.

They did so instantly, looking first at her, then at the brush all about
them. Something was moving. Figures began to detach themselves, breaking their concealment, moving into the light. There were hundreds of
them—small, squat creatures with hairy, gnarled limbs and bony features.
They looked as if they had grown out of the scrub, so like it were they, and
it was only the short pants and weapons that seemed to separate the two.
The weapons were formidable—short spears and strangely shaped throwing
implements with razor edges. The creatures held them threateningly as they
advanced.

"Urdas," Horner Dees said quietly. "Don't move."

No one did, not even Pe Ell who was crouched in much the same way
as the creatures who menaced him.

"Who are they?" Morgan asked of Dees, at the same time backing protectively toward Quickening.

"Gnomes," the other said. "With a little Troll thrown in. No one has
ever been sure of the exact mix. You don't find them anywhere south of
the Charnals. They're Northlanders as much as the Trolls. Tribal like the
Gnomes. Very dangerous."

The Urdas were all about them now, closing off any chance of escape.
They had thickly muscled bodies with short, powerful legs and long arms,
and their faces were blunt and expressionless. Morgan tried to read something of what they might be thinking in their yellow eyes, but failed.

Then he noticed that they were all looking at Quickening.

"What do we do?" he asked Dees in an anxious whisper, worried now.
Dees shook his head.

The Urdas moved to within a dozen feet of the company and stopped.
They did not threaten; they did not speak. They simply stood there, watching Quickening for the most part, but waiting as well.

Waiting for what? Morgan asked himself silently.

And at almost the same moment the brush parted, and a golden-haired
man stepped into view. Instantly the Urdas dropped to one knee, heads
bowed in recognition. The golden-haired man looked at the five beleaguered members of the surrounded company and smiled.

"The King has come," he said brightly. "Long live the King."

14

W ould you lay down your weapons, please?" the man called out to them cheerfully. "Just put them on the ground in front of you. Don't worry. You can pick them up again in a moment."
He sang:

> *"Nothing given freely is ever given up.*
> *It will be given back to you*
> *Through others' love and trust."*

The five from Rampling Steep stared at him.

"Please?" he said. "It will make things so much easier if you do."

Dees glanced at the others, shrugged, and did as he was asked. Neither Walker nor Quickening carried any weapons. Morgan hesitated. Pe Ell didn't move at all.

"This is only for the purpose of demonstrating your friendship," the man went on encouragingly. "If you don't lay down your weapons, my subjects won't allow me to approach. I'll have to keep shouting at you from over here."

He sang:

> *"High, low, wherever we may go,*
> *I'll have to keep on shouting out to you."*

Morgan, after a sharp glance from Dees, complied. It was hard to tell what Pe Ell might have done if Quickening hadn't turned to him and whispered, "Do as he says." Pe Ell hesitated even then before unstrapping his broadsword. The look on his hard face was unmistakable. The broadsword notwithstanding, Morgan was willing to bet that Pe Ell still had a weapon concealed on him somewhere.

"Much better," the stranger announced. "Now step back a pace. There!" He beckoned, and the Urdas came quickly to their feet. He was a man of average height and build, his movements quick and energetic, and his clean-shaven face handsome beneath his long blond hair. His blue eyes twinkled. He gestured at the Urdas and then at the weapons on the ground. The odd-looking creatures muttered agreeably and heads began to nod. He sang again, a short piece that the Urdas seemed to recognize, his voice full and rich, his handsome face beaming. When he finished, the circle parted to let him pass. He came directly up to Quickening, bowed low before her, took her hand in his own and kissed it. "My lady," he said.

He sang:

> *"Five travelers crossed field and stream*
> *And Eastland forests wide.*
> *They crossed the Charnal Mountain range*
> *To gain the Northland side.*
> *Tra-la-la-diddie-oh-day.*
>
> *Five travelers came from afar*
> *And entered Urda Land.*
> *They braved the dangers of the Spikes*
> *To meet King Carisman.*
> *Tra-la-la-diddie-oh-day."*

He bowed to Quickening again. "That is my name, Lady. Carisman. And yours?"

Quickening gave it to him and those of her companions as well. She seemed unconcerned that he knew. "Are you indeed a king?" she asked.

Carisman beamed. "Oh, yes, Lady. I am king of the Urdas, lord of all those you now survey and many, many more. To be honest, I did not seek out the job. It was thrust upon me, as they say. But come now. Time enough to tell that tale later. Pick up your weapons—carefully, of course. We mustn't alarm my subjects; they are very protective of me. I shall take you to my palace and we shall talk and drink wine and eat exotic fruits and fishes. Come now, come. It shall be a royal feast!"

Dees tried to say something, but Carisman was gone as swiftly as a feather caught by the wind, dancing away, singing some new song, and beckoning them to follow. The Tracker, Morgan, and Pe Ell retrieved their weapons and with Walker and Quickening in tow, started after. Urdas surrounded them on all sides, not pressing in on them, but staying uncomfortably close nevertheless. The odd creatures did not speak, but merely gestured to one another, their eyes shifting from Carisman to the travelers, inquisitive and cautious. Morgan returned the gaze of those closest and tried a smile. They did not smile back.

The gathering went down off the Spikes into the forested valley below, west of the ridgeline where the shadows were deepest. There was a narrow trail that wound through the trees, and the procession followed it dutifully, Carisman in the lead, singing as he went. Morgan had encountered some odd characters in his time, but Carisman struck him as odder than most. He could not help wondering why anyone, even the Urdas, would make this fellow their king.

Dees had dropped back a pace to walk with him, and he asked the old Tracker. "As I said, a tribal folk. Superstitious, like most Gnomes. Believe in spirits and wraiths and other nonsense."

"But Carisman?" Morgan questioned.

Dees shook his head. "I admit I can't figure it. Urdas usually don't want anything to do with outlanders. This one seems goofy as a week-old loon, but he's obviously found some way of gaining their respect. I never heard of him before this. Don't think anyone has."

Morgan peered over the heads of the Urdas at the prancing Carisman. "He seems harmless enough."

Dees snorted. "He probably is. Anyway, it isn't him you have to worry about."

They worked their way west toward the wall of the mountains, daylight fading rapidly now, dusk spreading until the whole of the forestland was enveloped. Morgan and Dees continued to exchange comments, but the other three kept their thoughts to themselves. Walker and Pe Ell were gaunt shadows, Quickening a burst of sunlight. The Urdas filtered out about them, appearing and disappearing in the heavy brush, strung out ahead, behind, and to either side. Carisman's words had suggested that they were guests, but Morgan couldn't shake the feeling that they were really prisoners.

After a little more than a mile, the trail ended at a clearing in which the village of the Urdas was settled. A stockade had been built to protect the village from raiders, and its gates opened now to let the hunters and those they shepherded pass through. A sea of women, children, and old people waited within, bonyfaced and staring, their voices a low, inaudible buzz. The village consisted of a cluster of small huts and open-sided shelters surrounding a lodge constructed of notched logs and a shingled roof. Trees grew inside the stockade, shading the village and providing supports for treeways and lifts. There were wells scattered about and smokehouses for curing meat. The Urdas, it appeared, had at least rudimentary skills.

The five from Rampling Steep were taken to the main lodge and led to a platform on which a rough-hewn chair draped with a garland of fresh flowers was situated. Carisman seated himself ceremoniously and beckoned his guests to take their places next to him on mats. Morgan and the others did as they were asked, keeping a wary eye on the Urdas, a large number of whom entered as well and took seats on the floor below the platform. When everyone was settled, Carisman came to his feet and sang some more, this time in a tongue that Morgan found impossible to identify. When he was finished, a handful of Urda women began to bring out platters of food.

Carisman sat down. "I have to sing to get them to do anything," he confided. "It is so tedious sometimes."

"What are you doing here anyway?" Horner Dees asked bluntly. "Where did you come from?"

"Ah," Carisman said with a sigh.

He sang:

> "There was a young tunesmith from Rampling,
> Who felt it was time to take wing.

> *He decided to hike,*
> *North into the Spikes,*
> *To the Urdas, who made him their king!"*

He grimaced. "Not very original, I'm afraid. Let me try again."
He sang:

> *"Come hither, my fellows, and lady, come nigh,*
> *There are worlds to discover more'n what meets the eye.*
> *Far reaches to travel and people to see,*
> *Wonders to gaze on and lives for to lead,*
> *A million adventures to try.*
>
> *Come hither, my fellows, and lady, come nigh,*
> *A tunesmith's a man who must sing for to fly.*
> *He searches the byways for songs telling truth,*
> *Seeks out hidden meanings and offers of proof,*
> *Of the reasons for being alive.*
>
> *Come hither, my fellows, and lady, come nigh,*
> *For life's to be found in the rivers and skies.*
> *In the forests and mountains that lie far away,*
> *In the creatures that frolic and gambol and play,*
> *And beg me my songs to apply."*

"Considerably better, don't you think?" he asked them, blue eyes dart-ing from one face to the next, anxiously seeking their approval.

"A tunesmith, are you?" Dees grunted. "From Rampling Steep?"

"Well, by way of Rampling Steep. I was there a day or so once several years back." Carisman looked sheepish. "The rhyme works, so I use it." He brightened. "But a tunesmith, yes. All my life. I have the gift of song and the wit to make use of it. I have talent."

"But why are you here, Carisman?" Quickening pressed.

Carisman seemed to melt. "Lady, chance has brought me to this place and time and even to you. I have traveled the better part of the Four Lands, searching out the songs that would give wings to my music. There is a rest-lessness in me that will not let me stay in any one place for very long. I have had my chances to do so, and even ladies who wished to keep me—though none was as beautiful as you. But I keep moving. I wandered first west, then east, and finally north. I passed through Rampling Steep and found myself wondering what lay beyond. Finally I set out across the mountains to see."

"And survived?" Horner Dees asked incredulously.

"Just barely. I have a sense of things; it comes from my music, I think. I was well provisioned, for I had traveled in rough country before. I found my way by listening to my heart. I had the good fortune of encountering favorable weather. When I was finally across—exhausted and close to starving, I admit—I was found by the Urdas. Not knowing what else to do, I sang for them. They were enchanted by my music and they made me their king."

"Enchanted by limericks and snippets of rhyme?" Dees refused to let go of his skepticism. "A bold claim, Carisman."

Carisman grinned boyishly. "Oh, I don't claim to be a better man than any other."

He sang:

> *"No matter how high or lofty the throne,*
> *What sits on it is the same as your own."*

He brushed the matter aside. "Eat now, you must be very hungry after your journey. There is as much food and drink as you want. And tell me what brings you here. No one from the Southland ever comes this far north—not even the trappers. I never see anyone except Trolls and Gnomes. What brings you?"

Quickening told him that they were on a quest, that they had come in search of a talisman. It was more than Morgan would have revealed, but it seemed to matter little to Carisman, who did not even bother asking what the talisman was or why they needed it but only wanted to know if Quickening could teach him any new songs. Carisman was quick and bright, yet his focus was quixotic and narrow. He was like a child, inquisitive and distracted and full of the wonder of things. He seemed to genuinely need approval. Quickening was the most responsive, so he concentrated his attention on her and included the others in his conversation mostly by implication. Morgan listened disinterestedly as he ate, then noticed that Walker wasn't listening at all, that he was studying the Urdas below the platform. Morgan began studying them as well. After a time he saw that they were seated in carefully defined groups, and that the foremost group consisted of a mixed gathering of old and young men to whom all the others deferred. Chiefs, thought Morgan at once. They were talking intently among themselves, glancing now and then at the six seated on the platform, but otherwise ignoring them. Something was being decided, without Carisman.

Morgan grew nervous.

The meal ended and the empty plates were carried away. There was a sustained clapping from the Urdas, and Carisman rose to his feet with a sigh. He sang once more, but this time the song was different. This time it was studied and intricate, a finely wrought piece of music filled with nuances and subtleties that transcended the tune. Carisman's voice filled the lodge, it soared and swept aside everything that separated it from the senses, reaching down through the body to embrace and cradle the heart. Morgan was astounded. He had never been so affected—not even by the music of the wishsong. Par Ohmsford could capture your feeling for and sense of history in his song, but Carisman could capture your soul.

When the tunesmith was finished, there was utter silence. Slowly he sat down again, momentarily lost in himself, still caught up in what he had sung. Then the Urdas began thumping their hands on their knees approvingly.

Quickening said, "That was beautiful, Carisman."

"Thank you, Lady," he replied, sheepish again. "I have a talent for more than limericks, you see."

The silver-haired girl looked suddenly at Walker. "Did you find it beautiful, Walker Boh?"

The pale face inclined in thought. "It makes me wonder why someone who possesses such abilities chooses to share them with so few." The dark eyes fixed Carisman.

The tunesmith squirmed uncomfortably. "Well." The words suddenly would not seem to come.

"Especially since you said yourself that there is a restlessness in you that will not allow you to stay in one place. Yet you stay here among the Urdas."

Carisman looked down at his hands.

"They will not let you leave, will they?" Walker said quietly.

Carisman looked as if he would sink into the earth. "No," he admitted reluctantly. "For all that I am, a king notwithstanding, I remain a captive. I am allowed to be king only so long as I sing my songs. The Urdas keep me because they believe my song is magic."

"And so it is," Quickening murmured so softly that only Morgan, seated next to her, heard.

"What about us?" Dees demanded sharply. He shifted his bulk menacingly. "Are we captives as well? Have you brought us here as guests or prisoners, King Carisman? Or do you even have a say in the matter?"

"Oh, no!" the tunesmith exclaimed, clearly distraught. "I mean, yes, I have a say in the matter. And, no, you are not prisoners. I need only speak with the council, those men gathered there below us." He pointed to the group that Walker and Morgan had been observing earlier. Then he hesitated as he caught the black look on Pe Ell's face and came hurriedly to his feet. "I shall speak to them at once. If need be, I shall sing. A special song. You shall not remain here any longer than you wish, I promise. Lady, believe me, please. Friends."

He rushed from the platform and knelt next to the members of the Urda council, addressing them earnestly. The five who waited to discover whether they were guests or prisoners looked at one another.

"I don't think he can do anything to help us," Horner Dees muttered.

Pe Ell edged forward. "If I put a knife to his throat they will release us quick enough."

"Or kill us on the spot," Dees replied with a hiss. The two glared at each other.

"Let him have his chance," Walker Boh said, looking calmly at the assemblage. His face was unreadable.

"Yes," Quickening agreed softly. "Patience."

They sat silently after that until Carisman returned, detaching himself from the council, stepping back onto the platform to face them. His face told them everything. "I . . . I have to ask you to stay the night," he said, struggling to get the words out, discomforted beyond measure. "The council wishes to . . . debate the matter a bit. Just a formality, you understand. I simply require a little time . . ."

He trailed off uncertainly. He had positioned himself as far as possible from Pe Ell. Morgan held his breath. He didn't think the distance separating the two offered the tunesmith much protection. He found himself wondering, almost in fascination, what Pe Ell would do, what he *could* in fact do against so many.

He would not find out on this occasion. Quickening smiled reassuringly at Carisman and said, "We will wait."

They were taken to one of the larger huts and given mats and blankets for sleeping. The door was closed behind them, but not locked. Morgan didn't think it mattered either way. The hut sat in the center of the village, and the village was enclosed by the stockade and filled with Urdas. He had taken the trouble of asking Dees about the strange creatures during dinner. Dees had told him that they were a tribe of hunters. The weapons they carried were designed to bring down even the swiftest game. Two-legged intruders, he said, would not prove much of a challenge.

Pe Ell stood looking out through chinks in the hut's mud walls. "They are not going to let us leave," he said. No one spoke. "It doesn't matter what that play-king says, they'll try to keep us. We had better get away tonight."

Dees sat back heavily against one wall. "You make it sound as if leaving were an option."

Pe Ell turned. "I can leave whenever I choose. No prison can hold me."

He said it so matter-of-factly that the others, save Quickening, just stared at him. Quickening was looking off into space. "There is magic in his song," she said.

Morgan remembered her saying something like that before. "Real magic?" he asked.

"Close enough to be called so. I do not understand its source; I am not even certain what it can do. But a form of magic nevertheless. He is more than an ordinary tunesmith."

"Yes," Pe Ell agreed. "He is a fool."

"We might think you one as well if you persist in suggesting we can get out of here without him," Horner Dees snapped.

Pe Ell wheeled on him. There was such rage in his face that Dees came to his feet much more quickly than Morgan would have thought possible. Walker Boh, a dark figure at the hut's far end, turned slowly. Pe Ell seemed to consider his options, then stalked to where Quickening stood looking at him from beside Morgan. It was all the Highlander could do to stand his ground. Pe Ell's black look dismissed him with barely a flicker of a glance and fell instead on the girl.

"What do we need any of them for?" he whispered, his voice a hiss of fury. "I came because you asked me to; I could easily have chosen otherwise."

"I know that," she said.

"You know what I am." He bent close, his gaunt face hawklike above her, his lean body taut. "You know I have the magic you need. I have all the magic you need. Be done with them. Let us go on alone."

Around him, the room seemed to have turned to stone, the others frozen into statues that could only observe and never act. Morgan Leah's hand moved a fraction of an inch toward his sword, then stopped. He would never be quick enough, he knew. Pe Ell would kill him before he could pull the blade clear.

Quickening seemed completely unafraid. "It is not yet time for you and I, Pe Ell," she whispered back, her voice soothing, cool. Her eyes searched his. "You must wait until it is."

Morgan did not understand what she was saying and he was reasonably certain that Pe Ell didn't either. The narrow face pinched and the hard eyes flickered. He seemed to be deciding something.

"My father alone has the gift of foresight," Quickening said softly. "He has foreseen that I shall have need of all of you when we find Uhl Belk. So it shall be—even though you might wish it otherwise, Pe Ell. Even though."

Pe Ell shook his head slowly. "No, girl. You are wrong. It shall be as I choose. Just as it always is." He studied her momentarily, then shrugged. "Nevertheless, what difference does it make? Another day, another week, it shall all come out the same in the end. Keep these others with you if you wish. At least for now."

He turned and moved away by himself, settling into a darkened corner.

The others stared after him in silence.

Night descended and the village of the Urdas grew quiet as its inhabitants drifted off to sleep. The five from Rampling Steep huddled within the darkened confines of their shelter, separated from each other by the privacy of their thoughts. Horner Dees slept. Walker Boh was a shapeless bundle in the shadows, unmoving. Morgan Leah sat next to Quickening, neither speaking, eyes closed against the faint light of moon and stars that penetrated from without.

Pe Ell watched them all and raged silently against circumstance and his own stupidity.

What was *wrong* with him? he wondered bleakly. Losing his temper like that, exposing himself, nearly ruining his chance of accomplishing what he had set out to do. He was always in control. *Always!* But not this time, not when he was giving way to frustration and impatience, threatening the girl and all of her precious charges as if he were some schoolboy bully.

He was calm now, able to analyze what he had done, to sift through his emotions and sort out his mistakes. There were many of both. And it was the girl who was responsible, who undid him each time, he knew. She was

the bane of his existence, an irritation and an attraction pulling him in opposite directions, a creature of beauty and life and magic that he would never
understand until the moment he killed her. His yearning to do so grew
stronger all the time, and it was becoming increasingly difficult to restrain. Yet
he knew he must if he expected to gain possession of the Black Elfstone. The
difficulty was in knowing how to withstand his obsession for her in the meantime. She incensed him, inflamed him, and left him twisted inside like fine
wire. Everything that seemed obvious and uncomplicated to him appeared to
be just the opposite to her. She insisted on having these fools accompany
them—the one-armed man, the Highlander, and the old Tracker. *Shades! Useless foils!* How much longer would he have to tolerate them?

He felt the anger begin again and moved quickly to quell it. *Patience.*
Her word, not his—but he had better try it on for size.

He listened to the sounds of the Urdas without, the guards, more
than a dozen of them, crouched down in the darkness about the hut. He
couldn't see them, but he could feel their presence. His instincts told him
they were there. There was no sign of the tunesmith yet—not that it made
any difference. The Urdas weren't about to set them free.

So many intrusions on what really matters!

His sharp eyes fixed momentarily on Dees. That old man. He was the
worst of the lot, the hardest to figure out. There was something about him . . .

He caught himself again. Be patient. Wait. Events would undoubtedly
continue to conspire to force him to do otherwise, but he must overcome
them. He must remain in control.

Except that it was so difficult here. This was not his country, these were
not his people, and the familiarity of surroundings and behavior, of people
and customs that he had always been able to rely upon before was missing
here. He was scaling a cliff he had never seen before and the footing was
treacherous.

Perhaps staying in control this time would prove impossible.

He shook his head uneasily. The thought stayed with him and would
not be dispelled.

It was after midnight when Carisman reappeared. Quickening brought
Morgan awake with a touch of her hand to his cheek. He came to his feet
and found the others already standing. The door unlatched and opened, and
the tunesmith slipped inside.

"Ah, you are awake. Good." He moved at once to stand next to Quickening, hesitant to speak, uncertain in their presence, like a boy forced to
confess something he would prefer to keep secret.

"What has the council decided, Carisman?" Quickening prodded him
gently, taking his arm and bringing him about to face her.

The tunesmith shook his head. "Lady, the best and the worst, I am
afraid." He glanced at the others. "All of you are free to go when you
choose." He turned back to Quickening. "Except you."

Morgan remembered at once the way the Urdas had looked at Quickening, recalling their fascination with her. "Why?" he demanded heatedly. "Why isn't she released as well?"

Carisman swallowed. "My subjects find her beautiful. They think she may be magic, like myself. They . . . wish her to marry me."

"Well now, this is an inventive tale!" Horner Dees snapped, his bristled face screwing up in disbelief.

Morgan seized Carisman by the tunic front. "I have seen the way you look at her, tunesmith! This is your idea!"

"No, no, I swear it is not!" the other cried in dismay, his handsome face contorted in horror. "I would never do such a thing! The Urdas . . ."

"The Urdas couldn't care less about . . ."

"Let him go, Morgan," Quickening said, interrupting, her voice low and steady. Morgan released his grip and stepped back instantly. "He speaks the truth," she said. "This is not his doing."

Pe Ell had shoved forward like a knife blade. "It doesn't matter whose doing it is." His eyes fixed Carisman. "She goes with us."

Carisman's face went pale, and his eyes shifted anxiously from one determined face to the next. "They won't let her," he whispered, his gaze dropping. "And if they don't, she will end up like me."

He sang:

> "Long ago, in times gone by, there was a fair, fair maiden.
> She wandered fields and forest glens,
> With all the world her haven.
> A mighty Lord a fancy took, demanded that she wed him.
> When she refused, he took her home,
> And locked her in his dungeon.
> She pined away for what she'd lost, a life beyond her prison.
> She promised everything she owned,
> If she could have her freedom.
> A fairy imp her plea did hear and quickly broke the door in.
> Yet freed her not as she had asked,
> But claimed her his possession.
>
> The moral is: If you offer to give up everything,
>   Be prepared to keep nothing."

Horner Dees threw up his hands in exasperation. "What is it you are trying to say, Carisman?" he snapped.

"That your choices often undo you. That seeking everything sometimes costs you everything." It was Walker Boh who answered. "Carisman thought that in becoming a king he would find freedom and has instead found only shackles."

"Yes," the tunesmith breathed, sadness flooding his finely chiseled features. "I don't belong here any more than Quickening. If you would take her when you go, then you must take me as well!"

"No!" Pe Ell cried instantly.

"Lady," the tunesmith begged. "Please. I have been here for almost five years now—not just several as I claimed. I am caged as surely as that maiden in my song. If you do not take me with you, I shall be kept captive until I die!"

Quickening shook her head. "It is dangerous where we go, Carisman. Far more dangerous than it is here. You would not be safe."

Carisman's voice shook. "It doesn't matter! I want to be free!"

"No!" Pe Ell repeated, circling away like a cat. "Think, girl! Yet another fool to burden us? Why not an army of them, then? Shades!"

Morgan Leah was tired of being called a fool and was about to say so when Walker Boh caught him firmly by the arm and shook his head. Morgan frowned angrily, but gave way.

"What do you know of the country north, Carisman?" Horner Dees asked suddenly, his bulk backing the tunesmith away. "Ever been there?"

Carisman shook his head. "No. It doesn't matter what's there. It is away from here." His eyes darted furtively. "Besides, you have to take me. You can't get away if I don't show you how."

That stopped them. Everyone turned. "What do you mean?" Dees asked cautiously.

"I mean that you will be dead a dozen times over without my help," the tunesmith said.

He sang:

> *"Sticks and stones will break your bones,*
> *But only if the spears don't.*
> *There's traps and snares placed everywhere,*
> *And none to warn if I don't.*
> *Fiddle-de-diddle-de-de."*

Pe Ell had him by the throat so quickly that no one else had time to intervene. "You'll tell everything you know before I'm done with you or wish you had!" he threatened furiously.

But Carisman held steady, even forced back as he was, the hard eyes inches from his own. "Never," he gasped. "Unless . . . you agree . . . to take me with you."

His face lost all its color as Pe Ell's hand tightened. Morgan and Horner Dees glanced uncertainly at each other and then at Quickening, hesitating in spite of themselves. It was Walker Boh who stepped in. He moved behind Pe Ell and touched him in a manner they could not see. The gaunt man jerked back, his face rigid with surprise. Walker was quickly by him, his arm coming about Carisman and lifting him away.

Pe Ell whirled, cold rage in his eyes. Morgan was certain he was going to attack Walker, and nothing good could come of that. But Pe Ell surprised him. Instead of striking out, he simply stared at Walker a moment and then turned away, his face suddenly an expressionless mask.

Quickening spoke, diverting them. "Carisman," she said. "Do you know a way out of here?"

Carisman nodded, swallowing to speak. "Yes, Lady."

"Will you show it to us?"

"If you agree to take me with you, yes." He was bargaining now, but he seemed confident.

"Perhaps it would be enough if we helped you escape the village?"

"No, Lady. I would lose my way and they would bring me back again. I must go to wherever it is that you are going—far away from here. Perhaps," he said brightly, "I may turn out to be of some use to you."

When pigs fly, Morgan thought uncharitably.

Quickening seemed undecided, strange for her. She looked questioningly at Horner Dees.

"He's right about the Urdas bringing him back," the old Tracker agreed. "Us, too, if we aren't quick enough. Or smart enough."

Morgan saw Pe Ell and Walker Boh glaring at each other from opposite corners of the hut—harsh, dark wraiths come from exacting worlds, their silent looks full of warning. Who would survive a confrontation between those two? And how could the company survive while they were at such odds?

Then suddenly an idea occurred to him. "Your magic, Quickening!" he burst out impulsively. "We can use your magic to escape! You can control all that grows within the earth. That is enough to make the Urdas give way. With or without Carisman, we have your magic!"

But Quickening shook her head and for an instant she seemed almost to dissolve. "No, Morgan. We have crossed the Charnals into the country of Uhl Belk, and I cannot use my magic again until after we find the talisman. The Stone King must not discover who I am. If I use the magic, he will know."

The hut went silent again. "Who is the Stone King?" Carisman asked, and they all looked at him.

"I say we take him," Horner Dees said finally, bluff and to the point as always. His bulky figure shifted. "If he really can get us out of here, that is."

"Take him," Morgan agreed. He grinned. "I like the idea of having a king on our side as well—even if all he can do is make up songs."

Quickening glanced at the silent antagonists behind her. Pe Ell shrugged his indifference. Walker Boh said nothing.

"We will take you, Carisman," Quickening said, "though I am afraid to guess what this choice might cost you."

Carisman shook his head emphatically. "No price is too great, Lady, I promise you." The tunesmith was elated.

Quickening moved toward the door. "The night flies. Let us hurry."

Carisman held up his hand. "Not that way, Lady."

She turned. "There is another?"

"Indeed." He was beaming mischievously. "As it happens, I am standing on it."

15

The Spikes and the lands surrounding were filled with tribes of Urdas and other species of Gnomes and Trolls. Since they were all constantly at war with one another, they kept their villages fortified. A lot of hard lessons had been learned over the years, and one of them was that a stockade needed more than one way out. Carisman's bunch had dug tunnels beneath the village that opened through hidden trapdoors into the forests beyond. If the village were threatened by a prolonged siege or by an army of overwhelming numbers, the inhabitants still had a means of escape.

One of the entrances to the tunnels that lay inside the village was under the floor of the hut in which the five from Rampling Steep had been placed. Carisman showed them where it lay, buried a good foot beneath the earthen floor, sealed so tightly by weather and time that it took Horner Dees and Morgan working together to pull it free. It had clearly never seen use and perhaps been all but forgotten. In any case, it was a way out and the company was quick to seize upon it.

"I would feel better about this if we had a light," Dees muttered as he stood looking down into the blackness.

"Here," Walker Boh whispered impatiently, moving forward to take his place. He slipped down into the blackness where the walls of the tunnel shielded his actions and made a snapping motion with his fingers. Light blazed up about his hand, an aura of brightness that had no visible source. The Dark Uncle has at least a little of his magic left, Morgan thought.

"Carisman, is there more than one passage down here?" Walker's voice sounded hollow. The tunesmith nodded. "Then stay close to me and tell me how we are to go."

They dropped into the hole one by one, Carisman following Walker, Quickening and Morgan after them, Dees and Pe Ell last. It was black in the tunnel, even with Walker's light, and the air was close and full of earth smells. The tunnel ran in a straight line, then branched in three directions. Carisman took them right. It branched again, and this time he took them left. They had gone far enough, Morgan thought, that they must be beyond the stockade walls. Still the tunnel continued. Tree roots penetrated its walls, tangling their arms and feet, slowing their progress. At times the roots grew so thick that they had to be severed to permit passage. Even when the passageway was completely clear, it was hard for Horner Dees to fit through. He grunted and huffed and pushed ahead determinedly. Other tunnels intersected and passed on. Dirt and silt from their movements began to choke the air, and it grew hard to breathe. Morgan buried his face in his tunic sleeve and would not allow himself to think about what would happen if the tunnel walls collapsed.

After what seemed an impossibly long time they slowed and then stopped altogether. "Yes, this is it," Morgan heard Carisman say to Walker. He listened as the two struggled to free the trapdoor that sealed them in. They labored in wordless silence, grunting, digging, and shifting about in the cramped space. Morgan and the others crouched down in the blackness and waited.

It took them almost as long to loosen the trapdoor as it had to navigate the tunnel. When it finally fell back, fresh air rushed in and the six scrambled up into the night. They found themselves in a heavily wooded glen, the limbs of the trees grown so thick overhead that the sky was masked almost completely.

They stood wordlessly for a moment, breathing in the clean air, and then Dees pushed forward. "Which way to the Spikes?" he whispered anxiously to Carisman.

Carisman pointed and Dees started away, but Pe Ell reached out hurriedly and yanked him back. "Wait!" he warned. "There will be a watch!"

He gave the old Tracker a withering look, motioned them all down and melted into the trees. Morgan sank back against the trunk of a massive fir, and the others became vague shadows through the screen of its shaggy limbs. He closed his eyes wearily. It seemed days since he had rested properly. He thought about how good it would feel to sleep.

But a touch on his shoulder brought him awake again almost immediately. "Easy, Highlander," Walker Boh whispered. The tall man slid down next to Morgan, dark eyes searching his own. "You tread on dangerous ground these days, Morgan Leah. You had better watch where you step."

Morgan blinked. "What do you mean?"

Walker's face inclined slightly, and Morgan could see the lines of tension and strain that creased it. "Pe Ell. Stay away from him. Don't taunt him, don't challenge him. Have as little to do with him as you can. If he chooses, he can strike you down faster than a snake in hiding."

The words were spoken in a whisper that was harsh and chilling in its certainty, a brittle promise of death. Morgan swallowed what he was feeling and nodded. "Who is he, Walker? Do you know?"

The Dark Uncle glanced away and back again. "Sometimes I am able to sense things by touching. Sometimes I can learn another's secrets by doing nothing more than brushing up against him. It happened that way when I took Carisman away from Pe Ell. He has killed. Many times. He has done so intentionally rather than in self-defense. He enjoys it. I expect he is an assassin."

A pale hand reached up to hold a startled Morgan in place. "Listen, now. He conceals a weapon of immense power beneath his clothing. The weapon he carries is magic. It is what he uses to kill."

"Magic?" Morgan's voice quivered in surprise despite his effort to keep it steady. His mind raced. "Does Quickening know?"

"She chose him, Highlander. She chose us all. She told us we possessed magic. She told us our magic was needed. Of course, she knows."

Morgan was aghast. "She deliberately brought an assassin? Is this how she plans to regain the Black Elfstone?"

Walker stared fixedly at him. "I think not," he said finally. "But I can't be sure."

Morgan slumped back in disbelief. "Walker, what are we doing here? Why has she brought us?" Walker did not respond. "I don't know for the life of me why I agreed to come. Or maybe I do. I am drawn to her, I admit; I am enchanted by her. But what sort of reason is that? I shouldn't be here. I should be back in Tyrsis searching for Par and Coll."

"We have had this discussion," Walker reminded him gently.

"I know. But I keep questioning myself. Especially now. Pe Ell is an assassin; what do we have to do with such a man? Does Quickening think us all the same? Does she think we are all killers of other men? Is that the use to which we are to be put? I cannot believe it!"

"Morgan." Walker spoke his name to calm him, then eased back against the tree until their heads were almost touching. Something in the way the Dark Uncle's body was bent reminded Morgan for a moment of how broken he had been when they had found him amid the ruins of his cottage at Hearthstone. "There is more to this than what you know," Walker whispered. "Or I, for that matter. I can sense things but not see them clearly. Quickening has a purpose beyond what she reveals. She is the daughter of the King of the Silver River—do not forget that. She has forbidden insight. She has magic that transcends any that we have ever seen. But she is vulnerable as well. She must walk a careful path in her quest. I think that we are here in part, at least, to see that she is able to keep to that path."

Morgan thought it over a moment and nodded, listening to the stillness of the night about them, staring out through the boughs of the old fir at the shadowy figures beyond, picking out Quickening's slim, ethereal form, a slender bit of movement that the night might swallow with no more than a slight shifting of the light.

Walker's voice tightened. "I have been shown a vision of her—a vision as frightening as any I have ever experienced. The vision told me that she will die. I warned her of this before we left Hearthstone; I told her that perhaps I should not come. But she insisted. So I came." He glanced over. "It is the same with all of us. We came because we knew we must. Don't try to understand why that is, Morgan. Just accept it."

Morgan sighed, lost in the tangle of his feelings and his needs, wishing for things that could never be, for a past that was lost and a future he could not determine. He thought of how far things had gone since the Ohmsfords had come to him in Leah, of how different they all now were.

Walker Boh rose, a rustle of movement in the silence. "Remember what I said, Highlander. Stay away from Pe Ell."

He pushed through the curtain of branches without looking back. Morgan Leah stared after him.

Pe Ell was gone a long time. When he returned, he spoke only to Horner Dees. "It is safe now, old man," he advised softly. "Lead on."

They departed the glen wordlessly, following Carisman as he led them back toward the ridgeline, a silent procession of wraiths in the forest night. No one challenged them, and Morgan was certain that no one would. Pe Ell had seen to that.

It was still dark when they again caught sight of the Spikes. They climbed to the crest of the ridgeline and turned north. Dees moved them forward at a rapid pace, the pathway clear, the spine of the land bare and open to the light of moon and stars, empty save where the skeletal trees threw the spindly shadow of their trunks and branches crosswise against the earth like spiders' webs. They followed the Spikes through the narrow end of the valley's funnel and turned upward into the hills beyond. Daybreak was beginning to approach, a faint lightening of the skies east. Dees moved them faster still. No one had to bother asking why.

By the time the sun crested the mountains they were far enough into the hills that they could no longer see the valley at all. They found a stream of clear water and stopped to drink. Sweat ran down their faces and their breathing was labored.

"Look ahead," Horner Dees said, pointing. A line of peaks jutted into the sky. "That's the north edge of the Charnals, the last we have to cross. There's a dozen passes that lead over and the Urdas can't know which one we will take. It's all rock up there, hard to track anything."

"Hard for you, you mean," Pe Ell suggested unkindly. "Not necessarily hard for them."

"They won't go out of their mountains." Dees ignored him. "Once we're across, we'll be safe."

They hauled themselves back to their feet and went on. The sun climbed into the cloudless sky, a brilliant ball of white fire that turned the earth beneath into a furnace. It was the hottest Morgan could remember it being since he had left Culhaven. The hills rose toward the mountains, and the trees began to give way to scrub and brush. Once Dees thought he saw something moving in the forestlands far behind them, and once they heard a wailing sound that Carisman claimed was Urda horns. But midday came and went, and there was no sign of pursuit.

Then clouds began to move in from the west, a large threatening bank of black thunderheads. Morgan slapped at the gnats that flew against his sweat-streaked face. There would be a storm soon.

They stopped again as midafternoon approached, exhausted from their flight and hungry now as well. There was little to eat, just some roots and wild vegetables and fresh water. Horner Dees went off to scout ahead, and Pe Ell decided to backtrack to a bluff that would let him study the land behind. Walker sat by himself. Carisman began speaking with Quickening again about his music, insistent upon her undivided attention. Morgan studied the tunesmith's handsome features, his shock of blond hair, and his uninhibited gestures and was annoyed. Rather than show what he was feeling, the Highlander moved into the shade of a spindly pine and faced away.

Thunder rumbled in the distance, and the clouds pushed up against the mountains. The sky was a peculiar mix of sunshine and darkness. The heat was still oppressive, a suffocating blanket as it pressed down against the earth. Morgan buried his face in his hands and closed his eyes.

Both Horner Dees and Pe Ell were back quickly. The former advised that the passage that would take them across the last of the Charnals lay less than an hour ahead. The latter reported that the Urdas were after them in force.

"More than a hundred," he announced, fixing them with those hard, unreadable eyes. "Right on our heels."

They resumed their march at once, pressing ahead more quickly, a sense of urgency driving them now that had not been present before. No one had expected the Urdas to catch up with them this fast, certainly not before they were across the mountains. If they were forced to stand and fight here, they knew, they were finished.

They worked their way upward into the rocks, scrambling through huge fields of boulders and down narrow defiles, struggling to keep their footing on slides that threatened to send them careening away into jagged, bottomless fissures. The clouds scraped over the mountain peaks and filled the skies from horizon to horizon. Heavy drops of rain began to fall, spattering against the earth and their heated skin. Darkness settled over everything, an ominous black that echoed with the sound of thunder as it rolled across the empty, barren rock. Dusk was approaching, and Morgan was certain they would be caught in the mountains at nightfall, a decidedly unpleasant prospect. His entire body ached, but he forced himself to keep going. He glanced ahead to Carisman and saw that the tunesmith was in worse shape, stumbling and falling regularly, gasping for breath. Fighting back against his own exhaustion, he caught up with the other man, put an arm about him, and helped him to go on.

They had just gained the head of the pass that Dees had been shepherding them toward when they caught sight of the Urdas. The rugged, shaggy creatures appeared out of the rocks behind them, still more than a mile off, but charging ahead as if maddened, screaming and crying out, shaking their weapons with an unmistakable promise of what they would do with those they were pursuing when they finally caught up with them. The company, after no more than a moment's hesitation, fled into the pass.

The pass was a knife cut that sliced upward through the cliffs, a narrow passageway filled with twists and turns. The company spread out, snaking its way forward. The rain began to fall in earnest now, turning from a slow spattering into a heavy downpour. The footing became slippery, and tiny streams began to flow down out of the rocks, cutting away at the earth beneath their feet. They passed from the shadow of the cliffs and found themselves on a barren slope that angled left into a high-walled defile that was as

black as night. Wind blew across the slope in frenzied gusts that sent silt flying into their faces. Morgan let go of Carisman and brought his cloak
across his head to protect himself.

It required a tremendous effort to gain the defile, the wind beating
against them so hard that they could progress only a little at a time. As they
reached the darkened opening, the Urdas reappeared, very close now, come
that last mile all too quickly. Darts, lances, and the razor-sharp throwing
implements whizzed through the air, falling uncomfortably close. Hurriedly
the company charged into the passageway and the protection of its walls.

Here, the rain descended in torrents and the light was almost extinguished. Jagged rock edges jutted out from the floor and walls of the narrow corridor and cut and scraped them as they passed. Time slowed to a
standstill in the howl of wind and the roll of the thunder, and it seemed as
if they would never get free. Morgan moved ahead to be with Quickening,
determined to see that she was protected.

When they finally worked their way clear of the defile, they found
themselves standing on a ledge that ran along a seam midway down a towering cliff face that dropped away into a gorge through which the waters of
the Rabb raged in a churning, white-foamed maelstrom. Dees took them
onto the ledge without hesitation, shouting something back that was meant
to be encouraging but was lost in the sound of the storm. The line spread
out along the broken seam, Dees in the lead, Carisman, Quickening, Morgan, and Walker Boh following, and Pe Ell last. The rain fell in sheets, the
wind tore at them, and the sound of the river's rush was an impenetrable
wall of sound.

When the foremost of the Urdas appeared at the mouth of the defile,
no one saw. It wasn't until their weapons began to shatter against the rocks
about the fleeing company that anyone realized they were there. A dart
nicked Pe Ell's shoulder and spun him about, but he kept his footing and
struggled on. The others began to advance more quickly, trying desperately
to distance themselves from their pursuers, hastening along the ledge,
booted feet slipping and sliding dangerously. Morgan glanced back and saw
Walker Boh turn and throw something into the storm. Instantly the air
flared with silver light. Darts and lances that were hurled into the brightness
fell harmlessly away. The Urdas, frightened by the Dark Uncle's magic, fell
back into the defile.

Ahead, the ledge broadened slightly and sloped downward. The far side
of the mountains came into view, a sweeping stretch of forested hills that
ran into the distance until it disappeared into a wall of clouds and rain. The
Rabb churned below, cutting back on itself, rushing eastward through the
rocks. The trail followed its bend, some fifty feet above its banks, the barren
rock giving way to the beginnings of earth and scrub.

Morgan looked around one final time and saw that the Urdas were not
following. Either Walker had frightened them off, or Horner Dees had
been right about them not leaving their mountains.

He turned back.

In the next instant the entire cliff face was rocked with tremors as parts of it gave way under the relentless pounding of the wind and rain. The trail in front of him, an entire section of earth and rock, disappeared completely and took Quickening with it. She fell back against the slope, grasping. But there was nothing to hold on to, and she began to slide in a cloud of silt and gravel toward the river. Carisman, directly in front of her, almost went, too, but managed to throw himself forward far enough to clutch a tangle of roots from some mountain scrub and was saved.

Morgan was directly behind. He saw that Quickening could not save herself and that there was no one who could reach her. He didn't hesitate. He jumped from the crumbling trail into the gap, hurtling down the mountainside after her, the trailing shouts of his companions disappearing almost instantly. He struck the waters of the Rabb with jarring force, went under, and came up again gasping in shock at the cold. He caught a flash of Quickening's silver hair bobbing in a shower of white foam a few feet away, swam to her, seized her clothing, and drew her to him.

Then the current had them both, and they were swept away.

It was all that Morgan Leah could do to keep himself and Quickening afloat in the churning river, and while he might have considered trying to swim for shore if he had been unencumbered he gave no thought of doing so here. Quickening was awake and able to lend some assistance to his effort, but it was mostly Morgan's strength that kept them away from the rocks and out of the deep eddies that might have pulled them down. As it was, the river took them pretty much where it chose. It was swollen by the rains and overflowing its banks, and its surface waters were white with foam and spray against the darkness of the skies and land. The storm continued to rage, thunder rumbling down the canyon depths, lightning flashing against the distant peaks, and the rains falling in heavy sheets. The cliff face they had tumbled down disappeared from view almost immediately and with it their companions. The Rabb twisted and turned through the mountain rocks, and soon they lost any sense of where they were.

After a time a tree that had been knocked into the river washed by and they caught hold of it and let it carry them along. They were able to rest a bit then, clutching the slippery trunk side by side, doing what they could to protect their bodies from the rocks and debris, searching the river and the shoreline for a means to extract themselves. They did not bother trying to speak; they were too exhausted to expend the effort and the river would likely have drowned out their words in any case. They simply exchanged glances and concentrated on staying together.

Eventually the river broadened, tumbling down out of the peaks into the hill country north, emptying into a forested basin where it pooled before being swept into a second channel that carried it south again. There was an island in the center of the basin, and the tree they were riding ran aground against it, spinning and bumping along its banks. Morgan and Quickening shoved away from their make-do raft and stumbled wearily ashore. Exhausted, their clothing hanging in tatters, they crawled through weeds and grasses for the shelter of the trees that grew there, a cluster of hardwoods dominated by a pair of monstrous old elms. Streams of water eddied and pooled on the ground about them as they fought their way along the island's rain-soaked banks, and the wind howled around their ears. Lightning struck the mainland shore nearby with a thunderous crack, and they flattened themselves while the thunder rolled past.

At last they gained the trees, grateful to discover that it was comparatively dry beneath the canopy of limbs and sheltered against the wind. They stumbled to the base of the largest of the elms and collapsed, sprawling next to each other on the ground, gasping for breath. They lay without moving for a time, letting their strength return. Then, after exchanging a long look that conveyed their unspoken agreement to do so, they pulled themselves upright against the elm's rough trunk and sat shoulder to shoulder, staring out into the rain.

"Are you all right?" Morgan asked her.

It was the first thing either of them had said. She nodded wordlessly. Morgan checked himself carefully for injuries, and finding none, sighed and leaned back—relieved, weary, cold, and unexplainably hungry and thirsty, too, despite being drenched. But there was nothing to eat or drink, so there was no point in thinking about it.

He glanced over again. "I don't suppose you could do anything about a fire, could you?" She shook her head. "Can't use magic of any kind, huh? Ah, well. Where's Walker Boh when you need him?" He tried to sound flippant and failed. He sighed.

She reached over and let her hand rest on his, and it warmed him despite his discomfort. He lifted his arm and placed it about her shoulders, easing her close. It brought them both some small measure of warmth. Her silver hair was against his cheek, and her smell was in his nostrils, a mix of earth and forest and something else that was sweet and compelling.

"They won't find us until this storm ends," she said.

Morgan nodded. "If then. There won't be any trail to follow. Just the river." He frowned. "Where are we, anyway? North or south of where we went into the river?"

"North and east," she advised.

"You know that?"

She nodded. He could feel her breathing, the slight movement of her body against him. He was shivering, but having her close like this seemed to make up for it. He closed his eyes.

"You didn't have to come after me," she said suddenly. She sounded uncomfortable. "I would have been all right."

He tried unsuccessfully to stifle a yawn. "I was due for a bath."

"You could have been hurt, Morgan."

"Not me. I've already survived attacks by Shadowen, Federation soldiers, Creepers, and other things I'd just as soon forget about. A fall into a river isn't going to hurt me."

The wind gusted sharply, howling through the branches of the trees, and they glanced skyward to listen. When the sound died away, they could hear the rush of the river again as it pounded against the shoreline.

Morgan hunched down within his sodden clothing. "When this storm blows itself out, we can swim to the mainland, get off this island. The river is too rough to try it now. And we're too tired to make the attempt in any case. But that's all right. We're safe enough right here. Just a little damp."

He realized that he was talking just to be doing something and went still again. Quickening did not respond. He could almost feel her thinking, but he hadn't a clue as to what she was thinking about. He closed his eyes again and let his breathing slow. He wondered what had become of the others. Had they managed to make it safely down that trail or had the collapse of the ledge trapped Walker and Pe Ell on the upper slope? He tried to envision the Dark Uncle and the assassin trapped with each other and failed.

It was growing dark now, dusk chasing away what little light remained, and shadows began to spread across the island in widening black stains. The rains were slowing, the sounds of thunder and wind receding in the distance, and the storm was beginning to pass. The air was not cooling as Morgan had expected, but instead was growing warm again, thick with the smells of heat and humidity. Just as well, he thought. They were too cold as it was. He thought about what it would feel like to be warm and dry again, to be secluded in his hunting lodge in the Highlands with hot broth and a fire, seated on the floor with the Ohmsfords, swapping lies of what had never been.

Or seated perhaps with Quickening, saying nothing because speaking wasn't necessary and just being together was enough, just touching . . .

The ache of what he was feeling filled him with both longing and fear. He wanted it to continue, wanted it to be there always, and at the same time he did not understand it and was certain that it would betray him.

"Are you awake?" he asked her, anxious suddenly for the sound of her voice.

"Yes," she replied.

He took a deep breath and breathed out slowly. "I have been thinking about why I'm here," he said. "Wondering about it since Culhaven. I haven't any magic anymore—not really. All I ever had was contained in the

Sword of Leah, and now it's broken and what magic remains is small and probably won't be of much help to you. So there's just me, and I . . ." He stopped. "I just don't know what it is that you expect of me, I guess."

"Nothing," she answered softly.

"Nothing?" He could not keep the incredulity from his voice.

"Only what you are able and wish to give," she answered vaguely.

"But I thought that the King of the Silver River said . . ." He stopped. "I thought that your father said I was needed. Isn't that what you said? That he told you we were needed, all of us?"

"He did not say what it was that you were to do, Morgan. He told me to bring you with me in my search for the talisman and that you would know what to do, that we all would." She lifted away slightly and turned to look at him. "If I could tell you more, I would."

He scowled at her, frustrated with the evasiveness of her answers, with the uncertainty he was feeling. "Would you?"

She almost smiled. Even rain-streaked and soiled by the river's waters, she was the most beautiful woman he had ever seen. He tried to speak and failed. He simply sat there, mute and staring.

"Morgan," she said softly. "My father sees things that are hidden from all others. He tells me what I must know of these things, and I trust him enough to believe that what he tells me is enough. You are here because I need you. It has something to do with the magic of your Sword. I was told by my father and told you in turn that you will have a chance to make the Sword whole again. Perhaps then it will serve us both in a way we cannot foresee."

"And Pe Ell?" he pressed, determined now to know everything.

"Pe Ell?"

"Walker says he is an assassin—that he, too, carries a weapon of magic, a weapon that kills."

She studied him for a long moment before she said, "That is true."

"And he is needed, too?"

"Morgan." His name was spoken as a caution.

"Tell me. Please."

Her perfect features lowered into shadow and lifted again, filled with sadness. "Pe Ell is needed. His purpose, as yours, must reveal itself."

Morgan hesitated, trying to decide what to ask next, desperate to learn the truth but unwilling to risk losing her by crossing into territory in which he was not welcome.

His face tightened. "I would not like to think that I had been brought along for the same reason as Pe Ell," he said finally. "I am not like him."

"I know that," she said. She hesitated, wrestling with some inner demon. "I believe that each of you—Walker Boh included—is here for a different reason, to serve a different purpose. That is my sense of things."

He nodded, anxious to believe her, finding it impossible not to do so. He said, "I just wish I understood more."

She reached up and touched his cheek with her fingers, letting them slide down his jaw to his neck and lift away again. "It will be all right," she said.

She lay back again, folding into him, and he felt his frustration and doubt begin to fade. He let them go without a fight, content just to hold the girl. It was dark now, daylight gone into the west, night settled comfortably over the land. The storm had moved east, and the rains had been reduced to mist. The clouds were still thick overhead but empty now of thunder, and a blanket of stillness lay across the land as if to cover a child preparing for sleep. In the invisible distance the Rabb continued to churn, a sullen, now sluggish flow that lulled and soothed with its wash. Morgan peered into the night without seeing, finding its opaque curtain lowered to enclose him, to wrap about him as if an invisible shroud. He breathed the clean air and let his thoughts drift free.

"I could eat something," he mused after a time. "If there were anything to eat."

Quickening rose without speaking, took his hands in hers, and pulled him up after her. Together, they walked into the darkness, picking their way through the damp grasses. She was able to see as he could not and led the way with a sureness that defied him. After a time she found roots and berries that they could eat and a plant that when properly cut yielded fresh water. They ate and drank what they found, crouched silently next to each other, saying nothing. When they were finished, she took him out to the riverbank where they sat in silence watching the Rabb flow past in the dim, mysterious half-light, a murky sheen of movement against the darker mainland.

A light breeze blew into Morgan's face, filled with the rich scent of flowers and grasses. His clothes were still damp, but he was no longer chilled. The air was warm, and he felt strangely light-headed.

"It is like this sometimes in the Highlands," he told her. "Warm and filled with earth smells after a summer storm, the nights so long you think they might never end and wish they wouldn't." He laughed. "I used to sit up with Par and Coll Ohmsford on nights like this. I'd tell them that if a man wished hard enough for it, he could just . . . melt into the darkness like a snowflake into skin, just disappear into it, and then stay as long as he liked."

He glanced over to judge her reaction. She was still beside him, lost in thought. He brought his knees up to his chest and wrapped his arms around them. A part of him wanted to melt into this night so that it would go on forever, wanted to take her with him, away from the world about them. It was a foolish wish.

"Morgan," she said finally, turning. "I envy you your past. I have none."

He smiled. "Of course you . . ."

"No," she interrupted him. "I am an elemental. Do you know what that means? I am not human. I was created by magic. I was made from the earth of the Gardens. My father's hand shaped me. I was born full-grown, a woman without ever having been a child. My purpose in being has been determined by my father, and I have no say in what that purpose is to be. I am not saddened by this because it is all I know. But my instincts, my human feelings, tell me there is more, and I wish that it were mine as it has been yours. I sense the pleasure you take in remembering. I sense the joy."

Morgan was speechless. He had known she was magic, that she possessed magic, but it had never occurred to him that she might not be . . . He caught himself. Might not be what? As real as he was? As human? But she was, wasn't she? Despite what she thought, she was. She felt and looked and talked and acted human. What else was there? Her father had fashioned her in the image of humans. Wasn't that enough? His eyes swept over her. It was enough for him, he decided. It was more than enough.

He reached out to stroke her hand. "I admit I don't know anything about how you were made, Quickening. Or even anything about elementals. But you are human. I believe that. I would know if you weren't. As for not having any past, a past is nothing more than the memories you acquire, and that's something you're doing right now, acquiring memories—even if they're not the most pleasant in the world."

She smiled at the idea. "The ones of you will always be pleasant, Morgan Leah," she said.

He held her gaze. Then he leaned forward and kissed her, just a brief touching of their lips, and lifted away. She looked at him through those black, penetrating eyes. There was fear mirrored there, and he saw it.

"What frightens you?" he asked.

She shook her head. "That you make me feel so much."

He felt himself treading on dangerous ground, but went forward nevertheless. "You asked me before why I came after you when you fell. The truth is, I had to. I am in love with you."

Her face lost all expression. "You cannot be in love with me," she whispered.

He smiled bleakly. "I'm afraid I have no choice in the matter. This isn't something I can help."

She looked at him for a long time and then shuddered. "Nor can I help what I feel for you. But while you are certain of your feelings, mine simply confuse me. I do not know what to do with them. I have my father's purpose to fulfill, and my feelings for you and yours for me cannot be allowed to interfere with that."

"They don't have to," he said, taking her hands firmly now. "They can just be there."

Her silver hair shimmered as she shook her head. "I think not. Not feelings such as these."

He kissed her again and this time she kissed him back. He breathed her in as if she were a flower. He had never felt so certain about anything in his life as how he felt about her.

She broke the kiss and drew away. "Morgan," she said, speaking his name as if it were a plea.

They rose and went back through the damp grasses to the sheltering trees, to the elm where they had waited out the storm earlier, and sank down again by its roughened trunk. They held each other as children might when frightened and alone, protecting against nameless terrors that waited just beyond the bounds of their consciousness, that stalked their dreams and threatened their sleep.

"My father told me as I left the Gardens of my birth that there were things he could not protect me against," she whispered. Her face was close against Morgan's, soft and smooth, her breath warm. "He was not speaking of the dangers that would threaten me—of Uhl Belk and the things that live in Eldwist or even of the Shadowen. He was speaking of this."

Morgan stroked her hair gently. "There isn't much of anything that you can do to protect against your feelings."

"I can close them away," she answered.

He nodded. "If you must. But I will tell you first that I am not capable of closing my feelings away. Even if my life depended on it, I could not do so. It doesn't make any difference who you are or even what you are. Elemental or something else. I don't care how you were made or why. I love you, Quickening. I think I did from the first moment I saw you, from the first words you spoke. I can't change that, no matter what else you ask of me. I don't even want to try."

She turned in his arms, and her face lifted to find his. Then she kissed him and kept on kissing him until everything around them disappeared.

When they woke the next morning the sun was cresting the horizon of a cloudless blue sky. Birds sang and the air was warm and sweet. They rose and walked to the riverbank and found the Rabb slow-moving and placid once more.

Morgan Leah looked at Quickening, at the curve of her body, the wild flow of her silver hair, the softness of her face, and the smile that came to his face was fierce and unbidden. "I love you," he whispered.

She smiled back at him. "And I love you, Morgan Leah. I will never love anyone again in my life the way I love you."

They plunged into the river. Rested now, they swam easily the distance that separated the island from the mainland. On gaining the far shore, they stood together for a moment looking back, and Morgan fought to contain the sadness that welled up within him. The island and their solitude and last night were lost to him except as memories. They were going back into the world of Uhl Belk and the Black Elfstone.

They walked south along the river's edge for several hours before encountering the others. It was Carisman who spied them first as he wandered the edge of a bluff, and he cried out in delight, summoning the rest. Down the steep slope he raced, blond hair flying, handsome features flushed. He skidded the last several yards on his backside, bounded up, and raced to intercept them. Throwing himself at Quickening's feet, he burst into song.

He sang:

"Found are the sheep who have strayed from the fold,
Saved are the lambs from the wolves and the cold,
Wandering far, they have yet found their way,
Now, pray we all, they are here for to stay.
Tra-la-la, tra-la-la, tra-la-la!"

It was a ridiculous song, but it made Morgan smile nevertheless. In moments, the others had joined them as well, gaunt Pe Ell, his dark anger at having lost Quickening giving way to relief that she had been found again; bearish Horner Dees, gruffly trying to put the entire incident behind them; and the enigmatic Walker Boh, his face an inscrutable mask as he complimented Morgan on his rescue. All the while, an exuberant Carisman danced and sang, filling the air with his music.

When the reunion finally concluded the company resumed its journey, moving away from the Charnals and into the forestlands north. Somewhere far ahead, Eldwist waited. The sun climbed into the sky and hung there, brightening and warming the lands beneath as if determined to erase all traces of yesterday's storm.

Morgan walked next to Quickening, picking his way through the slowly evaporating puddles and streams. They didn't speak. They didn't even look at each other. After a time, he felt her hand take his.

At her touch, the memories flooded through him.

They walked north for five days through the country beyond the Charnals, a land that was green and gently rolling, carpeted by long grasses and fields of wildflowers, dotted by forests of fir, aspen, and spruce. Rivers and streams meandered in silver ribbons from the mountains and bluffs, pooling in lakes, shimmering in the sunlight like mirrors, and sending a flurry of cooling breezes from their shores. It was easier journeying here than it had been through the mountains; the terrain was far less steep, the footing sure, and the weather mild. The days were sun-filled, the nights warm and sweet smelling. The skies stretched away from horizon to horizon, broad and empty and blue. It rained only once, a slow and gentle dampening of trees and grasses that passed almost unnoticed. The spirits of the company were high; anticipation of what lay ahead was tempered by renewed confidence and a sense of well-being. Doubts lay half-forgotten in the dark grottos to which they had been consigned. There was strength and quickness in their steps. The passage of the hours chipped away at uncertain temperaments with slow, steady precision and like a stonecutter's chisel

etched and shaped until the rough edges vanished and only the smooth surface of agreeable companionship remained.

Even Walker Boh and Pe Ell called an unspoken truce. It could never
be argued reasonably that they showed even the remotest inclination toward
establishing a friendship, but they kept apart amiably enough, each maintaining a studied indifference to the other's presence. As for the remainder
of the company, constancy was the behavioral norm. Horner Dees continued reticent and gruff, Carisman kept them all entertained with stories and
songs, and Morgan and Quickening feinted and boxed with glances and
gestures in a lovers' dance that was a mystery to everyone but them. There
was in all of them, save perhaps Carisman, an undercurrent of wariness and
stealth. Carisman, it seemed, was incapable of showing more than one face.
But the others were circumspect in their dark times, anxious to keep their
doubts and fears at bay, hopeful that some mix of luck and determination
would prove sufficient to carry them through to the journey's end.

The beginning of that end came the following day with a gradual
change in the character of the land. The green that had brightened the
forests and hills south began to fade to gray. Flowers disappeared. Grasses
withered and dried. Trees that should have been fully leafed and vibrant
were stunted and bare. The birds that had flown in dazzling bursts of color
and song just a mile south were missing here along with small game and the
larger hoofed and horned animals. It was as if a blight had fallen over everything, stripping the land of its life.

They stood at the crest of a rise at midmorning and looked out over
the desolation that stretched away before them.

"Shadowen," Morgan Leah declared darkly.

But Quickening shook her silvery head and replied, "Uhl Belk."

It grew worse by midday and worse still by nightfall. It was bad enough
when the land was sickened; now it turned completely dead. All trace of
grasses and leaves disappeared. Even the smallest bit of scrub disdained to
grow. Trunks lifted their skeletal limbs skyward as if searching for protection, as if beseeching for it. The country appeared to have been so thoroughly ravaged that nothing dared grow back, a vast wilderness gone empty
and stark and friendless. Dust rose in dry puffs from their boots as they
stalked the dead ground, the earth's poisoned breath. Nothing moved about
them, above them, beneath them—not animals, not birds, not even insects.
There was no water. The air had a flat, metallic taste and smell to it. Clouds
began to gather again, small wisps at first, then a solid bank that hung above
the earth like a shroud.

They camped that night in a forest of deadwood where the air was so
still they could hear each other breathe. The wood would not burn, so they
had no fire. Light from a mix of elements in the earth reflected off the ceiling of clouds and cast the shadows of the trees across their huddled forms
in clinging webs.

"We'll be there by nightfall tomorrow," Horner Dees said as they sat
facing each other in the stillness. "Eldwist."

Dark stares were his only reply.

Uhl Belk's presence became palpable after that. He huddled next to them there in the fading dusk, slept with them that night, and walked with them when they set out the following day. His breath was what they breathed, his silence their own. They could feel him beckoning, reaching out to gather them in. No one said so, but Uhl Belk was there.

By midday, the land had turned to stone. It was as if the whole of it, sickened and withered and gone lifeless, had been washed of every color but gray and in the process petrified. It was all preserved perfectly, like a giant piece of sculpture. Trunks and limbs, scrub and grasses, rocks and earth—everything as far as the eye could see had been turned to stone. It was a starkly chilling landscape that despite its coldness radiated an oddly compelling beauty. The company from Rampling Steep found itself entranced. Perhaps it was the solidity that drew them, the sense that here was something lasting and enduring and somehow perfectly wrought. The ravages of time, the changing of the seasons, the most determined efforts of man—it seemed as if none of these could affect what had been done here.

Horner Dees nodded and the members of the company went forward.

A haze hung about them as they walked across this tapestry of frozen time, and it was only with difficulty that they were able, after several hours, to distinguish something else shimmering in the distance. It was a vast body of water, as gray as the land they passed through, blending into its bleakness, a backdrop merging starkly into earth and sky as if the transition were meaningless.

They had reached the Tiderace.

Twin peaks came into view as well, jagged rock spirals that lifted starkly against the horizon. It was apparent that the peaks were their destination.

Now and again the earth beneath them rumbled ominously, tremors reverberating as if the land were a carpet that some giant had taken in his hands and shaken. There was nothing about the tremors to indicate their source. But Horner Dees knew something. Morgan saw it in the way his bearded face tightened down against his chest and fear slipped into his eyes.

After a time the land about them began to narrow on either side and the Tiderace to close about, and they were left with a shrinking corridor of rock upon which to walk. The corridor was taking them directly toward the peaks, a ramp that might at its end drop them into the sea. The temperature cooled, and there was moisture in the air that clung to their skin in faint droplets. Their booted feet were strangely noiseless as they trod the hard surface of the rock, climbing steadily into a haze. Soon they became a line of shadows in the approaching dusk. Dees led, ancient, massive, and steady. Morgan followed with Quickening, the tall Highlander's face lined with wariness, the girl's smooth and calm. Handsome Carisman hummed beneath his breath while his gaze shifted about him as rapidly as a bird's. Walker Boh floated behind, pale and introspective within his long cloak. Pe Ell brought up the rear, his stalker's eyes seeing everything.

The ramp began to break apart before them, an escarpment out of which strange rock formations rose against the light. They might have been carvings of some sort save for the fact that they lacked any recognizable form. Like pillars that had been hewn apart by weather's angry hand over thousands of years, they jutted and angled in bizarre shapes and images, the mindless visions of a madman. The company passed between them, anxious in their shadow, and hurried on.

They arrived finally at the peaks. There was a rift between them, a break so deep and narrow that it appeared to have been formed by some cataclysm that had split apart what had once been a single peak to form the two. They loomed to either side, spirals of rock that thrust into the clouds as if to pin them fast. Beyond, the skies were murky and misted, and the waters of the Tiderace crashed and rumbled against the rocky shores.

Horner Dees moved ahead and the others followed until all had been enveloped in shadows. The air was chill and unmoving in the gap, and the distant shrieks of seabirds echoed shrilly. What sort of creatures besides those of the sea could possibly live here? Morgan Leah wondered uneasily. He drew his sword. His whole body was rigid with tension, and he strained to catch some sign of the danger he sensed threatening them. Dees was hunched forward like an animal at hunt, and the three behind the Highlander were ghosts without substance. Only Quickening seemed unaffected, her head held high, her eyes alert as she scanned the rock, the skies, the gray that shrouded everything.

Morgan swallowed against the dryness in his throat. *What is it that waits for us?*

The walls of the break seemed to join overhead, and they were left momentarily in utter blackness with only the thin line of the passageway ahead to give them reassurance that they had not been entombed. Then the walls receded again, and the light returned. The rift opened into a valley that lay cradled between the peaks. Shallow, rutted, choked with the husks of trees and brush and with boulders many times the size of any man, it was an ugly catchall for nature's refuse and time's discards. Skeletons lay everywhere, vast piles of them, all sizes and shapes, scattered without suggestion of what creatures they might once have been.

Horner Dees brought them to a halt. "This is Bone Hollow," he said quietly. "This is the gateway to Eldwist. Over there, across the Hollow, through the gap in the peaks, Eldwist begins."

The others crowded forward for a better look. Walker Boh stiffened. "There's something down there."

Dees nodded. "Found that out the hard way ten years ago," he said. "It's called a Koden. It's the Stone King's watchdog. You see it?"

They looked and saw nothing, even Pe Ell. Dees seated himself ponderously on a rock. "You won't either. Not until it has you. And it won't matter much by then, will it? You could ask any of those poor creatures down there if they still had tongues and the stuff of life to use them."

Morgan scuffed his boot on a piece of deadwood as he listened. The deadwood was heavy and unyielding. Stone. Morgan looked at it as if understanding for the first time. Stone. Everything underfoot, everything surrounding them, everything for as far as the eye could see—it was all stone.

"Kodens are a kind of bear," Dees was saying. "Big fellows, live up in the cold regions north of the mountains, keep pretty much to themselves. Very unpredictable under any conditions. But this one?" He made his nod an enigmatic gesture. "He's a monster."

"Huge?" Morgan asked.

"A *monster*," Dees emphasized. "Not just in size, Highlander. This thing isn't a Koden anymore. You can recognize it for what it's supposed to be, but just barely. Belk did something to it. Blinded it, for one thing. It can't see. But its ears are so sharp it can hear a pin drop."

"So it knows we are here," Walker mused, edging past Dees for a closer look at the Hollow. His eyes were dark and introspective.

"Has for quite a while, I'd guess. It's down there waiting for us to try to get past."

"If it's still there at all," Pe Ell said. "It's been a long time since you were here, old man. By now it might be dead and gone."

Dees looked at him mildly. "Why don't you go on down there and take a look?"

Pe Ell gave him that lopsided, chilling smile.

The old Tracker turned away, his gaze shifting to the Hollow. "Ten years since I saw it and I still can't forget it," he whispered. He shook his grizzled head. "Something like that you don't ever forget."

"Maybe Pe Ell is right; maybe it is dead by now," Morgan suggested hopefully. He glanced at Quickening and found her staring fixedly at Walker.

"Not this thing," Dees insisted.

"Well, why can't we see it if it's all that big and ugly?" Carisman asked, peering cautiously over Morgan's shoulder.

Dees chuckled. His eyes narrowed. "You can't see it because it looks like everything else down there—like stone, all gray and hard, just another chunk of rock. Look for yourself. One of those mounds, one of those boulders, something that's down there that doesn't look like anything— that's it. Just lying there, perfectly still. Waiting."

"Waiting," Carisman echoed.

He sang:

> "Down in the valley, the valley of stone.
> The Koden lies waiting amid shattered bone.
> Amid all its victims,
> Within its gray home,
> The Koden lies waiting to make you its own."

"Be still, tunesmith," Pe Ell said, a warning edge to his voice. He scowled at Dees. "You got past this thing before, if we're to believe what you tell us. How?"

Dees laughed aloud. "I was lucky, of course! I had twelve other men with me and we just walked right in, fools to the last. It couldn't get us all, not once we started running. No, it had to settle for three. That was going in. Coming out, it only got one. Of course, there were just two of us left by then. I was the one it missed."

Pe Ell stared at him expressionlessly. "Like you said, old man—lucky for you."

Dees rose, as bearish as any Koden Morgan might have imagined, sullen and forbidding when he set his face as he did now. He faced Pe Ell as if he meant to have at him. Then he said, "There's all sorts of luck. Some you've got and some you make. Some you carry with you and some you pick up along the way. You're going to need all kinds of it getting in and out of Eldwist. The Koden, he's a thing you wouldn't want to dream about on your worst night. But let me tell you something. After you see what else is down there, what lies beyond Bone Hollow, you won't have to worry about the Koden anymore. Because the dreams you'll have on your worst nights after that will be concerned with other things!"

Pe Ell's shrug was scornful and indifferent. "Dreams are for frightened old men, Horner Dees."

Dees glared at him. "Brave words now."

"I can see it," Walker Boh said suddenly.

His voice was soft, almost a whisper, but it silenced the others instantly and brought them about to face him. The Dark Uncle was staring out across the broken desolation of the Hollow, seemingly unaware that he had spoken.

"The Koden?" Dees asked sharply. He came forward a step.

"Where?" Pe Ell asked.

Walker's gesture was obscure. Morgan looked anyway and saw nothing. He glanced at the others. None of them appeared to be able to find it either. But Walker Boh was paying no attention to any of them. He seemed instead to be listening for something.

"If you really can see it, point it out to me," Pe Ell said finally, his voice carefully neutral.

Walker did not respond. He continued to stare. "It feels . . ." he began and stopped.

"Walker?" Quickening whispered and touched his arm.

The pale countenance shifted away from the Hollow at last and the dark eyes found her own. "I must find it," he said. He glanced at each of them in turn. "Wait here until I call for you."

Morgan started to object, but there was something in the other man's eyes that stopped him from doing so.

Instead, he watched silently with the others as the Dark Uncle walked alone into Bone Hollow.

The day was still, the air windless, and nothing moved in the ragged expanse of the Hollow save Walker Boh. He crossed the broken stone in silence, a ghost who made no sound and left no mark. There were times in the past few weeks when he had thought himself little more. He had almost died from the poison of the Asphinx and again from the attack of the Shadowen at Hearthstone. A part of him had surely died with the loss of his arm, another part with the failure of his magic to cure his sickness. A part of him had died with Cogline. He had been empty and lost on this journey, compelled to come by his rage at the Shadowen, his fear at being left alone, and his wish to discover the secrets of Uhl Belk and the Black Elfstone. Even Quickening, despite ministering to his needs, both physical and emotional, had not been strong enough to give him back to himself. He had been a hollow thing, bereft of any sense of who and what he was supposed to be, reduced to undertaking this quest in the faint hope that he would discover his purpose in the world.

And now, here within this vast, desolate stretch of land, where fears and doubts and weaknesses were felt most keenly, Walker Boh thought he had a chance to come alive again.

It was the presence of the Koden that triggered this hope. Until now the magic had been curiously silent within him, a worn and tired thing that had failed repeatedly and at last seemed to have given up. To be sure, it was there still to protect him when he was threatened, to frighten off the Urdas when they came too close, to deflect their hurled weapons. Yet this was a poor and sorry use when he remembered what it had once been able to do. What of the empathy it had given him with other living things? What of his sense of emotions and thoughts? What of the knowledge that had always just seemed to come to him? What of the glimpses of what was to be? All of these had deserted him, gone away as surely as his old world, his life with Cogline and Rumor at Hearthstone. Once he had wished it would be so, that the magic would disappear and he would be left in peace, a man like any other. But it had become increasingly clear to him on this journey, his sense of who and what he was heightened by the passing of Cogline and his own physical and emotional devastation, that his wish had been foolish. He would never be like other men, and he would never be at peace without the magic. He could not change who and what he was; Cogline had known that and told him so. On this journey he had discovered it was true.

He needed the magic.

He required it.

Now he would test whether or not he could still call it his own. He had sensed the presence of the Koden before Pe Ell had. He had sensed what it was before Horner Dees had described it. Amid the strewn rock, hunched down and silent, it had reached out to him as creatures once had when he approached. He could feel the Koden call to him. Walker Boh was not certain of its purpose in doing so, yet knew he must respond. It was more than the creature's need that he was answering; it was also his own.

He moved directly through the jumble of boulders and petrified wood to where the Koden waited. It had not moved, not even an inch, since the company had arrived. But Walker knew where it lay concealed nevertheless, for its presence had brought the magic awake again. It was an unexpected, exhilarating, and strangely comforting experience to have the power within him stir to life, to discover that it was not lost as he had believed, but merely misplaced.

Or suppressed, he chided harshly. Certainly he had worked hard at denying it even existed.

Mist curled through the rocks, tendrils of white that formed strange shapes and patterns against the gray of the land. Far distant, beyond and below the peaks and the valley they cradled, Walker could hear the crash of the ocean waters against the shoreline, a dull booming that resonated through the silence. He slowed, conscious now that the Koden was just ahead, unable to dispel entirely his apprehension that he was being lured to his doom, that the magic would not protect him, and he would be killed. Would it matter if he was? he wondered suddenly. He brushed the thought away. Within, he could feel the magic burning like a fire stoked to life.

He came down from between two boulders into a depression, and the Koden rose up before him, cat-quick. It seemed to materialize out of the earth, as if the dust that lay upon the rock had suddenly come together to give it form. It was huge and old and grizzled, three times his own size, with great shaggy limbs and ragged yellow claws that curled down to grip the rock. It lifted onto its hind legs to show itself to him, and its twisted snout huffed and opened to reveal a glistening row of teeth. Sightless white eyes peered down at him. Walker stood his ground, his life a slender thread that a single swipe of one huge paw could sever. He saw that the Koden's head and body had been distorted by some dark magic to make the creature appear more grotesque and that the symmetry of shape that had once given grace to its power had been stripped away.

Speak to me, thought Walker Boh.

The Koden blinked its eyes and dropped down so close that the huge muzzle was no more than inches from the Dark Uncle's face. Walker forced himself to meet the creature's empty gaze. He could feel the hot, fetid breath.

Tell me, he thought.

There was an instant's time when he was certain that he was going to die, that the magic had failed him entirely, that the Koden would reach out and strike him down. He waited for the claws to rend him, for the end to come. Then he heard the creature answer him, the guttural sounds of its own language captured and transformed by the magic.

Help me, the Koden said.

A flush of warmth filled Walker. Life returned to him in a way he found difficult to describe, as if he had been reborn and could believe in himself again. A flicker of a smile crossed his face. The magic was still his.

He reached out slowly with his good arm and touched the Koden on its muzzle, feeling beneath his fingertips more than the roughness of its hide and fur, finding as well the spirit of the creature that was trapped beneath. The Dark Uncle read its history in that touch and felt its pain. He stepped close to study its massive, scarred body, no longer frightened by its size or its ugliness or its ability to destroy. It was a prisoner, he saw— frightened, angered, bewildered, and despairing in the manner of all prisoners, wanting only to be free.

"I will make you so," Walker Boh whispered.

He looked to discover how the Koden was bound and found nothing. Where were the chains that shackled it? He circled the beast, testing the weight and texture of the air and earth. The great head swung about, seeking to follow him, the eyes fixed and staring. Walker completed his circuit and stopped, frowning. He had found the invisible lines of magic that the Stone King had fashioned and he knew what it would take to set the creature free. The Koden was a prisoner of its mutation. It would have to be changed back into a bear again, into the creature it had been, and the stigma of Uhl Belk's touch cleansed. But Walker hadn't the magic for that. Only Quickening possessed such power, magic strong enough to bring back the Meade Gardens out of the ashes of the past, to restore what once was, and she had already said she could not use her magic again until the Black Elfstone was recovered. Walker stood looking at the Koden helplessly, trying to decide if there were anything he could do. The beast shifted to face him, its great, ragged bulk a shimmer of rock dust against the landscape.

Walker reached out once more, and his fingers rested on the Koden's muzzle. His thoughts became words. *Let us pass, and we will find a way to set you free.*

The Koden stared out at him from the prison of its ruined body, sightless eyes hard and empty. *Go,* it said.

Walker lifted his hand away long enough to beckon his companions forward, then placed it back again. The others of the company came hesitantly, Quickening in the lead, then Morgan Leah, Horner Dees, Carisman, and Pe Ell. He watched them pass without comment, his arm outstretched, his hand steady. He caught a glimpse of what was in their eyes, a strange mix of emotions, understanding in Quickening's alone, fear and awe and disbelief in the rest. Then they were past. They walked from the rubble of Bone Hollow to the break in the cliffs beyond which they turned to wait for him.

Walker took his hand away and saw the Koden tremble. Its mouth gaped wide, and it appeared to cry out soundlessly. Then it wheeled away from him and lumbered down into the rocks.

"I won't forget," the Dark Uncle called after it.

The emptiness he felt made him shiver. Pulling his cloak close, he walked from the Hollow.

Morgan and the others, all but Quickening, asked Walker Boh when he reached them what had happened. How had he managed to charm the

Koden so that they could pass? But the Dark Uncle refused to answer their questions. He would say only that the creature was a prisoner of the Stone King's magic and must be freed, that he had given his promise.

"Since you made the promise, you can worry about keeping it," Pe Ell declared irritably, anxious to dismiss the matter of the Koden now that the danger was behind them.

"We'll have trouble enough keeping ourselves free of the Stone King's magic," Horner Dees agreed.

Carisman was already skipping ahead, and Morgan suddenly found himself facing Walker Boh with no reply to give. It was Quickening who spoke instead, saying, "If you gave your promise, Walker Boh, then it must be kept." She did not, however, say how.

They turned away from Bone Hollow and passed into the break that opened out through the peaks to the Tiderace. The passage was shadowed and dark in the fading afternoon light, and a chill, rough-edged wind blew down off the slopes of the cliffs above, thrusting into them like a giant hand, shoving them relentlessly ahead. The sun had dropped into the horizon west, caught in a web of clouds that turned its light scarlet and gold. The smell of salt water, fish, and kelp filled the air, sharp and pungent.

Morgan glanced back once or twice at Walker Boh, still amazed at how he had been able to keep the Koden from attacking them, to walk right up to it as he had and touch it without coming to harm. He recalled the stories of the Dark Uncle, of the man before he had suffered the bite of the Asphinx and the loss of Cogline and Rumor, the man who had taught Par Ohmsford not to be frightened of the power of the Elven magic. Until now, he had thought Walker Boh crippled by the Shadowen attack on Hearthstone. He pursed his lips thoughtfully. Perhaps he had been wrong. And if wrong about Walker, why not wrong about himself as well? Perhaps the Sword of Leah could be made whole again and his own magic restored. Perhaps there was a chance for all of them, just as Quickening had suggested.

The defile opened suddenly before them, the shadows which had caged them brightened into gray, misty light, and they peeked through a narrow window in the cliffs. The Tiderace spread away below in an endless expanse, its waters roiling and white-capped as they churned toward the shoreline. The company moved ahead, back into the shadows. The trail they followed began to descend, to twist and turn through the rocks, damp and treacherous from the mist and the ocean spray. The walls split apart once more, this time forming ragged columns of stone that permitted brief glimpses of sky and sea. Underfoot, the rock was loose, and it felt as if everything was on the verge of breaking up.

Then they turned onto a slide so steep that they were forced to descend sitting and found themselves in a narrow passageway that curled ahead into a tunnel. They stooped to pass through, for the tunnel was filled with jagged rock edges. At its far end, the walls fell away, and the tunnel opened onto a shelf that lifted toward the sky. The company moved onto the shelf, discovered a pathway, and climbed to where it ended at a rampart formed of stone blocks.

They stood at the edge of the rampart and looked down. Morgan felt his stomach lurch. From where they stood, the land dropped away to a narrow isthmus that jutted into the sea. Connected to the isthmus was a peninsula, broad and ragged about the edges, formed all of cliffs against which the waters of the Tiderace pounded relentlessly. Atop the cliffs sat a city of towering stone buildings. The buildings were not of this time, but of the old world, of the age before the Great Wars destroyed the order of things and the new Races were born. They rose hundreds of feet into the air, smooth and symmetrical and lined with banks of windows that yawned blackly against the gray light. Everything was set close together, so that the city had the look of a gathering of monstrous stone obelisks grown out of the rock. Seabirds wheeled and circled about the buildings, crying out mournfully in the failing light.

"Eldwist," Horner Dees announced.

Far west, the sun was sinking into the waters of the sea, losing its brightness and its color with the coming of night, the scarlet and gold fading to silver. The wind howled down off the cliffs behind them in a steady crescendo, and it felt as if even the pinnacle of rock on which they stood was being shaken. They huddled together against its thrust and the fall of night and watched raptly as Eldwist turned black with shadow. The wind howled through the city as well, down the canyons of its streets, across the drops of its cliffs. Morgan was chilled by the sound of it. Eldwist was empty and dead. There was only its stone, hard and unyielding, unchanging and fixed.

Horner Dees called out to them over the sound of the wind as he turned away. He led them back to where a set of steps had been carved into the cliff face to lead downward to the city. The steps ran back against the wall, angling through the crevices and nooks, twisting once more into shadow. Night closed about as they descended, the sun disappearing, the stars winking into view in a sky that was clear and bright. Moonlight reflected off the Tiderace, and Morgan could see the stark, jutting peaks of the city lifting off the rocks. Mist rose in gauzy trailers, and Eldwist took on a surrealistic look—as if come out of time and legend. The seabirds flew away, the sound of their cries fading into silence. Soon there was only the roll of the waves as they slapped against the rocky shores.

At the base of the stairs they found an alcove sheltered by the rocks. Horner Dees brought them to a halt. "No sense in trying to go farther," he advised, sounding weary. The wind did not reach them here, and he talked in a normal tone of voice. "Too dangerous to try to go in at night. There's a Creeper down there . . ."

"A Creeper?" Morgan, who had been examining bits of grass and shrub that were perfectly preserved in stone, looked up sharply.

"Yes, Highlander," the other continued. "A thing that sweeps the streets of the city after dark, gathering up any stray bits and pieces of living refuse . . ."

A rumbling within the earth cut short the rest of what he was about to say. The source of the rumbling was Eldwist, and the members of the company turned quickly to look. The city stood framed against the night sky, all black save for where the light reflected off the stone. It was larger and more forbidding when viewed from below, Morgan thought as he peered into its shadows. More impenetrable . . .

Something huge surged out of the dark recesses he searched, a thing of such monstrous size as to give the momentary illusion that it dwarfed even the buildings. It rose from between the monoliths as if kindred, all bulk and weight, but long and sinewy like a snake as well, stone blocks turned momentarily liquid to reshape and re-form. Then jaws gaped wide—Morgan could see the jagged edge of the teeth clearly against the backdrop of the moon—and they heard a horrifying cry, like a strangled cough. The earth reverberated with that cry, and the members of the company from Rampling Steep dropped into a protective crouch—all but Quickening, who remained erect, as if she alone were strong enough to withstand this nightmare.

A second later it was gone, dropping away as quickly and smoothly as it had come, the rumble of its passing hanging faintly in the air.

"That was no Creeper," Morgan whispered.

"And it wasn't here ten years ago either," a white-faced Horner Dees whispered back. "I'd bet on it."

"No," Quickening said softly, turning to face them now. Her companions came slowly to their feet. "It is newly born," she said, "barely five years old. It is still a baby."

"A baby!" Morgan exclaimed incredulously.

Quickening nodded. "Yes, Morgan Leah. It is called the Maw Grint." She smiled sadly. "It is Uhl Belk's child."

18

The six that formed the company from Rampling Steep spent the remainder of the night huddled in the shelter of the cliffs, crouched silently in the darkness, hidden away from the Maw Grint and whatever other horrors lay in wait within Eldwist. They built no fire—indeed, there was no wood to be gathered for one—and they ate sparingly of their meager food. Food and water would be a problem in the days to come since there was little of either to be found in this country of stone. Fish would become the staple of their diet; a small stream of rainwater that tumbled down off the rocks behind would quench their thirst. If the fish proved elusive or the stream dried up, they would be in serious trouble.

No one slept much in the aftermath of the Maw Grint's appearance. For a long while no one even tried. Their uneasiness was palpable as they waited out the night. Quickening used that time to relate to the others what she knew of the Stone King's child.

"My father told me of the Maw Grint when he sent me forth from his Gardens," she began, her black eyes distant as she spoke, her silver hair gleaming brightly in the moonlight. They sat in a half-circle, their backs settled protectively against the rocks, their eyes shifting warily from time to time toward the forbidding shadow of the city. All was silent now, the Maw Grint disappeared as mysteriously as it had come, the seabirds gone to roost, and the wind faded away.

Quickening's voice was carefully hushed. "As I am the child of the King of the Silver River, so the Maw Grint is the child of Uhl Belk. Both of us were made by the magic, each to serve a father's needs. We are elementals, beings of earth's life, born out of the soil and not of woman's flesh. We are much the same, the Maw Grint and I."

It was such a bizarre statement that it was all Morgan Leah could do to keep from attacking it. He refrained from doing so only because there was nothing to be gained by voicing an objection and diverting the narration from its intended course.

"The Maw Grint was created to serve a single purpose," Quickening went on. "Eldwist is a city of the old world, one which escaped the devastation of the Great Wars. The city and the land on which it is settled mark the kingdom of Uhl Belk, his haven, his fortress against all encroachment of the world beyond. For a while, they were enough. He was content to burrow in his stone, to remain secluded. But his appetite for power and his fear of losing it were constant obsessions. In the end, they consumed him. He became convinced that if he did not change the world without, it would eventually change him. He determined to extend his kingdom south. But to do so he would have to leave the safety of Eldwist, and that was unacceptable. Like my father, his magic grows weaker the farther he travels from its source. Uhl Belk refused to take such a risk. Instead, he created the Maw Grint and sent his child in his place.

"The Maw Grint," she whispered, "once looked like me. It was human in form and walked the land as I do. It possessed a part of its father's magic as I do. But whereas I was given power to heal the land, the Maw Grint was given power to turn it to stone. A simple touching was all it took. By touching it fed upon the earth and all that lived and grew upon it, and everything was changed to stone.

"But Uhl Belk grew impatient with his child, for the transformation of the lands surrounding was not proceeding quickly enough to suit him. Surrounded by the waters of the Tiderace, which his magic could not affect, he was trapped upon this finger of land with only the way south open to him and only the Maw Grint to widen the corridor. The Stone King infused his child with increasingly greater amounts of his own magic, anxious for quicker and more extensive results. The Maw Grint began to change form as a result of the infusions of power, to transform itself into something more adaptable to what its father demanded. It became molelike. It began to tunnel into the earth, finding that change came quicker from beneath than above. It grew in size as it fed and changed again. It became a massive slug, a burrowing worm of immense proportions."

She paused. "It also went mad. Too much power, too quickly fed, and it lost its sanity. It evolved from a thinking, reasoning creature to one so mindless that it knew only to feed. It swept into the land south, burrowing deeper and deeper. The land changed quickly then, but the Maw Grint changed more quickly yet. And then one day Uhl Belk lost control of his child completely."

She glanced at the dark silhouette of the city and back again. "The Maw Grint began to hunt its father when it was not feeding off the land, aware of the power that the Stone King possessed and eager to usurp it. Uhl Belk discovered that he had fashioned a two-edged sword. On the one hand, the Maw Grint was tunneling into the Four Lands and changing them to stone. On the other, it was tunneling beneath Eldwist as well, searching for a way to destroy him. So powerful had the Maw Grint grown that father and son were evenly matched. The Stone King was in danger of being dispatched by his own weapon."

"Couldn't he simply change his son back again?" Carisman asked, wide-eyed. "Couldn't he use the magic to restore him to what he was?"

Quickening shook her head. "Not by the time he thought to do anything. By then it was too late. The Maw Grint would not let itself be changed—even though, my father tells me, a part of it realized the horror of what it had become and longed for release. That part, it seems, was too weak to act."

"So now it burrows the earth and sorrows over its fate," the tunesmith murmured.

He sang:

> *"Made in the shape of humankind,*
> *To serve the Stone King's dark design,*
> *The Maw Grint tunnels 'neath the land,*
> *A horror wrought by father's hand,*
> *Become a monster out of need,*
> *With no true hope of being freed,*
> *It hunts."*

"Hunts, indeed," Morgan Leah echoed. "Hunts us, probably."

Quickening shook her head. "It isn't even aware that we exist, Morgan. We are too small, too insignificant to catch its attention. Until we choose to use magic, of course. Then it will know."

There was a studied silence. "What was it doing when we saw it tonight?" Horner Dees asked finally.

"Crying out what it feels—its rage, frustration, hatred, and madness." She paused. "Its pain."

"Like the Koden, it is a prisoner of the Stone King's magic," Walker Boh said. His sharp eyes fixed the girl. "And somehow Uhl Belk has managed to keep that magic his own, hasn't he?"

"He has gained possession of the Black Elfstone," she replied. "He went out from Eldwist long enough to steal it from the Hall of Kings and replace it with the Asphinx. He took it back into his keep and used it against his child. Possession of the Elven magic shifted the balance of power back to Uhl Belk. Even the Maw Grint was not powerful enough to defeat the Stone."

"A magic that can negate the power of other magics," Pe Ell recited thoughtfully. "A magic that can turn them to its own use."

"The Maw Grint still threatens its father, but it cannot overcome the Elfstone. It lives because Uhl Belk wishes it to continue feeding on the land, to continue transforming living matter to stone. The Maw Grint is a useful, if dangerous, slave. By night, it tunnels the earth. By day, it sleeps. Like the Koden, it is blind—made so by the magic and the nature of what it does, burrowing within darkness, seldom seeing light." She looked again toward the city. "It will probably never know we are here if we are careful."

"So all we have to do is to steal the Elfstone." Pe Ell smiled. "Steal the Elfstone and let father and son feed on each other. Nothing complicated about it, is there?" He glanced sharply at Quickening. "Is there?"

She met his gaze without flinching, but did not answer. Pe Ell's smile turned cold as he leaned back into the shadows.

There was a moment of strained silence, and then Morgan said to Horner Dees, "What about this Creeper you mentioned?"

Dees was looking sullen as well. He leaned forward ponderously, his eyes narrowed suspiciously. "Maybe the girl can tell you more about it than me," he answered quietly. "I've a feeling there's a great deal she knows and isn't telling."

Quickening's face was devoid of expression, coldly perfect as she faced the old Tracker. "I know what my father told me, Horner Dees—nothing more."

"King of the Silver River, Lord of the Gardens of Life," Pe Ell growled from the shadows. "Keeper of dark secrets."

"As you say, there is a Creeper in the city of Eldwist," Quickening went on, ignoring Pe Ell, her eyes on Dees. "Uhl Belk calls it the Rake. The Rake has been there for many years, a scavenger of living things serving the needs of its master. It comes out after dark and sweeps the streets and walkways of the city clean. We will have to be careful to avoid it when we go in."

"I've seen it at work," Dees grunted. "It took half a dozen of us on the first pass ten years ago, another two shortly after. It's big and quick." He was remembering now, and his anger at Quickening seemed to dissipate. He shook his head doubtfully. "I don't know. It hunts you out, finds you, finishes you. Goes into the buildings if it needs to. Did then, anyway."

"So it would be wise for us to find the Black Elfstone quickly, wouldn't it?" Pe Ell whispered.

They fell silent then, and after a few moments drifted away from each other into the shadows. They spent the remainder of the night attempting to sleep. Morgan dozed, but never for long. Walker was seated at the edge of the rocks watching the city when the Highlander nodded off and was still there when he woke. They were all tired and disheveled—all but Quickening. She stood fresh and new in the weak light of the morning sunrise, as beautiful as in the moment of their first meeting. Morgan found himself disturbed by the fact. In that way, certainly, she was something more than ordinary. He watched her, then looked quickly away when she turned toward him, afraid she would see. It bothered him to think that there might be differences between them after all and, worse, that those differences might be substantial.

They ate breakfast with the same lack of interest with which they had eaten dinner the night before. The land was a stark and ominous presence that watched them through hidden eyes. Fog hung across the peninsula, rising from the cliffs on which the city rested to the peaks of the tallest towers, giving the impression that Eldwist sat within the clouds. The seabirds had returned, gulls, puffins, and terns, wheeling and calling out above the dark waters of the Tiderace. A dampness had settled into the air with dawn's coming, and the water beaded on the faces of the six.

Having been warned by Dees of what lay ahead, they gathered rainwater from pools high in the rocks, wrapped what little food they still possessed against the wet, and set out to cross the isthmus.

It took them longer than they expected. The distance was short, but the path was treacherous. The rock was crisscrossed with crevices, its surface broken apart by ancient upheavals, damp and slick beneath their feet from the ocean's constant pounding. The wind gusted sharply, blowing spray in their faces, chilling their skin. Progress was slow. The sun remained a hazy white ball behind the low-hanging clouds, and the land ahead was filled with shadows. Eldwist rose before them, a cluster of vague shapes, dark and forbidding and silent. They watched it grow larger as they neared, rising steadily into the bleak skies, the sound of the wind echoing mournfully through its canyons.

Sometimes, as they walked, they could feel a rumbling beneath their feet, far distant, but ominously familiar. Apparently the Maw Grint didn't always sleep during the daylight hours.

Midday neared. The isthmus, which had been so narrow at points that the rock dropped away to either side of where they walked into dark cauldrons and whirlpools, broadened finally onto the peninsula and the outskirts of the city. The cliffs on which Eldwist had been built lifted before them, and the company was forced to climb a broad escarpment. Winding through a jumble of monstrous boulders along a pathway littered with loose stone, with their feet constantly sliding out from under them, they struggled resolutely ahead.

It took them the better part of two hours to gain the heights. By then the sun was already arcing west.

They paused to catch their breath at the city's edge, standing together at the end of a stone street that ran between rows of towering, vacant-windowed buildings and narrowed steadily until it disappeared into mist and shadow. Morgan Leah had never seen a city such as this one, the buildings flat and smooth, all constructed of stone, all symmetrically arranged like squares on a checkerboard. Broken rock littered the street, but beneath the rubble he could see the hard, even surface. It seemed as if it ran on forever, as if it had no end, a long, narrow corridor that disappeared only when the mist grew too thick for the eye to penetrate.

They began to walk it, a slow and cautious passage, spreading out along its corridor, listening and watching like cats at hunt. Other streets bisected it from out of the maze of tall buildings, these in turn disappearing right and left into shadow. There were no protective walls about Eldwist, no watchtowers or battlements or gates, only the buildings and the streets that fronted them. There appeared to be nothing living there. The streets and buildings came and went as the company pressed deeper, and the only sounds were those of the ocean and the wind and the seabirds. The birds flew overhead, the only sign of movement, winging their way past the caps of the buildings, down into the streets, across intersections and catwalks. Some roosted on the window ledges high overhead. After a time, Morgan saw that some of those he had believed roosting had been turned to stone.

Much of the debris that lay strewn about had once been something other than stone although most of it was not unrecognizable. Odd-looking poles stood at every street corner, and it was possible to surmise that these might have once been some form of lamps. The carcass of a monstrous carriage lay on its side against one building, a machine whose bones had been stripped of their flesh. Scattered pieces of engines had survived time and weather, gear wheels and cylinders, flywheels and tanks. All had turned to stone. There were no growing things, no trees or shrubs, or even the smallest blade of grass.

They looked inside a few of the buildings and found the rooms cavernous and empty. Stairways ran upward into the stone shells, and they climbed one set all the way to the top so that they could look out across Eldwist and orient themselves. It was impossible to tell much, even as little as where the city began and ended. Clouds and mist obscured everything, revealing only glimpses of facings and roofs in a sea of swirling gray.

They did sight an odd dome at Eldwist's center, a structure unlike the tall obelisks that formed the balance of the city, and they chose to explore it next.

But coming down again into the streets they lost their sense of direction and turned the wrong way. They walked for the better part of an hour before deciding they had made a mistake; then they were forced to climb the stairs of another building in order to regain their bearings.

While they were doing so, the sun set. None of them had been paying any attention to how quickly the daylight had been fading.

When they emerged from their climb they were stunned to find the city in darkness.

"We'd better find a place to hide right now," Horner Dees admonished, glancing around uneasily. "The Rake will be out soon if it isn't already. It if finds us unprotected . . ."

He didn't have to finish the thought. For a moment they stared wordlessly at one another. None of them had bothered looking for a nighttime shelter.

Then Walker Boh said, "There was a small building several streets back with no windows on the lower levels, a small entry, a maze of corridors and rooms inside—like a warren."

"Safe enough for the moment," Pe Ell muttered, already heading down the street.

They began to backtrack through the city. It was so dark by now that they could barely find their way. The buildings loomed to either side in a wall made more solid by the thickening of the mist. The seabirds had again gone to roost, and the sound of ocean and wind had faded into a distant lull. The city was uncomfortably still.

Beneath them, the stone shell of the earth rumbled and shook.

"Something's awake and hungry," Pe Ell murmured and smiled coldly at Carisman.

The tunesmith laughed nervously, his handsome face white and drawn. He sang:

> "Slip away, slip away, slip away home,
> Run for your bedcovers, no more to roam,
> Steal away quick from the things of the night,
> Keep yourself hidden and well out of sight."

They crossed an intersection that was flooded with pale moonlight that had found a break in the clouds and was streaming down in a splash of white fire. Pe Ell stopped abruptly, bringing the rest of them up short as well, listened for a moment, shook his head, and moved on. The rumbling beneath them came and went, sometimes close, sometimes far, never in one spot at any given time, seemingly all around. Morgan Leah peered ahead through mist and shadows. Was this the same street they had been on before? It didn't look quite the same . . .

There was a loud click. Pe Ell, still in the lead, catapulted backward, careening into Horner Dees and Quickening, who were closest, the force of his thrust knocking them both from their feet. They tumbled down in a heap, inches from the edge of a gaping hole that had opened in the street.

"Get back against the buildings!" he snapped, leaping to his feet and sweeping Quickening up with him as he raced from the chasm's edge.

The others were only a step behind. Another section of the street gave way, this one behind them, falling with a crash into blackness. The rumbling beneath crescendoed into a roar that deafened them, and they could hear the passing of something massive below. Morgan crouched deep within a shadowed alcove, pressed up against the stone wall, fighting to keep from screaming against his fear. The Maw Grint! He saw Horner Dees next to him, his bearded face all but invisible as it turned away into the shadows. The thunder of the monster moving below peaked and then began to fade. Seconds later, it was gone.

The members of the little company came out of hiding then, one after another, white-faced and staring. They moved cautiously into the street, then started violently as the holes in the streets closed up again, the fallen sections lifting smoothly back into place.

"Trapdoors!" Pe Ell spat. There was fear and loathing in his face. Morgan caught sight of something white in his hand, a knife of some sort, its metal bright and shining. Then it was gone.

Pe Ell released Quickening from his grasp and turned away from them, moving back along the street, this time staying well up on the walkways that fronted the buildings. Wordlessly, eyes darting from one pool of shadows to the next, the others followed. They hastened down the walkway in single file, crossed the next intersection the same way, and hurried on. The rumbling sounded again, but far away now. The streets about them were quiet and empty once more.

Morgan Leah was still shaking. Those trapdoors had been placed there either to snare intruders or to let the Maw Grint into the city. Probably both. He swallowed against the dryness in his throat. They had been careless back there. They had better not be so again.

A heavy wall of mist blocked the way forward. Pe Ell hesitated as they approached it, then stopped. He looked back at Walker Boh, his eyes hard and penetrating. Some unspoken communication passed between them, a shared look that Morgan found almost feral. Walker glanced right. Pe Ell, after a moment's hesitation, turned that way.

They walked ahead, slowly now, listening to the silence again. The mist was all about them, fallen out of the clouds, seeped up from the stone, and come out of nowhere to envelop them. They moved with their hands stretched out to brush against the walls of the buildings for reassurance. Pe Ell was studying the path ahead carefully, aware now that the city was probably one vast collection of traps, that any part of the stone could drop away beneath their feet without warning.

Ahead, the mist began to clear.

Morgan thought he heard something, then decided he hadn't heard it, that he had sensed it instead. What?

They emerged from the shadow of the building next to them and the answer was waiting. The Rake stood in the center of the street, a huge, splay-legged metal monster with dozens of tentacles and feelers, pincers that gaped from its maw, and a whiplike tail. It was a Creeper like the one the outlaws of the Movement had faced at the Jut, comprised of metal and flesh, a hybrid nightmare of machine and insect. Except that this one was much bigger.

And much quicker. It came for them so fast that it was almost upon them before they had begun to scatter. Its wide, bent legs skittered like a centipede's. Tentacles swept out in a flurry of movement, the sound of metal scraping against stone a horrid rasp. The tentacles caught Dees and Carisman almost instantly, wrapping about them as they tried to flee. Pe Ell shoved Quickening across the walkway toward an open doorway, feinted as if to rush the monster, then darted away. Morgan drew his sword and would have attacked, having lost all sense of what he was doing at the thought of Quickening in danger, when Walker Boh caught hold of him and threw him back against the wall.

"Get inside!" the Dark Uncle cried, motioning toward a set of massive stone doors that gaped open.

Then Walker Boh threw back his cloak and his single arm came up. The Rake was almost on top of him when the arm lowered and a sheet of white light ignited. Morgan shrank back against the wall, blinded. He heard a harsh shriek and realized it was the Creeper. His vision cleared enough to see the creature's metal arms windmilling violently and caught a glimpse of Carisman and Horner Dees running from it. Then he was seized in an iron grip and thrust back through the black opening of the doorway.

It was Pe Ell who had yanked him inside. Quickening was already there. The white light of Walker's magic still burned through the darkness without, and they could hear the Rake thrashing against the building, the force of its attack so violent that stone chips were scattered everywhere. Walker burst into view, Carisman and Horner Dees running before him, stunned but freed. They stumbled across the floor and fell, then regained their feet instantly as the Rake tore the giant entry doors from their hinges, ripped the stone facing apart and shoved inside.

There was a broad staircase leading upward behind them, and they bolted for it. The Rake came after them, staggering slightly. If Walker's magic had done nothing else, it had momentarily disoriented the beast. Its tentacles lashed out wildly in an effort to snare its prey. The six dashed up the stairs. A single whiplash movement from below brought one arm across the steps before them, but Pe Ell's strange knife flashed into view, slicing across the arm and all but severing it. The arm withdrew. They raced upward, springing from one landing to the next, fleeing without looking back.

Finally, at a landing ten floors up, Walker brought them to a ragged halt. Behind them there was only silence. They stood in a knot, their breathing ragged as they listened.

"Perhaps it's given up," Carisman whispered, sounding hopeful.

"Not that thing," Horner Dees replied, his voice a muffled rasp as he fought to catch his breath. "That thing won't ever quit. I've seen what it can do."

Pe Ell thrust forward. "Since you claim to know so much about it, tell us what it might do here!" he snarled.

Dees shook his bearish head obstinately. "I don't know. We never made it as far as the buildings last time." Then he shuddered. "Shades! I can still feel those arms coming tight about me!" He glanced sideways at Quickening. "I should never have let you talk me into coming back here!"

"Hsssst!" Walker Boh was standing at the top of the stairs, head cocked. "There's something . . ." he started to say and stopped.

Pe Ell was next to him in a moment, crouched next to the stair railing. Suddenly he jerked upright. "It's outside!" he snarled and whirled about.

The once-glassed floor-to-ceiling latticework shattered into pieces across the landing as the Rake clawed its way in. Morgan was aghast. While the company had looked for it to come up the stairs, the Rake had climbed the wall!

For a second time, it almost had them. Tentacles whipped across the small space and knocked most of them from their feet. Pe Ell was too quick for it, however, and the strange knife materialized in his hand, shredding the nearest arm. The Creeper flinched away, then came for him. But the diversion had given Walker Boh time to act. A fistful of Cogline's black powder appeared in his hand. He threw it at the beast and fire exploded forth.

The company raced up the stairs once more—one floor, two, three. Behind them, the Creeper thrashed against the fire. Then everything went still. They could no longer hear it; but they all knew where it was. There were openings through the walls on each floor where the windows had fallen away over the years. The Creeper could attack through any of them. It would keep coming after them, and sooner or later it would have them.

"We'll have to stand and fight!" Morgan cried out to the others, snatching free his broadsword.

"Do that and we'll all die, Highlander!" Horner Dees shouted back.

Then Pe Ell brought them up short, lunging ahead and wheeling to face them. "Back down those stairs, the bunch of you! Now! Stay close and I'll see you out of this!"

No one stopped to argue, not even Walker. They retraced their steps in a rush, descending in leaps and bounds, eyes on the window openings at each floor. Two flights down they caught a glimpse of the Rake as it pulled itself level with the frame. Tentacles snaked out, falling short. As they darted away, they could hear the monstrous thing reverse itself against the stone and start after them.

Another three flights, still far from the ground, Pe Ell brought them to a halt once more. "Here! This is the spot!" He pushed them down a long, high-ceilinged corridor. Behind them, the Rake gained the landing and lumbered swiftly in pursuit. The creature seemed to elongate as it came, changing the shape of its body to allow it access. Morgan was terrified. This Creeper could adapt to any situation. Narrow passageways and long climbs were not nearly enough to stop it.

At the end of the corridor was an enclosed catwalk that crossed over to another building. "Get across as fast as you can!" Pe Ell snapped.

Morgan and the others did as they were told. But the Highlander despaired of escape this way. Narrow as the catwalk might be, it would not stop the Rake.

He reached the other side and turned with the others. Pe Ell was kneeling at the far end of the walk where it joined to the other building and sawing at the stone bracing with his strange knife. Morgan stared. Had Pe Ell lost his mind? Did he actually think his knife—any knife—could cut through stone? The Rake was almost on top of him before he was back on his feet. Cat-quick, he darted across the walk. He reached them just as the Rake eased into view, snakelike now as it entered the narrow tunnel opening.

And then the impossible happened. The bracing that Pe Ell had been sawing snapped and gave way. The catwalk lurched downward, held momentarily, then collapsed completely beneath the weight of the Rake. Down it plunged to the street, shattering into fragments, dust and debris rising to mix with the mist and the night.

The six from Rampling Steep stared downward, waiting. Then they heard something—a scraping movement, the sound of metal on stone.

"It's not dead!" Dees whispered in horror.

They stepped back hurriedly from the opening and slipped down to the ground floor, exiting from a door on the far side of the building onto the street. With Pe Ell and Walker in the lead, they made their way silently through the dark. Behind them, they could hear the Creeper beginning to search again.

Less than five blocks away they came upon the building Walker Boh had been seeking, a squat, virtually windowless bunker. They entered with anxious backward glances and peered about. It was indeed a warren, a maze of rooms and corridors with several sets of stairs and half a dozen entries. They climbed four stories, settled themselves in a central room away from any windows, and crouched down to wait.

The minutes passed and the Rake did not appear. An hour came and went. They ate a cold meal and settled back. No one slept.

In the silence, their breathing was the only sound.

Toward dawn, Morgan Leah grew restless. He found himself thinking of Pe Ell's knife, a blade that could cut through stone. The knife intrigued him. Like Pe Ell's presence on this journey, it was an unsolved mystery. The

Highlander took a deep breath. Despite Walker's warning to stay clear of the man, he decided to see what he could learn. Climbing to his feet, he moved to the darkened corner where the other sat with his back to the wall. He could see Pe Ell's eyes track him as he approached.

"What do you want?" Pe Ell asked coldly.

Morgan crouched down in front of him, hesitating in spite of his resolve. "I was curious about your knife," he admitted after a moment.

Their voices were barely audible whispers in the stillness. In the darkened room, no one else could hear.

Pe Ell's smile was cold. "You are, are you?"

"We all saw what it did."

Pe Ell had the knife out instantly, the blade held inches from Morgan's nose. Morgan held his breath and did not move. "The only thing you need to know about this," Pe Ell swore, "is that it can kill you before you can blink. You. Your one-armed friend. Anyone."

Morgan swallowed hard. "Even the Stone King?" He forced the question out, angry with himself for being frightened.

The blade disappeared back into the shadows. "Let me tell you something. The girl says you have magic about you. I don't believe it. You have nothing. One-arm is the only one among you who has magic, and his magic doesn't do anything! It doesn't kill. *He* doesn't kill. I can see it in his eyes. None of you matters in this business, whether you know it or not. You're nothing but a pack of fools."

He jabbed at Morgan with his finger. "Don't get in my way, Highlander. Any of you. And don't expect me to save you the next time that Creeper comes hunting. I'm all done with the lot of you." He withdrew his hand scornfully. "Now get away from me."

Morgan retreated wordlessly. He glanced briefly at Walker as he went, ashamed he had ignored the other's warning about Pe Ell. It was impossible to tell if the Dark Uncle had been watching. Dees and Carisman were asleep. Quickening was a faceless, barely distinguishable shadow.

Morgan sat cross-legged in a corner by himself, seething. He had learned nothing. All he had done was humiliate himself. His mouth tightened. One day he would have the use of his sword again. One day he would find a way to make it whole and recapture its magic—just as Quickening had said he would.

Then he would deal with Pe Ell.

He made himself a promise of it.

19

The company emerged from its concealment at daybreak. Clouds masked the skies over Eldwist from horizon to horizon, morning's arrival bleak and gray. A faint brightening of the damp, misty air was the best that dawn could manage, and night's shadows merely retreated into the city's alcoves and nooks to await their mistress' return.

There was no sign of the Rake. The six from Rampling Steep scanned the gloom cautiously. The buildings rose about them, massive and silent. The streets stretched away, canyons of stone. The only sounds were the howl of the wind, the crashing of the ocean, and the cries of the high-flying seabirds. The only movements were their own.

"As if it were never here," Horner Dees muttered as he shouldered his way past Morgan. "As if it were all a dream."

They began the search again for Uhl Belk. Rain fell through a curtain of smoky mist that tasted and smelled of the sea, and they were soaked through in minutes. A damp sheen settled across the stone walkways and streets, the walls of the buildings, the rubble and debris, a coating that mirrored the gloom and the shadows and played tricks with the light. The wind blew in sharp gusts, darting out of hiding at corners and alleyways, racing down the city's corridors with shrieks of delight, chasing itself endlessly. The morning wore on, a slow grinding of gears in some vast machine that could only be heard in the mind and felt in the wearing of the spirit. Time stole from them, they sensed. Time was a thief.

They found no trace of the Stone King. The city was vast and filled with hiding places, and even if they were sixty instead of six a thorough search could take weeks. None of them had any idea where to look for Uhl Belk or, worse, any idea what he looked like. Even Quickening could offer no help. Her father had not told her how the Stone King might appear. Did he look as they did? Was he human in form? Was he large or small? Morgan asked these questions as they trudged through the gloom, keeping well back on the walkways, close to the building walls. No one knew. They were searching for a ghost.

Midday passed. The buildings and streets of the city came and went in an endless procession of obelisks and gleaming black ribbons. The rain lessened, then increased. Thunder rumbled overhead, slow and ominous. The six ate a cold meal and drank a little in the dank, shadowed entry of one of the buildings while the rain turned into a downpour that flooded the streets with several inches of churning water. They peered outside and watched as the water gathered and flowed in small rivers to stone drains that swallowed it up.

They resumed walking when the rainfall lessened again and shortly afterward came upon the strange dome they had seen from the top of the building they had climbed the previous day. It sat amid the stone spires, a monstrous shell, its surface pitted and worn and cracked. They walked its circumference, searched for an entry, and found none. There were no doors, no stairs, no windows, nor openings of any kind. There were alcoves and niches and insets of varying sizes and shapes that gave its armor a sculpted look, but no way in or out. There were no footholds or ladders that would allow them to climb to its top. It was impossible to determine what it might have been used for. It sat there in the gloom and damp and defied them.

Mindful of time's rapid passing after yesterday's debacle, they returned early to their shelter. No one had much to say. They sat in the growing darkness, mostly apart from each other, mostly silent, and kept their thoughts to themselves.

There had been no sign of either the Maw Grint or the Rake that day. Nightfall brought them both out. They heard the Rake first, a skittering of metal legs on the stone street below, passing by without stopping as they held their collective breath. The Maw Grint came later, the sound of its approach a low rumbling that quickly became a roar. The monster burst forth, howling as it rose into the night. It was uncomfortably close; the stone of the building in which they hid shook with its cry. Then, just as quickly as it had come, it was gone again. No one made any attempt to try to catch a glimpse of it. Everyone stayed carefully put.

They slept better that night, perhaps because they were growing used to the city's night sounds, perhaps because they were so exhausted. They posted a watch and took turns standing it. The watch proved uneventful.

For three days afterward they continued their search. Fog and mist and rain hunted with them, persistent and unwelcome, and the city haunted their dreams. Eldwist was a stone forest filled with shadows and secrets, its towering buildings the trees that hemmed them in and closed them about. But unlike the green, living forests of the lands south the city was empty and lifeless. The girl and the men could form no affinity with Eldwist; they were trespassers here, unwanted and alone. Everything about the world in which they hunted was hard and unyielding. There were no recognizable signs, no familiar markings, and no changes in color or shape or smell or taste that would reveal to them even the smallest clue. There was only the enigma of the stone.

It began to affect the little company despite its resolve. Conversation diminished, tempers grew short, and there was a growing uncertainty as to what they were about. Horner Dees became more sullen and taciturn, his skills as a Tracker rendered useless, his experience from ten years previous used up. Pe Ell continued to distance himself, his eyes suspicious, his

movements furtive and tense, a prowling cat at the edges of a jungle determined not to be brought to bay. Carisman quit singing almost completely.
Morgan Leah found himself jumping at the smallest sound and was preoccupied with thoughts of the magic he had lost when the Sword of Leah
had shattered. Walker Boh was a voiceless ghost, pale and aloof, floating
through the gloom as if at any moment he might simply fade away.

Even Quickening changed. It was barely perceptible, a faint blurring of
her exquisite beauty, an odd shading of her voice and movements, and a
vague weariness in her eyes. Morgan, ever aware of what the girl was
about, thought that he alone could tell.

But once, as they paused in their search in the shadow of a carriage
husk, Walker Boh eased down beside the Highlander and whispered, "This
city consumes us, Morgan Leah. Can you feel it? It has a life beyond what
we understand, an extension of the Stone King's will, and it feeds on
us. The magic is all about. If we do not find Uhl Belk soon, we will be in
danger of being swallowed up entirely. Do you see? Even Quickening is
affected."

And she was, of course. Walker drifted away again, and Morgan was
left to wonder to what end they had been brought here. So much effort
expended to reach this place and it all seemed for nothing. They were being drained of life, sapped of energy and purpose and will. He thought
to speak of it to Quickening, but changed his mind. She knew what was
happening. She always did. When it was time to do something, she would
do it.

But it was Walker Boh who acted first. The fourth day of their hunt
for the Stone King had concluded in the same manner as the previous
three, without any of them having found even the smallest trace of their
quarry. They were huddled in the shadows of their latest shelter; Pe Ell had
insisted they change buildings in an effort to avoid discovery by the Rake,
who still hunted them each night. They had not eaten a hot meal or enjoyed a fire's warmth since their arrival in Eldwist, and their water supply
was in need of replenishing. Footsore and discouraged, they sat mired in
silence.

"We need to search the tunnels beneath the city," the Dark Uncle said
suddenly, his soft voice distant and cold.

The others looked up. "What tunnels?" Carisman wearily asked. The
tunesmith, less fit than the others, was losing strength.

"The ones that honeycomb the rock beneath the buildings," Walker
answered. "There are many of them. I have seen the stairways leading down
from the streets."

Bearish Horner Dees shook his shaggy head. "You forget. The Maw
Grint is down there."

"Yes. Somewhere. But it is a huge, blind worm. It won't even know of
us if we're careful. And if the Maw Grint hides within the earth, maybe the
Stone King hides there as well."

Morgan nodded. "Why not? They might both be worms. Maybe both are blind. Maybe neither likes the light. Goodness knows, there will be little enough of it down there. I think it is a good idea."

"Yes," Quickening agreed without looking at any of them.

Pe Ell stirred in the shadows and said nothing. The others muttered their assent. The darkness of their refuge went quickly still again.

That night Quickening slept next to Morgan Leah, something she had not done since their arrival in Eldwist. She came to him unexpectedly and burrowed close, as if she feared something would attempt to steal her away. Morgan reached around and held her for a time, listening to the sound of her breathing, feeling the pulse of her body against his own. She did not speak. After a time, he fell asleep holding her. When he awoke, she was gone again.

At dawn they departed their shelter and entered the catacombs beneath the city. A stairwell leading down from the building next to the one in which they were housed placed them on the first level. Other stairs ran deeper into the rock, spiraling down black holes of stone into emptiness. The tunnels on the first level were shaped from stone blocks and rails sat on beds of stone and cross ties as they disappeared into the dark. All had been turned to stone. There was no light beneath the city, so Walker Boh used one of Cogline's powders to coat the head of a narrow wedge of stone and create a firebrand. They moved ahead into the tunnels, following the line of the rails as they wound through the darkness. The rails passed platforms and other stairs leading up and down, and the tunnels branched and diverged. The air smelled musty, and loose stone crunched beneath their feet. After a time they came upon a giant carriage that lay upon its side, its wheels grooved to fit the rails, but broken and splintered now and fused to the axle and body by the magic's transformation. Once this carriage had ridden the rails, propelled in some mysterious way, carrying people of the old world from building to building, and from street to street. The members of the company paused momentarily to gaze upon the wreck, then hurried on.

There were other carriages along the way, once an entire chamber full of them, some still seated upon the rails, some fallen and smashed along the way. There were piles of debris fallen by the rails that could not be identified and bits and pieces of what had been iron benches on the platforms they passed. Once or twice they ascended the stairs back to the streets of the city to regain their bearings before going down again. Below, far from where they walked, they could hear the rumble of the Maw Grint. Farther down still there was the sound of the ocean.

After several hours of exploring the network of tunnels without encountering any sign of the Stone King, Pe Ell brought them up short. "This is a waste of time," he said. "There's nothing to be found at this level. We need to go farther down."

Walker Boh glanced at Quickening, then nodded. Morgan caught sight of the looks on the faces of Carisman and Horner Dees and decided the same look was probably on his own.

They descended to the next level, winding down the stairwell into a maze of sewers. The sewers were empty and dry, but there was no mistaking what they had once been. The pipes that formed them were more than twenty feet high. Like everything else, they had been turned to stone. The company began following them, the light of Walker's makeshift torch a silver flare against the black, and the sound of their boots thudding harshly in the stillness. Not more than a hundred yards from where they had entered the sewers, a giant hole had been torn in the side of the stone pipe, shattering it apart as if it were paper. Something massive had burrowed through the rock and out again, something so huge that the sewer pipe had been no more than a blade of grass in its path.

From down the black emptiness of the burrowed tunnel came the rumble of the Maw Grint. The company crossed quickly through the rubble-strewn opening and continued on.

For two hours they wandered the sewers beneath the city, searching in vain for the lair of the Stone King. They twisted and wound about, and soon any sense of direction was irretrievably lost. There were fewer stairs leading up from this level, and many of them were nothing more than ladders hammered into the walls of drains. They came across the burrowings of the Maw Grint several times in the course of their hunt, the massive, jagged openings ripping upward through the earth and then disappearing down into it again, chasms of blackness large enough to swallow whole buildings. Morgan Leah stared into those chasms, realized they must honeycomb the peninsula rock, and wondered why the entire city didn't simply collapse into them.

Shortly after midday they stopped to rest and eat. They found a set of steps leading up to the first level and climbed to where an abandoned platform offered a set of battered stone benches. Seated there, Walker's odd torch planted in the rubble so that its light spilled over them like a halo, they stared wordlessly into the shadows.

Morgan finished before the others and moved over to where a thin shaft of daylight knifed down a stairwell leading to the streets of the city. He seated himself and stared upward, thinking of better times and places, wondering despondently if he would ever find them again.

Carisman came over to sit beside him. "It would be nice to see the sun again," the tunesmith mused and smiled faintly as Morgan glanced over. "Even for just a moment."

He sang:

> "Darkness is for bats and cats and frightened little mice,
>   It's not for those of us who find the sunshine rather nice,
>   So stay away from Eldwist's murk and take this good advice,
>   Go someplace where your skin is warm instead of cold as ice."

He grinned rather sadly. "Isn't that a terrible piece of doggerel? It must be the worst song I've ever composed."

"Where did you come from, Carisman?" Morgan asked him. "I mean, before the Urdas and Rampling Steep. Where is your home?"

Carisman shook his head. "Anywhere. Everywhere. I call wherever I am my home, and I have been most places. I have been traveling since I was old enough to walk."

"Do you have a family?"

"No. Not that I know about." Carisman drew his knees up to his chest and hugged them. "If I am to die here, there is no one who will wonder what has become of me."

Morgan snorted. "You're not going to die. None of us are. Not if we're careful." The intensity of Carisman's gaze made him uncomfortable. "I have a family. A father and mother back in the Highlands. Two younger brothers as well. I haven't seen them now in weeks."

Carisman's handsome face brightened. "I traveled the Highlands some years back. It was beautiful country, the hills all purple and silver in the early light, almost red when the sun set. It was quiet up there, so still you could hear the sound of the birds when they called out from far away." He rocked slightly. "I could have been happy there if I had stayed."

Morgan studied him a moment, watched him stare off into space, caught up in some inner vision. "I plan to go back when we're done with this business," he said. "Why don't you come home with me?"

Carisman stared at him. "Would that be all right? I would like that."

Morgan nodded. "Consider it done. But let's not have any more talk about dying."

They were silent for a moment before Carisman said, "Do you know that the closest thing I ever had to a family was the Urdas? Despite the fact that they kept me prisoner, they took care of me. Cared about me, too. And I cared about them. Like a family. Strange."

Morgan thought about his own family for a moment, his father and mother and brothers. He remembered their faces, the sound of their voices, the way they moved and acted. That led him to think of the Valemen, Par and Coll. Where were they? Then he thought of Steff, dead several weeks now, already becoming a memory, fading into the history of his past. He thought of the promise he had made to his friend—that if he found a magic that could aid the Dwarves in their struggle to be free again, he would use it—against the Federation—against the Shadowen. A rush of determination surged through him and dissipated again. Maybe the Black Elfstone would prove to be the weapon he needed. If it could negate other magics, if it were indeed powerful enough to bring back disappeared Paranor by counteracting the spell of magic that bound it . . .

"They liked the music, you know, but it was more than just that," Carisman was saying. "I think they liked me as well. They were a lot like children in need of a father. They wanted to hear all about the world beyond their valley, about the Four Lands and the peoples that lived there. Most of them had never been anywhere beyond the Spikes. I had been everywhere."

"Except here," Morgan said with a smile.

But Carisman only looked away. "I wish I had never come here," he said.

The company resumed its search of the sewers of Eldwist and continued to find them empty of life. They discovered nothing—not the smallest burrowing rodent, not a bat, not even the insects that normally thrived underground. There was no sign of Uhl Belk. There was only the stone that marked his passing. They wandered for several hours and then began to retrace their steps. Daylight would be gone shortly, and they had no intention of being caught outside when the Rake began its nocturnal scavenging.

"It may be, however, that it doesn't come down into the tunnels," Walker Boh mused.

But no one wanted to find out, so they kept moving. They followed the twisting catacombs, recrossed the burrowings of the Maw Grint, and pushed steadily ahead through the darkness. Grunting and huffing were the only sounds to be heard. Tension lined their faces. Their eyes reflected their discouragement and discontent. No one spoke. What they were thinking needed no words.

Then Walker brought them to a sudden halt and pointed off into the gloom. There was an opening in the tunnel, one that they had somehow missed earlier, smaller than the sewers and virtually invisible in the dimness. Walker crouched down to peer inside, then disappeared into the dark.

A moment later he returned. "There is a cavern and a stairwell leading down," he reported. "It appears there is yet another set of tunnels below."

They followed him through the opening to the chamber beyond, a cave whose walls and floors were studded with jagged projections and rent with deep clefts. They found the stairwell and looked down into its gloom. It was impossible to see anything. They exchanged uneasy glances. Wordlessly, Walker moved to the head of the stairs. Holding the makeshift torch out in front of him, he started down. After a moment's hesitation, the others followed.

The stairs descended a long way, ragged and slick with moisture. The smell of the Tiderace was present here, and they could hear the trickle of seawater in the blackness. When they reached the end of the stairs, they found themselves standing in the middle of a broad, high tunnel in which the rock was crystallized and massive stone icicles hung from the ceiling in clusters, dripping water into black pools. Walker turned right, and the company moved ahead. The dampness chilled the air to ice, and the six pulled their cloaks tightly about them for warmth. Echoes of their footsteps reverberated through the stone corridor, chasing the silence.

Then suddenly there was something else, a sort of squealing that reminded Morgan Leah of a rusted iron lever being shifted after a long period of disuse. The members of the company stopped as one at its sound and stood in the faint silver glow of the torchlight, listening. The squealing continued; it was coming from somewhere behind them.

"Come," Walker Boh said sharply and began hurrying ahead. The others hastened after, spurred on by the unexpected urgency in his voice. Walker had recognized something in the sound that they had not. Morgan glanced over his shoulder as he went. What was back there?

They crossed a shallow stream of water that tumbled from a fissure in the rock wall, and Walker turned, motioning the rest of them past. The squealing sound was deafening now and coming closer. The Dark Uncle passed the torch to Morgan wordlessly, then lifted his arm and threw something into the black. A white fire flared to life, and the tunnel behind them was suddenly filled with light.

Morgan gasped. There were rats everywhere, a churning, scrambling mass of furred bodies. But these rats were giants, grown to three and four times their normal size, all claws and teeth. Their eyes were white and sightless, like everything else the company had encountered in Eldwist, and their bodies were sleek with the dampness of the sea. They looked ravenous. And maddened. They poured out of the rocks and came for the men and the girl.

"Run!" Walker cried, snatching the torch back from Morgan.

And run they did, charging frantically through the darkness with the sound of the squealing chasing after them in gathering waves, struggling to keep at the edges of the torchlight as they fought to escape the horror that pursued. The tunnel rose and fell in ragged slopes, and the rocks cut and scraped at them. They fell repeatedly, scrambled up again, and ran on.

A ladder! That was all that Morgan Leah could think. *We've got to find a ladder!*

But there was none. There were only the rock walls, the streams and pools of seawater, and the rats. And themselves, trapped.

Then from somewhere ahead came a new sound, the booming of waves against a shoreline, the pounding of the ocean against land.

They broke from the blackness of the tunnel into a faint, silvery brightness and staggered to a ragged halt. Before them a cliff dropped sharply into the Tiderace. The ocean churned and swirled below, crashing into the rocks, foaming white as it spilled over them. They were in an underground cavern so massive that its farthest reaches were lost in mist and shadow. Daylight spilled through clefts in the rock where the ocean had breached the wall. Other tunnels opened into the cavern as well, black holes far to the right and left. All were unreachable. The cliffs to either side were impassable. The drop below led to the rocks and the roiling sea. The only way left was back the way they had come.

Through the rats.

The rats were almost on top of the company now, their squeals rising up to overwhelm the thunder of the ocean's waters, their masses filling the lower half of the tunnel as they bit and clawed ahead. Morgan yanked out his broadsword, knowing even as he did so how futile the weapon would be. Pe Ell had moved to one side, clear of the others, and his strange silver knife was in his hand. Dees and Carisman were backed to the edge of the drop, crouched as if to jump.

Quickening stepped forward beside Morgan, her beautiful face strangely calm, her hands steady on his arm.

Then Walker Boh cast aside his torch and hurled a fistful of black powder into the horde of rats. Fire exploded everywhere, and the first rank was incinerated. But there were hundreds more behind that one, thousands of churning dark bodies. Claws scraped madly on the rocks, seeking to find a grip. Teeth and sightless eyes gleamed. The rats came on.

"Walker!" Morgan cried out desperately and shoved Quickening behind him.

But it wasn't the Dark Uncle who responded to Morgan's plea, or Pe Ell, or Horner Dees, or even Quickening. It was Carisman, the tunesmith.

He rushed forward, pushing past Morgan and Quickening, coming up beside Walker just as the rats burst through the tunnel opening onto the narrow ledge. Lifting his wondrous voice, he began to sing. It was a song that was different than any they had ever heard; it scraped like the rub of metal on stone, shrieked like the tearing of wood, and broke through the thunder of the ocean and the squeal of the rats to fill the cavern with its sound.

"Come to me!" Quickening cried out to the rest of them.

They bunched close at once, even Pe Ell, flattening themselves against one another as the tunesmith continued to sing. The rats poured out of the tunnel and swept toward them in a wave of struggling bodies. But then the wave split apart, flowing to either side of the tunesmith, passing by without touching any of them. Something in Carisman's song was turning them away. They twisted to either side, a churning mass. Onward they scrambled, heedless of everything, whether fleeing or being called it was impossible to tell, and tumbled into the sea.

Moments later, the last of them had been swallowed up or swept away. Carisman went still, then collapsed into Morgan's arms. The Highlander propped him up, and Quickening wiped cold seawater onto his face with the sleeve of her tunic. The others glanced about breathlessly, cautiously, scanning the dark tunnel opening, the empty rock, the waters of the sea.

"It worked," Carisman whispered in surprise as his eyes fluttered open again. "Did you see? It worked!" He struggled up and seized Quickening jubilantly by the arms. "I'd read something about it once, or heard about it maybe, but I had never thought I would . . . I mean, I had never tried such a thing before! Never! It was a cat song, Lady! A cat song! I didn't know what else to do, so I made those horrid rodents think we were giant cats!"

Everyone stared in disbelief. Only then did Morgan Leah appreciate how truly miraculous their escape had been.

20

With the destruction of the rats, they were able to retrace their steps through the tunnel that had brought them to the underground cavern, climb back into the sewers of Eldwist, climb from there to the level of tunnels above, and finally reach the streets of the city. It was already growing dark, and they hurried quickly through the descending gloom to gain the safety of their nighttime refuge. They only just succeeded. The Rake appeared almost at once, an invisible presence beyond the walls of the building, its armored legs scraping across the stone below, searching for them still. They sat huddled silently in the dark listening to it hunt until it had gone. Walker said he thought the creature could track by smell, only the rain and the number of trails they had left was confusing it. Sooner or later it would figure out where they were hiding.

Exhausted and aching and shaken by what had befallen them, they ate their dinner in silence and went quickly off to sleep.

The next morning Pe Ell, who following their escape from the tunnels had descended into a mood so black that no one dared approach him, announced that he was going out on his own.

"There are too many of us stumbling about to ever find anything," he declared, his voice calm and expressionless, his narrow face unreadable. He spoke to Quickening, as if only she mattered. "If there truly is a Stone King, he knows by now that we are here. This is his city; he can hide in it forever if he chooses. The only way to find him is to catch him off guard, sneak up on him, and surprise him. There will be none of that if we continue to hunt like a pack of dogs."

Morgan started to intervene, but Walker's fingers closed about his arm like iron bands.

Pe Ell glanced around. "The rest of you can keep bumbling about as long as you wish. But you'll do it without me. I've spent enough time shepherding you around. I should have gone off on my own from the first. If I had, this business would be finished by now." He turned back to Quickening. "When I have found Uhl Belk and the Black Elfstone, I will come back for you." He paused, meeting her gaze squarely. "If you are still alive."

He strode past them contemptuously and disappeared down the hall. His boots thudded softly on the stairs and faded into silence.

Horner Dees spit. "We're well rid of that one," he muttered.

"He is correct, though," Walker Boh said, and they all turned to look at him. "In one respect at least. We must divide ourselves up into groups if

511

we are ever to complete this search. The city is too large, and we are too easy to avoid while we stay together."

"Two groups then," Dees agreed, nodding his shaggy head. "No one goes out alone."

"Pe Ell doesn't seem worried about hunting alone," Morgan noted.

"He's a predator, sure enough," Dees replied. He looked at Quickening speculatively. "How about it, girl? Does he have any chance of finding Belk and the Elfstone on his own?"

But Quickening only said, "He will return."

They seated themselves to work out a strategy, a method by which the city could be searched from end to end. The buildings ran mostly north of where they were concealed, so it was decided to divide Eldwist in two with one group taking the east half and the other the west. The search would concentrate on the buildings and streets, not the tunnels. If nothing were found aboveground, they would change their approach.

"Pe Ell may be wrong when he says that the Stone King must know we are here," Quickening said in closing. She brought her slender fingers up in a quick, birdlike movement. "We are insignificant in his eyes, and he may not yet have even noticed us. We are the reason he keeps the Rake in service. Besides, the Maw Grint occupies his time."

"How do we divide ourselves up?" Carisman asked.

"You will go with me," Quickening answered at once. "And Walker Boh."

Morgan was surprised. He had expected her to choose him. The disappointment he felt cut deeply. He started to dispute her choice, but her black eyes fixed him with such intensity that he went instantly still. Whatever her reasons for making this decision, she did not want it questioned.

"That leaves you and me, Highlander," Horner Dees grunted and clapped one heavy hand on Morgan's shoulder. "Think we can manage to disappoint Pe Ell and keep our skins whole?"

His sudden laugh was so infectious that Morgan found himself smiling in response. "I'd bet on it," he replied.

They gathered up their gear and went down into the street. Sheets of gloom draped the buildings, hung from skies thick with clouds and mist. The air was damp and chill, and their breath exhaled in a haze of white. They wished each other well and began moving off in separate directions, Morgan and Horner Dees going west, Quickening, Walker, and Carisman east.

"Take care of yourself, Morgan," Quickening whispered, her exquisite face a mix of shadow and light beneath the sweep of her silver hair. She touched him softly on the shoulder and hurried after Walker Boh.

"Tra-la-la-la, a-hunting we will go!" Carisman sang merrily as they disappeared.

Rain began to fall in a steady drizzle. Morgan and Horner Dees slogged ahead with their cloaks pulled tightly about their shoulders and their heads bent. They had agreed that they would follow the street to its end, until they were at the edge of the city, then turn north to track the peninsula's shoreline. There had been little enough found within the core of the city; perhaps there was something outside—particularly if the Stone King's magic was ineffective against water. They kept to the walkways and glanced cautiously down the darkened corridors of the sidestreets they passed. Rainwater collected on the city's stone skin in puddles and streams, shimmering darkly in the gloom. Seabirds huddled in nooks and crevices, waiting out the storm. In the shadows, nothing moved.

It was nearing midmorning when they reached the Tiderace, the land ending in cliffs which dropped hundreds of feet into the sea. Craggy outcroppings of rock rose out of the churning waters, worn and pitted. Waves crashed against the cliffs, the sound of their pounding mixing with the wind as it swept off the water in a rising howl. Morgan and Dees melted back into the shelter of the outer buildings, seeking to protect themselves. Rain and ocean spray soaked them quickly through, and they were soon shivering beneath their clothes. For two hours they skirted the city's western boundaries without finding anything. By midday, when they stopped to eat, they were disgruntled and worn.

"There's nothing to be found out here, Highlander," Dees observed, chewing on a bit of dried beef—his last. "Just the sea and the wind and those confounded birds, shrieking and calling like madwomen."

Morgan nodded without answering. He was trying to decide whether he could eat a seabird if he had to. Their food supplies were almost exhausted. Soon they would be forced to hunt. What else was there besides those birds? Fish, he decided firmly. The birds looked too rangy and tough.

"You miss the Highlands?" Dees asked him suddenly.

"Sometimes." He thought about his home and smiled faintly. "All the time."

"Me, too, and I haven't seen them in years. Thought they were the most beautiful piece of work nature ever made. I liked how they made me feel when I was in them."

"Carisman said he liked it there, too. He said he liked the quiet."

"The quiet. Yes, I remember how quiet it was in those hills." They had found shelter in a building's shadowed entry. The big man shifted himself away from a widening stain where the rain had trickled down the wall and collected on the steps where they were seated, backs to the wall, facing out into the weather.

He leaned forward. "Let me tell you something," he said softly. "I know this fellow, Pe Ell."

Morgan looked over, intrigued. "From where?"

"From before. Long before. Almost twenty years. He was just a kid then; I was already old." Dees chuckled darkly. "Some kid. A killer even then. An assassin right from the beginning—as if that was what he was born to be and he couldn't ever be anything else but." He shook his grizzled head. "I knew him. I knew it was bad luck if you crossed him."

"Did you?"

"Cross him? Me? No, not me. I know well enough who to stand up to and who to back away from. Always have. That's how I've stayed alive. Pe Ell is the kind who once he takes a dislike to you will keep coming till you're dead. Doesn't matter how long it takes him or how he gets the job done. He'll just keep at it." He pointed at Morgan. "You better understand something. I don't know what he's doing here. I don't know why the girl brought him. But he's no friend to any of you. You know what he is? He's a Federation assassin. Their best, in fact. He's Rimmer Dall's favorite boy."

Morgan froze, the blood draining from his face. "That can't be."

"Can and is," Dees said emphatically. "Unless things have changed from how they used to be, and I doubt they have."

Morgan shook his head in disbelief. "How do you know all this, Horner?"

Horner Dees smiled, a wide, hungry grin. "Funny thing about that. I remember him even though he doesn't remember me. I can see it in his eyes. He's trying to figure out what it is I know that he doesn't. Have you seen the way he looks at me? Trying to figure it out. Been too long, I guess. He's killed too many men, has too many faces in his past to remember many of them. Me, I been gone a long time. I don't have so many ghosts to worry about." He paused. "Truth is, Highlander, I was one of them myself."

"One of them?" Morgan asked quietly.

The other gave a sharp laugh, like a bark. "I was with the Federation! I tracked for them!"

As quick as that Morgan Leah's perception of Horner Dees changed. The big, bearish fellow was no longer just a gruff, old Tracker whose best days were behind him; he was no longer even a friend. Morgan started to back away and then realized there was nowhere to back to. He reached for his broadsword.

"Highlander!" Dees snapped, freezing him. The big man clenched one massive fist, then relaxed it. "Like I said, that was long ago. I been gone from those people twenty years. Settle back. You haven't any reason to fear me."

He placed his hands in his lap, palms up. "Anyway, that's how I came to see the Highlands, believe it or not—in the service of the Federation. I was tracking Dwarf rebels for them, hunting the Rainbow Lake and Silver River country. Never found much. Dwarves are like foxes; they go to ground quick as a wink when they know they're being hunted." He smiled unexpectedly. "I didn't try very hard in any case. It was a worthless sort of job."

Morgan released his grip on the broadsword and sat back again.

"I was with them long enough to find out about Pe Ell," the other went on, and now his eyes were distant and troubled. "I knew most of what was happening back then. Rimmer Dall had me slated to be a Seeker. Can you imagine? Me? I thought that wolf's head stuff was nonsense. But I learned about Pe Ell while Dall was working on me. Saw him come and go once, when he didn't know it. Dall arranged for me to see because he liked putting one over on Pe Ell. It was a sort of game with the two of them, each trying to show up the other. Anyway, I saw him and heard what he did. A few others heard things, too. Everyone knew to stay away from him."

He sighed. "Just a little while after that, I quit the bunch of them. Left when no one was looking, came north through the Eastland, traveled about until I reached Rampling Steep, and decided that was where I'd live. Away from the madness south, the Federation, the Seekers, all of it."

"All of it?" Morgan repeated doubtfully, still trying to decide what to make of Horner Dees. "Even the Shadowen?"

Dees blinked. "What do you know of the Shadowen, Morgan Leah?"

Morgan leaned forward. Windblown mist had left Horner's face damp and shining, and droplets of water clung to his hair and beard. "I want to know something from you first. Why are you telling me all this?"

The other's smile was strangely gentle. "Because I want you to know about Pe Ell, and you can't know about him without knowing about me. I like you, Highlander. You remind me a little of myself when I was your age—kind of reckless and headstrong, not afraid of anything. I don't want there to be secrets about me that might come out in a bad way. Like if Pe Ell should remember who I am. I want you for a friend and ally. I don't trust anyone else."

Morgan studied him wordlessly for a moment. "You might do better with someone else."

"I'll chance it. Now, how about it? I've answered your question. You tell me how you know about the Shadowen."

Morgan drew up his knees and hugged them to his chest, making up his mind. Finally, he said, "My best friend was a Dwarf named Steff. He was with the Resistance. The woman he loved was a Shadowen, and she killed him. I killed her."

Horner Dees arched his eyebrows quizzically. "I was given to understand that nothing but magic could kill those things."

Morgan reached down and drew out the shattered end of the Sword of Leah. "There was magic in this Sword once," he said. "Allanon put it there himself—three hundred years ago. I broke it during a battle with the Shadowen in Tyrsis before the start of all this. Even so, there was still enough magic left to avenge Steff and save myself." He studied the blade speculatively, hefted it, waited in vain to feel its warmth, then looked back at Dees. "Maybe there's still some. Anyway, that's why Quickening brought me along. This Sword. She said there was a chance it could be restored."

Horner Dees frowned. "Are you to use it against Belk then?"

"I don't know," Morgan admitted. "I haven't been told anything except that it could be made whole again." He slipped the broken blade back into its scabbard. "Promises," he said and sighed.

"She seems like the kind who keeps hers," the other observed after a moment's thought. "Magic to find magic. Magic to prevail over magic. Us against the Stone King." He shook his head. "It's too complicated for me.

You just be sure you remember what I said about Pe Ell. You can't turn your back on him. And you mustn't go up against him either. You leave that to me."

"You?" Morgan declared in surprise.

"That's right. Me. Or Walker Boh. One-armed or not, he's a match for Pe Ell or I've misjudged him completely. You concentrate on keeping the girl safe." He paused. "Shouldn't be too hard, considering how you feel about each other."

Morgan flushed in spite of himself. "It's mostly me that's feeling anything," he muttered awkwardly.

"She's the prettiest thing I've ever seen," the old man said, smiling at the other's discomfort. "I don't know what she is, human or elemental or what, but she can charm the boots right off you. She looks at you, that face softens, she speaks the way she does, and you'll do anything for her. I should know. I wasn't ever going to come back to this place and here I am. She's done it to all of us."

Morgan nodded. "Even to Pe Ell. He's as much hers as the rest of us."

But Dees shook his head. "I don't know, Highlander. You look careful next chance you get. He's hers, but he isn't. She walks a fine line with that one. He could turn quick as a cat. That's why I tell you to look after her. You remember what he is. He's not here to do us any favors. He's here for himself. Sooner or later, he'll revert to form."

"I think so, too," Morgan agreed.

Dees gave a satisfied smirk. "But it won't be so easy for him now, will it? Because we'll be watching."

They packed up, tightened their cloaks against the weather, and stepped back out into the downpour. They continued to follow the shoreline as the afternoon lengthened, reaching the northernmost point of the peninsula without finding anything, and turned back again into the city. The rain finally ended, changing to a fine mist that hung like smoke against the gray sky and buildings. The air warmed. Shadows yawned and stretched in alleyways and nooks like waking spirits, and steam rose off the streets.

From somewhere underground the rumble of the Maw Grint sounded, a distant thunder that shook the earth.

"I'm beginning to think we're not ever going to find anything," Horner Dees muttered at one point.

They followed the dark corridors of the streets and searched the brume that lay all about, the doorways and windows that gaped open like mouths in search of food, and the flat, glistening walkways and passages. Everywhere the city lay abandoned and dead, stripped of life and filled with hollow, empty sounds. It walled them away with its stone and its silence; it wrapped about them with such persistence that despite memory and reason it seemed that the world beyond must have fallen away and that Eldwist was all that remained.

They grew weary with the approach of evening; the sameness of their surroundings dulled their senses and wore against their resistance. They be-

TERRY BROOKS

gan to stray a bit, to wander closer to the walkway's edge, to look upward more often at the stone heights that loomed all about, and to give themselves over to a dangerous and persistent wish that something—*anything*—would happen. Their boredom was acute, their sense of being unable to change or affect the things about them maddening. They had been in Eldwist almost a week. How much longer would they be forced to remain?

Ahead, the street deadended. They rounded the corner of the building they were following and discovered that the street widened into a square. At the square's center was an odd depression with steps leading down on all sides to a basin from which a statue rose, a winged figure with streamers and ribbons trailing from its body. Almost without thinking, they turned into the square, beguiled by its look, so different from anything else they had seen. *A park,* they thought to themselves without speaking. What was it doing here?

They were halfway across the street when they heard the catch that secured the trapdoor beneath them release.

They had no chance of saving themselves. They were standing in the center of the door when it dropped, and they plunged into the void beneath. They fell a long way, struck the side of a chute, and began to slide head-downward. The chute was rough, its surface littered with loose rock that cut and bit into their faces and hands. They clawed frantically in an attempt to slow their descent, heedless of the pain. Boots and knees dug in; hands and fingers grasped. The slide broadened and its slope decreased. They quit rolling, flattened themselves in a spread-eagle position, and came to a grinding halt.

Morgan lifted his head gingerly and peered about. He lay facedown on a slab of rock that stretched so far away into the shadows on either side that he could not see its end. Loose rock lay upon the slide like a carpet, bits and pieces of it still tumbling away. There was a faint glimmer of light from somewhere above, a narrow shaft that sought in vain to penetrate the gloom, so thin that it barely reached to where Morgan lay. He forced himself to look down. Horner Dees lay some twenty feet below him on his right, sprawled on his back with his arms and legs thrown wide, unmoving. Farther down, like a giant, hungry mouth, was a chasm of impenetrable blackness.

Morgan swallowed against the dust in his throat. "Horner?" he whispered hoarsely.

"Here," the other said, his voice a faint rasp.

"Are you all right?"

There was a grunt. "Nothing broken, I think."

Morgan took a moment to look about. All he could see was the slide, the shaft of light above, and the chasm below. "Can you move?" he called down softly.

There was silence for a moment, then the sound of rocks clattering away into the dark. "No," the reply came. "I'm too fat and old, Highlander. If I try to get up to you, I'll start sliding and won't be able to stop."

Morgan heard the strain in his voice. And the fear. Dees was helpless, laying on that loose rock like a leaf on glass; even the slightest movement would send him spinning away into the void.

Me, too, if I make any attempt to help, the Highlander thought darkly.

Yet he knew that he had to try.

He took a deep breath and brought his hand up slowly to his mouth. A shower of loose rock rattled away, but his body stayed in place on the slide. He brushed at the silt on his lips and closed his eyes, thinking. There was a rope in his backpack, a thin, strong coil, some fifty feet of it. His eyes opened again. Could he find a way to fasten it to something and haul himself up?

A familiar rumbling shook the earth, rising from below, shaking the carpet of rock about him so that small showers of it slid into the abyss. There was a thunderous huffing and a great, long sigh as if an enormous amount of air was being released.

Morgan Leah glanced down, cold to the bone. In the depths below, right beneath where they hung, the Maw Grint lay sleeping.

Morgan looked up again quickly. His breath came in short, frantic gasps, and he had to struggle to overcome an almost overpowering urge to claw his way out of there as fast as he could. The Maw Grint. That close. It was huge beyond belief; even his vague glimpse of it had been enough to tell him that. He couldn't begin to guess how much of it there was, where it began and ended, how far it stretched away.

He gripped at the rock until his hands hurt, fighting back against his fear and nausea. He had to get out of there! He had to find a way!

Almost without thinking about what he was doing, he reached beneath his stomach and began working free the broken remains of the Sword of Leah. It was a slow, agonizing process, for he was unable to lift up without fear of beginning his slide down again. And now, more than he had ever wanted anything, he did not want that.

"Don't try to move, Horner!" he called down softly, his voice dry and rough. "Stay where you are!"

There was no response. Morgan inched the Sword of Leah clear of its scabbard and out from under him, bringing it level with his face. The polished metal surface of the broken blade glittered brightly in the faint light. He pushed it above his head with one hand, then reached up with the other until he could grip it firmly with both. Turning the jagged end of the blade downward, he began to slide it into the rock. He felt it bite into the stone slab beneath.

Please! he begged.

Jamming the Sword of Leah into the stone, he hauled himself up. The blade held, and he pulled his face level with its handle. Bits of rock fell away beneath him, tumbling and sliding into the void. The Maw Grint did not stir.

Morgan freed the Sword, reached upward to jam it into the rock again, gripped it with every ounce of strength he possessed, and pulled himself level once more. He closed his eyes and lay next to it panting, then felt a rush of heat surge through his body. *The magic?* He opened his eyes quickly to see, searching the Sword's gleaming length. Nothing.

Holding himself in place with one hand, he used the other to dive into his pack and secure the length of rope and a grappling hook. A handful of cooking implements and a blanket worked free in the process and fell onto the chute. Ignoring them, the Highlander slipped the rope about his waist and shoulders and tied it in a harness.

"Horner!" he whispered.

The old Tracker looked up, and Morgan threw the rope to him. It fell across his body, and he seized it with both hands. He started to slip almost immediately, swinging over until he was beneath Morgan. Then the rope went taut, catching him. The shock to Morgan's body was staggering, an immense, wrenching weight that threatened to pull him down. But he had both hands fastened once more on the Sword of Leah, and the blade held firm.

"Climb to me!" he whispered down harshly.

Horner Dees began to do so, slowly, torturously, hand over hand up the rope and the slide. As he passed the cooking implements and blanket that had fallen from Morgan's pack, he kicked them free, and they tumbled farther down in a shower of rock.

This time the Maw Grint coughed and came awake.

It grunted, a huffing sound that reverberated against the stone walls. It lifted itself, its massive body thudding against the walls of the tunnel in which it slept, shaking the earth violently. It rolled and pitched and began to move. Morgan hung on to the pommel of his sword, and Dees clung to the slender rope, both gritting their teeth against the strain on muscle and bone. The Maw Grint shook itself, and Tracker and Highlander could hear a spraying sound and then a hiss of steam.

The Maw Grint slid away into the black and the sound of its passing faded. Morgan and Dees looked down cautiously.

An odd, greenish stain was working its way up the stone of the chute, just visible at the far edge of the shaft of light several dozen feet below Dees. It glistened darkly and steamed like a fire advancing through brush. They watched as it reached the blanket that had fallen from Morgan's pack. When it touched it, the rough wool turned instantly to stone.

Horner Dees began climbing again at once, a furious assault on the loose stone of the slide. When he was almost to Morgan, the Highlander stopped him, beckoned for slack on the rope, and began his own ascent, jamming the Sword blade down into the rock, pulling himself up, jamming and pulling, over and over again.

They went on that way for what seemed an endless span of time. Daylight beckoned them, drawing them like a beacon toward the surface of the city and safety. Sweat ran down Morgan's face and body until he was drenched in it. His breathing grew labored, and his entire body was wracked with pain. It grew so bad at one point that he thought he must quit. But he

could not. Below, the stain continued to advance, the poison given off by
the Maw Grint's body solidifying everything in its path. The blanket went
first, then the handful of cooking implements that hadn't fallen into the
abyss. Soon there was nothing left save Morgan and Horner Dees.

And it was gaining steadily on them.

They struggled on, hauling themselves upward foot by foot. Morgan's
mind closed down on his thoughts like an iron lid on a trunk of useless
relics, and all of his efforts became concentrated on the climb. As he labored, he felt the heat spread through him once more, stronger this time,
more insistent. He could feel it turning inside him like an auger, boring and
twisting at the core of his being. It reached from head to heels and back
again, from fingers to toes, through the muscles and bone and blood, until
it was all he knew. At some point—he never knew exactly when—he
looked at the Sword of Leah and saw it glowing as bright as day, the white
fire of its magic burning through the shadows. *Still there,* he thought in furious determination. *Still mine!*

Then suddenly there was a ladder, rungs lining the walls of the chute
above him, rising up from the darkness of their prison toward the fading
daylight and the city. The light, he saw, came from a narrow airshaft. He
scrambled toward it, jamming, hauling, releasing, starting all over again. He
heard Horner Dees calling to him from below, his hoarse voice almost a
sob, and looked down long enough to see the poison of the Maw Grint
inches from the old Tracker's boots. He reached down impulsively with one
hand and calling on a strength he didn't know he possessed, hauled upward
on the rope, pulling Dees clear. The other kicked and scrambled toward
him, bearded face a mask of dust and sweat. Morgan's hand released the
rope and closed over the bottommost rung of the ladder. Dees continued
to climb, digging his boots into the loose stone. The light was failing
quickly now, gone gray already, slipping rapidly into darkness. Below, the
Maw Grint's muffled roar shook the earth.

Then they were both on the ladder, scrambling upward, feet and hands
gripping, bodies pressing against the stone. Morgan jammed the Sword of
Leah back into his belt, safely in place. *Still magic!*

They burst from the airshaft into the street and fell on the walkway in
exhaustion. Together, they crawled to the doorway of the nearest building
and collapsed in the cool of its shadows.

"I knew . . . I was right . . . in wanting you for a friend," Horner Dees
gasped.

He reached over, this great bearish man, and pulled the Highlander
close. Morgan Leah could feel him shake.

21

Pe Ell spent the day sleeping.

After he walked out on Quickening and the others of the little company from Rampling Steep he went directly to a building less than a block away that he had chosen for himself two days earlier. Rounding the corner of the building so that he was out of sight of anyone who might be watching, he entered through a side door, climbed the stairs one floor, followed the hallways to the front of the building, and turned into a large, well-lighted chamber with windows that ran almost floor to ceiling and opened on the street below and the buildings across, one of which was where his once-companions were presently hiding.

He permitted himself a brief smile. They were such a pack of fools.

Pe Ell had a plan. He believed, as Quickening did, that the Stone King was hidden somewhere in the city. He did not believe the others of the company would find him even if they searched from now until next summer. He alone could do so. Pe Ell was a hunter by instinct and experience; the others were something less—each to a varying degree, but all hopeless. He had not lied when he told them he would be better off on his own. He would. Horner Dees was a Tracker, but a Tracker's skills were useless in a city of stone. Carisman and Morgan Leah had no skills worth talking about. Quickening disdained the use of her magic—maybe with good reason, although he wasn't convinced of that yet. The only one who might have been useful to him was Walker Boh. But the man with one arm was his most dangerous enemy, and he did not want to have to worry about watching his back.

His plan was simple. The key to finding Uhl Belk was the Rake. The Creeper was the Stone King's house pet, a giant watchdog that kept his city free of intruders. He turned it loose at night, and it swept the streets and buildings clean. What it missed one night, it went after the next. But only at night, not during the day. Why was that? Pe Ell asked himself. And the answer was obvious. Because like everything else that served the Stone King, willingly or not, it could not see. It hunted by using its other senses. The night was its natural ally. Daylight might even hinder it.

Where did it go during the day? Pe Ell then asked. Again, the answer seemed obvious. Like any house pet, it went back to its master. That meant that if Pe Ell could manage to follow the Rake to its daytime lair he had a good chance of finding the Stone King.

Pe Ell thought he could do so. The night was his ally as well; he had done most of his own hunting in the dark. His own senses were as sharp as those of the Creeper. He could hunt the Rake as easily as the Rake could hunt him. The Rake was a monster; there was no point in thinking he stood a chance against such a beast in a face-to-face confrontation, even with the aid of the Stiehl. But Pe Ell could be a shadow when he chose, and nothing could bring him to bay. He would take his chances; he would play cat and mouse with the Rake. Pe Ell was feeling many things, but fear wasn't one of them. He had a healthy respect for the Creeper, but he was not frightened of it. After all, he was the smarter of the two.

Come nightfall, he would prove it.

So he slept the daylight hours away, stretched out of sight just beneath the windows where he could feel the faint, hazy sunlight on his face and hear the sounds of anyone or anything passing in the street below.

When it grew dark, the shadows cooling the air to a damp chill, the light fading away, he rose and slipped down the stairs and out the door. He stood listening in the gloom for a long time. He had not heard the others of the company return from their daytime hunt; that was odd. Perhaps they had come into their shelter through another door, but he thought he would have heard them nevertheless. For a moment he considered stealing in for a quick look, but abandoned the idea almost immediately. What happened to them had nothing to do with him. Even Quickening no longer mattered as much. Now that he was away from her, he discovered, she had lost something of her hold over him. She was just a girl he had been sent to kill, and kill her he would if she was still alive when he returned from his night's hunt.

He would kill them all.

The cries of the seabirds were distant and mournful in the evening stillness, faint whimpers carried on the ocean wind. He could hear the dull pounding of the waters of the Tiderace against Eldwist's shores and the low rumble of the Maw Grint somewhere deep beneath the city.

He could not hear the Creeper.

He waited until it was as black as it would get, the skies obscured by clouds and mist, the gloom settled down about the buildings, spinning shadow webs. He had listened to and identified all of the dark's sounds by then; they were as familiar as the beating of his pulse. He began to move, just another shadow in the night. He slipped down the streets in quick, cautious dartings that carried him from one pool of darkness to the next. He did not carry any weapon but the Stiehl, and the Stiehl was safely sheathed within the covering of his pants. The only weapons he needed right now were instinct and stealth.

He found a juncture of streets where he could crouch in wait within a deeply shadowed entry that opened out of a tunnel stairwell and gave him a clear view of everything for almost two blocks. He settled himself back against the stone centerpost and waited.

Almost immediately, he began thinking of the girl.

Quickening, the daughter of the King of the Silver River—she was a maddening puzzle who stirred such conflicting feelings within him that he could barely begin to sort them out. It would have been better simply to brush them all aside and do as Rimmer Dall had said he must—kill her. Yet he could not quite bring himself to do so. It was more than defiance of Dall and his continued attempts to subvert him to the Shadowen cause, more than his determination that he would handle matters in his own way; it was the doubt and hesitation she roused in him, the feeling that somehow he wasn't as much in control of matters as he believed, that *she* knew things about him he did not. Secrets—she was a harborer of so many. If he killed her, those secrets would be lost forever.

He pictured her in his mind as he had done for so many nights during their journey north. He could visualize the perfection of her features, the way the light's movement across her face and body made every aspect seem more stunning than the one before. He could hear the music in her voice. He could feel her touch. She was real and impossible at once: an elemental by her own admission, a thing made of magic, yet human as well. Pe Ell was a man whose respect for life had long since been deadened by his killings. He was a professional assassin who had never failed. He did not understand losing. He was a wall that could not be breached; he was unapproachable by others save for those brief moments he chose to tolerate their presence.

But Quickening—this strange, ephemeral girl—threatened all of that. She had it in her, he believed, to ruin everything he was and in the end to destroy him. He didn't know how, but he believed it was so. She had the power to undo him. He should have been anxious to kill her then, to do as Rimmer Dall had asked. Instead, he was intrigued. He had never encountered anyone until now who he felt might threaten him. He wanted to rid himself of that threat; yet he wanted to get close to it first.

He stared out into the streets of Eldwist, down the corridors between the silent, towering buildings, and into the tunnels of endless gloom, unbothered by the seeming contradiction in his wants. The shadows reached out to him and drew him close. He was as much at home here as he had been at Southwatch, a part of the night, the emptiness, the solitude, the presence of death and absence of life. How little difference there was, he marveled, between the kingdoms of Uhl Belk and the Shadowen.

He relaxed. He belonged in the anonymity of darkness.

It was *she* and those who stayed with her that required the light.

He thought of them momentarily. It was a way to pass the time. He pictured each as he had pictured Quickening and considered the potential of each as a threat to him.

Carisman. He dismissed the tunesmith almost immediately.

Horner Dees. What was it about that old man that bothered him so? He hated the way the bearish Tracker looked at him, as if seeing right through skin and bone. He reflected on it momentarily, then shrugged it away. Dees was used up. He wielded no magic.

Morgan Leah. He disliked the Highlander because he was so obviously Quickening's favorite. She might even love him in her own way, although he doubted she was capable of real feeling—not her—not the elemental daughter of the King of the Silver River. She was simply using him as she was using them all, her reasons her own, carefully concealed. The Highlander was young and rash and probably would find a way to kill himself before he became a real problem.

That left Walker Boh.

As always, Pe Ell took an extra measure of time to ponder him. Walker Boh was an enigma. He had magic, but he didn't seem comfortable using it. Quickening had practically raised him from the dead, yet he seemed almost uninterested in living. He was preoccupied with matters of his own, things that he kept hidden deep down inside, secrets as puzzling as those of the girl. Walker Boh had a sense of things that surprised Pe Ell; he might even be prescient. Once, some years ago, Pe Ell had heard of a man who lived in the Eastland and could commune with animals and read the changes in the Lands before they came to pass. This man, perhaps? He was said to be a formidable opponent; the Gnomes were terrified of him.

Pe Ell rocked forward slowly and clasped his hands together. He would have to be especially careful of One-arm, he knew. Pe Ell wasn't frightened of Walker Boh, but neither was Walker Boh frightened of him.

Yet.

The minutes drifted away, the night deepened, and the streets remained empty and still. Pe Ell waited patiently, knowing the Rake would eventually come as it had come each night, searching for their hiding place, seeking them out, and determined to exterminate them as it had been trained to do. Tonight would be no exception.

He let himself consider for a time the implications of having possession of a magic like the Black Elfstone—a magic that could negate all other magics. Once he had it in his grasp—as he eventually would—what would he do with it? His narrow, sharp features crinkled with amusement. He would use it against Rimmer Dall for starters. He would use it to negate Dall's own magic. He would slip into Southwatch, find the First Seeker, and put an end to him. Rimmer Dall had grown more annoying than useful; Pe Ell no longer cared to tolerate him. It was time to sever their partnership once and for all. After that, he might use the talisman against the rest of the Shadowen, perhaps make himself their leader. Except that he really didn't want anything to do with them. Better, perhaps, simply to eliminate them all—or as many as he could reach. He smiled expectantly. That would be an interesting challenge.

He leaned back contentedly in the shadows of his shelter. He would have to learn how to use the magic of the Elfstone first, of course. Would that prove difficult? Would he have to rely on Quickening to instruct him? Would he have to find a way to keep her alive awhile longer? He shivered with anticipation. The solution would present itself when it was time. For now, he must concentrate on gaining possession of the Elfstone.

Almost an hour passed before he finally heard the approach of the Rake. The Creeper came from the east, its metal legs scraping softly on the stone as it slipped through the gloom. It came right toward Pe Ell, and the assassin melted back into the darkness of the stairwell until his eyes were level with the street. The creature looked enormous from this angle, its immense body balanced on iron-encased legs, its whiplike tail curled and ready, and its tentacles outstretched and sweeping the damp air like feelers. Steam rose from its iron shell, the heat of its body reacting to the cool air, condensation forming and dripping onto the street. It sent its tentacles snaking into doorways and windows, along the gutters below the walkways, down the sewers, and into the wrecks of the ancient skeletons of the toppled stone carriages. For an instant Pe Ell thought the beast would spy him out, but then something caught the Creeper's attention and it scuttled past and disappeared into the night.

Pe Ell waited until he could just barely hear it, then slipped from his hiding place in pursuit.

He tracked the Rake for the remainder of the night, down streets and alleyways, through the foyers and halls of massive old buildings, and along the edges of the cliffs that bounded the city west and north. The Creeper went everywhere, a beast at hunt, constantly on the move. Pe Ell stalked it relentlessly. Most of the time he could only hear it, not see it. He had to be very sure he did not get too close. If he did, the creature would sense his presence and come after him. Pe Ell made himself a part of the shadows, just another piece of an endless stone landscape, a thing of vapor and non-being that not even the Rake could detect. He kept on the walkways and close to the building walls, avoided the streets and their maze of trapdoors, and stayed clear of any open spaces. He did not hurry; he kept his pace steady. Playing cat and mouse required a careful exercise of patience.

And then suddenly, near dawn, the Rake disappeared. He had glimpsed it only minutes earlier as it skittered away down a street in the central section of the city, rather close to where the others of the company were hiding. He could hear its legs and tentacles scrape, its body turn, and then there was nothing. Silence. Pe Ell slowed, stopped, and listened. Still there was nothing. He moved ahead cautiously, following a narrow alleyway until it emerged into a street. Still concealed within the shadows of the alleyway, he peered out. Left, the street tunneled into the gloom past rows of buildings that stretched skyward, flat faced and unrevealing. Right, the street was bisected by a cross street and bracketed by twin towers with huge, shadowed foyers that disappeared into complete blackness.

Pe Ell searched the street both ways, listened again, and began to fume. How could he have lost it so suddenly? How could it have just disappeared?

He was aware again of a brightening of the air, a hint of the sun's pending emergence into the world beyond the clouds and mist and gloom of Eldwist. It was daybreak. The Rake would go into hiding now. Perhaps it already had. Pe Ell frowned, then scanned the impenetrable shadows of the buildings across the way. Was that its hiding place? he wondered.

He started from his own concealment for a look when that sixth sense he relied upon so heavily warned him what was happening. The Rake was in hiding all right, but not for the reason he had first imagined. It was in hiding because it was setting a trap. It knew the intruders were still loose in the city, somewhere close. It knew they would have to kill it or it would kill them. So on the chance that they had followed, it had set a trap. It was waiting now to see if anything fell into it.

Pe Ell felt a rush of cold determination surge through him as he shrank back into the gloom of the alleyway. Cat and mouse, that's all it was. He smiled and waited.

Long minutes passed and there was only silence. Pe Ell continued to wait.

Then abruptly the Rake emerged from the shadows of the building across the street to the left, dancing almost gracefully into view, body poised. Pe Ell held his breath as the monster tested the air, turning slowly about. Satisfied, it moved on. Pe Ell exhaled slowly and followed.

It was growing brighter now, and the night air evolved into a sort of gray haze that reflected the dampness so that it became even more difficult to see what lay ahead. Yet Pe Ell did not slow, relying on his hearing to warn him of any danger, always conscious of the sound of the Rake moving ahead. It was no longer worrying about pursuit. Its night's work was finished; it was headed home.

To the lair of the Stone King, Pe Ell thought, impatient for the first time since his hunt had begun.

He caught up with the Rake as it slowed before a flat-sided building with a shadowed alcove thirty feet high and twice that across. The Rake's feelers probed the stone at the top of the alcove, and a section of the wall within swung silently away, lifting into the gloom. Without a backward glance, the Rake slipped through the opening. When it was inside, the wall swung back into place.

Got you! Pe Ell thought fiercely.

Nevertheless, he stood where he was for almost an hour afterward, waiting to see if anything else would happen, making certain that this was not another trap. When he was sure that it was safe, he emerged and darted along the edge of the buildings, following the walkways until he stood before the hidden entry.

He took a long time to study it. The stone facing was flat and smooth. He could trace the seams of the opening from within the frame of the alcove, but he would never have noticed the door without first knowing it was there. Far above him, just visible against the gray of the stone, he could detect a kind of lever. A release, he thought triumphantly. A way in.

He stood there for a while longer, thinking. Then he moved away, searching the buildings across the street for a hiding place. Once safely concealed, he would sit down and figure out a way to trip that lever. Then he would sleep again until it was dark. When night came, he would wake and wait for the Rake to go out.

When it did, he would go in.

22

Night lay across the Westland in a humid, airless pall, the heat of the day lingering with sullen determination long after the sun's fiery ball had disappeared into the horizon. Darkness disdained to offer even the smallest measure of relief, empty of cool breezes, devoid of any suggestion of a drop in the temperature. The day's swelter was rooted in the earth, a stubborn presence that would not be dispelled, breathing fire out of its concealment like an underground dragon. Insects buzzed and hummed and flew in erratic, random bursts. Trees were heat-ravaged giants, drooping and exhausted. A full moon crawled across the southern horizon, gibbous and shimmering against the haze. The only sounds that broke the stillness were those dredged from the throats of hunted creatures an instant before their hunters silenced them forever.

Even on the hottest of nights, the game of life and death played on.

Wren Ohmsford and the big Rover Garth turned their horses down the rutted trail that led into the town of Grimpen Ward. It had taken them a week to journey there from the Tirfing, navigating hidden passes of the Irrybis that only the Rovers knew, following the trails of the Wilderun north and west, shying well clear of the treacherous Shroudslip, winding at last over Whistle Ridge and down into the dank mire of the Westland's most infamous lair.

When there was nowhere else to run or hide, it was said, there was always Grimpen Ward. Thieves, cutthroats, and misfits of all sorts came to the outlaw town to find refuge. Walled away by the Irrybis and the Rock Spur, swallowed up by the teeming jungle of the Wilderun, Grimpen Ward was a haven for renegades of every ilk.

It was also a deathtrap from which few escaped, a pit of vipers preying on one another because there was no one else, devouring their own kind with callous indifference and misguided amusement, feeding in a frenzy of need and boredom. Of those who came to Grimpen Ward seeking to stay alive, most ended up disappointed.

The town grew visible through the trees, and Wren and Garth slowed. Lights burned through the window glass of buildings black with grime, their shutters sagging and broken, their walls and roofs and porches so battered and ravaged by time and neglect that they seemed in immediate danger of collapse. Doors stood ajar in a futile effort to dispel the heat trapped within. Laughter broke sharply against the forest silence, rough, forced, desperate. Glasses clinked and sometimes shattered. Now and again, a scream sounded, solitary and disembodied.

Wren glanced at Garth and then signed, *We'll leave the horses hidden here.* Garth nodded. They turned their mounts into the trees, rode them some distance from the road until a suitable clearing was found, and tethered them in a stand of birch.

"Softly," Wren whispered, fingers moving.

They worked their way back to the roadway and continued down. Dust rose from beneath their boots and settled in a dark sheen on their faces. They had been riding all day, a slow journey through impossible heat, unable to force the pace without risking the health of their horses. The Wilderun was a morass of midsummer dampness and decay, the wood of the forests rotting into mulch, the ground soft and yielding and treacherous, the streams and drinking pools dried or poisoned, and the air a furnace that parched and withered. No matter how terrible the heat might be in other parts of the Four Lands, it was always twice as bad here. A stagnant, inhospitable cesspool, the Wilderun had long been regarded as a place to which the discards of the population of the Four Lands were welcome.

Bands of Rovers frequently came to Grimpen Ward to barter and trade. Accustomed to the vagaries and treacheries of Men, outsiders themselves from society, branded outlaws and troublemakers everywhere, the Rovers were right at home. Even so, they traveled in tight-knit families and relied on strength of numbers to keep themselves safe. Seldom did they venture into Grimpen Ward alone as Wren and Garth were doing.

A chance encounter with a small family of coin traders had persuaded the girl and her giant protector to accept the risk. Just a day after Garth's unsuccessful attempt to backtrack and trap their shadow, they had come upon an old man and his sons and their wives traveling north out of the passes, returning from a journey through the Pit. Eating with them, sharing tales, Wren had asked simply out of habit if any among them knew of the fate of the Westland Elves, and the old man had smiled, brokentoothed and wintry, and nodded.

"Not me, girl, you understand," he had rasped softly, chewing at the end of the pipe he smoked, his gray eyes squinting against the light. "But at the Iron Feather in Grimpen Ward they be an old woman that does. The Addershag, she's called. Haven't spoke to her myself, for I don't frequent the ale houses of the Ward, but word has it the old woman knows the tale. A seer, they say. Queer as sin, maybe mad." He'd leaned into the fire's glow. "They's making use of her someway, I hear. A pack of them snakes. Making her give them secrets to take others' money." He shook his head. "We stayed clear."

Later, they had talked it over, Wren and Garth, when the family was asleep and they were left alone. The reasons to stay out of the Wilderun were clear enough; but there were reasons to go in as well. For one, there was the matter of their shadow. It was back there still, just out of view and reach, carefully hidden away like the threat of winter's coming. They could not catch it and despite all their efforts and skill they could not shake it. It clung to them, a trailing spider's web floating invisibly in their wake. The

Wilderun, they reflected, might be less to its taste and might, with a bit of luck, bring it to grief.

For another, of course, there was the indisputable fact that this was the first instance since Wren had started asking about the Elves that she had received a positive response. It seemed unreasonable not to test its merit.

So they had come, just the two of them, defying the odds, determined to see what sort of resolution a visit to Grimpen Ward would bring. Now, a week's journey later, they were about to find out.

They passed down through the center of the town, eyes quick but thorough in their hunt. Ale houses came and went, and there was no Iron Feather. Men lurched past them, and a handful of women, tough and hard all, reeking of ale and the stale smell of sweat. The shouts and laughter grew louder, and even Garth seemed to sense how frantic they were, his rough face grim-set and fierce. Several of the men approached Wren, drunken, unseeing, anxious for money or pleasure, blind to the danger that mirrored in Garth's eyes. The big Rover shoved them away.

At a juncture of cross-streets, Wren caught sight of a cluster of Rovers working their way back toward their wagons at the end of an unlit road. She hailed them down and asked if they knew of the Iron Feather. One made a face and pointed. The band hurried off without comment. Wren and Garth continued on.

They found the ale house in the center of Grimpen Ward, a sprawling ramshackle structure framed of splitting boards and rusting nails, the veranda fronting painted a garish red and blue. Wide double doors were tied open with short lengths of rope; within, a crush of men sang and drank against a long bar and about trestle benches. Wren and Garth stepped inside, peering through the haze of heat and smoke. A few heads turned; eyes stared momentarily and looked away again. No one wanted to meet Garth's gaze. Wren moved up to the bar, caught the attention of the server, and signaled for ale. The server, a narrow-faced man with sure, steady hands brought the mugs over and waited for his money.

"Do you know a woman called the Addershag?" Wren asked him.

Expressionless, the man shook his head, accepted his money, and walked away. Wren watched him stop and whisper something to another man. The man slipped away. Wren sipped at her mug, found the ale unpleasantly warm, and moved down the serving bar, repeating her question as she went. No one knew of the Addershag. One grinned, leered, and made an unimaginative suggestion. Then he saw Garth and hurried off. Wren continued on. A second man reached out at her, and she flicked his arm away. When he reached again, she brought the heel of her hand into his face so hard he was knocked unconscious. She stepped around him, anxious to be done with this business. It was dangerous to continue on, even with Garth to protect her.

She reached the end of the serving bar and slowed. At the very back of the room a group of men occupied a table in the shadows. One of them beckoned, waited until he was certain she had seen, then beckoned again.

She hesitated, then moved forward, pushing through the crowd, Garth at her back. She came up to the table and stopped when she was just out of reach of the men seated there. They were a rough bunch—dirty, unshaven, their skin the color of paste, their eyes ferretlike and dangerous. Ale mugs sat before them, sweating.

The man who had beckoned said, "Who is it you're looking for, girl?"

"A seer called the Addershag," she answered and then waited, certain that he already knew who she was looking for and probably where she would look.

"What do you want with her?"

"I want to ask her about the Elves."

The man snorted. "There aren't any Elves."

Wren waited.

The man eased forward in his chair. He was thick-featured, and his eyes were empty of feeling. "Suppose I decided to help you. Just suppose. Would you do something for me in turn?" The man studied her face a moment and grinned insolently. "Not that. I just want you to talk to her for me, ask her something. I can tell what you are by your clothes. You're a Rover. See, the Addershag is a Rover, too." He paused. "Didn't know that, did you? Well, she doesn't feel like talking to us, but she might feel different about you, one of her own." His gaze on her was hard and sullen. All pretense was gone now, the game under way. "So if I take you to her, then you have to ask a question or two for me. That a deal?"

Wren knew already that the man was planning to kill her. It was simply a question of how and when he and his friends would try. But she also knew he might really be able to take her to the Addershag. She weighed the risks and rewards momentarily, then said, "Agreed. But my friend goes with me."

"Whatever you say." The man smirked. "Course, my friends go, too. So I'll feel safe. Everyone goes."

Wren looked at the man appraisingly. Heavyset, muscular, an experienced cutthroat. The others the same. If they got her in a tight place . . .

"Garth," she said, looking back at him. She signed quickly, screening her movements from the men at the table. Garth nodded. She turned back to the table. "I'm ready."

The speaker rose, the others with him, an anxious, hungry-looking bunch. There was no mistaking what they were about. The speaker began ambling along the rear wall toward a door leading out. Wren followed, cautious, alert. Garth was a step behind; the remainder of the table trailed. They passed through the door into an empty hall and continued toward a back entrance. The sounds of the ale house disappeared abruptly as the door closed.

The man spoke over his shoulder. "I want to know how she reads the gaming cards like she does. How she reads the dice roll. I want to know how she can see what the players are thinking." He grinned. "Something for you, girl; something for me. I have to make a living, too."

He stopped unexpectedly before a side door, and Wren tensed. But the man ignored her, reaching into his pocket to extract a key. He inserted it in the lock and twisted. The lock released with a click and the door swung open. There were stairs beyond leading down. The man groped inside and brought forth an oil lamp, lit it, and handed it to Wren.

"She's in the cellar," he said, motioning through the door. "That's where we're keeping her for the moment. You talk to her. Take your friend if you want. We'll wait here." His smile was hard and unpleasant. "Just don't come back up without something to trade for my helping you out. Understand?"

The men with him had crowded up behind them, and the reek of them filled the narrow hall. Wren could hear the ragged sound of their breathing.

She moved close to the speaker and put her face inches from his own. "What I understand is that Garth will remain here with you." She held his gaze. "Just in case."

He shrugged uncomfortably. Wren nodded to Garth, indicating the door and the gathering of men. Then holding the lamp before her, she started down the steps.

It was a shadowy descent. The stairway wound along a dirt wall shored up with timbers, the earth smell thick and pungent. It was cooler here, if only marginally. Insects skittered from underfoot. Strands of webbing brushed her face. The steps angled left along a second wall and ended. The cellar opened up before her in the lamplight.

An old woman sat slumped against the far wall, almost lost in the gloom. Her body was a dried husk, and her face had withered into a maze of lines and furrows. Ragged white hair tumbled down about her frail shoulders, and her gnarled hands were clasped before her. She wore a cloth shift and old boots. Wren approached and knelt before her. The ancient head lifted, revealing eyes that were milky and fixed. The old woman was blind.

Wren placed the oil lamp on the floor beside her. "Are you the seer they call the Addershag, old mother?" she asked softly.

The staring eyes blinked and a thin voice rasped, "Who wishes to know? Tell me your name."

"My name is Wren Ohmsford."

The white head tilted, shifting toward the stairway and the door above. "Are you with them?"

Wren shook her head. "I'm with myself. And a companion. Both of us are Rovers."

Aged hands reached out to touch her face, exploring its lines and hollows, scraping along the girl's skin like dried leaves. Wren did not move. The hands withdrew.

"You are an Elf."

"I have Elven blood."

"An Elf!" The old woman's voice was rough and insistent, a hiss against the silence of the ale house cellar. The wrinkled face cocked to one side as if reflecting. "I am the Addershag. I am the seer of the future and what it holds, the teller of truths. What do you wish of me?"

Wren rocked back slightly on the heels of her boots. "I am searching for the Westland Elves. I was told a week ago that you might know where to find them—if they still exist."

The Addershag cackled softly. "Oh, they exist, all right. They do indeed. But it's not to everyone they show themselves—to none at all in many years. Is it so important to you, Elf-girl, that you see them? Do you search them out because you have need of your own kind?" The milky eyes stared unseeing at Wren's face. "No, not you. Despite your blood, you're a Rover before everything, and a Rover has need of no one. Yours is the life of the wanderer, free to travel any path you choose, and you glory in it." She grinned, nearly toothless. "Why, then?"

"Because it is a charge I have been given—a charge I have chosen to accept," Wren answered carefully.

"A charge, is it?" The lines and furrows of the old woman's face deepened. "Bend close to me, Elf-girl."

Wren hesitated, then leaned forward tentatively. The Addershag's hands came up again, the fingers exploring. They passed once more across Wren's face, then down her neck to her body. When they touched the front of the girl's blouse, they jerked back as if burned and the old woman gasped. "Magic!" she howled.

Wren started, then seized the other's wrists impulsively. "What magic? What are you saying?"

But the Addershag shook her head violently, her lips clamped shut, and her head sunk into her shrunken breast. Wren held her a moment longer, then let her go.

"Elf-girl," the old woman whispered then, "who sends you in search of the Westland Elves?"

Wren took a deep breath against her fears and answered, "The shade of Allanon."

The aged head lifted with a snap. "Allanon!" She breathed the name like a curse. "So! A Druid's charge, is it? Very well. Listen to me, then. Go south through the Wilderun, cross the Irrybis and follow the coast of the Blue Divide. When you have reached the caves of the Rocs, build a fire and keep it burning three days and nights. One will come who can help you. Do you understand?"

"Yes," Wren replied, wondering at the same time if she really did. Rocs, did the old woman say? Weren't they supposed to have been a form of giant coastal bird?

"Beware, Elf-girl," the other warned, a stick-thin hand lifting. "I see danger ahead for you, hard times, and treachery and evil beyond imagining. My visions are in my head, truths that haunt me with their madness. Heed me, then. Keep your own counsel, girl. Trust no one!"

She gestured violently, then slumped back again, her blind gaze fixed and hard. Wren glanced down the length of her body and started. The Addershag's worn dress had slipped back from her boots to reveal an iron chain and clamp fastened to her leg.

Wren reached out and took the aged hands in her own. "Old mother," she said gently. "Let me get you free of this place. My friend and I can help you, if you'll let us. There is no reason for you to remain a prisoner."

"A prisoner? Ha!" The Addershag lurched forward, teeth bared like an animal at bay. "What I look and what I am are two very different things!"

"But the chain . . ."

"Holds me not an instant longer than I wish!" A wicked smile creased the wrinkled face until its features almost disappeared. "Those men, those fools—they take me by force and chain me in this cellar and wait for me to do their bidding!" Her voice lowered. "They are small, greedy men, and all that interests them is the wealth of others. I could give them what they want; I could do their bidding and be gone. But this is a game that interests me. I like the teasing of them. I like the sound of their whining. I let them keep me for a time because it amuses me. And when I am done being entertained, Elf-girl, when I tire of them and decide again to be free, why . . . this!"

Her stick hands freed themselves, then twisted sharply before Wren's eyes and were transformed into writhing snakes, tongues darting, fangs bared, hissing into the silence. Wren jerked away, shielding her face. When she looked again, the snakes had disappeared.

She swallowed against her fear. "Were . . . they real?" she asked thickly, her face flushed and hot.

The Addershag smiled with dark promise. "Go, now," she whispered, shrinking back into the shadows. "Take what I told you and use it as you will. And guard yourself closely, Elf-girl. Beware."

Wren hesitated, pondering whether she should ask answers to the rush of questions that flooded through her. She decided against it. She picked up the oil lamp and rose. "Goodbye, old mother," she said.

She went back through the darkness, squinting into the light of the oil lamp to find the stairs, feeling the sightless gaze of the Addershag follow after her. She climbed the steps swiftly and slipped back through the cellar doorway into the ale house hall.

Garth was waiting for her, facing the knot of men who had come with them from the front room. The sounds of the ale house filtered through the closed door beyond, muffled and raucous. The eyes of the men glittered. She could sense their hunger.

"What did the old woman tell you?" the leader snapped.

Wren lifted the oil lamp to shed a wider circle of light and shook her head. "Nothing. She doesn't know of the Elves or if she does, she keeps it to herself. As for gaming, she won't say a word about that either." She paused. "She doesn't seem any kind of a seer to me. I think she's mad."

Anger reflected in the other man's eyes. "What a poor liar you are, girl."

Wren's expression did not change. "I'll give you some good advice, cutthroat. Let her go. It might save your life."

A knife appeared in the other's hand, a glint of metal come out of nowhere. "But not yours . . ."

He didn't finish because Wren had already slammed the oil lamp onto the hallway floor before him, shattering the glass, spilling the oil across the wood, exploding the flames everywhere. Fire raced across the wooden planks and up the walls. The speaker caught fire, shrieked, and stumbled back into the unwilling arms of his fellows. Garth and Wren fled the other way, reaching the back door in seconds. Shoulder lowered, Garth hammered into the wooden barrier and it flew from its hinges as if made of paper. The girl and the big Rover burst through the opening into the night, howls of rage and fear chasing after them. Down between the buildings of the town they raced, swift and silent, and moments later emerged back onto the main street of Grimpen Ward.

They slowed to a walk, glanced back, and listened. Nothing. The shouts and laughter of the ale houses nearest them drowned out what lay behind. There was no sign of fire. There was no indication of pursuit.

Side by side, Wren and Garth walked back up the roadway in the direction they had come, moving through the revelers, the heat and the gloom, calm and unhurried.

"We're going south to the Blue Divide," Wren announced as they reached the edge of the town, signing the words.

Garth nodded and made no response.

Swiftly they disappeared into the night.

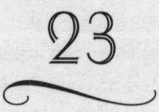

23

When Walker Boh, Quickening, and Carisman left Morgan and Horner Dees, they traveled only a short distance east through the darkened streets of Eldwist before slowing to a halt. Walker and the girl faced each other. Neither had said anything about stopping; it was as if they had read each other's mind. Carisman looked from one face to the other in confusion.

"You know where the Stone King is hiding," Quickening said. She made it a statement of fact.

"I think I do," Walker answered. He stared into the depthless black eyes and marveled at the assurance he found there. "Did you sense that when you chose to come with me?"

She nodded. "When he is found, I must be there."

She didn't explain her reasoning, and Walker didn't ask. He glanced into the distance, trying futilely to penetrate the gloom, to see beyond the mist and darkness, and to find something of what he was meant to do. But there was nothing to be found out there, of course. The answers to his questions lay somewhere within.

"I believe the Stone King hides within the dome," he said quietly. "I suspected as much when we were there several days ago. There appear to be no entrances, yet as I touched the stone and walked about the walls I sensed life. There was a presence that I could not explain. Then, yesterday, when we were beneath the earth, trapped in that underground cavern, I again sensed that presence—only it was above us this time. I took a quick calculation when we emerged from the tunnels. The dome is seated directly above the cavern."

He stopped momentarily and glanced about. "Eldwist is the creation of its master. Uhl Belk has made this city of the old world his own, changing to stone what wasn't already, expanding his domain outward symmetrically where the land allows it. The dome sits centermost, a hub in a wheel of streets and buildings, walls and wreckage."

His pale face turned to meet hers. "Uhl Belk is there."

He could almost see the life brighten in her eyes. "Then we must go to meet him," she said.

They started off again, following the walkway to the end of the block and then turning abruptly north. Walker led, keeping them carefully back from the streets, against the walls of the buildings, clear of the open spaces, and away from the danger of trapdoors. Neither he nor Quickening spoke; Carisman hummed softly. They watched the gloom like hawks, listened for strange sounds, and smelled and tasted the damp, stale air warily. A brief rain caught up with them and left them shedding water from their cloaks and hoods, their feet chilled within their boots.

Walker Boh thought of home. He had done so increasingly of late, driven by the constant, unrelenting pressure of being hemmed about by the city's stone and darkness to seek out something of what had once been pleasant and healing. For a time he had sought to banish all thoughts of Hearthstone; its memories cut at him like broken glass. The cottage that he had adopted as his home had been burned to the ground in the battle with the Shadowen. Cogline and Rumor had died there. He had barely escaped dying himself, and keeping his life had cost him his arm. He had once believed himself invulnerable to the intrusions of the outside world. He had been vain and foolish enough to boast that what lay beyond Hearthstone presented no danger to him. He had denied the dreams that Allanon had sent him from the spirit world, the pleas that Par Ohmsford had extended for his help, and in the end the charge he had been given to go in search of Paranor and the Druids. He had encased himself in imaginary walls and believed himself secure. When those walls began collapsing, he had found that they could not be replaced and those things he had thought secure were lost.

Yet there were older memories of Hearthstone that transcended the recent tragedies. There were all those years when he had lived in peace in the valley, the seasons when the world outside did not intrude and there was time enough for everything. There were the smells of flowers, trees, and freshwater springs; the sounds of birds in early spring and insects on warm summer nights; the taste of dawn on a clear autumn morning; the feeling of serenity that came with the setting sun and the fall of night. He could reach back beyond the past few weeks and find peace in those memories. He did so now because they were all he had left to draw on.

Yet even his strongest memories provided only a momentary haven. The harsh inevitabilities of the present pressed in about him and would not be banished. He might escape for brief moments into the past, into the world that had sheltered him for a time before he was swept away by the tide of events he had sought foolishly to ignore. Escape might soothe and strengthen the spirit, but it was transitory and unresolving. His mind darted away into his memories only to find the past forever beyond his reach and the present forever at hand. He was struggling with his life, he discovered. He was adrift, a castaway fighting to keep afloat amid the wreckage of his confusion and doubt. He could almost feel himself sinking.

They reached the dome at midmorning and began their search. Working together, not willing to separate if there was any chance at all that the Stone King waited within, they began to explore the dome's surface, walking its circumference, feeling along its walls, and searching even the ground it sat upon. It was perfectly formed, although its ageing shell was pitted and cracked, rising several hundred feet into the air at its peak, spreading from wall to wall several hundred feet more. Depressions that had the look of giant thumbprints decorated the dome's peak along its upper surface, laid open like the petals of a flower, separated by bands of stone that curved downward to the foundation. Niches and alcoves indented its walls at ground level, offering no way inside, leading nowhere. Sculpted designs marked its stone, most of them almost completely worn away by time's passage, no longer decipherable, the runes of a world that had long since passed away.

"I can feel a presence still," Walker Boh said, slowing, folding his cloak about him. He glanced skyward. It was raining again, a slow, persistent drizzle. "There's something here. Something."

Quickening stood close beside him. "Magic," she whispered.

He stared at her, surprised that she had been so quick to recognize a truth that had eluded him. "It is so," he murmured. His hand stretched forth, searching. "All about, in the stone itself."

"He is here," Quickening whispered.

Carisman stepped forward and stroked the wall tentatively. His handsome brow furrowed. "Why does he not respond? Shouldn't he come out long enough to see what we want?"

"He may not even know we are here. He may not care." Quickening's soft face lifted. "He may even be sleeping."

Carisman frowned. "Then perhaps a song is needed to wake him up!" He sang:

> *"Awake, awake, oh aged King of Stone,*
> *Come forth from your enfolding lair,*
> *We wait without, a worn and tired band,*
> *So lacking in all hope and care.*
>
> *Awake, awake, oh aged King of Stone,*
> *Be not afraid of what we bring,*
> *'Tis nothing more than finite spirit,*
> *A measure of the song I sing.*
>
> *Awake, awake, oh aged King of Stone,*
> *You who have seen all passing time,*
> *Share with us weak and mortal creatures,*
> *The truths and secrets of Mankind."*

His song ended, and he stood looking expectantly at the broad expanse of the dome. There was no response. He glanced at Quickening and Walker and shrugged. "Not his choice of music, perhaps. I shall think of another."

They moved away from the dome and into the shelter of an entry in a building that sat adjacent. Seating themselves with their backs to the wall so that they could look out at the dome, they pooled from their backpacks a collection of old bread and dried fruit for their lunch. They ate silently, staring out from the shadows into the gray rain.

"We are almost out of food," Walker said after a time. "And water. We will have to forage soon."

Carisman brightened. "I shall fish for us. I was a very good fisherman once—although I only fished for pleasure. It was a pleasing way to pass the time and compose. Walker Boh, what did you do before you came north?"

Walker hesitated, surprised by the question, unprepared to give an answer. What did he do? he asked himself. "I was a caretaker," he decided finally.

"Of what?" Carisman pressed, interested.

"Of a cottage and the land about it," he said softly, remembering.

"Of an entire valley and all the creatures that lived within it," Quickening declared, her eyes drawing Carisman's. "Walker Boh preserved life in the manner of the Elves of old. He gave of himself to replenish the land."

Walker stared at her, surprised once again. "It was a poor effort," he suggested awkwardly.

"I will not permit you to be the judge of that," the girl replied. "It is for others to determine how successful you have been in your work. You are too harsh in your criticism and lack the necessary distancing to be fair

and impartial." She paused, studying him, her black eyes calm and reasoning. "I believe it will be judged that you did all that you could."

They both knew what she was talking about. Walker was strangely
warmed by her words, and once again he experienced that sense of kinship.
He nodded without responding and continued to eat.

When they had finished their meal they stood facing the dome once
more, debating what approach to take next.

"Perhaps there is something to be seen from above," Quickening suggested. "An opening through the top of the dome or an aberration in the
stone that would suggest a way in."

Walker glanced about. There was an ornate building less than a block
distant that opened at its top into a belltower and gave a clear view of the
dome below. They crossed to it cautiously, forever wary of trapdoors, and
gained its entrance. Sculptures of winged angels and robed figures decorated
its walls and ceilings. They moved inside cautiously. The central chamber
was vast, the glass of its windows long disintegrated, the furnishings turned
to dust. They found the stairway leading to the belltower and began to
climb. The stairs had fallen away in spots, and only the bracing remained.
They maneuvered along its spans, working their way upward. Floors came
and went, most ragged with holes and cluttered with debris, all turned to
stone, their collapse preserved in perfect relief.

They gained the belltower without difficulty and walked to the windows facing out. The city of Eldwist spread away on all sides, misted and
gray, filled with the shadows of daylight's passing and night's approach. The
rain had diminished, and the buildings rose like stone sentries across the
span of the peninsula. The clouds had lifted slightly, and the choppy slate
surface of the Tiderace and the ragged cliffs of the mainland beyond the
isthmus could be seen in snatches through gaps in the lines of stone walls.

The dome sat directly below them, as closed and unrevealing at its top
as it had been at its bottom. There was nothing to see, no hint of an opening, no suggestion of a way in. Nonetheless, they studied it for some time,
hoping to discover something they had missed.

In the midst of their study a horn sounded, startling them.

"Urdas!" Carisman cried.

Walker and Quickening looked at each other in surprise, but Carisman
had already dashed to the south window of the tower and was peering in
the direction of the isthmus and the cliffs leading down.

"It must be them; that is their call!" he shouted, excitement and concern reflecting in his voice. He shaded his eyes against the glare of the
dampened stone. "There! Do you see them?"

Walker and Quickening hastened to join him. The tunesmith was
pointing to where the stairway descending the cliffs from the overlook was
barely visible through the mist. There were glimpses of movement to be
seen on the stairs, small, hunched figures crouched low as if to hide even
from the shadows. Urdas, Walker recognized, and they were coming down.

"What is it that they think they are doing!" Carisman exclaimed, obviously upset. "They cannot come here!"

The Urdas faded into a patch of fog and were lost from view. Carisman wheeled on his companions, stricken. "If they are not stopped, they will all be killed!"

"The Urdas are no longer your responsibility, Carisman," Walker Boh declared softly. "You are no longer their king."

Carisman looked unconvinced. "They are children, Walker! They have no understanding of what lives down here. The Rake or the Maw Grint, either one will destroy them. I can't imagine how they slipped past the Koden . . ."

"In the same way as Horner Dees did ten years ago," Walker cut him short. "With a sacrifice of lives. And still they come ahead. They are not as worried about themselves, it appears, as you are."

Carisman wheeled on Quickening. "Lady, you've seen the way they react to things. What do they know of the Stone King and his magic? If they are not stopped . . ."

Quickening seized his arms and held them. "No, Carisman. Walker Boh is right. The Urdas are dangerous to you now as well."

But Carisman shook his head vehemently. "No, Lady. Never to me. They were my family before I abandoned them."

"They were your captors!"

"They cared for me and protected me in the only way they knew how. Lady, what am I to do? They have come here to find me! Why else would they be taking such a risk? I think they have never come so far away from home. They are here because they think you stole me away. Can I abandon them a second time, this time to die for a mistake that I can prevent them from making?" Carisman pulled free, slowly, gently. "I have to go to them. I have to warn them."

"Carisman . . ."

The tunesmith was already backing toward the belltower stairs. "I have been an orphan of the storm all of my life, blown from one island to the next, never with family or home, always in search of somewhere to belong and someone to belong to. The Urdas gave me what I have of both, little as it may seem to you. I cannot let them die needlessly."

He turned and started quickly down the stairs. Quickening and Walker exchanged wordless glances and hurried after.

They caught up with him on the street below. "We'll come with you then," Walker said.

Carisman whirled about at once. "No, no, Walker! You cannot show yourselves to them! If you do, they might think I am threatened by you—perhaps even that I am a prisoner! They might attack, and you could be hurt! No. Let me deal with them. I know them; I can talk with them, explain what has happened, and turn them back before it is too late." His handsome features crinkled with worry. "Please, Walker? Lady?"

There was nothing more to be said. Carisman had made up his mind and would not allow them to change it. As a final concession they demanded that they be allowed to accompany him at least as far as was reasonable to assure that they would be close at hand in case of trouble. Carisman was reluctant to agree even to that much, concerned that he was taking them away from work that was more important, that he was delaying their search for the Stone King. Both Quickening and Walker refused to argue the point. They walked in silence, single file along the walkways, down the tunneled streets, traveling south through the city. He would meet the Urdas at the city's south edge, Carisman told them, sweeping back his blond hair, squaring himself for his encounter. Walker found him odd and heroic at once, a strange parody of a man aspiring to reality yet unable quite to grasp it. Give thought to what you are doing, he begged the tunesmith at one point. But Carisman's answering smile was cheerfully beguiling and filled with certainty. He had done all the thinking he cared to do.

When they neared the boundaries of the city, the rocky flats of the isthmus peeking through the gaps in the buildings, Carisman brought them to a halt.

"Wait for me here," he told them firmly. Then he made them promise not to follow after him. "Do not show yourselves; it will only frighten the Urdas. Give me a little time. I am certain I can make them understand. As I said, my friends—they are like children."

He clasped their hands in farewell and walked on. He turned at one point to make certain they were doing as he had asked, then waved back to them. His handsome face was smiling and assured. They watched the mist curl about him, gather him up, and finally cause him to disappear.

Walker glanced at the buildings surrounding them, chose a suitable one, and steered Quickening toward it. They entered, climbed the stairs to the top floor, and found a room where a bank of windows gaped open to the south. From there they could watch the Urdas approach. The gnarled figures were strung out along the isthmus, making their way cautiously past the crevices and ruts. There were perhaps twenty of them, several obviously injured.

They watched until the Urdas reached the edge of the city and disappeared into the shadow of the buildings.

Walker shook his head. "I find myself wishing we had not agreed to this. Carisman is almost a child himself. I cannot help thinking he would have been better off not coming with us at all."

"He chose to come," Quickening reminded him. Her face tilted into the light, out of a striping of shadows. "He wanted to be free, Walker Boh. Coming with us, even here, was better than staying behind."

Walker glanced through the windows a final time. The stone of the isthmus flats and the streets below glistened with the damp, empty and still. He could hear the distant thunder of the ocean, the cries of the seabirds, and the rushing of the wind down the cliffs. He felt alone.

"I wonder sometimes how many like Carisman there are," he said finally. "Orphans, as he called himself. How many left to roam the land, made outcasts by Federation rule, their magic not the gift it was intended to be, but a curse they must disguise if they would keep their lives."

Quickening seated herself against the wall and studied him. "A great many, Walker Boh. Like Carisman. Like yourself."

He eased down beside her, folding his cloak about him, lifting his pale face toward the light. "I was not thinking of myself."

"Then you must do so," she said simply. "You must become aware."

He stared at her. "Aware of what?"

"Of the possibilities of your life. Of the reasons for being who you are. If you were an elemental, you would understand. I was given life for a specific purpose. It would be terrifying to exist without that purpose. Is it not so for you?"

Walker felt his face tighten. "I have purpose in my life."

Her smile was unexpected and dazzling. "No, Walker Boh, you do not. You have thrust from you any sense of purpose and made yourself an outcast twice over—first, for having been born with the legacy of Brin Ohmsford's magic, and second, for having fallen heir to her trust. You deny who and what you are. When I healed your arm, I read your life. Tell me this is not so."

He took a deep breath. "Why is it that I feel we are so much alike, Quickening? It is neither love nor friendship. It is something in between. Am I joined to you somehow?"

"It is our magic, Walker Boh."

"No," he said quickly. "It is something more."

Her beautiful face masked all traces of the emotion that flickered in her eyes. "It is what we have come here to do."

"To find the Stone King and take back from him the stolen Black Elfstone. Somehow." Walker nodded solemnly. "And for me, to regain the use of my arm. And for Morgan Leah, to regain the magic of the Sword of Leah. All somehow. I have listened to your explanations. Is it true that you have not been told how any of this is to be accomplished? Or are there secrets that you hide from us as Pe Ell charges?"

"Walker Boh," she said softly. "You turn my questions into your own and ask of me what I would ask of you. We both keep something of the truth at bay. It cannot be so for much longer. I will make a bargain with you. When you are ready to confront your truth, I shall confront mine."

Walker struggled to understand. "I no longer fear the magic I was born with," he said, studying the lines of her face, tracing its curves and angles as if she were in danger of disappearing before he could secure a memory of her. "I listened once to my nephew Par Ohmsford admonish me that the magic was a gift and not a curse. I scorned him. I was frightened of the implications of having the magic. I feared . . ."

He caught himself, an iron grip that tightened on his voice and thoughts instantly. A shadow of something terrifying had shown itself to him, a shadow that had grown familiar to him over the years. It had no face, but it spoke with the voices of Allanon and Cogline and his father and even himself. It whispered of history and need and the laws of Mankind. He thrust it away violently.

Quickening leaned forward and with gentle fingers touched his face. "I fear only that you will continue to deny yourself," she whispered. "Until it is too late."

"Quickening . . ."

Her fingers moved across his mouth, silencing him. "There is a scheme to life, to all of its various happenings and events, to everything we do within the time allotted to us. We can understand that scheme if we let ourselves, if we do not become frightened of knowing. Knowledge is not enough if there is not also acceptance of that knowledge. Anyone can give you knowledge, Walker Boh, but only you can learn how to accept it. That must come from within. So it is that my father has sent me to summon you and Pe Ell and Morgan Leah to Eldwist; so it is that the combination of your magics shall free the Black Elfstone and begin the healing process of the Lands. I know that this is to be. In time, I shall know how. But I must be ready to accept its truths when that happens. It is so as well for you."

"I will . . ."

"No, you will not be ready, Walker," she anticipated him, "if you continue to deny truths already known to you. That is what you must realize. Now speak no more of it to me. Only think on what I have said."

She turned away. It was not a rebuff; she did not intend it that way. It was a simple breaking off, an ending of talk, done not to chastise but to allow him space in which to explore himself. He sat staring at her for a time, then turned introspective. He gave himself over to the images her words conjured. He found himself thinking of other voices in other times, of the world he had come from with its false measure of worth, its fears of the unknown, its subjugation to a government and rules it did not wish to comprehend. *Bring back the Druids and Paranor,* Allanon had charged him. And would that begin a changing back of the world, of the Four Lands, into what they had been? And would that make things better? He doubted, but he found his doubts founded more in a lack of understanding than in his fears. What was he to do? He was to recover the Black Elfstone, carry it to disappeared Paranor, and somehow, in some way, bring back the Keep. Yet what would that accomplish? Cogline was gone. All of the Druids were gone. There was no one . . .

But himself.

No! He almost screamed the word aloud. It bore the face of the thing he feared, the thing he struggled so hard to keep from himself. It was the terrifying possibility that had scratched and clawed around the edges of his self-imposed shield for as long as he could remember.

He would not take up the Druid cause!

Yet he was Brin Ohmsford's last descendent. He was bearer of the trust that had been left to her by Allanon. *Not in your lifetime. Keep it safe for gen-*

erations to come. One day it will be needed again. Words from the distant past, spoken by the Druid's shade after death, haunting, unfulfilled.

I haven't the magic! he wailed in desperation, in denial. *Why should it be me? Why?*

But he already knew. Need. Because there was need. It was the answer that Allanon had given to all of the Ohmsfords, to each of them, year after year, generation after generation. Always.

He wrestled with the specter of his destiny in the silence of his thoughts. The moments lengthened. Finally he heard Quickening say, "It grows dark, Walker Boh."

He glanced up, saw the failing of the light as dusk approached. He climbed to his feet and peered south into the flats. The isthmus was empty. There was no sign of the Urdas.

"It's been too long," he muttered and started for the stairs.

They descended quickly, emerged from the building, and began following the walkway south toward the city's edge. Shadows were already spreading into dark pools, the light chased west to the fringes of the horizon. The seabirds had gone to roost, and the pounding of the ocean had faded to a distant moan. The stone beneath their feet echoed faintly with their footsteps as if whispering secrets to break the silence.

They reached the fringe of the city and slowed, proceeding more cautiously now, searching the gloom for any signs of danger. There was no movement to be found. The mist curled its damp tendrils through vacant windows and down sewer grates, and there was a sense of a hidden presence at work. Ahead, the isthmus flats stretched out into the darkness, broken and ragged and lifeless.

They stepped clear of the building walls and stopped.

Carisman's body was slumped against a pillar of rock at the end of the street, pinned fast by a dozen spears. He had been dead for some time, the blood from his wounds washed away by the rain.

It appeared that the Urdas had gone back the way they had come.

They had taken Carisman's head with them.

Even children can be dangerous, Walker Boh thought bleakly. He reached over for Quickening's hand and locked it in his own. He tried to imagine what Carisman's thoughts had been when he realized his family had disowned him. He tried to tell himself that there was nothing he could have done to prevent it.

Quickening moved close to him. They stood staring at the dead tunesmith wordlessly for a moment more, then turned and walked back into the city.

24

They did not return to their normal place of concealment that night; it was already dusk when they departed the flats and the distance back through the city was too great to cover safely. Instead, they found a building close at hand, a low, squat structure with winding, narrow halls and rooms with doors opening through at both ends to provide a choice of escape routes if the Rake should appear. Settled deep within the stone interior of the building, shut away with barely enough light to see each other at arm's length, they ate their dinner of dried fruits and vegetables, stale bread, and a little water and tried to banish the ghost of Carisman from their presence. The dead tunesmith surfaced in memories, in unspoken words, and in the faint, soft roll of the ocean's distant waters. His face blossomed in the shadows they cast, and his voice whispered in the sound of their breathing. Walker Boh regarded Quickening without seeing her; his thoughts were of Carisman and of how he had let the tunesmith go when he could have stopped him from doing so. When Quickening touched him on the arm, he was barely aware of the pressure of her fingers. When she read his thoughts in the touch, he was oblivious. He felt drained and empty and impossibly alone.

Later, while she slept, he grew aware of her again. His self-reproach had exhausted itself, his sorrow had dried up; Carisman's shade was banished, consigned at last to the place and time in which it belonged. He sat in a box of darkness, the stone of the walls and ceiling and floor pressing in around him, the silence a blanket that would suffocate him, time the instrument by which he measured the approach of his own death. Could it be far away now for any of them? He watched the girl sleeping next to him, watched the rise and fall of her breast as she breathed, turned on her side, her face cradled in the crook of her arm, her silver hair fanned back in a sweep of brightness. He watched the slow, steady beat of her pulse along the slim column of her throat, searched the hollows of her face where the shadows draped and pooled, and traced the line of her body within the covering of clothes that failed to hide its perfection. She was a fragile bit of life whatever her magic, and he could not escape the feeling that despite the confidence she evidenced in her father and the command with which she had brought them north she was in peril. The feeling was elusive and difficult to credit, but it took life in his instincts and his prescience, born of the magic that he had inherited from Brin Ohmsford, magic that still ebbed and flowed within him as the tide of his belief in himself rose and fell. He could not disregard it. Quickening was at risk, and he did not know how to save her.

The night deepened and still he did not sleep. They were all at risk, of course. What he sensed of danger to the daughter of the King of the Silver River was possibly no more than what he sensed of danger to them all. It had caught up with Carisman. It would eventually catch up with Quickening as well. Perhaps what he feared was not that Quickening would die, but that she would die before she revealed the secrets she knew. There were many, he suspected. That she hid them so completely infuriated him. He was surprised at the anger his realization provoked. Quickening had brought him face to face with the darkest of his fears and then left him to stand alone against it. His entire life had been shadowed by his apprehension that Allanon's mysterious trust to the Ohmsfords, given over three hundred years ago to Brin and passed unused from generation to generation, might somehow require fulfillment by him. He had lived with the specter of it since childhood, aware of its existence as all of his family had been, finding it a ghost that would not be banished, that instead grew more substantial with the passing of the years. The magic of the Ohmsfords was alive in him as it had not been in his ancestors. The dreams of Allanon had come only to him. Cogline had made him his student and taught him the history of his art and of the Druid cause. Allanon had told him to go in search of the Druids and lost Paranor.

He shivered. Each step took him closer to the inevitable. The trust had been held for him. The phantom that had haunted him all these years had revealed a terrifying face.

He was to take the Black Elfstone and bring back Paranor.

He was to become the next Druid.

He could have laughed at the ridiculousness of the idea if he had not been so frightened of it. He despised what the Druids had done to the Ohmsfords; he saw them as sinister and self-serving manipulators. He had spent his life trying to rid himself of their curse. But it was more than that. Allanon was gone—the last of the real Druids. Cogline was gone—the last of those who had studied the art. He was alone; who was to teach him what a Druid must know? Was he to divine the study of magic somehow? Was he to teach himself? And how many years would that take? How many centuries? If the magic of the Druids was required to combat the Shadowen, such magic could not be drawn leisurely from the Histories and the tomes that had taught all the Druids who had gone before. Time did not permit it.

He clenched his teeth. It was foolish to think that he could become a Druid, even if he were willing, even if he wished it, even if the specter he had feared so for all these years turned out to be himself.

Foolish!

Walker's eyes glittered as he searched the shadows of the room for an escape from his distress. Where were the answers that he needed? Did

Quickening hide those answers? Were they a part of the truths she concealed? Did she know what was to become of him? He started to reach for her, intending to shake her awake. Then he caught himself and drew back. No, he reasoned. Her knowledge was as small and imperfect as his own. With Quickening, it was more a sensing of possibilities, a divining of what might be, a prescience like his own. It was a part of the reason he felt her to be kindred; there was that sharing of abilities and uses of the magics they wielded. He forced his thoughts to slow and his mind to open and he gazed upon her as if his eyes might swallow her up. He felt something warm and generous touch him, her sleep presence, unbidden and revealed. It reminded him of his mother's when he was small and still in need of her reassurance and comfort. She was in some way a rendering of his future self. She opened him up to the possibilities of what he might be. He saw the colors of his life, the textures and the patterns that might be woven, and the styles that might be tried. He was cloth to be cut and shaped, but he lacked the tools and understanding. Quickening was doing what she could to give him both.

He dozed then for a time, still upright against the chamber wall, his legs and arms folded tightly together against his body, his face tilted forward into his cloak. When he came awake again, Quickening was looking at him. They studied each other wordlessly for a moment, each searching the other's eyes, seeking out some reading of the other's needs.

"You are afraid, Walker Boh," the girl said finally.

Walker almost smiled. "Yes, Quickening. I have been afraid forever. Afraid of this—of what is happening now—all of my life. I have run from it, hidden from it, wished it away, begged that it would disappear. I have fought to contain it. Exercising a strict and unyielding control over my life was the technique that seemed to work best. If I could dictate my own fate, then it could have no power over me. The past would be left for others; the present would belong to me."

He let his legs unfold and straightened them gingerly before him. "The Druids have affected the lives of so many of the Ohmsfords, of the children of Shannara, for generations. We have been used by them; we have been made over to serve their causes. They have changed what we are. They have made us slaves of the magic rather than simply wielders. They have altered the composition of our minds and bodies and spirits; they have subverted us. And still they are not satisfied. Look at what they expect of us now! Look at what is expected of me! I am to transcend the role of slave and become master. I am to take up the Black Elfstone—a magic I do not begin to understand. I am to use it to bring back lost Paranor. And even that is not enough. I am to bring back the Druids as well. But there are no Druids. There is only me. And if there is only me, then . . ."

He choked on the words. His resolve faltered. His patience failed him. His anger returned, a raw and bitter echo in the silence.

"Tell me!" he begged, trying to contain his urgency.

"But I do not know," she whispered.

"You must!"

"Walker . . ."

There were tears in his eyes. "I cannot be what Allanon wants me to be—what he demands that I be! I cannot!" He took a quick, harsh breath to steady himself. "Do you see, Quickening? If I am to bring back the Druids by becoming one, if I must because there is no other way that the Races can survive the Shadowen, must I then be as they once were? Must I take control of the lives of those I profess to help, those others who are Ohmsfords, Par and Coll and Wren? For how many generations yet to come? If I am to be a Druid, must I do this? Can I do anything else?"

"Walker Boh." When she spoke his name her voice was soft and compelling. "You will be what you must, but you will still be yourself. You are not trapped in some spider's web of Druid magic that has predetermined your life, that has fated you to be but one way and one way only. There is always a choice. Always."

He had the sudden sense that she was talking of something else completely. Her perfect face strained against some inner torment, and she paused to reshape it, chasing quickly the furrows and lines. "You are frightened of your fate without knowing what it is to be. You are paralyzed by doubts and misgivings that are of your own making. Much has happened to you, Dark Uncle, and it is enough to make any man doubt. You have lost loved ones, your home, a part of your body and spirit. You have seen the specter of a childhood fear take form and threaten to become real. You are far from everything you know. But you must not despair."

His eyes were haunted. "But I do. I am adrift, Quickening. I feel myself slipping away completely."

She reached out her hand and took his own. "Then cling to me, Walker Boh. And let me cling to you. If we keep hold of each other, the drifting will stop."

She moved against him, her silver hair spilling across his dark cloak as her head lowered into his chest. She did not speak, but simply rested there, still holding his hand, her warmth mixing with his own. He lowered his chin to her hair and closed his eyes.

He slept then, and there were no dreams or sudden wakings, only a gentle cradling by soft, invisible threads that held him firm. His drifting ceased, just as she had promised it would. He was no longer plagued by troubling and uncertain visions; he was left at peace. Calm enfolded him, soothing and comforting. It had a woman's hands, and the hands belonged to Quickening.

He woke again at daybreak, easing from the chilly stone floor to his feet as his eyes adjusted to the thin gray light. From beyond the maze of rooms and corridors that buffered him from the outside world, he could hear the soft patter of rain. Quickening was gone. Vaguely worried, he searched until he found her standing at a bank of windows on the north wall, staring out into the haze. The stone buildings and streets shimmered wetly, reflecting their own images in grotesque parody, mirroring their deadness. Eldwist greeted the new day as a corpse, sightless and stiff. It stretched away into the distance, rows of buildings, ribbons of streets, a symmetry of design and construction that was flat and hard and empty of life. Walker stood next to Quickening and felt the oppressiveness of the city close about him.

Her black eyes shifted to find his own, her mane of silver hair the sole brightness in the gloom. "I held you as tightly as I could, Walker Boh," she told him. "Was it enough?"

He took a moment to answer. The stump of his missing arm ached and the joints of his body were stiff and slow to respond. He felt himself to be a large shell in which his spirit had shriveled to the size of a pebble. Yet he was strangely resolved.

"I am reminded of Carisman," he said finally, "determined to be free at any cost. I would be free as well. Of my fears and doubts. Of myself. Of what I might become. That cannot be until I have learned the secret of the Black Elfstone and the truth behind the dreams of the shade of Allanon."

Quickening's faint smile surprised him. "I would be free, too," she said softly. She seemed anxious to explain, then looked quickly away. "We must find Uhl Belk," she said instead.

They departed their shelter and went out into the rain. They walked the silent streets of Eldwist north through the shadows and gloom, hunched within the protection of their forest cloaks, lost in their private thoughts.

Quickening said, "Eldwist is a land in midwinter waiting for spring. She is layered in stone as other parts of the earth at times are layered in snow. Can you feel her patience? There are seeds planted, and when the snow melts those seeds can be brought to bloom."

Walker wasn't sure what she was talking about. "There is only stone in Eldwist, Quickening. It runs deep and long, from shore to shore, the length and breadth of the peninsula. There are no seeds here, nothing of the woodlands or the fields, no trees, no flowers, no grasses. Only Uhl Belk and the monsters that serve him. And us."

"Eldwist is a lie," she said.

"Whose lie?" he asked. But she wouldn't answer.

They followed the street for close to an hour, keeping carefully to the walkways, listening for the sound of anything moving. Except for the steady patter of the rain, there was only silence. Even the Maw Grint slept, it seemed. Water pooled and was channeled into streams, and it swept down the gutters in sluggish torrents that eddied and splashed and washed away the silt and dust the wind had blown in. The buildings watched in mute and indifferent testimony, unfeeling sentinels. Clouds and mist mixed and descended to wrap them about, easing steadily downward until they scraped the earth. Things began to disappear, towers first, then entire walls, then bits and pieces of the streets themselves. Walker and Quickening felt a changing in the world, as if a presence had been loosed. Phantasms came out to play, dark shadows risen from the earth to dance at the edges of their vision, never entirely real, never quite completely formed. Eyes watched, peering downward from the heights, staring upward through the stone.

Fingers brushed at their skin, droplets of rain, trailers of mist, and something more. Walker let himself become one with what he was feeling, an old trick, a blending of self with external sensations, all to gain a small measure of insight into the origin of what was unseen. He could sense a presence after a time, dark, brooding, ancient, a thing of vast power. He could hear it breathing. He could almost see its eyes.

"Walker," Quickening whispered.

A figure appeared out of the haze before them, cloaked and hooded as they were and uncomfortably close. Walker stepped in front of Quickening and stopped. The figure stopped as well. Wordlessly, they faced each other. Then the clouds shifted, changing the slant of the light, the shadows reformed, and a voice called out uncertainly. "Quickening?"

Walker Boh started forward again. It was Morgan Leah.

They clasped hands on meeting, and Quickening hugged the sodden and disheveled Highlander close, kissing his face passionately. Walker watched without speaking, already aware of the attraction shared by the two, surprised that Quickening would allow it to be. He watched the way her eyes closed when Morgan held her and thought he understood. She was letting herself feel because it was all still new. She was no older than the time of her creation, and even if her father had given her human feelings she would not have experienced them firsthand until now. He felt an odd twinge of sadness for her. She was trying so hard to live.

"Walker." Morgan moved over to him, one arm still wrapped about the girl. "I've been searching everywhere. I thought something had happened to you as well."

He told them what had befallen Horner Dees and himself, how they had been snared by the trapdoor and tumbled onto the slide, and how they had found themselves confronted by the horror of the Maw Grint slumbering directly below. His eyes were fierce and bright as he struggled to describe how he had somehow managed to release the magic of the Sword of Leah once again, magic he had feared lost. With its aid they had escaped. They had taken refuge for the night close by, then made their way at dawn to where they had left the others of the little company. But the building had been empty and there had been no sign of anyone's return. Worried for Quickening—for all of them, he hastened to add—he had left Dees to keep watch for them in case they returned and gone hunting alone.

"Horner Dees was prepared to come as well, but I refused to allow it. The truth is, he would never move again if he could arrange it—at least not until it was time to leave this place." The Highlander smiled broadly. "He's had enough of Eldwist and its traps; he wants the ale house at Rampling Steep again!" He paused then, looking past them speculatively. "Where's Carisman?"

It was their turn to speak, and Quickening did so, her voice steady and strangely comforting as she related the events that had led to the death of the tunesmith. Even so, Morgan Leah's face was lined with despair and anger by the time she had finished.

"He never understood anything, did he?" the Highlander said, the emotions he was holding inside threatening to choke him. "He just never understood! He thought his music was a cure for everything. Shades!"

He looked away a moment, shielding his expression, hands clasped on his hips defiantly, as if stubbornness might somehow change what had happened. "Where do we go now?" he asked finally.

Walker glanced at Quickening. "We believe that Uhl Belk hides within the dome." The girl spoke for him. "We were looking for a way in when the Urdas appeared. We are returning to continue the search."

Morgan turned, his face set. "Then I am coming with you. Horner will be better off resting right where he is. We can rejoin him at nightfall." The look he gave them was almost defiant. "That's the way it should be anyway. Just the three of us."

"Come if you wish, Morgan," Quickening soothed, and Walker nodded without comment.

They resumed walking, three rain-soaked figures nearly lost in the mist and shadows. Walker led, a lean and white-faced ghost against the gloom, leader now because Quickening had moved a step back to be with Morgan, content to follow. He hunched his narrow shoulders against the weather, felt the bite of the wind as it gusted momentarily, and felt the emptiness inside threaten to engulf him. He reached into that emptiness and tried to secure some part of his magic, a strength he could rely upon. It eluded him, like a snake in flight. He peered ahead through the thin curtain of the rain and watched the shadows chase after the light. The specter of his fate leered at him, a faint shimmer in a pool of water, a wisp of fog in a doorway, a darkening of stone where the dampness reflected like a mirror. In each instance, it wore the face of Allanon.

The street ended, and the dark bulk of the dome lifted before them like the shell of some sleeping crustacean. The three stepped down off the walkway and crossed to stand before it, dwarfed by its size. Walker stared at the dome without speaking, aware that Morgan and Quickening were waiting on him, conscious that something else was waiting on him as well. *It.* The presence he had sensed before was back again, stronger here, readier, more assured. And watching. Silently watching. Walker did not move. He felt eyes all around him, as if there were nowhere he might run that he could not be seen. The stone of the city was a hand that cradled him yet might close without warning to crush out his life. The presence wanted him to know that. It wanted him to know how insignificant he was, how futile his quest, and how purposeless his life. It bore down on him, pressed about like the mist and rain. Go home, he heard it whisper. Leave while you can.

He did not leave. He did not even step away. He had faced enough threats in his time, enough dark things that roamed the land, to know when he was being tested. The effort was not a crushing one; it was teasing and fey, as if designed to insinuate an opposite effect than the one indicated. Don't really leave, it seemed to say. Just remember that you were asked.

Walker Boh stepped forward to where the wall was broadest between the bands of stone. Death brushed up against him, a soft sprinkle of rain caught in the wind. It was odd, but he sensed Cogline close beside him, the old man's ghost risen from the ashes of Hearthstone, come to watch his student practice the craft he had taught him, come perhaps to judge how well he performed. You will never be free of the magic, he could hear the other say. He stared momentarily at the pitted, worn surface of the wall, watching the rainwater snake downward along its irregular paths, silver streamers that glistened like strands of Quickening's hair. He reached down again within himself for the magic and this time fastened on it. He drew its strength about him like armor, banded himself with it as if to match the stone of the shell before him, then reached out with his one remaining hand and pressed his fingers to the wall.

He felt the magic rise within him, flowing hot like fire, extending from his chest to his arm to the tips of his fingers to . . .

There was a shudder, and the stone before him drew back, flinching away as if human flesh that had been burned. There was a long, deep groan that was the sound of stone grating on stone and a thin shriek as if a life had been pressed between. Quickening crouched like a startled bird, her silver hair flung back, her eyes bright and strangely alive. Morgan Leah drew out the broadsword strapped across his back in a single swift motion.

The wall before them opened—not as a door would swing wide or a panel lift, but as a cloth torn asunder. It opened, stretched wide from foundation to apex, a mouth that sought to feed. When it was twenty feet across, it stopped, immobile once more, the stone edges smooth and fixed, imbued with the look of a doorway that had always been there and clearly belonged.

A way in, thought Walker Boh. Exactly what they had come searching for.

Quickening and Morgan Leah stood beside him expectantly. He did not look at either of them. He kept his eyes focused on the opening before him, on the darkness within, on its sea of impenetrable shadows. He searched and listened, but nothing revealed itself.

Still, he knew what waited.

Carisman's voice sang softly in his mind. *Come right in, said the spider to the fly.*

With the girl and the Highlander flanking him, Walker Boh complied.

25

Shadows enveloped them almost immediately, layers of darkness that began less than a dozen feet inside the opening to the dome and entirely concealed everything that lay beyond. They slowed on Walker's lead, waiting for their eyes to adjust, listening to the hollow echoes of their booted feet fade into the silence. Then there was only the sound of their breathing. Behind them, the faint gray daylight was a slender thread connecting them to the world without, and an instant later it was severed. Stone grated on stone once more, and the opening that had admitted them disappeared. No one moved to prevent it from happening; indeed, they had all expected as much. They stood together in the silence that followed, each conscious of the reassuring presence of the others, each straining to hear the sound of any foreign movement, each waiting for some small measure of sight to return. The sense of emptiness was complete. The interior of the dome had the feel of a monstrous tomb in which nothing living had walked in centuries. The air had a stale and musty smell, devoid of any recognizable scents, and it was cold, a bone-biting chill that entered through the mouth and nostrils and worked its way instantly to the pit of the stomach and lodged there. They began to shiver almost immediately. Even in the impenetrable darkness it seemed to Walker Boh that he could see the clouding of his breath.

The seconds dragged by, heartbeats in the unbroken stillness. The three waited patiently. Something would happen. Someone would appear. Unless they had been brought into the dome to be killed, Walker speculated in the silence of his thoughts. But he didn't think that was the case. In fact, he no longer believed as he had in the beginning that there was any active effort being made to eliminate them. The character of their relationship with Eldwist suggested on close study that the city functioned in an impersonal way to rid itself of intruders, but that it did not exert any special effort if it immediately failed. Eldwist did not rely on speed; it relied on the law of averages. Sooner or later intruders would make a mistake. They would grow incautious and either the trapdoors or the Rake would claim them. Walker was willing to wager that Quickening had guessed right, that until very recently the Stone King hadn't even been aware of their presence—or if he had, hadn't bothered himself about it. It wasn't until Walker had used magic against the shell of his enclosure that he had roused himself. Not even using magic against the Rake had made any difference to him. But now, Walker believed, he was curious—and that was why they had been brought inside . . .

Walker caught himself. He had missed something. Nothing was going to happen if they just stood there in the darkness, not if they waited all that day and all the next. The Stone King had brought them inside for a reason. He had brought them inside to see what they would do.

Or, perhaps, *could* do.

He reached out with his good arm to grip first Morgan and then Quickening and bent their heads gently to press close against his own. "Whatever happens, Quickening," he whispered, speaking only to the girl, his voice so soft it was barely audible, "remember your vow to do nothing to reveal that you have any use of the magic."

Then he released them, stepped away, brought up his hand, snapped his fingers, and sparked a single silver flame to life.

They looked about. They were standing in a tunnel that ran forward a short distance to an opening. Holding the flame before him, Walker led them forward. When they reached the tunnel's end, he extinguished the flame, summoned his magic a second time, and sent a scattering of silver fire into the darkness.

Walker inhaled sharply. The shower of light flew into the unknown, soaring through the shadows, chasing them as it went, and rising until everything about them lay revealed. They stood at the entrance to a vast rotunda, an arena ringed by row upon row of seats that lifted away into the gloom. The roof of the dome stretched high overhead, its rafters of stone arcing downward from peak to foundation. Lines of stairs ran upward to the rows of seats, and railings encircled the arena. The arena and stands, like the rafters, were stone, ancient and worn by time, hard and flat against the darkness that cloaked them. A string of shadowed tunnels similar to the one that had admitted them opened through the stands, black holes that burrowed and disappeared.

At the very center of the arena stood a massive stone statue, roughhewn and barely recognizable, of a man hunched over in thought.

Walker let the fire settle in place, its light extending. The dome was vast and empty, silent save for the sound of their footfalls, seemingly bereft of any life but their own. Out of the corner of his eye he saw Morgan start forward and reached out quickly to hold him back. Quickening moved over to take the Highlander's arm protectively in her own. Walker's gaze swept the arena, the black tunnels that opened onto it, the stands that surrounded it, the rafters and ceiling, and then the arena again. He stopped when he reached the statue. Nothing moved. But there was something there. He could feel it, more strongly now than before, the same presence he had sensed when he had stood without.

He started forward, slowly, cautiously. Morgan and Quickening trailed. He was momentarily in command of matters now, Quickening's deference in some way become an acknowledgment of her need. She was not to use magic. She was to rely on him. He discovered an unexpected strength of resolution in the fact that he had made her dependent on him. There was no time now for drifting, for self-doubts and fears, or for the uncertainties of who and what he was meant to be. A fiery determination burned through him. It was better this way, he realized, better to be in command, to accept responsibility for what was to happen. It had always been that way. At that moment he understood for the first time in his life that it always would.

The statue loomed directly before them, a massive chunk of stone that seemed to defy the light Walker had evoked to defuse the darkness. The thinker faced away from them, a gnarled and lumpish form, kneeling half-seated and half-slumped, one arm folded across his stomach, the second closed to a fist and cocked to brace his chin. It might have been intended that there be a cloak thrown about him or he might simply have been covered with hair; it was impossible to discern. There was no writing on the base he rested upon; indeed, it was a rather awkward pedestal that seemed to join the legs of the statue to the dome's floor as if the rock had simply melted away once upon a distant time.

They reached the statue and began to circle it. The face came slowly into view. It was a monster's face, ravaged and pocked, a mass of protuberances and knots, all misshapen in the manner of a sculpture partially formed and then abandoned. Eyes of stone stared blankly from beneath a glowering brow. There was horror written in the statue's features; there were demons captured in the shaping that could never be dislodged. Walker glanced away uneasily to search again the dome's shadows. The silence winked back at him.

Suddenly Quickening stopped, freezing in place like a startled deer. "Walker," she whispered, her voice a low hiss.

She was looking at the statue. Walker wheeled catlike to follow her gaze.

The eyes of the statue had shifted to fix on him.

He heard Morgan's blade clear its sheath in a rasp of metal.

The statue's misshapen head began moving, the stone grating eerily as it shifted, not breaking off or cracking, but rearranging somehow, as if become both solid and liquid. The grating echoed through the hollow shell of the dome like the shifting of massive mountain boulders in a slide. Arms moved and shoulders followed. The torso swiveled, the stone rubbing and grinding until the short hairs on Walker's neck were rigid.

Then it spoke, mouth opening, stone rubbing on stone.

—Who are you—

Walker did not reply, so astonished at what he was seeing that he could not manage to answer. He simply stood there, dumbfounded. The statue was alive, a thing of stone, frighteningly shaped by a madman's hand, lacking blood and flesh, yet somehow alive.

In the next instant he realized what he was seeing and even then he could not speak the creature's name. It was Quickening who spoke for him.

"Uhl Belk," she whispered.

—Who are you—

Quickening stepped forward, looking tiny and insignificant in the shadow of the Stone King, her silver hair swept back.

"I am called Quickening," she replied. Her voice, surprisingly strong and steady, reverberated through the stillness. "These are my companions, Walker Boh and Morgan Leah. We have come to Eldwist to ask you to return the Black Elfstone."

The head shifted slightly, stone crackling and grinding.

—The Black Elfstone belongs to me—

"No, Uhl Belk. It belongs to the Druids. You stole it from them. You stole it from the Hall of Kings and brought it into Eldwist. Now you must give it back."

There was a long pause before the Stone King spoke again.

—Who are you—

"I am no one."

—Have you magic to use against me—

"No."

—What of these others, do they have magic—

"Only a little. Morgan Leah once had use of a sword given him by the Druids which possessed the magic of the Hadeshorn. But it is broken now, the blade shattered, and its magic failed. Walker Boh once had the use of magic he inherited from his ancestors, from the Elven house of Shannara. But he lost the use of most of that magic when he suffered damage to his arm and his spirit. He has yet to gain it back. No, they have no magic that can harm you."

Walker was so astonished he could barely credit what he was hearing. In a matter of seconds, Quickening had undone them completely. She had revealed not only what it was that they had come to find but also that they lacked any reasonable chance of gaining possession of it. She had admitted that they were virtually powerless against this spirit creature, that they were unable to force it to comply with their demands. She had removed even the possibility that they might run a bluff. What was she thinking?

Uhl Belk was apparently wondering the same thing.

—I am to give up the Black Elfstone simply because you ask me to do so, give it up to three mortals of finite lives, a girl with no magic, a one-armed man, and a swordsman with a broken blade—

"It is necessary, Uhl Belk."

—I determine what is necessary in the Kingdom of Eldwist; I am the law and the power that enforces that law; there is no right but mine and therefore no necessity but mine; who would dare say no to me; not any of you; you are as insignificant as the dust that blows across the surface of my skin and washes into the sea—

He paused.

—The Black Elfstone is mine—

Quickening did not respond this time, but simply continued to stare into the Stone King's scarred eyes. Uhl Belk's massive body shifted again, moving as if mired in quicksand, the stone grinding resolutely, a wheel of time and certainty given the skin of substance.

—You—

He pointed to Walker, a finger straightening.

—The Asphinx claimed a part of you; I can sense its stink upon your body; yet somehow you still live; are you a Druid—

"No," Quickening answered instantly. "He is a messenger of the Druids, sent by them to recover the Black Elfstone. His Elven magic saved him from the poison of the Asphinx. His claim to the Black Elfstone is the rightful one, granted him by the Druids."

—The Druids are all dead—

Quickening said nothing, waiting for the Stone King, standing fearlessly beneath him. A sudden movement of one massive arm and she would be crushed. She seemed unconcerned. Walker glanced quickly at Morgan, but the Highlander's eyes were on the face of Uhl Belk, transfixed by the ugliness of it, hypnotized by the power he saw there. He wondered what he was expected to do. Anything? He wondered suddenly what he was doing there at all.

Then the Stone King spoke again, a slow rasping in the silence.

—I have been alive forever and I will live on long after you are dust; I was created by the Word and I have survived all that were given life with me save one and that one will soon be gone as well; I care nothing for the world in which I exist save for the preservation of that over which I was given dominion—eternal stone; it is stone that weathers all things, that is unchanging and fixed and therefore as close to perfection as life can achieve; I am the giver of stone to the world and the architect of what is to become; I use all necessary means to see that my purpose is fulfilled; therefore I took the Black Elfstone and made it mine—

The dome echoed with his words, and then the echoes died away into silence. The shadows were lengthening already as Walker's light began slowly to fail, the magic fading. Walker felt the futility of what they were about. Morgan's sword arm had lowered uselessly to his side; what purpose was there in trying to employ a weapon of iron against something as ancient and immutable as this? Only Quickening seemed to believe there was any hope.

—The Druids were as nothing compared to me; their precautions to hide and protect their magic were futile; I left the Asphinx to show my disdain for what they had attempted to do; they were believers in the laws of nature and evolution, foolish purveyors of the creed of change; they died and left nothing; stone is the only element of the earth's body that endures, and I shall live in that stone forever—

"Constant," Quickening whispered.

—Yes—

"Eternal."

—Yes—

"But what of your trust, Uhl Belk? What of that? You have disdained to be that which you were created—a balancing force, a preservationist of the world as it was created to be." Her voice was low and compelling, a web weaving images that seemed to take form and shimmer in the dead air before her. "I was told your story. You were given life to preserve life; that was the trust given you by the Word. Stone preserves nothing of life. You were not instructed to transform, yet you have taken it upon yourself to subvert everything, to alter forever the composition of life upon the land, to change living matter to stone—all this to create an extension of who and what you are. And look what it has done to you."

She braced herself against the anger already forming on the Stone King's brow. "Give back the Black Elfstone, Uhl Belk. Let us help you become free again."

The massive stone creature shifted on his bed of rock, joints grating, the sounds cracking through the arena as if some invisible audience sought to respond. Uhl Belk spoke, and his voice had a new and frightening edge to it.

—You are more than you pretend to be; I am not deceived; yet it does not matter; I care nothing for who you are or what you want; I admitted you to me so that I might examine you; the magic with which you touched me caught my attention and made me curious as to who you might be; but I need nothing from you; I need nothing from any living thing; I am complete; think of me as the land on which you walk and you as the tiniest of fleas that live upon me; if you should become a bother I will eliminate you in an instant; if you should survive this day you will probably not survive another—

The great brow knitted, and the gnarled face re-formed its ridges and lines.

—What am I if not the whole of your existence; look about you and I am everything you see; look where you stand within Eldwist and I am everything you touch; I have made myself so; I have made myself one with the land I create; I am free of all else and shall ever be—

Suddenly Walker Boh understood. Uhl Belk wasn't a living thing in the conventional sense of the words. He was a spirit in the same way as the King of the Silver River. He was more than the statue that crouched before them. He was everything they walked upon; he was the entire Kingdom of Eldwist. The stone was his skin, he had said—a part of his living self. He had found a way to infuse himself into everything he created, ensuring his permanency in a way that nothing else could.

But that meant he was a prisoner as well. That was why he didn't rise to greet them or come hunting for them or involve himself directly in any way in what they were about. That was why his legs were sunk down into the stone. Mobility was beyond him, an indulgence meant for lesser creatures. He had evolved into something greater; he had evolved into his own world. And it held him trapped.

"But you are not free, are you?" Quickening questioned boldly, as if reading Walker's thoughts. "If you were, you would give us the Black Elfstone, for you would have no real need of it." Her voice was hard and insistent. "But you cannot do that, can you, Uhl Belk? You need the Black Elfstone to stay alive. Without it, the Maw Grint would have you."

—No—

"Without it, the Maw Grint would destroy you."

—No—

"Without it . . ."

—No—

A stone fist crashed downward, barely missing the girl, shattering a portion of the ground next to her, sending jagged cracks along its surface for a hundred yards in every direction. The Stone King shuddered as if stricken.

"The Maw Grint is your child, Uhl Belk," Quickening continued, ramrod straight before him, as if it were she who had the size and the power and not the Stone King. "But your child does not obey you."

—You know nothing; the Maw Grint is an extension of me, as is everything in Eldwist an extension of me; it has no life except what I would give; it serves my purpose and no other, turning the lands adjoining and all that live within them to stone, the permanency of myself—

The girl's black eyes were bright and quick. "And the Black Elfstone?"

The Stone King's voice was resonant with some strange mix of emotions that refused to be identified.

—The Black Elfstone allows—

The jagged mouth ground closed and the Stone King hunched down into himself, limbs and body knotting together as though they might disappear into a single massive rock.

"Allows?" Quickening breathed softly.

The flat, empty eyes lifted.

—Watch—

The word reverberated like a splitting of the Stone King's soul. Rock grated and ground once more, and the wall of the dome behind them parted. Gray, hazy daylight spilled through as if to flee the steady curtain of rain that fell without. Clouds and mist drifted past, bending and twisting about the buildings that loomed beyond, cloaking them as if they were a gathering of frozen giants set patiently at watch. An eerie wail burst from the Stone King's mouth and it filled the emptiness of the city with a sound like a thin sheet of metal vibrating in the wind. It rose and died quickly, but its echo lingered as if it would last forever.

—Watch—

They heard the Maw Grint before they saw it, its approach signaled by a rumble deep beneath the city's streets that rose steadily as the creature neared, a low growl building to a roar that jolted everything and brought the three from Rampling Steep to their knees. The Maw Grint burst into view, shattering apart the stone that was Uhl Belk's skin, splitting it wide just beyond the wall of the dome, just without the opening through which they stared wide-eyed and helpless. They could see the Stone King flinch with pain. The Maw Grint rose and seemed to keep rising, a leviathan of impossible size that dwarfed even the buildings themselves, swaying like a snake, a loathsome cross between burrowing worm and serpent, as black as pitch with foul liquid oozing from a rock-encrusted body, eyeless, headless, its mouth a sucking hole that seemed intent on drinking first the rain and then the air itself. It shot into view with a suddenness that was terrifying and filled the void of the dome's opening like a wave of darkness that would collapse it completely.

Walker Boh went cold with disbelief and horror. The Maw Grint wasn't real; it was impossible even to imagine such a thing. For the first time in his life he wanted to run. He watched Morgan Leah stagger back and drop to his knees. He watched Quickening freeze in place. He felt himself lose strength and only barely managed to keep from falling. The Maw Grint writhed against the skyline, a great spineless mass of black ooze that nothing could withstand.

Yet the Stone King did not waver. A thick, gnarled hand lifted, the one that had cradled his chin when they had thought him a statue, and the fingers slowly began to open. Light burst forth—yet it was light the like of which none of them had ever seen. It sprayed in all directions at first and did not illuminate in the manner of ordinary light but instead turned everything it touched dark.

This is not light, Walker Boh realized as he fought to hold back a flood of sensations that threatened to overwhelm him. *This is the absence of light!*

Then the fingers of the Stone King spread wide, and they could see what he held. It was a perfectly formed gemstone, its center as black and impenetrable as night. The stone glittered as it reflected the thin streamers of gray daylight and let not even the smallest trace pass within. It looked tiny cradled in Uhl Belk's massive stone palm, but the darkness it cast stretched away into the farthest corners of the dome, into the deepest recesses, seeking out and enveloping the whole of Walker's scattered luminescence so that in a matter of seconds the only light remaining came from the rent in the dome's stone skin.

Walker Boh felt his own magic stir within him in recognition.

They had found the Black Elfstone.

Uhl Belk cried out then, a thundering howl that rose above even the sounds of the Maw Grint's coming, of the wind and the rain and the sea far beyond, and he thrust the Black Elfstone before him. The blackness gathered and tightened into a single band that shot forward to strike the Maw Grint. The Maw Grint did not resist. Instead, it simply hung there, transfixed. It shuddered—pained and pleasured both somehow, wracked with feelings that the humans crouched before it could only imagine. It twisted, and the blackness twisted in response. The blackness spread, widening, flowing out, then back again, until the Stone King was enveloped as well. They could hear him groan, then sob, again with feelings that were mixed in some veiled way, not clearly defined and not meant to be. The Elfstone's magic joined them, father and son, monsters each, a substanceless lock that bound them as surely as iron chains.

What is happening? Walker Boh wondered. *What is the magic doing to them?*

Then the nonlight disappeared, a line of shadow fading, steadily dissipating like ink soaking into and through white netting, the air brightening until the daylight returned and the link between the Stone King and the Maw Grint had vanished. The Maw Grint sank from sight, oozing back into the earth. The hole that it had made closed after it, the stone knitting into place, as smooth and hard as before, leaving the street whole again, creating the illusion that nothing at all had happened. The rain washed away all traces of the creature's coming, streams of water loosening the greenish film of poison secreted from its body and carrying it from sight.

Uhl Belk's fingers closed once more about the Black Elfstone, his eyes lidded, his face transformed in a way that Walker could not describe, as if he had been made over somehow, created anew. Yet he was more frightening looking than ever, his features harsher, less human, and more a part of the rock that encased him. He withdrew the Elfstone, his hand clasping it tightly to his body. His voice rumbled.

—Do you see—

They did not, not even Quickening. The puzzlement in her dark eyes was evident. They stood mute before the Stone King, all three, feeling tiny and uncertain.

"What has happened to you, Uhl Belk?" the girl asked finally.

Rain hammered down, and the wind ripped through the dome's rent.

—Go—

The massive pitted head began to turn away, the stone grating ominously.

"You must give us the Black Elfstone!" Quickening shouted.

—The Black Elfstone is mine—

"The Shadowen will take it from you—just as you took it from the Druids!"

Uhl Belk's voice was weary, disinterested.

—The Shadowen are children; you are all children; you do not concern me; nothing that you do can harm or affect me; look at me; I am as old as the world and I shall last as long; you shall be gone in the blink of an eye; take yourselves out of my city; if you remain, if you come to me again, if I am disturbed by you in any way, I shall summon the Rake to dispose of you and you shall be swept away at once—

The floor rippled beneath them, a shudder that sent them tumbling backward toward the opening in the wall. The Stone King had flinched the way an animal would in an effort to shed itself of some bothersome insect. Walker Boh rose, pulling Quickening back with him, beckoning to Morgan. There was nothing to be gained by staying. They would not have the Black Elfstone this day—if indeed ever. Uhl Belk was a creature evolved far beyond any other. He was right; what could they do that would harm or affect him?

Yet Quickening seemed unconvinced. "It is you who shall be swept away!" she shouted as they backed through the opening into the street. She was shaking. "Listen to me, Uhl Belk!"

The craggy face was turned again into shadow, the massive shoulders hunched down, the thinker's pose resumed. There was no response.

Standing outside in the rain they watched the wall seal over, the skin knit, the rent fade away as if it had never been. In moments the dome was an impenetrable shell once more.

Morgan moved to place his hands on Quickening's shoulders. The girl seemed unaware of him, a thing of stone herself. The Highlander leaned close and began whispering.

Walker Boh moved away from them. When he was alone, he turned once again to face Uhl Belk's haven. A fire consumed him and at the same time he felt detached. He was there and he was not. He realized that he no longer knew himself. He had become an enigma he could not solve. His thoughts tightened like a cinched cord. The Stone King was an enemy that none of them could defeat. He was not simply ruler of a city; he was the city itself. Uhl Belk had become Eldwist. He was a whole world, and no one could change an entire world. Not Allanon or Cogline or all of the Druids put together.

Rain streamed down his face. No one.

Yet he already knew that he was going to try.

26

Pe Ell had changed his mind twice before finally settling the matter. Now he slipped down the darkening street and ducked into the doorway of the building in which the others had concealed themselves with his misgivings comfortably stowed. Rain dripped from his cloak, staining the stone of the stairs he followed, tracking his progress in a steady, meandering trail. He paused at the landing to listen, heard nothing, and went on. The others were probably out searching. There or not, it made no difference to him. Sooner or later, they would return. He could wait.

He passed down the hallway without bothering to conceal his approach and stalked through the doorway of their hiding place. At first glance the room appeared empty, but his instincts warned him instantly that he was being watched and he stopped a dozen feet through. Shadows dappled the room in strange patterns, clustered about haphazardly as if stray children chased inside by the weather. The patter of the rain sounded steadily in the silence as Pe Ell stood waiting.

Then Horner Dees appeared, slipping noiselessly from the shadows of a doorway to one side, moving with a grace and ease that belied his bulky frame. He was scratched and bruised and his clothing was torn. He looked as if some animal had gotten hold of him. He fixed Pe Ell with his grizzled look, as rough and suspicious as ever, an aging bear come face-to-face with a familiar enemy.

"You constantly amaze me," Pe Ell said, meaning it, still curious about this troublesome old man.

Dees stopped, keeping his distance. "Thought we'd seen the last of you," he growled.

"Did you, now?" Pe Ell smiled disarmingly, then moved across the room to where a collection of withered fruits sat drying in a makeshift bowl. He picked one up and took a bite. It was bitter tasting, but edible. "Where are the others?"

"Out and about," Dees answered. "What difference does it make to you?"

Pe Ell shed his damp cloak and seated himself. "None. What happened to you?"

"I fell down a hole. Now what do you want?"

Pe Ell's smile stayed in place. "A little help."

It was difficult to tell if Horner Dees was surprised or not; he managed to keep his face from showing anything but seemed at a momentary loss for a response. He hunched down a few inches, as if settling himself against an attack, studied Pe Ell wordlessly, then shook his head.

"I know you, Pe Ell," he declared softly. "I remember you from the old days, from the time you were just beginning. I was with the Federation then, a Tracker, and I knew you. Rimmer Dall had plans for me as well; but I decided not to go along with them. I saw you once or twice, saw you come and go, heard the rumors about you." He paused. "I just want you to know."

Pe Ell finished the fruit and tossed the pit aside. He wasn't sure how he felt about this unexpected revelation. He guessed it really didn't matter. At least now he had an inkling of what it was that bothered him so about Dees.

"I don't remember you," he said finally. "Not that it matters." The hatchet face inclined away from the light. "Just so we understand each other, Rimmer Dall's plans for me didn't work out quite as he expected either. I do what I choose. I always have."

Dees rugged face nodded. "You kill people."

Pe Ell shrugged. "Sometimes. Are you frightened?"

The other man shook his head. "Not of you."

"Good. Then if we've finished with that topic of conversation, let's move back to the other. I need a little help. Care to lend me some?"

Horner Dees stood mute a moment, then moved over to seat himself. He settled down with a grunt and stared at Pe Ell without speaking, apparently assessing the offer. That was fine with Pe Ell. He had thought the matter through carefully before coming back, weighing the pros and cons of abandoning his plan of entering the Rake's shelter alone, of seeking assistance in determining whether or not the Stone King hid within. He had nothing to hide, no intention to deceive. It was always best to take a straight-forward approach when you could.

Dees stirred. "I don't trust you."

Pe Ell laughed tonelessly. "I once told the Highlander he was a fool if he did. I don't care if you trust me; I'm not asking for your trust. I'm asking for your help."

Dees was intrigued despite himself. "What sort of help?"

Pe Ell hid his satisfaction. "Last night I tracked the Rake to its lair. I watched it enter, saw where it hides. I believe it likely that where the Rake hides, the Stone King hides as well. When the Rake goes out tonight to patrol the streets of the city, I intend to go in for a look."

He shifted forward, bringing Dees into the circle of his confidence. "There is a catch that releases a door through which the Rake passes. If I trip it, I should be able to go in. The trouble is, what if the door closes behind me? How will I get out?"

Dees rubbed his bearded chin, digging at the thick whiskers as though they itched. "So you want someone to watch your back for you."

"It seems like a good idea. I had planned to go in alone, to confront the Stone King, kill him if need be, and take the Stone. That's still my plan, but I don't want to have to worry about the Rake crawling up my back when I'm not watching."

"So you want me to watch for you."

"Afraid?"

"You keep asking that. Fact is, I should be asking you. Why should you trust me? I don't like you, Pe Ell. I'd be just as happy if the Rake would get you. That makes me a poor choice for this job, don't you think?"

Pe Ell unfolded his legs and stretched his lean body back against the wall. "Not necessarily. You don't have to like me. I don't have to like you. And I don't. But we both want the same thing—the Black Elfstone. We want to help the girl. Doesn't seem likely either of us can do much alone—although I have a better chance than you do. The point is, if you give your word that you will keep watch for me, I think that's what you'll do. Because your word means something to you, doesn't it?"

Dees laughed dryly. "Don't tell me you're about to make a plea to my sense of honor. I don't think I could stomach that."

Pe Ell quit smiling. "I have my own code of honor, old man, and it means every bit as much to me as yours does to you. If I give my word, I keep it. That's more than most can say. I'm telling you I'll watch out for you if you watch out for me—just until this business is finished. After that, we each go back to watching out for ourselves." He cocked his head. "Time is slipping away. We have to be in place by sunset. Are you coming or not?"

Horner Dees took a long time to answer. Pe Ell would have been surprised and suspicious if he had not. Whatever else Dees was, he was an honest man, and Pe Ell was certain he would not enter into an arrangement he did not think he could abide by. Pe Ell trusted Dees; he wouldn't have asked the old man to watch his back if he didn't. Moreover, he thought Dees capable, the best choice of all, in some ways, not inexperienced like the Highlander or flighty like Carisman. Nor was he unpredictable like Walker Boh. Dees was nothing more nor less than what he appeared to be.

"I told the Highlander about you," Dees announced, watching. "He's told the others by now."

Pe Ell shrugged once more. "I don't care about that." And he didn't.

Dees hunched his heavy frame forward, squinting into the faint gray light. "If we get possession of the Stone, either of us, we bring it back to the girl. Your word."

Pe Ell smiled in spite of himself. "You would accept my word, old man?"

Dees' features were hard and certain. "If you try to break it, I'll find a way to make you sorry you did."

Pe Ell believed him. Horner Dees, for all of being old and used up, for the weathered look of him and the wear of the years, would be a dangerous adversary. A Tracker, a woodsman, and a hunter, Dees had kept himself alive for a long time. He might not be Pe Ell's equal in a face-to-face confrontation, but there were other ways to kill a man. Pe Ell smiled inwardly. Who should know better than he?

Pe Ell reached out his hand and waited for the old man to take it. "We have a bargain," he said. Their hands tightened, held momentarily and broke. Pe Ell came to his feet like a cat. "Now let's be off."

They went out the door of the room and down the stairs again, Pe Ell leading. The gloom without had thickened, the darkness growing steadily as nightfall approached. They hunched their cloaked shoulders against the rain and started away. Pe Ell's thoughts drifted to his bargain. It had been an easy one to make. He would return the Elfstone to the girl because not to do so would be to risk losing her completely and to face an eternity of being tracked by all of them.

Never leave your enemies alive to follow after you, he thought.

Better to kill them when you had the chance.

Daylight was fading rapidly by the time Walker, Morgan, and Quickening approached the building Pe Ell and Horner Dees had vacated less than an hour earlier. The rain was falling steadily, a dark curtain that shaded the tall, somber buildings of the city, that masked away the skies and the mountains and the sea. Morgan walked with his arm protectively encircling the girl's shoulders, his head lowered to hers, two shadowed and hooded figures against the mist. Walker stayed apart, leaving them to each other. He saw how Quickening leaned into the Highlander. She seemed to welcome his embrace, an uncharacteristic response. Something had happened to her during the confrontation with the Stone King that he had missed, and he was only now beginning to make sense of what it was.

A thick stream of rainwater clogged the gutter ahead, blocking the walkway's end like a moat, and he was forced to move outside and around it. He was leading still, choosing their path, his cloaked form darkened by rain and gloom. A wraith, perhaps, he thought. A Grimpond, he corrected. He had not thought of the Grimpond for a long time, the memory too painful to retrieve from the corner of his mind to which he had confined it. It was the Grimpond with its twisted riddles who had led him to the Hall of Kings and his encounter with the Asphinx. It was the Grimpond who had cost him his arm, his spirit, and something of what he had been. Wounded in body and spirit—that was how he saw himself. It would make the Grimpond glad if it knew.

He lifted his face momentarily and let the rain wash over it, cooling his skin. He hadn't thought it possible to be so hot in such dank weather.

It was the Grimpond's visions, of course, that haunted him—the three dark and enigmatic glimpses of the future, not accurate necessarily, lies twisted into half-truths, truths shaded by lies, but real. The first had already come to pass; he had sworn he would cut off his hand before he would take up the Druid cause and that was exactly what he had done. Then he had taken up the cause anyway. Ironic, poetic, terrifying.

The second vision was of Quickening. The third . . .

His good hand clenched. The truth was, he never got beyond thinking about the second. Quickening. In some way, he would fail her. She would reach out to him for help, he would have the chance to save her from falling, and he would let her die. He would stand there and watch her tumble away into some dark abyss. That was the Grimpond's vision. That was what would come to pass unless he could find a way to prevent it.

He had not, of course, been able to prevent the first.

Disgust filled him, and he banished his memory of the Grimpond back to the distant corner from which it had been set loose. The Grimpond, he reminded himself, was itself a lie. But, then, wasn't he a lie as well? Wasn't that what he had become, so determined to keep himself clear of Druid machinations, so ready to disdain all use of the magic except that which served to sustain his own narrow beliefs, and so certain that he could be master of his own destiny? He had lied to himself repeatedly, deceived himself knowingly, pretended all things, and made his life a travesty. He was mired in his misconceptions and pretenses. He was doing what he had sworn he would never do—the work of the Druids, the recovery of their magic, the undertaking of their will. Worse, he was committed to a course of action which could only result in his destruction—a confrontation with the Stone King to take back the Black Elfstone. Why? He was clinging to this course of action as if it were the only thing that would stop his drifting, as if it were all that was left that would keep him from drowning, the only choice that remained.

Surely it was not.

He peered through the damp at the city and realized again how much he missed the forestlands of Hearthstone. It was more than the city's stone, its harsh and oppressive feel, its constant mist and rain. There was no color in Eldwist, nothing to wash clean his sight, to brighten and warm his spirit. There were only shadings of gray, a blurring of shadows layered one upon another. He felt himself in some way a mirror of the city. Perhaps Uhl Belk was changing him just as he changed the land, draining off the colors of his life, reducing him to something as hard and lifeless as stone. How far could the Stone King reach? he wondered. How deep into your soul? Was there any limit? Could he stretch his arms out all the way to Darklin Reach and Hearthstone? Could he find a human heart? In time, probably. And time was nothing to a creature that had lived so long.

They crossed to the front entry of their after-dark refuge and began to climb the stairs. Because Walker led, he saw the stains of rainwater preceding him on the stone steps that his own trailing dampness masked to those following. Someone had entered and gone out again recently. Horner Dees? But Dees was supposedly already there and waiting for their return.

They moved down the maze of hallways to the room which served as their base of operations. The room was empty. Walker's eyes swept the trail of dampness to the shadows of the doors exiting through each wall; his ears probed the quiet. He crossed to where someone had seated himself and eaten.

His instincts triggered unexpectedly.

He could almost smell Pe Ell.

"Horner? Where are you?" Morgan was peering into other rooms and corridors, calling for the old Tracker. Walker met Quickening's gaze and said nothing. The Highlander ducked out momentarily, then back in again. "He said he would wait right here. I don't understand."

"He must have changed his mind," Walker offered quietly.

Morgan looked unconvinced. "I think I'll take a look around."

He went out the door they had come through, leaving the Dark Uncle and the daughter of the King of the Silver River staring at each other in the gloom.

"Pe Ell was here," she said, her black eyes locked on his.

He let the fire of her gaze warm him; he felt that familiar sense of kinship, of shared magics. "I don't sense a struggle," he said. "There is no blood, no disruption."

Quickening nodded soberly and waited. When he didn't speak further, she crossed to stand before him. "What are you thinking, Walker Boh?" she asked, discomfort in her eyes. "What have you been thinking all the way back, so lost within yourself?"

Her hands reached out to take his arm, to hold it tight. Her face lifted and the silver hair tumbled back, bathed in the weak gray light. "Tell me."

He felt himself laid bare, a thin, rumpled, battered life with barely enough strength remaining to keep from crumbling entirely. The ache in him stretched from his severed limb to his heart, physical and emotional both, an all-encompassing wave that threatened to sweep him away.

"Quickening." He spoke her name softly, and the sound of it seemed to steady him. "I was thinking you are more human than you would admit."

Puzzlement flashed across her perfect features.

He smiled, sad, ironic. "I might be a poor judge of such things, less responsive than I should be, a refugee from years of growing up a boy with no friends and few companions, of living alone too much. But I see something of myself in you. You are frightened by the feelings you have discovered in yourself. You admit to possessing the human emotions your father endowed you with when he created you, but you disdain to accept what you perceive to be their consequences. You love the Highlander—yet you try to mask it. You shut it away. You despise Pe Ell—yet you play with him as a lure would a fish. You grapple with your emotions, yet refuse to acknowledge them. You work so hard to hide from your feelings."

Her eyes searched his. "I am still learning."

"Reluctantly. When you confronted the Stone King, you were quick to state what had brought you. You told him everything; you hid nothing. There was no attempt at deception or ruse. Yet when Uhl Belk refused your demand—as you surely knew he would—you grew angry, almost . . ." He searched for the word. "Almost frantic," he finished. "It was the first time I can remember when you allowed your feelings to surface openly, without concern for who might witness them."

He saw a flicker of understanding in her eyes. "Your anger was real, Quickening. It was a measure of your pain. I think you wanted Uhl Belk to give you the Black Elfstone because of something you believe will happen if he does not. Is that so?"

She hesitated, torn, then let her breath escape slowly, wearily. "Yes."

"You believe that we will gain the Elfstone. I know that you do. You believe it because your father told you it would be so."

"Yes."

"But you also believe, as he told you, that it will require the magics of those you brought with you to secure it. No amount of talking, no manner of persuasion, will convince Uhl Belk to give it up. Yet you felt you had to try."

Her eyes were stricken. "I am frightened . . ." Her voice caught.

He bent close. "Of what? Tell me."

Morgan Leah appeared in the doorway. He slowed, watched Walker Boh draw back from Quickening, and completed his entrance. "Nothing," he said. "No sign of Horner. It's dark out now; the Rake will be about. I'll have to postpone any search until tomorrow." He came up to them and stopped. "Is something wrong?" he asked quietly.

"No," said Quickening.

"Yes," said Walker.

Morgan stared. "Which is it?"

Walker Boh felt the shadows of the room close about, as if darkness had descended all at once, intending to trap them there. They stood facing one another across a void, the Highlander, the Dark Uncle, and the girl. There was a sense of having reached an expected crossroads, of now having to choose a path which offered no return, of having to make a decision from which there was no retreat.

"The Stone King . . ." Quickening began in a whisper.

"We're going back for the Black Elfstone," Walker Boh finished.

Barely a mile away, at a window two floors up in a building fronting the lair of the Rake, Pe Ell and Horner Dees waited for the Creeper to emerge. They had been in position for some time, settled carefully back in the shadows with the patience of experienced hunters. The rain had stopped finally, turned to mist as the air cooled and stilled. A thin vapor rose off the stone of the streets in wisps that curled upward like snakes. From somewhere deep underground came the faint rumble of the Maw Grint awakening.

Pe Ell was thinking of the men he had killed. It was strange, but he could no longer remember who they were. For a time he had kept count, first out of curiosity, later out of habit, but eventually the number had grown so large and the passing of time so great that he simply lost track. Faces that had been clear in the beginning began to merge and then to fade altogether. Now it seemed he could remember only the first and the last clearly.

The fact that his victims had lost all sense of identity was disconcerting. It suggested that he was losing the sharpness of mind that his work required. It suggested that he was losing interest.

He stared into the blackness of the night and felt an unfamiliar weariness engulf him.

He forced the weariness away irritably. It would be different, he promised himself, when he killed the girl. He might forget the faces of these others from Rampling Steep, the one-armed man, the Highlander, the tunesmith, and the old Tracker; after all, killing them was nothing more than a matter of necessity. But he would never forget Quickening. Killing her was a matter of pride. Even now he could visualize her as clearly as if she were seated next to him, the soft curve and sweep of the skin over her bones, the tilting of her face when she spoke, the way her eyes drew you in, the weave and sway of her hands when they moved. Surely she was the most wondrous of creatures, spellbinding in a way that defied explanation. Hers was the magic of the King of the Silver River and therefore as old as the beginning of life. He wanted to drink in that magic when he killed her; he believed he could. Once he had done so, she would be a part of him, living inside, a presence stronger than even the most indelible memory, stirring within him as nothing else could.

Horner Dees shifted softly beside him, relieving cramped muscles. Still wrapped in his private thoughts, Pe Ell did not glance over. He kept his eyes fixed on the flat surface of the hidden entry across the street. The shadows that cloaked it remained still and unmoving.

What would happen when he slid the blade of the Stiehl into her body?

he wondered. What would he see in those depthless black eyes? What would he feel? The anticipation of the moment burned through him like fire. He had not thought of killing her for some time, waiting because he had no other choice if he was to secure the Black Elfstone, letting events take matters where they would. But the moment was close now, he believed. Once he had gained entry into the lair of the Rake, once he had discovered the hiding place of the Stone King, once he had secured possession of the Black Elfstone and disposed of Horner Dees . . .

He jerked upright.

Despite his readiness he was startled when across the way the stone panel lifted and the Rake emerged. He quickly dispensed with all further thoughts of Quickening. The Creeper's dark body glimmered where thin streamers of starlight managed to penetrate the blanket of clouds and reflect off the plates of armor. The monster stepped through the entry, then paused momentarily as if something had alarmed it. Feelers lifted and probed the air tentatively; the whiplike tail curled and snapped. The two in hiding shrank lower into the shadows. The Creeper remained motionless a moment longer, then, apparently satisfied, reached back and triggered the release overhead. The stone panel slid silently into place. The Rake turned and scuttled away into the mist and gloom, its iron legs scraping the stone like trailing chains.

Pe Ell waited until he was certain it was gone, then motioned for Horner Dees to follow him. Together they slipped down to the street, crossed, and stood before the Rake's lair. Dees produced the rope and grappling hook he was carrying and flung them toward a stone outcropping that projected above the secret entry. The grappling hook caught with a dull clank and held. Dees tested the rope, nodded, and passed the end to Pe Ell. Pe Ell climbed effortlessly, hand over hand, until he was level with the release. He triggered it, and the entry panel began to lift. Pe Ell dropped down quickly and with Horner Dees beside him, watched the black cave of the building's interior open into view.

Cautiously, they edged forward.

The entry ran back into deep shadow. Faint gray light slipped through the building's upper windows, seeped downward through gaps in the ruined floors, and illuminated small patches of the blackness. There was no sound from within. There was no movement.

Pe Ell turned to Dees. "Watch the street," he whispered. "Whistle if there's trouble."

He moved into the blackness, fading into it as comfortably as if he were one of its shadows. He was immediately at home, confident within its cloaking, his eyes and ears adjusting to its sweep. The walls of the building were bare and worn with age, damp in places where the rain had seeped through the mortar and run down the stone, tall and rigid against the faint light. Pe Ell slipped ahead, picking his way slowly, cautiously, waiting for something to show itself. He sensed nothing; the building seemed empty.

Something crunched underfoot, startling him. He peered down into the blackness. Bones littered the floor, hundreds of them, the remains of creatures the Rake had gathered in its nightly sweeps and carried back to its lair to consume.

The entry turned down a vast corridor to a larger hall and ended. No doors opened in, no passageways led out. The hall had once been an inner court and rose hundreds of feet through the building to a domed ceiling speckled with strange light patterns and the slow movement of shadows thrown by the clouds. The hall was silent. Pe Ell stared about in distress. He knew at once that there was nothing to discover—not the Stone King, not the Black Elfstone. He had guessed wrong. Anger and disappointment welled up within him, forcing him to continue his search even after he knew it was pointless. He started toward the far wall, scanning the mortared seams, the lines of floor and ceiling, desperate to find something.

Then Horner Dees whistled.

At almost the same moment Pe Ell heard the soft scrape of metal on stone.

He wheeled instantly and darted back through the darkened hall. The Rake had returned. There was no reason for it to have done so unless it had detected them. How? His mind raced, clawing back the layers of confusion. The Rake was blind, it relied on its other senses. It could not have seen them. Could it have smelled them? He had his answer instantly. Their scent about the doorway had alerted it; that was why it had paused. It had pretended to go out, waited, then circled back.

Pe Ell raged at his own stupidity. If he didn't get out of there at once, he would be trapped.

He burst into the darkened entry just in time to discover that he was too late. Through the raised door he caught a glimpse of the Rake rounding the corner of the building across the way, moving as fast as its metal legs would carry it toward its lair. The rope and Horner Dees were gone. Pe Ell melted into the darkest section of one wall, sliding forward soundlessly. He had to reach the entrance and get past the Creeper before it triggered the release. If he failed, he would be caught in the creature's lair. Even the Stiehl would not be enough to save him then.

The Rake rumbled up to the opening, iron claws rasping, and tentacles lashing out against the stone walls, beginning its probe within. Pe Ell slipped the Stiehl free of its sheath and crouched down against the dark. He would have to be quick. He was oddly calm, the way he was before a kill. He watched the monster fill the opening and start to move through.

At once he was up and running. The Rake sensed him instantly, its instincts even keener than Pe Ell's. A tentacle lashed out and caught him, inches from the door. The Stiehl whipped up, severing the limb, freeing the assassin once more. The Rake wheeled about, huffing. Pe Ell tried to run, but there were snaking arms everywhere.

Then the grappling hook shot out of the darkness behind the advancing Creeper, wrapping about its back legs. The rope securing it went taut, and the monster was jerked backward. Its limbs flailed, and its claws dug in.

For a moment its attention was diverted. That moment was enough. Pe Ell was past it in a split second, racing into the street, darting to safety. Almost immediately Horner Dees was running beside him, his bearish form laboring from the strain. Behind them, they heard the rope snap and the Rake start after in pursuit.

"Here!" Dees yelled, pulling Pe Ell left into a gaping doorway.

They ran through an entry, up several flights of stairs, down a hall, and out onto a back ramp that crossed to another building. The Creeper lumbered behind, smashing everything that blocked its way. The men hastened into the building at the end of the ramp and down a second set of stairs to the street again. The sounds of pursuit were beginning to fade. They slowed, rounded a corner, peered cautiously down the empty street, then followed the walkway south several blocks to where a cluster of smaller buildings offered an impassable warren into which they quickly crept. Safe within, they slid down wearily, backs to the wall, side by side, breathing heavily in the stillness.

"I thought you'd run," Pe Ell said, gasping.

Dees grunted, shook his head. "I would have, but I gave my word. What do we do now?"

Pe Ell's body steamed with sweat, but deep inside a cold fury was building. He could still feel the Rake's tentacle wrapped about his body. He could still feel it beginning to squeeze. He experienced such revulsion that he could barely keep from screaming aloud.

Nothing had ever come so close to killing him.

He turned to Horner Dees, watched the rough, bearded face furrow, the eyes glitter. Pe Ell's voice was chilly with rage. "You can do what you wish, old man," he whispered. "But I'm going back and kill that thing."

27

Morgan Leah was appalled. "What do you mean we're going back?" he demanded of Walker Boh. He was not just appalled; he was terrified. "Who gave you the right to decide anything, Walker? Quickening is leader of this company, not you!"

"Morgan," the girl said softly. She tried to take his hand, but he stepped quickly away.

"No. I want this settled. What's going on here? I leave the room for just a moment, just long enough to make sure Horner isn't . . . and when I come back I find you close enough to . . ." He choked on the words, his brown face flushing as the impact of what he was saying caught up with him. "I . . ."

"Morgan, listen to me," Quickening finished. "We have to recover the Black Elfstone. We have to."

The Highlander's fists clenched helplessly. He was aware of how foolish he looked, how young. He made a studied effort to control himself. "If we go back there, Quickening, we will be killed. We didn't know what we were up against before; now we do. Uhl Belk is too much for us. We all saw the same thing—a creature changed into something only vaguely human, armored in stone, and capable of brushing us aside like we were nothing. He's part of the land itself! How do we fight something like that? He'll swallow us whole before we have a chance even to get close!"

He forced his breathing to slow. "And that's only if he doesn't call the Maw Grint or the Rake first. We can't stand up to *them* let alone *him*. Think about it, will you? What if he chooses to use the Elfstone against us? Then what do we do—you without any magic at all that you can use, me with a broken sword that's lost most of its magic, and Walker with . . . I don't know, what? With what, Walker? What are you?"

The Dark Uncle was unfazed by the attack, his pale face expressionless, his eyes steady as they fixed on the Highlander. "I am what I always was, Morgan Leah."

"Less an arm!" Morgan snapped and regretted it immediately. "No, I'm sorry, I didn't mean that."

"But it is true," the other replied quietly.

Morgan looked away awkwardly for a moment, then back again. "Look at us," he whispered. "We're barely alive. We've trekked all the way to the end of the world and it's just about finished us. Carisman's already dead. Maybe Horner Dees as well. We're beaten up. We look like scare-crows. We haven't had a bath in weeks, unless you want to count getting rained on. We're dressed in rags. We've been running and hiding so long we don't know how to fight anymore. We're caught in this gray, dismal world where all we see is stone and rain and mist. I hate this place. I want to see trees and grass and living things again. I don't want to die here. I especially don't want to die when there is no reason for it! And that's exactly what will happen if we go looking for the Stone King. Tell me, Walker, what chance do we have?"

To his surprise, Walker Boh said, "A better chance than you think. Sit down a minute and listen."

Morgan hesitated, suspicion mirrored in his eyes. Then slowly he sat, his anger and frustration momentarily spent. He allowed Quickening to move next to him again, to wrap her arms about him. He let the heat of her body soak through him.

Walker Boh crossed his legs before him and pulled his dark cloak close. "It is true that we appear to be little more than beggars off some Southland city street, that we have nothing with which to threaten Uhl Belk, that we are as insignificant to him as the smallest insects that crawl upon the land. But that appearance may be an illusion we can use. It may give us the chance we need to defeat him. He sees us as nothing. He does not fear us. He disdains to worry about us at all. It is possible that he has already forgotten us. He believes himself invulnerable. Perhaps we can use that against him."

The dark eyes were intense. "He is not what he believes, Highlander. He has evolved beyond the spirit creature he was born, beyond anything he was intended to be. I believe he has evolved even beyond the King of the Silver River. But his evolution has not been a natural one. His evolution has been brought about by his usage of the Black Elfstone. It is ironic, but the Druids protected their magic better than Uhl Belk realizes. He thinks that he stole it easily and uses it without consequence. But he is wrong. Just by calling up the Elfstone's magic, he is destroying himself."

Morgan Leah stared. "What are you talking about?"

"Listen to him, Morgan," Quickening cautioned, her soft face bent close, her dark eyes expectant.

"I did not understand before today what it was that the Black Elfstone was intended to do," Walker Boh continued, hurrying now, anxious to complete his explanation. "I was given the Druid History by Cogline and told to read it. I learned that the Black Elfstone existed and that its purpose was to release Paranor from its spell and return it to the world of men. I learned from Quickening that the Black Elfstone's magic was conceived to negate the effects of other magics—thus the magic that sealed away Paranor could be dispelled. Such power, Highlander! How could such power exist? I kept wondering if it was possible, and if possible, why the Druids—who were so careful in such matters—took no better precautions to protect against its misuse. After all, the Black Elfstone was the only magic that could restore their Keep, that could initiate the process that would restore them to power. Would they let that magic slip away so easily? Would they allow it to be utilized by others, even a creature as powerful as Uhl Belk?

"I knew, of course, that they would not. But how could they prevent it? Today I discovered the answer to that question. I watched the Stone King summon the Maw Grint; I watched what passed between father and son. Did you see it? When Uhl Belk invoked the power of the Stone, there was a binding of the two, a bringing together. The magic was a catalyst. But what did it do? I wondered. It seemed to give life to them both. It was clearly addictive; they reveled in its use. The magic of the Black Elfstone was stronger than their own in the moment of its release. It was so strong that they could not resist what it was doing to them; in fact, they welcomed its coming."

He paused, and his voice lowered to a guarded whisper. The room's shadows cloaked them like conspirators. "This is what I believe must happen when the magic is invoked. Yes, it negates whatever magic it is directed against, just as the Druid History suggests, just as Quickening was told by her father. It confronts and steals away that magic's power. But it must do more. It cannot simply cause the magic to disappear. It cannot take a magic and change it into air. Something must happen to that magic. The laws of nature require it. What it does, I believe, is to absorb and transfer the effects of that other magic to the user of the Stone. When Uhl Belk turns the Black Elfstone on the Maw Grint he takes his child's magic and makes it his own; he takes the poison that transforms the land and its creatures to stone and alters himself as well. That is why he has evolved as he has. And perhaps even more important than that, each time he siphons off a part of the Maw Grint's magic, Uhl Belk is brought close again for a few moments to the son he created. Using the Black Elfstone to share the Maw Grint's magic has given them a bond they could not otherwise enjoy. They hate and fear each other, but they need each other as well. They feed on each other, a giving and taking that only the Black Elfstone can facilitate. It is as close as they can come to a father/son relationship. It is the only bond they can share."

He hunched forward. "But it is killing Uhl Belk. It is changing him to stone entirely. In time, he will disappear into the stone that encases him. He will become like any other statue—inanimate. He is doing it to himself without even realizing it. That is the way the Elfstone works; that is why he was able to steal it so easily. The Druids didn't care. They knew that anyone using it would suffer the consequences eventually. Magic cannot be absorbed without consequence. Uhl Belk is addicted to that magic. He needs the feeling of transformation, of adding to his stone body, to his land, to his kingdom of self. He could not stop now even if he tried."

"But how does this help us?" Morgan asked, impatient once more. He hunched forward curiously, caught up in the possibilities that Walker's explanation offered. "Even if you're right, what difference does it make? You're not suggesting that we simply wait until Uhl Belk kills himself, are you?"

Walker Boh shook his head. "We haven't time enough for that. The process may take years. But Uhl Belk is not as invulnerable as he believes. He has become largely dependent on the Black Elfstone, cocooned within his stone keep, changed mostly to stone himself, interested not so much in what is happening about him as in the feeding he requires so that his mutation can continue. He is largely stationary. Did you watch him when he tried to move? He cannot change positions quickly; he is welded to the rock of the floor. His magic is old and unused; most of what he does relates to feeding himself through use of the Stone. Fear of losing the Black Elfstone, of being deprived of his source of feeding, and of being left to the questionable mercy of his maddened child dominates his thinking. He has crippled himself with his obsessions. That gives us a chance to defeat him."

Morgan studied the other's face wordlessly for several long moments, thinking the matter through in spite of his reluctance to believe there was any possibility of succeeding, conscious of Quickening's eyes on him as he did so. He had always believed in Walker Boh's ability to reason matters through when others could not. He was the one who had suggested Par and Coll Ohmsford go to their uncle when they needed advice in dealing with the dreams of Allanon. He was frightened by what the Dark Uncle was suggesting, but not so big a fool as to discount it entirely.

Finally he said, "Everything you say may be so, Walker, but you have forgotten something. We still have to get inside the dome to have any chance of overcoming Uhl Belk. And he's not going to invite us in a second time. He's already made that clear. Since we haven't been able to find a way in on our own, how are we supposed to get close enough to do anything?"

Walker folded his hands before him thoughtfully. "Uhl Belk made a mistake when he admitted us to the dome. I was able to sense things that were hidden from me before, when I was forced to stand without. I was able to divine the nature of his fortress keep. He has settled himself above that cavern where the rats cornered us while we were searching the tunnels beneath the city. He places the Tiderace between himself and the Maw Grint's underground lair. But he miscalculated in doing so. The constant changing of the tide has worn and eroded portions of the stone on which he rests."

The Dark Uncle's eyes narrowed. "There is an opening that leads into the dome from beneath."

Another pair of eyes narrowed as well, these in disbelief as Horner Dees weighed the implications of Pe Ell's words in the dark silence of the building in which the two men were crouched. "Kill it?" he questioned finally, unable to keep himself from repeating the other's words. "Why would you want to do that?"

"Because it's out there!" Pe Ell snapped impatiently, as if that explained everything.

His stare challenged the Tracker, daring him to object. When Dees did not respond, Pe Ell bent forward like a hawk at hunt. "How long have we been in this city, old man—a week, two? I can't even remember anymore. It seems as if we've been here forever! One thing I do know. Ever since we arrived, that thing has been hunting us. Every night, everywhere we go! The Rake, sweeping up the streets, cleaning up the garbage. Well, I've had enough!"

He was stiff with rage, fighting back against the memory of that iron tentacle wrapped about him, struggling to control his revulsion. When he killed, it was quick and clean. Not a slow squeezing, not a death that choked and strangled. And nothing ever touched him. Nothing ever got close.

Not until now.

His failure to find the Stone King in the Rake's lair hadn't done anything to improve his disposition either. He had been certain that he would find Uhl Belk and the Black Elfstone. Instead, he had almost succeeded in getting himself killed.

His knife-blade face was set and raw with feeling. "I won't be hunted anymore. A Creeper can die like anything else." He paused. "Think about this. Once it's dead, maybe the Stone King will show himself. Maybe he'll come out to see what killed his watchdog. Then we'll have him!"

Horner Dees did not look convinced. "You're not thinking straight."

Pe Ell flushed. "Are you frightened once more, old man?"

"Of course. But that doesn't have anything to do with the matter. The fact is, you're supposed to be a professional killer, an assassin. You don't kill without a reason and never without being sure that the odds are in your favor. I don't see any evidence of that here."

"Then you're not looking hard enough!" Pe Ell was furious. "You already have the reason! Haven't you been listening? It doesn't have to be money and it doesn't have to be someone else's idea! Do you want to find Uhl Belk or not? As for the odds, I'll find a way to change them!"

Pe Ell rose and wheeled away momentarily to face the dark. He shouldn't care one way or the other what this old man thought; it shouldn't matter in the least. But somehow, for some reason, it did, and he refused to give Dees the satisfaction of thinking he was somehow misguided. He hated to admit that Horner Dees might have saved his life, even that he might have helped him escape. The old man was a thorn in his side that needed removing. Dees had come out of his past like a ghost, come out of a time he had thought safely buried. No one alive should know who he was or what he had done save Rimmer Dall. No one should be able to talk about him.

He found suddenly that he wanted Horner Dees dead almost as much as he wanted to dispose of the Rake.

Except that the Rake was the more immediate problem.

He turned back to the old Tracker. "I've wasted enough time on you," he snapped. "Go back to the others. I don't need your help."

Horner Dees shrugged. "I wasn't offering it."

Pe Ell started for the door.

"Just out of curiosity," Dees called after him, rising now as well, "how do you plan to kill it?"

"What difference does it make to you?" Pe Ell called over his shoulder.

"You don't have a plan, do you?"

Pe Ell stopped dead in the doorway, seized by an almost overpowering urge to finish off the troublesome Dees here and now. After all, why wait any longer? The others would never know. His hand dropped through the crease in his pants to close about the Stiehl.

"Thing is," Horner Dees said suddenly, "you can't kill the Rake even if you manage to get close enough to use that blade of yours."

Pe Ell's fingers released. "What do you mean?"

"I mean that even if you lay in wait for the thing, say you drop on it from above or sneak up on it from underneath—not likely, but say that you do—you still can't kill it quick enough." The sharp eyes glittered. "Oh, you can cut off a tentacle or two, maybe sever a leg, or even put out an eye. But that won't kill it. Where do you stab it that will kill it, Pe Ell? Do you know? I don't. Before you've taken two cuts, the Rake will have you. Damage the thing? A Creeper builds itself right back again, finds spare pieces of metal and puts what it's lost back in place."

Pe Ell smiled—mean, sardonic, empty of warmth. "I'll find a way."

Dees nodded. "Sure you will." He paused deliberately, his bearish frame shifting, changing his weight from one foot to the other. In the near darkness, he seemed like a piece of the wall breaking loose. "But not without a plan."

Pe Ell looked away in disgust, shook his head, then looked back again. He'd spent too much time trudging about this dismal city, this tomb of stone and damp. He'd been fighting too long to keep from being swallowed up in its belly. That coupled with prolonged exposure to Quickening's magic had eroded his instincts, dulled the edge of his sharpness, and twisted the clearness of his thought. He was at a point where the only thing that mattered was getting back to where he had started from, to the world beyond Eldwist, and to the life that he had so fully controlled.

But not without the Black Elfstone. He would not give it up.

And not without Quickening's life. He would not give that up either.

Meanwhile, Horner Dees was trying to tell him something. It never hurt to listen. He made himself go very still inside—everything, right down to his thoughts. "You have a plan of your own, don't you?" he whispered.

"I might."

"I'm listening."

"Maybe there's something to what you say about killing the Rake. Maybe that will bring Belk out of hiding. Something has to be tried." The admission came grudgingly.

"I'm still listening."

"It'll take the two of us. Same agreement as before. We look out for each other until the matter's done. Then it's every man for himself. Your word."

"You have it."

Horner Dees shuffled forward until he was right in front of Pe Ell, much closer than Pe Ell wanted him, wheezing like he'd run a mile, grinning through his shaggy beard, big hands knotting into fists.

"What I think we ought to do," he said softly, "is drop the Rake down a deep hole."

Morgan Leah stared at Walker Boh wordlessly for a moment, then shook his head. He was surprised at how calm his voice sounded. "It won't work. You said yourself that the Stone King isn't just a moving statue; he's made himself a part of the land. He's everything in Eldwist. You saw what he did when he finally decided to let us into the dome and then after, when he summoned the Maw Grint. He just split the rock wall apart. His own skin, Walker. Don't you think he'll know if we try to climb through that same skin from beneath? Don't you think he'll be able to feel it? What do you think will happen to us then? Squish!"

Morgan made a grinding motion with his palms. A dark flush crept into his face; he found that he was shaking.

Walker's expression never changed. "What you suggest is possible, but unlikely. Uhl Belk may be the heart and soul of the land he has created, but he is also, like it, a thing of stone. Stone feels nothing, senses nothing. Uhl Belk would not have even discovered we were here if he had been forced to rely on his external senses. It was our use of magic that alerted him. There may remain enough of him that is human to detect intruders, but he relies principally on the Rake. If we can avoid using magic we can enter the dome before he knows what we are about."

Morgan started to object, then cut himself short. Quickening was clutching his arm so hard it hurt. "Morgan," she whispered urgently. "We can do it. Walker Boh is right. This is our chance."

"Our chance?" Morgan looked down at her, fighting to keep his balance as the black eyes threatened to drown him, finding her impossibly beautiful all over again. "Our chance to do what, Quickening?" He forced his gaze away from her, fixing on Walker. "Suppose that you are right about all this, that we can get into the dome without Belk knowing it. What difference does it make? What are we supposed to do then? Use our broken magics, the three of us—a weaponless girl, a one-armed man, and a man with half a sword? Aren't we right back where we started with this conversation?"

He ignored Quickening's hands as they pulled at him. "I won't pretend with you, Walker. You can see what I'm thinking. You can with everyone. I'm terrified. I admit it. If I had the Sword of Leah whole again, I would stand a chance against something like Uhl Belk. But I don't. And I don't have any innate magic like you and Par. I just have myself. I've stayed alive this long by accepting my limitations. That's how I was able to fight the Federation officials who occupy my homeland; that's how I managed to survive against something far bigger and stronger. You have to pick and choose your battles. The Stone King is a monster with monsters to command, and I don't see how the three of us can do anything about him."

Quickening was shaking her head. "Morgan . . ."

"No," he interrupted quickly, unable to stop himself now. "Don't say anything. Just listen. I have done everything you asked. I have given up other responsibilities I should have fulfilled to come north with you in search of Eldwist and Uhl Belk. I have stayed with you to find the Black Elfstone. I want you to succeed in what your father has sent you to do. But I don't know how that can happen, Quickening. Do you? Can you tell me?"

She moved in front of him, her face lifting. "I can tell you that it will happen. My father has said it will be so."

"With my magic and Walker's and Pe Ell's. I know. Well, then, what of Pe Ell? Isn't he supposed to go with us? Don't we need him if we are to succeed?"

She hesitated before giving her answer. "No. Pe Ell's magic will be needed later."

"Later. And your own?"

"I have no magic until you recover the Elfstone."

"So it is left to Walker and me."

"Yes."

"Somehow."

"Yes."

Walker Boh stepped forward impatiently, his pale face hard. "Enough, Highlander. You make it sound as if this were some mystical process that required divine intervention or the wisdom of the dead. There is nothing difficult about what we are being asked to do. The Stone King holds the Black Elfstone; he must be made to give it up. We must sneak through the floor of the dome and surprise him. We must find a way to shock him, to stun him, to do something that will make him release his grip on the Stone, then snatch it from him. We don't have to stand against him in battle; we don't have to slay him. This isn't a contest of strength; it is a contest of will. And cleverness. We must be more clever than he."

The Dark Uncle's eyes burned. "We have not come all this way, Morgan Leah, just to turn around and go back again. We knew there were no answers to be given to our questions, that we would have to find a way to do everything that was required. We have done so. We need do so only one time more. If we don't, the Elfstone is lost to us. That means that the Four Lands are lost as well. The Shadowen have won. Cogline and Rumor died for nothing. Your friend Steff died for nothing. Is that what you wish? Is that your intent? Is it, Morgan Leah?"

Morgan pushed past Quickening and seized the front of the other's cloak. Walker seized his in turn. For an instant they braced each other without speaking, Morgan's face contorted with rage, Walker's smooth and intense.

"I am frightened, too, Highlander," Walker Boh said softly. "I have fears that go far beyond what we are being asked to do here. I have been charged by the shade of Allanon with using the Black Elfstone to bring back Paranor and the Druids. If using the Elfstone on the Maw Grint turns Uhl Belk to stone, what will using it on disappeared Paranor do to me?"

There was a long, empty silence in which the question hung skeletal and forbidding against the dark of the room. Then Walker whispered, "It doesn't matter, you see. I have to find out."

Morgan let the other's cloak slip from his fingers. He took a slow step back. "Why are we doing this?" he whispered in reply. "Why?"

Walker Boh almost smiled. "You know why, Morgan Leah. Because there is no one else."

Morgan laughed in spite of himself. "Brave soldiers? Or fools?"

"Maybe both. And maybe we are just stubborn."

"That sounds right." Morgan sighed wearily, pushing back the oppressiveness of the dark and damp, fighting through his sense of futility. "I just think there should be more answers than there are."

Walker nodded. "There should. Instead, there are only reasons and they will have to suffice."

Morgan's mind spun with memories of the past, of his friends missing and dead, of his struggle to stay alive, and of the myriad quests that had taken him from his home in the Highlands and brought him at last to this farthest corner of the world. So much had happened, most of it beyond his control. He felt small and helpless in the face of those events, a tiny bit of refuse afloat in the ocean, carried on tides and by whim. He was sick and worn; he wanted some form of resolution. Perhaps only death was resolution enough.

"Let me speak with him," he heard Quickening say.

Alone, they knelt at the center of the room in shadow, facing each other, their faces so close that Morgan could see his reflection in her dark eyes. Walker had disappeared. Quickening's hands reached out to him, and he let her fingers come to rest on his face, tracing the line of his bones.

"I am in love with you, Morgan Leah," she whispered. "I want you to know that. It sounds strange to me to say such a thing. I never thought I would be able to do so. I have fears of my own, different from yours and Walker Boh's. I am afraid of being too much alive."

She bent forward and kissed him. "Do you understand what I mean when I say that? An elemental gains life not out of the love of a man and a woman for each other but out of magic's need. I was created to serve a purpose, my father's purpose, and I was told to be wary of things that would distract me. What could distract me more, Morgan Leah, than the love I have for you? I cannot explain that love. I do not understand it. It comes from the part of me that is human and surfaces despite my efforts to deny it. What am I to do with this love? I tell myself I must disdain it. It is . . . dangerous. But I cannot give it up because the feeling of it gives me life. I become more than a thing of earth and water, more than a bit of clay made whole. I become real."

He kissed her back, hard and determined, frightened by what she was telling him, by the sound of the words, by the implications they carried. He did not want to hear more.

She broke away. "You must listen to me, Morgan. I had thought to keep to my father's path and not to stray. His advice seemed sound. But I find now that I cannot heed it. I must love you. It does not matter what is meant for either of us; we are not alive if we do not respond to our feelings. So it is that I will love you in every way that I am able; I will not be frightened any longer by what that means."

"Quickening . . ."

"But," she said hurriedly, "the path remains clear before us nevertheless and we must follow it, you and I. We have been shown where it leads, and we must continue to its end. The Stone King must be overcome. The Black Elfstone must be recovered. You and I and Walker Boh must see that these things are done. We must, Morgan. We must."

He was nodding as she spoke, helpless in the face of her persistence, his love for her so strong that he would have done anything she asked despite the gravest reservations. The tears started in his eyes, but he forced them back, burying his face in her shoulder, hugging her close. He combed her silver hair with his fingers; he stroked the curve of her back. He felt her slim arms go around him, and her body tremble.

"I know," he answered softly.

He thought then of Steff, dying at the hands of the girl he had loved, thinking her something she was not. Would it be so with him? he wondered suddenly. He thought, too, of the promise he had once made his friend, a promise they had all made, Par and Coll and he, that if any of them found a magic that would help free the Dwarves, they would do what they could to recover it and see that it was used. Surely the Black Elfstone was such a magic.

He felt a calm settle through him, dissipating the anger and foreboding, the doubt and uncertainty. The path was indeed laid out for him, and he had never had any choice but to follow it.

"We'll find a way," he whispered to her and felt her own tears dampen his cheek.

Standing in the blackness of the room beyond, Walker Boh looked back at the lovers as they embraced and felt the warmth of their closeness reach out to him like a lost child's tiny hands. He turned away. There could be no such love for him. He felt an instant's remorse and brushed it hastily aside. His future was a shining bit of certainty in the darkness of his present. Sometimes his prescience revealed a cutting edge.

He moved soundlessly through the building until he reached an open window high above the street and looked down into the roil of mist and gloom. The world of Eldwist was a maze of stone obstructions and corridors that glared back at him through a hard, wet sheen. It was harsh and certain and pointless and it reminded him of the direction of his life.

Yet now, at last, his life might become something more.

One puzzle remained. The Highlander had touched on it, brushed by it in his effort to understand how it was that they could stand against a being with the power of Uhl Belk. The puzzle had been with them since the beginning of their journey, a constant presence, and an enigma that refused to be revealed.

The puzzle was Quickening. The daughter of the King of the Silver River, created out of the elements of the Garden, given life out of magic—she was a riddle of words in another tongue. She had been sent to bring them all into Eldwist. But wouldn't a summons have done the job as well? Or even a dream? Instead the King of the Silver River had sent a living, breathing bit of wonder, a creature so beautiful she defied belief. Why? She was here for a reason, and it was a reason beyond that which she had revealed.

Walker Boh felt a dark place inside shiver with the possibilities.

What was it that Quickening had really been sent to do?

28

At dawn the three left their concealment and went down into the streets. The rain had ceased to fall, the clouds had lifted above the peaks of the buildings, and the light was gray and iron hard. Silence wrapped the bones of Eldwist like a shroud, the air windless, unmisted, and empty. Far distant, the ocean was a faint murmur. Their footfalls thudded dully and receded into echoes that seemed to hang like whispers against the skies. Unsuccessfully, they searched the city for life. There was no sign of either Horner Dees or Pe Ell. The Rake had retreated to its daylight lair. The Maw Grint slept within the earth. And in his domed fortress, Uhl Belk was a dark inevitability awaiting confrontation.

Yet Walker Boh was at peace.

He strode before Morgan and Quickening, surprised at the depth of his tranquillity. He had given so much of himself to the struggle to understand and control the purpose of his life, battling with the twin specters of legacy and fate. Now all that was cast aside. Time and events had rushed him forward to this moment, an implacable whirlwind that would resolve the purpose of his life for him. His meeting with the Stone King would settle the matter of who and what he was. Either he merited the charge that the shade of Allanon had given him or he did not. Either he was meant to possess the Black Elfstone and bring back Paranor and the Druids or he was not. Either he would survive Uhl Belk or he would not. He no longer questioned that his doubt must give way to resolution; he did not choose to mire himself further in the "what ifs" that had plagued him for so long. Circumstance had placed him here, and that was enough. Whether he lived or died, he would finally be free of the past. Was the Shannara magic alive within him, strong beyond the loss of his arm to the poison of the Asphinx, powerful enough to withstand the fury of the Stone King? Was the trust Allanon had given to Brin Ohmsford meant for him? He would find out. Knowledge, he thought with an irony that he could not ignore, was always liberating.

Morgan Leah was less certain.

Half-a-dozen steps back, his hand clasped in Quickening's, the Highlander was a fragile shell through which fears and misgivings darted like trapped flies. In contrast to Walker Boh, he already knew far too much. He knew that Walker was not the Dark Uncle of old, that the myth of his invincibility had been shattered along with his arm, and that he was swept along on the same tide of prophecies and promises as the rest of them. He knew that he himself was even less able, a man without a whole weapon, bereft of the magic that had barely sustained him through previous encounters with far lesser beings. He knew that there were only the two of them, that Quickening could not intervene, that she might share their fate but could not affect it. He could say that he understood her need to gain possession of the Black Elfstone, her belief in her father's promises, and her confidence in them—he could speak the words. He could pray that they would find some way to survive what they were undertaking, that some miracle would save them. But the fears and the misgivings would not be captured by words and prayers; they would not be allayed by false hope. They darted within like startled deer, and he could feel the beating of his heart in response to their flight.

What would he do, he wondered desperately, when the Stone King turned those empty eyes on him? Where would he find his strength?

He glanced covertly at Quickening, at the lines and shadows of her face, and at the darkly reassuring glitter of her eyes.

But Quickening walked beside him without seeing.

They passed down the empty streets toward the heart of the city, stalking like cats along the stone ribbon of the walkways, their backs to the building walls. They could almost feel the earth beneath them pulse with the Stone King's life; they could almost hear the sound of his breathing through the hush. An old god, a spirit, a thing of incomprehensible power—they could feel his eyes upon them. The minutes slipped away, and the streets and buildings came and went with a sameness that whispered of ages come and gone and lives before their own that had passed this way without effect. An oppressive certainty settled down about them, an unspoken voice, a barely remembered face, a feathered touch, all designed to persuade them of the futility of their effort. They felt its presence and reacted, each differently, each calling up what defenses could be found. No one turned back. No one gave way. Locked together by their determination to make an end of this nightmare, they continued on.

In the east, dawn's faint gray light brightened to a chilly silver mist that mingled with the clouds and left the city crystallized.

They caught their first glimpse of the dome shortly after and when Walker Boh, still leading, pressed them back into the shadows of the building they followed as if afraid the dome could see. He took them back along the walkway and down a secondary street, then over and down another, winding this way and that, twisting about through the maze. They slid along the dampness like a trail of water seeking its lowest level and never slowed. Their path meandered, but the dome drew closer beyond the walls that concealed them.

Finally Walker stopped, head lifting within the cowl of his dark cloak as if to sniff the air. He was lost within himself, casting about in the darkness of his mind, the magic working to lead him to where his eyes could not see. He started out again, taking them across a street, down an alleyway and out again, down another street to where a building entry opened onto a set of broad stairs. The stairs took them into the earth beneath the building, a dark and engulfing descent into a cavernous chamber where dozens of the ancient carriages of the old world sat resting on their stone tracks. Massive hulks, broken apart by time and age, the carriages gave the chamber the look of a boneyard. Light fell across the carcasses in narrow stripes, and dust motes decorated the air in a thin, choking haze.

The stairs went farther down, and the three continued their descent. They entered an anteroom with a circular portal set in the far wall, stepped through hesitantly, and found themselves back in the city's sewers. The sewers burrowed in three directions into the darkness, catacombs wrapped in silence and the smell of dead things. Walker's good hand lifted and silver light wrapped about it. He paused once more, as if testing the air. Then he took them left.

The tunnel swallowed them effortlessly, its stone walls massive and impenetrable, threatening to hold them fast forever. Silence was a stealthy, invisible watcher. They heard nothing of the Maw Grint—not a rumble, not even the tremor of its breathing. Eldwist had the feel of a tomb once more, deserted of life, a haven for the dead. They stretched ahead in a line, Walker leading, Quickening next, and Morgan last. No words were exchanged, no glances. They kept their eyes on the light that Walker held forth, on the rock of the tunnel floor they followed, and on the movement of the shadows they cast.

Walker slowed, then stopped. His lighted hand moved to one side, then the other. A faint glimmer caught the outline of a dark opening in the wall left and stairs beyond.

Once again they started down, following damp, slick, roughened steps through a wormhole in the earth. They began to smell the Tiderace, then to hear the faint roar of its waters against Eldwist's shore. They listened closely, guardedly for the squealing of the rats, but it did not come. When they reached the end of these stairs, Walker took them right into a narrow gap studded with stone projections honed razor-sharp by nature and time. They moved slowly, inching their way along, hunched up close to each other to keep within the circle of the light. The dampness spread up the walls before them, a dark stain. Things began moving in the light, skittering away. Morgan caught a glimpse of what they were. Sea life, he recognized in surprise. Tiny black crabs. Were they far enough down from Uhl Belk that such things could live? Were they close enough to the water?

Then they emerged once more into the subterranean cavern that lay beneath the city. Rock walls circled away from the ledge on which they stood and the ocean crashed wildly into the rocks below. Mist churned overhead, draping the cavern's farthest reaches with curtains of white. Daylight brightened the shadows where the rocks were cleft to form small, nearly colorless rainbows against the mist.

The ledge ran away to either side, dipping, climbing, jagged and uneven, disappearing into rock and shadow. Walker Boh cast both ways, feeling for the presence he knew he would find, sensing the pulse of its magic. His eyes lifted toward the unseen. Uhl Belk.

"This way," he said quietly, turning left.

Then the rumble of the Maw Grint's waking sounded, elevating from a stir to a roar, and the whole of Eldwist shook with fury.

The plan was simple, but then simple plans were the ones that usually worked best. The only trouble with this one, thought Pe Ell as he stood in the shadows of the building across from the Rake's lair, was that he was the one taking all the chances while Horner Dees remained safe and sound.

The plan, of course, had been the old man's.

Like Quickening, Walker, and Morgan Leah, they had gone out at dawn, slipping from their refuge back to the streets, greeting the cheerless gray light with squinted eyes and suspicious frowns. A brief exchange of glances and they had been off, going first to the Rake's lair, then tracing the route that Pe Ell would lure the Creeper down. When Dees had satisfied himself that Pe Ell had memorized it, they hooked the old man's harness in place, checked the leverage on the makeshift pulley, and parted company.

Pe Ell had backtracked to the Rake's lair, and now there he stood, waiting.

Stealth and speed were what he would need, first the one, then the other, and not too much of either—an assassin's tools.

He listened to the silence for a long time, judging the distance he must cover and measuring the retreat he would make. There would be no one to help him escape this time if things went wrong. His narrow face turned this way and that, lifted into the smell of the sea and the stone, knifed against the mist, sifted through the instincts that warned him the Creeper was still awake.

He smiled his cold, empty smile. The anger was gone. The anticipation of killing calmed him like Quickening's touch, soothed him, and gave him peace. He was still and settled within himself, everything ready, in place, as sharp as the edge of the Stiehl and as certain.

Noiselessly, he crossed the street to the door of the lair. He carried the grappling hook and rope firmly in hand. Standing before the door, he tossed the hook skyward to wrap about the same stone projection they had used the previous night. The grappling hook caught with a sharp clang and held. Pe Ell backed away, waiting. But the door remained closed. The Rake had either not heard or was preparing itself for whatever would happen next. Pe Ell had hoped that the noise of the hook would bring the beast out and save him the trouble of making the climb. But he knew that was asking too much.

He took a deep breath. This was where the plan became really dangerous.

He stepped forward, grasped the rope that dangled from the grappling hook, and began to climb. He went swiftly, hand over hand, strong enough that he did not require the use of his legs. Once up, he gripped the release that triggered the hidden entry to the lair, yanked violently on it, and immediately dropped away, skinning down the rope like a cat. The door was already coming up when he struck the ground. There was a whisper of sound from within, and he sprang back instantly. A tentacle barely missed catching him, whistling past his feet. The Rake was already moving, lumbering forward, a nest of tentacles outstretched and grasping.

In another instant the door to the lair was completely up. The Creeper rushed forth, skittering madly, wildly, heedless of the fact that it was no longer night. Enraged by Pe Ell's invasion, it gave immediate pursuit. The assassin raced away, darting just ahead of the maddened beast, racing into the shadows of the alleyway across the street. The Creeper followed, faster than Pe Ell had expected. For an instant he wondered if he had misjudged his chances. But there was no time to ponder the matter now, and the doubts evaporated in a surge of determination that propelled him forward.

Down the alleyway he ran and out into the adjoining street. He skidded to a halt. Careful of the traps, he thought. Careful you don't get caught in one yourself. That was what they had planned for the Rake, the old man and he—a long drop down a deep hole, a drop into the bowels of Eldwist. If he could stay alive that long.

The Creeper crashed through the entry of the building next to him, choosing its own route now, almost catching him by surprise. He barely eluded the closest tentacles, knife thin as he twisted away, gone almost before the beast could track him. He darted along the building's edge, the Rake in pursuit. The iron that armored the creature clanked and grated, thudded and scraped. He could feel the size of the thing looming over him, an avalanche waiting to fall. He went through one building, through a second, and emerged another street over. Close now, just two blocks more. But the beast? He turned, searching. He could hear it coming, but the sound seemed to project from everywhere at once. Where . . . ?

Out from the shadows of a darkly recessed entry the Creeper tore, iron arms slamming into the earth inches from Pe Ell as the assassin leaped free. Pe Ell howled in fury and dismay.

So quick!

He wanted to turn and fight, to see the monster react to the cold iron of the Stiehl as he slashed its body to ribbons. He wanted to *feel* the Creeper die. Instead he ran once more, racing along the stone paths of the city, down the streets, along the building walls, through shadows and gray light, a wisp of something darker than night. Tentacles rustled and slithered after him, catching at doors and windowframes, tearing them apart, leaving showers of stone dust scattered in their wake. The massive body hammered and careened, and the legs tore at the walk. The Rake seemed to pick up speed, coming faster still. If daylight bothered it, if blindness inhibited it, it showed nothing of it here. Pe Ell could feel its rage as if it were palpable.

The chase took them down another street and around a final corner. Pe Ell could sense that he was losing ground. Ahead, the street deadended at a stone park. A basin of steps led down to a statue of a winged figure with streamers and ribbons trailing from its body—and to a trap, the same trap that had snared the old man and the Highlander days before.

Horner Dees was waiting, secured in his harness, standing at the edge of the hidden door, bait for the trap. Pe Ell leaped sideways to a walkway and picked up speed as the Rake rounded the corner behind him, tentacles whipping. He went past Horner Dees on the fly, caught a glimpse of his rough face, pale beneath the heavy beard, and sprang onto the wall where the lines securing the harness were laid. He pulled them taut, hoisting Dees out over the hidden pit. He heard the Creeper rumble into the street, heard Horner Dees yell. The Rake became aware of the old man, deviated direction slightly, and charged. Dees tried to backpedal in spite of himself as the juggernaut bore down on him, metal parts shrieking.

Then the trapdoor dropped open, and the monster began to fall. It tumbled wildly down the stone ramp, its armored body rasping. It had been so eager to reach the Tracker that it had forgotten where it was. Now it was caught, sliding away, disappearing from view. Pe Ell howled with delight.

But suddenly the tentacles lashed out and began snaring stone projections—a corner of the basin stairs, a section of a crumbling wall, anything within reach. The sliding stopped. Dust rose into the air, obscuring everything. Pe Ell hesitated, forgetting momentarily to pull in on the harness that secured Dees. Then he heard the old man scream. Yanking frantically on the ropes, he found they would not move. Something was pulling from the other end, something far stronger than himself. He had waited too long. The Rake had Horner Dees.

Pe Ell never hesitated. He wasn't thinking of his promise; keeping his word had never much concerned him. He simply reacted. He dropped the ropes, leaped from the wall, and raced through the basin park into the street. He saw the old Tracker sliding across the stone toward the edge of the drop, hands grasping and feet kicking, a tentacle wrapped about his stout body. He caught up with Horner Dees just as the old man was about to be pulled from view. One slice of the Stiehl severed the tentacle that bound him; a second severed the ropes of the harness.

"Run!" he screamed, shoving the bulky form away.

A tentacle snaked about him, trying to pin his arms fast. He twisted, the Stiehl's blade glowing white with magic, and the tentacle dropped away. Pe Ell raced left, cutting at the tentacles that secured the Rake, severing its hold. There was dust everywhere, rising into the gray light, mingling with the mist until it was uncertain where anything lay. Pe Ell was moving on instinct. He darted and skipped through the tangle of arms, hacked at each, heard the scraping begin again, and the sliding resume.

Then there was a rush of metal and flailing arms and the Rake was gone. It dropped into the chute and fell, tumbling down into the chasm. Pe Ell smothered his elation, racing back the way he had come, searching for Dees. He found him crawling weakly along the basin stairs. "Get up!" he cried, hauling him to his feet in a frenzied lunge, propelling him ahead.

The earth behind them exploded, the street shattering apart, stone fragments flying everywhere. The two men stumbled and fell and turned to look.

The remaining pieces of Horner Dees' plan tumbled into place.

Out of the depths of Eldwist rose the Maw Grint, awakened by the impact of the Rake's fall, aroused and angered. The monster roared and shook itself as it lifted skyward, worm body glistening, all ridges and scales, so huge that it blocked even the faint gray daylight. The Rake dangled from its mouth, turning to stone as the poison coated it, its struggles beginning to lessen. The Maw Grint held it firm a moment, then tossed it as a dog might a rat. The Rake flew through the air and struck the side of a building. The wall collapsed with the impact, and the Rake shattered into pieces.

Back down into the tunnels slid the Maw Grint, its thunder already fading to silence. Clouds of dust settled in its wake, and the light brightened to slate.

Impulsively Pe Ell reached out and locked hands with Horner Dees. Their labored breathing was the only sound in the stillness that followed.

Underground, in the cavern beneath the Stone King's fortress dome, the rumble of the Maw Grint's waking disappeared into the pounding of the Tiderace against Eldwist's rocky shores. Morgan Leah's sun-browned face lifted to peer through the mists.

"What happened?" he whispered.

Walker Boh shook his head, unable to answer. He could still feel the tremors in the earth, lingering echoes of the monster's fury. Something had caused it to breach—something beyond normal waking. The creature's response had been different than when the Stone King had summoned it, more impatient, more intense.

"Is it sleeping again?" the Highlander pressed, anxious now, concerned with being trapped.

"Yes."

"And him?" Morgan pointed into the mists. "Does *he* know?"

Uhl Belk. Walker probed, reaching through the layers of rock in an effort to discover what might be happening. But he was too far away, the stone too secure to be penetrated by his magic. Not unless he used his touch, and if he did that the Stone King would be warned.

"He rests still," Quickening answered unexpectedly. She came forward to stand next to him, her face smooth and calm, her eyes distant. The wind rushed into her silver hair and scattered it about her face. She braced against its thrust. "Be at ease, Morgan. He does not sense the change."

But Walker sensed it, whatever it was, just as the girl had. Barely perceptible yet, but the effects were beginning to reach and swell. It was something beyond the passing of time and the erosion of rock and earth. The wind whispered it, the ground echoed with it, and the air breathed it. Born of the magic, the daughter of the King of the Silver River and the Dark Uncle had both felt its ripple. Only the Highlander was left unaware.

Walker Boh felt a rough, unexpected urgency clutch at him. Time was slipping away.

"We have to hurry," he said at once, starting away again. "Quickly, now. Come."

He took them left down the rocky outcropping of the ledge, across its ragged, slippery surface. They inched along with their backs to the wall, the ledge no more than several feet wide in places, the ocean's spray redampening its surface with each newly broken wave. Beyond where they stood the cavern spread away like some vast hidden world, and it seemed as if they could feel the eyes of its invisible inhabitants peering out at them.

The ledge ended at a cave that burrowed into darkness. Walker Boh lifted the magic of his silver light to the black and a staircase appeared, winding away, circling upward into the rock.

With Quickening and Morgan following shadowlike, the Dark Uncle began to climb.

29

When Morgan Leah was a boy he often played in the crystal-studded caves that lay east of the city. The caves had been formed centuries earlier, explored and forgotten by countless generations, their stone floors worn smooth by the passing of time and feet. They had survived the Great Wars, the Wars of the Races, the intrusions of living creatures of all forms, and even the earth fires that simmered just beneath their surface. The caves were pockets of bright luminescence, their ceilings thick with stalactites, floors dotted with pools of clear water and darkly shadowed sinkholes, and their chambers connected by a maze of narrow, twisting tunnels. It was dangerous to go into the caves; there was a very high risk of becoming lost. But for an adventure-seeking Highland boy like Morgan Leah, any prospect of risk was simply an attraction.

He found the caves when he was still very small, barely old enough to venture out on his own. There were a handful of boys with him when he discovered an entrance, but he was the only one brave enough to venture in. He went only a short distance that day, intimidated more than a little; it seemed a very real possibility that the caves ran to the very center of the earth. But the lure of that possibility was what called him back in the end, and before long he was venturing ever farther. He kept his exploits secret from his parents, as did all the boys; there were restrictions enough on their lives in those days. He played at being an explorer, at discovering whole worlds unknown to those he had left behind. His imagination would soar when he was inside the caves; he could become anyone and anything. Often he went into them alone, preferring the freedom he felt when the other boys were not about to constrict the range of his playacting, for their presence imposed limits he was not always prepared to accept. Alone, he could have things just as he wished.

It was while he was alone one day, just after the anniversary of the first year of his marvelous discovery, that he became lost. He was playing as he always played, oblivious of his progress, confident in his ability to find his way back because he had done so every time before, and all of a sudden he didn't know where he was. The tunnel he followed did not appear familiar; the caves he encountered had a different, foreign look; the atmosphere became abruptly and chillingly unfriendly. It took him a while to accept that he was really lost and not simply confused, and then he simply stopped where he was and waited. He had no idea what it was that he was waiting for at first, but after a time it became clear. He was waiting to be swallowed. The caves had come alive, a sleeping beast that had finally roused itself long enough to put an end to the boy who thought to trifle with it. Morgan would remember how he felt at that moment for the rest of his life. He would remember his sense of despair as the caves transformed from inanimate rock into a living, breathing, seeing creature that wrapped all about him, snakelike, waiting to see which way he would try to run. Morgan did not run. He braced himself against the beast, against the way it hunched down about him. He drew the knife he carried and held it before him, determined to sell his life dearly. Slowly, without realizing what he was doing, he disappeared into the character he had played at being for so many hours. He became someone else. Somehow that saved him. The beast drew back. He walked ahead challengingly, and as he did so the strangeness slowly vanished. He began to recognize something of where he was, a bit of crystallization here, a tunnel's mouth there, something else, something more, and all of a sudden he knew where he was again.

When he emerged from the caves it was night. He had been lost for several hours—yet it seemed only moments. He went home thinking that the caves had many disguises to put on, but that if you looked hard enough you could always recognize the face beneath.

He had been a boy then. Now he was a man and the beliefs of boyhood had long since slipped away. He had seen too much of the real world. He knew too many hard truths.

Yet as he climbed the stairs that curled upward through the rock walls of the cavern beneath Eldwist he was struck by the similarity of what he felt now and what he had felt then, trapped both times in a stone maze from which escape was uncertain. There was that sense of life in the rock, Uhl Belk's presence, stirring like a pulse in the silence. There was that sense of being spied upon, of a beast awakened and set at watch to see which way he would try to run. The weight of the beast pressed down upon him, a thing of such size that it could not be measured in comprehensible terms. A peninsula, a city and beyond, an entire world—Eldwist was all of these and Uhl Belk was Eldwist. Morgan Leah searched in vain for the disguise that had fooled him as a boy, for the face that he had once believed hidden beneath. If he did not find it, he feared, he would never get free.

They ascended in silence, those who had come from Rampling Steep, the only ones left who could face the Stone King. Morgan was so cold he was shivering, and the cold he felt derived from far more than the chill of the cavern air. He could feel the sweat bead along his back, and his mind raced with thoughts of what he would do when the stairs finally came to an end and they were inside the dome. Draw his sword, the one of ordinary metal, yet whole? Attack a thing that was nearly immortal with only that? Draw his shattered talisman, a stunted blade? Attack with that? What? What was it that he was expected to do?

He watched Quickening move ahead of him, small and delicate against Walker Boh's silver light, a frail bit of flesh and blood that might in a single sweep of Uhl Belk's stone hand scatter back into the elements that had formed it. Quickening gone—he tried to picture it. Fears assailed him anew, darts that pierced and burned. Why were they doing this? Why should they even try?

Walker slipped on the mist-dampened steps and grunted in pain as he struck his knee. They slowed while he righted himself, and Morgan waited for Uhl Belk to stir. Hunter and hunted—but which was which? He wished he had Steff to stand beside him. He wished for Par Ohmsford, for Padishar Creel. He wished for any and all of them, for even some tiny part of them to appear. But wishing was useless. None of them were there; none of them would come. He was alone.

With this girl he loved, who could not help.

And with Walker Boh.

An unexpected spark of hope flashed inside the Highlander. Walker Boh. He stared at the cloaked figure leading them, one-armed, escaped from the Hall of Kings, risen from the ashes of Hearthstone. A cat with many lives, he thought. The Dark Uncle of old, evolved perhaps from the invincible figure of the legends, but a miracle nevertheless, able to defy Druids, spirits, and the Shadowen and live on. Come here to Eldwist, to fulfill a destiny promised by the shade of Allanon or to die—that was what Walker Boh had elected to do. Walker, who had survived everything until now, Morgan reminded himself, was not a man who could be killed easily.

So perhaps it was not intended that the Dark Uncle be killed this time either. And perhaps—just perhaps—some of that immortality might rub off on him.

Ahead, Walker slowed. A flick of his fingers and the silver light vanished. They stood silently in the dark, waiting, listening. The blackness lost its impenetrability as their eyes adjusted, and their surroundings slowly took shape—stairs, ceiling, and walls, and beyond, an opening.

They had reached the summit of their climb.

Still Walker kept them where they were, motionless. When Morgan thought he could stand it no longer, they started ahead once more, slowly, cautiously, one step at a time, shadows against the gloom. The steps ended and a corridor began. They passed down its length, invisible and silent save

for their thoughts which seemed to Morgan Leah to hang naked and screaming and bathed in light.

When the corridor ended they stopped again, still concealed within its
protective shadow. Morgan stepped forward for an anxious look.

The Stone King's dome opened before them, vast and hazy and as
silent as a tomb. The stands that circled the arena stretched away in symmetrical, stair-step lines, a still life of shadows and half-light that lifted to
the ceiling, its highest levels little more than a vague suggestion against the
aged stone. Below, the arena was flat and hard and empty of movement.
The giant form of Uhl Belk crouched at its center, turned away so that
only a shading of the rough-hewn face was visible.

Morgan Leah held his breath. The silence of the dome seemed to
whisper the warnings that screamed inside his head.

Walker Boh moved back to stand beside him, and the pale, hollowed
face bent close so that the other's mouth was at his ear. "Circle left. I'll go
right. When I strike him, be ready. I shall try to cause him to drop the
Stone. Seize hold of it if he does. Then run. Don't look back. Don't hesitate. Don't stop for anything." The other's hand seized his wrist and held it.
"Be swift, Highlander. Be quick."

Morgan nodded voicelessly. For an instant Quickening's black eyes met
his own. He could not read what he saw there.

Then Walker was gone, slipping from the mouth of the corridor into
the arena, moving to his right along the front wall of the stands into the
gloom. Morgan followed, turning left. He pushed aside his dread and gave
himself over to the Dark Uncle's command. He passed across the stone like
a wraith, quick and certain, finding a surprising reassurance simply from
being in motion. But his fear persisted, a cornered beast within his skin.
Shadows seemed to circle about him as he went, and the dome's silence
hissed at him in his mind, a voiceless snake. His eyes fixed on the bulky
form at the arena's center; he found himself searching for even the smallest
movement. There was none. Uhl Belk was carved stone against the gray,
still and fixed. Quick, now, thought Morgan as he went. Quick as light. He
saw Walker at the far side of the arena, a lean and furtive figure, nearly invisible in the gloom. Another few moments, he thought. And then . . .

Quickening.

He suddenly realized that in his haste to obey Walker he had forgotten
about the girl. Where was she? He stopped abruptly, casting about for her
without success, scanning the risers, the tunnels, the shadows that issued
from everywhere. He felt something drop in his chest. Quickening!

Then he saw her—not safely concealed or well back from where they
crept, but fully revealed, striding out from the corridor into the arena directly toward the massive figure of Uhl Belk. His breath caught sharply in
his throat. What was she doing?

Quickening!

His cry was silent, but the Stone King seemed to hear, responding with an almost inaudible grunt, stirring to life, lifting away from his crouch, beginning to turn . . .

Brilliant white light flared across the canopy of the dome, so blinding that for an instant even Morgan had to look away. It was as if the sun had exploded through the clouds, the gray haze, the stone itself, to set fire to the air imprisoned there. Morgan saw Walker Boh with his single arm raised, thrust out from his dark robes, the magic bursting from his fingers. Uhl Belk howled in surprise, his massive body shuddering, arms raising to shield his eyes, his stone parts grinding with the effort.

Walker Boh leaped forward then, a shadow against the light, charging at the Stone King as the latter flailed ponderously at the painful brightness. Again his good arm raised, thrusting forth. An entire bag of Cogline's volatile black powder flew at Uhl Belk and exploded, hammering into the Stone King. Bits and pieces of the ragged body shattered into fragments. Fire burned along his arm to where his fist clenched the Black Elfstone.

But still he held the talisman fast.

And suddenly Morgan Leah found that he could not move. He was frozen where he stood. Just as had happened at the Jut when the Creeper had gained the heights under cover of darkness and the outlaws of the Movement had gone to meet its attack, he found himself paralyzed. All his fears and doubts, all his misgivings and terrors descended on him. They seized him with their clawed fingers and bound him up as surely as if he had been wrapped in chains. What could he do? How could he help? His magic was lost, his Sword blade shattered. He watched helplessly as Uhl Belk began to turn, to fight past Walker Boh's assault, and to brush back his magic. The Dark Uncle renewed his attack, but this time he struck without the element of surprise to aid him and the Stone King barely flinched. Already the brightness of Walker's false sun was beginning to fade and the gray of the dome's true light to return.

Walker Boh's words echoed tauntingly in Morgan's ears.

Be swift, Highlander. Be quick.

Morgan fought through his immobility and wrenched free from its scabbard the broadsword he wore strapped to his back. But his fingers refused to hold it; his hands would not obey. The broadsword slipped away, tumbling to the arena floor with a hollow clang.

The Stone King's breath hissed as one monstrous hand swept out to seize Walker Boh and crush the life from him. The Dark Uncle had gotten too close; there was no chance for him to escape. Then suddenly he was gone, reappearing first as two images, then four, and then countless more— Jair Ohmsford's favorite trick, three centuries ago. The Stone King grabbed at the images, and the images evaporated at his touch. The true Walker Boh sprang at the monster, scattered new fire into his face, and slid nimbly away.

The Stone King howled in rage, clawed at his face, and shook himself like an animal seeking to rid itself of flies. The whole of the arena shuddered in response. Fissures opened in jagged lines across the floor, the stands buckled and snapped, and a shower of dust and debris descended from the ceiling. Morgan lost his footing and fell, the impact of the stone jarring him to his teeth.

He felt pain, and with the coming of that pain the paralyzing chains fell away.

The Stone King's fist came up, and the fingers of his hand began to open. The nonlight of the Elfstone seeped through, devouring what remained of Walker Boh's fading magic. The Dark Uncle threw up a screen of fire to slow the magic's advance, but the nonlight enveloped it in a wave of blackness. Walker stumbled backward toward the shadows, chased by the nonlight, harried by the fissures and the cracking of stone.

Another few seconds and he would be trapped.

Then Quickening caught fire.

There was no other way to explain it. Morgan watched it happen and still couldn't believe what he was seeing. The daughter of the King of the Silver River, less than twenty feet away from Uhl Belk by now, standing exposed and unprotected beneath his shadow, elevated like a creature made of air, until she was level with the giant's head, then burst into flames. The fire was golden and pure, its blaze a cloaking of light, flaring all along her body and limbs, leaving her illuminated as if by the midday sun. She was, in that instant, more beautiful than Morgan had ever seen her, radiant and flawless and exquisite beyond belief. Her silver hair lifted away from her, feathering outward against the fire, and her eyes glistened black within the gold. She hung there revealed, all wondrous, impossible magic come to life.

She is trying to distract him, Morgan realized in disbelief. *She is giving herself away, revealing who she is, in an effort to distract him from us!*

The Stone King turned at the unexpected flaring of light, his already crumpled face twisting until his features virtually ceased to exist. The slash of his mouth gaped at the sight of her and his voice sounded in anguish.

—You—

Uhl Belk forgot about Walker Boh. He forgot about the Dark Uncle's magic. He forgot about everything but the burning girl. In a frenzy of grinding stone limbs and joints, he struggled to reach her, surging up against the stone floor that welded him fast, grappling futilely for her, then in desperation bringing the hand that cupped the Black Elfstone to bear against her. His voice was a terrifying moan become a frenzied roar. The earth shuddered with the urgency of his need.

Morgan acted then, finally, desperately, even hopelessly. Surging back to his feet, his eyes fastened on Quickening and on the monster who sought to destroy her, he attacked. He went without thought, without reason, driven by need and armored in determination he had not thought he could ever possess. He raced into the haze of dust and debris, leaping past the fissures and drops, speeding as if he were carried on the strong autumn winds of his homeland. One hand dropped to his waist, and he pulled forth the shattered blade of his ancestors, the jagged remnant of the Sword of Leah.

Though he was not aware of it, the Sword shone white with magic.

He screamed the battle cry of his homeland. "Leah! Leah!"

He reached the Stone King just as the other became aware of his presence and the hard, empty eyes began to turn. He sprang onto a massive bent leg, vaulted forward, seized the arm that extended the Black Elfstone, and drove the shattered blade of the Sword of Leah deep into its stone.

Uhl Belk screamed, not in surprise or anger this time, but in terrifying pain. White fire burst from the shattered blade into the Stone King's body, lines of flame that penetrated and seared. Morgan stabbed Uhl Belk again and yet again. The stone hands trembled and clutched, and the stricken monster shuddered.

The Black Elfstone tumbled from his fingers.

Instantly Morgan yanked free his Sword and scrambled down in an effort to retrieve it. But the Stone King's damaged arm blocked his way, swinging toward him like a hammer. He dodged wildly, desperate to escape its sweep, but it clipped him anyway and sent him tumbling back, arms and legs flying. He barely managed to keep hold of his weapon. He caught a brief glimpse of Quickening, an oddly clear vision, her face bright even though the magic of her fire had faded. He caught a snatch of dark motion as Walker Boh appeared next to her out of the shadows. Then he struck the wall, the force of the blow knocking the breath from him, jamming the joints of his body so that he thought he had broken everything. Even so, he refused to stay down. He staggered back to his feet, dazed and battered, determined to continue.

But there was nothing more to do. As quickly as that, the battle was ended. Walker Boh had gained possession of the fallen Elfstone. He braced the Stone King, the Druid talisman clutched menacingly in his raised hand. Quickening stood beside him, returned to herself, the magic she had summoned gone again. As his vision slowly cleared, as his sense of balance restored itself, Morgan saw her again in his mind, all on fire. He was still astonished at what she had done. Despite her vow she had used the magic, revealed herself to Uhl Belk, and risked everything to give them a chance to survive.

The questions whispered at him then, insidious tricksters.

Had she known that he would come to save her?

Had she known what his Sword would do?

The gloom of the dome's interior returned again with the fading of the magic, cloaking Uhl Belk's massive form in shadow. The Stone King faced them from a cloud of swirling dust, his body sagging as if melted by the heat of his efforts to defend himself, still joined to the stone of Eldwist in the chaining that had undone him. Try as he might, he had not been able to rise and break free. By choosing to become the substance of his kingdom he had rendered himself virtually immobile. His face was twisted into something unrecognizable, and when he spoke there was horror and madness reflected in his voice.

—Give the Elfstone back to me—

They stared up at him, the three from Rampling Steep, and it seemed none of them could find words to speak.

"No, Uhl Belk," Walker Boh replied finally, his own voice strained from the effort of his battle. "The Elfstone was never yours in the first place. It shall not be given back to you now."

—I shall come for you then; I shall take it from you—

"You cannot move from where you stand. You have lost this battle and with it the Elfstone. Do not think to try and steal it back."

—It is mine—

The Dark Uncle did not waiver. "It belongs to the Druids."

Dust geysered from the ravaged face as the creature's breath exploded in a hiss of despair.

—There are no Druids—

The accusation died away in a grating echo. Walker Boh did not respond, his face chiseled with emotions that seemed to be tearing him apart from within. The Stone King's arms rose in a dramatic gesture.

—Give the Black Elfstone back to me, human, or I shall command Eldwist to crush the life from you; give the talisman back now or see yourself destroyed—

"Attack me or those with me," Walker Boh said, "and I shall turn the Elfstone's magic against this city! I shall summon power enough to shatter the stone casing that preserves it and turn it and you to dust! Do not threaten further, Uhl Belk! The power is no longer yours!"

The silence that followed was profound. The Stone King's hand closed into a fist and the sound of grinding rose out of it.

—You cannot command me, human; no one can—

Walker's response was immediate. "Release us, Uhl Belk. The Black Elfstone is lost to you."

The statue straightened with a groan, and the sound of its voice was thick with weeping.

—It will come for me; the Maw Grint will come; my son, the monster I have made will descend upon me, and I shall be forced to destroy it; only the Black Elfstone kept it at bay; it will see me old and wearied and believe me without strength to defend against its hunger; it shall try to devour me—

Depthless hard eyes fixed on Quickening.

—Child of the King of the Silver River, daughter of he who was my brother once, give thought to what you do; you threaten to weaken me forever if you steal away the Stone; the Maw Grint's life is no less dear to me than your own to your father; without him there can be no expansion of my land, no fulfillment of my trust; who are you that you should be so quick to take what is mine; are you completely blind to what I have made; there is in the stone of my land a changeless beauty that your father's Gardens will never have; worlds may come and go but Eldwist will remain; it would be better for all worlds to be so; your father believes himself right in what he does, but his vision of life is no clearer than my own; am I not entitled to do what I see is right as the Word has given me to see right—

"You subvert what you touch, Uhl Belk," the girl whispered.

—And you do not; your father does not; all who live within nature do not; can you pretend otherwise—

Quickening's frail form eased a step closer to the giant, and the light that had radiated from her before flared anew.

"There is a difference between nurturing life and making it over," she said. "It was to nurture that you were charged when given your trust. You have forgotten how to do so."

The Stone King's hand brushed at the particles of light that floated from her body, an unconscious effort to shield himself. But then he drew his hand back sharply, the intake of his breath harsh with pain.

—No—

The word was an anguished cry. He straightened, caught by some invisible net that wrapped him and held him fast.

—Oh, child; I see you now; I thought that in the Maw Grint I had created a monster beyond all belief; but your father has done worse in you—

The rough voice gasped, choked as if it could not make the words come further.

—Child of change and evolution, you are the ceaseless, quicksilver motion of water itself; I see in truth what you have been sent to do; I have indeed been stone too long to have missed it; I should have realized when you came to me that you were madness; I am mired in the permanency I sought and have been as blind as those who serve me; the end of my life is written out before me by the scripting of my own hand—

"Uhl Belk." Quickening whispered the name as if it were a prayer.

—How can you give what has been asked after tasting so much—

Morgan did not understand what the Stone King was talking about. He glanced at Quickening and started in surprise. Her face was stricken with guilt, a mirror of the hidden secrets that he had always suspected but never wanted to believe she kept.

The Stone King's voice was a low hiss.

—Take yourself from me, child; go into the world again and do what you must to seal all our fates; your victory over me must seem hollow and bitter when the price demanded for it is made so dear—

Walker Boh was staring as well, his mouth shaped with a frown, his brow furrowed. He did not seem to understand what Uhl Belk was saying either. Morgan started to ask Quickening what was happening and hesitated, unsure of himself.

Then Uhl Belk's head jerked up with a sharp crack.

—Listen—

The earth began to shudder, a low rumbling that emanated from deep within, rising to the surface in gathering waves of sound. Morgan Leah had heard that rumble before.

—It comes—

The Maw Grint.

Walker began backing away, yelling at Morgan and Quickening to follow. He shouted at the Stone King, "Release us, Uhl Belk, if you would save yourself! Do so now! Quickly!"

Walker's arm lifted, threatening with the fist that held the Black Elf-stone. Uhl Belk barely seemed to notice. His face had become more haggard, more collapsed than ever, a parody of human features, a monster's face grown hideous beyond thought. The giant's voice hissed like a serpent's through the roar of the Maw Grint's approach.

—Flee, fools—

There was no anger in the voice—only frustration and emptiness. And something more, Morgan Leah thought in amazement. There was hope, just a glimmer of it, a recognition beyond the Highlander's understanding, a seeing of some possibility that transcended all else.

A section of the dome's massive wall split apart directly behind them, stone blocks grinding with the movement, gray daylight spilling through.

—Flee—

Morgan Leah broke for the opening instantly, chased by demons he did not care to see. He felt, rather than saw, the Stone King watch him go. Quickening and Walker followed. They gained the opening in a rush and were through, running from the fury of the Maw Grint's coming, racing away into the gloom.

30

It appeared that the Maw Grint had gone mad.

Twice before the three who fled had observed the monster's coming, once when it had surfaced as they stood on the overlook above the city and once when it had been summoned by Uhl Belk. There hadn't been a day since they had arrived in Eldwist that they hadn't heard the creature moving through the tunnels below them, astir at the coming of each sunset to prowl with the dark. Each time its approach had been prefaced with the same unmistakable deep, low rumbling of the earth. Each time the city had trembled in response.

But there had never been anything like this.

The city of Eldwist was like a beast shaking itself awake from a bad dream. Towers and spires rocked and trembled, shedding bits and pieces of loose stone amid a shower of choking dust. The streets threatened to buckle, stone cracking in jagged fissures, trapdoors dropping away as their catches released, supports and trestles snapping apart. Whole stairways leading downward to the tunnels crumbled and disappeared, and sky-bridges connecting one building to another collapsed. Against a screen of gray haze and clouds Eldwist shimmered like a vanishing mirage.

Racing to escape the Stone King's dome, Walker Boh barely gained the closest walkway before the tremors drove him to his knees. He pitched forward, his outstretched arm curling against his body to protect his hold on the Black Elfstone. He took the force of the fall on his shoulder, a sharp, jarring blow, and kept skidding. He struck the wall of the building ahead of him, and the breath left his body. For a moment he was stunned, bright pinpricks of light dancing before his eyes. When his vision cleared he saw Quickening and Morgan sprawled in the street behind him, knocked from their feet as well.

He rose with an effort and started away again, yelling for them to follow. As he watched them struggle up, his mind raced. He had threatened Uhl Belk with the Black Elfstone by saying that he would invoke its magic against the city if they were not released. The threat had been an idle one. He could not use the Elfstone that way without destroying himself. It was fortunate for them all that Uhl Belk still did not understand how the Druid magic worked. Even so they were not free yet. What would they do if the Maw Grint came after them? There was every reason to believe that it would. The magic of the Black Elfstone had provided a link between father and son, spirit lord and monster, that Walker Boh had broken. The Maw Grint already sensed that break; it had awakened in response. Once it discovered that the Elfstone was gone, that the Stone King no longer had possession of it, what was to prevent the beast from giving chase?

Walker Boh grimaced. There wasn't any question as to how such a chase would end. He couldn't use the Black Elfstone on the Maw Grint either.

A stone block large enough to bury him crashed into the street a dozen feet ahead, sending the Dark Uncle sprawling for the second time. Quickening darted past, her beautiful face oddly stricken, and raced away into the gloom. Morgan appeared, reached down as he caught up with Walker, and hauled him back to his feet. Together they ran on, sidestepping through the gathering debris, dodging the cracks and fissures.

"Where are we going?" the Highlander cried out, ducking his head against the dust and silt.

Walker gestured vaguely. "Out of the city, off the peninsula, back up on the heights!"

"What about Horner Dees?"

Walker had forgotten the Tracker. He shook his head. "If we can find him, we'll take him with us! But we can't stop to look! There isn't time!" He shoved the Elfstone into his tunic and reached out to grasp the other as they ran. "Highlander, stay close to Quickening. This matter is not yet resolved! She is in some danger!"

Morgan's eyes were white against his dust-streaked face. "What danger, Walker? Do you know something? What was Uhl Belk talking about back there when he spoke about her victory being hollow, about the price she was paying? What did he mean?"

Walker shook his head wordlessly. He didn't know—yet sensed at the same time that he should, that he was overlooking something obvious, forgetting something important. The street yawned open before them, a trapdoor sprung. He yanked the Highlander aside just in time, pulling him clear, propelling him back onto the walkway. The roaring of the Maw Grint was fading slightly now, falling back as the Stone King's fortressed dome receded into the distance.

"Catch up to her, Highlander!" Walker yelled, shoving him ahead. "Keep an eye out for Dees! We'll meet back at the building where we hid ourselves from the Rake!" He glanced over his shoulder and back again, shouting, "Careful, now! Watch yourself!"

But Morgan Leah was already gone.

Pe Ell and Horner Dees had only just reached the building to which the others now fled when the tremors began. Their battle with the Rake completed, they had come in search of the remainder of the company from Rampling Steep, each for his own reasons, neither sharing much of anything with the other. The truce they had called had ended with the destruction of the Rake, and they watched each other now with careful, suspicious eyes.

They whirled in surprise as the rumbling began to build, deeper and more pronounced than at any time before. The city shuddered in response.

"Something's happened," Horner Dees whispered, his bearded face lifting. "Something more."

"It's come awake again," Pe Ell cried with loathing. When they had left the Maw Grint it was sunk back down into the earth and gone still.

The street on which they faced shook with the impact of the creature's rising.

Pe Ell gestured. "Look upstairs. See if anyone is there."

Dees went without argument. Pe Ell stood rooted on the walk while the city's tremors washed over him. He was taut and hard within himself, the battle with the Rake still alive inside, driving through him like the rushing of his blood. Things were coming together now; he could sense the coalescing of events, the weaving of the threads of fate of the five from Rampling Steep. It would be over soon, he sensed. It would be finished.

Horner Dees reappeared at the building entry. "No one."

"Then wait here for their return," Pe Ell snapped, starting quickly away. "I'll look toward the center of the city."

"Pe Ell!"

The hatchet face turned. "Don't worry, old man. I'll be back." *Perhaps,* he added to himself.

He darted into the gloom, leaving the aging Tracker to call uselessly after him. Enough of Horner Dees, he thought bitterly. He was still rankled by the fact that he had saved the bothersome Tracker from the Rake, that he had acted on instinct rather than using common sense, that he had risked his life to save a man he fully intended to kill anyway.

On the other hand his plans for Dees and the other fools who had come with Quickening were beginning to change. He could feel those plans settling comfortably into place even now. Everything always seemed much clearer when he was moving. It was all well and good to anticipate the event, but circumstances and needs evolved, and the event did not always turn out as expected, the coming about of it not always as foreseen. Pe Ell revised his earlier assessment of the necessity of killing his companions. Quickening, of course, would have to die. He had already promised Rimmer Dall that he would kill her. More important, he had promised himself. Quickening's fate was unalterable. But why bother with killing the others? Unless they got in his way by trying to interfere with his plans for the girl, why expend the effort? If he somehow managed to gain possession of the Black Elfstone there was no possible harm they could cause him. And even if he was forced to abandon that part of his plan—as it now appeared he would have to—the old Tracker, the one-armed man, the Highlander, and the tunesmith offered no threat to him. Even if they escaped Eldwist to follow him he had little to fear. How would they find him? And what would they do if they did?

No, he need not kill them—though he would, he added, almost as an afterthought, if the right opportunity presented itself.

The tremors continued, long and deep, the growl of the earth protesting the coming of the monster worm. Pe Ell darted this way and that along the empty walkways, down streets littered with debris and past buildings weakened by ragged, wicked cracks that scarred their smooth surface. His sharp eyes searched the shadows for movement, seeking those who had come with him or even perhaps some sign of the elusive Stone King. He hadn't given up completely on the Black Elfstone. There was still a chance, he told himself. Everything was coming together, caught in a whirlpool. He could feel it happening . . .

Out of the haze before him raced Quickening, silver hair flying as she ran, her reed-thin body a quicksilver shadow. Pe Ell moved to intercept her, catching her about the waist with one arm before she realized what was happening. She gasped in surprise, stiffened, and then clung to him.

"Pe Ell," she breathed.

There was something in the way she spoke his name that surprised him. It was a measure of fear mingled with relief, an odd combination of dismay and satisfaction. He tightened his grip instinctively, but she did not try to break away.

"Where are the others?" he asked.

"Coming after me, escaped from Uhl Belk and the Maw Grint." Her black eyes fixed on him. "It is time to leave Eldwist, Pe Ell. We found the Stone King and we took the Black Elfstone away from him—Morgan, Walker Boh, and I."

Pe Ell fought to stay calm. "Then we are indeed finished with this place." He glanced past her into the gloom. "Who has the Elfstone now?"

"Walker Boh," she replied.

Pe Ell's jaw tightened. It would have to be Walker Boh, of course. It would have to be him. How much easier things would be if the girl had the Stone. He could kill her now, take it from her, and be gone before any of them knew what had happened. The one-armed man seemed to stand in his way at every turn, a shadowy presence he could not quite escape. What would it take to be rid of him?

He knew, of course, what it would take. He felt his plans begin to shift back again.

"Quickening!" a voice called out.

It was the Highlander. Pe Ell hesitated, then made up his mind. He clamped his hand about Quickening's mouth and hauled her into the shadows. Surprisingly, the girl did not struggle. She was light and yielding, almost weightless in his arms. It was the first time he had held her since he had carried her from the Meade Gardens. The feelings she stirred within him were distractingly soft and pleasant, and he forced them roughly aside. Later for that, he thought, when he used the Stiehl . . .

Morgan Leah burst into view, pounding along the walkway, shouting for the girl, searching. Pe Ell held Quickening close and watched the Highlander run past. A moment later, he was gone.

Pe Ell released his hand from the girl's mouth, and she turned to face him. There was neither surprise nor fear in her eyes now; there was only resignation. "It is almost time for us, Pe Ell," she whispered.

A flicker of doubt tugged at his confidence. She was looking at him in that strange way she had, as if he were transparent to her, as if everything about him were known. But if everything were known, she would not be standing there so calmly. She would be attempting to flee, to call after the Highlander, or to do something to save herself.

The rumbling beneath the city increased, then faded slightly, a warning of the slow, inevitable avalanche bearing down on them.

"Time for us to do what?" he managed hesitantly, unable to break away from her gaze.

She did not answer. Instead she glanced past him, her black eyes searching. He turned to stare with her and watched the dark form of Walker Boh materialize from out of the haze of dust and gray light.

Unlike the Highlander, the Dark Uncle had seen them.

Pe Ell swung the girl in front of him and unsheathed the Stiehl from its hiding place, the blade gleaming bright with the magic. The one-armed man slowed perceptibly, then came on.

"Pe Ell," he whispered softly, as if the name itself were venomous.

"Stand back from me, Walker Boh," Pe Ell ordered. The other stopped. "We've seen enough of each other to know what we are capable of doing. No need to test it. Better that we part now and go our separate ways. But first give me the Stone."

The tall man stood without moving, seemingly without life, eyes fixed on the assassin and his hostage. He appeared to be weighing something.

Pe Ell's smile was sardonic. "Don't be foolish enough to think you might be quicker than me."

"We might neither of us be quick enough to survive this day. The Maw Grint comes."

"It will find me gone when it does. Give me the Black Elfstone."

"If I do so, will that be enough to satisfy you?" the other asked quietly, his gaze intense, as if trying to read Pe Ell's thoughts.

Like the girl, Pe Ell thought. Two of a kind. "Pass it to me," he commanded, ignoring the question.

"Release Quickening."

Pe Ell shook his head. "When I am safely away. Then I promise that I will set her free." *Free, forever.*

They stood staring at each other wordlessly for a moment, hard looks filled with unspoken promises, with visions of possibilities that were dark and forbidding. Then Walker Boh reached down into his tunic and brought forth the Stone. He held it out in his palm, dark and glistening. Pe Ell smiled faintly. The Elfstone was as black as midnight, opaque and depthless, seamless and unflawed. He had never seen anything like it before. He could almost feel the magic pulsing within.

"Give it to me," he repeated.

Walker Boh reached down to his belt and worked free a leather pouch marked with brilliant blue runes. Carefully he used the fingers of his solitary hand to maneuver the Stone into the pouch and pull the drawstrings tight. He looked at Pe Ell and said, "You cannot use the Black Elfstone, Pe Ell. If you try, the magic will destroy you."

"Life is filled with risks," Pe Ell replied. Dust churned in the air about them, sifted by a faint sea breeze. The stone of the city shimmered, swept up in the earth's distant rumble, wrapped in a gauze of mist and clouds. "Toss it to me," he ordered. "Gently."

He used the hand with the Stiehl to keep tight hold of Quickening. The girl did not stir. She waited passively, her slender body pressed against him, so compliant she might have been sleeping. Walker held out the pouch with the Black Elfstone and carefully lobbed it. Pe Ell caught it and shoved it into his belt, securing the strings to his buckle.

"Magic belongs to those who are not afraid to use it," he offered, smiling, backing cautiously away. "And to those who can keep it."

Walker Boh stood rock-still against the roiling dust and tremors. "Beware, Pe Ell. You risk everything."

"Don't come after me, Walker Boh," Pe Ell warned darkly. "Better for you if you remain here and face the Maw Grint."

With Quickening securely in his grasp he continued to move away, following the line of the walkway until the other man vanished into the haze.

Walker Boh remained motionless, staring after the disappearing Pe Ell and Quickening. He was wondering why he had given up the Black Elfstone so easily. He had not wanted to, had resolved not to in fact, and had been prepared instead to attack Pe Ell, to go to the girl's rescue—until he looked into her eyes and saw something there that stopped him. Even now he wasn't sure what it was that he had seen. Determination, resignation, some private insight that transcended his own—something. Whatever it was, it had changed his mind as surely as if she had used her magic.

His head lowered and his dark eyes narrowed.

Had she, he wondered, used her magic?

He stood lost in thought. A light dusting of water sprinkled his face. It was beginning to rain again. He looked up, remembering where he was, what he was about, and hearing again the thunder caused by the movement of the Maw Grint beneath the city, feeling the vibration of its coming.

Cogline's voice was a whisper in his ear, reminding him gently to understand who he was. He had always wondered before. Now he thought he knew.

He summoned his magic, feeling it rise easily within him, strong again since his battle with the Stone King, as if that confrontation had freed him of constraints he had placed upon himself. It gathered at the center of his being, whirling like a great wind. The rune markings on the pouch in which the Black Elfstone rested would be its guide. With barely a lifting of his head he sent it winging forth in search of Pe Ell.

Then he followed after.

Pe Ell ran, dragging Quickening behind him. She came without resisting, moving obediently to keep pace, saying nothing, asking nothing, her eyes distant and calm. He glanced back at her only once and quickly turned away again. What he saw in those dark eyes bothered him. She was seeing something that he could not, something old and immutable, a part of her past or her future—he wasn't sure which. She was an enigma still, the one secret he had not yet been able to solve. But soon now he would, he promised himself. The Stiehl would give him an answer to what she hid. When her life was fading from her she would stand revealed. There would be no secrets then. The magic would not permit it. Just as it had been with all the others he had killed, there would be only truth.

He felt the first drops of rain strike his heated face.

He darted left along a cross street, angling away from the direction Morgan Leah had gone and Walker Boh would follow. There was no reason to give them any chance of finding him. He would slip quickly from the city onto the isthmus, cross to the stairs, gain the heights of the overlook, and then with time and privacy enough to take full advantage of the moment he would kill her. Anticipation washed through him. Quickening, the daughter of the King of the Silver River, the most wondrous magical creature of all, would be his forever.

Yet the flicker of doubt continued to burn within him. What was it that bothered him so? He searched for the answer, pausing briefly as he remembered what she had said about needing their magics, the magics of all three—the Highlander, Walker Boh, and himself. All three were required, the King of the Silver River had proclaimed. That was why she had recruited them, persuaded them to come, and kept them together through all the anger and mistrust. But it had been Walker Boh and the Highlander alone who had discovered the hiding place of Uhl Belk and secured the Black Elfstone. He had done nothing—except to destroy the Rake. Was that the use for which his magic had been intended? Was that the reason for his coming? It didn't seem enough somehow. It seemed there should be something more.

Pe Ell slid through the murk of Eldwist's deepening morning, holding the girl close to him as he went, thinking to himself that this whole journey had been a puzzle with too many missing pieces. They had come in search of the Stone King—yet the others, not Pe Ell, had found him. They had come to retrieve the Black Elfstone—yet the others, not Pe Ell, had done so. The magic of the Stiehl was the most deadly magic that any of them possessed—yet what purpose had it served?

Uneasiness stole through him like a thief, draining his elation at having both Quickening and the Stone.

Something was wrong and he didn't know what it was. He should feel in control of things and he did not.

They passed back onto a roadway leading south, winding their way down between the buildings, passing through the haze, two furtive shadows fleeing into light. Pe Ell slowed now, beginning to tire. He peered through the thin curtain of rain that hung before him, blinking uncertainly. Was this the way he had intended to come? Somehow, he didn't think so. He glanced right, then left. Wasn't this street the one he had been trying to avoid? Confusion filled him. He felt Quickening's eyes on him but would not allow himself to meet her gaze.

He steered them down another sidestreet and crossed to a broad plaza dominated by a tiered basin encircled by benches, some crumbling and split, and the remains of poles from which flags had once flown. He was working his way left toward an arched passageway between the buildings, intent on gaining the open street beyond, a street that would take him directly to the isthmus, when he heard his name called. He whirled, pulling the girl close, the blade of the Stiehl coming up to her throat.

Morgan Leah stood across the plaza from him, a lean and dangerous figure. Pe Ell stared. How had the Highlander found him? It was chance, he quickly decided. Nothing more. Dismay grappled with anger. Any misfortune that resulted from this encounter must not be his.

The Highlander did not appear to know what was happening. "What are you doing, Pe Ell?" he shouted through the forest of broken poles.

"What I wish!" Pe Ell responded, but there was a weariness in his voice that surprised him. "Get away, Highlander. I have no wish to hurt you. I have what I came for. Your one-armed friend has given me the Elfstone— here, in this pouch at my belt! I intend to keep it! If you wish the girl to go free, stand away!"

But Morgan Leah did not move. Haggard-looking and worn, just a boy really, he seemed both lost and unresolved. Yet he refused to give way. "Let her go, Pe Ell. Don't hurt her."

His plea was wasted, but Pe Ell managed a tired nod. "Go back, Highlander. Quickening comes with me."

Morgan Leah seemed to hesitate momentarily, then started forward. For the first time since he had seized her, Pe Ell felt Quickening tense. She was worried for the Highlander, he realized. Her concern enraged him. He pulled her back and brought the Stiehl against her throat, calling to the other man to stop.

And then suddenly Walker Boh appeared as well, materializing out of the gloom, close by Morgan Leah. He stepped forward unhurriedly and grasped the Highlander's arm, pulling him back. The Highlander struggled, but even with only one arm the other man was stronger.

"Think what you are doing, Pe Ell!" Walker Boh called out, and now there was anger in his voice.

How had the big man caught up to him so quickly? Pe Ell felt a twinge of uneasiness, a sense that for some unexplainable reason nothing was going right. He should have been clear of this madness by now, safely away. He should have had time to savor his victory, to speak with the girl before using the Stiehl, to see how much he could learn of her magic. Instead he was being harried unmercifully by the very men he had chosen to spare. Worse, he was in some danger of being trapped.

"Get away from me!" he shouted, his temper slipping, his control draining away. "You risk the girl's life by continuing this chase! Let me leave now or she dies!"

"Let her go!" the distraught Highlander screamed again. He had fallen to his knees, still firmly in the grip of the one-armed man.

Behind Pe Ell, still too far away to make any difference but closing on him steadily, came Horner Dees. The assassin was now ringed by his enemies. For the first time in his life he was trapped, and he sensed a hint of panic setting in. He jerked Quickening about to face the burly Tracker. "Out of my way, old man!" he bellowed.

But Horner Dees simply shook his head. "I don't think so, Pe Ell. I've backed away from you enough times. I've a stake in this business, too. I've given at least as much of myself as you. Besides, you've done nothing to earn what you claim. You simply seek to steal. We know who and what you are, all of us. Do as Morgan Leah says. Let the girl go."

Walker Boh's voice rose. "Pe Ell, if the Shadowen sent you to steal the Elfstone, take it and go. We won't stop you."

"The Shadowen!" Pe Ell laughed, fighting to contain his rage. "The Shadowen are nothing to me. I do for them what I wish and nothing more. Do you think I came all this way because of them? You are a fool!"

"Then take the Elfstone for yourself if you must."

The rage broke free. Caution disappeared in a red mist. "If I must! Of course, I must! But even the Elfstone isn't the real reason I came!"

"Then what is, Pe Ell?" Walker Boh asked tightly.

"She is!" Pe Ell yanked Quickening around once more, lifting her exquisite face above the point of his knife. "Look at her, Walker Boh, and tell me that you don't desire her! You cannot, can you? Your feelings, mine, the Highlander's—they're all the same! We came on this journey because of her, because of the way she looked at us and made us feel, because of the way she wove her magic all about us! Think of the secrets she hides! Think of the magic she conceals! I came on this journey to discover what she is, to claim her. She has belonged to me from the first moment of her life, and when I am finished here she shall belong to me always! Yes, the Shadowen sent me, but it was my choice to come—my choice when I saw what she could give me! Don't you see? I came to Eldwist to kill her!"

The air went still suddenly, the tremors and the thunder fading into a vague and distant moan, leaving the assassin's words sharp and clear against the silence. The stone of the city caught their sound and held the echo within its walls, a long, endless reverberation of dismay.

"I have to discover what she is," Pe Ell whispered, trying vainly to explain now, unable to think what else to do, stunned that he had been foolish enough to reveal so much, knowing they would never let him go now. How had he managed to lose control of matters so completely? "I have to kill her," he repeated, the words sounding harsh and bitter. "That is how the magic works. It reveals all truths. In taking life, it gives life. To me. Once the killing is done, Quickening shall be mine forever."

For an instant no one spoke, stunned by the assassin's revelation. Then Horner Dees said slowly, deliberately, "Don't be stupid, Pe Ell. You can't get away from all of us. Let her go."

It was uncertain then exactly what happened next. There was an explosion of shattered rock as the Maw Grint broke free of the tunnels and reared skyward against the buildings of the city somewhere close to where the Stone King hid within his fortressed dome. The monster rose like a bloated snake, swaying against the shroud of mist and damp, huffing as if to catch its breath, as if the air were being sucked from it. Pe Ell started, feeling the earth begin to shudder so violently that it seemed Eldwist would be shaken apart.

Then Quickening broke free, slipping from his grasp as if she were made of air. She turned to him, disdaining to run, standing right against him, her hands gripping the arm that held the Stiehl, her black eyes shackling him as surely as if he were chained. He could not move; he just stood there, frozen in place. He saw the symmetry of her face and body as if seeing it for the first time; he marveled at the perfection of her, at beauty that lay not just upon the surface of her wondrous form, but ran deep within. He felt her press forward—or did he? Which was it? He saw her mouth open with surprise and pain and relief.

He glanced down then and saw that the handle of the Stiehl was flush against her stomach, the blade buried in her body. He could not remember stabbing her, yet somehow he had. Confusion and disbelief surged through him. How had this happened? What of his plan to kill her where and when he chose? What of his intention to savor the moment of her dying? He looked quickly into her eyes, desperate to snare what was trapped there and about to be set free, anxious to capture her magic. He looked, and what he saw filled him with rage.

Pe Ell screamed. As if seeking to hide what he had discovered, he stabbed her again and again, and each time it was a frantic, futile attempt to deny what he was seeing. Quickening's body jerked in response, but her gaze remained steady, and the visions shimmering in her eyes remained fixed.

Pe Ell understood at last, and with understanding came a horror against which he had no defense. His thoughts collapsed, tumbling into a quagmire of despair. He shoved himself free of the girl and watched her slump to the street in a slow, agonizing fall, her black eyes never leaving him. He was aware of Morgan Leah crying out in fury, of Walker Boh racing forward, and of Horner Dees charging at him from the rear. They did not matter. Only the girl did. He stepped away, shaking with a cold that threatened to freeze him in place. Everything he had hoped for had been stolen from him. Everything he had wanted was lost.

What have I done?

He wheeled about and began to run. His cold turned abruptly to fire, but the words buzzed within his mind, a nest of hornets with sharp and anxious stingers.

What have I done?

He darted past Horner Dees with a quickness born of fear and despair, gone so fast that the old Tracker had no chance of stopping him. The stone street shuddered and quaked and was slick with rain, but nothing could slow his flight. Gloom shrouded him with its gray, friendless mantle, and he shrank to a tiny figure in the shadow of the city's ancient buildings, a speck of life caught up in a tangle of magic far older and harsher than his own. He saw Quickening's face before him. He felt her eyes watching as the Stiehl entered her body. He heard her sigh with relief.

Pe Ell fled through Eldwist as if possessed.

31

M organ Leah was the first to reach Quickening. He broke free of Walker with a strength that surprised the other, raced across the empty plaza as she tumbled to the stone, and caught her up almost before she was done falling. He knelt to hold her, turned her ashen face into his chest, and began whispering her name over and over again.

Walker Boh and Horner Dees hurried up from opposite sides, bent close momentarily, then exchanged a sober glance. The entire front of Quickening's shirt was soaked with her blood.

Walker straightened and peered through the gloom in the direction Pe Ell had gone. The assassin was already out of sight, gone into the maze of buildings and streets, fled back toward the isthmus and the cliffs beyond. Walker remembered the look he had seen on the other's face—a look filled with horror, disbelief, and rage. Killing Quickening clearly hadn't given him what he had been looking for.

"Walker!"

Morgan Leah's voice was a plea of desperation. Walker glanced down. "Help her! She's dying!"

Walker looked at the blood on her clothes, at the collapsed, broken body, at the face with its long hair spilled across the lovely features like a silver veil. *She's dying.* He whispered the words in the silence of his mind, marveling first that such a thing could be and second that he hadn't recognized much sooner its inevitability. He stared at the girl, as helpless and despairing as the Highlander, but beginning as well to catch a glimmer of understanding into the reason that it was happening.

"Walker, do something!" Morgan repeated, urgent, stricken.

"Highlander," Horner Dees said in response, taking hold of his shoulder gently. "What would you have him do?"

"What do you think I would have him do? Use his magic! Give her the same chance she gave him!"

Walker knelt. His voice was calm, low. "I can't, Morgan. I haven't the magic she needs." He reached out to touch the side of her throat, feeling for a pulse. It was there, faint, irregular. He could see her breathing. "She must do what she can to save herself."

Morgan stared at him momentarily, then began talking again to Quickening, urging her to wake, to speak to him. His words were jumbled, desperate, filled with need. The girl stirred sluggishly in response.

Walker looked again at Horner Dees. The old man shook his head slowly.

Then Quickening's eyes opened. They were clear and frightened, filled with pain. "Morgan," she whispered. "Pick me up. Carry me out of the city."

Morgan Leah, though he clearly thought to do otherwise, did not argue the matter. He lifted her effortlessly, carrying her as if she were weightless. He held her close against himself, infusing her with his warmth, whispering down to her as he went. Walker and Dees trailed after wordlessly. They moved across the plaza and into the street down which Pe Ell had fled.

"Stay back on the walkways," Walker cautioned hurriedly, and Morgan was quick to comply.

They had gone only a short distance when the earth began to rumble anew. All of Eldwist shook in response, the buildings cracking and splitting, shards of stone and clouds of dust tumbling down. Walker glanced back toward the heart of the city. The Maw Grint was moving again. Whatever the outcome of its confrontation with Uhl Belk, it had clearly decided on a new course of action. Perhaps it had put an end to its parent. Perhaps it had simply concluded that the Black Elfstone was more important. In any case, it was coming straight for them. Disdaining the use of its underground tunnels, it surged down the streets of Eldwist. Walls shattered and collapsed with its passing. The poison of its body spit wickedly. The air about it shimmered and steamed.

Those who remained of the company from Rampling Steep began to run southward toward the isthmus, fighting to keep their balance as the earth beneath them shuddered and quaked. Trapdoors sprang open all about, jarred loose by the tremors, and the debris of the crumbling buildings littered the pathway at every turn. Behind them, the Maw Grint huffed and grunted with the urgency of its movements and came on. Despite having to carry Quickening, Morgan set an exhausting pace, and neither Walker nor Horner Dees could maintain it. The old Tracker had already fallen fifty paces back by the time they broke clear of the city, his breathing short and labored, his bulky form lurching as he struggled to keep up. Walker was between the two, his own chest constricting with pain, his legs heavy and weak. He yelled once at Morgan to slow him down, but the Highlander was deaf to him, the whole of his attention focused on the girl. Walker glanced back at Dees, at the trembling of the buildings where the Maw Grint passed, closer to them now than before, at the shadow the monster cast against the graying light. He did not think they would escape. He could not help reflecting on how ironic it was that they were going to be killed for something they no longer even had.

The moments lengthened impossibly as they fled, receding into the pounding of their boots on the stone. The waves crashed against the shores of the isthmus to either side, the spray washing across their heated faces. The rocks grew slippery, and they stumbled and tripped as they ran. The clouds darkened, and it began to rain again. Walker thought again of the look on Pe Ell's face when he had stabbed Quickening. He revised his earlier assessment. What he had seen there was surprise. Pe Ell hadn't been ready for her to die. Had he even wanted to use the Stiehl? There was something in the movements of the two immediately before the stabbing that was troubling. Why hadn't Quickening simply run? She had been free of him for an instant, yet had turned back. Into the blade? Deliberately? Walker shivered. Had she done more than stand there and wait? Had she actually shoved herself against Pe Ell?

His jumbled thoughts seemed to crystallize, freezing to ice. Shades! Was that why Pe Ell had been summoned? Pe Ell, the assassin with magic in his weapon, magic that nothing could withstand—was that why he was there?

Ahead of him, Morgan Leah reached the base of the cliffs and the pathway leading up from the isthmus. Without slowing, he began to climb.

Behind them, the Maw Grint appeared, its monstrous head thrusting into view through the ruined buildings, lifting momentarily to test the air, then surging ahead. It oozed through the walls of the city like something without bones. It filled the whole of the isthmus with its bulk, hunching its way forward, a juggernaut of impossible size.

Walker scrambled up the pathway toward the summit of the cliffs, Horner Dees still lagging behind. He forced his thoughts of Quickening and Pe Ell aside. They made no sense. Why would Quickening want Pe Ell to kill her? Why would she want to die? There was no reason for any of it. He tried to concentrate on what he would do to slow the advance of the Maw Grint. He glanced back once more, watching the massive slug-thing work its way across the rock. Could he collapse the isthmus beneath it? No, the rock was too deep. The cliffs on top of it, then? No, again, it would simply tunnel its way free. Water would slow it, but all the water was behind them in the Tiderace. Nothing of Walker's magic or even Cogline's was strong enough to stop the Maw Grint. Running away was their only choice, and they could not run for long.

He reached the summit of the cliffs and found Morgan Leah waiting. The Highlander knelt gasping for breath on the ramp that overlooked the peninsula and Eldwist, his head lowered. Quickening was cradled in his arms, her eyes open and alert. Walker crossed to them and stopped. Quickening's face was chalk white.

Morgan Leah's eyes lifted. "She won't use her magic," he whispered in disbelief.

Walker knelt. "Save yourself, Quickening. You have the power."

She shook her head. Her black eyes glistened as they found Morgan's. "Listen to me," she said softly, her voice steady. "I love you. I will always love you and be with you. Remember that. Remember, too, that I would change things if I could. Now set me down and rise."

Morgan shook his head. "No, I want to stay with you . . ."

She touched him once on the cheek with her hand, and his voice trailed off, the sentence left hanging. Wordlessly, he laid her on the ground and backed away. There were tears running down his face.

"Take out your Sword, Morgan, and sheath it in the earth. Do so now."

Morgan drew out the Sword of Leah, gripped it in both hands, and jammed it into the rock. His hands remained tightly fixed about the hilt momentarily, then released.

He looked up slowly. "Don't die, Quickening," he said.

"Remember me," she whispered.

Horner Dees lumbered up beside Walker, panting. "What's going on?" he asked, bearded face close, rough voice hushed. "What's she doing?"

Walker shook his head. Her black eyes had shifted to find his. "Walker," she said, calling him.

He went to her, hearing the sounds of the Maw Grint advancing below, thinking they must run again, wondering like Dees what it was that she intended. He knelt beside her.

"Help me up," she said, her words quick and hurried, as if she sought to give voice to them while she still could. "Walk me to the edge of the cliffs."

Walker did not question what she asked. He put his arm about her waist and lifted her to her feet. She sagged against him weakly, her body shuddering. He heard Morgan cry out in protest, but a sudden glance from the girl silenced him. Walker held her up to keep her from falling as he maneuvered her slowly toward the drop. They reached the edge and stopped. Below, the Maw Grint hunched across the rock of the isthmus, an obscene cylinder of flesh, body rippling and poison oozing down. It was more than halfway to them now, its monstrous bulk steaming, the trail of its poison stretched back across the causeway to the city. Eldwist rose raggedly against the skyline, towers broken off, buildings split apart, walls crumbled and shattered. Dust and mist formed a screen against the dampness of the rain.

The dome where the Stone King made his lair stood intact.

Quickening turned and her face lifted. For an instant she was beautiful once more, as alive as she had been when she had brought Walker back from the dead, when she had restored his life and driven the poison of the Asphinx from his body. Walker caught his breath seeing her so, blinking against the momentary illusion. Her dark eyes fixed him.

"Dark Uncle," she whispered. "When you leave this place, when you go back into the world of the Four Lands, take with you the lessons you have learned here. Do not fight against yourself or what you might be. Simply consider your choices. Nothing is predetermined, Walker. We can always choose."

She reached up then and touched his face, her fingers cool against his cheek. Images flooded through him, her thoughts, her memories, and her knowledge. In an instant's time, she revealed herself completely, showing him the secrets she had kept hidden so carefully during the whole of their journey, the truth of who and what she was. He cried out as if he had been burned, staggered by what he saw. He clutched her tightly to him, and his pale face lowered into her hair in dismay.

Both Morgan and Horner Dees started forward, but Walker shouted for them to stand where they were. They stopped, hesitant, uncertain. Walker half-turned, still holding Quickening against him, his face an iron mask of concentration. He understood now; he understood everything.

"Walker." She spoke his name again. Her hand brushed him one final time, and a single image appeared.

It was the Grimpond's second vision.

Her eyes lifted to his. "Let me fall," she said softly.

He saw the vision clearly, himself standing at the summit of these cliffs with the Four Lands stretched out below and Quickening beside him, her black eyes beseeching as he shoved her away.

Here. Now. The vision come to pass.

He started to shake his head no, but her eyes stopped him, her gaze so intense it was threatening.

"Goodbye, Walker," she whispered.

He released her. He held her in the circle of his arm for just an instant more, then spun her away over the precipice. It was almost as if someone else was responsible, someone hidden inside himself, a being over which reason could not prevail. He heard Horner Dees gasp, horror-stricken. He heard Morgan scream out in disbelief. They rushed at him in a frenzy, grasped him roughly, and held him as Quickening tumbled away. They watched her fall, a small bundle of cloth with her silver hair streaming out behind her. They watched her shimmer.

Then, incredibly, she began to disintegrate. She came apart at the edges first, like fraying cloth, bits and pieces scattering away. Mute, awestruck, the three at the edge of the precipice stared downward as she disappeared. In seconds she was no more, her body turned to a dust that sparkled and shone as it was caught by the wind.

Below, the Maw Grint ceased its advance, its head lifting. Perhaps it knew what was about to happen; perhaps it even understood. It made no effort to escape, waiting patiently as the dust that had been Quickening settled over it. It shuddered then, cried out once, and began to shrink. It withered rapidly, its bulk shriveling away, disappearing back into the earth until nothing remained.

The dust blanketed the isthmus next and the rock began to change, turning green with grass and moss. Shoots sprang to life, vibrant and bright. The dust swept on, reaching the peninsula and Eldwist, and the transformation continued. Centuries of Uhl Belk's dark repression were undone in moments. The stone of the city crumbled—walls, towers, streets, and tunnels all collapsing. Everything gave way before the power of Quickening's magic, just as it had at the Meade Gardens in Culhaven. All that had existed before the Stone King had worked his change was brought to life again. Rocks shifted and reformed. Trees sprang up, gnarled limbs filled with summer leaves that shone against the gray skies and water. Patches of wildflowers bloomed, not in abundance as in Culhaven, for this had always been a rugged and unsettled place, but in isolated pockets, vibrant and rich. Sea grasses and scrub swept over the broken rock, changing the face of the land back into a coastal plain. The air came alive again, filled with the smell of growing things. The deadness of the land's stone armor faded into memory. Slowly, grudgingly, Eldwist sank from view, swallowed back into the earth, gone into the past that had given it birth.

When the transformation was complete, all that remained of Eldwist was the dome in which the Stone King had entombed himself—a solitary gray island amid the green of the land.

"There was nothing we could do to save her, Morgan," Walker Boh explained softly, bent close to the devastated Highlander to make certain he could hear. "Quickening came to Eldwist to die."

They were crouched down together at the edge of the cliffs, Horner Dees with them, speaking in hushed voices, as if the silence that had settled over the land in the aftermath of Quickening's transformation was glass that might shatter. Far distant, the roar of the Tiderace breaking against the shoreline and the cries of seabirds on the wing were faint and momentary. The magic had worked its way up the cliffs now and gone past them, cleansing the rock of the Maw Grint's poison, giving life back again to the land. Island breezes gusted at the clouds, forming breaks, and sunshine peeked through guardedly.

Morgan nodded wordlessly, his head purposefully lowered, his face taut.

Walker glanced at Horner Dees, who nodded encouragingly. "She let me see everything, Highlander, just before she died. She wanted me to know, so that I could tell you. She touched me on the cheek as we stood together looking down at Eldwist, and everything was revealed. All the se-crets she kept hidden from us. All of her carefully guarded mysteries."

He shifted a few inches closer. "Her father created her to counteract the magic of Uhl Belk. He made her from the elements of the Gardens where he lived, from the strongest of his magic. He sent her to Eldwist to die. In a sense, he sent a part of himself. He really had no other choice. Nothing less would be sufficient to overcome the Stone King in his own domain. And Uhl Belk had to be overcome there because he would never leave Eldwist—could not leave, in fact, although he didn't know it. He was already a prisoner of his own magic. The Maw Grint had become Uhl Belk's surrogate, dispatched in his stead to turn the rest of the Four Lands to stone. But if the King of the Silver River waited for the monster to get close enough to confront, it would have grown too huge to stop."

His hand came up to rest on Morgan's shoulder. He felt the other flinch. "She selected each of us for a purpose, Highlander—just as she said. You and I were chosen to regain possession of the Black Elfstone, stolen by Belk from the Hall of Kings. The problem Quickening faced, of course, was that her magic would not work while Uhl Belk controlled the Elfstone. As long as he could wield the Druid magic, he could siphon off her own magic and prevent the necessary transformation from taking place. He would have done so instantly if he had discovered who she was. He would have turned her to stone. That was why she couldn't use her magic until the very last."

"But she changed the Meade Gardens simply by touching the earth!" Morgan protested, his voice angry, defiant.

"The Meade Gardens, yes. But Eldwist was far too monstrous to change so easily. She could not have done so with a simple touching. She needed to infuse herself into the rock, to make herself a part of the land." Walker sighed. "That was why she chose Pe Ell. The King of the Silver River must have known or at least sensed that the Shadowen would send someone to try to stop Quickening. It was no secret who she was or how she could change things. She was a very real threat. She had to be elimi-nated. A Shadowen, it appears now, would lack the necessary means. So Pe Ell was sent instead. Pe Ell believed that his purpose was a secret, that killing Quickening was his own idea. It wasn't. Not ever. It was hers, right from the beginning. It was the reason she sought him out, because her father had told her to do so, to take with her to Eldwist the man and the weapon that could penetrate the armor of her magic and allow her to transform."

"Why couldn't she simply change by willing it?"

"She was alive, Morgan—as human as you and I. She was an elemental, but an elemental in human guise. I don't think she could be anything else in life. It was necessary for her to die before she could work her magic on Eldwist. No ordinary weapon could kill her; her body would protect her against common metals. It required magic equal to her own, the magic of a weapon like the Stiehl—and the hands and mind of an assassin like Pe Ell."

Walker's smile was brief, tight. "She summoned us to help her—because she was told to and because we were needed to serve a purpose, yes—but because she believed in us, too. If we had failed her, any of us, even Pe Ell, if we had not done what she knew we could do, Uhl Belk would have won. There would have been no transformation of the land. The Maw Grint would have continued its advance and Uhl Belk's kingdom would have continued to expand. Combined with the onslaught of the Shadowen, everything would have been lost."

Morgan straightened perceptibly, and his eyes finally lifted. "She should have told us, Walker. She should have let us know what she had planned."

Walker shook his head gently. "No, Morgan. That was exactly what she couldn't do. We would not have acted as we did had we known the truth. Tell me. Wouldn't you have stopped her? You were in love with her, Highlander. She knew what that meant."

Morgan stared at him tight-lipped for a moment, then nodded reluctantly. "You're right. She knew."

"There wasn't any other way. She had to keep her purpose in coming here a secret."

"I know. I know." Morgan's breathing was ragged, strained. "But it hurts anyway. I can almost believe she isn't gone, that she will find a way to come back somehow." He took a deep breath. "I need her to come back."

They were silent then, staring off in separate directions, remembering. Walker wondered momentarily if he should tell the other of the Grimpond's vision, of how he had spoken of that vision with Quickening yet she had brought him anyway, of how she must have known from the first how it would end yet had come nevertheless so that her father's purpose in creating her could be fulfilled. He decided against it. The Highlander had heard enough of secrets and hidden plans. There was nothing to be gained by telling him any more.

"What's become of Belk, do you think?" Horner Dees' rough voice broke the silence. "Is he still down there in that dome? Still alive?"

They looked as one over the cliff edge to where the last vestige of Eldwist sat amid the newborn green of the peninsula, closed about and secretive.

"I think a fairy creature like Uhl Belk does not die easily," Walker answered, his voice soft, introspective. "But Quickening holds him fast, a prisoner within a shell, and the land will not be changed to his liking again any time soon." He paused. "I think Uhl Belk might go mad when he understands that."

Morgan reached down tentatively and touched a patch of grass as if searching for something. His fingers brushed the blades gently. Walker watched him for a moment, then rose. His body ached, and his spirits were dark and mean. He was starved for real food, and his thirst seemed unquenchable. His own odyssey was just beginning, a trek back through the Four Lands in search of Pe Ell and the stolen Black Elfstone, a second confrontation to discover who should possess it, and if he survived all that, a journey to recover disappeared Paranor and the Druids . . .

His thoughts threatened to overwhelm him, to drain the last of his strength, and he shoved them away.

"Come, Highlander," Horner Dees urged, reaching down to take Morgan's shoulders. "She's gone. Be glad we had her for as long as we did. She was never meant to live in this world. She was meant for a better use. Take comfort in the fact that she loved you. That's no small thing."

The big hands gripped tight, and Morgan allowed himself to be pulled to his feet. He nodded without looking at the other. When his eyes finally lifted, they were hard and fixed. "I'm going after Pe Ell."

Horner Dees spat. "We're all going after him, Morgan Leah. All of us. He won't get away."

They took one final look down from the heights, then turned and began walking toward the defile that led back into the mountains. They had gone only a few steps when Morgan stopped suddenly, remembering, and looked over to where he had left the Sword of Leah. The Sword was still jammed into the rocks, its shattered blade buried from sight. Morgan hesitated a moment, almost as if thinking to leave the weapon where it was, to abandon it once and for all. Then he stepped over and fastened his hands on the hilt. Slowly, he began to pull. And kept pulling, far longer than he should have needed to.

The blade slid free. Morgan Leah stared. The Sword of Leah was no longer broken. It was as perfect as it had been on the day it had been given to him by his father.

"Highlander!" Horner Dees breathed in astonishment.

"She spoke the truth," Morgan whispered, letting his fingers slide along the blade's gleaming surface. He looked at Walker, incredulous. "How?"

"Her magic," Walker answered, smiling at the look on the other's face. "She became again the elements of the earth that were used by her father to create her, among them the metals that forged the blade of the Sword of Leah. She remade your talisman in the same way she remade this land. It was her final act, Highlander. An act of love."

Morgan's gray eyes burned fiercely. "In a sense then, she's still with me, isn't she? And she'll stay with me as long as I keep possession of the

Sword." He took a deep breath. "Do you think the Sword has its magic back again, Walker?"

"I think that the magic comes from you. I think it always has."

Morgan studied him wordlessly for a moment, then nodded slowly. He sheathed his weapon carefully in his belt. "I have my Sword back, but there is still the matter of your arm. What of that? She said that you, like the blade, would be made whole again."

Walker thought carefully a moment, then pursed his lips. "Indeed." With his good hand, he turned Morgan gently toward the defile. "I am beginning to think, Highlander," he said softly, "that when she spoke of becoming whole, she was not referring to my arm, but to something else altogether."

Behind them, sunlight spilled down across the Tiderace.

Her eyes!

They stared down at Pe Ell from the empty windows of the buildings of Eldwist, and when he was free of the city they peered up from the fissures and clefts of the isthmus rock, and when he was to the cliffs they peeked out from behind the misted boulders of the trail leading up. Everywhere he ran, the eyes followed.

What have I done?

He was consumed with despair. He had killed the girl, just as he had intended; he had gained possession of the Black Elfstone. Everything had gone exactly as planned. Except for the fact that the plan had never been his at all—it had been hers from the beginning. That was what he had seen in her eyes, the truth of why he was here and what he had been summoned to do. She had brought him to Eldwist not to face the Stone King and retrieve the Black Elfstone as he had believed; she had brought him to kill her.

Shades, to kill her!

He ran blindly, stumbling, sprawling, clawing his way back to his feet, torn by the realization of how she had used him.

He had never been in control. He had merely deluded himself into thinking he was. All of his efforts had been wasted. She had manipulated him from the first—seeking him out in Culhaven knowing who and what he was, persuading him to come with them while letting him think that he was coming because it was his choice, and keeping him carefully away from the others, turning him this way and that as her dictates required, using him! Why? Why had she done it? The question seared like fire. Why had she wanted to die?

The fire gave way to cold as he saw the eyes wink at him from left and right and all about. Had it even been his choice at the end to stab her? He couldn't remember making a conscious decision to do so. It had almost seemed as if she had impaled herself—or made his hand move forward those few necessary inches. Pe Ell had been a puppet for the daughter of the King of the Silver River all along; perhaps she had pulled the strings that moved him one final time—and then opened her eyes to him so that all her secrets could be his.

He tumbled to the ground when he reached the head of the cliff path, flinging himself into a cleft between the rocks, huddling down, burying his gaunt, ravaged face in his arms, wishing he could hide, could disappear. He clenched his teeth in fury. He hoped she was dead! He hoped they were all dead! Tears streaked his face, the anger and despair working through him, twisting him inside out. No one had ever done this to him. He could not stand what he was feeling! He could not tolerate it!

He looked up again, moments later, longer perhaps, aware suddenly that he was in danger, that the others would be coming in pursuit. Let them come! he thought savagely. But no, he was not ready to face them now. He could barely think. He needed time to recover himself.

He forced himself back to his feet. All he could think to do was run and keep running.

He reached the defile leading back through the cliffs, away from the ramp and any view of that hated city. He could feel tremors rock the earth and hear the rumble of the Maw Grint. Rain washed over him, and gray mist descended until it seemed the clouds were resting atop the land. Pe Ell clutched the leather bag with its rune markings and its precious contents close against his chest. The Stiehl rested once again in its sheath on his hip. He could feel the magic burning into his hands, against his thigh, hotter than he had ever felt it, fire that might never be quenched. What had the girl done to him? What had she done?

He fell, and for a moment was unable to rise. All the strength had left him. He looked down at his hands, seeing the blood that streaked them. Her blood.

Her face flashed before him out of the gloom, bright and vibrant, her silver hair flung back, her black eyes . . .

Quickening!

He managed to scramble back to his feet and ran faster still, slipping wildly, trying to fight against the visions, to regain his composure, his self-control. But nothing would settle into place, everything was jumbled and thrown about, madness loosed within him like a guard dog set free. He had killed her, yes. But she had made him do it, made him! All those feelings for her, false from the start, her creations, her twisting of him!

Bone Hollow opened before him, filled with rocks and emptiness. He did not slow. He ran on.

Something was happening behind him. He could feel a shifting of the tremors, a changing of the winds. He could feel something cold settling deep within. *Magic!* A voice whispered, teasing, insidious. *Quickening comes for you!* But Quickening was dead! He howled out loud, pursued by demons that all bore her face.

He stumbled and fell amid a scattering of bleached bones, shoved himself back to his knees, and realized suddenly where he was.

Time froze for Pe Ell, and a frightening moment of insight blossomed within.

The Koden!

Then, abruptly, it had him, its shaggy limbs enfolding him, its body smelling of age and decay. He could hear the whistle of its breath in his ear and could feel the heat of it on his face. The closeness of the beast was suffocating. He struggled to catch a glimpse of it and found he could not. It was there, and at the same time it wasn't. Had it somehow become invisible? He tried to reach for the handle of the Stiehl, but his fingers would not respond.

How could this be happening?

He knew suddenly that he was not going to escape. He was only mildly surprised to discover that he no longer cared.

An instant later, he was dead.

Less than an hour later the last three survivors of the company from Rampling Steep made their way into Bone Hollow and found Pe Ell's body. It lay midway through, sprawled loose and uncaring upon the earth, lifeless gaze fixed upon the distant sky. One hand clutched the rune-marked leather bag that contained the Black Elfstone. The Stiehl was still in its sheath.

Walker Boh glanced about curiously. Quickening's magic had worked its way through Bone Hollow, changing it so that it was no longer recognizable. Saw grass and jump weed grew everywhere in tufts that shaded and softened the hard surface of the rock. Patches of yellow and purple wildflowers bent to find the sun, and the bones of the dead had faded back into the earth. Nothing remained of what had been.

"Not a mark on him," Horner Dees muttered, his rough face creased further by the frown that bent his mouth, his voice wondering. He moved forward, bent down to take a close look, then straightened. "Neck might be broke. Ribs crushed. Something like that. But nothing that I can see. A little blood on his hands, but that belongs to the girl. And look. Koden tracks all around, everywhere. It had to have caught him. Yet there's not a mark on his body. How do you like that?"

There was no sign of the Koden. It was gone, disappeared as if it had never been. Walker tested the air, probed the silence, closed his eyes to see if he could find the Koden in his mind. No. Quickening's magic had set it free. As soon as the chains that bound it were broken, it had gone back into its old world, become itself again, a bear only, the memories of what had been done to it already fading. Walker felt a deep sense of satisfaction settle through him. He had managed to keep his promise after all.

"Look at his eyes, will you?" Horner Dees was saying. "Look at the fear in them. He didn't die a happy man, whatever it was that killed him. He died scared."

"It must have been the Koden," Morgan Leah insisted. He hung back from the body, unwilling to approach it.

Dees glanced pointedly at him. "You think so? How, then? What did it do, hug him to death? Must have done it pretty quick if it did. That knife of his isn't even out of its case. Take a look, Highlander. What do you see?"

Morgan stepped up hesitantly and stared down. "Nothing," he admitted.

"Just as I said." Dees sniffed. "You want me to turn him over, look there?"

Morgan shook his head. "No." He studied Pe Ell's face a moment without speaking. "It doesn't matter." Then his eyes lifted to find Walker's. "I don't know what to feel. Isn't that odd? I wanted him dead, but I wanted to be the one who killed him. I know it doesn't matter who did it or how it happened, but I feel cheated somehow. As if the chance to even things up had been taken away from me."

"I don't think that's the case, Morgan," the Dark Uncle replied softly. "I don't think the chance was ever yours in the first place."

The Highlander and the old Tracker stared at him in surprise. "What are you saying?" Dees snapped.

Walker shrugged. "If I were the King of the Silver River and it was necessary for me to sacrifice the life of my child to an assassin's blade, I would make certain her killer did not escape." He shifted his gaze from one face to the other and back again. "Perhaps the magic that Quickening carried in her body was meant to serve more than one purpose. Perhaps it did."

There was a long silence as the three contemplated the prospect. "The blood on his hands, you think?" Horner Dees said finally. "Like a poison?" He shook his head. "Makes as much sense as anything else."

Walker Boh reached down and carefully freed the bag with the Black Elfstone from Pe Ell's rigid fingers. He wiped it clean, then held it in his open palm for a moment, thinking to himself how ironic it was that the Elfstone would have been useless to the assassin. So much effort expended to gain possession of its magic and all for nothing. Quickening had known. The King of the Silver River had known. If Pe Ell had known as well, he would have killed the girl instantly and been done with the matter. Or would he have remained anyway, so captivated by her that even then he would not have been able to escape? Walker Boh wondered.

"What about this?" Horner Dees reached down and unstrapped the Stiehl from around Pe Ell's thigh. "What do we do with it?"

"Throw it into the ocean," Morgan said at once. "Or drop it into the deepest hole you can find."

It seemed to Walker that he could hear someone else speaking, that the words were unpleasantly familiar ones. Then he realized he was thinking of himself, remembering what he had said when Cogline had brought him the Druid History out of lost Paranor. Another time, another magic, he thought, but the dangers were always the same.

"Morgan," he said, and the other turned. "If we throw it away, we risk the possibility that it will be found again—perhaps by someone as twisted and evil as Pe Ell. Perhaps by someone worse. The blade needs to be locked away where no one can ever reach it again." He turned to Horner Dees. "If you give it to me, I will see that it is."

They stood there for a moment without moving, three worn and ragged figures in a field of broken stone and new green, measuring one another. Dees glanced once at Morgan, then handed the blade to Walker. "I guess we can trust you to keep your word as well as anyone," he offered.

Walker shoved the Stiehl and the Elfstone into the deep pockets of his cloak and hoped it was so.

They walked south the remainder of the day and spent their first night free of Eldwist on a barren, scrub-grown plain. A day earlier, the plain had been a part of Uhl Belk's kingdom, infected by the poison of the Maw Grint, a broken carpet of stone. Even with nothing more than the scrub to brighten its expanse, it felt lush and comforting after the deadness of the city. There was little to eat yet, a few roots and wild vegetables, but there was fresh water again, the skies were star filled, and the air was clean and new. They made a fire and sat up late, talking in low voices of what they were feeling, remembering in the long silences what had been.

When morning came they awoke with the sun on their faces, grateful simply to be alive.

They traveled down again through the high forests and crossed into the Charnals. Horner Dees took them a different way this time, carefully avoiding dead Carisman's tribe of Urdas, journeying east of the Spikes. The weather stayed mild, even in the mountains, and there were no storms or avalanches to cause them further grief. Food was plentiful again, and they began to regain their strength. A sense of well-being returned, and the harshest of their memories softened and faded.

Morgan Leah spoke often of Quickening. It seemed to help him to speak of her, and both Walker and Horner Dees encouraged him to do so. Sometimes the Highlander talked as if she were still alive, touching the Sword he carried, and gesturing back to the country they were leaving behind. She was there, he insisted, and better that she were there than gone completely. He could sense her presence at times; he was certain of it. He smiled and joked and slowly began to return to himself.

Horner Dees became his old self almost as quickly, the haunted look fading from his eyes, the tension disappearing from his face. The gruffness in his voice lost its edge, and for the first time in weeks the love he bore for his mountains began to work its way back into his conversation.

Walker Boh recovered more slowly. He was encased in an iron shell of fatalistic resignation that had stripped his feelings nearly bare. He had lost his arm in the Hall of Kings. He had lost Cogline and Rumor at Hearthstone. He had nearly lost his life any number of times. Carisman was dead. Quickening was dead. His vow to refuse the charge that Allanon had given him was dead. Quickening had been right. There were always choices. But sometimes the choices were made for you, whether you wanted it so or not. He might have thought not to be ensnared by Druid machinations, to turn his life away from Brin Ohmsford and her legacy of magic. But circumstances and conscience made that all but impossible. His was a destiny woven by threads that stretched back in time hundreds, perhaps thousands, of years, and he could not be free of them, not entirely, at least. He had thought the matter through since that night in Eldwist when he had agreed to return with Quickening to the lair of the Stone King in an effort to recover the Black Elfstone. He knew that by going he was agreeing that if they were successful he would carry the talisman back into the Four Lands and attempt to restore Paranor and the Druids—just as Allanon had charged him.

He knew without having to speak the words what that meant.

Make whatever choice you will, Quickening had advised.

But what choices were left to him? He had determined long ago to search out the Black Elfstone—perhaps from the moment he had first discovered its existence while reading the Druid History; certainly from the time of the death of Cogline. He had determined as well to discover what its magic would do—and that meant testing Allanon's charge that Paranor and the Druids could be restored. He might argue that he had been considering the matter right up until the moment Eldwist had met its end. But he knew the truth was otherwise. He knew as well that if the magic of the Black Elfstone was everything that had been promised, if it worked as he believed, then Paranor would be restored. And if that happened, then the Druids would come back into the Four Lands.

Through him.

Beginning with him.

And that reality provided the only choice left to him, the one he believed Quickening had wanted him to make—the choice of who he would be. If it was true that Paranor could be restored and that he must become the first of the Druids who would keep it, then he must make certain he did not lose himself in the process. He must make certain that Walker Boh survived—his heart, his ideas, his convictions, his misgivings—everything he was and believed. He must not evolve into the very thing he had struggled so hard to escape. He must not, in other words, turn into Allanon. He must not become like the Druids of old—manipulators, exploiters, dark and secretive conjurers, and hiders of truths. If the Druids must return in order to preserve the Races, in order to ensure their survival against the dark things of the world, Shadowen or whatever, then he must make them as they should be—a better order of Men, of teachers, and of givers of the power of magic.

That was the choice he could still make—a choice he must make if he were to keep his sanity.

It took them almost two weeks to reach Rampling Steep, choosing the longer, safer routes, skirting any possibility of danger, sheltering when it was dark, and emerging to travel on when it was light. They came on the mountainside town toward midday, the skies washed with a gray, cloudy haze left by a summer shower that suggested spun cotton pulled apart by too-anxious hands. The day was warm and humid, and the buildings of the town glistened like damp, squat toads hunched down against the rocks. The three travelers approached as strangers, seeing the town anew, the first since Eldwist. They slowed as one as they entered the solitary street that navigated the gathering of taverns, stables, and trading stores to either side, pausing to look back into the mountains they had descended, watching momentarily as the runoff from the storm churned down out of the cliffs into gullies and streams, the sound a distant rush.

"Time to say goodbye," Horner Dees announced without preliminaries and stuck out his hand to Morgan.

Morgan stared. There had been no talk of his leaving until now. "You're not coming on with us?"

The old Tracker snorted. "I'm lucky to be alive, Highlander. Now you want me to come south? How far do you expect me to push things?"

Morgan stammered. "I didn't mean . . ."

"Fact is, I shouldn't have gone with you the first time." The other cut him short with a wave of one big hand. "It was the girl who talked me into it. Couldn't say no to her. And maybe it was the sense of having left something behind when I fled the Stone King and his monsters ten years ago. I had to go back to find it again. So here I am, the only man to have escaped Eldwist and Uhl Belk twice. Seems to me that's enough for one old man."

"You would be welcome to come with us, Horner Dees," Walker Boh assured him, taking Morgan's part. "You're not as old as you pretend and twice as able. The Highlander and his friends can use your experience."

"Yes, Horner," Morgan agreed hurriedly. "What about the Shadowen? We need you to help fight them. Come with us."

But the old Tracker shook his bearish head stubbornly. "Highlander, I'll miss you. I owe you my life. I look at you and see the son I might have had under other circumstances. Now isn't that something to admit? But I've had enough excitement in my life and I'm not anxious for any more. I need the dark quiet of the ale houses. I need the comforts of my own place." He stuck out his hand once again. "Who's to say that won't change though? So. Some other time, maybe?"

Morgan clasped the hand in his own. "Any time, Horner." Then, forsaking the hand, he embraced the old man. Horner Dees hugged him back.

The journey went swiftly after that, time slipping away almost magically, the days and nights passing like quicksilver. Walker and Morgan came down out of the Charnals into the foothills south and turned west along their threshold toward the Rabb. They forded the north branch of the river and the land opened into grasslands that stretched away toward the distant peaks of the Dragon's Teeth. The days were long and hot, the sun burning out of cloudless skies as the intemperate weather of the mountains was left behind. Sunrise came early, and daylight stayed late, and even the nights were warm and bright. The pair encountered few travelers and no Federation patrols. The land grew increasingly infected by the Shadowen sickness, dark patches that hinted at the spread of the disease, but there was no sign of the carriers.

At week's end, the Dark Uncle and the Highlander reached the south entrance to the Jannisson Pass. It was nearing noon, and the pass stretched away through the juncture of the cliffs of the Dragon's Teeth and the Charnals, a broad empty corridor leading north to the Streleheim. It was here that Padishar Creel had hoped to rally the forces of the Southland Movement, the Dwarf Resistance, and the Trolls of Axhind and his Kelktic Rock in an effort to confront and destroy the armies of the Federation. The wind blew gently across the flats and down through the pass, and no one stirred.

Morgan Leah cast about wearily, a resigned look on his face. Walker stood silently beside him for a moment, then put his hand on the other's shoulder. "Where to now, Highlander?" he asked softly.

Morgan shrugged and smiled bravely. "South, I suppose, to Varfleet. I'll try to make contact with Padishar, hope that he's found Par and Coll. If that fails, I'll go looking for the Valemen on my own." He paused, studying the other's hard, pale face. "I guess I know where you're going."

Walker nodded. "To find Paranor."

Morgan took a deep breath. "I know this isn't what you wanted, Walker."

"No, it isn't."

"I could come with you, if you'd like."

"No, Highlander, you've done enough for others. It is time to do something for yourself."

Morgan nodded. "Well, I'm not afraid, if that's what you're thinking. I have the magic of the Sword of Leah again. I might be of some use."

Walker's fingers tightened on the other's shoulder and then dropped away. "I don't think anyone can help me where I'm going. I think I have to help myself as best I can. The Elfstone will likely be my best protection." He sighed. "Strange how things work out. If not for Quickening, neither of us would be doing what he is or even be who he is, would he? She's given us both a new purpose, a new face, maybe even a new strength. Don't forget what she gave up for you, Morgan. She loved you. I think that in whatever way she is able she always will."

"I know."

"Horner Dees said you saved his life. You saved my life as well. If you hadn't used the Sword, even broken as it was, Uhl Belk would have killed me. I think Par and Coll Ohmsford could ask for no better protector. Go after them. See that they are well. Help them in any way you can."

"I will."

They clasped hands and held tight for a moment, eyes locked.

"Be careful, Walker," Morgan said.

Walker's smile was faint and ironic. "Until we meet again, Morgan Leah."

Then Walker turned and walked into the pass, angling through sunlight into shadow as the rocks closed about. He did not look back.

For the remainder of that day and the whole of the one following Walker Boh traveled west across the Streleheim, skirting the dark, ancient forests that lay south, cradled by the peaks of the Dragon's Teeth. On the third day he turned down, moving into the shadowed woods, leaving the plains and the sunshine behind. The trees were massive, towering sentinels set at watch like soldiers waiting to be sent forth into battle, thick trunks grown close in camaraderie, and limbs canopied against the light. These were the forests that for centuries past had sheltered the Druid's Keep against the world beyond. In the time of Shea Ohmsford there had been wolves set at watch. Even after, there had been a wall of thorns that none could penetrate but Allanon himself. The wolves were gone now, the wall of thorns as well, and even the Keep itself. Only the trees remained, wrapped in a deep, pervasive silence.

Walker navigated the trails as if he were a shadow, passing soundlessly through the sea of trunks, across the carpet of dead needles, lost in the roil of his increasing indecision. His thoughts of what he was about to do were jumbled and rough-edged, and whispers of uncertainty that he had thought safely put to rest had risen to haunt him once again. All his life he had fought to escape Brin Ohmsford's legacy; now he was rushing willingly to embrace it. His decision to do so had been long in coming and repeatedly questioned. It had resulted from an odd mix of circumstance, conscience, and deliberation. He had given it as much thought as he was capable of giving and he was convinced that he had chosen right. But the prospect of its consequences was terrifying nevertheless, and the closer he came to discovering them, the deeper grew his misgivings.

By the time he arrived at the heart of the forests and the bluff on which Paranor had once rested, he was in utter turmoil. He stood for a long time staring upward at the few stone blocks that remained of what had once been the outbuildings, at the streaking of red light across the bluff's crest where the sunset cast its heated, withering glow. In the shimmer of the dying light he could imagine it was possible to see Paranor rise up against the coming night, its parapets sharply defined and its towers piercing the sky's azure crown like spears. He could feel the immensity of the Keep's presence, the sullen bulk of its stone. He could touch the life of its magic, waiting to be reborn.

He built a fire and sat before it, awaiting the descent of night. When it was fully dark, he rose and walked again to the bluff's edge. The stars were pinpricks of brightness overhead, and the woods about him were anxious with night sounds. He felt foreign and alone. He stared upward once more at the crest of the rise, probing from within with his magic for some sign of what waited. Nothing revealed itself. Yet the Keep was there; he could sense its presence in a way that defied explanation. The fact that his magic failed to substantiate what he already knew made him even more uneasy. Bring back lost Paranor and the Druids, Allanon had said. What would it take to do so? What beyond possession of the Black Elfstone? There would be more, he knew. There would have to be.

He slept for a few hours, though sleep did not come easily, a frail need against the whisper of his fears. He lay awake at first, his resolve slipping away, eroded and breached. The trappings of a lifetime's mistrust ensnared him, working free of the restraints under which he had placed them, threatening to take control of him once again. He forced himself to think of Quickening. What must it have been like for her, knowing what she was expected to do? How frightened she must have been! Yet she had sacrificed herself because that was what was needed to give life back to the land. He took strength in remembering her courage, and after a time the whispers receded again, and he fell asleep.

It was already daybreak when he awoke, and he washed and ate quickly, woodenly, anxious in the shadow of what waited. When he was done he walked again to the base of the bluff and stared upward. The sun was behind him, and its light spilled down upon the bluff's barren summit. Nothing had changed. No hint of what had been or what might be revealed itself. Paranor remained lost in time and space and legend.

Walker stepped away, returning to the edge of the trees, safely back from the bluff. He reached into the deep pockets of his cloak and lifted free the pouch that contained the Black Elfstone. He stared blankly at it, feeling the weight of its power press against him. His body was stiff and sore; his missing arm ached. His throat was as dry as autumn leaves. He felt the insecurities, doubts, and fears begin to rise within him, massing in a wave that threatened to wash him away.

Quickly, he dumped the Elfstone into his open palm.

He closed his hand instantly, frightened to look into its dark light. His mind raced. One Stone, one for all, one for heart, mind, and body—made that way, he believed, because it was the antithesis of all the other Elfstones created by the creatures of the old world of faerie, a magic that devoured rather than expended, one that absorbed rather than released. The Elfstones that Allanon had given to Shea Ohmsford were a talisman to defend their holder against whatever dark magic threatened. But the Black Elfstone was created for another reason entirely—not to defend, but to enable. It was conceived for a single purpose—to counteract the magic that had been called forth to spirit away the Druid's Keep, to bring lost Paranor out of limbo again. It would do so by consuming that magic—and transferring it into the body of the Stone's holder—himself. What that would do to him, Walker could only imagine. He knew that the Stone's protection against misuse lay in the fact that it would work the same way no matter who wielded it and for what purpose. That was what had destroyed Uhl Belk. His absorption of the Maw Grint's magic had turned him to stone.

Walker's own fate might be similar, he believed—yet it would also be more complex. But how? If use of the Black Elfstone restored Paranor, then what would be the consequence of transference to himself of the magic that bound the Keep?

Whosoever shall have cause and right shall wield it to its proper end.

Himself. Yet why? Because Allanon had decreed that it must be so? Had Allanon told the truth? Or simply a part of the truth? Or was he gamesplaying once more? What could Walker Boh believe?

He stood there, solitary, filled with indecision and dread, wondering what it was that had brought him to this end. He saw his hand begin to shake.

Then suddenly, unexpectedly, the whispers broke through his defenses in a torrent and turned to screams.

No!

He brought the Black Elfstone up almost without thinking, opened his hand, and thrust the dark gem forth.

Instantly the Elfstone flared to life, its magic a sharp tingling against his skin. Black light—the nonlight, the engulfing darkness. *Whosoever.* He watched the light gather before him, building on itself. *Shall have cause and right.* The backlash of the magic rushed through him, shredding doubt and fear, silencing whispers and screams, filling him with unimaginable power. *Shall wield it to its proper end.*

Now!

He sent the black light hurtling forth, a huge tunnel burrowing through the air, swallowing everything in its path, engulfing substance and space and time. It exploded against the crest of the empty bluff, and Walker was hammered back as if struck a blow by an invisible fist. Yet he did not fall. The magic rushed through him, bracing him, wrapping him in armor. The black light spread like ink against the sky, rising, broadening, angling first this way, then that, channeling itself as if there were runnels to be followed, gutters down which it must flow. It began to shape. Walker gasped. The light of the Black Elfstone was etching out the lines of a massive fortress, its parapets and battlements, and its towers and steeples. Walls rose and gates appeared. The light spread higher against the skies, and the sunlight was blocked away. Shadows cast down by the castle enveloped Walker Boh, and he felt himself disappear into them.

Something inside him began to change. He was draining away. No, rather he was filling up! Something, the magic, was washing through. *The other,* he thought, weak before its onslaught, helpless and suddenly terrified. It was the magic that encased lost Paranor being drawn down into the Elfstone!

And into him.

His jaw clenched, and his body went rigid. *I will not give way!*

The black light flooded the empty spaces of the image atop the bluff, coloring it, giving it first substance and then life—Paranor, the Druid's Keep, come back into the world of men, returned from the dark half-space that had concealed it all these years. It rose up against the sky, huge and forbidding. The Black Elfstone dimmed in Walker's hand; the nonlight softened and then disappeared.

Walker's hoarse cry ended in a groan. He fell to his knees, wracked with sensations he could not define and riddled with the magic he had absorbed, feeling it course through him as if it were his blood. His eyes closed and then slowly opened. He saw himself shimmering in a haze that stole away the definition of his features. He looked down in disbelief, then felt himself go cold. He wasn't really there anymore! He had become a wraith!

He forced his terror aside and climbed back to his feet, the Black Elfstone still clutched in his hand. He watched himself move as if he were someone else, watched the shimmer of his limbs and body and the shadings that overlapped and gave him the appearance of being fragmented. *Shades, what has been done to me!* He stumbled forward, scrambling to gain the bluff, to reach its crest, not knowing what else to do. He must gain Paranor, he sensed. He must get inside.

The climb was long and rugged, and he was gasping for breath by the time he reached the Keep's iron gates. His body reflected in a multitude of images, each a little outside of the others. But he could breathe and move as a normal man; he could feel as he had before. He took heart from that, and hastened to reach Paranor's gates. The stone of the Keep was real enough, hard and rough to his touch—yet forbidding, too, in a way he could not immediately identify. The gates opened when he leaned into them, as if he had the strength of a thousand men and could force anything that stood before him.

He entered cautiously. Shadows enfolded him. He stood in a well of darkness, and there was a whisper of death all about.

Then something moved within the gloom, detached, and took shape— a four-legged apparition, hulking and ominous. It was a moor cat, black as pitch with luminous gold eyes, there and not there, like Walker himself.

Walker froze. The moor cat looked exactly like . . .

Behind the cat, a man appeared, old and stooped, a translucent ghost, shimmering. As the man drew near, his features became recognizable.

"At last you've come, Walker," he whispered in an anxious, hollow voice.

The Dark Uncle felt the last vestiges of his resolve fade away.

The man was Cogline.

33

The King of the Silver River sat in the Gardens that were his sanctuary and watched the sun melt into the western horizon. A stream of clear water trickled across the rocks at his feet and emptied into a pond from which a unicorn drank, and a breeze blew softly through the maidenhair, carrying the scent of lilacs and jonquils. The trees rustled, their leaves a shimmer of green, and birds sang contented day-end songs as they settled into place in preparation for the coming of night.

Beyond, in the world of Men, the heat was sullen and unyielding against the fall of darkness, and a pall of weariness draped the lives of the people of the Four Lands.

So must it be for now.

The eyes that could see everything had seen the death of his child and the transformation of the land of the Stone King. The Maw Grint was no more. The city of Eldwist had gone back into the earth, returned to the elements that had created it, and the land was green and fertile again. The magic of his child was rooted deep, a river that flowed invisibly about the solitary dome in which Uhl Belk was imprisoned. It would be long before his brother could emerge into the light again.

Iridescent dragonflies buzzed past him without slowing and disappeared into the twilight's glow.

Elsewhere, the battle against the Shadowen went on. Walker Boh had invoked the magic of the Black Elfstone, as Allanon had charged him, and the Druid's Keep had been summoned out of the mists that had hidden it for three centuries. What would the Dark Uncle make, the King of the Silver River wondered, of what he found there? West, where the Elves had once lived, Wren Ohmsford continued her search to discover what had become of them—and, more important, though she did not yet realize it, what would become of herself. North, the brothers Par and Coll Ohmsford struggled toward each other and the secrets of the Sword of Shannara and the Shadowen magic. There were those who would help and those who would betray, and all of the wheels of chance that Allanon had set in motion could yet be stopped.

The King of the Silver River rose and slipped into the waters of the pond momentarily, reveling in the cool wetness, letting himself become one with the flow. Then he emerged and passed down the Garden pathways, through stands of juniper and hemlock onto a hillock of centauries and bluebells that reflected gold about the edges of their petals with the day's fading light. He paused there, staring out again into the world beyond.

His daughter had done well, he reflected.

But the thought was strangely bleak and empty. He had created an elemental out of the life of his Gardens and sent that elemental forth to serve his needs. She had been nothing to him—a daughter in name only, a child merely by designation. She had been only a momentary reality, and he had never intended that she be anything more.

Yet he missed her. Shaping her as he did, breathing his life into her, he had brought himself too close. The human feelings they had shared would not dissolve as easily as their human forms. She should have meant nothing to him, now that she was gone. Instead, her absence formed a void he could not seem to fill.

Quickening.

A child of the elements and his magic, he repeated. He would do the same again—yet perhaps not so readily. There was something in the ways of the creatures of the mortal Races that endured beyond the leaving of the flesh. There was a residue of their emotions that lingered. He could still hear her voice, see her face, and feel the touch of her fingers against him. She was gone from him, yet remained.

Why should it be so?

He sat there as darkness cloaked the land and wondered at himself.

THE ELF QUEEN
of SHANNARA

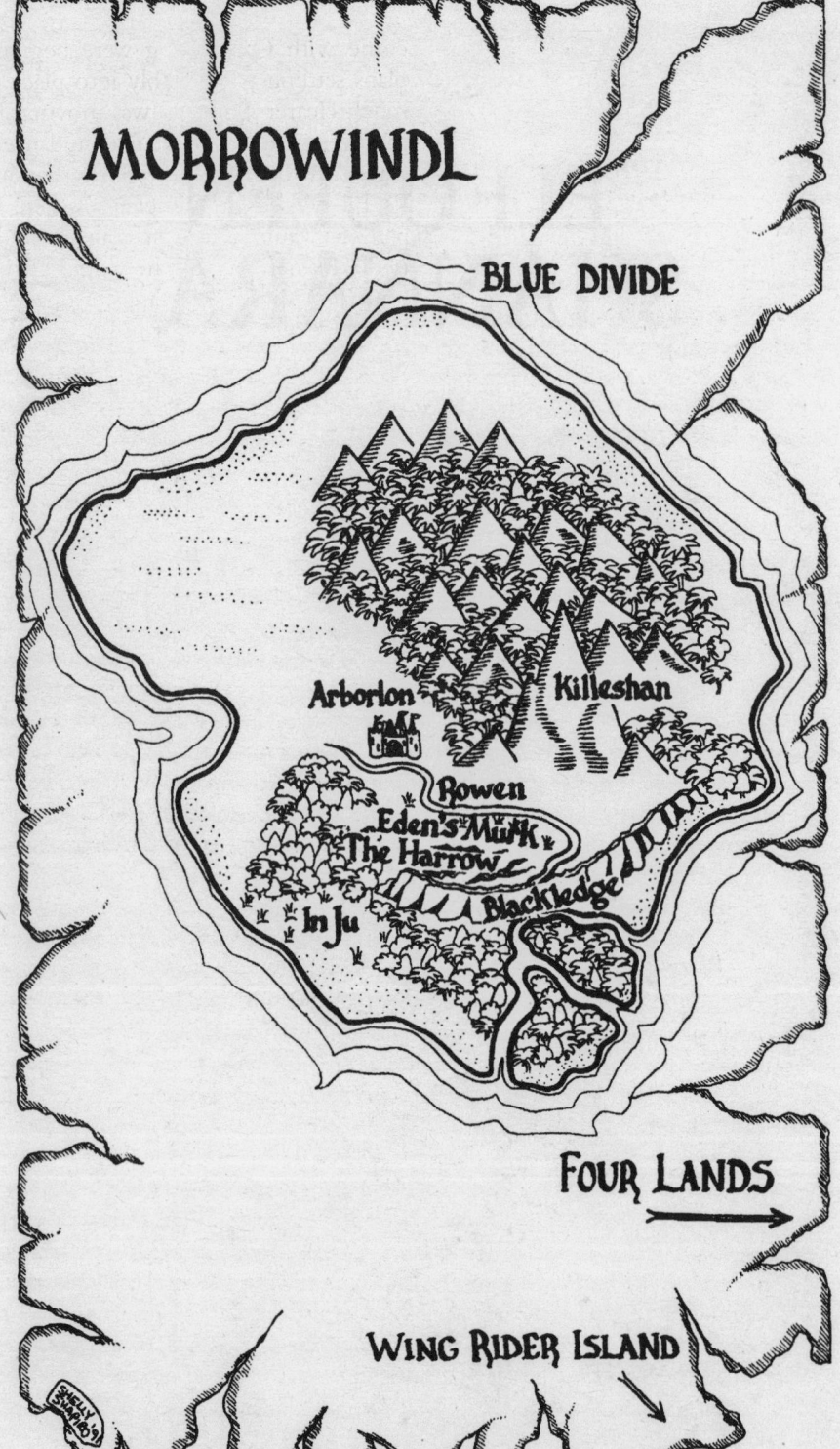

MORROWINDL

BLUE DIVIDE

Arborlon   Killeshan

Rowen
Eden's Murk
The Harrow
Blackledge
In Ju

FOUR LANDS →

WING RIDER ISLAND

For Diane,
who is missed

Fire.

It sputtered in the oil lamps that hung distant and solitary in the windows and entryways of her people's homes. It spat and hissed as it licked at the pitch-coated torches bracketing road intersections and gates. It glowed through breaks in the leafy branches of the ancient oak and hickory where glassed lanterns lined the treelanes. Bits and pieces of flickering light, the flames were like tiny creatures that the night threatened to search out and consume.

Like ourselves, she thought.

Like the Elves.

Her gaze lifted, traveling beyond the buildings and walls of the city to where Killeshan steamed.

Fire.

It glowed redly out of the volcano's ragged mouth, the glare of its molten core reflected in the clouds of vog—volcanic ash—that hung in sullen banks across the empty sky. Killeshan loomed over them, vast and intractable, a phenomenon of nature that no Elven magic could hope to withstand. For weeks now the rumbling had sounded from deep within the earth, dissatisfied, purposeful, a building up of pressure that would eventually demand release.

For now, the lava burrowed and tunneled through cracks and fissures in its walls and ran down into the waters of the ocean in long, twisting ribbons that burned off the jungle and the things that lived within it. One day soon now, she knew, this secondary venting would not be enough, and Killeshan would erupt in a conflagration that would destroy them all.

If any of them remained by then.

She stood at the edge of the Gardens of Life, close to where the Ellcrys grew. The ancient tree lifted skyward as if to fight through the vog and breathe the cleaner air that lay sealed above. Silver branches glimmered faintly with the light of lanterns and torches; scarlet leaves reflected the volcano's darker glow. Scatterings of fire danced in strange patterns through breaks in the tree as if trying to form a picture. She watched the images appear and fade, a mirror of her thoughts, and the sadness she felt threatened to overwhelm her.

What am I to do? she thought desperately. *What choices are left me?*

None, she knew. None, but to wait.

She was Ellenroh Elessedil, Queen of the Elves, and all she could do was to wait.

She gripped the Ruhk Staff tightly and glanced skyward with a grimace. There were no stars or moon this night. There had been little of either for weeks, only the vog, thick and impenetrable, a shroud waiting to descend, to cover their bodies, to enfold them all, and to wrap them away forever.

She stood stiffly as a hot breeze blew over her, ruffling the fine linen of her clothing. She was tall, her body angular and long limbed. The bones of her face were prominent, shaping features that were instantly recognizable. Her cheekbones were high, her forehead broad, and her jaw sharp-edged and smooth beneath her wide, thin mouth. Her skin was drawn tight against her face, giving her a sculpted look. Flaxen hair tumbled to her shoulders in thick, unruly curls. Her eyes were a strange, piercing blue and always seemed to be seeing things not immediately apparent to others. She seemed much younger than her fifty-odd years. When she smiled, which was often, she brought smiles to the faces of others almost effortlessly.

She was not smiling now. It was late, well after midnight, and her weariness was like a chain that would not let her go. She could not sleep and had come to walk in the Gardens, to listen to the night, to be alone with her thoughts, and to try to find some small measure of peace. But peace was elusive, her thoughts were small demons that taunted and teased, and the night was a great, hungering black cloud that waited patiently for the moment when it would at last extinguish the frail spark of their lives.

Fire, again. Fire to give life and fire to snuff it out. The image whispered at her insidiously.

She turned abruptly and began walking through the Gardens. Cort trailed behind her, a silent, invisible presence. If she bothered to look for him, he would not be there. She could picture him in her mind, a small, stocky youth with incredible quickness and strength. He was one of the Home Guard, protectors of the Elven rulers, the weapons that defended them, the lives that were given up to preserve their own. Cort was her shadow, and if not Cort, then Dal. One or the other of them was always there, keeping her safe. As she moved along the pathway, her thoughts slipped rapidly, one to the next. She felt the roughness of the ground through the thin lining of her slippers. Arborlon, the city of the Elves, her home, brought out of the Westland more than a hundred years ago—here, to this . . .

She left the thought unfinished. She lacked the words to complete it.

Elven magic, conjured anew out of faerie time, sheltered the city, but the magic was beginning to fail. The mingled fragrances of the Garden's flowers were overshadowed by the acrid smells of Killeshan's gases where they had penetrated the outer barrier of the Keel. Night birds sang gently from the trees and coverings, but even here their songs were undercut by the guttural sounds of the dark things that lurked beyond the city's walls in the jungles and swamps, that pressed up against the Keel, waiting.

The monsters.

The trail she followed ended at the northernmost edge of the Gardens on a promontory overlooking her home. The palace windows were dark, the people within asleep, all but her. Beyond lay the city, clusters of homes and shops tucked behind the Keel's protective barrier like frightened animals hunkered down in their dens. Nothing moved, as if fear made movement impossible, as if movement would give them away. She shook her head sadly. Arborlon was an island surrounded by enemies. Behind, to the east, was Killeshan, rising up over the city, a great, jagged mountain formed by lava rock from eruptions over the centuries, the volcano dormant until only twenty years ago, now alive and anxious. North and south the jungle grew, thick and impenetrable, stretching away in a tangle of green to the shores of the ocean. West, below the slopes on which Arborlon was seated, lay the Rowen, and beyond the wall of Blackledge. None of it belonged to the Elves. Once the entire world had belonged to them, before the coming of Man. Once there had been nowhere they could not go. Even in the time of the Druid Allanon, just three hundred years before, the whole of the Westland had been theirs. Now they were reduced to this small space, besieged on all sides, imprisoned behind the wall of their failing magic. All of them, all that remained, trapped.

She looked out at the darkness beyond the Keel, picturing in her mind what waited there. She thought momentarily of the irony of it—the Elves, made victims of their own magic, of their own clever, misguided plans, and of fears that should never have been heeded. How could they have been so foolish?

Far down from where she stood, near the end of the Keel where it buttressed the hardened lava of some long past runoff, there was a sudden flare of light—a spurt of fire followed by a quick, brilliant explosion and a shriek. There were brief shouts and then silence. Another attempt to breach the walls and another death. It was a nightly occurrence now as the creatures grew bolder and the magic continued to fail.

She glanced behind her to where the topmost branches of the Ellcrys lifted above the Garden trees, a canopy of life. The tree had protected the Elves from so much for so long. It had renewed and restored. It had given peace. But it could not protect them now, not against what threatened this time.

Not against themselves.

She grasped the Ruhk Staff in defiance and felt the magic surge within, a warming against her palm and fingers. The Staff was thick and gnarled and polished to a fine sheen. It had been hewn from black walnut and imbued with the magic of her people. Fixed to its tip was the Loden, white brilliance against the darkness of the night. She could see herself reflected in its facets. She could feel herself reach within. The Ruhk Staff had given strength to the rulers of Arborlon for more than a century gone.

But the Staff could not protect the Elves either.

"Cort?" she called softly.

The Home Guard materialized beside her.

"Stand with me a moment," she said.

They stood without speaking and looked out over the city. She felt impossibly alone. Her people were threatened with extinction. She should be doing something. Anything. What if the dreams were wrong? What if the visions of Eowen Cerise were mistaken? That had never happened, of course, but there was so much at stake! Her mouth tightened angrily. She must believe. It was necessary that she believe. The visions would come to pass. The girl would appear to them as promised, blood of her blood. The girl would appear.

But would even she be enough?

She shook the question away. She could not permit it. She could not give way to her despair.

She wheeled about and walked swiftly back through the Gardens to the pathway leading down again. Cort stayed with her for a moment, then faded away into the shadows. She did not see him go. Her mind was on the future, on the foretellings of Eowen, and on the fate of the Elven people. She was determined that her people would survive. She would wait for the girl for as long as she could, for as long as the magic would keep their enemies away. She would pray that Eowen's visions were true.

She was Ellenroh Elessedil, Queen of the Elves, and she would do what she must.

Fire.

It burned within as well.

Sheathed in the armor of her convictions, she went down out of the Gardens of Life in the slow hours of the early morning to sleep.

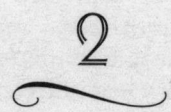

Wren Ohmsford yawned. She sat on a bluff overlooking the Blue Divide, her back to the smooth trunk of an ancient willow. The ocean stretched away before her, a shimmering kaleidoscope of colors at the horizon's edge where the sunset streaked the waters with splashes of red and gold and purple and low-hanging clouds formed strange patterns against the darkening sky. Twilight was settling comfortably in place, a graying of the light, a whisper of an evening breeze off the water, a calm descending. Crickets were beginning to chirp, and fireflies were winking into view.

Wren drew her knees up against her chest, struggling to stay upright when what she really wanted to do was lie down. She hadn't slept for almost two days now, and fatigue was catching up with her. It was shadowed and cool where she sat beneath the willow's canopy, and it would have been easy to let go, slip down, curl up beneath her cloak, and drift away. Her eyes closed involuntarily at the prospect, then snapped open again instantly. She could not sleep until Garth returned, she knew. She must stay alert.

She rose and walked out to the edge of the bluff, feeling the breeze against her face, letting the sea smells fill her senses. Cranes and gulls glided and swooped across the waters, graceful and languid as they flew. Far out, too far to be seen clearly, some great fish cleared the water with an enormous splash and disappeared. She let her gaze wander. The coastline ran unbroken from where she stood for as far as the eye could see, ragged, tree-grown bluffs backed by the stark, whitecapped mountains of the Rock Spur north and the Irrybis south. A series of rocky beaches separated the bluffs from the water, their stretches littered with driftwood and shells and ropes of seaweed.

Beyond the beaches, there was only the empty expanse of the Blue Divide. She had traveled to the end of the known world, she thought wryly, and still her search for the Elves went on.

An owl hooted in the deep woods behind her, causing her to turn. She cast about cautiously for movement, for any sign of disturbance, and found none. There was no hint of Garth. He was still out, tracking . . .

She ambled back to the cooling ashes of the cooking fire and nudged the remains with her boot. Garth had forbidden any sort of real fire until he made certain they were safe. He had been edgy and suspicious all day, troubled by something that neither of them could see, a sense of something not being right. Wren was inclined to attribute his uneasiness to lack of sleep. On the other hand, Garth's hunches were seldom wrong. If he was disturbed, she knew better than to question him.

She wished he would return.

A pool sat just within the trees behind the bluff and she walked to it, knelt, and splashed water on her face. The pond's surface rippled with the touch of her hands and cleared. She could see herself in its reflection, the distortion clearing until her image was almost mirrorlike. She stared down at it—at a girl barely grown, her features decidedly Elven with sharply pointed ears and slanted brows, her face narrow and high cheeked, and her skin nut-brown. She saw hazel eyes that seldom stayed fixed, an off-center smile that suggested she enjoyed some private joke, and ash-blond hair cut short and tightly curled. There was a tautness to her, she thought—a tension that would not be dispelled no matter how valiant the effort employed.

She rocked back on her heels and permitted herself a wry smile, deciding that she liked what she saw well enough to live with it awhile longer.

She folded her hands in her lap and lowered her head. The search for the Elves—how long had it been going on now? How long since the old man—the one who claimed he was Cogline—had come to her and told her of the dreams? Weeks? But how many? She had lost count. The old man had known of the dreams and challenged her to discover for herself the truth behind them. She had decided to accept his challenge, to go to the Hadeshorn in the Valley of Shale and meet with the shade of

Allanon. Why shouldn't she? Perhaps she would learn something of where she had come from, of the parents she had never known, or of her history.

Odd. Until the old man had appeared, she had been uninterested in her lineage. She had persuaded herself that it didn't matter. But something in the way he spoke to her, in the words he used—something—had changed her.

She reached up to finger the leather bag about her neck self-consciously, feeling the hard outline of the painted rocks, the play Elfstones, her only link to the past. Where did they come from? Why had they been given to her?

Elven features, Ohmsford blood, and Rover heart and skills—they all belonged to her. But how had she come by them?

Who was she?

She hadn't found out at the Hadeshorn. Allanon had come as promised, dark and forbidding even in death. But he had told her nothing. Instead, he had given her a charge—had given each of them a charge, the children of Shannara, as he called them, Par and Walker and herself. But hers? Well. She shook her head at the memory. She was to go in search of the Elves, to find them and bring them back into the world of Men. The Elves, who hadn't been seen by anyone in over a hundred years, who were believed by most never even to have existed, and who were presumed a child's faerie tale—she was to find them.

She had not planned to look at first, disturbed by what she had heard and how it had made her feel, unwilling to become involved, or to risk herself for something she did not understand or care about. She had left the others and with Garth once again her only companion had gone back into the Westland. She had thought to resume her life as a Rover. The Shadowen were not her concern. The problems of the races were not her own. But the Druid's admonition had stayed with her, and almost without realizing it she had begun her search after all. It had started with a few questions, asked here and there. Had anyone heard if there really were any Elves? Had anyone ever seen one? Did anyone know where they might be found? They were questions that were asked lightly at first, self-consciously, but with growing curiosity as time wore on, then almost an urgency.

What if Allanon were right? What if the Elves were still out there somewhere? What if they alone possessed whatever was necessary to overcome the Shadowen plague?

But the answers to her questions had all been the same. No one knew anything of the Elves. No one cared to know.

And then someone had begun following them—someone or something— their shadow as they came to call it, a thing clever enough to track them despite their precautions and stealthy enough to avoid being caught at it. Twice they had thought to trap it and failed. Any number of times they had tried to backtrack to get around behind it and been unable to do so. They had never seen its face, never even caught a glimpse of it. They had no idea who or what it was.

It had still been with them when they had entered the Wilderun and gone down into Grimpen Ward. There, two nights earlier, they had found the Addershag. A Rover had told them of the old woman, a seer it was said who knew secrets and who might know something of the Elves. They had found her in the basement of a tavern, chained and imprisoned by a group of men who thought to make money from her gift. Wren had tricked the men into letting her speak to the old woman, a creature far more dangerous and cunning than the men holding her had suspected.

The memory of that meeting was still vivid and frightening.

The old woman was a dried husk, and her face had withered into a maze of lines and furrows. Ragged white hair tumbled down about her frail shoulders. Wren approached and knelt before her. The ancient head lifted, revealing blind eyes that were milky and fixed.

"Are you the seer they call the Addershag, old mother?" Wren asked softly.

The staring eyes blinked and a thin voice rasped. "Who wishes to know? Tell me your name."

"My name is Wren Ohmsford."

Aged hands reached out to touch her face, exploring its lines and hollows, scraping along the skin like dried leaves. The hands withdrew.

"You are an Elf."

"I have Elven blood."

"An Elf!" The old woman's voice was rough and insistent, a hiss against the silence of the alehouse cellar. The wrinkled face cocked to one side as if reflecting. "I am the Addershag. What do you wish of me?"

Wren rocked back slightly on the heels of her boots. "I am searching for the Westland Elves. I was told a week ago that you might know where to find them—if they still exist."

The Addershag cackled. "Oh, they exist, all right. They do indeed. But it's not to everyone they show themselves—to none at all in many years. Is it so important to you, Elf-girl, that you see them? Do you search them out because you have need of your own kind?" The milky eyes stared unseeing at Wren's face. "No, not you. Why, then?"

"Because it is a charge I have been given—a charge I have chosen to accept," Wren answered carefully.

"A charge, is it?" The lines and furrows of the old woman's face deepened. "Bend close to me, Elf-girl."

Wren hesitated, then leaned forward tentatively. The Addershag's hands came up again, the fingers exploring. They passed once more across Wren's face, then down her neck to her body. When they touched the front of the girl's blouse, they jerked back as if burned and the old woman gasped. "Magic!" she howled.

Wren started, then seized the other's wrists impulsively. "What magic? What are you saying?"

But the Addershag shook her head violently, her lips clamped shut, and her head sunk into her shrunken breast. Wren held her a moment longer, then let her go.

"Elf-girl," the old woman whispered, "who sends you in search of the Westland Elves?"

Wren took a deep breath against her fears and answered, "The shade of Allanon."

The aged head lifted with a snap. "Allanon!" She breathed the name like a curse. "So! A Druid's charge, is it? Very well. Listen to me, then. Go south through the Wilderun, cross the Irrybis and follow the coast of the Blue Divide. When you have reached the caves of the Rocs, build a fire and keep it burning three days and nights. One will come who can help you. Do you understand?"

"Yes," Wren replied, wondering at the same time if she really did.

"Beware, Elf-girl," the other warned, a stick-thin hand lifting. "I see danger ahead for you, hard times, and treachery and evil beyond imagining. My visions are in my head, truths that haunt me with their madness. Heed me, then. Keep your own counsel, girl. Trust no one!"

Trust no one!

Wren had left the old woman then, admonished to leave even though she had offered to stay and help. She had rejoined Garth, and the men had tried to kill them then, of course, because that had been their plan all along. They had failed in their attempt and paid for their foolishness—perhaps with their lives by now if the Addershag had tired of them.

Slipping clear of Grimpen Ward, Wren and Garth had come south, following the old seer's instructions, still in search of the disappeared Elves. They had traveled for two days without stopping to sleep, anxious to put as much distance between themselves and Grimpen Ward as possible and eager as well to make yet another attempt to shake loose of their shadow. Wren had thought earlier that day they might have done so. Garth was not so certain. His uneasiness would not be dispelled. So when they had stopped for the night, needing at last to sleep and regain their strength, he had backtracked once more. Perhaps he would find something to settle the matter, he told her. Perhaps not. But he wanted to give it a try.

That was Garth. Never leave anything to chance.

Behind her, in the woods, one of the horses pawed restlessly and went still again. Garth had hidden the animals behind the trees before leaving. Wren waited a moment to be certain all was well, then stood and moved over again beneath the willow, losing herself in the deep shadows formed by its canopy, easing herself down once more against the broad trunk. Far to the west, the light had faded to a glimmer of silver where the water met the sky.

Magic, the Addershag had said. How could that be?

If there were still Elves, and if she was able to find them, would they be able to tell her what the old woman had not?

She leaned back and closed her eyes momentarily, feeling herself drifting, letting it happen.

When she jerked awake again, twilight had given way to night, the darkness all around save where moon and stars bathed the open spaces in a silver glow. The campfire had gone cold, and she shivered with the chill that had invaded the coastal air. Rising, she moved over to her pack, withdrew her travel cloak, and wrapped it about her for warmth. After moving back beneath the tree, she settled herself once more.

You fell asleep, she chided herself. *What would Garth say if he were to discover that?*

She remained awake after that until he returned. It was nearing midnight, the world about her gone still save for the lulling rush of the ocean waves as they washed onto the beach below. Garth appeared soundlessly, yet she had sensed he was coming before she saw him and took some small satisfaction from that. He moved out of the trees and came directly to where she hid, motionless in the night, a part of the old willow. He seated himself before her, huge and dark, faceless in the shadows. His big hands lifted, and he began to sign. His fingers moved swiftly.

Their shadow was still back there, following after them.

Wren felt her stomach grow cold and she hugged herself crossly.

"Did you see it?" she asked, signing as she spoke.

No.

"Do you know yet what it is?"

No.

"Nothing? Nothing about it at all?"

He shook his head. She was irritated by the obvious frustration she had allowed to creep into her voice. She wanted to be as calm as he was, as clear thinking as he had taught her to be. She wanted to be a good student for him.

She put a hand on his shoulder and squeezed. "Is it coming for us yet, Garth? Or waiting still?"

Waiting, he signed.

He shrugged, his craggy, bearded face expressionless, carefully composed. His hunter's look. Wren knew that look. It appeared when Garth felt threatened, a mask to hide what was happening inside.

Waiting, she repeated soundlessly to herself. Why? For what?

Garth rose, strode over to his pack, extracted a hunk of cheese and an aleskin, and reseated himself. Wren moved over to join him. He ate and drank without looking at her, staring off at the black expanse of the Blue Divide, seemingly oblivious of everything. Wren studied him thoughtfully. He was a giant of a man, strong as iron, quick as a cat, skilled in hunting and tracking, the best she had ever known at staying alive. He had been her protector and teacher from the time she was a little girl, after she had been brought back into the Westland and given over to the care of the Rovers, after her brief stay with the Ohmsford family. How had that all come about? Her father had been an Ohmsford, her mother a Rover, yet she could not remember either of them. Why had she been given back to the Rovers rather than allowed to stay with the Ohmsfords? Who had made that decision? It had never really been explained. Garth claimed not to know. Garth claimed that he knew only what others had told him, which was little, and that his only instruction, the charge he had accepted, was to look after her. He had done so by giving her the benefit of his knowledge, training her in the skills he had mastered, and making her as good at what he did as he was himself. He had worked hard to see that she learned her lessons. She had. Whatever else Wren Ohmsford might know, she knew first and foremost how to stay alive. Garth had made certain of that. But this was not training that a normal Rover child would receive—especially a girl-child—and Wren had known as much almost from the beginning. It led her to believe Garth knew more than he was telling. After a time, she became convinced of it.

Yet Garth would admit nothing when she pressed the matter. He would simply shake his head and sign that she needed special skills, that she was an orphan and alone, and that she must be stronger and smarter than the others. He said it, but he refused to explain it.

She became aware suddenly that he had finished eating and was watching her. The weathered, bearded face was no longer hidden by shadows. She could see the set of his features clearly and read what she found there. She saw concern etched in his brow. She saw kindness mirrored in his eyes. She sensed determination everywhere. It was odd, she thought, but he had always been able to convey more to her in a single glance than others could with a basketful of words.

"I don't like being hunted like this," she said, signing. "I don't like waiting to find out what is happening."

He nodded, his dark eyes intense.

"It has something to do with the Elves," she followed up impulsively. "I don't know why I feel that is so, but I do. I feel certain of it."

Then we should know something shortly, he replied.

"When we reach the caves of the Rocs," she agreed. "Yes. Because then we'll know if the Addershag spoke the truth, if there really are still Elves."

And what follows us will perhaps want to know, too.

Her smile was tight. They regarded each other wordlessly for a moment, measuring what they saw in each other's eyes, considering the possibility of what lay ahead.

Then Garth rose and indicated the woods. They picked up their gear and moved back beneath the willow. After settling themselves at the base of its trunk, they spread their bedrolls and wrapped themselves in their forest cloaks. Despite her weariness, Wren offered to stand the first watch, and Garth agreed. He rolled himself in his cloak, then lay down beside her and was asleep in seconds.

Wren listened as his breathing slowed, then shifted her attention to the night sounds beyond. It remained quiet atop the bluff, the birds and insects gone still, the wind a whisper, and the ocean a soothing, distant murmur. Whatever was out there hunting them seemed very far away. It was an illusion, she warned herself, and became all the more wary.

She touched the bag with its make-believe Elfstones where it rested against her breast. It was her good-luck charm, she thought, a charm to ward off evil, to protect against danger, and to carry her safely through whatever challenge she undertook. Three painted rocks that were symbols of a magic that had been real once but was now lost, like the Elves, like her past. She wondered if any of it could be recovered.

Or even if it should be.

She leaned back against the willow's trunk and stared out into the night, searching in vain for her answers.

3

At sunrise the following morning, Wren and Garth resumed their journey south in search of the caves of the Rocs. It was a journey of faith, for while both had traveled parts of the coastline neither had come across caves large enough to be what they were looking for or had ever seen a Roc. Both had heard tales of the legendary birds—great winged creatures that had once carried men. But the tales were only that, campfire stories that passed the time and conjured up images of things that might be but probably never were. There were sightings claimed, of course, as with every fairy-tale monster. But none was reliable. Like the Elves, the Rocs were apparently invisible.

Still, there didn't need to be Rocs in order for there to be Elves. The Addershag's admonition to Wren could prove out in any case. They had only to discover the caves, Rocs or no, build the signal fire, and wait three days. Then they would learn the truth. There was every chance that the truth would disappoint them, of course, but since they both recognized and accepted the possibility, there was no reason not to continue on. Their only concession to the unfavorable odds was to pointedly avoid speaking of them.

The day began clear and crisp, the skies unclouded and blue, the sunrise a bright splash across the eastern horizon that silhouetted the mountains in stark, jagged relief. The air filled with the mingled smells of sea and forest, and the songs of starlings and mockingbirds rose out of the trees. Sunshine quickly chased the chill left by the night and warmed the land beneath. The heat rose inland, thick and sweltering where the mountains trapped it, continuing to burn the grasses of the plains and hills a dusty brown as it had all summer, but the coastline remained cool and pleasant as a steady breeze blew in off the water. Wren and Garth kept their horses at a walk, following the narrow, winding coastal trails that navigated the bluffs and beaches fronting the mountains east. They were in no hurry. They had all the time they needed to get to where they were going.

There was time enough to be cautious in their passage through this unfamiliar country—time enough to keep an eye out for their shadow in case it was still following after them.

But they chose not to speak of that either.

Choosing not to speak about it, however, did not keep Wren from thinking about it. She found herself pondering the possibility of what might be back there as she rode, her mind free to wander where it chose as she looked out over the vast expanse of the Blue Divide and let her horse pick its way. Her darker suspicions warned her that what tracked them was something of the sort that had tracked Par and Coll on their journey from Culhaven to Hearthstone when they had gone in search of Walker Boh—a thing like the Gnawl. But could even a Gnawl avoid them as completely as their shadow had succeeded in doing? Could something that was basically an animal find them again and again when they had worked so hard to lose it? It seemed more likely that what tracked them was human—with a human's cunning and intelligence and skill: a Seeker, perhaps—sent by Rimmer Dall, a Tracker of extraordinary abilities, or an assassin, even, though he would have to be more than that to have managed to stay with them.

It was possible, too, she thought, that whoever was back there was not an enemy at all, but something else. "Friend" was hardly the right word, she supposed, but perhaps someone who had a purpose similar to their own, someone with an interest in the Elves, someone who . . .

She stopped herself. Someone who insisted on staying hidden, even knowing Garth and she had discovered they were being followed? Someone who continued playing cat and mouse with them so deliberately?

Her darker suspicions reemerged to push the other possibilities aside.

By midday they had reached the northern fringe of the Irrybis. The mountains split off in two directions, the high range turning east to parallel the northern Rock Spur and enclose the Wilderun, the low running south along the coastline they followed. The coastal Irrybis were thickly forested and less formidable, scattered in clusters along the Blue Divide, sheltering valleys and ridges, and forming passes that connected the inland hill country to the beaches. Nevertheless, travel slowed because the trails were less well defined, often disappearing entirely for long stretches. At times the mountains ran right up against the water, falling away in steep, impassable drops so that Wren and Garth were required to circle back to find another route. Heavy stands of timber blocked their path as well, forcing them to go around. They found themselves moving away from the beaches, higher into the mountain passes where the land was more open and accepting. They worked their way ahead slowly, watching as the sun drifted west to sink into the sea.

Night passed uneventfully, and they were awake again at daybreak and on their way. The morning chill again gave ground to midday heat. The ocean breezes that had cooled the previous day were less noticeable in the passes, and Wren found herself sweating freely. She shoved back her tousled hair, tied a scarf about her head, splashed water on her face, and forced herself to think about other things. She cataloged her memories as a child in

Shady Vale, trying to recall once again what her parents had been like. As usual, she found that she couldn't. What she remembered was vague and fragmented—bits and pieces of conversation, small moments out of time, or words or phrases out of context. All of what she recalled could as easily be identified with Par's parents as with her own. Had any of it come from her parents—or had it all come from Jaralan and Mirianna Ohmsford? Had she ever really known her parents? Had they ever been with her in Shady Vale? She had been told so. She had been told they had died. Yet she had no memory of it. Why was that so? Why had nothing about them stayed with her?

She glanced back at Garth, irritation mirrored in her eyes. Then she looked away again, refusing to explain.

They stopped to eat at midday and rode on. Wren questioned Garth briefly about their shadow. Was it still following? Did he sense anything? Garth shrugged and signed that he was no longer certain and that he no longer trusted himself on the matter. Wren frowned doubtfully, but Garth would say nothing further, his dark, bearded face unreadable.

The afternoon was spent crossing a ridgeline over which a raging forest fire had swept a year ago, leveling the land so thoroughly that only the blackened stumps of the old growth and the first green shoots of the new remained. From atop the spine of the ridge Wren could look back across the land for miles, her view unobstructed. There was nowhere that their shadow could hide, no space it could traverse without being seen. Wren looked for it carefully and saw nothing.

Yet she couldn't shake the feeling that it was still back there.

Nightfall brought them back along the rim of a high, narrow bluff that dropped away abruptly into the sea. Below where they rode, the waters of the Blue Divide crashed and boomed against the cliffs, and seabirds wheeled and shrieked above the white foam. They made camp in a grove of alder, close to where a stream trickled down out of the mountain rock and provided them with drinking water. To Wren's surprise, Garth built a fire so they could eat a hot meal. When Wren looked at him askance, the giant Rover cocked his head and signed that if their shadow was still following, it was also still waiting. They had nothing to fear yet. Wren was not so sure, but Garth seemed confident, so she let the matter drop.

She dreamed that night of her mother, the mother she could not remember and was uncertain if she had ever known. In the dream, her mother had no name. She was a small, quick woman with Wren's ash-blond hair and intense hazel eyes, her face warm and open and caring. Her mother said to her, *"Remember me."* Wren could not remember her, of course; she had nothing to remember her by. Yet her mother kept repeating the words over and over. *Remember me. Remember me.*

When Wren woke, a picture of her mother's face and the sound of her words remained. Garth did not seem to notice how distracted she was. They dressed, ate their breakfast, packed, and set out again—and the memory of the dream lingered. Wren began to wonder if the dream might be the resurrection of a truth that she had somehow kept buried over the years. Perhaps it really was her mother she had dreamed about, her mother's face she had remembered after all these years. She was hesitant to believe, but at the same time reluctant not to.

She rode in silence, trying in vain to decide which choice would end up hurting worse.

Midmorning came and went, and the heat grew oppressive. As the sun lifted from behind the rim of the mountains, the breezes off the ocean died away completely. The air grew still. Wren and Garth walked their horses to rest them, following the bluff until it disappeared completely and they were on a rocky trail leading upward toward a huge cliff mass. Sweat beaded and dried on their skin as they walked, and their feet became tired and sore. The seabirds disappeared, gone to roost, waiting for the cool of the evening to venture forth again to fish. The land and its hidden life grew silent. The only sound was the sluggish lapping of the waters of the Blue Divide against the rocky shores, a slow, weary cadence. Far out on the horizon, clouds began to build, dark and threatening. Wren glanced at Garth. There would be a storm before nightfall.

The trail they followed continued to snake upward toward the summit of the cliffs. Trees disappeared, spruce and fir and cedar first, then even the small, resilient stands of alder. The rock lay bare and exposed beneath the sun, radiating heat in thick, dull waves. Wren's vision began to swim, and she paused to wet her cloth headband. Garth turned to wait for her, impassive. When she nodded, they pressed on again, anxious to put this exhausting climb behind them.

It was nearing midday when they finally succeeded in doing so. The sun was directly overhead, white-hot and burning. The clouds that had begun massing earlier were advancing inland rapidly, and there was a hush in the air that was palpable. Pausing at the head of the trail, Wren and Garth glanced around speculatively. They stood at the edge of a mountain plain that was choked with heavy grasses and dotted with stands of gnarled, wind-bent trees that looked to be some variety of fir. The plain ran south between the high peaks and the ocean for as far as the eye could see, a broad, uneven collection of flats across which the sultry air hung thick and unmoving.

Wren and Garth glanced wearily at each other and started across. Overhead, the storm clouds inched closer to the sun. Finally they enveloped it completely, and a low breeze sprang up. The heat faded, and shadows began to blanket the land.

Wren slipped the headband into her pocket and waited for her body to cool.

They discovered the valley a short time after that, a deep cleft in the plain that was hidden until one was almost on top of it. The valley was broad, nearly half a mile across, sheltered against the weather by a line of knobby hills that lay east and a rise in the cliffs west and by broad stands of trees that filled it wall to wall. Streams ran through the valley; Wren could hear the gurgle even from atop the rim, rippling along rocks and down gullies. With Garth trailing, she descended into the valley, intrigued by the prospect of what she might find there. Within a short time they came upon a clearing. The clearing was thick with weeds and small trees, but devoid of any old growth. A quick inspection revealed the rubble of stone foundations buried beneath the undergrowth. The old growth had been cut away to make room for houses. People had lived here once—a large number of them.

Wren looked about thoughtfully. Was this what they were looking for? She shook her head. There were no caves—at least not here, but . . .

She left the thought unfinished, beckoned hurriedly to Garth, mounted her horse, and started for the cliffs west.

They rode out of the valley and onto the rocks that separated them from the ocean. The rocks were virtually treeless, but scrub and grasses grew out of every crack and crevice. Wren maneuvered to reach the highest point, a sort of shelf that overhung the cliffs and the ocean. When she was atop it, she dismounted. Leaving her horse, she walked forward. The rock was bare here, a broad depression on which nothing seemed able to grow. She studied it momentarily. It reminded her of a fire pit, scoured and cleansed by the flames. She avoided looking at Garth and walked to the edge. The wind was blowing steadily now and whipped against her face in sudden gusts as she peered down. Garth joined her silently. The cliffs fell away in a sheer drop. Pockets of scrub grew out of the rock in a series of thick clusters. Tiny blue and yellow flowers bloomed, curiously out of place. Far below, the ocean rolled onto a narrow, empty shoreline, the waves beginning to build again as the storm neared, turning to white foam as they broke apart on the rocks.

Wren studied the drop for a long time. The growing darkness made it difficult to see clearly. Shadows overlay everything, and the movement of the clouds caused the light to shift across the face of the rock.

The Rover girl frowned. There was something wrong with what she was looking at; something was out of place. She could not decide what it was. She sat back on her heels and waited for the answer to come.

Finally she had it. There were no seabirds anywhere—not a one.

She considered what that meant for a moment, then turned to Garth and signed for him to wait. She rose and trotted to her horse, pulled a rope free from her pack, and returned. Garth studied her curiously. She signed quickly, anxiously. She wanted him to lower her over the side. She wanted to have a look at what was down there.

Working silently, they knotted one end of the rope in sling fashion beneath Wren's arms and the other end about a projection close to the cliff edge. Wren tested the knots and nodded. Bracing himself, Garth began lowering the girl slowly over the edge. Wren descended cautiously, choosing hand and footholds as she went. She soon lost sight of Garth and began a prearranged series of tugs on the rope to tell him what she wanted.

The wind rushed at her, growing stronger now, pushing at her angrily. She hugged the cliff face to avoid being blown about. The clouds masked the sky overhead completely, building on themselves. A few stray drops of rain began to fall.

She gritted her teeth. She did not fancy being caught out in the open like this if the storm broke. She had to finish her exploration and climb up again quickly.

She backed down into a pocket of scrub. Thorns raked her legs and arms, and she pushed away angrily. Working through the brush, she continued down. Glancing over her shoulder, she could see something that had not been apparent before, a darkness against the wall, a depression. She fought to contain her excitement. She signaled Garth to give her more slack and dropped quickly along the rock. The darkness grew closer. It was larger than she had believed, a great black hole in the face. She peered through the gloom. She couldn't see what lay inside, but there were others as well, there, off to the side, two of them, and there, another, partially obscured by the brush, hidden by the rock . . .

Caves!

She signaled for more slack. The rope released, and she slid slowly toward the closest of the openings, eased toward its blackness, her eyes squinting . . .

Then she heard the sound, a rustling, from just below and within. It startled her, and for a moment she froze. She peered down again. Shadows shrouded everything, layers of darkness. She could see nothing. The wind blew shrilly, muffling other sounds.

Had she been mistaken?

She dropped another few feet, uncertain.

There, something . . .

She jerked frantically on the rope to halt her descent, hanging inches above the dark opening.

The Roc burst into view beneath her, exploding from the blackness as if shot from a catapult. It seemed to fill the air, wings stretched wide against the gray waters of the Blue Divide, across the shadows and clouds. It passed so close that its body brushed her feet and sent her spinning like a web-tangled piece of cotton. She curled into a ball instinctively, clinging to the rope as she would a lifeline, bouncing against the rough surface of the rock and fighting not to cry out, all the while praying the bird wouldn't see her. The Roc lifted away, oblivious to her presence or uncaring of it, a golden-hued body with a head the color of fire. It looked wild and ferocious, its plumage in disarray, its wings marked and scarred. It soared into the storm-filled skies west and disappeared.

And that's why there are no seabirds about, Wren confirmed to herself in a frightened daze.

She hung paralyzed against the cliff face for long moments, waiting to be certain that the Roc would not return, then gave a cautious tug on the rope and let Garth haul her to safety.

It began to rain shortly after she regained the summit of the cliffs. Garth wrapped her in his cloak and hustled her back to the valley where they found temporary shelter in a stand of fir. Garth built a fire and made soup to warm her. She stayed cold for a long time, shivering with the memory of hanging there helplessly as the Roc swept underneath, close enough to snatch her away, to make an end of her. Her mind was numb. She had thought to find the Roc caves in making her descent. She had never dreamed she would find the Rocs as well.

After she had recovered sufficiently to move again, after the soup had chased the chill from within her stomach, she began conversing with Garth.

"If there are Rocs, there might be Elves as well," she said, fingers translating. "What do you think?"

Garth made a face. *I think you almost got yourself killed.*

"I know," she admitted grudgingly. "Can we let that pass for now? I feel foolish enough."

Good, he indicated impassively.

"If the Addershag was right about the caves of the Rocs, don't you think there is a pretty fair chance she was right about the Elves as well?" Wren forged ahead. "I think so. I think someone will come if we light a signal fire. Right up on that ledge. In that pit. There have been fires there before. You saw. Maybe this valley was home to the Elves once. Maybe it still is. Tomorrow we'll build that signal fire and see what happens."

She ignored his shrug and settled back comfortably, her blankets wrapped close, her eyes bright with determination. The incident with the Roc was already beginning to recede into the back corners of her mind.

She slept until well after midnight, taking watch late because Garth chose not to wake her. She was alert for the remainder of the night, keeping her mind active with thoughts of what was to come. The rain ended, and by daybreak the summer heat was back, steamy and thick. They foraged for dry wood, cut pieces small enough to load, built a sled, and used the horses to haul their cuttings to the cliff edge. They worked steadily through the heat, careful not to overexert themselves or their animals, taking frequent rests, and drinking sufficient water to prevent heat stroke. The day stayed clear and sultry, the rains a distant memory. An occasional breeze blew in off the water but did little to cool them. The sea stretched away from the land in a smooth, glassy surface that from the cliff heights seemed as flat and hard as iron.

They saw nothing further of the Rocs. Garth believed them to be night birds, hunters that preferred the cover of darkness before venturing forth. Once or twice Wren thought she might have heard their call, faint and muffled. She would have liked to know how many nested in the caves and whether there were babies. But one brush with the giant birds was enough, and she was content to let her curiosity remain unsatisfied.

They built their signal fire in the stone depression on the rock ledge overlooking the Blue Divide. When sunset approached, Garth used his flint to ignite the kindling, and soon the larger pieces of wood were burning as well. The flames soared skyward, a red and gold glare against the fading light, crackling in the stillness. Wren glanced about in satisfaction. From this height, the fire could be seen for miles in every direction. If there were anyone out there looking, they would see it.

They ate dinner in silence, seated a short distance from the signal fire, their eyes on the flames, their minds elsewhere. Wren found herself thinking about her cousins, Par and Coll, and about Walker Boh. She wondered whether they had been persuaded, as she had, to take up the charges of Allanon. Find the Sword of Shannara, the shade had told Par. Find the Druids and lost Paranor, it had told Walker. And to her, find the missing Elves. If they did not, if any of them failed, then the vision it had shown them of a world turned barren and empty would come to pass, and the people of the races would become the playthings of the Shadowen. Her lean face tightened, and she brushed absently at a loose curl. The Shadowen—what were they? Cogline had spoken of them, she reflected, without actually revealing much. The history he had given them that night at the Hadeshorn was surprisingly vague. Creatures formed in the vacuum left with the failing of the magic at Allanon's death. Creatures born out of stray magic. What did that mean?

She finished her meal, rose, and walked out to the cliff edge. The night was clear and the sky filled with a thousand stars, their white light shimmering on the surface of the ocean to form a glittering tapestry of silver. Wren lost herself in the beauty of it for a time, basking in the evening cool, freed momentarily of her darker thoughts. When she came back to herself, she wished she knew better where she was going. What had once been a very certain, structured existence had turned surprisingly quixotic.

She moved back to the fire and rejoined Garth. The big man was arranging bedrolls carried up from the valley. They were to sleep by the fire and tend it until the three days elapsed or until someone came. The horses were tethered back in the trees at the edge of the valley. As long as it didn't rain, they would be comfortable enough sleeping in the open.

Garth offered to stand the first watch, and Wren agreed. She wrapped herself in her blankets at the edge of the fire's warmth and lay back. She watched the flames dance against the darkness, losing herself in their hypnotic motion, letting herself drift. She thought again of her mother, of her face and voice in the dream, and wondered if any of it was real.

Remember me.

Why couldn't she?

She was still mulling it over when she fell asleep.

She came awake again with Garth's hand on her shoulder. He had woken her hundreds of times over the years, and she had learned to tell from his touch alone what he was feeling. His touch now told her he was worried.

She rolled to her feet instantly, sleep forgotten. It was early yet; she could tell that much by a quick glance at the night sky. The fire burned on beside them, its glow undiminished. Garth was facing away, back toward the valley. Wren could hear something approaching—a scraping, a clicking, the sound of claws on rock. Whatever was out there wasn't bothering to hide its coming.

Garth turned to her and signed that everything had been completely still until just moments before. Their visitor must have drawn close at first on cat's feet, then changed its mind. Wren did not question what she was being told. Garth heard with his nose and his fingers and mostly with his instincts. Even deaf, he heard better than she did. *A Roc?* she suggested quickly, reminded of their clawed feet. Garth shook his head. *Then perhaps it was whoever the Addershag had promised would come?* Garth did not respond. He didn't have to. What approached was something else, something dangerous . . .

Their eyes locked, and abruptly she knew.

It was their shadow, come to reveal itself at last.

The scraping grew louder, more prolonged, as if whatever approached was dragging itself. Wren and Garth moved away from the fire a few steps, trying to put some of the light between themselves and their visitor, trying to put some of the darkness at their backs.

Wren felt for the long knife at her waist. Not much of a weapon. Garth gripped his hardened quarter staff. She wished she had thought to gather up hers, but she had left it with the horses.

Then a misshapen face pushed into the light, shoving out of the darkness as if tearing free of something. A muscled body followed. Wren went cold in the pit of her stomach. What stood before her wasn't real. It had the look of a huge wolf, all bristling gray hair, dark muzzle, and eyes that glittered with the fire's light. But it was grotesquely human, too. It had a human's forelegs with hands and fingers, though the hair grew everywhere, and the fingers ended in claws and were misshapen and thick with callouses. The head had something of a human cast to it as well—as if someone had fitted it with a wolf's mask and worked it like clay to make it fit.

The creature's head swung toward the fire and away again. Its hard eyes locked on them.

So this was their shadow. Wren took a slow breath. This was the thing that had tracked them relentlessly across the Westland, the thing that had followed after them for weeks. It had stayed hidden all that time. Why was it showing itself now?

She watched the muzzle draw back to reveal long rows of hooked teeth. The glittering eyes seemed to brighten. It made no sound as it stood before them.

It is showing itself now because it has decided to kill us, Wren realized, and was suddenly terrified.

Garth gave her a quick glance, a look that said everything. He had no illusions as to what was about to happen. He took a step toward the beast.

Instantly it came at him, a lunge that carried it into the big Rover almost before he could brace himself. Garth jerked his head back just in time to keep it from being ripped from his shoulders, whipped the quarter staff around, and flung his attacker aside. The wolf creature landed with a grunt, regained its footing in a scramble of clawed feet, and wheeled about, teeth bared. It came at Garth a second time, ignoring Wren completely. Garth was ready this time and slammed the end of the heavy quarter staff into the gnarled body. Wren heard the sound of bone cracking. The wolf thing tumbled away, came to its feet again, and began to circle. It continued to pay no attention to Wren, other than to make certain it could see what she was doing. It had apparently decided that Garth was the greater threat and must be dealt with first.

What are you? Wren wanted to scream. *What manner of thing?*

The beast tore into Garth again, barreling recklessly into the waiting staff. Pain did not seem to faze it. Garth flung it away, and it attacked again instantly, teeth snapping. Back it came, time after time, and nothing Garth did seemed to slow it. Wren crouched and watched, helpless to intervene without risking her friend. The wolf thing allowed her no opening and gave her no opportunity to strike. And it was quick, so swift that it was never down for more than an instant, moving with a fluid grace that suggested the agility of both man and beast. Certainly no wolf had ever moved like this, Wren knew.

The battle wore on. There were wounds to both combatants, but while Garth's blood streamed from the cuts he had suffered, the damage to the wolf creature seemed to heal almost instantly. Its cracked ribs should have slowed it, should have hampered its movements, but they did not. The blood from its cuts disappeared in seconds. Its injuries appeared not to concern it, almost as if . . .

And suddenly Wren remembered the story Par had told her of the Shadowen that he and Coll and Morgan Leah had encountered during their journey to Culhaven—that monstrous man thing, reattaching its severed arm as if pain meant nothing to it.

This wolf thing was a Shadowen!

The realization impelled her forward almost without thinking. She came at the creature with her long knife drawn, angry and determined as she bounded toward it. It turned, a hint of surprise reflected in its hard eyes, distracted momentarily from Garth. She reached it at the same instant that Garth did, and they had the beast trapped between them. Garth's staff hammered down across its skull, splintering with the force of the impact. Wren's blade buried itself in the bristling chest, sliding in smoothly. The creature jerked up and back, and for the first time made a sound. It shrieked, the cry of a woman in pain. Then it wheeled sharply and launched itself at Wren, bearing her down. It was enormously strong. Wren tumbled back, kicking up with her feet as she struggled to keep the hooked teeth from tearing her face. The wolf thing's momentum saved her, carrying it head over heels into the darkness. Wren scrambled to her feet. The long knife was gone, still buried in the beast's body. Garth's staff was ruined. He was already gripping a short sword.

The wolf thing came back into the light. It moved without pain, without effort, teeth bared in a terrifying grin.

The wolf thing.

The Shadowen.

Wren knew suddenly that they would not be able to kill it—that it was going to kill them.

She backed quickly to stand with Garth, frantic now, fighting to keep her reason. He withdrew his long knife and passed it to her. She could hear the ragged sound of his breathing. She could not bring herself to look at him.

The Shadowen came for them, hurtling forward in a rush. It shifted at the last instant toward Garth. The big Rover met its rush and turned it, but the force of the attack knocked him from his feet. Instantly the Shadowen was on him, snarling. Garth forced the sword between them, holding the wolf jaws back. Garth was stronger than any man Wren had ever known. But not stronger than this monster. Already she could see him weakening.

Garth!

She launched herself at the wolf thing, slamming the long knife into its body. It did not seem to notice. She clutched at the beast, struggling to dislodge it. Beneath, she could glimpse Garth's dark face, sweat stained and rigid. She screamed in fury.

Then the Shadowen shook itself, and she was thrown clear. She sprawled in a heap, weaponless, helpless. She hauled herself to her knees, aware suddenly that she was burning from the heat of the fire. The burning was intense—how long had it been there?—centered in her chest. She clawed at herself, thinking she had caught fire somehow. No, there were no flames, she realized, nothing at all except . . .

Her fingers flinched as they found the little leather bag with its painted rocks. The burning was there!

She yanked the bag free and almost without thinking about what she was doing poured the rocks into her palm.

Instantly they exploded into light, dazzling, terrifying. She found that she could not release them. The paint covering the rocks disappeared, and the rocks became . . . She could not bring herself to think the word, and there was no time for thinking in any case. The light flared and gathered like a living thing. From across the clearing, she saw the Shadowen's wolfish head jerk up. She saw the glitter of its eyes. She and Garth might still have a chance to survive, if . . .

She acted out of instinct, sending the light hurtling ahead with only a thought. It launched itself with frightening speed and hammered into the Shadowen. The wolf creature was flung away from Garth, twisting and shrieking. The light wrapped it about, fire everywhere, burning, consuming. Wren held her hand forth, commanding the fire. The magic terrified her, but she forced her terror down. Power coursed through her, dark and exhilarating, both at once. The Shadowen fought back, wrestling with the light, fighting to break free. It could not. Wren howled triumphantly as the Shadowen died, watching it explode and turn to dust and disappear.

Then the light disappeared as well, and she and Garth were alone.

W ren worked swiftly to bind Garth's wounds. No bones were broken, but he had suffered a series of deep lacerations on his forearms and chest, and he was cut and bruised from head to foot. He lay back against the earth as she knelt above him applying the healing salves and herbs that Rovers carried everywhere, his dark face calm. Iron Garth. The great, muscular body flinched once or twice as she cleaned and bandaged, stitched and bound, but that was all. Nothing showed on his face or revealed in his eyes the trauma and pain he had endured.

Tears came to her eyes momentarily, and she bent her head so he would not see. He was her closest friend, and she had very nearly lost him.

If not for the Elfstones . . .

And they were Elfstones. Real Elfstones.

Don't think about it!

She concentrated harder on what she was doing, blocking out her anxious, frightened thoughts. The signal fire burned on, flames leaping at the darkness, and wood crackling as it disintegrated with the heat. She labored in silence, yet she could hear everything about her—the fire's roar, the whistle of the wind across the rocks, the lapping of waves against the shore, the hum of insects far back in the valley, and the hiss of her own breathing. It was as if all of the night sounds had been magnified a hundredfold—as if she had been placed in a great, empty canyon where even the smallest whisper had an echo.

She finished with Garth and for a moment felt faint, a swarm of images swimming before her eyes. She saw again the wolf thing that was a Shadowen, all teeth and claws and bristling hair. She saw Garth, locked in combat with the monster. She saw herself as she rushed to help him, a vain attempt. She saw the fire's glow spread across them all like blood. She saw the Elfstones come to life, flaring with white light, with ancient power, filling the night with their brilliance, lancing out and striking the Shadowen, burning it as it struggled to break free . . .

She tried to rise and fell back. Garth caught her in his arms, having risen somehow to his knees, and eased her to the ground. He held her for a moment, cradled her as he might a child, and she let him, her face buried against his body. Then she pushed gently away, taking slow, deep breaths to steady herself. She rose and moved over to their cloaks, retrieved them and brought them back to where Garth waited. They wrapped themselves against the night's chill and sat staring at each other wordlessly.

Finally Wren lifted her hands and began to sign. *Did you know about the Elfstones?* she asked.

Garth's gaze was steady. *No.*

Not that they were real, not what they could do, nothing?

No.

She studied his face for a moment without moving. Then she reached into her tunic and drew out the leather bag that hung about her neck. She had slipped the Elfstones back inside when she had gone to help Garth. She wondered if they had transformed again, if they had returned to being the painted rocks they once were. She even wondered if she had somehow been mistaken in what she had seen. She turned the bag upside down and shook it over her hand.

Three bright blue stones tumbled free, painted rocks no longer, but glittering Elfstones—the Elfstones that had been given to Shea Ohmsford by Allanon over five hundred years ago and had belonged to the Ohmsford family ever since. She stared at them, entranced by their beauty, awed that she should be holding them. She shivered at the memory of their power.

"Garth," she whispered. She placed the Elfstones in her lap. Her fingers moved. "You must know something. You must. I was given into your care, Garth. The Elfstones were with me even then. Tell me. Where did they really come from?"

You already know. Your parents gave them to you.

My parents. She felt a welling up of pain and frustration. "Tell me about them. Everything. There are secrets, Garth. There have always been secrets. I have to know now. Tell me."

Garth's dark face was frozen as he hesitated, then signed to her that her mother had been a Rover and that her father had been an Ohmsford. They brought her to the Rovers when she was a baby. He was told that the last thing they did before leaving was to place the leather bag with its painted rocks about her neck.

"You did not see my mother. Or my father?"

Garth shook his head. He was away when they came and when he returned they were gone. They never came back. Wren was taken to Shady Vale to be raised by Jaralan and Mirianna Ohmsford. When she was five, the Rovers took her back again. That was the agreement the Ohmsfords had made. It was what her parents had insisted upon.

"But why?" Wren interrupted, bewildered.

Garth didn't know. He had never even been told who had made the bargain on behalf of the Rovers. She was given into his care by one of the family elders, a man who had died shortly after. No one had ever explained

why he was to train her as he did—only what was to be done. She was to
be quicker, stronger, smarter, and better able to survive than any of them.
Garth was to make her that way.

Wren sat back in frustration. She already knew everything that Garth
was telling her. He had told it all to her before. Her jaw tightened angrily.
There must be something more, something that would give her some insight
into where she had come from and why she was carrying the Elfstones.

"Garth," she tried again, insistent now. "What is it that you haven't told
me? Something about my mother? I dreamed of her, you know. I saw her
face. Tell me what you are hiding!"

The big man was expressionless, but there was hurt in his eyes. Wren
almost reached out to reassure him, but her need to know kept her from
doing so. Garth stared at her for long moments without responding. Then
his fingers signed briefly.

I can tell you nothing that you cannot see for yourself.

She flinched. "What do you mean?"

*You have Elven features, Wren. More so than any Ohmsford. Why do you
think that is?*

She shook her head, unable to answer.

His brow furrowed. *It is because your parents were both Elves.*

Wren stared in disbelief. She had no memory at all of her parents looking like Elves and she had always thought of herself as simply a Rover girl.

"How do you know this?" she asked, stunned.

*I was told by one who saw them. I was also told that it would be dangerous for
you to know.*

"Yet you choose to tell me now?"

Garth shrugged, as much as if to say, What difference does it make after
what has happened? How much more danger can you be in by knowing?
Wren nodded. Her mother a Rover. Her father an Ohmsford. But both of
them Elves. How could that be? Rovers weren't Elves.

"You're sure about this?" she repeated. "Elves, not humans with Elven
blood, but Elves?"

Garth nodded firmly and signed, *It was made very clear.*

To everyone but her, she thought. How had her parents come to be
Elves? None of the Ohmsfords had been Elves, only of Elven descent with
some percentage of Elven blood. Did this mean that her parents had lived
with the Elves? Did it mean that they had come from them and that this
was why Allanon had sent her in search of the Elves, because she herself was one?

She looked away, momentarily overwhelmed by the implications. She
saw her mother's face again as she had seen it in her dream—a girl's face, of
the race of Man, not Elf. That part of her that was Elf, those more distinctive features, had not been evident. Or had she simply missed seeing them?
What about her father? Funny, she thought. He had never seemed very important in her musings of what might have been, never as real, and she had
no idea why. He was faceless to her. He was invisible.

She looked back again. Garth was waiting patiently. "You did not know that the painted rocks were Elfstones?" she asked one final time. "You knew nothing of what they were?"

Nothing.

What if she had discarded them? she asked herself peevishly. What then of her parents' plans—whatever they were—for her? But she knew the answer to that question. She would never have given up the painted rocks, her only link to her past, all she had to remind her of her parents. Had they relied on that? Why had they given her the Elfstones in the first place? To protect her? Against what? Shadowen? Something more? Something that hadn't even existed when she was born?

"Why do you think I was given these Stones?" she asked Garth, genuinely confused.

Garth looked down a moment, then up again. His great body shifted. He signed. *Perhaps to protect you in your search for the Elves.*

Wren stared, blank faced. She had not considered that possibility. But how could her parents have known she would go in search of the Elves? Or had they simply known she would one day seek out her own heritage, that she would insist on knowing where she had come from and who her people were?

"Garth, I don't understand," she confessed to him. "What is this all about?"

But the big man simply shook his head and looked sad.

They kept watch together through the night, one dozing while the other stayed awake, until finally dawn's light brightened the eastern skies. Then Garth fell asleep until noon, his strength exhausted. Wren sat staring out at the vast expanse of the Blue Divide, pondering the implications behind her discovery of the Elfstones. They were the Elfstones of Shea Ohmsford, she decided. She had heard them described often enough, listened to stories of their history. They belonged to whomever they were given and they had been given to the Ohmsford family—and then lost again, supposedly. But perhaps not. Perhaps they had been simply taken away at some point. It was possible. There had been many Ohmsfords after Brin and Jair and three hundred years in which to lose track of the magic— even a magic as personal and powerful as the Elfstones. There had been a time when no one could use them, she reminded herself. Only those with sufficient Elven blood could invoke the magic with impunity. Wil Ohmsford had been damaged that way. His use of the Stones had caused him to absorb some of their magic. When his children were born, Brin and Jair, the magic had transformed itself into the wishsong. So perhaps one of the Ohmsfords had decided to take the Elfstones back to those who could use them safely—to the Elves. Was that how they had found their way to her parents?

The questions persisted, overwhelming, insistent, and unanswerable. What was it that Cogline had said to her when he had found her that first time in the Tirfing and persuaded her to come with him to the Hadeshorn to meet with Allanon? *It is not nearly so important to know who you are as who you might be.* She was beginning to see how that might be true in a way she had never envisioned.

Garth rose at noon and ate the vegetable stew and fresh bread she had prepared. He was stiff and sore, and his strength had not yet returned. Nevertheless, he thought it necessary that he make a sweep of the area to make certain that there wasn't another of the wolf things about. Wren had not considered the possibility. Both of them had recognized their attacker as a Shadowen—a thing once human that had become part beast, a thing that could track and hunt, that could hide and stalk, and that could think as well as they and kill without compunction. No wonder it had tracked them so easily. She had assumed it had come alone. It was an assumption she could not afford to make. She told Garth that she was the one who would go. She was better suited at the moment than he, and she had the Elfstones. She would be protected.

She did not tell him how frightened she was of the Elven magic or how difficult she would find it if she were required to invoke it again.

As she backtracked the country south and east, searching for prints, for signs, or for anything out of place, relying mostly on her instincts to warn her of any danger, she thought about what it meant to be in possession of such magic. She remembered when Par had kidded her about the dreams, saying that she had the same Elven blood as he and perhaps some part of the magic. She had laughed. She had only her painted rocks, she had said. She remembered the Addershag's touch at her breast where the Elfstones hung in their leather bag and the unbidden cry of "Magic!" She hadn't even thought of the painted rocks that time. All her life she had known of the Ohmsford legacy, of the magic that had belonged to them as the descendants of the Elven house of Shannara. Yet she had never thought to have use of the magic herself, never even desired it. Now it was hers as the Elfstones were hers, and what was she to do about it? She did not want the responsibility of the Stones or their magic. She wanted nothing of the legacy. The legacy was a millstone that would drag her down. She was a Rover, born and raised free, and that was what she knew and was comfortable with being—not any of this other. She had accepted her Elven looks without questioning what they might imply. They were part of her, but a lesser part, and nothing at all of the Rover she was. She felt as if she had been turned inside out by the discovery of the Elfstones, as if the magic by coming into her life was somehow taking life out of her and making her over. She did not like the feeling. She was not anxious to be changed into someone other than who she was.

She pondered her discomfort all that day and had not come close to resolving it on her return to the camp. The signal fire was a guiding beacon, and she followed its glow to where Garth waited. He was anxious for her— she could see it in his eyes. But he said nothing, passing her food and drink and sitting back quietly to watch her eat. She told him she had not found any trace of other Shadowen. She did not tell him that she was beginning to have second thoughts about this whole business. She had asked herself once before, once right at the beginning when she had decided she would try to learn something about who she was, What would happen if she did not like what she discovered? She had dismissed the possibility. She was worried now that she had made a very big mistake.

The second night passed without incident. They kept the signal fire burning steadily, feeding it new wood as the old was consumed, patiently waiting. Another day began and ended, and still no one appeared. They searched the skies and the land from horizon to horizon, but there was no sign of anyone. By nightfall, both were edgy. Garth, his superficial wounds already healed and the deeper ones beginning to close, prowled the camp-site like a caged animal, repeating meaningless tasks to keep from having to sit. Wren sat to keep from prowling. They slept as often as they could, rest-ing themselves because they needed to and because it was something to do. Wren found herself doubting the Addershag, questioning the old woman's words. How long had the Addershag been a captive of those men, chained and imprisoned in that cellar? Perhaps her memory had failed her in some way. Perhaps she had become confused. But she had not sounded feeble or confused. She had sounded dangerous. And what about the Shadowen that had tracked them the length and breadth of the Westland? All those weeks it had kept hidden, following at a distance. It had shown itself only after the signal fire had been lit. Then it had come forth to destroy them. Wasn't it reasonable to assume that its appearance had been brought about by what it was seeing them do, that it believed the signal fire posed some sort of threat and so must be stopped? Why else would it have chosen that moment to strike?

So don't give up, Wren kept telling herself, the words a litany of hope to keep her confidence from failing completely. Don't give up.

The third night dragged away, minutes into hours. They changed the watch frequently because by now neither could sleep for more than a short time without waking. More often than not they kept watch together— uneasy, anxious, worried. They fed deadwood into the flames and watched the fire dance against the night. They stared out over the black void above the Blue Divide. They sifted through the night sounds and their scat-tered thoughts.

Nothing happened. No one came.

It was nearing morning when Wren dozed off in spite of herself, some time during the final hour of her watch. She was still sitting up, her legs crossed, her arms about her knees, and her head dipped forward. It seemed only moments had passed when she jerked awake again. She glanced about warily. Garth was asleep a few feet away, wrapped in his great cloak. The fire continued to burn fiercely. The land was cloaked in a frost-tipped blan-ket of shadows and half-light, the sunrise no more than a faint silver light-ening at the rim of the mountains east. A scattering of stars still brightened the sky west, although the moon had long since disappeared. Wren yawned and stood up. Clouds were moving in from out on the ocean, low-hanging, dark . . .

She started. She was seeing something else, she realized, something blacker and swifter, moving out of the darkness for the bluffs, streaking directly for her. She blinked to make certain, then stepped back hurriedly and reached down for Garth. The big Rover was on his feet at once. Together they faced out across the Divide, watching the black thing take shape. It was a Roc, they realized after a few seconds more, winging its way toward the fire like a moth drawn by the flames. It swept across the bluff and wheeled back again, its outline barely visible in the faint light. It flew over them twice, turning each time, crossing and recrossing as if studying what lay below. Wren and Garth watched wordlessly, unable to do anything else.

Finally, the Roc plummeted toward them, its massive body whistling overhead, so close it might have snatched them up with its great claws if it had wished. Wren and Garth flattened themselves against the rocks protectively and stared as the bird settled comfortably down at the edge of the cliffs, a giant, black-bodied creature with a head as scarlet as fire and wings greater than those on the bird that Wren had barely escaped days earlier.

Wren and Garth climbed back to their feet and brushed themselves off.

There was a man seated astride the Roc, held in place by straps from a leather harness. They watched as the man released the straps and slid smoothly to the ground. He stood next to the bird and studied them momentarily, then started forward. He was small and bent, wearing a tunic, pants, boots, and gloves made of leather. He walked with an oddly rolling gait, as if not altogether comfortable with the task. His features were Elven, narrow and sharp, and his face was deeply lined. He wore no beard, and his brown hair was short cropped and peppered with gray. Fierce black eyes blinked at them with alarming rapidity.

He came to a stop when he was a dozen feet away.

"Did you light that fire?" he demanded. His voice was high-pitched and rough about the edges.

"Yes," Wren answered him.

"Why did you do that?"

"Because I was told to."

"Were you now? By whom, if you don't mind my asking?"

"I don't mind at all. I was told to light it by the Addershag."

The eyes blinked twice as fast. "By the what?"

"An old woman, a seer I spoke with in Grimpen Ward. She is called the Addershag."

The little man grunted. "Grimpen Ward. Ugh! No one in his right mind goes there." His mouth tightened. "Well, why did this Addershag tell you to light the fire, eh?"

Wren sighed impatiently. She had waited three days for someone to come and she was anxious to discover if this gnarled little fellow was the person she had been expecting or not. "Let me ask you something first," she replied. "Do you have a name?"

The frown deepened. "I might. Why don't you tell me yours first?"

Wren put her hands on her hips challengingly. "My name is Wren Ohmsford. This is my friend Garth. We're Rovers."

"Hah, is that so now? Rovers, are you?" The little man chuckled as if enjoying some private joke. "Got a bit of Elf in you, too, it looks."

"Got a bit in you as well," she replied. "What's your name?"

"Tiger Ty," the other said. "At least, that's what everyone calls me. All right now, Miss Wren. We've introduced ourselves and said hello. What are you doing out here, Addershag and what-all notwithstanding? Why'd you light that fire?"

Wren smiled. "Maybe to bring you and your bird, if you're the one who can take us to the Elves."

Tiger Ty grunted and spit. "That bird is a Roc, Miss Wren. He's called Spirit. Best of them all, he is. And there aren't any Elves. Everyone knows that."

Wren nodded. "Not everyone. Some think there are Elves. I've been sent to see if that's so. Can you and Spirit help?"

There was a long silence as Tiger Ty scrunched his face into a dozen different expressions. "Big fellow, your friend Garth, isn't he? I see you telling him what we're saying with your hands. Bet he hears better than we do, push come to shove." He paused. "Who are you, Miss Wren, that you would care to know whether there are Elves or not?"

She told him, certain now that he was the one for whom the signal fire was intended and that he was simply being cautious about what he revealed until he found out whom he was dealing with. She disclosed her background, revealing that she was the child of an Elf and a Rover, searching for some link to her past. She advised him of her meeting with the shade of Allanon and the Druid's charge that she go in search of the missing Elves, that she discover what had become of them, and that she return them to the world of Men so that they could take part in the battle against the Shadowen.

She kept quiet about the Elfstones. She was not yet ready to trust anyone with that information.

Tiger Ty shifted and fidgeted as she talked, his face worrying itself into a dozen different expressions. He seemed heedless of Garth, his attention focused on Wren. He carried no weapons save for a long knife, but with Spirit standing watch she supposed he had no need of weapons. The Roc was clearly his protector.

"Let's sit," Tiger Ty said when she had finished, pulling off his leather gloves. "Got anything to eat?"

They seated themselves beside the now-forgotten signal fire, and Wren produced a collection of dried fruit, a little bread, and some ale. They ate and drank in silence, Wren and Garth exchanging occasional glances, Tiger Ty ignoring them both, absorbed in the task of eating.

When they were finished, Tiger Ty smiled for the first time. "A good start to the day, Miss Wren. Thanks very much."

Wren nodded. "You're welcome. Now tell me. Was our fire meant for you?"

The leathery face furrowed. "Well, now. Depends, you know. Let me ask you, Miss Wren. Do you know anything of Wing Riders?"

Wren shook her head no.

"Because that's what I am, you see," the other explained. "A Wing Rider. A flyer of the skylanes, a watcher of the Westland coast. Spirit is my Roc, trained by my father, given to me when I became old enough. One day he'll go to my son, if my son proves out. There's some question about it just now. Fool boy keeps winging about where he's not supposed to. Doesn't pay attention to what I tell him. Impetuous. Anyway, Wing Riders have flown their Rocs along the Blue Divide for hundreds of years. This very spot, right here—and back there in the valley—was our home once. It was called the Wing Hove. That was in the time of the Druid Allanon. You see, I know a few things."

"Do you know the Ohmsford name?" Wren asked impulsively.

"There was a tale about an Ohmsford some several hundred years ago when the Elves fought demons released out of the Forbidding. Wing Riders fought in that war, too, they say. But there was an Ohmsford, I'm told. Relation of yours?"

"Yes," she said. "Twelve generations removed."

He nodded thoughtfully. "So that's you, is it? A child of the house of Shannara?"

Wren nodded. "I suppose that's why I've been sent to find the Elves, Tiger Ty."

Tiger Ty looked doubtful. "Wing Riders are Elves, you know," he said carefully. "But we're not the Elves you're looking for. The Elves you're looking for are Land Elves, not Sky Elves. Do you understand the difference?"

She shook her head no once more. He explained then that the members of the Wing Hove were Sky Elves and considered themselves a separate people. The majority of the Elves were called Land Elves because they had no command of the Rocs and therefore could not fly.

"That's why they didn't take us with them when they left," he finished, eyebrows arched. "That's why we wouldn't have gone with them in any case."

Wren felt her pulse quicken. "Then there are still Elves, aren't there? Where are they, Tiger Ty?"

The gnarled little man blinked and squinched up his leathery face. "Don't know if I should tell you that," he opined. "Don't know if I should tell you anything. You might be who you say. Then again, you might not. Even if you are, maybe it's not for you to know about the Elves. The Druid Allanon sent you, you say? Told you to find the Elves and bring them back? Tall order, if you ask me."

"I could use a little help," Wren admitted. "What would it hurt you to give it to me, Tiger Ty?"

He ceased his ruminations and rocked back thoughtfully. "Well, now, you've got a point there, Miss Wren," he replied, nodding in agreement with himself. "Besides, I sort of like what I see in you. My son could use a little of what you've got. On the other hand, maybe that's what he's already got too much of! Humph!"

He cocked his head and his sharp eyes fixed her. "Out there," he said, pointing to the Blue Divide. "That's where they are, the ones that are left." He paused, scowling. "It's a long story, so make certain you listen close because I don't intend to repeat myself. You, too, big fellow." He indicated Garth with a menacing finger.

Then he took a deep breath and sat back. "Long time ago, better than a hundred years, the Land Elves held a council and decided to migrate out of the Westland. Don't ask me why; I don't pretend to know. The Federation, mostly, I'd guess. Pushing in, taking over, pretending everything that ever was or ever would be belonged to them. And blaming everything on the magic and saying it was all the fault of the Elves. Lot of nonsense. Land Elves didn't like it in any case and decided to leave. Problem was, where could they go? Wasn't as if there was anywhere a whole people could move to without upsetting someone already settled in. Eastland, Southland, Northland—all taken. So they asked us. Sky Elves get around more than most, see places others don't even know exist. So we said to them, well, there's some islands out there in the Blue Divide that no one lives on, and they thought it over, talked about it, took a few flights out on the Rocs with Wing Riders, and came to a decision. They picked a gathering spot, built boats—hundreds of them, all in secret—and off they went."

"All of them?"

"Every last one, so I'm told. Sailed away."

"To live on the islands?" Wren asked, incredulous.

"One island." Tiger Ty held up a single finger for emphasis. "Morrowindl."

"That was its name? Morrowindl?"

The other nodded. "Biggest of all the islands, better than two hundred miles across, ideal for farming, something like the Sarandanon already planted. Fruits, vegetables, trees, good soil, shelter—everything. Hunting was good, too. The Land Elves had some notion about starting over, taking themselves out of the old world, and beginning again in the new. Isolate themselves all over again, let the other races do what they wanted with themselves. Wanted their magic back, too—that was part of it."

He cleared his throat. "As I said, that was a long time ago. After a while, we migrated, too. Not so far, you understand—just to the islands offshore, just far enough away to keep the Federation from hunting us. Elves are Elves to them. We'd had enough of that kind of thinking. Not so many of us to make the move, of course; not like the Land Elves. We needed less space and could settle for the smaller islands. That's where we still are, Miss Wren. Out there, couple miles offshore. Only come back to the mainland when it's necessary—like when someone lights a signal fire. That was the agreement we made."

"Agreement with whom?"

"With the Land Elves. A few who remained behind of the other races knew to light the fire if there was need to talk to us. And a few of the Elves came back over the years. So some knew about the fire. But most have long since died. This Addershag—I don't know how she found out."

"Back up a moment, Tiger Ty," Wren requested, holding out her hands placatingly. "Finish your story about the Land Elves first. What happened to them? You said they migrated more than a hundred years ago. What became of them after that?"

Tiger Ty shrugged. "They settled in, made a home, raised their families, and were happy. Everything worked out the way they thought it would—at first. Then about twenty years ago, they started having trouble. It was hard to tell what the problem was; they wouldn't discuss it with us. We only saw them now and again, you see. Still didn't mix much, even after we'd migrated out, too. Anyway, everything on Morrowindl began to change. It started with Killeshan, the volcano. Dormant for hundreds of years and suddenly it came awake again. Started smoking, spitting, erupted once or twice. Clouds of vog—you know, volcanic ash—started filling the skies. The air, the land, the water about—it was all different." He paused, a hard look darkening his face. "They changed, too—the Land Elves. Wouldn't admit it, but we saw that something was different. You could see it in the way they behaved when we were about—guarded, secretive about everything. Armed to the teeth everywhere they went. And strange creatures began appearing on the island, monstrous things, things that had never been there before. Just appeared, just out of nothing. And the land began to grow sick, changing like everything else."

He sighed. "The Land Elves began to die off then, a few at a time, more after a while. They had lived all over the island once; they quit doing that and moved into their city, all jammed together like rats in a sinking ship. They built fortifications and reinforced them with magic. Old magic, you know, brought back out of time and the old ways. Sky Elves want nothing to do with it, but we've never used the magic anyway like them."

He sat back. "Ten years ago, they disappeared completely."

Wren started. "Disappeared?"

"Vanished. Still on Morrowindl, mind. But gone. Island was a mass of ash and mist and steamy heat by then, of course. Changed so completely it might have been a different place entirely." He tightened his frown. "We couldn't get in to find out what had happened. Sent half a dozen Wing Riders. Not a one came back. Not even the birds. And no one came out. No one, Miss Wren. Not in all that time."

Wren was silent for a moment, thinking. The sun was up now, warm light cascading down from atop the Irrybis, the cloudless morning sky bright and friendly. Spirit remained perched on the cliff edge, oblivious to them. The Roc was a statue frozen in place. Only his sharp, searching eyes registered life.

"So if there are any Elves left," Wren said finally, "any Land Elves, that is, they're still on Morrowindl somewhere. You're sure about that, Tiger Ty?"

The Wing Rider shrugged. "Sure as I can be. I suppose they could have disappeared to somewhere else, but it's odd that they didn't get word to us."

Wren took a deep breath. "Can you take us to Morrowindl?" she asked.

It was an impulsive request, born out of a fierce and quixotic determination to discover a truth that was apparently hidden not only from herself but from everyone else as well. She recognized how selfish she was being. She had not even considered asking Garth for his thoughts; she had not even bothered to remember how badly he had been injured in their fight with the Shadowen. She couldn't bring herself to look at him now. She kept her eyes fastened on Tiger Ty.

There was no mistaking what he thought of the idea. The little man scowled fiercely. "I *could* take you to Morrowindl," he said. "But I won't."

"I have to know if there are any Elves left," she insisted, trying to keep her voice level. Now she risked a quick glance at Garth. The big Rover's face registered nothing of what he was thinking. "I have to discover if they can be brought back into the world of Men. It was Allanon's charge to me, and I guess I believe it important enough to carry it out."

"Allanon, again!" Tiger Ty snapped irritably. "You'd risk your life on the word of a shade? Do you have any idea what Morrowindl is like? No, of course you don't! Why do I even ask? You didn't hear a word I said, did you? You think you can just walk in and look around and walk out again? Well, you can't! You wouldn't get twenty feet, Miss Wren—you or your big friend! That whole island is a death trap! Swamp and jungle, vog choking off everything, Killeshan spitting fire. And the things that live there, the monsters? What sort of chance do you think you'll have against them? If a Wing Rider and his Roc couldn't land and come out again, you sure as demon's blood can't either!"

"Maybe," Wren agreed. "But I have to try." She glanced again at Garth, who signed briefly, not a rebuke, but a caution. *Are you certain about this?* She nodded resolutely, saying to Tiger Ty, "Don't you want to know what's happened to them? What if they need help?"

"What if they do?" he growled. "What are the Sky Elves supposed to do? There's only a handful of us. There were thousands of them. If they couldn't deal with what's there, what chance would we have? Or you, Miss Rescuer?"

"Will you take us?" she repeated.

"No, I will not! Forget the whole business!" He rose in a huff.

"Very well. Then we'll build a boat and reach Morrowindl that way."

"Build a boat! What do you know about building boats! Or sailing them for that matter!" Tiger Ty was incensed. "Of all the foolish, pigheaded . . . !"

He stormed off toward Spirit, then stopped, kicked at the earth, wheeled, and came back again. His seamed face was crimson, his hands knotted into fists.

"You mean to do this thing, don't you?" he demanded. "Whether I help you or not?"

"I have to," she answered calmly.

"But you're just . . . You're only . . ." He sputtered, seemingly unable to complete the thought.

She knew what he was trying to say and she didn't like it. "I'm stronger than you think," she told him, a hard edge to her voice now. "I'm not afraid."

Tiger Ty stared long and hard at her, glanced briefly at Garth, and threw up his hands. "All right, then!" He leveled a scorching glare at her. "I'll take you! Just to the shoreline, mind, because unlike you I'm good and scared and I don't fancy risking my neck or Spirit's just to satisfy your curiosity!"

She met his gaze coolly. "This doesn't have anything to do with satisfying my curiosity, Tiger Ty. You know that."

He dropped down in front of her, his sun-browned face only inches from her own. "Maybe. But you listen. I want your promise that after you see what you're up against, you'll rethink this whole business. Because despite the fact that you're a bit short of common sense, I kind of like you and I'd hate to see anything bad happen to you. This isn't going to turn out the way you think. You'll see that soon enough. So you promise me. Agreed?"

Wren nodded solemnly. "Agreed."

Tiger Ty stood up, hands on hips, defiant to the end. "Come on, then," he muttered. "Let's get this over with."

5

Tiger Ty was anxious to be off, but he was forced to wait almost an hour while Wren and Garth went back down into the valley to gather up the gear and weapons they would carry with them on their journey and to provide for their horses. The horses were tethered, and Garth released them so that they could graze and drink as they needed. The valley provided grass and water enough on which to survive, and the horses were trained not to wander. Wren sorted through their provisions, choosing what they would need and be able to carry. Most of their supplies were too cumbersome, and she stashed them for when they returned.

If they returned, she thought darkly.

What had she done? Her mind spun with the enormity of the commitment she was making, and she was forced to wonder, if only in the privacy of her own thoughts, whether she would have cause to regret her brashness.

When they regained the cliffs, Tiger Ty was waiting impatiently. Bidding Spirit to stand, he helped Wren and Garth climb atop the giant bird and fasten themselves in place with the straps of the harness. There were foot loops, knotted hand grips, and a waist restraint, all designed to keep them safely in place. The Wing Rider spent long moments telling them how the Roc would react once in flight and how flying would make them feel. He gave them each a bit of bitter-tasting root to chew on, advising that it would keep them from being sick.

"Not that a couple of seasoned veterans of the Rover life should be bothered by any of this," he chided, managing a grin that was worse than his scowl.

He clambered aboard in front of them, settled himself comfortably, pulled on his heavy gloves, and without warning gave a shout and whacked Spirit on the neck. The giant bird shrieked in response, spread his wings, and lifted into the air. They cleared the edge of the cliffs, dipped sharply downward, caught a current of wind, and rose skyward. Wren felt her stomach lurch. She closed her eyes against what she was feeling, then opened them again, aware that Tiger Ty was looking over his shoulder at her, chuckling. She smiled back bravely. Spirit flattened out above the Blue Divide, wings barely moving, letting the wind do the work. The coastline behind them grew small, then lost definition. Soon it was nothing more than a thin dark line against the horizon.

Time slipped away. They saw nothing below them save for a scattering of rocky atolls and the occasional splash of a large fish. Seabirds wheeled and dived in small white flashes, and clouds lay along the western horizon like strips of gauze. The ocean stretched away, a vast, flat blue surface streaked with the foaming crests of waves that rolled endlessly toward distant shores. After a time Wren was able to dismiss her initial uneasiness and settle back. Garth was less successful in adjusting. He was seated immediately behind her, and whenever she glanced back at him she found his dark face rigid and his hands clutched about the restraining straps. Wren quit looking at him and concentrated on the sweep of the ocean ahead.

She soon began thinking about Morrowindl and the Elves. Tiger Ty did not seem the sort to exaggerate the danger she faced if she persisted in trying to penetrate the island. It was true enough that she was determined to discover what had become of the Elves; it was also true that her discovery would serve little purpose if she didn't survive to do something about it. And what exactly did she expect to do? Suppose the Elves were still there on Morrowindl? Suppose they were alive? If no one had gotten in or out in ten years, how was her appearance going to change anything? Why, whatever their present circumstances, would the Elves even consider what Allanon had sent her to propose—that they abandon life outside the Four Lands and return?

She had no answers to these questions, of course. It was pointless to try to find any. She had made her decisions up to now based strictly on instinct—to search for the Elves in the first place, to seek out the Addershag in Grimpen Ward and then to follow her directions, to persuade Tiger Ty to convey them to Morrowindl. She could not help but wonder if her instincts had misled her. Garth had stayed with her, virtually without argument, but Garth could be doing so out of loyalty or friendship. He might have resolved to see this matter through, but that didn't mean he had any better sense of what they were about than she did. She scanned the empty expanse of the Blue Divide, feeling small and vulnerable. Morrowindl was an island in the middle of the ocean, a tiny speck of earth amid all that water. Once she and Garth were there, they would be isolated from everything familiar. There would be no way off again without the aid of a Roc or a boat, nor was it certain there would be anyone on the island who could help them. There might no longer be any Elves. There might be only the monsters . . .

Monsters. She considered for a moment the question of what sort of monsters were there. Tiger Ty had failed to say. Were they as dangerous as the Shadowen? If so, then that would explain why the Elves had disappeared. Enough of these monsters could have trapped them, she supposed, or even destroyed them. But how had the Elves let such a thing happen? And if the monsters hadn't trapped them, then why did the Elves still remain on Morrowindl? Why hadn't even one of them escaped to seek help?

There were so many questions once again. She closed her eyes and willed them away.

It was approaching noon when they passed over a cluster of small islands that looked like emeralds floating in the sea, brilliant green against the blue. Spirit circled for a moment under Tiger Ty's direction, then descended toward the largest, choosing a narrow bluff thick with grasses to land upon. Once the great bird was settled, his riders released their safety straps and climbed down. Wren and Garth were stiff and sore already, and it took a few moments for them to get their limbs working again. Wren rubbed her aching joints and glanced around. The island appeared to be formed of a dark, porous rock on which vegetation grew as if on rich soil. The rock lay everywhere, crunching beneath their feet when they walked on it. Wren reached down and picked up a piece, finding it surprisingly light.

"Lava rock," Tiger Ty said with a grunt, seeing the puzzled look on her face. "All these islands are part of a chain formed by volcanoes sometime in the past, hundreds, maybe thousands of years ago." He paused, made a face, and then pointed. "The islands the Sky Elves live upon are just south. Course, we're not going there, you understand. I don't want anyone to discover I'm taking you to Morrowindl. I don't want them finding out how stupid I am."

He moved over to a grassy knoll and seated himself. After pulling off his gloves and boots, he began massaging his feet. "We'll have something to eat and drink in a minute," he muttered.

Wren said nothing. Garth had stretched out full length in the grass and his eyes were closed. He was happy, she thought, to be on the ground again. She put down the rock she had been examining and moved over to sit with Tiger Ty.

"You spoke of monsters on Morrowindl," she said after a minute. A soft breeze ruffled her hair, blowing curls across her face. "Can you tell me anything about them?"

The sharp eyes fastened on her. "There's all kinds, Miss Wren. Big and little, four-legged and two, flying, crawling, and stalking. There's those with hair, those with scales, and those with skin. Some come out of your worst nightmares. Some, they say, aren't living things. They hunt in packs, some of them. Some burrow in the earth and wait." He shook his gray-peppered head. "I've only seen one or two myself. Most I've just heard described. But they're there right enough." He paused, considering. "Odd though, isn't it, that there's so many different kinds? Odd, too, that there weren't any at first and then all of a sudden they just started to appear."

"You think the Elves had something to do with it." She made it a statement of fact.

Tiger Ty pursed his lips thoughtfully. "I have to think that. It has to have something to do with their recovery of the magic—their return to the old ways. They wouldn't say so, wouldn't admit to a thing, the few I talked to. Ten years ago, that was. More, I guess. They claimed it all had something to do with the volcano and the changes in the earth and climate. Imagine that."

He smiled disarmingly. "That's the way it is, you know. Nobody wants to tell you the truth. Everybody wants to keep secrets." He paused to rub his chin. "Take yourself, for instance. I don't suppose you want to tell me what happened back there at the Wing Hove, do you? While you were waiting for me to spy your fire?" He watched her face. "See, I'm pretty quick to pick up on things. I don't miss much. Like your big friend over there, all bandaged up the way he is. Scratched and marked from a fight, a recent one, a bad one. You have a few marks yourself. And there was a dark scar on the rocks, the kind made from a very hot fire. Wasn't where the signal fire usually burns and it was new. And the rock was scraped pretty bad a place or two. From iron dragging, I'd guess. Or claws."

Wren had to smile in spite of herself. She regarded Tiger Ty with new-found admiration. "You're right—you don't miss much. There was a fight, Tiger Ty. Something tracked us for weeks, a thing we call a Shadowen." She saw recognition in his eyes instantly. "It attacked us when we lit the signal fire. We destroyed it."

"Did you now?" the little man sniffed. "Just the two of you. A Shadowen. I know a little of the Shadowen. Way I understand it, it would take something special to destroy one of them. Fire, maybe. The kind that comes from Elven magic. That would account for the burn on the rock, wouldn't it?"

He waited. Wren nodded slowly. "It might."

Tiger Ty leaned forward. "You're like the rest of them somehow, aren't you, Miss Wren. You're an Ohmsford like the others. You have the magic, too."

He said it softly, speculatively, and there was a curiosity mirrored in his eyes that hadn't been there before. He was right again, of course. She did have the magic, a discovery she had pointedly avoided thinking about since she had made it because to do otherwise would be to acknowledge that she had some responsibility for its possession and use. She continued to tell herself that the Elfstones did not really belong to her, that she was merely a caretaker and an unwilling one at that. Yes, they had saved Garth's life. And her own. And yes, she was grateful. But their magic was dangerous. Everyone knew that. She had been taught all of her life to be self-sufficient, to rely upon her instincts and her training, and to remember that survival was dependent principally on your own abilities and thought. She did not want a reliance on the magic of the Elfstones to undermine that.

Tiger Ty was still looking at her, waiting to see if she was going to respond. Wren met his gaze boldly and did not.

"Well," he said finally, and shrugged his disinterest. "Time to get a bite to eat."

The island was thick with fruit trees, and they made a satisfactory meal from what they picked. Afterward, they drank from a freshwater stream they found inland. Flowers grew everywhere—bougainvillea, oleander, hibiscus, orchids, and many more—massive bushes filled with their blooms, the colors bright through the green, the scents wafting on the air at every turn. There were palms, acacia, banyan, and something called a ginkgo. Strange birds perched in the branches of armored, spiny recops, their plumage a rainbow's blend. Tiger Ty described it all as they walked, pointing, identifying and explaining. Wren stared about in amazement, not permitting her gaze to linger anywhere for more than a few seconds, anxious that she not miss anything. She had never seen such beauty, a profusion of incredibly wonderful living things. It was almost overpowering.

"Was Morrowindl like this?" she asked Tiger Ty at one point.

He gave her a brief glance. "Once," he replied, and did not elaborate.

They climbed back atop Spirit shortly afterward and resumed their flight. It was easier now, a bit more familiar, and even Garth seemed to have discovered a way to make the journey bearable. They flew west and north, angling away from the sun as it passed overhead. There were other islands, small and mostly rocky, though all sustained at least a sprinkling of growth. The air was warm and soothing against their skin, and the sun burned down out of a cloudless sky, brightening the Blue Divide until it glistened.

They saw massive sea animals that Tiger Ty called whales and claimed were the largest creatures in the ocean. There were birds of all sizes and shapes. There were fish that swam in groups called schools and leapt from the water in formation, silver bodies arcing against the sun. The journey became an incredible learning experience for Wren, and she immersed herself in its lessons.

"I have never seen anything like this!" she shouted enthusiastically at Tiger Ty.

"Wait until we reach Morrowindl," he grunted back.

They descended a second time for a brief rest at midafternoon, choosing a solitary island with wide, white-sand beaches and coves so shallow the water was a pale turquoise. Wren noticed that Spirit had not eaten all day and asked about it. Tiger Ty said the Roc consumed meat and hunted on its own. It required food only once every seven days.

"A very self-sustaining bird, the Roc," the Wing Rider said with undisguised admiration. "Doesn't ask much more than to be left alone. More than you can say about most people."

They continued their journey in silence, both Wren and Garth beginning to tire now, stiff from sitting in the same position all day, worn from the constant rocking motion of the flight, and from gripping the knotted hand restraints until their fingers cramped. The waters of the Blue Divide passed steadily beneath, an endless progression of waves. They had been out of sight of the mainland for hours, and the ocean seemed to stretch away forever. Wren felt dwarfed by it, reduced by its size to something so insignificant she threatened to disappear. Her earlier sense of isolation had increased steadily with the passing of the hours, and she found herself wondering for the first time if she would ever see her home again.

It was nearing sunset when at last they came in sight of Morrowindl. The sun had drifted west to the edge of the horizon, its light growing soft, changing from white to pale orange. A streaking of purple and silver laced a long line of odd-shaped clouds that paraded across the sky like strange animals. Silhouetted against this panorama was the island, dark and misted and forbidding. It was much larger than any other landmass they had encountered, rising up like a wall as they approached. Killeshan lifted its jagged mouth skyward, steam seeping from its throat, slopes dropping away into a thick blanket of fog and ash, disappearing for hundreds of feet until they surfaced again at a shoreline formed of rocky projections and ragged cliffs. Waves crashed against the rocks, white foaming caldrons that threw their spray skyward.

Spirit flew closer, winging down toward the shroud of vog. A stench filled the air, the smell of sulfur escaped from beneath the earth where the volcano's fire burned rock to ash. Through the clouds and mist they could see valleys and ridges, passes and defiles, all heavily forested, a thick, strangling jungle. Tiger Ty glanced back over his shoulder and gestured. They were going to circle the island. Spirit wheeled right at his command. The north end of the island was engulfed in driving rain, a monsoon that inundated everything, creating vast waterfalls that tumbled down cliffs thousands of feet high. West the island was as barren as a desert, all exposed lava rock except for a scattering of brightly flowering shrubs and stunted, gnarled, wind-blown trees. South and east the island was a mass of singular rock formations and black-sand beaches where the shoreline met the waters of the Blue Divide before rising to disappear into jungle and mist.

Wren stared down at Morrowindl apprehensively. It was a forbidding, inhospitable place, a sharp contrast to the other islands they had seen. Weather fronts collided and broke apart. Each side of the island offered a different set of conditions. The whole of it was shadowed and clouded, as if Killeshan were a demon that breathed fire and had wrapped itself in the cloak of its own choking breath.

Tiger Ty wheeled Spirit about one final time, then took him down. The Roc settled cautiously at the edge of a broad, black-sand beach, claws digging into the crushed lava rock, wings folding reluctantly back. The giant bird turned to face the jungle, and his piercing eyes fixed on the mist.

Tiger Ty ordered them to dismount. They released their harness straps and slid to the beach. Wren looked inland. The island rose before her, all rock and trees and mist. They could no longer see the sun. Shadows and half-light lay over everything.

The Wing Rider faced the girl. "I suppose you're still set on this? Stubborn as ever?"

She nodded wordlessly, unwilling to trust herself to speak.

"You listen, then. And think about changing your mind while you do. I showed you all four sides of Morrowindl for a reason. North, it rains all the time, every day, every hour of the day. Sometimes it rains hard, sometimes drizzles. But the water is everywhere. Swamps and pools, falls and drops. If you can't swim, you drown. And there's nests of things waiting to pull you down in any case."

He gestured with his hand. "West is all desert. You saw. Nothing but open country, hot and dry and barren. You could walk it all the way to the top of the mountain, you probably think. Trouble is, you wouldn't get a mile before you ran crosswise of the things that live under the rock. You'd never see them; they'd have you before you could think. There's thousands of them, all sizes and shapes, most with poison that will kill you quick. Nothing gets through."

His frown etched the lines of his seamed face even deeper. "That leaves south and east, which it happens are pretty much the same. Rock and jungle and vog and a lot of very unpleasant things that live within. Once off this beach, you won't be safe again until you're back. I told you once that it was a death trap in there. I'll tell you again in case you didn't hear me.

"Miss Wren," he said softly. "Don't do this. You don't stand a chance."

She reached out impulsively and took his gnarled hands in her own. "Garth and I will look out for each other," she promised. "We've been doing so for a long time."

He shook his head. "It won't be enough."

She tightened her grip. "How far must we travel to find the Elves? Can you give us some idea?"

He released himself and pointed inland. "Their city, if it's still there, sits halfway down the mountain in a niche that's protected from the lava flows. Most of the flows run east and some of those tunnel under the rock to the sea. From here, it's maybe thirty miles. I don't know what the land's like in there anymore. Ten years changes a lot of things."

"We'll find our way," she said. She took a deep breath to steady herself, aware of how impossible this effort was likely to prove. She glanced at Garth, who stared back at her stone-faced. She looked again at Tiger Ty. "I need to ask one thing more of you. Will you come back for us? Will you give us sufficient time to make our search and then come back?"

Tiger Ty folded his arms across his chest, his leathery face managing to look both sad and stern. "I'll come, Miss Wren. I'll wait three weeks—time enough for you to make it in and get out again. Then I'll look for you once a week four weeks running." He shook his head. "But I have to tell you that I think it will be a waste of time. You won't be back. I won't ever see you again."

She smiled bravely. "I'll find a way, Tiger Ty."

The Wing Rider's eyes narrowed. "Only one way. You better be meaner and stronger than anything you run up against. And—" He jabbed at her with a bony finger. "—you better be prepared to use your magic!"

He wheeled abruptly and stalked to where Spirit waited. Without pausing, he pulled himself up the harness loops and settled into place. When he had finished fastening the safety straps, he looked back at them.

"Don't try going in at night," he advised. "The first day, at least, travel when it's light. Keep Killeshan's mouth to your right as you climb." He threw up his hands. "Demon's blood, but this is a foolish thing you're doing!"

"Don't forget about us, Tiger Ty!" Wren called in reply.

The Wing Rider scowled at her for an instant, then kicked Spirit lightly. The Roc lifted into the air, wings spreading against the wind, rising slowly, wheeling south. In seconds, the giant bird had become nothing more than a speck in the fading light.

Wren and Garth stood silently on the empty beach and watched until the speck had disappeared.

They remained on the beach that first night, heeding the advice of Tiger Ty to wait until it was daybreak before starting in. They chose a spot about a quarter of a mile north from where the Wing Rider had dropped them to set up their camp, a broad, open expanse of black sand where the tide line ended more than a hundred feet from the jungle's edge. It was already twilight by then, the sun gone below the horizon, its failing light a faint shimmer against the ocean's waters. As darkness descended, pale silver light from moon and stars flooded the empty beach, reflecting off the sand as if diamonds had been scattered, brightening the shoreline for as far as the eye could see. They quickly ruled out having a fire. Neither light nor heat was required. Situated as they were on the open beach, they could see anything trying to approach, and the air was warm and balmy. A fire would only succeed in drawing attention to them, and they did not want that.

They ate a cold meal of dried meat, bread, and cheese and washed it down with ale. They sat facing the jungle, their backs to the ocean, listening and watching. Morrowindl lost definition as night fell, the sweep of jungle and cliffs and desert disappearing into blackness until at last the island was little more than a silhouette against the sky. Finally even that disappeared, and all that remained was a steady cacophony of sounds. The sounds were indistinguishable for the most part, faint and muffled, a scattering of calls and hoots and buzzings, of birds and insects and animals, all lost deep within the sheltering dark. The waters of the Blue Divide rolled in steady cadence against the island's shores, washing in and retreating again, a slow and steady lapping. A breeze sprang up, soft and fragrant, washing away the last of the day's lingering heat.

When they had finished their meal, they stared wordlessly ahead for a time—at the sky and the beach and the ocean, at nothing at all.

Already Morrowindl made Wren feel uneasy. Even now, cloaked in darkness, invisible and asleep, the island was a presence that threatened. She pictured it in her mind, Killeshan rising up against the sky with its ragged maw open, a patchwork of jungled slopes, towering cliffs, and barren deserts, a chained giant wrapped in vog and mist, waiting. She could feel its breath on her face, anxious and hungry. She could hear it hiss in greeting.

She could sense it watching.

It frightened her more than she cared to admit, and she could not seem to dispel her fear. It was an insidious shadow that crept through the corridors of her mind, whispering words whose meanings were unintelligible but whose intent was clear. She felt oddly bereft of her skills and her training, as if all had been stripped from her at the moment she had arrived. Even her instincts seemed muddled. She could not explain it. It made no sense. Nothing had happened, and yet here she was, her confidence shredded and scattered like straw. Another woman might have been able to take comfort from the fact that she possessed the legendary Elfstones—but not Wren. The magic was foreign to her, a thing to be mistrusted. It belonged to a past she had only heard about, a history that had been lost for generations. It belonged to someone else, someone she did not know. The Elfstones, she thought darkly, had nothing to do with her.

The words brought a chill to the pit of her stomach. They, of course, were a lie.

She put her hands over her face, hiding herself away. Doubts crowded in on every side, and she wondered briefly, futilely, whether her decision to come to Morrowindl had been wrong.

Finally she took her hands away and edged forward until she was close enough in the darkness to see clearly Garth's bearded face. The big man watched unmoving as she lifted her hands and began to sign.

Do you think I made a mistake by insisting we come here? she asked him.

He studied her for a moment, then shook his head. *It is never a mistake to do something you feel is necessary.*

I did feel it necessary.

I know.

"But I did not come just to discover if the Elves are still alive," she said, fingers moving. "I came to find out about my parents, to learn who they were and what became of them."

He nodded without replying.

"I didn't use to care, you know," she went on, trying to explain. "It didn't use to make any difference. I was a Rover, and that was enough. Even after Cogline found us and we went east to the Hadeshorn and met with the Shade of Allanon, even when I began asking about the Elves, hoping to learn something of what had happened to them, I wasn't thinking about my parents. I didn't have any idea where it was all leading. I just went along, asking my questions, learning finally of the Addershag, then of the signal fire. I was just following a trail, curious to see where it would lead."

She paused. "But the Elfstones, Garth—that was something I hadn't counted on. When I discovered that they were real—that they were the Elfstones of Shea and Wil Ohmsford—everything changed. So much power—and they belonged to my parents. Why? How did my parents come by them in the first place? What was their purpose in giving them to me? You see, don't you? I won't ever have any answers unless I find out who my parents were."

Garth signed, *I understand. I wouldn't be here with you if I didn't.*

"I know that," she whispered, her throat tightening. "I just wanted to hear you say it."

They were silent for a moment, eyes turned away. Something huge splashed far out in the water. The sound reverberated momentarily and disappeared. Wren pushed at the rough sand with her boot.

Garth, she signed, catching his eye. *Is there anything about my parents that you haven't told me?*

Garth said nothing, his face expressionless.

"Because if there is," she signed, "you have to tell me now. You cannot let me continue with this search not knowing."

Garth shifted, his head lowering into shadow. When he lifted it again, his fingers began to move. *I would not keep anything from you that was not necessary. I keep nothing from you now about your parents. What I know, I have told you. Believe me.*

"I do," she affirmed quietly. Yet the answer troubled her. Was there something else he kept from her, something he considered necessary? Did she have the right to demand to know what it was?

She shook her head. He would never hurt her. That was the important thing. Not Garth.

We will discover the truth about your parents, he signed suddenly. *I promise.*

She reached out briefly to take his hands, then released them. "Garth," she said, "you are the best friend I shall ever have."

She kept watch then while he slept, feeling comforted by his words, reassured that she was not alone after all, that they were united in their purpose. Hidden by the darkness, Morrowindl continued to brood, sinister and threatening. But she was not so intimidated now, her resolve strengthened, her purpose clear. It would be as it had been for so many years—she and Garth against whatever waited. It would be enough.

When Garth woke at midnight, she went quickly to sleep.

Sunrise brightened the skies with pale silver, but Morrowindl was a black wall that shut that light away. The island stood between the dawn on the one hand and Garth and Wren on the other as if seeking to lock the Rovers permanently in shadow. The beach was still and empty, a black line that stretched away into the distance like a scattered bolt of mourning crepe. Rocks and cliffs jutted out of the green tangle of the jungle, poking forth like trapped creatures seeking to breathe. Killeshan thrust skyward in mute silence, steam curling from fissures down the length of its lava-rock skin. Far distant to the north, a glimpse of the island's desert side revealed a harsh, broken surface over which a blanket of sulfuric mist had been thrown and on which nothing moved.

The Rover girl and her companion washed and ate a hurried breakfast, anxious to be off. The day's heat was already beginning to settle in, chasing the ocean's breezes back across her waters. Seabirds glided and swooped about them, casting for food. Crabs scuttled about the rocks cautiously, seeking shelter in cracks and crevices. All about, the island was waking up.

Wren and Garth shouldered their packs, checked the readiness of their weapons, glanced briefly at each other, and started in.

The beach faded into a short patch of tall grass that in turn gave way to a forest of towering acacia. The trunks of the ancient trees rose skyward like pillars, running back until distance gave them the illusion of being a wall. The floor of the forest was barren and cleared of scrub; storms and risen tides had washed away everything but the giant trees. Within the acacia, all was still. The sun was masked yet in the east, and shadows lay over everything. Wren and Garth walked slowly, steadily ahead, watchful for any form of danger. They passed out of the acacia and into a stand of bamboo. They skirted it until they found a narrowing of the growth and used short swords to hack their way through. From there they proceeded along a meadow where the grasses were waist-high and wildflowers grew in colorful profusion amid the green. Ahead, the forest rose along the slopes of Killeshan, trees and brush amid odd formations of lava rock, all of it disappearing finally into the vog.

The first day passed without incident. They traveled through open country whenever they could find it, choosing a path that let them see what they were walking into. They camped that night in a meadow, comfortably settled on high ground that again gave them a clear view in all directions. The second day passed in the same manner as the first. They made good progress, navigating rivers and streams and climbing ravines and foothills without difficulty. There was no sign of the monsters that Tiger Ty had warned them about. There were brightly colored snakes and spiders that were most certainly poisonous, but the Rovers had dealt with their cousins in other parts of the world and knew enough to avoid any contact. They heard the harsh cough of moor cats, but saw nothing. Once or twice predatory birds flew overhead, but after a series of cursory passes these hunters soon sped away in search of easier prey. It rained frequently and heavily, but never for very long at one time, and except for threatening to trap them in dry riverbeds with an unexpected flash flood or to drop them into newly formed sinkholes, the rain did little more than cool them off.

All the while the haze blanketing Killeshan's slopes drew closer, a promise of harsher things to come.

The third day began in the same way as the two before, shadowed and still and brooding. The sun rose and was visible briefly through the trees ahead, a warm and inviting beacon. Then abruptly it disappeared as the lower edges of the vog descended. The haze was thin and untroubling at first, not much more than a thickening of the air, a graying of the light. But slowly it began to deepen, gathering in patches that screened away everything more than thirty feet from where they walked. The country grew rougher as the shoreline lowlands and grassy foothills gave way to slides and drops, and the lava rock turned crumbly and loose. Footing grew uncertain and the pace slowed.

They ate a hurried, troubled, silent lunch and started out again cautiously. They tied thick hides about their legs above the boot tops and below the knees to protect against snakes. They pulled on their heavy cloaks and wrapped them close. The heat of the lower slopes was absent here, and the air—which they had thought would turn warm as they moved closer to Killeshan—grew cold. Garth took the lead, deliberately shielding Wren. Shadows moved all about them in the mist, things that lacked shape and form but were there nevertheless. The familiar sounds of birds and insects died away, fading into an expectant hush. Dusk fell early, a draining away of light, and rain began to fall in steady sheets.

They made their camp at the foot of an ancient koa that fronted a small clearing. With their backs to the tree, they ate their dinner and watched the light deepen from smoke to charcoal. The rain slowed to an intermittent drizzle, and mist began to creep down the mountainside in probing tendrils. Already the forest was beginning to turn to jungle, the trees thickly grown and tangled with vines, the ground damp and soft and yielding. Slugs and beetles crawled through brush and rotting logs. The ground was dry beneath the koa, but the dampness in the air seemed to penetrate everywhere. There was no possibility of a fire. Wren and Garth hunched within their cloaks and pushed closer to each other. The night settled down about them, turning the world an inky black.

Wren offered to stand the first watch, too edgy to sleep. Garth acquiesced without comment. He pulled up his knees, put his head on his crossed arms, and was asleep almost immediately.

Wren sat staring into the blackness. The trees and mist screened away any light from moon and stars, and even after her eyes had adjusted it was impossible to see more than a dozen feet from where she kept watch. Shadows drifted at the periphery of her vision, brief, quick, and suggestive. Sounds darted out of the haze to challenge and tease—the shrill call of night birds, the click of insects, scrapes and rustlings, huffings and snarls. The low cough of hunting cats came from somewhere distant. She could smell faintly the sulfur fumes of Killeshan, wafting on the air, mingling with the thicker, more pungent scents of the jungle. All around her an invisible world was waking up.

Let it, she thought defiantly.

The air grew still as even the drizzle faded away and only fog remained. Time slipped away. The sounds slowed and softened, and there was a sense that everything out there in the blackness lay in wait, that everything watched. She was aware that the shadows at the edge of the encroaching mist had faded away. Garth was snoring softly. She shifted her cramped body but made no effort to rise. She liked the feel of the tree against her back and Garth pressing close. She hated how the island made her feel— exposed, vulnerable, unprotected. It was the newness, she told herself. It was the unfamiliarity of the terrain, the isolation from her own country, the memory of Tiger Ty's warning that there were monsters here. It would take time to adjust . . .

She left the thought unfinished as she saw the silhouette of something huge appear at the edge of the mist. It walked upright on two legs momentarily, then dropped down on four. It stopped and she knew it was looking at her. The hair on the back of her neck prickled, and she edged her hand down until her fingers closed about the long knife at her waist.

She waited.

The thing that watched did not move. It seemed to be waiting with her.

Then she saw another of the shadows appear, similar to the first. And another. And a fourth. They gathered in the darkness and went still, invisible eyes glittering. Wren took slow, deep breaths. She thought about waking Garth, but told herself over and over that she would wait just one more minute, just long enough to see what would happen.

But nothing happened. The minutes crawled past, and the shadows stayed where they were. Wren wondered how many were out there. Then she wondered if they were behind her where she couldn't see them, sneaking up until they were close enough to . . .

She turned quickly and looked. There was nothing there. At least, nothing within the limited range of her vision.

She turned back again. She knew suddenly that the things in the darkness were waiting to see what she would do, trying to ascertain how dangerous she might be. If she sat there long enough they would grow impatient and decide to test her. She wondered how much time she had. She wondered what it would take to discourage them. If the monsters were here already, only three nights off the beach, they would be there every night from here on in, watching and waiting. And there would be others. There were bound to be.

Wren's blood pumped through her, racing as quickly as her thoughts. Together, Garth and she were a match for most things. But they could not afford to fight everything they came across.

The shadows had begun to move again, restless. She heard murmurings, not words exactly, but something. She could feel movement all about her, something other than the shadows, things she could not see. The inhabitants of the jungle had discovered them and were gathering. She heard a growl, low and menacing. Beside her, Garth shifted in his sleep, turning away.

Wren's face felt hot.

Do something, she whispered to herself. *You have to do something.*

She knew without looking that the shadows were behind her now.

She felt a burning against her breast.

Almost without thinking, she reached down into her tunic and removed the leather bag with the Elfstones. Swiftly, unwilling to think about what she was doing, she shook the Stones into her hand and quickly closed her fingers about them. She could feel the shadows watching.

Just a hint of what they can do, she told herself. *That should be enough.*

She stretched forth her hand and let her fingers open slightly. The blue light of the Elfstones brightened. It gathered, a cold fire, and issued forth in thin streamers to probe the darkness.

Instantly the shadows were gone. They disappeared so swiftly and so completely that they might never have been there. The sounds died into a hush. The world became a vacuum, and she and Garth were all that remained within it.

She closed her fingers tightly again and withdrew her hand. The shadows, whatever they were, knew something of Elven magic.

Her instincts had told her that they would.

She was filled with a sudden bitterness. The Elfstones were not a part of her life, she had insisted. Oh, no—not her life. They belonged to someone else, not to her. How quick she had been to tell herself so. And how quick to turn to them the moment she felt threatened.

She slipped the Stones back into their container and shoved it within her tunic again. The night was peaceful and still; the mist was empty of movement. The things that lived on Morrowindl had gone in search of easier prey.

It was after midnight when she woke Garth. Nothing further had appeared to threaten them. She did not tell Garth what had happened. She wrapped herself in her cloak and leaned back against him.

It was a long time before she fell asleep.

They set out again at dawn. Vog lay thick across the slopes of Killeshan, and the light was thin and gray. Dampness filled the air; it seeped up through the ground on which they walked, penetrated the clothing they wore, and left them shivering. After a time, the sun began to burn through the mist, and some of the chill faded. Travel was slow and difficult, the land uneven and broken, a series of ravines and ridges choked by the jungle's growth. Last night's hush persisted, a sullen stillness that isolated the pair and spun webs of uneasiness all about them.

At the edge of their vision, the shadows persisted, furtive, cautious, a gathering of quick and formless ghosts that were there until the instant you looked for them and then were gone. Garth seemed oblivious to their presence, but Wren knew he was not. As she stole a furtive glance at his dark face from time to time she could see the calm that reflected in his eyes. She marveled that her giant friend could keep everything so carefully closed away. Her own eyes searched the haze relentlessly, for even now she was unsure how much the things that hid there feared the Elfstones, how long the magic would continue to keep them at bay. Her fingers strayed constantly to her tunic and the leather bag beneath, seeking reassurance that her protection was still there.

The day wore slowly down. They passed through forests of koa and banyan, old and shaggy with moss and vines, along slides where the lava rock was crusted and broken off into loose pieces that crumbled and skidded away as they tried to find footing, down ravines where the brush was thorny and across the sweep of valleys over which heavy clouds stretched in an impenetrable blanket of gray. All the while they continued to climb, working their way up Killeshan's slopes, catching brief glimpses of the volcano through breaks in the vog, the summit lifting away, seemingly never closer.

They began to recognize more and more of the dangers of the island. There were certain plants, bright colored and intricately formed, that snared and trapped anything that came within reach. There were sinkholes that could swallow you up in a moment's time if you were unfortunate enough to step in one. There were strange animals that showed themselves briefly and disappeared again, hunters all, scaled and spiked, clawed and sharp-toothed. No monsters appeared, but Wren suspected they were there, watching and waiting, the specters that whispered from the mist.

Night came and they slept, and this time the shadows did not approach, but stayed carefully hidden. A moor cat prowled close, but Garth blew into a thick stalk of grass, producing a whistling sound the big cat apparently did not care for, and it faded back into silence. Wren dreamed of home, of the Westland when she was young and everything was new, and she woke with the memories clear and bright.

"Garth, I used the Elfstones again," she told him at breakfast, the two of them huddled close against the chill gloom. "Two nights ago when the shadows first appeared."

I know, he replied, his eyes fixing her as he signed. *I was awake.*

"How much did you see?" she whispered, shaking her head in disbelief.

Enough. The magic frightens you, doesn't it?

She smiled wistfully. "Everything we do frightens me."

They walked through the silence of the dawn, lost in thought. The land flattened out before them and the jungle stretched away. The vog was thicker here, steady and unmoving before them. The air was still. They crossed an open space and found themselves at the edge of a swamp. Cautiously they skirted its reed-lined borders, searching for firmer ground. When they were successful, they started ahead again. The swamp persisted. Time after time, they were forced to change direction, seeking safer passage. The bog was a dull, flat shimmer of dampness stretched across masses of grass and weeds, and trees poked out of it like the limbs of drowned giants. Winged insects buzzed about, glittering and iridescent. Garth produced an ill-smelling salve that they used to coat their faces and arms, a shield against bites and stings. Snakes slithered in the mud. Spiders crawled everywhere, some larger than Garth's fist. Webs and moss and vines trailed from branches and brush, clinging and deadly. Bats flew through the cathedral ceilings of the trees, their squeaking sharp and chilling.

At one point they encountered a giant web concealed overhead and set like a snare to fall on whatever passed beneath. A less skilled pair of hunters might have missed it and been caught, but Garth spotted the trap at once. The strands of the webbing were as thick as Wren's fingers, and so close to transparent that they were invisible if you were not looking for them. She poked at one with a reed, and the reed was instantly stuck fast. Wren and Garth peered about cautiously for a long time without moving. Whatever it was that had spun that webbing was not something they wanted to meet.

Satisfied at last that the webmaker was not about, they pressed on.

It was nearing noon when they heard the scraping sound. They slowed and then stopped. The sound was rough and frantic, much too loud for the stillness of the swamp, almost a thrashing. It came from their left where shadows lay across a thicket of scrub with brilliant red flowers. With Garth leading, they skirted the scrub right, following a ridge of solid ground to a clearing of koa, moving silently, listening as the scraping sound continued. Almost immediately they saw strands of the clear webbing trailing earthward from the tops of the trees. The strands shook as something tugged against them from within the brush. It was apparent what had happened. Garth beckoned to Wren, and they continued cautiously on.

Amid the koa, they stopped again. A series of snares had been laid through the trees, one large and several small. One of the smaller snares had been tripped, and the scraping sound came from the creature it had entangled as it struggled to break free. The creature was unlike anything either Wren or Garth had ever seen. As large as a small hunting dog, it appeared to be a cross between a porcupine and a cat, its barrel-shaped body covered with black and tan ringed quills and supported by four short, thick legs while its squarish head, hunched virtually neckless between its shoulders, narrowed abruptly into the blunt, furry countenance of a feline. Wrinkled paws ended in powerful clawed fingers that dug at the earth, and its stubby, quilled tail whipped back and forth in a frantic effort to snap the lines of webbing that had wrapped about it.

The effort was futile. The more it thrashed, the more the webbing caught it up. Finally the creature paused, its head lifted, and it saw them. Wren was astonished by the creature's eyes. They had lids and lashes and were colored a brilliant blue. They were not the eyes of an animal; they were eyes like her own.

The creature's body sagged, exhausted from its struggle. The quills laid back sleekly, and the strange eyes blinked.

"Pfftttt!" The creature spit—very like the cat it in part, at least, resembled. "Don't suppose you would consider helping me," the creature softly rasped. "After all, you share some—arrgggh—responsibility for my predicament."

Wren stared, then glanced hurriedly over at Garth, who for once appeared as surprised as she was. How could this creature talk? She turned back again. "What do you mean, I share some responsibility?"

"Rrrowwwggg. I mean, you're an Elf, aren't you?"

"Well, no, as a matter of fact I'm not. I'm a . . ." She hesitated. She had been about to say she was a Rover. But the truth was she was at least part Elf. Wasn't that how the creature had identified her—by her Elven features? She frowned. How did it know of Elves anyway?

"Who are you?" she asked.

The creature appraised her silently for a moment, blue eyes unblinking. When he spoke, its voice was a low growl. "Stresa."

"Stresa," she repeated. "Is that your name?"

The creature nodded.

"My name is Wren. This is my friend Garth."

"Hssttt. You are an Elf," Stresa repeated, and the cat face furrowed. "But you are not from Morrowindl."

"No," she responded. She put her hands on her hips, puzzled. "How did you know that?"

The blue eyes squinted slightly. "You don't recognize me. You don't know what I am. Hrrrrowwl. If you lived on Morrowindl, you would."

Wren nodded. "What are you, then?"

"A Splinterscat," the creature answered. He growled deep in his throat. "That is what we are called, the few of us who remain. Part of this and part of that, but mostly something else altogether. Puurrft."

"And how is it that you know about Elves? Are there still Elves living here?"

The Splinterscat regarded her coolly, patient within his snare. "If you help me get free," he replied, his rough voice a low purr, "I will answer your questions."

Wren hesitated, undecided.

"Fffppht! You had better hurry," he advised. "Before the Wisteron comes."

Wisteron? Wren glanced again at Garth, signing to indicate what Stresa had said. Garth made a brief response.

Wren turned back. "How do we know you won't hurt us?" she asked the Splinterscat.

"Harrrwl. If you are not from Morrowindl and you have come this far, then you are more dangerous than I," he answered, coming as close as he probably could to laughing. "Hurry, now. Use your long knives to cut the webbing. The edge of the blade only; keep the flat turned away." The strange creature paused, and for the first time she saw a hint of desperation in its eyes. "There isn't much time. If you help me—hrroww—perhaps I can help you in return."

Wren signed to Garth, and they moved over to where the Splinterscat was bound, careful to avoid triggering any of the snares still in place. Working quickly, they sliced through the strands entangling the creature and then backed away. Stresa stepped over the fallen webbing gingerly and eased past them to where the ground was firm. He spread his quills and shook himself violently. Both Wren and Garth flinched at the sudden movement, but no quills flew at them. The Splinterscat was merely shaking loose the last of the webbing clinging to his body. He began preening himself, then stopped when he remembered they were watching.

"Thank you," he said in his low, rough voice. "If you had not freed me, I would have died. Grrwwll. The Wisteron would have eaten me."

"The Wisteron?" Wren asked.

The Splinterscat laid back its quills, ignoring the question. "You should already be dead yourself," he declared. The cat face furrowed once more. "Pffftt!" he spit. "You are either very lucky or you have the protection of magic. Which is it?"

Wren took a moment to respond. "You promised to answer my questions, Stresa. Tell me of the Elves."

The Splinterscat bunched itself up and sat down. He was bigger than he had looked in the snare, more the size of a dog than the cat or porcupine he looked. "The Elves," he said, the growl creeping back into his voice, "live inland, high on the slopes of Killeshan in the city of Arborlon—hrrowggh—where the demons have them trapped."

"Demons?" Wren asked, immediately thinking of those that had been shut away within the Forbidding by the Ellcrys. They had already broken free once in the time of Wil Ohmsford. Had they done so again? "What do these demons look like?" she pressed.

"Sssssttt! Like lots of different things. What difference does it make? The point is, the Elves made them and now they can't get rid of them. Pfft! Too bad for the Elves. The magic of the Keel fails now. It won't be long before everything goes."

The Splinterscat waited while Wren wrestled with this latest news. There was still too much she didn't understand. "The Elves *made* the demons?" she repeated in confusion.

"Years ago. When they didn't know any better."

"But . . . made them from what?"

Stresa's tongue licked out, a dark violet against its brown face. "Why did you come here—grrwll? Why are you looking for the Elves?"

Wren felt Garth's cautionary hand on her shoulder. She turned and saw him gesture off into the jungle.

"Hssttt, yes, I hear it, too," Stresa announced, rising hurriedly. "The Wisteron. It begins to hunt, to check its snares for food. We have to get away from here quickly. Once it discovers I've escaped, it will come looking for me." The Splinterscat shook out its quills. "Hhgggh. Since you don't appear to know your way, you had better follow me."

He started off abruptly. Wren hurried to catch up, Garth trailing. "Wait a moment! What sort of creature is this Wisteron?" she asked.

"Better for you if you never find out," Stresa replied enigmatically, and all of his quills stood on end. "This swamp is called the In Ju. The Wisteron makes its home here. The In Ju stretches all the way to Blackledge—and that is a long way off. Phffaghh."

He shambled away, moving far more quickly than Wren would have expected. "I still don't understand how you know so much about the Elves," she said, hastening after. "Or how it is that you can talk, for that matter. Does everything on Morrowindl talk?"

Stresa glanced back, a cat look, sharp and knowing. "Rraarggh—did I forget to tell you? The reason I can talk is that the Elves made me, too. Hssssttt." The Splinterscat turned away. "Enough questions for now. Better if we keep still for a while."

He moved rapidly into the trees, as silent as smoke, leaving Wren with Garth to follow, pondering her confusion and disbelief.

They fled swiftly, silently through the In Ju. The Splinterscat led, his brownish quilled body shambling through brush and into grasses, under brambles and over logs as if they were all one, a single obstacle that required the same amount of effort to surmount. Wren and Garth followed, forced to skirt the heavier undergrowth, to pick their way more cautiously, to test the ground before they walked upon it. They managed to keep pace only because Stresa had sufficient presence of mind to look back for them now and again and wait until they caught up.

None of them spoke as they hastened on, but they all listened carefully for sounds of the Wisteron's pursuit.

The jungle grew darker and webs began to appear everywhere. Many were trailers from snares long since sprung or worn away, yet an equal number were triggers to nets stretched through the treetops, across brush, even over pits in the earth. The webbing was clear and invisible except where leaves or dirt had become attached and gave color and definition, and even then it was hard to detect. Wren soon gave up searching for anything else, concentrating solely on the dangerous nets. A spider would spin webs such as these, she thought to herself, and pictured the Wisteron so in her mind.

They had been fleeing for only a handful of minutes when she finally heard it moving. The sound reached her clearly—brush and scrub thrashing, the limbs of trees snapping, bark scraping, and water splashing and churning. The Wisteron was big and it was making no effort to hide its coming. It sounded as if a juggernaut were rolling over everything, implacable, inescapable. The In Ju was a monstrous green cathedral in which the silence had been snatched away. Wren was suddenly very afraid.

They passed through a broad clearing in which a lake had formed, forcing them to change direction. After a moment's hesitation, they skirted right along a low ridge on which a thick patch of brambles grew. Stresa tunneled ahead, oblivious. Wren and Garth followed bravely, ignoring the scrapes and cuts they received, the sounds of the Wisteron's coming growing louder behind them.

Then abruptly the sounds disappeared.

Stresa stopped instantly, freezing in place. The Rovers did so as well. Wren listened, motionless. Garth put his hands against the earth. All was still. The trees hovered motionless about them, the misted half-light a curtain of gauze. The only sound was a rustling of the wind . . . Except that there was no wind. Wren went cold. The air was as still as death. She looked quickly at Stresa. The Splinterscat was looking up.

The Wisteron was moving through the trees.

Garth was on his feet again, his long knife sliding free. Wren searched the canopy of limbs and branches overhead in a frantic, futile effort to catch sight of something. The rustling was closer, more recognizable, no longer the whisper of wind against leaves but the movement of something huge.

Stresa began to run, an odd-shaped chunk of prickly earth skimming toward a stand of koa, silent somehow, but frantic as well. Wren and Garth went, too, unbidden, unquestioning. Wren was sweating freely beneath her clothes, and her body ached from the effort to remain still. She moved in a crouch, afraid now to look back, to look up, or to look anywhere but ahead to where the Splinterscat raced. The rustling of leaves filled her ears, and there was a snapping of branches. Birds darted through the cavernous forest, spurts of color and movement that were gone in the blink of an eye. The jungle shimmered damp and frozen about her, a still life in which only they moved. The koa rose ahead, massive trunks trailing yards of mossy vines, great hoary giants rooted in time.

Wren started unexpectedly. Nestled against her breast, the Elfstones had begun to burn.

Not again, she thought desperately, *I won't use the magic again,* but knew even as she thought it she would.

They reached the shelter of the koa, moving hurriedly within, down a hall formed of trunks and shadows. Wren looked up, searching for snares. There were none to be seen. She watched Stresa scurry to one side toward a gathering of brush and push within. She and Garth followed, stooping to make their way past the branches, pulling their packs after them, clutching them close to mask any sound.

Crouched in blackness and breathing heavily, they knelt against the jungle floor and waited. The minutes slipped by. The leafy branches of their shelter muffled any sound from without, so they could no longer hear the rustling. It was close within their concealment, and the stench of rotting wood seeped up from the earth. Wren felt trapped. It would be better to be out in the open where she could run, where she could see. She felt a sudden urge to bolt. But she glanced at Garth and saw the calm set of the big man's face and held her ground. Stresa had eased back toward the opening, flattened against the earth, head cocked, stubby cat's ears pricked.

Wren eased down next to the creature and peered out.

The Splinterscat's quills bristled.

In that same instant she saw the Wisteron. It was still in the trees, so distant from where they hid that it was little more than a shadow against the screen of vog. Even so, there was no mistaking it. It crept through the branches like some massive wraith . . . No, she corrected. It wasn't creeping. It was stalking. Not like a cat, but something far more confident, far more determined. It stole the life out of the air as it went, a shadow that swallowed sound and movement. It had four legs and a tail and it used all five to grasp the branches of the trees and pull itself along. It might have been an animal once; it still had the look of one. But it moved like an in-

sect. It was all misshapen and distorted, the parts of its body hinged like giant grapples that allowed it to swing freely in any direction. It was sleek and
sinewy and grotesque beyond even the wolf thing that had tracked them
out of Grimpen Ward.

The Wisteron paused, turning.

Wren's breath caught in her throat, and she held it there with a single-
mindedness that was heartstopping. The Wisteron hung suspended against
the gray, a huge, terrifying shadow. Then abruptly it swung away. It passed
before her like the promise of her own death, hinting, teasing, and whispering silent threats. Yet it did not see her; it did not slow. On this afternoon, it had other victims to claim.

Then it was gone.

They emerged from hiding after a time to continue on, edgy and furtive,
traveling mostly because it was necessary to do so if they ever wanted to get
clear of the In Ju. Even so, they had not succeeded when darkness fell and
so spent that night within the swamp. Stresa found a large hollow in the
trunk of a dead banyan, and the Rovers reluctantly crawled in at the Splinterscat's urging. They were not anxious to be confined, but it was better
than sleeping out in the open where the creatures of the swamp could
creep up on them. In any event, it was dry within the trunk, and the chill
of night was less evident. The Rovers wrapped themselves in their heavy
cloaks and sat facing the opening, staring out into the murky dark, smelling
rot and mold and damp, watching the ever-present shadows flit past.

"What is it that's moving out there?" Wren asked Stresa finally, unable
to contain her curiosity any longer. They had just finished eating. The
Splinterscat seemed capable of devouring just about anything—the cheese,
bread, and dried meats they carried in equal measure with the grubs and
insects he foraged on his own. At the moment he was sitting just to one
side of the opening in the banyan, gnawing on a root.

He glanced up alertly. "Out there?" he repeated. The words were so guttural Wren could barely understand them. "Grrrssst. Nothing much, really.
Some ugly, little creatures that wouldn't dare show their faces in other circumstances. They creep about now—hhhrrgg—because all the really dangerous things—except the wwwssst Wisteron—are at Arborlon, waiting for the
Keel to give out."

"Tell me about the Keel," she urged. Her fingers signed to Garth,
translating the Splinterscat's words.

Stresa put down the root. The purr was back in his rough voice. "The
Keel is the wall that surrounds the city. It was formed of the magic, and
the magic keeps the demons out. Hggghhhh. But the magic weakens, and
the demons grow stronger. The Elves don't seem to be able to do anything
about either." The Splinterscat paused. "How did you find out about the
demons? Hssttt. What is your name again? Grrllwren? Wren? Who told you
about Morrowindl?"

Wren leaned back against the banyan trunk. "It's a long story, Stresa. A

Wing Rider brought us here. He was the one who warned us about the demons, except that he called them monsters. Do you know about Wing Riders?"

"Ssttppft! The Elves with the giant birds—yes, I know. They used to come here all the time. Not anymore. Now when they come, the demons are waiting. They pull them down and kill them. Fffftt—quick. That's what would have happened to you as well if they weren't all at Arborlon—or at least most of them. The Wisteron doesn't bother with such things."

Arborlon, Wren was thinking, had been the home city of the Elves when they had lived in the Westland. It had disappeared when they did. Had they rebuilt it on Morrowindl? What had they done with the Ellcrys? Had they brought it with them? Or had it died out once again as it had in the time of Wil Ohmsford? Was that why there were demons on Morrowindl?

"How far are we from the city?" she asked, pushing the questions aside.

"A long way yet," Stresa answered. The cat face cocked. "The In Ju runs to a mountain wall called Blackledge that stretches all the way across the south end of the island. Beyond that lies a valley where the Rowen flows. Rrwwwn. Beyond that sits Arborlon, high on a bluff below Kille-shan's mouth. Is that where you are trying to go?"

Wren nodded.

"Ppffahh! Whatever for?"

"To find the Elves," Wren answered. "I have been sent to give them a message."

Stresa shook his head and fanned his quills away from his body an inch or so. "I hope the message is important. I don't see how you will ever man-age to deliver it with demons all about the city—if the city is even there anymore. Ssstt."

"We will find a way." Wren wanted to change the subject. "You said earlier that the Elves made you, Stresa. And the demons. But you didn't ex-plain how."

The Splinterscat gave her an impatient look. "Magic, of course!" he rasped. "Hrrrwwll! Elven magic allows you to do just about anything. I was one of the first, long before they decided on the demons or any of the oth-ers. That was almost fifty years ago. Splinterscats live a long time. Ssppptt. They made me to guard the farms, to keep away the scavengers and such. I was very good at it. We all were. Pfftt. We could live off the land, required very little looking after, and could stay out for weeks. But then the demons came and killed most of us off, and the farms all failed and were aban-doned, and that was that. We were left to fend for ourselves—grrrsssst— which was all right because we had gotten pretty used to it by then. We could survive on our own. Actually, it was better that way. I would hate to be shut up inside that city with demons—hssstt—all about." The creature gave a low growl. "I hate even to think about it."

Wren was still trying to figure out what the Elves were doing using magic again. Where had the magic come from? They hadn't had the use of magic when they had lived in the Westland—hadn't had it since the time of faerie except for their healing powers. The real magic had been lost for years. Now, somehow, they had gotten it back again. Enough, it appeared, to allow them to create demons. Or to summon them, perhaps. A black choice, if ever there was one. What could have possessed them to do such a thing?

She wondered suddenly what her parents had to do with all of this. Were they involved in using the magic? If they were, then why had they given the Elfstones—the most powerful magic of all—to her?

"If the Elves . . . created these demons with their magic, why can't they destroy them?" she asked, curious still about where these so-called demons had come from and whether they were really demons at all. "Why can't they use their magic to free themselves?"

Stresa shook his head and picked up the root again. "I haven't any idea. No one has ever explained any of it to me. I never go to the city. I haven't spoken to an Elf in years. You are the first—and you're not wholly elf, are you? Prruufft. Your blood is mixed. And your friend is something else altogether."

"He is human," she said.

"Ssspttt. If you say so. I haven't seen anyone like him before. Where does he come from?"

Wren realized for the first time that Stresa probably didn't know that there was anyone out there other than Elves and Wing Riders or any place other than the islands.

"We both come from the Westland, which is part of a country called the Four Lands, which is where all the Elves came from years ago. There are lots of different kinds of people there. Garth and I are just one of them."

Stresa studied her thoughtfully. His quilled body bunched as his legs inched together. "After you find the Elves—rrrgggghh—and deliver your message, what will you do then? Will you go back to where you came from?"

Wren nodded.

"The Westland, you called it. Is it anything like—grwwl—Morrowindl?"

"No, Stresa. There are things that are dangerous, though. Still, the Westland is nothing like Morrowindl." But even as she finished speaking, she thought, Not yet anyway, but for how long with the Shadowen gaining strength?

The Splinterscat chewed on the root for a moment, then remarked, "Pfftt. I don't think you can get to Arborlon on your own." The strange blue eyes fixed on Wren.

"No?" she replied.

"Pft, pft. I don't see how. You haven't any idea how to scale Black-ledge. Whatever happens you have to avoid the hrrrwwll Harrow and the

Drakuls. Below, in the valley, there's the Revenants. Those are just the worst of the demons; there are dozens of others as well. Ssspht. Once they discover you . . ."

The quilled body bristled meaningfully and smoothed out again. Wren was tempted to ask about the Drakuls and the Revenants. Instead, she glanced at Garth for an opinion. Garth merely shrugged his indifference. He was used to finding his own way.

"Well, what do you suggest we do?" she asked the Splinterscat.

The eyes blinked. The purr lifted from the creature's throat. "I would suggest that we make a bargain. I will guide you to the city. If you get past the demons and deliver your message and get out again, I will guide you back. Hrrrwwll." Stresa paused. "In return, you will take me with you when you leave the island."

Wren frowned. "To the Westland? You want to leave Morrowindl?"

The Splinterscat nodded. "Sppppttt. I don't like it here much anymore. You can't really blame me. I have survived for a long time on wits and experience and instinct, but mostly on luck. Today my luck ran out. If you hadn't happened along, I would be dead. I am tired of this life. I want to go back to the way things were before. Perhaps I can do that where you live."

Perhaps, Wren thought. Perhaps not.

She looked at Garth. The big man's fingers moved swiftly in response. *We don't know anything about this creature. Be careful what you decide.*

Wren nodded. Typical Garth. He was wrong, of course—they did know one thing. The Splinterscat had saved them from the Wisteron as surely as they had saved him. And he might prove useful to have along, particularly since he knew the dangers of Morrowindl far better than they did. Agreeing to take him with them when they left the island was a small enough trade-off.

Unless Garth's suspicions should prove correct and the Splinterscat was playing some sort of game.

Don't trust anyone, the Addershag had warned her.

She hesitated a moment, thinking the matter through. Then she shrugged the warning aside. "We have a bargain," she announced abruptly. "I think it is a good idea."

The Splinterscat spread his quills with a flourish. "Hrrwwll. I thought you would," he said, and yawned. Then he stretched out full length before them and placed his head comfortably on his paws. "Don't touch me while I'm sleeping," he advised. "If you do, you will end up with a face full of quills. I would feel badly if our partnership ended that way. Phfftt."

Before Wren could finish communicating the warning to Garth, Stresa's eyes were closed, and the Splinterscat was asleep.

Wren took the early watch, then slept soundly until dawn. She woke to Stresa's stirrings—the rustle of quills, the scrape of claws against wood. She rose, her mind fuzzy and her eyes dry and scratchy. She felt weak and unsettled, but ignored her discomfort as Garth passed her the aleskin and some bread. Their food was being depleted rapidly, she knew; much of it had simply gone bad. They would have to forage soon. She hoped that Stresa, despite his odd eating habits, might be of some help in sorting out what was edible. She chewed a bit of the bread and spit it out. It tasted of mold.

Stresa lumbered outside, and the Rovers followed, crawling from the hollow trunk and pushing themselves to their feet, muscles cramped and aching. Daybreak was a faint gray haze seeping through the treetops, barely able to penetrate the darkness beneath. Vog swirled through the jungle as if soup stirred within a cooking pot, but the air at ground level was still and lifeless. Things moved in the fetid waters of the bogs and sinkholes and on the deadwood that bridged them, a shifting of shapes and forms against the gloom. Sounds wafted dully from the shadows and hung waiting in challenge.

They started walking through the half-light, Stresa in the lead, a shambling, rolling mass of spikes. They continued slowly, steadily through the morning hours, the vog enfolding them at every turn, a colorless damp wrapper smelling of death. The light brightened from gray to silver, but remained faint and diffuse as it hovered about the edges of the trees. Strands of the Wisteron's webbing wrapped about branches and vines, and snares hung everywhere, waiting to fall. The monster itself did not appear, but its presence could be felt in the hush that lay over everything.

Wren's discomfort increased as the morning wore on. She felt queasy now and she had begun to sweat. At times she could not see clearly. She knew she had contracted a fever, but she told herself it would pass. She walked on and said nothing.

The jungle began to break apart shortly after midday, the ground turning solid again, the swamp fading back into the earth, and the canopy of the trees opening up. Light shone in bold patches through sudden rifts in the screen of the vog. The hush faded in an undercurrent of buzzings and clicks. Stresa mumbled something, but Wren couldn't make out what it was. She had been unable to focus her thoughts for some time now, and her vision was so clouded that even the Splinterscat and Garth were just shadows. She stopped, aware that someone was talking to her, turned to find out who, and collapsed.

She remembered little of what happened next. She was carried for a short time, barely conscious of the motion, burdened with a lethargy that threatened to suffocate her. The fever burned through her, and she knew somehow that she would not be able to shake it off. She fell asleep, woke to discover she was lying wrapped in blankets, and promptly fell asleep again. She came awake thrashing, and Garth held her and made her drink something bitter and thick. She vomited it up and was forced to drink it again. She heard Stresa say something about water, felt a cool cloth on her forehead, and slept once more.

She dreamed this time. Tiger Ty was there, standing next to Stresa, the two of them looking down on her, bluff and craggy Wing Rider and sharp-eyed Splinterscat. They spoke in a similar voice, rough and guttural, commenting on what they saw, speaking of things she didn't understand at first, and then finally of her. She had the use of magic, they said to each other. It was clear she did. Yet she refused to acknowledge it, hiding it as if it were a scar, pretending it wasn't there and that she didn't need it. Foolish, they said. The magic was all she had. The magic was the only thing she could trust.

She awakened reluctantly, her body cool again, and the fever gone. She was weak, and so thirsty it felt as if all the liquids in her body had been drained away. Pushing back the covers that wrapped her, she tried to rise. But Garth was there instantly, pressing her down again. He brought a cup to her lips. She drank a few swallows—it was all she could manage—and lay back. Her eyes closed.

When she came awake next, it was dark. She was stronger now, her vision unclouded, and her sense of what was happening about her clear and certain. Gingerly she pushed herself up on one elbow and found Garth staring into her eyes. He sat cross-legged beside her, his dark, bearded face creased and worn from lack of sleep. She glanced past him to where Stresa lay curled in a ball, then looked back again.

Are you better? he signed.

"I am," she answered. "The fever is gone."

He nodded. *You have been asleep for almost two days.*

"So long? I didn't realize. Where are we?"

At the foot of Blackledge. He gestured into the darkness. *We left the In Ju after you collapsed and made camp here. The Splinterscat recognized the sickness that infected you and found a root that would cure it. I think without his help, you might have died.*

She grinned faintly. "I told you it was a good idea to have him come along."

Go back to sleep. There are several hours still until dawn. If you are well enough, we'll go on then.

She lay back obediently, thinking that Garth must have kept watch by himself for the entire time she was sick, that Stresa would not have bothered, comfortable within the protection of his own armor. A sense of gratitude filled her. Garth was always there for her. She resolved that her giant friend would have the sleep he deserved when it was night again.

She slept well and woke rested, anxious to resume their journey. She changed clothes, although nothing she carried was clean by now, washed, and ate breakfast. At Garth's insistence, she took a few moments to exercise her muscles, testing her strength for what lay ahead. Stresa looked on, by turns curious and indifferent. She stopped long enough to thank the Splinterscat for his help in chasing the fever. He claimed not to know what she was talking about. The root he had provided for her did nothing more than to help her sleep. What had saved her was her Elven magic, he growled, and spread his quills and trundled off to find something to eat.

It took them all of that day and most of the next to climb Blackledge, and it would have taken them much longer—if indeed they could have done it at all—without Stresa. Blackledge was a towering wall of rock that ran along the Southwest slope of Killeshan. It lay midway up the ascent and appeared to have been formed when an entire section of the volcano had split away and then dropped several thousand feet into the jungle. The cliff face, once sheer, had eroded over the years, turned pitted and craggy, and grown thick with scrub and vines. There were only a few places where Blackledge could be scaled, and Stresa knew them all. The Splinterscat chose a section of the cliff where the rock wall had separated, and a fissure sliced down to less than a thousand feet above the jungle floor. Within the fissure lay a pass that ran back into a valley. It was there, across the Rowen, Stresa announced, that the Elves would be found.

Resolutely he led them up.

The climb was hard and slow and seemingly endless. There were no passes or trails. There were, in fact, very few places that presented any kind of purchase at all, none of them offering more than a brief respite. The lava rock was knife-edge sharp beneath their hands and feet and would break away without warning. The Rovers wore heavy gloves and cloaks to protect their skin and to keep the spiders from biting and the scorpions from stinging. The vog rolled down the rock face as if poured from its edge, thick and stinking of sulfur and soot. Most of what grew on the rock was thorny and tough and had to be cut away. Every inch of the climb was a struggle that drained their strength. Wren had felt rested when she began. Before it was even midday, she was exhausted. Even Garth's incredible stamina was quickly depleted.

Stresa had no such problem. The Splinterscat was tireless, lumbering up the cliff face at a slow, steady pace, powerful claws finding adequate footing, digging into the rock, pulling the bulky body ahead. Spiders and scorpions did not seem to affect Stresa; if one got close enough, he simply ate it. He led the way, choosing the approaches that would be easiest for his human companions, frequently stopping to wait until they could catch up. He detoured briefly to bring back a branch laden with a sweet red berry that they quickly and gratefully consumed. When it was nightfall and they were still only halfway up the slope, he found a ledge on which they could spend the night, clearing it first of anything that might threaten them and then, to their utter astonishment, offering to keep watch while they slept. Garth, having spent the previous two nights standing guard over the feverish Wren, was too exhausted to argue. The girl slept the better portion of the night, then relieved the Splinterscat several hours before dawn, only to discover that Stresa preferred talk to sleep in any event. He wanted to know about the Four Lands. He wanted to hear of the creatures that lived within them. He told Wren more about life on Morrowindl, a harrowing account of the daily struggle to survive in a world where everything was always hunting or being hunted, where there were no safe havens, and where life was usually short and bitter.

"Rrrwwll. Wasn't like that in the beginning," he growled softly. "Not until the Elves made the demons and everything turned bad. Phhhfft. Foolish Elves. They made their own prison."

He sounded so bitter that she decided not to pursue the matter. She was still uncertain as to whether or not the Splinterscat knew what he was talking about. The Elves had always been healers and caretakers—never creators of monsters. She found it hard to believe they could have turned a paradise into a quagmire. She kept thinking there must be more to this story than what Stresa knew and she must reserve judgment until she had learned it all.

They resumed their climb at daybreak, pulling themselves up the rocks, scrambling and clawing against the cliff face, and peering up through the swirling mist. It rained several times, and they were left drenched. The heat lessened as they worked their way higher, but the dampness persisted. Wren was still weak from her bout with the swamp fever, and it took all of her strength and concentration to continue putting one foot in front of the other and to reach out with her hand for one more pull up. Garth helped her when he could, but there was seldom room to maneuver, and they were forced to make the ascent one behind the other.

They saw caves in the cliffs from time to time, dark openings that yawned silent and empty. Stresa pointedly steered his charges away from them. When Wren questioned him about what lay within, the Splinterscat hissed and declared rather pointedly that she didn't want to know.

Midafternoon finally brought them to the bottom of the fissure and the narrow defile that lay beyond. They stood on flat, solid ground again, aching and worn, and looked back across the south end of the island to where it dropped away in a rolling, misted carpet of green jungle and black lava rock to the azure-blue sweep of the ocean. Blackledge rose above them to either side, craggy and misted, stretching in an unbroken wall until it disappeared into the horizon. Seabirds circled against the sky. Sunlight appeared momentarily through a break in the clouds, blinding in its intensity, turning the muted colors of the land below vibrant and bright. Wren and Garth squinted against its glare, enjoying the warmth of it against their faces. Then it faded, gone as suddenly as it had appeared; the chill and damp returned, and the island's colors became dull again.

Turning away into the shadow of the fissure, they began to climb toward the mouth of the narrow pass. Then they were inside. The cliff rock rose all about them, a hulking, brooding presence, and wind blew down out of Killeshan's heights in rough, quick gusts like the sound of something breathing. It was cold in the pass, and the Rovers wrapped themselves tightly in their cloaks. Rain descended in sudden bursts and was gone again, and the vog spilled down off the rocks in opaque waves.

Twilight had descended by the time they reached the fissure's end. They stood at the rim of a valley that stretched away toward the final rise of Killeshan, a green-etched bowl settled beneath a distant stretch of forestline that lifted to the barren lava rock of the high slopes beyond. The valley was broad and misted, and it was difficult to see what lay within. The faint shimmer of a ribbon of water was visible east, winding through stands of acacia-dotted hills and ridgelines laced with black streamers of pitted rock. Across the sweep of the valley, all was still.

They made camp in the shelter of the pass under an overhang that fronted the valley. Night fell quickly, and with the sky so completely screened away the world about them turned frighteningly black. The silence of dusk slowly gave way to a jumble of rough sounds—the intermittent, barely perceptible rumble of Killeshan, the hiss of steam from cracks in the earth where the heat of the volcano's core broke through, the grunts and growls of hunting things, the sudden screams as something died, and the frantic whispers as something else fled. Stresa curled into a ball and lay facing out at the blackness, less quick to sleep this night. Wren and Garth sat next to him, anxious, uneasy, wondering what lay ahead. They were close now; the Rover girl could sense it. The Elves were not far. She would find them soon. Sometimes, through the black and the haze, she thought she could catch the glimmer of fires like eyes winking in the night. The fires were distant, across the valley, high on the slopes below the treeline's final stretch. They looked lonely and isolated, and she wondered if the perception was an accurate one. How far had the Elves come in their move away from the Four Lands? Too far, perhaps? So far that they could not get back again?

She fell asleep finally with the questions still on her mind.

They set out again at daybreak. Morrowindl had become a gray, misted world of shadows and sounds. The valley fell away sharply below them as they walked, and it was as if they were descending into a pit. The trail was rocky and slick with damp, and the green that had seemed so predominant in the previous night's uncertain light revealed itself now as nothing more than small patches of beleaguered moss and grass crouched amid long stretches of barren rock. Tendrils of steam laced with the stench of sulfur rose skyward to blend with the vog, and pockets of intense heat burned through the soles of their boots and seared the skin of their faces. Stresa set a slow pace, picking his way carefully, lumbering from side to side amid the rocks and their islands of green. Several times he stopped and turned back again altogether, choosing a different way. Wren could not tell what it was that the Splinterscat saw; everything was invisible to her. She felt bereft of her skills once more, a stranger in a hostile, secretive world. She tried to relax herself. Ahead, Stresa's bulky form rolled with the motion of his walk, daggerlike quills rising and falling rhythmically. Behind, Garth stalked as if at hunt, dark face intense, unreadable, hard. How very alike they were, she thought in surprise.

They had come down off a small rise into a stand of brush when the thing attacked. It launched itself out of the haze with a shriek, a bristling horror with claws and teeth bared, slashing in a desperate frenzy. It had legs and a body and a head—there was no time to tell more. It bypassed Stresa and came for Wren, who barely managed to bring her arms up before it was upon her. Instinctively she rolled, taking the weight of the thing as she did and then thrusting it away. It slashed and bit, but the heavy gloves and cloak protected her. She saw its eyes, yellow and maddened; she felt its fetid breath. Shaking free, she scrambled to her feet, seeing the thing wheel back again out of the corner of her eye.

Then Garth was there, short sword cutting. A glitter of iron and the creature's arm was gone. It fell, screaming, tearing at the earth. Garth stepped in swiftly and severed its head, and it went still.

Wren stood there shaking, still uncertain what the thing was. A demon? Something else? She looked down at the bloodied, shapeless husk. It had all happened so fast.

"Phfftt! Listen!" Stresa sharply hissed. "Others come! Ssstttfttp. This way! Hurry!"

He lumbered swiftly off. Wren and Garth were quick to follow, tunneling after him into the gloom.

Already they could hear the sounds of pursuit.

The chase began slowly, gathering momentum as it careened downward into the valley. Wren, Garth, and the Splinterscat were alone at first, sought after but not yet found, and their hunters were nothing more than scattered bits of noise still distant and indistinct. They slipped ahead swiftly, watchfully, without panic or fear. The landscape about them was dreamlike, by turns barren and empty where black lava had buried the foliage beneath its glistening rocky carpet and lush where patches of acacia and heavy grass fought from small islands within the wilderness to reclaim what had been taken. Vog hung over everything, a vast, loosely woven shroud, swirling and shifting, creating the illusion that everything it touched was alive. Overhead, visible in small patches through the haze, the skies were iron-gray and sunless.

Stresa chose a rambling, circuitous route, taking them first one way and then the other, his thick quilled body rolling and lurching so that it constantly seemed as if he were about to tip over. He favored neither the open sweep of the lava rock nor the canopied cover of the brush-grown forest, veering from one to the other impartially, whether selecting his path from intuition or experience, it was impossible to tell. Wren could hear his heavy breathing, a growl in his throat that turned to a hiss when he came across something he didn't like. Once or twice he looked back at them as if to make certain they were still there. He did not speak, and they kept silent as well.

It was chance alone that led to their discovery. They had come upon a stretch of open rock, and the creature was lying in wait. It rose up almost in front of them, thrusting out of the earth where it had burrowed, hissing and shrieking, a sort of birdlike thing on legs with a great hooked beak and claws at its wing tips. Talons swept downward to rip at Stresa, but the Splinterscat's backside hunched and rippled instantly and a flurry of razor-sharp quills flew into the attacker. The creature screamed in pain and tumbled back, tearing at its face.

"Sssttt! Quick!" the Splinterscat snapped, hurrying away.

They fled swiftly, the cries of their attacker fading behind them. But now others were alerted and began to close. The sounds were all about, snarls and growls and huffings, slicing through the haze, out of the shadows. Garth drew his short sword. They slipped down a shallow ravine and something flung itself out of the brush. Wren ducked as the thing flew past and saw the glitter of Garth's blade as it swept up. The thing fell away and was still. They climbed from the ravine onto a new stretch of lava rock, then raced for a cluster of trees. A flurry of small, four-legged creatures that resembled boars tore from the cover and bore down on them. Stresa crouched and shivered, and a shower of quills flew into the attackers. Squeals filled the air, and clawed forefeet tore at the earth. Stresa veered past them, quills lifting like spikes. One or two made a vain attempt to rise, but Garth kicked them aside.

Then they were into the trees, pushing through damp grasses and vines, feeling the wet slap of the foliage against their faces and arms. *Just give us a few minutes more,* Wren was thinking when a coiled body dropped out of the trees, wrapped about Garth, and lifted him away. She wheeled back, her sword drawn, and caught a final glimpse of the big man as he was pulled from view, half carried, half dragged, thrashing powerfully to break free.

"Garth!" she cried out.

She started after him instantly, but had only taken a dozen steps before Stresa slammed into her from behind, sweeping her legs from beneath her, knocking her to the ground, crying "Down, girl! Ssstt. Stay!"

She heard a hissing sound like dozens of snakes, then a ripping as the foliage overhead was sliced apart. Stresa pushed forward until he was next to her.

"That was foolish!" he spit roughly. "Look. Phffttt! See what almost got you?"

Wren looked. There was an odd-shaped bush that was as quilled as the Splinterscat, needles pointing in every direction. As she stared in disbelief, leaves folded about the needles to hide them, and the bush took on a harmless look once more.

"Hssssst! That's a Darter!" Stresa breathed. "Poisonous! Touch it, disturb it in any way, and it flings its needles! Death, if they prick you!"

The Splinterscat fixed her with his bright eyes. Wren could no longer see or hear Garth. Anger and frustration filled her, their bitter heat churning in her stomach. Where was he? What had been done to him? She had to find him! She had to . . .

Then Stresa was up and moving again, and she was moving with him. They pushed through the heavy foliage, searching the haze, listening. And suddenly she could hear struggling sounds again, and ahead there was a flash of movement. Stresa lumbered forward, bristling; Wren was a step behind. There was a grunt of pain and a thrashing. Garth rose up momentarily and then disappeared from view.

"Garth!" Wren shouted, and rushed forward heedlessly.

The big Rover was sprawled on the earth when she reached him, scratched and bruised, but otherwise unhurt. Whatever it was that had latched onto him had apparently tired of the struggle. Garth permitted the girl a momentary hug, then gently disentangled himself and stumbled back to his feet.

Stresa got them moving again at once, back through the trees, through the heavy undergrowth and out onto the lava rock. A cluster of shadows passed overhead and disappeared, silent, formless. The sounds of pursuit continued to build around them, rough and anxious. They scurried along a flat to a ridge that dropped into a pit of swirling mist. Stresa took them quickly past, down a slide to the streambed that had gone almost dry.

A new horror lumbered out of the mist, a being vaguely manlike, but with multiple limbs and a face that seemed all jaws and teeth. Stresa curled into a ball, quills jutting out in every direction, and the monster lurched past without slowing. Wren swung her sword defensively and jumped aside, barely avoiding a clutch of anxious fingers. Garth stood his ground and let the thing come to him, then cut at it so fast Wren could barely follow the movement of his blade. Blood flew from the beast, but it barely slowed. Grunting, it reached for Garth. The giant Rover leapt back and aside, then came at it again. Wren attacked from the rear, but one monstrous arm swung about and sent her flying. She kept her grip on the sword, rose, and saw the thing almost on top of her. Garth swept under it in a rush, caught her up and yanked her away. They were running again, flying along the glistening black rock, the crunch of it sharp beneath their boots. Garth slowed without stopping and swung her down. Her feet struck and instantly she was running with him. She saw Stresa ahead, somehow back in the lead. She heard the growling and huffing of the creature behind.

Then something exploded out of the shadows on her left and struck at her. Pain rushed along her arm, and she saw blood stain her sleeve. There was a tearing of teeth and claws. She screamed and pushed at whatever was clinging to her. It was too close for her to use her sword. Garth materialized out of nowhere, grasping her attacker with his bare hands and tearing it free. She saw its ugly, twisted face and gnarled body as it dropped. With a howl, she swung at it with her sword, and it flew apart.

"Grrrlll!" Stresa was next to them. "We have to hide! Sssttt! They are too many!"

Behind, too close to consider, the monster tracking them gave a triumphant roar. They fled from it again, back into the mist, through the tangle of shadows and half-light, stumbling and clawing their way across the rock. Wren was bleeding heavily. She could see blood on Garth as well, but wasn't sure if it was his or her own. Her mouth was dry and her chest burned as she gulped in air. Her strength was beginning to fail.

They topped a rise and suddenly Stresa, still leading, tumbled abruptly from view. Hurrying to where he had fallen, they found him sprawled awkwardly at the bottom of a short drop.

"Here! A hiding place!" he called out suddenly, spitting and hissing as he regained his feet.

They scrambled down the open side of the drop—the other was a mass of boulders—and saw where he was looking. Beneath an overhang was a split in the rock leading back into darkness.

"Sssstttppp! Inside, quickly. Go, it's safe enough!" the Splinterscat urged. When they failed to respond, he rushed at them threateningly. "Hide! I'll lead the thing away and come back for you! Hrrgggll! Go! Now!"

He whirled about and disappeared. Garth hesitated only a moment, then plunged into the cleft. Wren was a step behind. They brought up their hands awkwardly as the darkness closed about, groping to find their way. The split opened back into the lava for some distance, burrowing down into the earth. When they were inside far enough that they could barely see the light from without, they crouched down to wait.

Seconds later they heard the sounds of their pursuer. The monster approached without slowing and lumbered past. The sounds faded.

Wren reached for Garth and squeezed his arm. Her eyes were beginning to adjust, and she could just barely make him out in the dark. She sheathed her short sword, removed her leather jacket, and tore away the sleeve of her tunic. She could see the dark streaks of the claw marks down her arm. She medicated the wounds with a healing salve and bound them with the last clean scarf she carried. The stinging disappeared after a time, turning to a dull, throbbing ache. She sat back wearily, listening to the sound of her own breathing mesh with Garth's in the silence.

Time slipped away. Stresa did not return. Wren allowed her eyes to close and her thoughts to drift. How far were they from the river now? she wondered. The Rowen lay between themselves and Arborlon, and once they had crossed it they would reach the Elves. She considered momentarily what that meant. She had barely allowed herself time to think about the fact that the Elves even existed, that they were not simply rumor or legend, but real and alive, and that against all odds, she had found them. Or almost found them, at least. Another day, two at the most . . .

She let her eyes open again and that was when she saw the creature.

At first she thought she must be mistaken, that the shadows were playing tricks on her. But there was sufficient light for her to trust what she was seeing. It crouched motionless on a shelf of rock several feet behind Garth. It was small, barely a dozen inches high, she guessed, although it was hard to be certain when it was hunched down that way. It had large, round eyes that stared fixedly and huge ears pointing off a tiny head with a fox face. It had a spindly body and looked vaguely spiderlike at first glance—so much so that Wren had to fight down a moment's revulsion as she recalled the encounter with the Wisteron. But it was small and helpless looking, and it had tiny hands and feet like a human. It stared at her, and she stared back. She knew instinctively that the odd creature had chosen this cleft as a hiding place just as they had. It had frozen in place to avoid being seen, but now it was discovered and was trying to decide what to do.

Wren smiled and kept still. The creature watched, eyes searching. Casually Wren caught Garth's attention, brought her hands up slowly, and told him what was going on. She asked him to ease over next to her. He did so, and they sat together studying the creature. After a while, Wren reached into her pack and extracted a few scraps of food. She took a bite of some cheese and passed what remained to Garth. The big man finished it. The creature's tongue licked out.

"Hello, little one," Wren said softly. "Are you hungry?"

The tongue reappeared.

"Can you talk?"

No response. Wren leaned forward with a bit of cheese. The creature did not move. She eased a little closer. The creature stayed motionless. She hesitated, not certain what to do next. When the creature still did not move, she stretched out her hand cautiously and gently tossed the cheese toward the ledge.

Faster than the eye could follow, the creature's hand shot out and caught the cheese in midair. After hauling in its catch, the creature sniffed it, then gobbled it down.

"Hungry indeed, aren't you?" Wren whispered.

There was a shuffling at the entrance to their hiding place. The creature on the rock vanished instantly into the shadows. Wren and Garth turned, swords drawn.

"Hhrrrrgghh," Stresa muttered as he eased slowly into view, puffing and grunting. "Demon wouldn't give up the hunt. Ffphtt. Took much longer than I thought to lose it." He shook his quills until they rattled.

"Are you all right?" Wren asked.

The Splinterscat bristled. "Of course I'm all right. Do you see anything wrong with me? Ssstttt! I'm winded, that's all."

Wren glanced furtively at the ledge. The strange creature was back again, watching.

"Can you tell me what that is?" she asked, nodding in the direction of the creature.

Stresa peered into the gloom and then snorted. "Ssspptt. That's just a Tree Squeak! Completely harmless."

"It looks frightened."

The Splinterscat blinked. "Tree Squeaks are frightened of everything. That's what keeps them alive. That and their quickness. Fastest things on Morrowindl. Smart, too. Smart enough not to let themselves get trapped. You can be certain there is another way out of this crevice or this one wouldn't even be here. Rrrwwlll. Look at it stare. Seems to have taken an interest in you."

Wren kept her eyes on the little creature. "Did the Elves make the Tree Squeaks, too?"

Stresa settled himself comfortably in place, paws tucked in. "The Tree Squeaks were always here. But the magic has changed them like everything else. See the hands and feet? Used to be paws. They communicate, too. Watch."

He made a small chirping sound. The Tree Squeak cocked its head. Stresa tried again. This time the Tree Squeak responded, a soft, low squeaking.

Stresa shrugged. "It's hungry." The Splinterscat lost interest, his blunt head lowering onto its forepaws. "We'll rest until midday, then go on. The demons sleep when its hottest. Best time for us to be about."

His eyes closed, and his breathing deepened. Garth glanced purposefully at Wren and settled back as well, finding a smooth spot amid the rough edges of the lava rock. Wren was not ready to sleep. She waited a bit, then reached into her pack for another chunk of cheese. She nibbled at it while the Tree Squeak watched, then gently eased across the floor of the crevice until she had closed the distance between them. When she was no more than an arm's length away, she broke off a bit of the cheese and held it out to the Tree Squeak. The little creature took it gingerly and ate it.

A short time later the Tree Squeak was curled up in her lap. It was still there when she finally fell asleep.

Garth's hand on her shoulder, firm and reassuring, brought her awake again. She blinked and glanced about. The Tree Squeak was back on its ledge, watching. Garth signed that it was time to go. She rose cautiously in the cleft's narrow confines and pulled on her pack. Stresa waited by the entrance, quills spread, sniffing the air. It was hot within their shelter, the air still and close.

She looked around briefly to where the Tree Squeak crouched. "Goodbye, little one," she called softly.

Then they moved out of the darkness and into the misty light. Midday had come and gone while they slept. The vog that shrouded the valley seemed denser than before, its smell sulfuric and rank, and its taste gritty with ash and silt. Heat from Killeshan's core rose through the porous rock and hung stubborn and unmoving in the air, trapped within the valley's windless expanse as if captured in a kettle. The mist reflected whitely the diffused sunlight, causing Wren to squint against its glare. Shadowy stands of acacia rose against the haze, and ribbons of black lava rock disappeared into other worlds.

Stresa took them forward, making his way cautiously through the vog's murk, angling from one point to the next, sniffing as he went. The day had gone uncomfortably silent. Wren listened suspiciously, remembering that Stresa had said the demons would sleep now, mistrusting the information all the same. They worked their way deeper into the valley's bowl, past islands of jungle grown thick with vines and grasses, down ridges and drops carpeted with scrub, and along the endless strips of barren, crusted lava rock that unraveled like black bands through the mist.

The afternoon wore quickly on. In the haze about them, nothing moved. There were things out there, Wren knew—she could feel their presence. There were creatures like the one that had almost caught them that morning and others even worse. But Stresa seemed aware of where they were and made certain to avoid them, leading his charges on, confident in his choice of paths as he picked his way through the treacherous maze. Everything shifted and changed as they went, and there was a sense of nothing being permanent, of the whole of Morrowindl being in continual flux. The island seemed to break apart and reform about them, a surreal landscape that could be anything it wished and was not bound by the laws of nature that normally governed. Wren grew increasingly uneasy, used to the dependable terrain of plains and mountains and forests, to the sweep of country not hemmed about by water and settled upon a furnace that could open on a whim and consume everything that lived on it. Killeshan's breath steamed through fissures in the lava rock, small eruptions that stank of burning rock and gases and left shards of debris to drift upon the air. Incongruous amid the lava rock and weeds, isolated clusters of flowering bushes grew, fighting to survive against the heat and ash. Once, Wren thought to herself, this island must have been very beautiful, but it was difficult to imagine it so now.

It was late in the day when they finally reached the Rowen, the light gone gray and faint. The creatures within the haze had begun to stir again, their rumblings and growls causing the three companions to grow increasingly more watchful. They came upon the river at a point where its far shore was hidden by a screen of mist and its near fell sharply away to a rush of waters that were murky and rough, choked with silt and debris, clouded so thick that nothing of what lay beneath the surface showed.

Stresa stopped at the shore's edge, casting left and right uncertainly, sniffing the heavy air.

Wren knelt next to the Splinterscat. "How do we get across?" she asked.

"At the Narrows," the other answered with a grunt. "Ssspptt. The trouble is, I'm not sure where they are. I haven't been this way in a long time."

Wren glanced back at Garth, who watched impassively. The light was failing rapidly now, and the sound of the demons rising from their sleep was growing louder. The air remained still and thick as the heat of midday cooled to a damp swelter.

"Rrrwwll. Downstream, I think," Stresa ventured, sounding none too sure.

Then Wren saw something move in the mist behind them and started. Garth had his short sword out instantly. A small figure inched into view, and Wren came to her feet in surprise. It was the Tree Squeak. It circled away from Garth and came up to her, taking hold of her arm tentatively.

"What are you doing here, little one?" she murmured, and stroked its furry head.

The Tree Squeak pulled itself up on her shoulder and chittered softly at Stresa.

The Splinterscat grunted. "It says the crrrwwwll crossing is upstream, just a short distance from here. Phffttt. It says it will show us the way."

Wren frowned doubtfully. "It knows what we're looking for?"

"Ssssttt. Seems to." Stresa hunched his quills anxiously. "I don't like standing about in the open like this. Let's take a chance and do what it says. Maybe it knows something."

Wren nodded. With Stresa still leading, they started upstream, following the ragged curve of the Rowen's bank. Wren carried the Tree Squeak, who clung to her possessively. It must have followed them all the way from that cleft in the lava rock, she realized. Apparently it hadn't wanted to be left behind. Perhaps the small kindnesses she had shown had won it over. She stroked the wiry body absently and wondered how much kindness anything encountered on Morrowindl.

Moments later Stresa stopped abruptly and drew them back into the concealment of a cluster of rocks. Something huge and misshapen passed before them on its way to the river, a silent shadow in the haze. Patiently they waited. The volume of coughs and grunts continued to grow as the dusk deepened. When they went forward again, even their breathing had slowed to a whisper.

Then the shoreline moved away from where they walked, sloping downward into the river's swift waters, turning the swirling surface to broken rapids. The haze lifted sufficiently to reveal a narrow bridge of rocks. Quickly they crossed, crouched low against the water, darting for the cover of the mist beyond. When they were safely gathered on the far shore, the Tree Squeak again chittered to Stresa.

"Go left, it says," the Splinterscat translated, the words a low growl in its throat.

They did as the Tree Squeak advised, moving into the vog. The last of the daylight faded away and darkness closed about. The only light came from far ahead, an odd white glow that shimmered faintly through the haze. They were forced to slow, to grope ahead in the darker pockets, to pause and listen and then judge where it was safe to venture. The demons seemed to be ahead of them—massed, Wren was willing to bet, between themselves and their destination.

She discovered soon enough that she had guessed right. The company crested a rise on a slide of lava rock thick with withered scrub, and abruptly the mist cleared. Quickly they flattened themselves into the brush. Hunched close together in the shadows, they stared out at what lay before them.

Arborlon stood on a rise less than a mile ahead and was itself the source of the strange glow. The glow emanated from a massive wall that ringed the city, pulsing faintly against the mist and clouds. All about, the demons pressed close, shadows that slipped in and out of the vog and mist, faceless, formless wraiths caught momentarily in the glare of fires that burned from fissures in the earth where spouts of molten lava had broken through. Jets of steam filled the air with ash and heat and turned the charred earth into a ghostly, fiery netherworld. Demon growls disappeared into rumblings that rose from deep within the earth where the volcano's molten core churned and tossed. In the distance, looming high above the city and the wraiths that besieged it, Killeshan's maw steamed, jagged and threatening, a fire monster waiting to feast.

Wren's eyes shifted from the besieged city to the ruined landscape in shock. That the Elves could have allowed themselves to be trapped in a world such as this was beyond belief. She felt herself go hollow with fear and loathing. How could this have come about? The Elves were healers, trained from the moment of their birth to restore life, to keep the land and its living things whole. What had prevented that here? Arborlon was an island within its walls—its people somehow preserved, somehow still able to sustain themselves—while the world without had become a nightmare.

She bent close to Stresa. "How long have things been like this?"

The Splinterscat hissed. "Fffpphtt! Years. The Elves have been barricaded away for as long as any of us can remember, hiding behind their magic. Ssstttppp! See the light that rises from the wall that shields them? Mmssst. That is their protection!"

The Tree Squeak chittered softly, causing her to turn. Stresa grunted. "Hwrrrll. The Squeak says the light weakens and the magic fails. Not much time left before it goes out completely."

Wren stared out again at the carnage. Not much time, she repeated to herself. Shades, there could be little doubt of that. She experienced a sudden sense of futility. What was the point of her search now? She had come to Morrowindl to find the Elves and return them to the world of Men— Allanon's charge to her at the Hadeshorn. But how could the Elves ever return out of this? Surely they would have done so long ago if it were at all possible. Yet here they remained, ringed all about. She took a deep breath. Why had Allanon sent her here? What was she supposed to do?

A great sadness filled her. What if the Elves were lost? The Elves were all that was left of the world of faerie, all that remained of the first people, of the magic that had given life when life began. They had done so much to bring the Four Lands into being when the Great Wars ended and the old ways were lost. All of the children of Shannara had come from Elven blood; all of the struggles that had been waged to preserve the Races had been won by them. It seemed impossible that it could all be relegated to history's scroll, that nothing would remain of the Elves but the stories.

Myths and legends, she reflected—*the way it is now.*

She thought again of the promise she had made to herself to learn the truth about her parents, to find out who they were and why they had left her. And what of the Elfstones? She had vowed to discover why they had been given to her. Her fingers lifted to trace the outline of the leather bag about her neck. She had not thought of the Elfstones since they had begun their ascent of Blackledge. She had not even thought to use the magic when they were threatened. She shook her head. But then why should she? Look how much good the magic had done the Elves.

She felt Garth's hand on her shoulder and saw the questioning look in his eyes. He was wondering what she intended to do. She found herself wondering the same thing.

Go home, a voice whispered inside her. *Give this madness up.*

Part of her agreed. It was madness, and she had no reason to be here beyond foolish curiosity and stubborn insistence. Look at how little her skills and her training could help her in this business. She was lucky she had gotten this far. She was lucky even to be alive.

But here she was nevertheless. And the answers to all her questions lay just beyond the light.

"Stresa," she whispered, "is there a way to get into the city?"

The Splinterscat's eyes shone in the dark. "Wrroowwll, Wren of the Elves. You are determined to go down there, are you?" When she failed to respond, he said, "Within a ravine that—hrrwwll—lies close to where the demons prowl, there are tunnels hidden. Sssstttpht. The tunnels lead into the city. The Elves use them to sneak away—or did once upon a time. That was how they let us out to keep watch for them. Phhffft. Perhaps there is still one in use, do you think?"

"Can you find it?" she asked softly.

The Splinterscat blinked.

"Will you show it to me?"

"Hssstttt. Will you remember your promise to take me with you when this is finished?"

"I will."

"Very well." The cat face furrowed. "The tunnels, then. Which of us goes? Ssttpht."

"Garth, you, and me."

The Tree Squeak chittered instantly.

Stresa purred. "I thought as much. The Squeak plans on going, too. Rwwwll. Why not? It's only a Squeak."

Wren hesitated. She felt the Tree Squeak's fingers clutch tightly at her arm. The Squeak chittered once more.

"Sssttt." Stresa might have been laughing. "She says to tell you that her name is Faun. She has decided to adopt you."

"Faun." Wren repeated the name and smiled faintly. "Is that your name, little one?" The round eyes were fixed on her, the big ears cocked forward. It seemed odd that the Tree Squeak should even have a name. "So you would adopt me, would you? And go where I go?" She shook her head ruefully. "Well, it is your country. And I probably couldn't keep you from going if I tried."

She glanced at Garth to make certain he was ready. The rough face was calm and the dark eyes fathomless. She took a last look down at the madness below, then pushed back the fear and the doubt and told herself with as much conviction as she could muster that she was a Rover girl and that she could survive anything.

Her fingers passed briefly across the hard surface of the Elfstones.

If it becomes necessary . . .

She blocked the thought away. "Lead us in, Stresa," she whispered. "And keep us safe."

The Splinterscat didn't bother to reply.

Wren Ohmsford could not remember a time when she had been afraid of much of anything. It simply wasn't her nature. Even when she was small and the world was still new and strange and virtually everyone and everything in it was either bigger and stronger or quicker and meaner, she was never frightened. No matter the danger, whatever the uncertainty, she remained confident that somehow she would find a way to protect herself. This confidence was innate, a mix of iron-willed determination and self-assurance that had given her a special kind of inner strength all her life. As she grew, particularly after she went to live with the Rovers and began her training with Garth, she acquired the skill and experience needed to make certain that her confidence was never misplaced, that it never exceeded her ability.

All that had changed when she had come in search of the Elves. Twice since she had begun that search she had found herself unexpectedly terrified. The first time had been when the Shadowen that had tracked them all through the Westland had finally shown itself on the first night of the signal fire, and she had discovered to her horror that she was powerless against it. All of her training and all of her skill availed her nothing. She should have known it would be like that; certainly Par had warned her when he had related the details of his own encounter with the dark creatures. But for some reason she had thought it would be different with her—or perhaps she simply hadn't considered what it would be like at all. In any case, there she had been, bereft of Garth—Garth, whom she had believed stronger and quicker than anything!—face to face with something against which no amount of confidence and ability could prevail.

She would have died that night if she had not been able to call upon the magic of the Elfstones. The magic alone had been able to save them both.

Now, as she made her way forward with the others of her little company through the darkness and vog of Morrowindl, as they crept slowly ahead into a nightmare world of shadows and monsters, she found herself terrified anew. She tried to rationalize it away; she tried to argue against it. Nothing helped. She knew the truth of things, and the truth was the same as it had been that night at the ruins of the Wing Hove when she had confronted the Shadowen. Confidence, skill, experience, and Garth's protective presence, however formidable in most instances, were of little reassurance here. Morrowindl was a cauldron of unpredictable magic and unreasoning evil, and the only weapon she possessed that was likely to prove effective against it was the Elfstones. Magic alone kept the Elves alive inside the walls of Arborlon. Magic, however misguided, had apparently summoned the evil that besieged them. Magic had changed forever the island and the things that lived upon it. There was no reason for Wren to think that she could survive on Morrowindl for very long without using magic of her own.

Yet use of the Elfstones was as frightening to her as the monsters the magic was intended to protect against. Look at her; as a Rover girl, she had spent her entire life learning to depend upon her own skills and training and to believe that there was nothing they could not overcome. That was how Garth had schooled her and what life with the Rovers had taught her, but more important it was what she had always believed. The world and the things in it were governed by a set of behavioral laws; learn those laws and you could withstand anything. Reading trail signs, understanding habits, knowing another's weaknesses and strengths, using your senses to discover what was there—those were the things that kept you alive. But magic? What was magic? It was invisible, a force beyond nature's laws, an unknown that defied understanding. It was power without discernible limits. How could you trust something like that? The history of her family, of Ohmsfords ten generations gone, suggested you could not. Look what the magic had done to Wil and Brin and Jair. What certainty was there if she was forced to rely on something so unpredictable? What would using the magic do to her? True, it had been summoned easily enough in her confrontation with the Shadowen. It had flowed ever so smoothly from the Stones, come almost effortlessly, striking at the mere direction of her thoughts. There had been no sense of wrongness in its use—indeed, it was as if the power had been waiting to be summoned, as if it belonged to her.

She shivered at the recognition of what that meant. She had been given the Elfstones, she knew, in the belief that one day she would need them. Their power was intended to be hers.

She tightened her resolve against such an idea. She didn't want it. She didn't want the magic. She wanted her life to stay as it was, not to be irrevocably changed—for it would be so—by power that exceeded her understanding and, she believed, her need.

Except, of course, now—here on Killeshan's slopes, surrounded by demons, by things formed of magic and dark intention, set upon a landscape of fire and mist, where in a second's time she could be lost, unless . . .

She cut the thought short, refusing to complete it, focusing instead on Stresa's quilled bulk as the Splinterscat tunneled his way through the gloom.

Shadows wafted all about as the vog shifted and reformed, cloaking and lifting clear from islands of jungle scrub and bare lava rock, as if the substance
of a kaleidoscopic world that could not decide what it wanted to be.
Growls sounded, disembodied and directionless, low and threatening as
they rose and fell away again. She crouched down in the haze, a frantic inner voice shrieking at her to disappear, to burrow into the rock, to become
invisible, to do anything to escape. She ignored the voice, looking back for
Garth instead, finding him reassuringly close, then thinking in the next instance that it made no difference, that he was not enough, that nothing was.

Stresa froze. Something skittered away through the shadows ahead,
claws clicking on stone. They waited. Faun hung expectantly upon her
shoulder, head stretched forward, ears cocked, listening. The soft brown
eyes glanced at her momentarily, then shifted away.

What phase of the moon was it? she wondered suddenly. How
long had it been since Tiger Ty had left them here? She realized that she
didn't know.

Stresa started forward again. They topped a rise stripped of everything
but stunted, leafless brush and angled downward into a ravine. Mist pooled
on the rocky floor, and they groped their way ahead uncertainly. Stresa's
quills shimmered damply, and the air turned chill. There was light, but it
was difficult to tell where it was coming from. Wren heard a cracking
sound, as if something had split apart, then a hiss of trapped steam and gases
being released. A shriek rose and disappeared. The growls quieted, then
started again. Wren forced her breathing to slow. So much happening and
she could see none of it. Sounds came from everywhere, but lacked identity. There were no signs to read, no trails to follow, only an endless landscape of rock and fire and vog.

Faun chittered softly, urgently.

At the same moment, Stresa came to a sudden halt. The Splinterscat's
quills fanned out, and the bulky form hunched down. Wren dropped into
a crouch and reached for her short sword, starting as Garth brushed up
against her. There was something dark in the haze ahead. Stresa backed
away, half turned, and looked for another way to go. But the ravine was
narrow here, and there was no room to maneuver. He wheeled back,
bristling.

The dark image coalesced and began to take on form. Something on
two legs walked toward them. Garth fanned out to one side, as silent as the
shadows. Wren eased her sword clear of its sheath and quit breathing.

The figure emerged from the haze and slowed. It was a man, clad all in
close-fitting, earth-colored clothes. The clothes were wrinkled and worn,
streaked with ash and grime, and free of any metal clasps or buckles. Soft
leather boots that ended just above the ankle were scuffed and had the tops
folded down one turn. The man himself was a reflection of his clothes, of
medium height but appearing taller than otherwise because he was so angular. His face was narrow with a hawk nose and a seamed, beardless face,
and his dark hair was mostly captured in an odd, stockinglike cap. Overall,

he had the appearance of something that was hopelessly creased and faded from having been folded up and put away for so long.

He didn't seem surprised to see them. Nor did he seem afraid. Saying nothing, he put a finger to his lips, glanced over his shoulder momentarily, and then pointed back the way they had come.

For a minute, no one moved, still not certain what to do. Then Wren saw what she had missed before. Beneath the cap and the tousled hair were pointed ears and slanted brows.

The man was an Elf.

After all this time, she thought. *After so much effort.* Relief flooded through her and at the same time a strangeness that she could not identify. It seemed odd somehow to finally come face to face with what she had worked so hard to find. She stood there, staring, caught up in her emotions.

He gestured again, a bit more insistent than before. He was older than he had first appeared, but so weathered that it was impossible for Wren to tell how much of his aging was natural and how much the result of hard living.

Coming back to herself at last, she caught Garth's attention and signed for him to do as the Elf had asked. She rose and started back the way she had come, the others following. The Elf passed them a dozen steps along the way, a seemingly effortless task, and beckoned for them to follow. He took them back down the ravine and out again, drawing them across a bare stretch of lava rock and finally into a stand of stunted trees. There he crouched down with them in a circle.

He bent close, his sharp gray eyes fixing on Wren. "Who are you?" he whispered.

"Wren Ohmsford," she whispered back. "These are my friends— Garth, Stresa, and Faun." She indicated each in turn.

The Elf seemed to find this humorous. "Such odd company. How did you get here, Wren?"

He had a gentle voice, as seamed and worn as the rest of him, as comfortable as old shoes.

"A Wing Rider named Tiger Ty brought Garth and me here from the mainland. We've come to find the Elves." She paused. "And you look to me to be one of them."

The lines on the other's face deepened with a smile. "There are no Elves. Everyone knows that." The joke amused him. "But if pressed, I suppose that I would admit to being one of them. I am Aurin Striate. Everyone calls me the Owl. Maybe you can guess why?"

"You hunt at night?"

"I can see in the dark. That is why I am out here, where no one else cares to go, beyond the walls of the city. I am the queen's eyes."

Wren blinked. "The queen?"

The Owl dismissed the question with a shake of his head. "You have come all this way to find the Elves, Wren Ohmsford? Whatever for? Why should you care what has become of us?" The eyes crinkled above his smile. "You are very lucky I found you. You are lucky for that matter that you are even still alive. Or perhaps not. You are Elven yourself, I see." The smile faded. "Is it possible . . . ?"

He trailed off doubtfully. There was something in his eyes that Wren could not make out. Disbelief, hope, what? She started to say something, but he gestured for her to be silent. "Wren, I will take you inside the city, but your friends will have to wait here. Or more accurately, back by the river where it is at least marginally safe."

"No," Wren said at once. "My friends come with me."

"They cannot," the Owl explained, his voice staying patient and kind. "I am forbidden to bring any but the Elven into the city. I would do otherwise if I could, but the law cannot be broken."

"Phfft. I can wait at the—hrwwll—river," Stresa growled. "I've done what I promised in any case."

Wren ignored him. She kept her gaze fixed on the Owl. "It is not safe out here," she insisted.

"It is not safe anywhere," the other replied sadly. "Stresa and Faun are used to looking after themselves. And your friend Garth seems fit enough. A day or two, Wren—that would be all. By then, perhaps you can persuade the Council to let them come inside. Or you can leave and rejoin them."

Wren didn't know what sort of Council he was talking about, but irrespective of what was decided about Stresa and Faun she was not going to leave Garth. The Splinterscat and the Tree Squeak might be able to survive on their own, but this island was as foreign and treacherous for Garth as it was for her and she was not about to abandon him.

"There has to be another . . ." she started to say.

And suddenly there was a shriek and a wave of multilimbed things came swarming out of the mist. Wren barely had time to look up before they were upon her. She caught a glimpse of Faun streaking into the night, of Stresa's quilled body flexing, and of Garth as he rose to defend her, and then she was knocked flying. She got her sword up in time to cut at the closest attacker. Blood flew and the creature tumbled away. There were bodies everywhere, crooked and black, bounding about as they ripped and tore at the members of the little company. Stresa's quills flew into one and sent it shrieking away. Garth threw back another and battled to her side. She stood back to back with him and fought as the things came at them. She couldn't see them clearly, only glimpses of their misshapen bodies and the gleaming eyes. She looked for the Owl, but he was nowhere to be found.

Then abruptly she caught sight of him, a shadow rising from the earth as he cut two of the attackers down before they knew what was happening. In the next instant he was gone again, then back at another place, a pair of long knives in his hands, though Wren couldn't remember having seen any weapons on him before. The Elf was like smoke as he slipped among the attackers, there and gone again before you could get a fix on him.

Garth pressed forward, his massive arms flinging the attackers aside.

The demons held their ground momentarily, then fell back, bounding away to regroup. Howls rose out of the darkness all about.

Aurin Striate materialized at Wren's side. His words were harsh, urgent. "Quick. This way, all of you. We'll worry about the Council later."

He took them across the stretch of lava rock and back into the ravine. Sounds of pursuit came from everywhere. They ran in a low crouch along the rocky basin, angling through boulders and cuts, the Owl leading, a phantom that threatened at every turn to disappear into the night.

They had gone only a short distance when something small and furry flung itself onto Wren's shoulder. She gasped, reeled away protectively, then straightened as she realized it was Faun, returned from wherever she had run off to. The Tree Squeak burrowed into her shoulder, chittering softly.

Seconds later the demons caught up with them, swarming out of the haze once more. They swept past Stresa, who curled into a ball instantly, quills pointing every which way, and flung themselves on the humans. Garth took the brunt of the attack, a wall that refused to buckle as he flung the creatures back one after another. Wren fought next to him, quick and agile, the blade of the short sword flicking left and right.

Against her chest, nestled in their leather bag, the Elfstones began to burn.

Again the attackers drew back, but not so far this time and not so readily. The night and the fog turned them to shadows, but their howls were close and anxious as they waited for others to join them. The Elf and his charges gathered in a knot, fighting for breath, their weapons glistening damply.

"We have to keep running," the Owl insisted. "It is not far now."

A dozen feet away, Stresa uncurled, hissing. "Ssssttppht! Run if you must, but this is enough for me! Phhfft!" He swung his cat head toward Wren. "I'll be waiting—rwwwll—Wren when you return. At the river I'll be. Don't forget your promise!"

Then abruptly he was gone, slipping away into the dark, having become one of the shadows about him.

The Owl beckoned, and Wren and Garth began to run once again, still following the curve of the ravine. There was movement all about them in the mist, swift and furtive. Jets of steam gushed from the earth through cracks in the lava, and the stench of sulfur filled the air. A slide of rocks blocked their way, and they scrambled past it hurriedly. Ahead, Arborlon glowed behind its protective wall, a shimmer of buildings and towers amid forest trees. In the mixed light of the city's magic and the volcano's fire, Killeshan's barren, ravaged slope was dotted with islands of scrub and trees that had somehow escaped the initial devastation and were now reduced to a slow suffocation from the heat. Vog hung across the landscape in a ragged curtain, and the monsters that hid within it passed through its ashen haze like bore worms through earth.

A depression lay ahead, a continuation of the ravine they had been following. The Owl had them hurrying toward it when the demons attacked again. They flew at them from both sides this time, materializing out of the gloom as if risen from the earth. The Owl was knocked sprawling, and Wren went down in a flurry of claws and teeth. Only Garth remained standing, and there were demons all over him, clinging, tearing, trying to bring him down. Wren kicked out violently and freed herself. Faun had already disappeared, quick as a thought, back into the night. Wren's sword slashed blindly, cut into something, held momentarily, then jerked free. She scrambled up and was borne back again, hammered against the rock. She could feel gashes open on the back of her head and neck. Pain brought tears to her eyes. She rolled clear and came to her feet, demons circling all about. Night and mist had swallowed up the Owl. Garth was down, the demons atop him a writhing mass of black limbs. She screamed and struggled to reach him, but crooked hands clutched roughly at her and held her back.

The Elfstones seared her chest like fire.

Burdened by the weight of her attackers, she began to fall. She knew instinctively that this time she would not be able to get back up, that this was the end for all of them.

She could hear herself scream soundlessly somewhere deep inside.

Reason fled before her need, and fear gave way to rage. There were bodies all about her, claws and teeth ripping, and fetid breath against her skin. Her fingers plunged into her tunic and yanked the Stones free.

They flared to life instantly, an eruption of light and fire. The leather bag disintegrated. The magic exploded through cracks in the Rover girl's fingers, too impatient and too willful to wait for her hand to open. It swept the air like a scattering of knives, cutting apart the black things, turning them to dust almost before their screams died away. Wren was suddenly free again. She stumbled to her feet, with the Elfstones stretched forth now, the fire and the light racing from within her, joining with the magic until there was no distinction. She threw back her head as the power ripped through her—harsh, defiant, and exhilarating. She was transformed, and her fears of what would become of her in the wake of the magic's use dissipated and were lost. It made no difference who or what she had been or how she had lived her life. The magic was everything. The magic was all that mattered.

She turned its power on the mass of bodies atop Garth and it hammered into them. In seconds, they disintegrated. Some withstood the fury of the attack a few moments longer than the others—those that were larger and more hardened—but in the end they all died. Garth rose, bloodied, his clothes in tatters, and his dark, bearded face ashen. What was he staring at? she wondered vaguely. She marveled at the look on his face as she used the power of the Stones to sweep the landscape clean. The Owl reappeared out of the haze, and there was awe etched on his leathery face as well. And fear. They were both so afraid . . .

Suddenly she understood. She closed her fingers in shock, and the magic was gone. The exhilaration and the fire left her, draining away in an instant, and it was as if she had been stripped naked and set out for everyone to see. Weariness flooded through her. She felt ashamed. The magic had snared her, taken her for its own, destroyed her resolution to withstand its lure, and buried all her promises that she would not give way to it, that she would not become another of the Ohmsfords it had claimed.

Ah, but she had needed its power, hadn't she? Hadn't it kept her alive—kept them all alive? Hadn't she wanted it, even gloried in it? What else could she have done?

Garth was next to her, holding her by the shoulders, keeping her upright, his dark eyes intense as he looked into her own. She nodded vaguely that she was aware of him, that she was all right. But she wasn't, of course. The Owl was there as well, saying "Wren, you are the one that she has waited for, the one who was promised. You are welcome indeed. Come quickly now, before the dark things regroup and attack again. Hurry!"

She followed obediently, wordlessly, her body a foreign thing that swept her along as she watched from somewhere just without. Heat and exhaustion worked through her, but she felt detached from them. She saw the landscape revert to a sea of vog through which a strange array of shadows floated. Trees lifted skyward in clusters, leafless and bare, brittle stalks waiting to crumble away. Ahead, glistening like something trapped behind a rain-streaked window, was the city of the Elves, a jeweled treasure that shimmered with promise and hope.

A lie, the thought struck her suddenly, incongruously, and she was surprised with the intensity of it. *It is all a lie.*

Then the Owl led them through a tangle of brush and down a narrow defile where the shadows were so thick it was all but impossible to see. He crouched down, worked at a gathering of rocks, and a trapdoor lifted. Swiftly they scrambled inside, the air hot and stifling. The Elf reached up and pulled the trapdoor back into place and secured it. The darkness lasted only a moment, and then there was a hint of the city's strange light through the tunnel that lay ahead. The Owl took them down its length, saying nothing, lean and shadowy against the faint wash of brightness. Wren felt the sense of detachment fading now; she was back inside herself, returned to who and what she was. She knew what had happened, what she had done, but she would not let herself dwell on it. There was nothing to do but to go forward and to complete the journey she had set herself. The city lay ahead—Arborlon. And the Elves, whom she had come to find. That was what she must concentrate on.

She realized suddenly that Faun had not come back to her. The Tree Squeak was still outside, fled into that fiery netherworld . . . She shut her eyes momentarily. Stresa was there as well, gone of his own choice. She feared for them both. But there was nothing she could do.

They worked their way down the tunnel for what seemed an endless amount of time, crouched low in the narrow passageway, wordless as they went. The light brightened the farther they went until it was as clear as daylight within the rock. The world without faded entirely—the vog, the heat, the ash, and the stench—all gone. Suddenly the rock disappeared as well, turning abruptly to earth, black and rich, a reminder for Wren of the forests of the Westland, of her home. She breathed the smell in deeply, wondering that it could be. The magic, she thought, had preserved it.

The tunnel ended at a set of stone stairs that led upward to a heavy, iron-bound door set in a wall of rock. As they reached the door, the Owl turned suddenly to face them.

"Wren," he said softly, "listen to me." The gray eyes were intense. "I know I am a stranger to you, and you have no particular reason to trust anything I say. But you must rely on me at least this once. Until you speak with the queen, and only when you are alone with her, should you reveal that you have possession of the Elfstones. Tell no one else before. Do you understand?"

Wren nodded slowly. "Why do you ask this of me, Aurin Striate?"

The Owl smiled sadly, the creases in his worn face deepening. "Because, Wren, though I would wish it otherwise, not everyone will welcome your coming."

Then, turning, he tapped sharply on the door, waited, and tapped again—three and then two, three and then two. Wren listened. There was movement on the other side. Heavy locks released, sliding free.

Slowly the door swung open, and they stepped through.

I have come home.

It was Wren's first thought—vivid, startling, and unexpected.

She was inside the city walls, standing in an alcove that opened beneath the shadow of the parapets. Arborlon stretched away before her, and it was as if she had returned to the Westland, for there were oaks, hickories and elm, green bushes and grass, and earth that smelled of growing things and changes of season, streams and ponds, and life at every turn. An owl hooted softly, and there was a flutter of wings close at hand as a smaller bird darted away from its hidden perch. Some others sang. Whippoorwills! Fireflies glimmered in a stand of hemlock and crickets chirped. She could hear the soft rush of water from a river where it tumbled over the rocks. She could feel the whisper of a gentle night wind against her cheek. The air smelled clean, free of the stench of sulfur.

And there was the city itself. It nestled within the greenery—clusters of homes and shops, streets and roadways below and skypaths overhead, wooden bridges that connected across the tangle of streams, lamps that lit windows and flickered in welcome, and people—a handful not yet gone to

sleep—walking perhaps to ease their restlessness or to marvel at the sky. For
there was sky again, clear and cloudless, brilliant with stars and a three-
quarter moon as white as new snow. Beneath its canopy, everything glimmered faintly with the magic that emanated from the walls. Yet the glow
was not harsh as it had seemed to Wren from without, and the walls, despite their height and thickness, were so softened by it that they appeared
almost ephemeral.

Wren's eyes darted from place to place, finding flower gardens set out
in well-tended yards, hedgerows that lined walkways, and street lamps of
intricately wrought iron. There were horses, cows, chickens, and animals of
all sorts in pens and barns. There were dogs curled up asleep in doorways
and cats on sills. There were colored flags and umbrellas astride entries and
awnings hung from shop fronts and barter carts. The houses and shops were
white and clean, edged with fresh-painted borders in a myriad of colors.
She could not see it all, of course, only the closest parts of the city. Yet
there was no mistaking where she was or how it made her feel.

Home.

Yet as quickly as the pleasing rush of familiarity and sense of belonging
swept over her, it disappeared. How could she come home to a place she
had never been, had never seen, and hadn't even been certain existed until
this moment?

The vision blurred then and seemed to shrink back into the night's
shadows as if seeking to hide. She saw what she had missed before—or perhaps simply what she had not allowed herself to see in her excitement. The
walls teemed with men, Elves in battle dress with weapons in hand, their
lines of defense stretched across the battlements. An attack was under way.
The struggle was oddly silent, as if the magic's glow somehow muffled the
sounds. Men fell, some to rise again, and some to disappear. The shadows
that attacked suffered casualties as well, some burned by the light that
sparked and fizzled as a dying fire might, and some cut down by the defenders. Wren blinked. Within the walls, the city of the Elves seemed somehow less bright and more worn. The houses and shops were a little darker,
a little less carefully tended than she had first imagined, the trees and bushes
not as lush, and the flowers paler. The air she breathed was not so clean after all—there was a hint of sulfur and ash. Beyond the city, Killeshan
loomed dark and threatening, and its mouth glowed blood-red against the
night.

She was aware suddenly of the Elfstones still clenched tightly in her
hand. Without looking down at them, she slipped them into her pocket.

"Come this way, Wren," Aurin Striate said.

There were guards at the door through which they had entered, hard-
faced young men with distinctly Elven features and eyes that seemed tired
and old. Wren glanced at them as she passed and was chilled by the way
they stared back at her. Garth edged close against her shoulder and blocked
their view.

The Owl took them out from beneath the parapets and over a rampway bridging a moat that encircled the city inside its walls. Wren looked back, squinting against the light. There was no water in the moat; there seemed to be no purpose in having dug it. Yet it was clearly meant to be some sort of defense for the city, bridged at dozens of points by ramps that led to the walls. Wren glanced questioningly at Garth, but the big man shook his head.

A roadway opened through the trees before them, winding ahead into the center of the city. They started down it, but had gone only a short distance when a large company of soldiers hurried past, led by a man with hair so sun-bleached it was almost white. The Owl pulled Wren and Garth aside into the shadows, and the man went past without seeing them.

"Phaeton," the Owl said, looking after him. "The queen's anointed on the field of battle, her savior against the dark things." He said it ironically, without smiling. "An Elven Hunter's worst nightmare."

They went on wordlessly, turning off the roadway to follow a series of side streets that took them through rows of darkened shops and cottages. Wren glanced about curiously, studying, considering, taking everything in. Much was as she had imagined it would be, for Arborlon was not so different, apart from its size, from Southland villages like Shady Vale—and except, of course, for the continuing presence of the protective wall, still a shimmer in the distance, a reminder of the struggle being waged. When, after a time, the glow disappeared behind a screen of trees, it was possible to think of the city as it must have once been, before the demons, before the beginning of the siege. It would have been wonderful to live here then, Wren thought, the city forested and secluded as it had been above the Rill Song, reborn out of its Westland beginnings into this island paradise, its people with a chance to begin life anew, free of the threat of oppression by the Federation. No demons then, Killeshan dormant, and Morrowindl at peace—a dream come out of imagining.

Did anyone still remember that dream? she wondered.

The Owl took them through a grove of ash and willowy birch where the silence was a cloak that wrapped comfortably about. They reached an iron fence that rose twenty feet into the air, its summit spiked and laced with sharpened spurs, and turned left along its length. Beyond its forbidding barrier, tree-shaded grounds stretched away to a sprawling, turreted building that could only be the palace of the Elven rulers. The Elessedils, in the time of her ancestors, Wren recalled. But who now? They skirted the fence to where the shadows were so deep it was difficult to see. There the Owl paused and bent close. Wren heard the rasp of a key in a lock, and a gate in the fence swung open. They stepped inside, waited until the Owl locked the gate anew, and then crossed the dappled lawn to the palace. No one appeared to challenge them. No one came into view. There were guards, Wren knew. There must be. They reached the edge of the building and stopped.

A figure detached itself from the shadows, lithe as a cat. The Owl turned and waited. The figure came up. Words were exchanged, too low for Wren to hear. The figure melted away again. The Owl beckoned, and they slipped through a gathering of spruce into an alcove. A door was already ajar. They stepped inside into the light.

They stood in an entry with a vaulted ceiling and wood-carved lintels and jams that shone with polish. Cushioned benches had been placed against facing walls and oil lamps bracketed arched double doors opened to a darkened hallway beyond. From somewhere down that hallway, deep within the bowels of the palace, Wren could hear movement and the distant sound of voices. Following the Owl's lead, Wren and Garth seated themselves on the benches. In the light Wren could see for the first time how ragged she looked, her clothing ripped and soiled and streaked with blood. Garth looked even worse. One sleeve of his tunic was gone entirely and the other was in shreds. His massive arms were clawed and bruised. His bearded face was swollen. He caught her looking at him and shrugged dismissively.

A figure approached, easing silently out of the hallway, coming slowly into the light. It was an Elf of medium height and build, plain looking and plainly dressed, with a steady, penetrating gaze. His lean, sun-browned face was clean-shaven, and his brown hair was worn shoulder length. He was not much older than Wren, but his eyes suggested that he had seen and endured a great deal more. He came up to the Owl and took his hand wordlessly.

"Triss," Aurin Striate greeted, then turned to his charges. "This is Wren Ohmsford and her companion Garth, come to us from out of the Westland."

The Elf took their hands in turn, saying nothing. His dark eyes locked momentarily with Wren's, and she was surprised at how open they seemed, as if it would be impossible for them ever to conceal anything.

"Triss is Captain of the Home Guard," the Owl advised.

Wren nodded. No one spoke. They stood awkwardly for a moment, Wren remembering that the Home Guard was responsible for the safety of the Elven rulers, wondering why Triss wasn't wearing any weapons, and wondering in the next instant why he was there at all. Then there was movement again at the far end of the darkened hallway, and they all turned to look.

Two women appeared out of the shadows, the most striking of the two small and slender with flaming red hair, pale clear skin, and huge green eyes that dominated her oddly triangular face. But it was the other woman, the taller of the two, who caught Wren's immediate attention, who brought her to her feet without even being aware that she had risen, and who caused her to take a quick, startled breath. Their eyes met, and the woman slowed, a strange look coming over her face. She was long-limbed and slender, clothed in a white gown that trailed to the floor and was gathered about her narrow waist. Her Elven features were finely chiseled with high cheekbones and a wide, thin mouth. Her eyes were very blue and her hair flaxen, curling down to her shoulders, tumbled from sleep. Her skin was smooth across her face, giving her a youthful, ageless appearance.

Wren blinked at the woman in disbelief. The color of the eyes was wrong, and the cut of the hair was different, and she was taller, and a dozen other tiny things set them apart—but there was no mistaking the resemblance.

Wren was seeing herself as she would look in another thirty years.

The woman's smile appeared without warning—sudden, brilliant, and effusive. "Eowen, see how closely she mirrors Alleyne!" she exclaimed to the red-haired woman. "Oh, you were right!"

She came forward slowly, reaching out to take Wren's hands in her own, oblivious to everyone else. "Child, what is your name?"

Wren stared at her in bewilderment. It seemed somehow as if the woman should already know. "Wren Ohmsford," she answered.

"Wren," the other breathed. The smile brightened even more, and Wren found herself smiling in response. "Welcome, Wren. We have waited a long time for you to come home."

Wren blinked. What had she said? She glanced about hurriedly. Garth was a statue, the Owl and Triss impassive, and the red-haired woman intense and anxious. She felt suddenly abandoned. The light of the oil lamps flickered uncertainly, and the shadows crept close.

"I am Ellenroh Elessedil," the woman said, hands tightening, "Queen of Arborlon and the Westland Elves. Child, I barely know what to say to you, even now, even after so much anticipation." She sighed. "Here, what am I thinking? Your wounds must be washed and treated. And those of your friend as well. You must have something to eat. Then we can talk all night if we need to. Aurin Striate." She turned to the Owl. "I am in your debt once again. Thank you, with all my heart. By bringing Wren safely into the city, you give me fresh hope. Please stay the night."

"I will stay, my Lady," the Owl replied softly.

"Triss, see that our good friend is well looked after. And Wren's companion." She looked at him. "What is your name?"

"Garth," Wren answered at once, suddenly frightened by the speed with which everything was happening. "He doesn't speak." She straightened defensively. "Garth stays with me."

The sound of boots in the hall brought them all about once again. A new Elf appeared, dark-haired, square-faced, and rather tall, a man whose smile was as ready and effortless as that of the queen's. He came into the room without slowing, self-assured and controlled. "What's all this? Can't we enjoy a few hours' sleep without some new crisis? Ah, Aurin Striate is here, I see, come in from the fire. Well met, Owl. And Triss is up and about as well?"

He stopped, seeing Wren for the first time. There was an instant's disbelief mirrored on his face, and then it disappeared. His gaze shifted to the queen. "She has returned after all, hasn't she?" The gaze shifted back to Wren. "And as pretty as her mother."

Wren flushed, conscious of the fact that she was doing so, embarrassed by it, but unable to help herself. The Elf's smile broadened, unnerving her further. He crossed quickly and put his arm protectively about her. "No, no, please, it is true. You are every bit your mother." He gave her a companionable squeeze. "If a bit dusty and tattered about the edges."

His smile drew her in, warming her and putting her instantly at ease. There might not have been anyone else in the room. "It was a rather rough journey up from the beach," she managed, and was gratified by his quick laugh.

"Rough indeed. Very few others would have made it. I am Gavilan Elessedil," he told her, "the queen's nephew and your cousin." He cut himself short when he saw her bewildered look. "Ah, but you don't know about that yet, do you?"

"Gavilan, take yourself off to sleep," Ellenroh interrupted, smiling at him. "Time enough to introduce yourself later. Wren and I need to talk now, just the two of us."

"What, without me?" Gavilan assumed an injured look. "I should think you would want to include me, Aunt Ell. Who was closer to Wren's mother than I?"

The queen's gaze was steady as it fixed on him. "I was." She turned again to Wren, moving Gavilan aside, placing herself next to the girl. Her arms came about Wren's shoulders. "This night should be for you and I alone, Wren. Garth will be waiting for you when we are done. But I would like it if we spoke first, just the two of us."

Wren hesitated. She was reminded of the Owl telling her that she must say nothing of the Elfstones except to the queen. She glanced over at him, but he was looking away. The red-haired woman, on the other hand, was looking intently at Gavilan, her face unreadable.

Garth caught her attention, signing, *Do as she asks.*

Still Wren did not reply. She was on the verge of learning the truth about her mother, about her past. She was about to discover the answers she had come seeking. And suddenly she did not want to be alone when it happened.

Everyone was waiting. Garth signed again. *Do it.* Rough, uncompromising Garth, harborer of secrets.

Wren forced a smile. "We'll speak alone," she said.

They left the entryway and went down the hall and up a set of winding stairs to the second floor of the palace. Garth remained behind with Aurin Striate and Triss, apparently untroubled that he was not going with her, comfortable with their separation even knowing Wren was clearly not. She caught Gavilan staring after her, saw him smile and wink and then disappear another way, a sprite gone back to other amusing games. She liked him instinctively, just as she had the Owl, but not in the same way. She wasn't really sure yet what the difference was, too confused at the moment by everything happening to be able to sort it out. She liked him because he made her feel good, and that was enough for now.

Despite the queen's admonishment to the others about wanting to speak with Wren alone, the red-haired woman trailed after them, a wraith white faced against the shadows. Wren glanced back at her once or twice, at the strangely intense, distant face, at the huge green eyes that seemed lost in other worlds, at the flutter of slender hands against a plain, soft gown. Ellenroh did not seem to notice she was there, hastening along the darkened corridors of the palace to her chosen destination, forgoing light of any sort save the moon's as it flooded through long, glassed windows in silver shafts. They passed down one hallway and turned into another, still on the second floor, and finally approached a set of double doors at the hall's end. Wren started at a hint of movement in the darkness to one side—one that another would not have seen but did not escape her. She slowed deliberately, letting her eyes adjust. An Elf stood deep in the shadows against the wall, still now, watchful.

"It is only Cort," the queen softly said. "He serves the Home Guard." Her hand brushed Wren's cheek. "You have our Elf eyes, child."

The doors led into the queen's bedchamber, a large room with a domed ceiling, latticed windows curved in a bank along the far wall, a canopied bed with the sheets still rumpled, chairs and couches and tables in small clusters, a writing desk, and a door leading off to a wash chamber.

"Sit here, Wren," the queen directed, leading her to a small couch. "Eowen will wash and dress your cuts."

She looked over at the red-haired woman, who was already pouring water from a pitcher into a basin and gathering together some clean cloths. A minute later she was back, kneeling beside Wren, her hands surprisingly strong as she loosened the girl's clothes and began to bathe her. She worked wordlessly while the queen watched, then finished by applying bandages where they were needed and supplying a loose-fitting sleeping gown that Wren gratefully accepted and slipped into—the first clean clothes she had enjoyed in weeks. The red-haired woman crossed the room and returned with a cup of something warm and soothing. Wren sniffed at it tentatively, discovered traces of ale and tea and something more, and drank it without comment.

Ellenroh Elessedil eased down on the couch beside her and took her hand. "Now, Wren, we shall talk. Are you hungry? Would you like something to eat first?" Wren shook her head, too tired to eat, too anxious to discover what the queen had to tell her. "Good, then." The queen sighed. "Where shall we begin?"

Wren was suddenly conscious of the red-haired woman moving over to sit down across from them. She glanced at the woman doubtfully— Eowen, the queen had called her. She had assumed that Eowen was the queen's personal attendant and had been brought along solely for the purpose of seeing to their comfort and would then be dismissed as the others had. But the queen had not dismissed her, appearing barely aware of her presence in fact, and Eowen gave no indication that she thought she was expected to leave. The more Wren thought about it the less Eowen seemed simply an attendant. There was something about the way she carried herself, the way she reacted to what the queen said and did. She was quick enough to help when asked, but she did not show the deference to Ellenroh Elessedil that the others did.

The queen saw where Wren was looking and smiled. "I'm afraid I've gotten ahead of myself again. And failed to show proper manners as well. This is Eowen Cerise, Wren. She is my closest friend and advisor. She is the reason, in fact, that you are here."

Wren frowned slightly. "I don't understand what you mean. I am here because I came in search of the Elves. That search came about because the Druid Allanon asked me to undertake it. What has Eowen to do with that?"

"Allanon," the Elf Queen whispered, momentarily distracted. "Even in death, he keeps watch over us." She released Wren's hand in a gesture of confusion. "Wren, let me ask you a question first. How did you manage to find us? Can you tell us of your journey to reach Morrowindl and Arborlon?"

Wren was anxious to learn about her mother, but she was not the one in control here. She concealed her impatience and did as the queen asked. She told of the dreams sent by Allanon, the appearance of Cogline and the resulting journey to the Hadeshorn, the charges of the Druid shade to the Ohmsfords, her return with Garth to the Westland and search for some hint of what had become of the Elves, their subsequent arrival at Grimpen Ward and talk with the Addershag, their escape to the ruins of the Wing Hove, the coming of Tiger Ty and Spirit, and the flight to Morrowindl and the journey in. She left out only two things—any mention of the Shadowen that had tracked them or the fact that she possessed the Elfstones. The Owl had been quite clear in his warning to say nothing of the Stones until she was alone with the queen, and unless she spoke of the Stones she could say nothing of the Shadowen.

She finished and waited for the queen to say something. Ellenroh Elessedil studied her intently for a moment and then smiled. "You are a cautious girl, Wren, and that is something you must be in this world. Your story tells me exactly as much as it should—and nothing more." She leaned forward, her strong face lined with a mix of feelings too intricate for Wren to sort out. "I am going to tell you something now in return and when I am done there will be no more secrets between us."

She picked up Wren's hands once more in her own. "Your mother was called Alleyne, as Gavilan told you. She was my daughter."

Wren sat without moving, her hands gripped tightly in the queen's, surprise and wonder racing through her as she tried to think what to say.

"My daughter, Wren, and that makes you my grandchild. There is one thing more. I gave to Alleyne, and she in turn was to give to you, three painted stones in a leather bag. Do you have them?"

Wren hesitated, trapped now, not knowing what she was supposed to do or say. But she could not lie. "Yes," she admitted.

The queen's blue eyes were penetrating as they scanned Wren's face, and there was a faint smile on her lips. "But you know the truth of them now, don't you? You must, Wren, or you would never have gotten here alive."

Wren forced her face to remain expressionless. "Yes," she repeated quietly.

Ellenroh patted her hands and released them. "Eowen knows of the Elfstones, child. So do a few of the others who have stood beside me for so many years—Aurin Striate, for one. He warned you against saying anything, didn't he? No matter. Few know of the Elfstones, and none have seen them used—not even I. You alone have had that experience, Wren, and I do not think you are altogether pleased, are you?"

Wren shook her head slowly, surprised at how perceptive the queen was, at her insight into feelings Wren had thought carefully hidden. Was it because they were family and therefore much alike, their heredity a bonding that gave each a window into the other's heart? Could Wren, in turn, perceive when she chose what Ellenroh Elessedil felt?

Family. She whispered the word in her mind. *The family I came to find. Is it possible? Am I really the grandchild of this queen, an Elessedil myself?*

"Tell me the rest of how you came to Arborlon," the queen said softly, "and I will tell you what you are so anxious to know. Do not be concerned with Eowen. Eowen already knows everything that matters."

So Wren related the balance of what had occurred on her journey, all that involved the wolf thing that was Shadowen and the discovery of the truth about the painted stones that her mother had given her as a child. When she was done, when she had told them everything, she folded her arms protectively, feeling chilled by her own words, at the memories they invoked. Then, impulsively, she rose and walked to where her discarded clothing lay. Searching hurriedly through the tattered pieces, she came upon the Elfstones, still tucked inside where she had left them after entering the city. She carried them to the queen and held them forth. "Here," she offered. "Take them."

But Ellenroh Elessedil shook her head. "No, Wren." She closed Wren's fingers over the Elfstones and guided her hand to a pocket of the sleeping gown. "You keep them for me," she whispered.

For the first time, Eowen Cerise spoke. "You have been very brave, Wren." Her voice was low and compelling. "Most would not have been able to overcome the obstacles you faced. You are indeed your mother's child."

"I see so much of Alleyne in her," the queen agreed, her eyes momentarily distant. Then she straightened, fixing her gaze on Wren once more. "And you have been brave indeed. Allanon was right in choosing you. But it was predetermined that you should come, so I suppose that he was only fulfilling Eowen's promise."

She saw the confusion in Wren's eyes and smiled. "I know, child. I speak in riddles. You have been very patient with me, and it has not been easy. You are anxious to hear of your mother and to discover why it is that you are here. Very well."

The smile softened. "Three generations before my own birth, while the Elves still lived within the Westland, several members of the Ohmsford family, direct descendants of Jair Ohmsford, decided to migrate to Arborlon. Their decision, as I understand it, was prompted by the encroachment of the Federation on Southland villages like Shady Vale and the beginnings of the witch hunt to suppress magic. There were three of these Ohmsfords, and they brought with them the Elfstones. One died childless. Two married, but when the Elves chose to disappear only one of the two went with them. The second, I was told, a man, returned to Shady Vale with his wife. That would have been Par and Coll Ohmsfords' great-grandparents. The Ohmsford who remained was a woman, and she kept with her the Elfstones."

Ellenroh paused. "The Elfstones, Wren, as you know, were formed in the beginning by Elven magic and could be used only by those with Elven blood. The Elven blood had been bred out of the Ohmsfords in the years since the death of Brin and Jair, and they were of no particular use to those Ohmsfords who kept custody of them. They decided therefore at some point and by mutual agreement that the Stones belonged back with the people who had made them—or, more properly, I suppose, with their descendants. So when the three who came from Shady Vale married and began their new lives, it was natural enough for them to decide that the Elfstones, a trust to the Ohmsford family from Allanon since the days of their ancestor Shea, should remain with the Elves no matter what became of them personally.

"In any case, the Elfstones disappeared when the Elves did, and I suppose I need to say a word or two about that." She shook her head, remembering. "Our people had been receding farther into the Westland forests for years. They had become increasingly isolated from the other Races as the Federation expansion worked its way north. Some of that was their own doing, but an equal share was the result of a growing belief, fostered by the Federation's Coalition Council, that the Elves were different and that different was not good. The Elves, after all, were the descendants of faerie people and not really human. The Elves were the makers of the magic that had shaped the world since the advent of the First Council at Paranor, and no one had ever much trusted either the magic or its users. When the things you call Shadowen began to appear—there was no name for them then—the Federation was quick to place the blame for the sickening of the land on the Elves. After all, that was where the magic had originated, and wasn't it magic that was causing all the problems? If not, why were the Elves and their homeland not affected? It all multiplied as such things do until finally our people had had enough. The choice was simple. Either stand up to the Federation, which meant giving them the war they were so actively seeking, or find a way to sidestep them completely. War was not an attractive prospect. The Elves would stand virtually alone against the strongest army in the Four Lands. Callahorn had already been absorbed and the Free Corps disbanded, the Trolls were as unpredictably tribal as ever, and the Dwarves were hesitant to commit.

"So the Elves decided simply to leave—to migrate to a new territory, resettle, and wait the Federation out. This decision wasn't arrived at easily; there were many who wanted to stand and fight, an equal number who thought it better to wait and see. After all, this was their homeland they were being asked to abandon, the birthplace of Elves since the cataclysm of the Great Wars. But, in the end, after much time and deliberation, it was agreed that the best choice was to leave. The Elves had survived moves before. They had established new homelands. They had perfected the art of seeming to disappear while in fact still being there."

She sighed. "It was so long ago, Wren, and I wasn't there. I can't be certain now what their motives were. The move began a slow gathering together of Elves from every corner of the Westland so that villages simply ceased to exist. Meanwhile, the Wing Riders found this island, and it suited the needs of the Land Elves perfectly. Morrowindl. When it was settled that this is where they would come, they chose a time and just disappeared."

She seemed to deliberate as to whether to explain further, then shook her head. "Enough of what brought us here. As I said, one among the Ohmsfords stayed. Two generations passed with children being born, and then my mother married the King of the Elessedils, and the Ohmsford and Elessedil families merged. I was born and my brother Asheron after me. My brother was chosen to be king, but he was killed by the demons—one of the first to die. I became queen then instead. I married and your mother was born, Alleyne, my only child. Eventually the demons killed my husband as well. Alleyne was all I had left."

"My mother," Wren echoed. "What was she like?"

The queen smiled anew. "There was no one like her. She was smart, willful, pretty. She believed she could do anything—some part of her wanted to try, at least." She clasped her hands and the smile faded. "She met a Wing Rider and chose him for her husband. I didn't think it a good idea—the Sky Elves have never really bonded with us—but what I thought didn't really matter, of course. This was nearly twenty years ago, and it was a dangerous time. The demons were everywhere and growing stronger. We were being forced back into the city. Contact with the outside world was becoming difficult.

"Shortly after she was married, Alleyne became pregnant with you. That was when Eowen told me of her vision." She glanced at the other woman, who sat watching impassively, green eyes huge and depthless. "Eowen is a seer, Wren, perhaps the best that ever was. She was my playmate and confidante when I was a child, even before she knew she had the power. She has been with me ever since, advising and guiding me. I told you that she was the reason you are here. When Alleyne became pregnant,

Eowen warned me that if my daughter did not leave Morrowindl before you were born, both of you would die. She had seen it in a vision. She told me as well that Alleyne could never return, but that one day you must and that your coming would save the Elves."

She took a deep breath. "I know. I felt as you must now. How can this be true? I did not want Alleyne to go. But I knew that Eowen's visions were never wrong. So I summoned Alleyne and had Eowen repeat what she had told to me. Alleyne did not hesitate, although I know she was inwardly reluctant. She said she would go, that she would see to it that the baby was kept safe. She never mentioned herself. That was your mother. I still had possession of the Elfstones, passed down to me through the union of my parents. I gave them to Alleyne to keep her safe, first changing their appearance with a bit of my own magic to see to it that they would not be immediately recognizable or appear to have any value.

"Alleyne was to return to the Westland with her husband. She was to journey from there to Shady Vale and reestablish contact with the descendants of the Ohmsfords who had gone back when the Elves had come to Morrowindl. I never knew if she did. She disappeared from my life for nearly three years. Eowen could only tell me that she—and you—were safe.

"Then, a little more than fifteen years ago now, Alleyne decided to return. I don't know what prompted that decision, only that she came. She gave you the leather bag with the Elfstones, placed you in the care of the Ohmsfords in Shady Vale, and flew back with her husband to us."

She shook her head slowly, as if the idea of her daughter's return were incomprehensible even now. "By then, the demons had overrun Morrowindl; the city was all that was left to us. The Keel had been formed of our magic to protect us, but the demons were everywhere without. Wing Riders were coming in less and less frequently. The Roc Alleyne and her husband were riding came down through the vog and was struck by some sort of missile. He landed short of the city gates. The demons . . ."

She stopped, unable to continue. There were tears in her eyes. "We could not save them," she finished.

Wren felt a great hollowness open within. In her mind, she saw her mother die. Impulsively she leaned forward and put her arms around her grandmother, the last of her family, the only tie that remained to her mother and her father, and hugged her close. She felt the queen's head lower to her shoulder and the slender arms come about her in reply. They sat in silence for a long time, just holding each other. Wren tried to conjure up images of her mother's face in her mind and failed. All she could see now was her grandmother's face. She was conscious of the fact that however deep her own loss, it would never match the queen's.

They pulled away from each other finally, and the queen smiled once more, radiant, bracing. "I am so glad you have come, Wren," she repeated. "I have waited a very long time to meet you."

"Grandmother," Wren said, the word sounding odd when she spoke it. "I still don't understand why I was sent. Allanon told me that I was to find the Elves because there could be no healing of the Lands until they returned. And now you tell me Eowen has foretold that my coming will save the Elves. But what difference does my being here make? Surely you would have returned long ago if you were able."

The smile faded slowly. "It is more complicated than that, I am afraid."

"How can it be more complicated? Can't you leave, if you choose?"

"Yes, child, we can leave."

"If you can leave, why don't you? What is it that keeps you? Do you stand because you must? Are these demons come from the Forbidding? Has the Ellcrys failed again?"

"No, the Ellcrys is well." She paused, uncertain.

"Then where did these demons come from?"

There was a barely perceptible tightening of the queen's smooth face. "We are not certain, Wren."

She was lying. Wren knew it instinctively. She heard it in her grandmother's voice and saw it in the sudden lowering of Eowen's green eyes. Shocked, hurt, angry as well, she stared at the queen in disbelief. *No more secrets between us?* she thought, repeating the other's own words. *What are you hiding?*

Ellenroh Elessedil seemed not to notice her grandchild's distress. She reached out again and embraced her warmly. Though tempted, Wren did not push away, thinking there must be a reason for this secrecy and it would be explained in time, thinking as well that she had come too far to discover the truth about her family and give up on finding it out because some part of it was slow in coming. She forced her feelings aside. She was a Rover girl, and Garth had trained her well. She could be patient. She could wait.

"Time enough to speak more of this tomorrow, child," the queen whispered in her ear. "You need sleep now. And I need to think."

She drew back, her smile so sad that it almost brought tears to Wren's eyes. "Eowen will show you to your room. Your friend Garth will be sleeping right next door, should you need him. Rest, child. We have waited a long time to find each other and we must not rush the greeting."

She came to her feet, bringing Wren up with her. Across from them, Eowen Cerise rose as well. The queen gave her grandchild a final hug. Wren hugged her back, masking the doubts that crowded within. She was tired now, her eyes heavy, and her strength ebbing. She felt warm and comforted and she needed to rest.

"I am glad to be here, Grandmother," she said quietly, and meant it.

But I will know the truth, she added to herself. *I will know it all.*

She let Eowen Cerise lead her from the bedchamber and into the darkened hallway beyond.

11

When Wren awoke the following morning she found herself in a room of white-painted walls, cotton bedding with tiny flowers sewn into the borders, and tapestries woven of soft pastel threads that shimmered in the wash of brilliant light flooding through breaks in lace curtains that hung in folds across the floor-to-ceiling windows.

Sunlight, she marveled, in a land where beyond the walls of the city and the power of the Elven magic there was only darkness.

She lay back, drowsy still, taking time to gather her thoughts. She had not seen much of the room the night before. It had been dark, and Eowen had used only candlelight to guide her. She had collapsed into the down-stuffed bed and been asleep almost immediately.

She closed her eyes momentarily, trying to connect what she was seeing to what she remembered, this dreamlike, translucent present to the harsh, forbidding past. Had it all been real—the search to find where the Elves had gone, the flight to Morrowindl, the trek through the In Ju, the climb up Blackledge, the march to the Rowen and then Arborlon? Lying there as she was, swathed in sunlight and soft sheets, she found it hard to believe so. Her memory of what lay without the city's walls—the darkness and fire and haze, the monsters that came from everywhere and knew only how to destroy—seemed dim and far away.

Her eyes blinked open angrily, and she forced herself to remember. Events paraded before her, vivid and harsh. She saw Garth as he stood with her against the Shadowen at the edge of the cliffs above the Blue Divide. She pictured once more how it had been that first night on the beach when Tiger Ty and Spirit had left them. She thought of Stresa and Faun, forced herself to remember how they looked and talked and acted, and what they had endured in helping her travel through this monstrous world, friends who had helped her only to be left behind.

Thinking of the Splinterscat and the Tree Squeak was what finally brought her awake. She pushed herself into a sitting position and looked slowly around. She was here, she assured herself, in Arborlon, in the palace of the Elf Queen, in the home of Ellenroh Elessedil, her grandmother. She took a deep breath, wrestling with the idea, working to make it be real. It was, of course—yet at the same time it didn't yet seem so. It was too new, she supposed. She had come looking to find the truth about her parents; she could not have guessed the truth would prove so startling.

She remembered what she had said to herself when Cogline had first approached her about the dreams: What she learned by agreeing to travel to the Hadeshorn to speak with Allanon might well change her life.

She could not have imagined how much.

It both intrigued and frightened her. So much had happened to bring her to Morrowindl and the Elves, and now she was faced with confronting a world and a people she did not really know or understand. She had discovered last night just how difficult things might prove to be. If even her own grandmother would choose to lie to her, how much trust could she put in any of the others? It rankled still that there were secrets being kept from her. She had been sent to the Elves for a purpose, but she still didn't know what it was. Ellenroh, if she knew, wasn't saying—at least not yet. And she wasn't saying anything about the demons either—only that they hadn't come through the Forbidding and that the Ellcrys hadn't failed. But they had come from somewhere, and the queen knew where that was, Wren was certain. She knew a lot of things she wasn't telling.

Secrets—there was that word again.

Secrets.

She let the matter drop with a shake of her head. The queen was her grandmother, the last of her family, the giver of life to her mother, and a woman of accomplishment and beauty and responsibility and love. Wren shook her head. She could not bring herself to think ill of Ellenroh Elessedil. She could not disparage her. She was too like her, perhaps—physically, emotionally, and in word and thought and act. She had seen it for herself last night; she had felt it in their conversation, in the glances they exchanged, and in the way they responded to each other.

She sighed. It was best that she do as she had promised, that she wait and see.

After a time, she rose and walked to the door that led to the adjoining chamber. Almost immediately the door opened and Garth was there. He was shirtless, his muscled arms and torso wrapped in bandages, and his dark bearded face cut and bruised. Despite the impressive array of injuries, the big Rover looked rested and fit. When she beckoned him in, he reached back into his own room for a tunic and hastily slipped it on. The clothes that had been provided him were too small and made him look decidedly outsized. She hid her smile as they moved over to sit on a bench by the lace-curtained window, happy just to see him again, taking comfort from his familiar presence.

What have you learned? he signed.

She let him see her smile now. Good, old, dependable Garth—right to the point every time. She repeated her previous night's conversation with the queen, relating what she had been told of the history of the Elessedils and Ohmsfords and of her mother and father. She did not voice her suspicion that Ellenroh was shading the truth about the demons. She wanted to keep that to herself for now, hoping that given a little time her grandmother would choose to confide in her.

Nevertheless, she wanted Garth's opinion about the queen.

"What did you notice about my grandmother that I missed?" she asked him, fingers translating as she spoke.

Garth smiled faintly at the implication that she had missed anything. His response was quick. *She is frightened.*

"Frightened?" Wren had indeed missed that. "What do you think frightens her?"

Difficult to say. Something that she knows and we don't, I would guess. She is very careful with what she says and how she says it. You saw as much.

He paused. *She may be frightened for you, Wren.*

"Because my mother was killed by coming back here, and now I am at risk as well? But I was supposed to return according to Eowen's vision. They have been expecting me. And what do you make of this vision anyway? How am I supposed to save the Elves, Garth? Doesn't that seem silly to you? After all, it was all we could do just to stay alive long enough to reach the city. I don't see what difference my being here can make."

Garth shrugged. *Keep your eyes and ears open, Rover girl. That's how you learn things.*

He smiled, and Wren smiled in return.

He left her then so that she could dress. As he closed the door separating their rooms, she stood staring after him for a moment. It occurred to her suddenly that there were enormous inconsistencies in the stories told by her grandmother and Garth concerning her parents. Admittedly, Garth's version was secondhand and the queen's based entirely on events that had taken place before the departure from Arborlon, so perhaps inconsistencies were to be expected. Still, neither had commented on what each must have viewed as the other's obvious mistakes. There was no mention of Wing Riders by Garth. There was no mention of Rovers by the queen. There was nothing from either about why her parents had not traveled first to Shady Vale and the Ohmsfords but had gone instead to the Westland.

She wondered if she should say anything about it to Garth. Given the importance of her other concerns, she wondered if this one really mattered.

She found clothing set out for her to wear, garments that fit better than Garth's—pants, a tunic, stockings, a belt, and a pair of fine-worked leather ankle boots. She slipped the clothing on, going over in her mind as she did so the revelations of the night before, considering anew what she had learned. The queen seemed decided on the importance of Wren's arrival in Arborlon, certain in her own mind at least that Eowen's vision would prove accurate. Aurin Striate, too, had mentioned that they had been waiting for her. Yet no one had said why, if, in fact, anyone knew. There hadn't been any mention in the dream of what it was that Wren's presence was supposed to accomplish. Maybe it would take another vision to find out.

She grinned at her own impudence and was pulling on her boots when the grin abruptly faded.

What if the importance of her return was that she carried with her the

Elfstones? What if she was expected to use the Stones as a weapon against the demons?

She went cold with the thought, remembering anew how she had been forced to use them twice now despite her reluctance to do so, remembering the feeling of power as the magic coursed through her, liquid fire that burned and exhilarated at the same time. She was aware of their addictive effect on her, of the bonding that took place each time they were employed, and of how they seemed so much a part of her. She kept saying she would not use them, then found herself forced to do so anyway—or persuaded, perhaps. She shook her head. The choice of words didn't matter; the results were the same. Each time she used the magic, she drifted a little farther from who and what she was and a little closer to being someone she didn't know. She lost power over herself by using the power of the magic.

She jammed her feet into the boots and stood up. Her thinking was wrong. It couldn't be the Elfstones that were important. Otherwise, why hadn't Ellenroh simply kept them here instead of giving them to Alleyne? Why hadn't the Stones been used against the demons long ago if they could really make a difference?

She hesitated, then reached over to her sleeping gown and extracted the Elfstones from the pocket in which she had placed them the night before. They lay glittering in her hand, their magic dormant, harmless, and invisible. She studied them intently, wondering at the circumstances that had placed them in her care, wishing anew that Ellenroh had agreed last night to take them back.

Then she brushed aside the bad feelings that thinking of the Elfstones conjured up and shoved the troublesome talismans deep into her tunic pocket. After slipping a long knife into her belt, she straightened confidently and walked from the room.

An Elven Hunter had been posted outside her door, and after pausing to summon Garth, the sentry escorted them downstairs to the dining hall and breakfast. They ate alone at a long, polished oak table covered in white linen and decorated with flowers, seated in a cavernous room with an arched ceiling and stained-glass windows that filtered the sunlight in prismatic colors. A serving girl stood ready to wait upon them, making the self-sufficient Wren feel more than a little uncomfortable. She ate in silence, Garth seated across from her, wondering what she was supposed to do when she was finished.

There was no sign of the queen.

Nevertheless, as the meal was being completed, the Owl appeared. Aurin Striate looked as gaunt and faded now as he had in the shadows and darkness of the lava fields without, his angular body loose and disjointed as he moved, nothing working quite as it should. He was wearing clean clothes and the stocking cap was gone, but he still managed to look somewhat creased and rumpled—it seemed that was normal for him. He came up to the dining table and took a seat, slouching forward comfortably.

"You look a whole lot better than you did last night," he ventured with a half smile. "Clean clothes and a bath make you a pretty girl indeed, Wren. Rest well, did you?"

She smiled back at him. She liked the Owl. "Well enough, thanks. And thanks again for getting us safely inside. We wouldn't have made it without you."

The Owl pursed his lips, glanced meaningfully at Garth, and shrugged. "Maybe so. But we both know that you were the one who really saved us." He paused, stopped short of mentioning the Elfstones, and settled back in his chair. His aging Elven features narrowed puckishly. "Want to take a look around when you're done? See a little of what's out there? Your grandmother has put me at your disposal for a time."

Minutes later, they left the palace grounds, passing through the front gates this time, and went down into the city. The palace was settled on a knoll at the center of Arborlon, deep in the sheltering forests, with the cottages and shops of the city all around. The city was alive in daylight, the Elves busy at their work, the streets bustling with activity. As the three edged their way through the crowds, glances were directed toward them from every quarter—not at the Owl or Wren, but at Garth, who was much bigger than the Elves and clearly not one of them. Garth, in typical fashion, seemed oblivious. Wren craned her neck to see everything. Sunlight brightened the greens of the trees and grasses, the colors of the buildings, and the flowers that bordered the walkways; it was as if the vog and fire without the walls did not exist. There was a trace of ash and sulfur in the air, and the shadow of Killeshan was a dark smudge against the sky east where the city backed into the mountain, but the magic kept the world within sheltered and protected. The Elves were going about their business as if everything were normal, as if nothing threatened, and as if Morrowindl outside the city might be exactly the same as within.

After a time they passed through the screen of the forest and came in sight of the outer wall. In daylight, the wall looked different. The glow of the magic had subsided to a faint glimmer that turned the world beyond to a soft, hazy watercolor washed of its brightness. Morrowindl—its mountains, Killeshan's maw, the mix of lava rock and stunted forest, the fissures in the earth with their geysers of ash and steam—was misted almost to the point of invisibility. Elven soldiers patroled the ramparts, but there were no battles being fought now, the demons having slipped away to rest until nightfall. The world outside had gone sullen and empty, and the only audible sounds came from the voices and movement of the people within.

As they neared the closest bridgehead, Wren turned to the Owl and asked, "Why is there a moat inside the wall?"

The Owl glanced over at her, then away again. "It separates the city from the Keel. Do you know about the Keel?"

He gestured toward the wall. Wren remembered the name now. Stresa had been the first to use it, saying that the Elves were in trouble because its magic was weakening.

"It was built of the magic in the time of Ellenroh's father, when the demons first came into being. It protects against them, keeps the city just as it has always been. Everything is the same as it was when Arborlon was brought to Morrowindl over a hundred years ago."

Wren was still mulling over what Stresa had said about the magic growing weaker. She was about to ask Aurin Striate if it was so when she realized what he had just said.

"Owl, did you say when Arborlon was *brought* to Morrowindl? You mean when it was built, don't you?"

"I mean what I said."

"That the buildings were brought? Or are you talking about the Ellcrys? The Ellcrys is here, isn't it, inside the city?"

"Back there." He gestured vaguely, his seamed face clouded. "Behind the palace."

"So you mean—"

The Owl cut her short. "The city, Wren. The whole of it and all of the Elves that live in it. That's what I mean."

Wren stared. "But . . . It was rebuilt, you mean, from timbers the Elves ferried here . . ."

He was shaking his head. "Wren, has no one told you of the Loden? Didn't the queen tell you how the Elves came to Morrowindl?"

He was leaning close to her now, his sharp eyes fixed on her. She hesitated, saying finally, "She said that it was decided to migrate out of the Westland because the Federation—"

"No," he cut her short once more. "That's not what I mean."

He looked away a moment, then took her by the arm and walked her to a stone abutment at the foot of the bridge where they could sit. Garth trailed after them, his dark face expressionless, taking up a position across from them where he could see them speak.

"This isn't something I had planned on having to tell you, girl," the Owl began when they were settled. "Others could do the job better. But we won't have much to talk about if I don't explain. And besides, if you're Ellenroh Elessedil's grandchild and the one she's been waiting for, the one in Eowen Cerise's vision, then you have a right to know."

He folded his angular arms comfortably. "But you're not going to believe it. I'm not sure I do."

Wren smiled, a trifle uncomfortable with the prospect. "Tell me anyway, Owl."

Aurin Striate nodded. "This is what I've been told, then—not what I necessarily know. The Elves recovered some part of their faerie magic more than a hundred years back, before Morrowindl, while they were still living in the Westland. I don't know how they did it; I don't really suppose I care. What's important to know is that when they made the decision to migrate, they supposedly channeled what there was of the magic into an Elfstone called the Loden. The Loden, I think, had always been there, hidden away, kept secret for the time when it would be needed. That time didn't come for hundreds of years—not in all the time that passed after the Great Wars.

But the Elessedils had it put away, or they found it again, or something, and when the decision was made to migrate, they put it to use."

He took a steadying breath and tightened his lips. "This Elfstone, like all of them, I'm told, draws its strength from the user. Except in this case, there wasn't just a single user but an entire race. The whole of the strength of the Elven nation went into invoking the Loden's magic." He cleared his throat. "When it was done, all of Arborlon had been picked up like . . . like a scoop of earth, shrunk down to nothing, and sealed within the Stone. And that's what I mean when I say Arborlon was brought to Morrowindl. It was sealed inside the Loden along with most of its people and carried by just a handful of caretakers to this island. Once a site for the city was found, the process was reversed and Arborlon was restored. Men, women, children, dogs, cats, birds, animals, houses and shops, trees, flowers, grass— everything. The Ellcrys, too. All of it."

He sat back and the sharp eyes narrowed. "So now what do you say?"

Wren was stunned. "I say you're right, Owl. I don't believe it. I can't conceive of how the Elves were able to recover something that had been lost for thousands of years that fast. Where did it come from? They hadn't any magic at all in the time of Brin and Jair Ohmsford—only their healing powers!"

The Owl shrugged. "I don't pretend to know how they did any of it, Wren. It was long before my time. The queen might know—but she's never said a word about it to me. I only know what I was told, and I'm not sure if I believe that. The city and its people were carried here in the Loden. That's the story. And that's how the Keel was built, too. Well, it was actually constructed of stone by hand labor first, but the magic that protects it came out of the Loden. I was a boy then, but I remember the old king using the Ruhk Staff. The Ruhk Staff holds the Loden and channels the magic."

"You've seen this?" Wren asked doubtfully.

"I've seen the Staff and its Stone many times," the Owl answered. "I saw them used only that once."

"What about the demons?" Wren went on, wanting to learn more, trying to make sense of what she was hearing. "What of them? Can't the Loden and the Ruhk Staff be used against them?"

The Owl's face darkened, changing expression so quickly that it caught Wren by surprise. "No," he answered quietly. "The magic is useless against the demons."

"But why is that?" she pressed. "The magic of the Elfstones I carry can destroy them. Why not the magic of the Loden?"

He shook his head. "It's a different kind of magic, I guess."

He didn't sound very sure of himself. Quickly Wren said, "Tell me where the demons came from, Owl?"

Aurin Striate looked uncomfortable. "Why ask me, Wren Elessedil?"

"Ohmsford," she corrected at once.

"I don't think so."

There was a strained silence as they faced each other, eyes locked. "They came out of the magic, too, didn't they?" Wren said finally, unwilling to back off.

The Owl's sharp gaze was steady. "You ask the queen, Wren. You talk with her."

He rose abruptly. "Now that you know how the city got here, according to legend at least, let's finish looking around. There's three sets of gates in the Keel, one main and two small. See over there . . ."

He started off, still talking, explaining what they were seeing, steering the conversation away from the questions no one seemed to want to answer. Wren listened halfheartedly, more interested in the tale of how the Elves had come to Morrowindl. It required such incredible magic to gather up an entire city, reduce it to the size of an Elfstone, and seal it inside for a journey that would carry it over an ocean. She still could not conceive of it. Elven magic recovered from out of faerie, from a time that was barely remembered—it was incredible. All that power, and still no way to break free of the demons, no way to destroy them. Her mouth tightened against a dozen protestations. She really didn't know what to believe.

They spent the morning and the early part of the afternoon walking through the city. They climbed to the ramparts and looked out over the land beyond, dim and hazy, empty of movement save where Killeshan's steam erupted and the vog swirled. They saw Phaeton again, passing from the city to the Keel, oblivious to them, his strong features scarred and rough beneath his sun-bleached hair. The Owl watched stone faced and was turning to continue their walk when Wren asked him to tell her about Phaeton. The queen's field commander, Aurin Striate answered, second in command only to Barsimmon Oridio and anxious to succeed him.

"Why don't you like him?" Wren asked bluntly.

The Owl cocked one eyebrow. "That's a hard one to explain. It's a fundamental difference between us, I suppose. I spend most of my time outside the walls, prowling the night with the demons, taking a close look at where they are and what they're about. I live like them much of the time, and when you do that you get to know them. I know the kinds and their habits, more about them than anyone. But Phaeton, he doesn't think any of that matters. To him, the demons are simply an enemy that needs to be destroyed. He wants to take the Elven army out there and sweep them away. He's been after Barsimmon Oridio and the queen to let him do exactly that for months. His men love him; they think he's right because they want to believe he knows something they don't. We've been shut away behind the Keel for almost ten years. Life goes on, and you can't tell by just looking or even by talking to the people, but they're all sick at heart. They remember how they used to live and they want to live that way again."

Wren considered momentarily bringing up the subject of how the demons got there and why they couldn't simply be sent back again, but decided against it. Instead she said, "You think that there isn't any hope of the army winning out there, I gather."

The Owl fixed her with a hard stare. "You were out there with me, Wren—which is more than Phaeton can say. You traveled up from the beach to get here. You faced the demons time and again. What do you think? They're not like us. There's a hundred different kinds, and each of them is dangerous in a different way. Some you can kill with an iron blade and some you can't. Down along the Rowen there's the Revenants—all teeth and claws and muscle. Animals. Up on Blackledge there's the Drakuls—ghosts that suck the life out of you, like smoke, nothing to fight, nothing to put a sword to. And that's only two kinds, Wren." He shook his head. "No, I don't think we can win out there. I think we'll be lucky if we can manage to stay alive in here."

They walked on a bit farther and then Wren said, "The Splinterscat told me that the magic that shields the city is weakening."

She made it a statement of fact and not a question and waited for an answer. For a long time the Owl did not respond, his head lowered toward his stride, his eyes on the ground before him.

Finally, he looked over, just for a moment, and said, "The Scat is right."

They went down into the city proper for a time, wandering into the shops and poring over the carts that dominated the marketplace, perusing the wares and studying the people buying and selling them. Arborlon was a city that in all respects but one might have been any other. Wren gazed at the faces about her, seeing her own Elven features reflected in theirs, the first time she had ever been able to do that, pleased with the experience and with the idea that she was the first person to be able to do so in more than a hundred years. The Elves were alive; the Elves existed. It was a wondrous discovery, and it still excited her to have been the one to have made it.

They had a quick meal in the marketplace—some thin-baked bread wrapped about seared meat and vegetables, a piece of fresh fruit that resembled a pear, and a cup of ale, and then continued on. The Owl took them behind the palace into the Gardens of Life. They walked the pathways in silence, losing themselves in the fragrance of the flower beds and in the scents of the hundreds of colorful blooms that lay scattered amid the plants and bushes and trees. They came upon a white-robed Chosen, one of the caretakers of the Ellcrys, who nodded and passed by. Wren found herself thinking of Par Ohmsford's tale of the Elven girl Amberle, the most famous Chosen of all. They climbed to the summit of the hill on which the Gardens had been planted and stood before the Ellcrys, the tree's scarlet leaves and silver branches vibrant in the sunlight, so striking that it seemed they could not be real. Wren wanted to touch the tree, to whisper something to it, and to tell it perhaps that she knew and understood who and what it had endured. She didn't, though; she just stood there. The Ellcrys never spoke to anyone, and it already knew how she felt. So she simply stared at it, thinking as she did how terrible it would be if the Keel failed completely and the demons overran the Elves and their city. The Ellcrys would be

destroyed, of course, and when that happened all of the monsters imprisoned within the Forbidding, the things out of faerie shut away for all these
years, would be released into the world of mortal Men once more. Then,
she thought darkly, Allanon's vision of the future would truly come to pass.

They went back to the palace after that to rest until dinner. The Owl
left them inside the front entry, saying he had business to attend to, offering
nothing more.

"I know you have more questions than you know what to do with,
Wren," he said in parting, his lean face creasing solemnly. "Try to be patient. The answers will come all too soon, I'm afraid."

He went back down the walkway and out the gates. Wren stood with
Garth and watched him go, saying nothing. The big Rover turned to her
after a moment, signing. He was hungry again and wanted to go back to
the dining hall to see if he could find the kitchen and a bite to eat. Wren
nodded absently, still thinking about the Elves and their magic, thinking
as well that the Owl never had answered her question about why there was
a moat inside the Keel. Garth disappeared down the hallway, footsteps
echoing into silence. After a moment she wheeled about and started for
her room. She wasn't sure what she would do once she got there other than
to think matters through, but maybe that was enough. She climbed the
main stairs, listening to the silence, caught up in the spin of her thoughts,
and was starting down the hallway at their head when Gavilan Elessedil
appeared.

"Well, well, cousin Wren," he greeted brightly, flamboyant in a yellow
and blue cross-hatch weave with a silver chain belt. "Been up and about the
city, I understand. How are you today?"

"Fine, thanks," Wren answered, slowing to a halt as he came up to her.

He reached for her hand and lifted it to his lips, kissing softly. "So tell
me. Are you glad you came or do you wish you had stayed home?"

Wren smiled, blushing in spite of her resolve not to. "A little of each, I
suppose." She took her hand away.

Gavilan's eyes twinkled. "That sounds as it should be. Some sour and
some sweet. You came a long way to find us, didn't you? It must have been
a very compelling search, Wren. Have you learned what you came to
discover?"

"Some of it."

The handsome face turned grave. "Your mother, Alleyne, was someone you would have liked very much. I know that the queen has told you
about her, but I want to say something, too. She cared for me as a sister
would when I was growing up. We were very close. She was a strong and
determined girl, Wren—and I see that in you."

Wren smiled anew. "Thank you, Gavilan."

"It is the truth." The other paused. "I hope you will think of me as
your friend rather than simply your cousin. I want you to know that if you
ever need anything, or want to know anything, please come to me. I will
be happy to help if I can."

Wren hesitated. "Gavilan, could you describe my mother for me? Could you tell me what she looked like?"

Her cousin shrugged. "Easily done. Alleyne was small like you. Her hair was colored the same. And her voice . . ." He trailed off. "Hard to describe. It was musical. She was quick-witted and she laughed a lot. But I suppose I remember her eyes best. They were just like yours. When she looked at you, you felt as if there wasn't anyone or anything more important in all the world."

Wren was thinking of the dream, the one in which her mother was bending close to her, looking very much as Gavilan had described her, saying *Remember me. Remember me.* It no longer seemed just a dream to her now. She felt that once, long ago, it must have really happened.

"Wren?"

She realized that she was staring off into space. She looked back at Gavilan, wondering all at once if she should ask him about the Elfstones and the demons. He seemed willing enough to talk with her, and she was drawn to him in a way that surprised her. But she didn't really know him yet, and her Rover training made her cautious.

"These are difficult times for the Elves," Gavilan offered suddenly, bending close. Wren felt his hands come up to take her shoulders. "There are secrets of the magic that—"

"Good day, Wren," Eowen Cerise greeted, appearing at the head of the stairs behind her. Gavilan went still. "Did you enjoy your walk about the city?"

Wren turned, feeling Gavilan's hands drop away. "I did. The Owl was an excellent guide."

Eowen approached, her green eyes shifting to fix Gavilan. "How do you find your cousin, Gavilan?"

The Elf smiled. "Charming, strong-minded—her mother's daughter." He glanced at Wren. "I have to be on my way. Lots to do before dinner. I will talk with you then."

He gave a short nod and walked away, loose, confident, a bit jaunty. Wren watched him go, thinking that he masked a lot with his well-met attitude, but that what lay beneath was rather sweet.

Eowen met her gaze as she turned back. "Gavilan makes us all feel like young girls again." Her flaming red hair was tucked within a netting, and she was wearing a loose, flower-embroidered shift. Her smile was warm, but her eyes, as always, seemed cool and distant. "I think we are all in love with him."

Wren flushed. "I don't even know him."

Eowen nodded. "Well, tell me about your walk. What have you learned of the city, Wren? What did Aurin Striate tell you about it?"

They began to walk the length of the hallway toward Wren's bedchamber. Wren told Eowen what the Owl had said, hoping secretly that the seer would reveal something in return. But Eowen simply listened, nodded encouragingly, and said nothing. She seemed preoccupied with other things, although she paid close enough attention to what Wren was saying that she did not lose the threads of the conversation. Wren finished her narrative as they reached the door to her sleeping room and turned so that they were facing each other.

A smile flickered on Eowen's solemn face. "You have learned a great deal for someone who has been in the city less than a day, Wren."

Not nearly as much as I would like to learn, Wren thought. "Eowen, why is it that no one will tell me where the demons come from?" she asked, throwing caution to the winds.

The smile disappeared, replaced by a palpable sadness. "The Elves don't like to think about the demons, much less talk about them," she said. "The demons came out of the magic, Wren—out of misunderstanding and misuse. They are a fear and a shame and a promise." She paused, saw the disappointment and frustration mirrored in Wren's eyes, and reached out to take her hands. "The queen forbids me, Wren," she whispered. "And perhaps she is right. But I promise you this. Some day soon, if you still wish it, I will tell you everything."

Wren met her gaze, saw honesty reflected in her eyes, and nodded. "I will hold you to that, Eowen. But I would like to think my grandmother would choose to tell me first."

"Yes, Wren. I would like to think so, too." Eowen hesitated. "We have been together a long time, she and I. Through childhood, first love, husbands, and children. All are gone. Alleyne was the worst for both of us. I have never told your grandmother this—though I think she suspects—but I saw in my vision that Alleyne would try to return to Arborlon and that we could not stop her. A seer is blessed and cursed with what she sees. I know what will happen; I can do nothing to change it."

Wren nodded, understanding. "Magic, Eowen. Like that of the Elfstones. I wish I could be shed of it. I don't trust what it does to me. Is it any different for you?"

Eowen tightened her grip, her green eyes locking on Wren's face. "We are given our destiny in life by something we can neither understand nor control, and it binds us to our future as surely as any magic."

She released Wren's hands and stepped away. "As we speak the queen determines the fate of the Elves, Wren. It is your coming that prompts this. You would know what difference your being here makes? Tonight, I think, you shall."

Wren started in sudden realization. "You have had a vision, haven't you, Eowen? You've seen what is to be."

The seer brought up her hands as if not knowing whether to ward the accusation off or to embrace it. "Always, child," she whispered. "Always." Her face was anguished. "The visions never leave."

She turned away then and disappeared back down the hall. Wren stood watching after her as she had watched after the Owl, prophets wandering toward an uncertain future, visions themselves of what the Elves were destined to be.

Dinner that night was a lengthy, awkward affair marked by long periods of silence. Wren and Garth were summoned at dusk and went down to find Eowen and the Owl already waiting. Gavilan joined them a few minutes later. They were seated close together at one end of the long oak table, an impressive array of food was laid out before them, serving people were placed at their beck and call, and the dining hall was brightly lit against the coming night. They spoke little, working hard when they did to avoid wandering into those areas that had already been designated as swampy ground. Even Gavilan, who did most of the talking, chose his topics carefully. Wren could not tell whether her cousin was intimidated by the presence of Eowen and the Owl or whether something else was bothering him. He was as bright and cheerful as before, but he lacked any real interest in the meal and seemed preoccupied. When they spoke, it was mostly to discuss Wren's childhood with the Rovers and Gavilan's memories of Alleyne. The meal passed tediously, and there was an unmistakable sense of relief when it was finally finished.

Although everyone kept looking for her, Ellenroh Elessedil did not appear.

The five were rising and preparing to go their separate ways when an anxious messenger burst into the room and held a hurried conversation with the Owl.

The Owl dismissed him with a scowl and turned to the others. "The demons have mounted an attack against the north wall. Apparently they've succeeded in breaking through."

They scattered quickly then, Eowen to find the queen, Gavilan to arm himself, the Owl, Wren and Garth to discover for themselves what was happening. The Owl led as the latter three rushed through the palace, out the front gates, and down into the city. Wren watched the ground fly beneath her feet as she ran. The dusk had turned to darkness, and the Keel's light flared wildly through the screen of the trees. They passed down a series of side streets, Elves running in every direction, shouting and calling out in alarm, the whole of the city mobilizing at the news of the assault. The Owl avoided the crowds that were already forming, skirting the heart of the city, hastening east along its backside until the trees broke apart and the Keel loomed before them. The wall was swarming with Elven soldiers as hundreds more crossed the bridges to join them, all rushing toward a place in the glow where the light had dimmed to almost nothing and a massive knot of fighters battled in near darkness.

Wren and her companions continued on until they were less than two hundred yards from the wall. There they were stopped as lines of soldiers surged forward in front of them.

Wren gripped Garth's arm in shock. The magic seemed to have failed completely where the Keel had been breached, and the stone of the wall had been turned to rubble. Hundreds of dark, faceless bodies jammed into the gap, fighting to break through as the Elves fought to keep them out.

The struggle was chaotic, bodies twisting and writhing in agony as they were crushed by those pressing from behind. Shouts and screams filled the air, and there was no muffling of the sounds of battle between Elf and demon on this night. Swords hacked and claws rent, and the dead and wounded lay everywhere about the break. For a time the demons seemed to have succeeded, their numbers so great that those in the vanguard were actually inside the city. But the Elves counterattacked ferociously and drove them back again. Back and forth the battle surged about the breach with neither side able to gain an advantage.

Then the cry of "Phaeton, Phaeton" sounded, and the white-blond head of the Elven commander appeared at the forefront of a newly arrived company of soldiers. Sword arm raised, he led a rush for the wall. The demons were thrust back, shrieking and howling, as the Elves hammered into them. Phaeton stood foremost in the attack, miraculously untouched as his men fell all around him. The Elves on the ramparts joined the counterattack, striking from above, and spears and arrows rained down. The Keel's glow brightened, knitting together momentarily across the gap in the damaged wall.

Then the demons mounted yet another assault, a huge mass of them, scrambling through at every turn. The Elves held momentarily, then started to fall back once more. Phaeton leapt before them, sword lifted. The battle stalled as the combatants on each side struggled to take control. Wren watched in horror as the carnage mounted, the dead and dying and injured lying everywhere, the struggle so intense that no one could reach them. Crowds of Elves had formed all about Wren and her companions, old people, women and children, all who were not soldiers in the Elven army, and a curious silence hung over them as they watched, their voices stunned into silence by what they were seeing.

What if the demons break through? Wren thought suddenly. *No one will have a chance. There is no place for these people to run. Everyone will be killed.*

She glanced about frantically. *Where is the queen?*

And suddenly she was there, surrounded by a dozen of her Home Guard, the crowd parting before her. Wren caught sight of Triss, hard-faced and grim as he led his Elven Hunters. The queen walked straight and tall in their midst, seemingly unconcerned by the turmoil raging about her, smooth face calm, and eyes directed ahead. She moved past the edges of the crowd toward the nearest bridge spanning the moat. In one hand she carried the Ruhk Staff, the Loden shimmering white hot at its tip.

What is she going to do? Wren wondered, and was suddenly frightened for her.

The queen walked to the center of the bridge, where it arched above the waters of the moat, and stood where she could be seen by all. Shouts rose, and the soldiers at the wall began to cry out her name, taking heart. The Elves who fought with Phaeton in the breach renewed their efforts. The defense gathered strength and surged forward. Again the demons were pushed back. The clang and rasp of iron weapons rose and with it the screams of the dying.

Then suddenly Phaeton went down. It was impossible to see what had happened—one moment he was there, leading the way, and the next he was gone. The Elves cried out and charged forward to protect him. The demons gave way grudgingly, thrown back by the rush. The battle surged into the gap once more, and this time went beyond as the demons were pushed down the other side and back through the light. Again the magic that protected the Keel began to knit, the lines of the magic weaving together.

Then the demons started back a third time. The Elves, exhausted, reeled away.

Ellenroh Elessedil raised the Ruhk Staff and pointed. The Loden flared abruptly. Warnings were shouted, and the Elves poured back through the breach. Light exploded from the Loden, lancing toward the Keel as the magic of the Elfstone gathered force. It reached the wall as the last of the Elven soldiers threw themselves clear. Stone rubble lifted piece by piece, grinding and scraping as it came, and the wall began to rebuild itself. Demons were caught in the whirlwind and buried. Stones layered themselves one on top of the other and mortar filled the gaps, the magic working and guiding, the power of the Loden reaching out. Wren caught her breath in disbelief. The wall rose, closing off the black hole that had been hammered through it, reconstructing itself until it was whole again.

In seconds the magic had done its work, and the demons were shut without once more.

The queen stood motionless at the center of the bridge while new companies of Elven soldiers raced past her to man the battlements. She waited until a messenger she had dispatched returned from the carnage. The messenger knelt briefly and rose to speak. Wren watched the queen nod once, turn and come back across the bridge. The Home Guard cleared a path for her once more, but this time she came directly toward Wren, able to find her somehow in the swelling crowds. The Rover girl was frightened by what she saw in her grandmother's face.

Ellenroh Elessedil swept up to her, robes billowing out like banners flown from the Ruhk Staff she held pressed to her body, the Loden still glimmering with wicked white light.

"Aurin Striate," the queen called out as she reached them, her eyes fixing momentarily on the Owl. "Go ahead of us, if you will. Summon Bar and Eton from their chambers—if they are still there. Tell them . . ." Her breath seemed to catch in her throat, and her hand tightened about the Ruhk Staff. "Tell them that Phaeton died in the attack, an accident, killed by an arrow from his own bowmen. Tell them that I wish a meeting in the chambers of the High Council at once. Go now, quickly."

The Owl melted into the crowd and was gone. The queen turned to

Wren, one arm coming up to encircle the girl's slender shoulders, the other gesturing with the Staff toward the city. They began to walk, Garth a step behind, the Home Guard all around.

"Wren," the Elf Queen whispered, bending near. "This is the beginning of the end for us. We go now to determine if we can be saved. Stay close to me, will you? Be my eyes and ears and good right arm. It is for this that you have come to me."

Saying no more, she clutched Wren to her and hurried on into the night.

The chambers of the Elven High Council were situated not far from the palace within an ancient grove of white oak. The building was framed by massive timbers and walled with stone, and the council room itself, which formed the principal part of the structure, was a cavernous chamber shaped like a hexagon, its ceiling braced with beams that rose from the joinder of the walls to a center point like a sheltering star. Heavy wooden doors opened from one wall and faced a three-step dais on which rested the throne of the Elven Kings and Queens, and flanking the throne were standards from which pennants hung that bore the personal insignia of the ruling houses. To either side, set against the remaining walls, were rows of benches, a gallery for observers and participants in public meetings. At the center of the room was a broad stretch of flooring dominated by a round table and twenty-one seats. When the High Council was in session, it sat here, and the king or queen sat with it.

Ellenroh Elessedil entered the chamber with a flourish, robes sweeping out behind her, the Ruhk Staff carried before her, and Wren, Garth, Triss, and a handful of the Home Guard trailing after. Gavilan Elessedil was already seated at the council table and rose hurriedly as the queen appeared. He wore chain mail and his broadsword hung from the back of his chair. The queen went to him, embraced him warmly, and moved on to the head of the table.

"Wren," she said, turning. "Sit next to me."

Wren did as she was asked. Garth drifted off to one side and made himself comfortable in the gallery. The chamber doors closed again, and two of the Home Guard took up positions to either side of the entry. Triss moved over to sit at the table next to Gavilan, his lean, hard face distant. Gavilan straightened in his chair, smiled uneasily at Wren, smoothed out his tunic sleeves nervously, and looked away. Ellenroh folded her hands before her and did not speak, clearly waiting for whoever else was expected.

Wren surveyed the chamber, peering into dark corners where the lamplight failed to penetrate. Polished wood gleamed faintly in the gloom behind Garth, and images cast by the flames of the lamp danced at the edges of the light. At her back, the pennants hung limp and unmoving, their insignia cloaked in heavy folds. The chamber was still, and only the soft scrape of boots and the rustle of clothing disturbed the silence.

Then she saw Eowen, seated far back in the gallery opposite Garth, nearly invisible in the shadows.

Wren's eyes shifted instantly to the queen, but Ellenroh gave no indication that she knew the seer was there, her gaze fastened on the council chamber doors. Wren looked back at Eowen momentarily, then off into the shadows. She could feel the tension in the air. Everyone seated in that room knew something was going to happen, but only the queen knew what. Wren took a deep breath. It was for this moment, the queen had told her, that she had come to Arborlon.

Be my eyes and ears and good right arm.

Why?

The doors to the council chamber opened and Aurin Striate entered with two other men. The first was old and heavyset, with graying hair and beard and slow, ponderous movements that suggested he was not a man to let things stand in his way. The second was of average size, clean-shaved, his eyes hooded but alert, his movements light and easy. He smiled as he entered. The first scowled.

"Barsimmon Oridio," the queen greeted the first. "Eton Shart. Thank you both for coming. Aurin Striate, please stay."

The three men seated themselves, eyes fastened on the queen. They were all looking at her now, waiting.

"Cort, Dal," she addressed the guards at the door. "Wait outside, please."

The Elven Hunters slipped through the doors and were gone. The doors closed softly.

"My friends." Ellenroh Elessedil sat straight backed in her chair, her voice carrying easily through the silence as she spoke. "We can't pretend any longer. We can't dissemble. We can't lie. What we have struggled for more than ten years to prevent is upon us."

"My Lady," Barsimmon Oridio began, but she silenced him with a glance.

"Tonight the demons broke through the Keel. The magic has been failing now for months—probably for years—and the things without have been stealing its strength for themselves. Tonight the balance shifted sufficiently to enable them to create a breach. Our hunters fought valiantly to prevent it, doing everything they could to throw back the assault. They failed. Phaeton was killed. In the end, I was forced to use the Ruhk Staff. If I had not done so, the city would have fallen."

"My Lady, that is not so!" Barsimmon Oridio could keep silent no longer. "The army would have rallied. It would have prevailed. Phaeton took too many chances or he would still be alive!"

"He took those chances to save us!" Ellenroh was stone faced. "Do not speak unkindly of him, Commander. I forbid it." The big man's scowl deepened. "Bar." The queen spoke gently now, the warmth in her voice evident. "I was there. I saw it happen."

She waited until his fierce eyes lowered, then turned her gaze again to the table at large. "The Keel will not protect us much longer. I have used the Ruhk Staff to strengthen it, but I cannot do so again or we risk losing its power altogether. And that, my friends, I cannot allow. I have called you together then to tell you that I have decided on another course of action."

She turned to Wren. "This is my granddaughter, Wren, the child of Alleyne, sent to us out of the old world as Eowen Cerise foresaw. She appears, the foretelling promises, in order that the Elves should be saved. I have waited for her to come for many years, not really believing that she would or that if she did she could do anything for us. I did not want her to come, in truth, because I was afraid that I would lose her as I lost Alleyne."

She reached over and touched Wren's cheek softly with her fingers. "I am still afraid. But Wren is here despite my fears, having crossed the vast expanse of the Blue Divide and braved the terrors of the demons to sit now with us. I can no longer doubt that she is meant to save us, just as Eowen foretold." She paused. "Wren neither fully believes nor understands this yet." Her eyes were warm as they found Wren's own. "She has come to Arborlon for reasons of her own. The shade of Allanon summoned her and dispatched her to find us. The Four Lands, it seems, are beset by demons of their own, creatures called Shadowen. We are needed, the shade insists, if the Four Lands are to be preserved."

"What happens in the Four Lands is not our problem, my Lady," Eton Shart advised calmly.

She turned to face him. "Yes, First Minister, that is exactly what we have said for more than a hundred years, haven't we? But what if we are wrong? What if our problem is also theirs? What if, contrary to what we have believed, the fates of all are linked together and survival depends on the forging of a common bond? Wren, tell those gathered how you came to find me. Tell them everything that was told to you by the Druid's shade and the old man. Tell them as well of the Elfstones. It will be all right now. It is time they knew."

So Wren related once more the story of how she and Garth had come to Arborlon, beginning with the dreams and ending with her discovery of who she was. She spoke hesitantly of the Elfstones, uncertain still that she should reveal their presence. But the queen nodded encouragingly when she began, so she left nothing out. When she was finished, there was silence. Those seated at the table exchanged uncertain glances. Gavilan stared at her as if seeing her for the first time.

"Now do you understand why I think it impossible to ignore any longer what takes place beyond Morrowindl?" the queen asked quietly.

"My Lady, I believe we understand," the Owl said, "but we need to hear now what you propose to do."

Ellenroh nodded. "Yes, Aurin Striate, you do." The room went still once more. "There is nothing left for us here on Morrowindl," she said finally. "Therefore, it is time for us to leave, to return to the old world, and to become a part of it once again. Our days of disappearance and isolation are finished. It is time to use the Loden."

Gavilan was on his feet instantly. "Aunt Ell, no! We can't just give up! How do we know the Loden even works after all this time? It's just a story! And what about the Keel's magic? If we leave, it's lost! We can't do such a thing!"

Wren heard Barsimmon Oridio growl in agreement.

"Gavilan!" Ellenroh was furious. "We are in council. You will address me properly!"

Gavilan flushed. "I apologize, my Lady."

"Now sit down!" the queen snapped. Gavilan sat. "It seems to me that we owe our present predicament to indecision. We have failed to act for too long. We have allowed fate to dictate our choices for us. We have struggled with the magic even after it became apparent to all of us that we could no longer depend upon it."

"My Lady!" a pale-faced Eton Shart cautioned hurriedly.

"Yes, I know," Ellenroh responded. She did not look directly at Wren, but there was a flicker of movement in her eyes that told the girl that the warning had been given because of her.

"My Lady, you are asking that we give up the magic entirely?"

The queen's nod was curt. "It no longer serves much purpose to retain it, does it, First Minister?"

"But, as young Gavilan says, we have no way of knowing if the Loden will do as we expect."

"If it fails, we have lost nothing. Except, perhaps, any chance of escape."

"But escape, my Lady, is not necessarily the answer we are looking for. Perhaps help from another source . . ."

"Eton." The queen cut him short. "Consider what you are suggesting. What other source is there? Do you propose to summon more magic still? Do we use what we have in another way, convert it to some further horror, perhaps? Or are we to seek help from the very people we abandoned to the Federation years ago?"

"We have the army, my Lady," a glowering Barsimmon Oridio declared.

"Yes, Bar, we do. For the moment. But we cannot regenerate those lives that are lost. That magic we lack. Every new assault takes more of our Hunters. The demons materialize out of the very air, it seems. If we stay, we won't have an army much longer."

She shook her head slowly, her smile ironic. "I know what I am asking. If we return Arborlon and the Elves to the world of Men, to the Four Lands and their Races, the magic will be lost. We will be as we were in the old days. But maybe that is enough. Maybe it will have to be."

Those seated about the table regarded her in silence, their faces a mix of anger, doubt, and wonder.

"I don't understand about the magic," Wren said finally, unable just to continue sitting there while the questions piled up inside. "What do you mean when you say the magic will be lost if you leave Morrowindl?"

Ellenroh turned to face her. "I keep forgetting, Wren, that you are not versed in Elven lore and know little yet of the origins of the magic. I will try to make this simple. If I invoke the Loden, as I intend to do, Arborlon and the Elves will be gathered within the Elfstone for the journey back to the Westland. When that happens, the magic that shields the city falls away. The only magic left then is that which comes from the Loden and protects what is carried within. When Arborlon is restored, that magic ceases as well. The Loden, you see, has only one use, and once put to that use, its magic fades."

Wren shook her head in confusion. "But what about the way it restored the Keel where the demons breached it? What of that?"

"Indeed. I appropriated some of the same magic that the Loden requires to transport the city and its people. In short, I stole some of its power. But using that power to shore up the Keel drains what is needed for the Elfstone's primary use." Ellenroh paused. "Wren, you are aware by now that the Elves recaptured some of the magic they had once wielded in the time of faerie. They did so after discovering that the magic had its source in the earth and its elements. Even before we came to Morrowindl, years ago, long before my time, a decision was made to attempt a recovery." She paused. "That effort was not entirely successful. Eventually it was abandoned completely. What magic was left went into the formation of the Keel. But the magic exists only so long as there is need. Once the city is gone, the need is gone. When that happens, the magic disappears."

"And cannot be reinstated once you return to the Westland?"

Ellenroh's face turned to stone. "No, Wren. Never again."

"You assume . . ." Gavilan began.

"Never!" Ellenroh snapped, and Gavilan went still.

"My Lady." Eton Shart drew her attention gently. "Even if we do what you suggest and invoke the power of the Loden, what chance do we have of getting back to the Westland? The demons are all about. As you say, we have barely been able to hold our own within the walls of the city. What happens when those walls are gone? Will even our army be enough to get us to the beaches? And what happens to us then without boats and guides?"

"The army cannot hold the beaches for long, my Lady," Barsimmon Oridio agreed.

"No, Bar, it can't," the queen said. "But I don't propose to use the army. I think our best chance is to leave Morrowindl as we came to it—just a handful of us carrying the Loden and the rest safely captured inside."

There was stunned silence.

"A handful, my Lady?" Barsimmon Oridio was aghast. "They won't stand a chance!"

"Well, that's not necessarily true," Aurin Striate quietly mused.

The queen smiled. "No, Aurin, it isn't. After all, my granddaughter is proof of that. She came through the demons with no one to help her but her friend Garth. The truth of the matter is that a small party stands a far better chance of getting clear than an entire army. A small party can travel quickly and without being seen. It would be a hazardous journey, but it could be done. As for what would happen once that party reached the beaches, Wren has already made those arrangements for us. The Wing Rider Tiger Ty will be there with his Roc to convey at least one of us and the Loden to safety. Other Wing Riders can remove the rest. I have thought this through carefully and I believe it is the answer to our problem. I think, my friends, it is the only answer."

Gavilan shook his head. He was calm now, his handsome face composed. "My Lady, I know how desperate things have become. But if this gamble you propose fails, the entire Elven nation will be lost. Forever. If the party carrying the Loden is killed, the power of the Elfstone cannot be invoked and the city and its people will be trapped inside. I don't think it is a risk we can afford to take."

"Isn't it, Gavilan?" the queen asked softly.

"A better risk would be to summon further magic from the earth," he replied. His hands lifted to ward off her sharp protest. "I know the dangers. But this time we might be successful. This time the magic might be strong enough to keep us safe within the Keel, to keep the dark things locked without."

"For how long, Gavilan? Another year? Two? And our people still imprisoned within the city?"

"Better that than their extinction. A year might give us the time we need to find a method to control the earth magic. There must be a way, my Lady. We need only discover it."

The queen shook her head sadly. "We have been telling ourselves that for more than a hundred years. No one has found the answer yet. Look at what we have done to ourselves. Haven't we learned anything?"

Wren did not comprehend entirely what was being said, but she understood enough to realize that somewhere along the line the Elves had run into problems with the magic they had summoned. Ellenroh was saying they should have nothing further to do with it. Gavilan was saying they needed to keep trying to master it. Without being told as much, Wren was certain that the demons were at the heart of the dispute.

"Owl." The queen addressed Aurin Striate suddenly. "What do you think of my plan?"

The Owl shrugged. "I think it can be done, my Lady. I have spent years outside the city walls. I know that it is possible for a single man to go undetected by the demons, to travel among them. I think a handful could do the same. As you say, Wren and Garth came up from the beaches. I think they could go down again as well."

"Are you saying that you would give the Loden to this girl and her friend?" Barsimmon Oridio exclaimed in disbelief.

"A good choice, don't you think?" Ellenroh replied mildly. She glanced at Wren, who was thinking that she was the last person the queen should consider. "But we would have to ask them first, of course," Ellenroh continued, as if reading her mind. "In any case, I think more than two are needed."

"How many, then?" the Elven commander demanded.

"Yes, how many?" Eton Shart echoed.

The queen smiled, and Wren knew what she was thinking. She had them considering the proposal now, not simply arguing against it. They hadn't agreed to anything, but they were at least weighing the merits.

"Nine," the queen said. "The Elven number for luck. Just enough to make sure the job is done right."

"Who would go?" Barsimmon Oridio asked quietly.

"Not you, Bar," the queen replied. "Nor you either, Eton. This is a journey for young men. I wish you to stay with the city and our people. This will all be new for them. The Loden is only a story, after all. Someone must keep order in my absence, and you will do best."

"Then you intend to be one of those who makes the journey?" Eton Shart said. "This journey for young men?"

"Don't look so disapproving, First Minister," Ellenroh chided gently. "Of course I must go. The Ruhk Staff is in my charge and the power of the Loden mine to invoke. More to the point, I am Queen. It is up to me to see to it that my people and my city are brought safely back into the Westland. Besides, the plan is mine. I cannot very well advocate it and then leave it for someone else to carry out."

"My Lady, I don't think . . ." Aurin Striate began doubtfully.

"Owl, please do not say it." Ellenroh's frown left the other silent. "I am certain I can repeat word for word every objection you are about to make, so don't bother making them. If you feel it necessary, you can relate them to me as we go along since I expect you to make the journey as well."

"I wouldn't have it any other way." The Owl's seamed face was clouded with doubt.

"There is no one better able to survive outside the walls than you, Aurin Striate. You will be our eyes and ears out there, my friend."

The Owl nodded wordlessly in acknowledgment.

Ellenroh glanced about. "Triss, I'll need you and Cort and Dal to safeguard the Loden and the rest of us. That's five. Eowen will go. We may have need of her visions if we are to survive. Gavilan." She looked hopefully at her nephew. "I would like you to go as well."

Gavilan Elessedil surprised them all with a brilliant smile. "I would like that, too, my Lady."

Ellenroh beamed. "You can go back to calling me 'Aunt Ell,' Gavilan, after tonight."

She turned finally to Wren. "And you, child. Will you go with us, too? You and your friend Garth? We need your help. You have made the journey from the beach and survived. You know something of what is out there, and that knowledge is valuable. And you are the one the Wing Rider has promised to come back for. Am I asking too much?"

Wren was silent for a moment. She didn't bother looking over at Garth. She knew that he would go along with whatever she decided. She knew as well that she had not come all the way to Arborlon to be shut away, that Allanon had not dispatched her here to hide, and that she had not been given possession of the Elfstones only to forbear any use of them. The reality was harsh and demanding. She had been sent as more than a messenger, to do more than simply learn about who she was and from where she had come. Her part in this business—whether she liked it or not—was just beginning.

"Garth and I will come," she answered.

She believed her grandmother wanted to reach over and hug her then, but the queen remained straight backed in her chair and simply smiled instead. What Wren saw in her eyes, though, was better than any hug.

"Are we really agreed on doing this, then?" Eton Shart asked suddenly from the other end of the table.

The room was silent as Ellenroh Elessedil rose. She stood before them, pride and confidence reflected in her finely sculpted features, in the way she held herself, and in the glitter of her eyes. Wren thought her grandmother beautiful at that moment, the ringlets of her flaxen hair tumbling to her shoulders, the robes falling to her feet, and the lines of her face and body smooth and soft against the mix of shadows and light.

"We are, Eton," she replied softly. "I asked you to meet with me to hear what I had decided. If I could not persuade you, I told myself, I would not proceed. But I think I would have gone ahead in any case—not out of arrogance, not out of a sense of certainty in my own vision of what must be, but out of love for my people and fear that if they were lost the fault would be mine. We have a chance to save ourselves. Eowen foretold in her vision that this would be. Wren by coming has said that now is the time. All that we are and would ever be is at risk whatever choice we make, but I would rather the risk be taken in doing something than nothing. The Elves will survive, my friends. I am certain of it. The Elves always do."

She looked from face to face, her smile radiant. "Do you stand with me in this?"

They rose then, one by one, Aurin Striate first, Triss, Gavilan, Eton Shart, and Barsimmon Oridio after a brief hesitation and with obvious misgiving. Wren came to her feet last of all, so caught up in what she was seeing that she forgot for a moment that she was a part of it.

The queen nodded. "I could not ask for better friends. I love you all." She gripped the Ruhk Staff before her. "We will not delay. One day to advise our people, to prepare ourselves, and to make ready for what lies ahead. Sleep now. Tomorrow is already here."

She turned away from them then and walked from the room. In silence, they watched her go.

Wren was standing just outside the High Council doors, staring absently at patches of bright, star-filled sky and thinking that she could barely remember her life before the beginning of her search for the Elves, when Gavilan came up to her. The others had already gone, all but Garth, who lounged against a tree some distance off, looking out at the city. Wren had searched for Eowen, hoping to speak with her, but the seer had disappeared. Now she turned as Gavilan approached, thinking to speak with him instead, to ask him the questions she was still anxious to have answered.

The ready smile appeared immediately. "Little Wren," he greeted, ironic, a bit wistful. "Do you see our future as Eowen Cerise does?"

She shook her head. "I'm not sure I want to see it just now."

"Hmmm, yes, you might be right. It doesn't promise to be as soft and gentle as this night, does it?" He folded his arms comfortably and looked into her eyes. "What will we see once we're outside these walls, can you tell me? I've never been out there, you know."

Wren pursed her lips. "Demons. Vog, fire, ash, and lava rock until you reach the cliffs, then swamp and jungle, and then there's mostly vog. Gavilan, you shouldn't have agreed to come."

He laughed. "And you should? No, Wren, I want to die a whole man, knowing what's happened, not wondering from within the shield of the Loden's magic. If it even works. I wonder. No one really knows, not even the queen. Perhaps she'll invoke it and nothing will happen."

"You don't believe that, though, do you?"

"No. The magic always works for Ellenroh. Almost always, at least." The hands dropped away wearily.

"Tell me about the magic, Gavilan," she asked impulsively. "What is it about the magic that doesn't work? Why is it that no one wants to talk about it?"

Gavilan shoved his hands in the pockets of his coat, seeming to hunch down within himself as he did so. "Do you know, Wren, what it will be like for the Elves if Aunt Ell invokes the Loden's magic? None of them were alive when Arborlon was brought out of the Westland. None of them have ever seen the Four Lands. Only a few remember what it was like when Morrowindl was clean and free of the demons. The city is all they know. Imagine what it will be like for them when they are taken away from the island and put back into the Westland. Imagine what they will feel. It will terrify them."

"Perhaps not," she ventured.

He didn't seem to hear her. "We will lose everything we know when that happens. The magic has sustained us for our entire lives. The magic does everything for us. It cleans the air, shelters against the weather, keeps our fields fertile, feeds the plants and animals of the forest, and provides us with our water. Everything. What if these things are lost?"

She saw the truth then. He was terrified. He had no concept of life beyond the Keel, of a world without demons where nature provided everything for which the Elves now relied upon the magic.

"Gavilan, it will be all right," she said quietly. "Everything you enjoy now was there once before. The magic only provides you with what will be there again if nature's balance is restored. Ellenroh is right. The Elves will not survive if they remain on Morrowindl. Sooner or later, the Keel will fail. And it may be that the Four Lands, in turn, cannot survive without the Elves. Perhaps the destiny of the Races is linked in some way, just as Ellenroh suggested. Perhaps Allanon saw that when he sent me to find you."

His eyes fixed on hers. The fear was gone, but his look was intense and troubled. "I understand the magic, Wren. Aunt Ell thinks it is too dangerous, too unpredictable. But I understand it and I think I could find a way to master it."

"Tell me why she fears it," Wren pressed. "What is it that causes her to think it dangerous?"

Gavilan hesitated, and for a moment he seemed about to answer. Then he shook his head. "No, Wren. I cannot tell you. I have sworn I wouldn't. You are an Elf, but . . . It is better if you never find out, believe me. The magic isn't what it seems. It's too . . ."

He brought up his hands as if to brush the matter aside, frustrated and impatient. Then abruptly his mood changed, and he was suddenly buoyant. "Ask me something else, and I will answer. Ask me anything."

Wren folded her arms angrily. "I don't want to ask you anything else. I want to know about this."

The dark eyes danced. He was enjoying himself. He stepped so close to her that they were almost touching. "You are Alleyne's child, Wren. I'll give you that. Determined to the end."

"Tell me, then."

"Won't give it up, will you?"

"Gavilan."

"So caught up in wanting an answer you won't even see what's right in front of your face."

She hesitated, confused.

"Look at me," he said.

They stared at each other without speaking, eyes locked, measuring in ways that transcended words. Wren could feel the warmth of his breath and could see the rise and fall of his chest.

"Tell me," she repeated stubbornly.

She felt his hands come up to grip her arms, their touch light but firm. Then his face lowered to hers, and he kissed her.

"No," he whispered, gave her a quick, uncertain smile, and disappeared into the night.

13

By noon of the following day everyone in Arborlon knew of Ellenroh Elessedil's decision to invoke the power of the Loden and return the Elves and their home city to the Westland. The queen had sent word at first light, dispatching select messengers to every quarter of her besieged kingdom—Barsimmon Oridio to the officers and soldiers of the army, Triss to the Elven Hunters of the Home Guard, Eton Shart to the remainder of the High Council and from there to the officials who served in the administrative bureaus of the government, and Gavilan to the market district to gather together the leaders in the business and farming communities. By the time Wren had awakened, dressed, eaten breakfast, and gone out into the city, the talk was of nothing else.

She found the Elves' response remarkable. There was no panic, no sense of despair, and no threats or accusations against the queen for making her decision. There was uncertainty, of course, and a healthy measure of doubt. None among the Elves had been alive when Arborlon had been carried out of the Westland, and while all had heard the story of the migration to Morrowindl, few had given much thought to migrating out again. Even with the city ringed by the demons and life drastically altered from what it was in the time of Ellenroh's father, concern for the future had not embraced the possibility of employing the Loden's magic. As a result the people talked of leaving as if the idea was an entirely new one, a prospect freshly conceived, and for the most part the conversations that Wren listened in on suggested that if Ellenroh Elessedil believed it best, then certainly it must be so. It was a tribute to the confidence that the Elves placed in their queen that they would accept her proposal so readily—especially when it was as drastic as this one.

"It will be nice to be able to go out of the city again," more than one said. "We've lived behind walls for too long."

"Travel the roads and see the world," others agreed. "I love my home, but I miss what lies beyond."

There was more than one mention of life without the constant threat of demons, of a world where the dark things were just a memory and the young could grow without having to accept that the Keel was all that allowed them to survive and there could never be any kind of existence beyond. Some expressed concern about how the magic worked, or if it even would, but most seemed satisfied with the queen's assurance that life within the city would go on as always during the journey, that the magic would protect and insulate against whatever happened without, and that it would be as before except that in place of the Keel there would be a darkness that none could pass through until the magic of the Loden was recalled.

She ran across Aurin Striate in the market center. The Owl had been up since dawn gathering together the supplies the company of nine would require to make the journey down Killeshan's slopes to the beaches. His task was made difficult mostly by the queen's determination that they would take only what they could carry on their backs and that stealth and quickness would serve them best in their efforts to elude the demons.

"The magic, as I understand it, works like this," he explained as they walked back toward the palace. "There's both a wrapping about and a carrying away when it is invoked. Once in place, it protects against intrusions from without, like a shell. At the same time, it removes you to another place—city and all—and keeps you there until the spell is released. There is a kind of suspension in time. That way you don't feel anything of what's happening during the journey; you don't have any sense of movement."

"So everything just goes on as before?" Wren queried, trying to envision how that could happen.

"Pretty much. There isn't any day or night, just a grayness as if the skies were cloudy, the queen tells me. There's air and water and all the things you need to survive, all wrapped carefully away in this sort of cocoon."

"And what happens once you get to where you are going?"

"The queen removes the Loden's spell, and the city is restored."

Wren's eyes shifted to find the Owl's. "Assuming, of course, that what Ellenroh has been told about the magic is the truth."

The Owl sighed. "So young to be so skeptical." He shook his head. "If it isn't the truth, Wren, what does any of this matter? We are trapped on Morrowindl without hope, aren't we? A few might save themselves by slipping past the dark things, but most would perish. We have to believe the magic will save us, girl, because the magic is all we have."

She left him as they neared the palace gates, letting him go on ahead, tired eyed and stoop shouldered, his thin, rumpled shadow cast against the earth, a mirror of himself. She liked Aurin Striate. He was comfortable and easy in the manner of old clothes. She trusted him. If anyone could see them through the journey that lay ahead, it was the Owl.

She turned away from the palace and wandered absently toward the Gardens of Life. She had not looked for Garth when she had risen, slipping from her room instead to search out the queen. But Ellenroh was nowhere to be found once again, and so she had decided to walk out into the city by herself. Now, her walk completed, she found that she still preferred to be alone. She let her thoughts stray as she entered the deserted Gardens, making her way up the gentle incline toward the Ellcrys, and her thoughts, as they had from the moment she had come awake, gravitated stubbornly toward Gavilan Elessedil. She stopped momentarily, picturing him. When she closed her eyes she could feel him kissing her. She took a deep breath and let it out slowly. She had only been kissed once or twice in her life— always too busy with her training, aloof and unapproachable, caught up in

other things, to be bothered with boys. There had been no time for relationships. She had had no interest in them. Why was that? she wondered
suddenly. But she knew that she might as well inquire as to why the sky was
blue as to question who she had become.

She opened her eyes again and walked on.

When she reached the Ellcrys, she studied it for a time before seating
herself within its shade. Gavilan Elessedil. She liked him. Maybe too much.
It seemed instinctual, and she distrusted the unexpected intensity of her
feelings. She barely knew him, and already she was thinking of him more
than she should. He had kissed her, and she had welcomed it. Yet it angered
her that he was hiding what he knew about the magic and the demons, a
truth he refused to share with her, a secret so many of the Elves harbored—
Ellenroh, Eowen, and the Owl among them. But she was bothered more
by Gavilan's reticence because he had come to her to proclaim himself a
friend, he had promised to answer her questions when she asked them, he
had kissed her and she had let him, and despite everything he had gone
back on his word. She smoldered inwardly at the betrayal, and yet she
found herself anxious to forgive him, to make excuses for him, and to give
him a chance to tell her in his own time.

But was it any different with Gavilan than it had been with her grandmother? she asked herself suddenly. Hadn't she used the same reasoning
with both?

Perhaps her feelings for each were not so very different.

The thought troubled her more than she cared to admit, and she
shoved it hastily away.

It was still and calm within the Gardens, secluded amid the trees and
flower beds, cool and removed beneath the silken covering of the Ellcrys.
She let her eyes wander across the blanket of colors that formed the Gardens, studying the way they swept the earth like brush strokes, some short
and broad, some thin and curving, borders of brightness that shimmered in
the light. Overhead, the sun shone down out of a cloudless blue sky, and
the air was warm and sweet smelling. She drank it in slowly, carefully, savoring it, aware as she did so that it would all be gone after tonight, that when
the magic of the Loden was invoked she would be cast adrift once more
in the wilderness dark of Morrowindl. She had been able to forget for a
time the horror that lay beyond the Keel, to block away her memories of
the stench of sulfur, the steaming fissures in the crust of lava rock, the swelter of Killeshan's heat rising off the earth, the darkness and the vog, and the
rasps and growls of the demons at hunt. She shivered and hugged herself.
She did not want to go back out into it. She felt it waiting like a living
thing, crouched down patiently, determined it would have her, certain she
must come.

She closed her eyes again and waited for the bad feelings to subside,
gathering her determination a little at a time, calming herself, reasoning
that she would not be alone, that there would be others with her, that they
would all protect one another, and that the journey down out of the

mountains would pass quickly and then they would be safe. She had climbed unharmed to Arborlon, hadn't she? Surely she could go back down again.

And yet her doubts persisted, nagging whispers of warning that echoed in the Addershag's warning at Grimpen Ward. *Beware, Elf-girl. I see danger ahead for you, hard times, and treachery and evil beyond imagining.*

Trust no one.

But if she did as the Addershag had advised, if she kept her own counsel and gave heed to no one else, she would be paralyzed. She would be cut off from everyone and she did not think she could survive that.

How much had the Addershag seen of her future? she wondered grimly. How much had she failed to reveal?

She pushed herself to her feet, took a final look at the Ellcrys, and turned away. Slowly she descended the Gardens of Life, stealing as she went faint memories of their comfort and reassurance, brightness and warmth, tucking them away for the time when she would need them, for when the darkness was all about and she was alone. She wanted to believe it would not happen that way. She hoped the Addershag was wrong.

But she knew she could not be certain.

Garth caught up with her shortly after that and she remained with him for what was left of the day. They spoke at length about what lay ahead, listing the dangers they had already encountered and debating what they would require to make a journey back through the madness that lay without. Garth seemed relaxed and confident, but then he always seemed that way. They agreed that whatever else happened, they would stay close to each other.

She saw Gavilan only once and only for a moment. It was late that afternoon and he was leaving the palace on yet another errand as she came across the lawn. He smiled at her and waved as if everything was as it should be, as if the whole world were set right, and in spite of her irritation at his casual manner she found herself smiling and waving back. She would have spoken with him if she could have managed it, but Garth was there and several of Gavilan's companions as well, and there was no opportunity. He did not reappear after that, although she made it a point to look for him. As dusk approached she found herself alone in her room once more, staring out the windows at the dying light, thinking that she ought to be doing something, feeling as if she were trapped and wondering if she should be fighting to get free. Garth was secluded once again in the adjoining room, and she was about to seek out his company when her door opened and the queen appeared.

"Grandmother," she greeted, and she could not mask entirely the relief in her voice.

Ellenroh swept across the room wordlessly and took her in her arms, holding her close. "Wren," she whispered, and her arms tightened as if she were afraid that Wren might flee.

She stepped back finally, smiled past a momentary mask of sadness, then took Wren's hand and led her to the bed where they seated themselves. "I have ignored you shamefully all day. I apologize. It seemed that every time I turned around I was remembering something else that needed doing, some small task I had forgotten that had to be completed before tonight." She paused. "Wren, I am sorry to have gotten you involved in this business. The problems we made for ourselves should not be yours as well. But there is no help for it. I need you, child. Do you forgive me?"

Wren shook her head, confused. "There is nothing to forgive, Grandmother. When I decided to bring Allanon's message to you I chose to involve myself. I knew that if you heeded that message I would be coming with you. I never thought of it in any other way."

"Wren, you give me such hope. I wish that Alleyne was here to see you. She would have been proud. You have her strength and her determination." The smooth brow furrowed. "I miss her so much. She has been gone for years, and still it seems that she has only stepped away for a moment. I sometimes find myself looking for her even now."

"Grandmother," Wren said quietly, waiting until the other's eyes were locked on her own. "Tell me about the magic. What is it that you and Gavilan and Eowen and the Owl and everyone else knows that I don't? Why does it frighten everyone so?"

For a moment Ellenroh Elessedil did not respond. Her eyes went hard, and her body stiffened. Wren could see in that instant the iron resolve that her grandmother could call upon when she was in need, a casting that belied the youthful face and slender form. A silence settled between them. Wren held her gaze steady, refusing to look away, determined to put an end to the secrets between them.

The queen's smile, when it came, was unexpected and bitter. "As I said, you are like Alleyne." She released Wren's hands as if anxious to establish a boundary between them. "There are some things I would like to tell you that I cannot, Wren. Not yet, in any case. I have my reasons, and you will have to accept my assurance that they are good ones. So I will tell you what I can and there the matter must rest."

She sighed and let the bitterness of her smile drift away. "The magic is unpredictable, Wren. It was so in the beginning; it remains so now. You know yourself from the tales of the Sword of Shannara and the Elfstones that the magic is not a constant, that it does not always do what is expected, that it reveals itself in surprising ways, and that it evolves with the passage of time and use. It is a truth that seems to continually elude us, one that must be constantly relearned. When the Elves came into Morrowindl, they decided to recover the magic, to rediscover the old ways, and to model themselves after their forefathers. The problem, of course, was that the model had long since been broken and no one had kept the plans. Recovery of the magic was accomplished more easily than expected, but mastering it once in hand was something else again. Attempts were made; many failed. In the course of those attempts, the demons were let into being. Inadvertent and unfortunate, but a fact just the same. Once here, they could not be dispatched. They flourished and reproduced and despite every effort employed to destroy them, they survived."

She shook her head, as if seeing those efforts parade before her eyes. "You would ask me why they cannot be sent back to wherever they came from, wouldn't you? But the magic doesn't work that way; it will not permit so easy a solution. Gavilan, among others, believes that further experimentation with the magic will produce better results, that trial and error will eventually give us a way to defeat the creatures. I do not agree. I understand the magic, Wren, because I have used it and I know the extent of its power. I am afraid of what it can do. There are no limits, really. It dwarfs us as mortal creatures; it lacks the restraints of our humanity. It is greater than we are; it will survive after we are all long dead. I have no faith in it beyond that which has been gleaned out of experience and is required by necessity. I believe that if we continue to test it, if we continue to believe that the solution to our problems lies in what it can do, then some new horror will find its way into our lives and we will wish that the demons were all that we had to deal with."

"What of the Elfstones?" Wren asked her quietly.

Ellenroh nodded, smiled, and looked away. "Yes, child, what of the Elfstones? What of their magic? We know what it can do; we have seen its results. When Elven blood fails, when it is not strong enough as it was not strong enough in Wil Ohmsford, it creates unexpected results. The wishsong. Good and bad, both." She looked back again. "But the magic of the Elfstones is known and it is contained. No one believes or suggests that it could be subverted to another use. Nor the Loden. We have some understanding of these magics and will employ them because we must if we are to survive. But there is much greater magic waiting to be discovered, child—magic that lives beneath the earth, that can be found in the air, and that cries out for recognition. That is the magic that Gavilan would gather. It is the same magic that the Druid called Brona sought to harness more than a thousand years ago—the same magic that convinced him to become the Warlock Lord and then destroyed him."

Wren understood her grandmother's fear of the magic, could see the dangers as she saw them, and could share with her as could no one else the feelings that invocation of the magic aroused—in the Elfstones, in the Loden—power that could overwhelm, that could subvert, and that could swallow you up until you were lost.

"You said that you wanted the Elves to go back to the way they were before they recovered the magic," she said, thinking back to the previous night when Ellenroh had addressed the High Council. "But can that happen? Won't some among the Elves simply bring it back again, perhaps find it in another way?"

"No." Ellenroh's eyes were suddenly distant. "Not again. Not ever again."

She was leaving something out. Wren sensed it immediately—sensed as well that it was not something Ellenroh would discuss. "And what of the magic you have already invoked, that which protects the city?"

"It will all disappear once we leave—all but that required to fulfill the Loden's use and to carry the Elves and Arborlon back into the Westland. All but that."

"And the Elfstones?"

The queen smiled. "There are no absolutes, Wren. The Elfstones have been with us for a long time."

"I could cast them away once we are safe."

"Yes, child, you could—should you choose to do so."

Wren felt something unspoken pass between them, but she could not identify its meaning. "Will the magic of the Loden really do as you believe, Grandmother? Will it carry the Elves safely out of Morrowindl?"

The queen's smooth face lowered momentarily, shaded with doubt and something more. "Oh, the magic is there, certainly. I have felt it in my use of the staff. I have been told its secret and I know it to be the truth." Her face lifted abruptly. "But it is we, Wren, who must do the carrying. It is we who must see to it that those who have been gathered up by the Loden's spell—our people—are restored to the world again, that they are given a new chance at life. Magic alone is not enough. It is never enough. Our lives, and ultimately the lives of all those who depend upon us, are forever our responsibility. The magic is only a tool. Do you understand?"

Wren nodded somberly. "I will do anything I can to help," she said softly. "But I tell you now that I wish the magic dead and gone, all of it, every last bit, everything from Shadowen to demons to Loden to Elfstones. I would see it all destroyed."

The queen rose. "And if it were, Wren, what then would take its place? The sciences of the old world, come back to life? A greater power still? It would be something, you know. It will always be something."

She reached down and pulled Wren up with her. "Call Garth now and come with me to dinner. And smile. Whatever else might come of this, we have found each other. I am very glad that you are here."

She hugged Wren close once more, holding her. Wren hugged her back and said, "I'm glad, too, Grandmother."

All of the members of the inner circle of the High Council were in attendance at dinner that night—Eton Shart, Barsimmon Oridio, Aurin Striate, Triss, Gavilan, and the queen, together with Wren, Garth, and Eowen Cerise—all those who had been present when the decision was made to invoke the Loden's power and abandon Morrowindl. Even Cort and Dal were there, standing watch in the halls beyond, barring any from entering, including the service staff once the food was on the table. Comfortably secluded, those gathered discussed the arrangements for the coming day. Talk was animated and direct with discussions about equipment, supplies, and proposed routes dominating the conversation. Ellenroh, after consulting with the Owl, had decided that the best time to attempt an escape was just before dawn when the demons were weary from the night's prowl and anxious for sleep and a full day's light lay ahead for travel. Night was the most dangerous time to be out, for the demons always hunted then. It would take the company of nine a bit more than a week to reach the beaches if all went smoothly. If any of them doubted that it would really happen that way, at least they kept it to themselves.

Gavilan sat across from Wren, one place removed, and smiled at her often. She was aware of his attention and politely acknowledged it, but directed her talk to her grandmother and the Owl and Garth. She ate something, but later she couldn't remember what, listening to the others talk, glancing frequently at Gavilan as if studying him might somehow reveal the mystery of his attraction, and thinking distractedly about what the queen had told her earlier.

Or, more to the point, what she hadn't told her.

The queen's revelations, on close examination, were a trifle threadbare. It was all well and good to say that the magic had been recovered; but where had it been recovered from? It was fine to admit that recovery had somehow triggered the release of the demons that besieged them; but what was it about the magic that had freed them? And from where? Wren still hadn't heard a word about what had gone wrong with usage of the magic or why it was that no magic was available to undo the wrong that had been done. What her grandmother had given her was a sketch without shadings or colors or background of any kind. It wasn't enough by half.

And yet Ellenroh had insisted that it must be.

Wren sat with her thoughts buzzing inside like gnats. The conversations flowed heatedly about her as faces turned this way and that, the light failed without as the darkness closed down, and time passed by with silent footsteps, a retreat from the past, a stealthy approach toward a future that might change them all forever. She felt disconnected from everything about her, as if she had been dropped into place at the dinner table quite unexpectedly, an uninvited guest, an eavesdropper on the lives of those about her. Even Garth's familiar presence failed to comfort her, and she said little to him.

When dinner ended, she went straight to her room to sleep, stripped off her clothing, slipped beneath the bed coverings, and lay waiting in the dark for things to change back again. They refused. Her breathing slowed, her thoughts scattered, and at last she fell asleep.

Even so, she was awake again and dressed before the knock on the door that was meant to rouse her. Gavilan stood there, clothed in drab hunter's garb with weapons strapped all about, the familiar grin shelved, looking like someone else entirely.

"I thought you might like to walk down to the wall with me," he said simply.

Her smile in response brought a trace of his own. "I would," she agreed.

With Garth in tow, they departed the palace and moved through the dark, deserted streets of the city. Wren had thought the people would be awake and watchful, anxious to observe what would happen when the magic of the Loden was invoked. But the homes of the Elves were dark and silent, and those who watched did so from the shadows. Perhaps Ellenroh had not told them when the transformation would occur, she thought. She became aware of someone following them and glanced back to find Cort a dozen paces behind. Triss must have dispatched him to make certain they reached their appointed gathering spot on time. Triss would be with the queen or Eowen Cerise or Aurin Striate—or Dal would. All of them shepherded down to the Keel, to the door that led out into the desolation beyond, into the harsh and barren emptiness that they must traverse in order to survive.

They arrived without incident, the darkness unbroken, the dawn's light still hidden beneath the horizon. All were gathered—the queen, Eowen, the Owl, Triss, Dal, and now the four of them. Only nine, Wren thought, suddenly aware of how few they were and how much depended on them. They exchanged hugs and hand clasps and furtive words of encouragement, a handful of shadows whispering into the night. All wore hunter's garb, loose fitting and hardy, protection against the weather and, to some small measure, the dangers that waited without. All carried weapons, save for Eowen and the queen. Ellenroh carried the Ruhk Staff, its dark wood glimmering faintly, the Loden a prism of colors that winked and shimmered even in the near black. Atop the Keel, the magic was a steady glow that illuminated the battlements and reached heavenward. Elven Hunters patrolled the walls in groups of half a dozen, and sentries stood at watch within their towers. From without, the growls and hissings were sporadic and distant, as if the things emitting them lacked interest and would as well have slept.

"We'll give them a surprise before this night is over, won't we?" Gavilan whispered in her ear, a tentative smile on his face.

"Just so long as they're the ones who end up being surprised," she whispered back.

She saw Aurin Striate by the door leading down into the tunnels and moved over to stand beside him. His rumpled body shifted in the gloom. He glanced at her and nodded.

"Eyes and ears sharp, Wren?"

"I guess so."

"Elfstones handy?"

Her mouth tightened. The Elfstones were in a new leather bag strung about her neck—she could feel their weight resting against her chest. She had managed to avoid thinking about them until now. "Do you think I'll need them?"

He shrugged. "You did last time."

She was silent for a moment, considering the prospect. Somehow she had thought she might escape Morrowindl without having to call on the magic again.

"It seems quiet out there," she ventured hopefully.

He nodded, his slender frame draping itself against the stone. "They won't be expecting us. We'll have our chance."

She leaned back next to him, shoulders touching. "How good a chance will it be, Owl?"

He laughed tonelessly. "What difference does it make? It is the only chance we have."

Barsimmon Oridio materialized out of the blackness, went directly to the queen, spoke to her in hushed tones for a few minutes, and then disappeared again. He looked haggard and worn, but there was determination in his step.

"How long have you been going out there?" she asked the Owl suddenly, not looking at him. "Out with them."

There was a hesitation. He knew what she meant. She could feel his eyes fixing on her. "I don't know anymore."

"What I want to know, I guess, is how you made yourself do it. I can barely make myself go even this once, knowing what's out there." She swallowed against the admission. "I mean, I can do it because it's the only choice, and I won't have to do it again. But you had a choice each time, before this. You must have thought better of it more than once. You must not have wanted to go."

"Wren." She turned when he spoke her name and faced him. "Let me tell you something you haven't learned yet, something you learn only by living awhile. As you get older, you find that life begins to wear you down. Doesn't matter who you are or what you do, it happens. Experience, time, events—they all conspire against you to steal away your energy, to erode your confidence, to make you question things you wouldn't have given a second thought to when you were young. It happens gradually, a chipping away that you don't even notice at first, and then one day it's there. You wake up and you just don't have the fire anymore."

He smiled faintly. "Then you have a choice. You can either give in to what you're feeling, just say 'okay, enough is enough' and be done with it, or you can fight it. You can accept that every day you're alive you're going to have to face it down, that you're going to have to say to yourself that you don't care what you feel, that it doesn't matter what happens to you because sooner or later it is going to happen anyway, that you're going to do what you have to because otherwise you're defeated and life doesn't have any real purpose left. When you can do that, little Wren, when you can accept the wearing down and the eroding, then you can do anything. How did I manage to keep going out nights? I just told myself I didn't matter all that much—that those in here mattered more. You know something? It's not so hard really. You just have to get past the fear."

She thought about it a minute and then nodded. "I think you make it sound a lot easier than it is."

The Owl lifted off the wall. "Do I?" he asked. Then he smiled anew and walked away.

Wren drifted back over to stand with Garth. The big Rover pointed to the ramparts of the Keel. Elven Hunters were coming down off the heights—furtive, silent figures easing out of the light and down into the shadows. Wren glanced eastward and saw the first faint tinge of dawn against the black.

"It is time," Ellenroh said suddenly, and motioned them toward the wall.

They moved quickly, Aurin Striate in the lead, pulling open the doorway that led down into the tunnels, pausing at the entry to look back at the queen. Ellenroh had moved away from the wall to the bridgehead, stopping just before she reached its ramp to plant the butt end of the Ruhk firmly in the earth. From somewhere within Arborlon a bell tolled, a signal, and those few Elven Hunters who remained atop the Keel slipped hurriedly away. In seconds, the wall was deserted.

Ellenroh Elessedil glanced back at the eight who waited just once, then turned to face the city. Her hands clasped the polished shaft of the Ruhk, and her head lowered.

Instantly the Loden began to glow. The brightness grew rapidly to white fire, flaring outward until the queen was enveloped. Steadily the light continued to spread, rising up against the darkness, filling the space within the walls until all of Arborlon was lit as bright as day. Wren tried to watch what was happening, but the intensity of the light grew until it blinded her and she was forced to look away. The white fire flooded to the parapets of the Keel and began to churn. Wren could feel it happen more than she could see it, her eyes closed against the glare. Without, the demons began to shriek. There was a rush of wind that came out of nowhere and grew into a howl. Wren dropped to her knees, feeling Garth's strong arm come up about her shoulders and hearing Gavilan's voice call to her. Images formed in her mind, triggered by Ellenroh's summoning, wild and erratic visions of a world in chaos. The magic was racing past her, a brushing of fingers that whispered and sang.

It ended in a shriek, a sound that no voice could have made, and then the light rushed away, whipping back into the black, withdrawing as if sucked down into a whirlpool. Wren's eyes jerked up, following the motion, trying to see. She was just quick enough to catch the last of it as it disappeared into the Loden's brilliant orb. She blinked once, and it was gone.

The city of Arborlon was gone as well—the people, the buildings, the streets and walkways, the gardens and lawns, the trees, everything from wall to wall within the Keel, disappeared. All that remained was a shallow crater in the earth—as if a giant hand had simply scooped Arborlon up and spirited it away.

Ellenroh Elessedil stood alone at the edge of what had once been the moat and was now the lip of the crater, leaning heavily on the Ruhk Staff, her own energy drained. Above her, the Loden was a prism of many-colored fire. The queen stirred herself, tried to move and failed, stumbled, and fell to her knees. Triss raced back for her instantly, lifted her as if she were a weary child, and started back again. It was then that Wren realized that the magic that had protected the Keel had faded as well, just as her grandmother had forewarned, its glow vanished completely. Overhead, the sky was enveloped in a haze of vog and the sunrise was a sullen lightening of the eastern skies barely able to penetrate the night's blackness. Wren drew a breath and found the stench of sulfur had returned. All that had been of Arborlon's shelter had vanished.

The silence of a moment earlier gave way to a cacophony of demon howls and shrieks as the realization of what had happened set in. The sound of bodies scrambling onto the walls and of claws digging in rose from every quarter.

Triss had reached them, the queen and the Ruhk Staff clutched in his arms.

"Inside, quickly!" the Owl shouted, hurrying ahead.

Hastening to follow after him, the others of the little company charged with the safe delivery of Arborlon and its Elves disappeared through the open door and down into the black.

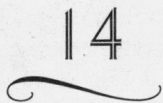

In a world of light and shadows where truths were a shimmer of inconsistency, of life stolen out of substance and made over into transparency, of nonbeing and mist, Walker Boh was brought face to face with the impossible.

"I have been waiting a long time, Walker, hoping you would come," the ghost before him whispered.

Cogline—he had been dead weeks now, killed by the Shadowen at Hearthstone, destroyed by Rimmer Dall—and Rumor with him. Walker had seen it happen, sick almost beyond recovery from the poison of the Asphinx, crouched helplessly in his bedroom as the old man and the moor cat fought their last battle. He had seen it all, the final rush of the monsters created of the dark magic, the fire of the old man's magic as it flared in retaliation, and the explosion that had consumed everyone within reach. Cogline and Rumor had disappeared in the conflagration along with dozens of their attackers. None had survived save Rimmer Dall and a handful who had been thrown clear.

Yet here was Cogline and the cat, come somehow into Paranor, shades out of death.

Except that Walker Boh found them as real as he was, a reflection of himself in this twilight world into which the Black Elfstone had dispatched him, ghostlike and yet alive when they should not have been. Unless he was dead as well and a reflection of them instead. The contradictions overwhelmed him. His breath caught sharply in his throat and he could not speak. Who was alive and who was not?

"Walker." The old man spoke his name, and the sound of it drew him back from the precipice on which he was poised.

Cogline approached, slowly, carefully, seeming to realize the fear and confusion that his presence had generated in his pupil. He spoke softly to Rumor, and the moor cat sat back on his haunches obediently, his luminous eyes bright and interested as they fixed on Walker. Cogline's body was as fragile and sticklike as ever beneath the gathering of worn robes, and the gray, hazy light passed through him in narrow streamers. Walker flinched as the old man reached out to touch him on the shoulder, the skeletal fingers trailing down to grip his arm.

The grip was warm and firm.

"I am alive, Walker. And Rumor, too. We are both alive," he whispered. "The magic saved us."

Walker Boh was silent a moment, staring without comprehension into the other's eyes, searching for something that would give meaning to the other's words. Alive? How could it be? He nodded finally, needing to respond in some fashion, to get past the fear and confusion, and asked hesitantly, "How did you get here?"

"Come sit with me," the other replied.

He led Walker to a stone bench that rested against a wall, both an odd glimmer of hazy relief against the shadows, wrapped in mist and gloom. Sound was muffled within the Keep, as if an unwelcome guest forced to tread lightly in order not to draw attention. Walker glanced about, disbelieving still, searching the maze of walkways that disappeared ahead and behind, catching glimpses of stone walls and parapets and towers rising up about him, as empty of life as tombs set within the earth. He sat beside the old man, feeling Rumor rub up against him as he did.

"What has happened to us?" he asked, a measure of steadiness returning, his determination to discover the truth pushing back the uncertainty. "Look at us. We are like wraiths."

"We are in a world of half-being, Walker," Cogline replied softly. "We are somewhere between the world of mortal men and the world of the dead. Paranor rests there now, brought back out of nonbeing by the magic of the Black Elfstone. You found it, didn't you? You recovered it from wherever it was hidden and carried it here. You used it, as you knew you must, and brought us back.

"Wait, don't answer yet." He cut short Walker's attempt to speak. "I get ahead of myself. You must know first what happened to me. Then we will speak of you. Rumor and I have had an adventure of our own, and it has brought us to this. Here is what happened, Walker. Some weeks earlier when I spoke with the shade of Allanon, I was warned that my time within the world of mortal men was almost gone, that death would come for me when next I saw the face of Rimmer Dall. When that happened, I was to hold the Druid History to me and not to give it up. I was told nothing more. When the First Seeker and his Shadowen appeared at Hearthstone, I remembered Allanon's words. I managed to slow them long enough to retrieve the book from its hiding place. I stood with it clasped to my breast on the porch of the cottage, Rumor pressed back up against me, as the Shadowen reached to tear me apart.

"You thought it was my magic that enveloped me. It was not. When the Shadowen closed about me, a magic contained within the Druid History came to my defense. It released white fire, consuming everything about it, destroying everything that was not a part of me, except for Rumor, who sought to protect me. It did not harm us, but instead caught us up and carried us away as quick as the blink of an eye. We fell unconscious, a sleep that was as deep as any I have ever known. When we came awake again, we were here within Paranor, within the Druid's Keep."

He bent close. "I cannot know for certain what happened when the magic was triggered, Walker, but I can surmise. The Druids would never leave their work unprotected. Nothing of what they created would ever be left for use by those who lacked the right and the proper intent. It was so, I am certain, of their Histories. The magic that protected them was such that any threat would result in their return to the vault within the Keep that had sheltered them all those years. That was what happened to the History I held. I have looked within the vaults and found the History back among the others, safely returned. Allanon must have known this would happen— and known that anyone holding the History would be carried away as well—back into Paranor, back into the Druid's sanctuary.

"But not," he finished, "back into the world of mortal men."

"Because the Keep had been sent elsewhere three hundred years ago," Walker murmured, beginning to understand now.

"Yes, Walker, because the Keep had been sent from the Four Lands by Allanon and would remain gone until the Druids brought it back again. So the book was returned to it and Rumor and I sent along as well." He paused. "It appears that the Druids are not done with me yet."

"Are you trapped here, then?" Walker asked softly.

The other's smile was tight. "I am afraid so. I lack the magic to free us. We are a part of Paranor now, just as the Histories are, alive and well, but ghosts within a ghost castle, caught in some twilight time and place until a stronger magic than mine sets us free. And that is why I have been waiting for you." The bony fingers tightened about Walker's arm. "Tell me now. Have you brought the Black Elfstone? Will you show it to me?"

Walker Boh remembered suddenly that he still had hold of the Stone, the talisman clasped so tightly in his hand that the edges had embedded themselves in the flesh of his palm. He held his hand out tentatively, and his fingers slipped open one by one. He was cautious, afraid that the magic would overwhelm him. The Black Elfstone gleamed darkly in the hollow of his palm, but the magic lay dormant, the nonlight sealed away.

Cogline peered down at the Stone wordlessly for long moments, not attempting more, his narrow, seamed face reflecting wonder and hesitation. Then he looked up again and said, "How did you find it, Walker? What happened after Rumor and I were taken away?"

Walker told him then of the coming of Quickening, the daughter of the King of the Silver River, and of how she had healed his arm. He related all that had happened on the journey north to Eldwist, of the struggle of Quickening and her companions to survive in that land of stone, of the search for Uhl Belk, of the encounters with the Rake and the Maw Grint, and of the ultimate destruction of the city and those who sought to preserve it.

"I came here alone," he concluded, his gaze distant as the memories of what had befallen him recalled themselves. "I knew what was expected of me. I accepted that the trust Allanon had bequeathed to Brin Ohmsford had been meant for me." He glanced over. "You always told me that I first needed to accept in order to understand, and I suppose I have done as you advised. And as Allanon charged. I used the Black Elfstone and brought back the Druid's Keep. But look at me, Cogline. I appear as you do, a ghost. If the magic has achieved what was intended, then why—"

"Think, Walker," the other interrupted quickly, a pained look in his ancient eyes. "What was your charge from Allanon? Repeat it to me."

Walker took a deep breath, his pale face troubled. "To bring back Paranor and the Druids."

"Yes, Paranor and the Druids—both. You realize what that means, don't you? You understand?"

Walker's brow knotted with frustration and reluctance. "Yes, old man." He breathed harshly in response. "I must become a Druid if Paranor is to be restored. I have accepted that, though it shall be as I wish it and not as a shade three hundred years dead intends." His words were angry now and quick. "I will not be as they were, those old men who—"

"Walker!" Cogline's anger was as intense as his own, and he went still immediately. "Listen to me. Do not proclaim what you will do and how you will be until you understand what is required of you. This is not simply a matter of accepting a charge and carrying it out. It was never that. Acceptance of who you are and what you must do is just the first of many steps your journey requires. Yes, you have recovered the Black Elfstone and summoned its magic. Yes, you have gained entry into disappeared Paranor. But that is only the beginning of what is needed."

Walker stared. "What do you mean? What else is there?"

"Much, I am afraid," the other whispered. A sad smile eased across the wrinkled features, seamed wood splitting with age. "You came to Paranor much in the same way as Rumor and I. The magic brought you. But the magic gives you entry on its own terms. We are here at its sufferance, alive under the conditions it dictates. You have already noted how you seem— almost a ghost, having substance and life yet not enough of either to be as other mortal men. That should tell you something, Walker. Look about you. Paranor appears the same—here and yet not here, vague in its form, not come fully to life."

The thin mouth tightened. "Do you see? We are none of us—Rumor, you and I, Paranor—returned yet to the world of Men. We are still in a limbo existence, somewhere between being and nonbeing, and we are waiting. We are waiting, Walker, for the magic to restore us fully. Because it has not done that yet, despite your use of the Black Elfstone and your entry into the Keep. Because it has not yet been mastered."

He reached down and gently closed Walker's fingers back around the Black Elfstone, then slowly sat back, a frail bundle of sticks against the shadows.

"In order for Paranor to be restored to the world of men, the Druids must come again. More precisely, one Druid, Walker. You. But acceptance of what this means is not enough to let you become a Druid. You must do more if the magic is to be yours, if it is to belong to you. You must become what you are charged with being. You must transform yourself."

"Transform myself?" Walker was aghast. "It would seem that I have done so already! What further transformation is required? Must I disappear altogether? No, don't answer that. Let me puzzle this through a moment on my own. I have the legacy of Allanon, possession of the Black Elfstone, and still I must do more if any of this is to mean anything. Transform myself, you say? How?"

Cogline shook his head. "I don't know. I know that if you do not do so you will not become a Druid and Paranor will not be restored to the world of Men."

"Am I trapped here if I fail?" Walker demanded furiously.

"No. You can leave whenever you choose. The Black Elfstone will see you clear."

There was an uncertain moment of angry silence as the two men faced each other, vague shadows seated on the stone bench beneath the castle walls. "And you?" Walker asked finally. "And Rumor? Can you come away with me?"

Cogline smiled faintly. "We gained life at a cost, Walker. We are tied to the magic of the Druid Histories, irrevocably bound. We must remain with them. If they are not restored into the world of men, then we cannot be brought back either."

"Shades." Walker breathed the word like a curse. He felt the weight of Paranor's stone settle down about him. "So I can gain my own freedom, but not yours. I can leave, but you must stay." His own smile was hard and ironic. "I would never do that, of course. Not after you gave up your own life so that I could keep mine. You knew that, didn't you? You knew it from the start. And Allanon surely knew. I am trapped at every turn, aren't I? I posture about who I will be and what I will do, how I will control my own destiny, and my words are meaningless."

"Walker, you are not bound to us," Cogline interjected quickly. "Rumor and I fought to save you because we wished to."

"You fought because it was necessary if I was to carry out Allanon's charge, Cogline. There is no escaping why I am alive. And if I refuse to carry it out now, or if I fail, everything that has gone before will have been pointless!" He fought to control himself as his voice threatened to become a shout. "Look at what is being done to me!"

Cogline waited a moment, then said quietly, "Is it really so bad, Walker? Have you been so misused?"

There was a pause as Walker glared at him. "Because I have nothing to say about what is to become of me? Because I am fated to be something I despise? Because I must act in ways I would not otherwise act? Old man, you astonish me."

"But not sufficiently to provoke you to answer?"

Walker shook his head in disgust. "Answers are pointless. Any answer I might give would only come back to haunt me later. I feel I am betrayed by my own thoughts in this business. Better to deal with what is given than what might be, isn't it?" He sighed. The cold of the stone seeped into him, felt now for the first time. "I am as trapped here as you are," he whispered.

Cogline leaned back against the castle wall, looking momentarily as if he might disappear into it. "Then make your escape, Walker," he said quietly. "Not by running from your fate, but by embracing it. You have insisted from the beginning that you would not allow yourself to be manipulated by the Druids. Do you suppose that I feel any different? We are both victims of circumstances set in motion three hundred years ago, and we would neither of us be so if we had the choice. But we don't. And it does no good to rail against what has been done to us. So, Walker, do something to turn things to your advantage. Do as you are fated, become what you must, and then act in whatever ways you perceive to be right."

Walker's smile was ironic. "So you would have me transform myself. How do I do that, Cogline? You have yet to tell me."

"Begin with the Druid Histories. All of the secrets of the magic are said to be contained within." The old man's hand gripped his arm impulsively. "Go up into the Keep and take the Histories from their vault, one by one, and see for yourself what they can teach. The answers you need must lie therein. It is a place to start, at least."

"Yes," Walker agreed, inwardly mulling over the possibility that Cogline was right, that he might gain what he sought not by pushing his fate away but by turning it to his own use. "Yes, it is a start."

He rose then, and Cogline with him. Walker faced the old man in silence for a moment, then reached out with his good arm and gently embraced him. "I am sorry for what has been done to you," he whispered. "I meant what I said back at Hearthstone before Rimmer Dall came—that I was wrong to blame you for any of what has happened, that I am grateful for all you have done to help me. We shall find a way to get free, Cogline. I promise."

Then he stepped back, and Cogline's answering smile was a momentary ray of sunlight breaking through the gloom.

So Walker Boh went up into the Keep, following the lead of Cogline and Rumor, three specters at haunt in a twilight world. The castle of the Druids was dark and heavy, shimmering like an image reflected in a pool of water adrift with shadows. The stone of the walls and floors and towers was cold and empty of life, and the hallways wound about like tunnels beneath the earth, dark and dank. There were bones scattered here and there along the carpeted, tapestried halls, the remains of those Gnomes who had died when Allanon had invoked the magic that sent the Keep out of the Four Lands three hundred years earlier. Piles of dust marked the end of the Mord Wraiths trapped there, and all that remained of what they had been was a whisper of a memory sealed away by the walls.

Passageways came and went, stairways that ran straight and curved about, a warren of corridors burrowing back into the stone. The silence was pervasive, thick and deep as leaves in late autumn in the forest, rooted in the castle walls and inexorable. They did not challenge it, wordless as they passed through its curtain, focusing instead on what lay ahead, on the path they followed to the paths that waited. Doors and empty chambers came and went about them, stark and uninviting within their trappings of gloom. Windows opened into grayness, a peculiar haze that shaded everything beyond so that the Keep was an island. Walker searched for something of the forestland that ringed the empty hill on which Paranor had stood, but the trees had disappeared; or he had, he amended—come out of the Four Lands into nothingness. Color had been drained from the carpets and tapestries and paintings, from the stone itself, and even from the sky. There was only the gloom, a kind of gray that defied any brightening, that was empty and dead.

Yet there was one thing more. There was the magic that held Paranor sealed away. It was present at every turn, at once invisible and suddenly revealed, a kind of swirling, greenish mist. It hovered in the shadows and along the edges of their vision, wicked and certain, the hiss of its being a whisper of killing need. It could not touch them, for they were protected by other magic and were at one with the Keep itself. But it could watch. It could tease and taunt and threaten. It could wait with the promise of what would happen when their protection was gone.

It was odd that it should be such an obvious presence; Walker Boh felt it immediately. It was as if the magic were a living thing, a guard dog set at prowl through the Keep, searching out intruders and hunting them down so that they might be destroyed. Its presence reminded him of the Rake in Eldwist, a Creeper that scoured its master's grounds and swept them clean of life. The magic lacked the substance of the Rake, but its feel was the same. It was an enemy, Walker sensed, that would eventually have to be faced.

Within the Druid library, behind the bookcases where the vault was concealed, they found the Histories, banks of massive, leather-bound books set within the walls of the Keep, the magic that had once hidden them from mortal eyes faded with the passing of the Keep from the world of men. Walker studied the books for a time, deliberating, then chose one at random, seated himself, and began to read. Cogline and Rumor kept him company, silent and unobtrusive. Time passed, but the light did not change. There was no day or night in Paranor. There was no past or future. There was only the here and now.

Walker did not know how long he read. He did not grow tired and did not find himself in need of sleep. He did not eat or drink, being neither hungry nor thirsty. Cogline told him at one point that in the world into which Paranor had been dispatched, mortal needs had no meaning. They were ghosts as much as they were two men and a moor cat. Walker did not question. There was no need.

He read for hours or days or even weeks; he did not know. He read at first without comprehending, simply seeing the words flow in front of his eyes, a narrative that was as distant and removed as the life he had known before the dreams of Allanon. He read of the Druids and their studies, of the world they had tried to make after the cataclysm of the Great Wars, of the First Council at Paranor, and of the coming together of the Races out of the holocaust. What should it mean to him? he wondered. What difference did any of it make now?

He finished one book and went on to another, then another, working his way steadily through the volumes, constantly searching for something that would tell him what he needed to know. There were recitations of spells and conjurings, of magics that could aid in small ways, of healings by touch and thought, of the succor of living things, and of the work that was needed to make the land whole again. He read them, and they told him nothing. How was he supposed to transform himself from what he was into what he was expected to be? Where did it say what he was supposed to do? The pages turned, the words ran on, and the answers stayed hidden.

He did not finish in one sitting, even though he was free of the distractions of his mortal needs and did not sleep or eat or drink. He left to walk about periodically, to think of other things, and to let his mind clear itself of all that the Histories related. Sometimes Cogline went with him, his shadow; sometimes it was Rumor. They might have been back at Hearthstone, walking its trails, keeping each other company, living in the seclusion of the valley once more. But Hearthstone was gone, destroyed by the Shadowen, and Paranor was dark and empty of life, and no amount of wishing could change what had gone before. There was no returning to the past, Walker thought to himself more than once. Everything that had once been was lost.

After a time, he began to despair. He had almost finished reading the Druid Histories and still he had discovered nothing. He had learned everything of who and what the Druids were, of their teachings and their beliefs, and of how they had lived and what they had sought to accomplish, and none of it told him anything about how they acquired their skills. There was no indication of where Allanon had come from, how he had learned to be a Druid or who had taught him, or what the subject matter of his teachings had been. The books were devoid of any reference to the conjuring that had sealed away the Keep or what it might require to reverse the spell.

"I cannot fathom it, Cogline," Walker Boh admitted finally, frustrated beyond hope as the last of the volumes sat open on his lap before him. "I have read everything, and none of it has helped. Is it possible that there are volumes missing? Is there something more to be tried?"

But Cogline shook his head. The answers, if they existed in written form, would be found here. There were no other books, no other sources of reference. Everything was contained in the Histories. All of the Druid studies began and ended there.

Walker went out alone then for a time, stalking the halls in anger, feeling betrayed and cheated, a victim of Druid whim and conceit. He thought bitterly of all that had been done to him because of who he was, of all that he had been forced to endure. His home had been destroyed. He had lost an arm and barely escaped with his life. He had been lied to and tricked repeatedly. He had been made to feel responsible for the fate of an entire world. Self-pity washed through him, and then his mouth tightened in admonishment. Enough, he chided himself. He was alive, wasn't he? Others had not been so fortunate. He was still haunted by Quickening's face; he could not forget how she had looked when he had let her fall. *Remember me,* she had pleaded with Morgan Leah—but she had been speaking to him as well. *Remember me*—as if anyone who had known her could ever forget.

Absently he turned down a corridor that led toward the center of the Keep and the entrance to the black well that had given birth to the magic that sealed away Paranor. His mind was still on Quickening, and he recalled once again the vision the Grimpond had shown him of her fate. Bitterness welled up within him. The vision had been right, of course. The Grimpond's visions were always right. First the loss of his arm, then the loss of Quickening, then . . .

He stopped suddenly, startled into immobility, a statue staring blankly into space at the center of the cavernous passageway. *He had forgotten. There was a third vision.* He took a steadying breath, picturing it in his mind. He stood within an empty, lifeless castle fortress, stalked by a death he could not escape, pursued relentlessly . . .

He exhaled sharply. *This castle?* He closed his eyes, trying to remember. Yes, it might have been Paranor.

He felt his pulse quicken. In the vision, he felt a need to run, but could not. He stood frozen as Death approached. A dark-robed figure stood behind him, holding him fast, preventing his escape.

Allanon.

He felt the silence grow oppressive. What had become of this third vision? he wondered. When was it supposed to happen? Was it meant to happen here?

And suddenly he knew. The certainty of it shocked him, but he did not doubt. The vision would come to pass, just as the others had, and it would come to pass here. Paranor was the castle, and the death that stalked him was the dark magic called forth to seal the Keep. Allanon did indeed stand behind him, holding him fast—not physically, but in ways stronger still.

But there was more, some part of things that he had not yet divined. It was not foreordained that he should die. That was the obvious meaning of the Grimpond's vision, what the Grimpond wanted Walker to think. The visions were always deceptive. The images were cleverly revealed, lending themselves to more than one interpretation. Like pieces to a puzzle, you had to play with them to discover how they fit.

Walker's eyes prowled the dark shadows that lay all about, hunting. What if he could find a way to turn the Grimpond's cleverness to his own use? What if this time he could decipher the vindictive spirit's foretelling in advance of its happening? And suppose—he hardly dared let himself hope—deciphering the vision could provide him with the key to understanding his fate within the Druid's Keep?

A fire began to build within him—a burning determination. He did not have the answers he needed yet, but he had something just as good. He had a way to discover what they were.

He thought back to his entry into Paranor, to his meeting with Cogline and Rumor. The missing pieces were there, somewhere. He retraced his reading of the Druid Histories, seeing again the words on the pages, feeling anew the weight of the books, the texture of the bindings. Something was there, something he had missed. He closed his eyes, picturing himself, following all that had happened, relating it to himself in his mind, a sequence of events. He searched it, standing solitary in that hall, wrapped in shadows and silence, feeling the edges of his confusion begin to draw away, hearing sounds that were new and welcome begin to whisper to him. He went down inside himself, reaching for the darker places where the secrets hid themselves. His magic rose to greet him. He could see anything if he searched hard and long enough, he told himself. He dropped away into the stillest, calmest part of himself, letting everything fall away.

What had he overlooked?

Whosoever shall have the cause and the right shall wield it to its proper end.

His eyes snapped open. His hand came up slowly along his body, groping. His fingers found what they were seeking, carefully tucked within his clothing, and they closed tightly about it.

The Black Elfstone.

Clutching the talisman protectively, his mind awash with new possibilities, he hurried away.

15

Wren Ohmsford crouched wordlessly with her companions in the darkness of the tunnels beneath the Keel while the Owl worked in silence somewhere ahead, striking flint against stone to produce a spark that would ignite the pitch-coated torch he balanced on his knees. The magic that had illuminated the tunnel when Wren had come into the city was gone now, disappeared with Arborlon and the Elves into the Loden. Triss had been the last to enter, carrying Ellenroh from the bridge, and he had closed the door tightly behind, shutting them away from the madness that raged without, but trapping them as well with the heat and the stench of Killeshan's fire.

A spark caught in the darkness ahead, and a dark orange flame flared to life, casting shadows everywhere. Heads turned to where the Owl was already starting away.

"Be quick," he whispered back to them, his voice rough and urgent. "It won't take long for the dark things to find that door."

They crept swiftly after him, Eowen, Dal, Gavilan, Wren, Garth, Triss carrying Ellenroh, and Cort trailing. Beyond, burrowing down into the earth with the tenacity of moles, the howls and shrieks of the demons tracked them. Sweat beaded on Wren's skin, the heat of the tunnels intense and stifling. She brushed at her eyes, blinked away the stinging moisture, and worked to keep pace. Her thoughts strayed as she labored, and she remembered Ellenroh, standing at the center of the bridgehead, invoking the Loden, calling forth the light that would sweep up all of Arborlon and carry it down into the gleaming depths of the Stone. She could see the city disappear, vanishing as if it never were—buildings, people, animals, trees, grass, everything. Now Arborlon was their responsibility, theirs to protect, cradled within a magic that was only as strong as the nine men and women to whom it had been entrusted.

She pushed past trailing roots and spider's webs, and the enormity of the task settled on her like a weight. She was only one, she knew, and not the strongest. Yet she could not escape the feeling that the responsibility was inevitably hers alone, an extension of Allanon's charge, the reason for which she had come in search of the Elves.

She shook the feeling aside, crowding up against Gavilan in her haste to keep moving.

Then abruptly the earth shuddered.

The line stopped, and heads lowered protectively as silt broke free of the tunnel roof in a shower. The ground shook again, the tremors building steadily, rocking the earth as if some giant had seized the island in both hands and was struggling to lift it free.

"What's happening?" Wren heard Gavilan demand. She dropped to her knees to keep from being thrown off balance, feeling Garth's steadying hand settle on her shoulder.

"Keep moving!" the Owl snapped. "Hurry!"

They ran now, crouched low against a pall of loose dirt that hung roiling in the air. The tremors continued, a rumbling from beneath, the sound rising and falling, a quaking that tossed them against the tunnel walls and left them struggling to remain upright. The seconds sped away, fleeing as quickly as they did, it seemed, from the horror following. A part of the tunnel collapsed behind them, showering them with dirt. They could hear a cracking of stone, a splitting apart of the lava rock, as if the earth's crust were giving way. There was a heavy thud as a great boulder dropped through a crevice and struck the tunnel floor.

"Owl, get us out of here!" Gavilan called out frantically.

Then they were climbing free again, scrambling from the tunnel through an opening in the earth, clawing their way into the weak morning light. Behind them, the tunnel collapsed completely, falling away in a rush of air, silt exploding through the opening they had fled. The tremors continued to roll across Morrowindl's heights, ripping its surface, causing the rock to grate and crumble. Wren hauled herself to her feet with the others and stood in the shelter of a copse of dying acacia, looking back at where they had been.

The Keel was swarming with demons, their black bodies everywhere as they sought to scale the hated barrier. The magic was gone, but the tremors that had replaced it proved an even more formidable obstacle. Demons flew from the heights, screaming as they fell, shaken free like leaves from an autumn tree in a windstorm. The Keel cracked and split as the mountainside shuddered beneath it, chunks of stone tumbling away, the whole of it threatening to collapse. Fires spurted out of the earth from within, the crater from which Arborlon had been scooped by the magic become a cauldron of heat and flames. Steam hissed and spurted in geysers. High on Killeshan's slopes, the crust of the mountain's skin had ruptured and begun to leak molten rock.

"Killeshan comes awake," Eowen said softly, causing them all to turn. "The disappearance of Arborlon shifted the balance of things on Morrowindl; a void was created in the magic. The disruption reaches all the way to the core of the island. The volcano is no longer dormant, no longer stable. The fires within will burn more fiercely, and the gases and heat will build, until they can no longer be contained."

"How long?" the Owl snapped.

Eowen shook her head. "Hours here on the high slopes, days farther down." Her eyes were bright. "It is the beginning of the end."

There was an instant of uncertain silence.

"For the demons, perhaps, but not for us." It was Ellenroh Elessedil who spoke, back on her feet again, recovered from the strain of invoking the Loden's magic. She freed herself from Triss's steadying grip and walked through them, drawing them after in her wake until she turned to face them. She looked calm and assured and unafraid. "No hesitation now," she admonished. "We go quickly, quietly, down to the shores of the Blue Divide and off the island, back to where we belong. Keep together, keep your eyes sharp. Owl, take us out of here."

Aurin Striate turned away at once, and the others went with him. There were no questions asked—Ellenroh Elessedil's presence was that strong. Wren glanced back once to see her grandmother come up beside Eowen, who seemed to have lapsed into a trance, put her arms about the seer, and lead her gently away. Behind them, the glare of the volcano's fire turned the Keel and the demons the color of blood. It seemed as if everything had disappeared in a wash of red.

Shadows against the hazy light, the company crept down off the slopes of Killeshan through the rugged mix of lava rock, deadwood, and scrub. All of the sounds were behind them now where the demons converged on an enemy that they were just beginning to discover was no longer there. Ahead there was only the steady rush of the Rowen as its gray waters churned toward the sea. The tremors chased after, shudders that rippled along the stretches of lava rock and shook the trees and brush; but their impact diminished the farther the company went. Vog clouded the air before them, turning the brightness of early-morning haze and the shape of the land indistinct. Wren's breathing steadied, and her body cooled. She no longer felt trapped as she had in the tunnel, and the intensity of the heat had lessened. She began to relax, to feel herself merge with the land, her senses reaching out like invisible feelers to search out what was hidden.

Even so, she failed to detect the demons that lay in wait for them before the attack. There were more than a dozen, smallish and gnarled, crooked like deadwood, rising up with a rending of brush and sticks to seize at them. Eowen went down, and the Owl disappeared in a flurry of limbs. The others rallied, striking out at their attackers with whatever came to hand, bunching together about Eowen protectively. The Elven Hunters fought with grim ferocity, dispatching the demons as if they were nothing more than shadows. The fight was over almost before it began. One of the black things escaped; the rest lay still upon the ground.

The Owl reappeared from behind a ridge, one sleeve shredded, his thin face clawed. He beckoned them wordlessly, turning away from the path they had been following, taking them swiftly down from the summit of a rise to a narrow gully that wound ahead into the fog. They watched closely now, alert for further attacks, reminded that the demons would be everywhere, that not all of them would have gone to the Keel. The sky overhead turned a peculiar yellow as the sun ascended the sky yet struggled unsuccessfully to penetrate the vog. Wren crept ahead with long knives in both hands, her eyes sweeping the shadows cautiously for any sign of movement.

They were nearing the Rowen when Aurin Striate brought them to a sudden halt. He dropped into a crouch, motioning them down with him, then turned, gestured for them to remain where they were, and disappeared ahead into the haze. He was gone for less than five minutes before reappearing. He shook his head in warning and motioned them left. Keeping low, they slipped along a line of rocks to where a ridge hid them from the Rowen. From there they worked their way parallel to the river for more than a mile, then resurfaced cautiously atop a rise. Wren peered out at the sluggish gray surface of the river, empty and broad before her as it stretched away into the distance.

Nothing moved.

The Owl rejoined them, his leathery face furrowed. "The shallows are filled with things we don't want anything to do with. We'll cross here instead. It's too broad and too wide to swim. We'll have to ferry over. We'll build a raft big enough to hold on to—that will have to do."

He took the Elven Hunters with him to gather wood, leaving Gavilan and Garth with the women. Ellenroh came over to Wren and gave her a brief hug and a reassuring smile. All was well, she was saying, but there were worry lines etched in her brow. She moved quietly away.

"Feel the earth with your hands, Wren," Eowen whispered suddenly, crouching next to her. Wren reached down and let the tremors rise into her body. "The magic comes apart all about us—everything the Elves sought to build. The fabric of our arrogance and our fear begins to unravel." The rust-colored hair tumbled wildly about the distant green eyes, and Eowen had the look of someone awakening from a nightmare. "She will have to tell you sometime, Wren. She will have to let you know."

Then she was gone as well, moving over to join the queen. Wren was not sure exactly what she had been talking about, but assumed she was referring to Ellenroh, and that, as the Rover girl already knew, there were secrets still unrevealed.

The vog swirled about, screening off the Rowen, snaking through the cracks and crevices of the land, changing the shape of everything as it passed. Cort and Dal returned hauling lengths of deadwood, then disappeared again. The Owl passed through the gloom heading toward the river, stick-thin and bent as if at hunt. Everything moved as if not quite there, a shading of some half-forgotten memory that could trick you into believing things that never were.

A sudden convulsion rocked the earth underfoot, causing Wren to gasp in spite of herself and to reach down hurriedly to regain her balance. The waters of the Rowen seemed to surge sharply, gathering force in a wave that crashed against the shoreline and rolled on into the distance.

Garth touched her shoulder. *The island shakes itself apart.*

She nodded, thinking back to Eowen's declaration that the impending cataclysm was the result of a disruption in the magic. She had thought the seer was referring solely to Ellenroh's use of the Loden, but now it occurred to her that the seer meant something more. The implication of what she had just told Wren was that the disruption of the magic was broader than simply the taking away of Arborlon, that at some time in the past the Elves had sought to do something more and failed and that what was happening now was a direct result.

She stored the information away carefully for a time when she could make use of it.

Garth moved down to help the Elven Hunters, who were beginning to lash together the logs for the raft. Gavilan was speaking in low tones with Ellenroh, and there was a restless anger reflected in his eyes. Wren watched him carefully for a moment, measuring what she saw now against what she had seen before, the hard-edged tension and the careless disregard, two images in sharp contrast. She found Gavilan intriguing, a complex mix of possibilities and enticements. She liked him; she wanted him close. But there was something hidden in him that bothered her, something she had yet to define.

"Just a few more minutes," the Owl advised, passing by her like a shadow and fading back into the mist.

She started to climb to her feet, and something small and quick darted from the undergrowth and threw itself on her. She tumbled back, flailing desperately, then realized in shock that the thing clinging to her was Faun. She laughed in spite of herself and hugged the Tree Squeak close.

"Faun," she cooed, nuzzling the odd little creature. "I thought something terrible had happened to you. But you're all right, aren't you? Yes, little one, you're just fine."

She was aware of Ellenroh and Gavilan looking over, puzzlement registered on their faces, and she quickly climbed to her feet again, waving to them reassuringly, smiling in spite of herself.

"Hrrwwwll. Have you forgotten your promise?"

She turned abruptly to find Stresa staring up at her from the edge of the gloom, quills all on end.

She knelt hurriedly. "So you are all right as well, Mr. Splinterscat. I was worried for you both. I couldn't come out to see if you were safe, but I hoped you were. Did you find each other after I left?"

"Yes, Wren of the Elves," the Splinterscat replied, his words cool and measured. "Pffttt. The Squeak came scampering back at dawn, fur all wild and ragged, chittering about you. It found me down by the river where I was waiting. So, now—your promise. You remember your promise, don't you?"

Wren nodded solemnly. "I remember, Stresa. When I left the city, I was to take you with me to the Westland. I will keep that promise. Did you worry I would not?"

"Hssst, pfftt!" The Splinterscat flattened its quills. "I hoped you were someone whose word meant something. Not like—" He cut himself short.

"Grandmother," Wren called out to the queen, and Ellenroh moved over to join her, curly hair blowing across her face like a veil. "Grandmother, these are my friends, Stresa and Faun. They helped Garth and me find our way to the city."

"Then they are friends of mine as well," Ellenroh declared.

"Lady," Stresa replied stiffly, not altogether charmed, it seemed.

"What's this?" Gavilan came up next to them, amusement dancing in his eyes. "A Scat? I thought they were all gone."

"There are a few of us—sssttt—no thanks to you," Stresa announced coldly.

"Bold fellow, aren't you?" Gavilan couldn't quite conceal his disapproval.

"Grandmother," Wren said quickly, putting an end to the exchange, "I promised Stresa I would take him with us when we left the island. I must keep that promise. And Faun must come as well." She hugged the furry Tree Squeak, who hadn't even looked up yet from her shoulder, still burrowed down against her, clinging like a second skin.

Ellenroh looked doubtful, as if taking the creatures along presented some difficulty that Wren did not understand. "I don't know," she answered quietly. The wind whistled past her, gathering force in the gloom. She gazed off at the Elven Hunters, at work now on loading backpacks and supplies onto the raft, then said, "But if you gave your promise . . ."

"Aunt Ell!" Gavilan snapped angrily.

The queen's gaze was icy as it fixed on him. "Keep silent, Gavilan."

"But you know the rules . . ."

"Keep silent!"

The anger in Gavilan's face was palpable. He avoided looking at either her or Wren, shifting his gaze instead to Stresa. "This is a mistake. You should know best, Scat. Remember who made you? Remember why?"

"Gavilan!" The queen was livid. The Elven Hunters stood up abruptly from their work and looked back at her. The Owl reappeared from out of the mist. Eowen moved to stand next to the queen.

Gavilan held his ground a moment longer, then wheeled away and stalked down to the raft. For a moment, no one else moved, statues in the mist. Then Ellenroh said, to no one in particular, her voice sounding small and lost, "I'm sorry."

She walked off as well, sweeping Eowen up in her wake, her youthful features so stricken that it kept Wren from following after.

She looked instead at Stresa. The Splinterscat's laugh was bitter. "She doesn't want us off the island. Ffﬂttt. None of them do."

"Stresa, what is going on here?" Wren demanded, angry herself now, bewildered at the animosity Stresa's appearance had generated.

"Rrrwwll. Wren Ohmsford. Don't you know? Hssst. You don't, do you? Ellenroh Elessedil is your grandmother, and you don't know. How strange!"

"Come, Wren," the Owl said, passing by once more, touching her lightly on the shoulder. "Time to be going. Quick, now."

The Elven Hunters were shoving the raft down to the water's edge, and the others were hastening after. "Tell me!" she snapped at Stresa.

"A ride down the rwwlll Rowen is not my idea of a good time," the

Splinterscat said, ignoring her. "I'll sit directly in the middle, if you please. Hsssttt. Or if you don't, for that matter."

A renewed series of shudders shook the island, and in the haze behind them Killeshan erupted in a shower of crimson fire. Ash and smoke belched out, and a rumbling rose from deep within the earth.

They were all calling for Wren now, and she ran to them, Stresa a step ahead, Faun draped about her neck. She was furious that no one would confide in her, that arguments could be held in her presence about things of which she was being kept deliberately ignorant. She hated being treated this way, and it was becoming apparent that unless she forced the issue no one was ever going to tell her anything about the Elves and Morrowindl.

She reached the raft as they were pushing it out into the Rowen, meeting Gavilan's openly hostile gaze with one of her own, shifting deliberately closer to Garth. The Elven Hunters were already in water up to their knees, steadying the raft. Stresa hopped aboard without being asked and settled down squarely in the middle of the backpacks and supplies, just as he had threatened he would do. No one objected; no one said anything. Eowen and the queen were guided to their places by Triss, the queen clutching the Ruhk Staff tightly in both hands. Wren and Garth followed. Together, the members of the little company eased the raft away from the shoreline, leaning forward so that its logs could bear the weight of their upper bodies, their hands grasping the rope ties that had been fashioned to give them a grip.

Almost immediately the current caught them up and began to sweep them away. Those closest to the shore kicked in an effort to move clear of the banks, away from the rocks and tree roots that might snag them. Killeshan continued to erupt, fire and ash spewing forth, the volcano rumbling its discontent. The skies darkened with this new layer of vog, clouding farther against the light. The raft moved out into the center of the channel, rocking with the motion of the water, picking up speed. The Owl shouted instructions to his companions, and they tried in vain to maneuver the raft toward the far bank. Geysers burst through the lava rock on the shoreline behind them, rupturing the stone skin of the high country, sending steam and gas thrusting skyward. The Rowen shuddered with the force of the earth's rumblings and began to buck. The waters turned choppy and small whirlpools began to form. Debris swirled past, carried on the crest of the river. The raft was buffeted and tossed, and those clinging to it were forced to expend all of their efforts just to hang on.

"Tuck in your legs!" the Owl shouted in warning. "Tighten your grip!"

Downriver they swept, the shoreline passing in a blur of jagged trees and scrub, rugged lava fields, and mist and haze. The volcano disappeared behind them, screened away by a bend in the river and the beginnings of the valley into which it poured. Wren felt things jab and poke at her, slam up against her and spin away, and whip past as if yanked by an invisible rope. Her hands and fingers began to ache with the strain of holding on to the rope stays, and her body was chilled numb by the icy mountain waters. The river's rush drowned out the roar of the volcano, but she could still feel it shudder beneath her, waking up, recoiling with sickness, and splitting apart with convulsions. Cliffs appeared in front of them, rising like impassable walls. Then they were in their midst, the rock miraculously dividing to let the Rowen tumble through a narrow defile. For a few minutes the rapids were so severe that it seemed they must break apart on the rocks. Then they were clear again, the channel broadening out once more, the cliffs receding into the distance. They spun through a series of wide, sluggish riffs and emerged in a lake that stretched away into the green haze of a jungle.

The river slowed and quieted. The raft quit spinning and began to float lazily toward the center of the lake. Mist hung thick upon its gleaming surface, screening the shoreline to either side, transforming it into a deep green mask of silence. From somewhere distant, Killeshan's angry rumble sounded.

At the center of the raft, Stresa lifted his head tentatively and looked about. The Splinterscat's sharp eyes shifted quickly to find Wren. "Sssppptttt! We must get away from here!" he urged. "This is not a good—ssspp—place to be! Over there is Eden's Murk!"

"What are you muttering about, Scat?" Gavilan growled irritably.

Ellenroh shifted her grip on the Ruhk Staff where it lay across the raft. "Owl, do you know where we are?"

Aurin Striate shook his head. "But if the Splinterscat says it is unsafe . . ."

The waters behind him erupted thunderously, and a huge, crusted black head reared into view. It rose into the brume slowly, almost languorously, balanced atop a thick, sinuous body of scales and bumps that rippled and flexed against the half-light. Tendrils trailed from its jaws like feelers twisting to find food. Teeth bared as its greenish mouth widened, crooked and double rowed. It coiled until it towered over them, no more than fifty feet away, and then it hissed like a snake that has been stepped upon.

"A serpent!" Eowen cried softly.

The Elven Hunters were already moving, hastily changing positions so that they were bunched between the monster and their charges. Weapons drawn, they began to scull the raft toward the opposite shore. It was a futile attempt. The serpent swam soundlessly in pursuit, expending almost no effort to overtake them, dipping its head threateningly, jaws agape. Wren worked next to Garth to help push the raft ahead, but the riverbank seemed a long way off. At the center of the raft, Stresa's spines stuck out in all directions, and his head disappeared.

The serpent hit them with its tail when they were still a hundred yards from shore, swinging it up into them from underneath, lifting the raft and the nine who clung to it clear of the water, spinning them into the air. They flew for a short distance and landed with a *whump* that knocked the breath from their bodies. Grips loosened, and people and packs tumbled away. Eowen splashed frantically, went under, and was pulled back to the surface by Garth. The raft had begun to come apart from the force of the landing, ties loosening, logs splitting. The Owl yelled at them to kick, and they did, frantically, furiously, for there was nothing else they could do.

The serpent came at them again, sliding out of the Rowen with a huffing that sprayed water everywhere. Its cry was a deep, booming cough as it launched itself, body flexing and coiling, huge and monstrous as it descended. Wren and Garth broke free of the raft as the beast struck, dragging Ellenroh and Faun with them. Wren saw Gavilan dive, watched the others scatter, and then the serpent struck and everything disappeared in an explosion of water. The raft flew apart, hammered into kindling. Wren went under, Faun clinging desperately to her. She resurfaced, sputtering for air. Heads bobbed in the water, waves generated by the attack washing over them. The serpent's head reared into the haze once more, but this time Triss and Cort had hold of it, swords stabbing and hacking furiously. Scales and dark blood flew, and the monster cried out in fury. Its body thrashed in an effort to shake loose its attackers, and then it dove. As it went under, Triss buried his sword in the scaly head and broke away. Cort was still attacking, his youthful face grimly set.

The serpent's body convulsed, scattering everyone. Stray logs from the shattered raft were sent spinning.

One flew at Wren and caught her a glancing blow along the side of her head. She had a momentary vision of the serpent diving, of Garth hauling Eowen toward the shore, and of Ellenroh and the Owl clinging to other stray bits of the raft, and then everything went black.

She drifted, unfeeling, unfettered, numb to her soul. She could tell that she was sinking, but she didn't seem to be able to do anything about it. She held her breath as the water closed over her, then exhaled when she could hold it no longer and felt the water rush in. She cried out soundlessly, her voice lost to her. She could feel the weight of the Elfstones about her neck; she could feel them begin to burn.

Then something caught hold of her and began to pull, something that fastened first on her tunic, then slipped down about her body. A hand first, then an arm—she was in the grip of another person. Slowly she began to ascend again.

She surfaced, sputtering and choking, struggling to breathe as she coughed out the water in her lungs. Her rescuer was behind her, pulling her to safety. She laid back weakly and did not resist, still stunned from the blow and the near drowning. She blinked away the water in her eyes and looked back across the Rowen. It spread away in a choppy silver sheen, empty now of everything but debris, the serpent disappeared. She could hear voices calling—Eowen's, the Owl's, and one or two more. She heard her own name called. Faun was no longer clinging to her. What had become of Faun?

Then the shore came into view on either side, and her rescuer ceased swimming and stood up, hauling her up as well and turning her about. She was face to face with Gavilan.

"Are you all right, Wren?" he asked breathlessly, worn from the strain of hauling her. "Look at me."

She did, and the anger she had felt toward him earlier faded when she saw the look on his face. Concern and a trace of fear were mirrored there, genuine and unforced.

She gripped his hand. "It's okay. Everything's fine." She took a deep, welcome breath of air. "Thank you, Gavilan."

He looked surprisingly uncomfortable. "I said I was here to help you if you needed it, but I didn't expect you to take me up on my offer so soon."

He helped her from the water to where Ellenroh was waiting to fold her into her arms. She hugged Wren anxiously and whispered something barely audible, words that didn't need to be heard to be understood. Garth was there as well, and the Owl, drenched and sorry-looking, but unharmed. She saw most of their supplies stacked at the water's edge, soaked through but salvaged. Eowen sat disheveled and worn beneath a tree where Dal was looking after her.

"Faun!" she called, and immediately heard a chittering. She looked out across the Rowen and saw the Tree Squeak clinging to a bit of wood several dozen yards away. She charged back out into the water until she was almost up to her neck, and then her furry companion abandoned its float and swam quickly to reach her, scrambling up on her shoulder as she hauled it to shore. "There, there, little one, you're safe as well now, aren't you?"

A moment later Triss stumbled ashore, one side of his sunbrowned face scraped raw, his clothing torn and bloodied. He sat long enough for the Owl to check him over, then rose to walk back down to the river with the others. Standing together, they looked out over the empty water.

There was no sign of either Cort or Stresa.

"I didn't see the Scat after the serpent struck the raft that last time," Gavilan said quietly, almost apologetically. "I'm sorry, Wren. I really am."

She nodded without answering, unable to speak, the pain too great. She stood rigid and expressionless as she continued to search futilely for the Splinterscat.

Twice now I've left him, she was thinking.

Triss reached down to tighten the stays on the sword he had picked up from the supplies they had salvaged. "Cort went down with the serpent. I don't think he was able to get free."

Wren barely heard him, her thoughts dark and brooding. *I should have looked for him when the raft sank. I should have tried to help.*

But she knew, even as she thought it, that there was nothing she could have done.

"We have to go on," the Owl said quietly. "We can't stay here."

As if to emphasize his words, Killeshan rumbled in the distance, and the haze swirled sluggishly in response. They hesitated a moment longer, bunched close at the riverbank, water dripping from their clothing, silent and unmoving. Then slowly, one after another, they turned away. After picking up the backpacks and supplies and checking to be certain that their weapons were in place, they stalked off into the trees.

Behind them, the Rowen stretched away like a silver-gray shroud.

The company had gone less than a hundred yards from the Rowen's edge when the trees ended and the nightmare began. A huge swamp opened before them, a collection of bogs thick with sawgrass and weeds and laced through with sparse stretches of old-growth acacia and cedar whose branches had grown tight about one another in what appeared to be a last, desperate effort to keep from being pulled down into the mud. Many were already half fallen, their root systems eroded, their massive trunks bent over like stricken giants. Through the tangle of dying trees and stunted scrub, the swamp spread away as far as the eye could see, a vast and impenetrable mire shrouded in haze and silence.

The Owl brought them to an uncertain halt, and they stood staring doubtfully in all directions, searching for even the barest hint of a pathway. But there was nothing to be found. The swamp was a clouded, forbidding maze.

"Eden's Murk," the Owl said tonelessly.

The choices available to the company were limited. They could retrace their steps to the Rowen and follow the river upstream or down until a better route showed itself, or they could press on through the swamp. In either case, they would eventually have to scale the Blackledge because they had come too far downstream to regain the valley and the passes that would let them make an easy descent. There was not enough time left them to try going all the way back; the demons would be everywhere by now. The Owl worried that they might already be searching along the river. He advised pressing ahead. The journey would be treacherous, but the demons would not be so quick to look for them here. A day, two at the most, and they should reach the mountains.

After a brief discussion, the remainder of the company agreed. None of them, with the exception of Wren and Garth, had been outside the city in almost ten years—and the Rover girl and her protector had passed through the country only once and knew little of how to survive its dangers. The Owl had lived out there for years. No one was prepared to second-guess him.

They began the trek through Eden's Murk. The Owl led, followed by Triss, Ellenroh, Eowen, Gavilan, Wren, Garth, and Dal. They proceeded in single file, strung out behind Aurin Striate as he worked to find a line of solid footing through the mire. He was successful most of the time, for there were still stretches where the swamp hadn't closed over completely. But there were times as well when they were forced to step down into the oily water and mud, easing along patches of tall grass and scrub, clutching with their hands to keep from losing their footing, feeling the muck suck eagerly in an effort to draw them in. They traveled slowly, cautiously through the gloom, warned by the Owl to stay close to the person ahead, peering worriedly into the haze whenever the water bubbled and the mud belched.

Eden's Murk, despite the pall of silence that hung over it, was a haven for any number of living things. Most were never seen and only barely heard. Winged creatures flew like shadows through the brume, silent in their passage, swift and furtive. Insects buzzed annoyingly, some iridescent and as large as a child's hand. Things that might have been rats or shrews skittered about the remaining trees, climbing catlike from view an instant after they were spied. There were other creatures out there as well, some of them massive. They splashed and growled in the stillness, hidden by the gloom, hunters that prowled the deeper waters. No one ever saw them, but it was never for lack of keeping watch.

The day wore on, a slow, agonizing crawl toward darkness. The company stopped once to eat, huddled together on a trunk that was half drowned by the swamp, backs to one another as their eyes swept the screen of vog. The air turned hot and cold by turns, as if Eden's Murk had been built of separate chambers and there were invisible walls all about. The swamp water, like the air, could be chilly or tepid, deep in some spots and shallow in others, a mix of colors and smells, none of which were pleasant, all of which pulled and dragged at the life above. Now and again the earth would shudder, a reminder that somewhere behind them Killeshan continued to threaten, gases and heat building within its core, lava spurting from its mouth to run burning down the mountainside. Wren pictured it as she slogged along with the others—the air choked with vog, the land a carpet of fire, everything enveloped by gathering layers of steam and ash. Already the Keel would be gone. What of the demons? she wondered. Would they have fled as well, or were they too mindless to fear even the lava? If they had fled, where would they have gone?

But she knew the answer to that last question. There was only one place for any of them to go.

They will be driven from their siege back across the Rowen, Garth signed grimly when she asked for his opinion. They walked together momentarily across a rare stretch of earth where the swamp was still held more than an arm's length at bay. *They will start back toward the cliffs, just as we have done. If we are too slow, they will be all about us before we can get clear.*

Perhaps they won't come this far downriver, she suggested hopefully, fingers flicking out the signs. *They may keep to the valley because it is easier.*

Garth didn't bother to respond. He didn't have to. She knew as well as he did that if the demons kept to the valley in their descent of the Black-ledge, they would reach the lower parts of the island quicker than the company and be waiting on the beaches.

She thought often of Stresa, trying to remember when she had last seen the Splinterscat after the serpent's attack, trying to recall something that would give her even the faintest hope that he had escaped. But she could think of nothing. One moment he had been there, crouched amid the baggage, and the next he was gone along with everything else. She grieved silently for him, unable to help herself, more attached to him than she should have been, than she should have allowed herself to become. She clutched Faun tightly and wondered at herself, feeling oddly drawn away from who and what she had once been, a stranger to everything, no longer so self-assured by her training, so confident in her skills, so certain that she was a Rover first and always and that nothing else mattered.

More often than she cared to admit, her fingers stole beneath her tunic to find the Elfstones. Eden's Murk was immense and implacable, and it threatened to erode her courage and her strength. The Elfstones reassured her; the Elven magic was power. She hated herself for feeling so, for needing to rely on them. A single day out of Arborlon, and already she had begun to despair. And she was not alone. She could see the uneasiness in all of their eyes, even Garth's. Morrowindl did something to you that transcended reason, that buried rational thought in a mountain of fear and doubt. It was in the air, in the earth, in the life about them, a kind of madness that whispered insidious warnings and stole life with casual disregard. She again tried to picture the island as it had once been and again failed to do so. She could not see past what it was, what it had become.

What the Elves and their magic had made it.

And she thought once more of the secrets they were hiding—Ellenroh, the Owl, Gavilan, all of them. Stresa had known. Stresa would have told her. Now it would have to be someone else.

She touched Eowen on the shoulder at one point and asked in a whisper, "Are you able to see anything of what is to happen to us? Do you have use of the sight?"

But the pale, emerald-eyed woman only smiled sadly and replied, "No, Wren, the sight is clouded by the magic that runs through the core of the island. Arborlon gave me shelter to see. Here there is only madness. Perhaps if I am able to get beyond the cliffs to where the sun's light and the sea's smell reach . . ." She trailed off.

Then darkness descended in a slow setting of gray veils, one after another, that gradually screened away the light. They had been walking since midmorning and still there was no sign of Blackledge, no hint of the swamp's end. The Owl began to look for a place where they could spend the night, cautioning them to be especially careful now as shadows dappled the land and played tricks with their eyes. The day's silence gradually gave way to a rising tide of night sounds, a mix rough-edged and sharp, rising out of the darker patches to echo through the gloom. Bits and pieces of foliage began to glow with a silver phosphorescence, and flying insects glimmered and faded as they skipped across the mire.

Aurin Striate's lank form knifed steadily ahead, bent against the encroaching dark. Wren saw Ellenroh slip past Triss momentarily, leaning forward to say something to the Owl. The company was crossing a stretch of weeds grown waist high, and the fading light glimmered dully off the surface of the swamp to their left.

Abruptly the water geysered as something huge surfaced to snare unsuspecting prey, jaws closing with a snap as it sank again from sight. Everyone jumped, and for an instant all were distracted. Wren saw the Owl turn halfway back, warning with his hands. She saw something else, something half hidden in the gloom ahead. There was a flicker of movement.

A second later, she heard a familiar hissing sound.

Garth couldn't have heard it, of course, yet something warned him of the danger, and he launched himself atop Wren and Eowen both and threw them to the ground. Behind them, Dal dropped instinctively. Ahead, the Owl wrapped himself about Ellenroh Elessedil, shoving her back into Triss and Gavilan. There was a ripping, thrusting sound as a hail of needles sliced through the grasses and leaves. Wren heard a surprised grunt. Then they were all flat upon the earth, deep in the grasses, breathing heavily in the sudden stillness.

A Darter!

The name scraped like rough bark on bare skin as she screamed it in her mind. She remembered how close one had come to killing her on the way in. Garth's arm loosened about her waist, and she signed quickly to him as the hard, bearded face pushed up next to her own.

Ahead, she heard her grandmother sob.

Frantic now, forgetting everything else, she scrambled forward through the tall grass, the others crawling hurriedly after her. She passed Gavilan, who was still trying to figure out what was going on, and caught up with Triss as the Captain of the Home Guard reached the queen.

Ellenroh was half lying, half bent over the Owl, cradling him in the crook of one arm as she wiped his sweating face. The Owl's scarecrow frame looked as if all the sticks had been removed and nothing remained but the clothing that draped them. His eyes were open and staring, and his mouth worked desperately to swallow.

Dozens of the Darter's poisonous needles stood out from his body. He had taken the full brunt of the plant's attack.

"Aurin," the queen whispered, and his eyes swung urgently to find her. "It's all right. We're all here."

Her own eyes lifted to meet Wren's, and they stared at each other in helpless disbelief.

"Owl." Wren spoke softly, her hand reaching out to touch his face.

Aurin Striate's breath quickened sharply. "I can't . . . feel a thing," he gasped.

Then his breathing stopped altogether, and he was dead.

Wren didn't sleep at all that night. She wasn't sure any of them did, but she kept apart from the others so she had no real way of knowing. She sat alone with Faun curled in her lap at the base of a shaggy cedar, its trunk overgrown with moss and vines, and stared out into the swamp. They were less than a hundred yards from where the attack had occurred, huddled down against the vog and the night, encircled by the sounds of things they could not see, too devastated by what had happened to worry about going farther until morning.

She kept seeing the Owl's face as he lay dying.

It was just a fluke, she knew, just bad luck. It was nothing they could have foreseen and there was nothing they could have done to prevent it. She had come across only one other Darter until now, one other on the whole of Morrowindl she had traveled through. What were the chances that she should find another here? What were the odds that of all of them it should end up striking down Aurin Striate?

The improbability of it haunted her.

Would things have turned out differently if Stresa had been there watching out for them?

There was no solid ground in which to bury the Owl, nothing but marshland where the beasts that lived in Eden's Murk would dig him up for food, so they found a patch of quicksand and sank him to where he could never be touched.

They ate dinner then, what they could manage to eat, talking quietly about nothing, not even able to contemplate yet what losing the Owl meant. They ate, drank more than a little ale, and dispersed into the dark. The Elven Hunters set a watch, Triss until midnight, Dal until dawn, and the silence settled down.

Just a fluke, she repeated dismally.

She had so many fond memories of the Owl, even though she had known him only a short time, and she clung to them as a shield against her grief. The Owl had been kind to her. He had been honest, too—as honest as he could be without betraying the queen's trust. What he could share of himself, he did. He had told her that very morning that he had been able to survive outside of Arborlon's walls all these years because he had accepted the inevitability of his death and by doing so had made himself strong against his fear of it. It was a necessary way to be, he had told her. If you are always frightened for yourself you can't act, and then life loses its purpose. You just have to tell yourself that, when you get right down to it, you don't matter all that much.

But the Owl had mattered more than most. Alone with her thoughts, the others either asleep or pretending to be, she allowed herself to acknowledge exactly how much he had mattered. She remembered how Ellenroh had cried in her arms when Aurin Striate was gone, like a little girl again, unashamed of her grief, mourning someone who had been much more than a faithful retainer of the throne, more than a lifetime companion, and more than just a friend. She had not realized the depth of feeling that her grandmother bore for the Owl, and it made her cry in turn. Gavilan, for once, was at a complete loss for words, taking Ellenroh's hands and holding them without speaking, impulsively hugging Wren when she most needed it, doing nothing more than just being there. Garth and the Elven Hunters were stone faced, but their eyes reflected what lay behind their masks. They would all miss Aurin Striate.

How much they would miss him would become evident at first light, and its measure extended far beyond any emotional loss. For the Owl was the only one among them who knew anything about surviving the dangers of Morrowindl outside the walls of Arborlon. Without him, they had no one to serve as guide. They would have to rely on their own instincts and training if they were to save themselves and all those confined within the Loden. That meant finding a way to get free of Eden's Murk, descending the Blackledge, passing through the In Ju, and reaching the beaches in time to meet up with Tiger Ty. They would have to do all that without any of them knowing the way they should travel or the dangers they should watch out for.

The more Wren thought about it, the more impossible it seemed. Except for Garth and herself, none of the others had any real experience in wilderness survival—and this was strange country for the Rovers as well, a land they had passed through only once and then with help, a land filled with pitfalls and hazards they had never encountered before. How much help would any of them be to the others? What chance did they have without the Owl?

Her brooding left her hollow and bitter. So much depended on whether they lived or died, and now it was all threatened because of a fluke.

Garth slept closest to her, a dark shadow against the earth, as still as death in slumber. He puzzled her these days—had done so ever since they had arrived on Morrowindl. It wasn't something she could easily define, but it was there nevertheless. Garth, always enigmatic, had become increasingly remote, gradually withdrawing in his relationship with her—almost as if he felt that she didn't need him any more, that his tenure as teacher and hers as student were finished. It wasn't in any specific thing he had done or way he had behaved; it was more a general attitude, evinced in a pulling back of himself in little, unobtrusive ways. He was still there for her in all the ways that counted, protective as always, watching out and counseling. Yet at the same time he was moving away, giving her a space and a solitude she had never experienced before and found somewhat disconcerting. She was strong enough to be on her own, she knew; she had been so for several years now. It was simply that she hadn't thought that where Garth was concerned she would ever find a need to say good-bye.

Perhaps the loss of the Owl called attention to it more dramatically than would have otherwise been the case. She didn't know. It was hard to think clearly just now, and yet she knew she must. Emotions would only distract and confuse, and in the end they might even kill. Until they were clear of Morrowindl and safely back in the Westland, there could be little time wasted on longings and needs, on what-ifs and what-might-have-beens, or on what once was and could never be again.

She felt her throat tighten and the tears spring to her eyes. Even with Faun sleeping in her lap, Garth a whisper away, her grandmother found again, and her identity known, she felt impossibly alone.

Sometime after midnight, when Triss had given over the watch to Dal, Gavilan came to sit with her. He didn't speak, just wrapped the blanket he had carried over around her and positioned himself at her side. She felt the warmth of his body through the damp and the chill of the swamp night, and it gave her comfort. After a time, she leaned against him, needing to be touched. He took her in his arms then, cradled her to his chest, and held her until morning.

At first light, they resumed their trek through Eden's Murk. Garth led now, the most experienced survivalist among them. It was Wren who suggested that he lead and Ellenroh who quickly approved. No one was Garth's equal as a Tracker, and it would take a Tracker's skill to get them free of the swamp.

But even Garth could not unravel the mystery of Eden's Murk. Vog hung over everything, shutting out the sky, wrapping everything close about so that nothing was visible beyond a distance of fifty feet. The light was gray and weak, diffused by the mist, reflected by the dampness, and scattered so that it seemed to come from everywhere. There was nothing from which to take direction, not even the lichen and moss that grew in the swamp, which seemed clustered like fugitives against the coming of night, as confused and lost as those of the company who sought their aid. Garth set a course and stayed with it, but Wren could tell that the signs he needed were not to be found. They traveled without knowing what direction they were taking, without being able to chart their progress. Garth kept his thoughts to himself, but Wren could read the truth in his eyes.

Travel was steady, but slow, in part because the swamp was all but impassable and in part because Ellenroh Elessedil was ill. The queen had caught a fever during the night, and it had spread through her with such rapidity that she had gone from headaches and dizziness to chills and coughing in a matter of hours. By midday, when the company stopped for a quick meal, her strength was failing badly. She could still walk, but not without help. Triss and Dal shared the task of supporting her, arms wrapped securely about her waist to hold her up as they traveled. Eowen and Wren both checked her for injuries, thinking that perhaps she had been scratched by the spikes of the Darter and poisoned. But they found nothing. There was no ready explanation for the queen's sickness, and while they administered to her as best they could, neither had a clue as to what remedy might help.

"I feel foolish," she confided to Wren at one point, her wan features bathed in a sheen of sweat. They sat together on a log, eating a little of the cheese and bread that was their meal, wrapped in their great cloaks. "I was fine when I went to sleep, then woke sometime during the night feeling . . . odd." She laughed dryly. "I do not know any other way to describe it. I just didn't feel right."

"You will be better again after another night's sleep," Wren assured her. "We are all worn down."

But Ellenroh was beyond simple weariness, and her condition worsened as the day wore on. By nightfall, she had fallen so often that the Elven Hunters were simply carrying her. The company had spent the afternoon wallowing about in a chilly bottomland, a pocket of cold that had strayed somehow into the broad stretch of the swamp's volcanic heat and become trapped there, sending down roots into the mire, turning water and air to ice. Ellenroh, already on the verge of exhaustion, was weakened further. What little strength remained to her seemed to seep quickly away. When they stopped finally for the night, she was unconscious.

Wren watched Eowen bathe her crumpled face as Gavilan and the Elven Hunters set camp. Garth was at her elbow, his dark face impassive but his eyes clouded with doubt. When she met his gaze squarely, he gave a barely perceptible shake of his head. His fingers gestured. *I cannot read the signs. I cannot even find them.*

The admission was a bitter one. Garth was a proud man and he did not accept defeat easily. She looked into his eyes and touched him briefly in response. *You will find a way,* she signed.

They ate again, mostly because it was necessary, huddled together on a small patch of damp earth that was dryer than anything about it. Ellenroh slept, wrapped in two blankets, shaking with cold and fever, mumbling from time to time, and tossing within her dreams. Wren marveled at her grandmother's strength of will. Not once while she had struggled with her illness had she relaxed her hold on the Ruhk Staff. She clutched it to her still, as if she might with her own body protect the city and people the Loden's magic enclosed. Gavilan had offered more than once to relieve her of the task of carrying the staff, but she had steadfastly refused to give it up. It was a burden she had resolved to shoulder, and she would not be persuaded to lay it down. Wren thought of what it must have cost her grandmother to become so strong—the loss of her parents, her husband, her daughter, her friends—almost everyone close to her. Her whole life had been turned about with the coming of the demons and the walling away of the city of Arborlon. All that she remembered as a child of Morrowindl was gone. Nothing remained of the promise she must have once felt for the future save the possibility that the Elves and their city might, through her resolve and trust, be reborn into a better world.

A world of Federation oppression and Shadowen fear, a world in which, like Morrowindl, use of magic had somehow gone awry.

Wren's smile was slow, bitter, and ironic.

She was struck suddenly by the similarities between the two, the island and the mainland, Morrowindl and the Four Lands—different, yet afflicted with the same sort of madness. Both worlds were plagued with creatures that fed on destruction; both were beset with a sickness that turned the earth and the things that lived upon it foul. What was Morrowindl if not the Four Lands in an advanced state of decay? She wondered suddenly if the two were somehow connected, if the demons and the Shadowen might have some common origin. She wondered again at the secrets that the Elves were keeping from her of what had happened on Morrowindl years ago.

And again she asked herself, *What am I doing here? Why did Allanon send me to bring the Elves back into the Four Lands? What is it that they can do that will make a difference, and how will any of us ever discover what that something is?*

She finished eating and sat for a time with her grandmother, studying the other's face in the fading light, trying to find in the ravaged features some new trace of her mother, of the vision she had claimed from that now long-ago, distant dream when her mother had pleaded, *Remember me. Remember me.* Such a fragile thing, her memory, and it was all that she had of either parent, all that remained of her childhood. As she sat there with her grandmother's head cradled in her lap, she contemplated asking Garth to tell her something more of what had been, though she no longer had any real expectation that there was anything else to be told, knowing only that she was empty and alone and in need of something to cling to. But Garth stood watch, too far away to summon without disturbing the others and too distanced from her to be of any real comfort, and she turned instead to the familiar touch of the Elfstones within their leather pouch, running the tips of her fingers over their hard, smooth surfaces, rolling the Stones idly beneath the fabric of her tunic. They were her mother's legacy to her and her grandmother's trust, and despite her misgivings as to their purpose in her life she could not give them up. Not here, not now, not until she was free of the nightmare into which she had so willingly journeyed.

I chose this, she whispered to herself, the words bitter and harsh. *I came because I wanted to.*

To learn the truth, to discover who and what she was, to bring past and future together once and for all.

And what do I know of any of that? What do I understand?

Eowen came to sit next to her, and she realized how tired she had grown. She gave her grandmother over to the red-haired seer and crept silently away to her own bed. Wrapped in her blankets, she lay staring out into the impenetrable night, the swamp a maze that would swallow them all and care nothing for what it had done, the world a blanket of indifference and deceit, of dangers as numerous as the shadows gathered about, and of sudden death and the taunting ghosts of what might have been. She found herself thinking of the years she had trained with Garth, of what he had taught her, of what she had learned. She would need all of it if she were to survive, she knew. She would need everything she could summon of strength, experience, training and resolve, and she would need more than a little luck.

And one thing more.

Her fingers brushed against the Elfstones once more and fell away as if burned. Their power was hers to summon and command whenever she chose. Twice now she had called upon them to save her. Both times she had done so either out of ignorance or desperation. But if she used them again, she sensed, if she employed them a third time now that she knew the magic was there and understood what wielding it meant, she risked giving up everything she was and becoming something else entirely. Nothing would ever be the same for her again, she cautioned herself. Nothing.

Yet, as she considered the failure of strength, experience, training, and resolve to come to her aid, as she lamented the apparent absence of any luck, it seemed that the power of the Stones was all that was left to her, the only resource that remained.

She turned her head into the blankets and fell asleep in a spider's web of doubt.

W ren dreamed, and her dreams were of Ohmsfords come and gone, a kaleidoscopic, fragmented rush of images that exploded out of memory. They careened into her like an avalanche and swept her away, tossed and tumbled in a slide that would not end. A spectator with no voice, she watched the history of her ancestors take shape in bits and flashes of time, saw events unfold that she had never seen but only heard described, the legends of the past carried forward in the words of the stories Par and Coll Ohmsford told.

Then she was awake, sitting bolt upright, startled from her sleep with a suddenness that was frightening. Faun, curled at her throat, skittered hurriedly away. She stared into blackness, listening to the sound of her heartbeat in her throat, to the rush of her breathing. All around her, the others of the little company slept, save whoever among them kept guard, a dim, faceless shape at the edge of their camp.

What was it? she thought wildly. *What was it that I saw?*

For something in her dreams had brought her awake, something so unnerving, so unexpected, that sleep was no longer possible.

What?

The memory, when it came, was shocking and abrupt. Her hand flew at once to the small leather bag tucked within her tunic.

The Elfstones!

In her dreams of Ohmsford ancestors, she had caught a singular glimpse of Shea and Flick, one brief image out of many, one story out of all those told about the search for the Sword of Shannara. In that image, the brothers were lost with Menion Leah in the lowlands of Clete at the start of their journey toward Culhaven. No amount of skill or woodlore seemed able to help them, and they might have died there if Shea, in desperation, had not discovered that he possessed the ability to invoke the power of the Elfstones given him by the Druid Allanon—the same Elfstones she carried now. In that image, dredged up by her dreams out of a storehouse of tales only barely remembered, she uncovered a truth she had forgotten—that the magic could do more than protect, it could also seek. It could show the holder a way out of the darkest maze; it could help the lost be found again.

She bit her lip hard against the sharp intake of breath that caught in her throat. She had known once, of course—all of them had, all of the Ohmsford children. Par had sung the story to her when she was little. But it had been so long ago.

The Elfstones.

She sat frozen within the covering of her blankets, stunned by her revelation. She had possessed the power all along to get them free of Eden's Murk. The Elfstones, if she chose to invoke the magic, would show the way clear. Had she truly forgotten? she wondered in disbelief. Or had she simply blocked the truth away, determined that she would not be made to rely on the magic, that she would not become subverted by its power?

And what would she do now?

For a moment she did nothing, so paralyzed with the fears and doubts that using the Elfstones raised that she could only sit there, clutching her blankets to her like a shield, voicing within her mind the choices with which she had suddenly been presented in an effort to make sense of them.

Then abruptly she was on her feet, the blankets and the fears and doubts cast aside as she made her way on cat's feet to where her grandmother lay sleeping. Ellenroh Elessedil's breathing was shallow and quick, and her hands and face were cold. Her hair curled damply about her face, and her skin was tight against her bones. She lay supine within blankets that swaddled her like a burial shroud.

She's dying, Wren realized in dismay.

The choices fell away instantly, and she knew what she must do. She crept to where Garth slept, hesitated, then moved on past Triss to where Gavilan lay.

. She touched his shoulder lightly and his eyes flickered open. "Wake up," she whispered to him, trying to keep her voice from shaking. *Tell him first,* she was thinking, remembering his kindness of the previous night. *He will support you.* "Gavilan, wake up. We're getting out of here. Now."

"Wren, wait, what are you . . . ?" he began futilely for she was already hastening to rouse the others, anxious that there be no delays, so worried and distracted that she missed the fear that sprang demonlike into his eyes. "Wren!" he shouted, scrambling up, and everyone came awake instantly.

She stiffened, watching the others rise up guardedly—Triss and Eowen, Dal come back from keeping watch at the campsite's edge, and Garth, hulking against the shadows. The queen did not stir.

"What do you think you are doing?" Gavilan demanded heatedly. She felt his words like a slap. There was anger and accusation in them. "What do you mean we're getting out? Who gave you the right to decide what we do?"

The company closed about the two as they came face to face. Gavilan was flushed and his eyes were bright with suspicion, but Wren stood her ground, her look so determined that the other thought better of whatever it was he was about to say next.

"Look at her, Gavilan," Wren pleaded, seizing his arm, turning him towards Ellenroh. Why couldn't he understand? Why was he making this so difficult? "If we stay here any longer, we will lose her. We haven't a choice anymore. If we did, I would be the first to take advantage of it, I promise you."

There was a startled silence. Eowen turned to the queen, kneeling anxiously beside her. "Wren is right," she whispered. "The queen is very sick."

Wren kept her eyes fixed on Gavilan, trying to read his face, to make him understand. "We have to get her out of here."

Triss pushed forward hurriedly. "Do you know a way?" he asked, his lean features lined with worry.

"I do," Wren answered. She glanced quickly at the Captain of the Home Guard, then back again at Gavilan. "I don't have time to argue about this. I don't have time to explain. You have to trust me. You have to."

Gavilan remained stubbornly unconvinced. "You ask too much. What if you're wrong? If we move her and she dies . . ."

But Triss was already gathering up their gear, motioning Dal to help. "The choice has been made for us," he declared quietly. "The queen has no chance if we don't carry her from this swamp. Do what you can, Wren."

They collected what remained of their supplies and equipment, and built a hasty litter from blankets and poles on which they placed the queen. When they were finished, they turned expectantly to Wren. She faced them as if she were condemned, thinking that she had no choice in this matter, that she must forget her fears and doubts, her resolutions, the promises she had made herself regarding use of the magic and the Elfstones, and do what she could to save her grandmother's life.

She reached down into her tunic and pulled free the leather bag. A quick loosening of the drawstrings, and the Elfstones tumbled into her hand with a harsh, blue glitter.

Feeling small and vulnerable, she walked to the edge of the campsite and stood staring out for a moment into the shadows and mist. Faun tried to scramble up her leg, but she reached down gently and shooed the Tree Squeak away. Vog swirled everywhere, a vile stench of sulfur and ash clinging to its skirts. A mix of haze and steam rose off the swamp's fetid waters. She was at the edge of her life, she sensed, brought there by circumstance and fate, and whatever happened next, she would never be the same. She longed for what once had been, for what might have been, for an escape she could not hope to find.

Frightened that she might change her mind if she considered the matter longer, she held forth the Elfstones and willed them to life.

Nothing happened.

Oh, Shades!

She tried again, concentrating, letting herself form the words carefully in her mind, thinking each one in order, picturing the power that lay within stirring, rising up. She had the Elven blood, she thought desperately. She had summoned the power before . . .

And then abruptly the blue fire flared, exploding out of the Stones as if a stopper had been pulled. It coalesced about her hand, brilliant and stunning, brightening the swamp as if daylight had at last broken through into the mire. The members of the company reeled away, crouching guardedly, shielding their eyes. Wren stood erect, feeling the power of the Stones flow through her, searching, studying, and deciding if it belonged. A pleasant, seductive warmth enveloped her. Then the light shot away to her right, scything through the mist and haze and the dying trees and scrub and vines, shooting across the empty waters hundreds of yards, farther than the eye should have been able to see, to fix upon a rock wall that lifted away into the night.

Blackledge!

As quickly as it had come, the light was gone again, the power of the Elfstones dying, returned from whence it had come. Wren closed her fingers about the Stones, drained and exhilarated both at once, swept clean somehow by the magic, invigorated but left weak. Shaking in spite of her resolve, she slipped the talismans back into their pouch. The others straightened uncertainly, eyes shifting to find her own.

"There," she said quietly, pointing in the direction that the light had taken.

For an instant, no one spoke. Wren's mind was awash with what she had done, the magic's rush still fresh within her body, warring now with the guilt she felt for betraying her vow. But she had not had a choice, she reminded herself quickly; she had only done what was needed. She could not let her grandmother die. It was this one time only; it need not happen again. This once, because it was her grandmother's life and her grandmother was all she had left . . .

The words dissipated with Eowen's soft voice. "Hurry, Wren," she urged, "while there is still time."

They set off at once, Wren leading until Garth caught up to her and she motioned him ahead, content to let someone else take charge. Faun returned from the darkness, and she scooped the little creature up and placed it on her shoulder. Dal and Triss bore the litter with the queen, and she dropped back to walk beside it. She reached down and took her grandmother's hand in her own, held it for a moment, then squeezed it gently. There was no response. She laid the hand carefully back in place and walked ahead again. Eowen passed her, the white face looking lost and frightened in the shadows, the red hair flaring against the night. Eowen knew how sick Ellenroh was; had she foreseen what would happen to the queen in her visions? Wren shook her head, refusing to consider the possibility. She walked alone for a time until Gavilan slipped up beside her.

"I'm sorry, Wren," he said softly, the words coming with difficulty. "I should have known you would not act without reason. I should have had more trust in your judgment." He waited for her response, and when it did not come, said, "It is this swamp that clouds my thinking. I can't seem to focus as I should . . ." He trailed off.

She sighed soundlessly. "It's all right. No one can think clearly in this place." She was anxious to make excuses for him. "This island seems to breed madness. I caught a fever on the way in and for a time I was incoherent. Perhaps a touch of that fever has captured you as well."

He nodded distractedly, as if he hadn't heard. "At least you see the truth now. Magic has made Morrowindl and its demons, and magic is what will save us from them. Your Elfstones and the Ruhk Staff. You wait. You will understand soon enough."

And he dropped back again, his departure so abrupt that Wren was once again unable to ask the questions that his comments called to mind—questions of how the demons had been made, what it was the magic had done, and how things had come to such a state. She half turned to follow him, then decided to let him go. She was too tired for questions now, too worn to hear the answers even if he would give them—which he probably would not. Biting back her frustration, she forced herself to continue on.

It took them all night to get free of Eden's Murk. Twice more Wren was forced to call upon the power of the Elfstones. Torn each time by conflicting urges both to shun its flow and welcome it, she felt the magic boil through her like an elixir. The blue light seared the blackness and cut away the haze, showing them the path to Blackledge, and by dawn they had climbed free of the mire and stood at last upon solid ground once more. Before them, Blackledge lifted away into the haze, a towering mass of craggy stone jutting skyward out of the jungle. They chose a clearing at the base of the rocks and set the litter with Ellenroh carefully at its center. Eowen bathed the queen's face and hands and gave her water to drink.

Ellenroh stirred and her eyes flickered open. She studied the faces about her, glanced down to the Ruhk Staff still clutched between her fingers, and said, "Help me to sit up."

Eowen propped her forward gently and gave her the cup. Ellenroh drank it slowly, pausing frequently to breathe. Her chest rattled, and her face was flushed with fever.

"Wren," she said softly, "you have used the Elfstones."

Wren knelt beside her, wondering, and the others crowded close as well. "How did you know?"

Ellenroh Elessedil smiled. "It is in your eyes. The magic always leaves its mark. I should know."

"I would have used them sooner, Grandmother, but I forgot what it was that they could do. I'm sorry."

"Child, there is no need to apologize." The blue eyes were kind and warm. "I have loved you so much, Wren—even before you came to me, ever since I knew from Eowen that you had been born."

"You need to sleep, Ellenroh," the seer whispered.

The queen closed her eyes momentarily and shook her head. "No, Eowen. I need to speak with you. All of you."

Her eyes opened, worn and distant. "I am dying," she whispered. "No, say nothing. Hear me out." She fixed them with her gaze. "I am sorry, Wren, that I cannot be with you longer. I wish that I could. We have had too short a time together. Eowen, this is hardest for you. You have been my friend all of my life, and I would stay to keep you well if I could. I know what my dying means. Gavilan, Triss, Dal—you did for me what you could. But my time is here. The fever is stronger than I am, and while I have tried to break free of it, I find I cannot. Aurin Striate waits for me, and I go to join him."

Wren was shaking her head deliberately, angrily. "No, Grandmother, don't say this, don't make it so!"

The soft hand found her own and gripped it. "We cannot hide from the truth, Wren. You, of all people, should know this. I am weakened to the bone. The fever has cut me apart inside, and there is almost nothing left holding me together. Even magic would not save me now, I'm afraid—and none of us possesses magic that would help in any case. Be strong, Wren. Remember what we share of flesh and blood. Remember how much alike we are—how much like Alleyne."

"Grandmother!" Wren was crying.

"A medicine," Gavilan whispered urgently. "There must be some medicine we can give you. Tell us!"

"Nothing." The queen's eyes seemed to drift from face to face and away again, seeking something that wasn't there. She coughed and stiffened momentarily. "Am I still your queen?" she asked.

They murmured yes, all of them, an uncertain reply. "Then I have one last command to give you. If you love me, if you care for the future of the Elven people, you will not question it. Say that you will obey."

They did, but furtive looks passed from one to the other, questioning what they were about to hear.

"Wren." Ellenroh waited until her granddaughter had moved to where she could see her clearly. "This is yours now. Take it."

She held out the Ruhk Staff and the Loden. Wren stared at her in disbelief, unable to move. "Take it!" the queen said, and this time Wren did as she was bidden. "Now, listen to me. I entrust the magic to your care, child. Take the Staff and its Stone from Morrowindl and carry them back into the Westland. Restore the Elves and their city. Give our people back their life. Do what you must to keep your promise to the Druid's shade, but remember as well your promise to me. See that the Elves are made whole. Give them a chance to begin again."

Wren could not speak, stunned by what was happening, struggling to accept what she was hearing. She felt the weight of the Ruhk Staff settle in her hands, the smoothness of its haft, cool and polished. *No,* she thought. *No, I don't want this!*

"Gavilan. Triss. Dal." The queen whispered their names, her voice breaking. "See that she is protected. Help her to succeed in what she has been given to do. Eowen, use your sight to ward her against the demons. Garth . . ."

She was about to speak to the big man, but trailed off suddenly, as if she had come upon something she could not face. Wren glanced back at her friend in confusion, but the dark face was chiseled in stone.

"Grandmother, I should not be the one to carry this." Wren started to object, but the other's hand gripped her sharply in reproof.

"You are the one, Wren. You have always been the one. Alleyne was my daughter and would have been queen after me, but circumstances forced us apart and took her from me. She left you to act in her place. Never forget who you are, child. You are an Elessedil. It was what you were born and what you were raised, whether you accept it or not. When I am dead, you shall be Queen of the Elves."

Wren was horrified. *This can't be happening,* she kept telling herself, over and over. *I am not what you think! I am a Rover girl and nothing more! This isn't right!*

But Ellenroh was speaking again, drawing her attention back once more. "Give yourself time, Wren. It will all come about as it should. For now, you need only concern yourself with keeping the Staff and its Stone safe. You need only find your way clear of this island before the end. The rest will take care of itself."

"No, Grandmother," Wren cried out urgently. "I will keep the Staff for you until you are well again. Just until then and not one moment more. You will not die. Grandmother, you can't!"

The queen took a long, slow breath. "Let me rest now, please. Lay me back, Eowen."

The seer did as she was asked, her green eyes frightened and lonely as they followed the queen's face down. For a moment they all remained motionless, staring silently at Ellenroh. Then Triss and Dal moved away to settle their gear and set watch, whispering as they went. Gavilan walked off muttering to himself, and Garth slipped from view as well. Wren was left staring at the Ruhk Staff, gripped now in her own hands.

"I don't think that I should . . ." she started to say and couldn't finish. Her eyes lifted to find Eowen's, but the red-haired seer turned away. Alone now with her grandmother, she reached out to touch the other's hand, feeling the heat of the fever burning through her. Her grandmother slept, unresponsive. *How could she be dying? How could such a thing be so? It was impossible!* She felt the tears come again, thinking of how long it had taken to find her grandmother, the last of her family, how much she had gone through and how little time she had been given.

Don't die, she prayed silently. *Please.*

She felt a scratching against her legs and looked down to discover Faun, wide-eyed and skittish, peering up. She released Ellenroh's hand long enough to lift the little creature into her arms, ruffle its fur, and let it snuggle into her shoulder. The Ruhk Staff lay balanced on her lap like a line drawn in the gray light between herself and the sickened queen.

"Not me," she said softly to her grandmother. "It shouldn't be me."

She rose then, carrying both the Tree Squeak and the Staff up with her, and turned to find Garth. The big Rover was resting against a section of the cliff wall a dozen paces off. He straightened as she came up to him. The hard look she gave him made him blink.

"Tell me the truth now," she whispered, signing curtly. "What is there between you and my grandmother?"

His gaze was impassive. *Nothing.*

"But the way she looked at you, Garth—she wanted to say something and was afraid!"

You were a child given into my care by her daughter. She wanted to be certain I did not forget. That was what she thought to tell me. But she saw that it was not necessary.

Wren faced him unmoving a moment longer. Perhaps, she thought darkly. But there are secrets here . . .

Trust no one, the Addershag had warned.

But she couldn't do that. She couldn't be like that.

She broke off the confrontation and moved away, still stunned at the whirlwind of events that had surrounded her, at the way in which she was being rushed along without having any control over what was happening. She glanced again at her grandmother, feeling torn at the prospect of losing her and at the same time angry at the responsibilities she had been asked to assume. Wren Ohmsford, Queen of the Elves? It was laughable. She didn't care who she was or what her family background might be, her whole life was defined by how she perceived herself, and she perceived herself as a Rover. She couldn't just wish all that away, forget all the years she had spent growing up, accept what had happened in these last few weeks as if it were a mandate she could not refuse. How could her grandmother say that she had been raised as an Elessedil? Why would the Elves want her as their queen in any case? She wasn't really one of them, her birthright notwithstanding.

Almost without thinking about it, she stalked over to where Gavilan sat back against a moss-grown stump and squatted down beside him.

"What am I to do about this?" she demanded almost angrily, thrusting the Ruhk Staff in his face.

He shrugged, his eyes distant and empty. "What you were asked to do, I expect."

"But this isn't mine! It doesn't belong to me! It shouldn't have been given to me in the first place!"

His voice was bitter. "I happen to agree. But what you and I want doesn't count for much, does it?"

"That isn't true. Ellenroh would never have done this if she weren't so sick. When she's better . . ." She stopped as he looked pointedly away. "When she's better," she continued, snapping off each word like a broken stick, "she will realize this is all a mistake."

His gaze was flat. "She's not going to get better."

"Don't say that, Gavilan. Don't."

"Would you rather I lied?"

Wren stared at him, unable to speak.

Gavilan's face was hard. "All right, then. I realize that you didn't plan for any of this to happen, that the Elves aren't your people, that none of this really has anything to do with you, and that all you wanted to do was to find Ellenroh and deliver your message. You don't want to be Queen of the Elves? Fair enough. You don't have to. Give the Staff to me."

There was a long, empty silence as they stared at each other.

"The Elessedil blood flows through my body as well," he pointed out heatedly. "These are my people, and Arborlon is my city. I can do what is needed. I have a better grasp of things than you. And I am not afraid to use the magic."

Suddenly Wren understood what was happening. Gavilan had expected to be given the Ruhk Staff; he had expected Ellenroh to name him as her successor. If Wren had not appeared, it probably would have happened that way. In fact, Wren's coming to Arborlon had changed everything for Gavilan. She felt a momentary pang of dismay, but it gave way almost instantly to wariness. She remembered how Gavilan and Ellenroh had quarreled about the Loden. Gavilan favored use of the magic to change things back to how they had once been, to set things right again. Ellenroh believed it was time to give the magic up, to return to the Westland and live as the Elves had once lived. That conflict surely must have influenced Ellenroh's decision to give the Staff to Wren.

Gavilan seemed to sense her uncertainty. "Think about it, Wren. If the queen dies, her burden need not be yours. If you had not returned, it never would have been." He folded his arms defensively. "In any case, it is up to you. If you wish it, I will help. I told you that when we first met, and the offer still stands. Whatever I can do."

She didn't know what to say. "Thank you, Gavilan," she managed.

She moved away from him then, feeling decidedly uneasy about what he had suggested. As much as she wanted to be free of the responsibility of the Staff, she was not at all sure she should give it over to him. The magic was a trust; it should not be relinquished too quickly, not when the consequences of its use were so enormous. Ellenroh could have given the Staff to Gavilan, but had chosen not to. Wren was not prepared to question the queen's judgment without thinking the matter through.

But she cared for Gavilan; she relied on his friendship and support. That complicated things. She understood his disappointment, and she knew that he was right when he said that the Elves were his people and Arborlon his city and that she was an outsider. She believed that Gavilan wanted what was best as much as she did.

A harsh, desperate determination took root inside her. *None of this matters, because Grandmother will recover, because she must recover, she will not die, she will not!* The words were a litany in her mind, repeating over and over. Her breathing was ragged and angry, and her hands were shaking.

She shook her head and fought back her tears.

Finally she sat down again next to her grandmother. Numb with grief, she stared down at the ravaged face. *Please, get well. You must get well.*

Weariness stole over her like a thief and left her drained.

They remained camped at the cliff wall all that day, letting Ellenroh sleep, hoping that her strength would return. While Wren and Eowen took turns caring for the queen, the men kept watch. Time slipped away, and Wren watched it escape with a quickness that was frightening. They had been gone from Arborlon for three days now, but it seemed like weeks. All about them, the world of Morrowindl was gray and hazy, a bleak landscape of shadows and half-light. Beneath, the earth rumbled with Killeshan's discontent. How much time remained to them? How much before the volcano exploded and the island broke apart? How much before the demons found them? How much before Tiger Ty and Spirit decided that there was no point in searching any longer, that they were irretrievably lost?

She bathed Ellenroh's face and whispered and sang to her, trying to dispel the fever, searching for some small sign that her grandmother was mending and the sickness would pass. She stayed clear of the others, save for Eowen, and even when she was close to the seer she spoke little. Her mind was restless, however, and filled with misgivings to which she could not give voice. The Ruhk Staff was a constant reminder of how much was at stake. Thoughts of the Elves plagued her; she could see their faces, hear their voices, and imagine what they must be thinking, more trapped than she was, more powerless. It terrified her to be so inextricably tied to them. She could not shake the feeling that she was all they had, that they must rely on her alone and no one else in the company mattered. Their lives were her charge, and while she might wish it otherwise, the fact of it could not be easily changed.

Night fell, and Ellenroh's condition grew worse.

Wren sat alone at one point and cried without being able to stop, hollow with losses that suddenly seemed to press about her at every turn. Once she would have told herself that none of it mattered—that the absence of parents and family, of a history, of a life beyond the one she lived was of no consequence. Coming to Morrowindl and finding Arborlon and the Elves had changed that forever. What had once seemed of so little importance had inexplicably become everything. Even if she survived, she would never be the same. The realization of what had been done to her left her stunned. She had never felt more alone.

She slept then for a time, too exhausted to stay awake longer, her emotions gone distant and numb, and woke again with Garth's hand on her shoulder. She rose instantly, frightened by what he might have come to tell her, but he quickly shook his head. Saying nothing, he simply pointed.

From no more than six feet away, a bulky, spiked form stood staring at her with eyes that gleamed like a cat's. Faun was dancing about in front of it, chittering wildly.

Wren stared. "Stresa?" she whispered in disbelief. She scrambled up hurriedly, throwing her blanket aside, her voice shaking. "Stresa, is that really you?"

"Come back from the dead, rwwlll Wren of the Elves," the other growled softly.

Wren would have thrown her arms about the Splinterscat if she could have managed to find a way, but settled instead for a quick gasp of relief and laughter. "You're alive! I can't believe it!" She clapped her hands and hugged herself. "Oh, I am so glad to see you! I was certain you were gone! What happened to you? How did you escape?"

The Splinterscat moved forward several paces and seated himself, ignoring Faun, who continued to dart about excitedly. "The—ssppht—serpent barely missed me when it destroyed the raft. I was dragged beneath the surface and towed by the current all the way back—hsstttt—across the Rowen. Phhhffft. It took me several hours to find another crossing. By then, you had gone into Eden's Murk."

Faun skittered too close, and the spines rose threateningly. "Foolish Squeak. Hsssttt!"

"How did you find us?" Wren pressed. Garth was seated next to her now, and she signed her words as she spoke.

"Ha! Ssspptt! Not easily, I can tell you. I tracked you, of course—hsssstt—but you have wandered in every direction since you entered. Lost your way, I gather. I wonder that you managed to find the cliffs at all."

She took a deep breath. "I used the magic."

The Splinterscat hissed softly.

"I had to. The queen is very sick."

"Sssttt. And so the Ruhk Staff is yours now?"

She shook her head hurriedly. "Just until Ellenroh is better. Just until then."

Stresa said nothing, yellow eyes agleam.

"I'm glad that you're back," she repeated.

He yawned disinterestedly. "Phhfft. Enough talk for tonight. Time to get some rrwwoll rest."

He made a leisurely turn and ambled off to find a place to sleep, looking for all the world as if nothing unusual had happened, as if tonight were just like any other night. Wren stared after him for a moment, then exchanged a long look with Garth. The big Rover shook his head and moved away.

Wren pulled the blanket back around her shoulders and cradled Faun in her arms. After a moment, she realized that she was smiling.

18

Ellenroh Elessedil died at dawn. Wren was with her when she woke for the last time. The darkness was just beginning to lighten, a pale violet tinge within the mist, and the queen's eyes opened. She stared up at Wren, her gaze calm and steady, seeing something beyond her granddaughter's anxious face. Wren took her hand at once, holding it with fierce determination, and for just an instant there appeared the faintest of smiles. Then she breathed once, closed her eyes, and was gone.

Wren found it odd when she could not cry. It seemed as if she had no tears left, as if they had been used up in being afraid that the impossible might happen, and now that it had she had nothing left to give. Drained of emotion, she was yet left feeling curiously unprotected in her sense of loss, and because she had no one she wanted to turn to and nowhere else to flee she took refuge within the armor of responsibility her grandmother had given her for the fate of the Elves.

It was well that she did. It appeared no one else knew what to do. Eowen was inconsolable, a crumpled, frail figure as she huddled next to the woman who had been her closest friend. Red hair fallen down about her face and shoulders, body shaking, she could not manage even to speak. Triss and Dal stood by helplessly, stunned. Even Gavilan could not seem to summon the strength to take charge as he might have before, his handsome face stricken as he stared down at the queen's body. Too much had happened to destroy their confidence in themselves, to shatter any belief that they could carry out their charge to save the Elven people. Aurin Striate and the queen were both gone—the two they could least afford to lose. Trapped within the bottomland of Eden's Murk on the wrong side of Blackledge, they were consumed with a growing premonition of disaster that was in danger of becoming self-fulfilling.

But Wren found within herself that morning a strength she had not believed she possessed. Something of who and what she had once been, of the Rover girl she had been raised, of the Elessedil and Shannara blood to which she had been born, caught fire within her and willed that she should not despair.

She rose from the queen and stood facing them, the Ruhk Staff gripped in both hands, placed in front of her like a standard, a reminder of what bound them.

"She's gone," Wren said quietly, drawing their eyes, meeting them with her own. "We must leave her now. We must go on because that is what we have sworn we would do and that is what she would want. We have been asked to do something that grows increasingly difficult, something we all wish we had not been asked to do, but there is no point in questioning our commitment now. We are pledged to it. I don't presume to think I can be the woman my grandmother was, but I shall try my best. This Staff belongs in another world, and we are going to do everything we can to carry it there."

She stepped away from the queen. "I only knew my grandmother a short time, but I loved her the way I would have loved my mother had I been given the chance to know her. She was all I had of family. She was the best she could be for all of us. She deserves to live on through us. I do not intend to fail her. Will you help me?"

"Lady, you need not ask that," Triss answered at once. "She has given the Ruhk Staff to you, and while you live the Home Guard are sworn to protect and obey you."

Wren nodded. "Thank you, Triss. And you, Gavilan?"

The blue eyes lowered. "You command, Wren."

She glanced at Eowen, who simply nodded, still lost within her grief.

"Carry the queen back into the Eden's Murk," Wren directed Triss and Dal. "Find a sinkhole and give her back to the island so that she can rest." The words fought their way clear, harsh and biting. "Take her."

They bore the Queen of the Elves into the swamp, found a stretch of mire a hundred feet in, and eased her down. She disappeared swiftly, gone forever.

In silence, they retraced their steps. Eowen was crying softly, leaning on Wren's arm for support. The men were voiceless wraiths turned silver and gray by the shadows and mist.

When they reached the base of Blackledge, Wren faced them once again. "This is what I think. We have lost a third of our number and have barely gotten clear of Killeshan's slopes. Time slips away. If we don't move quickly, we won't get off the island, any of us. Garth and I know something of wilderness survival, but we are almost as lost as the rest of you here on Morrowindl. There is only one of us remaining who stands a chance of finding the way."

She turned to look at Stresa. The Splinterscat blinked.

"You brought us safely in," she said quietly. "Can you take us out again?"

Stresa stared at her for a long moment, his gaze curious. "Hrrwlll, Wren of the Elves, bearer of the Ruhk Staff, I will take a chance with you, though I have no particular reason to help the Elves. But you have promised me passage to the larger world, and I hold you to your promise. Yes, I will guide you."

"Do you know the way, Scat," Gavilan asked warily, "or do you simply toy with us?"

Wren gave him a sharp glance, but Stresa simply said, "Stttsst. Come along and find out, why don't you?" Then he turned to Wren. "This is not country through which I have traveled often. Here the Blackledge is impassable. Hssstt. We will need to—rrwwlll—travel south for a distance to find a pass through which to climb. Come."

They gathered what remained of their gear, shouldered it determinedly, and set out. They walked through the morning gloom, into the heat and the vog, following the line of the cliffs along the boundary of Eden's Murk. At noon they stopped to rest and eat, a gathering of hard-faced, silent men and women, their furtive, uneasy eyes scanning the mire ceaselessly. The earth was silent today, the volcano momentarily at rest. But from within the swamp there was the sound of things at hunt, distant cries and howls, the splashing of water, the grunting of bodies locked in combat. The sounds followed after them as they trudged on, an ominous warning that a net was being gathered in about them.

By midafternoon, they had found the pass that Stresa favored, a steep, winding trail that disappeared into the rocks like a serpent's tongue into its maw. They began their ascent quickly, anxious to put distance between themselves and the sounds trailing after, hopeful that the summit could be reached before nightfall.

It was not. Darkness caught them somewhere in midclimb, and Stresa settled them quickly on a narrow ledge partially in the shelter of an overhang, a perch that would have looked out over a broad expanse of Eden's Murk had it not been for the vog, which covered everything in a seemingly endless shroud of dingy gray.

Dinner was consumed quickly and without interest, a watch was set, and the remainder of the company prepared to settle in for the night. The combination of darkness and mist was so complete that nothing was visible beyond a few feet, giving the unpleasant impression that the entire island had somehow fallen away beneath them, leaving them suspended in air. Sounds rose out of the haze, guttural and menacing, a cacophony that was both disembodied and directionless. They listened to it in silence, feeling it track them, feeling it tighten about.

Wren tried to think of other things, wrapping her blanket close, chilled in spite of the heat given off by the swamp. But her thoughts were disjointed, scattered by a growing sense of detachment from everything that was real. She had been stripped of the certainty of who and what she was and left with only a vague impression of what she might be—and that a thing beyond her understanding and control. Her life had been wrenched from its certain track and settled on an empty plain, there to be blown where it would like a leaf in the wind. She had been given trusts by the shade of Allanon and by her grandmother, and she knew not enough of either to understand how they were to be carried out. She recalled why it was that she had accepted Cogline's challenge to go to the Hadeshorn in the first place, all those weeks ago. By going, she had believed, she might learn something of herself; she might discover the truth. How strange that belief seemed now. Who she was and what she was supposed to do seemed to change as rapidly as day into night. The truth was an elusive bit of cloth that would not be contained, that refused to be revealed. It fluttered away at each approach she made, ragged and worn, a shimmer of color and light. Still, she was determined that she would follow the threads left hanging in its wake, thin remnants of brightness that would one day lead to the tapestry from which they had come unraveled.

Find the Elves and bring them back into the world of Men.

She would try.

Save my people and give them a new chance at life.

Again, she would try.

And in trying, perhaps she would find a way to survive.

She dozed for a time, her back against the cliff wall, legs drawn up to her chest and arms wrapped guardedly about the polished length of the Ruhk Staff. Faun was asleep at her feet in the blanket's folds. Stresa was a featureless ball curled up within the shadows of a rocky niche. She was aware of movement about her as the watch changed; she even considered asking to take a turn, but let the thought pass. She had slept little in two nights and needed to regain her strength. There was time enough to take the watch another night. She rested her cheek against her knees and lost herself in the darkness behind her eyes.

Later that night, she was never sure when, she was roused by the rough scrape of a boot on rock as someone approached. She lifted her head slightly, peering out from the shelter of the blanket. The night was black and thick with vog, the haze creeping down the mountainside and settling onto the ledge like a snake at hunt. A figure appeared out of the gloom, crouched low, movements quick and furtive.

Wren's hand slowly reached for the handle of her knife.

"Wren," the figure said quietly, calling her name.

It was Eowen. Wren lifted her head in recognition and watched the other creep forward and settle down before her. Eowen was wrapped in her hooded cloak, her red hair wild and tossed, her face flushed, and her eyes wide and staring as if she had just witnessed something terrifying. Her mouth tightened as she started to speak, and then she began to cry. Wren reached out to her and pulled her close, surprised at the other's vulnerability, a softening of strength that until the queen's death had never once been in evidence.

Eowen stiffened, brushed at her eyes, and breathed deeply of the night air in an effort to compose herself. "I cannot seem to stop," she whispered. "Every time I think of her, every time I remember, I start to grieve anew."

"She loved you very much," Wren told her, trying to lend some comfort, remembering her own love as she did so.

The seer nodded, lowered her eyes momentarily, and then looked up again. "I have come to tell you the truth about the Elves, Wren."

Wren stayed perfectly still, saying nothing, waiting. She felt a cold, fathomless pit open within.

Eowen glanced back at the misty night, at the nothingness that surrounded them, and sighed. "I had a vision once, long ago now, in which I saw myself with Ellenroh. She was alive and vibrant, all aglow against a pale background that looked like dusk in winter. I was her shadow, attached to her, bound to her. Whatever she did, I did as well—moved as she did, spoke when she spoke, felt her happiness and her pain. We were joined as one. But then she began to fade, to disappear, her color to wash, her lines to blur. She disappeared—yet I remained, a shadow still, alone now, in search of a body to which I might attach myself. Then you appeared—I didn't know you then, but I knew who you were, Alleyne's daughter, Ellenroh's grandchild. You faced me, and I approached. As I did, the air about me went dark and forbidding. A mist fell across my eyes, and I could see only red, a brilliant scarlet haze. I was cold to the bone, and there was no life left within me."

She shook her head slowly. "The vision ended then, but I took its meaning. The queen would die, and when she did I would die as well. You would be there to witness it—perhaps to partake in it."

"Eowen." Wren breathed the seer's name softly, appalled.

The seer turned back quickly and the green eyes clouded. "I am not frightened, Wren. A seer's visions are both gift and curse, but always the rule of her life. I have learned neither to fear nor deny what I am shown, only to accept. I accept now that my time in this world is almost gone, and I would not die without telling you the truth that you are so desperate to know."

She hugged the cloak to her shoulders. "The queen could not do so, you know. She could not bring herself to speak. She wanted to. Perhaps in time she would have. But it was the horror of her life that the magic of the Elves had done so much harm and caused so much hurt. I was loyal to Ellenroh in life, but I am released now by her death—in this at least. You must know, Wren. You must know and judge as you will, for you are indeed your mother's daughter and meant to be Queen of the Elves. The Elessedil blood marks you plainly, and while you question still that such a thing could be so, be certain that it is. I have seen it in my visions. You are the hope of all of the Elves, now and in the future. You have come to save them, if they are fated to be saved. Seeing that you accept the trust of the Ruhk Staff and the Loden, knowing that the Elfstones will protect you, I find that all that remains left undone is the telling of that which has been hidden from you—the secret of the rebirth of the Elven magic and of the poisoning of Morrowindl."

Wren shook her head quickly. "Eowen, I have not yet decided about the trust . . ." she began.

"Decisions are made for us for the most part, Wren Elessedil." Eowen cut her short. "I understand that better than you. I understood it better than the queen, I think. She was a good person, Wren. She did the best she could, and you must not blame her in any way for what I will tell you. You must reflect on what I say; if you do so, you will see that Ellenroh was trapped from the beginning and all of the decisions it might seem she made of her own will were in fact made for her. If she kept the truth secret from you, it was because she loved you too well. She could not bear to think of losing you. You were all she had left."

The pale face reflected like a ghost's in the haze, the voice gone back again to a whisper.

"Yes, Eowen," Wren replied softly. "And she was all I had."

The seer's slender hands reached out to take her own, the skin as cold as ice. Wren shivered in spite of herself. "Then heed what I say, daughter of Alleyne, Elf-kind found. Heed carefully."

Emerald eyes glittered like frosted leaves at sunrise. "When the Elves first came to Morrowindl, the island was innocent and unspoiled. It was a paradise beyond anything they could have imagined, all clean and new and safe. The Elves remembered what they had left behind—a world already beginning to spoil, sickening where the Shadowen had crawled to birth and feed, buckling under the weight of Federation oppression and the advance of armies that knew only to obey and never to question. It was an old story, Wren, and the Elves had endured it for countless generations. They wanted no more of it; they wanted it to be gone.

"So they began to scheme of how they might keep their newfound world and themselves protected. The Federation might one day choose to extend itself even beyond the boundaries of the Four Lands. The Shadowen surely would. Only magic could protect them, they felt, and the magic they relied upon now came not out of Druid lore or new world teachings but out of the rediscovered power of their beginnings. Such magic was vast and wild, still in its infancy for this generation, and they forgot the lessons of the Druids, of the Warlock Lord and his Skull Bearers, and of all those who had fallen victim before. They would not succumb, they must have told themselves. They would be smarter, more careful, and more deft in their use."

She took another deep breath, and her hands released Wren's to brush back the tangle of her hair. "Some among them had . . . experience in making things with the magic. Living creatures, Wren—new species that could serve their needs. They had found a way to extract the essence of nature's creatures and with use of the magic could nurture it so that as it grew it became a variation of the thing on which it had been modeled. They could make dogs from dogs and cats from cats, only bigger, stronger, quicker, smarter. But that was only the beginning. They quickly progressed to combining life forms, creating animals that evidenced the most desirable traits of both. That was how the Splinterscats came to be—and dozens of other species. They were the first experiments of the magic's new use, beasts that could think and speak as well as humans, beasts that could forage and hunt and stand guard against any enemy while the Elves remained safe.

"It was all right in the beginning, it seemed. The creatures flourished and served as they were intended to do, and all was well. But as time passed, some among the wielders began to advance new ideas for use of the magic. They had been successful once, the argument went. Why not again? If animals could be formed of the magic, why not something even more advanced? Why not duplicate themselves? Why not build an army of men that would fight in their place in the event of an attack while they remained safe behind the walls of Arborlon?"

Eowen shook her head slowly, delicate features twisting at some inner horror. "They made the demons then—or the things that would become the demons. They took parts of themselves, flesh and blood to begin with, but then memories and emotions and all the invisible pieces of their spirits, and they gave them life. These new Elves—for they were Elves, then—were made to be soldiers and hunters and guardians of the realm, and they knew nothing else and had no need or desire but to serve. They seemed ideal. Those who made them sent them forth to establish watch on the coasts of the island. They were self-sufficient; there was no need to feel concern for them."

Her voice dropped to a whisper. "For a time, they were almost forgotten, I am told—as if they were of no further consequence."

Again she reached for Wren's hands, clasping them tight. "Then the changes began. Little by little, the new Elves started to alter, their appearance and personality to change. It happened away from the city and out of the sight and mind of the people, and so there was no one to stop it or to warn against it. Some of the first creatures created by the magic, like the Splinterscats, came to the Elves and told what was happening, but they were ignored. They were just animals after all, despite their abilities, and their cautions were dismissed.

"The new Elves, already changing to demons, began to stray from their posts, to disappear into the jungles, to hunt and kill everything they came across. The Splinterscats and the others were the first victims. The Elves of Arborlon were next. Efforts were made to put an end to these monsters, but the efforts were scattered and misdirected, and the Elves still did not accept that the trouble lay not with just a few but with all of their creations. By the time they realized how badly they had misjudged the magic's effect, the situation was out of control.

"By then, Ellenroh was Queen. Her father had infused the Keel with the magic of the Loden to provide a shield behind which the Elves could hide, and in truth they seemed safe enough. But Ellenroh wasn't so sure. Determined to put an end to the demons, she took her Elven Hunters into the jungles to search them out. But the magic had worked too well in its specific intent, and the demons were too strong. Time and again, they threw the Elves back. The war went on for years, a terrible, endless struggle for supremacy of the island that ravaged Morrowindl and made living on her soil a nightmare beyond reason."

The hands tightened, hard and unyielding. "Finally, all other choices stripped from Ellenroh by the magic's intractability and the demons' savagery, she called the last of the Elves into the city. That was ten years ago. It marked the end of any contact with the outside world."

"But why couldn't the same magic that made these creatures be used to eliminate them?" Wren demanded.

"Oh, Wren, it was far too late for that." Eowen rocked as if comforting a child. "The magic was gone!" Her eyes had a distant, ravaged look. "All magic has a source. It is no different with Elven magic. Most of it comes from the earth, a weaving together of the life that resides there. The island was the source of the magic used to create the demons and the others before them—its earth, air, and water, the elements of its life. But magic is precious and not without its limits. Time replenishes what is used, but slowly. What the Elves did not realize was that the demons, as they changed, began to have need of the magic themselves. Created from it, they now discovered they required it in order to survive. They began to systematically siphon it from the earth and the things that lived upon it, killing whatever they fed upon. They devoured it faster than it could regenerate. The island began to change, to wither, to sicken and die. It was as if it could no longer protect itself from the creatures that ravaged it, demon and Elf alike. By the time the Elves recognized the truth, not enough magic remained to make a difference. The demons had grown too numerous to be destroyed. Everything beyond the city was abandoned to them. Morrowindl survived, if barely, but it had been subverted, changed so that it was either wasteland or carnivorous jungle, so that almost everything that lived upon it killed as swiftly and surely as the demons. Nature was no longer in balance. Killeshan came awake and boiled within its cauldron. And finally the island's magic began to dry up altogether, and that compelled the demons to lay siege to Arborlon. The scent of the Keel's magic was irresistible. It drew them as a magnet would iron, and they became determined to feed on it."

Wren paled. "And now they will come for us as well, won't they? We have the Keel's magic, all of the magic of Arborlon and the Elves, stored within the Loden, and they will seek it out."

"Yes, Wren. They must." Eowen's voice was a hiss. "But that is not the worst of what I have to tell you. There is more. Listen to me. It is bad enough that the Elves made the monsters that would destroy them, that they subverted Morrowindl beyond any possible salvation, that perhaps they have destroyed themselves as a people. Ellenroh could scarcely bear to think of it, of the part she played in stealing away the island's magic, or of her own failure to set things right again. But what devastated her was knowing why the Elves had come to Morrowindl in the first place. Yes, it was to escape the Federation and the Shadowen and all that they represented, to isolate themselves from the madness, to begin again in a new world. But, Wren, it was the Elves who ruined the old!"

Wren stared, disbelieving. "The Elves? How could that be? What are you saying, Eowen?"

The hands released her own and clasped together with white-knuckled determination, as if nothing less could persuade the red-haired seer to continue. "After the demons had claimed virtually all of Morrowindl, after it was clear that the island was lost and the Elven people had been made prisoners of their own folly, the queen had ferreted out and brought before her those who still sought to play with the power, foolish men and women who could not seem to learn from their mistakes, who persisted in thinking the magic could be mastered. Among them were those who had created the demons. She had them thrown from the walls of the city. She did so not because of what they had done but because of what they were attempting to do. They were attempting to use the magic in another way, a way that had been employed almost three hundred years earlier in the days following the death of Allanon and the disappearance of the Druids from the Four Lands."

She took a deep breath. "Not all of those who sought to reclaim the old ways went with us to Morrowindl. Not all of those who were Elves came out of the Four Lands. A handful of the magic-wielders remained behind, disowned by their people, cast out by the Elessedil rulers." Her voice lowered until it was almost inaudible. "That handful, Wren, created monsters of another sort."

There was a long, terrible silence as the seer and the Rover girl faced each other in the gloom. The cold in Wren's stomach began to snake into her limbs. "Shades!" she whispered in horror, realizing the truth now, a truth that had been hidden all this time from those summoned to the Hadeshorn by the shade of Allanon. "You're saying that the Elves made the Shadowen!"

"No, Wren." Eowen's voice choked as she struggled to finish. "The Elves didn't *make* the Shadowen. The Elves *are* the Shadowen."

Wren's breath caught in her throat, a knot that threatened to strangle her. She remembered the Shadowen at the Wing Hove, the one that had stalked her for so long, the one that in the end would have killed her if not for the Elfstones. She tried to picture it as an Elf and failed.

"Elves, Wren." Eowen's husky voice drew her attention back again. "My people. Ellenroh's. Your own. Just a few, you understand, but Elves still. There are others now, I expect, but in the beginning it was only Elves. They sought to be something better, I think, something more. But it all went wrong, and they became . . . what they are. Even then, they refused to change, to seek help. Ellenroh knew. All of the Elves knew, once upon a time at least. It was why they left, why they abandoned their homeland and fled. They were terrified of what their brethren had done. They were appalled that the magic had been so misused. For it was an inaccurate and changeable magic at best, and what they created was not always what they desired."

She smiled bitterly. "Do you see now why the queen could not reveal to you the truth of things? Do you understand the burden she carried? She was an Elessedil, and her forefathers had allowed this to happen! She had aided in the misuse of the magic herself, albeit because it was all she could do if she wished to save her people. She couldn't tell you. I can barely stand doing it myself! I wonder even now if I have made a mistake . . ."

"Eowen!" Wren seized the other's hands and would not let go. "You were right to tell me. Grandmother should have done so in the beginning. It is a terrible, awful thing, but . . ."

She trailed off helplessly, and her eyes locked on the seer's. *Trust no one,* the Addershag had warned. Now she understood why. The secrets of three hundred years lay scattered at her feet, and only death's presence had given them away.

Eowen started up, freeing her hands. "I have given you enough of truth this night," she whispered. "I wish it could have been otherwise."

"No, Eowen . . ."

"Be kind, Wren Elessedil. Forgive the queen. And me. And the Elves, if you can. Remember the importance of the trust you have been given. Carry the Loden back into the Four Lands. Let the Elves begin anew. Let them help set matters right again."

She turned, ignoring Wren's hushed plea to stay, and disappeared from view.

Wren sat awake after that until dawn, watching the mist swirl against the void, staring out into the impenetrable night. She listened to the movements of those on watch, to the breathing of those who slept, to the empty whisper of her thoughts as they wrestled with the truth that Eowen had left her.

The Shadowen are Elves.

The words repeated themselves, a whispered warning. She was the only one who knew, the only one who could warn the others. But she had to get off Morrowindl first. She had to survive.

The night seemed to close about her. She had wanted the truth. Now she had it. It was a bitter, wrenching triumph, and the cost of attaining it had yet to be fully measured.

Oh, Grandmother!

Her hands gripped the Ruhk Staff, and frustration, anger, and sadness rushed through her. She had found her birthright, discovered her identity, learned the history of her life, and now she wished that it would all disappear forever. It was vile and tainted and marked with betrayal and madness at every turn. She hated it.

And then, when the darkness of her mood had reached a point where it appeared complete, where it seemed that nothing worse could happen, a thought that was blacker still whispered to her.

The Shadowen are Elves—and you carry the entire Elven nation back into the Four Lands.

Why?

The question hung like an accusation in the silence of her mind.

19

Wren was still struggling with the ambiguity of what her grand-mother had given her to do when the rest of the company awoke at sunrise.

On the one hand, thousands of lives depended on her carrying the Lo-den and the Ruhk Staff safely from the island of Morrowindl back into the Westland. The whole of the Elven nation, all save the Wing Riders who resided on the coastal islands far away and had not migrated with the Land Elves to Morrowindl, had been gathered up by the magic and enclosed, there to remain until Wren—or, she supposed, another of the company, should she die as Ellenroh had—set them free. If she failed to do so, the Elves would perish, the oldest Race of all, the last of the faerie people, an entire history from the time of the world's creation gone.

On the other hand, perhaps it was best.

She shivered every time she repeated Eowen's words: *The Elves* are *the Shadowen*. The Elves, with their magic, and with their insistence on recov-ering their past, had turned themselves into monsters. They had created the demons. They had devastated Morrowindl and initiated the destruction of the Four Lands. Practically every danger that threatened could be traced to them. It might be better, given that truth, if they ceased to exist altogether.

She did not think she was overstating her concerns. Once the Elves were restored to the Westland, there was nothing to prevent them from be-ginning anew with the magic, from trying to recall it yet again so that it could be used in some newly terrible and destructive way. There was noth-ing that said that Ellenroh had disposed of all those who sought to play with its power, that some one or two had not survived. It would be easy enough for those few to begin to experiment once again, to create new forms of monsters, new horrors that Wren did not care to envision. Hadn't the Elves already proved that they were capable of anything?

Like the Druids, she thought sadly, victims of a misguided need to know, of an injudicious self-confidence, of a foolish belief that they could master something which by its very nature was dependably unreliable.

How had they let it all come to this, these people with so many years of experience in using the magic, these faerie folk brought into the new world out of the devastation of the old by lessons they could not have failed to learn? Surely they must have had some small inkling of the dangers they would encounter when they began to make nature over in their own ill-conceived image. Surely they must have realized something was wrong. Yet time's passage had rendered the Elves as human as the other Races, changed them from faerie creatures to mortals, and altered their perceptions and their knowledge. Why shouldn't they be as prone to make mistakes as anyone else—as anyone else had, in fact, from Druids to Men?

The Elves. She was one of them, of course, and worse, an Elessedil. However she might wish it otherwise, she was consumed with guilt for what their misjudgments had wrought and with remorse for what their folly had cost. A land, a nation, countless lives, a world's sanity and peace— they had set in motion the events that would destroy it all. Her people. She might argue that she was a Rover girl, that she shared nothing with the Elves beyond her bloodline and appearance, but the argument seemed hollow and feckless. Responsibility did not begin and end with personal needs—Garth had taught her that much. She was a part of everything about her, and not only survival but the measure of her life was directly related to whether she accepted that truth. She could not back away from the unpleasantnesses of the world; she could not forget its pain. Once upon a time, the Elves had been foremost among Healers, their given purpose to keep the land whole and instill in others the wisdom of doing so. What had happened to that commitment? How had the Elves become so misdirected?

She ate without tasting her food and she spoke little, consumed by her thoughts. Eowen sat across from her, eyes lowered. Garth and the other men moved past them unseeing, focused on the trek before them. Stresa was already gone, scouting ahead to make certain of his path. Faun was a ball of fur in her lap.

What am I to do? she asked herself in despair. *What choice am I to make?*

The climb up the Blackledge resumed, and still she could not settle on an answer. The day was dark and hazy like all the ones before, the sun screened away by the vog, the air thick with heat and ash and the faint stench of sulfur. Swamp sounds rose behind them out of Eden's Murk, a jumbled collection of screams and cries, fragmented and distant for the most part, scattered in the mist. Below, things hunted and foraged and struggled to stay alive for another day. Above, there was only silence, as if nothing more than clouds awaited. The trail was steep and winding, and it cut back upon itself frequently, a labyrinthine maze of ledges, drops, and defiles. Sporadic showers swept across them, quick and furious, the rain dampening the earth and rock to slickness and then fading back into the heat.

Time passed, and Wren's thoughts drifted. She found herself missing things she had never even considered before. She was young still, barely a woman, and she was struck by the possibility that she might never have a husband or children and that she would always be alone. She found herself envisioning faces and voices and small scenes out of an imagined life where these things were present, and without reason and to no particular purpose she mourned their loss. It was the discovery of who and what she was that triggered these feelings, she decided finally. It was the trust she carried, the responsibilities she bore that induced this sense of solitude, of aloneness.

There was nothing for her beyond fleeing Morrowindl, beyond determining the fate of the Elven people, beyond coming to terms with the horror of what she had discovered. Nothing of her life seemed simple anymore, and the ordinary prospects of things like a husband and children were as remote as the home she had left behind.

She made herself consider the possibility then, a tentative conjecture brought on by a need to establish some sense of purpose for all that had come about, that what she might really have been given to do—by Allanon's shade, by Ellenroh, and by choice and chance alike—was to be for her people both mother and wife, to accept them as her family, to shepherd them, to guide and protect them, and to oversee their lives for the duration of her own. Her mind was light and her sense of things turned liquid, for she had barely slept at all now in three days and her physical and emotional strength had been exhausted. She was not herself, she might argue, and yet in truth she had perhaps found herself. There was purpose in everything, and there must be a purpose in this as well. She had been returned to her people, given responsibility over whether they lived or died, and made their queen. She had discovered the magic of the Elfstones and assumed control of their power. She had been told what no one else knew—the truth of the origin of the Shadowen. Why? She gave a mental shrug. Why not, if not to make some difference? Not so much where the Shadowen were concerned, although there could be no complete separation of problems and solutions, as Allanon had indicated in making his charges to the children of Shannara. Not so much in the future of the Races, for that was too broad an undertaking for one person and must inevitably be decided by the efforts of many and the vagaries of fortune. But for the Elves, for their future as a people, for the righting of so many wrongs and the correcting of so many mistakes—in this she might find the purpose of her life.

It was a sobering thought, and she mulled it through as the ascent of Blackledge wore on, lost within herself as she considered what an undertaking of such magnitude would require. She was strong enough, she felt; there was little she could not accomplish if she chose. She had resolve and a sense of right and wrong that had served her well. She was conscious of the fact that she owed a debt—to her mother, who had sacrificed everything so that her child would have a chance to grow up safely; to her grandmother, who had entrusted her with the future of a city and its people; to those who had already given their lives to help preserve her own; and to those who were prepared to do so, who trusted and believed in her.

But even that was not enough by itself to persuade her. There must be something more, she knew—something that transcended expectations and conscience, something more fundamental still. It was the existence of need. She already knew, deep within herself, that genocide was abhorrent and that she must find some other solution to the dilemma of the future of the Elves and their magic. But if they lived, if she was successful in restoring them to the Westland, what would become of them then if she was to walk away? Who would lead them in the fight that lay ahead? Who would guide and counsel them? Could she leave the matter to chance, or even to the dictates of the High Council? The need of the Elven people was great, and she did not think she could ignore it even if it meant changing her own life entirely.

Even so, she remained uncertain. She was torn by the conflict within herself, a war between choices that refused to be characterized as simply right or wrong. She knew as well that none of the choices might be hers to make, for while leadership had been bestowed upon her by Ellenroh, ultimately it was the Elves who would accept or reject it. And why should they choose to follow her? A Rover, an outsider, a girl barely grown—she had much to answer for.

Her reasonings fell apart about her like scraps of paper tumbled by the wind, a collapse of distant plans in the face of present needs. She looked about her at the rock and scrub, at the screen of Vog, and at the dark, bent forms of those who traveled with her. Staying alive was all she could afford to worry about for now.

The trek continued until it was nearing midday, and then Stresa brought them to an uncertain halt. Wren pushed forward from behind Garth to discover what was happening. The Splinterscat stood at the mouth of a cavern that burrowed ahead into the rock. To the right, the trail they followed continued sharply up the slope of the cliff face and disappeared into a tangle of vegetation.

"See, Wren of the Elves," the Splinterscat said softly, bright eyes fixing on her. "We have a choice now. Phhfft! The trail winds ahead to the summit, but it is slow and difficult from here—sssppptt—not clear at all. The tunnel opens into a series of lava tubes formed by the pphhhtt fire of the volcano years ago. I have traveled them. They, too, lead to the summit."

Wren knelt. "Which is your choice?"

"Rwwll. There are dangers both ways."

"There are dangers everywhere." She dismissed his demurral. About her, the haze swirled and twisted against the island's thick growth, as if seeking its own way. "We rely on you to lead us, Stresa," she reminded him. "Choose."

The Splinterscat hissed his discontent. "The tunnels, then. Phhfftt!" The bulky body swung about and back again. The spikes lifted and fell. "We need light."

While Triss went off in search of suitable torch wood, the remainder of the company rummaged through backpacks and pockets for rags and tinder. Gavilan had the latter, Eowen the former. They placed them carefully inside the tunnel entrance and sat down to eat while waiting for Triss to return.

"Did you sleep?" Eowen asked softly, seating herself beside Wren. She kept her gaze carefully averted.

"No," Wren answered truthfully. "I couldn't."

"Nor I. It was as difficult to speak the words as it was to hear them."

"I know that."

The red hair shimmered damply as the pale face lifted into view. "I have had a vision—the first since leaving Arborlon."

Wren turned to meet the seer's gaze and was frightened by what she saw there. "Tell me."

Eowen shook her head, a barely perceptible movement. "Only because it is necessary to warn you," she whispered. She leaned in so that only Wren could hear. "In my vision, you stood alone atop a rise. It was clear that you were on Morrowindl. You held the Ruhk Staff and the Elfstones, but you could not use them. The others, those here, myself included, were black shadows cast upon the earth. Something approached you, huge and dangerous, yet you were not afraid—it was as if you welcomed it. Perhaps you did not realize that it threatened. There was a glint of bright silver, and you hastened to embrace it."

She paused, and her breath seemed to catch in her throat. "You must not do that, Wren. When it happens, remember."

Wren nodded, feeling numb and empty inside. "I will remember."

"I'm sorry," Eowen whispered. She hesitated a moment, like a hunted creature brought to bay with nowhere left to flee, then rose and swiftly moved away. *Poor Eowen,* Wren thought. She looked after the seer a moment, thinking. Then she beckoned to Garth. The big man came at once, eyes questioning, already reading her concern. She shifted so that only he could see her.

Eowen has had a vision of her own death, she signed, not bothering to speak the words this time. Garth showed nothing. *Watch out for her, will you? Try to keep her safe?*

Garth's fingers gestured. *I don't like what I see in her eyes.*

Wren sighed, then nodded. *Neither do I. Just do the best you can.*

Triss returned a few moments later bearing two hunks of dry wood that he had managed to salvage from somewhere on the rain-soaked slopes. He glanced over his shoulder as he approached. "There is movement below," he advised them, passing one of the pieces to Dal. "Something is climbing toward us."

For the first time since they had escaped the swamp, they experienced a sense of urgency. Until now, it had almost been possible to forget the things that hunted them. Wren thought instantly of the Loden's magic, wondering if the demons could indeed scent it, if the smell of the Keel's recovered magic was strong enough to draw them even when it was not in use.

They bound the strips of cloth in place about the wood and used the tinder to set it afire. When the brands were burning, they started ahead into the tunnels. Stresa led, a night creature comfortable in darkness, his burly body trundling smoothly ahead into the gloom. Triss followed close behind with one torch, while Dal trailed the company with the other. In between walked Wren, Gavilan, Eowen, and Garth. The air in the lava tube was cool and stale, and water dripped off the ceiling. In places, a narrow stream meandered along the gnarled floor. There were no projections, no obstructions; the passage of the red-hot lava years earlier had burned everything away. Stresa had explained to her while they waited for Triss how the pressure of heat and gases at the volcano's core forced vents in the earth, carving tunnels through the underground rock to reach the surface, the lava burning its way free. The lava burned so hot that the passageways formed were smooth and even. These tubes would run for miles, curling like giant worm burrows, eventually creating an opening through Morrowindl's skin that in turn would release the pressure and allow the lava to flow unobstructed to the sea. When the volcano cooled, the lava subsided and the tubes it had formed remained behind. The one they followed now was part of a series that cut through miles of Blackledge from crown to base.

"If I don't get us lost, we'll be atop the rrwwllll ridge by nightfall," the Splinterscat had promised.

Wren had wanted to ask him where he had learned about the tubes, but then decided the Splinterscat's knowledge had probably come from the Elves and it would only make him angry to talk about it. In any event, he seemed to know where he was going, nose thrust forward, pushing out at the edge of the torchlight as if seeking to drag them along in his wake, never hesitating once, even when he reached divergent passageways and was forced to choose. They twisted and wound ahead through the cool rock, climbing steadily, hauling themselves and their packs through the gloom, and brushing at the drops of water that fell on their faces and hands with cold, stinging splats. Their booted feet echoed hollowly in the deep stillness, and their breathing was an uneven hiss. They listened carefully for the sounds of pursuit, but heard nothing.

At one point they were forced to descend a particularly steep drop to a cross vent where the lava had cut through to a hollow core within the mountain and left a yawning hole that fell away into blackness. Farther on, there was a cavern where the lava had gathered and pooled for a time, forming a series of passageways that crisscrossed like snakes. In each instance, Stresa knew what to do, which tunnel to follow, and where the passage lay that would take them to safety.

The hours slipped away, and the trek wore on. Wren let Faun ride on her shoulder. The Tree Squeak's bright eyes darted left and right, and its voice was a low murmur in her ear. She quit thinking for a time and concentrated instead on putting one foot in front of the other, on studying the hypnotically swaying shadows they cast in the torchlight, on these and a dozen other mundane, purposeless musings that served to give her weary mind and emotions a much needed rest.

It was nightfall when they finally emerged from the tunnels, exiting the smokey blackness to stand amid a copse of thin-limbed ash and scrub backed up against the cliff face. Before them, a ledge spread away into the mist; behind, the mountain sloped upward to a broken, empty ridgeline. Overhead, the sky was murky and clouded, and a light rain was falling.

They moved away from the tunnels into a stretch of acacia near the rim of Blackledge, and there settled in for the night. They spread their gear and ate a hurried meal, then wrapped themselves in their cloaks and blankets and prepared for sleep. It was cold atop the mountain, and the wind blew at them in sharp gusts. Far distant, Wren could hear Killeshan's rumble and see the red glow of its fire shimmering through the haze. The earth had begun to tremble again, a slow, ominous vibration that loosened rock and earth and sent them tumbling, that caused the trees to sway and leaves to whisper like startled children.

Wren sat back against a half-fallen acacia whose exposed roots maintained a tenuous grip on the mountain rock. The Ruhk Staff rested on her lap, momentarily forgotten. Faun burrowed into her shoulder for a time as the tremors continued, then disappeared down inside her blanket to hide. She watched the small, solid figure of Dal slip past to take the first watch. Her eyes were heavy as she stared out at the dark, but she found she was not yet ready to sleep. She needed to think awhile first.

She had been sitting there for only a few moments when Gavilan appeared. He came out of the darkness rather suddenly, and she started in spite of herself.

"Sorry," he apologized hurriedly. "Can I sit with you awhile?"

She nodded wordlessly, and he settled himself next to her, his own blanket wrapped loosely about his shoulders, his hair tangled and damp. His handsome face was etched with fatigue, but a hint of the familiar smile appeared.

"How are you feeling?"

"I'm all right," she answered.

"You look very tired."

She smiled.

"Would that we had known," he murmured.

She glanced over. "Known what?"

"Everything. Anything! Something that would have prepared us better for what we're going through." His voice sounded odd to her, almost frenetic. "It is almost like being cast adrift in an ocean without a map and being told to navigate to safety and at the same time to refrain from using the little bit of drinking water we are fortunate enough to carry with us."

"What do you mean?"

He turned. "Think about it, Wren. We have in our possession both the Loden and the Elfstones—magic enough to accomplish almost anything. Yet we seem afraid to invoke that magic, almost as if we were restrained from doing so. But we aren't, are we? I mean, what is to prevent it? Look at how much better things became when you used the Elfstones to find a way out of Eden's Murk. We should be using that magic every step of the way! If we did, we might be to the beach by now."

"It doesn't work that way, Gavilan. It doesn't do just anything . . ."

But he wasn't listening. "Even worse is the way we ignore the magic contained in the Loden. Yes, it is needed to preserve the Elves and Arborlon for the journey back. But all of it? I don't believe it for a moment!" He let his hand come to rest momentarily on the Ruhk Staff. His words were suddenly fervent. "Why not use the magic against these things that hunt us? Why not just burn a path right through them? Or better still, why not make something that will go out there and destroy them!"

Wren stared at him, unable to believe what she was hearing. "Gavilan," she said quietly. "I know about the demons. Eowen told me."

He shrugged. "It was time, I suppose. Ellenroh was the only reason no one told you sooner."

"However that may be," she continued, her voice lowering, taking on a firmness, "how can you possibly suggest using the magic to make anything else?"

His face hardened. "Why? Because something went wrong when it was used before? Because those who used it hadn't the ability or strength or sense of what was needed to use it properly?"

She shook her head, voiceless.

"Wren! The magic has to be used! It has to be! That is why it is there in the first place! If we don't make use of it, someone else will, and then what? This isn't a game we play. You know as much. There are things out there so dangerous that . . ."

"Things the Elves made!" she said angrily.

"Yes! A mistake, I agree! But others would have made them if we had not!"

"You can't know that!"

"It doesn't matter. The fact remains we made them for a good cause! We have learned a lot! The making is in the soul of the wielder of the power! It simply requires strength of purpose and channeling of need! This time we can do it right!"

He broke off, waiting for her response. They faced each other in silence. Then Wren took a deep breath and reached down to remove his hand from the Staff. "I don't think you had better say anything more."

His smile was bitter, ironic. "Once you were angry because I hadn't said enough."

"Gavilan," she whispered.

"Do you think this will all go away if we don't talk about it, that everything will somehow just work out?"

She shook her head slowly, sadly.

He bent to her, his hands closing firmly on her own. She didn't try to pull away, both fascinated and repelled by what she saw in his eyes. She felt something like grief well up inside. "Listen to me, Wren," he said, shaking his head at something she couldn't see. "There is a special bond between us. I felt it the moment I first saw you, the night you came to Arborlon, still wondering what it was that you had been sent to do. I knew. I knew it even then, but it was too early to speak of it. You are Alleyne's daughter and you have the Elessedil blood. You have courage and strength. You have done more already than anyone had a right to expect from you.

"But, Wren, none of this is your problem. The Elves are not your people or Arborlon your city. I know that. I know how foreign it must all feel. And Ellenroh never understood that you couldn't ask people to accept responsibility for things when the responsibility was never theirs to begin with. She never understood that once she sent you away, she could never have you back the same. That was how she lost Alleyne! Now, look. She has given you the Ruhk Staff and the Loden, the Elves and Arborlon, the whole of the future of a nation, and told you to be queen. But you don't really want any part of it, do you?"

"I didn't," she admitted. "Once."

He missed her hesitation. "Then give it up! Be finished with it! Let me take the Staff and the Stone and use them as they should be used—to fight against the monsters that track us, to destroy the ones that have turned Morrowindl into this nightmare!"

"Which set of monsters?" she asked softly.

"What?"

"Which set? The demons or the Elves? Which do you mean?"

He stared at her, uncomprehending, and she felt her heart break apart inside. His eyes were clear and angry, his face intense. He seemed so convinced. "The Elves," she whispered, "are the ones who destroyed Morrowindl."

"No," he answered instantly, without hesitation.

"They made the demons, Gavilan."

He shook his head vehemently. "Old men made them in another time. A mistake like that wouldn't happen again. I wouldn't let it. The magic can be better used, Wren. You know that to be true. Haven't the Ohmsfords always found a way? Haven't the Druids? Let me try! I can stand against these things; I can do what is needed! You don't want the Staff; you said so yourself! Give it to me!"

She shook her head. "I can't."

Gavilan stiffened, and his hands drew away. "Why not, Wren? Tell me why not."

She couldn't tell him, of course. She couldn't find the words, and even if she had been able to find the words, she wouldn't have been able to speak them.

"I have given my promise," she said instead, wishing he would let the matter die, that he would give up his demand, that he would see how wrong it was for him to ask.

"Your promise?" he snapped. "To whom?"

"To the queen," she insisted stubbornly.

"To the queen? Shades, Wren, what's the worth of that? The queen is dead!"

She hit him then, struck him hard across the face, a blow that rocked his head back. He remained turned away for a moment and then straightened. "You can hit me again if it will make you feel any better."

"It makes me feel terrible," she whispered, curling up inside, turning to ice. "But that was a wrong thing to say, Gavilan."

He regarded her bitterly for a moment, and she found herself wishing that she could have him back as he was when they were still in Arborlon, when he was charming and kind, the friend she needed, when he had kissed her outside the High Council, when he had cared for her.

The handsome face tightened with determination. "You have to let me use the Loden's magic, Wren."

She shook her head firmly. "No."

He thrust forward aggressively, almost as if to attack her. "If you don't, we won't survive. We can't. You haven't the—"

"Don't, Gavilan!" she interjected, her hand flying to cover his mouth. "Don't say it! Don't say anything more!"

The sudden gesture froze them both momentarily, and the wind that blew past them in a sudden gust caused Wren to shiver. Slowly she took her hand away. "Go to sleep," she urged, fighting to keep her voice from breaking. "You're tired."

He rocked back slightly, a small motion only, one that moved him just inches away from her—yet she could feel the severing of ties between them as surely as if they were ropes cut with a knife.

"I'll go," he said quietly, the anger in his voice undiminished. He rose and looked down at her. "I was your friend. I would be still if you would let me."

"I know," she said.

He stayed where he was momentarily, as if undecided about what to do next, whether to stay or go, whether to speak or keep silent. He looked back through the darkness into the haze. "I won't die here," he whispered.

Then he wheeled and stalked away. Wren sat where she was, looking after him until he could no longer be seen. Tears came to her eyes, but she brushed them quickly away. Gavilan had hurt her, and she hated it. He made her question everything she had decided, made her wonder if she had any idea at all what she was doing. He made her feel stupid and selfish and naive. She wished that she had never gone to speak with the shade of Allanon, never come to Morrowindl, never discovered the Elves and their city and the horror of their existence—that none of it had ever happened.

She wished she had never met her grandmother.

No! she admonished herself sharply. *Don't ever wish that!*

But deep down inside, she did.

20

Daybreak arrived, a stealthy apparition cloaked iron-gray against the shadow of departing night as it crept uncertainly out of yesterday in search of tomorrow. The company rose to greet it, weary-eyed and disheartened, the weight of time's passage and shortening odds a mantle of chains that threatened to drag them down. Pulling cloaks and packs and weapons across their shoulders, they set out once more, wrapped in the silence of their separate thoughts, grim-faced against a rising wall of fear and doubt.

If I could sleep but one night, Wren was thinking as she tried to blink away her exhaustion. *Just one.*

There had been little rest for her last night, restless again as she lay awake in the stillness, beset by demons of all shapes and kinds, demons that bore the faces of those who had been or were closest, friends and family, the tricksters of her life. They whispered words to her, they teased and taunted, they warned of secrets she could not know, they gave her trails to follow and burdens to carry, and then they faded from her side like the morning mist.

Her hands clasped the Ruhk Staff and she leaned upon it for support as she climbed. *Trust no one,* the Addershag hissed again from out of memory.

The climb was short, for they had emerged from the lava tubes close to the summit at the end of yesterday's trek, with the ridgeline already in view. They reached it quickly this day, scrambling up the final stretch of broken trail to stand atop the wall, pausing to look back into the mists that cloaked the country they had passed through—almost as if they expected to find something waiting there. But there was nothing to see, the whole of it shrouded in clouds and fog, a world and a life vanished into the past. They could see it still in their minds, picture it as if it were drawn on the air before them. They could remember what it had cost them to come through it, what it had taken from them, and how little it had given back. They stared a moment longer, then quickly turned away.

They walked then through narrow stretches of rocks separated by trees that stretched from the edge of Blackledge like fingers until everything abruptly ended at a ragged tangle of ravines and ridges that split and folded back on themselves, huge wrinkles in the land's skin. A lava flow had passed this way some years back, come down out of Killeshan's maw to sweep the crest of Blackledge clean. Everything had been burned away save a scattering of silvered tree trunks standing bare and skeletal, some fallen away at strange angles, some propped against one another in hapless despair. Scrub grew out of the lava in gnarled clumps, and patches of moss darkened the shady side of roughened splits.

Stresa brought them to the edge of this forbidding world, lumbering to a halt atop a small rise, spines lifting guardedly. The company stared out bleakly at what lay ahead, listening for and hearing nothing, looking at and seeing nothing, feeling death's presence at every turn. The devastation spread away before them, a vast and empty landscape wrapped in gray silence.

On Wren's shoulder, Faun sat up stiffly and leaned forward, ears pricked. She could feel the Tree Squeak shiver.

"What is this place?" Gavilan asked.

A heavy rumble distracted them momentarily, causing them to glance north to where Killeshan's bulk loomed darkly, seemingly as close to them now as it had been on their leaving Arborlon. The rumble receded and died.

Stresa swung slowly about. "This is the Harrow," he said. "Hssttt! This is where the Drakuls live."

A form of demon—or Shadowen—Wren recalled. Stresa had mentioned them before. Dangerous, he had intimated.

"Drakuls," Gavilan repeated, weary recognition in his voice.

Killeshan rumbled again, more insistent than before, an unnecessary reminder of its presence, of the anger it bore them for having stolen the magic away, for having disrupted the balance of things. Morrowindl shuddered in response.

"Tell me about the Drakuls," Wren instructed the Splinterscat quietly.

Stresa's dark eyes fixed on her. "Demons, like the others. Phhfftt! They sleep in daylight, come out at night to feed. They drain the life out of the living things they catch—the blood, the fluids of the body. They make— hssstt—some into creatures like themselves." The blunt nose twitched. "They hunt as wraiths, but take form to feed. As wraiths, they cannot be harmed." He spit distastefully.

"We will go around," Triss announced at once.

Stresa spit again, as if the taste wouldn't go away. "Around! Phaaww! There is no 'around'! North, the Harrow runs back toward Killeshan, miles and miles—back toward the valley and the demons that hunt us. Rwwlll. South, the Harrow stretches to the cliffs. The Drakuls hunt its edges, too. In any case, we would never—hrraaggh—get around it before nightfall and we must if we are to live. Crossing in daylight is our only chance."

"While the Drakuls sleep?" Wren prompted.

"Yes, Wren of the Elves," the Splinterscat growled softly. "While they sleep. And even so—hsssttt—it will not be entirely safe. The Drakuls are present even then—as voices out of air, as faces on the mist, as feelings and hunches and fears and doubts. Phhfftt. They will try to distract and lure, try to keep us within the Harrow until nightfall."

Wren stared off into the blasted countryside, into the haze that hung from the skies to the earth. *Trapped again,* she thought. *The whole island is a snare.*

"There is no other passage open to us?"

Stresa did not answer—did not need to.

"And on the other side of the Harrow?"

"The In Ju. And the beaches beyond."

Triss had moved up beside her. His lean face was intense. "Aurin Striate used to speak of the Drakuls," he advised softly. His gaze fixed on her. "He said there was no defense against them."

"But they sleep now," she replied, just as softly.

The gray eyes shifted away. "Do they?"

A new rumble shook the island, deep and forbidding, rising like a giant coming awake angry, thunderous as the tremors built upon themselves. Cracks appeared in the ground about them and rock and silt fell away into the void. Steam and ash belched out of the Killeshan, showering skyward in towering geysers, arcing away into the gloom. Fire trailed ominously from the volcano's lip, a trickle only, just visible in the haze.

Garth caught Wren's attention, a simple shifting of his shoulders. His fingers moved. *Be quick, Wren. The island begins to shake itself apart.*

She glanced at them in turn—Garth, as enigmatic and impassive as ever; steady Triss, her protector now, given over to his new charge; Dal, restless as he stared out into the haze—she had never even heard him speak; Eowen, a white shadow against the gray, looking as if she might disappear into it; and Gavilan, uneasy, unpredictable, haunted, lost to her.

"How long will it take us to cross?" she asked Stresa. Faun scrambled down off her shoulder and moved away, picking at the earth.

"Half a day, a little more," the Splinterscat advised.

"A lifetime if you are wrong, Scat," Gavilan intoned darkly.

"Then we will have to hurry," Wren declared, and called Faun back to her shoulder. She brought the Ruhk Staff before her, a reminder. "We have no choice. Let's be off. Stay close to each other. Keep watch."

They struck out across the flats, winding down into the maze of depressions, through the tangle of tree husks, cautious eyes scanning the blasted land about them. Stresa took them along as quickly as he could, but travel was slow, the terrain broken and uneven, filled with twists and turns that prevented either rapid or straight passage. The Harrow swallowed them after only moments, gathering about them almost magically until there was nothing else to be seen in any direction. Mist swirled and spun in the wind currents, steam rose out of cracks in the earth that burrowed all the way to Killeshan's core, and vog drifted down from where it spewed out of the volcano. Nothing moved in the land; it was still and empty all about. Shadows played, black lines cast earthward by the skeletal trees, iron bars against the light. All the while the earth beneath rumbled ominously, and there was a sense of something dangerous awakening.

The voices began in the first hour. They lifted out of nothingness, whispers on the air that might have come from anywhere. They called compellingly, and for each of the company the words were different. Each would look at the others, thinking that all must have heard, that the voices were unmistakable. They asked, anxious, intense: *Did you hear that? Did you hear?* But none had, of course—only the speaker, called specifically, purposefully, drawn on by some mirror of self, by a reflection of sense and feeling.

The images came next, faces out of the air, figures that quickly formed and just as quickly faded in the shifting haze, visions of things peculiar to whomever they addressed—personifications of longings, needs, and hopes. For Wren, they took the form of her parents. For Triss and Eowen, it was the queen. For the others, something else. The images worked the fringes of their consciousness, struggling to break through the barriers they had erected to keep them at bay, working to turn them from their chosen path and lead them away.

It went on relentlessly. The voices were never loud, the images never clear, and the whole of the experience not unpleasant, not threatening, not even real—a false memory of what had never been. Stresa, familiar with the danger, started them talking to each other to ward off the attack—for there was no mistaking what it was. The Drakuls stalked them even in sleep, some part of what they were rising up to follow after, seeking to delay or detain, to turn aside or lead astray, to keep them within the Harrow until nightfall.

Time slowed, as cautious and measured as the haze through which they walked, as bleak as the landscape that stretched ahead. The depressions deepened, and in places the lifeless trees formed a barrier that could not be crossed, but had to be got around. Wren called to the others as they trudged ahead, pushing past the voices, casting through the faces, working to keep them all together, to keep them moving. Noon approached, and the day darkened. Clouds massed overhead, heavy with rain. It began to drizzle, then to pour. The wind quickened, and the rain blew into them in sheets. It would sweep across in a curtain, fade away to scattered drops, and start the cycle over again. It lasted for a time and was gone. The earth's heat returned, and the mist began to thicken. It closed about them, and soon nothing was visible beyond a dozen feet. They stayed close then, so close they were tripping over each other, bumping together as if made sightless, feeling their way through the gloom.

"Stresa! How much farther?" Wren shouted through the cacophony of voices that whirled about her ears.

"Spptptt! Close, now," the reply came. "Just ahead."

They passed down into a particularly deep ravine, a jagged knife cut across the surface of the lava rock, all shadows and shifting haze. Wren knew it was dangerous, almost called them back, but saw, too, that it sliced directly across their pathway out, that it was the only way they could go. She descended into the gloom, the Ruhk Staff gripped before her like a shield. Faun chittered wildly on her shoulder, another sound to blend with the others, the unseen voices that buzzed and raged and filled her subconscious with a growing need to scream. She saw Triss a step ahead, with

Stresa a faint dark spot beyond. She heard footsteps behind, someone following, the others . . .

And then the hands had her, abrupt, startling, as hard as iron. They reached up from nowhere, materializing from out of the mist, closed about her legs and ankles, and yanked her from the pathway. She yelled in fury and struck downward with the butt of the Ruhk Staff. White fire burst from the earth, flaring out in all directions, the magic of the talisman responding. It shocked her, stunned her that the magic should come so easily. There were shouts from the others, cries of warning. Wren wheeled about wildly, and the hands that had fastened on her fell away. Something moved in the mist—things, dozens of them, faceless, formless, yet there. The Drakuls, she realized, awake somehow when they should not have been. Perhaps it was dark enough here in this cut, black enough to pass for night. She cried out to the others, summoned them to her, and led them toward the ravine's far slope. The figures swirled all about, grasping, touching, nonsubstantive, yet somehow real. She saw faces drained of life, pale images of her own, eyes empty and unseeing, teeth that looked like the fangs of animals, sunken cheeks and temples, and bodies wasted away to nothing. She fought through them, for they seemed centered on her, drawn to her as if she were the one who mattered most to them. It was the magic, she realized. Like all the Shadowen, it was the magic that drew them first.

Drakul wraiths materialized in front of her and Garth bounded past, short sword hacking. The images dissipated and reformed, unharmed. Wren wheeled about as she reached the floor of the ravine. *One, two* . . . She counted frantically. All six were there. Stresa was already scrambling ahead, and she turned to follow him. They went up the slope in a tangle, clawing their way over the rain-slick lava rock, past the scrub and fallen trees. The images followed, the voices, the phantoms come from sleep, undead monsters trailing after. Wren fought them off with anger and repulsion, with the fury of her movement, conscious of Faun clinging to her neck as if become a part of her, of the heat of the Ruhk Staff in her hands as its magic sought to break free again. Magic that could do anything, she lamented, that could create anything—even monsters like these. She recoiled inwardly at the prospect, at the horror of a truth she wished had never been, a truth she feared would rise up to haunt her if she were to keep the promise she had made to her grandmother to save the Elves.

Over the top of the ravine the members of the little company stumbled and began to run. The gloom was thick and shifted like layers of gauze before them, but they did not slow, racing ahead heedlessly, calling words of encouragement to each other, fighting back against their pursuers. The Drakuls hissed and spit like cats, the venom of their thoughts a fire that burned inside. Yet it was only voices and images now and no longer real, for the Drakuls could not leave the darkness of their shelter to venture into the Harrow while it was yet daylight. Slowly their presence faded, drawing away like the receding waters of some vast ocean, gone back with the tide.

The company began to slow, their breathing heavy in the sudden stillness, their boots scraping as they came to a ragged halt.

Wren looked back into the haze. There was nothing there but the mist and the faint shadow of the scrub land and tree bones beyond, empty and stark. Faun poked her head up tentatively. Stresa lumbered over to join them, panting, tongue licking out. The Splinterscat spit. "Hsssttt! Stupid wraiths!"

Wren nodded. In her hands, the heat of the Ruhk Staff dissipated and was gone. She felt her own body cool in response. A small measure of relief welled up within.

Then abruptly Garth crowded forward, startled by something she had missed, intense and anxious as he searched the mist. Wren followed his gaze, frightened without yet knowing why. She saw the others glance at one another uneasily.

Her heart jumped. *What was wrong?*

She saw it then. There were only five of them. Eowen was missing.

At first she thought such a thing impossible, that she must be mistaken. She had counted all six when they had climbed from the ravine. Eowen had been among them; she had recognized her face . . .

She stopped herself. Eowen. She saw the red-haired seer in her mind, trailing after—too pale, too ephemeral. Almost as if she wasn't really there—which, of course, she hadn't been. Wren experienced a sinking feeling in the pit of her stomach, an aching that threatened to break free and consume her. What she had seen had been another image, one more clever and calculated than the others, an image designed to make them all believe they were together when in fact they were not.

The Drakuls had Eowen.

Garth signed hurriedly. *I was watching out for her as I promised I would. She was right behind us when we climbed from the ravine. How could I lose her?*

"You didn't," Wren replied instantly. She felt an odd calm settle over her, a resignation of sorts, an acceptance of the inevitability of chance and fate. "It's all right, Garth," she whispered.

She felt the ground open beneath her, a hole into which she must surely fall. She waited for the feeling to pass, for stability to take hold. She knew what she had to do. Whatever else happened, she could not abandon Eowen. To save her, she would have to go back into the Harrow, back among the Drakuls. She could send the others, of course; they would go if she asked. But she would never do that—would never even consider it. Tracker skills, Rover experience, Elven Hunter training—all would be useless against the Drakuls. Only one thing would make any difference.

She took a few uncertain steps and stopped. Reason screamed at her to reconsider. She was aware of the others coming forward one by one to stand with her, their eyes following her own as she peered out into the Harrow's gloom.

"No!" Stresa warned. "Phffft! It's already growing dark!"

She ignored him, turning instead to Gavilan. Wordlessly she took his measure, then held forth the Ruhk Staff. "It is time for you to be a friend to me again, Gavilan," she told him quietly. "Take the Staff. Hold it for me until my return. Keep it safe."

Gavilan stared at her in disbelief, then cautiously reached for the talisman. His hands closed over it, tightened about it, and drew it away. She did not allow her eyes to linger on his, frightened of what she would find there. He was all that remained of her family; she had to trust him.

Triss and Dal had dropped their packs and were cinching their weapons belts. Garth already had his short sword out.

"No," she told them. "I am going back alone."

They started to protest, the words quick and urgent, but she cut them off instantly. "No!" she repeated. She faced them. "I am the only one who stands a chance of finding Eowen and bringing her out again. Me." She reached within her tunic and pulled forth the pouch with the Elfstones. "Magic to find her and to protect me—nothing less will do. If you come with me, I shall have to worry about protecting you as well. These things can't be hurt by your weapons, and this one time at least you cannot help me."

She put a hand on Triss's arm, gentle but firm. "You are pledged to watch over me, I know. But I am ordering you to watch over the Loden instead—to stay with Gavilan, you and Dal, to see to it that whatever else happens, the Elves are kept safe."

The hard, gray eyes narrowed. "I beg you not to do this, Lady. The Home Guard serve the queen first."

"And the queen, if that is what in truth I am, believes you will serve best by staying here. I order it, Triss."

Garth was signing angrily. *Do what you wish with them. But I have no purpose in remaining. I come with you.*

She shook her head, and her fingers moved as she spoke. "No, Garth. If I am lost, they will need you to see them safely to the beaches and to Tiger Ty. They will need your experience. I love you, Garth, but you can do nothing to help me here. You must stay."

The big man looked at her as if she had struck him.

"This is the time we always knew would come," she told him, quiet and insistent, "the time for which you have worked so hard to train me. It is too late now for any further lessons. I have to rely on what I know."

She took Faun from her shoulder and placed her on the ground beside Stresa. "Stay, little one," she commanded, and stepped away.

"Rrrwwlll! Wren, of the Elves, take me!" Stresa snapped, spines bristling. "I can track for you—better than any of these others!"

She shook her head once more. "The Elfstones can track better still. Garth will see you safely to the Westland, Stresa, if I should fail to return. He knows of my promise to you."

She removed her pack, dropped her weapons—all but the long knife at her waist. The four men, the Splinterscat, and the Tree Squeak watched in silence. Carefully she shook the Elfstones from their pouch, dropping them into her open hand. Her fingers closed.

Then, before she could think better of it, she turned and stalked into the mist.

She walked straight ahead for a time, simply concentrating on putting one foot in front of the other, distance between herself and those who would keep her safe. She crossed the bare lava rock, a solitary hunter, feeling herself turn cold within, numb from the intensity of her determination. Eowen spoke to her out of memory, telling her of the vision she had seen so long ago, the vision of her own death. *No,* Wren swore silently. *Not now, not while I still breathe.*

The Drakuls began to whisper to her, urging her on, calling her to them. Within, fury battled back against fear. *I will come to you, all right—but not as you would have me!*

She passed through a line of silvered trunks, wood stakes barren and stark, a gate into the netherworld of the dead. She saw faces appear, gaunt and empty, skulls within the mist. She brought up the Elfstones, held them forth, and summoned their power. It came at once, obedient to her will, blazing to life with blue fire and streaking out into the haze. It took her left along a flat where nothing grew, where no trace of what had been survived. Ahead, far in the distance, she could see a gathering of white forms, bodies shifting, turning as if to greet her. Voices reached out, cries and whispers, a summons to death.

The blue fire faded, and she walked blindly on.

Wren, she heard Eowen call.

She shut her sense of urgency away, forcing herself to move cautiously, watching everything around her, the movement of shadows and mist, the hint of life coming awake. Stresa had been right. It was growing dark now, the afternoon lengthening toward evening, the light beginning to fail. She knew she would not reach Eowen before nightfall. It was what the Drakuls intended; it was what they had planned all along. Eowen's magic drew them like her own—but it was hers that they wanted, that was most powerful, that would feed them best. Eowen was bait for the trap that was meant to snare her.

She shut her eyes momentarily against the inevitability of it. She should have known all along.

The voices grew louder, more insistent, and she saw figures begin to take form at the edges of her vision, faint and ethereal in the mist. A ravine opened before her—the one in which she had lost Eowen? she wondered. She didn't know and didn't care. She went down into it without slowing, following the magic's lead, feeling the iron of it fill her now with its heat, fired in the forge of her soul. She didn't know how much time had passed—an hour, more? She had lost all track of time, all sense of everything but what she had come to do. Queen of the Elves, keeper of the Ruhk Staff and Loden, bearer of Druid magic, and heir to the blood of Elessedils and Ohmsfords alike—she was all these and she was none, made instead of something more, something undefinable.

Nothing, she told herself, could stand against her.

The darkness closed about as she reached the bottom of the ravine, the faint light above lost in mist and shadows. The Drakuls appeared boldly now, skeletal forms come slowly into view, gaunt and stripped of all life but that which their Shadowen existence gave them. They were hesitant still, afraid of the magic and at the same time eager for it. They looked upon her with hungry eyes, anxious to taste her, to make her their own. She felt the Elfstones burn against her palm in warning, but still she did not summon their magic. She walked ahead boldly, the living among the dead.

Wren, she heard Eowen call again.

A wall of pale bodies blocked her way. They were human of a sort, shaped as such, but twisted, pale imitations of what they had been in life. They turned to meet her, no longer apparitions that shimmered and threatened to dissolve at a breath of wind, but things taking on the substance of life.

"Eowen!" she cried out.

One by one the Drakuls stood away, and there was Eowen. She lay cradled in their arms, as white-skinned as they save for her fire-red hair and emerald eyes. The eyes glittered as they sought Wren's own, alive with horror. Eowen's mouth was open as if she were trying to breathe—or scream.

The mouths of the Drakuls were fastened to her body, feeding.

For an instant Wren could not move, stricken by the sight, trapped in a web of indecision.

Then Eowen's head jerked up, and her lips parted in a snarl to reveal gleaming fangs.

Wren howled in dismay, and the Drakuls came for her. She brought the Elfstones up with the quickness of thought, called forth their power in rage and terror, and turned the fire of the magic on everything in sight. It swept through her attackers like a scythe, incinerating them. Those who had taken solid form, those feeding and Eowen with them, were obliterated. The others, wraiths still, vanished. Flames engulfed everything. Wren scattered fire in every direction, feeling the magic course through her, hot and raw. She howled, exultant as the fire burned the ravine from end to end. She gave herself over to its heat—anything to block away the image of Eowen. She embraced it as she would a lover. Time and place disappeared in the rush of sensations.

She began to lose control.

Then, a bare instant before she would have disappeared into the power completely, she realized what was happening, remembered who she was, and made a last, desperate attempt to recover herself. Frantically she clamped her fingers about the Stones. The fire continued to leak through. Her hand tightened, and her body convulsed. She doubled over with the effort, falling to her knees. Finally, the magic swept back within her, raked her one final time with the promise of its invincibility, and was gone.

She crouched in the mist, fighting to regain mastery of herself, seeing once more with her mind's eye a picture of the Drakuls and Eowen as they disappeared into flames, consumed by the Elfstone magic.

Power! Such power! How she longed to have it back!

Shame swept through her, followed by despair.

She lifted her eyes wearily, already knowing what she would find, fully cognizant now of what she had done. Before her, the ravine stretched away, empty. Smoke and ash hung on the air. Her throat tightened as she tried to breathe. She had not had a choice, she knew—but the knowledge didn't help. Eowen had been one of them, brought to her death as Wren watched, her own prophecy fulfilled. Though Wren had tried, she could not change the outcome of the seer's vision. Eowen had told her once that her life had been built around her visions and she had come to accept them—even the one that foretold her death.

Wren felt tears fill her eyes and run down her cheeks.

Oh, Eowen!

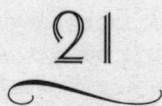

At Southwatch time drifted away like a cloud across the summer blue, and Coll Ohmsford could only watch helplessly as it passed him by. His imprisonment continued unchanged, his life an uneasy compendium of boredom and tension. His thoughts were unfettered, but led him nowhere. He dreamed of the past, of the life he had enjoyed in the Vale, and of the world that lay without the black walls of his confinement, but his dreams had turned tattered and faded. No one came for him. He began to accept that no one would.

He spent his days in the exercise yard, sparring with Ulfkingroh, the gnarled, scarred, taciturn fellow into whose care Rimmer Dall had given him. Ulfkingroh was as tough as nails and he worked Coll until the Valeman thought he would drop. With padded cudgels, heavy staffs, blunted swords, and bare hands, they exercised and trained as if fighters preparing for battle, sometimes all day, frequently until they were sweating so hard that the dust they raised in the yard ran from their bodies in black stripes. Ulfkingroh was a Shadowen, of course—but he didn't seem like one. He seemed like any normal man, albeit harder and more sullen. At times, Coll almost liked him. He spoke little, content to let his expertise with weapons do his talking for him. He was a skilled and experienced fighter, and it became a point of pride with him that he pass what he knew on to the Valeman. Coll, for his part, made the best of his situation, taking advantage of the one diversion he was allowed, learning what he could of what the other was willing to teach, playing at battle as if it meant something, and keeping fit for the time when it really would.

Because sooner or later, he promised himself over and over again, he would have his chance to escape.

He thought of it constantly. He thought of little else. If no one knew he was there, if no one would come to save him, then clearly it was up to him to save himself. Coll was resourceful in the manner of all Valemen; he was confident he would find a way. He was patient as well, and his patience was perhaps the more important attribute. He was watched whenever he was out of his cell, whenever he went down the dark halls of the monolith to the exercise yard and whenever he went back up again. He was allowed to spend as much time sparring with Ulfkingroh as he wished and allowed as well to visit with the rugged fellow to the extent that he was able to engage the other in conversation, but always he was watched. He could not afford to make a mistake.

Still, he never doubted that he would find a way.

He saw Rimmer Dall only twice after the First Seeker visited him in his cell. Each time it was from a distance, an unexpected glimpse that lasted only a moment before the other was gone. Each time the cold eyes were all he could remember afterward. Coll looked for him everywhere at first until he realized it was becoming something of an obsession and that he had to stop it. But he never stopped thinking of what the big man had told him, of how Par was a Shadowen, too, of how the magic would consume him if he did not accept the truth of his identity, and of how in his madness he was a danger to his brother. Coll did not believe what Rimmer Dall had told him—yet he could not bring himself to disbelieve either. The truth, he decided, lay somewhere in between, in that gray area amid the speculations and lies. But the truth was hard to decipher, and he would never learn it there. Rimmer Dall had his own reasons for what he was doing and he was not about to reveal them to Coll. Whatever they were, whatever the reality of the Shadowen and their magic, Coll was convinced that he had to reach his brother.

So he trained in the exercise yard by day, lay awake sorting out chances and possibilities by night, and all the while fought back against the insidious possibility that nothing would come of any of it.

Then one day, several weeks after he had been released from his cell, while sparring once again with Ulfkingroh in the exercise yard, he caught sight of Rimmer Dall passing down a walkway between two alcoves. At first it looked as if part of him had been cut away. Then he realized that the First Seeker was carrying something draped over one arm—something that at first seemed like nothing because it was so black it had the appearance of a piece of a new moon's night. Coll stopped in his tracks, then backed away, staring. Ulfkingroh glared in irritation, then glanced back over his shoulder to see what had caught the Valeman's eye.

"Huh!" he grunted when he saw what Coll was looking at. "There's nothing there that concerns you. Put up your hands."

"What is it he carries?" Coll pressed.

Ulfkingroh braced his staff against the ground and leaned on it with exaggerated patience. "A cloak, Valeman. It's called a Mirrorshroud. See how black it is? See how it steals away the light, just like a spill of black ink? Shadowen magic, little fellow." The rough face tightened about a half smile. "Know what it does?" Coll shook his head. "You don't? Good! Because you're not supposed to! Now put up your hands!"

They went back to sparring, and Coll, who was no little fellow and every bit as big and strong as Ulfkingroh, gained a measure of revenge by striking the other so hard he was knocked from his feet and left stunned for several minutes after.

That night Coll lay awake thinking about the Mirrorshroud and wondering what it was for. It was the first tangible piece of Shadowen magic he had ever seen. There were other magics, of course, but they were hidden from him. The biggest and most important was something kept deep in the bowels of the tower that hummed and throbbed and sometimes almost sounded as if it were screaming, something huge and very frightening. He envisioned it as a dragon that the Shadowen had managed to chain, but he knew he was being too simplistic. Whatever it was, it was far more impressive and terrible than that. There were other things as well, concealed behind the doors through which he was never allowed, secreted in the catacombs into which he could never pass. He could sense their presence, the brush of it against his skin, the whisper of it in his mind. Magic, all of it, Shadowen conjurings and talismans, things dark and evil.

Or not, if you believed Rimmer Dall. But he did not believe the First Seeker, of course. He never had believed him.

Still, he could not help wondering.

Two days later, while he was taking a break in the yard, the sweat still glistening on his body like oil, the First Seeker appeared out of the shadows of a door and came right up to him. Over one arm he carried the Mirrorshroud like a fold of stolen night. Ulfkingroh started to his feet, but Rimmer Dall dismissed him with a wave of his gloved hand and beckoned Coll to follow. They walked from the light back into the cooler shadows, out of the midday sun, away from its glare. Coll squinted and blinked as his eyes adjusted. The other man's face was all angles and planes in the faint gray light, the skin dead and cold, but the sharp eyes certain.

"You train hard, Coll Ohmsford," he said in that familiar whispery voice. "Ulfkingroh loses ground on you every day."

Coll nodded without speaking, waiting to hear what the other had really come to tell him.

"This cloak," Rimmer Dall said, as if in answer. "It is time that you understood what it is for."

Coll could not hide his surprise. "Why?"

The other glanced away as if thinking through his answer. The gloved hand lifted and fell again, a black scythe. "I told you that your brother was in danger, that you in turn were in danger, all because of the magic and what it might do. I had thought to use you to bring your brother to me. I let it be known you were here. But your brother remains in Tyrsis, unwilling to come for you."

He paused, looking for Coll's response. Coll kept his face an expressionless mask.

"The magic he hides within himself," the First Seeker whispered, "the magic that lies beneath the wishsong, begins to consume him. He may not even realize it yet. He may not understand. You've sensed that magic in him, haven't you? You know it is there?"

He shrugged. "I had thought to reason with him when I found him. I think now that he may refuse to listen to me. I had hoped that having you at Southwatch would make a difference. It apparently has not."

Coll took a deep breath. "You are a fool if you think Par will come here. A bigger fool if you think you can use me to trap him."

Rimmer Dall shook his head. "You still don't believe me, do you? I want to protect you, not use you. I want to save your brother while there is still time to do so. He is a Shadowen, Coll. He is like me, and his magic is a gift that can either save or destroy him."

A gift. Par had used that word so often, Coll thought bleakly. "Let me go to him then. Release me."

The big man smiled, a twisting at the corners of his mouth. "I intend to. But not until I have confronted your brother one more time. I think the Mirrorshroud will let me do so. This is a Shadowen magic, Valeman—a very powerful one. It took me a long time to weave it. Whoever wears the cloak appears to those he encounters as someone they know and trust. It masks the truth of who they are. It hides their identity. I will wear it when I go in search of your brother." He paused. "You could help me in this. You could tell me where I might find him, where you think he might be. I know he is in Tyrsis. I don't know where. Will you help me?"

Coll was incredulous. How could Rimmer Dall even think of asking such a thing? But the big man seemed so sure of himself, as if he were right after all, as if he knew the truth far better than Coll.

Coll shook his head. "I don't know where to find Par. He could be anywhere."

For a long moment Rimmer Dall did not respond, but simply stood looking at the Valeman, measuring him carefully, the hard eyes fixed on him as if the lie could be read on his face.

"I will ask again another time," he said finally. The heavy boots scraped on the stone of the walkway. "Return to your sparring. I will find him on my own, one way or the other. When I do, I will release you."

He turned and walked away. Coll stared after him, looking not at the man now but at the cloak he carried, thinking, *If I could just get my hands on that cloak for five seconds . . .*

He was still thinking about it when he woke the next day. A cloak that when worn could hide the identity of the wearer from those he encountered, making him appear to be someone they trusted—here at last was a way out of Southwatch. Rimmer Dall might envision the Mirrorshroud as a subterfuge that would allow him to trap Par, but Coll had a far better use for the magic. If he could find a way to get possession of the cloak long enough to put it on . . . His excitement at the prospect would not allow him to finish the thought. How could he manage it? he wondered, his mind racing as he dressed and paced the length of his cell, waiting for his breakfast.

It occurred to him then, for just a moment, that it was extraordinarily careless of Rimmer Dall to show him such a magic when the Shadowen had been so careful to keep all their other magics hidden. But then the First Seeker had been anxious for his help in locating Par, hadn't he, and the cloak was useless unless they found Par, wasn't it? Probably Dall had hoped to persuade Coll simply by letting him know he possessed such magic.

Then the first suspicion was abruptly crowded aside by a second. What if the cloak was a trick? How did he know that the Mirrorshroud could do what was claimed? What proof did he have? He started sharply as the metal food tray slid through the slot at the bottom of his door. He stared at it helplessly a moment, wondering. But why would the First Seeker lie? What did he stand to gain?

The questions besieged and finally overwhelmed him, and he brushed them aside long enough to eat his breakfast. When he was finished, he went down to the exercise yard to train with Ulfkingroh. He needed to talk with Rimmer Dall again, to find out more about the cloak and to discover the truth of its magic. But he could not afford to seem too interested; he could not let the First Seeker surmise his true motive. That meant he had to wait for Rimmer Dall to come to him.

But the First Seeker did not appear that day or the next, and it was not until three days later as sunset approached that he materialized from the shadows as Coll was trudging wearily back to his cell and fell in beside him.

"Have you given further thought to helping me find your brother?" he asked perfunctorily, his face lowered within the cowl of his black cloak.

"Some," Coll allowed.

"Time passes swiftly, Valeman."

Coll shrugged casually. "I have trouble believing anything you tell me. A prisoner is not often persuaded to confide in his jailor."

"No?" Coll could almost feel the other's dark smile. "I would have thought it was just the opposite."

They walked in silence for a few paces, Coll's face burning with anger. He wanted to strike out at the other, having him this close, alone in these dark halls, just the two of them. He fought down the temptation, knowing how foolish it would be to give in to it.

"I think Par would see through the magic of the Mirrorshroud," he said finally.

Dall glanced over. "How?"

Coll took a deep breath. "His own magic would warn him."

"So you think I would fail to get close enough even to speak with him?" The whispery voice was hoarse and low.

"I wonder," Coll replied.

Dall stopped and turned to face him. "How would it be if I tested the magic on you? Then you could make your own judgment."

Coll frowned, hiding the elation that surged abruptly within. "I don't know. It might not make any difference whether it works with me."

The gloved hand lifted, a lean blackness stealing the light from the air. "Why not let me try? What harm can it do?"

They went down the hallway and up a dozen flights of stairs until they were only several floors below the cell where Coll was kept imprisoned. At a door marked with a wolf's head and red lettering that Coll could not decipher, Rimmer Dall produced a key, inserted it in a heavy lock, and pushed the door back. Inside was a single window through which a narrow band of sunlight shone on a tall wooden cabinet. Rimmer Dall walked to the cabinet, opened its double doors, and took out the Mirrorshroud.

"Look away from me for a moment," he ordered.

Coll turned his head, waiting.

"Coll," a voice came.

He turned back. There was his father, Jaralan, tall and stooped, thick shouldered, wearing his favorite leather apron, the one he used for his woodworking. Coll blinked in disbelief, telling himself that it wasn't his father, that it was Rimmer Dall, and still it was his father he saw.

Then his father reached up to remove the apron, which instantly became the Mirrorshroud, and Rimmer Dall stood before him once more.

"Who did you see?" the First Seeker asked softly.

Coll could not bring himself to answer. He shook his head. "I still think Par will recognize you."

Rimmer Dall studied him a moment, the big, rawboned face flat and empty, the strange eyes as hard as stone. "I want you to think about something," he said finally. "Do you remember those pitiful creatures in the Pit at Tyrsis, the ones driven mad by Federation imprisonment, their magic consuming them? That is what will happen to your brother. It may not happen today or tomorrow or next week or even next month, but it will happen eventually. Once it does, there will be no help for him."

Coll fought to keep the fear from his eyes.

"I want you to think about this as well. All Shadowen have the power to invade and consume. They can inhabit the bodies of other creatures and become them for as long as it is needed." He paused. "I could become you, Coll Ohmsford. I could slip beneath your skin as easily as a knife blade and make you my own." The harsh whisper was a hiss against the silence. "But I don't choose to do that because I don't want to hurt you. I spoke the truth when I told you I wanted to help your brother. You will have to decide for yourself whether or not to believe me, but think about what I have just told you as you do."

He turned, shoved the Mirrorshroud back into its locker, and closed the door. Whether he was angry or frustrated or something else was difficult to tell, but his walk was purposeful as he led Coll from the room and pulled the door closed behind them. Coll listened automatically for the click of the lock and did not hear it. Rimmer Dall was already moving away, so Coll went after him without slowing. The First Seeker took him to a stairway and pointed up.

"Your quarters lie that way. Think carefully, Valeman," he warned. "You play with two lives while you delay."

Coll turned wordlessly and started up the stairs. When he glanced back over his shoulder a dozen steps later, Rimmer Dall was gone.

It was still light, if barely, when he went out once again, passing along the hallway to the stairs, then winding his way downward through the shadows toward the exercise yard. He had left his tunic there; he had forgotten it earlier. He didn't require it, of course, but it provided the excuse he needed to discover whether the door to the room that held the Mirrorshroud had been left unlocked.

His breathing was rapid and harsh-sounding in the silence of his descent. It was a reckless thing he was attempting to do, but his desperation was growing. If he did not get free soon, something bad was going to happen to Par. His conviction of this was based mostly on supposition and fear, but it was no less real for being so. He knew he wasn't thinking as clearly as he should; if he had been, he would never have even considered taking this risk. But if the lock had not released back into place, if the room was still open and the Mirrorshroud still in its locker, waiting . . .

Footsteps sounded from somewhere below, and he froze against the stair wall. The steps grew momentarily louder and then disappeared. Coll wiped his hands on his pants and tried to think. Which floor was it? Four, he had counted, hadn't he? He worked his way ahead again, then stepped onto the fourth landing down and with his body pressed against the stone, peered around the corner.

The hallway before him stood empty.

He took a deep breath to steady himself and stepped from hiding. Down the hall he crept, swift and silent, casting anxious glances ahead and behind as he went. The Shadowen were always watching him. Always. But there were none now, it seemed, none that he could see. He kept going. He checked each door as he passed it. A wolf's head with red lettering below—where was it?

If he was caught . . .

Then the door he was searching for was before him, the wolf's eyes glaring into his own. He stepped up to it quickly, put his ear close and listened. Silence. Carefully he reached out and turned the handle.

It gave easily. The door opened before him and he was through.

The room was empty save for the wooden cabinet, a tall, shrouded coffin propped against the far wall. He could hardly believe his good fortune.

Swiftly he went to the cabinet, opened it, and reached inside. His hands closed about the Mirrorshroud. Cautiously he took it out, lifting it toward the graying light. The fabric was soft and thick, the cloak as light as dust. Its blackness was disconcerting, an inkiness that looked as if it could swallow you whole. He held the cloak before him momentarily, studying it, weighing a final time the advisability of what he was about to do.

Then quickly he swung it over his shoulders and let it settle into place. He could barely feel it, a presence no greater than the shadow he cast in the failing daylight. He tied its cords about his neck and lifted the hood into place. He waited expectantly. Nothing seemed different. Everything was the same. He wished suddenly for a mirror in which to study himself, but there was none.

After closing the locker behind him, he crossed the room and stepped out into the hallway.

He hadn't taken a dozen steps when a Shadowen appeared from out of the stairwell.

Coll felt his heart sink. He had no weapons, no means of protection, and no time or place in which to hide. He kept walking toward his discoverer, unable to think what else to do.

The Shadowen went by him without slowing. A brief nod, a barely perceptible lifting of the dark face, and the other was past, moving away as if nothing had happened.

Coll felt a rush of elation coupled with relief. The Shadowen hadn't recognized him! He could scarcely believe it. But there was no time to revel in his good fortune. If he was ever to escape Southwatch and Rimmer Dall, it must be now.

Down he went through the corridors and stairwells of the monolith, skirting well-lit places in favor of darker ones, knowing only one way to go but determined to be noticed as little as possible, cloak or no cloak. His hands clutched the dark folds protectively, and his eyes searched the shadows as the daylight faded to dusk. He reached the exercise yard unchallenged. Weapons and armor stood stacked in racks and hung on pegs, metal edges and fastenings glinting dully. Ulfkingroh was nowhere to be seen. Coll helped himself to a brace of long knives, which he stuffed beneath his cloak. He circled the open area for the doors that led to the outer courts. A pair of Shadowen appeared and went past in the manner of the one before, oblivious. Coll felt his muscles tighten with tension, but his confidence in the Mirrorshroud was growing.

Momentarily he considered going down into the bowels of Southwatch to discover what the Shadowen were hiding there. But the risk was too great, he decided. Better to get clear as quickly as possible. Whatever else, he must be free.

He hastened along the corridors that led to the outer courts, another of twilight's shadows. He reached the courts without challenge, passed through, and almost before he realized it stood before an outer door. He glanced around hurriedly. No one was in sight.

He released the lock, pushed the door open, and stepped out.

He stood within an alcove that sheltered him from the coming night. Beyond, the Rainbow Lake spread away in a glimmer of silver, the surrounding forests a dark, irregular mass that buzzed and hummed with life, the smell of leaves, earth, and grasses wafting sweetly on the summer air.

Coll Ohmsford took a deep breath and smiled. He was free.

He would have preferred to wait until it was completely dark, but he couldn't chance the delay. It wouldn't be long before he was missed. Crouching low against the sawgrass, he sprinted from the shadows of the wall into the trees.

From the window of a darkened room thirty feet up, Rimmer Dall watched him go.

There was never any question in Coll Ohmsford's mind as to where he would go. He worked his way through the trees that separated Southwatch from the Mermidon, chose a quiet narrows a mile or so upstream, swam the river, and began his trek toward Tyrsis and his brother. He did not know how he would find Par once he reached the city; he would worry about that later. His most immediate concern was that the Shadowen were already searching for him. They seemed to materialize within moments of his escape, black shadows that slipped through the night like wraiths at haunt, silent and spectral. But if they saw him, and he was certain they must have, the Mirrorshroud disguised him from them. They passed without slowing, without interest, disappearing as anonymously as they had come.

But so many of them!

Oddly enough, the cloak seemed to give him a heightened sense of who and where they were. He could feel their presence before he saw them, know from which direction they approached, and discern in advance how many there were. He did not try to hide from them; after all, if the cloak's magic failed, they would search him out in any case. Instead, he tried to appear as an ordinary traveler, keeping to the open grasslands, to the roads when he found them, walking easily, casually, trying not to look furtive.

Somehow it all worked. Though the Shadowen were all about, obviously hunting him, they could not seem to tell who he was.

He slept for a few hours before dawn and resumed his journey at daybreak. He thought on more than one occasion to remove the cloak, but the presence of so many of the black things kept him from doing so. Better to be safe, he told himself. After all, as long as he wore the cloak, he would not be found out.

He passed other travelers on the road as he went. None seemed interested in what they saw of him. A few offered greetings. Most simply passed him by.

He wondered how he appeared to them. He must not have seemed someone they recognized or they would have said something. He must have seemed an ordinary traveler. It made him wonder why Rimmer Dall had looked like his father in the cloak. It made him wonder why the magic acted differently toward him.

The first day passed swiftly, and he camped in a small copse of ash still within view of the Runne. The sun collapsed behind the Westland forests in a splash of red-gold, and the warm night air was scented by grassland wildflowers. He built a fire and ate wild fruit and vegetables. He had a craving for meat, but no real way to catch any. The stars came out, and the night sounds died.

Again the Shadowen appeared, hunting him. Sometimes they came close—and again he was reluctant to remove the cloak. He did so long enough to wash, careful to keep concealed within the trees, and then quickly put it back on again. He was finding it more comfortable to wear now, less constricting and less unfamiliar. He was actually growing to like the sense of invisibility it gave him.

He went on again at first light, striding out across the grasslands, fixing on the dark edges of the Dragon's Teeth where they broke the blue skyline north. Just this side of those mountains lay Tyrsis and Par. The heat of this new day seemed more intense, and he found the light uncomfortable. Perhaps he would begin traveling at night, he decided. The darkness seemed somehow less threatening. He took shelter at midday in a cluster of rocks, crouching back within their shadows, hidden. His mind wandered, scattering to things that were forgotten almost as soon as they were remembered. He hunched down, his cowled head lowered between his knees, and he slept.

Nightfall took him from his shelter. He hunted down a rabbit, spying it out in the dark and chasing it to its den as if he were a cat. He dug down to it with his hands, wrung its neck, carried it back to his rock-walled shelter, and ate it before it was finished cooking over the little fire. He sat staring at the bones afterward, wondering what creature it had been.

Stars and moon brightened in the darkening sky. Somewhere distant, an owl hooted. Coll Ohmsford no longer searched for the Shadowen that hunted him. Somehow, they no longer mattered.

When the night had settled comfortably in about him, he rose, kicked out the fire, and crept from his place of concealment like an animal. Far distant still, but growing closer, was the city. He could smell it in the wind.

There was a rage inside him that he could not explain. There was a hunger. Somehow, though he could not yet determine how, it was tied to Par.

Swiftly he passed north toward the mountains. In the moonlight his eyes glinted blood-red.

22

Nightfall.

Wren Ohmsford walked back across the Harrow through the deepening gloom, empty of feeling. Shadows layered the lava rock, cast by the bones of the ravaged trees and the shifting mists. Daylight had faded to a tinge of brightness west, a candle's slender glow against the dark. The Harrow stretched silent and lifeless all about, a mirror of herself. The magic of the Elfstones had scoured her clean. The death of Eowen had hardened her to iron.

Who am I? she asked herself.

She chose her path without really thinking about it, moving in the direction from which she had come because that was the only way she knew to go. She stared straight ahead without seeing; she listened without hearing.

Who am I?

All of her life she had known the answer to that question. The fact of it had been her one certainty. She was a Rover girl, free of the constraints of personal history, of the ties and obligations of family, and of the need to live up to anyone's expectations but her own. She had Garth to teach her what she needed to know and she could do with herself as she pleased. The future stretched away intriguingly, a blank slate on which her life could be written with any words she chose.

Now that certainty was gone, disappeared as surely as her youthful misconceptions of who and what she would be. She would never be as she had been or had thought she would be. Never. She had lost it all. And what had she gained? She almost laughed. She had become a chameleon. Just look at her; she could be anyone. She couldn't even be sure of her name. She was an Ohmsford and an Elessedil both. Choose either—it would fit. She was an Elf and a human. She was the child of several families, one who birthed her, two more who raised her.

Who am I?

She was a creature of the magic, heir to the Elfstones, keeper of the Ruhk Staff and the Loden. She bore them all, trusts she had been given to hold, responsibilities she had been empowered to manage. The magic was hers, and she hated the very thought of it. She had never asked for it, certainly never wanted it, and now could not seem to get rid of it. The magic was a shadow within, a dark reflection of herself that rose on command to do her bidding, a trickster that made her feel as nothing else could and at the same time stole away her reason and sanity and threatened to take her over completely. The magic even killed for her—enemies to be sure, but friends as well. *Eowen. Hadn't the magic killed Eowen?* She bit down against her despair. It destroyed—which was all right because that was what she expected it to do, but at the same time was all wrong because it was indiscriminate and even when it chose properly it emptied her a little further of things like compassion, tenderness, remorse, and love, the soft that balanced the hard. It burned away the complexity of her vision and left her stripped of choices.

As she was now, she realized.

A wind had come up, slow and erratic at first, now quick and rough as it gusted across the flats, causing the spines of the trees to shiver and the ravines to hum and moan. It blew across her shoulders, pushing her sideways in the manner of a thoughtless stranger in a crowd. She lowered her head against it, another distraction to be suffered, another obstacle to be overcome. The light west had disappeared, and she was cloaked in darkness. It wasn't so far to go, she told herself wearily. The others were just ahead at the Harrow's edge, waiting.

Just ahead.

She laughed. What did it matter whether they were there or not? What did any of it matter? Her life would do with her as it chose, just as it had been doing ever since she had come in search of herself. No, she corrected, longer ago than that. Forever, perhaps. She laughed again. Come in search of herself, her family, the Elves, the truth—such foolishness! She could hear the mocking sounds of her own voice as the thoughts chased after one another.

A voice that echoed in the wind.

What matter? it whispered.

What difference?

Her thoughts returned unbidden to Eowen, kind and gentle, doomed in spite of her seer's gifts, fated to be swallowed up by them. What good had it done Eowen to know her future? What good would it do any of them? What good, in fact, even to try to determine it? Useless, she raged, because in the end it would do with you what it chose in any case. It would make you what it wished, take you where it willed, and leave you in its own good time.

All about her, the wind voice howled. *Let go!*

She heard it, nodded in recognition, and began to cry. The words caressed her like a mother's hands, and she welcomed their touch. Everything seemed to be fading away. She was walking—where? She didn't stop, didn't pause to wonder, but simply kept moving because movement helped, taking her away from the hurt, the anguish. She had something to do—what? She shook her head, unable to determine, and brushed at her tears with the back of her hand.

The hand that held the Elfstones.

She looked down at it wonderingly, surprised to discover the Stones were still there. The magic pulsed within her fist, within the fingers tightly wrapped about, its blue glow seeping through the cracks, spilling out into the dark. Why was it doing that? She stared blankly, vaguely aware that something was wrong. Why did it burn so?

Let go, the wind voice whispered.

I want to! she howled in the silence of her mind.

She slowed, looking up from the pathway her feet had been following, from the emptiness of the ground. The Harrow had taken on a different cast, one of brightness and warmth. There were faces all about, strangely alive against the haze, filled with understanding of her need. The faces were familiar, of friends and family, of all those who had loved and supported her, living and dead, come out of her imagination into life. She was surprised when they appeared, but pleased as well. She spoke to them, a word or two, tentative, curious. They glanced her way and whispered in reply.

Let go.

Let go.

The words repeated insistently in her mind, a glimmer of hope. She slowed and finally stopped, no longer knowing where she was and no longer caring. She was so tired. Her life was a shambles. She could not even pretend that she had any control over it. It rode her as a rider would a horse, but without pause or rest, without destination, endlessly into night.

Let go.

She blinked, then smiled. Understanding flooded through her. Of course. So simple, really. Let go of the magic. Let go, and the weariness and confusion and sense of loss would pass. Let go, and she would have a chance to start over again, to regain possession of her life, to return to who and what she had been. Why hadn't she seen it before?

Something tugged at her in warning, some part of her deep within that had become buried in the sound of the wind's voice. Curious, she tried to uncover it, but feathery touches on her skin distracted her. There was a burning against the skin of her palm from the Elfstones, but she ignored it. The touches were more intriguing, more inviting. She lifted her face to find their source. The faces were all about her now, milling at the edge of the darkness and the mist, taking on form. She knew them, didn't she? Why couldn't she remember?

Let go.

She cocked the hand that grasped the Elfstones in response, barely conscious of the act, and a sliver of blue light escaped the cracks of her fingers, lancing into the dark. Instantly the faces were gone. She blinked in confusion. What was she doing? Why had she stopped walking? She glanced about in alarm, seeing the darkness and the mist of the Harrow, realizing she was lost somewhere within, that she had strayed. The Drakuls were there, watching. She could feel their presence. She swallowed against her fear. What had she been thinking?

She started moving again, trying to sort out what had happened. She was dimly aware that for a time she had lost track of everything, that she must have wandered aimlessly. She remembered bits and pieces of her thoughts, like the fragments of dreams on waking. She had been about to do something, she thought worriedly. But what?

The minutes passed. Far ahead, lost in the howl of the wind, she heard the call of her name. It was there, hanging momentarily in a lull, then gone. She moved toward it, wondering if she was still going in the right direction. If she was unable to determine so soon, she would have to use the Elfstones. The thought was anathema. She never wanted to use them again. All she could see in her mind's eye was their fire exploding into the monster that had once been Eowen and turning her to ash.

Again she began to cry and again quickly stopped herself. There was no use in it, no point. Leafless trees and fire-washed lava rock spread away from her, an endless, changeless expanse. The Harrow seemed to go on forever. She was lost, she decided, become turned about somehow. She stopped and glanced around wearily. Exhaustion flooded through her, and in anguish and despair she closed her eyes.

The wind whispered. *Let go.*

Yes, she replied silently, *I want to.*

The spell of the words folded about her like a warm cloak, wrapped her and held her close. She resisted but a moment, then gave herself over to it. When she opened her eyes, the faces were back again, surrounding her in a circle of faint light and feathery touches. She saw that she was at the edge of a ravine—a familiar place, it seemed. Once again, everything began to fade. She forgot that she was trying to escape the Harrow, that the faces about her were something other than what they appeared to be. The haze of the mist crept into her mind and settled there, thick and murky. Her ice-bound thoughts melted and ran like liquid through her body; she could feel their cold. She was so tired, so weary of everything.

Let go.

The hand that clutched the Elfstones lowered, and the faces clustered about her began to take on shape and size. Lips brushed her throat.

Let go.

She let her eyes close again. Her fingers loosened. It would all be so easy. Let the Elfstones fall, and she would escape the magic's chain forever.

"Lady Wren!"

The shout was an anguished howl, and for a moment's time it didn't register. Then her eyes snapped open, and her body tensed. The strange sleep that had almost claimed her hovered close, a whisper of insistent need. Through its fog, beyond its pall, she saw two figures crouched at the edge of the light. They held swords in their hands, the metal glinting faintly.

"Phffft! Don't move, Wren of the Elves!" she heard another cry out in warning. Stresa.

"Stay where you are, Lady Wren," the first cautioned frantically. Triss.

The Captain of the Home Guard inched forward, his weapon held before him. She saw his face now, lean and hard, filled with determination. Behind him was Garth, a larger form, darker, inscrutable. Leading them both, spines bristling, was the Splinterscat.

A cold place opened in the pit of her stomach. What were they doing here? What had happened to bring them? She felt a surge of fear strike her, a sense that something was about to happen and she had not even been aware of it.

She forced back the lassitude, the calm, and the whisper of the wind and made herself see again. The cold turned to ice. The light surrounding her emanated from the things that clustered close. Drakuls, all about. They were so close she could feel their breath—or seem to. She could see their dead eyes, their gaunt, nearly featureless faces, and their ivory fangs. There were dozens of them, pressed about her, parted only at the point where Triss and Garth and Stresa sought to approach, a window into the dark of the Harrow. Their hands and fingers clutched her, held her fast, bound her in ropes of hunger. They had lured her to them, lulled her almost to slumber as they must have done Eowen. Turned from phantoms to things of substance, they were about to feed.

For an instant Wren hung suspended between being and nonbeing, between life and death. She could feel the draw of two choices, very different, each compelling. One would have her break free of the soothing, deadly bonds that held her, would have her rise up in revulsion and fury and fight for her life because that was what her instincts told her she must do. The other would have her do as the wind voice had whispered and simply let go because that was the only way she would ever be free of the magic. Time froze. She weighed the possibilities as if detached from them, a judging that seemed to bring into focus the whole of her existence, past, present, and future. She could see her rescuers creep nearer, their gestures unmistakable. She could feel the Drakuls draw a fraction of an inch closer. Neither seemed to matter. Each was a distant, slow-moving reality that could change in the blink of an eye.

Then fangs brushed her throat—a whisper of hunger and need.

Drakuls.

Shadowen.

Elves.

An evolution of horror—and only she knew.

If I do not escape Morrowindl and return to the Four Lands, who else will ever know?

"Lady Wren!" Triss called softly to her, his voice pleading, desperate, angry and lost.

She stepped back from the precipice and took a long, deep breath. She could feel the strength of her body return, a rising up out of lethargy. But she would still be too slow. She flexed gently, almost imperceptibly, seeking to discover if she could move, testing the limits of her freedom. There were none; the hands that secured her held her so fast that she might as soon have been chained to the earth.

One chance, then. One hope. Her mind focused, hard and insistent, reaching deep within. Her fingers slipped open.

Now.

Blue fire exploded into the night, racing up her body to sheathe her in flames. The fangs jerked back, the hands fell away, the Drakuls shrieked in fury, and she was free. She stood within a cylinder of fire, the magic's heat racing over her, wrapping her about as she waited for the pain to begin, anticipated what it would feel like to be burned to ash. *Better that than to become one of them,* the thought flashed through her mind, the corner of her life's need turned and become a certainty she would not question again. *Just let it be quick!*

The fire pillared over her, rising up against the black, searing the curtain of the vog. The Drakuls flung themselves into the flames, desperately trying to reach her, moths bereft of reason. They died in sudden bursts of light, incinerated as quick as thought. Wren watched them come at her, reach for her, become entangled in the fire and disappear. Her eyes snapped open seeking the Elfstones. She found them in the cup of her open hand, white with magic, as brilliant as small suns.

Yet she did not burn. The fire raged about her, swallowed her attackers, and left her untouched.

Oh, yes!

Now the exhilaration began, the sense of power that the magic always gave her. She felt invincible, indestructible. The fire could not hurt her, would not—and she must have known as much. She flung her hands out, carrying the fire away from her in a sweep, into the maelstrom of Drakuls that circled about her. They were engulfed and consumed, shrieking in despair. *For you, Eowen!* She watched them perish and felt nothing beyond the joy that use of the magic gave her, the Drakuls reduced to things of no consequence, as insignificant to her as dust. She embraced the magic's power and let it carry her beyond reason, beyond thought.

Use it, she told herself. *Nothing else matters.*

For an instant, she was lost completely. Forgotten were Triss and Garth, the need to escape Morrowindl and return to the Four Lands, the truths she had learned and planned to tell, the history of who and what she was, and the lives that had been given into her trust, everything. Forgotten was any purpose beyond the wielding of the Elfstones.

Then some small, ragged corner of her conscience reclaimed her once again, a whisper of sanity that reached past the mix of fear and exhaustion and despair that threatened to turn determination to madness. She saw Triss and Garth and Stresa as they fought the Drakuls turning now on them, back to back as the circle closed. She heard their cries to her and heard the voice within herself that echoed in reply. She sensed the island of self on which she had retreated beginning to sink into the fire.

Down came the hand with the Elfstones, the pillar of flames dying to a flare of light that curled about her hand, brought under control once more. She saw the darkness and the mist again, the ragged slopes of the ravine, the lava rock, jagged and black. She smelled the night, the ash and fire and heat. She wheeled toward the Drakuls and hissed at them as a snake might. They backed away in fear. She moved toward her friends, and the attackers that ringed them fell away. She carried death in her hand, certain annihilation for things who understood all too well what annihilation meant. They shimmered about her, losing substance. She stalked into their midst, unafraid, swinging the light of her magic this way and that, threatening, menacing, alive with deadly promise. The Drakuls did not challenge; in an instant they faded and were gone.

She came then to where Garth and Triss stood crouched, weapons in hand, uncertainty in their eyes. She stopped before Stresa, who stared up at her as if she were a thing beyond comprehension. She closed her fingers tight about the Elfstones, and the fire winked out.

"Help me walk from the ravine," she whispered, so weary she was in danger of collapse, knowing she could not, realizing that the Drakuls still watched.

Triss had his arm about her instantly. "Lady, we thought you lost," he said as he turned her gently about.

"I was," she answered, her smile tight.

Slowly, a step at a time, eyes sweeping the island night, they began to climb.

It took them until midnight to get clear of the Harrow. The Drakuls had drawn Wren deep into their lair, far from the pathway she had thought to follow, turning her about so completely after discovering Eowen that she had ended up wandering across the flats in the wrong direction. Stresa had managed to track her, but it hadn't been easy. They had come in search of her at nightfall, despite her command that they were not to do so, worried by then because she had been gone so long, determined to make certain that she was safe, even at the risk of their own lives. They knew they had no effective protection against the Drakuls, but that no longer mattered. Both Garth and Triss were decided. Dal was left to keep watch over Gavilan and the Ruhk Staff. Stresa had come because no one else could find Wren's trail in the dark. They might not have found her even then if the Drakuls hadn't been so preoccupied with their quarry. Even a handful of the wraiths would have been enough to disrupt the rescue effort. But Wren, bearer of the Elfstone magic, was a lure for the Drakuls, and all had joined in the hunt, anxious to share in the feeding, Shadowen to the end. Stresa had been able to track her unhindered. They had found her, it seemed, just in time.

Wren told them in turn of Eowen's fate, of how the Drakuls had subverted her, of how she had been made one of them. She described the seer's death, unwilling to gloss past it, needing to hear the words, to give voice to her grief. It felt as if she were speaking from some hollow place within, wrapped in a haze of emptiness and exhaustion. She was so tired.

Yet she would not slow; she would not rest. She disdained all help once clear of the ravine. She walked because she would not let herself be carried, because that would be another demonstration of weakness and she had shown weakness enough for one night. She was dismayed by what had happened to her, appalled at how easily she had been misled by the wind voice, how close she had come to dying, and how willing she had been to allow it to happen—Wren Elessedil, called Queen of the Elves, bearer of the trust of a people, heir of so much magic. She could still remember how inviting the wind voice had made it seem for her to give up her life. She had been so ready, welcoming the peace she had supposed she would find. All of her life she had been strong in the face of death, never giving way to the possibility of it finding her, always certain that she would fight for her last breath. What had happened in the Harrow had shaken her confidence more than she cared to admit. She had failed to resist as she had always told herself she would. She had let exhaustion and despair work through her so thoroughly that she was as hollowed out as wormwood and as quick to crumble. She saw the way the magic pulled her, first one way, then the other, the Drakul's, her own. Just as Eowen had been a prisoner of her visions, so Wren was now becoming a prisoner of the Elven magic. She hated herself for it. She despised what she had become.

I am nothing of what I believed, she thought in despair. *I am a lie.*

She talked to keep from thinking of it, speaking of what she had seen as she wandered the Harrow, of how the wind voice of the Drakuls had lulled her, of how Eowen—so vulnerable to visions and images—must have become ensnared. She rambled at times, the sound of her voice helping to distract her from dark thoughts, keeping her awake, keeping her moving. She thought of the dead on this nightmare journey, of Ellenroh and Eowen in particular. She was consumed by their loss, ravaged by feelings of helplessness at having been unable to save them and by guilt at being inadequate for the task they had left her. She clutched the Elfstones tightly in her hand, unable to persuade herself to put them away, frightened that the Drakuls would come again. They did not. Not even the wind voice whispered in the darkness now, gone back into the earth, leaving her alone. She gazed out into the black and felt it a mirror of the void within. She was heartsick for what she had become and what she feared she yet might be. The world was a place she no longer understood. She could not even decide which was the greater evil—the monsters or the monster makers. Shadowen or Elves—which should bear the blame? Where was the balance to life that should come from lessons learned and experience gained? Where was the sense that the madness would pass, that a purpose would be revealed for everything that was happening? She had no answers. The magic had caught them all up in a whirlwind, and it would drop them where it chose.

This night, it picked a darker hole than she would have imagined could exist. They came off the Harrow bone weary and numb, relieved to be clear, anxious to be gone. They would rest until dawn, then continue on.

The greater part of Blackledge was behind them now, left in the shadow of Killeshan's vog. Ahead, between themselves and the beaches, there was only the In Ju. They would pass through the jungle quickly, two days if they hurried, and reach the shores of the Blue Divide in two more. Quick, now, they urged themselves silently. Quick, and get free.

They reached the spot where their companions had been left, a clearing within a cluster of lava rocks in the shadow of a fringe of barren vines and famished scrub. Faun raced through the darkness, come out of hiding from some distance off, chittering wildly, springing to Wren's shoulder and hunkering there as if no other haven existed. Wren's hands came up reassuringly. The Tree Squeak was shivering with fear.

They found Dal then, sprawled at the clearing's far edge, a lifeless tangle of arms and legs, his skull split wide. Triss bent close and turned the Elven Hunter over.

He looked up, stunned. Dal's weapons were still sheathed.

Wren glanced away in despair, a dark certainty already taking hold. She didn't have to look further to know that Gavilan Elessedil and the Ruhk Staff were gone.

23

Par Ohmsford crouched in the shadow of the building wall, as dark as the night about him within the covering of his cloak, listening to the sounds of Tyrsis as she stirred restlessly beneath her blanket of summer heat, waiting for morning. The air was still and filled with the city's smells, sweet, sticky, and cloying. Par breathed it in reluctantly, wearily, peering out from his shelter into the pools of light cast by the street lamps, watchful for things that didn't belong, that crept and hunted, that searched relentlessly.

The Federation.

The Shadowen.

They were both out there, stalkers that never seemed to sleep and that refused to quit. For almost a week now Damson and he had been running from them, ever since they had fled the Mole's underground hideout and made their way back through the sewers of the city to the streets. A week. He could barely sort through the debris of its passing, his memory in fragments, a jumble of buildings and rooms, of closets and crawlways, and of one concealment after another. They had not been able to rest anywhere for more than a few hours, always discovered somehow just when they had thought themselves safe, forced to run again, to flee the dark things that sought to claim them.

How was it, Par wondered for what must have been the thousandth time, that they were always found so quickly?

At first he had attributed it to luck. But luck would only take you so far, and the regularity of their discovery had soon ruled out any possibility that it was luck alone. Then he had thought that it might be his magic, traced somehow by Rimmer Dall—for it was the Seekers that came most often, sometimes in Federation guise, but more often revealed as the monsters they were, dark shadows cloaked and hooded. But he hadn't used his magic since they had escaped the sewers, and if he hadn't used it, how could it be traced?

"They have infiltrated the Movement," Damson had declared, tight-lipped and wan before leaving him only hours earlier to search anew for a hiding place about which their pursuers did not know. "Or they have caught one of us and extracted all of our secrets. There is no other explanation."

But even she had been forced to admit that no one other than Padishar Creel knew all the hiding places she used. No one else could have betrayed them.

Which led, in turn, to the disquieting possibility that despite their hopes to the contrary, the fall of the Jut had yielded the Federation the catch it had been so anxious to make.

Par let his head fall back to rest against the rough, heated stone, his eyes closing momentarily in despair. Coll dead. Padishar and Morgan missing. Wren and Walker Boh. Steff and Teel. The company. Even the Mole—there had been no word of him since they had fled his subterranean chambers. There was no sign of him, nothing to reveal what had happened. It was maddening. Everyone he had started out with weeks ago—his brother, his cousin, his uncle, and his friends—had disappeared. It sometimes seemed as if everyone he came in contact with was doomed to fall off the face of the earth, to be swallowed by some netherworld blackness and never resurface again.

Even Damson . . .

No. His eyes snapped open again, anger reflected in the glimmer from the lamps. *Not Damson. He would not lose her. It would not happen again.*

But how much longer could they keep running like this? How long before their enemies finally ran them to earth?

There was sudden movement at the corner of the wall ahead where it turned the building to follow the street west toward the bluff, and Damson appeared. She scurried through the shadows in a crouch and came up next to him, breathless and flushed.

"Two other safe holes are discovered," she said. "I could smell the stench of the things that watch for us even before I saw them." Her long red hair was tangled and damp against her face and neck, tied back by a cloth band about her forehead. Her smile, when it came, was unexpected. "But I found one they missed."

Her hand reached out to brush his cheek. "You look so tired, Par. Tonight you will sleep well. This place—I remembered it, actually. A cellar beneath an old gristmill that was once something else, I forget what. It hasn't been used in more than a year—not by anyone. Once, Padishar and I . . ." She stopped, the memory retrieved at the verge of its telling and drawn back again—too painful, her eyes said, to relate. "They will not know of this one. Come with me, Valeman. We'll try again."

They hurried off into the night, twin shadows that appeared and faded again as quick as the blink of an eye. Par felt the weight of the Sword of Shannara against his back, flat and hard, its presence a reminder of the travesty his quest had become and of the confusions that plagued him. Was this, in fact, the ancient talisman he had been sent to find, or some trick of Rimmer Dall's meant to bring him to his destruction? If it was the Sword, why had he not been able to make it work when face to face with the First Seeker? If it was a fake, what had become of the real Sword?

But the questions, as always, yielded no answers, only further questions, and as always, he quickly abandoned them. Survival was all that counted for the moment, evasion of the black things and, more important, escape from the city. For their flight had been that of rats in a maze, trapped behind walls from which they could not break free. All efforts at getting clear of Tyrsis to regain the open country beyond had been thwarted. The gates were carefully watched, all the exits guarded, and Damson lacked sufficient skill, in the absence of the Mole, to navigate the tunnels beneath the city that provided the only other means of escape. So there was nothing left for them but to continue to run and hide, to scurry from one hole to the next, and to wait for an opportunity to arise or a means to present itself that would at last set them free.

They turned down a side street dappled with shards of light cast through the slats of shutters closed against windows high on a back wall, hearing laughter and the clink of drinking glasses from the alehouse within. Garbage littered the street, damp and stinking. Tyrsis wore her cheapest perfume in this quarter, and the smell of her body was rank and shameless where the poor and the homeless had been crowded away by the occupiers. Once a proud lady, she was used up and cast off now, a chattel to be treated as the Federation wished, a spoil of a war that had been over before it had begun.

Damson paused, searched carefully the empty swath of a lighted crossing, listened momentarily for sounds that didn't belong, then took him swiftly across. They passed down a second side street, this one as silent and musty as an unopened closet, then through an alcove and into an alley that connected to another street. Par was thinking of the Sword of Shannara again, wondering how he could discover if it was real and what test he could put it to that would determine the truth.

"Here," Damson whispered, turning him abruptly through the broken opening of an ancient board wall.

They stood in a barnlike room thick with gloom, the rafters overhead barely visible in the faint light of other buildings where it seeped through cracks in the split, dry boards of the walls. Machines hunkered down like animals crouched to spring, and rows of bins yawned empty and black. Damson steered him across the room, their boots crunching on stone and straw in the deep silence. Close to the back wall she stopped, reached down, seized an iron ring embedded in the floor, and pulled free a trapdoor. A glimmer of light showed stairs leading down into blackness.

"You first," she ordered, motioning. "Just inside, then stop."

He did as he was told, listened to the sound of her footsteps as she followed, then of the trapdoor as it closed behind them. They stood listening for a moment, then she pushed carefully past and fumbled quietly in the dark. A spark struck, a flame appeared, and the pitch of a torch caught and began to burn. Light filled the chamber in which they stood, weak and hazy, revealing a low cellar filled with old iron-banded casks and disintegrating crates. She gestured for him to follow, and they moved ahead through the debris. The cellar stretched on for a time, then ended at a passageway. Damson bent low against the black, thrust the torch ahead of her, and entered. The passage took them down a series of intersecting corridors to a room that had once been a sleeping chamber. A worn bed was positioned against one wall, a table and chairs against another. A second passage led out the other side and back into blackness. Where the torchlight ended, Par could just make out the beginning of a set of ancient stairs.

"We should be safe here for tonight, maybe longer," she advised, turning now so that the light caught her features, the bright gleam of her green eyes, the softness of her smile. "It's not much, is it?"

"If it's safe, it's everything," he replied, smiling back. "Where do the stairs lead?"

"Back to the street. But the door is locked from the outside. We would have to break it down if we needed to escape that way, if we were unable to use the cellar entry. Still, that's at least a measure of protection against being trapped. And no one will think to look where the lock is old and rusted and still in place."

He nodded, took the torch from her hand, looked about momentarily, then carried it to a ruined lamp bracket and jammed it in place. "Home it is," he declared, unslinging the Sword of Shannara and leaning it against the bed. His eyes lingered momentarily on the crest graven in its hilt, the upraised hand with its burning torch. Then he turned away. "Anything to eat in the cupboard?"

She laughed. "Hardly." Impulsively she went to him, put her arms about his waist, held him momentarily, then kissed his cheek. "Par Ohmsford." She spoke his name softly.

He hugged her, stroked her hair, felt the warmth of her seep through him. "I know," he whispered.

"It will be all right for you and me."

He nodded without speaking, determined that it would be, that it must.

"I have some fresh cheese and bread in my pack," she said, pulling away. "And some ale. Good enough for refugees like us."

They ate in silence, listening to the muffled tick of cooling iron nails embedded in the building's walls, tightening as the night grew deeper. Once or twice there were voices, so distant the words were indistinguishable, carried from the street through the padlocked door and down the ancient stairs. When they had finished, they carefully packed away what was left, extinguished the torch, wrapped themselves in their blankets, lay close together on the narrow bed, and quickly fell asleep.

Daybreak brought a glimmer of light creeping through cracks and crevices, cool and hazy, and the sounds of the city grew loud and distinct as people began to venture forth on a new day's business. Par woke refreshed for the first time in a week, wishing he had water in which to wash, but grateful simply to be shed momentarily of his weariness. Damson was bright-eyed and lovely to look upon, tousled and at the same time perfectly ordered, and Par felt as if the worst might at last be behind them.

"The first order of business is to find a way out of the city," Damson declared between bites of her breakfast, seated across from him at the little table. Her forehead was lined with determination. "We can't go on like this."

"I wish we could find out something about the Mole."

She nodded, her eyes shifting away. "I've looked for him when I've been out." She shook her head. "The Mole is resourceful. He has stayed alive a long time."

Not with the Shadowen hunting for him, Par almost said, then thought better of it. Damson would be thinking the same thing anyway. "What do I do today?"

She looked back at him. "Same as always. You stay put. They still don't know about me. They only know about you."

"You hope."

She sighed. "I hope. Anyway, I have to find a way for us to get past the walls, out of Tyrsis to where we can discover what's happened to Padishar and the others."

He folded his arms across his chest and leaned back. "I feel useless just sitting around here."

"Sometimes waiting is what works best, Par."

"And I don't like letting you go out alone."

She smiled. "And I don't like leaving you here by yourself. But that's the way it has to be for now. We have to be smart about this."

She pulled on her street cloak, her magician's garb, for she still appeared regularly in the marketplace to do tricks for the children, keeping up the appearance that everything was the same as always. A pale shaft of light penetrated the gloom of the passageways that had brought them, and with a wave back to him she disappeared into it and was gone.

He spent the remainder of the morning being restless, prowling the narrow confines of his shelter. Once, he climbed to the top of the stairs leading back to the street where he tested the lock that fastened the heavy wooden door and found it secure. He wandered back through the tunnels that branched from the gristmill cellar and discovered that each dead-ended at a storage hold or bin, all long empty and abandoned. When noon came, he took his lunch from the remains of yesterday's foodstuffs, still cached in Damson's backpack, then stretched out on the bed to nap and fell into a deep sleep.

When he finally woke, the light had gone silver, and the day was fading rapidly into dusk. He lay blinking sleepily for a moment, then realized that Damson had not returned. She had been gone almost ten hours. He rose quickly, worried now, thinking that she should have been back long ago. It was possible that she had come in and gone out again, but not likely. She would have woken him. He would have woken himself. He frowned darkly, uneasily, twisted his body from side to side to ease the kinks, and wondered what to do.

Hungry, in spite of his concern, he decided to eat something, and finished off the last of the cheese and bread. There was a little ale in the stoppered skin, but it tasted stale and warm.

Where was Damson?

Par Ohmsford had known the risks from the beginning, the dangers that Damson Rhee faced every time she left him and went out into the city. If the Mole was captured, they would make him talk. If the safe holes were compromised, she might be, too. If Padishar was taken, there were no secrets left. He knew the risks; he had told himself he had accepted them. But faced for the first time since escaping from the sewers that the worst had happened, he found he was not prepared after all. He found that he was terrified.

Damson. If anything had happened to her . . .

A scuffing sound caught his attention, and he left the thought unfinished. He started, then wheeled about, searching for the source of the noise. It was behind him, at the top of the stairs, at the door leading to the street.

Someone was playing with the lock.

At first he thought it must be Damson, forced for some reason to try to enter through the back. But Damson did not have a key. And the sound he was hearing was of a key scraping in the lock. The fumbling continued, ending in a sharp *snick* as the lock released.

Par reached down for the Sword of Shannara and strapped it quickly across his back. Whoever was up there, it was not Damson. He snatched up the backpack, thinking to hide any trace of his being there. But his bootprints were everywhere, the bed was mussed, and small crumbs of food littered the table. Besides, there was no time. The intruder had lifted the lock from its hasp and was opening the door.

Daylight flooded through the opening, an oblique shaft of wan gray. Par backed hastily from the room into the tunnels. He left the torch. He no longer needed it to find his way. The morning's explorations had left him with a clear vision of which way to go, even in the near dark. Boots thudded softly on the wooden steps, too heavy and rough to be Damson's.

He went down the tunnel in a noiseless crouch. Whoever had entered would know he had been there, but would not know how long ago. They would wait for him to return, thinking to catch him unprepared. Or Damson. But he could wait for Damson somewhere close to the entrance to the old mill and warn her before she entered. Damson would never come through the back entrance with the lock sprung. His thoughts raced through his mind in rapid succession, propelling him on through the darkness, silent and swift. All he had to do was escape detection, to get back through the cellar and out the door to the street.

He could no longer hear footsteps. Good. The intruder had stopped to view the room, was wondering who had been there, how many of them there had been, and why they had come. More time for Par to get away, a better chance for him to escape.

But when he reached the cellar, he moved too quickly toward the stairs leading up and stumbled into an empty wooden crate, tripped, and fell. The rotting wood cracked and splintered beneath him, the sound reverberating sharply through the silence.

As he pulled himself back to his feet, furious, breathless, he could hear the sound of footsteps coming toward him.

He broke for the stairs, no longer bothering to hide his flight. The footsteps gave chase. Not Shadowen, he thought—they would be silent in their coming. Federation, then. But only one. Why just one?

He gained the stairs and scrambled up. The trapdoor was a faint silhouette above. He wondered suddenly if others might be waiting above, if he was being driven into a trap. Should he stand his ground and face the one rather than allow himself to be herded toward the others? But it was all speculation, and besides there wasn't time left to decide. He was already at the trapdoor.

He shoved upward against it. The trapdoor did not move.

Shafts of fading daylight found their way through gaps in the heavy wooden boards and danced off his sweat-streaked face, momentarily blinding him. Lowering his head, he shoved upward a second time. The door was solidly in place. He squinted past the light, trying to see what had happened.

Something large and bulky was sitting atop the front edge of the trapdoor.

In desperation, he threw himself against the barrier, but it refused to budge. He backed down the steps, casting a quick glance over his shoulder. His heart was beating so loudly in his ears he could barely manage to hear the muffled voice that called his name.

"Par? Par Ohmsford?"

A man, someone he knew it seemed, but he wasn't sure. The voice was familiar and strange all at once. The speaker was still back in the tunnels, lost in the darkness. The gristmill cellar stretched low and tight to the dark opening, dust motes dancing on the air in the gloom, a haze that turned everything to shadow. Par looked at the trapdoor once more, then back again at the cellar.

He was trapped.

The line of his mouth tightened. Sweat was running down his body in the wake of his exertion and fear, and his skin was crawling.

Who was back there?

Who was it who would know his name?

He thought again of Damson, wondering where she was, what had become of her, whether she was safe. If she had been taken, then he was the only one left she could depend upon. He could not let himself be captured because then there would be no one to help her. Or him. Damson. He saw her flaming red hair, the quirk of her mouth as she smiled at him, and the brightness of her green eyes. He could hear her voice, her laughter. He could feel her touching him. He remembered how she had worked to save his life, to keep him from the madness that had claimed him when Coll had died.

The feelings he experienced in that instant were overwhelming, so intense he almost cried them out.

Anger and determination replaced his fear. He reached back and started to draw free the Sword of Shannara, then let it slip back into its sheath. The Sword was meant for other things. He would use his magic, use it even though it frightened him now, an old friend who had turned unexpectedly strange and unfamiliar. The magic was unreliable, quixotic, and dangerous.

And of questionable use, he realized suddenly, if what he faced was human.

His thoughts scattered, leaving him bereft of hope. He reached back a second time and pulled free the Sword. It was his only weapon after all.

A shadow appeared at the mouth of the tunnel, breath hissing softly in the sudden silence, a cloaked form, dark and featureless in the failing light. A man, it looked, taller than Par and broader as well.

The man stepped clear of the dark and straightened. He started forward and then abruptly stopped, seeing Par crouched on the cellar stairs, weapon in hand. The long knife in his own hand glinted dully. For an instant they faced each other without moving, each trying to identify the other.

Then the intruder's hands reached up slowly and slid back the hood of his dusty black cloak.

24

Triss straightened, his movements leaden and stiff. They stared wordlessly at one another, the Captain of the Home Guard, Wren, and Garth, faceless in Morrowindl's vog-shrouded night. They stood like statues about the crumpled form of Dal, as if sentinels set at watch, frozen in time. They were all that remained of the company of nine who had set out from beneath Killeshan's shadow to bear Arborlon and the Elves from their volcanic grave to life anew within the forests of the Westland. Three, Wren emphasized through her anguish, for Gavilan was lost to them as surely as her own innocence.

How could she have been so stupid?

Triss shifted abruptly, breaking his bonds. He walked away, bent down to examine the earth, stood again, and shook his head. "What could have done this? There must be tracks . . ." He trailed off.

Wren and Garth exchanged glances. Triss still didn't understand. "It was Gavilan," she said softly.

"Gavilan?" The Captain of the Home Guard turned. He stared at her blankly.

"Gavilan Elessedil," she repeated, speaking his full name, hoping that the saying of it would make what had happened real for her. Against her shoulder, Faun still shivered. "He's killed Dal and taken the Ruhk Staff."

Triss did not move. "No," he said at once. "Lady Wren, that could not happen. You are wrong. Gavilan is an Elf, and no Elf would harm another. Besides, he is a prince of the Elessedil blood! He is sworn to serve his people!"

Wren shook her head in despair. She should have seen it coming. She should have read it in his eyes, his voice, his changing behavior. It was there, and she had simply refused to recognize it. "Stresa," she called.

The Splinterscat lumbered up from out of the dark, spines prickling belligerently. "Hsssttt! I warned you about him!"

"Thank you for reminding me. Just tell me what the signs say. Your eyes are sharpest, your nose better able to measure. Read them for me, please."

Her words were gentle and filled with pain. The Splinterscat saw and edged quietly away. They watched as he began to skirt the clearing, sniffing, scanning, pausing frequently, then continuing on.

"He could not have done this," Triss murmured anew, the words hard-edged with disbelief. Wren did not reply. She looked away at nothing. The Harrow was a gray screen behind them, the In Ju a black hole ahead. Killeshan was a distant rumble. Morrowindl hunched over them like an animal with a bone.

Then Stresa was back. "Nothing—phhhfft—has passed through the place we stand in the last few hours except us. Sssttt. Our tracks come out from the Harrow, go in, then come out again—over there. Just us—no monsters, no intruders, nothing." He paused. "There." He swiveled in the opposite direction. "A newer set of tracks depart, west, toward the In Ju. His scent. I'm sorry, Wren Elessedil."

She nodded, her own last vestige of hope shredded. She looked pointedly at Triss.

"Why?" he asked, a worn and defeated whisper.

Because he was terrified, she thought. Because he was a creature of order and comfort, of walls and safe havens, and this was all too much for him, too overwhelming. Because he thought them all dead and was afraid that he would die too if he didn't run. Or because he was greedy and desperate and wanted the power of the Ruhk Staff and its magic for himself.

"I don't know," she said wearily.

"But Dal . . . ?"

"What difference does it make?" she interrupted, more angry than she should have been, regretting her harshness immediately. She took a deep breath. "What matters is that he has taken the Ruhk Staff and the Loden, and we have to get them back. We have to find him. Quickly."

She turned. "Stresa?"

"No," the Splinterscat said at once. "Hssstt. It is too dangerous to track at night. Stay here until daybreak."

She shook her head deliberately. "We don't have that much time."

"Rrrwwll Wren Elessedil. We had best find it then, if we want to stay alive!" Stresa's rough voice deepened to a growl. "Only a fool would venture down off the Blackledge and into the In Ju at night."

Wren felt her anger building. She did not care to be challenged just now. She could not permit it. "I have the Elfstones, Stresa!" she snapped. "The Elven magic will protect us!"

"The Elven magic you—hssstt—are so anxious not to use?" Stresa's words were a taunt. "Phhffft. I know you cared for him, but . . ."

"Stresa!" she screamed.

". . . the magic will not protect against what you cannot see," the other finished, calm, unruffled. "Ssstttpp! We must wait until morning."

The silence was immense. Inside, Wren could hear herself shriek. She looked up as Garth stepped in front of her. *Remember your training, Wren. Remember who you are.*

What she could remember at the moment was the look she had seen in Gavilan Elessedil's eyes when she had given him the Ruhk Staff. She met Garth's gaze squarely. What she saw in his eyes stayed her anger. Reluctantly she nodded. "We'll wait until morning."

She kept watch then while the others slept, her own exhaustion forgotten, buried in her anger and despair over Gavilan. She could not sleep while feeling so unsettled, her mind racing and her emotions in disarray. She sat alone with her back against a stand of rocks while the men curled up in sleep a dozen feet away and Stresa hunkered down at the clearing's edge, perhaps asleep, perhaps not. She stared into blackness, stroking Faun absently, thinking thoughts darker than the night.

Gavilan. He had been so charming, so comfortable when she had met him. She had liked him—perhaps more than liked him. She had harbored expectations for them that even now she could not bring herself to admit. He had promised to be a friend to her, to look after her, to give her what answers he could to the questions she asked, and to be there when she needed him. He had promised so much. Perhaps he could have kept those promises if they had not been forced to leave the protection of the Keel. For she had not been mistaken in assessing Gavilan's weakness; he was not strong enough for what lay beyond the safety of Arborlon's walls. The changes in him had been apparent almost immediately. His charm had faded into worry, then edginess, and finally fear. He had lost the only world he had ever known and been left naked and unprotected in a waking nightmare. Gavilan had been as brave as he could manage, but everything he had known and relied upon had been stripped away. When the queen had died and the Staff had been entrusted to Wren, it had just been too much. He had counted himself the queen's logical successor, and with the power of the Elven magic he still believed he could accomplish anything. He was committed to it; he had made it his cause. He was convinced that he could save the Elves, that he was destined to do so, that the magic would give him the means.

Let me have the Staff, she could still hear him plead.

And she had foolishly given it to him.

Tears came to her eyes. He probably panicked, she thought. He probably decided that she was dead, that they were all dead, and that he was alone. He tried to leave, and Dal stopped him, telling him, no, wait, underestimating the depth of his fear, his madness. He would have heard the sounds of the Drakuls, the whispers, and the lures. They would have affected him. He killed Dal then because . . .

No! She was crying, unable to stop. She let herself, furious that she should try to make excuses for him. But it hurt so to admit the truth, harsh and unavoidable—that he had been weak, that he had been greedy, that he had rationalized instead of reasoned, and that he had killed a man who was there to protect him. Stupid! Such madness! But the stupidity and the madness were everywhere, all about them, a mire as vast and impenetrable as Eden's Murk. Morrowindl fostered it, succored it within each of them, and for each there was a threshold of endurance that once crossed signaled an end to sanity. Gavilan had crossed that threshold, unable to help himself perhaps, and now he was gone, faded into mist. Even if they found him, what would be left?

She bit at her wrist, making herself feel pain. They must find him, of course—even though he no longer mattered. They must regain possession of the Ruhk Staff and the Loden or everything they had gone through to get clear of Morrowindl and all of the lives that had been given up—her grandmother's, the Owl's, Eowen's, and those of the Elven Hunters— would have been for nothing. The thought burned through her. She could not tolerate it. She would not permit them to fail. She had promised her grandmother. She had promised herself. It was the reason she had come— to bring the Elves back into the Westland and to help find a way to put an end to the Shadowen. Allanon's charge—hers now as well, she admitted in black fury. Find yourself, and she had. Discover the truth, and she had. Too much of both, but she had. Her life was revealed now, past, present, and future, and however she felt about it she would not let it be taken away without her consent.

I don't care what it takes, she vowed. *I don't care!*

She was sleeping when Triss touched her shoulder and brought her awake again. "Lady Wren," he whispered gently. "Go lie down. Rest now."

She blinked, accepting the blanket he slipped about her. "In a minute," she replied. "Sit with me first."

He did so, a silent companion, his lean brown face strangely untroubled, his eyes distant. She remembered how he had looked when she had told him of Gavilan's treachery. *Treachery, wasn't that what it was?* That look was gone now, washed away by sleep or by acceptance. He had found a way to come to terms with it. Triss, the last of those who had come out of Arborlon's old life—how alone he must feel.

He looked over at her, and it seemed as if he could read her thoughts. "I have been Captain of the Home Guard for almost eight years," he ventured after a moment. "A long time, Lady Wren. I loved your grandmother, the queen. I would have done anything for her." He shook his head. "I have spent my whole life in service to the Elessedils and the Elven throne. I knew Gavilan as a child; we were children together. I grew to manhood with him. We played. My family and his still wait within the Loden, friends, . . ." He drew a deep breath, groping for words, understanding. "I knew him. He would not have killed Dal unless . . . Could it be that something happened to change him? Could one of the demons have done something to him?"

She had not considered that possibility. It could have happened. There had been opportunity enough. Or why not something else, a poison, for instance, or a sickening like that which had killed Ellenroh? But she knew in her heart that it was none of those, that it was simply a wearing away of his spirit, a breaking apart of his resolve.

"It could have been a demon," she lied anyway.

The strong face lifted. "He was a good man," he said quietly. "He cared about people; he helped them. He loved the queen. She would have named him king one day, perhaps."

"If not for me."

He turned away, embarrassed. "I should not have said that. You are queen." He looked back again. "Your grandmother would not have given the Staff to you if she had not believed it best. She would have given it to Gavilan instead. Perhaps she saw something in him that the rest of us missed. Yours is the strength the Elven people need."

She faced him. "I didn't want any part of this, Triss. None of it."

He nodded, smiled faintly. "No. Why would you?"

"I just wanted to find out who I was."

She saw a flicker of despair in his dark eyes. "I don't pretend to understand what brought you to us," he told her. "I only know that you are here and you are Queen of the Elves." He kept his eyes fixed on her. "Don't abandon us," he said quietly, urgently. "Don't leave us. We need you."

She was amazed at the strength of his plea. She placed her hand on his arm reassuringly. "Don't worry, Triss. I promise I won't run away. Ever."

She left him then, went over to where Garth slept and curled up next to her big friend, needing both his warmth and bulk for comfort this night, wanting to retreat into the past, to recover the protection and safety it had once offered, to recapture what was irretrievably lost. She settled instead for what was there and finally slept.

At dawn she was awake, more rested than she had a right to expect. The light was faint and gray through the haze, and the world about them was still and empty feeling, smelling of rot. Killeshan's rumble was distant and faint, yet steady now for the first time since they had begun their journey, a slow building of tremors that promised bigger things to come. Time was running out, Wren knew—quicker now, swifter with the passing of each hour. The volcano's fire was beginning to build at the core of the island toward a final conflagration, and when it exploded everything would be swept away.

They set out immediately, Stresa leading, Garth a step behind, Wren following with Faun, and Triss trailing. Wren was calmer now, less distraught. Gavilan, she reasoned, had nowhere to go. He might run for the beaches in search of Tiger Ty and Spirit, but how likely was he to find his way through the In Ju? He was not a Tracker and had no experience in wilderness survival. He was already half mad with fear and despair. How far could he get? He would likely travel in circles, and they would find him quickly.

Yet in the back of her mind lurked the specter of his somehow managing to get clear of the jungle, finding his way down to the beach, convincing Tiger Ty that everyone else was dead, and having himself and the Ruhk Staff carried safely away while the rest of the company was left behind. The possibility infuriated her, the more so when she considered the possibility that Gavilan didn't really think her dead at all and had simply decided to strike out on his own, convinced of the rightness of his cause and the inevitability of his rule.

Unable to ponder the matter further, she brushed it roughly aside.

Blackledge began to drop away from the Harrow almost immediately, but it was not as steep here as where Garth and she had climbed up. The cliff face was craggy and thick with vegetation, and it was not difficult for them to find a pathway down. They descended quickly, Stresa keeping Gavilan's scent firmly before them as they went. Broken limbs and crushed leaves marked clearly the Elven Prince's passing; Wren could have followed the trail alone, so obvious was it. Time and again they discovered places where the fleeing man had fallen, apparently heedless of his safety, anxious only to escape. He must be frantic, Wren thought sadly. He must be terrified.

They reached the edge of the In Ju at midday and paused to eat. Stresa was gruffly confident. They were only a few hours behind Gavilan, he advised. The Elven Prince was staggering badly now, clearly exhausted. Unless something happened to change things, they would catch him before nightfall.

Stresa's prediction was prophetic—but not in the way they had hoped. Shortly after they resumed tracking Gavilan's futile efforts to circumvent the In Ju, it began to rain. The air had grown hotter with the descent off the mountain, a swelter that built slowly and did not recede. When the rain commenced, it was a dampness that layered the air, a thick moisture that hung like wet silk draped against their skin, beading on their leather clothing. After a time, the dampness turned to mist, then drizzle, and finally a torrent that washed over them with ferocious determination. They were blinded by it and forced to take shelter beneath a giant banyan. It swept through quickly and took Gavilan's scent with it. Stresa searched carefully in the aftermath, but all trace was gone.

Garth studied the damp green tangle of the jungle. He beckoned Wren. *The marks of his passing are still evident. I can track him.*

She let Garth assume the lead with Stresa a half step behind, the former searching for signs of their quarry's passing, the latter keeping watch for Darters and other dangers. *Their quarry,* Wren thought, repeating the words. Gavilan had been reduced to that. She felt pity for him in spite of herself, thinking he should have stayed within the city, reasoning she should have done more to keep him safe, still wishing for what could never be.

They progressed more slowly now. Gavilan had given up his efforts to bypass the In Ju and plunged directly in. What signs they found—broken twigs and small branches, vegetation disturbed, an occasional print—suggested he had abandoned any attempt at stealth and was simply trying to reach the beaches by the shortest possible route. Speed over caution was a poor choice, Wren thought to herself. They tracked him steadily, without difficulty, and at each turn Wren expected to find him, the chase concluded and the inevitable confirmed. But somehow he kept going, evading the pitfalls that were scattered everywhere, the bogs and sinkholes, the Darters, the things that lay in wait for the unwary, and the traps and the monsters made of the Elven magic he so foolishly thought to wield. How he managed to stay alive, Wren could only wonder. He should have been dead a dozen times over. A step either way, and he would have been. She found herself wishing it would happen, that he would make that one mistake and that the madness would cease. She hated what they were doing, hunting him like an animal, chasing after him as if he were prey. She wanted it to stop.

At the same time, she dreaded what it would take to make that happen.

When they began to catch sight of the Wisteron's webbing, she despaired. *Not like that,* she found herself pleading with whatever fate controlled such things. *Give him a quick end.* Trip lines were strung all about, draped from the trees, looped along the vines, and attached in deadly nets. Stresa retook the lead from Garth in order to guide them past the snares, pausing often to listen, to sniff the air, and to judge the safety of the land ahead. The jungle thickened into a maze of green fronds and dark trunks that crisscrossed one another in jigsaw fashion. Shadows moved slowly and ponderously about them, but the sounds they made were anxious and hungry.

The afternoon shortened toward evening, and it grew dark. Far distant, screened by the mountain they had descended, Killeshan rumbled. Tremors shook the island, and the jungle's green haze shivered with the echo. Explosions began to sound, muffled still, but growing stronger. Whole trees trembled with the reverberations, and steam geysered out of swamp pools, hissing with relief. As the light darkened, Wren could see through the ever-present haze of vog and mist the sky above Killeshan turn red.

It has begun, she thought as Garth's worried eyes met her own.

She wondered how much time was left to them. Even if they regained the Staff, it was still another two days to the beach. Would Tiger Ty be there waiting? How often had he promised he would come? Once a week, wasn't it? What if a whole week must pass before he was scheduled to return? Would he see the volcano's glare and sense the danger to them?

Or had he given up his vigil long ago, convinced that she had failed, that she had died like all the others and that there was no point in searching further?

She shook her head in stern admonishment. No, not Tiger Ty. She judged him a better man than that. He would not give up, she told herself. Not until there was no hope left.

"Phhffttt! We have to stop soon," Stresa warned. "Hssstt. Find shelter before it grows any darker, before the Wisteron hunts!"

"A little farther," Wren suggested hopefully.

They went on, but Gavilan Elessedil was not to be found. His ragged trail stretched before them, worming ahead into the In Ju, a line of bent and broken stalks and leaves disappearing into the shadows.

Finally, they quit. Stresa found shelter for them in the hollow stump of a banyan toppled by age and erosion, a massive trunk with entries through its base and a narrow cleft farther up. They blocked off the larger and set themselves to keep watch at the smaller. Nothing of any size could reach them. It was dark and close within their wood coffin and as dry as winter earth. Night descended, and they listened to the jungle's hunters come awake, to the sounds of coughing roars, of sluggish passage, and of prey as it was caught and killed. They huddled back to back with Stresa hunched down before them, spikes extended back toward the faint light. They took turns standing guard, dozing because they were too tired to stay awake but too anxious to sleep. Faun lay cradled in Wren's arms, as still as death. She stroked the little creature affectionately, wondering at how it could have survived in such a world. She thought of how much she hated Morrowindl. It was a thief that had stolen everything from her—the lives of her grandmother and her friends, the innocence she had harbored of the Elves and their history, the love and affection she had discovered for Gavilan, and the strength of will she had thought she would never lose. It was the loss of the latter that bothered her most, her confidence in who and what she was and in the certainty that she could determine her own fate. So much was gone, and Morrowindl, this once paradise made into a Shadowen nightmare, had taken it all. She tried to picture life beyond the island and failed.

She could not think past escape, for escape was still uncertain, still a fate that hung in the balance. She remembered how once she had thought that traveling to find Allanon and speak with his shade might be the beginning of a great adventure. The memory was ashes in her mouth.

She slept for a time, dreamed of dark and terrible things, and came awake sweating and hot. At watch, she found her thoughts straying once again to Gavilan, to small memories of him—the way he had touched her, the feel of his mouth kissing hers, and the wonder he had invoked in her through nothing more than a chance remark or a passing glance. She smiled as she remembered. There was so much of him she had liked; she hurt for the loss of him. She wished she could bring him back to her and return him to the person he had been. She even wished she could find a way to make the magic do what nature could not—to change the past. It was foolish, senseless thinking, and it teased her mercilessly. Gavilan was lost to her. He had fallen prey to Morrowindl's madness. He had killed Dal and stolen the Ruhk Staff. He had turned himself into something unspeakable. Gavilan Elessedil, the man she had been so attracted to and cared so much for, was no more.

At daybreak they rose and set out anew. They did not have to bother with breakfast because there was nothing left to eat. Their supplies were exhausted, those that hadn't been lost or abandoned. There was a little water, but not more than enough for another day. While they traveled the In Ju, they would find nothing to sustain them. One more reason to get clear quickly.

Their search that day was over almost before it began. In less than an hour, Gavilan's trail abruptly ended. They crested a ravine, slowed on Stresa's warning hiss, and stopped. Below, amid the wreckage of small plants and grasses trampled almost flat in what must have been a frantic struggle, lay the shreds of one of the Wisteron's webs.

Stresa eased down into the ravine, sniffed cautiously about, and climbed out again. The dark, bright eyes fixed on Wren. "Hssssttt. It has him, Wren Elessedil."

She closed her eyes against the horrific vision the Splinterscat's words evoked. "How long ago?"

"Ssspptt. Not long. Maybe six hours. Just after midnight, I would guess. The net snared the Elf Prince and held him until the Wisteron came. Rwwlll. The beast carried him away."

"Where, Stresa?"

The other pricked his ears. "Its lair, I expect. It has one deep within a hollow at the In Ju's center."

She felt a new weariness steal through her. Of course, a lair—there would have to be. "Any sign of the Ruhk Staff?"

The Splinterscat shook his head. "Gone."

So unless Gavilan had abandoned it—something he would never do—it was still with him. She shuddered in spite of her resolve. She was remembering her brief encounter with the Wisteron on her way in. She was remembering how just its passing had made her feel.

Poor, foolish Gavilan. There was no hope for him now.

She looked at the others, one by one. "We have to get the Ruhk Staff back. We can't leave without it."

"No, Lady Wren, we can't," Triss echoed, hard-eyed.

Garth stood, his great hands limp at his sides.

Stresa shook out his quills and his sharp-nosed face lifted to her own. "Rrwwll Wren of the Elves, I expected nothing less of you. Hssttt. But you will have to—ssppppptt—use the Elf Magic if we are to survive. You will have to, against the Wisteron."

"I know," she whispered, and felt the last vestige of her old life drop away.

"Chhttt. Not that it will make any difference. Phhfftt. The Wisteron is—"

"Stresa," she interrupted gently. "You needn't come."

The silence of the moment hung against the screen of the jungle. The Splinterscat sighed and nodded. "Phhfft. We have come this far together, haven't we? No more talk. I will take you in."

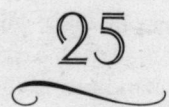

In the long, deep silence of Paranor's endless night, in the limbo of her gray, changeless twilight, Walker Boh sat staring into space. His hand was closed into a fist on the table before him, his fingers locked like iron bands about the Black Elfstone. There was nothing more to do—no other options to consider, no further choices to uncover. He had thought every-thing through to the extent that it was possible to do so, and all that re-mained was to test the right and wrong of it.

"Perhaps you should take a little more time," Cogline suggested gently.

The old man sat across from him, a frail, skeletal ghost nearly transpar-ent where caught against the light. Increasingly so, Walker thought in de-spair. White, wispy hair scattered like dust motes from the wrinkled face and head, robes hung like laundry set to dry on a line, and eyes flickered in dull glimmerings from out of dark sockets. Cogline was fading away, disap-pearing into the past, returning with Paranor to the place from which it had been summoned. For Paranor would not remain within the world of Men unless there was a Druid to tend it, and Walker Boh, chosen by time and fate to fill those dark robes, had yet to don them.

His eyes drifted over to Rumor. The moor cat slouched against the far wall of the study room in which they were settled, black body as faint and ethereal as the old man's. He looked down at himself, fading as well, though not as quickly. In any event, he had a choice; he could leave if he chose, when he chose. Not so Cogline or Rumor, who were bound to the Keep for all eternity if Walker did not find a way to bring it back into the world of Men.

Strangely enough, he thought he had found that way. But his discovery terrified him so that he was not certain he could act on it.

Cogline shifted, a rattle of dry bones. "Another reading of the books couldn't hurt," he pressed.

Walker's smile was ironic. "Another reading and there won't be anything left of you at all. Or Rumor or the Keep or possibly even me. Paranor is disappearing, old man. We can't pretend otherwise. Besides, there is nothing left to read, nothing to discover that I don't already know."

"And you're still certain that you're right, Walker?"

Certain? Walker was certain of nothing beyond the fact that he was most definitely not certain. The Black Elfstone was a deadly puzzle. Guess wrong about its workings and you would end up like the Stone King, enveloped by your own magic, destroyed by what you trusted most. Uhl Belk had thought he had mastered the Stone's magic, and it had cost him everything.

"I am guessing," he replied. "Nothing more."

He allowed his hand to open, and the Elfstone to come into the light. It lay there in the cup of his palm, smooth-faced, sharp-edged, opaque and impenetrable, power unto itself, power beyond anything he had ever encountered. He remembered how it had felt to use the Stone when he had brought back the Keep, thinking it would end then, that the retrieval out of limbo where Allanon had sent it was all that was required. He remembered the surge of power as it joined him to the Keep, the entwining of flesh and blood with stone and mortar, the reworking of his body so that he was as much ghost as man, changing him so that he could enter Paranor, so that he could discover the rest of what he must do.

A metamorphosis of being.

Within, he had encountered Cogline and Rumor and heard the tale of how they had survived the attack of the Shadowen by being caught up in the protective shield of the Druid Histories' magic and spirited into Paranor. Though Walker had brought Paranor out of the limbo place into which Allanon had dispatched it, it would not be fully returned until he had found a way to complete his transformation, to become the Druid it was decreed he must be. Until then, Paranor was a prison that only he could leave—a prison rapidly drawing back into the space from which it had come.

"I am guessing," he repeated, almost to himself.

He had read and reread the Druid Histories in an effort to discover what it was that he must do and found nothing. Nowhere did the Histories relate how one became a Druid. Despairing, he had thought the cause lost to him when he had remembered the Grimpond's visions, two of which had come to pass, the third of which, he realized, would happen here.

He faced the old man. "I stand within a castle fortress empty of life and gray with disuse. I am stalked by a death I cannot escape. It hunts me relentlessly. I know I must run from it, yet cannot. I let it approach, and it reaches for me. A cold settles within, and I can feel my life ending. Behind me stands a dark shadow holding me fast, preventing my escape. The shadow is Allanon."

The words were a familiar litany by now. Cogline nodded patiently. "Your vision, you said. The third of three."

"Two came to pass already, but neither as I anticipated. The Grimpond loves to play games. But this time I shall use that gamesplaying to my advantage. I know the details of the vision; I know that it will happen here within the Keep. I need only decipher its meaning, to separate the truth from the lie."

"But if you have guessed wrong . . ."

Walker Boh shook his head defiantly. "I have not."

They were treading familiar ground. Walker had already told the old man everything, testing it out on someone who would be quick to spot the flaws he had missed, putting it into words to see how it would sound.

The Black Elfstone was the key to everything.

He repeated from memory that brief, solitary passage inscribed in the Druid Histories:

Once removed, Paranor shall remain lost to the world of Men for the whole of time, sealed away and invisible within its casting. One magic alone has the power to return it—that singular Elfstone that is colored Black and was conceived by the faerie people of the old world in the manner and form of all Elfstones, combining nevertheless in one stone alone the necessary properties of heart, mind, and body. Whosoever shall have cause and right shall wield it to its proper end.

He had assumed until now that the Black Elfstone was meant to restore Paranor to its present state of half-being and to gain him entry therein. But the language of the inscription didn't qualify the extent of the Elfstone's use. One magic alone, it said, had the power to restore Paranor. One magic. The Black Elfstone. There wasn't any other magic mentioned, not anywhere. There wasn't another word about returning Paranor to the world of Men in all the pages of all the Druid Histories.

Suppose, then, that the Black Elfstone was all that was required, but that it must be used not just once, but twice or even three times before the restoration process was complete.

But used to do what?

The answer seemed obvious. The magic that Allanon had released into the Keep three hundred years ago was a sort of watchdog set loose to do two things—to destroy the Keep's enemies and to dispatch Paranor into limbo and keep it there until it was properly summoned out again. The magic was a living thing. You could feel it in the walls of the castle; you could hear it stir in its bowels. It watched and listened. It breathed. It was there, waiting. If the Keep was to be restored to the Four Lands, the magic Allanon had loosed must be locked away again. It was reasonable to assume that only another form of magic could accomplish this. And the only magic at hand, the only magic even mentioned in the Druid Histories where Paranor was concerned, was the Black Elfstone.

So far, so good. Druid magic to negate Druid magic. It made sense; it was the Black Elfstone's stated power, the negation of other magics. One magic, the inscription read. And Walker must wield it, of course. He had done so once, proved that he could. *Whosoever shall have cause and right.* Himself. Use the Black Elfstone against the watchdog magic and secure it. Use the Black Elfstone and bring Paranor all the way back.

But there was still something missing. There was no explanation of how the Black Elfstone would work. It was infinitely more complicated than simply calling up the magic and letting it run loose. The Black Elfstone negated other magics by drawing them into itself—and into its holder. Walker Boh had already been changed when he had used the Elfstone to bring Paranor back and gain entry, turned from a whole man into something incorporeal. What further damage might he do to himself if he used the Elfstone on the watchdog? What further transformation might take place?

And then, abruptly, he realized two things.

First, that he was still not a Druid and would not become one until he had established his right to do so—that his right would not come from study, or learning, or wisdom gleaned from a reading of the Druid Histories, that it was not foreordained, not predetermined by the bestowal of Allanon's blood trust to Brin Ohmsford three hundred years earlier, but that it would come at the moment he found a way to subdue the watchdog that guarded the Keep and brought Paranor fully back into the world of Men, because that was the test that Allanon had set him.

Second, that the third vision the Grimpond had shown him, the one that would take place within Paranor, the one where he was confronted by a death he could not escape, held fast by the ghost of Allanon, was a glimpse of that moment.

His arguments were persuasive. The Druids would not commit to writing a process as inviolate as this one when there was a better way. Only Walker Boh could use the Black Elfstone. Only he had the right. Somehow, in some way, that use would trigger the required transformation. When it was necessary to know, Walker would discover what was needed. So much of the Druid magic relied on acceptance—use of the Elfstones, of the Sword of Shannara, even of the wishsong. It was only reasonable that it would be the same here.

And the Grimpond's vision only cemented his thinking. There would have to be a confrontation of the sort depicted. A literal reading of the vision suggested that such a confrontation would result in Walker's death, that Allanon by sending him here had bound him so that he must die, and that whatever he might try to do to escape would be futile. But that was too simplistic. And it made no sense. Why would Allanon send him all this way to certain death? There had to be another interpretation, another meaning.

The one he favored was the one that ended one life and began another, that established him once and for all as a Druid.

Cogline was not so sure. Walker had guessed wrong on both of the Grimpond's previous visions. Why was he so convinced that he was not guessing wrong here as well? The visions were never what they seemed, devious and twisted bits of half-truth concealed amid lies. He was taking a terrible gamble. The first vision had cost him his arm, the second Quickening. Was the third to cost him nothing? It seemed more reasonable to believe that the vision was open to a number of interpretations, any one of which could come to pass in the right set of circumstances, including Walker's death. Moreover, it bothered Cogline that Walker had no clear idea of how use of the Black Elfstone was to effect his transformation, how it was to subdue the Druid watchdog, how Paranor itself was to be brought fully alive—or how any of this was to work. It could not possibly be as easy as Walker made it sound. Nothing involving use of the Elven magic ever was. There would be pain involved, enormous effort, and the very real possibility of failure.

So they had argued, back and forth, for longer than Walker cared to admit, until now, hours later, they were too tired to do anything but exchange a final round of perfunctory admonishments. Walker's mind was made up, and they both knew it. He was going to test his theory, to seek out and confront the thing that Allanon had let loose within Paranor and use the magic of the Black Elfstone to resecure it. He was going to discover the truth about the Black Elfstone and put an end to the last of the Grimpond's hateful visions.

If he could make himself rise from this table, take up the talisman, and go forth.

Though he had sought to keep it hidden from Cogline with hard looks and confident words, his terror bound him. So much uncertainty, so many guesses. He forced his fingers to close again over the Black Elfstone, to grip so hard he could feel pain.

"I will go with you," Cogline offered. "And Rumor."

"No."

"We might be able to help in some way."

"No," Walker repeated. He looked up, shaking his head slowly. "Not that I wouldn't like you to. But this isn't something you can help me with, either of you. It isn't something anyone can help me with."

He could feel an ache where his missing arm should be, as if it were somehow there and he simply couldn't see it. He shifted uneasily, trying to relieve muscles that had tightened and cramped while he had stayed seated with the old man, arguing. The movement gave him impetus, and he forced himself to rise. Cogline stood with him. They faced each other in the half-light, in the fading transparency of the Keep.

"Walker." The old man spoke his name quietly. "The Druids have made us both their creatures. We have been twisted and turned in every direction, made to do things we did not wish to do and become involved in matters we would rather have left alone. I would not presume to argue with you now the merits of their manipulation. We are both beyond the point where it matters."

He leaned forward. "But I would tell you, would ask you to remember, that they choose their paladins wisely." His smile was worn and sad. "Luck to you."

Walker came around the table, wrapped his good arm about the old man, and hugged him tight. He held him momentarily, then released him and stepped away.

"Thank you," he whispered.

There was nothing more to be said. He took a deep breath, walked over to scratch Rumor between his cocked ears, gazed into the luminous eyes, then turned and disappeared out the door.

With slow, cautious steps, moving through the vast, empty hallways as if the walls might hear him coming, as if his intentions could be divined, he proceeded toward the center of the Keep. Shadows hung about him in colorless folds, a sleep-shroud that cloaked his thoughts. He buried himself in the sanctuary of his mind, drawing his determination and strength of will about him in protective layers, summoning from deep within the resolve that would give him a chance at life.

For the truth of things was that he had no real idea what would happen when he confronted the Druid watchdog and called upon the Black Elfstone's magic to subdue it. Cogline was right; there would be pain and the process would be more complex and difficult than he wanted to admit. There would be a struggle, and he might not emerge the victor. He wished he had some better idea of what it was he faced. But there was no point in wishing for what could never be, for what had never been. The Druid ways had been secretive forever.

He turned down the main hallway, heading now to the doors that opened into the Keep—and to the well in which the watchdog slumbered. Or perhaps simply laired, for it seemed to the Dark Uncle that the magic was awake and watching, following him with its eyes as he moved through the castle, trailing along in a ripple of changing light, an invisible presence. Allanon's shade was there as well, a tightening at his back, a cramping of the muscles in his shoulders where the great hands gripped. He was held fast already, he thought to himself. He was propelled to this confrontation as much as if he were deadwood carried on the crest of a river in flood, and he could not turn aside from it.

Speak to me, Allanon, he pleaded silently. *Tell me what to do.*

But no answer came.

The doors of empty rooms and the dark tunnels of other halls and corridors came and went. He felt again the ache of his missing arm and wished that he were whole again, if only for the moment of this confrontation. He gripped the Black Elfstone tightly in his good hand, feeling its smooth facets and sharp edges press reassuringly against his flesh. He could summon the power within, but he could not predict what it would do. *Destroy you,* the thought came unbidden. He breathed slowly, deeply, to calm himself. He tried to remember the passage on the Stone's usage from the Druid History, but his memory suddenly failed him. He tried to remember what he had read in all the pages of all those books and could not. Everything was melting away within, lost in the rush of fear and doubt that surged through him, anxious and threatening. Don't give way to it, he admonished himself. Remember who you are, what has been promised you, what you have told yourself will happen.

The words were dead leaves caught in a strong wind.

Ahead, a broad alcove opened into the stone of the walls, arched and shadowed so deeply that it was as black as night. There, a set of tall iron doors stood closed.

The entry to the well of the Druid's Keep.

Walker Boh came up to the doors and stopped. All around him he could hear a whispering of voices, taunting, teasing in the manner of the Grimpond, telling him to go back, urging him to go on, a maddening whirl of conflicting exhortations. Memories stirred from somewhere within— but they were not his own. He could feel their movement along his spine, a reaching out of fingers that coiled and tightened. Before him, he could see a trace of wicked green light probe at the cracks and crevices of the door frame. Beyond, he could sense movement.

In that instant, he almost bolted. Had he been able to do so, he would have thrown down the Black Elfstone and run for his life, the whole of his resolve and purpose abandoned. His fear was manifest; it was so palpable that it seemed he could reach out and touch it. It did not wear the face he had expected. His fear was not of the confrontation, of the vision's promise, or even of dying. It was of something beyond that, something so intangible he was unable to define it and at the same time was certain it was there.

But Allanon's shade held him fast, just as in the vision, a contrivance of fate and time and manipulation of centuries gone combining to assure that Walker Boh fulfilled the purpose the Druids had set for him.

He reached forward with his closed fist, seeing his hand as if it belonged to another person, watching as it pushed against the iron doors.

Soundlessly they swung open.

Walker stepped through, his body numb and his head light and filled with small, terror-filled cries of warning. *Don't,* they whispered. *Don't.*

He stopped, breathless. He stood on a narrow stone landing within the well of the Keep. Stairs coiled upward along the wall of the tower like a spike-backed serpent. Weak gray light filtered through slits cut in the stone, piercing the shadows. There was nothing below where he stood but emptiness—a vast, yawning abyss out of which rose the hollow echo of the iron doors as they thudded closed behind him. He listened to his heart pound in his ears. He listened to the silence beyond.

Then something stirred in the abyss. Breath released from a giant's lungs, quick and angry. Greenish light flared, dimmed again, turned to mist, and began to swirl sluggishly.

Walker Boh felt the vastness of the Keep settle down about him, a monstrous weight he could not escape. Tons of stone ringed him, and the blackness it sealed away was a death shroud. The mist rose, a dark and ancient magic, the Druid watchdog roused and come forth to investigate. It came for him in a sweeping, lifting motion, curling along the stone, eating away at the dark, a morass that would swallow him without a trace.

Still he would have run but for the certainty that it was too late, that he had begun something that must be finished, that time and events had caught up with him at last, and now here, alone, he would have to resolve the puzzle of his Druid-shaped life. He made himself move forward to the landing's edge, frail flesh a drop of water against the ocean of the power below. It hissed at him as if it saw, a whisper of recognition. It seemed to gather itself, a tightening of movement.

Walker brought up the hand with the Black Elfstone.

Wait.

The voice rose out of the mist. Walker froze. The voice belonged to the Grimpond.

Do you know me?

The Grimpond? How could it be the Grimpond? Walker blinked rapidly. The mist had begun to take form at its center, a pillar of swirling green that bore upward into the light, that lifted through the shadows, steady, certain, until it was even with him, hanging in air and silence.

Look.

It became a human figure all cloaked and hooded and faceless. It grew arms and hands that stretched to embrace Walker. Fingers curled and flexed.

Who am I?

A face appeared, shadows and light shifting within the mist. Walker felt as if his soul had been torn away.

The face he saw was his own.

Within the dark seclusion of the vault that housed the Druid Histories, Cogline lurched to his feet. Something was happening. Something. He could feel it in the air, a vibration that stirred the shadows. The wrinkled face tightened in concentration; the aged eyes stared into space. The silence was unbroken, vast and changeless, time suspended, and yet . . .

Across the room from him, Rumor's head snapped up and the moor cat gave a deep, low, angry growl. He moved into a crouch, turning first this way, then that, as if seeking an enemy that had made itself invisible. He, too, sensed something. Cogline's eyes flickered right and left. On the table before him, the pages of the open book began to tremble.

It begins, the old man thought.

He gathered his robes close in an unconscious motion, thinking of all that had brought him to this place and time, of all that had gone before.

After so many years, what price? he wondered. But the price would be paid not by him, but by Walker Boh.

I must do what I can, he decided.

He focused deep within, one of those few skills he retained from his once-Druid past. He retreated down inside until he was free enough to leave. He could travel short distances so, see within small worlds. He sped through the castle corridors, still within his mind, seeing and hearing everything. He swept through the darkness, through the gray half-light, to the tower of the Keep.

There he found Walker Boh face to face with immortality and death, frozen by indecision. He realized what was happening.

His voice was surprisingly calm.

Walker. Use the Stone.

Walker Boh heard the old man's voice, a whisper in his mind, and he felt his body respond. His arm straightened, and he tensed.

The thing before him laughed. *Do you still not know me?*

He did—and didn't. It was many things at once, some of which he recognized, some of which he didn't. The voice, though—there could be no mistake. It was the Grimpond's, taunting, teasing, calling his name.

You have found your third vision, haven't you, Dark Uncle?

Walker was appalled. How could this be happening? How could the Grimpond be both this thing he had come to subdue and the avatar imprisoned in Darklin Reach? How could it be in two places at once? It didn't make sense! The Druids hadn't created the Grimpond. Their magics were diverse and opposed. Yet the voice, the movement, and the feel of the thing . . .

The shadow before him was growing larger, approaching.

I am your death, Walker Boh. Are you prepared to embrace me?

And abruptly the vision was back in Walker's mind, as clear as the moment it had first appeared to him—the shade of Allanon behind him, holding him fast, the dark shadow before him, the promise of his death, and the castle of the Druids all about.

Why don't you flee? Flee from me!

It was all he could do to keep from screaming. He groped away from it, beseeching help from any quarter. Cogline's voice was gone, buried in black fear. Resolve and purpose were scattered in pieces about him. Walker Boh was disintegrating while still alive.

Yet some small part of him did not give way, held fast by memory of what had brought him, by the promise he had made himself that he would not die willingly or in ignorance. Cogline's face was still there, the eyes frantic, the lips moving, trying to speak. Walker reached down inside for the one thing that had sustained him over the years, for that core of anger that burned at the thought of what the Druids had done to him. He fanned it until it blazed. He cupped it to his face and let it sear him. He breathed it in until the fear was forced to give way, until there was only rage.

Then an odd thing happened. The voice of the thing before him changed. The voice became his own, frantic, desperate.

Flee, Walker Boh!

The voice was no longer coming from the mist; it was coming from himself! He was calling his own name, urging himself to flee!

What was happening?

And suddenly he understood. He wasn't listening to the thing before him; he was listening to himself. It was his own voice he had been hearing all along, a trick of his subconscious—a trick, he realized in fury, of the Grimpond. The wraith had implanted in Walker's mind, along with that third vision, a suggestion of his death, a voice to convince him of it, and a certainty that it was the Grimpond itself who came forth in another form to deliver it. Revenge on the descendants of Brin Ohmsford—it was what the Grimpond had been after from the first. If Walker listened to that voice, faltered in his resolve, and turned away from the purpose that had brought him . . .

No!

His fingers opened and the Black Elfstone flared to life.

The nonlight streaked forth, spreading like ink across the shadowed well of the Keep to embrace the mist. *No more games!* Walker's shout was a euphoric, silent cry within his mind. The Grimpond—so insidious, so devious—had almost undone him. *Never again. Never . . .*

Then everything began to happen at once.

Nonlight and mist meshed and joined. Back through the tunnel of the magic's dark flooded the mist, a greenish, pulsing fury. Walker had only an instant to catch his breath, to question what had gone wrong, and to wonder if perhaps he had failed to outsmart the Grimpond after all—and then the Druid magic was on him. It exploded within, and he screamed in helpless dismay. The pain was indescribable, a fiery incandescence. It felt as if another being had entered him, carried within by the magic, drawn out of the concealment of the mist. A physical presence, it burrowed into bone and muscle and flesh and blood until it was all that Walker could bear. It expanded and raged until he thought he would be torn apart. Then the sense of it changed, igniting a different kind of pain. Memories flooded through him, vast and seemingly endless. With the memories came the feelings that accompanied them, emotions charged with horror and fear and doubt and regret and a dozen other sensations that rolled through Walker Boh in an unstoppable torrent. He staggered back, trying to resist, to fling them away. His hand fought to close over the Black Elfstone in an effort to shut this attack off, but his body would no longer obey him. He was gripped by the magics—those of both Elfstone and mist—and they held him fast.

Like Allanon and the specter of death in the third version!

Shades! Had the Grimpond been right after all?

He was seeing other places and times, viewing the faces of men and women and children he did not know, witnessing events transpire and fade, and above all feeling a wrenching series of emotions emanate from the being inside. Walker's sense of where he was disappeared. He was transported into the mind of his invader. A man? Yes, a man, he realized, a man who had lived countless lifetimes, centuries, far longer than any normal human, someone so different . . .

The images abruptly changed. He saw a gathering of black robes, dark figures concealed behind castle walls, closeted in chambers where the light barely reached, hunched over ancient books of learning, writing, reading, studying, discussing . . .

Druids!

And then he realized the truth—a jarring, shocking recognition that cut through the madness with a razor's edge.

The being that the mist had carried within him was Allanon—his memories, his experiences, his feelings, and his thoughts, everything but the flesh and blood he had lost in death.

How had Allanon managed this? Walker asked himself in disbelief, fighting to breathe against the rush of memories, against the suffocating blanket of the other's thoughts. But he already knew the answer to that. A Druid's magic allowed almost anything. The seeds had been planted three hundred years ago. Why, then? And that answer, too, came swiftly, a red flare of certainty. This was how the Druid lore was to be passed on to him. All that Allanon had known and felt was stored within the mist, his knowledge kept safe for three hundred years, waiting for his successor.

But there was more, Walker sensed. This was how he was to be tested as well. This was how it was to be determined if he should become a Druid.

His speculation ended as the images continued to rush through him, recognizable now for what they were, the whole of the Druid experience, all that Allanon had gleaned from his predecessors, from his studies, from the living of his own life. Like footprints in soft earth, they embedded in Walker's mind, their touch fiery and harsh, each a coal laid against his skin. The words and impressions and feelings descended in an avalanche. It was too much, too fast. *I don't want this!* he screamed in terror, but still the feeding continued, relentless, purposeful—Allanon's self transferring into Walker. He fought back against it, groping through the maze of images for something solid. But the black light of the Elfstone was a funnel that refused to be stoppered, drawing in the greenish mist, absorbing it, and channeling it into his body. Voices spoke words, faces turned to look, scenes changed, and time rushed away—a composite of all the years Allanon had been alive, struggling to protect the Races, to assure that the Druid lore wasn't lost, that the hopes and aspirations the First Council had envisioned centuries ago were carried forth and preserved. Walker Boh became privy to it all, learned what it had meant to Allanon and those whose lives he had touched, and experienced for himself the impact of life through almost ten centuries.

Then abruptly the images ceased, the voices, the faces, the scenes out of time—everything that had assailed him. They vanished in a rush, and he was standing alone again within the Keep, a solitary figure slumped against the stone-block wall.

Still alive.

He lifted away unsteadily, looking down at himself, making certain he was whole. Within, there was a rawness, like skin reddened from too much sun, the implant of all that Druid knowledge, of all that Allanon had intended to bequeath. His spirit felt leavened and his mind filled. Yet his command over the knowledge was disjointed, as if it could not be brought to bear, not called upon. Something was wrong. Walker could not seem to focus.

Before him, the Black Elfstone pulsed, the nonlight a bridge that arced into the shadows, still joined with what remained of the mist—a roiling, churning mass of wicked green light that hissed and sparked and gathered itself like a cat about to spring.

Walker straightened, weak and unsteady, frightened anew, sensing that something more was about to happen and that the worst was still to come. His mind raced. What could he do to prepare himself? There wasn't time enough left . . .

The mist launched itself into the nonlight. It came at Walker and enveloped him in the blink of an eye. He could see its anger, hear its rage, and feel its fury. It exploded through the new skin of his knowledge, a geyser of pain. Walker shrieked and doubled over. His body convulsed, changing within the covering of his robes. He could feel the wrenching of his bones. He closed his eyes and went rigid. The mist was within, curling, settling, feeding.

He experienced a rush of horror.

All of his life, Walker Boh had struggled to escape what the Druids had foreordained for him, resolved to chart his own course. In the end, he had failed. Thus he had gone in search of the Black Elfstone and then Paranor with the knowledge that if he should find them it would require that he become the next Druid, accepting his destiny yet promising himself that he would be his own person whatever was ordained. Now, in an instant's time, as he was wracked by the fury of what had hidden within the mist, all that remained of his hopes for some small measure of self-determination was stripped away, and Walker Boh was left instead with the darkest part of Allanon's soul. It was the Druid's cruelest self, a composite of all those times he had been forced by reason and circumstance to do what he abhorred, all those situations when he had been required to expend lives and faith and hope and trust, and all those years of hardening and tempering of spirit and heart until both were as carefully forged and as indestructible as the hardest metal. It was a rendering of the limits of Allanon's being, the limits to which he had been forced to journey. It revealed the weight of responsibility that came with power. It delineated the understanding that experience bestowed. It was harsh and ragged and terrible, an accumulation of ten normal lifetimes, and it inundated Walker like floodwaters over the wall of a dam.

Down into blackness the Dark Uncle spiraled, hearing himself cry out, hearing as well the Grimpond's laughter—imagined or real, he could not tell. His thoughts scattered before the flaying of his spirit, of his hopes, and of his beliefs. There was nothing he could do; the force of the magic was too powerful. He gave way before it, a monstrous strength. He waited to die.

Yet somehow he clung to life. He found that the torrent of dark revelation, while testing his endurance in ways he had not believed possible, had failed nevertheless to destroy him. He could not think—there was too much pain for that. He did not try to see, lost within a bottomless pit. Hearing availed him nothing, for the echo of his cry reverberated all about him. He seemed to float within himself, fighting to breathe, to survive. It was the testing he had anticipated—the Druid rite of passage. It battered him senseless, filled him with hurt, and left him broken within. Everything washed away, his beliefs and understandings, all that had sustained him for so long. Could he survive that loss? What would he be if he did?

Through waves of anguish he swam, buried within himself and the force of the dark magic, borne to the edge of his endurance, an inch from drowning. He sensed that his life could be lost in the tick of a moment's passing and realized that the measure of who and what he was and could be was being taken. He couldn't stop it. He wasn't sure he even cared. He drifted, helpless.

Helpless.

To be ever again who he had thought he would. To fulfill any of the promises he had made to himself. To have any control over his life. To determine if he would live or die.

Helpless.

Walker Boh.

Barely aware of what he was doing, separated from conscious reasoning, driven instead by emotions too primal to identify, the Dark Uncle thrashed clear of his lethargy and exploded through the waves of pain, through nonlight and dark magic, through time and space, a bright speck of fiery rage.

Within, he felt the balance shift, the weight between life and death tip.

And when he broke at last the surface of the black ocean that had threatened to drown him, the only sound he heard, as it burst from his lungs, was an endless scream.

26

It was late morning. The last three members of the company of nine worked their way cautiously through the tangle of the In Ju, following after the bulky, spiked form of Stresa, the Splinterscat, as he tunneled steadily deeper into the gloom.

Wren breathed the fetid, damp air and listened to the silence.

Distant, far removed from where they labored, Killeshan's rumble was a backdrop of sound that rolled across earth and sky, deep and ominous. Tremors snaked through Morrowindl, warning of the eruption that continued to build. But in the jungle, everything was still. A sheen of wetness coated the In Ju from the ground up, soaking trees and scrub, vines and grasses, a blanket that muffled sound and hid movement. The jungle was a vault of stunning green, of walls that formed countless chambers leading one into the other, of corridors that twisted and wound about in a maze that threatened to suffocate. Branches intertwined overhead to form a ceiling that shut out the light, canopied over a patchwork floor of swamp and quicksand and mud. Insects buzzed invisibly and things cried out from the mist. But nothing moved. Nothing seemed alive.

The Wisteron's webbing was everywhere by now, a vast networking that layered the trees like strips of gauze. Dead things hung in the webbing, the husks of creatures drained of life, the remains of the monster's feedings. They were small for the most part; the Wisteron took the larger offerings to its lair.

Which lay somewhere not far ahead.

Wren watched the shadows about her, made more anxious by the lack of any movement than by the silence. She walked in a dead place, a wasteland in which living things did not belong, a netherworld she traversed at her peril. She kept thinking she would catch sight of a flash of color, a rippling of water, or a shimmer of leaves and grasses. But the In Ju might have been sheathed in ice, it was so frozen. They were deep within the Wisteron's country now, and nothing ventured here.

Nothing save themselves.

She held the Elfstones clutched tightly in her hand, free now of their leather bag, ready for the use to which she knew they must be put. She harbored no illusions as to what would be required of her. She bore no false hope that use of the Elfstones might be avoided, that her Rover skills might be sufficient to save them. She did not debate whether it was wise to employ the magic when she knew how its power affected her. Her choices were all behind her. The Wisteron was a monster that only the Elfstones could overcome. She would use the magic because it was the only weapon they had that would make any difference in the battle that lay ahead. If she allowed herself to hesitate, if she fell prey yet again to indecision, they were all dead.

She swallowed against the dryness in her throat. Odd that she should be so dry there and so damp everywhere else. Even the palms of her hands were sweating. How far she had come since her days with Garth when she had roamed the Tirfing in what seemed now to have been another life, free of worry and responsibility, answerable only to herself and the dictates of time.

She wondered if she would ever see the Westland again.

Ahead, the gloom tightened into pockets of deep shadow that had the look of burrows. Mist coiled out and wound through the tree limbs and vines like snakes. Webbing cloaked the high branches and filled the gaps between—thick, semitransparent strands that shimmered with the damp. Stresa slowed and looked back at them. He didn't speak. He didn't have to. Wren was aware of Garth and Triss at either shoulder, silent, expectant. She nodded to Stresa and motioned for him to go on.

She thought suddenly of her grandmother, wondering what Ellenroh would be feeling if she were there, imagining how she would react. She could see the other's face, the fierce blue eyes in contrast to the ready smile, the imposing sense of calm that swept aside all doubt and fear. Ellenroh Elessedil, Queen of the Elves. Her grandmother had always seemed so much in control of everything. But even that hadn't been enough to save her. What then, Wren wondered darkly, could she rely upon? The magic, of course—but the magic was only as strong as the wielder, and Wren would have much preferred her grandmother's indomitable strength just now to her own. She lacked Ellenroh's self-assurance; she lacked her certainty. Even determined as she was to recover the Ruhk Staff and the Loden, to carry the Elven people safely back into the Westland, and to fulfill the terms of the trust that had been given her, she saw herself as flesh and blood and not as iron. She could fail. She could die. Terror lurked at the fringes of such thoughts, and it would not be banished.

Triss bumped up against her from behind, causing her to jump. He whispered a hasty apology and dropped back again. Wren listened to the pounding of her blood, a throbbing in her ears and chest, a measure of the brief space between her life and death.

She had always been so sure of herself . . .

Something skittered away on the ground ahead, a flash of dark movement against the green. Stresa's spines lifted, but he did not slow. The forest opened through a sea of swamp grass into a stand of old-growth acacia that leaned heavily one into the other, the ground beneath eroded and mired. The company followed the Splinterscat left along a narrow rise. The movement came again, quick, sudden, more than one thing this time. Wren tried to follow it. Some sort of insect, she decided, long and narrow, many legged.

Stresa found a patch of ground slightly broader than his body and turned to face them.

"Phhhfft. Did you see?" he whispered roughly. They nodded. "Scavengers! Orps, they are called. Hsssst! They eat anything. Hah, everything! They live off the leavings of the Wisteron. You'll see a lot more of them before we're finished. Don't be frightened when you do."

"How much farther?" Wren whispered back, bending close.

The Splinterscat cocked its head. "Just ahead," he growled. "Can't you smell the dead things?"

"What's back there?"

"Sssssttt! How would I know that, Wren of the Elves? I'm still alive!"

She ignored his glare. "We'll take a look. If we can talk, we will. If not, we will withdraw and decide what to do."

She looked at Garth and Triss in turn to be certain they understood, then straightened. Faun clung to her like a second skin. She was going to have to put the Tree Squeak down before she went much farther.

They burrowed ahead through the grasses and into the collapsing trees. Orps appeared from everywhere now, scattering at their approach. They looked like giant silverfish, quick and soundless as they disappeared into earth and wood. Wren tried to ignore them, but it was difficult. The surface water of the swamp bubbled and spit about them, the first sound they had heard in some time. Killeshan's reach was lengthening. They passed out of the grasses and through the trees, the gloom settling down about them in layers. It went still again, the air empty and dead. Wren breathed slowly, deeply. Her hand tightened about the Elfstones.

Then they were through the stand of acacia and moving across a mud flat to a cluster of huge fir whose limbs wrapped about one another in close embrace. Strands of webbing hung everywhere, and as they neared the far side of the flats Wren caught sight of bones scattered along the fringe of the trees. Orps darted right and left, skimming the surface of the flats, disappearing into the foliage ahead.

Stresa had slowed their pace to a crawl.

They gained the edge of the flats, eased down through an opening in the trees on hands and knees, and froze.

Beyond the trees lay a deep ravine, an island of rock suspended within the swamp. The fir trees lifted from its bedding in a jumble of dark trunks that looked as if they had been lashed together with hundreds of webs. Dead things hung in the webs, and bones littered the ravine floor. Orps crawled over everything, a shimmering carpet of movement. The light was gray and diffuse above the ravine, filtered down to faint shadows by the vog and mist. The smell of death hung over everything, captured within the rocks and trees and haze. It was quiet within the Wisteron's lair. Except for the scurrying Orps, nothing moved.

Wren felt Garth's hand grip her shoulder. She glanced over and saw him point.

Gavilan Elessedil hung spread-eagle in a hammock of webbing across from them, his blue eyes lifeless and staring, his mouth open in a silent scream. He had been gutted, his torso split from chest to stomach. Within the empty cavity, his ribs gleamed dully. All of his body fluids had been drained. What remained was little more than a husk, a grotesque, frightening parody of a man.

Wren had seen much of death in her short life, but she was unprepared for this. *Don't look!* she admonished herself frantically. *Don't remember him like this!* But she did look and knew as she did that she would never forget.

Garth touched her a second time, pointing down into the ravine. She peered without seeing at first, then caught sight of the Ruhk Staff. It lay directly beneath what remained of Gavilan, resting on the carpet of old bones. Orps crawled over it mindlessly. The Loden was still fixed to its tip.

Wren nodded in response, already wondering how they could reach the talisman. Her gaze shifted abruptly, searching once more.

Where was the Wisteron?

Then she saw it, high in the branches of the trees at one end of the ravine, suspended in a net of its own webbing, motionless in the haze. It was curled into a huge ball, its legs tucked under it, and it had the curious appearance of a dirty cloud. It was covered with spiked hair, and it blended with the haze. It seemed to be sleeping.

Wren fought down the rush of fear that seeing it triggered. She glanced hurriedly at the others. They were all looking. The Wisteron shifted suddenly, a straightening out of its surprisingly lean body, a stretching of several limbs. There was a flash of claws and a hideous insectlike face with an odd, sucking maw. Then it curled up again and went still.

In Wren's hand, the Elfstones had begun to burn.

She took a last despairing look at Gavilan, then motioned to the others and backed out of the trees. Wordlessly they retraced their steps across the flats until they had gained the cover of the acacia, where they knelt in a tight circle.

Wren searched their eyes. "How can we get to the Staff?" she asked quietly. The image of Gavilan was fixed in her mind, and she could barely think past it.

Garth's hands lifted to sign. *One of us will have to go down into the ravine.*

"But the Wisteron will hear. Those bones will sound like eggshells when they're stepped on." She put Faun down next to her. The dark eyes stared upward intently into her own.

"Could we lower someone down?" Triss asked.

"Phhhfft! Not without making some sound or movement," Stresa snapped. "The Wisteron isn't—ssstttt—asleep. It only pretends. It will know!"

"We could wait until it does sleep, then," Triss pursued. "Or wait until it hunts, until it leaves to check its nets."

"I don't know that we have enough time for that . . ." Wren began.

"Hssstt! It doesn't matter if there is enough time or not!" Stresa interjected heatedly. "If it goes to hunt or to check its nets, it will catch our scent! It will know we are here!"

"Calm down," Wren soothed. She watched the spiky creature back off a step, its cat face furrowed.

"There has to be a way," Triss whispered. "All we need is a minute or two to get down there and out again. Perhaps a diversion would work."

"Perhaps," Wren agreed, trying unsuccessfully to think of one.

Faun was chittering softly at Stresa, who replied irritably. "Yes, Squeak, the Staff! What do you think? Phfftt! Now be quiet so I can think!"

Use the Elfstones, Garth signed abruptly.

Wren took a deep breath. "As a diversion?" They were where she had known they must come all along. "All right. But I don't want us to separate. We'll never find each other again."

Garth shook his head. *Not as a diversion. As a weapon.*

She stared.

Kill it before it can kill us. One quick strike.

Triss saw the uncertainty in her eyes. "What is Garth suggesting?" he demanded.

One quick strike. Garth was right, of course. They weren't going to get the Ruhk Staff back without a fight; it was ridiculous to suppose otherwise. Why not take advantage of the element of surprise? Strike at the Wisteron before it could strike at them. Kill it or at least disable it before it had a chance to hurt them.

Wren took a deep breath. She could do it if she had to, of course. She had already made up her mind to that. The problem was that she was not at all certain the magic of the Elfstones was sufficient to overcome something as large and predatory as the Wisteron. And the magic depended directly on her. If she lacked sufficient strength, if the Wisteron proved too strong, she would have doomed them all.

On the other hand, what choice did she have? There was no better way to reach the Staff.

She reached down absently to stroke Faun and couldn't find her. "Faun?" Her eyes broke from Garth's, her mind still preoccupied with the problem at hand. Orps darted away as she shifted. Water pooled in the depressions left by her boots.

Through the cover of the trees in which they knelt, across the mud flats, she caught sight of the Tree Squeak entering the ravine.

Faun!

Stresa spotted her as well. The Splinterscat whirled, spines jutting forth. "Foolish sssttt Squeak! It heard you, Wren of the Elves! It asked what you wished. I paid no attention—phfftt—but . . ."

"The Staff?" Wren lurched to her feet, horror clouding her eyes. "You mean she's gone for the Staff?"

She was moving instantly then, racing from the trees onto the flats, running as silently as she could. She had forgotten that Faun could communicate with them. It had been a long time since the Tree Squeak had even tried. Her chest tightened. She knew how devoted the little creature was to her. It would do anything for her.

It was about to prove that now.

Faun! No!

Her breath came in quick gasps. She wanted to cry out, to call the Tree Squeak back. But she couldn't; a cry would wake the Wisteron. She reached the far edge of the flats, Orps racing away in every direction, dark flashes against the damp. She could hear Garth and Triss following, their breathing harsh. Stresa had gotten ahead of her somehow, the Splinterscat once again quicker than she expected; he was already burrowing through the trees. She followed, crawling hurriedly after, her breath catching in her throat as she broke free.

Faun was halfway down the side of the ravine, slipping smoothly, soundlessly across the rocks. Strands of webbing lay across Faun's path, but she avoided them easily. Above, the Wisteron hung motionless in its net, curled tight. The remains of Gavilan hung there as well, but Wren refused to look on those. She focused instead on Faun, on the Tree Squeak's agonizing, heartstopping descent. She was aware of Stresa a dozen feet away, flattened at the edge of the rocks. Garth and Triss had joined her, one to either side, pressed close. Triss gripped her protectively, trying to draw her back. She yanked her arm free angrily. The hand that gripped the Elfstones came up.

Faun reached the floor of the ravine and started across. Like a feather, the Squeak danced across the carpet of dry bones, carefully choosing the path, mincing like a cat. She was soundless, as inconsequential as the Orps that scattered at its coming. Above, the Wisteron continued to doze, unseeing. The vog's gray haze passed between them in thick curtains, hiding the Tree Squeak in its folds. *Shades, why didn't I keep hold of her?* Wren's blood pounded in her ears, measuring the passing of the seconds. Faun disappeared into the vog. Then the Squeak was visible again, all the way across now, crouched above the Staff.

It's too heavy, Wren thought in dismay. *She won't be able to lift it.*

But somehow Faun managed, easing it away from the layers of human deadwood, the sticks of once-life. Faun cradled it in her tiny hands, the Staff three times as long as she was, and began to walk a tightrope back, using the Staff as a pole. Wren came to her knees, breathless.

Triss nudged Wren urgently, pointing. The Wisteron had shifted in its hammock, legs stretching. It was coming awake. Wren started to rise, but Garth hurriedly pulled her back. The Wisteron curled up again, legs retracting. Faun continued toward them, tiny face intense, sinewy body taut. She reached the near side of the ravine again and paused.

Wren went cold. *Faun doesn't know how to climb out!*

Then abruptly Killeshan coughed and belched fire, miles distant, so far removed that the sound was scarcely a murmur in the silence. But the eruption triggered shock waves deep beneath the earth, ripples that spread outward from the mountain furnace like the rings that emanate from the splash of a stone. Those tremors traveled all the way to the In Ju and to the Wisteron's island lair, and swiftly a chain reaction began. The shock waves gathered force, turned quickly to heat, and the heat exploded from the mud flats directly behind Wren in a fountain of steam.

Instantly the Wisteron was awake, legs braced in its webbing, head swiveling on a thick, boneless stalk as its black mirrored eyes searched. Faun, caught unprepared for the tremors and explosion, bolted up the side of the ravine, lost her grip, and immediately fell back again. Bones clattered as the Ruhk Staff tumbled down. The hiss of the Wisteron matched that of the geyser. It spun down its webbing with blinding speed, half spider, half monkey, and all monster.

But Garth was faster. He went over the side of the ravine with the swiftness of a shadow cast by a passing cloud at night. Down the rocky outcropping he bounded, as nimble as light, dropping the last dozen feet without slowing. He landed in a crash of broken bones, stretched for the Ruhk Staff, and snatched it up. Faun was already scrambling for the safety of his broad back. Garth whirled to start up again, and the Wisteron's shadow closed over him as the creature spun down its webbing to smash him flat.

Wren came to her feet, her hand opened and her arm thrust forth, and she summoned the Elfstone power. As quick as thought it responded, streaking forth in a blinding rope of fire. It caught the Wisteron still descending, hammered into it like a massive fist, and sent it spinning away. Wren felt all of her strength leave her as the blow struck. In her urgency to save Garth, she held nothing back. The exhilaration swept through her in an instant and was gone. She gasped in shock, started to collapse, and Triss caught her about the waist. Stresa yelled at them to run.

Garth heaved up out of the ravine, his face sweat-streaked and grim, the Ruhk Staff in one hand, Faun in the other. The Tree Squeak flew to Wren, shivering. On hands and knees they crawled frantically back through the trees, rose, and began to run across the mud flats.

Wren shot a frantic glance over one shoulder.

Where was the Wisteron?

It appeared an instant later. It did not come through the trees as she had expected, but over them. It cleared the topmost limbs, surged into view in a cloud of gray, and dropped on them like a stone. Triss flung himself at Wren and knocked her from its path or she would have been crushed. Stresa turned into a ball of needles and was knocked flying. The Wisteron hissed, one clawed foot bristling with the Splinterscat's spines, and landed in a crouch. Garth dropped the Staff and turned to face it, broadsword drawn. Using both hands, the big Rover slashed at the Wisteron's face, missing as the beast drew back. It spit at Garth, a steaming spray that burned through the air like fire. "Poison!" Stresa screamed from what sounded like the bottom of a well, and Garth went down, flat against the mud.

The moment he dropped, the Wisteron charged.

Wren scrambled up again, arms extending. The Elfstones flared, and the magic responded. Fire exploded into the Wisteron from behind, sending it tumbling away in a cloud of smoke and steam. Howling in triumph, she went after it, a red haze across her vision, the power of the magic surging through her once again. She could not think; she could only react. Gathering the magic within herself, she attacked. The fire struck the Wisteron over and over, pounding it, burning it. The monster hissed and screeched, twisted away, and fought to stand upright. Out of the corner of her eye, Wren saw Garth stagger back to his feet. One hand snatched up the fallen Ruhk Staff, the other the broadsword. The big man was caked with mud. Wren saw him, then forgot him, the magic a veil that enveloped and swept away. The magic was an elixir that filled her with wonder and excitement and white heat. She was invincible; she was supreme!

But then abruptly her strength deserted her once again, drained in an instant's time, and the fire died in her hand. She closed her fingers protectively and dropped to one knee. Garth and Triss were both there at once, dragging her away, hauling her as if she were a child, racing back across the flats. Faun came out of nowhere to scramble up her leg and burrow in her shoulder. Stresa was still screaming in warning, the words unintelligible, the voice rising from somewhere back in the old growth.

Then the Wisteron shot out of the haze, burned and smoking, its sinewy body stretched out like a wolf's in flight. It slammed into them and everyone went sprawling. Wren lurched to her hands and knees in the monster's shadow, half dazed, still weak, mud in her eyes and mouth. In desperation, her protectors fought to save her. Garth stood astride her, broadsword swinging in a deadly arc. Bits and pieces of the Wisteron flew as it pressed the big Rover back. Triss appeared, hacking wildly, cutting one of the monster's legs out from under it with a bone-jarring blow. Shouts and cries filled the fetid air.

But the Wisteron was the largest and strongest of all Morrowindl's demons, of any Shadowen birthed in the lapse of the Elven magic's use, and it was the equal of them all. It whipped its tail against Triss and knocked him thirty feet to land in a crumpled heap. When Garth missed in a quick cut at its head, the beast sliced through clothing and flesh with one black-clawed limb and ripped the broadsword away. Garth had his short sword out in an instant, but a second blow sent him reeling back, tumbling over Wren to land helplessly on his back.

They would have been lost then if not for Faun. Terrified for Wren, who lay exposed now in the Wisteron's path, the Tree Squeak launched itself directly into the monster's face, a shrieking ball of fur, tiny hands tearing and ripping. The Wisteron was caught by surprise, flinched instinctively, and drew back. It reached for the Tree Squeak, anxious to crush this insignificant threat, but Faun was too quick, already scrambling along the monster's ridged back. The Wisteron twisted about in an effort to catch it, incensed.

Get up! Wren told herself, fighting to stand. The Elfstones were white heat in her tightened hand.

Then Garth was back, ragged and bloodied, broadsword flashing against the light. One massive stroke knocked the Wisteron back on two legs. A second almost severed one arm. The Wisteron hissed and writhed, curling back on itself. Faun leapt free and dashed away. Garth swung the broadsword in a deadly arc, blade sweeping, cutting, rending the air.

Wren staggered to her feet, the white heat of the Elfstones transferring from her hand to her chest, then deep into her heart.

Before her lay the Ruhk Staff, fallen from Garth's hand.

Abruptly the Wisteron spun about and spit a stream of liquid poison at Garth. This time the big man wasn't quick enough, and it struck him in the chest, burning like acid. He dropped to the mud in agony, rolling to cleanse himself.

The Wisteron was on him instantly. One clawed limb pinned him to the earth and began to press.

With both hands cupped about the Elfstones, Wren called forth the fire one final time. It exploded out of her with such force that it rocked her backward like the blow of a fist. The Wisteron was struck full on, picked up like deadwood and spun helplessly away. Fire enveloped it, a raging inferno. Wren pressed forward, the white heat of the magic reflecting in her eyes. Still the Wisteron struggled to break free, fighting to reach the girl. Between them, Garth raised himself to his hands and knees, blood everywhere, the broken blade of the broadsword gripped in one hand. For Wren, everything slowed to a crawl, a dream that was happening only in her mind. Triss was a vague shape stumbling back out of the mist, Stresa a voice without a body, Faun a memory, and the world a shifting, endless haze. Garth's dark eyes looked up at her from his ragged, broken form. At her feet lay the Ruhk Staff and the Loden, the last hope of the Elven people, their vessel of safekeeping, their chance at life. She shrugged it all away and buried herself in the power of the Elfstones, in the magic of her blood, shaping it, directing it, and knowing in some dark, secretive place that her own chance at life had come down to this.

Before her, the Wisteron surged back to its feet.

Help me! she cried out in the silence of her mind.

Then she directed the fire against the mud on which the Wisteron stood, melting it to soup, to a mire as liquid and yielding as quicksand. The Wisteron lurched forward and sank to its knees. The mud bubbled and spit like Killeshan's flow, sucking at the thing that floundered within it. The Wisteron hissed and spit and struggled to break free. But its weight was significant and drew it down; its legs could find no footing. The Elfstone fire burned about it, coring the mud deeper and deeper, pooling it in a bottomless pit. The Wisteron thrashed frantically, steadily sinking. It shrieked, a sound that froze the air to silence.

Then the mud closed over it, the roiling surface glazing orange and yellow with fire, and it was gone.

27

Wren's fingers closed over the Elfstones, mechanical appendages that seemed to belong to someone else. The fire flared once in response and died. She stood frozen in place for a moment, unable to find the strength to make herself move—light-headed, floating, a half step out of time. The magic spit and hissed within her, making small dashes along her arms and legs that caused her to gasp and shiver. She had trouble breathing; her chest was constricted, and her throat was dry and raw.

Before her, the flames that seared the surface of the mud flats diminished to small blue tongues and died into steam. Garth was still braced on hands and knees, head lowered and chest heaving. All about, the In Ju was cavernous and still.

Then Faun darted out of nowhere, scrambled up her arm, and nuzzled into her neck and shoulder, squeaking softly. She closed her eyes against the warm fur, remembering how the little creature had saved her, thinking it was a miracle that any of them were still alive.

She moved finally, forcing herself to take one step and then another, driven by her fear for Garth and by the sight of all that blood. She forced aside the last traces of exhilaration that were the magic's leavings, groped past her craving to savor the power anew, slipped the Elfstones into her pocket, and knelt hurriedly beside her friend. Garth lifted his head to look at her. His face was muddied almost beyond recognition, but the dark eyes were bright and certain.

"Garth," she whispered.

He was ripped open from shoulder to ribs on his left side, and his chest was burned black by the poison. Caked mud had helped to slow the flow of blood, but the wounds needed cleaning or they would become infected.

She eased Faun down gently, then put her arms around Garth and tried to help him to his feet. She could barely move him.

"Wait," a voice called out. "I'll help."

It was Triss, stumbling out of the mist, looking only marginally better off than Garth. He was streaked with mud and swamp water. His left arm hung limp; he carried his short sword in his right. One side of his face was a sheet of blood.

But the Captain of the Home Guard seemed unaware of his injuries. He draped Garth's arm about his shoulders and with a heave brought the big man to his feet. With Wren supporting from the other side, they recrossed the mud flats toward the old-growth acacia.

Stresa lumbered into view, quills sticking out in every direction. "This way! Phhffft! In here! In the shade!"

They bore Garth to a patch of dry earth that lay in the cradle of a cluster of tree roots and laid him down again. Wren worked quickly to cut away his tunic. She had only a little fresh water left, but used almost all of it to clean his wounds. The rest she gave to Triss for his face. She used sewing thread and a needle to stitch the gash closed and bound the big man with strips of cloth torn from the last of her extra clothing. Garth watched her work, silent, unmoving, as if trying to memorize her face. She signed to him once or twice, but he merely nodded and did not sign back. She did not like what she saw.

Then she worked on Triss. The face wound was superficial, merely a deep abrasion. But his left arm was broken. She set it, cut splints of wood and bound them with his belt. He winced once or twice as she worked, but did not cry out. He thanked her when she was done, solemn, embarrassed. She smiled at him.

Only then did she remember the Ruhk Staff, still lying somewhere out in the mud. Hurriedly she went back for it, leaving the cover of the old growth, crossing the flats once again. Orps scurried away at her approach, flashing bits of silver light. The air was empty and still, but the sound of Killeshan's rumble echoed ominously from beyond the wall of the mist, and the earth shivered in response. She found the Ruhk Staff where it had fallen and picked it up. The Loden sparkled like a cluster of small stars. So much given up on its behalf, she thought, on behalf of the Elven people, trapped inside. She experienced a dark moment of regret, a sudden urge to toss it aside, to sink it as deep within the mud as the Wisteron. The Elves, who had done so much damage with their magic, who had created the Shadowen with their ambition and who had abandoned the Four Lands to a savagery for which they were responsible, might be better gone. But she had made her decision on the Elves. Besides, she knew it was not the fault of these Elves, not of this generation, and it was wrong to hold an entire people accountable for the acts of a few in any case. Allanon must have counted on her thinking like that. He must have foreseen that she would discover the truth and decide for herself the wisdom of his charge. *Find the Elves and return them to the Four Lands.* She had wondered why many times. She thought now she was beginning to see. Who better than the Elves to right the wrong that had been done? Who better to lead the fight against the Shadowen?

She trudged back across the flats, numbness setting in, the last traces of the magic's euphoria fading away. She was tired and sad and oddly lost. But she knew she could not give in to these feelings. She had the Ruhk Staff back again, and the journey to the beaches and the search for Tiger Ty lay ahead. And there were still the demons.

Stresa was waiting at the edge of the trees. The rough voice was a whisper of warning. "Hsstt. He is badly hurt, Wren of the Elves. Your big friend. Be warned. The poison is a bad thing. Phffttt. He may not be able to come with us."

She brushed past the Splinterscat, irritated, abrupt. "He'll manage," she snapped.

With help from Triss, she got Garth to his feet once more and they started out. It was past midday, the light faint and hazy through the screen of vog, the heat a blanket of sweltering damp. Stresa led, working his way doggedly through the jungle's maze, choosing a path that gave those following a chance to maneuver with Garth. The In Ju seemed empty, as if the death of the Wisteron had killed everything that lived within it. But the silence was mostly a response to the earth tremors, Wren thought. The creatures of Morrowindl sensed that all was not well, and for the moment at least they had suspended their normal activities and gone into hiding, waiting to discover what would happen.

She watched Garth's face as they walked, saw the intensity of his eyes, the mask of pain that stretched his skin tight across his bones. He did not look at her, his gaze fixed purposefully on the path ahead. He was keeping upright through sheer determination.

It was twilight by the time they cleared the In Ju and passed into the forested hill country beyond. They found a clearing with a spring, and she cleaned her giant friend's wounds anew. There was nothing to eat; all of their provisions had been consumed or lost, and they were uncertain which of the island's roots and tree fruit was safe. They had to make do with spring water. Triss found enough dry wood to make a fire, but it began to rain almost immediately, and within seconds everything was soaked. They huddled back within the shelter of a broad-limbed koa, shoulder to shoulder against the encroaching dark. After a time, Stresa moved out to where he could keep watch, muttering something about being the only one left who was fit for the job. Wren didn't argue the point; she was half-inclined to agree. The light faded steadily from silver to gray to black. The forest was transformed, suddenly alive with movement as the need for food brought its creatures forth to hunt, but nothing that went abroad made any attempt to approach their refuge. Mist seeped through the trees and grasses in lazy tendrils. Water dripped softly from the leaves. Faun squirmed in Wren's arms, burrowing deep into her shoulder.

At midnight, Killeshan erupted. Fire belched out in a shower of sparks and flaming debris, and ash and smoke spewed forth. The sound it made was terrifying, a booming that shattered the night stillness and brought everyone awake with a start. The initial explosion turned quickly to a series of rumbles that built one upon the other until the entire island was shaking. Even from as far away as they were, the eruption was visible, a deep red glow against the black that lifted skyward and seemed to hang there. Close at hand, the earth split in small rents and steam rose in geysers, hissing and burning. In the shadows beyond, the island's creatures raced wildly about, fleeing without direction or purpose, frightened by the intensity of the tremors, by the sound and the glare. The company huddled back against the koa, fighting the urge to join them. But flight in such blackness was dangerous, Wren knew, and Stresa was quick to remind her that they must stay put until daylight.

The eruptions continued all night long, one after the other, a series of thundering coughs and fiery convulsions that threatened to rend Morrowindl from end to end. Fires burned high on Killeshan's slopes as lava flows began their descent to the sea. Cliffs slid away in a roar of broken stone, avalanches that tore free whole mountainsides. Giant trees snapped at their centers and tumbled to the earth.

Wren closed her eyes and tried unsuccessfully to sleep.

Toward dawn, Stresa rose to scout the area leading out and Triss took the Splinterscat's place at watch. Wren was left alone with Garth. The big man slept fitfully, his face bathed in sweat, his body wracked with convulsions. He was running a fever, and the heat of his body was palpable. As she watched him twist and turn against his discomfort, she found herself thinking of all they had been through together. She had worried about him before, but never as much as now. In part, her concern was magnified by her sense of helplessness. Morrowindl remained a foreign world to her, and her knowledge of it was too little. She could not help thinking that there must be something more that she could do for her big friend if she only knew what. She was reminded of Ellenroh, stricken by a fever similar to Garth's, a fever that none of them had understood. She had lost her grandmother; she did not intend to lose her best friend. She reassured herself over and over that Garth was strong, that he possessed great endurance. He could survive anything; he always had.

It was growing light, and she had just closed her eyes against her fatigue and depression when the big man surprised her by touching her gently on the arm. When she lifted her head to look at him, he began to sign.

I want you to do something for me.

She nodded, and her fingers repeated her words. "What?"

It will be difficult for you, but it is necessary.

She tried to see his eyes and couldn't. He was turned too far into the shadows.

I want you to forgive me.

"Forgive you for what?"

I have lied to you about something. I have lied repeatedly. Ever since I have known you.

She shook her head, confused, anxious, weary to the bone. "Lied about what?"

His gaze never faltered. *About your parents. About your mother and father. I knew them. I knew who they were and where they came from. I knew everything.*

She stared, not quite ready to believe what she was hearing.

Listen to me, Wren. Your mother understood the impact of Eowen's prophecy far better than the queen. The prophecy said that you must be taken from Morrowindl if you were to live, but it also said that you would one day return to save the Elves. Your mother correctly judged that whatever salvation you could provide your people would be tied in some way to a confrontation with the evil they had created. I did not know this at the time; I have surmised it since. What I did know was that your mother was determined that you be raised to be strong enough to withstand any danger, any foe, any trial that was required of you. That was why she gave you to me.

Wren was stunned. "To you? Directly to you?"

Garth shifted, pushing himself into a sitting position, giving his hands more freedom. He grunted with the effort. Wren could see blood soaking through the bandages of his wounds.

She came with her husband to the Rovers, sent by the Wing Riders. She came to us because she was told that we were the strongest of the free peoples, that we trained our children from birth to survive because survival is the hardest part of every Rover's life. We have always been an outcast people and as such have found it necessary to be stronger than any other. So your mother and your father came to us, to my family, a tribe of several hundred living on the plains below the Myrian, and asked if there were someone among us who could be trusted in the schooling of their daughter. They wished her to be trained in the Rover way, to begin learning as soon as she was old enough how to survive in a world where everyone and everything was a potential enemy. I was recommended. We talked, your parents and I, and I agreed to be your teacher.

He coughed, a deep, racking sound that tore from the depths of his chest. His head lowered momentarily as he gasped for breath.

"Garth," she whispered, frightened now. "Tell me about this later, after you have rested."

He shook his head. *No. I want this finished. I have carried it with me for too long.*

"But you can hardly breathe, you can barely . . ."

I am stronger than you think. His hand closed over her own momentarily and released. *Are you afraid I might be dying?*

She swallowed against her tears. "Yes."

Does that frighten you so? After all I have taught you?

"Yes."

The dark eyes blinked, and he gave her a strange look. *Then I will not die until you are ready for me to do so.*

She nodded wordlessly, not understanding what he meant, wary of the look, anxious only that he live, whatever bargain it required.

His breath exhaled in a thick rattle. *Good. Your mother, then. She was everything you have been told—strong, kind, determined, devoted to you. But she had decided that she must return to her people. She had made up her mind before she left Morrowindl, I think. Your father acquiesced. I don't know the reason for their decision; I only know that your mother was bound in countless ways to her own mother and to her people, and your father was desperately in love with her. In any case, it was agreed that you should be sent to live with the Ohmsfords in Shady Vale until you were five—the beginning age for training a Rover child—and then given back to me. You were to be told that your mother was a Rover and your father an Ohmsford and that your ancestors were Elves. You were to be told nothing else.*

Wren shook her head in disbelief. "Why, Garth? Why keep it all a secret from me?"

Because your mother understood how dangerous it was to try to influence the workings of a prophecy. She could have tried to keep you safe, to prevent you from returning to Morrowindl. She could have stayed with you and told you what was foreordained. But what harm might she have caused by interfering so? She knew enough of prophecies to recognize the threat. It was better, she believed, that you grow to womanhood without knowing the specifics of what Eowen had foretold, that you find your destiny on your own, however it was meant to be. It was given to me to prepare you.

"So you knew everything? All of it? You knew about the Elfstones?"

No. Not about the Elfstones. Like you, I thought them painted rocks. I was told to make certain that you knew where they came from, that they were your heritage from your parents. I was to see to it that you never lost them. Your mother was convinced, I suppose, that like your destiny, the power of the Elfstones would reveal itself when it was time.

"But you knew the rest, all the time I was growing up? And after, when I went to the Hadeshorn, when I was sent in search of the Elves?"

I knew.

"And didn't tell me?" There was a hint of anger in her voice now, the first. The impact of what he was telling her was beginning to set in. "Never a word, even when I asked?"

I could not.

"What do you mean, you could not?" She was incensed. "Why?"

Because I promised your mother. She swore me to secrecy. You were to know nothing of your true heritage, nothing of the Elessedils, Arborlon, or Morrowindl, nothing of the prophecy. You were to discover it on your own or not, as fate decreed. I was not to aid you in any way. I was to go with you when it came time if I chose. I was to protect you as best I could. But I was to tell you nothing.

"Ever?"

The big man's breath rattled in his chest, and his fingers hesitated. *I swore an oath. I swore that I would tell you nothing until the prophecy came to pass, if it ever did—nothing until you had come back into Arborlon, until you had discovered the truth for yourself, until you had done whatever it was you were fated to do to help your people. I promised.*

She sank back on her heels, despair washing through her. *Trust no one,* the Addershag had warned. *No one.* She had believed she realized the impact of those words. She had thought she understood.

But this . . .

"Oh, Garth," she whispered in dismay. "I trusted you!"

You lost nothing by doing so, Wren.

"Didn't I?"

They faced each other, silent, motionless. Everything that had happened to Wren since Cogline had first come to her those many weeks past seemed to gather and settle on her shoulders like an enormous weight. So many harrowing escapes, so many deaths, so much lost—she felt it all, the whole of it, come together in a single moment, in this truth terrible and unexpected.

Had you known before coming, it might have changed everything. Your mother understood that. Your father as well. Perhaps I would have told you if I could, but my promise bound me. The big frame shifted, and the sharply etched bones of the other's face lifted into the light. *Tell me, if you can, that I should have done otherwise. Tell me, Wren, that I should have broken my promise.*

Her mouth was a tight, bitter line. "You should have."

He held her gaze, dark eyes flat and expressionless.

"No," she admitted finally, tears in her eyes. "You shouldn't have." She looked away, empty and lost. "But that doesn't help. Everyone has lied to me. Everyone. Even you. The Addershag was right, Garth, and that's what hurts. There were too many lies, too many secrets, and I wasn't part of any of them."

She cried silently, head lowered. "Someone should have trusted me. My whole life has been changed, and I have had nothing to say about it. Look what's been done!"

One big hand brushed her own. *Think, Wren. The choices have all been yours. No one has made them for you; no one has shown you the way. Had you known the truth of things, had you understood the expectations held for you, would it have been the same? Could you say the choices were yours in that case?*

She looked back, hesitant.

Would it have been better to know you were Ellenroh Elessedil's granddaughter, that the Elfstones you thought painted rocks were real, that when you grew to womanhood you would one day be expected to travel to Morrowindl and, because of a prophecy given before you were born, save the Elves? How free would you have been to act then? How much would you have grown? What would you have become?

She took a deep breath. "I don't know. But perhaps I should have been given the chance to find out."

The light was stronger now as dawn broke somewhere beyond the pall of the mist and trees. Faun lifted her head from out of Wren's lap where she had lain motionless. Triss had come back from the edge of the dark; he stood watching them in silence. The night sounds had died away, and the frantic movement had ceased. In the distance, the sounds of Killeshan's eruption continued unabated, steady and ominous. The earth shook faintly, and the fire of the lava rose skyward into gray smoke and ash.

Garth stirred, his hands moving. *Wren,* he signed. *I did what I was asked, what I promised. I did the best I could. I wish it had not been necessary to deceive you. I wish I had been able to give you the chance you ask for.*

She looked at him for a long time, and finally nodded. "I know."

The strong, dark face was rigid with concentration. *Don't be angry with your mother and father. They did what they thought they had to do, what they believed was right.*

She nodded again. She did not trust herself to speak.

You must find a way to forgive us all.

She swallowed hard. "I wish . . . I wish I didn't hurt so much."

Wren, look at me.

She did so, reluctantly, warily.

We are not finished yet. There is one thing more.

She felt a chill settle in the pit of her stomach, an ache of something sensed but not yet fully realized. She saw Stresa appear out of the trees to one side, lumbering heavily, winded and damp. He slowed as he approached them, aware that something was happening, a confrontation perhaps, a revelation, a thing inviolate.

"Stresa," Wren greeted quickly, anxious to avoid hearing any more from Garth.

The Splinterscat swung his blunt cat face from one human to the other. "We can go now," he said. "In fact, we should. The mountain is coming down. Sooner or later it will reach here."

"We must hurry," she agreed, rising. She snatched up the Ruhk Staff, then looked down anxiously at her injured friend. "Garth?"

We need to speak alone first.

Her throat tightened anew. "Why?"

Ask the others to go ahead a short distance and wait for us. Tell them we won't be long.

She hesitated, then looked at Stresa and Triss. "I need a moment with Garth. Wait for us up ahead. Please."

They stared back at her without speaking, then nodded reluctantly, Triss first, lean face expressionless, and Stresa with sharp-eyed suspicion.

"Take Faun," she asked as an afterthought, disengaging the Tree Squeak from its perch on her shoulder and setting it gently on the ground.

Stresa hissed at the little creature and sent it racing off into the trees. He looked back at her with sad, knowing eyes. "Call, rwwwlll Wren of the Elves, if you need us."

When they had gone, the sound of their footsteps fading, she faced Garth once more, the Staff gripped tightly in both hands. "What is it?"

The big man beckoned. *Don't be frightened. Here. Sit next to me. Listen a moment and don't interrupt.*

She did as he asked, kneeling close enough that her leg was pressed up against his body. She could feel the heat of his fever. Mist and pale light obscured him in a shading of gray, and the world about was fuzzy and thick with heat.

She lay the Ruhk Staff down beside her, and Garth's big hands began to sign.

Something is happening to me. Inside. The Wisteron's poison, I think. It creeps through me like a living thing, fire that sears and deadens. I can feel it working about, changing me. It is a bad feeling.

"I'll wash the wounds again, rebind them."

No, Wren. What is happening now is beyond that, beyond anything you can do. The poison is in my system, all through me.

Her breath was hurried, angry. "If you are too weak, we will carry you."

I was weak at first, but the weakness is passing now. I am growing stronger again. But the strength is not my own.

She stared at him, not really understanding, but frightened all the same. She shook her head. "What are you saying?"

He looked at her with fierce determination, his dark eyes hard, his face all angles and planes, chiseled in stone. *The Wisteron was a Shadowen. Like the Drakuls. Remember Eowen?*

She shuddered, jerked back and tried to rise. He grabbed her and held her in place, keeping their eyes locked. *Look at me.*

She tried and couldn't. She saw him and at the same time didn't, aware of the lines that framed him but unable to see the colors and shadings between, as if doing so would reveal the truth she feared. "Let me go!"

Then everything broke within her, and she began to cry. She did so soundlessly, and only the heaving of her shoulders gave her away. She closed her eyes against the rage of feelings within, the horror of the world about her, the terrible price it seemed to require over and over again. She saw Garth even there, etched within her mind—the dark confidence and strength radiating from his face, the smile he reserved exclusively for her, the wisdom, the friendship, and the love.

"I can't lose you," she whispered, no longer bothering to sign, the words a murmur. "I can't!"

His hands released her, and her eyes opened. *Look at me.*

She took a deep breath and did so.

Look into my eyes.

She did. She looked down into the soul of her oldest and most trusted friend. A wicked red glimmer looked back.

It already begins, he signed.

She shook her head in furious denial.

I can't let it happen, Wren. But I can't do it alone. Not and be sure. You have to help me let go.

"No."

One hand slipped down to his belt and pulled free the long knife, its razor-sharp blade glinting in the half-light. She shuddered and drew back, but he grabbed her wrist and forced the handle of the knife into her palm.

His hands signed, quick, steady. *There is no more time left to us. What we've had has been good. I do not regret a moment of it. I am proud of you, Wren. You are my strength, my wisdom, my skill, my experience, my life, everything I am, the best of me. And still your own person, distinct in every way. You are what you were meant to be—a Rover girl become Queen of the Elves. I can't give you anything more. It is a good time to say good-bye.*

Wren couldn't breathe. She couldn't see clearly. "You can't ask this of me! You can't!"

I have to. There is no one else. No one I could depend upon to do it right.

"No!" She dropped the knife as if it had burned her skin. "I would rather," she choked, crying, "be dead myself!"

He reached down for the knife and carefully placed it back in her hand.

She shook her head over and over, saying no, no. He touched her, drawing her eyes once more to his own. He was shivering now, just cold perhaps, but maybe something more. The red glow was more pronounced, stronger.

I am slipping away, Wren. I am being stolen from myself. You have to hurry. Do it quickly. Don't let me become . . . He couldn't finish, his great, strong hands shaking now as well. *You can do it. We have practiced often enough. I can't trust myself. I might . . .*

Wren's muscles were so tight she could barely move. She glanced over her shoulder, thinking to call Stresa back, or Triss, desperate for anyone. But there was no one who could help her, she knew. There was nothing anyone could do.

She turned quickly back. "There must be an antidote that will counteract the poison, mustn't there?" Her words were frantic. "I'll ask Stresa! He'll know! I'll get him back!"

The big hands cut her short. *Stresa already knows the truth. You saw it in his eyes. There isn't anything he can do. There never was. Let it go. Help me. Take the knife and use it.*

No!

You have to.

No!

One hand swept up suddenly as if to strike her, and instinctively she reacted with a block to counter, the hand with the knife lifting, freezing, inches above his chest. Their eyes locked. For an instant, everything washed away within Wren but the terrible recognition of what was needed. The truth stunned her. She caught her breath and held it.

Quick, Wren . . . She did not move. He took her hand and gently lowered it until the knife blade was resting against his tunic, against his chest. *Do it.*

Her head shook slowly, steadily from side to side, a barely perceptible movement.

Wren. Help me.

She looked down at him, deep into his eyes, and into the red glare that was consuming him, that rose out of the horror growing within. She remembered standing next to him as a child when she had first come to live with the Rovers, barely as tall as his knee. She remembered herself at ten, whip-thin, leather-tough, racing to catch him in the forest. She remembered their games, constant, unending, all directed toward her training.

She felt his breath on her face. She felt the closeness of him and thought of the comfort it had given her as a child.

"Garth," she whispered in despair, and felt the great hands come up to tighten over her own.

Then she thrust the long knife home.

28

S he fled then. She ran from the clearing into the trees, numb with grief, half blind with tears, the Ruhk Staff clutched before her in both hands like a shield. She raced through the shadows and half-light of the island's early morning, oblivious to Killeshan's distant rumble, to Morrowindl's shudder in response, lost to everything but the need to escape the time and place of Garth's death, even knowing she could never escape its memory. She tore past brush and limbs with heedless disregard, through tall grasses and brambles, along ridges of earth encrusted with lava rock, and over dead-wood and scattered debris. She sensed none of it. It was not her body that fled; it was her mind.

Garth!

She called out to him endlessly, chasing after her memories of him, as if by catching one she might bring him back to life. She saw him race away, spectral, phantasmagoric. Parts of him appeared and faded in the air before her, blurred and distant images from times gone by. She saw herself give chase as she had so many times when they had played at being Tracker and prey, when they had practiced the lessons of staying alive. She saw herself that last day in the Tirfing before Cogline had appeared and everything had changed forever, skirting the shores of the Myrian, searching for signs. She watched him drop from the trees, huge, silent, and quick. She felt him grapple for her, felt herself slip away, felt her long knife rise and descend. She heard herself laugh. *You're dead, Garth.*

And now he really was.

Somehow—it was never entirely clear—she stumbled upon the others of the little company, the few who remained alive, Triss, the last of the Elves, the last besides herself, and Stresa and Faun. She careened into them, spun away angrily as if they were hindrances, and kept going. They came after her, of course, running to catch up, calling out urgently, asking what was wrong, what had happened, where was Garth?

Gone, she said, head shaking. Not coming.

But it was okay. It was all right.

He was safe now.

Still running, she heard Triss demand again, *What is wrong?* And Stresa reply, *Hsssstt, can't you see?* Words, whispered furtively, passed between them, but she didn't catch their meaning, didn't care to. Faun leapt from the pathway to her arm, clinging possessively, but she shook the Tree Squeak off roughly. She didn't want to be touched. She could barely stand to be inside her own skin.

She broke free of the trees.

"Lady Wren!" she heard Triss cry out to her.

Then she was scrambling up a lava slide, clawing and digging at the sharp rock, feeling it cut into her hands and knees. Her breath rasped heavily from her throat, and she was coughing, choking on words that wouldn't come. The Ruhk Staff fell from her hands, and she abandoned it. She cast everything away, the whole of who and what she was, sickened by the thought of it, wanting only to flee, to escape, to run until there was no-where left to go.

When she collapsed finally, exhausted, stretched flat on the slide, sobbing uncontrollably, it was Triss who reached her first, who cradled her as if she were a child, who soothed her with words and small touches and gave her a measure of the comfort she needed. He helped her to her feet, turned her about, and took her back down to the forest below. Carrying the Ruhk Staff in one arm and supporting her with the other, he guided her through the morning hours like a shepherd a stray lamb, asking nothing of her but that she place one foot before the other and that she continue to walk with him. Stresa took the lead, his bulky form becoming the point of reference on which she focused, the steadily changing object toward which she moved, first one foot, then the other, over and over again. Faun returned for another try at scrambling up her leg and onto her arm, and this time she welcomed the intrusion, pressing the Tree Squeak close, nuzzling back against the little creature's warmth and softness.

They traveled all day like this, companions on a journey that required no words. The few times they paused to rest, Wren accepted the water Triss gave her to drink and the fruit he pressed into her palm and did not bother to ask where it came from or if it was safe to eat. The daylight dimmed as clouds massed from horizon to horizon, as the vog thickened beneath. Killeshan stormed behind them, the eruptions unchecked now, fire and ash and smoke spewing skyward in long geysers, the smell of sulfur thick in the air, the island shaking and rocking. When darkness finally descended, the crest of the mountain was bathed in a blood-red corona that flared anew with each eruption and sent trailers of fire all down the distant slopes where the lava ran to the sea. Boulders grated and crunched as the molten rock carried them away, and trees burned with a sharp, crackling despair. The wind died to nothing, a haze settled over everything, and the island became a fire-rimmed cage in which the inhabitants bumped up against one another in frightened, angry confusion.

Stresa settled them that night in a cleft of rock that sheltered on three sides amid a grove of wiry ironwood stripped all but bare of foliage. They huddled in the dark with their backs to the wall and watched the holocaust beyond grow brighter. They were still a day from the beaches, a day from any rendezvous with Tiger Ty, and the destruction of the island was imminent. Wren came back to herself enough to realize the danger they were in. Sipping at the cup of water Triss gave her, listening to the sound of his voice as he continued to speak quietly, reassuringly, she remembered what it was that she was supposed to do and that it was Tiger Ty alone who could help her to do it.

"Triss," she said finally, unexpectedly, seeing him for the first time, speaking his name in acknowledgment, making him smile in relief.

Shortly after, the demons appeared, Morrowindl's Shadowen, the first of those that had escaped Killeshan's fiery flow, fled down out of the hills toward the beaches, lost and confused and ready to kill anything they came upon. They stumbled out of the fiery gloom, a ragged collection of mis-shapen horrors, and attacked unthinkingly, responding to instinct and to their own peculiar madness. Stresa heard them coming, sharp ears picking out the sound of their approach, and warned the others seconds before the attack. Sword drawn, Triss met the rush, withstood it, and very nearly turned it aside, almost a match for the things even with only one useful arm. But the demons were crazed past fear or reason, driven from their high country by something beyond understanding. These humans were a lesser threat. They rallied and attacked anew, determined to exact some measure of revenge from the source at hand.

But now Wren was facing them, consumed by her own madness, cold and reasoned, and she sent the magic of the Elfstones scything into them like razors. Too late, they realized the danger. The magic caught them up and they vanished in bursts of fire and sudden screams. In seconds nothing remained but smoke and ash.

Others came all during the night, small bunches of them, launching out of the darkness in frenzied rushes that carried them to quick and certain deaths. Wren destroyed them without feeling, without regret, and then burned the forest about until it was as fiery as the slopes above where the lava rivers steamed. As morning approached, the whole of their shelter for fifty yards out was barren and smoking, a charnel house of bodies blackened beyond recognition, a graveyard in which only they survived. There was no sleep, no rest, and little respite against the assaults. Dawn found them hollow-eyed and staring, gaunt and ragged figures against the coming light. Triss was wounded in half a dozen new places, his clothing in rags, all of his weapons lost or broken but his short sword. Wren's face was gray with ash, and her hands shook with the infusion of the Elfstones' power. Stresa's quills fanned out in every direction, and it did not seem as if they would ever settle back in place. Faun crouched next to Wren like a coiled spring.

As the light crept out of the east, silver sunrise through the haze of fire and smoke, Wren told them finally what had become of Garth, needing at last to tell, anxious to rid herself of the solitary burden she bore, the bitter knowledge that was hers alone. She told them quietly, softly, in the silence that followed the last of the attacks. She cried again, thinking that perhaps she would never stop. But the tears were cleansing this time, as if finally washing away some of the hurt. They listened to her wordlessly, the Captain of the Home Guard, the Splinterscat, and the Tree Squeak, gathered close so that nothing would be missed, even Faun, who might or might not have understood her words, nestled against her shoulder. The words flowed from her easily, the dam of her despair and shame giving way, and a kind of peace settled deep within her.

"Rwwlll Wren, it was what was needed," Stresa told her solemnly when she had finished.

"You knew, didn't you?" she asked in reply.

"Hssstt. Yes. I understood what the poison would do. But I could not tell you, Wren of the Elves, because you would not have wanted to believe. It had to come from him."

And the Splinterscat was right, of course, although it no longer really mattered. They talked a bit longer while the light seeped slowly past the gloom, brightening the world about them, their world of black ruin in which smoke still curled skyward in wispy spirals and the earth still trembled with the fury of Killeshan's discontent.

"He gave his life for you, Lady Wren," Triss offered solemnly. "He stood over you when the Wisteron would have claimed you and fought to keep you safe. None of us would have fared as well. We tried, but only Garth had the strength. Keep that as your memory of him."

But she could still feel herself pushing against the handle of the long knife as it slipped into his heart, still feel his hands closing over hers, almost as if to absolve her of responsibility. She would always feel them there, she thought. She would always see what had been in his eyes.

They started out again soon after, crossing the charred battleground of the night gone past to the fresh green landscape of the day that lay ahead, passing toward the last of the country that separated them from the beach. The tremors underfoot were constant still, and the fires of the lava rivers were burning closer, streaming down the mountainside above. Things fled about them in all directions, and even the demons did not pause to attack. Everything raced to escape the burning heat, driven by Killeshan's fury toward the shores of the Blue Divide. Morrowindl was turning slowly into a cauldron of fire, eating away at itself from the center out. Cracks were beginning to appear everywhere, vast fissures that opened into blackness, that hissed and spit with steam and heat. The world that had flourished in the wake of the Elven magic's use was disappearing, and within days only the rocks and the ashes of the dead would remain. A new world was evolving about the little company as it fled, and when it was complete nothing of the old would be left upon it.

They passed down into the meadows of tall grasses that bounded the final stretches of old growth bordering the shoreline. The grasses had already begun to curl and die, smoked and steamed by heat and gases, the life seared out of them. Scrub brush broke apart beneath their boots, dried and lifeless. Fires burned in hot spots all about, and to their right, across a deep ravine, a thin ribbon of red fire worked its way relentlessly through a patchwork of wildflowers toward a stand of acacia that waited in helpless, frozen anticipation. Clouds of black soot roiled down out of the heights of the In Ju, where the jungle burned slowly to the waterline, the swamp beneath already beginning to boil. Rock and ash showered down from somewhere beyond their vision like hail out of clouds, thrown by the volcano's continuing explosions. The wind shifted and it grew harder to see. It was midday, and the sky was as raw and gray and hazy as autumn twilight.

Wren's head felt light and substanceless, a part of the air she breathed. Her bones were loose within her body, and the fire of the Elfstones' magic still flared and sparked like embers cooling. She searched the land about her and could not seem to focus. Everything drifted in the manner of clouds.

"Stresa, how much farther?" she asked.

"A ways," the Splinterscat growled without turning. "Phhfftt. Keep walking, Wren of the Elves."

She did, knowing that her strength was failing and wondering absently if it was from so much use of the magic or from exhaustion. She felt Triss move close, one arm coming about her shoulders.

"Lean on me," he whispered, and took her weight against his own.

The meadows passed away with the sweep of the sun west, and they reached the old growth. Already it was aflame to the south, the topmost branches burning, smoke billowing. They pushed through rapidly, skidding and slipping on moss and leaves and loose rock. The trees were silent and empty, the pillars of a hall roofed in low-hanging clouds and mist. Growls and snarls rose up out of the haze, distant, but all about.

The trek wore on. Once something huge moved in the shadows off to one side, and Stresa wheeled to face it, spines lifting. But nothing appeared, and after a moment they moved on. The sound of water crashing against rocks sounded ahead, the rise and fall of the ocean. Wren found herself smiling, clasping the Ruhk Staff tight against her breast. There was still a chance for them, she thought wearily. There was still hope that they might escape.

Then finally, as daylight faded behind them and sunset brightened into silver and red ahead, they broke clear of the trees and found themselves staring out from a high bluff over the vast expanse of the Blue Divide. Smoke and ash clouded the air close at hand, but beyond its screen the horizon was ablaze with color.

The company staggered forward and stopped. The bluff fell away sharply to a shoreline jagged with rocks. There were no beaches anywhere and no sign of Tiger Ty.

Wren leaned heavily on the Staff, searching the sky. It stretched away, a vast and empty expanse.

"Tiger Ty!" she whispered in despair.

Triss released her and moved away, searching the bluff. "Down there," he signaled after a moment, pointing north. "There's a beach, if we can get to it."

But Stresa was already shaking his grizzled head. "Ssssttt! We'll have to go back through the woods, back into the smoke and the things it hides. Not a smart idea with darkness coming. Phffftt!"

Wren watched helplessly as the sun settled down against the ocean's edge and began to disappear. In minutes it would be dark. They had come so far, she thought, and whispered, "No," so that only she could hear.

She laid down the Staff and slipped free the Elfstones. Holding them forth, she sent the white magic streaking across the sky from end to end, a flare of brightness against the gray twilight. The light shimmered like fire and disappeared. They all stood looking after it, watching the dark approach, watching the sun paint the sky with color as it sank from view.

Behind them, the hunters began to gather, the demons come down from the heights, the black things either tracking them or drawn by the magic. Their shadows pushed against the edges of the twilight, growling, snarling, edging steadily closer. Wren and her companions were trapped on the bluff, caught against the drop into the ocean. Wren felt the rattle of her bones, of her breath, of her failing strength. It was too much to expect that Tiger Ty would be there for them after all this time, too much to hope for. Yet she refused to let go of the only hope left to them. Once more she would use the magic, if need be. Once more, for good measure. Because there wasn't enough left in any case to keep them alive another night. There was not enough strength left in her to use it, not enough left in any of them to matter.

Triss stepped out to confront the shadows in the trees, lean and hard, broken arm hanging stiff, sword arm bent and ready. "Keep behind me," he ordered.

The seconds slipped quickly away. The colors in the western sky faded into gray. Twilight deepened to a pale shade of ash.

"There!" Stresa warned.

Something launched itself out of the dark, a massive form, hammering into Triss, throwing him down. Another rushed in behind it, and Stresa showered it with quills. Wren swung the Elfstones up and sent the magic streaking forth, burning the things closest. They screamed and hastily withdrew. Triss lay unconscious on the earth.

Wren sagged to her knees, exhausted.

"Sssttt stand up!" Stresa growled desperately.

A handful of misshapen forms detached themselves anew and began to inch forward.

"Stand up!"

Then a shriek split the near silence, a sound like the tearing out of a human life, and a huge shadow swept the bluff. Claws raked the edges of the trees and sent the attackers scattering into the dark. Wren stared upward in disbelief, speechless. *Had she seen . . . ?* The shadow swung away, black wings knifelike against the sky, and another shriek emitted from its throat.

"Spirit!" Wren screamed in recognition.

Back swung the Roc and plummeted to the bluff edge where it settled with a mad beating of wings. A small, wiry form leapt down, yelling and shouting wildly.

"Ho, this way, quick now! They won't stay frightened long!"

Tiger Ty!

And when Wren pulled Triss to his feet and staggered forward to meet the little man, she found the Tiger Ty she remembered from all those weeks ago, wrinkled and smiling within his brown skin, a scarecrow of bones and leather, rough hands ready and bright eyes quick. He looked at her, at her companions, at the Ruhk Staff she carried, and he laughed.

"Wren Elessedil," he greeted. "You are as good as your word, girl! Come back out of death to find me, come back to spit in my face, to prove you could do it after all! Shades, you must be tough as nails!"

She was too happy to see him to disagree.

He hurried them atop Spirit then—but only after a sharp glance at Stresa and a pointed warning to the Splinterscat that he had best keep his quills to himself. Muttering something about Wren's choice of traveling companions, he wrapped the Splinterscat in a leather coverlet and boosted him up. Although Stresa remained still and compliant, his eyes darted anxiously. Wren bound Faun to her back, mounted Spirit, and pulled a semiconscious Triss up in front of her where she could hold him in place. Her hands full, she jammed the Ruhk Staff beneath her legs in the harness. They worked swiftly, Tiger Ty and she, chased by the snarls and growls that rose from the darkness of the trees, driven by their fear of the things hidden there. Twice black forms darted from the shadows as if to attack, but each time Spirit's angry shriek sent them scrambling away again.

It seemed to take them forever, but finally they were settled. With a quick last check of the harness straps, Tiger Ty sprang atop the Roc.

"Up, now, old bird!" he yelled urgently.

With a final cry, Spirit spread his great wings and lifted away. A handful of demons broke cover, racing to catch them in a last desperate effort, flinging themselves across the bluff. Several caught hold of the Roc's feathers, dragging the great bird down. But Spirit shook himself, twisted and raked wildly with his claws, and the attackers fell away into the dark. As the Roc swept out over the Blue Divide and began to rise, Wren glanced back a final time. Morrowindl was a furnace glowing against the night, all mist and steam and ash, Killeshan's mouth spitting out streams of molten rock, rivers of fire running to the sea.

She closed her eyes and did not look back again.

She was never sure how long they flew that night. It might have been hours; it might have been only minutes. She clung to Triss and the restraining straps as she fought to stay awake, exhausted to the point of senselessness. Faun's arms were wrapped about her neck, warm and furry, and she could feel the Tree Squeak's worried breath against her neck. Somewhere behind, Stresa rode in silence. She heard Tiger Ty call back to her once or twice, but his words were lost in the wind, and she did not bother to try to answer. A vision of Morrowindl in those last minutes floated spectrally before her eyes, harsh and unyielding, a nightmare that would never recede into sleep.

When they landed, whatever time had passed, it was still night, but the sky was clear and bright about her. Spirit settled down on a small atoll green with vegetation. The sweet smell of flowers wafted on the air. Wren breathed the scents gratefully as she slid down the Roc's broad back, reaching up in numb response for Triss and then Stresa. Imagine, she thought dizzily—a moon and stars, a night bright with their light, no mist or haze, no fire.

"This way, over here, girl," Tiger Ty advised gently, taking her arm.

He led her to a patch of soft grass where she lay down and instantly fell asleep.

The sun was red against the horizon when she woke again, a scarlet sphere rising from the ocean's crimson-colored waters into skies black with thunderheads. The storm and its fire seemed settled in a single patch of earth and sky. She raised herself on her elbow and peered at the strange phenomenon, wondering how it could be.

Then Tiger Ty, keeping watch at her side, whispered, "Go back to sleep, Miss Wren. It's still night. That's Morrowindl out there, all afire, burning up from the inside out. Killeshan's let go with everything. Won't be anything left soon, I'd guess."

She did go back to sleep, and when she woke again it was midday, the sun sitting high in a cloudless blue expanse overhead, the air warm and fragrant, and the birdsong a bright trilling against the rush of the ocean on the rocks. Faun chittered from somewhere close by. She rose to look, and found the Tree Squeak sitting on a rock and pulling at a vine so it could nibble its leaves. Triss still slept, and Stresa was nowhere to be seen. Spirit sat out at the edge of the cliff, his fierce eyes gazing out at the empty waters.

Tiger Ty appeared from behind the bird and ambled over. He handed her a sack with fruit and bread and motioned her away from the sleeping Triss. She rose, and they walked to sit in the shade of a palm.

"Rested now?" he asked, and she nodded. "Eat some of this. You must be starved. You look as if you haven't eaten in days."

She ate gratefully, then accepted the ale jug he offered and drank until she thought she would burst. Faun turned to watch, eyes bright and curious.

"You seem to have gathered up some new friends," Tiger Ty declared as she finished. "I know the Elf and the Splinterscat by name, but what's this one called?"

"Her name is Faun. She's a Tree Squeak." Wren's eyes locked on his. "Thanks for not leaving us, Tiger Ty. I was counting on you."

"Ha!" he snorted. "As if I would miss the chance of finding out how things had worked out! But I admit I had my doubts, girl. I thought your foolishness might have outstripped your fire. Looks like it almost did."

She nodded. "Almost."

"I came back looking for you every day after the volcano blew. Saw it erupt twenty miles out. I said to myself, she's got something to do with that, you mark me! And you did, too, didn't you?" He grinned, face crinkling like old leather. "Anyway, we circled about once a day, Spirit and me, searching for you. Had just finished last night's swing when we saw your light. Might have left, otherwise. How did you do that, anyway?" He pursed his lips, then shrugged. "No, hold off, don't tell me. That's the Land Elf magic at work or I miss my guess. It's better I don't know."

He paused. "In any case, I'm very glad you're safe."

She smiled in acknowledgment, and they sat silently for a moment, looking at the ground. Fishing birds swooped and dove across the open waters like white arrows, wings cocked back, and long necks extended. Faun came down from her perch to crawl up Wren's arm and burrow into her shoulder.

"I guess your big friend didn't make it," Tiger Ty said finally.

Garth. The pain of the memory brought tears to her eyes. She shook her head. "No. He didn't."

"I'm sorry. I think maybe you'll feel his loss a long time, won't you?" The shrewd eyes slid away. "Some kinds of pain don't heal easily."

She didn't speak. She was thinking of her grandmother and Eowen, of the Owl and Gavilan Elessedil, of Cort and Dal, all lost in the struggle to escape Morrowindl, all a part of the pain she carried with her. She stared out over the water into the distance, searching the skyline. She found what she was searching for finally, a dark smudge against the horizon where Morrowindl burned slowly to ash and rock.

"And what of the Elves?" Tiger Ty asked. "You found them, I guess, judging from the fact that one of them came with you."

She looked back at him again, surprised by the question, forgetting momentarily that he had not been with her. "Yes, I found them."

"And Arborlon?"

"Arborlon as well, Tiger Ty."

He stared at her a moment, then shook his head. "They wouldn't listen, would they? They wouldn't leave." He announced it matter-of-factly, undisguised bitterness in his voice. "Now they're all gone, lost. The whole of them. Foolish people."

Foolish, indeed, she thought. But not lost. Not yet. She tried to tell Tiger Ty about the Loden, tried to find the words, but couldn't. It was too hard to speak of any of it just now. She was still too close to the nightmare she had left behind, still floundering through the harsh emotions that even the barest thought of it invoked. Whenever she brought the memories out again, she felt as if her skin was being flayed from her body. She felt as if fire was searing her, burning down to her bones. The Elves, victims of their own misguided belief in the power of the magic—how much of that belief had been bequeathed to her? She shuddered at the thought. There were truths to be weighed and measured, motives to be examined, and lives to be set aright. Not the least of those belonged to her.

"Tiger Ty," she said quietly. "The Elves are here, with me. I carry them . . ." She hesitated as he stared at her expectantly. "I carry them in my heart." Confusion lined his brow. Her eyes lowered, searching her empty hands. "The problem is deciding whether they belong."

He shook his head and frowned. "You're not making sense. Not to me."

She smiled. "Only to myself. Be patient with me awhile, would you? No more questions. But when we get to where we're going, we'll find out together whether the lessons of Morrowindl have taught the Elves anything."

Triss awoke then, stirring sluggishly from his sleep, and they rose to tend him. As they worked, Wren's thoughts took flight. Like a practiced juggler she found herself balancing the demands of the present against the needs of the past, the lives of the Elves against the dangers of their magics, the beliefs she had lost against the truths she had found. Silent in her deliberation, her concentration complete, she moved among her companions as if she were there with them when in fact she was back on Morrowindl, watching the horror of its magic-induced evolution, discovering the dark secrets of its makers, reconstructing the bits and pieces of the frantic, terrifying days of her struggle to fulfill the charges that had been given her. Time froze, and while it stood statuelike before her, carved out of a chilling, silent introspection, she was able to cast away the last of the tattered robes that had been her old life, that innocence of being that had preceded Cogline and Allanon and her journey to her past, and to don at last the mantle of who and what she now realized she had always been meant to be.

Good-bye Wren that was.

Faun squirmed against her shoulder, begging for attention. She spared what little she could.

An hour later, Splinterscat, Tree Squeak, Captain of the Elven Home Guard, Wing Rider, and the girl who had become the Queen of the Elves were winging their way eastward atop Spirit toward the Four Lands.

It took the remainder of the day to reach the mainland. The sun was a faint melting of silver on the western horizon when the coastline finally grew visible, a jagged black wall against the coming night. Darkness had fallen, and the moon and stars appeared by the time they descended onto the bluff that fronted the abandoned Wing Hove. Their bodies were cramped and tired, and their eyes were heavy. The summer smells of leaves and earth wafted out of the forest behind them as they settled down to sleep.

"Phffttt! I could grow to like this land of yours, Wren of the Elves," Stresa said to her just before she fell asleep.

They flew out again at dawn, north along the coastline. Tiger Ty rode close against Spirit's sleek head, eyes forward, not speaking to anyone. He had given Wren a long, hard look when she had told him where she wanted to go and he had not glanced her way since. They rode the air currents west across the Irrybis and Rock Spur and into the Sarandanon. The land gleamed beneath them, green forests, black earth, azure lakes, silver rivers, and rainbow-colored fields of wildflowers. The world below appeared flawless and sculpted; from this high up, the sickness that the Shadowen had visited on it was not apparent. The hours slipped by, slow and lazy and filled with memories for the Roc's riders. There was an ache in the heart on such perfect days, a longing that they could last forever stitched against the knowledge that tomorrow would be different, that in life few promises were given.

They landed at noon in a meadow on the south edge of the Sarandanon and ate fruit and cheese and goat's milk provided by Tiger Ty. Birds flitted in the trees, and small animals disappeared along branches and into burrows. Faun watched everything as if she were seeing it for the first time. Stresa sniffed the air, cat's face wrinkling and twitching. Triss was well enough to sit and stand alone now, though bandaged and splinted still, his strong face scarred and bruised. He smiled often at Wren, but his eyes remained sad and distant. Tiger Ty continued to keep to himself. Wren knew he was mulling over what she was about, wanting to ask but unwilling to do so. She found him a curious man.

They continued their journey when their meal was finished, sweeping down the valley toward the Rill Song. By midafternoon they were following the river's channel north in a slow, steady glide toward sunset.

It was approaching twilight when they reached the Carolan. The rock wall rose in stark relief from the eastern shore of the river to a vast, empty bluff that jutted outward from a protective wall of towering hardwood and sheltering cliffs that rose higher still. The bluff was rocky and bare, a rugged stretch of earth on which only isolated patches of scrub grass grew.

It was atop the Carolan that Arborlon had been built. It was from here more than a hundred years ago that the city had been taken away.

Tiger Ty directed Spirit downward, and the giant Roc dropped smoothly to the center of the bluff. The riders dismounted, one after the other, Wren and Tiger Ty working side by side in silence to unwrap Stresa and set him on the ground. They stood clustered together for a moment, staring across the empty plain at the forest dark east and the cliff drop west. The country beyond was hazy with shadows, and the skies were faintly tinged with purple and gold.

"Ssssttt! What is this place?" Stresa questioned uncomfortably, staring about at the ravaged bluff.

"Home," Wren answered distantly, lost somewhere deep within herself.

"Home! Sssppph!" The Splinterscat was aghast.

"What are we doing here, if you don't mind my asking?" Tiger Ty snapped, unable to contain himself any longer.

"What Allanon's shade asked of me," she said.

She reached up along Spirit's harness and pulled free the Ruhk Staff. The walnut haft was marred and dirtied and the once gleaming surface dulled and worn. Fastened in the clawed grips at one end, the Loden shone with dull, worn persistence in the fading light.

She put the Staff butt downward against the earth and gripped it before her with both hands. Her eyes fixed on the Stone, and her thoughts traveled back to Morrowindl again, to the long, endless days of mist and darkness, of demon Shadowen, of monsters and pitfalls, and of horror born of the Elven magic. The island world rose up out of memory and gathered her in, a frantic, doomed lover too dangerous for any to hold. The faces of the dead paraded before her—Ellenroh Elessedil, to whom the care of the Elves had been given and who in turn had given it to her; Eowen, who had seen too much of what was to be; Aurin Striate, who had been her friend; Gavilan Elessedil, who could have been; Cort and Dal, her protectors; and Garth, who had been, in the end, all of these. She greeted them silently, reverently, promising each that a measure of what had been given would be returned, that she would keep the trust that had been passed on to her, and that she would respect what it had cost to keep it safe.

She closed her eyes and sealed away the past, then opened them again to stare into the faces of those gathered about her. Her smile was, for an instant, her grandmother's. "Triss, Stresa, Tiger Ty, and you, little Faun—you are my best friends now, and if you can, I would like you to stay with me, to be with me, for as long as you are able. I will not hold you—not even you, Triss. I do not charge you in any way. I ask that you decide freely."

No one spoke. There was uncertainty in their eyes, a hint of confusion. Faun edged forward and pulled at her leg anxiously.

"No, little one," she said. She beckoned to the others. "Walk with me."

They moved across the Carolan—the girl, the Elf, the Wing Rider, his Roc, and the two creatures from Morrowindl—trailing their shadows in the dust behind them. Birdsong rose from the trees and cliff rocks as darkness fell, and the Rill Song churned steadily below.

When they reached the cliff edge, she turned, then stepped away several paces so that the others were behind her. She was facing back across the bluff toward the forest, back into the closing night. Above the trees, stars were coming out, bright pinpoints against the deepening black. Her hands tightened on the Ruhk Staff. She had anticipated this moment for days, and now that it was here she found herself neither anxious nor excited, but only weary. Once, she had wondered if she would be able to invoke the Loden's magic when it was time—what she would decide, how she would feel. She had wondered without cause, she thought. She felt no hesitation now. Perhaps she had always known. Or perhaps all the wondering had simply resolved itself somewhere along the way. It didn't matter, in any case. She was at peace with herself. She even knew how the magic worked, though her grandmother had never explained. Because it hadn't been necessary? Because it was instinctive? Wren wasn't sure. It was enough that the magic was hers to call upon and that she had determined at last to do so.

She breathed the warm air as if drawing in the fading light. She listened to the sound of her heart.

Then she jammed the Ruhk Staff into the earth, twisting it in her hands, grinding it into the soil. Earth magic, Eowen had told her. All of the Elven magic was earth magic, its power drawn from the elements within. What came from there must necessarily be returned.

Her eyes fixed on the gleaming facets of the Loden. The world around her went still and breathless.

Her hands loosened their grip on the Staff, her fingers light and feathery on the gnarled, polished wood, a lover's caress. She need only call for them, she knew. Just think it, nothing more. Just will it. Just open your mind to the fact of their existence, to their life within the confines of the Stone. Don't debate it, don't question it. Summon them. Bring them back. Ask for them.

Yes.

I do.

The Loden flared brightly, a fountain of white light against the darkness, springing forth like fire, then building with blinding intensity. Wren felt the Ruhk Staff tremble in her hands and begin to heat. She tightened her grip on it, her eyes squinting against the brightness, then lowering into shadow. The light rose and began to spread. There was shape and movement within. And suddenly there was wind, a wind that seemed to come from nowhere, whipping across the bluff, sweeping up the light and carrying it across the barren expanse to the trees and rocks and back again, spreading it from end to end. The wind roared, yet lacked strength and impact as it raced past, all sound and brightness as it swallowed the light.

Wren tried to glance back at her companions to make certain they were safe, that the magic had not harmed them, but she could not seem to turn her head. Her hands were clutched tight about the Ruhk Staff now, and she was joined to it, enmeshed in the workings of the magic, given over to that alone.

The light filled the bluff plain, building on itself, rising up until the trees and cliffs that bracketed it had disappeared entirely, until the skies had folded into it and everything was colored silver. There was a wrenching sound, a rending of earth and rock, and a settling of something heavy. Through the slits of her eyes she could see the shapes in the light growing large and taking form as buildings and trees, roadways and paths, and lawns and parks appeared. Arborlon was coming back into being. She watched it materialize as if seeing it from behind a window streaked with rain, hazy and indistinct. At its center, like a gleaming arch of silver and scarlet in the mist, was the Ellcrys. She felt her strength begin to fail, the power of the magic stealing it away for its own use, and she found herself fighting to stand upright. White light whirled and spun like clouds before a storm, gathering in force until it seemed it must explode everything about it in a roar of thunder.

Then it began to fade, dimming steadily, wanning back into darkness like water into sand.

It was finished then, Wren knew. She could see Arborlon within the haze, could even pick out the people standing in clusters at the edges of the brightness as they peered to see what lay without. She had done what her grandmother had asked of her, what Allanon had asked, and had accomplished all with which she had been charged by others—but not yet that with which she had charged herself. For it would never be enough simply to restore the Elves and their city to the Westland. It would never be enough to give them back to the Four Lands, a people returned out of self-imposed exile. Not after Morrowindl. Not when she knew the truth about the Shadowen. Not while she lived with the horror of the possibility that the magic might be misused again. The lives of the Elves had been given to her on others' terms; she would give them back again on her own.

She clamped her hands about the Ruhk Staff and sent what was left of its magic soaring out into the light, burning downward into the earth, all of it that remained, all that could ever be. She drained it in a final fury that sent a crackle of fire exploding through the shimmering air. It swept out like lightning, flash after flash. She did not let up. She expended it all, emptying the Staff and the Stone, burning the power away until the last of it flared a final time and was gone.

Darkness returned. A haze hung on the night air momentarily, then dissipated into motes of dust and began to settle. She followed its movement, seeing grass now beneath her feet where there hadn't been grass before, smelling the scents of trees and flowers, of burning pitch, of cooking foods, of wood and iron, and of life. She looked past the dark line of the Ruhk Staff to the city, to Arborlon returned, buildings lit by lamps, streets and tree lanes stretching its length and breadth like dark ribbons.

And the people, the Elves, stood before her, thousands of them, gathered at the city's edge, staring wide-eyed and wondering. Elven Hunters stood at the forefront, weapons drawn. She faced them, saw their eyes fix on her, on the Staff she held. She was aware of Tiger Ty's mutter of disbelief, of Triss coming up to stand next to her, and of Stresa and Faun. She could feel their heat against her back, small touches flicking against her skin.

Barsimmon Oridio and Eton Shart emerged from the crowd and came slowly forward. When they were a dozen feet away, they stopped. Neither seemed able to speak.

Wren took her weight off the Ruhk Staff and straightened. For the first time she glanced up at the Loden. The gleaming facets had disappeared into darkness. The magic had gone back into the earth. The Loden had turned to common stone.

She brought the Ruhk Staff close to her face and saw that it was charred and brittle and dead. After taking it firmly in both hands, she brought it down across raised knee, snapped it in two, and cast the remains to the ground.

"The Elves are home," she said to the two who stood openmouthed before her, "and we won't ever leave again."

Triss stepped past her, his body still splinted and bandaged, but his eyes filled with pride and determination. He walked to where he could be seen, standing close to the Commander of the Elven armies and the First Minister, and called out. "Home Guard!"

They appeared instantly, dozens of them, gathering before their captain in row after row. There was a murmuring in the crowd, an anticipation.

Then Triss turned back to face Wren, dropped slowly to one knee, and placed his right hand over his heart in salute. Behind him, the lamps of the city flickered like fireflies in the dark. "Wren Elessedil, Queen of the Elves!" he announced. "The Home Guard stand ready to serve!"

His Elven Hunters followed his lead to a man, kneeling and repeating the words in a jumbled rush. Some among the crowd did the same, then more. Eton Shart went down, then after a moment's hesitation Barsimmon Oridio as well. Whether they did it out of recognition of the truth or simply in response to Triss, Wren never knew. She stood motionless as they knelt before her, the whole of the Elven nation, her charge from Ellenroh, her people found.

There were tears in her eyes as she stepped forward to greet them.

The Druid's Keep shuddered one final time, a massive stone giant stirring in sleep, and went still.

Cogline waited, braced against the heavy reading table, eyes closed, head bowed, making sure his strength had returned. He stood once more within the vault that sealed away the Druid Histories, come back to himself after his search to find Walker Boh, after leaving his body in the old Druid way. He had found Walker and warned him but been unable to remain—too weak now, too old, a jumble of bones filled with stiffness and pain. It had taken all of his strength just to do as much as he had.

He waited, and the tremors did not return.

Finally he pushed himself upright, released his grip on the table, let his eyes open, and looked carefully around. The first thing he saw was himself—his hands and arms, then his body, all of him—made whole again. He caught his breath, rubbed his hands together experimentally, and touched himself to be certain that what he was seeing was real. The transparency was gone; he was flesh and blood once more. Rumor crowded up against him, big head shoving into his scarecrow body so hard it threatened to knock the old man down. The moor cat was himself again as well, no longer faint lines and shadows, no longer wraithlike.

And the room—it stone walls were hard and clear, its colors sharply detailed, and its lines and surfaces defined by substance and light.

Cogline took a long, slow breath. Walker had done it. He had brought Paranor back into the world of Men.

He went out from the little room through the study beyond to the halls of the Keep. Rumor padded after. Sunlight filled the corridors, streaming through the high windows, motes of dust dancing in the glow. The old man caught a glimpse of white clouds against a blue sky. The smell of trees and grasses wafted on the summer air.

Back.

Alive.

He began to search for Walker, moving through the corridors of the Keep, his footsteps scraping softly on the stone. Ahead, he could hear the faint rush of something rising from within the castle's bowels, a low rumbling sound, a huffing like . . . And then he knew. It was the fire that fed the Keep from the earth's core, fire that had been cold and dead all this time, now alive again with Paranor's return.

He turned into the hall that ran to the well beneath the Keep.

In the shadows ahead, something moved.

Cogline slowed and stopped. Rumor dropped to a crouch and growled. A figure materialized out of the gloom, come from a place where the sunlight could not reach, all black and featureless. The figure approached, the light beginning to define it, a man hooded and cowled, tall and thin against the gloom, moving slowly but purposefully.

"Walker?" Cogline asked.

The other did not reply. When he was less than a dozen feet away, he stopped. Rumor's growl had died to heavy breathing. The man's arm reached up and drew back the hood.

"Tell me what you see," Walker Boh said.

Cogline stared. It was Walker, and yet it was not. His features were the same, but he was bigger somehow, and even with his white skin he seemed as black as wet ashes, the cast of him so dark it seemed any light that approached was being absorbed. His body, even beneath the robes, gave the impression of being armored. His right arm was still missing. His left hand held the Black Elfstone.

"Tell me," Walker asked him again.

Cogline stared into his eyes. They were flat and hard and depthless, and he felt as if they were looking right through him.

"I see Allanon," the old man answered softly.

A shudder passed through Walker Boh and was gone. "He is part of me now, Cogline. That was what he left to guard the Keep when he sent it from the Four Lands; that was what was waiting for me in the mist. They were all there, all of the Druids—Galaphile, Bremen, Allanon, all of them. That was how they passed on their knowledge, one to the next—a kind of joining of spirit with flesh. Bremen carried it all when he became the last of the Druids. He passed it on to Allanon, who passed in turn to me."

His eyes were bright; there were fires there that Cogline could not define. "To me!" Walker Boh cried out suddenly. "Their teachings, their lore, their history, their madness—all that I have mistrusted and avoided for so long! He gave it all to me!"

He was trembling, and Cogline was suddenly afraid. This man he had known so well, his student, at times his friend, was someone else now, a man made over as surely as day changed to night.

Walker's hand tightened about the Black Elfstone as he lifted it before him. "It is done, old man, and it can't be undone. Allanon has his Druid and his Keep back in the world of Men. He has his charge to me fulfilled.

And he has placed his soul within me!" The hand lowered like a weight pressing down against the earth. "He thinks to make the Druids over through me. Brin Ohmsford's legacy. He gives me his power, his lore, his understanding, his history. He even gives me his face. You look at me, and you see him."

A distant look came into the dark eyes. "But I have my own strength, a strength I gained by surviving the rite of passage he set for me, the horror of seeing what becoming a Druid means. I have not been made over completely, even in this."

He stared hard at Cogline, then stepped forward and placed his arm about the thin shoulders. "You and I, Cogline," he whispered. "The past and the future, we are all that remain of the Druids. It will be interesting to see if we can make a difference."

He turned the old man slowly about, and together they began to walk back along the corridor. Rumor stared after them momentarily, sniffed at the floor where Walker Boh's feet had trod as if trying to identify his scent, then padded watchfully after.

THE TALISMANS OF SHANNARA

For All My Friends at Del Rey Books,
Then and Now:
What a Time We've Had!

Dusk settled down about the Four Lands, a slow graying of light, a gradual lengthening of shadows. The swelter of the late summer's day began to fade as the sun's red fireball sank into the west and the hot, stale air cooled. The hush that comes with day's end stilled the earth, and leaves and grass shivered with expectation at the coming of night.

At the mouth of the Mermidon where it emptied into the Rainbow Lake, Southwatch rose blackly, impenetrable and voiceless. The wind brushed the waters of the lake and river, yet did not approach the obelisk, as if anxious to hurry on to some place more inviting. The air shimmered about the dark tower, heat radiating from its stone in waves, forming spectral images that darted and flew. A solitary hunter at the water's edge glanced up apprehensively as he passed and continued swiftly on.

Within, the Shadowen went about their tasks in ghostly silence, cowled and faceless and filled with purpose.

Rimmer Dall stood at a window looking out on the darkening countryside, watching the color fade from the earth as the night crept stealthily out of the east to gather in its own.

The night, our mother, our comfort.

He stood with his hands clasped behind his back, rigid within his dark robes, cowl pulled back from his rawboned, red-bearded face. He looked hard and empty of feeling, and had he cared he would have been pleased. But it had been a long time since his appearance had mattered to the First Seeker—a long time since he had bothered even to wonder. His outside was of no consequence; he could be anything he chose. What burned within mattered. That gave him life.

His eyes glittered as he looked beyond what he was seeing to what one day would be.

To what was promised.

He shifted slightly, alone with his thoughts in the tower's silence. The others did not exist for him, wraiths without substance. Below, deep within the bowels of the tower, he could hear the sounds of the magic at work, the deep hum of its breathing, the rumble of its heart. He listened for it without thinking now, a habit that brought reassurance to his troubled mind. The power was theirs, brought from the ether into substance, given shape and form, lent purpose. It was the gift of the Shadowen, and it belonged to them alone.

Druids and others notwithstanding.

He tried a faint smile, but his mouth refused to put up with it and it disappeared in the tight line of his lips. His gloved left hand squirmed within the clasp of the bare fingers of his right. Power for power, strength for strength. On his breast, the silver wolf's-head insignia glittered.

Thrum, thrum, came the sound of the magic working down below.

Rimmer Dall turned back into the grayness of the room—a room that until recently had held Coll Ohmsford prisoner. Now the Valeman was gone—escaped, he believed; but let go in fact and made prisoner another way. Gone to find his brother, Par.

The one with the real magic.

The one who would be his.

The First Seeker moved away from the window and seated himself at the bare wooden table, the weight of his big frame causing the spindly chair to creak. His hands folded on the table before him and his craggy face lowered.

All the Ohmsfords were back in the Four Lands, all the scions of Shannara, returned from their quests. Walker Boh had come back from Eldwist despite Pe Ell, the Black Elfstone regained, its magic fathomed, Paranor brought back into the world of men, and Walker himself become the first of the new Druids. Wren Elessedil had come back from Morrowindl with Arborlon and the Elves, the magic of the Elfstones discovered anew, her own identity and heritage revealed. Two out of three of Allanon's charges fulfilled. Two out of three steps taken.

Par's was to be the last, of course. Find the Sword of Shannara. Find the Sword and it will reveal the truth.

Games played by old men and shades, Rimmer Dall mused. Charges and quests, searches for truth. Well, he knew the truth better than they, and the truth was that none of this mattered because in the end the magic was all and the magic belonged to the Shadowen.

It grated on him that despite his efforts to prevent it, both the Elves and Paranor were back. Those he had sent to keep the Shannara scions from succeeding had failed. The price of their failure had been death, but that did little to assuage his annoyance. Perhaps he should have been angry—perhaps even a little worried. But Rimmer Dall was confident in his power, certain of his control over events and time, assured that the future was still his to determine. Though Teel and Pe Ell had disappointed him, there were others who would not.

Thrum, thrum, the magic whispered.

And so . . .

Rimmer Dall's lips pursed. A little time was all that was needed. A little time to let events he had already set in motion follow their course, and then it would be too late for the Druid dead and their schemes. Keep the Dark Uncle and the girl apart. Don't let them share their knowledge. Don't let them join forces.

Don't let them find the Valemen.

What was needed was a distraction, something that would keep them otherwise occupied. Or better still, something that would put an end to them. Armies, of course, to grind down the Elves and the free-born alike, Federation soldiers and Shadowen Creepers and whatever else he could muster to sweep these fools from his life. But something more, something special for the Shannara children with all their magics and Druid charms.

He considered the matter for a long time, the gray twilight changing to night about him. The moon rose in the east, a scythe against the black, and the stars brightened into sharp pinpricks of silver. Their glow penetrated the darkness where the First Seeker sat and transformed his face into a skull.

Yes, he nodded finally.

The Dark Uncle was obsessed with his Druid heritage. Send him something to play against that weakness, something that would confuse and frustrate him. Send him the Four Horsemen.

And the girl. Wren Elessedil had lost her protector and adviser. Give her someone to fill that void. Give her one of his own choosing, one who would soothe and comfort her, who would ease her fears, then betray her and strip her of everything.

The others were no serious threat—not even the leader of the free-born and the Highlander. They could do nothing without the Ohmsford heirs. If the Dark Uncle was imprisoned in his Keep and the Elf Queen's brief reign ended, the Druid shade's carefully constructed plans would collapse about him. Allanon would sink back into the Hadeshorn with the rest of his ghost kin, consigned to the past where he belonged.

Yes, the others were insignificant.

But he would deal with them anyway.

And even if all his efforts failed, even if he could do nothing more than chase them about, harry them as a dog would its prey, still that would be sufficient if in the end Par Ohmsford's soul fell to him. He needed only that to put an end to all of the hopes of his enemies. Only that. It was a short walk to the precipice, and the Valeman was already moving toward it. His brother would be the staked goat that would bring him, that would draw him like a wolf at hunt. Coll Ohmsford was deep under the spell of the Mirrorshroud by now, a slave to the magic from which the cloak was formed. He had stolen it to disguise himself, never guessing that Rimmer Dall had intended as much, never suspecting that it was a deadly snare to turn him to the First Seeker's own grim purpose. Coll Ohmsford would hunt his brother down and force a confrontation. He would do so because the cloak would let him do nothing less, settling a madness within him that only his brother's death could assuage. Par would be forced to fight. And because he lacked the magic of the Sword of Shannara, because his conventional weapons would not be enough to stop the Shadowen-kind his brother had become, and because he would be terrified that this was yet another trick, he would use the wishsong's magic.

Perhaps he would kill his own brother, but this time kill him in truth, and then discover—when it was too late to change things back—what he had done.

And perhaps not. Perhaps he would let his brother escape and be led to his doom.

The First Seeker shrugged. Either way, the result would be the same. Either way the Valeman was finished. Use of the magic and the series of shocks that would surely result from doing so would unbalance him. It would free the magic from his control and let him become Rimmer Dall's tool. Rimmer Dall was certain of it. He could be so because unlike the Shannara scions and their mentor he understood the Elven magic, his magic by blood and right. He understood what it was and how it worked. He knew what Par did not—what was happening to the wishsong, why it behaved as it did, how it had slipped its leash to become a wild thing that hunted as it chose.

Par was close. He was very close.

The danger of grappling with the beast is that you will become it.

He was almost one of them.

Soon it would happen.

There was, of course, the possibility that the Valeman would discover the truth about the Sword of Shannara before then. Was the weapon he carried, the one Rimmer Dall had given up so easily, the talisman he sought or a fake? Par Ohmsford still didn't know. It was a calculated risk that he would not find out. Yet even if he did, what good would it do him? Swords were two-edged and could cut either way. The truth might do Par more harm than good . . .

Rimmer Dall rose and walked again to the window, a shadow in the night's blackness, folded and wrapped against the light. The Druids didn't understand; they never had. Allanon was an anachronism before he had even become what Bremen intended him to be. Druids—they used the magic like fools played with fire: astounded at its possibilities, yet terrified of its risks. No wonder the flames had burned them so often. But that did not prevent them from refusing their mysterious gift. They were so quick to judge others who sought to wield the power—the Shadowen foremost—to see them as the enemy and destroy them.

As they had destroyed themselves.

But there was symmetry and meaning in the Shadowen vision of life, and the magic was no toy with which they played but the heart of who and what they were, embraced, protected, and worshipped. No half measures in which life's accessibility was denied or self-serving cautions issued to as-sure that none would share in the use. No admonitions or warnings. No gamesplaying. The Shadowen simply were what the magic would make them, and the magic when accepted so would make them anything.

The tree-tips of the forests and the cliffs of the Runne were dark humps against the flat, silver-laced surface of the Rainbow Lake. Rimmer Dall gazed out upon the world, and he saw what the Druids had never been able to see.

That it belonged to those strong enough to take it, hold it, and shape it. That it was meant to be used.

His eyes burned the color of blood.

It was ironic that the Ohmsfords had served the Druids for so long, carrying out their charges, going on their quests, following their visions to truths that never were. The stories were legend. Shea and Flick, Wil, Brin and Jair, and now Par. It had all been for nothing. But here is where it would end. For Par would serve the Shadowen and by doing so put an end forever to the Ohmsford-Druid ties.

"Par. Par. Par."

Rimmer Dall whispered his name soothingly to the night. It was a litany that filled his mind with visions of power that nothing could withstand.

For a long time he stood at the window and allowed himself to dream of the future.

Then abruptly he wheeled away and went down into the tower's depths to feed.

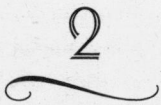

The cellar beneath the gristmill was thick with shadows, the faint streamers of light let through by gaps in the floorboards disappearing rapidly into twilight. Chased from his safe hole through the empty catacombs, pinned finally against the blocked trapdoor through which he had thought to escape, Par Ohmsford crouched like an animal brought to bay, the Sword of Shannara clutched protectively before him as the intruder who had harried him to this end stopped abruptly and reached up to lower the cowl that hid his face.

"Lad," a familiar voice whispered. "It's me."

The cloak's hood was down about the other's shoulders, and a dark head was laid bare. But still the shadows were too great . . .

The figure stepped forward tentatively, the hand with the long knife lowering. "Par?"

The intruder's features were caught suddenly in a hazy wash of gray light, and Par exhaled sharply.

"Padishar!" he exclaimed in relief. "Is it really you?"

The long knife disappeared back beneath the cloak, and the other's laugh was low and unexpected. "In the flesh. Shades, I thought I'd never find you! I've been searching for days, the whole of Tyrsis end to end, every last hideaway, every burrow, and each time only Federation and Shadowen Seekers waiting!"

He came forward to the bottom of the stairs, smiling broadly, arms outstretched. "Come here, lad. Let me see you."

Par lowered the Sword of Shannara and came down the steps in weary gratitude. "I thought you were . . . I was afraid . . ."

And then Padishar had his arms about him, embracing him, clapping him on the back, and then lifting him off the floor as if he were sackcloth.

"Par Ohmsford!" he greeted, setting the Valeman down finally, hands gripping his shoulders as he held him at arm's length to study him. The familiar smile was bright and careless. He laughed again. "You look a wreck!"

Par grimaced. "You don't look so well-kept yourself." There were scars from battle wounds on the big man's face and neck, new since they had parted. Par shook his head, overwhelmed. "I guess I knew you had escaped the Pit, but it's good seeing you here to prove it."

"Hah, there's been a lot happen since then, Valeman, I can tell you that!" Padishar's lank hair was tousled, and the skin about his eyes was dark from lack of sleep. He glanced about. "You're alone? I didn't expect that. Where's your brother? Where's Damson?"

Par's smile faded. "Coll . . ." he began and couldn't finish. "Padishar, I can't . . ." His hands tightened about the Sword of Shannara, as if by doing so he might retrieve the lifeline for which he suddenly found need. "Damson went out this morning. She hasn't come back."

Padishar's eyes narrowed. "Out? Out where, lad?"

"Searching for a way to escape the city. Or in the absence of that, another hiding place. The Federation have found us everywhere. But you know. You've seen them yourself. Padishar, how long have you been looking for us? How did you manage to find this place?"

The big hands fell away. "Luck, mostly. I tried all the places I thought you might be, the newer ones, the ones Damson had laid out for us during the previous year. This is an old one, five years gone since it was prepared and not used in the last three. I only remembered it after I'd given up on everything else."

He started suddenly. "Lad!" he exclaimed, his eyes lighting on the Sword in Par's hands. "Is that it? The Sword of Shannara? Have you found it, then? How did you get it out of the Pit? Where . . . ?"

But suddenly there was a scuffling of boots on wooden steps from the darkness behind, a clanking of weapons, and a raising of voices. Padishar whirled. The sounds were unmistakable. Armed men were descending the back stairs to the room Par had just vacated, come through the same door that had brought Padishar. Without slowing, they swept into the tunnels beyond, guided by torches that smoked and sputtered brightly in the near black.

Padishar wheeled back, grabbed Par's arm, and dragged him towards the trapdoor. "Federation. I must have been followed. Or they were watching the mill."

Par stumbled, trying to pull back. "Padishar, the door—"

"Patience, lad," the other cut him short, hauling him bodily to the top of the stairs. "We'll be out before they reach us."

He slammed into the door and staggered back, a look of disbelief on his rough face.

"I tried to warn you," Par hissed, freeing himself, glancing back toward the pursuit. The Sword of Shannara lifted menacingly. "Is there another way out?"

Padishar's answer was to throw himself against the trapdoor repeatedly, using all of his strength and size to batter through it. The door refused to budge, and while some of its boards cracked and splintered beneath the hammering they did not give way.

"Shades!" the outlaw leader spit.

Federation soldiers emptied out of the passageway into the room. A black-cloaked Seeker led them. They caught sight of Padishar and Par frozen on the trapdoor steps and came for them. Broadsword in one hand, long knife in the other, Padishar wheeled back down the steps to meet the rush. The first few to reach him were cut down instantly. The rest slowed, turned wary, feinting and lunging cautiously, trying to cripple him from the side. Par stood at his back, thrusting at those who sought to do so. Slowly the two backed their way up the stairs and out of reach so that their attackers were forced to come at them head on.

It was a losing fight. There were twenty if there was one. One good rush and it would be all over.

Par's head bumped sharply against the trapdoor. He turned long enough to shove at it one final time. Still blocked. He felt a well of despair open up inside. They were trapped.

He knew he would have to use the wishsong.

Below, Padishar launched himself at their attackers and drove them back a dozen steps.

Par summoned the magic and felt the music rise to his lips, strangely dark and bitter-tasting. It hadn't been the same since his escape from the Pit. Nothing had. The Federation soldiers rallied in a counterattack that forced Padishar back up the stairs. Sweat gleamed on the outlaw's strong face.

Then abruptly something shifted above and the trapdoor flew open. Par cried out to Padishar, and heedless of anything else they rushed up the steps, through the opening, and into the mill.

Damson Rhee was there, red hair flying out from her cloaked form as she sped toward a gap in the sideboards of the mill wall, calling for them to follow. Dark forms appeared suddenly to block her way, yelling for others. Damson wheeled into them, quick as a cat. Fire sprang from her empty hand, scattering into shards that flew into her attackers' faces. She went spinning through them, the street magic flicking right and left, clearing a path. Par and Padishar raced to follow, howling like madmen. The soldiers tried in vain to regroup. None reached Par. Fighting as if possessed, Padishar killed them where they stood.

Then they were outside on the streets, breathing the humid night air, sweat streaking their faces, breath hissing like steam. Darkness had fallen in a twilight haze of grit and dust that hung thickly in the narrow walled corridors. People ran screaming as Federation soldiers appeared from all directions, shouting and cursing, throwing aside any who stood in their way.

Without a word, Damson charged down an alleyway, leading Padishar and Par into a blackened tunnel stinking of garbage and excrement. Pursuit was instant, but cumbersome. Damson took them through a cross alley and into the side door of a tavern. They pushed through the dimly lit interior, past men hunched over tables and slumped in chairs, around kegs, and past a serving bar, then out the front door.

A shabby, slat-board porch with a low-hanging roof stretched away to either side. The street was deserted.

"Damson, what kept you?" Par hissed at her as they ran. "That trap-door . . ."

"My fault, Valeman," she snapped angrily. "I blocked the door with some machinery to hide it. I thought it would be safer for you. I was wrong. But I didn't bring the soldiers. They must have found the place on their own. Or followed Padishar." The big man started to speak, but she cut him short. "Quick, now. They're coming."

And from out of the shadows in front and behind them, the dark forms of Federation soldiers poured into the street. Damson spun about, cut back toward the far row of buildings, and took them down an alleyway so tight it was a close squeeze just to pass through. Howls of rage chased after them.

"We have to get back to the Tyrsian Way!" she gasped breathlessly.

They burst through an entry to a market, skidding on food leavings, grappling with bins. A pair of high doors barred their way. Damson struggled futilely to free the latched crossbar, and finally Padishar shattered it completely with a powerful kick.

Soldiers met them as they burst free, swords drawn. Padishar swept into them and sent them flying. Two went down and did not move. The rest scattered.

Sudden movement to Par's left caused him to turn. A Seeker rose up out of the night, wolf's head gleaming on his dark cloak. Par sent the wish-song's magic into it in the form of a monstrous serpent, and the Seeker tumbled back, shrieking.

Down the street they ran, cutting crosswise to a second street and then a third. Par's stamina was being tested now, his breathing so ragged it threatened to choke him, his throat dry with dust and fear. He was still weak from his battle in the Pit, not yet fully recovered from the damage caused by the magic's use. He clutched the Sword of Shannara to his breast protectively, the weight of it growing with every step.

They rounded a corner and paused in the lee of a stable entry, listening to the tumult about them grow.

"They couldn't have followed me!" Padishar declared suddenly, spitting blood through cracked lips.

Damson shook her head. "I don't understand it, Padishar. They've known all the safe holes, been there at each, waiting. Even this one."

The outlaw chief's eyes gleamed suddenly with recognition. "I should have seen it earlier. It was that Shadowen, the one who killed Hirehone, the one that pretended to be the Dwarf!" Par's head jerked up. "Somehow he discovered our safe holes and gave them all away, just as he did the Jut!"

"Wait! What Dwarf?" Par demanded in confusion.

But Damson was moving again, drawing the other two after, charging down a walkway and through a square connecting half-a-dozen cross streets. They pushed wearily on through the heat and gloom, moving closer to the Tyrsian Way, to the city's main street. Par's mind whirled with questions as he staggered determinedly on. A Dwarf gave them away? Steff or Teel—or someone else? He tried to spit the dryness from his throat. What had happened at the Jut? And where, he wondered suddenly, was Morgan Leah?

A line of soldiers appeared suddenly to block the way ahead. Damson quickly pushed Padishar and Par into the building shadows. Crowded against the darkened wall, she pulled their heads close.

"I found the Mole," she whispered hurriedly, glancing right and left as new shouts rose. "He waits at the leatherworks on Tyrsian Way to take us down into the tunnels and out of the city."

"He escaped!" breathed Par.

"I told you he was resourceful." Damson coughed and smiled. "But we have to reach him if he's to do us any good across the Tyrsian Way and down a short distance from those soldiers. If we get separated, don't stop. Keep going."

Then before anyone could object, she was off again, darting from their cover into an alleyway between shuttered stores. Padishar managed a quick, angry objection, and then charged after her. Par followed. They emerged from the alleyway into the street beyond and turned toward the Tyrsian Way. Soldiers appeared before them, just a handful, searching the night. Padishar flew at them in fury, broadsword swinging with a glint of wicked silver light. Damson took Par left past the fighters. More soldiers appeared, and suddenly they were everywhere, surging from the dark in knots, milling about wildly. The moon had gone behind a cloud bank, and the streetlamps were unlit. It was so dark that it was impossible to tell friend from foe. Damson and Par struggled through the melee, twisting free of hands that sought to grab them, shoving away from bodies that blocked their path. They heard Padishar's battle cry, then a furious clash of blades.

Ahead, the night erupted suddenly in a brilliant orange flash as something exploded at the center of the Way.

"The Mole!" Damson hissed.

They charged toward the light, a pillar of fire that flared into the darkness with a *whoosh*. Bodies rushed past, going in every direction. Par was spun about, and suddenly he was separated from Damson. He turned back to find her and went down in a tangle of arms and legs as a fleeing soldier collided with him. The Valeman struggled up, calling her name frantically. The Sword of Shannara reflected the orange fire as he turned first one way and then the other, crying out.

Then Padishar had him, appearing out of nowhere to lift him off his feet, sling him over one shoulder, and break for the safety of the darkened buildings. Swords cut at them, but Padishar was quick and strong, and no one was his match this night. The leader of the free-born launched himself through the last of the milling Federation soldiers and onto the walkway that ran the length of the buildings on the far side of the Way. Down the walk he charged, leaping bins and kegs, kicking aside benches, darting past the supporting posts of overhangs and the debris of the workday.

The leatherworks sat silent and empty-seeming ahead. Padishar reached it on a dead run and went through the door as if it weren't there, blunt shoulder lowering to hammer the portal completely off its hinges.

Inside, he swung Par down and wheeled about in fury.

There was no sign of Damson.

"Damson!" he howled.

Federation soldiers were closing on the leatherworks from every direction.

Padishar's face was streaked red and black with blood and dust. "Mole!" he cried out in desperation.

A furry face poked out of the shadows at the rear of the factory. "Over here," the Mole's calm voice advised. "Quickly, please."

Par hesitated, still looking for Damson, but Padishar snatched hold of his tunic and dragged him away. "No time, lad!"

The Mole's bright eyes gleamed as they reached him, and the inquisitive face lifted expectantly. "Lovely Damson . . . ?" he began, but Padishar quickly shook his head. The Mole blinked, then swung away wordlessly. He took them through a door leading to a series of storage rooms, then down a stairway to a cellar. Along a wall that seemed sealed at every juncture, he found a panel that released at a touch, and without a backward glance he took them through.

They found themselves on a landing joined to a stairway that ran down the city's sewers. The Mole was home again. He trundled down into the dank, cool catacombs, the light barely sufficient to enable Padishar and Par to follow. At the bottom of the stairs he passed a sooty blackened torch to the outlaw leader, who knelt wordlessly to light it.

"We should have gone back for her!" Par hissed at Padishar in fury.

The other's battle-scarred face rose from the shadows, looking as if it were chiseled from stone. The look he gave Par was terrifying. "Be silent, Valeman, before I forget who you are."

He sparked a flint and produced a small flame at the pitch-coated torch head, and the three started down into the sewer tunnels. The Mole scurried steadily ahead through the smoky gloom, picking his way with a practiced step, leading them deeper beneath the city and away from its walls. The shouts of pursuit had died completely, and Par supposed that even if the Federation soldiers had been able to find the hidden entry, they would have quickly lost their way in the tunnels. He realized suddenly that he was still holding the Sword of Shannara and after a moment's deliberation slipped it carefully back into its sheath.

The minutes passed, and with every step they took Par despaired of ever seeing Damson Rhee again. He was desperate to help her, but the look on Padishar's face had convinced him that for the moment at least he must hold his tongue. Certainly Padishar must be as anxious for her as he was.

They crossed a stone walkway that bridged a sluggish flow and passed into a tunnel whose ceiling was so low they were forced to crouch almost to hands and knees. At its end, the ceiling lifted again, and they navigated a confluence of tunnels to a door. The Mole touched something that released a heavy lock, and the door opened to admit them.

Inside they found a collection of ancient furniture and old discards that if not the same ones the Mole had been in danger of losing in his flight from the Federation a week ago were certainly duplicates. The stuffed animals sat in an orderly row on an old leather couch, button eyes staring blankly at them as they entered.

The Mole crossed at once, cooing softly, "Brave Chalt, sweet Everlind, my Westra, and little Lida." Other names were murmured, too low to catch. "Hello, my children. Are you well?" He kissed them one after the other and rearranged them carefully. "No, no, the black things won't find you here, I promise."

Padishar passed the torch he was carrying to Par, crossed to a basin, and began splashing cold water on his sweat-encrusted face. When he was finished, he remained standing there. His hands braced on the table that held the basin, and his head hung wearily.

"Mole, we have to find out what happened to Damson."

The Mole turned. "Lovely Damson?"

"She was right next to me," Par tried to explain, "and then the soldiers got between us—"

"I know," Padishar interrupted, glancing up. "It wasn't your fault. Wasn't anybody's. Maybe she even got away, but there were so many . . ." He exhaled sharply. "Mole, we have to know if they have her."

The Mole blinked lazily and the sharp eyes gleamed. "These tunnels go beneath the Federation prisons. Some go right into the walls. I can look. And listen."

Padishar's gaze was steady. "The Gatehouse to the Pit as well, Mole."

There was a long silence. Par went cold all over. Not Damson. Not there.

"I want to go with him," he offered quietly.

"No." Padishar shook his head for emphasis. "The Mole will travel quicker and more quietly." His eyes were filled with despair as they found Par's own. "I want to go as much as you do, lad. She is . . ."

He hesitated to continue, and Par nodded. "She told me."

They stared at each other in silence.

The Mole crossed the room on cat's feet, squinting in the glare of the light from the torch Par still held. "Wait here until I come back," he directed.

And then he was gone.

3

It had been a long and arduous journey that brought Par Ohmsford from his now long-ago meeting at the Hadeshorn with the shade of Allanon to this present place and time, and as he stood in the Mole's underground lair staring at the ruins and discards of other people's lives he could not help wondering how much it mirrored his own.

Damson.

He squeezed his eyes shut against the tears that threatened to come. He could not face what losing her would cost. He was only beginning to realize how much she meant to him.

"Par," Padishar spoke his name gently. "Come wash up, lad. You're exhausted."

Par agreed. Physically, emotionally, and spiritually. He was beaten down in every way possible, the strength drained from him, the last of his hope shredded like paper under a knife.

He found candles set about and lit them off the torch before extinguishing it. Then he moved to the basin and began to wash, slowly, ritualistically, cleansing himself of grime and sweat as if by doing so he was erasing all the bad things that had befallen him in his search for the Sword of Shannara.

The Sword was still strapped to his back. He stopped halfway through his bathing and removed it, setting it against an old bureau with a cracked mirror. He stared at it as he might an enemy. The Sword of Shannara—or was it? He still didn't know. His charge from Allanon had been to find the Sword, and though once he had believed he had done so, now he was faced with the possibility that he had failed. His charge had been all but forgotten in the aftermath of Coll's death and the struggle to stay alive in the catacombs of Tyrsis. He wondered how many of Allanon's charges had been forgotten or ignored. He wondered if Walker or Wren had changed their minds.

He finished washing, dried himself, and turned to find Padishar seated at a three-legged table whose missing limb had been replaced by an up-ended crate. The leader of the free-born was eating bread and cheese and washing it down with ale. He beckoned Par to a place that had been set for him, to a waiting plate of food, and the Valeman walked over wordlessly, sat down, and began to eat.

He was hungrier than he had thought he would be and consumed the meal in minutes. All about him, the candles sputtered and flared in the near darkness like fireflies on a moonless night. The silence was broken by the distant sound of water dripping.

"How long have you known the Mole?" he asked Padishar, not liking the empty feeling the quiet fostered within him.

Padishar pursed his lips. His face was scratched and cut so badly that he looked like a badly formed puzzle. "About a year. Damson took me to meet him one day in the park after nightfall. I don't know how she met him." He glanced over at the stuffed animals. "Peculiar fellow, but taken with her, sure enough."

Par nodded wordlessly.

Padishar leaned back in his chair, causing it to creak. "Tell me about the Sword, lad," he urged, moving the ale cup in front of him, twisting it between his fingers. "Is it the real thing?"

Par smiled in spite of himself. "Good question, Padishar. I wish I knew."

Then he told the leader of the free-born what had befallen him since they had struggled together to escape the Pit—how Damson had found the Ohmsford brothers in the People's Park, how they had met the Mole, how they had determined to go back down into the Pit a final time to gain possession of the Sword, how he had encountered Rimmer Dall within the vault and been handed what was said to be the ancient talisman with no struggle at all, how Coll had been lost, and finally how Damson and he had been running and hiding throughout Tyrsis ever since.

What Par didn't tell Padishar was how Rimmer Dall had warned him that, like the First Seeker, Par, too, was a Shadowen. Because if it was the truth . . .

"I carry it, Padishar," he finished, dismissing the prospect, gesturing instead toward the dusty blade where it leaned against the bureau, "because I keep thinking that sooner or later I'll be able to figure out whether or not it is real."

Padishar frowned darkly. "There's a trick being played here somewhere. Rimmer Dall's no friend to anyone. Either the blade is a fake or he has good reason to believe that you can't make use of it."

If I'm a Shadowen . . .

Par swallowed against his fear. "I know. And so far I can't. I keep testing it, trying to invoke its magic, but nothing happens." He paused. "Only once, when I was in the Pit, after Coll . . . I picked up the Sword from where I had dropped it, and the touch of it burned me like live coals. Just for a minute." He was thinking it through again, remembering. "The wishsong's magic was still live. I was still holding that fire sword. Then the magic disappeared, and the Sword of Shannara became cool to the touch again."

The big man nodded. "That's it, then, lad. Something about the wishsong's magic interferes with use of the Sword of Shannara. It makes some sense, doesn't it? Why not a clash of magics? If it's so, Rimmer Dall could give you the Sword and never have to worry one whit."

Par shook his head. "But how would he know it would work that way?" He was thinking now that it was more likely the First Seeker knew the Sword was useless to a Shadowen. "And what about Allanon? Wouldn't he know as well? Why would he send me in search of the Sword if I can't use it?"

Padishar had no answers to any of these questions, of course, so for a moment the two simply stared at each other. Then the big man said, "I'm sorry about your brother."

Par looked away momentarily, then back again. "It was Damson who kept me from . . ." He caught his breath sharply. "Who helped me get past the pain when I thought it was too much to bear." He smiled faintly, sadly at the other. "I love her, Padishar. We have to get her back."

Padishar nodded. "If she's lost, lad. We don't know anything for sure." His voice sounded uncertain, and his eyes were worried and distant.

"Losing Coll is as much as I can stand." Par would not let his gaze drop.

"I know. We'll see her safely back, I promise."

Padishar reached for the ale jug, poured a healthy measure into his own cup, and, as an afterthought, added a small amount to Par's. He drank deeply and set the cup down carefully. Par saw that he had said as much as he wanted to on the matter.

"Tell me of Morgan," Par asked quietly.

"Ah, the Highlander." Padishar brightened immediately. "Saved my life in the Pit after you and your brother escaped. Saved it again—along with everyone else's—at the Jut. Bad business, that."

And he proceeded to relate what had happened—how the Sword of Leah had been shattered in their escape from the Pit and its Shadowen, how the Federation had tracked them to the Jut and laid siege, how the Creepers had come, how Morgan had divined that Teel was a Shadowen, how the Highlander, Steff, and he had tracked Teel deep into the caves behind the Jut where Morgan had faced Teel alone and found just enough of his broken Sword's magic to destroy her, how the free-born had slipped away from the Federation trap, and how Morgan had left them then to go back to Culhaven and the Dwarves so that he might keep his promise to the dying Steff.

"I gave him my promise that I would go in search of you," Padishar concluded. "But I was forced to lie quiet at Firerim Reach first while my broken arm mended. Six weeks. Still tender, though I don't show it. We were supposed to meet Axhind and his Rock Trolls at the Jannisson two weeks past, but I got word to them to make it eight." He sighed. "So much time lost and so little of it to lose. It's one step forward and two back. Anyway, I finally healed enough to keep my end of the bargain and come find you." He laughed wryly. "It wasn't easy. Everywhere I looked the Federation was waiting."

"Teel, then, you think?" Par asked.

The other nodded. "Had to be, lad. Killed Hirehone after stealing his identity and his secrets. Hirehone was trusted; he knew the safe holes. Teel—

the Shadowen—must have gotten that information from him, drained it from his mind." He spat. "Black things! And Rimmer Dall would pretend to be your friend! What lies!"

Or worse, the truth, Par thought, but didn't say it. Par feared that his affinity with the First Seeker, whatever its nature, let Rimmer Dall glean the secrets he would otherwise keep hidden—even those he was not immediately privy to, those kept by his friends and companions.

It was a wild thought. Too wild to be believed. But then much of what he had encountered these past few weeks was of the same sort, wasn't it?

Better to believe that it was all Teel, he told himself.

"Anyway," Padishar was saying, "I've set guards to watch the Reach ever since we settled there, because Hirehone knew of it as well, and that means the Shadowen may know too. But so far all's been quiet. A week hence we keep the meeting with the Trolls, and if they agree to join we have an army to be reckoned with, the beginning of a true resistance, the core of a fire that will burn right through the Federation and set us free at last."

"At the Jannisson still?" Par asked, thinking of other things.

"We leave as soon as I return with you. And Damson," he added quickly, firmly. "A week is time enough to do it all." He didn't sound entirely sure.

"But Morgan's not come back yet?" Par pressed.

Padishar shook his head slowly. "Don't worry about your friend, lad. He's tough as leather and swift as light. And determined. Wherever he is, whatever he's doing, he'll be fine. We'll see him one day soon."

Oddly enough, Par was inclined to agree. If ever there was someone who could find a way out of any mess, it was Morgan Leah. He pictured his friend's clever eyes, his ready smile, the hint of mischief in his voice, and found that he missed him very much. Another of his journey's casualties, lost somewhere along the way, stripped from him like excess baggage. Except the analogy was wrong—his friends and his brother had given their lives to keep him safe. All of them, at one time or another. And what had he given them in return? What had he done to justify such sacrifice?

What good had he accomplished?

His eyes fell once more upon the Sword of Shannara, tracing the lines of the upraised hand with its burning torch. Truth. The Sword of Shannara was a talisman for truth. And the truth he most needed to discover just now was whether this blade for which so much had been given up was real.

How could he do that?

Across from him Padishar stretched and yawned. "Time to get some rest, Par Ohmsford," he advised, rising. "We need our strength for what lies ahead."

He moved to the couch on which the stuffed animals were seated, gathered them up perfunctorily, and plopped them down on a nearby chair. Turning back to the couch, he settled himself comfortably on the worn leather cushions, boots hanging off one end, head cradled in the crook of one arm. In moments he was snoring.

Par stayed awake for a time watching him, letting the dark thoughts settle in his mind, keeping his resolve from scattering like leaves in a wind storm. He was afraid, but the fear was nothing new. It was the eroding of hope that unsettled him most, the crumbling of his certainty that whatever happened he would find a way to deal with it. He was beginning to wonder if that was so anymore.

He rose finally and went to the chair where Padishar had dumped the stuffed animals. Carefully he gathered them up—Chalt, Lida, Westra, Everlind and the others—and carried them to where the Sword of Shannara leaned up against the bureau. One by one, he arranged them about the Sword, placing them at watch—as if by doing so they might aid him in keeping the demons from his sleep.

When he was finished, he walked to the back of the Mole's lair, found some discarded cushions and old blankets, made himself a pallet in a corner dominated by a collection of old paintings, and lay down.

He was still listening to the sound of water dripping when he finally drifted off to sleep.

When he woke again, he was alone. The couch where Padishar had been sleeping was empty and the Mole's chambers were silent. All of the candles were extinguished save for one. Par blinked against the sharp pinprick of light, then peered about into the gloom, wondering where Padishar had gone. He rose, stretched, walked to the candle, used it to light the others, and watched the darkness shrink to scattered shadows.

He had no idea how long he had slept; time lost all meaning within these catacombs. He was hungry again, so he made himself a meal from some bread, cheese, fruit, and ale, and consumed it at the three-legged table. As he ate, he stared fixedly across the room at the Sword of Shannara, propped in the corner, surrounded by the Mole's children.

Speak to me, he thought. Why won't you speak to me?

He finished eating, shoving the food in his mouth without tasting it, drinking the ale without interest, his eyes and his mind focused on the Sword. He pushed back from the table, walked over to the blade, lifted it away from its resting place, and carried it back to his chair. He balanced it on his knees for a time, staring down at it. Then finally he pulled it free of its scabbard and held it up before him, turning it this way and that, letting the candlelight reflect off its polished surface.

His eyes glittered with frustration.

Talisman or trickster—which are you?

If the former, something was decidedly wrong between them. He was the descendant of Shea Ohmsford and his Elven blood was as good as that of his famous ancestor; he should have been able to call up the power of the Sword with ease. If it was the Sword in truth, of course. Otherwise . . . He shook his head angrily. No, this was the Sword of Shannara. It was. He could feel it in his bones. Everything he knew of the Sword, everything he had learned of it, all the songs he had sung of it over the years, told him that this was it. Rimmer Dall would not have given him an imitation; the First Seeker was too eager that Par accept his guidance in the matter of his magic to risk alienating him with a lie that would eventually be discovered. Whatever else Rimmer Dall might be, he was clever—far too clever to play such a simple game . . .

Par left the thought unfinished, not as certain as he wanted to be that he was right. Still, it felt right, his reasoning sound, his sense of things balanced. Rimmer Dall wanted him to accept that he was a Shadowen. A Shadowen could not use the Elven magic of the blade because . . .

Because why?

The truth would destroy him, perhaps, and his own magic would not allow it?

But when the Sword of Shannara had burned him in the Pit after he had destroyed Coll and the Shadowen with him, hadn't it been the *blade's* magic that had reacted to his rather than the other way around? Which magic was resisting which?

He gritted his teeth, his hands clenching tightly about the Sword's carved handle. The raised hand with its torch pressed against his palm, the lines sharp and clear. What was the problem between them? Why couldn't he find the answer?

He shoved the blade back into its scabbard and sat unmoving in the candle-lit silence, thinking. Allanon had given him the charge to find the Sword of Shannara. Him, not Wren or Walker, and they had Elven Shannara blood as well, didn't they? Allanon had sent him. Familiar questions repeated themselves in his mind. Wouldn't the Druid have known if such a charge was pointless? Even as a shade, wouldn't he have been able to sense that Par's magic was a danger, that Par himself was the enemy?

Unless Rimmer Dall was right and the Shadowen weren't the enemy— the Druids were. Or perhaps they were all enemies of a sort, combatants for control of the magic, Shadowen and Druid, both fighting to fill that void that had been created at Allanon's death, that vacuum left by the fading of the last real magic.

Was that possible?

Par's brow furrowed. He ran his fingers along the Sword's pommel and down the bindings of the scabbard.

Why was the truth so difficult to discover?

He found himself wondering what had become of all the others who had started out on the journey to the Hadeshorn. Steff and Teel were dead. Morgan was missing. Where was Cogline? What had become of him after the meeting with Allanon and the giving of the charges? Par found himself wishing suddenly that he could speak with the old man about the Sword. Surely Cogline would be able to make some sense of all this. And what of Wren and that giant Rover? What of Walker Boh? Had they changed their minds and gone on to fulfill their charges as he had?

As he thought he had.

His eyes, staring into the space before him, lowered again to the Sword. There was one thing more. Now that he had possession of the blade—perhaps—what was he supposed to do with it? Giving Allanon the benefit of the doubt on who was good and who was bad and whether Par was doing the right thing, what purpose was the Sword of Shannara supposed to serve?

What truth was it supposed to reveal?

He was sick of questions without answers, of secrets being kept from him, of lies and twisted half-truths that circled him like scavengers waiting to feast. If he could break just a single link of this chain of uncertainty and confusion that bound him, if he could sever but a single tie . . .

The door slipped open across the room, and Padishar appeared through the opening. "There you are," he announced cheerfully. "Rested, I hope?"

Par nodded, the Sword still balanced on his knees. Padishar glanced down at it as he crossed the room. Par let his grip loosen. "What time is it?" he asked.

"Midday. The Mole hasn't come back. I went out because I thought I might be able to learn something about Damson on my own. Ask a few questions. Poke my nose in a few holes." He shook his head. "It was a waste of time. If the Federation has her, they're keeping it quiet."

He slumped down on the sofa, looking worn and discouraged. "If he isn't back by nightfall, I'll go out again."

Par leaned forward. "Not without me."

Padishar glanced at him and grunted. "I suppose not. Well, Valeman, perhaps we can at least avoid another trip down into the Pit . . ."

He stopped, aware suddenly of what that implied, then looked away uncomfortably. Par lifted the Sword of Shannara from his knees and placed it next to him on the floor. "She told me that you were her father, Padishar."

The big man stared at him wordlessly for a moment, then smiled faintly. "Love seems to cause all sorts of foolish talk."

He rose and walked to the table. "I'll have something to eat now, I think." He wheeled about abruptly, and his voice was as hard as stone. "Don't ever repeat what you just said. Not to anyone. Ever."

He waited until Par nodded, then turned his attention to putting together a meal. He ate from the same scraps of food as the Valeman, adding a bit of dried beef he scavenged from a food locker. Par watched him without comment, wondering how long father and daughter had kept their secret, thinking how hard it must have been for both of them. Padishar's chiseled features lowered into shadow as he ate, but his eyes glittered like bits of white fire.

When he was finished, he faced Par once more. "She promised—she swore—never to tell anyone."

Par looked down at his clasped hands. "She told me because we both needed to have some reason to trust the other. We were sharing secrets to gain that trust. It was right before we went down into the Pit that last time."

Padishar sighed. "If they find out who she is—"

"No," Par interrupted quickly. "We'll have her back before then." He met the other's penetrating gaze. "We will, Padishar."

Padishar Creel nodded. "We will, indeed, Par Ohmsford. We will, indeed."

It was several hours later when the Mole appeared soundlessly through the entryway, sliding out of the dark like one of its shadows, eyes blinking against the candlelight. His fur stood on end, bristling from his worn clothes and giving him the look of a prickly scrub. Wordlessly he moved to extinguish several of the lights, leaving the larger part of his chambers shrouded once more in the darkness with which he was comfortable. He scooted past to where his children sat clustered on the floor, cooed softly to them for a moment, gathered them up tenderly, and carried them back to the sofa.

He was still arranging them when Padishar's patience ran out.

"What did you find out?" the big man demanded heatedly. "Tell us, if you think you can spare the time!"

The Mole shifted without turning. "She is a prisoner."

Par felt the blood drain from his face. He glanced quickly at Padishar and found the big man on his feet, hands clenched.

"Where?" Padishar whispered.

The Mole took a moment to finish settling Chalt against a cushion and then turned. "In the old Legion barracks at the back of the inner wall. Lovely Damson is kept in the south watchtower, all alone." He shuffled his feet. "It took me a long time to find her."

Padishar came forward and knelt so that they were at eye level. The scratches on his face were as red as fire. "Have they . . ." He groped for the words. "Is she all right?"

The Mole shook his head. "I could not reach her."

Par came forward as well. "You didn't see her?"

"No." The Mole blinked. "But she is there. I climbed through the tower walls. She was just on the other side. I could hear her breathe through the stone. She was sleeping."

The Valeman and the leader of the free-born exchanged a quick glance. "How closely is she watched?" Padishar pressed.

The Mole brought his hands to his eyes and rubbed gently with his knuckles. "Soldiers stand watch at her door, at the foot of the stairs leading up, at the gate leading in. They patrol the halls and walkways. There are many." He blinked. "There are Shadowen as well."

Padishar sagged back. "They know," he whispered harshly.

"No," Par disagreed. "Not yet." He waited for Padishar's eyes to meet his own. "If they did, they wouldn't let her sleep. They're not sure. They'll wait for Rimmer Dall—just as they did before."

Padishar stared at him wordlessly for a moment, a glimmer of hope showing on his rough features. "You might be right. So we have to get her out before that happens."

"You and me," Par said quietly. "We both go."

The leader of the free-born nodded, and an understanding passed between them that was more profound than anything words could have expressed. Padishar rose and they faced each other in the gloom of the Mole's shabby chambers, resolve hardening them against what most certainly lay ahead. Par pushed aside the unanswered questions and the confusion over the Sword of Shannara. He buried his doubts over the use of his own magic. Where Damson was concerned, he would do whatever it took to get her free. Nothing else mattered.

"We will need to get close to her," Padishar declared softly, looking down at the Mole. "As close as we can without being seen."

The Mole nodded solemnly. "I know a way."

The big man reached out to touch his shoulder. "You will have to come with us."

"Lovely Damson is my best friend," the Mole said.

Padishar nodded and took his hand away. He turned to Par.

"We'll go after her now."

The man in the high castle was Walker Boh, and he walked its parapets and battlements, its towers and keeps, all of the corridors and walkways that defined its boundaries like the wraith he had been and the outcast he felt. Paranor, the castle of the Druids, was returned, come back into the world of men, brought alive by Walker and the magic of the Black Elfstone. Paranor stood as it had three hundred years before, lifting out of the dark forest where wolves prowled and thorns the size of lance-points bristled protectively. It rose out of the earth, set upon a bluff where it could be seen across the whole of the valley it dominated, from the Kennon to the Jannisson, from one ridgeline of the Dragon's Teeth to the other, spires and walls and gates. As solid as the stone from which it had been built more than a thousand years earlier, it was the Keep of legends and folk tales made whole once more.

But shades, Walker Boh thought in his despair, what it had cost!

"It was waiting for me down in the tower well, the essence of the Druid magic he had set at watch," Walker explained to Cogline that first night, the night he had emerged from the Keep with Allanon's presence at haunt within. "All those years it had been waiting, his spirit or some part of that spirit, concealed in the serpentine mist that had destroyed the Mord Wraiths and their allies and sent Paranor out of the land of men to wait for the time it would be summoned back again. Allanon's shade had been waiting as well, it seems, there within the waters of the Hadeshorn, knowing that the need for the Keep and its Druids would one day prove inexorable, that the magic and the lore they wielded must be kept at hand against the possibility that history's evolution would take a different path than the one he had prophesied."

Cogline listened and did not speak. He was still in awe of what had happened, of whom Walker Boh had become. He was afraid. For Walker was Walker still, but something more as well. Allanon was there, become a part of him in the transformation from man to Druid, in the rite of passage that had taken place in the Keep's dark hold. Cogline had ventured, in his spirit form, just long enough to pull Walker back from the madness that threatened to engulf him before he could come to grips with the change that was taking place. In those few seconds Cogline had felt the beginnings of Walker's change—and he had fled in horror.

"The Black Elfstone drew the mist into itself and thereby into me," Walker whispered, the words a familiar repetition by now, as if saying them would make them better understood. His stark visage lowered into the cowl of his robe, a mask still changing. "It brought Allanon within. It brought all of the Druids within—their history and lore and magic, their knowledge, their secrets, all that they were. It spun them through me like threads on a loom that weaves a new cloth, and I could feel myself invaded and helpless to prevent it."

The face within the cowl swung slightly toward the old man. "I have all of them inside me, Cogline. They have made a home within me, determined that I should have their knowledge and their power and that I should use it as they did. It was Allanon's plan from the beginning—a descendant of Brin to carry forth the Druid lineage, one that would be chosen when the need arose, one who would serve and obey."

Iron fingers fastened suddenly on Cogline's shoulder and made him wince. "Obey, old man! That is what they intend of me, but not what they shall have!" Walker Boh's words were edged with bitterness. "I can feel them working about inside, living things! I can sense their presence as they whisper their words and try to make me heed. But I am stronger than they are, made so by the very process that they used to change me. I survived the trial they set for me, and I will be what I choose, be they living within my body and mind, be they shades or memories of the past, be they what they will! If I must be this . . . this *thing* they have made of me, I shall at least give it my voice and my heart!"

So they walked, Cogline as cold as death listening to the tormented Walker Boh, Walker as hot as the fires that had begun to burn anew within the furnaces below Paranor's stone walls, his fury made over into the strength that sustained him against what was happening.

For the change continued even now as they walked the castle corridors,

the old man and the becoming Druid, shadowed by the silent presence of
Rumor the moor cat, as black-browed as his masters. The change swirled
through Walker like smoke in the wind, stirred by the hands of the Druids
gone, their spirits alive within the one who would permit the magic to live
again. It came as knowledge revealed in bits and pieces and sometimes in
sharp bursts, knowledge gained and preserved through the years, all that the
Druids had discovered and shaped in their order, the whole of what had
sustained them through the years of the Warlock Lord and the Skull Bearers, through the Demons within the Forbidding, through the Ildatch and
the Mord Wraiths, through all the trials of dark evil set to challenge hu-
mankind. The magic revealed itself little by little, peeking forth from the
jumble of hands and eyes and whispered words that roiled in Walker Boh's
mind and gave him no peace.

He did not sleep at all for three days. He tried, exhausted to the point
of despair, but when he endeavored to let himself go, to slip away into the
comfort of the rest he so desperately needed, some new facet of the change
lurched alive and brought him upright as if he were a puppet on strings,
making him aware of its need, of its presence, of its determination to be
heard. Each time he would fight it, not to prevent it from being, for there
was no sense in that, but to assure that it was not accepted without question, that the knowledge was perused and studied, that he recognized its
face and was cautioned thereby against blind use. The Druids were not his
maker, he reminded himself over and over again. The Druids had not given
him his life and should not be allowed to dictate his destiny. *He* would do
that. *He* would decide the nature of his life, power of magic or no, and in
doing so would be accountable only to himself.

Cogline and Rumor stayed with him, as exhausted as he was, but
frightened for him and determined that he would not be left alone to face
what was happening. Cogline's was the voice that Walker needed to hear
now and again in response to his own, a caution and reassurance to blunt
his lamentations of disgust. Rumor was the shaggy dark certainty that some
things did not change, a presence as solid and dependable as the coming of
day after night, the promise that there could be a waking from even the
worst of nightmares. Together they sustained him in ways he could not begin to describe and that they in turn could not begin to understand. It was
enough that they sensed that the bond was there.

Three days passed, then, before the change finally ran its course and the
transformation was made complete. All at once the hands stopped molding,
the eyes disappeared, and the whispers faded. Within Walker Boh, everything
suddenly went still. He slept then and did not dream, and when he woke he
knew that while he was changed in ways he was only beginning to discover,
still he was in the deepest part of himself the same person he had always
been. He had preserved the heart of the man who mistrusted the Druids
and their magics, and while the Druids now lived within him and would
have their voice in the way he conducted his life, nevertheless they would
be ruled by beliefs that had preceded their coming and would survive their

stay. Walker rose in the solitude of his sleeping chamber, alone in the darkness that the windowless room provided, at peace with himself for the first time he could remember, the long, terrible journey to fulfill the charge he had been given ended, the ordeal of the transformation set for him finished at last. Much had come undone and more than a little had been lost, but what mattered above all else was that he had survived.

He went out then to Cogline and found him sitting close by with the moor cat curled at his feet, worry lines etched in his aging face, uncertainty reflected in his eyes. He came up to the old man and raised him to his feet as if he were a child grown impossibly strong with the change, made over by the hands and eyes and voices until he was as ten men. He put his good arm about the frail old body and held his mentor gently.

"I am well again," he whispered. "It is over and I am safe."

And the old man gripped him back and cried into his shoulder.

They talked then as they had of old, two men who had experienced more than their share of surprises in life, joined by the common bond of the Druid magic and by the fates that had brought them to this time and place. They spoke of Walker's change, of the feelings it had generated, of the knowledge it had brought, and of the needs it might fulfill. They were whole again, flesh-and-blood men, and Paranor was returned. It was the beginning of a new era in the world of the Four Lands, and they were at the first moment in time that would determine how that era evolved. Walker Boh was uncertain even now how he was to wield the Druid magic—or even that he should. There was the Shadowen threat to consider, but the nature and extent of that threat remained a mystery. Walker had been given the Druid lore, but not an insight into what he was expected to do with it—especially as regarded the Shadowen.

"My transformation has left me with certain insights that weren't there before," Walker confided. "One is that the use of Druid magic will prove necessary if the Shadowen threat is to be ended. But whose insight is it— mine or Allanon's? Can I trust it, I wonder? Is it a truth or a fiction?"

The old man shook his head. "I think you must discover that for yourself. I think Allanon wants it that way. Hasn't it always been left to the Ohmsfords to discover the truth of things on their own? Gamesplaying, you once called it. But isn't it really much more than that? Isn't it the nature of life? Experience comes from doing, not from being told. Experiment and discover. Seek and find. It is not the machinations of the Druids that compel us to do so; it is our need to know. It is, in the end, the way we learn. I think it must be your way as well, Walker."

What should be done first, they decided, was to find out what had become of the other scions of Shannara—Par, Coll, and Wren. Had they fulfilled the charges they had been given? Where were they and what secrets had they uncovered in the weeks that had passed since their meeting at the Hadeshorn?

"Par will have found the Sword of Shannara or be searching for it,"

Walker declared. They sat within the Druid study, the Histories spread out before them, perused this time for particulars that Walker remembered from his previous readings and now understood differently with the knowledge his transformation had wrought. "Par was driven in his quest. He was all iron and determination. Whatever the rest of us chose to do, he would not have given up."

"Nor Wren either, I think," the old man offered thoughtfully. "There was as much iron in her, though it was not so apparent." He met Walker's gaze boldly. "Allanon's shade sensed what would drive each of you, and I think no one ever really stood a chance of being able to walk away."

Walker leaned back in the chair that cushioned him, lean face shadowed by lank dark hair and beard, the eyes so penetrating it seemed that nothing could hide from them. "From the time of Shea Ohmsford, the Druids have made us their own, haven't they?" he mused, cool and distant. "They found in us something that could be shackled, and they have held us prisoner ever since. We are servants to their needs—and paladins to the races."

Cogline felt the air in the room stir, a palpable response to the flow of magic that rose from Walker's voice. He had sensed it more than once since Walker had come out of the Keep, a measure of the power bestowed on him. More Druid than man, he was a manifestation of the dark arts and lore that once, long ago, the old man had studied and rejected in favor of forms of the old-world sciences. Opportunity lost, he thought. But sanity gained. He wondered if Walker would find peace in his own evolution.

"We are just men," he said cautiously.

And Walker replied, smiling, "We are just fools."

They talked late into the night, but Walker remained undecided on a course of action. Find the others of his family, yes—but where to begin and how to go about it? Use of his newfound magic was an obvious choice, but would that use reveal him to the Shadowen? Did his enemies know what had happened yet—that he had become a Druid and that Paranor had been brought back? How strong was the Shadowen magic? How far could it reach? He should not be too quick to test it, he kept repeating. He was still learning about his own. He was still discovering. He should not be hasty about what he chose to do.

The debate wore on, and as it did so it began to dawn on Walker that something was different between Cogline and himself. He thought at first that his reluctance to commit to a course of action was simply indecision—even though that was very unlike him. He soon realized it was something else altogether. While they talked as they had of old, there was a distance between them that had never been there before, not even when he had been angry with and mistrustful of the old man. The relationship between them had changed. Walker was no longer the student and Cogline the teacher. Walker's transformation had left him with knowledge and power far superior to Cogline's. Walker was no longer the Dark Uncle hiding out in Darklin Reach. The days of living apart from the races and forswearing his birthright were gone forever. Walker Boh was committed to whom and what he had become—a Druid, the only Druid, perhaps the single most powerful individual alive. What he did could affect the lives of everyone. Walker knew that. Knowing, he accepted that his decisions must be his own and the making of them could never again be shared, because no one, not even Cogline, should have to bear the weight of such a terrible responsibility.

When they parted finally to sleep, exhausted anew from their efforts, Walker found himself besieged by a mix of feelings. He had grown so far beyond the man he had been that in many ways he was barely recognizable. He was conscious of the old man staring after him as he retreated down the hall to his sleeping room and could not shake the sense that they were drawing apart in more ways than one.

Cogline. The Druid-who-never-was made companion to the Druid-who-would-be—what must he be feeling?

Walker didn't know. But he accepted reluctantly that from this night forward things would never be the same between them again.

He slept then, and his dreams were tenuous and filled with faces and voices he could not recognize. It was nearing dawn when he woke, an urgency gripping him, whispering insidiously at him, bringing him out of his sleep like a swimmer out of water, thrusting to the surface and drawing in huge gulps of air. For a moment he was paralyzed by the suddenness of his waking, frozen with uncertainty as his heart pounded within his chest and his eyes and ears struggled to make sense of the darkness surrounding him. At last he was able to move, swinging his legs down off the bed, steadied by the feeling of the solid stone beneath his feet. He rose, aware that he was still wearing the dark robes in which he had fallen asleep, the clothing he had been too tired to remove.

Something stirred just outside his door, a soft padding, a rubbing against the ancient wood.

Rumor.

He went to the door and opened it. The big cat stood just without, staring up at him. It circled away anxiously and came back again, big head swinging up, eyes gleaming.

It wants me to follow, Walker thought. Something is wrong.

He wrapped himself in a heavy cloak and went out from his sleeping chamber into the tomblike silence of the castle. Stone walls muffled the sound of his feet as he hurried down the ancient corridors. Rumor went on ahead, sleek and dark in the gloom, padding soundlessly through the shadows. Without slowing, they passed the room in which Cogline slept. The trouble did not lie there. The night faded about them as they went, dawn rising out of the east in a shimmer of silver that seeped through the castle windows in wintry, clouded light. Walker barely noticed, his eyes fixed on the movement of the moor cat as it slid through the overlapping shadows. His ears strained to hear something, to catch a hint of what was waiting. But the silence persisted, unbroken.

They climbed from the main hall to the battlement doors and went out into the open air. The dawn was chill and empty-feeling. Mist lay over the whole of the valley, climbing the wall of the Dragon's Teeth east and stretching west to the Streleheim in a blanket that shrouded everything between. Paranor lay wrapped within its upper folds, its high towers islands thrusting out of a misty sea. The mist swirled and spun, stirred by winds that came down off the mountains, and in the weak light of the early dawn strange shapes and forms came alive.

Rumor padded down the walkway, sniffing the air as he went, tail switching uneasily. Walker followed. They circled the south parapet west without slowing, seeing nothing, hearing nothing. They passed open stairwells and tower entryways, ghosts at haunt.

On the west battlement, Rumor slowed suddenly. The hair on the moor cat's neck bristled, and his dark muzzle wrinkled in a snarl. Walker moved up beside him and quickly placed a reassuring hand on the coarse hair of his back. Rumor was facing out now into the gloom. They stood just above the castle's west gate.

Walker peered into the mist. He could sense it, too.

Something was out there.

The seconds slipped away, and nothing showed. Walker began to grow impatient. Perhaps he should go out for a look.

Then suddenly the mist drew back, seemed to pull away as if in revulsion, and the riders appeared. There were four of them, gaunt and spectral in the faint light. They came slowly, purposefully, as gray as the gloom that had hidden their approach. Four riders atop their mounts, but none was human, and the animals they rode were loathsome parodies, all scales and claws and teeth. Four riders, each markedly different from the other, each with a mount that was a mirror of itself.

Walker Boh knew at once that they were Shadowen. He knew as well that they had come for him.

Coolly, dispassionately, he studied them.

The first was tall and lean and cadaverous. Bones pressed out against skin shrunk tight against it, the skeletal frame hunched forward like a cat at hunt. The face was a skull in which the jaw hung open slackly and the eyes stared out, too wide and too blank to be seeing. It wore no clothes, and its naked body was neither that of a man nor of a woman, but something in between. Its breath clouded the air before it, a vile green mist.

The second lacked any semblance of identity. It was human-shaped, but had no skin or bones. It was instead a raging cloud of darkness, buzzing and shrieking within its form. The cloud had the look of flies or mosquitoes trapped behind glass, gathered so thick that they shut out the light. The wicked sounds that issued from this rider seemed to warn that it hid within its spectral form an evil too dreadful to imagine.

The third was more immediately recognizable. Armored head to foot, it bristled with spikes and cutting edges and weapons. It wore maces and knives, swords and battle-axes, and carried a huge pike strung with skulls and finger bones laced together in a chain. A helmet hid its face, but the eyes that peered out through the visor slit were as red as fire.

The last rider was cloaked and hooded and as invisible as the night. No face could be seen within the concealing cowl. No hands showed to grip the reins of its sinewy mount. It rode hunched forward like a very old man, all bent and gnarled, a creature crippled by age and time. But there was no sense of weakness about it, nothing to suggest that it was anything of what it appeared. This rider rode steady and sure, and what crippled it was neither time nor age but the weight of the burden it bore for the lives it had taken.

Slung across its back was a scythe.

Walker Boh went cold with recognition. Far back in the Druid Histories, recorded from the old world of Men, there was mention of these four. He knew who they were, whom they had been created to be. Now Shadowen had taken on their guises, assumed the identities of the dark things of old.

His chest tightened. Four riders. The Four Horsemen of the legends, the slayers of mortal men come out of a time so distant it had been all but forgotten. But he had read the tales, he repeated to himself, and he knew what they were.

Famine. Pestilence. War. Death.

Walker's hand lifted away from Rumor, and the cat began to growl deep in his chest. Shadowen, Walker thought in a mix of awe and fear, created to be something that never was, that was only a manifestation of abstracts, of killing ways, come now to destroy me.

He wondered anew at who and what the Shadowen were, at the source of power that would let them be anything they chose. His transformation had given him no insight into this. He was as ignorant of their origins now as he had been at the start of things. Yes, they were as dark as the shade of Allanon had forewarned. Yes, they were an evil that used magic as a weapon to destroy. But who were they? Where had they come from? How could they be destroyed?

Where could he find the answers to his questions?

He watched the Four Horsemen advance, settled atop their lurching, writhing mounts, things that vaguely resembled horses but were intended to be much more. Breath steamed on the morning air like poisonous vapor. Claws scraped and crunched on the rock. Heads lifted and muzzles drew back to show hooked, yellowed teeth. Steadily, the Horsemen came on.

When they reached the gates, they stopped. They made no move to pass through. They showed no interest in advancing. In a line they faced the gate and waited. Walker waited with them. The minutes passed and the light brightened slowly, the gloom taking on a whiteness as the dawn neared.

Then at last the sun crested the mountains east, a faint glimmer above the dark peaks, and at the gates below, the rider Famine suddenly advanced. When it was next to the barrier, it lifted its skeletal hand and knocked. The sound was a dimly heard, echoing, hollow thud—the shudder that life makes as it departs the body for the final time. Walker cringed in spite of himself, revolted by how it made him feel.

Famine backed away then, and one by one the Four Horsemen turned right, spreading out in a thin line to circle the castle walls. Around they went, passing beneath Walker one by one as he watched them return and disappear again, keeping carefully apart in their movement so that there was always one at each wall, one at each corner of the compass.

A siege, Walker realized. The knock was a challenge, and if he did not come out to answer it, they intended to keep him trapped within. Rimmer Dall and the Shadowen had discovered that Paranor was back and that Walker had accepted the mantle of Allanon. The Horsemen had been sent in response.

Walker folded his arms within his cloak. *We'll see who traps whom,* he thought darkly.

He stood looking down for a while longer on the apparitions below, then went to wake Cogline.

5

The sewers beneath Tyrsis were dank and chill in a twilight dark that seeped along gutters and down grates like spilled ink. Daylight had gone west, and the night hovered in shadows that lengthened from buildings and walls, a ghost come to life. Footsteps and voices faded homeward, and the weariness of day's end was a sigh echoed by the hot summer wind as it settled into pockets of still, suffocating heat in the runnels of the city's streets and byways, an airless blanket laid over the catacombs below.

Padishar Creel, Par Ohmsford, and the Mole groped their way slowly and steadily through those catacombs, three of the shadows that grew out of night's coming, as silent as the dust stirred by the boots passing in the streets above. They breathed through their mouths, the sewer smells oppressive and rank within the twisting conduits, the city's waste a sluggish flow at the edges of their feet. At times they climbed iron ladders and stone steps, at times they crawled through narrow tunnels, all the while working their way outward from the city's center toward its walls and the bluff face, the watchtower where Damson Rhee was held prisoner, and the confrontation that waited.

"We will not return without her," Padishar had declared. "Whatever proves necessary to free her, we will do. Once we have her, we will not give her up again.

"Mole," he had whispered, kneeling before the strange little fellow. "You will guide us in and, if possible, out again. But you will not fight, do you understand? Keep yourself clear and safe. Because, Mole, once we have freed Damson"—there was no suggestion, Par noted, that they would not— "you alone will know how to see her safely away again. Agreed?" And the Mole had nodded solemnly.

"Par, yours is a harder task still," the leader of the free-born had continued, turning next to the Valeman. "If we encounter the Shadowen, you must use your magic to keep them from us. The Highlander was able to do so with his sword when we were trapped in the Pit. This time it will be up to you. I lack any means to defend against these monsters. If we encounter them, lad, don't hesitate."

Par had already decided that use of the wishsong in this endeavor was a foregone conclusion, so he was quick to give Padishar his promise. What he could not promise—and what he did not tell the other—was that he was no longer certain he could control the magic. It had already proved unreliable, already shown that it could take on a life of its own, unleashing power that might well consume him. But such fears as recognition of this danger generated paled against his feelings for Damson Rhee. Buried by the struggle they had shared to escape the city and its hunters, and by the fact that he had felt her safe with him, his feelings had surfaced instantly with the report of her taking, and now they raged within him like a fire unchecked. He loved her. Perhaps he had loved her from the first, but certainly since she had held him together after Coll's death. She was as much a part of him as anything separate could possibly be, and he could not stand the thought of losing her. He would give anything to see her safe again. He would give everything. If it meant risking the fury of a magic that could change him irrevocably, that could even destroy him, then so be it. If Rimmer Dall was right about who and what he was, then there was nothing he could do to save himself in any case. He would not shy from the dangers of the magic where Damson's safety was at stake. He would do what he must.

So they had set out, each determined that Damson was worth losing everything, knowing the risk was such that everything could well be lost. Now the sewers stretched away in narrow, winding tunnels before them, the darkness closing fast about the little light that remained. Soon they would be forced to use torchlight to see, and that would be especially dangerous as they neared the city's walls. For there the dark things would likely be at watch below ground as well as above, and torchlight would be seen coming from a long way off.

They hurried on, the Mole's sharp eyes and steady senses choosing their way unerringly, sorting out which paths were safe, avoiding the ones that might impede them. As they went, they could hear the sounds of the city above drifting down in trickles and snatches, bits and pieces of a life as disconnected from their own as the living from the dead. Par's thoughts drifted. It felt somehow as if they were entombed within the stone of the bluff on which Tyrsis had been built, specters at haunt just out of sight of the people they had once been. It seemed to the Valeman, on reflection, that he was indeed more ghost than human, that in his flight from the Shadowen and the other dangers encountered on this journey he had become transformed in a way that he did not entirely understand and as a result had been stripped of substance and left ethereal. He moved now in a shadow existence, increasingly bereft of friends and family, left trapped in a tangle of magics that were causing him to disintegrate. There should have been a way to save himself, he knew, but somehow he could not seem to discover what it was.

They reached a broad confluence of pipes and slowed behind the Mole's cautious signal. Huddled close at the bottom of a well from which a stone stairway climbed, they held their last council.

"The stairway leads to a cellar within the inner wall," whispered the Mole. His nose was damp and gleaming. "From there we must climb to a hall, follow it to an entryway that leads outside again, cross to another door, enter, and follow a second hall to a hidden passageway that will take us up through the watchtower to where Damson waits."

He looked from Padishar to Par and back again, intent.

The big man nodded. "Federation guards?"

The Mole blinked. "Everywhere."

"Shadowen?"

"In the tower, somewhere."

Padishar gave Par a wry smile. "Somewhere. Very incisive." He hunched his big shoulders. "All right. Remember what I said, the both of you. Remember what you are to do—and not to do." He glanced at Par. "If I fall, you go on—if you can. If not, get to Firerim Reach and find help there. Promise me."

Par nodded, thinking as he did that the promise was a lie, that he would never turn back, not until Damson was safe, no matter what.

Padishar reached back over his shoulder and tightened the straps that secured the broadsword to his back, then checked the long knives and short sword strapped about his waist. The handle of yet another long knife protruded from one boot. All were carefully sheathed and wrapped in cloth to keep the metal from rattling or reflecting light. Par wore only the Sword of Shannara. The Mole carried no weapons at all.

Padishar looked up again. "All right, then. Let's go in."

In single file they climbed the stairs, crouching low against the stone, easing their way toward the faint light that shone above. A grate came into view, bars of iron that cast a web of shadows down the steps and onto their bodies. There was silence above, an empty, hollow nothingness.

On reaching the grate, the Mole paused to listen, his head cocked in the manner of an animal at hunt—or at risk—then reached up and with surprising strength lifted the grate away almost soundlessly. Stepping from the well, he carried the grate overhead as the other two climbed swiftly free, then set it carefully back in place.

They stood in a cellar that was one in a series of interconnected rooms, all in a line that ran away to either side as far as the eye could see. Stores were stacked everywhere, crates of weapons, tools, clothes, and sundry goods, all carefully labeled and piled back against the thick stone walls on wooden pallets. Barrels were housed in an adjoining chamber, and barely visible through the gloom the rusting frames of old beds formed a maze of metal bones. High on the walls, just below the cellar ceiling and just above the ground without, a row of narrow, barred windows let in thin streamers of dusk's fading light.

The Mole took them ahead through the maze of cellar rooms, past the stacks of stores, and around the tangle of crates to where a second set of stairs climbed to a heavy wooden door. They went up the stairs cautiously, and Par felt the hairs on the back of his neck prickle with the possibility that unseen eyes watched their every move. He peered left and right, overhead and all about, but saw nothing.

At the door they stopped again while the Mole used a small metal implement to spring the lock. In seconds they were through, moving swiftly into the hallway beyond. They were inside the citadel's inner wall now, the second line of defense to the city and the location of the barracks that housed most of the Federation garrison. The corridor was straight and narrow, and riddled with doors and windows that might give them away to anyone. But no one appeared in the moments it took them to reach the entry the Mole sought, and they were through another door almost before Par had time to take a steadying breath.

Now they stood in a shadowed alcove that looked out across the courtyard that lay between the inner and outer walls of the city. Federation soldiers stood watch at gates and on ramparts, dim shapes in the growing dark. Lights flickered from the windows of the sleeping quarters and guardhouses and off the battlements and gates. Booted feet scraped in the stillness. Voices rose in low murmurs. Somewhere, a whetstone was sharpening metal. Par felt his stomach tighten. The sounds of activity were all about.

They clung to the shadows of the alcove for long minutes, listening and watching, waiting before trying to go on. Par could hear Padishar's breathing as the big man hunched next to him against the wall. His own breathing punctuated the rapid beating of his heart. Stirrings of the wishsong's magic rose out of the depths of his chest, down deep where emotions have their beginnings, and he fought to keep it under control. He found himself thinking again about what would happen when he tried to use the magic. It was there, and he would use it—of that he was certain. But whether it would obey him was another matter entirely, and it occurred to him suddenly that if it should indeed overwhelm him and cause him to become the thing that Rimmer Dall had warned he must be, what was to prevent him from turning on his friends?

Damson, he decided. Damson and what she meant to him would keep the magic in hand.

Then the Mole was moving again, sliding away from the darkened entry along the roughened stone of the great wall. Padishar followed instantly, and Par found himself hurrying to keep up almost before he knew what he was doing. They inched swiftly through the blackness, shying when light from the torches brightened their path in soft pools, trying to blend into the stone, to think of themselves as invisible so that they would in fact become so. Federation soldiers continued to move all about, impossibly loud, uncomfortably close, and each moment it seemed certain to Par that they must be discovered.

But seconds later they were before another door, this one unlocked, and then through it to the light beyond . . .

A startled Federation soldier stood before them, pike held casually in his hands as he prepared to go out on watch. His mouth gaped open, and for a second he froze. His hesitation cost him his life. Padishar was on him instantly. One hand came up to cover his mouth. The blade of a long knife flashed in the other and then disappeared. Par saw the soldier's eyes widen in surprise. He saw the pain and then the emptiness. The soldier slumped into Padishar's arms like a rag doll. The pike fell away, and the quick hands of the Mole caught it before it could strike the floor. In a hall of stone and old wood lit by fire that flickered at the ends of pitch-coated torches fixed in the mortared walls, the intruders stood breathless and unmoving with the dead soldier clutched between them and listened to the silence.

Then Padishar lifted the body in his arms, carried it back into the shadows of a niche, and shoved it from view. Par watched it happen as if from a great distance, removed somehow from the event, as cold as the stone about him. He tried not to look. He could still hear the sound the soldier made when he died. He could still see the look in his eyes.

They went down the passageway swiftly, wary of other soldiers who might appear, listening for the silence to be disturbed. But they met no one else, and almost before Par realized it they were through a small, iron-bound door that was barely visible even from within the shadowed niche in which it was set.

The door closed behind them, and they stood in a blackness as complete as moonless night. Par could smell wood and dust and feel the roughness of boards beneath his feet. There was a moment's pause as the Mole rummaged about. Then a flint struck—once, twice—and a candle's thin flame cast its small glow. They were in a closet of some sort, barely six feet square, crammed with odd supplies and debris. The Mole moved things carefully aside, freeing a space at the back of the cubicle, and then pushed against the wall. A section of it that had been invisible to the naked eye came away in the form of a small door swinging inward.

Quickly they moved through. A narrow space opened between walls of stone and wood shoring, so low-ceilinged that Padishar was forced to crouch to avoid bumping his head. One big hand came up guardedly. Par saw blood on the hand and felt suddenly the nearness of his own death, as if it were something the dead soldier's eyes had foretold.

The Mole slid past him and began to lead them down through the walls, edging past stone projections, iron nails, and jagged wood splinters. Cobwebs brushed at their faces and small rodents ran squeaking through the dark ahead. The candle's flame was a dim glow against the black.

They began to climb, finding rungs hammered into the shoring and steps cut in the rock, a mix of ladders and ramps that wound up through the walls. They were in the tower now, working their way toward its apex and Damson's prison. From time to time they would hear voices, muffled and faint. It grew steadily warmer and more airless, and Par began to sweat. Their passageway became smaller and more difficult to navigate, and Padishar was having trouble squeezing through.

Then abruptly the Mole stopped, frozen in place. The leader of the free-born and the Valeman went still as well, crouched in the near blackness, listening. There was only the silence to be heard, but Par sensed something nevertheless—the feel of something alive and moving, just through the walls, just on the other side. Within him, the magic of the wishsong stirred like a hungry cat, and its fire purred anxiously. Par closed his eyes and concentrated on muting its sound.

What he sensed beyond the wall was one of the Shadowen.

He felt his breath catch in his throat as an image formed in his mind of the black thing, a vision brought to life by his magic. It stole along a corridor within the tower, hooded and cloaked, fingers testing the air like tentacles in search of prey. Could it sense them as well? Did it know they were there? The magic rustled like a snake inside Par Ohmsford, coiling, tensing, gathering force. Par muffled it and would not let go. Too soon! It was too soon!

The air whispered in his ear as if it were alive. He gritted his teeth and held on.

Then the Shadowen was gone, fading like a momentary thought, dark and evil and full of hate. The wishsong's magic cooled, easing down once again. Par felt some of the tautness let go, and the muscles in his chest and stomach relaxed. He was aware of Padishar looking at him, of the uneasiness mirrored on the other's face. Padishar reached back to grip his shoulder questioningly. Par felt the iron in the other's fingers, and stole some of its strength. He managed a quick, reassuring nod.

They continued on, climbing still, edging ahead through the gloom. Everywhere it was still, the small sounds of Federation voices and boots gone completely. The night was a blanket of silence in which every living thing seemed to have drifted off to sleep. Deceptive, Par thought as he labored on. Dangerous.

A moment later they stopped again, this time at a stretch of mortared stone wall framed by heavy timbers that buttressed one end of a floor overhead. The Mole handed the candle to Padishar and began to explore the stone with his fingers. Something clicked beneath his careful touch, and a section of the wall gave way. A seam of light appeared, faint and smoky.

The Mole turned back to Padishar. His voice was hushed. "They keep her one flight down through the second door somewhere." He hesitated. "I could show you."

"No," Padishar said at once. "Wait here. Wait for us to come back."

The Mole studied him a moment and then nodded reluctantly. "Second door," he repeated.

With both hands braced against it, he pushed the portal in the wall all the way open. Padishar and Par Ohmsford stepped cautiously through.

They stood on a landing in a stairwell where the steps both climbed and descended. A door across from them was closed and barred, the metal thick with rust. Torches rested in iron brackets hammered into the stone, their glow tracing the line of the worn steps, their acrid smoke rising into the tower's gloom.

Everything was silent.

Behind them, the hidden door swung closed again.

Par glanced at Padishar. The big man was looking about guardedly. There was renewed uneasiness in his eyes. He shook his head at something unseen.

They began the descent, backs against the wall, ears straining to catch any threatening sounds. The stairs curled in serpentine fashion along the wall, the patches of torchlight just barely meeting at the turns. A hint of night sky was visible now and again through the slits in the stone, high and beyond reach from where they passed. Par's stomach was churning. He thought he heard something on the steps above, a small scraping of boots, a rustle of clothing. He blinked and wiped the sweat from his face. There was only silence.

They reached the next landing. There was a single door, unguarded, unlocked. They opened it and passed through easily. Par didn't like it. If this was where Damson was being kept, there should have been guards. He glanced again at Padishar, but the big man was looking ahead, down a dimly lit corridor that ran to the promised second door. They moved to it swiftly, and as they did Par felt the magic of the wishsong again stir suddenly to life. He gasped at the swiftness of its coming, almost doubling over with the heat it generated, like a furnace door being opened.

Something was wrong.

He grasped Padishar's arm. The big man turned, startled. Par jerked about, sensing movement behind, a dark presence . . . The Shadowen! They were—

And the door behind them flew open with a crash. Three black-cloaked Seekers surged through, Shadowen forms hunched and twisted within the concealing garb, weapons glinting in the torchlight. Padishar's broadsword scraped free of its scabbard. Par reached back for the Sword of Shannara, then jerked his hands away as if from live coals. He would be burned if he touched it! Burned, he knew!

"Padishar!" he gasped.

The big man wheeled toward the door behind them, but it, too, swung wide, and two more of the black-cloaked monsters appeared. Both ends of the corridor were blocked now, and Par Ohmsford and Padishar Creel were trapped.

"The Mole!" Padishar swore, certain they had been betrayed.

But Par did not hear him. The Seekers rushed to seize them, and the magic of the wishsong exploded in the sound of his warning cry, filling the tower with fury. It enveloped him like a whirlwind, pressing him back against an astonished Padishar. He fought to contain it, but it overpowered him effortlessly. Then it broke away in shards of white-hot fire that flew at the Shadowen. The black figures threw up their arms, but the wishsong's magic tore through them and they were turned to ash. Par screamed, unable to help himself, and the wishsong broke through the walls like a flood through a dam, shattering mortared seams and blowing holes through the stone. Padishar flinched away, then grabbed at Par in desperation and hauled him bodily through the second door, slamming it shut behind them.

Par dropped to his knees, the wishsong silent once more.

"I . . . I can't breathe!" he gasped.

Padishar yanked him to his feet. "Par! Shades, lad! What's happening to you? What's wrong?"

Par shook his head in despair. The magic's evolution continued unchecked within him. Substantive again, not imaginary. Brin's magic, not Jair's. A fire he could not control, smoldering, waiting . . .

His hands clasped the other's arms and his breath returned, a cooling within that stilled the madness. "Find Damson!" he hissed. "Maybe she's here, Padishar! Find her!"

There were shouts all about, the cries of Federation soldiers rushing along the ramparts and into the watchtower. Padishar grasped Par's tunic and dragged the Valeman after him as he hurried along a hall studded with heavy wooden doors, all locked and barred.

"Damson!" the big man called frantically.

Behind them, beyond the door through which they had fled, Par thought he heard the whisper of Shadowen robes.

"They're coming!" he warned, feeling the heat of the wishsong's magic beginning to build again.

"Damson!" Padishar Creel howled.

There was a muffled reply from behind one of the doors. Releasing Par, the leader of the free-born rushed on, calling out his daughter's name. The reply came again, and he skidded to a stop. The broadsword rose and fell, hacking at one of the doors. Shouts rose from a stairwell at the far end of the corridor. Padishar hammered at the door with several jarring strokes, then threw himself at what remained, his shoulder lowered. The door flew off its hinges and Padishar disappeared inside.

Par rushed to the opening and stopped. Padishar was back on his feet, bloodied and dazed, and Damson Rhee was hugging him, red hair dusty and tangled, her pale face smudged with dirt. Her eyes were all fire as they swept up to find the Valeman.

"Par," she breathed softly, and rushed to hold him.

The hallway behind was filled with the sound of armed men. Par turned to meet the attack, but Padishar Creel was past him in an instant and into the corridor. There was a chilling clash of weapons.

"Par!" the big man called. "Take her and run!"

Without thinking, Par grabbed Damson's arm and pulled her after him through the door. Padishar stood toe to toe with a knot of Federation soldiers. More appeared in the stairwell beyond. The leader of the free-born threw back the foremost by sheer strength alone and spun about in fury.

"Drat you, boy—run! Now! Remember our agreement!"

Then the soldiers were on him again, and he was fighting for his life. Two went down, then another, but there were more to take their place. Too many, Par thought. Too many to stand against. He felt his chest tighten. He must help his friend. But that would mean using the wishsong's magic, the fire he could not control. It would mean seeing those men ripped to pieces. It would mean chancing that Padishar would be ripped to pieces as well.

And he had given the big man his promise.

"Padishar," he heard Damson breathe in his ear and felt her start toward the big man.

Instantly he had hold of her and was dragging her back the way they had come, away from the fighting. He had made his choice. "Par!" she screamed in anger, but he shook his head no. They reached the closed door. Were there Shadowen behind it? Par could not hear them; he could not hear anything above the sounds of the battle behind him.

"We can't leave him!" Damson was screaming.

He pulled her close. "We have to." Before him, the wooden door loomed, hiding what lay behind, forbidding and silent. He braced himself, summoning the wishsong's magic because this time there was no choice. The magic stirred, anxious.

Please, he thought, *let me keep control of it just this once!*

He flung open the door, ready to send the magic careening down the corridor beyond, white-hot and deadly. Silence greeted him. Moonlight flooded down through cracks in the shattered stone. Debris littered the floor. The passage was empty.

He cast a final look back at the embattled Padishar Creel, a solitary barrier against the flood of Federation soldiers seeking to break past. There was no hope for Padishar, he knew. It had been a trap from the beginning. And the trap was about to close.

Yet there was still time to save Damson.

As they had agreed they would, whatever the cost.

With Damson still clinging to his arm, he charged ahead into the empty corridor, leaving Padishar Creel behind.

6

They were through the stairwell door and back out on the landing in seconds. A haze of sound and fury rose from the corridor behind them, where Padishar held the Federation soldiers at bay.

Par wheeled back and kicked the tower door shut.

Which way?

From below, he could hear the thudding of boots and the shouts of men as they ascended the stairs. They could not go down.

"Let go of me!" Damson cried furiously, and yanked free of him. Her green eyes were bright with tears and anger. "You left him!"

Par was barely listening. They had to go up, back the way they had come, back to where the Mole waited. Unless Padishar had been right and the Mole had indeed betrayed them. It was possible. The Mole might have been taken days ago when the Federation had first found them in his lair. But, no, if he had been taken then, he would not have helped them escape when they had fled the gristmill; he would have let the Federation have them and been done with the matter. But what if he had been caught when he had gone in search of Damson this last time—taken and subverted, made over into a Shadowen?

Damson was tearing at him. "We have to go back, Par! He needs us! He's my father!" Her teeth bared. "He came back for you!"

Par wheeled on her, grasped her arms, and dragged her so close that he could feel the heat of her breath on his face. "I'll only say this once. I gave him my promise. Whatever else happened, you were to be gotten safely away. He's given himself up for you, Damson, and it is not going to be for nothing! Now, run!"

He spun her about and shoved her up the stairwell. They raced up the steps, listening to the sounds of pursuit grow closer. Par's face was grim with purpose. If the Mole had betrayed them, they were finished whichever way they ran. If he had not, then their only chance was to find him.

They reached the next landing, and Par cast about in vain for the hidden door. He could not remember where it was; he hadn't paid that much attention when he had come through. Now everything looked the same.

"Mole!" he shouted in desperation.

Immediately the wall split apart to his left, and the Mole's furry face peered out. "Here! Here, lovely Damson!" he called frantically.

They hurried through the opening, and the Mole pushed the wall closed behind them. "Padishar?" he inquired anxiously, and the way he spoke and the look that came into his damp eyes suggested to Par for reasons he would never be able to explain that no betrayal had taken place.

"They have him," the Valeman answered, forcing himself to look directly at Damson. She turned aside instantly.

"Come away, then," the Mole urged, the candle in his hand as he scurried ahead of them. "Hurry."

They went back down into the tower walls, winding and twisting their way through the gloom, listening to the cries of soldiers filter through the stone in a muffled cacophony. They reached the closet and passed quickly into the hallway beyond. Outside, soldiers ran past the barracks windows, headed for the watchtower and the gates. Torchlight sparked and flared as it was brought to bear against the darkness, and the sound of bolts being thrown and crossbars being dropped into their metal fitting was deafening. Pressed against the wall in a pool of darkness, the Mole held his charges in place for a moment, then beckoned them ahead. They ran in a crouch through the empty corridor to the door that had brought them and pushed through to the courtyard without.

Darkness had fallen, and the moon and stars were hidden by clouds that hung low and sullen across the bluff. Fire cast its smoky light through the gloom with little effect. Figures charged about everywhere, but it was impossible to make out their faces.

"This way!" the Mole whispered hoarsely.

They moved left along the wall, hurrying because everyone else was hurrying as well. They slipped through the dark, just three more bodies in the confusion, another three for which no one had time or interest.

They were almost to the door leading back to the city's underground when they were challenged. A shout brought them about, and a dark figure came striding out of the gloom. For an instant Par thought it was Padishar, miraculously escaped, but then he saw the markings of a Federation captain on a dark uniform. All three froze at his approach, uncertain what to do. The captain reached them, his dark bearded face coming into the light.

Then Damson stepped forward, smooth and relaxed, smiling at him. A confused look appeared on his face. She gave him an instant more, then hit him three times across the face with the blade of her hand, the blows so quick that Par could barely see them. She stepped into him, drew his arm across her shoulder, and threw him down. He wheezed and tried to cry out, but a final blow to the throat silenced him for good.

Damson rose and pushed past Par to where the Mole was already disappearing through the door. Par remembered in that instant how easily she had overcome him that night in the People's Park when he had believed her responsible for the Federation trap that had ensnared Padishar and the others. She might have done so again in the watchtower, he realized. She could have forced him to go back if she had wished. Why hadn't she?

They were inside the inner wall again, hurrying back down to the cellars that had brought them. The sounds without were fading now, muffled behind the layers of stone block. They reached the trapdoor and passed through, descending the steps to the tunnels below. From there, they moved swiftly through the gloom, away from the city's walls and back toward its center. Soon they were deep within the sewers and everything was silent.

"Let's . . . let's just rest a moment," Par suggested finally, out of breath from running, needing to think, to decide what to do next.

"Here," the Mole offered, directing them to a platform that served as a base for a ladder climbing to the streets at a confluence of tunnels and pipes. Overhead, light shone dimly through a grate. The streets were still and empty of life. "I will go back and make certain we are not followed."

He disappeared into the dark, leaving them the candle. The Valeman and the girl watched him go, then settled themselves gingerly in place, backs to the wall, side by side with the candle before them. Par felt drained. He stared at the darkness beyond the candle's flame, exhaustion spreading through him. He could hear Damson breathing, could feel the heat of her body.

"You know what they'll do to him," she said finally. He didn't respond, looking straight ahead. "They'll make him one of them. They'll use him."

If they manage to take him alive, Par thought. And maybe not even then. Rimmer Dall is unpredictable.

"Why didn't you make me go back for him?" he asked her.

There was a long silence before she spoke. "I would never do that to you."

He didn't say anything for a moment, letting the import of the words sink in. "I'm sorry about Padishar," he said finally. "I didn't want to leave him either."

"I know," she said quietly.

She said it in such a matter-of-fact way that he looked over at her to make certain he had heard her correctly. Her eyes met his. "I know," she repeated. The pain in her voice was palpable. "It wasn't your fault. Padishar made you promise to save me first. He would have made me promise as well if our positions had been reversed." She looked away again. "I was just angry when I saw . . ." She shook her head.

"Are you all right?"

She nodded wordlessly, and her eyes closed.

"Do they know who you are?"

She glanced over again. "No. Why would they?"

He took a deep breath. "The Mole. That was a trap back there, Damson. They were waiting for us. They had some reason to believe we would come for you. What better reason than if they knew that you were Padishar Creel's daughter? Padishar thinks the Mole gave us away."

There was new anger in her eyes. "Par, the Mole saved us! Saved you, anyway. I was just unlucky. The Federation recognized me from the streets, and they knew I had helped you escape the gristmill." She hesitated. "That was a trap as well, wasn't it? They knew . . ." She paused again, uncertain of where she was going.

"It could have been the Mole," Par pressed. "He could have been taken when he came to look for you. Or sometime before."

"And helped us escape anyway?" she asked incredulously. "Why? What would be the point? The Federation would have had us all if he hadn't gotten us out of the watchtower."

"I know. I was thinking that, too." He shook his head. "But they keep finding us, Damson. How do they do that? The Shadowen seem to have an ear to every wall. It's insidious. Sometimes it seems as if there isn't anyone left to trust."

Her smile was bitter. "There isn't, Par. Not anyone. Didn't you realize that? There's only you and me. And can we even trust each other?"

He stared at her in shock. A sadness came into her eyes, and she reached out quickly, put her arms about him, and drew him close.

"I'm sorry," she said, and he could feel her crying.

"I thought I might have lost you for good," he whispered into her hair. He felt her nod slightly. "I'm so tired of all this. I just want it to end."

They clung to each other in silence, and Par let himself drift with the feel of her, closing his eyes, letting the weariness seep away. He wished suddenly that he were back in the Vale, returned home again to his family and his old life, that Coll were alive, and that none of this had ever happened. He wished he had it all to do over again. He would not be so eager to go in search of Allanon. He would not be so quick to undertake his search for the Sword of Shannara.

And he would not be tricked into believing that his magic was a gift.

He thought then of how much a part of him the wishsong had once been and how alien it seemed now. It had broken free of his control again when he had called upon it in the watchtower. Despite his preparations, despite his efforts. Could he even say, in fact, that he had summoned it— or had it simply come on its own when it sensed those Shadowen? Surely it had done as it chose in any case, lancing out like knives to cut them apart. Par felt himself shudder at the memory. He would never have wished for that. The magic had destroyed the black things without thought, without compunction. His brow furrowed. No, not the magic. Him. He had destroyed them. He had not wanted to, perhaps, but he had done so nevertheless. Par didn't like what that suggested. The Shadowen were what they were, and perhaps it was true that they would not hesitate the span of a breath to kill him. But that did not change who and what he was. He could still see the eyes of that soldier Padishar had killed. He could see the life fade from them in an instant's time. It made him want to cry. He hated the fact that it was necessary and that he was a part of it. Understanding the reasons for it did not make it any more palatable. Yet what sort of hypocrite was he, despairing for a single life one moment and putting an end to half-a-dozen the next?

He didn't want to know the answer to that question. He didn't think he could bear it. What he recognized was that the magic of the wishsong had changed somehow within him and in so doing had changed him as well. It made him think more closely of Rimmer Dall's claim that he, too, was a Shadowen. After all, what was the difference between them?

"Damson?"

The Mole's tentative voice whispered from out of the black and parted her from him as she looked up. Funny, he thought, how the Mole only speaks to her.

The little fellow slipped into the light, blinking and squinting. "They do not follow. The tunnels are empty."

Damson looked back at Par. "What do we do now, Elf-boy?" she whispered, reaching up to brush back his hair. "Where do we go?"

Par smiled and took the hand in his own. "I love you, Damson Rhee," he told her quietly, his words so soft they were lost in the rustle of his clothing.

He rose. "We get out of this city. We try to find help. From Morgan or the free-born or someone. We can't continue on alone." He looked down at the hunched form of the Mole. "Mole, can you help us get away?"

The Mole glanced at Damson. "There are tunnels beneath the city that will take you to the plain beyond. I can show you."

Par turned back to Damson. For a moment she did not speak. Her green eyes were filled with unspoken thoughts. "All right, Par, I'll go," she said at last. "I know we can't stay. Time and luck are running out for us here in Tyrsis." She stepped close. "But now you must give me your promise—just as you gave it to Padishar. Promise that we will come back for him—that we won't leave him to die."

She does not give a moment's consideration to the possibility that he might already be dead. She believes him stronger than that. And so do I, I guess.

"I promise," he whispered.

She leaned close and kissed him on the mouth, hard. "I love you, too, Par Ohmsford," she said. "I'll love you to the end."

It took them the remainder of the night to navigate the maze of tunnels that lay beneath Tyrsis, the ancient passageways that had served long ago as bolt holes for the city's defenders and now served as their escape. The tunnels crisscrossed over and back again, sometimes broad and high enough for wagons to pass through, sometimes barely large enough for the Mole and his charges. At places the rock was dry and dusty and smelled of old earth and disuse; at times it was damp and chill and stank of sewage. Rats squealed at their coming and disappeared into the walls. Insects skittered away like dry leaves blown across stone. The sound of their boots and their breathing echoed hollowly down the passageways, and it seemed that they could not possibly go undetected. But the Mole chose their path carefully, frequently taking them away from the most direct route, choosing on the basis of things that he alone sensed and knew. He did not speak to them; he guided them ahead through his silent netherworld like the specter at haunt he had become. Now and again he would pause to look back at them or to study something he found on the tunnel floors or to consider the gloom that pressed in about them, distracted and distant in his musings. Par and Damson would stop with him, waiting, watching, and wondering what he was thinking. They never asked. Par wanted to, but if Damson thought it wise to keep silent he was persuaded to do so as well.

At last they reached a place where the darkness ahead was broken by a hazy silver glow. They stumbled toward it through a curtain of old webbing and dust, scrambling up a rocky slide that narrowed as it went until they were bent double. Bushes blocked the way forward, so thick that the Mole was forced to cut a path for them using a long knife he had somehow managed to conceal within his fur. Pushing aside the severed branches, the three crawled through the last of the concealing foliage and emerged into the light.

They came to their feet then and looked about. The mountains sheltering the bluff on which Tyrsis was settled rose behind them, a jagged black wall against the light of the dawn breaking east, the shadow of its peaks stretching away north and west across the plains like a dark stain until it disappeared into the trees of the forests beyond. The air was warm and smelled of grasses dried by the summer sun. Birdsong rose from the concealment of the trees, and dragonflies darted over small pools of weed-grown water formed by streams that ran down out of the rocks behind them.

Par looked over at Damson and smiled. "We're out," he said softly, and she smiled back.

He turned to the Mole, who blinked uncertainly in the unfamiliar light. Impulsively, he reached down. "Thank you, Mole," he said. "Thank you for everything."

The Mole's face furrowed, and the blinking grew more rapid. A hand came up tentatively, touched Par's, and withdrew. "You are welcome," was the soft reply.

Damson came over, knelt before the Mole, and put her arms about him. "Good-bye for now," she whispered. "Go somewhere safe, Mole. Stay well away from the black things. Keep hidden until we return."

The Mole's arms lifted and his wrinkled hands stroked the girl's slim shoulders. "Always, lovely Damson. Always, for you."

She released him then, and the Mole's fingers brushed her face gently. Par thought he saw tears at the corners of the little fellow's bright eyes. Then the Mole turned from them and disappeared back into the gloom.

They stared after him for a moment, then looked at each other.

"Which way?" Par asked.

She laughed. "That's right. You don't know where Firerim Reach is, do you? I forget sometimes, you seem so much a part of things."

He smiled. "Hard to remember when you didn't have me to look after, isn't it?"

She gave him a questioning look. "I'm not complaining. Are you?"

He moved over to her and held her for a moment. He didn't say anything; he simply stood with his arms about her, his cheek against her auburn hair, and his eyes closed. He thought about all they had come through, how many times their lives had been at risk, and how dangerous their journey had been. So little distance traveled to come so far, he mused. So little time to have discovered so much.

Still holding her, he stroked her back in small circles and said, "I'll tell you something. It sometimes seems as if I'm frightened all the time. Ever since Coll and I first left Varfleet, all those weeks ago, I've been afraid. Everything that happens seems to cost something. I never know what I'm going to lose next, and I hate it. But what frightens me most, Damson Rhee, is the possibility that I might lose you."

He tightened his arms about her, pressing her close. "What do you think about that?" he whispered.

Her response was to tighten her arms back.

They walked through the early morning without saying much after that, leaving behind the city of Tyrsis, moving north across the plains to the forested threshold of the Dragon's Teeth. The day warmed quickly, crystals of night's dew faded with the sun's rise, and dampness dried away into stirrings of dust. They saw no one for a long time, and then only peddlers and families coming in from their farms to market in the city. Par found himself thinking of home again, of his parents and Coll, but it all seemed to be something that had happened a long time ago. He might wish that things were as they had been and that all that had happened since his encounter with Cogline had not—but he knew he might as well wish the day become night and the sun the moon. He looked at Damson walking beside him, at the soft strong lines of her face and the movement of her body, and let what might have been slide quickly away.

At midday they crossed the Mermidon into the forests beyond and stopped to eat. They foraged for fresh water, berries, roots, and vegetables, and made do. It was cool and silent within the trees while the day's heat suffocated the surrounding land in an airless, sweltering blanket. After eating, they decided to sleep for a time, weary from their night's efforts and anxious to take advantage of their refuge. It was only several hours further to the Kennon Pass, Damson advised, where they would cross through the Dragon's Teeth into the valley that had once been Paranor's home. From there they would travel north and east to the Jannisson Pass and Firerim Reach. In another two days, she promised, they should reach the free-born.

But they slept longer than they had planned, lulled by the coolness and the soothing sound of the wind in the trees, and it was nearing sunset when they came awake again. They rose and set out at once, anxious to make up as much time as they could. If the moon was out, they could navigate the pass at night. Otherwise, they would have to wait until morning. In either case, they wanted to reach the Kennon by nightfall.

So they traveled swiftly, unhindered by heavy stands of scrub or grasses in woods that were well traveled and spacious, feeling rested and fit after their sleep. The sun drifted west, edging down into the trees until it was a bright flare of gold and crimson through the screen of the leaves and branches. The moon appeared in skies that were clear and blue, and the day birds began to grow silent in response to the coming of night. Par felt at ease for the first time in days, at peace with himself. He was relieved to be out of Tyrsis, clear of her sewers and cellars, free of the confinement of her walls, safe from the things that had hunted him there. He looked over at Damson often and smiled when he did. He thought of Padishar and tried to keep from being sad. His thoughts scattered through the trees and across the carpet of the earthen floor like small creatures at play. He let them wander where they chose, content to let them go.

Not once did it occur to him that it might be wise to hide his trail.

Sunset burned like fire across the plains below Tyrsis as day inched toward night and the heat began to dissipate. Shadows lengthened and grew, taking on strange and suggestive shapes, coming alive with the dark. They rose out of gullies and ravines, from forests and solitary groves, stretching this way and that as if to flex their limbs on waking from the sleep that prepared them for going abroad to hunt.

One of those shadows moved with insidious purpose along the empty stretches running north to the Mermidon, a faint darkness hidden within the long grasses through which it passed. As the light failed it grew bolder, rising up now and again to sniff the air before lowering back to the earth to keep the scent it followed fresh. It ate as it went, sustaining itself with whatever it found, roots and berries, insects and small animals, anything it came across that was unable to escape. For the most part its attention was focused on the trail it followed, on the smell of the one it hunted so diligently, the one that was the source of its madness.

At the Mermidon it lifted to its hindquarters, a hunched-over, gnarled form wrapped in a shining black cloak that somehow resisted the dust and grime that coated its wearer. Hands skinned and scraped so badly they bled clutched at the cloak so that it would not wash free as it forded that river at a shallows. The cloak never left it, not for a moment. The cloak sustained it in some way, it knew. The cloak was what protected it.

Yet it seemed a source of the madness as well. Some part of the creature's mind whispered that this was so. It whispered it to the creature in warning, over and over again.

But most of what worked in the creature's thoughts assured it that the cloak was good and necessary to its survival, and that the madness was caused instead by the one it tracked. By him. (My brother?) The name would not come. Only the face. The madness buzzed within its head, through its ears, and out its mouth like a swarm of gnats, itching and biting and consuming its reason until it could think of nothing else.

Earlier that day, in the shadow of late afternoon, come abroad in the hated light because the madness drove it from its den with increasing frequency, it had found at last the scent of the one it hunted. (His name? What was his name?) Prowling the base of the bluff night after night for more than a week now, it had grown increasingly desperate, needing to find him, to search him out so that relief would come, so that the madness would end.

But how? How would it end?

It didn't know. Somehow it would happen. When it found the cause. When it . . . hurt him like he was hurting it . . .

The thought drifted before its eyes, unclear. But there was pleasure in the thought, in the taste and feel of it.

Teeth and eyes gleamed in the brightening moonlight.

On the far side of the river, the creature picked up the trail easily and again began to track. Fresh it was. As clear as the stench of something dead and left to rot in the sun. Not far it was. Another few hours, perhaps less . . .

A shudder passed through the creature. Anticipation. Need. The seeds of the madness in flower.

Coll Ohmsford put his nose to the ground like the animal he had become and disappeared into the trees.

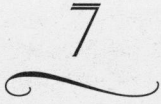

Dusk was edging into night by the time Par and Damson reached the base of the Dragon's Teeth and the trail that wound upward through the cliffs to the Kennon. Moonlight flooded down from the north, and the skies were clear and bright with stars. The day's heat had cooled, and there was a breeze blowing out of the mountains.

Somewhere in the trees of the forest behind, an owl hooted softly and was still.

Because there was light enough to navigate the trail and they were well rested, the Valeman and the girl pushed on. The night was well suited for travel, even in the mountains, and they made good time climbing from the lower slopes into the pass. As they went, night descended and the silence deepened, the forest and its inhabitants falling away behind them in a pool of black, the rocks closing about and becoming silhouettes that rose jagged and stark against the sky. Their boots scraped and crunched on the loose stone and their breathing grew labored, but beyond those immediate sounds the world was still and empty-feeling.

Time passed, and midnight approached. They were well into the pass now, approaching its apex, the point where the trail would start down again into the valley beyond. The light ahead seemed brighter than the light behind, a phenomenon for which neither the Valeman nor the girl could account, and they exchanged more than one questioning glance. It was not until they had reached the top of the pass, deep within the mountain peaks, the way forward a long, broad corridor through the rock, that they realized that what they were seeing was not the light of moon or stars, but the blaze of watch fires burning directly ahead.

Now the glance they exchanged was a wary one. Why were there watch fires burning here? Who had set them?

They proceeded more cautiously than before, keeping well into the shadows on the dark side of the pass, stopping frequently to listen for what might be waiting ahead. Even so, they almost missed seeing the guards posted on a rise several hundred yards further on, positioned so as to give them a clear view of anyone trying to slip past. The guards were soldiers, and they wore Federation uniforms. Par and Damson melted instantly into the shadows and out of view.

"What are they doing here?" the girl whispered in Par's ear.

The Valeman shook his head. There was no reason for them to be here that he could figure out. The free-born were nowhere near the Kennon. Firerim Reach was far to the east. There was only the valley beyond, and there was nothing in the valley, hadn't been anything there for that matter since . . .

His mind froze and his eyes went wide.

Since Paranor had disappeared.

He took a deep breath and held it, remembering Allanon's charge to Walker Boh. Was it possible that Walker had . . . ?

He did not finish the thought. He would not let himself. He knew he was jumping to conclusions, that the presence of the soldiers in the pass could be for any number of reasons.

Yet something inside whispered that he was right. The soldiers were there because Paranor was back.

He bent hurriedly to Damson. She stared at him in surprise, seeing the excitement in his eyes. "Damson." He breathed her name. "We have to get past those guards. Or at least . . ." His mind raced. "At least we have to get far enough into the rocks to see what's beyond, what's down in the valley. Can we do that? Is there a way? Another way?"

He was speaking so fast that his words were tumbling over one another. Walker Boh, he was thinking. The Dark Uncle. He had almost forgotten about Walker—had all but given up on him since their separation at the Hadeshorn. But Walker was unpredictable. And Allanon had believed in him, enough so that he had determined that the charge to find Paranor should be his.

Shades! His heart was pumping so fast it seemed to jump inside his chest. What if . . . ?

Damson's hand on his arm startled him. "Come with me."

They retraced their steps through the pass to a cut in the rocks where a narrow trail led upward. Slowly, they began to climb. The trail twisted and wound about, sometimes doubling back on itself, sometimes angling so steeply that they were forced to proceed on hands and knees, pulling themselves upward by gripping rocks and bits of scrub. The minutes slipped by and still they climbed, sweating freely now, breathing through their mouths, their muscles beginning to ache. Par did not question where they were going. These mountains had been the stronghold of the free-born for years. No one knew them better. Damson would know what she was about.

At last the trail flattened again and angled forward toward the glow from the watch fires. They were high in the peaks now, well above the pass. The air blew chilly and sharp here, and sound was muffled. They went forward in a crouch as the rocks to either side gave way to a narrow bluff. The wind whipped against them violently, and the light of the fires spread against the screen of the night sky like a misted autumn sunset.

The trail ended at a drop that fell away hundreds of feet along a cliff face. Below and halfway up lay the north entrance to the Kennon Pass. It was there that the watch fires burned, dozens of them, steady and bright within the shelter of the rocks. Sleeping forms lay all about, wrapped in blankets. Horses were tethered on a picket line. Sentries patrolled at every juncture. The Federation had blocked the pass completely.

Almost afraid of what he would find—or wouldn't find—Par lifted his gaze beyond the Federation encampment to the valley beyond. For a moment he couldn't see anything, his vision weakened from staring at the fires, the blackness into which he peered a sweeping curtain that shrouded the whole of the horizon. He waited for his eyes to adjust, keeping them focused on the dark. Slowly the valley began to take shape. In the softer light of moon and stars, the silhouettes of mountains and forests etched themselves against the skyline; lakes and rivers glimmered in dull flashes of silver, and the fuzzy deep gray of nighttime meadows and grassy hills were a patchwork against the black.

"Par!" Damson whispered suddenly, and her fingers tightened on his arm. Leaning into him with excitement, her hand lifted hurriedly to point.

And there was Paranor.

She had seen it first—far out in the valley, washed in moonlight and centered on a great rise. Par caught his breath and leaned forward, stretching out as far as he could from the edge of the drop to make certain that he was not deceived, that he was not mistaken . . .

No. There was no mistake. It was indeed the Druid's Keep, come back out of time and history, come back from dreams of what might once have been into the world of men. Par still couldn't believe it. No one living had ever seen Paranor. Par himself had only sung about it, envisioning it from the stories he had heard, from the tales of generations of Ohmsfords now long dead. Gone for all those years, gone for so long that it was only legend to most, and suddenly here it was, returned to the Four Lands—here, as real as life, walls and ramparts, towers and parapets, rising up out of the earth phoenixlike amid the dark girdle of the forests that encircled it protectively below.

Paranor. Somehow Walker Boh had found a way to bring it back.

Par's smile stretched ear to ear as he reached for Damson and hugged her until he feared she would break in two. She hugged him back as fiercely, laughing softly as she did. Then they broke apart, stared downward a final time at the dark bulk of the castle, and wormed their way back along the bluff into the shelter of the rocks.

"Did you see it?" Par exclaimed when they were safely away again. He hugged her once more. "Walker did it! He brought back Paranor! Damson, it's happening! The charges Allanon gave us are coming to pass! If I really do have the Sword of Shannara and if Wren has found the Elves . . . !" He caught himself. "I wonder what's happened to Wren? I wish I knew something more, confound it! And where's Walker? Do you think he's down there, inside the castle? Is that why the Federation has blocked the pass—to keep him there?" His hands gestured excitedly against her back. "And what about the Druids? What do you think, Damson? Has he found them?"

She shook her head, grinning at him. "We won't know for a while, I'm afraid. We're still stuck on the wrong side of the pass." The smile faded, and she loosened his arms gently. "There's no way around those soldiers, Par. Not unless you want to use your magic to disguise us. What do you think? Do you want to do that? Could you?"

Cold blossomed in the pit of his stomach. The wishsong again. There was no escape from it. He could feel its magic stir inside him in anticipation of the possibility that it might be needed again, that it might be given a new release . . .

Damson saw the change that came into his face and pulled him quickly to his feet. "No, you won't use the magic. Not if you don't have to, and you don't. We can go another way east below the mountains and then north across the Rabb. A little longer journey perhaps, but just as sure."

He nodded, relief washing through him. Her instincts were right. He was frightened of using the magic. He didn't trust it anymore. "All right," he agreed, forcing a smile. "That's what we'll do."

"Come on, then." She pulled at his hand. "Let's go back the way we came. We can sleep a few hours and then start out again." Her smile was brilliant. "Think of it, Par. Paranor!"

They retraced their steps along the narrow pathway, easing down out of the rocks to the main pass, and then began the trek south. They traveled swiftly, excited by what they had found, anxious to convey the news to others. But after the first rush of euphoria had passed, Par found himself having second thoughts. Perhaps he was being premature in celebrating the return of Paranor. Allanon's shade had never explained what purpose would be served in fulfilling the charges he had given. Paranor was back, but what difference did it make? Were the Druids back as well? If so, would they help in the battle against the Shadowen?

Or would they, as Rimmer Dall had suggested, prove to be the real enemy of the races?

As they twisted and wound their way along the trail toward the dark belt of the forests below, Par's mood darkened steadily. Walker had been wary of Allanon's motives. He had been the first to warn against the Druids. What had happened then to make him change his mind? Why had he agreed to bring back Paranor? Par wished he could speak with him, just for a moment. He wished he could talk to almost anyone from the original company who had come with him to the Hadeshorn. He was tired of feeling alone and abandoned in this. He was weary of having questions with no answers.

They reached the base of the Dragon's Teeth two hours later and moved back into the shelter of the trees. Behind them, the glow of the Federation watch fires had long since faded into the rocks, and the excitement of discovering Paranor had turned to insistent doubt. Par kept his thoughts to himself, but Damson's occasional glance suggested she was not fooled by his silence. It seemed to Par that they were so close and knew each other so well by now that words weren't necessary for communication. Damson could read his thoughts. She knew what he was thinking; he could see it in her eyes.

She took the lead as they entered the trees, turning them east along the base of the mountains, guiding them through heavier undergrowth to where the trees spread apart and there were grassy clearings and small streams in which to set camp. The night was filled with small, delicate sounds, a balance of contentment that no predator disturbed. The wind had died away, and the air before them turned frosty with their breath as they walked. The moon had disappeared below the horizon, and they were left with starlight to show them the way.

They did not go far, no more than a mile, before Damson settled on a glade beside a small spring for their resting place. A few hours, she advised; they would start out again before daybreak. They wrapped themselves in blankets that had been provided by the Mole from one of his underground caches and lay close to each other in the dark, staring up into the trees. Par cradled the Sword of Shannara in the crook of one arm, its length resting against his body, wondering again what purpose his talisman was meant to serve, wondering how he was ever supposed to find out.

Wondering still, at the very back of his mind, if it was really what he believed it to be.

"I think it is a good thing," Damson whispered just before he fell asleep. "I don't think you should worry."

He wasn't sure what she was talking about, and although he was tempted he didn't ask.

He woke while it was still dark, the sunrise a faint glimmering of silver far east, barely visible through the tops of the trees. It was the silence that woke him, the sudden absence of all sound—the birds and insects gone still, the animals frozen to ice, the whole of the immediate world turned empty and dead. He sat up with a start, as if waking from a bad dream. But it was the silence that had interrupted his slumber, and he was struck with the thought that no dream could ever be as terrifying.

Shadows cloaked the glade, deep and melting pools of damp. Gloom hung across the air like smoke, and there was a faint hint of mist through the trees. Par's hands were on the Sword of Shannara, the blade clutched before him as if to ward off his fear. He glanced about hurriedly, saw nothing, looked about some more, then came to his feet warily. Damson was awake as well now, sleepy-eyed as she lifted from her blanket, stifling a yawn.

Still as death, Par thought. His eyes shifted anxiously.

What was wrong? Why was it so quiet?

Then something moved in the deepest of the glade's shadows, a shifting of blackness barely discernible to the naked eye, the kind of motion that comes when clouds drift across the face of the moon. Except that there were no clouds or moon, nothing but the night sky and its fading stars.

Damson stood up beside him. "Par?" she whispered questioningly.

He did not avert his eyes from the movement. It began to take shape, an insidious coalescence that lent definition to what moments before had been nothing but the night.

A figure appeared, stunted and crouched, all black and faceless beneath a concealing cloak and hood.

Par stared. There was something about this intruder that was familiar, something he could almost put a name to. It was in the way it moved, or held itself, or breathed. But how could that be?

The figure approached, not walking as a man or animal would, but slouching like something that was neither and still both. It hunched its way out of the deep gloom and came toward them, the sound of its breathing suddenly audible. *Huff, huff,* a rasping cough, a hiss. Black-cloaked and hooded, it stayed hidden in its silky covering of night until all at once its head lifted and the light caught the faint glimmer of its crimson eyes.

Par felt Damson's fingers close on his arms.

It was Shadowen.

A weary and futile acceptance came with the Valeman's recognition of his enemy. He must fight again after all. He must call upon the wishsong once more. There was no end to it, he thought dully. Wherever he went, they found him. Each time he thought he had used the magic for the last time, he was required to use it one time more. And one time after that. Forever.

The Shadowen advanced, a humping of black cloth and a dragging of limbs. The thing seemed barely able to make itself move, and it clung to its cloak as if it could not bear to let go. The cloak, too, was an odd thing—all shiny black and as clean as new cloth despite the ragged, soiled appearance of the thing that wore it. Par felt the wishsong's magic begin building within him, unbidden, rising up on its own, the core of a fire that would not stay quenched. He let it come, knowing the futility of trying to stop it, realizing that there was no other choice. He did not even try to look for a way to escape the glade. Running, after all, was pointless. The Shadowen would simply track them. It would keep coming until it was stopped.

Until he killed it.

He winced at the words and thought, *Not again!*—seeing the face of that soldier in the watchtower, seeing all their faces, all the dead from all the encounters . . .

The creature stopped. Within the cloak, its head shook violently, as if it were beset by demons that only it could see. It made a sound; it might have been crying.

Then its face lifted into the light, and Par Ohmsford felt the world fall away beneath him.

He was looking at Coll.

Ravaged, twisted, bruised, and dirtied, the face before him was still Coll's.

For a moment, he thought he was going mad. He heard Damson's gasp of disbelief, felt himself take an involuntary step backward, and watched his brother's lips part in a twisted effort to speak.

"Par?" came the plea.

He gave a low, despairing cry, cut it short immediately, and with a supreme effort steadied himself. No. No, this had been tried once, tried and failed. This was not Coll. This was just a Shadowen pretending to be his brother, a trick to deceive him . . .

Why?

He groped for an answer. To drive him mad, of course. To make him . . . to force him to . . .

He clenched his teeth. Coll was dead! He had seen him die, destroyed in the fire of the wishsong's magic—Coll, who had become one of them, a Shadowen, like this one . . .

Something whispered at the back of his mind, a warning that took no discernible form, words that lacked meaning beyond their intent. *Caution, Valeman! Beware!*

His hands still clenched the Sword of Shannara. Without thinking, still lost in the horror of what he was seeing, he brought the blade and scabbard up before him like a shield.

Instantly, the Shadowen was on him, closing the distance between them in the blink of an eye, moving far more swiftly than should have been possible for such a twisted body. It sprang into him, giving forth an anguished shriek, and Coll's face rose up, large and terrifying, until it was right against his own and he could smell the stench of it. Gnarled hands closed about the handle of the Sword of Shannara and tried to wrench it free. Down the Valeman and the Shadowen went in a tangle of arms and legs. Par heard Damson cry out, and then he was rolling away from her, fighting for possession of the Sword. His hands shifted from the scabbard to the pommel, trying to gain leverage, to twist the blade free. He was face to face with his adversary as he fought. He could see into the depth of his brother's eyes . . .

No! No, it wasn't possible!

They tumbled into the trees, into grasses that whipped and sawed at their hands and faces. The scabbard to the Sword slid free, and now there was only the razor-sharp metal of the blade between them, jerking back and forth like a deadly pendulum as they struggled. Par became tangled in the folds of the strange, glimmering cloak, and the feel of it against his skin was repulsive, like the touch of something living. Thrashing wildly, he flung the trailing cloth away. He kicked out, and the Shadowen grunted as Par's knee jammed into its body. But it would not let go, hands clasped about the blade in a death grip. Par was furious. The Shadowen seemed to have no purpose other than to hang onto the Sword. Its eyes were fixed on the blade. Its face was slack and empty. Par's hands shifted to grasp what re-mained of the handle, coming tight against those of his adversary, feeling the rough, sweating skin. Their fingers intertwined as each sought to break the other's grip, their bodies thrashing and twisting . . .

Par gasped. A tingling sensation entered his fingers and spread into his hands and arms. He jerked backward in surprise—felt the Shadowen jerk as well. A flush of warmth surged through him, an odd pulse of heat that was centered in the palms of his hands.

His eyes snapped down.

The blade of the Sword of Shannara had begun to give off a faint blue glow.

Par's eyes widened. What was happening? Shades! Was it the magic? The magic of the Sword of—

The talisman flared sharply, and the blue light turned to white fire that blazed as bright as the midday sun. In its terrifying glow, he saw the face of the Shadowen change, the slackness disappearing as the features tightened in shock. Par wrenched wildly at the blade, but the Shadowen hung on.

From what seemed like a long way off, he heard Damson call his name once.

Then the Sword's light was surging through him, the white fire flaring like blood down the limbs of his body, cool but insistent as it took posses-sion. It surrounded him and then drew him away, outward from himself into the blade and then into the body of the Shadowen. He fought to resist the abduction, but found himself powerless. He entered the dark-cloaked figure, feeling the other shudder at the intrusion. Par tried to cry out and could not. He tried to break free and failed. Down into the Shadowen he went, raging and despairing all at once. The Shadowen was all around him, was there before him, eyes and mouth wide with disbelief, features con-torted into something . .

Someone . . .

Coll! Oh, it was Coll!

He might have whispered the words. He might have shrieked them aloud. He could not tell. There, in the dark center of his adversary's soul, the lies fell away before the power of the Sword of Shannara and became the truth. This was no Shadowen he fought, no dark demon with his brother's face, but his brother in fact. Coll, come back from the dead, come back to life, as real as the talisman they both clasped. Par saw the other shudder with some recognition of his own, realizing in the next instant that it was a recognition of what he had become. He saw his brother's tears, heard his wail of despair, and saw him convulse as if stricken with poison. His brother's mind shut down, too devastated by the revelation of what he had become to witness anything more. But Par saw the rest of it, all that his brother could not. He saw the truth of the cloak that wrapped Coll, a thing called the Mirrorshroud, Shadowen-made, stolen by his brother so that he could escape his imprisonment at Southwatch. He saw Rimmer Dall smile darkly, looming above them both from within a vortex of images. But most terrible of all, he saw the madness that engulfed his brother, that drove him in search of Par, in search of the perceived cause of his pain, determined to put an end to both . . .

Then Coll thrashed uncontrollably and tore free, his hands releasing their grip on the Sword of Shannara. The images ceased instantly, the white fire dying. Par tumbled backward, his head striking the base of a tree with stunning force. Through a spinning dark haze he watched his brother, Shadowen-consumed, still wrapped within the hateful cloak, rise up like a netherworld specter. For an instant he crouched there, hands pressed against his hooded head as if to crush the images still locked within, shrieking against his madness. In the next he was gone, fled into the trees, crying as he went until the cries were just an echo in his horrified brother's mind.

Damson was there then, helping Par to his feet, holding him up until she was sure he could stand alone. Her eyes were anxious and frightened, and he was conscious of the way she moved her body to shelter him. Soft streaks of morning light dappled their faces as they clung to each other. Together they stared out into the forest gloom, as if somehow they might catch a final glimpse of the creature who fled from them.

"It was Coll." Par breathed the words as if they were anathema. "Damson, it was Coll!"

She stared at him in disbelief, not daring a reply.

"And this!" He brought up the Sword of Shannara, still clasped in his scraped, raw hands. "This is the Sword."

"I know," she whispered, more certain of this second declaration. "I saw."

He shook his head, still trying to comprehend. "I don't know what happened. Something triggered the magic. I don't know what. But something. It was there, buried inside the Sword." He wheeled to face her. "I couldn't bring it out alone, but when both of us held the blade, when we struggled . . ." His fingers tightened on her arms. "I saw him, Damson—as clearly as I see you. It was Coll."

Damson held herself rigid. "Par, Coll is dead."

"No." The Valeman shook his head adamantly. "No, he is not dead. That was what I was supposed to think. But that wasn't Coll I killed in the Pit. It was someone or something else. That"—he gestured toward the trees— "was Coll. The Sword showed me, Damson. It showed me the truth. Coll was imprisoned at Southwatch and escaped. But he's been changed by that cloak he wears. There is some sort of malevolent magic in it, something that subverts you if you wear it. It's Coll, but he's turning into a Shadowen!"

"Par, I saw his face, too. And it looked a little like Coll, but not enough that—"

"You didn't see everything," he cut her short. "I did, because I was holding the Sword, and the Sword of Shannara reveals the truth! Remember the legends?" He was so excited he was shouting. "Damson, this is the Sword of Shannara! It is! And that was Coll!"

"All right, all right." She nodded quickly, trying to calm him. "It was Coll. But why was he chasing us? Why did he attack you? What was he trying to do?"

Par's lips tightened. "I don't know. I didn't have time to find out. And Coll doesn't know what's happening either. I could see what he was thinking for a moment—as if I was inside his mind. He realized what had been done to him, but he didn't know what to do about it. That was why he ran, Damson. He was horrified at what he had become."

She stared at him. "Did he know who you were?"

"I don't know."

"Or how to help himself? Did he know enough to take off the cloak?"

Par took a deep breath. "I don't think so. I'm not even sure he can." His face was stricken. "He looked so lost, Damson."

She put her arms around him then, and he held her as if she were a rock without which the sea of his uncertainty might wash him away. All about them darkness was fading as sunrise brightened the skies east. Birds were coming awake with cheerful calls, and a faint scattering of dampness sparkled on the grass.

"I have to go after him," Par said into her shoulder, feeling her stiffen at the words. "I have to try to help him." He shook his head despairingly. "I know it means breaking my promise to go back for Padishar. But Coll's my brother."

She moved so that she could see his face. Her eyes searched his and did not look away. "You've made up your mind about this, haven't you?" She looked terrified. "This is probably a trap, you know."

His smile was bitter. "I know."

She blinked rapidly. "And I can't come with you."

"I know that, too. You have to continue on to Firerim Reach and get help for your father. I understand."

There were tears in her eyes. "I don't want to leave you."

"I don't want to leave you either."

"Are you sure it was Coll? Absolutely sure?"

"As sure as I am that I love you, Damson."

She brought her arms about him again. She didn't speak, but buried her face in his shoulder. He could feel her crying. He could feel himself breaking apart inside. The euphoria of finding Paranor was gone, the discovery itself all but forgotten. The sense of peace and contentment he had experienced so briefly on getting free of Tyrsis was buried in his past.

He pulled away again. "I'll come back to you," he said quietly. "Wherever you are, I'll find you."

She bit at her lower lip, nodding. Then she fumbled through her clothing, reaching down the front of her tunic. A moment later she pulled forth a thin, flat metal disk with a hole in it through which a leather cord had been threaded and then tied about her neck. She looked at the disk a moment, then at him.

"This is called a Skree," she said. "It is a kind of magic, a street magic. It was given to me a long time ago." There was fire in the look she gave him. "It can only be used once."

Then she took the disk in both hands and snapped it in two as easily as she might a brittle stick. She handed the loose half to him. "Take it and bind it about your neck. Wear it always. The halves will seek each other out. When the metal glows, it will tell us we are close. The brighter it becomes, the closer we will be."

She pressed the broken half of the disk into his hands. "That is how I will find you again, Par. And I will never stop looking."

He closed his fingers about the disk. He felt as if a pit had opened beneath him and was about to swallow him up. "I'm sorry, Damson," he whispered. "I don't want to do this. I would keep my promise if I could. But Coll's alive, and I can't—"

"No." She put her fingers against his lips to silence him. "Don't say anything more. I understand. I love you."

He kissed her and held her against him, memorizing the touch and feel of her until he was certain the memory was burned into him. Then he released her, retrieved the scabbard for the Sword, picked up his blanket, rolled it up, and slung it over his shoulder.

"I'll come back to you," he repeated. "I promise I will."

She nodded without speaking and would not look away, so he turned from her instead and hurried off into the trees.

It was nearing midafternoon of the day following the separation of Par and Damson when Morgan Leah at last came in sight of the borderland city of Varfleet. The summer was drifting toward autumn now, and the days were long and slow and filled with heat that arrived with the sun and lingered on until well after dark. The Highlander stood on a rise north of the city and looked down at the jumble of buildings and crooked streets and thought that nothing would ever be the same for him again.

It had been more than two weeks since he had parted company with Walker Boh—the Dark Uncle gone in search of Paranor, the Black Elfstone his key to the gates of time and distance that locked away the castle of the Druids, and the Highlander come looking for Padishar Creel and the Ohmsford brothers.

Two weeks. Morgan sighed. He should have reached Varfleet in two days, even afoot. But then nothing much seemed to work out the way he expected it these days.

What had befallen him was ironic considering what he had survived during the weeks immediately preceding. On leaving Walker, he had followed the Dragon's Teeth south along the western edge of the Rabb. He reached the lower branch of its namesake river by sunset of his second day out and made camp close by, intent on crossing at sunrise and completing his journey the next day. The plains were sweltering and dusty, and there were pockets of the same sickness that marked the Four Lands everywhere, patches of blight where everything was poisoned. He thought that he had avoided these, that he had kept well clear in his passing. But when he woke at dawn on that third morning he was hot and feverish and so dizzy that he could barely walk. He drank some water and lay down again, hoping the sickness would pass. But by midday he was barely able to sit up. He forced himself to his feet, recognizing then how sick he was, knowing it was necessary that he find help immediately. His stomach was cramping so badly he could not straighten up, and his throat was on fire. He did not feel strong enough to cross the river, so instead he wandered upstream onto the plains. He was hallucinating when he came upon a farmhouse settled in a shady grove of elm. He staggered to the door, barely able to move or even speak, and collapsed when it opened.

For seven days he slept, drifting in and out of consciousness just long enough to eat and drink the small portions of food and water he was offered by whoever it was who had taken him in. He did not see any faces, and the voices he heard were indistinct. He was delirious at times, thrashing and crying out, reliving the horrors of Eldwist and Uhl Belk, seeing over and over again the stricken face of Quickening as she lay dying, feeling again the anguish he had experienced as he stood helplessly by. Sometimes he saw Par and Coll Ohmsford as they called to him from a great distance, and always he found that try as he might he could not reach them. There were dark things in his dreams as well, faceless shadows that came at him unexpectedly and from behind, presences without names, unmistakable nevertheless for who and what they were. He ran from them, hid from them, tried desperately to fight back against them—but always they stayed just out of his reach, threatening in ways he could not identify but could only imagine.

His fever broke at the end of the first week. When at last he was able to open his eyes and focus on the young couple who had cared for him, he saw in their faces an obvious relief and realized how close he had come to not waking at all. His sickness had left him drained of strength, and for several days after he had to be fed by hand. He managed to stay awake for short periods and to speak a little when he did. The young wife with the straw-blond hair and the pale blue eyes looked after him while her husband worked in the fields, and she smiled with concern when she told him that his dreams must have been bad ones. She gave him soup and bread with water and a small ration of ale. He accepted it gratefully and thanked her repeatedly for looking after him. Sometimes her husband would appear, standing next to her and looking down at him, bluff and red-faced from the sun, with kind eyes and a broad smile. He mentioned once that Morgan's sword was safely put aside, that it had not been lost. Apparently that had been part of the nightmares as well.

At the end of the two weeks Morgan was taking his meals with them at their dinner table, growing stronger daily, close to returning to normal. His memories lingered, however—the feeling of pain and nausea, the sense of helplessness, the fear that the sickness was the door to the darkness that would come at the end of his life. The memories stayed, for Morgan had come close to dying too often in the past few weeks to be able to put them aside easily. He was marked by what he had experienced and endured as surely as if scarred in battle, and even the farmer and his wife could see in his eyes and face what had been done to him. They never asked for an explanation, but they could see.

He offered to pay them for their care and predictably they refused. When he said good-bye to them seventeen days later, he slipped half of what money remained to him into the pocket of the wife's worn apron when she wasn't looking. They watched after him as parents might a child until he was out of sight.

And so not only was his arrival at Varfleet and his search for Padishar and Par and Coll considerably delayed, but he was left as well with a renewed sense of his own mortality. Morgan Leah had come down out of Eldwist and the Charnals still grappling with Quickening's death, devastated by the loss he felt with her passing, in awe of her strength in carrying out her father's wish that she give up her own life in order that the land should be restored. An elemental that had become more human than her father had anticipated, she remained for Morgan an enigma for which he did not believe he would ever find a resolution. Coupled with this realization was the undeniable pride and strength he had found in helping to defeat Uhl Belk and in regaining anew the magic of the Sword of Leah. When the Sword had been made whole again, somehow so had he. Quickening had given him that. In the loss of Quickening, Morgan realized, he had somehow found himself. The contradictions between what had been lost and gained had warred within him as he traveled south with Walker and Horner Dees, a conflict that would never be entirely settled, and it was not until the sickness had overtaken him that their raging was forced to give way to the more basic need of finding a way to stay alive.

Now, staring down at the city, come back out of several nightmare worlds, out of the lives he had expended in those worlds, so distant that they might have been lived by someone else, Morgan reflected that he stood at the beginning of yet another life. He found himself wondering if those who had known him in the old life would ever recognize now who he was.

He entered Varfleet as just another traveler come down out of the north, a Southlander weathered and seasoned from troubles that were his own business, and he was pretty much ignored by the people of the city, who, after all, had troubles of their own to worry about. He passed through the poorer sections where families lived in makeshift shelters and children begged in the streets, conscious again of how little the ill-named Federation Protectorate had done to help anyone in Callahorn. He passed into the city proper, where the smells of cooking and sewage mingled unpleasantly, the merchants hawked their wares in strident voices from carts and shopfronts, and the tradesmen serviced the needs of those who could afford the price. Federation soldiers patrolled the streets, a threatening presence wherever they went, looking as uncomfortable as the people they were charged with policing. If you stripped away the weapons and uniforms, the Highlander thought darkly, it would be hard to tell who was who.

He found a clothing shop and used most of his remaining money to buy pants, a tunic, a well-made forest cloak, and some new boots. His own clothing was frayed and soiled and worn beyond help, and he left it all behind in the shop when he departed, taking only his weapons. He asked for directions to the Whistledown, not certain even now what it was, and was told by the shopkeeper that it was a tavern that could be found at the center of the city on Wyvern Split.

Making his way through the crowds and the midday heat, Morgan recalled anew the instructions that Padishar Creel had given him weeks ago. He was to go to the Whistledown and show the hawk ring to a woman named Matty Roh. She would know how to find Padishar. Morgan fingered the hawk ring where it was buried in his pocket, safely tucked away for the time he would need it. He mused on how often he had doubted that such a time would come. The rough outline of the hawk emblem pressed against his skin as he twisted it about, bringing back memories of the outlaw chief. He wondered if Padishar Creel had been forced to come back from the dead as often as he had these past few weeks. The possibility brought a bitter smile to his lips.

He found Wyvern Split and turned down its length toward a square ringed by taverns, inns, and pleasure houses. Not a very attractive part of the city, but a busy one. He shifted the Sword of Leah from where it was draped across his back, adjusting the straps, feeling sad and weary and at the same time buoyed—an odd mix, but somehow a proper one. Sickness and loss had worn him down, but surviving both had strengthened his resolve. There was not much out there, he believed, that he could not get through. He needed that conviction. For weeks he had watched his friends and companions slip away, some lost to fortune, some to the machinations of others. He had seen his own plans repeatedly altered, his course turned aside time and again to serve a higher—or at least a different—purpose. He had done what he had believed right in each case, and he had no reason to second-guess himself. But he was tired of having his life rearranged like furniture in a room where each time he turned to look everything was in a different place. He had honored Steff's dying wish and gone back to Culhaven to rescue Granny Elise and Auntie Jilt. He had given himself then to Quickening and her journey to Eldwist. Now it was time to do what he had been promising himself he would do since escaping Tyrsis and the Pit. It was time to find Par and Coll, to give them what protection he could, to see to it that he stayed with them until . . .

He gave a mental shrug. Well, until they no longer needed him, he guessed—whenever that might be.

And where were they now? he wondered for what must have been the hundredth time. What had become of them since their own escape?

Thinking of them made him uneasy. It always did. Too much time had passed since he had left them. The danger of the Shadowen was too great for the Valemen to have been left out there alone. He hoped Padishar had found them by now. He hoped that they'd had an easier time of things than he had.

But he wouldn't have cared to place a bet on it.

He arrived at the square and saw the Whistledown off to the left in the far corner. A weather-beaten wooden sign carved with a flute and a foaming tankard over the name announced its location. It was a slat-boarded building like all the others clustered about it, sharing a common wall with the ones on either side, looming three stories against the skyline, with curtained windows on the second and third floors where there were either living quarters for the owners and their families or sleeping rooms for hire. The square was thronged with people coming and going from this place to that, more than a few meandering from tavern to tavern, some so drunk they could hardly stand. Morgan avoided them, moving aside to let those he encountered pass, smelling the sweat and dirt of their bodies and the stench of the streets. Wyvern Split, he thought, was a cesspool.

He reached the Whistledown's open doors, stepped through, and was surprised to find that the inside of the ale house bore an entirely different look. Although it was plain and sparsely furnished, the floors were scrubbed clean, the wood trim on the serving bar was polished to a high sheen, the tables and chairs and stools were neatly arranged, and the smell of cedar chips and lacquer was everywhere. Ale casks gleamed in their racks against the wall behind the serving counter, and there were glass doors and metal trim on the tankard cupboard. A pair of heavy swinging doors at the end of the serving counter hung closed. A massive stone fireplace dominated the wall to the left of the counter, and a narrow staircase leading to the upper floors took up most of the wall to the right. Serving bowls and cleaning cloths were stacked on the counter itself.

But it was something else that caught Morgan's eye and held it, something so obviously out of place that he had to take a second look to be certain he was not mistaken about what he was seeing.

There were bunches of wildflowers arranged in large vases on shelves bracketing the ale casks and tankard cupboard.

Flowers—here, of all places! He shook his head.

The swinging doors opened and a boy with a broom pushed through. He was tall and lean with short-cropped black hair and fine, almost delicate features. He moved with fluid grace as he swept down the length of the serving counter, almost as if dancing, working the broom in front of him, lost in thought. He whistled softly, unaware yet of Morgan.

Morgan shifted his stance enough to announce that he was there, and the boy looked up at once.

"We're closed," he said. Cobalt eyes fixed on the Highlander, a frank, almost challenging stare. "We open at dusk."

Morgan stared back. The boy's face was smooth and hairless, and his hands were long and thin. The clothes he wore were loose and shapeless, hanging on him as if on sticks, belted at his narrow waist and tied at his ankles. He wore shoes instead of boots, low-cut, stitched leather things that molded to his feet.

"Is this the Whistledown?" Morgan asked, deciding he had better make sure.

The boy nodded. "Come back later. Go take a bath first."

Morgan blinked. Take a bath? "I'm looking for someone," he said, beginning to feel uncomfortable under the other's steady gaze.

The boy shrugged. "I can't help you. There's no one here but me. Try across the street."

"Thanks, but I'm not looking for just anyone . . ." Morgan began.

But the boy was already turning away, working the broom back up the floor against the counter. "We're closed," he repeated, as if that settled the matter.

Morgan started forward, a hint of irritation creeping into his voice. "Wait a minute." He reached for the other's shoulder. "Hold on a minute. Did you say you were the only one . . . ?"

The boy wheeled about smoothly as Morgan touched him, the broom came up, and the blunt end jabbed the Highlander hard below the rib cage. Morgan doubled over, paralyzed, then dropped to one knee, gasping.

The boy came up beside him and bent close. "We're closed, I told you. You should pay better attention." He helped Morgan to his feet, surprisingly strong for being so lean, and guided him to the door. "Come back later when we open."

And the next thing Morgan knew he was back outside on the street, leaning against the slat-board wall of the building, arms clasped about his body as if he were in danger of falling apart—which was not too far off the mark in terms of how he felt. He took several deep breaths and waited for the ache in his chest to subside.

This is ridiculous, he thought angrily. A boy!

He managed to straighten finally, rubbed at his chest, adjusted the shoulder straps of his sword where they had begun to chafe, and walked back through the Whistledown's doors.

The boy, who was sweeping behind the counter now, did not look pleased to see him. "What seems to be your problem?" he asked Morgan pointedly.

The Highlander walked to the counter and glared. "What seems to be my problem? I didn't have a problem until I came in here. Don't you think you were a little quick with that broom?"

The boy shrugged. "I asked you to leave and you didn't. What do you expect?"

"How about a little help? I told you I was looking for someone."

The boy sighed wearily. "Everyone is looking for someone—especially the people who come in here." His voice was low and smooth, an odd mix. "They come in here to drink and to feel better. They come in here to find company. Fine. But they have to do it when we're open. And we're not open. Is that plain enough for you?"

Morgan felt his temper begin to slip. He shook his head. "I'll tell you what's plain to me. What's plain to me is that you don't have any manners. Someone ought to box your ears."

The boy set the broom down and put his slim hands on the counter. "Well, it won't be you who does it. Now turn around and go back out that door. And forget what I said before. Don't come back later. Don't come back at all."

For a moment Morgan considered reaching over the counter, taking hold of the boy by the scruff of his neck, and pulling him across. But the memory of that broom handle was too recent to encourage precipitous action, and besides, the boy didn't look the least bit afraid of him.

Keeping his anger in check, he folded his arms across his chest and held his ground. "Is there anyone else here that I can talk to besides you?" he asked.

The boy shook his head.

"The owner, maybe?"

The boy shook his head.

"No?" Morgan decided to take a chance. "Is the owner's name Matty Roh?"

There was a flicker of recognition in the cobalt eyes, there for an instant and then gone. "No."

Morgan nodded slowly. "But you know who Matty Roh is, don't you?" He made it a statement of fact.

The boy's gaze was steady. "I'm tired of talking to you."

Morgan ignored him. "Matty Roh. That's who I came here to find. And I came a long way. Which is why I need a bath, as you so rudely pointed out. Matty Roh. Not some nameless companion for some unmentionable purpose, thanks just the same." His voice was taking on a sharper edge. "Matty Roh. You know the name; you know who she is. So if you want to be rid of me, just tell me how to find her and I'll be on my way."

He waited, arms folded, feet planted. The boy's expression never changed; his gaze never moved off Morgan. But his hands slipped down behind the serving counter and came up again holding a thin-bladed sword. The way they held it suggested a certain familiarity.

"Now, what's this?" Morgan asked quietly. "Am I really that unwelcome?"

The boy was as still as stone. "Who are you? What do you want with Matty Roh?"

Morgan shook his head. "That's between her and me." Then he added, "I'll tell you this much. I'm not here to cause trouble. I just need to speak with her."

The boy studied him for a long time, gaze level and fixed, body still. He stood behind the serving counter like a statue, and Morgan had the uneasy feeling that he was poised between fleeing and attacking. Morgan watched the eyes and the hands for a hint of which way the boy would go, but there was no movement at all. From outside, the sounds of the street drifted in through the open doors and hung shrill and intrusive in the silence.

"I'm Matty Roh," the boy said.

Morgan Leah stared. He almost laughed aloud, almost said something about how ridiculous that was. But something in the boy's voice stopped him. He took a closer look at the other the fine, delicate features, the slim hands, the lean body concealed beneath the loose-fitting clothing, the way he held himself. He remembered how the boy had moved. None of it seemed quite right for a boy. But for a girl . . .

He nodded slowly. "Matty Roh," he said, his surprise still evident. "I thought you were a . . . that you were . . ."

The girl nodded. "That's what you were supposed to think." Her hand did not move off the sword. "What do you want with me?"

For a moment Morgan did not respond, still grappling with the idea that he had mistaken a girl for a boy. Worse, that he had let her make him look like such a fool. But you mustered the defenses available to you when you lived in a place like Wyvern Split. The girl was clever. He had to admit her disguise was a good one.

He reached into his tunic pocket and drew forth the ring with the hawk emblem and held it out. "Recognize this?"

She took a quick look at the ring, and her hand tightened on the sword. "Who are you?" she asked.

"Morgan Leah," he said. "We both know who gave me the ring. He told me to come to you when I needed to find him."

"I know who you are," she declared. Her gaze stayed level, appraising. "Do you still carry a broken sword, Morgan Leah?"

An image of Quickening as she lay dying flashed in his mind. "No," he said quietly. "It was made whole again." He pushed back the pain the memory brought and forced himself to reach over his shoulder and touch the sword's hilt. "Do you want to have a look?"

She shook her head no. "I'm sorry I gave you such a bad time. But it's difficult to know who to trust. The Federation has spies everywhere—Seekers more often than not."

She picked up her own sword and slipped it back under the counter. For a moment she didn't appear to know what to do next. Then she said, "Would you like something to eat?"

He said he would, and she took him through the swinging doors in back into a kitchen where she seated him at a small table, scooped some stew into a serving bowl from a kettle hung over a cooking fire in the hearth, cut off several slices of bread, poured ale into a mug, and brought it all over to where he waited. He ate and drank eagerly, hungrier than he had been in days. There were wildflowers in a vase on the table, and he touched them experimentally. She watched him in silence, the same serious expression on her face, studying him with that frank, curious gaze. The kitchen was surprisingly cool, with a breeze blowing in through the open back door and venting up the chimney of the fireplace. Sounds from the streets continued to drift in, but the Highlander and the girl ignored them.

"It took you a long time to get here," she said when he had finished his meal. She carried his dishes to a sink and began to wash them. "He expected you sooner than this."

"Where is he now?" Morgan asked. They were taking great pains to avoid saying Padishar Creel's name—as if mention of it might alert the Federation spies set at watch.

"Where did he say he would be?" she countered.

Still testing, Morgan thought. "At Firerim Reach. Tell me something. You're being pretty careful about me. How am I supposed to know I can trust you? How do I know you really are Matty Roh?"

She finished with the dishes, set them to dry on the counter, and turned to face him. "You don't. But you came looking for me. I didn't come looking for you. So you have to take your chances."

He rose. "That's not very reassuring."

She shrugged. "It isn't meant to be. It isn't my job to reassure you. It's my job to make sure you're who you say you are."

"And are you sure?"

She stared at him. "More or less."

Her stare was impenetrable. He shook his head. "When do you think you might know?"

"Soon."

"And what if you decide I'm lying? What if you decide I'm someone else?"

She came forward until she was directly across the table from him, until the blue of her eyes was so brilliant that it seemed to swallow all the light.

"Let's hope you don't have to find out the answer to that question," she said. She held his gaze challengingly. "The Whistledown stays open until midnight. When it closes, we'll talk about what happens next."

As she turned away, he could have sworn she almost smiled.

9

Morgan spent the rest of the day in the kitchen with an old woman who came in to do the cooking but devoted most of her time to sipping ale from a metal flask and stealing food from the pots. The old woman barely gave him a glance and then only long enough to mutter something undecipherable about strange men, so he was left pretty much to himself. He took a bath in an old tub in one of the back rooms (because he wanted to and not because Matty Roh had suggested it, he told himself), carrying steaming water in buckets heated over the fire until he had enough to submerse himself. He languished in the tub for some time, letting more than just the dirt and grit soak away, staying long after the water had cooled.

After the Whistledown had opened for business he left the kitchen and went out into the main room to have a look around. He stood at the serving counter and watched the citizens of Varfleet come and go. The crowd was a well-dressed one, men and women both, and it was immediately clear that the Whistledown was not a workingman's tavern. Several of the tables were occupied by Federation officers, some with their wives or consorts. Talk and laughter was restrained, and no one was particularly boisterous. Once or twice soldiers from Federation patrols paused long enough for a quick glance inside, but then passed on. A strapping fellow with curly dark hair drew ale from the casks, and a serving girl carried trays of the foaming brew to the tables.

Matty Roh worked, too, although it was not immediately apparent to Morgan what her job was. At times she swept the floor, at times she cleared tables, and occasionally she simply went about straightening things up. He watched her for some time before he was able to figure out that what she was really doing was listening in on the conversations of the tavern patrons. She was always busy and never seemed to stand about or to be in any one place for more than a moment, a very unobtrusive presence. Morgan couldn't tell if anyone knew she was a girl or not, but in any case they paid almost no attention to her.

After a time she came up to the counter carrying a tray full of empty glasses and stood next to him. As she reached back for a fresh cleaning rag she said, "You're too obvious standing here. Go back into the kitchen." And then she turned back to the crowd.

Irritated, he nevertheless did as he was told.

At midnight the Whistledown closed. Morgan helped clean up, and then the old cook and the counterman said good-night and went out the back door. Matty Roh blew out the lamps in the front room, checked the locks on the doors, and came back into the kitchen. Morgan was waiting at the little table for her, and she came over and sat down across from him.

"So what did you learn tonight?" he asked, half joking. "Anything useful?"

She gave him a cool stare. "I've decided to trust you," she announced.

His smile faded. "Thanks."

"Because if you're not who you say you are, then you are the worst Federation spy I've ever seen."

He folded his arms defensively. "Forget the thanks. I take it back."

"There is a rumor," she said, "that the Federation have captured Padishar at Tyrsis." Morgan went still. The cobalt eyes stayed fastened on him. "It had something to do with a prison break. I overheard a Federation commander talking about it. They claim to have him."

Morgan thought about it a moment. "Padishar's hard to trap. Maybe a rumor is all it is."

She nodded. "Maybe. It wasn't so long ago that they claimed to have killed him at the Jut. They said the Movement was finished." She paused. "In any case, we'll learn the truth at Firerim Reach."

"We're going?" Morgan asked quickly.

"We're going." She rose. "Help me pack some food. I'll get us some blankets. We'll slip away before it gets light. It will be better if we aren't seen leaving."

He stood up with her and moved over to the pantry. "What about the tavern?" he asked. "Doesn't someone have to look after it?"

"The tavern will stay closed until I return."

He glanced up from stuffing a loaf of bread into a sack. "You lied to me, didn't you? You are the owner."

She met his gaze and held it. "Try not to be so stupid, Highlander. I didn't lie to you. I'm the manager, not the owner. The owner is Padishar Creel."

They finished putting together supplies and sleeping gear, strapped everything across their backs, and went out the back door into the night. The air was warm and filled with the smells of the city as they hurried down empty streets and alleyways, keeping close watch for Federation patrols. The girl was as silent as a ghost, a knife-lean figure cutting smoothly through the building shadows. Morgan noticed that she wore the sword she'd kept hidden beneath the counter, the narrow blade strapped across her back beneath her other gear. He wondered, rather unkindly, if she'd brought her broom. At least her odd shoes were gone, replaced by more serviceable boots.

They passed from the city into the land beyond and marched north to the Mermidon where they crossed at a shallows and turned east. They followed the line of the Dragon's Teeth, and by daybreak they were traveling north again across the Rabb. They walked steadily until sunset, pausing long enough at midday to eat and to wait out the worst of the afternoon heat. The plains were dusty and dry and empty of life, and the journey was uneventful. The girl spoke little, and Morgan was content to leave things that way.

At sunset they made camp close against the Dragon's Teeth beside a tributary of the Rabb, settling themselves in a grove of ash that climbed into the rocks like soldiers on the march. They ate their evening meal as the sun disappeared behind the mountains, its hazy mix of red and gold melting across the plains and sky. When they were finished, they sat watching the dusk deepen and the river's waters turn silver in the light of the moon and stars.

"Padishar told me you saved his life," the girl said after a time.

She hadn't spoken a word all through dinner. Morgan looked over, surprised by the suddenness of the declaration. She was watching him, her strange blue eyes depthless.

"I saved my own in the bargain," he replied, "so it wasn't an entirely selfless act."

She folded her arms. "He said to keep watch for you and to take good care of you. He said I'd know you when I saw you."

Her expression never changed. Morgan grinned in spite of himself. "Well, he makes mistakes like everyone else." He waited for a response and, when there was none, said, a bit huffy, "You may not believe this but I can take pretty good care of myself."

She looked away, shifting to a more comfortable position. Her eyes gleamed in the starlight. "What is it like where you come from?"

He hesitated, confused. "What do you mean?"

"The Highlands, what are they like?"

He thought for a moment she was teasing him, then decided she wasn't. He took a deep breath and stretched out, remembering. "It is the most beautiful country in the Four Lands," he said, and proceeded to describe it in detail—the hills with their carpets of blue, lavender, and yellow grasses and flowers, the streams that turned frosty at dawn and blood-red at dusk, the mist that came and went with the changing seasons, the forests and the meadows, the sense of peace and timelessness. The Highlands were his passion, the more so since his departure weeks earlier. It reminded him again how much home meant to him, even a home that was really no longer his now that the Federation occupied it—though in truth, he thought, it was still more his than theirs because he kept the feel of it with him in his mind and its history was in his blood and that would never be true for them.

She was silent for a time when he finished, then said, "I like how you describe your home. I like how you feel about it. If I lived there, I think I would feel the same."

"You would," he assured her, studying the profile of her face as she stared out across the Rabb, distracted. "But I guess everyone feels that way about their home."

"I don't," she said.

He straightened up again. "Why not?"

Her forehead furrowed. It produced only a slight marring of her smooth features but gave her an entirely different look, one at once both introspective and distant. "I suppose it's because I have no good memories of home. I was born on a small farm south of Varfleet, one of several families that occupied a valley. I lived there with my parents and my brothers and one sister. I was the youngest. We raised milk cows and grain. In summer, the fields would be as gold as the sun. In fall, the earth would be all black after it was plowed." She shrugged. "I don't remember much other than that. Just the sickness. It seems a long time ago, but I guess it wasn't. The land went bad first, then the stock, and finally my family. Everything began to die. Everyone. My sister first, then my mother, my brothers, and my father. It was the same with the people who lived on the other farms. It happened all at once. Everyone was dead in a few months. One of the women on the other farms found me and took me to Varfleet to live with her. We were the last. I was six years old."

She made it all sound as if it were nothing out of the ordinary. There was no emotion in her voice. She finished and looked away. "I think there might be some rain on the way," she said.

They slept until dawn, ate a breakfast of bread, fruit, and cheese, and began their trek north again. The skies were clouding when they woke, and a short time after they crossed the Rabb it began to rain. Thunderheads built up, and lightning streaked the blackness. When the rain began to come down in torrents, they took shelter in the lee of an old maple set back against a rocky rise. Brushing water from their faces and clothes, they settled back to wait out the storm. The air cooled slightly, and the plains shimmered with the damp.

Shoulder to shoulder, they sat with their backs against the maple, staring out into the haze, listening to the sound of the rain.

"How did you meet Padishar?" Morgan asked her after they had been quiet for a time.

She brought her knees up and wrapped her arms about them. Water beaded on her skin and glistened in her black hair. "I apprenticed to Hirehone when I was old enough to work. He taught me to forge iron and to fight. After a while I was better than he was at both. So he brought me into the Movement, and that's how I met Padishar."

Memories of Hirehone crowded Morgan's mind. He let them linger a moment and then banished them. "How long have you been looking after the Whistledown?"

"A couple of years. It offers an opportunity to learn things that can help the free-born. It's a place to be for now."

He glanced over. "But not where you want to end up, is that what you're saying?"

She gave him a flicker of a smile. "It's not for me."

"What is?"

"I don't know yet. Do you?"

He thought about it. "I guess I don't. I haven't let myself think beyond what's been happening these past few weeks. I've been running so fast I haven't had time to stop and think."

She leaned back. "I haven't been running. I've been standing in place, waiting for something to happen."

He shifted to face her. "I was like that before I came north. I spent all of my time thinking of ways to make life miserable for the Federation occupiers—all those officers and soldiers living in the home that had belonged to my family, pretending it was theirs. I thought I was doing something, but I was really just standing in place."

She gave him a curious glance. "So now you're running instead. Is that any better?"

He smiled and shrugged. "At least I'm seeing more of the country."

The rains slowed, the skies began to clear, and they resumed their journey. Morgan found himself sneaking glances at Matty Roh, studying the expression on her face, the lines of her body, and the way she moved. He thought her intriguing, suggestive of so much more than what she allowed to show. On the surface she was cool and purposeful, a carefully fixed mask that hid stronger and deeper emotions beneath. He believed, for reasons he could not explain, that she was capable of almost anything.

It was nearing midday when she turned him into the rocks and they began to follow a trail that ran upward into the hills fronting the Dragon's Teeth. They entered a screen of trees that hid the mountains ahead and the plains behind, and when they emerged they were at the foot of the peaks. The trail disappeared with the trees, and they were soon climbing more rugged slopes, picking their way over the rocks as best they could. Morgan found himself wondering, rather uncharitably, if Matty Roh knew where she was going. After a while they reached a pass and followed it through a split in the rocks into a deep defile. The cliff walls closed about until there was only a narrow ribbon of clouded blue sky visible overhead. Birds took flight from their craggy perches and disappeared into the sun. Wind whistled in sudden gusts down the canyon's length, a shrill and empty sound.

When they stopped for a drink from the water skin, Morgan glanced at the girl to see how she was holding up. There was a sheen of sweat on her smooth face, but she was breathing easily. She caught him looking, and he turned quickly away.

Somewhere deep in the split Matty Roh took them into a cluster of massive boulders that appeared to be part of an old slide. Behind the concealing rocks they found a passageway that tunneled into the cliff wall. They entered and began to climb a spiraling corridor that opened out again onto a ledge about halfway up. Morgan peered down cautiously. It was a straight drop. A narrow trail angled upward from where they stood, the cut invisible from below, and they followed the pathway to the summit of the cliff and along the rim to another split, this one barely more than a crack in the rocks, so narrow that only one person at a time could pass through.

Matty Roh stopped at the opening. "They'll come for us in a moment," she announced, slipping the water skin from her shoulder and passing it to him so that he could drink.

He declined the offering. If she didn't need a drink, neither did he. "How will they know we're here?" he asked.

That flicker of a smile came and went. "They've been watching us for the past hour. Didn't you see them?"

He hadn't, of course, and she knew it, so he just shrugged his indifference and let the matter drop.

Shortly afterward a pair of figures emerged from the shadows of the split, bearded, hard-faced men with longbows and knives. They greeted Matty Roh and Morgan perfunctorily, then beckoned for them to follow. Single file, they entered the split and passed along a trail that wound upward into a jumble of rocks that shut away any view of what lay ahead. Morgan climbed dutifully, unable to avoid noticing that Matty Roh continued to look as if she were out for a midday stroll.

Finally they reached a plateau that stretched away north, south, and west and offered the most breathtaking views of the Dragon's Teeth and the lands beyond that Morgan had ever seen. Sunset was approaching, and the skies were turning a brilliant crimson through the screen of mist that clung to the mountain peaks. Hence the name Firerim Reach, thought Morgan. East, the plateau backed up against a ridge grown thick with spruce and cedar. It was here that the outlaws were encamped, their roofed shelters crowded into the trees, their cooking fires smoldering in stone-lined pits. There were no walled fortifications as there had been at the Jut, for the plateau dropped away into a mass of jagged fissures and deep canyons, its sheer walls unscalable by one man let alone any sort of sizable force. At least, that was the way it appeared from where Morgan stood, and he assumed it was the same on all sides of the quarter-mile or so stretch of plain. The only way in appeared to be the way they had come. Still, the Highlander knew Padishar Creel well enough to bet there was at least one other.

He turned as a familiar burly figure lumbered up to meet them, black-bearded and ferocious-looking with his missing eye and ear and his scarred face. Chandos embraced Matty Roh warmly, nearly swallowing her up in his embrace, and then reached out for Morgan.

"Highlander," he greeted, taking Morgan's hand in his own and crushing it. "It's good to have you back with us."

"It's good to be back." Morgan extracted his hand painfully. "How are you, Chandos?"

The big man shook his head. "Well enough, given everything that's happened." There was an angry, frustrated look in his dark eyes. His jaw tightened. "Come with me where we can talk."

He took Morgan and Matty Roh from the rim of the cliffs across the bluff. The guards who had brought them in disappeared back the way they had come. Chandos moved deliberately away from the encampment and the other outlaws. Morgan glanced questioningly at Matty Roh, but the girl's face was unreadable.

When they were safely out of earshot, she said immediately to Chandos, "They have him, don't they?"

"Padishar?" Chandos nodded. "They took him two nights earlier at Tyrsis." He turned and faced Morgan. "The Valeman was with him, the smaller one, the one Padishar liked so well—Par Ohmsford. Apparently the two of them went into the Federation prisons to rescue Damson Rhee. They got her out, but Padishar was captured in the attempt. Damson's here now. She arrived yesterday with the news."

"What happened to Par?" Morgan asked, wondering at the same time why there had been no mention of Coll.

"Damson said he went off in search of his brother—something about the Shadowen," Chandos brushed the question aside. "What matters at the moment is Padishar." His scarred face furrowed. "I haven't told the others yet." He shook his head. "I don't know if I should or not. We're supposed to meet with Axhind and his Trolls at the Jannisson at the end of the week. Five days. If we don't have Padishar with us, I don't think they'll join up. I think they'll just turn around and go right back the way they came. Five thousand strong!" His face flushed, and he took a steadying breath. "We need them if we're to have any kind of chance against the Federation. Especially after losing the Jut."

He looked at them hopefully. "I was never much at making plans. So if you've any ideas at all . . ."

Matty Roh shook her head. "If the Federation has Padishar, he won't stay alive very long."

Chandos scowled. "Maybe longer than he'd like, if the Seekers get their hands on him."

Morgan recalled the Pit and its inhabitants momentarily and quickly forced the thought away. Something about all this didn't make sense. Padishar had gone looking for Par and Coll weeks ago. Why had it taken him so long to find them? Why had the Ohmsford brothers remained in Tyrsis all that time? And when Par and Padishar had gone into the prisons to rescue Damson Rhee, where was Coll? Did the Shadowen have Coll as well?

It seemed to Morgan that there was an awful lot unaccounted for.

"I want to speak with Damson Rhee," he announced abruptly. He had wondered about her at the beginning, and suddenly he was beginning to wonder about her all over again.

Chandos shrugged. "She's sleeping. Walked all night to get here."

Images of Teel danced in Morgan's head, whispering insidiously. "Then let's wake her."

Chandos gave him a hard stare. "All right, Highlander. If you think it's important. But it will be your doing, not mine."

They crossed to the encampment and passed through the cooking fires and the free-born at work about them. The sun had dropped further in the west, and it was nearing dinnertime. There was food in the cooking kettles, and the smells wafted on the summer air. Morgan scarcely noticed, his mind at work on other matters. Shadows crept out of the trees, lengthening as dusk approached. Morgan was thinking about Par and Coll, still in Tyrsis after all this time. They had escaped the Pit weeks ago. Why had they stayed there? he kept wondering. Why for so long?

As the questions pressed in about him, he kept seeing Teel's face—and the Shadowen that had hidden beneath.

They reached a small hut set well back in the trees, and Chandos stopped. "She's in there. You wake her if you want. Come have dinner with me when you're finished, the both of you."

Morgan nodded. He turned to Matty Roh. "Do you want to come with me?"

She gave him an appraising look. "No. I think you should do this on your own."

It seemed for a moment as if she might say more, but then she turned and walked off into the trees after Chandos. She knew something she wasn't telling, Morgan decided. He watched her go, thinking once again that Matty Roh was a good deal more complex than what she revealed.

He looked back at the hut, momentarily undecided as to how he should go about bracing Damson Rhee. Suspicions and fears shouldn't be allowed to get in the way of common sense. But he couldn't shake the image of Teel as a Shadowen. It could easily be the same with this girl. The trick was in finding out.

He reached back over his shoulder to make certain that the Sword of Leah would slide free easily, took a deep breath, then walked up to the door and knocked. It opened almost immediately, and a girl with flaming red hair and emerald eyes stood looking out at him. She was flushed, as if she had just awakened, and her dark clothing was disheveled. She was tall, though not as tall as Matty, and very pretty.

"I'm Morgan Leah," he said.

She blinked, then nodded. "Par's friend, the Highlander. Yes, hello. I'm Damson Rhee. I'm sorry, I've been sleeping. What time is it?" She peered up at the sky through the trees. "Almost dusk, isn't it? I've slept too long."

She stepped back as if to go inside, then stopped and turned to face him again. "You've heard about Padishar, I suppose. Did you just get here?"

He nodded, watching her face. "I wanted to hear what happened from you."

"All right." She did not seem surprised. She glanced over her shoulder, then came out into the light. "Let's talk out here. I'm tired of being shut away. Tired of being inside where there's no light. How much did Chandos tell you?"

She moved away from the hut into the trees, a very determined stride, and he was swept along in her wake. "He told me that Padishar had been taken by the Federation when he and Par came to rescue you. He said

Par had left you to go find Coll—that it had something to do with the Shadowen."

"Everything has something to do with the Shadowen, doesn't it?" she whispered, her head lowering wearily.

She walked over to one end of a crumbling log and sat down. Morgan hesitated, still guarded, then sat with her. She turned slightly so that she was facing him. "I have a very long story to tell you, Morgan Leah," she advised.

She began with finding Par and Coll after they had escaped the Pit in Tyrsis. She told of how they had decided to go back down into the Shadowen breeding ground one final time, how they had enlisted the help of the Mole and found their way through the tunnels beneath the city to the old palace. From there the brothers had gone off together in search of the Sword of Shannara. Par had come back alone, carrying with him what he believed to be the talisman, half-mad with grief and horror because he had killed his brother. She had nursed him for weeks in the Mole's underground home, slowly bringing him back to himself, carefully bringing him out of his dark nightmare. From there they had fled from safe house to safe house, the Sword of Shannara in tow, hiding from the Seekers and the Federation, looking for a way to escape the city. Finally Padishar had found them, but in the process of yet another escape from the Federation, Damson herself had been taken. Padishar and Par had come back to rescue her, and that in turn had led to Padishar's capture. Fleeing the city completely, because at last there was a way to do so and there was nothing they could do for Padishar without help, they had come north through the Kennon.

She touched his arm impulsively. "And what we saw, Morgan Leah, from high in the pass, far off in the distance beyond the Federation watch fires, but as clear as I see you, was Paranor. It is back, Highlander, returned out of the past. Par was certain of it. He said it meant that Walker Boh had succeeded!"

Then, growing subdued again, she described their journey back out of the pass and their fateful encounter with Coll—or the thing Coll had become, wrapped in that strange, shimmering cloak, hunched and twisted as if his bones had been rearranged. In the struggle that followed the power of the Sword of Shannara had somehow been invoked, revealing what Par now thought to be the truth about the brother he believed dead.

"He went after Coll, of course," she finished. "What else could he do? I did not want him to go, not without me—but I did not have the right to stop him." She searched Morgan's eyes. "I am not as certain as he that it is Coll he tracks, but I realize that he must find out one way or the other if he is ever to be at peace."

Morgan nodded. He was thinking that Damson Rhee had given up an awful lot of herself to help Par Ohmsford, that she had risked more than he would have expected anyone to risk besides himself and Coll. He was thinking as well that the story she had told him had a feeling of truth to it, that it seemed right in the balance of things. The doubts he had brought with him coming in began to fade away. Certainly Par's persistence in going after the Sword of Shannara was in character, as was this new search to find his brother. The problem now was that Par was more alone than ever, and Morgan was reminded once again of his failure to watch out for his friend.

He realized Damson was studying him, a hard, probing look, and without warning his suspicions flared anew. Damson Rhee—was she the friend that Par believed or the enemy he sought so desperately to escape? Certainly she could have been the reason he'd had so many narrow escapes, the reason the Shadowen had almost trapped him so many times. But then, too, wasn't she also the reason he had escaped?

"You're not certain of me, are you?" she asked quietly.

"No," he admitted. "I'm not."

She nodded. "I don't know what I can do to convince you, Morgan. I don't know that I even want to try. I have to spend whatever energy is left me finding a way to free Padishar. Then I will go in search of Par."

He looked away into the trees, thinking of the dark suspicions that the Shadowen bred in all of them, wishing it could be otherwise. "When I was at the Jut with Padishar," he said, "I was forced to kill a girl who was really a Shadowen." He looked back at her. "Her name was Teel. My friend Steff was in love with her, and it cost him his life."

He told her then of Teel's betrayals and the eventual confrontation deep within the catacombs of the mountains behind the Jut where he had killed the Shadowen who had been Teel and saved Padishar Creel's life.

"What frightens me," he said, "is that you could be another Teel and Par could end up like Steff."

She did not respond, her gaze distant and lost. She might have been looking right through him. There were tears in her eyes.

He reached back suddenly and drew out the Sword of Leah. Damson watched him without moving, her green eyes fixing on the gleaming blade as he placed it point downward in the earth between them, his hands fastened on the pommel.

"Put your hands on the flat of the blade, Damson," he said softly.

She looked at him without answering, and for a long time she did not move. He waited, listening to the distant sounds of the free-born as they gathered for dinner, listening to the silence closer at hand. The light was fading rapidly now, and there were shadows all about. He felt oddly removed from everything about him, as if he were frozen in time with Damson Rhee.

Not this girl, he found himself praying. *Not again.*

At last she reached out and touched the Sword of Leah, her palms tight against the metal. Then she deliberately closed her fingers about the edge. Morgan watched in horror as the blade cut deep into her flesh, and her blood began to trickle down its length.

"A Shadowen couldn't do that, could it?" she whispered.

He reached down quickly and pried her fingers away. "No," he said. "Not without triggering the magic." He lay the talisman aside, tore strips of cloth from his cloak, and began to bind her hands. "You didn't have to do that," he reproached her.

Her smile was faint and wistful. "Didn't I? Would you have been sure of me otherwise, Morgan Leah? I don't think so. And if you're not sure of me, how can we be of help to each other? There has to be trust between us." She fixed him with her gentle eyes. "Is there now?"

He nodded quickly. "Yes. I'm sorry, Damson."

Her bound hands reached up to clasp his own. "Let me tell you something." The tears were back in her eyes. "You said that your friend Steff was in love with Teel? Well, Highlander, I am in love with Par Ohmsford."

He saw it all then, the reason she had stayed with Par, had given herself so completely to him, following him even into the Pit, watching over him, protecting him. It was what he would have done—had tried to do—for Quickening. Damson Rhee had made a commitment that only death would release.

"I'm sorry," he said again, thinking how inadequate it sounded.

Her hands tightened on his and did not let go. They faced each other in the dusk without speaking for a long time. As he held her hands, Morgan was reminded of Quickening, of the way she had felt, of the feelings she had invoked in him. He found that he missed her desperately and would have given anything to have her back again.

"Enough testing," Damson whispered. "Let's talk instead. I'll tell you everything that's happened to me. You do the same about yourself. Par and Padishar need us. Maybe together we can come up with a way to help."

She squeezed his hands as if there were no pain in her own and gave him an encouraging smile. He bent to retrieve the Sword of Leah, then started back with her through the trees toward the glow of the cooking fires. His mind was spinning, working through what she had told him, sorting out impressions from facts, trying to glean something useful. Damson was right. The Valeman and the leader of the free-born needed them. Morgan was determined not to let either down.

But what could he do?

The smell of food from the cooking fire reached out to him enticingly. For the first time since he had arrived, he was hungry.

Par and Padishar.

Padishar first, he thought.

Chandos had said five days.

If the Seekers didn't reach him first . . .

It came to him in a rush, the picture so clear in his mind he almost cried out. He reached over impulsively and put his arm around Damson's shoulders.

"I think I know how to free Padishar," he said.

10

Five days the Four Horsemen circled the walls of Paranor, and five days Walker Boh stood on the castle battlements and watched. Each dawn they assembled at the west gates, shadows come from the gloom of fading night. One would approach, a different one each time, and strike the gates once in challenge. When Walker failed to appear they would resume their grim vigil, spreading out so that there was one at each compass point, one at each of the main walls, riding in slow, ceaseless cadence, circling like birds of prey. Day and night they rode, specters of gray mist and dark imaginings, silent as thought and certain as time.

"Incarnations of man's greatest enemies," Cogline mused when he saw them for the first time. "Manifestations of our worst fears, the slayers of so many, given shape and form and sent to destroy us." He shook his head. "Can it be that Rimmer Dall has a sense of humor?"

Walker didn't think so. He found nothing amusing about any of it. The Shadowen appeared to possess boundless raw power, the kind of power that would let them become anything. It was neither subtle nor intricate; it was as straightforward and relentless as a flood. It seemed able to build on itself and to sweep aside anything that it found in its path. Walker did not know how powerful the Horsemen were, but he was willing to bet that they were more than a match for him. Rimmer Dall would have sent nothing less to deal with a Druid—even one newly come to the position, uncertain of his own strength, of the extent of his magic, and of the ways it might be made to serve him. At least one of Allanon's charges to the Ohmsfords had been carried out, and it posed a threat that the Shadowen could not afford to ignore.

Yet the purpose of the charges remained a mystery that Walker could not solve. Standing atop Paranor's walls, watching the Four Horsemen circle below, he pondered endlessly why the charges had been given. What was it that the Sword of Shannara was supposed to accomplish? What purpose would it serve to have the Elves brought back into the world of men? What was the reason for returning Paranor and the Druids? Or one Druid at least, he mused darkly. One Druid, made over out of bits and pieces of others. He was an amalgam of those who had come and gone, of their memories, of their strengths and weaknesses, of their lore and history, of their magic's secrets. He was an infant in his life as a Druid, and he did not yet know how he was supposed to act. Each day he opened new doors on what others before him had known and passed on, knowledge that revealed itself in unexpected glimpses, light coming from the darkened corners of his mind as if let in through shuttered windows thrown wide. He did not understand it all, sometimes doubted it, often questioned its worth. But the flow was relentless, and he was forced to measure and weigh each new revelation, knowing it must have had worth once, accepting that it might again.

But what role was he supposed to play in the struggle to put an end to the Shadowen? He had become the Druid that Allanon had sought, and he had made himself master of Paranor. Yet what was he supposed to do with this? Surely he had magic now that might be used against the Shadowen—just as the Druids had used magic before to give aid to the Races. He possessed knowledge as well, perhaps more knowledge than any man alive, and the Druids had used this as a weapon, too. But it seemed to Walker that his newfound power lacked any discernible focus, that he needed first to understand the nature of his enemy before he could settle on a way to defeat it.

Meanwhile, here he was, trapped within his tower fortress where he could not help anyone.

"They do not try to enter," Cogline observed at one point after three days of vigilance atop the castle walls. "Why do you think that is?"

Walker shook his head. "Perhaps they do not need to. As long as we remain locked within, their purpose is served."

The old man rubbed his whiskered chin. He had grown older since his release from the half life to which the magic of the Druid Histories had consigned him. He was lined and wrinkled anew, more stooped than before, slower in his walk and speech, frail beyond what his years allowed. Walker did not like what he saw, but said nothing. The old man had given much for him, and what he had given had clearly taken its toll. But he did not complain or choose to talk of it, so there was no reason for Walker to do so either.

"It may be that they are afraid of the Druid magic," Walker continued after a moment, his good hand lifting to rest on the battlement stone. "Paranor has always been protected from those that would enter uninvited. The Shadowen may know of this and choose to stay without because of it."

"Or perhaps they wait until they have tested the nature and extent of that magic," Cogline said softly. "They wait to discover how dangerous you are." He looked at Walker without seeing him, eyes focused somewhere beyond. "Or until they simply grow tired of waiting," he whispered.

Walker considered ways in which he might defeat these Shadowen, turning those ways over and over in his mind like artifacts hiding clues to the past. The Black Elfstone was an obvious choice, secreted now in a vault deep within the catacombs of the Keep. But the Elfstone would exact its own price if called upon, and it was not a price that Walker was willing to pay. There was no reason to think that the Elfstone would not work against the Four Horsemen, draining their magic away until nothing remained but ashes. But the nature of the Elfstone required that the stolen magic be transferred into the holder, and Walker had no wish to have the Shadowen magic made part of him.

There was also the S.
sin Pe Ell at Eldwist, the we. he strange killing blade taken from the assas-
not relish the prospect of using a... at could kill anything. But Walker did
history of the Stiehl, and thought .. s weapon, especially one with the
were plenty at hand that could be used aga. pons were required, there
What he needed most, he knew, was a pla... dowen.
could remain safely within Paranor's walls, hoping
out; he could go out and face them; or he could try to three choices. He
out being seen. The first offered only the faintest possibility o Shadowen
besides, time was not something of which he had an abundance in with-
The second seemed incontestably foolhardy.

That left the third.

Five days after the Four Horsemen laid siege to Paranor, Walker Boh decided to attempt an escape.

Underground.

He told Cogline of his plan at dinner that night—a dinner comprising some few small stores left over from three centuries gone and frozen in time with the castle, sorely depleted stores that reinforced the importance of breaking the siege. There were tunnels beneath the castle that opened into the forests beyond, concealments known only to Druids past and now to him. He would slip through such a tunnel that night and emerge behind where the Horsemen patrolled the walls. He would be clear of them and gone before they knew he had escaped.

Cogline frowned and looked doubtful. It seemed entirely too easy to him. Surely the Shadowen would have thought of such a possibility.

But Walker had made up his mind. Five days of standing about was long enough. Something had to be tried, and this was the best he could come up with. Cogline and Rumor would remain within the Keep. If the Horsemen attempted an assault before Walker returned, they should slip out the same way he had gone. Cogline reluctantly agreed, bothered by something he refused to discuss, so agitated that Walker came close to pressing for an explanation. But the old man's enigmatic behavior was nothing new, so in the end Walker let the matter drop.

He waited for midnight, watching from the walls until late to make certain that the Shadowen kept to their rounds. They did, spectral shapes in the dark below, circling ceaselessly. The fog that had blanketed the valley for the better part of four days had lifted that dawn, and now with the coming of night Walker Boh saw something new in the valley. Far west, where the Dragon's Teeth turned north into the Streleheim, there were watch fires at the mouth of the Kennon Pass. An army was camped there, blocking all passage. The Federation, Walker thought, staring out across the trees of the forest below, across the hills beyond, to the light. Perhaps their presence in the pass was unrelated to that of the Shadowen at Paranor, but Walker didn't think so. Knowingly or not, the Federation served the Shadowen cause—a tool for Rimmer Dall and others in the Coalition Council

soldiers in the Kennon had
hierarchy—and it was safe to assume th.. ..n wasn't worried for a moment that
something to do with the Four H... ..w. any hindrance to him.

Not that it mattered. ne left the castle walls and went down through
Federation soldiers. thes as black as night, loose-fitting and serviceable,
When mi.eapons. He left Cogline and Rumor peering after him as
the Kee..ne fire pit. His memories were Allanon's and those of Druids
a. before, and he found he knew his way as well as if the Keep had always
been his home. Doors hidden within the castle stone opened at his
touch, and passageways were as familiar as the haunts of Hearthstone in the
days before the dreams of Allanon. He found the tunnels that ran beneath
the rock on which Paranor rested and worked his way down into the earth.
All about him he could hear the steady thrum of the fires contained in the
furnaces beneath the Keep, throbbing steadily within their core of rock
deep below the castle walls, the only sound within the darkness and silence.

It took him over an hour to make his way through. There were numerous passageways beneath the castle, all intertwined and leading from a single
door that only he could open. He chose the one that led west, seeking to
exit within the sheltering trees of the forests that lay between the Horsemen and the Kennon Pass, certain that once free of the Shadowen he could
slip past the Federation soldiers easily. When he reached the concealed
opening, he paused to listen. There was no sound above him. There was no
movement. Still, he felt uneasy, as if sensing that despite appearances all was
not well.

He went out from the tunnel into the black of the forest, rising from
the earth like a shadow within a covering of brush and rocks. Through gaps
in the canopy of limbs overhead he could see the stars and a hint of the
waning moon. It was silent within the trees, as if nothing lived there. He
searched for a hint of the presence of the gray wolves and did not find it.
He listened for the small sounds of insects and birds, and they were missing.
He sniffed the air and smelled an odd mustiness.

He breathed deeply and stepped out into the open.

He heard, rather than saw, the sweep of the scythe arcing toward him,
and flung himself aside just before it struck. Death grunted with the effort
of the swing, a cloaked black shape to one side. Walker rolled to his feet,
seeing another shape materialize to his right. War, all in armor, blade edges
and spikes glinting wickedly, hurled a mace that thudded into the tree next
to him and caused the trunk to split apart. Walker whirled away, careening
wildly past the skeletal arms of Famine, white bones reaching, clutching.
They were all there, all of them, he realized in despair. Somehow they had
found him out.

He darted away, hearing the buzz and hiss of Pestilence, feeling dry
heat and smelling sickness close beside. He leaped a small ravine, his fear giving him unexpected strength, a fiery determination building within him.

The Horsemen came after, dismou.. [obscured]
of night broken free like the edges of .. [obscured]
movement as he might the rustle of leaves in a .. [obscured]
There was nothing else—no footsteps, no breathing, .. [obscured]
or bone.

Walker raced through the trees, no longer sure in which direction he
was running, seeking only to elude his pursuers. He was suddenly lost in the
darkness of the forest corridors, fleeing to no purpose but to escape, any advantage of surprise lost. The Shadowen came on, a swift and certain pursuit.
He was aware of their movements out of the corner of his eye. They had
him flushed now, and they were hunting him as dogs would a fox.

No!

He whirled then and brought his magic to bear, throwing up a wall of
fire between himself and his pursuers, sending the flames back into their
faces like white-hot spikes. War and Pestilence shrank away, slowed, but
Famine and Death came on, unaffected. Of course, Walker thought as he
ran anew. Famine and Death. Fire would not harm them.

He crossed a stream and swerved right toward the rise of Paranor, towers and walls sharp-edged against the night. He had been running that way
without knowing it, and now saw it as his only chance of escape. If he
could gain the castle before they caught him . . .

Cogline! Was the old man watching?

Something rose out of the night before him, serpentine and slick with
moisture. Claws reached for him and teeth gleamed. It was one of the
Shadowen mounts, set there to cut him off. He slipped beneath its grasp, a
bit of night that could not be held, the magic making him as swift and
ephemeral as the wind. The serpent thing hissed and slashed wildly, sending
gouts of earth flying. Walker Boh was behind it by then, racing away with
the quickness of thought. Ahead the castle of the Druids loomed—his sanctuary, his haven from these things—

A black motion to his left sent him skidding away as Famine lashed out
with a sword carved of bone, a dull white gleaming that tore at the edges of
his clothing. Walker lost his footing and went down, tumbling along a
slope, rolling wildly through brush and long grass and into a slick of standing water. Something rushed past, just missing him with a click of jaws.
Another of the serpents. Walker came to his feet, flinging fire and sound in
all directions in a desperate effort to shield himself. He had the satisfaction
of hearing something shriek in pain, of hearing something else grunt as if
clubbed, and then he was moving again. Trees rose off to one side, and he
disappeared into them, searching out the concealment of the deep shadows.
His breathing was ragged and uneven, and his body ached. To his dismay,
he found himself moving away from the castle again, turned aside from the
safety he had hoped to gain.

A shadow flitted off to his left, swift and silent, a black cloak and a glint
of an iron blade. *Death.* Walker was tiring, worn from his flight, from being

...on so often. The Shadowen had hemmed him in ... He did not think he could reach the castle before they ...p to him. He sought to change directions back again, but saw ...ovement between himself and the Keep and heard a hiss of anticipation and the sudden rustle of scales through the grasses and brush. Walker could barely keep his panic in check, feeling it as a growing tightness in his throat. He had been too quick to assume, too sure of himself. He should have known it would not be this easy. He should have anticipated better.

Branches slapped at his face and arms as he forced his way into a stretch of deep woods. Behind, the serpent closed. It seemed as if he could feel its breath on his neck, the touch of claws and teeth on his body. He increased his pace, broke free of the underbrush into a clearing, and found Death waiting, cloaked and hooded, scythe lifted. The Shadowen struck at him, missed as he veered sideways, swung a second time, and Walker caught hold of the scythe to deflect it. Instantly a cold numbed his hand and arm, hollow and bone-chilling, and he jerked away in pain, thrusting the scythe and its wielder aside as he did so. Something else moved in from the right, but he was running again, throwing himself back into the forest, slipping past rows of dark trunks as if turned substanceless, all the while feeling the numbness settle deeper.

So cold!

His strength was failing now, and he was no closer to safety than before. Think, he admonished himself furiously. *Think!* Shadows moved all about, the skeletal shape of Famine, the hideous buzz of Pestilence, the rumble of War in his unbreachable armor, the silent rush of Death, and with them the serpents they commanded.

Then suddenly a memory triggered, and Walker Boh grasped for the thread of hope it offered. There was a trapdoor hidden in the earth just ahead and beneath it a tunnel leading back into Paranor. The trapdoor was Allanon's memory, come alive in the terror and anguish of the moment, recalled just in time. *There, left!* Walker swerved, lurching ahead, hand and arm feeling as dead as the one he had lost. *Don't think about it!* He threw himself into a covering of brush, whipping past leafy barriers, down a ravine, and across a narrows.

There!

His hand dropped to the earth, clawing for the hidden door with nerveless fingers. It was here, he thought, here in this patch of ground. Sounds approached from behind, closing. He found an iron ring, grasped it, and heaved upward. The door came away with a thud, falling back. Walker tumbled through the opening and down the stairs beyond, then scrambled back to his feet. There were shadows at the entry, coming through. He raised his damaged hand and arm, fighting through the numbness and chill, and called for the magic. Fire exploded up the stairs and filled the opening. The shadows disappeared in a ball of light. There was a rending of earth and stone, and the entire entrance collapsed.

Walker lurched away into the tunnel, choking and coughing from the dust and smoke. Twice he glanced back to make certain that nothing followed.

But he was alone.

He was besieged by doubts and fears as he made his way back to the Keep through the tunnels, assailed by demons that bore the faces of his enemies. It seemed as if he could hear his Shadowen pursuers even here, come down into the earth to finish what they had started. Death, War, Pestilence, and Famine—what was rock and earth to them? Could they not penetrate anywhere? What was to keep them out?

But they did not come, for, notwithstanding the forms and identities they had assumed, they were not invincible and not truly the incarnations they pretended to be. He had heard them cry out in pain; he had felt their substance. The numbness in his hand and arm was beginning to recede, and he welcomed the tingling gratefully, feeling anew the pain of loss of his other limb, wishing he could live that part of his life over again.

He wondered how much more of himself he would be forced to cede before this struggle was over. Wasn't he lucky just to be alive? How narrow his escape from the Shadowen had been this time!

And then suddenly it occurred to him that perhaps he hadn't really escaped anything. Perhaps he had been *allowed* to escape. Perhaps the Horsemen had only been toying with him. Hadn't they had enough chances to kill him if they wanted to? It seemed on reflection that they might have been trying to scare him rather than kill him, to instill enough fear in him that he would be unable to function at all once he was back within the Druid's Keep.

But he discarded the idea almost immediately. It was ridiculous to think that they wouldn't have killed him if they could. They had simply tried and failed. He had possessed enough skill and magic to save himself even in the confusion of an ambush, and he would take what comfort he could from that.

Aching and worn, he reentered Paranor's walls and made his way back into the Keep. Cogline would be waiting. He would have to confess his failure to the old man. The thought troubled him, and he was aware that it was his preconception of the invincibility of the Druids that stood in the way of acceptance. But he could not afford pride. He was a novice still. He was just beginning to learn.

Slowly the fears and doubts dropped away, and the demons disappeared. There would be another day, he promised another time and place in which to deal with the Horsemen.

When it came, he would be ready.

Morgan Leah explained his plan to rescue Padishar Creel to Damson Rhee and Chandos during dinner. He pulled them aside where they would not be overheard, huddling on the open bluff about their food and drink, listening to the night sounds and watching the stars brighten in the darkening sky while they talked. He first had Damson relate again the particulars of her own escape from the city, letting her tell the story as she chose, glancing back and forth between the girl and the fierce-looking free-born. When she had finished, he set his empty plate aside—he had consumed everything while she talked—and leaned forward intently.

"They will expect a rescue attempt," he advised softly, glancing at each in turn. "They know we won't just give up on him. They know how important he is to us. But they will not expect us to come at them the same way. They will expect a different approach this time—a major effort involving a large number of men maybe, a diversion of some sort perhaps leading to an all-out assault. They will expect us to try to catch them off guard. So we have to give them something other than what they're looking for before they realize what it is they're seeing."

Chandos snorted. "Are you making any sense, Highlander?"

Morgan permitted himself a quick grin. "Above all else, we have to get in and out again quick. The longer this takes, the more dangerous it becomes. Bear with me, Chandos. I just want you to understand the reasoning behind what I'm about to suggest. We have to think the way they do in order to anticipate their plan to trap us and find a way to avoid it."

"You're sure there will be a trap, then?" the big man asked, rubbing his bearded chin. "Why won't they just dispose of Padishar and be done with it? Or why not do to him what they did to Hirehone?" He glanced quickly at Damson, who was tight-lipped.

Morgan clasped a hand on the other's broad shoulder. "I can't be sure of anything. But think about it for a moment. If they dispose of Padishar, they lose any chance of getting their hands on the rest of us. And they want us all, Chandos. They want the free-born wiped out." He faced Damson. "Eventually, they will use Padishar the same way they used Hirehone. But they won't do that right away. First of all, they know we will be looking for it. If Padishar comes back, what's the first thing we'll ask ourselves? Is it really Padishar—or is it another of the Shadowen? Second, they know we found a way to discover the truth about Teel. And they know we might do it again with Padishar. Third, and most important, we have the use of magic and they want it. Rimmer Dall has been chasing Par Ohmsford from the beginning and it must have something to do with his magic. Same with Walker Boh. And the same with me."

He leaned forward. "They'll try to use Padishar to bring us to them because they know we won't attempt a rescue without bringing the magic along, that we won't challenge theirs without being able to call on ours. They want that magic—just like they want all the magic—and this is their best chance to get it."

Chandos frowned. "So you figure it's the Shadowen that we'll really be up against?"

Morgan nodded. "It's been the Shadowen right from the beginning. Teel, Hirehone, the Creepers, Rimmer Dall, the Gnawl, that little girl Par encountered on Toffer Ridge everywhere we've gone, the Shadowen have been there waiting. They control the Federation and the Coalition Council as well; they have to. Of course it's the Shadowen we'll be up against."

"Tell us your plan," Damson urged quietly.

Morgan leaned back again, folding his arms comfortably. "We go back into Tyrsis through the tunnels—the same way Damson escaped. We dress ourselves in Federation uniforms, just as Padishar did at the Pit. We go up into the city, to the watchtower or prisons or wherever they have Padishar. We enter in broad daylight and set him free. We go in one way and out another. We do it all in a matter of a few minutes."

Chandos and Damson both stared at him. "That's it? That's the whole plan?" Chandos demanded.

"Wait a minute," Damson interrupted. "Morgan, how do we get back into the tunnels? I can't remember the way."

"No, you can't," Morgan agreed. "But the Mole can." He took a deep breath. "This plan depends mostly on him. And you persuading him to help." He paused, studying her green eyes. "You will have to go back into the city and find him, then come down through the catacombs to lead us in. You will have to find out where Padishar is being held so that we can go right to him. The Mole knows all the secret passageways, all the tunnels that lie beneath the city of Tyrsis. He can find a way for us to go. If we just appear at their door, they won't have time to stop us. It's the best chance we have—do what they expect us to do, but not in the way they're anticipating."

Chandos shook his head. "I don't know, Highlander. They know about Damson; they'll be looking for her."

Morgan nodded. "But she's the only one the Mole will trust. She has to go in first, through the gates. I'll go with her." He looked at her. "What do you think, Damson Rhee?"

"I think I can do it," she declared quietly. "And the Mole will help— if they haven't caught up with him yet." She frowned doubtfully. "They have to be hunting for him down in those same tunnels we'll be coming through."

"But he knows them better than the soldiers do," Morgan said. "They've been trying to catch him for weeks now and haven't been able to do so. We just need another few days." He looked at the girl and the big man in turn. "It is the best chance we're going to get. We have to try."

Chandos shook his head once more. "How many of us will this take?"

"Two dozen, no more."

Chandos stared at him, wide-eyed. "Two dozen! Highlander, there's five thousand Federation soldiers quartered in Tyrsis, and who knows how many Shadowen! Two dozen men won't stand a chance!"

"We'll stand a better chance than two hundred—or two thousand, if we had that many to muster, which we don't, do we?" The big man's jaw tightened defensively. "Chandos, the smaller the company, the better the chance of hiding it. They'll be looking for something larger; they'll expect it. But two dozen men? We can be on top of them before they know who we are. We can disguise two dozen among five thousand a lot more easily than two hundred. Two dozen is all we need if we get close enough."

"He's right," Damson said suddenly. "A large force would be heard in the tunnels. There would be nowhere for them to hide in the city. We can slip two dozen in and hide them until the attempt." She looked directly at Morgan. "What I don't know is whether two dozen will be enough to free Padishar when the time comes."

Morgan met her gaze. "Because of the Shadowen?"

"Yes, because of the Shadowen. We don't have Par with us this time to keep them at bay."

"No," Morgan agreed, "you have me instead." He reached back over his shoulder, drew out the Sword of Leah, brought it around in front of him, and jammed it dramatically into the earth. It rested there, quivering slightly, polished surface smooth and silver in the starlight. He looked at them. "And I have this."

"Your talisman," Chandos muttered in surprise. "I thought it was broken."

"It was healed when I went north," Morgan replied softly, seeing Quickening's face appear and then fade in his mind. "I have the magic back again. It will be enough to withstand the Shadowen."

Damson glanced from one face to the other, confused. Perhaps Par hadn't told her about the Sword of Leah. Perhaps he hadn't had time in the struggle to escape Tyrsis and reach the free-born. And no one knew about Quickening save for Walker Boh.

Morgan did not care to explain, and he did not try. "Can you find the men?" he asked Chandos instead.

The black eyes fixed him. "I can, Highlander. Twenty times that for Padishar Creel." He paused. "But you're asking them to place a lot of faith in you."

Morgan jerked his sword free of the earth and slid it back into its sheath. In the distance, along the bluff edge, free-born patrolled in the darkness. Behind, back against the trees, cooking fires burned low, and the clank and rattle of cookware was beginning to diminish as the meal ended and thoughts turned to sleep. Pipes were lit, small bits of light against the black, fireflies that wavered in the concealment of the trees. The sound of voices was low and easy.

Morgan looked at the big man. "If there were a better choice, Chandos, I would take it gladly." He held the other's dark gaze. "What's it to be, yes or no?"

Chandos looked at Damson, his gold earring a small glitter as his head turned. "What do you say?"

The girl brushed back her fiery hair, the look in her eyes a determined one, edged with flashes of anger and hope. "I say we have to try something or Padishar is lost." Her face tightened. "If it was us instead of him, wouldn't he come?"

Chandos rubbed at the scarred remains of his ear. "In your case, he already did, didn't he?" He shook his head. "Fools to the end, we are," he muttered to no one in particular. "All of us." He looked back at Morgan. "All right, Highlander. Two dozen men, myself included. I'll pick them tonight."

He rose abruptly. "You'll want to leave right away, I expect. First light, or as soon thereafter as we can put together supplies for the trip." He gave Morgan a wry look. "We don't have to live off the land by any chance, do we, Highlander?"

Morgan and Damson stood up with him. Morgan extended his hand to the free-born. "Thank you, Chandos."

The big man laughed. "For what? For agreeing to a madman's scheme?" He clasped Morgan's hand nevertheless. "Tell you what. If this works, it'll be me thanking you a dozen times over."

Muttering, he trudged off toward the cooking fires, carrying his empty plate, shaggy head lowered into his barrel chest. Morgan watched him go, thinking momentarily of times gone by and of places and companions left behind. The thoughts were haunting and filled with regrets for what might have been, and they left him feeling empty and alone.

He felt Damson's shoulder brush up against his arm and turned to face her. The emerald eyes were thoughtful. "He may be right about you," she observed quietly. "You may be a madman."

He shrugged. "You backed me up."

"I want Padishar free. You seem to be the only one with a plan." She arched one eyebrow. "Tell me the truth—is there any more to this scheme than what you've revealed?"

He smiled. "Not much. I hope to be able to improvise as I go along."

She didn't say anything, just studied him a moment, then took his arm and steered him out along the bluff face. They walked without saying anything for a long time, crossing from the edge of the trees to the cliffs and back again, breathing the scent of wildflowers and grasses on the wind that skipped down off the ridges of the peaks beyond. The wind was warm and soothing, like silk against Morgan's skin. He lifted his face to it. It made him want to close his eyes and disappear into it.

"Tell me about your sword," she said suddenly, her voice very quiet. Her gaze was steady despite the sudden shifting of his eyes away from her. "Tell me how it was healed—and why you hurt so much, Morgan. Because you do in some way, don't you? I can see it in your eyes. Tell me. I want to hear."

He believed her, and he discovered all at once that he did want to talk about it after all. He let himself be pulled down onto a flat-surfaced rock. Sitting next to her in the darkness, both of them facing out toward the cliffs, he began to speak.

"There was a girl named Quickening," he said, the words thick and unwieldy sounding as he spoke them. He paused and took a deep, steadying breath. "I loved her very much."

He hoped she didn't see the tears that came to his eyes.

He spent the night rolled into a blanket at the edge of the trees, body wedged within the roots of an ancient elm, head cradled by his rolled-up travel cloak. The makeshift bedding proved less than satisfactory, and he woke stiff and sore. As he shook the leaves and dust out of the cloak he realized that he had not seen Matty Roh since the night before, that he hadn't actually seen her even at dinner, although he had been pretty preoccupied with his plan for rescuing Padishar—his great and wonderful plan that on reflection in the pale first light of dawn appeared pretty makeshift and decidedly lacking in common sense. Last night it had seemed pretty good. This morning it just looked desperate.

But he was committed to it now. Chandos would have already begun preparations for the journey back to Tyrsis. There was nothing to be gained by second-guessing.

He stretched and headed for the little stream that ran down out of the rocks behind him some distance back in the trees. The cold water would help to unclog his brain, chase the sleep from his eyes. He had talked with Damson Rhee until well after midnight. He had told her everything about Quickening and the journey north to Eldwist. She had listened without saying much, and somehow it had brought them closer together. He found himself liking her more, found himself trusting her. The suspicions that had been there earlier had faded. He began to understand why Par Ohmsford and Padishar Creel had gone back for her after the Federation had taken her prisoner. He thought that he would have done the same.

Nevertheless, there was something she wasn't telling him about her relationship with the Valeman and the leader of the free-born. It was neither a deception nor a lie; it was simply an omission. She had been quick enough to acknowledge that she was in love with Par, but there was something else, something that predated her feelings for the Valeman, that formed the backbone for everything that had led to her own involvement in trying to recover the Sword of Shannara from the Pit. Morgan wasn't sure what it was, but it was there in the fabric of her tale, in the way she spoke of the two men, in the strength of her conviction that she must help them. Once or twice Morgan had almost been able to put his finger on what it was that she was keeping to herself, but each time the truth skittered just out of reach.

In any case, he felt better for having told someone about Quickening, for having given some release to the feelings he had kept bottled up inside since his return. He'd slept well after that, a dreamless rest cradled in the crook of that old tree, able to let go a little of the pain that had dogged him for so many weeks.

He heard the sound of the stream ahead, a small rippling against the silence. He crossed a clearing, pushed through a screen of brush, and found himself staring at Matty Roh.

She sat across from him at the edge of the stream, her pants rolled up and her bare feet dangling in the water. The moment he appeared she jerked away, reaching for her boots. Her feet came out of the water in a flash of white skin, disappearing into the shadow of her body almost immediately. But for just an instant he had a clear view of them, hideously scarred, the toes missing or so badly deformed that they were almost unrecognizable. Her black hair shivered in the light with the urgency of her movements as she turned her face away from him.

"Don't look at me," she whispered harshly.

Embarrassed, he turned away at once. "I'm sorry," he apologized. "I didn't know you were here."

He hesitated, then started away, following the stream toward the rocks, the picture of her feet uncomfortably clear in his mind.

"You don't have to leave," she called after him, and he stopped. "I . . . I just need a minute."

He waited, looking out into the trees, hearing voices now from just beyond where he stood, a snatch of laughter here, a quick murmur there.

"All right," she said, and he turned back again. She was standing by the stream with her pants rolled down and her boots on. "I'm sorry I snapped at you like that."

He shrugged and walked over to her. "Well, I didn't mean to surprise you. I'm still a little bit asleep, I guess."

"It wasn't your fault." She looked embarrassed as well.

He knelt by the stream and splashed water on his face and hands, used soap to wash himself, and rubbed himself dry again on a soft cloth. He could have used a bath, but didn't want to take the time. He was conscious of the girl watching him as he worked, a silent shadow at his side.

He finished and rocked back on his heels, breathing deeply the morning air. He could smell wildflowers and grasses.

"You're leaving for Tyrsis to rescue Padishar," she said suddenly. "I want to go with you."

He looked up at her in surprise. "How did you know about the rescue?"

She shrugged. "Doing what I've trained myself to do—keeping my eyes and ears open. Can I come?"

He stood up and faced her. Her eyes were level with his. He was surprised all over again at how tall she was. "Why would you want to do that?"

"Because I'm tired of standing about, of doing nothing more than listening in on other people's conversations." Her gaze was steady and determined. "Remember our conversation on the trail? I said I was waiting for something to happen? Well, it has. I want to go with you."

He wasn't sure he understood and didn't know what to say in any case. It was bad enough that Damson Rhee had to go back with them. But Matty Roh as well? On a journey as dangerous as this one would undoubtedly be?

She stepped back a pace, measuring him. "I would hate to think that you were stupid enough to be worried about me," she said bluntly. "The fact of the matter is I can take care of myself a lot better than you can. I've been doing it for a much longer time. You might remember how things went back at the Whistledown when you tried to grab me."

"That doesn't count!" he snapped defensively. "I wasn't ready—"

"No, you weren't," she cut him short. "And that is the difference between us, Highlander. You aren't trained to be ready, and I am." She stepped close again. "I'll tell you something else. I'm a better swordsman than anyone this side of Padishar Creel—and maybe as good as he is. If you don't believe me, ask Chandos."

He stared at her, at the piercing cobalt eyes, at the thin line of her lips, at the slender shoulders squared and set, everything thrust forward combatively, daring him to challenge her.

"I believe you," he said, and meant it.

"Besides," she said, not relaxing herself an inch, "you need me to make your plan work."

"How do you know about—"

"You're the wrong one to go into Tyrsis with Damson," she interrupted, ignoring his unfinished question. "It should be me."

". . . the plan?" he finished, trailing off. He put his hands on his hips, frustrated. "Why should it be you?"

"Because I won't be noticed and you will. You're too obvious, Highlander. You look exactly like what you are! Anyway, your face is known to the Federation and mine isn't. And if anything goes wrong, you don't know your way around Tyrsis, and I do. I've been there many times. Most important of all, they won't be looking for two women. We'll walk right past them, and they won't give us a second glance."

She squared up to him again. "Tell me I'm wrong," she challenged.

He smiled in spite of himself. "I guess I can't do that." He looked away into the trees, hoping the answer to her demand lay there. It didn't. He looked back again. "Why don't you ask Chandos? He's in charge, not me."

Her expression did not change. "I don't think so. At least not in this case." She paused, waiting. "Well? Can I go?"

He sighed, suddenly weary. Maybe she was right. Maybe having her along would be a good idea. She certainly gave a convincing argument. Besides, hadn't he just finished telling himself that his plan needed help? Perhaps Matty Roh was a little of what was needed.

"All right," he agreed. "You can come."

"Thanks." She turned away and started back toward the camp, her cloak slung over one shoulder.

"But Chandos has to agree, too!" he called after her, still looking for a way out.

"He already has!" she shouted back in reply. "He said to ask you."

She gave him a quick smile over her shoulder as she disappeared into the trees.

Chandos was terse and withdrawn at breakfast, and Morgan left him alone, choosing to sit instead with Damson Rhee. The long table they occupied was crowded and the men were boisterous, so the Highlander and the girl didn't say much to each other, concentrating on their food and the conversation around them. Matty Roh appeared briefly, passing next to Morgan without looking at him, on her way to someplace else. She paused long enough to say something to Chandos, which caused him to scowl deeply. Morgan didn't hear what she said but had no trouble imagining what it might be.

When the meal was concluded Chandos pushed to his feet, bellowed at everyone still seated to get to work, and called Damson and Morgan aside. He took them out of the trees and onto the open bluff once more, waiting until they were out of earshot to speak. Dark-visaged and gruff, he announced that during the night word had arrived through the free-born network that the Elves had returned to the Westland. This news was several days old and not entirely reliable, and he wanted to know what Morgan and the girl thought.

"I think it's possible," Morgan said at once. "Returning the Elves to the Westland was one of the charges given to the Ohmsfords."

"If Paranor is back, the Elves could be back as well," agreed Damson.

"And that would mean that all the charges have been fulfilled," Morgan added, growing excited now. "Chandos, we have to know if it's true."

The big man's scowl returned. "You'll want another expedition, I suppose—as if one wasn't enough!" He sighed wearily. "All right, I'll send someone to check it out, a messenger to let them know they have friends in Callahorn. If they're there, we'll find them."

He went on to add that he had chosen the men for the journey to Tyrsis and that supplies and weapons were being assembled as they spoke. Everything should be in place by midmorning, and as soon as it was they would depart.

As he turned to leave, Morgan asked impulsively, "Chandos, what's your opinion of Matty Roh?"

"My opinion?" The big man laughed. "I think she gets pretty much anything she wants." He started away again, then called back, "I also think you'd better watch your step with her, Highlander."

He went on, disappearing into the trees, yelling orders as he went.

Damson looked at Morgan. "What was that all about?"

Morgan told her about his meeting with Matty at Varfleet and their journey to Firerim Reach. He told her about the girl's insistence that she be included in their effort to rescue Padishar. He asked Damson if she knew anything about Matty Roh. Damson did not. She had never met her before.

"But Matty's right about two women attracting less attention," she declared. "And if she was able to persuade both you and Chandos that she should go on this journey, I'd say you'd both better watch out for her."

Morgan left to put together his pack for the trek south, strapped on his weapons, and went back out on the bluff. Within an hour the company that Chandos had chosen was assembled and ready to leave. It was a hard and capable-looking bunch, some of them men who had fought side by side with Padishar against the Creeper at the Jut. A few recognized Morgan and nodded companionably. Sending one man on ahead to scout for any trouble, Chandos led the rest, Morgan and Damson and Matty Roh with them, down off Firerim Reach toward the plains beyond.

They walked all day, descending out of the Dragon's Teeth to the Rabb, then turning south to cross the river and continue on toward Varfleet. They traveled quickly, steadily through the heat, the sky clear and cloudless, the sun burning down in a steady glare, causing the air above the dusty grasslands to shimmer like water. They rested at midday and ate, rested again at midafternoon, and by nightfall had reached the flats that led up into the Valley of Shale. A watch was set, dinner was eaten, and the company retired to sleep. Morgan had walked with Damson during the day, and bedded down close to her that night. While she probably neither needed nor wanted it, he had assumed a protective attitude toward her, determined that if he could not do anything for Par or Coll just at the moment, at least he could look after her.

Matty Roh had kept to herself most of the day, walking apart from everyone, eating alone when they rested, choosing to keep her own company. No one seemed all that surprised that she was along; no one seemed to question why she was there. Several times Morgan thought to speak with her, but each time he saw the set of her face and the deliberate distance she created between herself and others, and decided not to.

At midnight, restless from dreams and the anticipation of what lay ahead, he awoke and walked down to the edge of the grove of trees in which they had sheltered to look up at the sky and out across the plains. She appeared suddenly at his elbow. Silent as a ghost, she stood next to him as if she might have been expected all along. Together, they stared out across the empty stretch of the Rabb, studying the outline of the land in the pale starlight, breathing the lingering swelter of the day in the cooling night.

"The country I was born in looked like this," she said after a time, her voice distant. "Flat, empty grasslands. A little water, a lot of heat. Seasons that could be harsh and beautiful at the same time." She shook her head. "Not like the Highlands, I expect."

He didn't say anything, just nodded. A stray bit of wind ruffled her black hair. Somewhere in the distance, a wolf howled, its cry fading unanswered into silence.

"You don't know what to make of me, do you?"

He shrugged. "I suppose I don't. You're a pretty confusing person."

Her smile in response was there and gone in an instant. Her delicate features were shadowed and gave her a gaunt look in the dim light. She seemed to be working something through.

"When I was five years old," she said after a moment, "just before I reached my sixth birthday, not long after my sister died, I was out playing in a field near the house with my older brother. It was a pasture, left fallow that year. There were milk cows in it, grazing. I remember seeing one of the cows lying on its side down in a depression. It had a funny look about it, and I walked down to see what was wrong. The cow was looking at me, its eyes wide and staring, very frightened. It didn't seem to be able to cry out. It was dying, half in and half out of some sort of muddy sinkhole that I had never seen there before. Its body was being eaten away."

She folded her arms across her chest as if she was cold. "I don't know why, but I wanted a closer look. I walked right up to it, didn't stop until I was no more than several yards away. I should have called for my brother, but I was little and I didn't think to do so. I looked at the cow, wondering what had happened. And suddenly I felt this burning on the soles of my feet. I looked down and saw that I was standing in some of the same mud that the cow had gotten into. The mud was streaked with greenish lines and bubbling. It had eaten right through my shoes. I turned and ran, crying now, calling out for help. I ran as fast as I could, but the pain was faster. It went all through my feet. I remember looking down and seeing that some of my toes were gone."

She shivered at the memory. "My mother washed me as best she could, but it was too late. Half my toes were gone, and my feet were scarred and burned as if they had been set on fire. I developed a fever. I was in bed for two weeks. They thought I was going to die. But I didn't; I lived. They died instead. All of them."

Her smile was bitter and ironic. "I just thought you should know after this morning. I don't like people to see what happened to me." She looked at him briefly, then turned away again. "But I wanted you to understand."

She stood with him a moment longer, then said good-night and disappeared back into the trees. He stared after her for a long time, thinking about what she had said. When he returned to the campsite and rolled himself back into his blanket, he could not sleep. He could not stop thinking about Matty Roh.

They set out again at dawn, shadows in the faint gray light that seeped out of the east. The day was overcast, and by midday it had begun to rain. The company trudged on through the forested hill country north of Varfleet and the Mermidon, following the line of the Dragon's Teeth west. Twice the scout came back to warn of Federation patrols and they were forced to take cover until the patrols had passed. The land was gray and shone damply through the rain, and they encountered no one else. Morgan walked with Matty Roh, moving up next to her unbidden, staying with her through the day. She said nothing to discourage him and did not move away. She spoke little, but she seemed comfortable with his presence. When they stopped to eat lunch, she shared with him the small bit of fruit she was carrying.

By nightfall, they had crossed the Mermidon and come in sight of Tyrsis. The city glowed bleakly from the bluff heights as they stared up at it from across the approaching plains. Rain continued to fall, steady and unrelenting, turning the dusty earth to mud. Damson and Matty Roh would not attempt to enter the city until morning, when they could mingle with the usual tradesmen come up for the day from the surrounding villages. Chandos sent the scout on ahead to see if he could learn anything useful from travelers departing the city. The rest of the company bedded down in a grove of old maples, finding to their displeasure that dry spaces were few and far between.

It was nearing midnight when the scout returned. Morgan was still awake, huddled with Chandos and Matty Roh, all of them listening as Damson described what she knew of the tunnels beneath Tyrsis and the Federation prisons. The scout bent to whisper something to Chandos, furtive and quick. Chandos turned ashen. He dismissed the scout and turned to the Highlander and the girls.

The Federation had announced its intention to execute Padishar Creel. The execution would be public. It would take place at noon on the day after tomorrow.

Chandos got up and walked away, shaking his head. Morgan sat with Damson and Matty Roh in stunned silence. He had guessed wrong. The Federation had decided to rid itself of Padishar once and for all. The leader of the free-born had less than two days to live.

Morgan's eyes met Damson's, then Matty's. They were all thinking the same thing. Whatever rescue plan they tried, they had better get it right the first time.

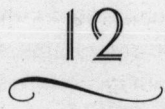

12

Wind blew across Wren Elessedil's face, cooling it against the heat of the midday sun. Her short cropped hair whipped from side to side with its passing, and the whistling rush past her ears drowned out all other sounds. There was a cadence to it that lulled and soothed de-

spite its thrust, that wrapped about in the manner of a warm cloak on a
cold night. She smiled at the feeling, closed her eyes, and gave herself over
to its embrace.

Wren was seated astride the giant Roc Spirit, flying high over the Westland forests south and east of Arborlon, approaching the Mermidon where
it brushed the vast swamp they called the Shroudslip and edged down into
the plains of the Tirfing. Tiger Ty sat in front of her, straddling Spirit's
neck where it joined the shoulders, just forward of the great wings. Both
Wing Rider and Elf Queen were strapped tightly to the bird's harness, securely fastened against the possibility of a fall. The sky was bright and cloudless, the sun's light bathing the land from horizon to horizon in melted
gold. Below, where the earth stretched away in a patchwork maze of green
and brown, it was hot and humid in the long, slow days of late summer,
and everything seemed to stand still. But here, high above the heat, where
the wind blew steady and cool, Wren soared through space and time unchecked, and there was within her that sense of escape that flight inevitably
generated.

Her eyes opened and there was bitterness in her smile. Certainly she
had spent enough time seeking escape in one form or another to recognize
the feeling, she thought.

It was ten days now since her return to the Four Lands. The nightmare
of Morrowindl was behind her and beginning to fade into the recesses of
her memory. Her sleep was still haunted by dreams of what had been—by
the monsters that had pursued the little company down Killeshan's ruptured
mountain slopes to the beaches, by the faces of those who had died in the
attempt, by the fear and anguish she had felt, and by the terrible sense of
loss that she did not think would ever leave her. She still woke from those
dreams, shaking and cold in spite of the summer heat, leaving her bed to
walk alone through the palace halls, a driven spirit. Even now Morrowindl,
gone back into the ocean in that fiery conflagration, whispered to her from
out of the past, from out of its watery grave, its voice a constant reminder
of how she had gotten to where she was and what it had cost her.

But there was little time to dwell on what had been, for the demands of
the present overshadowed everything. She was Queen of the Elves, entrusted with the safety and welfare of her people. It was the charge that Ellenroh had given her; it was the charge she had accepted. But not all those
for whom she had been given responsibility believed in her. It was not easy
convincing the Elves that she was the one who should lead them. After the
first rush of euphoria over finding themselves free of Morrowindl and
returned once again to the Westland faded, they began to question. Who
was this barely grown girl who had declared herself their queen—this girl
who was not even a pure-blooded Elf, but a mix of Elf and Man? Who had
decided that she should lead them, should govern them, should make decisions that would affect their lives? It was claimed that she was the granddaughter of Ellenroh, the daughter of Alleyne, a child of the Elessedils and

the last of them left to rule. But she was a stranger, too, come out of nowhere, unknown and untested. Who was she, that she should be queen?

Eton Shart and Barsimmon Oridio were among those who continued
to doubt—her first minister and the general of her armies, men she could
not afford to lose. They did not say so to her face or even publicly, but their
aloofness was obvious. They had served Ellenroh long and faithfully, and
they had not expected to lose her. Worse, they had not expected to find
someone they barely knew assuming her place. Certainly not an outsider,
and a girl at that. Wren understood their reticence; she also understood that
she could not permit it to continue unresolved.

Triss and the Home Guard were her real support. Triss had come with
her out of Morrowindl, had seen her struggle with the power of the Elfstones, with the demons that pursued them, and with the responsibility she
had been given. He accepted her as queen because he had been there when
Ellenroh had named her and had exacted his pledge of loyalty. Triss had declared her queen to the High Council, to the army, and especially to the
Home Guard, who were charged with her protection. The Home Guard,
unlike the other branches of the Elven government, had accepted her instantly and without reservation. Having lost Ellenroh, they were now
fiercely committed to her. Nothing would harm this queen, they swore.
This queen would have their full protection. It was the kind of support she
desperately needed, and Triss, as captain of the Home Guard, made certain
that she had it.

Still, Home Guard support alone would not be enough in the long
run. She needed to win over both the High Council and the army if she
was to be accepted as queen. That meant she needed to win over Eton
Shart and Barsimmon Oridio, and she did not know how to do that. Despite her efforts to convince them of the merits of accepting her, they remained distant and aloof, polite but decidedly cool. Time was running out.
Ten days the Elves had been back in the Westland, and by now the Federation and the Shadowen knew. For more than a century the Federation had
claimed that the Elves were the source of the land's sickening, and here at
last was an opportunity to put things right. No matter that it was the wrong
set of Elves, she mused; the Federation was hardly likely to worry about
making any distinction between good and bad. Eradicate them all and the
problem was solved.

Which was why she was flying south with Tiger Ty. The effort to begin that eradication was already under way.

Tiger Ty touched Spirit lightly along the neck, and the Roc responded
by swinging downward toward a bluff that faced out across the river. The
bird descended easily, gracefully, and in moments they were settled on a
grassy bank at the edge of a forest of broad-leaved trees. Wren disengaged
herself from the straps and climbed down, stretching her cramped muscles.
She was still not used to riding the giant Rocs, though she had done so several times now since her return. The Wing Riders had begun to come back

into the Westland as well, resettling themselves in the old Wing Hove south of the Irrybis. Wren had gone to speak to them, asking for their support, telling them of the danger they all faced if the Shadowen weren't stopped. Tiger Ty, a respected member of the community, had spoken in her behalf, adding his own rough assessment of her character. A girl who's got more sand than a dozen of us, he'd said. A girl with sharp edges, but quick-thinking and smart. A girl who's got use of the magic, but uses it with caution and respect. The Land Elves—and the Wing Riders—could do worse.

She smiled at the memory. The Wing Riders had agreed to help. Almost thirty of them were already settled at Arborlon, made a part of her personal command.

"Something to eat?" Tiger Ty asked, strolling up to her in that rolling gait he used, bowlegged and spindly. He was as grizzled and nut-brown as ever, but no longer as gruff. When he spoke to her these days there was something new in his voice—something that almost suggested deference.

She nodded, then seated herself on the grass across from him. She accepted a hunk of cheese, an apple, and a cup of ale poured from a stoppered skin. She crossed her legs and was taking a bite of the cheese when she felt a stirring against her breast. A furry face poked out of her tunic, and Faun appeared, sniffing the air tentatively.

"Ha! The Squeak doesn't miss a thing, does she?" Tiger Ty laughed, cut off a bite of his cheese, and passed it to the little creature. Faun took it from him cautiously, slipped clear of Wren's clothing, plopped down on the grass, and began to eat.

"She likes you," Wren observed.

Tiger Ty snorted. "Shows you Tree Squeaks don't have the sense of tree stumps!"

They ate in silence, finished, and sat back contentedly, staring out from the bluff across the river to where the plains of the Tirfing stretched away in an unbroken wave of dusty grasses.

"How much farther?" Wren asked after a moment.

Tiger Ty shrugged. "Another hour at most. They were traveling pretty fast when I spotted them."

A Federation army, sighted by the patrolling Wing Rider, had brought Wren out of Arborlon in spite of the objections of Triss and the Home Guard. It was necessary, she felt, to have a close look at the enemy before she brought her plan of action before the High Council and its skeptics.

She took a final drink from her cup, finishing the last of the ale. If things had been difficult up to now, she had a feeling that they were about to get a whole lot worse.

They climbed back aboard Spirit, fastened themselves in place, and lifted off into the dazzling blue. Faun was inside her tunic, snuggled down comfortably against her body. Spirit gained height, then settled into a flat glide that swept them down the snaking length of the Mermidon to where it bypassed the Shroudslip. There they left the river and began to follow the line of the Irrybis where it bordered the Tirfing east. Time slipped quickly past, and it seemed only moments later that Tiger Ty lifted one arm to point south.

A huge column of dust rose into the swelter of summer heat that hung over the plains. Tiger Ty glanced back at her and she nodded.

The Federation army.

They continued due south, following a line parallel to the army, keeping in the shadow of the cliffs. Tiger Ty would circle back around and come in from behind the army with the sun at his back. That way they would not be seen. As yet, no one knew anything about the Wing Riders. Wren had decided it would be better if things remained that way.

Swiftly they sped south, and when the column of dust was well behind them they banked left across the plains. They continued to circle until the sun was directly behind them, then swung back toward the dust. They rose higher than before, trying to place as much glare as possible at their backs in case anyone was scanning the sky.

Minutes later, the Federation army came in sight.

It was a huge, sprawling, dark stain against the sun-scorched grasslands, three companies deep, column after column of black-and-red-garbed soldiers and horsemen, great iron-and-wood fighting machines, siege equipment, wagons and supplies. The army seemed to stretch on forever, the dust of its wake obscuring everything for miles. Wren felt her heart sink at the size of the enemy. The Elves could barely muster a tenth of the fighting men the Federation had assembled, and it was reported that there were another five thousand soldiers garrisoned in Tyrsis. If they were forced to confront this army head on, the Elves would be annihilated.

Which was the general idea, of course, she thought disconsolately.

She counted lines and columns and companies carefully as Tiger Ty took Spirit close to the back of the army and then banked the Roc sharply away again, heading south once more, still within the protective glare of the sun. There had been no shouts or pointed arms from below. Apparently they had not been seen.

It took them most of the remainder of the day to make the return flight, and Wren used the time to think about what she would say to the High Council that night. She found herself thinking that it would be nice if she could just keep on flying, traveling to a place so far away that the Federation would never find her. But there was no such place, of course. For even if the Federation couldn't reach her, the Shadowen could. They had proved that on Morrowindl. The Shadowen sickness was everywhere, and no one would be safe again until a cure was found.

It was nearing sunset when Arborlon, the home city of the Elves, came in sight again, a shading of wood colors, metal stays, and spots of bright clothing amid the green. Spirit swung wide above the Rill Song, the river's blue waters turned diamond-tipped in the fading light, and settled gently down onto the grassy bluffs of the Carolan. Wren was barely out of her restraining straps and on the ground again before the Home Guard, Triss in the lead, were hurrying down from the city proper to make certain she was safe. She gave them a reassuring wave and a welcoming smile, then bent quickly to Tiger Ty.

"Not a word of what we saw," she whispered. "Not yet."

The Wing Rider's fierce black eyes locked on her. "Until you meet with the High Council?"

She nodded. "Until."

"They won't like what you have to tell them—not that that's anything new. Wooden-headed mules!"

She smiled, quick and furtive. "You know me. I just keep chipping away."

The rough face grimaced. "Do you meet with them tonight?"

"Probably within the hour."

"Mind if I sit in? Help do a little of that chipping? I pride myself on my woodcutting."

The look she gave him was filled with gratitude. "Thanks, Tiger Ty. The Wing Riders should be represented in this, too. You can most certainly sit in."

She turned away then as Triss and the others of the Home Guard reached her, relief reflected in their hard faces.

"My lady, you are well?" Triss asked quietly, his usual greeting. He was still scraped and bruised from their battle with the Wisteron on Morrowindl. His broken left arm was splinted and cradled in a cloth sling. But there was strength again in his lean face, and confidence and determination mirrored in his eyes. He had managed to put Morrowindl's ordeal behind him better than she.

"Fine," she answered, her usual reply. "I want you to call together the members of the High Council, Triss. All of them, within the hour."

"Yes, my lady," he acknowledged, and turned away, disappearing across the bluff.

Wren gave a short wave to Tiger Ty, then started after Triss, angling toward the Gardens of Life and the Elessedil palace. Lights were coming on in the treelanes and streets of the city as the shadows deepened, and the air was filled with the tantalizing aroma of cooking. She reached inside her tunic and brought Faun out to sit on her shoulder as she walked. She breathed the forest air, reaching out beyond the food smells for the tree and grass scents that lay beyond. A breeze wafted up from the river, cool and soothing in the dying heat of the day.

Home Guard fanned out around her. They would stay with her now everywhere she went, disappearing completely with the darkness, invisible protectors against any threat. She smiled. They worried so for her safety, and yet she was better able than they to protect against danger, better trained and better equipped. They thought themselves necessary, and she did not do anything to discourage that belief. But she always knew where they were, could always sense them out there watching over her, even in the deepest night. She had been trained to be aware of such things since she was a child. Her teacher had been the best.

Garth. The memories rushed through her, and she forced them away. Garth was gone.

She reached the entrance to the Gardens of Life. The Black Watch stood at attention as she approached, protectors of the Ellcrys, the tree of the Forbidding. Their eyes followed her as she passed, though she did not acknowledge them. She went into the Gardens, into their seclusion, listening to the chirps and clicks of insects come awake in the growing darkness, smelling the flowers and grasses more strongly here, the rich scent of black earth. She climbed the hill to where the Ellcrys stood and stopped in front of her. She did this every night, a ritual of sorts. At times she would do nothing but stand there, looking and thinking. At times she would reach out and touch the tree, as if to let it know that she was there. Coming to the Ellcrys seemed to renew her own strength, to give her a fresh determination to carry through with her life. The kinship she felt with the tree, with the woman it had been, with the strength of commitment embodied in the tale of how it had come into being, was sustaining. *From flesh and blood to leaves and limbs, from woman to tree, from mortal life to life everlasting.*

On her shoulder Faun rubbed against her neck as if to reassure her that everything was all right.

A cure for the Races, she mused, changing subjects if not moods, thinking again of the army that approached, of the Shadowen threat she must find a way to end. It would take more than the Elves to accomplish this, she knew. Allanon had told the Ohmsfords as much when he had sent them to fulfill their separate charges—Par to find the Sword of Shannara, Walker Boh to find the Druids and Paranor, and Wren to find the Elves. Had Par and Walker succeeded as she had? Were all the charges now fulfilled? She knew that she had to find out. Somehow she had to make contact with the others who had gathered at the Hadeshorn. On the one hand she must discover what had become of them and on the other apprise them of what had happened to her. They must be told the truth of the Shadowen, that the Shadowen were Elves who had recovered the old magic of faerie and become subverted by it in the same way as the Warlock Lord and his Skull Bearers nearly five hundred years earlier. How they had recovered this magic and how it sustained them remained a mystery. But the knowledge she held must be passed on to the others. She felt it instinctively. Until that was done, any cure for the Shadowen sickness would remain out of reach.

What to do? Already some among the Elves had gone out from Arborlon into the far reaches of the Westland to establish new homes. Farmers had begun to settle in the Sarandanon, the fertile valley that had served as the breadbasket of the Elven nation for centuries. Trappers and hunters had begun ranging north to the Breakline and south to the Rock Spur. Craftsmen were anxious to open new markets for their wares. Everywhere, there was a push to reclaim old homesteads and towns. Most important of all, Healers and their acolytes had gone forth to seek out those places in which the Westland's sickness was worst in an attempt to stem its spread—carrying on an Elven tradition that had lasted since the beginning of time. For the Elves had always been healers, a people who believed that they were one with the earth into which they were born, the purveyors of the philosophy that something must be given back to the world that sustained them. As with the Gnome Healers at Storlock, who cared for the earth's people, the Elven Healers were committed in turn to the people's earth.

But they and the farmers, trappers, hunters, traders, and others were at risk in the Westland unless the Elven army protected them against the threat mounting from without. If the Queen of the Elves could not find a way to keep the Federation at bay long enough to put an end to the Shadowen . . .

She left the thought hanging, turning away from the Ellcrys in disgust. So much was needed, and try as she might she could not provide it alone.

The sky was streaked scarlet above the trees west, a vivid smear against the mountainous horizon that had the look of blood. Or at least that was the image that flashed in Wren Elessedil's mind.

Your memories never leave you, she thought—even those you wish would, even those you wish had never been.

She walked down out of the Gardens, eyes on the ground in front of her. She wondered about Stresa. It had been days since she had seen the Splinterscat. Unlike Faun, Stresa was more comfortable in the wild and preferred the woods to the city. He had made his home somewhere close to Arborlon and would appear unexpectedly from time to time, but consistently refused to think about living with her in the Elessedil family home. Stresa was content with his new country, happy in his solitary life, and he had promised more than once that he would be there if she ever needed him. The trouble was that she needed him more than she cared to admit. But Stresa had gone through a lot for her already and was happy now; she did not have the right to place fresh demands on him just to assuage her own insecurity.

Still, she missed him greatly. Stresa, that strange and unpredictable creature from the world that had cost the Elves so much, would always be her friend.

It was dark now, the sun disappeared entirely beneath the horizon west, the stars a scattering of pinprick lights, the moon a fading crescent east above the treetops, the night's sounds gentle and soothing and filled with the promise of sleep. Would that it were so for her, she thought. Sleep would come hard this night, harder than most, for she must meet with the High Council and determine the fate of the Elves. And of herself, perhaps, as well.

She walked from the Gardens, passing the Black Watch once more, listening to the barely discernible sounds of the Home Guard shadowing her. Sometimes she found herself wishing she were a Rover girl again and nothing more, her life made simple anew, all of the constraints of her stewardship lifted, her freedom restored. She would give up being queen. She would give up the Elfstones, those three blue talismans that nestled within the leather bag hung about her neck, the symbol of the magic that had been bequeathed to her by her mother, of the power she had been given to wield. She would shed her life as if it were a season's skin grown old, and she would become . . .

What? What would she become, she wondered?

In truth, she no longer knew—maybe because it no longer mattered.

When she walked into the chambers of the High Council barely a quarter of an hour later, those she had summoned were waiting, seated about the council table at which the queen presided. She entered with Tiger Ty trailing (he had remained outside until now, uncertain of his welcome in her absence) and walked directly to her seat at the head of the table. Everyone rose in deference, but she perfunctorily waved them back into their seats.

The room was cavernous. High walls of stone and wood supported a star-shaped ceiling formed of massive oak beams. The High Council was dominated at the far end by a dais which supported the throne of the Elven Kings and Queens and which was flanked by the standards of the ruling Elven houses and at its center by the ancient twenty-one-chair round table. Benches forming gallery seats for public viewing when the full Council was in session ran the length of either wall.

There were six members present this night besides herself, the full complement of the High Council's inner circle. Triss was there, as Captain of the Home Guard; Eton Shart as First Minister; Barsimmon Oridio as General of the Elven Armies; Perek Arundel as Minister of Trade; Jalen Ruhl as Minister of Home Defense; and Fruaren Laurel as Minister of Healing. Only Laurel was new, appointed on the Council's recommendation when Wren told them she wanted a minister responsible for overseeing efforts to heal the Elven Westland. Laurel was cooperative and hardworking, a woman in her middle years with a steady, likeable disposition; but like Wren she was unproven. She held a secondary position in the eyes of the remainder of the Council. Wren liked her but wasn't sure she could be counted on in a fight.

She would find out tonight.

She stood in front of her chair and faced the High Council. "I asked Wing Rider Tiger Ty to sit in on this session of the Council since the subject matter directly concerns his people." She made it a statement of fact and did not ask approval. She beckoned the gnarled Wing Rider forward from where he stood by the door. "Sit there, please," she said, indicating a vacant seat by Fruaren Laurel.

Tiger Ty sat. The chamber went very still as those assembled waited for Wren to speak. The doors leading in were closed, sealed by the Home Guard on Wren's orders until such time as she permitted them to be opened again. Torches burned in brackets affixed to the stone of the walls and in free-standing stanchions at the front and back of the room. Smoke rose toward the ceiling and dispersed through air loops high overhead. The smoke left a faint coppery taste to the chamber air.

Wren straightened. She had not bothered to change her clothes, deciding she would not make the concession to the dictates of formality. They would have to accept her as she was. She had left Faun in her chambers. She would have wished for Cogline or Walker Boh or any of those who had stood with her once and were now dead or scattered, but wishing for help from any quarter was pointless. If she was to succeed this night in what she intended to do, she would have to do it on her own.

"Ministers, Council Members, my friends," she began, looking from face to face, her voice measured and calm. "We have all come a very long way from where we were only weeks ago. We have seen a great many changes take place in the life of the Elven people. None of us could have foreseen what would happen; maybe some of us wish things had turned out differently. But here we are, and there is no going back. Morrowindl is behind us forever, and the Four Lands are before us. When we agreed to come back, we knew what would be waiting for us—a struggle with the Federation, with the Shadowen, with Elven magic hideously subverted, with our past brought forward to become our future. We knew what would be waiting, and now we must face it."

She paused, her gaze steady. "Yesterday the Wing Riders spotted a Federation army coming up from the deep Southland. Today, with Tiger Ty, I flew south to have a look for myself. We found the army within the Tirfing, a day's march above the Myrian. The army is ten times ours and travels with siege and war machines and supplies to sustain it well into another month. It comes north and west. It comes in search of us. If I were to guess, I would say it would reach us in another ten days."

She stopped, waiting for a response. Her eyes traveled from face to face.

"Ten times ours?" Barsimmon Oridio repeated doubtfully. "How accurate is your estimation, my lady?"

Wren had been anticipating this. She gave him a count, column by column, company by company, machines and wagons, foot soldiers and horsemen, leaving nothing out. When she was finished, the general of her armies was pale.

"An army of that size will wipe us out," said Eton Shart quietly. As always, he was composed, his hands folded on the table before him, his expression unreadable.

"If we engage it," Jalen Ruhl amended. The minister of defense was slight and stoop-shouldered, his voice a deep rumble in his narrow chest. "The Westland is a big place."

"Are you suggesting we hide?" Barsimmon Oridio demanded incredulously.

"Hiding won't work," Eton Shart interjected shortly. "We can't leave the city or we give up the Ellcrys. If the Ellcrys is destroyed, the Forbidding comes down. Better we all perish than that happen."

There was a long pause as the ministers glanced at each other doubtfully.

"A concession of some sort, perhaps?" Perek Arundel suggested, ever the compromiser. He was handsome in a soft way, rather vain, but shrewd and quick-thinking. He looked about. "There must be a way to make peace with the Coalition Council."

Again Eton Shart shook his head. "It was tried before. The Coalition Council is a puppet of the Shadowen. Any compromise will involve occupation of the Westland and agreement to serve the Federation. I don't think we came all the way back from Morrowindl to embrace a lifetime of that."

He looked at Wren. "What are your thoughts, my lady? I am certain you have assessed the situation on your own."

Again she was ready. "It seems our choices are these. Either we fortify Arborlon and await the Federation army here or we take our army out to meet them."

"Go out to meet them?" Barsimmon Oridio was aghast. His heavy frame shifted combatively, and his aged face furrowed. "You have said yourself they have ten times our strength. What point would there be in forcing a battle?"

"It would give us the advantage of not letting them dictate time and place and circumstance," she replied. She was still standing, keeping her vantage point so that she could continue to look down at them and they up at her. "And I said nothing about forcing a battle."

Again there was silence. Barsimmon Oridio flushed. "But you said that—"

"She said we could go out and meet them," Eton Shart interrupted. He was sitting forward now, interested. "She did not say anything about fighting them." His gaze stayed on Wren. "But what would we do once we were out there, my lady?"

"Harass them. Draw them off. Hit and run. Whatever it takes to delay them. Fight them if we get a chance to hurt them badly, but avoid a direct confrontation where we would lose."

"Delay them," the first minister repeated thoughtfully. "But sooner or later they will catch up to us—or reach Arborlon. Then what?"

"We would be better off spending the time setting traps, fortifying the city, and gathering in supplies," Perek Arundel offered. "We withstood the demons when the Ellcrys failed two hundred years ago. We can withstand the Federation as well."

Barsimmon Oridio grunted and shook his head. "Study your history, Perek. The gates to the city were taken and we were overrun. If the young girl Chosen hadn't transformed into the Ellcrys anew, it would have been over for us." He swung his heavy head away. "Besides, we had allies in that fight—not many, but a few, some Dwarves and the Legion Free Corps."

"Perhaps we shall have allies again," Wren declared suddenly, bringing all eyes back to her. "There are free-born in the mountains north of Callahorn, a sizable number, the Dwarf Resistance in the Eastland, and the Troll nations north. Some of them might be persuaded to help us."

"Not likely," the general of her armies said gruffly, incisively, declaring the matter at an end. "Why should they?"

Wren had brought the discussion to where she wanted it; she had the Council listening to her, looking for an answer to what seemed an unsolvable dilemma.

She straightened. "Because we'll give them a reason, Bar." She used his nickname easily, familiarly, the way Ellenroh had. "Because we'll give them something they didn't have before. Unity. The Races united against their enemies in a common cause. A chance to destroy the Shadowen."

Eton Shart smiled faintly. "Words, my lady. What do they mean?"

She faced him. He was her biggest hurdle in this business. She had to have his support. "I'll tell you what they mean, Eton. They mean that for the first time in three centuries we have a chance to win." She paused for emphasis. "Do you remember what brought me in search of the Elves, First Minister? Let me tell the story once again."

And she did, all of it, from the journey to the Hadeshorn and the Shade of Allanon to the search for Morrowindl and Arborlon. She repeated Allanon's charges to the Ohmsfords. She had shown no one the Elfstones save Triss, but she brought them out now as she finished her tale, dumped them in her hand, and held them out to be seen.

"This is my legacy," she said, shifting the hand with the Elfstones from face to face. "I did not want it, did not ask for it, and more than once have wished it gone. But I promised my grandmother I would use it on behalf of the Elves and I will. Magic to combat magic. The Shadowen must deal with me and with the others the shade of Allanon has called upon—my kindred in some instances, but whoever is destined to wield the Sword of Shannara and the Druid power. I think all the talismans have been brought back, not just the Elfstones—all the magics that the Shadowen fear. If we can combine their power and unite the men and women of the free-born and the Resistance and perhaps even the Trolls of the Northland, we have the chance we need to win this fight."

Eton Shart shook his head. "There are a great many conditions attached to all of this, my lady."

"Life is filled with conditions, First Minister," she replied. "Nothing is guaranteed. Nothing is assured. Especially for us. But remember this. The Shadowen come from us, and their magic is ours. We created them. We gave them life through our misguided efforts to recapture something that was best left in the past. Like it or not, they are our responsibility. Ellenroh knew this when she decided we must come back into the Four Lands. We are here, First Minister, to set things right. We are here to put an end to what we started."

"And you will lead us in this, of course?"

He put just enough emphasis on the question to convey his own doubts that she possessed the strength and ability to do so. Wren fought down her anger.

"I am Queen," she pointed out quietly.

Eton Shart nodded. "But you are very young, my lady. And you have not ruled long. You must expect some hesitation from those of us who have helped govern longer."

"What I expect is your support, First Minister."

"Unconditional support for anyone would be foolish."

"A reluctance to acknowledge that there may be wisdom in youth would be foolish as well. Get to the point."

Eton Shart's bland face tightened. There was an uncomfortable shifting about the table. No one was looking at him. He was as alone in this as Wren.

"I am not questioning you . . ." he began.

"Yes, you are, First Minister," she snapped.

"You must remember that I was not there when you were named Queen, my lady, and I—"

"Stop right there!" She was furious now, and she did not bother to hide it. "You are right, Eton Shart. You were not there. You were not there to see Ellenroh Elessedil die. Or Gavilan. Or the Owl. Or Eowen Cerise. You were not there to see Garth give his life for ours in our fight against the Wisteron. You did not have to help him die, First Minister, as I did, because to let him live would have condemned him to become one of the Shadowen!"

She steadied herself with an effort. "I gave up everything to save the Elves—my past, my freedom, my friends, everything. I do not begrudge that. I did it because my grandmother asked it of me, and I loved her. I did it because the Elves are my people, and while I have been gone from them a long time I am still one of them. One of you, First Minister. I am finished explaining myself. I have nothing to answer for to you or anyone. Either I am Queen or I am not. Ellenroh believed me so. That was enough for me; it ought to be enough for you. This debate ends here."

She let her gaze rest heavily on Eton Shart. "We must be friends and allies, First Minister, if we are to have any chance against the Federation and the Shadowen. There must be trust between us, not doubt. It will not always be easy, but we must work to understand each other. We must support and encourage, not belittle and deride. There is no room in our lives for anything less. Though we might wish it otherwise, we must accept what fate has decreed for us."

She took a deep breath, looking away to the others. "As Ellenroh once did, I ask for your support. I think we must go out to meet the Federation army and deal with it as we determine best. I think we shall discover that there are others who will help us. Hiding will gain us nothing. Isolating ourselves is exactly what the Federation hopes for. We must not give them the satisfaction of finding us frightened and alone. We are the oldest people on the earth, and we must act the part. We must provide leadership for the people of the other, younger Races. We must give them hope."

She looked at them. "Who stands with me?"

Triss rose at once. Tiger Ty rose with him, looking decidedly awkward. Then, to her pleasant surprise, Fruaren Laurel, who had not said a word the entire time, stood up as well.

She waited. Four stood, four remained seated. Of the four who stood, only three were members of the High Council. Tiger Ty was only an emissary of his people. If nothing changed, Wren lacked the support she needed.

She turned her gaze on Eton Shart, then held out her hand to him, a gesture at once conciliatory and challenging. He stared at her in surprise, eyes questioning. He hesitated momentarily, undecided, then reached out to accept her hand and rose. "My lady," he acknowledged, and bowed. "As you say, we must stand together."

Barsimmon Oridio rose, too. "Better a gamecock than a plucked chicken," he grumbled. He shook his head, then looked at Wren with something akin to admiration in his aging eyes. "Your grandmother would have advised us in the same way, my lady."

Jalen Ruhl and Perek Arundel stood up reluctantly, casting helpless glances at each other as they did so. They were not persuaded, but they did not care to stand alone against her. Wren gave them a gracious nod. She would take what she could get.

"Thank you," she said quietly. She squeezed Eton Shart's hand and released it. "Thank you all. Let us remember in the days that come what we have committed to this night. Let us remember to let our belief and trust in each other sustain us."

She looked about the table, at each face, at the way their eyes were fixed on her. For that moment, at least, she had bound them to her, and she was indeed their queen.

13

Walker Boh deliberated for two days before he again tried to escape the Shadowen siege of Paranor.

Perhaps he wouldn't have gone even then, but he found himself slipping into a dangerous state of mind. The more he thought about various ways of breaking free, the more it seemed he needed to consider further. Each plan had its flaws, and each flaw became magnified as it was held up this way and that for examination. Nothing he conceived seemed exactly right, and the harder he worked at discovering a foolproof method of gaining his escape, the more he began to doubt himself. Finally it became apparent that if he allowed himself to go on, he would lose all confidence and in the end be unable to act at all.

It was all part of a game that the Shadowen were playing with him, he was afraid.

His first encounter with the Four Horsemen had left him physically battered, but those injuries were not the ones that troubled him. It was the psychological damage that refused to mend, that lingered within like a fever. Walker Boh had always been in control of his life, able to manipulate events around him and to keep intrusions at bay. He had accomplished this mostly by isolating himself within the familiar confines of Darklin Reach, where the dangers to be faced and problems to be solved were familiar and within the purview of his enormous capabilities. He had command of magic, intelligence coupled with extraordinary insight, and other assorted abilities that ranged from the intuitive to the acquired—all of which were far superior to those of anyone against whom he chose to direct them.

But that was changed. He had crossed out of Darklin Reach and come into the outside world. This was his home now, the cottage at Hearthstone reduced to ashes, the life he had known gone into another time. He had traveled a road that had altered his existence as surely as dying. He had taken up Allanon's charge and followed it through to its conclusion. He had re-covered the Black Elfstone and brought back Paranor. He had become the first of the new Druids. He was someone entirely different than the person he had been only weeks ago. That change had given him new insight, strength, knowledge, and power. But it had also exposed him to new re-sponsibilities, expectations, challenges, and enemies. It remained to be de-cided if the former would be sufficient to overcome the latter. For the moment at least, the matter was unresolved. Walker Boh might fall and be lost forever—or he might find a way to climb back to safety. He was a man hanging from a precipice.

The Shadowen knew this. They had come for him as soon as they had discovered that Paranor was returned. Walker was still a child in his role as Druid, and now was the time when he would be most vulnerable. Besiege him, frustrate him, distract his development, kill him if possible, but cripple him at all costs—that was the plan.

And the plan was working. Walker had come back into Paranor, after his first aborted attempt at escape, aware of several very unpleasant truths. First, he did not possess sufficient power to break free in a head-to-head confrontation. The Four Horsemen were his equal and more, their magic a match for his own. Second, he could not slip past them undetected. Third, and worst of all, their experience was superior to his own—and they did not fear him. They had come looking for him. They had done so openly, without subterfuge. They had challenged him, daring him to come out and fight them. They circled Paranor in open disdain of what he might do. He was a prisoner in his own castle, reduced to trying to come up with a plan that would let him be free, and the Four Horsemen were betting he couldn't do it. It was possible, he was forced to admit, that they were right.

"You are working too hard at this," Cogline advised him finally, finding him back on the walls, staring down at the wraiths circling below. He looked gaunt and pale, ragged and worn. "Look at you, Walker. You barely sleep. You take no notice of your appearance—you have not bathed since your return. You do not eat."

A frail hand rubbed at the whiskers of the old man's chin. "Think, Walker. This is what they want. They are afraid of you! If they weren't, they would simply force the gates and finish this business. But that won't be necessary if you can be made to doubt yourself, to panic, to forgo the caution and resolve that got you this far. If that happens, they will have won. Sooner or later, they think, you will do something foolish, and then they will have you."

It was the most that Cogline had said to him since his return. Walker stared at him, at the ancient, weather-beaten face, at the stick-thin body, at the arms and legs jutting from his robes like poles. Cogline had welcomed him back with reassurances, but mostly he had seemed removed and distant— just as he had for those few days before Walker had first tried to go out. Something was happening with Cogline, some secret conflict, but Walker had been too preoccupied with his own problems then, as he was now, to take time to decipher what it was.

Nevertheless, he let the old man lead him down from the parapets to the inner shell of the castle and a hot meal. He ate without enthusiasm, drank a little ale, and decided that a bath was a good idea after all. He sat in the steaming water, letting it cleanse him inside and out, feeling the heat soothe and relax his body and mind. Rumor kept him company, curled up against the side of the tub as if to share its warmth. While Walker dried himself and dressed again, he pondered the enormous calm of the moor cat, the facade that all cats assumed as they regarded the world about them, considering it in their own impenetrable way. A little of that calm would be useful, he thought.

Then his thoughts shifted abruptly.

What was wrong with Cogline?

He left his own troubles behind with the bathwater and went out to find the old man. He came on him in the library, reading once more the Druid Histories. Cogline looked up as he entered, startled by his appearance or by something it suggested—Walker could not tell which.

Walker sat beside him on a carved, cushioned bench. "Old man, what is it that bothers you?" he asked quietly. He reached out to place a reassuring hand on the other's thin shoulder. "I see the worry in your eyes. Tell me."

Cogline shrugged in an exaggerated manner. "I worry for you, Walker. I know how strange everything seems to you since . . . well, since all this began. It cannot be easy. I keep thinking there must be something I can do to help."

Walker looked away. *Since the Black Elfstone,* he thought. *Since Allanon made himself a part of me, come in through the magic left to keep Paranor safe until the Druids' return. Strange is hardly the word for it.*

"You need not worry for me," he replied, his smile ironic. *At least not about that.* The warring within of the past and the present had faded as the two assimilated, and the lives and knowledge of the Druids had become his own. He thought of the way the magic had churned through him, burning away defenses until there had been nothing left for him to do but to accept it as his own.

"Walker." Cogline was staring at him, focused now. "I do not think Allanon would have put you through this if he did not believe that it would leave you with sufficient power to stand against the Shadowen."

"You have more faith than I."

Cogline nodded solemnly. "I always have, Walker. Didn't you know that? But my faith will be yours as well one day. It simply takes time. I have been given that time and used it to learn. I have been alive a long time now, Walker. A long time. Faith is a part of what gives me the strength to go on."

Walker took his hand away. "I had faith in myself. I had it when I knew who and what I was. But that has changed, old man. I am someone and something else entirely, and I am being asked to place my faith in a stranger. It is hard for me to do that."

"Yes," Cogline agreed. "But it will happen—if you give it time."

"If I have the time to give," Walker Boh finished.

He went out again. Rumor trailed, a black shadow slipping from lamplight to lamplight in the gloom, head swaying rhythmically, tail switching. Walker was aware of him without thinking of him, his thoughts turned again to the Shadowen without.

There must be a way . . .

Strength alone was not enough. The power of the Druid magic was impressive, but it had never been enough by itself even for those Druids come and gone. Knowledge was necessary as well. Cleverness. Resolve. Unpredictability. This last most of all, perhaps—an intangible that was the special province of survivors. Did he have it? he wondered suddenly. What did he have besides what the Druid magic had given him that he could call upon? He had made much out of the fact that nothing done to him by the Druids would change who he was. But was that so? If so, then what part of himself could he call upon now to enable him to believe in himself once again?

And wasn't that the key to everything? That he believe in himself enough that he should not despair?

He went back up to the battlements, Rumor trailing. The night was clear and bright with stars, and the air smelled clean and fresh. He breathed it deeply as he walked atop the walls, not looking down at what waited there, letting his thoughts slip free as he went, unburdened. He found himself thinking about Quickening, the daughter of the King of the Silver River, the elemental who had given everything to restore life to a land of stone, to give the earth a chance to heal. He pictured her face and listened in his memory to her voice. He felt the slight weight of her that last time as he carried her to the edge of Eldwist, the sense of sureness that had emanated from her, the sense of power. Dying, she was fulfilling her promise. It was what she had wanted. But she had bequeathed some part of her life to him, a sense of purpose and need, a resolve that he would do in life what she could only do in death.

He stopped, staring out at the night. How far he had traveled, he thought in genuine amazement. How long a journey it had been. All to reach this point, to arrive at this place and time.

He paused in his meandering, faced inward to the castle spires, to the walls and towers that loomed over him, rising darkly into the night. Was this where his life was supposed to end? he wondered suddenly. Was this where the journey finally stopped?

It had been a pointless struggle if that was so.

He turned and looked down over the wall. One of the Horsemen was passing directly below, a faint luminescence against the dark. Death, he thought, but it was hard to tell. It made no difference in any case. Names notwithstanding, identities assumed aside, they were all Death in one form or another. Shadowen killers lacking use and purpose beyond their ability to destroy. Why had they allowed themselves to become so? What choice had made them thus?

He watched that rider fade and waited for the next. All night they would patrol and at dawn assemble once more before the gates to issue their challenge anew . . .

He caught himself. All together, before the gates.

A glimmer of hope flickered in his mind. What if he were to answer that challenge?

His face grim-set, he wheeled from the wall and went down the battlements in search of Cogline.

Dawn arrived with a silvering of the eastern skies that hinted of mist and heat. The air was still and sultry even this early, a remnant of yesterday's swelter, a promise that this summer did not intend to give way easily to autumn. Birds sounded their calls in snappish, weary tones, as if unwilling to herald the morning's start.

The Four Horsemen were assembled before the gates, lined up in the grayness on their nightmare mounts. The serpents clawed distractedly at the earth as their riders sat mutely before Paranor's high walls, specters without voice, lives without balance. As the light crested the tips of the Dragon's Teeth, War urged his monstrous carrier forward, lifted his armored hand, and struck the gate with a hollow thud. The sound lingered in the silence that followed, an echo that disappeared into the trees and the gloom. The gate shuddered and went still.

War started to turn away.

Walker Boh was waiting. He was already outside the walls, come through a hidden door in a tower barely fifty feet away. He was cloaked by his magic in a spell of invisibility, shrouded in the touch and look and smell of ancient stone so that he appeared just another part of Paranor. They had not been looking for him. Even if they had, he believed he would not have been discovered.

He brought up his good arm, the magic already summoned, gathered within until it was white-hot, and he sent it hurtling toward the Shadowen.

The magic exploded into War and cut the unsuspecting wraith entirely in half. The serpent mount bolted, War's legs and lower torso still clinging to it, and disappeared.

Walker struck again. The magic hammered into the remaining three, catching them bunched tightly together and entirely unprepared. Fire exploded everywhere, engulfing them. The serpents reared and clawed in fury, wheeling about in an effort to escape. Walker sent the fire in front of their eyes so that they could not see and into their nostrils so that they could not smell, so that it clogged their senses and drove them mad. The Shadowen slammed up against one another, blinded and confused.

I've got them! Walker thought in elation.

His strength was draining from him fast, but he did not relent. He dropped the spell of invisibility, saving as much of himself as he could, and pressed the attack further, willing the magic into fire, willing the fire to consume. One of the Horsemen broke free, steaming and spitting like embers kicked by a boot. It was Pestilence, the strange body come apart into a buzzing swarm of darkness, all of its shape and definition lost. Famine had gone down, horse and rider writhing on the earth in a desperate effort to extinguish the flames that were consuming them. Death spun out of control, wheeling in a frenzy.

Then the impossible happened. Through smoke and flame, come back from where it had fled stricken and ruined, War reappeared atop its serpent mount.

But War had become whole again.

Walker stared in disbelief. He had severed the Horseman at the midpoint of its body, seen the top half fall away, and now War was back together, looking as if nothing had been done to it at all.

It charged Walker, closing the distance between them, armored body leaning forward eagerly, metal gleaming in the faint dawn light. Walker could hear the thunder of the clawed feet, the rasp of breathing, the shriek of armor, and the whistle of air giving way before its coming.

It wasn't possible!

Instinctively Walker shifted the magic to meet the attack, gathering it in one final burst. It caught the Horseman and its mount in a whirlwind of fire and spun them away, sweeping them off the pathway circling the castle and down into the trees where they disappeared with a crash.

But there was no time to follow up the attack. The remaining Horsemen had recovered themselves. Death pivoted toward him, gray-cloaked and hooded, gleaming scythe lowered. Pestilence followed, hissing like a sackful of snakes, its body taking shape as it came. Walker cut Death's serpent's legs from beneath it and sent both tumbling in a heap. By then Pestilence was almost on top of him. He jumped aside, cat quick. But the Horseman's outstretched fingers grazed him as it passed.

Instantly a wave of nausea swept through Walker. He dropped to his knees, weakened and dazed. *Just a touch had been all!* He swung about to track Pestilence and sent a new lance of fire into the Shadowen's dark back. Pestilence broke apart in a swarm of black flies.

Everything seemed to slow down for Walker Boh. He watched Famine approach in a heavy, sluggish, lurching rush. He tried to respond, but his strength seemed to have deserted him. He was aware of the day beginning, of new light brightening the eastern horizon, diffusing in thick, syrupy streamers across the trailing robes of departing night. He could feel the air, could taste and smell it, the scents of fresh leaves and grasses mingling with dust and heat. Paranor was a monstrous stone shadow at his elbow, close enough to touch and yet impossibly far.

He should not have dropped his cloak of invisibility. He had lost any advantage he had possessed.

He sent fire lancing into Famine and turned its attack aside, the Horseman's skeletal body hunching and breaking apart from the blow.

Dead, but not really, Walker thought, feeling himself turning feverish and hot.

The horsemen swarmed back from all directions, serpents rising up and converging on him. Why wouldn't they die? How could they keep coming? The questions rolled thickly off his tongue, and he was aware suddenly that he was speaking them aloud, that a sort of delirium was settling in. He was impossibly weak as he stumbled back toward the wall, mustering his strength to face the renewed rush. His plan was falling apart. He had misjudged something. What was it?

He lifted his arm and sent the fire sweeping in all directions, scattering it into his attackers in a desperate effort to keep them at bay. But his strength was depleted now, expended in his initial attack, siphoned away by Pestilence. The magic barely slowed the Shadowen, who broke through its screen and came on. War threw a jagged-edged mace at him, and he watched it hurtle toward him, unable to act. At the last moment he summoned magic enough to deflect it, but still the iron struck him a glancing blow, spinning him backward into Paranor's stone with such force that the breath was knocked from him.

The blow saved his life.

As he clawed at the stone of Paranor's wall to keep himself from falling, he found the seam of the hidden door. For an instant his head cleared, and he remembered that he had left himself a way to escape if things went wrong. He had forgotten it in the rage of battle, in the grip of the fever and delirium. He still had a chance. The Four Horsemen were bearing down on him, closing impossibly fast. The fingers of his hand raced along the hidden door's seam, numb and bloodied. If only he had two hands, two arms! If only he was whole! The thought was there and gone in an instant, the despair that summoned it banished by his fury.

There was a shriek of metal and claws.

His fingers closed on the release.

The door swung inward, carrying him with it, a shapeless bundle of robes. As it did, he threw back into the space it left shards of fire as sharp as razors. He heard them tear into his pursuers, thought that perhaps he heard the Shadowen scream somewhere inside his mind.

Then he was in musty, cool darkness, the sound and fury shut away with the closing of the door, the battle over.

Cogline found him in the passageway beneath the castle's ramparts, curled in a ball, so exhausted he could not bring himself to move. With considerable effort, the old man brought Walker to his bed and laid him in it. He undressed him, sponged him with cool, clean water, gave him medicines, and wrapped him in blankets to sleep. He spoke words to Walker, but Walker could not seem to decipher them. Walker replied, but what he said was unclear. He knew that he was alive, that he had survived to fight another day, and that was all that mattered.

Shivering, aching, bone-weary from his struggle, he let himself be settled in and left in darkness to rest. He was conscious of Rumor curling up beside him, keeping watch against whatever might threaten, ready to summon Cogline if need required it. He swallowed against the dryness in his throat, thinking that the sickness would pass, that he would be well again when he woke. Determined that he would be.

His eyes closed, but as they did so his mind locked tightly on a final, healing thought.

The battle had been lost this day. The Four Horsemen had broken him again. But he had learned something from his defeat—something that ultimately would prove their undoing.

He took a long slow breath and let it out again. Sleep swept through his body in warm, relaxing waves.

The next time he faced the Shadowen, he promised himself before drifting off, sheathing his oath in layers of iron resolve, he would put an end to them.

14

While Walker Boh was fighting to break free of the Four Horsemen at Paranor, Wren Elessedil was convincing the Elven High Council to engage the Federation army marching north to destroy them, and Morgan Leah was leading Damson and a small company of free-born to rescue Padishar Creel at Tyrsis, Par Ohmsford was tracking his brother, Coll.

It was an arduous, painstaking effort. When Damson and he had separated, he had begun his search immediately, aware that Coll was only minutes ahead of him, thinking that if he was quick enough, he would surely catch up to him. Sunrise had broken, the darkness that might have hampered his efforts fading to scattered shadows and patches of mist that lingered in the trees. Coll was fleeing in mindless disregard of everything but the vision shown him by the Sword of Shannara. He was confused and terrified; his pain had been palpable. In such a state, how much effort would he make to conceal his flight? How far could he run before exhaustion overtook him?

The answer was not the one Par had anticipated. Although he was able to follow his brother's tracks easily enough, the trail clear amid a wreckage of brush and grasses, he found himself unable to gain ground. Despite everything—or perhaps because of it—Coll seemed to have discovered within himself unexpected strength. He was running from Par, not just hastening away, and he was not pausing to rest. Nor was he running in a straight line. He was charging all over the place, starting out in one direction and then within moments reversing himself, not for any discernible reason, but seemingly out of whim. It was as if he had gone mad, as if demons pursued him, shut inside his head so that he could not determine from where they came.

And, indeed, Par thought as he followed after, it must seem so to Coll.

By nightfall, he was exhausted. His face and arms were streaked with dust and sweat, his hair was matted in clumps, and his clothes were filthy. Having discarded everything else to lighten his load and give him more speed, he was carrying only the Sword of Shannara, a blanket, and a water skin. Nevertheless, he could still barely walk. He wondered how Coll had managed to stay ahead of him. His fear should have exhausted him hours ago. The Mirrorshroud and its Shadowen magic must be driving his brother like a whip would an animal. The thought made Par despair. If Coll did not slow, if he did not regain even some small measure of his judgment, the exertion would kill him. Or if the exertion didn't, then some mistake brought on by careless disregard for personal safety would. There were dangers in this country that could kill a man even when he was employing a healthy measure of caution and common sense. At the moment, it seemed, Coll Ohmsford was possessed of neither.

When he stopped finally, Par found himself just west of where the Mermidon divided, one tributary running east toward the Rabb, the other turning south toward Varfleet and the Runne. Follow the second branch far enough and you would reach the Rainbow Lake. You would also reach Southwatch. That was the direction that Coll had been traveling when it had grown too dark to follow his trail farther. The more Par considered the matter, the more it seemed that his brother had been following that path all along—albeit in a meandering way. Back to Southwatch and the Shad-owen. It made sense, if the magic of the cloak was subverting Coll.

Par wrapped up in his blanket and propped himself against the rough surface of an old shagbark hickory to think things through. The Sword of Shannara lay on the ground next to him, and his fingers traced the outline of the carved hilt with its raised hand and burning torch. If the Shadowen magic was controlling his brother, Coll might not have any idea at all what he was doing. He might have come looking for Par without knowing why; he might be fleeing now in the same condition. Except that the Sword had shown Coll the same vision it had shown Par, so that meant Coll had seen the truth about himself. Par had felt a bonding in those moments; Coll had been joined to him long enough for both to see. Had that changed things in any way? Having seen the truth about himself, was he trying to shake free of the Shadowen magic?

Par closed his eyes tightly against the strain of his weariness. He needed to sleep but was unwilling to do so until he had figured out what was hap-pening. Damson had warned him that the pursuit was probably some sort of trap. Coll did not just happen on them. He had been sent by the Shad-owen. Why? To hurt him or to kill him? Par wasn't sure. How had Coll managed to find him? How long had he been searching? The questions buzzed through his mind like angry hornets, intrusive and demanding, stingers poised. *Think!* Perhaps the magic of the cloak had let Coll find him—had driven Coll to find him. The magic had infected his brother, had turned him into the Shadowen thing, all the while Coll believing it was helping him escape his captors, fooled into donning it so that it could begin its work, tricked . . .

Par took a deep breath. He could barely breathe at all, picturing Coll as one of them, one of the things in the Pit, the things that were living even when they were already dead.

He drank some water because water was all he had. How long had it been since he had eaten? he wondered. Tomorrow he would have to forage or hunt. He needed to regain his strength. No food and little rest would eventually catch up to him. He could not afford to be foolish if he was to be of any use to his brother.

He forced his thoughts back to Coll, wrapping the blanket closer in the gathering night. It was cool in the trees by the river, the summer heat ban-ished to other realms. If Coll had not come to kill him, why had he come? Not for any good reason surely. Coll was not Coll now.

Par blinked. To steal the Sword of Shannara perhaps?

The idea was intriguing, but it made no sense. Why would Rimmer Dall hand the Sword over to Par only to dispatch Coll later to steal it back? Unless Coll was someone else's tool. But that made even less sense. There was only one enemy here, despite all of the First Seeker's protestations. Rimmer Dall had gone to a great deal of trouble to make Par think he had killed his brother. The Shadowen had sent Coll for a reason, but it was not to steal back the Sword of Shannara.

Par let himself consider for a moment how odd it was that the Sword had finally revealed itself to him. He had tried everything to trigger the magic, and until then nothing had worked. He had always believed that it really was the talisman, that it was not a fake, even though Rimmer Dall had given it to him willingly. He had sensed its power, even when it did not respond to him. But the doubts had persisted, and more than once he had despaired. Now suddenly, unexpectedly, the magic had been brought to life, all because of his struggle with Coll.

And Par didn't have a clue as to why.

He slid down the tree trunk until he was resting on his back, staring up through the leafy boughs of the hickory at the clear, starlit sky. He just needed to get comfortable, he told himself. Just needed to ease a little of the aching of his body. He could think better if he did that. He knew he could.

He fell asleep telling himself so.

When he woke it was dawn, and Coll was staring down at him. His brother was crouched atop a mound of rocks not twenty feet off, twisted and hunched like a scavenger. He was wrapped in the Mirrorshroud, the folds glimmering wickedly in the faint silver light as if dew were woven through the fabric. Coll's face was haggard and drawn, and his eyes, always so calm and steady, were darting about with fear and loathing.

Par was so startled that he couldn't bring himself to move. It had never occurred to him that his brother might circle back—would even have the presence of mind to do so. Why had he come? To attack him anew, to try to kill him perhaps? He stared at Coll, into his stricken face and sunken eyes. No, Coll was there for something else. He looked as if he wished to approach, as if he wanted to speak, as if he was seeking something from Par. And maybe he is, Par thought suddenly. The Sword of Shannara had given Coll his first glimpse of truth since he had donned the Mirrorshroud. Perhaps he wanted more.

He lifted slowly and started to hold out his hand.

Instantly Coll was gone, leaping from the rock into the shadows beyond and bounding away into the trees.

"Coll!" Par screamed after him. The echo faded and died. The sound of Coll's running disappeared into silence, lost as the distance between them widened anew.

Par foraged for berries and roots, convinced as he ate a meager breakfast that if he didn't find real food by nightfall he would be in serious trouble. He ate quickly, thinking of Coll all the while. There had been such terror in his brother's eyes and such fury. At Par, at himself, at the truth? There was no way to know. But Coll was aware of him still, was actively seeking him out, and there was still a chance to catch up with him.

What would he do, though, when he did? Par hadn't thought that far ahead. Use the Sword of Shannara again, he answered himself, almost without thinking. The Sword was Coll's best hope for getting free of the

Mirrorshroud. If Coll could be made to see the nature of the magic that possessed him, perhaps a way could be found to throw the cloak and its magic off. Perhaps Par could manage to tear it off him if nothing else. But the Sword was the key. Coll hadn't recognized anything until the Sword's magic engaged him, but the truth had shown in his eyes then. Par would use the talisman again, he told himself. And this time he wouldn't stop until Coll was free.

He picked up his blanket and set out again. The day was sultry and still, the heat growing quickly to a sticky swelter that left Par's clothing damp with sweat. He picked up Coll's trail and followed it to the Mermidon and across, heading north, then back again south. This time his brother continued in a direct line for several hours, traveling the east bank into the Runne Mountains. He passed Varfleet across the river, seeing trawlers and ferries maneuvering sluggishly on the broad expanse, thinking that it would be good to have a boat, thinking a second later that a boat was useless while he was tracking prints on dry land. He remembered when Coll and he had fled Varfleet weeks earlier and come south down the Mermidon, the beginning of everything. He remembered how close they had been then, despite their arguments over the direction of their lives and the purpose of Par's magic. It all seemed to have happened a very long time ago.

Toward midafternoon he came upon a small landing with a fishing dock and trading post several miles downriver of Varfleet. The post was ramshackle and cluttered, its tenants a taciturn, recalcitrant bunch with scarred, callused working hands and sun-browned faces. He was able to trade his ring for fishing line and hooks, flint, bread, cheese, and smoked fish. He carried everything just beyond sight of the landing, plopped down, and ate half of the foodstuffs without stopping for breath. When he was finished, he resumed his trek south, feeling decidely better about himself. The line and hooks would allow him to fish, and the flint would give him a fire. He was beginning to realize that catching up to Coll would take a lot longer than he had expected.

He found himself thinking again about why Coll had come in search of him—or more accurately, why he had been sent. If it wasn't to kill him or to steal the Sword, that didn't leave much. Perhaps Coll's coming was intended to provoke some sort of response from him. Damson's warning whispered once again—the chase was probably a Shadowen trap. But how could the Shadowen know their meeting would trigger the magic of the Sword of Shannara and reveal the truth about who Coll was, that Par would be able to see him as anything but a Shadowen? Coll might have been sent as a lure to draw Par after—that certainly seemed like Rimmer Dall—but again, how could the Shadowen know that Par would discover his brother's identity?

Unless he wasn't supposed to find out . . .

Par stopped abruptly. He was passing beneath a huge old oak. It was shady there and cool. He could feel a breeze waft in off the Mermidon. He could hear the sound of the river's sluggish flow. He could smell the water and the woods.

. . . *until it was too late.*

He felt his throat tighten. What if he had this whole business backward? What if Coll wasn't supposed to kill him? What if he was supposed to kill Coll?

Why?

Because . . .

He struggled with the answer. It was almost there, just on the edge of his reasoning. A whisper of words, straining to be recognized, to be understood.

He could not quite reach them.

He started off again, frustrated. He was on the right track, even if he didn't have all the particulars straight yet. It was Coll out there, leading him on, fleeing without knowing why, coming back at night to make certain Par was following. It was the Sword of Shannara Par carried, and its magic that had told him the truth. It was the Shadowen who had orchestrated this whole business, who were playing with them as if they were children set at a game, made to perform for the enjoyment of others.

It has to do with the magic of the wishsong, Par thought suddenly. It has to do with that.

It would come to him, he knew. He just needed to keep thinking about it. He just needed to keep reasoning it through.

He had not found Coll by sunset of the second day, and he made camp in a rock-sheltered niche that protected his back while allowing him to see whatever approached from the front. He did not build a fire. A fire would obscure his night vision when it grew dark. He ate a little more of his provisions, wrapped himself in his blanket, and settled back against the rocks to wait.

The night deepened and the stars came out. Par watched the shadows define and take shape in the pale light. He listened to the sluggish flow of the river against the rocks and the cries of the night birds circling its waters. He breathed the cooling, damp air, and allowed himself to wonder for the first time in two days about Damson Rhee. It was strange being without her after the time they hid together in Tyrsis, the two of them fighting to stay free. He worried for her, but reassured himself by deciding that she was probably better off than he was. By now she would have reached the freeborn and be engaged in an effort to rescue Padishar. By now she was safe.

Or as safe as either of them could be until this business was finished.

Thoughts of Damson, Padishar, Morgan Leah, Wren, and Walker Boh crowded into his mind, fragments of his memories of those who had been lost along the way. It sometimes seemed to him that he was destined to lose everyone. So much effort expended and so little gained—the weight of it bore down on him.

He drew his knees up to his chest protectively, tightening himself into a ball. The Sword of Shannara pressed against his back; he had forgotten to unstrap it. The Sword, his charge from Allanon, his chance for life, his sole hope for someday getting free of the Shadowen—a lot had been given up for it. He wondered anew what purpose the talisman was supposed to serve. Surely something wondrous, for magic like this was created for nothing less. But how was he supposed to discover that purpose—especially here, lost somewhere in the Runne, chasing after poor Coll? He should be searching for Walker Boh and for Wren, the others who had been given charges by Allanon.

But that was wrong, of course. He should be doing exactly what he was; he should be searching for his brother so that he could help him. If he lost Coll, who had stood by him through so much, who had given up everything, lost him after losing him once already, after having found him again . . .

He shook his head. He would not lose Coll. He would not allow that to happen.

The minutes slipped away, and Par Ohmsford continued to wait. Coll would come. He was certain of it. He would come as he had the night before. Perhaps he would only sit and stare at Par, but at least he would be there, nearby.

He reached into his tunic and brought out the broken half of Skree that Damson had given to him. He had wrapped it tight with a leather cord and hung it about his neck. If Damson was close, the Skree was supposed to brighten. He inspected it thoughtfully. The metal reflected dully in the pale starlight, but did not glow. Damson was far away.

He looked at the Skree a moment longer, then slipped it back into his tunic. Another bit of magic to keep him safe, he thought ruefully. The wishsong, the Sword of Shannara, and the Skree. He was well equipped with talismans. He was awash in them.

But his bitterness served no purpose, so he tried to brush it away. He took off the Sword and set it on the ground beside him. Somewhere out on the Mermidon a fish splashed. From the trees behind him came the low hoot of an owl, sudden and compelling.

A heritage of magic, he thought, unable to help himself, the darkness of his mood inexorable, *and all it does is make me wonder if Rimmer Dall is right—if I am indeed a Shadowen.*

The thought lingered as he stared out into the night.

The thing that was a mix of Shadowen and Coll Ohmsford stared out from its concealment in the trees some fifty feet from where the one who tracked it sat waiting for it to appear.

But I will not, no, it thought to itself. *I will stay here, safe within the dark, where I belong, where the shadows protect me from . . .*

What? It could not remember. This other creature? The strange weapon it carried? No, something else. The cloak it wore? It fingered the material uncertainly, feeling something unpleasant stir at the tips of its fingers as it did so, aware again of the vision it had witnessed when it had struggled with the other, the one who was . . . who was . . . It could not remember. Someone it had known. Once, long ago. Confusion beset it; the confusion never left, it seemed.

The Shadowen/Coll thing shifted silently, eyes never leaving the figure wedged into the rocks.

It thinks it can see me from there, but it is wrong. It can see nothing I do not wish it to see—not while I wear the cloak, not while I have the magic. I come to it when I wish, and I go away when I choose. It cannot see me. It cannot catch me. It hunts me, but I take it where I wish. I take it south, south to, to . . .

But it wasn't sure, the confusion clouding its thoughts again, distracting it. It could think better if it took off the cloak, it sometimes seemed. But no, that would be foolish. The cloak protected it, the Mirrorshroud, given to it by—no, stolen, taken from—no, tricked away by someone . . . dangerous . . .

The thoughts came and went, fragmented and fleeting. They spun like eddies in a river, touching down against silt and rock for just an instant before moving on.

Tears of frustration came to its eyes, and it brought one soiled hand up to brush them away. Sometimes it remembered things from before, from when it did not wear the cloak, from when it was someone else. The memories made it sad, and it seemed that something bad had been done to it to cause the memories to make it feel that way.

I saw, for a moment, in the light in my mind, in that vision, I saw something about myself, about who I was, am, could be. I want to see it again!

It fled now from the thing it had hunted once, frightened of it without knowing why. The cloak reassured, but even the cloak did not seem enough to protect it against this other. And flight from its pursuer always seemed to bring it back around to where that pursuer waited, a circle of running it could not understand. If it ran from its pursuer, why did the running bring it back again? Sometimes the cloak soothed and sheltered against the pursuer and the memories, but sometimes it felt as if the cloak were fire against its skin, burning away its identity, making it into something terrible.

Take off the cloak!

No, foolish, foolish! The cloak protects!

And so the battle raged within the tormented thing that was both Coll and Shadowen, driving it this way and that, wearing it down and building it up again, pulling and pushing both at once until there was nothing of reason and peace left within it.

Help me, it pleaded silently. *Please, help me.*

But it did not know who it was asking for help or what form that help should take. It stared down through the darkness at the one who tracked it, thinking that its hunter would sleep soon. What should it do then? Should it go down there, creeping, creeping, silent as clouds drifting in the sky, and touch it, touch . . .

The thought would not complete. The cloak seemed to fold more tightly about it, distracting it. Yes, creep down perhaps, show its hunter that it was not afraid (but it was!), that it could do as it wished in the night, in its cloak, in the safety of the magic . . .

Help me.

It choked on the words, trying to shriek them aloud, unable to do so. It closed its eyes against the pain and forced itself to think.

Take something from it, something it needs, that it treasures. Take something that will make it . . . hurt as I do. Reason jarred loose a familiar memory. *I know this one, know from when, when we were, we were . . . brothers! This one can help, can find a way . . .*

But the Coll/Shadowen thing was not certain of this, and the thought faded away with the others, lost in the teeming fragments that jostled and fought for consideration in the confused mind. It was both drawn to and repelled by the one it watched, and the conflict would not resolve itself no matter how much effort was expended.

Tears came again, unbidden, unwanted. The soiled, scraped hands knotted and tightened. The ravaged face fought to shape itself into something recognizable. For a second Coll was back, recovered out of the web of dark magic that imprisoned him.

Need to act, to do something that will let the other know!

Need to take something away!

I must!

Par was asleep when he felt the tearing at his neck. He jerked and thrashed wildly in an effort to stop it, not knowing what it was or who was causing it. Something was choking him, closing off his throat so that he could not breathe. There was a weight atop him, climbing on him, wrapping about.

A *Shadowen!*

Yet the wishsong had not warned him, so it could not be that. He summoned the magic now, desperate to save himself. He felt it build with agonizing slowness. Something was breathing on his face and neck. There was a flash of teeth, and he felt coarse hair rub against his skin. His hand reached out to brace himself so that he might shove upward against his attacker. His hand brushed the handle of the Sword of Shannara, and the metal burned him like fire.

Then the pressure on his throat abruptly released, the weight on his body lifted, and through a haze of colored light and gloom he saw a crumpled, hunched form race away into the night.

Coll! It had been Coll!

He came to his feet, bewildered and frightened, fighting for air and balance. What was going on? Had Coll been sent to kill him after all? Had he tried to choke him to death? He watched the dark form disappear into the shadows, lost in the rocks and trees almost instantly. There was no mistake. It had been Coll. He was certain of it.

But what was his brother trying to do?

He thought suddenly of the Sword, glanced hurriedly down, and found it lying untouched next to where he stood. Not the Sword, he thought. What then?

He groped at his neck, aware suddenly of new pain. His hand came away wet with blood. He felt again. He found a collar of bruised, torn flesh. He touched it gingerly, questioningly.

And then he realized that the Skree was gone.

His brother had stolen it. He must have seen Par hold it up while he was hiding out there in the dark. He must have come down after Par had fallen asleep, crept up on him, pinned him to the ground, yanked at the leather cord about his neck so that he choked, bitten it through when nothing else worked, and carried off Damson's talisman.

Why?

So that Par would follow him, of course. So that Par would have to give chase.

The Valeman stood staring after his brother, after the thing his brother had become, stunned. In the silence of his mind it seemed he could hear the other cry out to him.

Help me, Coll was saying.

Help me.

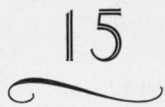

When it grew light enough to see, Par went after his brother. Sunrise was early, the day clear and bright, and the trail Coll left easy to follow once again. Par redoubled his efforts, pushing himself harder than before, determined that this time Coll would not get away. They were deep within the Runne Mountains by now, hemmed in by canyon walls as they followed the Mermidon south, and there was little room for deviation. Nevertheless, Coll continued to wander away from the riverbank as if searching for a way out. Sometimes he would get almost half a mile before the mountains blocked his path. Once he was able to climb to a low ridge and follow it south for several miles before it dead-ended at another cliff face and turned him aside. Each time Par was forced to follow so as not to lose the trail, afraid that if he simply kept to the riverbank Coll would double back. The effort of the pursuit drained him of his strength, and the muggy, windless air made him light-headed. The day passed, sunset came, and still he had not found Coll.

He fished for his dinner that night, using the hook and line from the trading center, cooked and ate his catch, and left what remained—a more than generous portion—on a flat rock several dozen feet off from where he slept. He was awake most of the night, hearing and seeing things that weren't there, dozing infrequently and fitfully. He did not see Coll once. When he woke, he found the fish gone—but it might have been eaten by wild animals. He didn't think so, but there was no way to be sure.

For the next three days he continued his pursuit, working his way downriver, edging steadily closer to the Rainbow Lake and Southwatch. He began to worry that he was not going to catch up to Coll until it was too late. Somehow his brother was managing to keep just ahead of him, even with his diminished capacity to reason, even in his half-Shadowen state. Coll was not thinking clearly, not choosing the easiest or quickest paths, not bothering to hide his tracks, not doing anything but somehow managing to keep just out of reach. It was frustrating and troubling at once. It seemed inevitable that he would find Coll too late to help him—or perhaps even to help himself, if the Shadowen discovered them. If Rimmer Dall found Coll first, what was Par supposed to do then? Use the Sword of Shannara? He had tried that once to no avail. Use the magic of the wish-song? He had tried that as well and found it dangerously unpredictable. Still, he might have no choice. He would have to use the wishsong if that was the only way he could free his brother. The price he would have to pay was not a consideration.

He thought often now of how the wishsong had evolved and what it seemed to be doing to him when he summoned it. He tried to think what he might do to protect himself, to keep the magic under control, to prevent it from getting away from him entirely. The power was building in a manner he could not comprehend, evolving just as it had with Wil Ohmsford years ago, manifesting itself in new and frightening ways that suggested something fundamental was changing inside Par as well. When he considered the extent of that evolution, he was terrified. At one time it had been the magic of Jair Ohmsford, a wishsong that could form images out of air, images that seemed real but were only imaginings imprinted on the minds of those who listened. Now it seemed more the magic of Jair's sister, Brin, magic that could change things in truth, that could alter them irrevocably. But with Par it could create as well. It could make things out of nothing, like that fire sword in the Pit, or the shards of metal and wind in the watchtower at Tyrsis. Where had power like that come from? What could have made the magic change so drastically?

What frightened him most, of course, was that the answer to all of his questions about the source of his magic was the same, a faint and insidiously confident whisper in his mind, the words spoken to him by Rimmer Dall when he had faced the First Seeker in the vault that had housed the Sword of Shannara.

You are a Shadowen, Par Ohmsford. You belong with us.

Six days into his pursuit, four after the theft of the Skree, the afternoon heat so intense it seemed to color the air and burn the lungs, Coll's trail turned sharply into the river and disappeared.

Par stopped at the water's edge, scanned the ground in disbelief, backtracked to make certain he had not been deceived, and then sat down in a patch of shade beneath a spreading poplar to gather his thoughts.

Coll had gone into the river.

He stared out across its waters, over the sluggish, broad surface to the tree-lined bank beyond. The Mermidon turned out of the Runne where they were now, closing on the Rainbow Lake. The mountains continued south along the east bank, but the west flattened out into hilly grasslands and scattered groves of hardwoods. If Coll had been thinking clearly, he might have chosen to cross where travel was easier. But Coll was in the thrall of the Mirrorshroud. Par decided he couldn't be sure of anything. In any event, if Coll had crossed, he must cross as well.

He stripped off his clothing, used the fishing line and some deadwood to create a makeshift raft, lashed his clothing, blanket, pack, and the Sword of Shannara in place, and slipped into the river. The water was cold and soothing. He pushed off into the current, swimming with it at an angle toward the far shore. He took his time and was across about a mile down. He climbed out, dried himself, dressed, lashed the Sword and his gear to his back, and set off to find Coll's trail again.

But the trail was nowhere to be found.

He searched upriver and down until it was dark and discovered nothing. Coll had disappeared. Par sat in the dark staring out at the river's flat, glittery surface and wondered if his brother had drowned. Coll was a good swimmer under normal circumstances, but maybe his strength had finally given out. Par forced himself to eat, drank from his water skin, rolled himself into his blanket, and tried to sleep. Sleep would not come. Thoughts of Coll tugged and twisted at him, memories of the past, the weight of all that had come about since the beginning of the dreams. Par was assailed by conflicting emotions. What was he supposed to do now? What if Coll was really gone?

Sunrise was a deep red glow out of the east shadowed by a gathering of clouds west. The clouds rolled across the horizon, coming into Callahorn like a wall. Daylight was pale and thin, and the air turned dead still. Par rose and started out again, heading south along the river, still searching for his brother. He was tired and discouraged, and on the verge of quitting. He kept wondering what he was doing, chasing after a ghost, chasing after a Shadowen thing, being led on like a dumb animal. How did he know it was really Coll? Maybe Damson had been right. Couldn't the Shadowen have fooled him in some way? What if Rimmer Dall had tampered with the Sword, or changed its magic so that it deceived? Suppose this was all some sort of elaborate trap. Was there any way to tell?

He quit thinking altogether after a while because there were no possibilities left that he hadn't considered and he was wearing himself out to no good purpose. He simply kept walking, following the river as it meandered south through the hill country, scanning the ground mechanically, everything inside beginning to shut down into a black silence.

To the west, the clouds began to darken as they neared, and a sudden wind gusted ahead of them in warning. Birds flew screaming into the mountains east, flashes of white disappearing into the shadows.

Ahead, only miles downriver, Southwatch appeared, its black obelisk etched against the skyline. Par watched it grow steadily larger as he approached, a fortress standing firm in the path of the coming storm. Par's eyes swept its walls and towers as he edged closer to stands of trees and rocks to gain cover. Nothing showed itself. Nothing moved.

Then suddenly, unexpectedly, he came upon Coll's trail again. He found it at the river's edge where his brother had emerged after having been carried south for what must have been at least seven or eight miles. He was certain it was Coll, even before he found a bootprint that confirmed it. The trail set off west into the hills and the coming storm.

But the trail was hours old. Coll had come ashore yesterday and set out at once. Par was at least a day behind.

Nevertheless, he began to track, grateful to have found any trail at all, relieved to know that his brother was still alive. He trudged inland from the river, the light failing rapidly now as the storm neared, the air turning slick and damp, and the grasses whipping wildly against his legs. Clouds roiled and tumbled overhead, filling the skies to overflowing. Par glanced back to where he had last seen Southwatch, but the Shadowen tower had disappeared into the gloom.

Rain began to fall in scattered drops, cool on his heated skin, then stinging as the wind gusted sharply and blew them into his face.

Moments later he crested a rise and saw Coll.

His brother was sprawled motionless on a stretch of dusty grass, facedown beneath a leafless, storm-ravaged oak that rose out of the center of a shallow vale. At first glance he appeared to be dead. Par started forward hurriedly, his heart sinking. *No,* was all he could think. *No.* Then he saw Coll stir, saw his arm move slightly, rearranging itself. A leg followed, drawing up, then relaxing again. Coll wasn't dead; he was simply exhausted. He had finally run himself out.

Par came down off the rise into the teeth of a wind that howled and bucked as it swept out of the enveloping black. The sound of his approach was lost in its shriek. He bent his head and pushed forward. Coll had gone still again. He did not hear Par. Par would reach him before Coll knew he was there.

And then what? he wondered suddenly. What would he do then?

He reached back over his shoulder deliberately and pulled out the Sword of Shannara. Somehow he would find a way to call forth the talisman's magic once more, to hold his brother fast while it worked its way through him, forcing him to see the truth, shredding the Shadowen cloak, freeing him for good.

At least, that's what he hoped would happen. He breathed in the smell and taste of the storm. Well, he would have his chance. Coll would not be as strong now as he was before. And Par would not be the one caught off guard.

As he closed on Coll, coming underneath the ruined oak's skeletal limbs, thunder—the storm's first—rumbled out of the black. Coll started at the sound, rolled onto his back, and stared upward at his brother ten feet away.

Par stopped, uncertain. Coll looked at him from within the shadows of the Mirrorshroud's velvet-black hood, his eyes blank and uncomprehending. A hand lifted weakly to pull the cloak closer about his hunched body. He whimpered and drew his knees up.

Par held his breath and started forward again, a step, another, the wind thrusting at him, billowing his clothes out from his body, whipping his hair from side to side. He kept the Sword of Shannara as still as he could against his body, unable to hide it now, hoping to keep it from becoming Coll's point of focus.

A jagged streak of lightning darted across the sky followed by a deafening peal of thunder that reverberated from horizon to horizon.

Coll came to his knees, eyes wide and frightened. For a second his hands relaxed their grip on the cloak, letting it fall away, and his face gained back a measure of its old look. Coll Ohmsford was there again in that moment's time, staring out at his brother as if he had never gone away. There was recognition in his face, a stunned, grateful relief that smoothed away pain and despair. Par felt a surge of hope. He wanted to call out to his brother, to assure him everything would be all right, to tell him he was safe now.

But in the next instant Coll was gone. His face disappeared back into the Shadowen thing that the Mirrorshroud had made, and a twisted, cunning visage took its place. Teeth bared, and his brother went into a crouch, snarling.

He's going to flee again! Par thought in anguish.

But instead Coll rushed him, bounding to his feet and closing the distance between them almost before Par could bring up the Sword of Shannara in defense. Coll's hands closed over Par's, grappling with the handle of the talisman, twisting at it to wrest it free. Par hung on, lurching forward and back as he fought with his brother for control of the blade. Rain poured down on them, a torrent of such ferocity that Par was left almost blinded. Coll was right up against him, pressed so close he could feel his brother's heartbeat. Their hands were locked above their heads as they wrenched at the Sword, swinging it this way and that, the metal glistening wetly.

Lightning struck north, a flash of intense light followed by a huge clap of thunder. The ground shook.

Par tried to summon the magic of the Sword but couldn't. It had come easily enough before—why wouldn't it come now? He tried to fight past his brother's madness, past the fury of his attack. He tried to block out his fear that nothing would help, that the power was somehow lost again.

Across the slick, wind-swept grasses the Ohmsford brothers struggled, fighting for possession of the Sword of Shannara, grunts and shouts lost in the sound of the storm. Over and over Par sought unsuccessfully to summon the magic. Despair washed through him. He was losing this battle, too. Coll was bigger than he was, and his size and weight were wearing Par down. Worse, his brother seemed to be growing stronger as his own strength failed. Coll was all over him, kicking and clawing, fighting as if he had gone completely mad.

But Par would not give up. He clung desperately to the Sword, determined not to lose it. He let his brother shove him back, muscle him about, thrust him this way and that, hoping the efforts would tire Coll, slow him down, weaken him enough that Par could find a way to knock him unconscious. If he could manage that, he might have a chance.

Lightning flashed again, quick and startling. In its momentary glare Par caught a glimpse of shadowy forms gathering on the rise above the vale, dozens of them, twisted and gnarled and stooped, the gleam of their eyes like blood.

Then they were gone again, swallowed in the black storm night. Distracted, Par blinked away the rain that ran into his eyes, trying to peer past Coll's struggling form. What had he just seen out there? Again the lightning flashed, just as Coll thrust out wildly and toppled him to the sodden grass. He saw nothing this time, fighting to keep the breath in his lungs as he struck the ground. Coll threw himself on Par, howling. But Par let his brother's momentum work against him, tumbling the other over his head and twisting himself free.

He came to his feet, dazed and searching. The gloom was so thick he could barely see the ravaged oak. The rise was invisible.

Coll came at him again, but this time Par was ready. Breaking through the other's guard, he struck Coll sharply on the head with the hilt of the Sword. Coll dropped to his knees, stunned. He groped at the air in front of him, as if grasping for something that only he could see. A trickle of red ran down his face from where the blow had broken the skin, blood diffusing and turning pink as it mingled with the rain. His features began to change, losing their Shadowen cast, turning human again. Par started to strike, trembling in despair and exhaustion, then stopped as he saw the other's eyes fix on him in wonder.

It was his brother looking at him. It was Coll.

He dropped to his knees in the slick grass and mud, facing Coll. His brother's lips were moving, the words he was speaking lost in the howl of the wind and rain. He was shivering with cold and something more. He began shaking his head slowly beneath the glistening cover of the Mirrorshroud, twisting within the dark folds as if it were the hardest thing he had ever had to do. *Coll.* Par mouthed his name. Coll's hands came up to grasp the folds of the Shadowen cloak, shook violently, and then dropped away. *Coll.*

Desperate to help his brother before the chance was gone, Par impulsively jammed the Sword of Shannara into the earth before him and reached past it to take hold of Coll's hands. Coll did not resist, his eyes empty and dull. Par guided Coll's hands to the pommel of the Sword and fastened the chill, shaking fingers in place, holding them there with his own. *Please, Coll. Please stay with me.* Coll was staring at him, seeing him now and at the same time seeing right through him. The Sword of Shannara bound them, held them fast, fingers intertwined, pressed against the raised torch carved into the handle and against each other.

Par saw the distorted reflection of his face in the rain-streaked surface of the blade. "Coll!" he screamed.

His brother's eyes snapped up. *Please let the magic come,* Par begged. *Please!*

Coll's eyes were fixed on him, searching for more.

"Coll, listen to me! It's Par! It's your brother!"

Coll blinked. There was a hint of recognition. There was a glint of light. Beneath his own hands, Par could feel Coll's tighten on the Sword's hilt.

Coll!

Light flared down the length of the Sword's smooth blade, quick and blinding, a white fury that engulfed everything in a moment's time. Fire followed, cool and brilliant as it burned outward from the Sword and into Par's body. He felt it extend and weave, drawing him out of himself and into the talisman, there to find Coll waiting, there to join them as one. He felt himself twist through the metal and out again to somewhere far beyond. The world from which he had been drawn disappeared—the damp and the mud, the dark and the sound. There was whiteness and there was silence. There was nothing else.

Just Coll and himself. Just the two of them.

Then he was aware of the shimmering black length of the Mirror-shroud wrapping about his brother's head and body, writhing like a snake. The cloak was alive, working itself this way and that, twisting violently against the pull of something invisible, something that was threatening to tear it apart.

Par could hear it hiss.

The Sword of Shannara. The magic of the Sword.

He let his thoughts flow deep into his brother's mind, down into the darkness that had settled there and was now fighting hard to remain. *Listen to me, Coll. Listen to the truth.* He forced his brother's mind to open, casting aside the Shadowen magic he found waiting there, heedless of his own safety, oblivious to everything but the need to set his brother free. The magic of the sword armored and sustained him. *Listen to me.* His voice cracked like a whip in his brother's mind. He assembled his words and gave them shape and form, images that matched the intensity of the wishsong when it told the tales of three hundred years gone. The truth of who and what Coll had become released in a rush that could not be slowed or turned aside, flooding inward. Coll saw how he had been subverted. He saw what the cloak had done to him. He saw the way in which he had been turned against his brother, sent to fulfill some dark intent of which neither of them was aware. He saw everything that had been so carefully hidden by the Shadowen magic.

He saw as well what was needed in order that he should be free of it.

The pain of those revelations was intense and penetrating. Par could feel it reverberate through his brother, the waves washing back upon himself. His brother's life was laid bare before him, a stark and unrelenting series of truths that cut to the bone. Par fought his panic and the pain and faced them unflinching, steady because his brother needed him to be so. He could hear Coll's silent scream of anguish at what he was being shown. He could see that anguish reflected in Coll's eyes, deep and harsh. He did not turn away. He did not soften. The truth was the Sword of Shannara's white fire, burning and cleansing, and it was their only hope.

Coll reared back and screamed then, the sound bringing them out of the white silence and back into the black, howling fury of the storm, kneeling together in the mud and wet grasses beneath that ancient oak, beneath the dark, roiling clouds. There was swirling, misty gloom all about, as if the last of the daylight had been stripped away. Rain blew into their faces, blinding them to everything but a shimmer of each other grasping as one the glittering length of the Sword. Lightning struck, brilliant and searing, and then thunder sounded in a tremendous blast.

Coll Ohmsford's hands wrenched free of the Sword, tearing loose Par's as well. Coll rose, a stricken look on his face. But it was *his* face Par saw, his *brother's* face, and nothing of the Shadowen horror that had sought to claim it. Coll reached back in a frenzy and tore loose the Mirrorshroud. He ripped it away and threw it to the earth. The Mirrorshroud landed in a heap amid the dampness and muck and at once began to steam. It shuddered and twisted, then began to bubble. Green flames sprang from its shimmering folds, burning wildly. The fire spread, inexorable, consuming, and in seconds the Mirrorshroud was turned to ash.

Par came wearily to his feet and faced his brother, seeing in Coll's eyes what he had been searching for. Coll had come back to him. The Sword of Shannara had shown him the truth about the Mirrorshroud—that it was Shadowen-sworn, that it had been created to subvert him, that the only way he could ever be free was to take off the cloak and throw it away. Coll had done so. The Sword had given him the strength.

But even in that moment of supreme elation, when the struggle had been won and Coll had been returned to him, Par felt something uneasy stir within. There should have been more, a voice whispered. The magic should have done something more. Remember the tales of five hundred years gone? Remember the first Ohmsford? Remember Shea? The magic had done something different for Shea when he had summoned it. It had shown him the truth about himself, revealed first all that he had sought to hide away, to disguise, to forget, to pretend did not exist. It had shown to Shea Ohmsford the truth about himself, the harshest truth of all, in order that he might be able to bear after any other truth that was required of him.

Why had nothing of this truth been shown to him? Why had everything been of Coll alone?

Lightning flashed again, and Par's thoughts disintegrated in the movement of the dark forms on the rise surrounding them, forms so clearly revealed this time that there could be no mistaking what they were. Par turned, seeing them crouched and waiting everywhere, twisted and dark, red eyes gleaming. He felt Coll edge close, felt his brother take up a protective stance at his back. Coll was seeing them now as well.

A strange mix of despair and fury washed through Par Ohmsford. The Shadowen had found them.

Then Rimmer Dall descended from the ranks, the raw, harsh features lifted into the rain, the eyes as hard as stone and as red as blood. A dozen steps from them, he stopped. Without saying a word, he lifted his gloved hand and beckoned. The gesture said everything. They must come with him. They belonged to him. They were his now.

Par heard the First Seeker's voice in his mind, heard it as surely as if the other had spoken. He shook his head once. He would not come. Neither he nor Coll. Not ever again.

"Par," he heard his brother speak his name softly. "I'm with you."

There was a sudden rasp of the Sword of Shannara's blade against the pull of the earth as Coll slowly drew it free. Par turned slightly. Coll was holding the talisman in both hands, facing out at the Shadowen.

Fiercely determined that nothing would separate them again, Par Ohmsford summoned the magic of the wishsong. It responded instantly, anxious for its release, eager for its use. There was something terrifying about the voracious intensity of its coming. Par shuddered at the feelings it sent through him, at the hunger it unleashed inside. He must control it, he warned himself, and despaired that he could do so.

Across the darkness that separated them, Par could see Rimmer Dall smile. All about the crest of the rise, he could see the Shadowen begin to edge down, the rasp of claws and teeth sliding through the wind's quick howl, the glint of red eyes turning the rain to steam. How many were there? Par wondered. Too many. Too many even for the wishsong's volatile magic. He cast about desperately, looking for a place to break through. They would have to run at some point. They would have to try to reach the river or the woods, someplace they would have a chance to hide.

As if such a place existed. As if there were any chance for them at all.

The magic gathered at his fingertips in a white glow that seethed with fury. Par felt Coll press up against him, and they stood back to back against the closing circle.

Lightning flashed and thunder rolled across the blackness, booming into the wind's rush. In the distance, trees swayed, and leaves torn from their limbs scattered like frightened thoughts. Run, Par thought. Run now, while you can.

And then a light flared at the base of the ancient oak, a brightness sure and steady, seeming to grow out of the air. It came forward into the gloom, swaying gently, barely more than a candle's flicker through the curtain of the rain. The movement of the Shadowen froze into stillness. The wind faded to a dull rush. Par saw the smile on Rimmer Dall's face disappear. His cold eyes shifted to where the light approached, easing out of the murk to reveal the small, slender form that directed it.

It was a boy carrying a lamp.

The boy came toward Par and Coll without slowing, the lamp held forth to guide his way, eyes dark and intense, hair damp against his forehead, features smooth and even and calm. Par felt the magic of the wishsong begin to fade. He did not feel threatened by this boy. He did not feel afraid. He glanced hurriedly at Coll and saw wonder mirrored in his brother's dark eyes.

The boy reached them and stopped. He did not spare even the slightest glance for the monsters that snarled balefully in the gloom beyond the fringes of his lamp. His eyes remained fixed on the brothers.

"You must come with me now, if you are to be made safe," he said quietly.

Rimmer Dall rose up like a dark spirit, throwing off the protection of his robes so that his arms were left free, the one with the dark glove stretching out as if to tear away the light. "You don't belong here!" he hissed in his stark, whispery voice. "You have no power here!"

The boy turned slightly. "I have power wherever I choose. I am the bearer of the light of the Word, now and always."

Rimmer Dall's eyes were on fire. "Your magic is old and used up! Get away while you can!"

Par stared from one face to the other. What was going on? Who was this boy?

"Par!" he heard Coll gasp.

And he saw the boy begin to change suddenly into an old man, frail and bent with age, the lamp held away from him as if to hold it closer would burn.

"And your magic," the old man whispered to Rimmer Dall, "is stolen, and in the end it will betray you."

He shifted again toward Par and Coll. "Come away now. Don't be frightened. There are small things that I can still do for you, and this is one." The seamed face regarded them. "Not frightened, are you? Of an old man? Of an old friend of so many of your family? Do you know me? You do, don't you? Of course. Of course you do." One hand reached out and brushed theirs. It was the feel of old paper or dried leaves. Something sparked within as he did so. "Speak my name," he said.

And abruptly they knew. "You are the King of the Silver River," they whispered together, and the lamplight reached out to gather them in.

Instantly the Shadowen attacked. They came down off the slope in a black tide, their shrieks and howls shattering the odd calm that the King of the Silver River had brought with him. They came in a gnashing of teeth and a tearing of claws, rending the air and earth in fury. Before them came

Rimmer Dall, transformed into something indescribable, a shadow so swift that it cut through the space separating him from the Ohmsfords in an instant's time. Iron bands wrapped about Par's throat and Coll's chest, tightening and suffocating. There was a feeling of being swallowed whole into the blackness it caused, of falling away into a pit that was too deep to measure. For an instant they were lost, and then the voice of the King of the Silver River reached out to gather them in, cradling them like the hands of a mother holding her child, freeing them from the iron bands and carrying them up from the darkness.

Rimmer Dall's voice was the grate of iron on stone, and the voice of the King of the Silver River disappeared. Again the blackness closed and the bands took hold. Par struggled desperately to get free. He could feel the terrible sway of magics wielded by the combatants, the strengths of the First Seeker and the ancient spirit as they fought for control of Coll's life and his. His brother had become separated from him somehow; he could no longer feel him pressing close. For a moment he could see Coll, could make out the other's familiar features, and then even that was gone.

"Par, I have to tell you—" he heard his brother call out.

Inside, the magic of the wishsong was building, and his brother's words disappeared in its rush.

The lamp of the King of the Silver River cut against the Shadowen dark, forcing it away. Par reached toward the light, stretching out his hands. But the darkness surged back again, a shriek of desperation and anger. It scythed across the light and shut Par away.

In terror Par released his magic. It roared out of him like floodwaters in a spring storm, a torrent that could not be slowed. Par felt the magic explode everywhere, white-hot and fierce, burning everything. It swept about him in a fury, and Par could do nothing to stop it.

He felt himself change, felt himself shift away from his body, turn his face aside and mask who and what he was. The change was terrifying and real; it was as if his skin was being shed.

He saw the lamp of the King of the Silver River disappear. He saw the darkness close about.

Then his strength gave out, consciousness left him completely, and he saw nothing at all.

When Barsimmon Oridio advised Wren, following the High Council's decision to engage the approaching Federation force rather than wait for it in Arborlon, that it would take at least a week to assemble and provision the whole of their army, she determined to set forth with as many men as he could have ready in two days to act as a vanguard. Predictably, the old warrior balked, challenging the sense of taking a small force against so many, questioning what would happen if it was trapped and forced to fight. She listened patiently, then explained that the purpose of the vanguard was not to engage the enemy, but to monitor it and perhaps to slow it by letting it discover the presence of another army in the field. There was no reason to worry, she assured. Bar could select the commander of the vanguard, and she would be bound by his decisions. Bar fussed and fumed, but in the end he gave in, satisfying himself with her promise that she would wait until he arrived with the bulk of the army before attempting any sort of offensive engagement.

Word went out to the Elves who had settled the surrounding countryside of the approach of the Federation army and of the danger that it posed. Those who wished could come to Arborlon, which would serve as a defense for the Elven people. Those who chose to remain where they were should be prepared to flee if the Federation broke through. Wing Riders were dispatched to the farthest points and to the Wing Hove. Runners were used elsewhere. Families from the settlements nearest the city began to drift in almost immediately. Wren settled them in camps scattered across the bluff and away from the defenses that were being built. There could be no closing away of the city behind walls this time. The Elfitch had been destroyed in the demon attack in Elventine Elessedil's time, and the Keel had been left behind on Morrowindl. Bulwarks would be constructed, but they would be neither tall nor high nor unbroken. The cliffs of the Carolan and waters of the Rill Song offered some natural protection against an attack from the west, and there were high mountains north and south, but the Federation was most likely to come at them from the east through the Valley of Rhenn. Whatever defenses were to be employed would have to be settled there.

Wren spoke with her ministers and the commanders of her army at length about what form those defenses might take. There were heavy woods all the way east from the city to the plains, much of them impassable for a force the size of the one that approached. It was agreed that the Federation army would seek to use its size to crush the Elves, and scattering itself through the trees would not seem an attractive alternative to its commanders. Therefore it would come through the Rhenn and follow the main road west to the city, there to deploy. But even that approach would not be easy. It had been many years since the road had been used regularly—barely at all since the Elves had disappeared from the Westland. Much of it had been reclaimed by the forest. It was more trail than road these days. It was narrow and winding and filled with places where a small force could hold out for a time against a much larger one. Fortifications would be built at as many of these places as time allowed, using pitfalls and traps to hinder any advance. Meanwhile, the main Elven army would attempt to slow the Federation forces on the grasslands east, relying on its cavalry, bowmen, and Wing Riders to offset the superior numbers of Southland infantry. If that failed, a last stand would be made at the Rhenn.

One team of builders was dispatched to begin work on the defenses for the approach east while a second set about fortifying the Carolan. An attack from the west was unlikely, but there was no point in leaving anything to chance.

Meanwhile, the enormous job of outfitting and provisioning the Elven army commenced under the direction of Barsimmon Oridio. Wren stayed out of the old soldier's way, content to have him busily engaged in something besides questioning her. Out of everyone's hearing she quietly advised Triss that she wanted a large contingent of Home Guard to go on her expedition as well and Tiger Ty that she wanted a dozen Wing Riders. Both forces would be under her personal command. It was fine to leave battlefield tactics to men like Bar, but a major confrontation was the last thing she wanted. She had thought the matter through very carefully. Harass, harry, and delay, she had told the Council—that was what the Elves could reasonably hope to accomplish. Garth had taught her everything there was to know about that kind of fighting. She had not said anything to the Council, but the week required to assemble the Elven army might prove too long a delay. The vanguard, in truth, was simply a screen that would allow her to act more quickly. The Federation army needed to be disrupted now, at once. Unconventional tactics were called for, and the Home Guard and Wing Riders were perfect for the job.

On the morning of the third day, she set out with a force that consisted of a little more than a thousand men—eight hundred infantry made up essentially of bowmen, three hundred cavalry, a hundred of the Home Guard under the command of Triss, and the dozen Wing Riders she had requested of Tiger Ty. The Wing Riders were directed by a seasoned veteran named Erring Rift, but Tiger Ty was there as well, insisting that no one but he should take the queen skyward should she wish to do any further scouting. Barsimmon Oridio had appointed a lean, hard-faced veteran named Desidio, to lead the expedition. Wren knew him to be reliable, tough, and smart. It was a good choice. Desidio was experienced enough to do what was needed and to not do anything more. That was fine with Wren. The Home Guard were hers, and the Wing Riders were independent and could follow who they chose. It would make for a good balance.

That she was going at all was a point of some debate among the ministers, but she had made it clear from the first night that a Queen of the Elves must always lead if she expects anyone to follow. She had intended from the beginning to go out with the army, she reminded them, and there was no point in waiting about to do it. She had spent a lifetime learning to survive, and she possessed the power of the Elfstones to protect her. She had less reason than most to worry. She did not intend to make excuses.

In the end she got her way because no one was prepared to go up against her on the matter. Some, she thought rather uncharitably, seeing the black looks on the faces of Jalen Ruhl and Perek Arundel, might be hoping her rash insistence would come back to haunt her.

She left Eton Shart in charge of the Council and the city. The ministers would not cross him, and the Elves knew and respected him. He would be able to guide them in whatever way was necessary, and she had confidence that he would know what to do. Her first minister might not yet be convinced that she was the queen her people needed, but he had given his pledge of support and she believed he would not break it. Of the others she was less certain, though Fruaren Laurel seemed committed to her now. But they would all toe the line for Eton Shart.

Barsimmon Oridio was there to see her off, declaring that he would follow within a few days, reminding her of her promise to wait for him. She smiled and winked, and that unnerved him enough that he stalked away. She was aware of Triss on one side, stone-faced, and Desidio, eyeing her covertly from the other. Tiger Ty had already set out, flying Spirit away at daybreak to scout the Federation's progress. The remainder of the Wing Riders would leave at sunset to link up with them at their campsite near the Rhenn. The Elven Hunters marched out to the waves and cheers of the people of the city, young and old come down to see them off, waving banners and ribbons and calling out their wishes for success. Wren glanced about doubtfully. It all felt very strange. Their departure was festive and gay, and it forecast nothing of the injury and death that was certain to follow.

They traveled swiftly that first day, strung out along the narrow roadway to avoid clogging, scouts dispersed into the trees at regular intervals to warn of impending danger. They were in their own country and so paid less heed to the precautions they might otherwise have observed. Wren rode with Triss and the Home Guard, screened front and back by Hunters, carefully protected against anything that might threaten. It made her smile to think how different things were from when she was a simple Rover girl. Now and again she had to suppress an urge to leap down off her horse and race away into the cool green stillness of the trees, returning to the life from which she had come, returning to its peace.

Faun had been left at home, closed within Wren's room on the second floor of the Elessedil home. The Streleheim was no place for a forest creature, she had reasoned. But the Tree Squeak had a mind of its own and was not always persuaded by what Wren believed was best. So by the time the vanguard stopped to rest and water the horses at midday, there was Faun, streaking from the foliage in a dark blur to throw herself on her startled mistress. In seconds the little creature had burrowed down into the folds of Wren's riding cloak and was comfortably settled. Wren shrugged obligingly and accepted what she could obviously not change.

The late summer heat was sticky and damp, and by day's end men and horses alike were sweating freely. They camped in a canopied stretch of oak and hickory several miles from the Rhenn, close by a stream and pool so

that they could wash and drink, but back within the shade and concealment of the forest. Desidio sent a patrol of horsemen ahead into the pass to
make certain that all was well, then sat down with Wren and Triss to discuss
how they would proceed. Tiger Ty would bring news of the Federation
army's location when he returned, and presuming the army was still proceeding northward through the Tirfing, the Elves might then travel south
across the open plains, relying on scouts to prevent them from running into
an ambush, or might keep within the fringe of the trees where they would
not be so easily seen. Wren listened patiently, glanced at Triss, then said she
preferred that they travel in the open so as to make better time. Once they
had made contact with the Federation, they could then use the forest in
which to hide while they decided what to do next. Desidio gave her a
sharp look at the words "decide what to do next," but then nodded his
agreement, rose, and walked away.

They had just finished eating dinner when Tiger Ty winged down
through the trees, dusty and hot and tired. He settled Spirit a short distance
down the trail, where the giant Roc was less likely to disturb the horses,
then strode determinedly back toward the camp. Wren and Triss walked
out to greet him and were joined by Desidio. The Wing Rider was brief
and to the point. The Federation army had reached the Mermidon and begun crossing. By tomorrow sometime, they would have completed the task
and be on their way north. They were making very good time.

Wren accepted the news with a frown. She had hoped to catch up to
them on the far side of the river and keep them there. That had been wishful thinking, it seemed. Events were moving more quickly than she wanted
them to.

She thanked Tiger Ty for the report and sent him off to get something
to eat.

"You are thinking that the Elven army is too far away," Desidio said
quietly, his lean face pinched with thought.

She nodded. "They are still the best part of a week even from here."
Her green eyes fixed him. "I don't think we can allow the Federation to get
that close to Arborlon before we try to stop them."

They stared at each other. "You heard the general," Desidio said.
"We're to wait for the main army." His face showed nothing.

She shrugged. "I heard. But General Oridio isn't here. And you are."

The dark eyebrows lifted inquiringly. "You have something in mind,
my lady?"

She held his gaze. "I might. Would you be willing to listen, when it's
time?"

Desidio rose. "You are the queen. I must always listen."

When he had departed, she gave Triss a doubtful smile. "He knows
what I am up to, don't you think?"

Triss eased his splinted arm away from his body and then let it settle
back again. In another day the splint would be gone. Triss was impatient for

that to happen. He considered her question and shook his head. "I don't think anyone knows what you are up to, my lady," he said softly. "That's why they are frightened of you."

She accepted the observation without comment. Triss could tell her anything. What they had shared coming out of Morrowindl allowed for that. She looked off into the trees. Dusk was spreading shadows in dark pools that ate up the light. Sometimes, since Garth had died, she found herself wondering if they might be trying to swallow her as well.

Moments later the sound of horses' hoofs drew her attention back toward the camp. The scouts dispatched to the Rhenn had returned, and they had brought someone with them. They thundered to a stop, sawing on the reins of their snorting, lathered mounts. The horses had been ridden hard. Triss rose quickly, and Wren came up with him. The riders and their charge—one man—had dismounted and were making their way through a cluster of Elven Hunters to where Desidio waited, a gaunt shadow against the firelight. There was an exchange of words, and then Desidio and the unidentified man turned and came toward her.

She got a closer look as the pair neared and saw that it wasn't a man with Desidio after all. It was a boy.

"My lady," her commander said as he approached. "A messenger from the free-born."

The boy came into the light. He was blond and blue-eyed and very fair-skinned beneath the browning from sun and wind. He was small and quick-looking, compact without being heavily muscled. He smiled and bowed rather awkwardly.

"I am Tib Arne," he announced. "I have been sent by Padishar Creel and the free-born to give greetings to the Elven people and to offer support in the struggle against the Federation." His speech sounded very rehearsed.

"I am Wren Elessedil," she replied, and offered her hand. He took it, held it uncertainly for a moment, and released it. "How did you find us, Tib?"

He laughed. "You found me. I came west out of Callahorn in search of the Elves, but you made my job easy. Your scouts were waiting at the mouth of the valley when I entered." He glanced about. "It seems I have arrived just in time for something."

"What sort of help do the free-born offer?" she asked, ignoring his observation. He was too quick by half.

"Me, for starters. I am to be your ready and willing servant, your link to the others until they arrive. The free-born assemble in the Dragon's Teeth for a march west. They should be here within the week. Five thousand or more with their allies, my queen."

Wren saw Triss lift his eyebrows. "Five thousand strong?" she repeated.

Tib shrugged. "So I was told. I'm just a messenger."

"And a rather young one at that," she observed.

His smile was quick and reassuring. "Oh, not so young as I look. And I do not travel alone. I have Gloon for protection."

Wren smiled back. "Gloon."

He nodded, then stuck his fingers in the corners of his mouth and gave a shrill whistle that silenced everything about them. Up came his right arm, and now Wren saw that he wore a thick leather glove that ran to his elbow.

Then down out of the darkness hurtled a shadow that was darker still, a whistle of sound and fury that sliced through the air like black lightning. It landed on the boy's glove with an audible thud, wings spread and cocked, feathers jutting out like spikes. In spite of herself, Wren shrank away. It was a bird, but a bird like no other she had ever seen. It was big, larger than a hawk or even an owl, its feathers slate gray with red brows and a crest that bristled menacingly. Its beak was yellow and sharply hooked. Its claws were two sizes too large for the rest of its body, and its body was squat and blocky, all sinew and muscle beneath its feathers. It hunched its head down into its shoulders like a fighter and stared at Wren through hard, wicked eyes.

"What is that?" she asked the boy, wondering suddenly where Faun was hiding—hoping she was hiding well.

"Gloon? He's a war shrike, a breed of hunting bird that comes out of the Troll country. I found him as a baby and raised him. Trained him to hunt." Tib seemed quite proud. "He makes sure nothing happens to me."

Wren believed it. She didn't like the look of the bird one bit. She forced her eyes away from it and fixed on the boy. "You must eat and rest here for tonight, Tib," she offered. "But shouldn't you go back in the morning and let the free-born know where we are? We need them to get here as quickly as they can."

He shook his head. "They come already and nothing I can do will move them along any quicker. When they get closer, they will send a message— another bird. Then I will send Gloon." He smiled. "They will find us, don't worry. But I am to stay with you, my queen. I am to serve you here."

"You might serve best by going back," the implacable Desidio observed.

Tib blinked and looked confused. "But . . . but I don't want to go back!" he blurted out impulsively. He suddenly seemed as young as he looked. "I want to stay here. Something is going to happen, isn't it? I want to be part of it." He glanced quickly at Wren. "You're Elves, my queen, and no one has seen Elves before, ever! I . . . I wasn't the first choice for this journey. I had to argue a long time to win the job. Don't make me leave right away. I can help in some way, I know I can. Please, my queen? I've come a long way to find you. Let me stay awhile."

"And Gloon as well, I suppose?" She smiled.

He smiled back instantaneously. "Oh, Gloon will stay hidden until he is called." He threw up his hand, and the war shrike streaked upward and disappeared. Tib watched him go, saying, "He looks after himself, mostly."

Wren glanced at Desidio, who shook his head doubtfully. Tib didn't seem to see, his eyes still directed skyward.

"Tib, why don't you get something to eat and then go to bed," Wren advised. "We'll talk about the rest of it in the morning."

The boy looked at her, blinked, stifled a yawn, nodded, and trotted off dutifully behind Desidio. Tiger Ty passed them coming up from the cooking fire with a plate of food and cast a sharp glance back at the boy on reaching Wren.

"Was that a war shrike I saw?" he growled. "Nasty bird, those. Hard to believe that boy could train one. Most of them would as soon take your head off as look at you."

"That dangerous?" Wren asked, interested.

"Killers," the Wing Rider answered. "Hunt anything, even a moor cat. Don't know how to quit once they've started something. It's rumored that in the old days they were used to hunt men—sent out like assassins. Smart and cruel." He shook his head. "Nasty, like I said."

She glanced at Triss. "Maybe we don't want it around, then."

Tiger Ty started away. "I wouldn't." He stretched. "Time for sleep. The others flew in an hour ago, in case you didn't see. We'll scout things out again tomorrow morning. Night."

He ambled off into the dark, gnarled, bowlegged, rocking from side to side like some old piece of furniture that had been jostled in passing. Wren and Triss watched him go without comment. When he was gone, they looked at each other.

"I'm sending Tib back," she said.

Triss nodded. Neither of them spoke after that.

Wren slept, curled into her light woolen blanket at the edge of the firelight, dreaming of things that were forgotten as quickly as they were gone. Twice she woke to the sounds of the night, tiny chirpings and buzzings, small movements in the brush, and the rustle of things unseen far overhead in the branches of the trees. It was warm and the air was still, and the combination did not make for a sound sleep. Home Guard slept around her; Triss was less than a dozen feet away. At the edges of her vision she saw others on patrol, vague shadows against the darkness. Curled in the crook of her arm, Faun stirred fitfully. The night edged away in a crawl, and she swam listlessly through sleep and waking.

She was just settling in for yet another try, the deepest part of the night reached, when a prickly face poked into view directly in front of her. She jumped in fright.

"Hssst! Easy, Wren Elessedil!" said a familiar voice.

Hurriedly she pushed herself up on one elbow. "Stresa!"

Faun squeaked in recognition, and the Splinterscat hissed it into silence. Lumbering close, it sat back on its haunches and regarded her with those strange blue eyes. "It didn't seem phhttt a good idea to let you go off on your own."

She smiled in spite of herself. "You nearly scared me to death! How did you get past the guards?"

The Splinterscat's tongue licked out, and she could have sworn that it smiled. "Really, now, Elf girl. They are only men. Sssstt! If you want to give me a challenge phffttt put me back on Morrowindl." The eyes blinked, luminous. "On second thought, don't. I like it here, in your world."

Wren hugged Faun into her body as the Tree Squeak tried to squirm away. "I'm glad you're here," she told Stresa. "I worry about you sometimes."

"Worry about me. Phaagg! Whatever for? After Morrowindl, nothing much frightens me. This is a good world you live in, Wren of the Elves."

"But not so good where we're going. Do you know?"

"Hsssttt. I heard. More of the dark things, the same as Morrowindl's. But how bad are these, Elf girl? Are they things like the rrowwwll Wisteron?"

The Splinterscat's nose was damp and glistening in the starlight. "No," she answered. "Not yet, at least. These are men, but many more than we are and determined to destroy us."

Stresa thought about it for a moment. "Still, better than the monsters."

"Yes, better." She breathed the hot night air in a sigh. "But some of these men make monsters, too."

"So nothing changes, does it?" The Splinterscat ruffled its quills and rose. "I'll be close to you hssttt but you won't see me. If you need me, though phhfftt I'll be there."

"You could stay," she suggested.

Stresa spit. "I'm happier in the forest. Safer, too. Rowwlll. You'd be safer as well, but you won't go. I'll have to be your eyes. Hssstt! What I see, you'll know about first." The tongue licked out. "Watch yourself, Wren Elessedil. Don't forget the lessons of Morrowindl."

She nodded. "I won't."

Stresa turned and started away. "Send the Squeak ssttt if you need me," he whispered back, and then was gone.

She stared after him into the darkness for a time, Faun cradled in her arms, small and warm. Finally she lay back again, smiled, and closed her eyes. She felt better for knowing that the Splinterscat was there for her.

In seconds she was asleep once more. She did not wake again until morning.

17

At daybreak, the vanguard of the Elven army prepared to set out again. Wren summoned Tib Arne and advised him that she was sending him back to the free-born to make certain that they knew he had found them and to urge them to come as quickly as possible. She assured him that it was important that he go or she would have honored his request to stay. She told him he was welcome to return when the message was delivered. Tib pouted a bit and expressed his disappointment, but in the end he agreed that she was right and promised to do his best to hurry the free-born to their aid. Desidio gave him a pair of Elven Hunters to act as escorts and protectors—despite his repeated protests that he needed no one—and the trio set out through the valley to the Streleheim Plains. Gloon did not make an appearance, and Wren was just as glad.

It took the Elves the better part of two days to close the gap between themselves and the Federation. They traveled swiftly and steadily, using the open grasslands to speed their passage, relying on the Wing Riders and the cavalry scouts to keep from being discovered. The Wing Riders brought back regular reports of the Southland army's progress, which had slowed. One day had been used in crossing the Mermidon and a second in repairs to equipment caused by water damage. The Federation had not traveled far beyond the north bank of the Mermidon when, by midafternoon of the second day, the Elves found themselves within striking distance.

The Wing Riders brought word of the contact, two of them, speeding out of the sun where it hung against the sky in a blazing white heat. The Elves were spread out along the edges of the Westland forests not far from where the Mermidon bent back upon itself coming out of the Pykon. When Wren was informed that the approaching army was no more than five miles distant and closing, she had Desidio order the Elves back into the shelter of the trees to wait for nightfall. There, in the cool of the shade, she called together the expedition's commanders.

"We have a choice to make," she informed them.

They were five in all, Triss, Desidio, Tiger Ty, Erring Rift, and herself. Rift was a tall, stoop-shouldered Elf with a shaggy black beard and thinning hair and eyes like chips of obsidian. As the leader of the Wing Riders, his presence was essential. Tiger Ty was there as a personal courtesy and because Wren trusted his judgment. They were gathered in a loose circle under an aging shagbark hickory, nudging at nut shells and twigs with their boots as they listened to her speak.

"We've found them," she continued, "but that's not enough. Now we have to decide what to do about it. I think we all realize what sort of progress they are making. A massive army, but moving at a decent rate of speed—much quicker than we had anticipated. Five days, and they have already crossed the Mermidon and gotten here. Our own army is at least a week away from where we sit. The Federation is not going to wait on us. Left alone, they will reach the Rhenn in that week's time, and we will be making our first stand in the place where we had hoped to make our last."

"The heat might slow them some on these open grasslands," Desidio observed.

"A fire would slow them worse," Rift suggested. He rubbed at his beard. "Set properly, the wind would carry it right into them."

"And right into the Westland forests as well," Triss finished.

"Or the wind could shift it into us," Wren shook her head. "Too risky, except as a last resort. No, I think we have a better choice."

"An engagement," Desidio declared quietly. "What you have planned for all along, my lady. What I am forbidden by order of the general to do."

Wren smiled and faced him squarely. "I told you there would come a time when it was necessary for you to hear me out. The time is now, Commander. I know what your orders are. I know what I promised General Oridio. I also know what I didn't promise him."

She shifted her weight and leaned forward. "If we sit here and do nothing, the Federation will reach the Rhenn before we do and bottle us up. Arborlon will be finished. There will be no time for anyone to come to our aid, free-born or otherwise. We need to slow this army down, to give our own time to come forward where it can be effective. Orders are orders, Commander, but in the field events dictate how closely those orders must be adhered to."

Desidio said nothing.

"We both promised that the vanguard would not be taken into battle against the Federation army until General Oridio arrived. Very well, we'll keep that promise. But nothing binds the actions of the Home Guard, which I command, or the Wing Riders, who are free to act on their own. I think we should consider ways in which they might be used against this enemy."

"A dozen Wing Riders and a hundred Home Guard?" Desidio raised his eyebrows questioningly.

"More than enough for what I think she's got in mind," Tiger Ty interjected defensively. "Let's hear her out."

Desidio nodded. Erring Rift was rubbing his chin harder, eyes intent. Triss looked as if they were discussing the weather.

"We are too small to engage the Federation army openly," she said, her eyes sweeping their faces. "But we have speed and quickness and surprise on our side, and these could be valuable weapons in a night attack designed to disrupt and confuse. Wing Riders can strike from anywhere, and the Home Guard are trained to be present without being seen. What if we were to come at them in the dark, when they do not expect it? What if we strike at them where they are vulnerable?"

Triss nodded. "Their wagons and supplies."

Erring Rift clapped his hands. "Their siege machines!"

"Set fire to them," Tiger Ty whispered eagerly. "Burn them to the ground while they sleep!"

"More than that," Wren interjected quickly, drawing them back to her. "Confuse them. Frighten them. At night, they cannot see. Let's take advantage of that. Do all you've suggested, but make them think there is an entire army out there doing it. Come at them all at once from a dozen directions and be gone again before they can determine what has happened. Leave them with the impression that they are besieged on all sides. They won't proceed so quickly after that. Even after they repair the damage, they will be working harder at looking for us and that will slow them down."

Erring Rift laughed. "Spoken like a true Rover girl!" he exclaimed enthusiastically, then added, rather quickly, "My lady."

"And what is to be my part in this?" Desidio asked quietly. "And that of the vanguard?"

Wren might have been mistaken, but she thought she caught a hint of anticipation in the other's voice, as if perhaps he was actually hoping she had something in mind. She did not wish to disappoint him.

"Supplies and siege machines will be kept to the army's rear. The Wing Riders and Home Guard will come from that direction. If you can see your way clear, Commander, a strike by your archers and cavalry along the front and flank would provide no small amount of additional confusion."

Desidio considered. "They may be more awake than you think. They may be better prepared."

"Within the borders of their own protectorate? Without having seen a single Elf during the entire course of their march north?" She shook her head. "By now, they are wondering if there is anyone at all to find."

"There may be Shadowen," Triss said quietly.

Wren nodded. "But the Shadowen will be disguised as men and will not wish to reveal themselves to the army. Remember, Triss—they manipulate by staying hidden. If they show themselves, they lose their anonymity and panic their army. I don't think they will risk it. I don't think they will have time even to think about it if we catch them off guard."

"We will only be able to do that once."

She smiled faintly. "So we had better make the most of it, hadn't we?" She looked at Desidio. "Can you help us?"

He gave her a rueful look. "What you mean is, can I go against my orders from General Oridio?" He sighed. "They are explicit, but then there is a certain amount of independent thinking permitted a commander in the field. Besides, you are correct in your assessment of how matters stand if we do nothing."

He looked to the others. "You are all committed to this?" They nodded, each of them. He looked back again at Wren. "Then I must do what I can to save you from yourselves, even if it means taking the field. The general will not approve, but he will accept the logic, I hope. He knows I have no authority over the Wing Riders or the Home Guard and certainly none over you, my lady." He paused, then added ruefully, "I confess I am surprised at how easily I am persuaded by you."

"You are persuaded by reason, Commander," she corrected. "There is a difference."

There was an exchange of looks. "Is the matter settled?" Tiger Ty asked gruffly.

"Except for strategy," Wren replied. "I leave that to you. But understand that I will be going with you. No, Tiger Ty, no arguments. Look to Triss—he doesn't even bother trying anymore."

The Wing Rider gave her a black look and bit back whatever objection he had been about to make.

"When do we do it, my lady?" Erring Rift asked. His black eyes sparkled.

Wren came to her feet. "Tonight, of course. As soon as they are sleeping." She stepped around them and began walking away. "I'm going to wash up and have something to eat. Let me know when your plan is in place."

She smiled in satisfaction at the silence that followed after her and did not look back.

The day closed with the western horizon colored red and purple and the clouds forming and reforming in a slowly changing panorama. The heat lingered on as the sun disappeared and the colors faded, a fetid dampness in the windless air that caused clothes to stick and skin to itch. The Elves ate early and tried to sleep, but even in the shade of the forests there was little comfort to be found. As midnight approached, Desidio's Elven Hunters were awakened, told to dress and arm, and taken from the trees onto the grasslands, slipping silently toward the rise north that overlooked the sleeping Federation army.

Wren went with them, anxious for a look at ground level before she took to the air with the Wing Riders. She went out with a detachment of Home Guard, Desidio and Triss leading, all of them dressed for concealment in green and brown forest colors with high boots, belts, and gloves for protection against brush and scrub. She was wearing a backpack to carry Faun (who would not be left behind) and had strung a leather pouch about her neck to keep the Elfstones close. A brace of long knives were strapped about her waist and a dagger was in one boot. Armed for anything, she thought. They rode a short distance onto the plains, then dismounted and made their way on foot to where the forward lines of Elven Hunters crouched in the dark.

Alone with Triss and Desidio, she crept forward to where she could look down on the Federation encampment.

Their army was enormous. Even though she had seen it from the air with Tiger Ty, she was not prepared for how huge it looked now. It sprawled in a maze of hundreds of cooking fires for as far as the eye could see, a wash of light that crowded out the stars with its brilliance. Talk and laughter drifted off the plains as clear as if the voices came from only yards away. Outlined against the sky by the firelight were the huge siege machines, great skeletal bulks of wooden bones and iron joints, rising up like misshapen giants. Wagons huddled in clusters, piled with stores and weapons, and the smell of oil and pitch drifted on the wind. Even though it was by now after midnight, there were many who still did not sleep, wandering from fire to fire, spurred by the clink of glasses and tin cups, drawn by calls and shouts and the promise of drink and companionship.

Wren glanced at Triss. The Federation was at ease with itself, satisfied that its size and strength would ward it from any danger. She mouthed the word "guards" questioningly. Triss shrugged, pointed left and then right, picking out the sentries that the Federation commanders had placed. They were few and widely scattered. She had been right in her assessment; the Southlanders were not expecting trouble.

They slipped back down the rise until they were out of view of the camp, then rose and retraced their steps through the lines of bowmen and cavalry. When they were safely away, she drew Triss and Desidio close.

"Get as close as you can, Commander," she whispered to the latter. "Wait for the Wing Riders to strike at them from the rear. Look for the fires, then attack. Archers followed by cavalry, as we planned, then quickly away. Take no chances. Don't let them see any more of you than necessary. We want them to use their imaginations as to how many of us there are."

Desidio nodded. He knew his job better than she, but she was the queen and he was not about to tell her so. She smiled faintly, took his hand in her own to express her confidence, then turned with Triss and crept away. Their escort was waiting, and they remounted and rode back into the forests.

The Wing Riders and the main body of the Home Guard were waiting in a clearing. A dozen baskets had been woven from branches and tied together with leather cords, each large enough to hold a dozen men. The Elven Hunters climbed aboard, armed with longbows and short swords, dark and silent forms in the night. Each basket would be carried by a Roc onto the plains behind the Federation army. Wren hurried to Tiger Ty, who was already seated atop Spirit, and pulled herself up behind him, securing the straps that would hold her in place. Triss climbed into the basket set in front. Erring Rift gave a low whistle, and one by one the Rocs rose skyward, claws fastened to straps that held the baskets at four corners, lifting them gently, carefully away from the earth, carrying them up through the trees and into the darkened skies.

Wind rushed in cool waves across Wren Elessedil's face as Spirit cleared the trees and swept east toward the plains. The fires of the Federation army became visible almost immediately, and their sweep seemed even larger from here. Erring Rift took the lead aboard his Roc Grayl, turning the formation south along the line of the forests and as far away from the light as he could manage. They flew silently down the tree line, watching the fires widen and then shrink again as they passed beyond their glow and back into the darkness. When they were far enough down, Rift led them back again toward the light, swinging wide onto the plains so that they would come up from the center rear.

Wren clung to Tiger Ty with one hand to steady herself and to maintain contact. The Wing Rider was solid and steady in his seat, hunched over as he flew, face turned away. Neither of them spoke.

When they were as close as they could safely manage without being seen, the Rocs settled earthward. The baskets were lowered, and the straps released. The Home Guard scattered from the carriers and disappeared into the night. The Rocs rose again, Wren still riding behind Tiger Ty, and swept wide in an arc that carried them out and away. A few minutes for Triss to dispose of the sentries, and then it would be time.

The Rocs swung back again, leveled out, and headed directly into the Federation camp, picking up speed as they went. This was the most dangerous part—so dangerous that Tiger Ty was forbidden to do more than to carry the Queen of the Elves as an observer. Whatever else might happen, she was to come away safe. They sped toward the Federation encampment, flattening out some fifty feet above the ground as they passed over the first of the fires.

Then down they went, dark arrows out of the night, all but Spirit. Eleven strong, the Rocs hurtled into the Federation camp, streaking toward the watch fires. At the last instant they were spotted, and howls of surprise rose from the men below. The warnings came too late. Wings extended, the Rocs skimmed the watch fires, choosing those that were close to dying, and snatched up bunches of the burning embers with their hardened claws. Why bring fire for the burning when there was fire already at hand? Erring Rift had argued. Away flew the Rocs, wheeling right and left toward the siege machines. The Federation soldiers were turning out of their blankets and bedding in swarms, trying to decipher from the jumble of words being shouted at them by those already awake what was happening. By now the Rocs had reached the siege machines and supply wagons. Burning brands tumbled from their claws onto the dry, seasoned wood. The wind fanned the embers in falling, and the wood burst instantly into flames. Some of the brands were dropped onto dusty canvas tarpaulins, some onto the shingle-roofed cabins atop the giant scaling towers, some into the vats of pitch that served to coat the missiles of the catapults.

Fire roared into the air from a dozen quarters, licking hungrily. Shouts turned to screams of fury and cries for water, but the flames were everywhere at once. The Rocs swept down on those who tried to smother the flames early, driving them away.

Then the Home Guard attacked from out of the night, longbows sending a hail of arrows into the milling Federation soldiers, dropping them as they struggled for their weapons, killing them before they knew what was happening. Swordsmen appeared, materializing all along the encampment's edges, cutting loose war horses and pack animals and driving them into the night, spilling sacks of grain and overturning water casks, and shredding whoever stood in their way.

The Federation army was in total disarray. Men charged about wildly, striking out at anyone or anything they encountered, frequently themselves. Officers tried to restore order, but no one was certain who was who, and the effort was swept away in the tide of confusion.

Now Desidio's Elven Hunters struck from the front, bowmen first, raining arrows into the camp, one volley after another. Then the cavalry swept out of the night with a terrifying howl. From high overhead Wren watched the Elven horses cut a swath through the front ranks of the Federation, charging deep into the camp and then out again, scattering watch fires and men, sending soldiers and retainers fleeing into the darkness.

But the Federation army was huge, and the attacks barely scratched its edges. Already ranks of men had formed at its center, where calm still prevailed, and were beginning a slow, steady march outward toward the source of the trouble. Hundreds of foot soldiers armed with shields and short swords trooped through the melee, shoving aside or trampling their own men, seeking out the intruders. In moments they were at the camp's perimeter, the light of burning wagons and siege machines reflecting off their armored bodies like blood.

Wren searched the darkness to discover what had become of her Elves. The Rocs were already winging south again, and Tiger Ty had turned Spirit to follow. She scanned the camp over her shoulder as they sped away into the dark, and there was no sign of Desidio's Hunters or the Home Guard. The Federation soldiers were advancing from out of the firelight, searching in vain for an enemy that had already vanished. Behind, the entire siege and pack train was in flames, pyramids of fire that burned hundreds of feet into the night sky and gave off a heat so intense that Wren could feel it even from where she flew. The stench of ash and smoke was thick in her nostrils, and the cries of the injured filled her ears. Men lay everywhere, bloodied and still.

We have our victory, she thought, but felt the intensity of her initial satisfaction diminish.

Away they flew, Spirit trailing the others momentarily before catching up. Spread out, they descended to where the makeshift baskets waited, found the Home Guard already in place, snatched up the retaining straps, lifted the baskets into the air, and sped away west toward the forests. It was all accomplished in a few moments, and then they were passing over the trees, far from the madness of the Federation camp, back into the shelter from which they had come.

When they set down again within the forest, Wren summoned her commanders to discover the extent of their own losses. The Rocs had passed through the strike unscathed. All of the Home Guard were safely returned save one. Only three of the Elven Hunters had been lost, cavalry pulled from their horses. There were a number of injuries, but only one was serious. The attack had been a complete success.

Wren thanked Triss, Desidio, and Erring Rift, and ordered the vanguard to pack up. They would slip north now before the Federation could begin to search for them, choosing a new spot within the Westland forests to hide. Come morning, they would scout the damage to the enemy and decide what to do next. Tonight had been a good beginning, but the end was still far from sight.

Quickly the Elves prepared to move out. Whispers of satisfaction and handclasps passed from man to man as they worked. The Elves had fought their first battle in their homeland in more than a hundred years and won.

Morrowindl's long night was finally behind them, and some small part of the rage and frustration that they had lived with all their lives had been released. For many, there was a renewed sense of being set free.

Wren Elessedil understood. As Queen of the Elves that night in more than name, as her grandmother's hope of what she could be and Garth's promise of what she would be, something in her had been set free as well. She could feel the way the Elves looked at her. She could sense their respect. She belonged to them now. She was one of them.

Within an hour, all was ready. In stealth and silence, the Elves of Morrowindl's past melted away into the night.

A fter an hour's steady march, the Elves spent the remainder of that night in a forest just north of the Pykon that was backed up against the larger mass of Drey Wood and faced south toward the plains on which the Federation camp was settled. All night they could see the fires from the burning siege machines and supply wagons lighting the horizon in a bright glow, and in the still of their forest concealment they could hear faint shouts and cries.

They slept fitfully and rose again at dawn to wash, eat, and be dispatched to their duties. Desidio sent riders north to Arborlon with news of the attack and Wren's personal request to Barsimmon Oridio that the balance of the army proceed south as soon as possible. Cavalry patrols were dispatched in all directions with orders to make certain that no other Southland force was in the field besides the one they knew about. Special attention was to be given to the garrisons within the cities of Callahorn. Wing Riders flew south to assess the extent of the damage inflicted in last night's strike, with a particular eye toward determining how soon the column would be able to move again. The day was clouded and gray, and the Rocs would fly unseen against the dark backdrop of the Westland mountains and forest. The remainder of the Elves, after seeing to the care and feeding of their animals and the cleaning and repair of their battle gear, were sent back to sleep until midday.

Wren spent the morning with her commanders—Desidio, Triss, and Erring Rift. Tiger Ty had flown south, determined that any assessment made of the condition of the Federation army should be subject to his personal verification. Wren was both tired and excited, flushed with energy and taut with fatigue, and she knew that she needed a few hours' sleep herself before she would be clear-headed again. Nevertheless, she wanted her commanders—and especially Desidio, now that she had won him over—to start considering what their small force should do next. To a great extent, that depended on what the Federation did. Still, there were only so many possibilities, and Wren wanted to steer the thinking regarding those possibilities in the right direction. With luck the Southlanders would be unable to start moving again for several days, and that would give the main body of the Elven army time to reach the Rhenn. But if they did begin to move, it would be up to Wren and the vanguard to find a way to slow them once more. Under no circumstances did she intend that they should do nothing. Standing fast was out of the question. They had won an important victory over their larger foe with last night's strike, and she did not intend to lose the advantage that victory had established. The Federation would be looking over its collective shoulder now; she wanted to keep it looking for as long as possible. It was important that her commanders think the same way she did.

She was satisfied she had accomplished this when they were done conferring, and she went off to sleep. She slept until it was nearing midday and woke to find Tiger Ty and the Wing Rider patrol returned. The news they carried was good. The Federation army was making no attempt to advance. All of its siege equipment and most of its supplies had been reduced to ashes. The camp was sitting exactly where they had left it last night, and all of the army's efforts seemed to be directed toward caring for the injured, burying the dead, and culling through what remained of their stores. Scouts were patrolling the perimeter and foraging parties were canvassing the countryside, but the main body of the army was still picking itself up off the ground.

Still, Tiger Ty wasn't satisfied.

"It's one thing to find them regrouping today," he declared to Wren, out of hearing of the others. "You expect them to sit tight after an attack like that one. They suffered real damage, and they need to lick their wounds a bit. But don't be fooled. They'll be doing what we're doing—thinking about how to react to this. If they're still sitting there tomorrow, it'll be time for a closer look. Because they'll be up to something by then. You can depend on it."

Wren nodded, then led him off to join Triss for lunch. Triss, apprised of Tiger Ty's thinking, agreed. This was a seasoned army they faced, and its commanders would work hard at finding a way to take back the momentary advantage the Elves had won.

They had just finished eating when an Elven patrol rode in with a battered and disheveled Tib Arne in tow. The patrol had been scouting the low end of the Streleheim toward Callahorn when they had come across the boy wandering the plains in search of the Elves. Finding him alone and injured, they had picked him up and brought him directly here.

Tib was cut and bruised about the face, and covered from head to foot with dirt and dust. He was very distressed and could barely speak at first. Wren brought him over to sit, and cleaned off his face with a damp cloth. Triss and Tiger Ty stood close to listen to what he had to say.

"Tell me what happened," she urged him after she had calmed him down sufficiently to speak.

"I am sorry, my queen," he apologized, shamefaced now at his loss of control. "I have been out there for a day and a night with nothing to eat or drink and I haven't had any sleep."

"What happened to you?" she repeated.

"We were attacked, myself and the men you sent with me, not far from the Dragon's Teeth. It was night when they came, more than a dozen of them. We were camped, and they charged out at us. The men you sent, they fought as hard as they could. But they were killed. I would have been killed as well, but for Gloon. He came to my aid, striking at my attackers, and I ran away into the dark. I could hear Gloon's shriek, the shouts of the men fighting him, and then nothing. I hid in the darkness all night, then started back to find you. I was afraid to go on without Gloon, afraid that there were other patrols searching for me."

"The shrike is dead?" Tiger Ty asked abruptly.

Tib dissolved into tears. "I think so. I didn't see him again. I whistled for him when it was light, but he didn't come." He looked at Wren, stricken. "I'm sorry I failed you, my lady. I don't know how they found us so easily. It was as if they knew!"

"Never mind, Tib," she comforted him, placing her hand on his shoulder. "You did your best. I'm sorry about Gloon."

"I know," he murmured, composing himself once more.

"You'll stay here with us now," she told him. "We'll find another way to get word to the free-born, or if not, we'll just wait for them to find us."

She ordered food and drink for the boy, wrapped him in a woolen blanket, then pulled Tiger Ty and Triss aside. They stood beneath a towering oak with acorn shells carpeting the forest floor and clouds screening away the skies overhead and leaving the light faint and gray.

"What do you think?" she asked them.

Triss shook his head. "Those were experienced men that went with the boy. They shouldn't have been caught unprepared. I think they were either very unlucky or the boy is right and someone was waiting for them."

"I'll tell you what I think," Tiger Ty said. "I think it's pretty hard to kill a war shrike even when you can see it, let alone when you can't."

She looked at him. "What does that mean?"

His frown deepened. "It means that there's something about all this that bothers me. Don't you think this boy is an odd choice for the job of carrying word to us about the free-born?"

She stared at him wordlessly for a moment, considering. "He's young, yes. But he would be less likely to be noticed because of it. And he seems confident enough about himself." She paused. "You don't trust him, Tiger Ty?"

"I'm not saying that." The other's brows knitted fiercely. "I just think we ought to be careful."

She nodded, knowing better than to dismiss Tiger Ty's suspicion out of hand. "Triss?"

The Captain of the Home Guard was tugging at the bindings on his broken arm. The sling had come off yesterday before the attack, and all that remained was a pair of narrow splints laced about his forearm.

He did not glance up as he tightened a loosening knot. "I think Tiger Ty is right. It doesn't hurt to be careful."

She folded her arms. "All right. Assign someone to keep an eye on him." She turned to Tiger Ty. "I have something important I want you to do. I want you to pick up where Tib left off. Take Spirit and fly east. See if you can find the free-born and lead them here, just in case they're having trouble reaching us. It may take you several days, and you'll have to track them without much help from us. I don't have any idea where to tell you to start, but if there are five thousand of them they shouldn't be hard to find."

Tiger Ty frowned anew. "I don't like leaving you. Send someone else."

She shook her head. "No, it has to be you. I can trust you to make certain the search is successful. Don't worry about me. Triss and the Home Guard will keep me safe. I'll be fine."

The gnarled Wing Rider shook his head. "I don't like it, but I'll go if you tell me to."

On the chance that he might encounter Par or Coll Ohmsford or Walker Boh or even Morgan Leah in his travels, she gave him a brief description of each and a means by which he could be certain who they were. When she had finished, she gave him her hand and wished him well.

"Be careful, Wren of the Elves," he cautioned gruffly, keeping her hand firmly tucked in his own for a moment. "The dangers of this world are not so different from Morrowindl's."

She smiled, nodded, and he was gone. She watched him gather a pack of stores and blankets together, strap them atop Spirit, board, and wing off into the gray. She stared skyward for a long time after he was lost from sight. The clouds were turning darker. It would be raining by nightfall.

We'll need better shelter, she thought. We'll need to move.

"Call Desidio over," she ordered Triss.

A heavy enough rain would mire the whole of the grasslands on which the Federation camped. It was too much to hope for, but she couldn't help herself.

Just give us a week, she begged, eyes fixed on the roiling gray. Just a week.

The first drop of rain splashed on her face.

The Elven vanguard assembled, packed up, and moved back into the heavy trees within Drey Wood, there to wait for the storm to pass. It began to rain more heavily as the day edged toward nightfall, and by dusk it was pouring. The Wing Riders had tethered their Rocs apart from the horses, and the men had stretched canvas sheets between trees to keep themselves and their stores dry. The patrols had come in, returned from everywhere but Arborlon, with word that nothing was approaching from any direction and there was no sign of any other Federation force.

They ate a hot meal, the smoke concealed by the downpour, and retired to sleep. Wren was preoccupied with dozens of possibilities of what
might happen next and thought she would be awake for hours, but she fell
asleep almost instantly, her last conscious thought of Triss and the two
Home Guard who stood watch close by.

It was still raining when she awoke, as steady as before. The skies were
clouded, and the earth was sodden and turning to mud. It rained all that
day and into the next. Scouts went forth to check on the Federation army's
progress and returned to advise that there was none. As Wren had hoped,
the grasslands were soggy and treacherous, and the Southland army had
pulled up its collective collar and was waiting out the storm. She remembered Tiger Ty's admonition not to be fooled into thinking that the Federation was doing nothing simply because it was not moving, but the weather
was so bad that the Wing Riders did not wish to fly and there was little to
discover while they were grounded.

Word arrived from Arborlon that the main body of the Elven army was
still several days from being ready to begin its march south. Wren ground
her teeth in frustration. The weather wasn't helping the Elves either.

She spent some of her time with Tib, curious to know more about
him, wondering if there was any basis for Tiger Ty's suspicions. Tib was
open and cheerful, except when Gloon was mentioned. Encouraged by her
attention, he was eager to talk about himself. He told her he had grown up
in Varfleet, subsequently lost his parents to the Federation prisons, had been
recruited by the free-born to help in the Resistance, and had lived with the
outlaws ever since. He carried messages mostly, able to pass almost anywhere because he looked as if he wasn't a danger to anyone. He laughed
about that, and made Wren laugh, too. He said he had traveled north once
or twice to the outlaw strongholds in the Dragon's Teeth, but hadn't gone
there to live because he was too valuable in the cities. He spoke glowingly
of the free-born cause and of the need to free the Borderlands from Federation rule. He did not speak of the Shadowen or indicate that he knew
anything about them. She listened carefully to everything he said and heard
nothing that suggested Tib was anything other than what he claimed.

She asked Triss to speak with the boy as well so that he might decide.
Triss did, and his opinion was the same as her own. Tib Arne seemed to be
who and what he claimed. Wren was persuaded. After that, she let the matter drop.

The rain ended on the third day, disappearing at midmorning as clouds
dispersed and skies cleared into bright sunlight. Water dripped off leaves
and puddled in hollows, and the air turned steamy and damp. Desidio sent
riders back to the plains, and Erring Rift dispatched a pair of Wing Riders
south. The Elves moved out of the deep forest to the edge of the grasslands
and settled down to wait.

The scouts and the Wing Riders returned at midday with varying reports. The Elven Hunters had found nothing, but the Wing Riders reported
that the Federation camp was being struck, and the army was preparing to

move. As it was already midday, it was uncertain as to what this meant since the army could not hope to progress more than a few miles before dusk. Wren listened to all the reports, had them repeated a second time, thought the matter through, then summoned Erring Rift.

"I want to go up for a look," she advised him. "Can you choose someone to take me?"

The black-bearded Rift laughed. "And have to face Tiger Ty if something goes wrong? Not a chance! I'll take you myself, my queen. That way if anything bad happens at least I won't be around to answer for it!"

She told Triss what she was about, declined his offer to accompany her, and moved to where Rift was strapping himself onto Grayl. Tib caught up with her, wide-eyed and anxious, and asked if he might go as well. She laughed and told him no, but spurred by his mix of eagerness and disappointment promised that he might go another time.

Minutes later she was winging her way southward atop Grayl, peering down at the damp canopy of the forests below and the windswept carpet of the grasslands east. Mist rose off the land in steamy waves, and the air shimmered like bright cloth. Grayl sped quickly down the forest line past the Pykon until they were within sight of the Federation army. Rift guided the Roc close against the backdrop of trees and mountains, keeping between the Southlanders and the glare of the midafternoon sun.

Wren peered down at the sprawling camp. The report had been right. The army was mobilizing, packing up goods, forming up columns of men, and preparing to move out. Some soldiers were already under way, the lead-most divisions, and they were heading north. Whatever else the Elf attack might have done, it had not discouraged the army's original purpose. The march to Arborlon was under way once more.

Grayl swept past, and as Rift was about to swing the giant Roc back again, Wren caught his arm and gestured for them to continue on. She was not sure what she was looking for, only that she wanted to be certain she wasn't missing anything. Were there riders coming up from the Southland cities, reports being exchanged, reinforcements being sent? Tiger Ty's warning whispered in her ear.

They flew on, following the muddy ribbon of the Mermidon where it flowed south out of the Pykon along the plains before turning east above the Shroudslip toward Kern. The grasslands stretched away south and east, empty and green and sweltering in the summer heat. The wind blew across her face, whipping at her eyes until they teared. Erring Rift hunched forward, hands resting on Grayl's neck, as steady as stone, guiding by touch.

Ahead, the Mermidon swung sharply east, narrowed, and then widened again as it disappeared into the grasslands. The river was sluggish and swollen by the rains, clogged with debris from the mountains and woodlands, churning its way steadily on through its worn channel.

On the river's far bank a glint of sunlight reflected off metal as something moved. Wren blinked, then touched Rift's shoulder. The Wing

Rider nodded. He had seen it, too. He slowed Grayl's flight and guided the Roc closer to the concealment of the trees by the northern edge of the Irrybis.

Another glint of light flashed sharply, and Wren peered ahead carefully. There was something big down there. No, several somethings, she corrected. All of them moving, lumbering along like giant ants . . .

And then she got a good look at them, hunched down at the riverbank as they prepared to cross at a narrows, coming out of the Tirfing on their way north.

Creepers.

Eight of them.

She took a quick breath, seeing clearly now the armored bodies studded with spikes and cutting edges, the insect legs and mandibles, the mix of flesh and iron formed of the Shadowen magic.

She knew about Creepers.

Rift swung Grayl sharply back into the trees, away from the view of the things on the riverbank, away from the revealing sunlight. Wren glanced back over her shoulder to make certain she had not made a mistake. Creepers, come out of the Southland, sent to give aid to the Federation army that marched on Arborlon—it was the Shadowen answer to her disruption of the Federation army's march. She remembered the history Garth had taught her as a child, a history that the people of the Four Lands had whispered rather than told for more than fifty years, tales of how the Dwarves had resisted the Federation advance into the Eastland until the Creepers had been sent to destroy them.

Creepers. Sent now, it seemed, to destroy the Elves.

A pit opened in the center of her stomach, chill and dark. Erring Rift was looking at her, waiting for her to tell him what to do. She pointed back the way they had come. Rift nodded and urged Grayl ahead. Wren stole a final look back and watched the Creepers disappear into the heat.

Gone for the moment, she thought darkly.

But what would the Elves do when they reappeared?

W alker Boh blinked.

It was a crystalline clear day, the kind of day in which the sunlight is so bright and the colors so brilliant that it almost hurts the eyes to look. The skies were empty of clouds from horizon to horizon, a deep blue void that stretched away forever. Out of that void and those skies blazed the sun at midday, a white-hot glare that could only be seen by squinting and quickly looking away again. It flooded down upon the Four Lands, bringing out the colors of late summer with startling clarity, even the dull browns of dried grasses and dusty earth, but especially the greens of the forests and grasslands, the blues of the rivers and lakes, and the iron grays and burnt coppers of the mountains and flats. The sun's heat rose in waves in those quarters where winds did not cool, but even there everything seemed etched and defined with a craftsman's precision, and there was the sense that even a sharp cry might shatter it all.

It was a day for living, where all the promises ever made might find fulfillment and all the hopes and dreams conceived might come to pass. It was a day for thinking about life, and thoughts of death seemed oddly out of place.

Walker's smile was faint and bitter. He wished he could find a way to make such thoughts disappear.

He stood alone outside Paranor's walls, just at their northwest corner beneath a configuration in the parapets that jutted out to form a shallow overhang, staring out across the sweep of the land. He had been there since sunrise, having slipped out through the north gates while the Four Horsemen were gathered at the west sounding their daily challenge. Almost six hours had passed, and the Shadowen hadn't discovered him. He was cloaked once again in a spell of invisibility. The spell had worked before, he had argued to Cogline while laying out his plan. No reason it shouldn't work again.

So far, it had.

Sunlight washed the walls of the Dragon's Teeth, chasing even the most persistent of shadows, stripping clean the flat, barren surface of the rocks. He could see north above the treeline to the empty stretches of the Streleheim. He could see east to the Jannisson and south to the Kennon. Streams and ponds were a glimmering of blue through the trees that circled the Keep, and songbirds flew in brilliant bursts of color that surprised and delighted.

Walker Boh breathed deeply the midday air. Anything was possible on a day like this one. Anything.

He was dressed in loose-fitting gray robes cinched about his waist, the hood pulled down so that his black hair hung loose to his shoulders. He was bearded, but trimmed and combed. Nothing of this was visible, of course. To anyone passing, and particularly to the Shadowen, he was just another part of the wall. Rest and nourishment had restored his strength. The wounds he had suffered three days earlier were mostly healed, if not forgotten. He did not give thought to what had befallen him then except in passing. He was focused on what was to happen now, this day, this hour.

It was the tenth day of the Shadowen siege. It was the day he meant for that siege to end.

He glanced back over his shoulder along the castle wall as another of the Four Horsemen circled into view. It was Famine, edging around the turn that would take it along the north wall, skeletal frame hunched over its serpent mount, looking neither left nor right as it proceeded, lost in its own peculiar form of madness. Gray as ashes and ephemeral as smoke, it slouched along the pathway. It passed within several feet of Walker Boh and did not look up.

Today, the newest of the Druids thought to himself.

He looked out again across the valley, thinking of other times and places, of the history that had preceded him, of all the Druids who had come to Paranor and made it their home. Once there had been hundreds, but they had all died save one when the Warlock Lord had trapped them there a thousand years ago. Bremen alone had survived to carry on, a solitary bearer of hope for the Races and wielder of the Druid magic. Then Bremen had passed away, and Allanon had come. Now Allanon was gone, and there was only Walker Boh.

The empty sleeve of his missing arm was drawn back and pinned against his body. He reached across to test the fitting, to touch experimentally his shoulder and the scarred flesh that ended only inches below. He could barely remember any more what it had been like to have two arms. It seemed odd to him that it should be so difficult. But much had happened to him in the weeks since his encounter with the Asphinx, and it might be argued that he could not be expected to remember anything of his old life, so completely had he changed. Even the anger and mistrust he had felt for the Druids had dissipated, useless now to one who had become their successor. The Druids he had despised belonged to the past. Gone, too, was the fury he had borne for the Grimpond, relegated to that same past. The Grimpond had tried its best to destroy him and failed. It would not have another chance. The Grimpond was a shadow in a shadowland. It could never come out, and Walker would never go back to see it. The past had carried away Pe Ell and the Stone King as well. Walker had found the strength to survive all of the enemies that had been set against him, and now they were memories that barely mattered in the scheme of his life's present demands.

Walker breathed the air, closed his eyes, and drifted away into a place deep inside him. War was passing now, all sharp edges and spikes, glinting armored plates and black breathing holes. Walker ignored the Shadowen. Settling into the silence and the calm that lay within, he played out once more what was to happen. Step by step, he went over the plan he had formed while he lay healing, taking himself through the events he would precipitate and the consequences he would control. There would be nothing left to chance this time. There would be no testing, no halfway measures, no quarter given. He would succeed, or he would . . .

He almost smiled.

Or he would not.

He opened his eyes and glanced skyward. The midday was past now, edging on toward afternoon. But the light was not yet at its brightest and the heat not yet at its greatest, and so he would wait a little longer still.

Light and heat would serve him better than it would the Shadowen, and that was why he was out there at midday. Before, he had thought to slip away in darkness. But darkness was the ally of the Horsemen, for they were creatures born of it and took their strength therefrom. Walker, with his Druid magic, would find his strength in brightness.

It was to be a testing of strengths, after all, that would determine who lived and died this day.

Strengths of all kinds.

He remembered his last conversation with Cogline. It was nearing dawn and he was preparing to go out. There was movement on the steps leading down through the gate towers to the entry court where he was positioned, and Cogline appeared. His stick-thin body slipped from the stairwall shadows in a soft flutter of robes and labored breathing. The seamed, whiskered face glanced at Walker briefly from beneath the edges of his frayed cowl, then looked away again. He approached and stopped, turning toward the door that led out.

"Are you ready?" he asked.

Walker nodded. They had discussed it all—or as much of it as Walker was willing to discuss. There was nothing more to say.

The old man's hands rested on the stone bulwarks that shielded and supported the iron-bound entry, so thin that they seemed almost transparent. "Let me come with you," he said quietly.

Walker shook his head. "We have discussed this already."

"Change your mind, Walker. Let me come. You will have need of me."

He sounded so sure, Walker recalled thinking. "No. You and Rumor will wait here. Stay by the door—let me back in if this fails."

Cogline's jaw tightened. "If this fails, you won't need me to let you back in."

True, Walker thought. But that didn't change things. He wasn't going to let the old man and the moor cat go out there with him. He wasn't going to be responsible for their lives as well. It would be enough that he would have to worry about keeping himself whole.

"You think I can't look after myself," the old man said, as if reading his thoughts. "You forget I took care of myself for years before you came along—before there were any Druids. I took care of you as well, once."

Walker nodded. "I know that."

The old man fidgeted. "Could be I was meant to take care of you again, you know. Could be you'll have need of me out there." He turned his face within the cowl to look at Walker. "I'm an old man, Walker. I've lived a long time—lived a full life. It doesn't matter so much what happens to me anymore."

"It matters to me."

"It shouldn't. It shouldn't matter a whit." Cogline was emphatic. "Why should it matter? Since when did you like me all that much anyway? I was the one who dragged you into this business. I was the one who persuaded you to visit the Hadeshorn, then to read the Druid History. Have you forgotten?"

Walker shook his head. "No, I haven't forgotten any of it. But it was me who made the choices that mattered—not you. We've talked all this out, too. You were as much a pawn of the Druids as I was. Everything was decided three hundred years ago when Allanon bestowed the blood trust on Brin Ohmsford. You are not to blame for any of it."

Cogline's eyes turned filmy and distant. "I am to blame for everything that has happened in my life and yours as well, Walker Boh. I chose early on to take up the Druid way and chose after to discard it. I chose the old sciences to learn, to recover in small part. I made myself a creature of both worlds, Druid and Man, taking what I needed, keeping what I coveted, stealing from both. I am the link between the past and the present, the new and the old, and Allanon was able to use me as such. How much of what I am has made your own transformation possible, Walker? How far would you have gone without me there to prod you on? Do you think for a moment that I wasn't aware of that? Or that Allanon was blind to it? No, I cannot be absolved from my blame. You cannot absolve me by taking it upon yourself."

Walker remembered the vehemence in the other's voice, the hard edge it had revealed, the insistence it had conveyed. "Then I shall not attempt to absolve you, old man," he replied. "But neither shall I absolve myself. You did not make the choices for me; nor did you hinder me in making them. Yes, there were compelling reasons to choose as I did, but those reasons were not suggested by you before I had considered them myself. Besides, I could claim as you do, if I wished. Without me, what part would you have had in all of this? Would you have been more than a messenger to Par and Wren if you had not been tied to me as well? I don't think that you can say so."

The old man's face was lowered into shadow by then, seeing the other's inflexibility, hearing his resolve.

"You will help me best by waiting here," Walker finished, reaching out to touch the other's arm. "Always before, you have understood the importance of knowing when to act and when not to. Do so again for me now."

It had ended there, Cogline standing with him until the sound of the Shadowen challenge had reverberated through Paranor's stone walls and Walker had gone out into the gloomy dawn to meet it.

Strengths of all kinds, he repeated as he stood now in the lee of the castle wall and listened to the approach of the next of the circling Shadowen. He would need especially a resolve of the sort that Cogline possessed—a fierce determination not to give in to the hardest and most certain of life's dictates—if he was to survive this day. Famine, Pestilence, War, and Death the Four Horsemen of the Apocalypse, come to claim his soul. But on this day he was Fate, and Fate would determine the destiny of all.

He looked up as Pestilence appeared, then straightened perceptibly. It was time.

Walker Boh waited in the shadow of the wall, an invisible presence, while the Horseman approached. It came disinterestedly, lethargically, borne on its serpent mount, a swarm of buzzing, plague-ridden insects gathered in the shape of a man. Pestilence lacked features and therefore expression, and Walker could not tell what it was seeing or thinking. It passed without slowing, serpent claws scraping roughly on the path. Walker fell into step behind it. The spell of invisibility kept him from being seen, and the sound of the serpent's own passage kept him from being heard. Walker had considered using the spell of invisibility to slip clear of the Shadowen entirely. But they had been quick enough to find him when he had tried to escape through Paranor's underground tunnels, even though he had been as silent as thought, and he believed that they could sense him when he was far enough from the Keep, from his sanctuary and the source of his Druid power. Even invisibility might not protect him then. Better, he had decided, to use his advantage where it could be relied upon and put an end to the Horsemen once and for all.

In the wake of Pestilence he circled the castle walls, the silence of midday broken only by the scrabble of serpent claws and the buzzing of caged insects. They moved out of the cooler north wall and down along the west, passing the gates at which each morning the Horsemen gathered to issue challenge to him. He had chosen the north wall in which to hide, aware that he would be out there for hours in the heat, hoping that the castle's lee shadows might give him some protection. But the south wall was where he would fight these Shadowen—south, where the sunlight was strongest. Already it was brightening ahead as they passed from the last shade offered by the castle ramparts and edged out into the light.

They rounded the corner of the south wall, a towering, flat expanse of burning stone that faced out across a broad sweep of forestland towards the densely clustered peaks of the Dragon's Teeth. A worn, dusty stretch of bluff offered what passageway there was below the wall, barren save for a smattering of scrub and a few stunted trees that fell away in a steep slide toward the cooler woodlands. The heat rose in a swelter that threatened to suck the air from Walker's lungs, but he held himself steady against the burning rush, trailing Pestilence at the same distance, catching sight momentarily of Famine far ahead disappearing into the shadows formed by the parapet arch beneath the eastern fasthold.

The seconds slipped away. Walker could feel the tension build inside. Be patient, he reminded himself. Wait until it is time.

Within, his magic began to come together.

When Pestilence was midway between the near watchtower and the south gates, Walker Boh struck. Still concealed within the spell of invisibility, he unleashed a thunderbolt at Pestilence that sent both rider and mount tumbling to the earth. The Horseman tried to rise, and Walker struck again, the magic a cool heat lancing from his hands, slamming the Shadowen backward in shock. Already Walker could hear the sound of the others coming, a shriek in his mind. Already he could feel their anger.

Famine appeared first, wheeling through the arch of the fasthold that had momentarily swallowed it, closer to the struggle than the others. Skeletal frame hunched low, bony hands stretched forth, the Horseman charged ahead. But there was a cloud of dust and smoke in its way, stirred by Walker in anticipation of its coming, and it could not see clearly what was happening. When it broke through the screen, it found itself right on top of its prey. Walker Boh was struggling with Pestilence, grappling with the Shadowen, trying to wrest it from atop its writhing serpent, fighting to keep either from rising.

Famine swept past, finger bones raking Walker across the face.

Missing him completely.

Catching Pestilence instead. And being caught by the other in turn.

Both of the Horsemen screamed as the magic of each attacked the other. Pestilence fell back, weakened by hunger and want. Famine lurched away, sickened and retching.

Fire exploded out of the stone walls between them, dealing Famine a ferocious blow that sent the Shadowen reeling.

Now War appeared, come around the west end of the wall, the huge mace raised overhead as the Horseman thundered to the fray. Its serpent breathed flames, and there was a glimmer of fire in the eye slits beneath the armor. It saw Walker Boh clearly, saw the Druid grappling with Famine, and it attacked at once. It might have heard Famine scream in warning, but if it did it failed to heed. It brought the mace down with a crunching blow, intending to finish Walker Boh with a single pass. But Walker had disappeared, and the blow struck Famine instead, hammering right through the Shadowen and deep into his serpent. Famine wailed in anguish and collapsed in a pile of bones. Serpent and rider lay unmoving in the dust.

War wheeled back, and suddenly there were plague flies all over it, stinging and biting past weapons and armor. War shrieked, but the strike was quick and certain. Pestilence had seen Walker Boh dodge the blow that had felled Famine, seen him launch himself onto War and begin to strangle the Shadowen. Pestilence, dazed and battered, had reacted out of instinct, sending fever and sickness in a swift counterattack. But somehow things had gone awry; it was not Walker Boh who was struck, but the Horseman War.

Flattened against the castle wall, Walker withdrew the image of himself into a cloud of dust behind the thrashing War and sent a bolt of fire into Pestilence that threw the Shadowen from his mount completely. The entire stretch of bluff was a haze of dust and heat thrown up by the twisting, snarling serpents and their maddened riders. The images were an old trick, one that a young Jair Ohmsford had perfected three centuries ago in his battle with the Mord Wraiths. Walker had remembered and used the trick to good purpose this day, sending the Shadowen wheeling this way and that, overlaying an image of himself on first one and then another, all the while keeping his back firmly planted against the castle wall.

Mirrors and light, but it was proving to be enough.

Stricken with a dozen killing fevers, War wheeled its serpent about. Walker Boh had appeared again, straddling the fallen Pestilence, trying to smother the Shadowen. War charged, half-blinded and crazed, a great battle-axe drawn. It was on the Druid in seconds, and the axe swept down, cutting him apart.

Except that he wasn't there again, and the blade sliced through Pestilence and his serpent instead.

From his place against the castle wall, Walker sent fire hammering into War. The Shadowen went down, separated from his mount. When the mount tried to rise, Walker burned it to ash.

The mounts, he had discovered, did not share their riders' resiliency. And the Four Horsemen, while able to recover from his magic, were not immune to their own. He had not missed the way they had attacked him each time out—one at a time, one after the other, never all at once. A sustained rush would have finished him, and there had been none. The Four Horsemen were deadly not only to their enemies, but to one another. Flawed imitations of the legends, their magics were anathema. He had counted on that. He had depended on it like he had depended on the midday light and heat weakening these things born of darkness. He had been right.

There was a desperate thrashing from where War lay writhing within its armor, fighting the sickness that raged through it. Famine and Pestilence were unmoving heaps. Their serpents lay still beside them, greenish ichor seeping from their bodies into the ground. The hazy air was clearing, dust and grit settling to the earth. Patches of sky and mountain and forest were coming back into view.

Walker stepped away from the wall. One left. Where was—

The weighted black cord whistled out of the haze with a hawk's shriek, slamming into Walker and whipping about him as he sagged from the blow. Tangled, he dropped to his knees, then fell onto his back. Instantly Death appeared, riding out of the sunlight's glare, the great scythe lifted. Walker gulped air into his stinging lungs. How could it have found him? How could it have seen where he was? The Horseman was bearing down on him, its serpent's claws scrabbling viciously on the rocky earth. Walker lunged back to his knees, fighting to get free. It must have come up more cautiously than the others. It must have seen him burn War's serpent, traced the fire to its source, and guessed where he was hiding.

Walker dropped the spell of invisibility, useless to him now that he had been discovered, and summoned the Druid fire in a blinding whirlwind that cut Death's cord to ribbons. Just as the Horseman reached him, Walker struggled to his feet, threw up a protective shield, and deflected the scythe as it swept down. Even so, the force of the blow knocked him sprawling. He lurched to his feet again as the Shadowen wheeled back. Walker braced. There was no one left to fight this battle for him; he had taken the image trick as far as it would go. This time he must stand alone.

He summoned the fire again. Death against Fate. Walker crouched.

The Horseman swept past a second time, and Walker sent the fire burning into it. Death reeled away, the scythe's blade deflected just enough that it missed. But the air turned chilly at its passing, and Walker felt a wave of nausea rush through him.

Back around swung the Shadowen, and Walker counterattacked at once, the Druid fire lancing from his extended hand. Up came the scythe, catching the fire and shattering it. Death urged the serpent forward, sending it at Walker once more. Again and again Walker struck out, but the fire would not penetrate the Horseman's defenses. Death was almost on top of him now, the serpent hissing balefully through the dust and heat, the scythe glinting. Walker realized suddenly that Death had changed the form of its attack and meant simply to ride him down. Instantly he shifted the focus of the Druid fire, striking the serpent's legs, cutting them out from underneath, striking next the writhing body until everything was a mass of smoking flesh.

The serpent shuddered, twisted aside, lost its balance, and went tumbling forward. Walker threw himself out of the way as the monstrous beast slid past, engulfed in flames, screaming in fury. The tail thrashed wildly, catching Walker across the chest and slamming him down against the earth. Dust rose in clouds to mingle with the smoke from the serpent's charred body, and everything disappeared in a blinding haze.

Battered and bloodied, his robes torn, Walker forced himself to his feet. To one side the serpent lay dying, its breathing an uneven rasp in the sudden silence. Walker peered about, searching the haze.

Then Death appeared behind him, scythe swinging wickedly for his head. Walker threw up the Druid fire and blocked the strike, then straightened to meet Death's rush. His good hand locked on the handle of the scythe, and his body pressed up against Death's. Paralyzing cold surged through him. The Shadowen's cowled head lowered as they lurched back and forth across the bluff, the strange red eyes fixing him, drawing him slowly in. Walker turned his face aside quickly and sent the Druid fire spinning out from his hand and down the scythe's haft. Death jerked back, cowl lifting to the light, empty within save for the crimson eyes. One hand left the scythe and struck out at Walker, knocking him backward. Walker shrank from the blow, feeling the cold spread through him anew. His magic was failing him. Again Death struck out, a vicious blow to his throat. Walker released his hold on the scythe and fell away.

Death strode forward purposefully, a terrible blackness against the haze. Walker rolled to his knees, pain washing through him as he clutched at his chest, fighting for breath.

The blade of the scythe rose and fell.

Then suddenly Cogline was between them, come out of nowhere, a scarecrow figure, worn robes flapping and wispy hair flying. He caught the handle of the scythe and turned the blow aside, sending the blade slicing deep into the earth beside Walker. Walker twisted away and tried to regain his feet, yelling at the old man. But Cogline had thrown himself on the

Shadowen and forced him further back. Death had one hand on Cogline's throat and the other on the handle of the blade, lifting it to strike. The old man was determined, fighting with every ounce of strength he possessed, but the Shadowen was too much. Slowly Cogline was forced back, the hand on his throat bending him away, the other hand shifting to get a better grip on the scythe. *Get away!* Walker pleaded in a silent mouthing, unable to speak the words. *Cogline, get away!*

Walker staggered to his feet, fighting through his exhaustion and pain, reaching down inside for the last of his strength.

Cogline's stick-thin frame was bending like deadwood in a high wind, crumpling beneath the Shadowen onslaught. Then suddenly he cried out, his hand snatched a handful of the black powder he carried from his robe, and he threw it at the Horseman with a curse.

At the same instant, the scythe swept down.

The powder exploded through Death in a flash of fire and sound, catching Cogline as well, sending both flying. Walker flinched away from the blast and the sudden glare and the glimpse of tattered bodies. Then he was stumbling forward, summoning the magic as he went, building the Druid fire in his fist. He saw Death rise from the dust, black-cloaked form singed and smoking, bits of flame spurting from the ends of its sleeve. The scythe lay shattered on the ground beside it, and its red eyes flared as it reached for what remained.

Walker sent the fire lancing into the Shadowen, down through the faceless hood, down into what lived inside. Death lurched back, stricken. Walker kept coming, the fire hammering with relentless purpose, burning and burning more. Death reeled away, trying to flee. But there was no escape. Walker caught up to it, jammed his fist into the twisting cowl, and sent everything he had left down inside.

Death shuddered once and exploded in flames.

Walker fell back, yanking his arm clear and twisting away from the light and the heat. His allies, light and heat, he thought dazedly—what he knew the Shadowen could not survive. He looked back once. Death burned in tatters on the dusty ground, lifeless and still.

Walker Boh went back then to where Cogline lay sprawled on the earth in a crumpled heap. Gently he turned the old man over, kneeling to straighten out his arms and legs and to place the blackened, singed head in his lap. Cogline's hair and beard were mostly burned away. There was blood leaking from his mouth and nostrils. He had been too close to the fire to escape what it would do. Walker felt a tightening in his chest. The old man had known that, of course. He had known it and used the powder anyway.

Cogline's eyes opened, startlingly white against the blackened skin. "Walker?" he breathed.

Walker nodded. "I'm here. It's over, old man. They are finished—all of them."

A rattle of breath ended in a gasping for air. "I knew you would need me."

"You were right. I did."

"No." Cogline's hand reached up and gripped his arm possessively. "I *knew*, Walker." He coughed up blood, and his voice strengthened. "I was told. By Allanon. At the Hadeshorn, when he warned me that my time was gone, that my life was ending. Remember, Walker? I told you only part of what I learned that day. The part about the Druid Histories. There was more that I kept secret from you. You would have need of me, I was told. I would be given a little time, here, in Paranor, to be with you. I would stay alive long enough to be of use once more."

He coughed, doubling over with pain. "Do you understand?"

Walker nodded. He recalled how distant and withdrawn the old man had seemed within the Druid's Keep. Something had changed, he had thought, but consumed by his struggle to escape the Shadowen he had not taken time to discover what. Now it was clear. Cogline had known his life was almost over. Allanon had given him a reprieve from death, but not a pass. The magic of the Druid Histories had saved him at Hearthstone so that he could die at Paranor. It was a trade the old man had been willing to make.

Walker glanced down at the ruined body. Where the scythe had cut through him, there was frost woven in silver streaks through the fabric of his robes.

"You should have told me," he insisted quietly. There were tears in his eyes. He did not know when they had come. Some part of him remembered being able to cry once, a long time ago. He did not understand why he was able to do so now, but did not think after this that he would ever do so again.

Cogline shook his head, a slow and painful movement. "No. A Druid doesn't tell what he doesn't have to." He coughed again. "You know that."

Walker Boh couldn't speak. He simply stared down at the old man.

Cogline blinked. "You told me that I always knew when to act and when not to." He smiled. "You were right."

He swallowed once more. Then his eyes fixed and he quit breathing. Walker kept staring down at him, kneeling in the dust and heat, listening to the silence as it stretched away unbroken, thinking in bitter consolation that Allanon had used the old man for the last time.

He closed Cogline's sightless eyes.

It remained to be seen if the Druid had used him well.

20

Walker Boh buried Cogline in the woods below Paranor, laying him to rest in a glade cooled by a stream that meandered through a series of shallow rapids, a glade sheltered by oaks and hickories whose leafy branches dappled a carpet of wildflowers and green grasses with shadowy patterns that would shift and change each day with the sun's passage west. It was a setting that reminded Walker of the hidden glens at Hearthstone where they had both loved to walk. He chose a place near the center of the glade where the spires of Paranor could be clearly seen. Cogline, who to the end had thought of himself as a Druid gone astray, had come home for good.

When he was finished with the old man, Walker stayed in the clearing. He was battered and worn, but the wounds that were deepest were those he couldn't see, and it gave him a measure of comfort to stand amid the ancient trees and breathe the forest air. Birds sang, a wind rustled the leaves and grasses, the stream rippled, and the sounds were soothing and peaceful. He didn't want to go back into Paranor just yet. He didn't want to go up past the blackened, charred remains of the Four Horsemen and their serpent mounts. What he wanted was to wipe away everything that had happened in his life like chalk from a board and start over. There was a bitterness within him that he could not resolve, which gnawed and scratched at him with the persistence of a hungry animal and refused to be chased. The bitterness had many sources—he did not care to list them. Mostly, of course, he was bitter with himself. He was always bitter with himself these days, it seemed, a stranger come out of nowhere, a man whose identity he barely recognized, an all-too-willing pawn for the wants and needs of old men a thousand years gone.

He sat in the glade by the stream, staring back across the clearing and the patch of fresh-turned earth where Cogline lay, and forced himself to remember the old man. His bitterness needed a balm; perhaps memories of the old man would provide it. He took a moment to splash handfuls of the stream's cold water on his face, cleansing it of the dirt and ash and blood, then positioned himself in a patch of sun and let his thoughts drift.

Walker remembered Cogline as a teacher mostly, as the man who had come to him when his life had been jumbled and confused, when he had abandoned the Races to live in isolation at Hearthstone where he would not be stared at and whispered about, where he would not be known as the Dark Uncle. The magic had been a mystery to Walker then, the legacy of the wishsong come down through the years from Brin Ohmsford in a tangle of threads he could not unravel. Cogline had shown him ways in which he could control the magic so that he no longer would feel helpless before it. Cogline had taught him how to focus his life so that he was master of the white heat that roiled within. He removed the fear and the confusion, and he gave back to Walker a sense of purpose and self-respect.

The old man had been his friend. He had cared about him, had looked after him in ways that on reflection Walker knew were the ways that a father looked after a son. He had instructed and guided and been present when he was needed. Even when Walker was grown, and there was that distance between them that comes when fathers and sons must regard themselves as equals without ever quite believing it, Cogline stayed close in whatever ways Walker would allow. They had fought and argued, mistrusted and accused, and challenged each other to do what was right and not what was easy. But they had never given up on or forsaken each other; they had never despaired of their friendship. It helped Walker now to know that was so.

Sometimes it was easy to forget that the old man had lived other lives before this one, some of which Walker still barely knew about. Cogline had been young once. What had that been like? The old man had never said. He had studied with the Druids—with Allanon, with Bremen, with those who had gone before, perhaps, though he had never really said. How old was Cogline? How long had he been alive? Walker realized suddenly that he didn't know. Cogline had been an old man when Kimber Boh was a child and Brin Ohmsford came into Darklin Reach in search of the Ildatch. That was three hundred years ago. Walker knew about Cogline then; the old man had talked about that period of time, about the child he had raised, about the madness he had feigned and then embraced, about how he had led Brin and her companions to the Maelmord to put an end to the Mord Wraiths. Walker had heard those stories; yet it was such a small piece of the old man's life to know—one day of a year's time. What of all the rest? What parts of his life had Cogline failed to reveal—what parts that were now lost forever?

Walker shook his head and stared out across the trees at Paranor. Parts that the old man had not minded losing, he decided. Walker could not begrudge that Cogline had chosen to keep them secret. It was that way with everyone's life. All people kept parts of who and what they were and how they had lived to themselves, things that belonged only to them, things that no one else was meant to share. At death, those things were dark holes in the memories of those who lived on, but that was the way it must be.

He pictured the old man's whiskered face. He listened for the sound of his voice in the silence. Cogline had lived a long time. He had lived any number of lives. He had lived longer than he should have, spared at Hearthstone to come into Paranor and see it brought back again, and he had died in the way he chose, giving up his own life so that Walker could keep his. It would be wrong for Walker to regret that gift, because in regretting it he was necessarily diminishing its worth. Cogline had lived to see him transformed into the Druid the old man had never become. He had lived to see him through growing up to the dreams of Allanon and the fulfillment of Brin Ohmsford's trust. Whether it was for good or bad, Walker had gotten safely through because of Cogline.

He felt some of the bitterness beginning to fade. The bitterness was wrong. Regrets were wrong. They were chains that bound you tight and dragged you down. Nothing good could come of them. What was needed was balance and perspective if the future was to have meaning. Walker could remember and should. But memories were for shaping what would come, for taking the possibilities that lay ahead and turning them to the uses for which they were intended. He thought again of the Druids and their machinations, of the ways they had shaped the history of the Races. He had despised their efforts. Now he was one of them. Cogline had lived and died so that he could be so. The chance was his to do better what he had been so quick to criticize in those who had gone before. He must make the most of that chance. Cogline would expect him to do so.

The sun was slipping beneath the canopy of the forest west when he rose and stood a final time before the ground in which the old man lay. He was better reconciled to what had happened than before, more at peace with the hard fact of it. Cogline was gone. Walker remained. He would take strength and courage and resolve from the old man's example. He would carry his memory in his heart.

With the light turning crimson and gold and purple in the haze of summer heat, he made his way back through the darkening forests to Paranor.

That night he dreamed of Allanon.

It was the first time he had done so since Hearthstone. His sleep was deep and sound, and the dream did not wake him though he thought afterward it might have come close once or twice. He was exhausted from his struggle, and he had eaten little. He had bathed, changed, then drank a cup of ale as he sat within the study that Cogline had favored. Rumor lay curled up at his feet, the luminous eyes glancing toward him now and then as if to ask what had become of the old man. When he had grown so tired he could barely hold himself upright, he had gone to his sleeping chamber, crawled beneath the blankets, and let himself drift away.

The dream seemed to come instantly. It was night, and he walked alone upon the shiny black rock that littered the floor of the Valley of Shale. The sky was clear and filled with stars. A full moon shone white as fresh linen against the jagged ridge of the Dragon's Teeth. The air smelled clean and new as it had of old, and a wind brushed his face with a cooling touch. Walker was dressed in black, robe and cowl, belt and boots, a Druid passing in the wake of Druids gone before. He did not question who he was, come out of the darkness of the Black Elfstone, come through the fire of the transformation in the well of the Keep, come back into the world of men.

He was master of Paranor and servant to the Races. It was a strange, exhilarating feeling. The feeling seemed to belong.

Languid moments slipped past in the dream and then he neared the Hadeshorn, its waters black and still in the night. Like glass the lake shone in the moonlight, smooth and polished, reflecting the sky and the stars. The stone crunched beneath his feet as he walked, but beyond that single sound there was only silence. It was as if he were alone in the world, the last man to walk it, keeper of a solitary vigil over the emptiness that remained.

He reached the Hadeshorn and stopped, standing perfectly still at its edge. The wind died as he did so, and the silence pressed in about him. He reached up and pulled back the hood of his cloak; he did not know why. Head bared, he waited.

The wait lasted only a moment. Almost instantly the Hadeshorn began to churn, its waters boiling as if heated in a kettle. Then they began to swirl, a slow and steady clockwise sweep that extended from shoreline to shoreline. Walker recognized what was happening. He had seen it happen before. The Hadeshorn hissed, and spray lifted in geysers that towered above the surface and fell away in a tumble of diamonds. Wailing began, the sound of voices trapped in a faraway place, begging for release. The valley shuddered as if recognizing the cries, as if cringing away from them. Walker Boh held his ground.

Then Allanon appeared, rising out of the black waters to a chorus of cries, a cloaked and hooded gray ghost come out of the netherworld to speak with the man who had been chosen as his successor. He shimmered as he rose, translucent in the moonlight, the flesh and bone of his mortal body faded into dust long ago, a pale image of who he had been. He ascended from the depths until he stood upon the surface of the waters, there to settle into stillness facing out at Walker Boh.

"Allanon," the Dark Uncle greeted in a voice he did not recognize as his own.

—You have done well, Walker Boh—

The voice was deep and sonorous, welling up from far inside some cavernous space within the shade.

Walker Boh shook his head. "Not so well. Only adequately. I have done what I must. I have given up who I was for who you would have me be. I was angry at first that it should be so, but I have put that anger behind me."

The waters of the Hadeshorn roiled and hissed anew as the shade came forward, gliding on the surface without seeming to move. It stopped when it was within ten feet of Walker.

—Life is a time for making choices, Walker Boh. Death is a time for remembering how we chose. Sometimes the memories are not always pleasant—

Walker nodded. "I know that it must be so."

—Are you sad for Cogline—

Walker nodded again. "But that, too, is behind me. The choices he made were good ones. Even this last."

The shade's arm lifted, trailing a glitter of spray that fell away like silver dust.

—I could not save him. Even Druids do not have the power to stay death. I was told by Bremen when my time was near. Cogline was told by me. I gave him what help I could—a chance to come back into the Four Lands with Paranor restored—a chance to help you one last time in your battle with the Shadowen. It was all I could do—

Walker did not speak, staring at the apparition, staring right through him, looking far away at events come and gone, at Cogline's final stand. Death had claimed the old man, but it had claimed him on his terms.

—If I could, I would give you back all those you have lost, Walker Boh. But I cannot. I can give you nothing of what is gone and nothing of what will yet be lost. A Druid's life sees many passings—

In his dream the valley was darkened by a wash of mistiness that swept like rain through a forest or clouds across the sun. It was a slow, soft passage, and it carried with it a sense that lives had come into being and run their course, all in a matter of seconds. There were faces, all unknown; there were voices that called out in laughter and pain. Time stretched away, hours to days, days to years, and Walker was there, unchanged, through it all, constantly left behind, eternally alone.

—It will be like that for you. Remember—

But Walker did not need to remember. He had Allanon's memories for that. The transformation had given them to him. He had the memories of all the Druids who had gone before. He knew what his life would be like. He understood what he was facing.

—Remember—

The shade's whisper brought time to a halt again, the Valley of Shale back into focus, and the flow of Walker's thoughts to bear on the dream's intent once more.

"Why am I here, Allanon?" he asked.

—You are complete now, Walker Boh. You have become what you were intended to be, and there is nothing more that remains to be done. You bear the Druid mantle; you will wear it in my stead. Carry it now from Paranor into the Four Lands. You are needed there—

"I know."

Spray hissed and sang. Allanon's hooded face lowered.

—You do not know. You are transformed, Walker Boh, but that is only the beginning. You have become a Druid, yes—but becoming is not being. Yours is the responsibility of the Races, of their well-being, Dark Uncle. Those from whom you once sought to isolate yourself must now be your charge. They wait—

"To be free of the Shadowen."

—For you to show them *how* to be free. For you to set them on the path. For you to guide them from the darkness—

Walker Boh shook his head, confused. "But I don't know the way any better than they do."

The surface of the Hadeshorn steamed, and the air was filled with mist. The dampness settled on Walker's face like the chill of an early winter's morning. It was death to touch the waters of the Hadeshorn, but not for him. For the Druids had discovered secrets long ago that enabled them to transcend death.

Allanon's voice was dark and certain.

—You will find the way. You have the strength and the wisdom of all those who have gone before. You have the magic of the ages. Take yourself out from Paranor and find the other children of Shannara. Each of you was sent to fulfill a charge. Each of you has done so. You are bearers of talismans, Walker Boh. Those talismans shall sustain you—

Walker shook his head in confusion. "What talisman do I bear?"

The shade of Allanon shimmered momentarily in a wailing of cries that rose out of the lake, threatening to disappear.

—The most powerful talisman of all: the Druid mantle which you have assumed. It can never be seen, but it is always there and it is yours alone. Its power increases as you wield it; it strengthens with each use. Think, Walker Boh. Before you fought and destroyed the Horsemen, you were less than what you are now. So shall it be with each challenge you face and overcome. You are in your infancy, and you are just beginning to discover what it is to be a Druid. With time, you will grow—

"But for now . . . ?"

—The charges are enough. The charges yield talismans, and the talismans yield magic. Magic combined with knowledge shall see the end of the Shadowen. It was thus when I first spoke to you. It is thus now. If I could, I would give you more, Walker Boh. But I have given you all I can, all that I know. Remember, Dark Uncle. I am gone from your world and placed within another. I am without substance. I am now of other things. I see imperfectly from where I stand. I see only shadows of what would be and must rely on those. Yours is the vision that can be relied upon. Go, Walker. Find the scions of Shannara and discover what they have done. In their stories and in your own you will find what you need. You must believe—

Walker said nothing then, thinking for a moment that he was being asked once again to proceed on faith alone. But, of course, that was what he had been doing ever since the dreams had first appeared to him and he had been persuaded to travel to the Hadeshorn and Allanon. Was it really so difficult to accept that faith must guide him anew?

He looked at the pale figure before him, all lines about transparency, all memories of life gone before. "I believe," he said to Allanon's shade, and meant it.

—Walker Boh—

The shade's voice was soft and filled with regrets that words could not speak.

—Find the children of Shannara. You have the Druid sight. You have the wisdom they need. Do not fail them—

"No," Walker said hoarsely. "I will not."

—Put an end to the Shadowen before they destroy the Four Lands completely. I feel their sickness spreading even here. They steal the earth's life. Stop them, Walker Boh—

"Yes, Allanon, I will."

—Bend to me then, Dark Uncle. Bend to me one final time before you go. Sleep carries us towards daybreak, and we must travel different paths. Hear the last of what I would tell you, and let your wisdom and your reason divine what remains concealed from us both. Bend to me, Walker Boh, and listen—

The shade approached, steam upon the waters of the Hadeshorn in human shape, a cloaking of mist and gray light, a wraith formed of sounds come out of terrifying darkness.

Tense and uncertain, Walker Boh waited, eyes lowered to the boiling waters, to the reflection of stars and sky, until both disappeared in the blackness of shadow.

Then he felt the other's touch against his skin, and he shuddered uncontrollably.

He came awake at sunrise, the light a faint creeping from the hallway beyond his darkened room. He lay without moving for a time, thinking of the dream and what it had shown him. Allanon had sent the dream so that he would have a place to begin his new life. The dream had reinforced his intention to seek out Par and Wren, but it had also given him reason to believe in himself. He could accept who and what he had become if there was at least a chance that he could bring the ravaged lands and their people safely out of the Shadowen thrall.

Find the children of Shannara. Do not fail them.

He rose then from his bed, washed, dressed, and ate breakfast on the castle battlements looking out over the land in the light of the new day. He thought again of Cogline, of all that the old man had taught him. He recited to himself the litany of rules and understandings that his transformation from mortal man to Druid had given him, the whole of the history of the Druids come and gone. He worked his way carefully through the teachings of his magic's use—some already put to the test, some that remained untried.

Last of all, he recounted the events of the dream and the secrets it had shown him. And there had been secrets—a few, important ones, there at the last, when Allanon had touched him. What he had learned was already beginning to suggest answers to his heretofore-unanswered questions. The whole of the history of the Four Lands since the time of the First Council at Paranor formed a pattern for what was happening now. The events of weeks past gave color and shape to that pattern. But it was the dream and the insights with which it provided him that thrust that pattern into the light where it could be clearly seen.

What was missing still was the reason that Wren had been charged with bringing back the Elves.

What was missing was the reason Par had been sent to find the Sword of Shannara.

Most of all what was missing was the truth behind the secret of the Shadowen power.

He rose finally and went down into the depths of the castle, Rumor trailing silently, a shadow at his back. He would take the moor cat with him, he decided. Cogline had given him the cat, after all; it was his responsibility to see that it was looked after. It could not be left locked up within the Keep, and the closeness they shared might prove useful. He smiled as he examined his thinking. The truth was that Rumor would provide a little of the companionship he would miss without Cogline.

Down into the well of the Keep he descended, there to place his hands on the walls of stone, reaching inward to the life that rested there. The magic came to him, obedient to his summons, and he set in place a bar to any but himself so that none could enter until he returned.

Then he closed Paranor's gates and went out into the world again. He went down from the bluff and into the forests where the heat was screened away and it was shady and cool. Rumor went with him, grateful to be free again of the confining walls, slipping into the shadows to forage and track, returning now and again to Walker's side to be certain he was still there. They traveled north of the place where Cogline lay, and Walker did not turn aside. He had said goodbye already to the old man; it was best to leave it at that.

The day eased away toward nightfall, the sun's fiery glare slipping west toward the Dragon's Teeth, the heat dissipating slowly into the cool of the evening shadows. Walker and the moor cat traveled steadily on. Ahead, the watch fires of the Federation soldiers camped within the Kennon Pass were lit, meals were consumed, and guards sent to their posts.

By midnight Walker and the cat had slipped by them unseen and were on their way south.

21

The rains that had inundated the Westland Elves and the pursuing Federation army were still thunderheads on the western horizon the morning the two ragged scrapwomen led their elderly blind father through the gates of Tyrsis with the other tradesmen, merchants, drummers, peddlers, and itinerant hucksters who had come in from the outlying communities to barter their wares. As with most of the others that sought entry, they had spent the night camped before the gates, anxious to enter early so as to secure the best stalls in the open market where the trading and bartering took place. They shuffled along as quickly as they could manage, the women slowed by the old man as he groped his way uncertainly, supported on either side, his feet directed carefully along the dusty way.

Federation guards lined the entries through the outer and inner walls, checking everyone who passed, pulling aside those who seemed suspicious. It was unusual for them to worry about who was entering the city, for the emphasis in the past had been directed toward worrying about who might leave. But Padishar Creel, the leader of the free-born, was to be executed at noon of the following day, and the Federation was concerned that an attempt would be made to rescue him. It was believed that such a rescue would fail, no matter how well conceived, because the city garrison was at full strength, some five thousand men strong, and security measures were extraordinary. Still, nothing was to be left to chance, so the guards at the gates had been given explicit instructions to make certain of everyone.

They chose to pull aside the scrapwomen and the old man. It was a random selection, an approach the guard commander had settled on early, a compromise between stopping everyone, which would take forever, and no one, which would seem a dereliction of his duty. The three were ordered to stand apart from the throng, to occupy a space in the center of the court between the city's walls, there to wait for questioning. Scattered glances from the crowd were directed their way, furtive and suspicious. Better you than me, they seemed to say. Dust rose with the crowd's passing, and even now, before the heat of the day had settled in, the air had a hot, sticky feel to it.

"Names," the duty officer said to the scrapwomen and the old man.

"Asra, Wintath, and our father, Criape," the one with the ragged, tangled reddish hair said. Sores dappled the skin of her face, and she smelled like old rubbish.

The officer glanced at the other woman, who promptly opened her mouth to reveal blackened teeth and a raw, red throat in which the tongue was missing. The officer swallowed.

"She can't speak," the first said, grinning.

"What's your village?"

"Spekese Run," said the woman. "Know of it?"

The officer shook his head. He studied the piles of rags they carried strapped to their backs. Worthless stuff. He glanced at the old man, whose head was lowered into his cowl. Couldn't see much of his face. The officer stepped forward and pushed back the cowl. The old man's head jerked up and his blackened lids snapped back to reveal a thick, milky fluid where his eyes should have been. The officer gagged.

"On with you." He beckoned, moving quickly away to question the next unfortunate.

The women and the old man shuffled off obediently, slipping back into the crowd, passing through the cordon of guards that lined the gates of the inner wall, moving on from there into the city. They were well off the Tyrsian Way and into the side streets where there were no Federation guards before Matty Roh spit out the dyed fruit skin pasted to the inside of her mouth and said, "I told you this was too risky!"

"We got through, didn't we?" Morgan snapped irritably. "Stop complaining and get me where I can wash this stuff out of my eyes!"

"Be silent, the both of you!" Damson Rhee ordered, and hurried them on.

Tempers were short by now. They had fought bitterly about who was to come into the city, a fight precipitated by the news of Padishar Creel's impending execution. A day and a half was not nearly enough time to effect a rescue, but it was all they had to work with and Morgan had decided that his original plan needed changing. Instead of Matty and Damson going into the city and finding the Mole on their own, he would enter as well. At best they had today and tonight to track down the Mole, bring Chandos and the others of the free-born in through the underground tunnels, devise a rescue plan for Padishar, and set it in motion. Morgan insisted that he needed to get inside the city immediately in order to determine what must be done. He could not afford to wait for nightfall and the Mole to get a look at things. Damson and Matty were equally insistent that any attempt to sneak him past the guards would jeopardize them all. It would be hard enough for just the two of them, but doubly dangerous if they were forced to take him in as well. Why couldn't he do his thinking where he was? Hadn't he spent enough time in the city by now to know where everything was?

So it had gone, but in the end Morgan won the argument by pointing out that he couldn't do any thinking at all until he knew where Padishar was being kept, and he couldn't know that unless he went into the city. The price for his victory was an implacable demand by both women that he leave his Sword behind. A disguise would possibly work, but not if he carried that weapon. Chances of discovery were simply too great. Despite his protests, neither woman would budge. The Sword of Leah had stayed behind with Chandos.

Damson took them down an alleyway to a side door in an abandoned building, pushed open the door, and guided them inside. The interior was close and airless, and dust hung in the air in visible layers. She closed the door behind them. They moved across the room to a second door and from there into another room, equally stifling. A tiny courtyard opened beyond, and they crossed through the early morning shadows and the faint scent of wildflowers inexplicably growing in one sun-drenched corner of the otherwise withered yard to an open-fronted shed filled with old tools and workbenches. Damson left her companions there and went off with a tin bowl. When she returned, the bowl was filled with water, and the three sat down to wash themselves off.

When they were scrubbed clean again, they dug through the bundles of rags and pulled out their good clothes. Stripping off the old, they redressed and sat down on a pair of the workbenches to discuss what would happen next.

"I'll go out first to try to make contact with the Mole," Damson said, still combing out the knots from her tangled red hair. Carefully she tied it all back and tucked it into a scarf. "There are signs I can leave that he will understand. When that's done, I'll come back and we'll see what we can discover about Padishar. Then I'll have to put you somewhere while I go wait for the Mole. He might not come if he sees all of us—he doesn't know either of you and he will be very careful after what's happened. If he comes, he and I will go after Chandos and the rest, and we will meet up with you again by dawn. If he doesn't come—"

"Don't say it," Morgan cut her short. "Just do the best you can."

Damson looked at Matty. "How well do you know the city?"

"Well enough to stay out of trouble."

Damson nodded. "If anything happens to me, you will have to get Morgan out of here."

"Wait a minute!" Morgan exclaimed. "I'm not going to—"

"You are going to do what you are told. Your plans count for nothing if I fail. If the Federation has the Mole or if they capture me, there isn't anything more to be done."

Morgan stared at her, silenced by the anger and determination he found in her green eyes.

Matty took his arm and moved him back a step. "I'll look after him," she promised.

Damson nodded, and her face softened a shade. She rose, wrapped her cloak about herself, gave them a short nod, and disappeared back the way she had come. Morgan stared after her, feeling helpless. She was right. There was nothing he could do if she failed. The success of any plan he devised depended on the girl and the Mole bringing Chandos and the free-born into the city. Without the free-born or the magic of his Sword, he would not be able to help Padishar. Such a slender thread for events to hang upon, he thought grimly.

"Care for something to eat?" Matty Roh asked cheerfully, her dark eyes questioning, and offered him an apple.

They waited within the shade of the storage shed, secluded and alone in the little, closed-about courtyard until almost midday. The air grew steamy and thick with heat, and the sun burned a slow trail across the stones and withered grass, climbing the north wall east to west like the spread of spilled paint. Morgan dozed for a time, weary from the long march in and the uncertain night sleeping before the gates in his uncomfortable disguise. He found himself thinking of Par and Coll and the days before the Shadowen and Allanon, of the times they had spent hunting and fishing in the Highlands, of his own boyhood, of the long slow days when life had seemed an exciting game. He thought of Steff and Granny Elise and Auntie Jilt. He thought of Quickening. They were memories of a past that lost a little of its color with the passing of every day. They all seemed to have disappeared from his life a very long time ago.

The sun was directly overhead when Damson Rhee finally returned. She was flushed with the heat and covered with dust, but there was excitement in her eyes.

"They have Padishar within the same watchtower where they held me," she announced, dropping down on one of the benches and peeling off her cloak. She took a long drink from the cup of water Matty Roh offered her. "It seems to be common knowledge. They plan to take him to the main gates at noon tomorrow and hang him in view of the city."

"How is he?" Morgan asked quickly. "Did anyone say?"

She shook her head, swallowing. "No one has seen him. But talk among the soldiers is that he'll walk to his end."

She glanced at Matty Roh. The other woman frowned. "Common knowledge, is it?" She gave Damson a thoughtful look. "I don't much trust common knowledge. Common knowledge often ends up meaning 'false rumor' in my experience."

Damson hesitated. "Everyone seemed so sure." She cut herself short. "But I guess we have to make certain, don't we?"

Matty Roh leaned forward, elbows on knees, chin in hands, her boyish face intense. "You've told me how they used you to trap Padishar." Morgan stared. This was the first he'd heard of that. How much more had Damson told her that he didn't know? "It worked once, so chances are pretty good they'll try it again. But they'll change the rules. They'll make sure no one gets away this time. Instead of using live bait, maybe they'll use . . . common knowledge."

Morgan nodded. He should have thought of that. "A decoy. They expect a rescue attempt, so they misdirect it. They keep Padishar somewhere else."

Matty nodded solemnly. "I would guess."

Damson came back to her feet. "I've left signs for the Mole that he can't miss. If he's coming, he'll come tonight. I've got until then to go back out and try to find where Padishar really is."

"I'm coming as well." Morgan rose and reached for his cloak.

"No." Matty Roh's voice was sudden and firm. She stood up and came between them. "Neither of you is going." She reached for her cloak. "I am." She looked at Morgan. "You might be recognized, now that you've shed your disguise, and you can't go where you might learn anything in any case. You are better off staying here." She turned to Damson. "And you can't afford to risk yourself further. After all, they know who you are, too. It was chancy enough going out this morning. Whatever happens, you have to stay safe until you can meet the Mole and bring the others in. You can't do that if you're discovered and find yourself in Padishar Creel's company. Besides, I'm better at this sort of thing than you are. I know how to listen, how to find things out. Discovering secrets is what I do."

They stared at her without speaking for a moment. When Morgan started to object, Damson silenced him with a look. "She's right. Padishar would agree."

Again Morgan tried to speak, but Damson overrode him, saying, "We'll wait here for you, Matty. Be careful."

Matty nodded and slung her cloak over her shoulder. Her slim face was tight and smooth across the set of her jaw. "Don't wait if I'm not back by dark." She gave Morgan a quick, ironic smile. "Keep me safe in your thoughts, Highlander."

Then she was across the courtyard and through the door of the room beyond and gone.

They waited for Matty Roh all day, hunched down in the shelter of the shed, trying to take what small comfort they could from the shade it provided. The sun passed slowly west, the heat building in its wake, the air still and dusty within the airless court.

To help pass the time, Morgan began telling Damson how Padishar and he had fought together against the Federation at the Jut. But talking of it did not ease his boredom as he had hoped. Instead it brought back a memory he had hoped forgotten—not of Steff or Teel or the Creeper or even his shattering battle within the catacombs, but of the terrible, frightening sense of incompleteness he had felt when deprived of the magic of the Sword of Leah. Discovering its magic again after years of dormancy through generations of his family had opened doors that he could not help but feel had been better left closed. The magic had saddled him with such dependency, an elixir of power that was stronger than reason or self-denial, that was insidious in its intent to dominate, that was absolute in its need to command. He remembered how that power had bound him, how he had suffered its loss afterward, how it had stripped him of his courage and resolve when he had needed both—until now, in possession of that power once more, he was terrified of what its renewed use would cost him. It made him think again of Par, cursed, not blessed, with the magic of the wishsong, a magic potentially ten times stronger than that of the Sword of Leah, a magic with which he had been forced to contend since his birth, and which now had evolved in some frightening way so that it threatened to consume him completely. Morgan thought he had been lucky in a way the Valeman had not. There had been many to give aid to the Highlander—Steff, Padishar, Walker, Quickening, Horner Dees, and now Damson and Matty Roh. Each had brought a measure of reason and balance to his life, keeping him from losing himself in the despair that might otherwise have claimed him. Some had been taken from him forever, and some were distanced by events. But they had been there when he had needed them. Whom had Par been able to rely upon? Coll, stripped away by Shadowen trickery? Padishar, gone as well? Walker or Wren or any of the others who had started out on this endless jurney? Cogline? Himself? Certainly not himself. No, there had been only Damson and the Mole—and mostly only Damson. Now she was gone, too, and Par was alone again.

One thought led to another, and although he had started talking of Padishar and the Jut, he found himself turned about in the end, speaking once more of what haunted him most, of Par, his friend, whom he had failed, he felt, over and over again. He had promised Par he would stay with him; he had sworn to come north as his protector. He had failed to keep that promise, and he found himself wishing that he might have another chance, just one, to make up for what he had given away.

Damson spoke of the Valeman as well, and the timbre of her voice betrayed her feelings more surely than any words, a whisper of her own sense of loss, of her own perceived failing. She had chosen Padishar Creel over Par, and while the choice could be justified, there was no comfort for her in the knowledge.

"I am tired of making choices, Morgan Leah," she whispered to him at one point. They had not spoken for a time, lying back within their shelter, sipping at warm water to keep their bodies from dehydrating. Her hand gestured futilely. "I am tired of being forced to choose, or constantly having to make decisions I do not want to make, because whatever I decide, I know I am going to hurt someone." She shook her head, lines of pain etched across her brow. "I am just plain tired, Morgan, and I don't know if I can go on anymore."

There were tears in her eyes, generated by thoughts and feelings hidden from him. He shook his head. "You will go on because you must, Damson. People depend on you to do so. You know that. Padishar now. Par later." He straightened. "Don't worry, we'll find him, you and I. We won't stop until we do. We can't be tired before then, can we?"

He sounded condescending to himself and didn't like it. But she nodded in response and brushed away the tears, and they went back to waiting for Matty Roh.

Nightfall came, and she still hadn't returned. Shadows blotted away the light, and the sky was darkening quickly and filling with stars. West, beyond where they could see, the storm front continued to approach, and within the walls of the city the air began to cool with its coming.

Damson rose. "I can't wait any longer, Highlander. I have to go now if

I am to find the Mole and still have time to bring the free-born into the city." She pulled on her cloak and tied it about her. "Wait here for Matty. When she comes, find out what you can that will help us."

"When she comes," Morgan repeated. "Assuming she does."

She reached down to touch him lightly on the shoulder. "Whatever happens, I will come back for you as quickly as I can."

He nodded. "Good luck, Damson. Be careful."

She smiled and disappeared across the darkening courtyard into the shadows. The sound of her footsteps echoed on the stone and faded away into silence.

Morgan sat alone in the gloom and listened to the sounds of the city slowly quiet and die. Overhead, clouds moved across the stars and began to screen them away. The night darkened, and a strange hush settled over the bluff. Padishar, he thought, hang on, we're coming. Somehow, we're coming.

He tried sleeping and could not. He tried thinking of something he could do, but everything involved going out from his hiding place, and if he did that he might not get back again. He would have to wait. Rescue plans crowded his mind, but they were as ephemeral as smoke, based on speculation, not on fact, and useless. He wished he had brought the Sword of Leah so that he would not feel so defenseless. He wished he had made better choices in his efforts to aid his friends. He wished himself into a dark corner and was forced to stop wishing for fear that he would find himself paralyzed by regrets.

It was nearing midnight when he heard the scrape of boots on the stone of the courtyard and looked up from his light doze to see Matty Roh materialize in the fading starlight. He jerked upright, and she hushed him to silence. She crossed to where he waited and sat next to him, breathing heavily.

"I ran the last mile," she said. "I was afraid you would be gone."

"No." He waited. "Are you all right?"

She looked at him, and her eyes were haunted. "Damson?"

"Gone in search of the Mole, then off to bring Chandos and the rest through the tunnels. She'll meet us back here by dawn."

The smile she gave was anxious and searching. "I'm glad you're here."

He smiled back, but the smile seemed wrong, and he let it drop. "What happened, Matty?"

"I found him."

Morgan took a deep breath. "Tell me," he urged softly, sensing she should not be rushed. There was a sheen of sweat on her skin, and that strange look in her eyes.

She bent so that their shoulders touched. Her boyish, delicate features were taut, and there was an urgency that radiated as surely as light. "I began at the ale houses, looking and listening. I made some easy friends, soldiers, a junior officer. I got what I could from them and kept moving. Padishar's name was mentioned, but just in passing, in connection with the execution. Night came, and I still hadn't learned where they were keeping him."

She swallowed, reached for the water tin, scooped out a cup, and drank deeply. He could feel the strength in her slim body as it moved against his own.

She turned back. "I was certain they were keeping him somewhere people would avoid. The watchtower was a ruse, so where else would he be? There are prisons, but word would leak from there. It had to be someplace else, a place no one would want to go."

Morgan paled. "The Pit."

She nodded. "Yes." She kept her eyes fixed on him. "I went into the People's Park and found the Gatehouse heavily guarded. Why would that be? I wondered. I waited until an officer emerged, one highly placed, one who shares. I followed him, then sat with him to drink. I let him persuade me to go with him to a private place. When I had him alone, I put a knife to his throat and asked him questions. He was evasive, but I was able to persuade him to admit what I already knew—that Padishar was being held in his cells."

"But he is alive?"

"Alive so that he can be executed publicly. They don't want rumors floating about afterwards that he might have escaped. They want everyone to see him die."

They stared at each other in the dark. The Pit, Morgan was thinking, a sinking feeling in his stomach. He had hoped never to go back there again, never even to come close. He thought of the things that lived there, the Shadowen misfits, the monsters trapped by the barrier of magic that had shattered the Sword of Leah . . .

He brushed the thought aside. The Pit. At least he knew what he was up against. He could devise a plan with that.

"Did you learn anything else?" he asked quietly.

She shook her head. He could see the pulse beat at her throat, the black helmet of her hair a frame about her delicate face.

"And the officer?"

There was a long silence as she looked into his eyes, seeing something beyond and far away. Then she gave him an empty smile.

"When I was finished with him, I cut his throat."

They sat without speaking after that, side by side on the workbench, still touching, looking out at the darkness. Several times Morgan thought to rise and move away, but he was afraid that she would mistake the reason for it and so stayed where he was. The sound of laughter penetrated the silence of the open court from somewhere without, harsh and unwelcome, and it seemed to rub raw even further nerves that were already frayed. Morgan did not know how much time passed. He should say something, he knew. He should confront the dark image of her words. But he did not know how to do so.

A dog barked in the distance, a long staccato peal that died away with jarring sharpness.

"You don't like it that I killed him," she said finally. It was not a question; it was a statement of fact.

"No, I don't."

"You think I should have done something else?"

"Yes." He didn't like making the admission. He didn't like the way he sounded. But he couldn't help himself.

"What would you have done?"

"I don't know."

She put her hands on his shoulders and turned him until they were facing. Her eyes were pinpricks of blue light. "Look at me." He did. "You would have done the same thing."

He nodded, but was not convinced.

"You would have, because if you stop to think about it, there wasn't any other choice. This man knew who I was. He knew what I was up to. He couldn't have mistaken that. If I had let him live, even if I had tied him up and hidden him away somewhere, he might have escaped. Or been found. Or anything. If that had happened, we would have been finished. Your plans, whatever they might be, wouldn't stand a chance. And I have to return to Varfleet. If he ever saw me there, he would know. Do you see?"

He nodded again. "Yes."

"But you still don't like it." Her rough, low voice was a whisper. She shook her head, her black hair shimmering. There was an unmistakable sadness in her voice. "I don't either, Morgan Leah. But I learned a long time ago that there are a lot of things I have to do to survive that I don't like. And I can't help that. It has been a long time since I have had a home or a family or a country or anything or anyone but myself to rely on."

He stopped her, suddenly ashamed. "I know."

She shook her head. "No, you don't."

"I do. What you did was necessary, and I shouldn't find fault. What bothers me is the idea of it, I suppose. I think of you in another way, a different way."

She smiled sadly. "That is only because you really don't know me, Morgan. You see me one way, for a short time, and that is how I am for you. But I am a good many more things than what you have seen. I've killed men before. I've killed them face to face and out of hiding. I've done it to stay alive." There were tears in her eyes. "If you can't understand that . . ."

She stopped, bit down on her lip, rose abruptly, and moved away. He did not try to stop her. He watched her walk to the far side of the courtyard and seat herself on the stones with her back against the wall in the deep shadows. She stayed there, motionless in the dark. Time slipped away, and Morgan's eyes grew heavy. He had not slept since the previous night and then poorly. Dawn would be there before he knew it, and he would be exhausted. He had not yet devised a plan for rescuing Padishar Creel—had not even considered the matter. He felt bereft of ideas and hope.

Finally he spread his cloak on the floor of the shed, made a pillow with the rags that the three of them had carried in, and lay down. He tried to think about Padishar, but he was asleep almost at once.

Sometime during the night he was awakened by a stirring next to him. He felt Matty Roh curl up against him, her body pressing close against his own. One slender arm reached around him, and her hand found his.

They lay together like that for the remainder of the night.

It was nearing dawn when Damson's touch on his shoulder brought him awake. There was a lightening in the spaces between the shadows that told of day's coming, faint and silvery lines against the building walls surrounding where he lay. He blinked the sleep from his eyes and recognized who it was crouching next to him. He was still tangled with Matty, and he nudged her gently awake. Together they rose stiffly, awkwardly, to their feet.

"They're here," Damson said simply. Her eyes revealed nothing of what she thought, finding them together. She gestured over her shoulder. "The Mole has them hidden in a cellar not far away. He found me last night shortly after I left you, took me through the tunnels, and together we brought Chandos and the others in. We're ready. Did you find Padishar?"

Morgan nodded, fully awake now. "Matty found him." He looked back at the elfin face. "I wouldn't have been able to, I don't think."

Damson smiled gratefully at the tall girl and clasped her slender hands in her own. "Thank you, Matty. I was afraid this was all going to be for nothing."

Matty's cobalt eyes glinted like stone. "Don't thank me yet. We still have to get him out. He's being held in the Gatehouse cells at the Pit."

Damson's jaw tightened. "Of course. They would take him there, wouldn't they?" She wheeled back. "Morgan, how are we going to—"

"We'd better hurry," he said, cutting her short. "I'll tell you when we reach the others."

If I can think of something by then, he added silently. But the beginnings of an idea were forming in the back of his mind, a plan that had come to him all at once upon waking. He threw on his cloak, and together the three of them abandoned the tiny court, went back through the rooms that led in, and stepped out into the street.

It was silent and empty there, the street a black corridor that sliced through building walls until it disappeared into a tangle of crossroads and alleyways. They moved quickly ahead, skimming along the stone in tandem with their shadows, pressing through the blackness of the dying night. Morgan's mind was working now, turning over possibilities, examining ways, considering alternatives. They would execute Padishar at midday. He would be hanged at the city gates. To do that, they would have to transport him from the Gatehouse at the Pit to the outer wall. How would they do that? They would take him down the Tyrsian Way, which was broad and easily watched. Would he walk? No, too slow. On horseback or in a wagon? Yes, standing in a wagon so that he could be seen by everyone . . .

They turned into a passage that ran back between two buildings to a dead end. There was a door halfway down, and they entered. Inside, it was black, but they groped their way to a door on the far wall that opened to a flicker of lamplight. Chandos stood in the door, sword in hand, black beard bristling. He looked ferocious in the shadows, all bulk and iron. But his smile was quick and welcoming, and he guided them down the steps into the cellar below where the others waited.

There were greetings and handshakes, a sense of anticipation, of readiness. It had taken the little band of twenty-four almost the entire night to come into Tyrsis through the tunnels, but they seemed fresh and eager, and there was determination in their eyes. Chandos handed Morgan the Sword of Leah, and the Highlander strapped it across his back. He was as anxious as they.

He looked for the Mole and could not find him. When asked about him, Damson said he was keeping watch.

"I'll need him to show me where the tunnels run beneath the streets," he announced. "And I'll need you to draw a map of the city so that he can do that."

"Have you a plan, Highlander?" Chandos asked, pressing close.

Good question, Morgan thought. "I do," he replied, hoping he was right.

Then he drew them close and told them what it was.

The dawn was gray and oppressive, the thunderheads moved close to the edge of Callahorn, roiling black clouds that cast their dark shadow east to the Runne. It was hot and windless in the city of Tyrsis as its citizens woke to begin their day's work, the air thick with the taste of sweat and dust and old smells. Men and women glanced skyward, anxious for the impending rain to begin so that it might give them some small measure of relief.

As morning slid toward midday, excitement over the impending execution of the outlaw Padishar Creel began to build. Crowds gathered at the city gates in anticipation, irritable and weary from the heat, anxious for any distraction. Shops closed, vendors cleaned out their stalls, and work was set aside in what soon became a carnival atmosphere. There were clowns and tricksters, sellers of drink and sweets, hucksters and mimes, and cordons of Federation soldiers everywhere, dressed in their black and scarlet uniforms as they lined the Tyrsian Way from inner to outer wall. It grew darker with midday's approach as the thunderheads crowded the skies from horizon to horizon and rain began to fall in a thin haze.

At the center of the city, the People's Park sat silent and deserted. Wind from the approaching storm rustled the leaves of the trees and stirred the banners at the Gatehouse entrance. A wagon had arrived, drawn by a team of horses and surrounded by Federation guards. Canvas stretched over metal hoops covered its wooden bed, and iron bound its wheels and sides. The horses stamped and grew lathered in their traces, and the heat brought a sheen of sweat to the faces of the uniformed men. Eyes searched the trees and pathways of the Park, the walls that ringed the Pit, and the shadows that gathered in clumps all about. The iron heads of pikes and axes glinted dully. Voices were kept low and furtive, as if someone might hear.

Then the Gatehouse doors swung open, and a team of soldiers emerged with Padishar Creel in tow. The leader of the free-born had his arms bound tightly behind him and his mouth securely gagged. He walked unsteadily, his gait halting and painful. There was blood on his face and bruises and cuts everywhere. He lifted his head despite his obvious pain, and his eyes were hard and fierce as he surveyed his captors. Few met that gaze, keeping their attention trained elsewhere, waiting until he was past to sneak a furtive glance. The outlaw was taken to the back of the wagon and pushed inside. Canvas flaps were drawn in place, the wagon was turned about, and the soldiers began to assemble in lines on either side. When all was in readiness, the procession began to move slowly ahead.

It took a long time to complete the journey out of the park, the horses held carefully in check, the lines of soldiers surrounding the wagon in a solid wall. There were more than fifty of them, armed and hard-faced, spearing a path through the trees and out onto the Tyrsian Way. The few people they encountered were moved quickly back, and the wagon lurched slowly into the city. Buildings rose to either side, and heads leaned out of windows. The soldiers deployed, teams moving ahead to search doorways and alcoves, to check cross streets and alleys, to move aside any obstruction they found. Rain was falling steadily now, spattering on the stones of the roadway, staining them dark and beginning to puddle. Thunder boomed from somewhere distant, a long steady peal that echoed through the city walls. The rain fell harder, and it grew increasingly difficult to see.

The wagon had reached a commons where a series of cross streets intersected when the woman appeared. She was crying hysterically, calling out to the soldiers to stop. Her clothes were in disarray and there were tears on her face. They had the outlaw leader with them, didn't they? They were taking him to be hanged, weren't they? Good, she cried out vehemently, for he was responsible for the deaths of her husband and son, good men who had fought in the Federation cause. She wanted to see him hang. She wanted to make certain she was there when it happened.

The procession lurched to an uncertain stop as others appeared to take up the cry, stirred by the woman's fiery speech. Hang the outlaw leader, they cried out angrily. They pressed forward, a ragged bunch, throwing up their hands and gesturing wildly. The soldiers held them away with pikes and spears, and the unit's commanding officer ordered them to move back.

No one noticed the sewer grate slide away from its seating under where the wagon was stopped or saw the shadowy forms that slid out of the darkness one by one to crouch beneath.

Hang him here and now! the crowd was crying, continuing to press up against the soldiers massed before it. The Federation officer had drawn his sword and was shouting angrily for his men to clear the way.

Then abruptly the forms beneath the wagon sprang up on all sides, some onto the driver's seat, some into the bed. The drivers and the officer were thrown to the street, clutching their throats. More soldiers were thrown out the back to land in crumpled heaps, bloodied and still. The soldiers surrounding the wagon turned instinctively to see what was happening, and in an instant's time half fell dying as the free-born who at that point made up the bulk of the crowd killed them with the daggers they had kept hidden. Screams and shouts rose up, and the soldiers surged back and forth wildly, trying to bring their weapons to bear.

Morgan Leah appeared on the driver's seat of the wagon, snatched up the reins, and shouted at the horses. The wagon lurched forward, the horses wild-eyed. Soldiers flung themselves at the Highlander, trying to claw their way up to stop him, but Matty Roh was there instantly, her blade swift and deadly as it cut them down. The wagon broke through the leading edge of the column, the team trampling some men beneath its hoofs, the wagon wheels crushing more. Morgan sawed on the reins and turned the team onto a side street. Behind, the fighting continued, men grappling with one another and striking out with their weapons. The Federation column was decimated. No more than a handful still stood, and those few had backed themselves against a building wall and were battering at the doors.

Damson Rhee raced up, finished now with her deception as the grieving widow. She reached for the seat rail and pulled herself aboard as the wagon rolled past. The free-born were charging after them as well, swiftly closing the gap between themselves and the wagon. For a second it seemed that Morgan's plan was going to work. Then something moved in the shadows to one side, and Morgan, distracted momentarily, turned to look. As he did, the wagon struck a water-filled hole, an axle broke, a wheel flew off, and the traces snapped. The wagon lurched wildly to one side, and a split second later it upended, sending everyone sprawling into the street.

Morgan lay in a tangle with Damson and Matty Roh. Slowly they picked themselves up, muddied and bruised. The wagon was ruined, the canvas shredded and the wooden box splintered and cracked. In the distance, the terrified team disappeared into the gloom. Chandos crawled from beneath the wreckage with his burly arms wrapped about Padishar. The outlaw leader had freed his hands and removed the gag. There was fire in his eyes as he tried to stand on his own.

"Don't stop!" he rasped. "Keep moving!"

The others of the free-born reached them, their clothing bloodstained and torn. There were fewer than before, and some were wounded. Shouts and cries trailed after them, and a fresh body of soldiers surged into the square.

"Hurry! This way!" Damson called urgently, and began to run.

They slogged after her down the muddied street through a maze of rain-soaked buildings. Mist rose off the damp, heated stone as the air cooled and everything farther than twenty feet away disappeared in a haze. More Federation soldiers appeared, surging out of side streets with their weapons drawn. The free-born met them head-on and thrust them back, struggling to get clear. Matty Roh battled at the forefront of the charge, cat-quick and deadly as she opened a path for the rest. Chandos and Morgan fought on either side of Padishar, who, though game enough to try, lacked sufficient strength to protect himself. He fell continually, and finally Chandos was forced to pick him up and carry him.

They reached a bridge that spanned a dry riverbed and stumbled across wearily. Without the wagon to carry them, they were tiring quickly. Almost half of those who had come into the city to rescue Padishar were dead. Several of those who remained were wounded so badly they could no longer fight. Federation soldiers were coming at them from everywhere, summoned from the gates where news of the escape had carried. The little party fought valiantly to go on, but time was running out. Soon there would be too many soldiers to avoid. Even the mist and the rain would not hide them then.

A body of horsemen charged out of the mist, appearing so swiftly that there was no chance to get clear. Morgan saw Matty fling herself aside and tried to do the same. Bodies went flying as the free-born were overrun. The horses stumbled and went down in the melee and their riders went flying as well. Screams and shouts rose from the struggling mass. Chandos was gone, buried in a pile of bodies. Padishar lurched to one side and fell to his knees. Morgan rose and stood centermost on the bridge, virtually alone, and swung the Sword of Leah at everything that came within reach. He gave his family's battle cry, *"Leah, Leah,"* seeking strength in the sound of it, and fought to rally those who were left to stand with him.

For a second he thought they were lost.

Then Chandos surged back into view, bloodied and terrible, thrusting Federation soldiers aside like deadwood as he stumbled to where Padishar leaned against the bridge wall and pulled the leader of the free-born back to his feet. Damson was calling out from somewhere ahead, urging them on. Matty Roh reappeared, darted at the last Federation soldier standing, killed him with a single pass, and sped on. Morgan and the free-born followed, skidding in the mix of rain and blood that coated the bridge surface.

On the low end of the causeway they found Damson waiting in the open doors of a large warehouse, gesturing for them to hurry. They struggled to reach her, hearing the sounds of pursuit—booted feet pounding through the mud, weapons clanging against armor, curses and shouts of rage. They entered the gloom-filled building in a rush, and Damson slammed and barred the doors behind them. The Mole poked his head out of a trapdoor that was all but lost in the shadows at the building's rear and disappeared again.

"Down into the tunnels!" Damson ordered, pointing after the Mole. "Quick!"

The free-born hastened to comply, those who were able giving what support they could to the injured. Chandos went first, half dragging, half carrying Padishar Creel, and disappeared from sight. The shouts of their pursuers reached the doors of the warehouse, and a violent pounding began. Pikes and spears slammed into the barrier, splitting the wood. Morgan paused, halfway to the tunnel. Matty Roh stood alone before the impending rush, sword held ready.

"Matty!" he called out.

The last of the free-born dropped through the trapdoor. Battle-axes split the crossbar that braced the warehouse entrance, and the heavy doors sagged. Matty Roh backed away slowly, reluctant even now to give ground. She seemed small and vulnerable before the crush that surely faced her, but held herself as if made of iron.

"Matty!" Morgan shouted again, then raced back for her. Seizing her arm, he dragged her toward the tunnel entry just as the warehouse doors gave way, and Federation soldiers poured into the room. Foremost were Seekers, hooded and cloaked, the wolf's-head insignia gleaming on their uniforms. Their cries at seeing him were hisses of delight.

Morgan turned to face them, standing before the tunnel entrance. It was too late to flee. If he tried, they would cut him down from behind and then catch the others as well. If he stayed, he could slow the rush and the others would gain a few precious moments. Matty Roh crouched at his elbow. He thought momentarily to tell her to run, but a furtive glance at her face told him he would be wasting his time.

The rush came from three sides, but Morgan and the girl fought with a ferocity born of desperation and threw it back. The Sword of Leah turned to blue fire as it met the Seeker strike, hammering past the Shadowen defense and turning the black things to ash. Some of the Federation soldiers saw what was happening and fell back with whispered cries and oaths. Matty Roh attacked at the first indication of a weakening in the ranks, her slender sword snaking out so quickly that it could barely be seen, her movements fluid and efficient as she followed her weapon into the crush. Morgan went with her, fighting to cover her back, impelled by the sudden rush of magic that surged from the Leah talisman into his limbs. He howled out his battle cry anew, *"Leah, Leah,"* and threw himself at the men before him. The Seekers died immediately, and the soldiers who had followed them in tripped and fell over one another in their haste to get away. Matty Roh was crying out as well, a shriek that pierced the cacophony of screams rising from the dead and wounded. Morgan felt light-headed, empty of thought, of needs and wants, of everything but the magic's fire.

Then suddenly the Federation attack gave way completely, and the last of those who still lived fled back through the warehouse doors into the streets of Tyrsis. Morgan whirled in fury, driven by the magic, and the Sword of Leah radiating fire. Swinging the talisman like a scythe, he cut into the upright beams that braced the ceiling supports, cut so deep that he severed them, and the entire building began to collapse.

"Enough!" Matty screamed, catching hold of his arm and pulling him away.

He fought her for an instant, then realized what he was doing and gave in. They rushed for the trapdoor and scrambled to safety just as the ceiling gave way and buried everything in a thunderous crash.

Below, they ran through the blackness of the tunnels, charging ahead recklessly, heedless of where they were going. Light glimmered in the distance, faint and beckoning, and they raced wildly to reach it. The strange wholeness that Morgan felt when using the Sword's magic began to dissipate, opening a pit within that widened into a hunger, into a familiar sense of loss, into the beginnings of a desperate need. He fought against it, warning himself that he must not let the magic rule him as it had before, calling up images of Par and Walker and finally Quickening to strengthen his resolve. He reached out for Matty and caught hold of her hand. Her grip tightened on his own, as if she sensed his fear, and she held him fast.

Don't let me go, he prayed silently. Don't let me fall.

Dust and dampness filled his lungs, and he coughed against the air's thickness, fighting to catch his breath. His weariness weighed him down, chains on his limbs and body. They ran on, the light stronger now, closer. Matty's ragged breathing matched the pounding of their boots on the stone. The blood pulsed in his ears.

Then they were within the light, a shaft of brightness from a drainage-grate opening in the street above. Rain cascaded down through the gaps and formed a silver curtain, and thunder rolled across the skies. Matty collapsed against one wall, pulling him down with her. They sat with their backs against the cool stone, gasping.

She turned to him, and her cobalt eyes were wild and fierce and her waiflike features were shining. She looked as if she wanted to howl with glee. She looked as if she had discovered something that she had believed forever lost.

"That was wonderful!" she breathed, and laughed like a child.

When she saw the astonishment mirrored on his face, she leaned over quickly and kissed him hard on the mouth. She held the kiss for a long time, her arms wrapping about him and holding him fast.

Then she released him, laughed again, and pulled him to his feet. "Come on, we have to catch the others! Come on, Morgan Leah! Run!"

They continued down the tunnel, the sounds of the storm trailing after them into the black. They did not run far, slowing quickly to a walk as their wind gave out. Their eyesight adjusted to the gloom, and they could pick out the movement of rats. Rainwater sloshed down the grates in an increasingly heavy flow, and soon they were ankle-deep. From light shaft to light shaft they made their way, listening for the sounds of those who might be following as well as for those they sought. They heard shouts and cries from the streets, the gallop of horses, the rumble of wagons, and the thudding of booted feet. The city was swarming with soldiers hunting for them, but for now the sounds were all aboveground.

Still there was no sign of Damson and the free-born.

Finally they reached a divergence in the passageway that forced them to choose. Morgan did the best he could, but there was nothing to help him decide. If the rainwater hadn't flooded the sewer floor, there might have been tracks. They pressed on, side by side, Matty Roh holding onto him as if frightened she might lose him to the dark. The distance between the grates began to widen until the tunnel was so black they could barely see.

"I think we missed a turn," Morgan said softly, angrily.

They backtracked and tried again. The new passage angled sharply one way and then another, and again the distance between grates widened and the light began to fail. They found a blackened torch wedged in the rock wall and managed to light it using a strip of cloth and Matty's fire-making stones. It took a long time to get a flame in the dampness, and by the time they had the torch burning, they could hear movement in the watery corridors behind them.

"They've dug through—or found another way," the girl whispered, and gave him a secretive smile. "But they won't catch us—or if they do, they'll wish they hadn't. Come on!"

They pushed ahead into tunnels that grew increasingly narrow. The grates finally disappeared entirely and the torch became their only light. The hours wore on, and it became obvious that they were hopelessly lost. Neither said so, but both knew. Somehow they had chosen the wrong direction. It was still possible that they would find their way clear, but Morgan didn't care for the odds. Even Damson, who lived in the city and came down into the tunnels often, did not feel she could navigate the maze of corridors without the Mole. He wondered what had become of her and the others of the free-born. He wondered if they thought Matty and he were dead.

They found another torch, this one in better condition, and took it with them as a spare. When the pitch-coated length of the first was burned away, Morgan used the stub to light the spare and they continued on. They were angling deeper into the bluff and could no longer see or hear the rain. Sounds grew muffled and then disappeared; there was only their breathing and their footsteps. Morgan tried to set a direct course, but the tunnels intersected and cut back so often that he gave it up. Time ticked away, but there was no way to be certain how much of it had passed. They grew hungry and thirsty, but there was nothing to eat or drink.

Finally Morgan stopped and turned to Matty. "We're not getting anywhere. We have to try something else. Let's find our way back up to the first level. Maybe we can slip out into the city tonight and sneak through the gates tomorrow."

It was a faint hope at best—the Federation would be looking for them everywhere—but anything was better than wandering around hopelessly in the dark. Night would be coming soon, and Morgan kept thinking about the Shadowen that Damson had told him prowled the tunnels closest to the Pit. Suppose they stumbled into one of those. It was too dangerous for them to remain down here any longer.

They worked their way back toward the bluff face, choosing tunnels that angled upward, winding about with their torch slowly burning away. They knew they were running out of time; if they did not regain the streets of the city soon, their light would be used up and they would be stuck there in the dark. But now they were hearing continual sounds in the distance, the movement of men through water and damp, the whisper of voices. Their hunters were out in force, and they were no closer than before to finding a way past them.

It was a long time before they reached the sewers again and caught a glimpse of daylight through a street grating. The light was thin and fading now, the day easing quickly toward dark. The rain had turned to a slow drizzle, and the city was silent and empty feeling. They walked until they found a ladder leading up, and Morgan took a deep breath and climbed. When he peered out from between the bars he saw Federation soldiers stationed across from him, grim and silent in the gloom. He climbed back down noiselessly, and they continued on.

Their torch burned out, the daylight turned to dark—the skies so clouded that almost no light showed down into the tunnels, and the sound of their hunters faded away and was replaced by the scurrying of rats and the drip of runoff. All of the grate openings they checked were under watch. They kept moving because there was nothing else for them to do, afraid that if they stopped they might not be able to start again.

Morgan was beginning to despair when the eyes appeared in front of him. Cat's eyes, they gleamed in the darkness and then disappeared.

Morgan came to an immediate stop. "Did you see that?" he whispered to Matty Roh.

He felt, rather than saw, her nod. They stood frozen for a long time, not wanting to move until they knew what was out there. Those eyes had not belonged to any rat.

Then there was a whisper of water disturbed and a scrape of boots.

"Morgan?" someone called softly. "Is that you?"

It was Damson. Morgan answered, and an instant later she was hugging him, then Matty, telling them she had been looking for them for hours, searching the tunnels from end to end, trying to find their trail.

"Alone?" Morgan asked incredulously. He was so relieved to see her he was almost giddy. "Do you have any food or water?"

She gave them both an aleskin and bread and cheese from her pack. "I had the Mole to help me," she said, keeping her voice at a whisper. "When you collapsed the ceiling to the warehouse, a part of the tunnel went with it. Maybe you didn't even notice. At any rate, we were cut off from you, and you ended up going the wrong way." She shook back her fiery hair and sighed. "We had to get Padishar and the others out first. There was no time to look for you then. When they were safe, the Mole and I came back for you."

In the darkness to one side, the Mole's bright eyes blinked and gleamed. Morgan was dumbfounded. "But how did you find us? We were completely lost, Damson. How could you. . . ?"

"You left a trail," she said, clutching at his arm to slow his argument.

"A trail? But the rainwater washed everything away!"

She smiled, although she was clearly trying not to. "Not in the earth, Morgan—in the air." He shook his head in confusion. "Mole?" she called. "Tell him."

The Mole's furry face eased into the light. He blinked almost sleepily, and his nose twitched as he sniffed at the Highlander. "Your smell is very strong," he said. "All through the tunnels. Lovely Damson is right. You were easy to track."

Morgan stared. He could hear Matty Roh's smothered laughter, and he turned bright red.

They rested only long enough to eat, then set out again, this time with the Mole as their guide. There were no encounters with either Federation soldiers or Shadowen wraiths and their passage was smooth and easy. As he walked, Morgan's thoughts wandered into the past and out again, a slow, deliberate journey of self-evaluation. He looked at himself and the ways he had changed. When he was done, he found he was not displeased. The lessons he had learned were important ones, and he was better for having traveled the road that had brought him north from Leah.

When they emerged from the side of the mountain north, the skies were clear once more and filled with light from the moon and stars. The air was rain-washed and smelled of the forest, and the breeze that blew out of the west was cool and soft as down. They stood together in grasses still damp with the storm, looking out across the plains and hills to the Dragon's Teeth and the horizon beyond.

Morgan glanced at Matty Roh and found her studying him, smiling slightly, her thoughts private and secretive and strangely compelling. She was plain and pretty, reticent and forward, and a dozen other contradictions, a paradox of moods and behavior he did not understand but wanted to. He saw her in fragments of memory—as the boy he had believed her to be at the Whistledown, as the girl with the ruined feet and shattered past at Firerim Reach, as the deadly quick swordswoman standing against the Federation and the Shadowen at Tyrsis, and as the quixotic waif who could be either demon or sprite at a moment's passing.

He could not help himself. He smiled back at her, trying to share a secret that only she knew.

Damson was kneeling before the Mole. "Won't you come with us this time?" she was asking him. The Mole was shaking his head. "It grows more dangerous for you every time you go back."

The Mole considered. "I am not afraid for myself, lovely Damson. I am afraid only for you."

"The monsters, the Shadowen, are in the city," she reminded him gently.

He gave her a small shrug and a serious look. "The monsters are everywhere."

Damson sighed, nodded, reached out carefully, put her arms around the little fellow, and hugged him. "Goodbye, Mole. Thank you for everything. Thank you for Padishar. I owe you so much."

The Mole blinked. His bright eyes glistened.

She released him and rose. "I will come back for you when I can," she said. "I promise."

"When you find the Valeman?" The Mole suddenly looked embarrassed.

"Yes, when I find Par Ohmsford. We will both come back."

The Mole brushed at his face. "I will wait for you, lovely Damson. I will always wait for you."

Then he turned and disappeared back into the rocks, melting away like one of night's shadows. Morgan stood with Matty Roh and stared after him, not quite believing he was really gone. The night was still and cool, empty of sound and filled with memories that jumbled together like words spoken too fast, and it seemed as if everything was a dream that could end in the blink of a waking eye.

Damson turned to look at him. "I'm going after Par," she announced quietly. "Chandos has taken Padishar and the others back to Firerim Reach where they will rest a day or two before making their journey north to meet with the Trolls. I have done what I can for him, Morgan. He doesn't need me for anything more. But Par Ohmsford does, and I intend to keep my promise to him."

Morgan nodded. "I understand. I'm going with you."

Matty Roh looked inexplicably defiant. "Well, I'm going, too," she declared. She searched first one face and then the other for an objection, found none, and then asked in a more reasonable tone, "Who is Par Ohmsford?"

Morgan almost laughed. He had forgotten that Matty knew only a little of what was going on. There was no reason, he guessed, that she shouldn't know it all. She had earned the right by coming with them into Tyrsis after Padishar Creel.

"Tell her on the way," Damson interjected suddenly, and gave an uneasy glance over her shoulder. "We're too exposed, standing about out here. Don't forget they're still hunting for us."

Within moments they were moving east away from the bluff and toward the Mermidon. An hour's walk would bring them to the shelter of the forests and a few hours' sleep. It was the best that they could hope for this night.

As they traveled, Morgan told again the story of Par Ohmsford and the dreams of Allanon. The three figures receded slowly into the distance, midnight came and went, and the new day began.

23

They spent what remained of the night in an arbor of white oaks bordering the Mermidon a few miles below the Kennon Pass. It was cool and shady where they slept, protected from the late summer heat that gathered early on the open grasslands, and they did not wake until well after sunrise. They washed and ate from the supplies that Damson carried, listening to the steady flow of the river and an effervescent birdsong. Morgan rubbed sleep from his eyes and tried to remember everything that had happened the previous day, but it was already growing vague in his mind, a memory that seemed to have been stored away a long time ago. That Padishar Creel was safe again, however distant the event, was all that mattered, he told himself wearily, and he let the matter slide into the distance of yesterday.

He pulled on his boots as he munched on bread and cheese and considered what lay ahead. Today was a hot, sultry expectation that shimmered through the dappled shadows of the leaves and branches, and it might take him anywhere. The past was a reminder of the vicissitudes of life, chance playing off opportunity and giving back what she would. The hardships and losses that Morgan had experienced had tempered him like iron run through the fire, and a vacuum had formed around him that he did not think anything would ever get past again, a dead place where hurt and disappointment and fear could not survive, a shield that let him keep everything away so that he might go on when sometimes he did not think he could. The problem, of course, was that it kept other things away as well—hope and caring and love among them. He could admit them when he chose, but there was always the danger that the other feelings would come in as well. When you let in one, you always risked letting in the others. It was his legacy from Steff and Quickening, from the Jut and Eldwist, from Druid wraiths and Shadowen. It was a truth that haunted him.

He brushed aside the musings and speculation, finished off his meal, and stood and stretched.

"Ready?" Damson Rhee asked. She was flushed from cold water splashed on her skin, and her fiery hair was brushed out so that it shone. She was pretty and vital and filled with a determination that radiated like heat from a flame. Morgan looked at her and thought again how lucky Par was to have someone like that in love with him.

Matty Roh finished washing off her plate and handed it over to Damson to pack. "Where do we go from here?" she asked in her customarily blunt fashion. "How do we go about finding Par Ohmsford?"

Damson shoved the plate in with the others. "We track him." She tightened the stays on the pack and stood up. "With this."

She reached down inside her tunic front and pulled out what looked to be half of a medallion threaded on a leather thong. Morgan and Matty bent close. The medallion—a metal disk, actually—had no markings or insignia, and the jagged sharpness of the straight edge indicated that it had been broken recently.

"It is called a Skree," Damson explained, holding it up to the light where it gleamed a copper gold. "I gave the other half to Par when we separated. The disk was fashioned out of one metal, one forging, and can only be used once. The halves draw the holders to each other. They give off light when they are brought close."

Matty Roh looked skeptical. "How close do you have to be?" Her black hair was short and straight about her elfin face, and her eyes were deep and searching. She looked fresh-scrubbed and new—younger than she was, Morgan thought, and nothing of who she could be.

Damson smiled. "The Skree is a street magic. I have seen it work; I know what it can do." The smile tightened. "Shall we try it out?"

She held it outstretched in her palm and faced west, north, and then east. The Skree did nothing. Damson glanced at them quickly. "He was traveling south," she explained. "I saved that for last."

She pointed her hand south. The coppery face of the Skree might have pulsed faintly, but Morgan really wasn't sure. Damson, however, nodded in satisfaction.

"He's a long way away, it seems." Her smile was hesitant as she let her eyes meet theirs. "You have to know how to read it." She stuffed the disk back inside her tunic. "We had better start walking."

She reached down for her pack and swung it over her shoulders. Matty Roh gave Morgan a sideways glance and a shake of her head that said, *Did you see something I missed?* Morgan shrugged. He wasn't sure.

They set out into the heat, following the Mermidon on its winding path east toward Varfleet, keeping as much as they could to the shade of the trees. A breeze blew off the water and helped cool them, but the surrounding countryside was empty and still. The peaks of the Dragon's Teeth north were barren and gray with the summer's swelter, and the mix of hills and low mountains south were burned out and dry. The sun lifted in the cloudless sky, and the heat beat down in waves. Dead animals lay scattered on the open plains, their twisted bodies rotting. Vast stretches of Callahorn's woods had been sickened and the earth beneath left bare. Pools of stagnant, dull-green water stood listless and stinking. Trees were ravaged and withered like the carcasses of creatures hung out to dry. Often the stretches of ruined earth lasted for miles. Morgan could smell the decay in the air. This was more than the summer heat and dryness; this was the Shadowen poisoning that he had witnessed time and again since coming north, a devastation of the land that the dark things were somehow causing. And it was growing worse.

Midday faded into afternoon, and they skirted Varfleet to the north, still following the Mermidon as it began to bend south. They encountered a handful of peddlers and other tradesmen on their way, but the heat kept most would-be travelers out of the sun, so they had the river road pretty much to themselves. They spotted their first Federation patrol as they neared Varfleet and stepped back into the trees to let it pass.

Damson used the Skree again while they waited, and the result was the same. The disk glowed faintly when pointed south—or it might have been nothing more than a glimmer of sunlight. Again Morgan and Matty Roh exchanged a surreptitious look. It was hot, and they were tired. They were wondering if this was leading somewhere or if Damson was just being hopeful. There were other ways to track Par if the disk wasn't working, but neither of them was ready to challenge Damson on the matter just yet.

They needed a boat to travel down the Mermidon to the Rainbow Lake, she advised, tucking the Skree away once more. It would be quicker by three times than trying to make the journey afoot. Matty shrugged and said she would go into the city, since it was less dangerous for her to do so than for them, and she would meet them here again as soon as she had found what they needed. She put down the bedroll she had been carrying and disappeared into the swelter.

Morgan sat with Damson in the shade of an ancient willow close by the riverbank where they could see anyone approaching from either direction. The river was muddy and clogged with debris in the wake of last night's storm, and they watched it flow past in sluggish, deliberate fashion, a bearer of discards and old news. Morgan's eyes were heavy with lack of sleep, and he closed them against the light.

"You're still not certain of me, are you?" he heard Damson ask after a time.

He looked over at her. "What do you mean?"

"I saw the look you exchanged with Matty when I used the Skree."

He sighed. "That doesn't mean I'm not certain of you, Damson. It means I didn't see anything and that worries me."

"You have to know how to use it."

"So you said. But what if you're wrong? You can't blame me for being skeptical."

She smiled ironically. "Yes, I can. Somewhere along the way we have to start trusting each other, all three of us. If we don't, we're going to get into a lot of trouble. You think about it, Morgan."

He did and was still thinking on it when dusk settled over the borderlands and Matty trudged back out of the haze with a tired look on her face.

"We have a boat," she announced, dropping wearily into the shadow of the willow and reaching for the water cup Damson offered. She splashed water on her dust-streaked face and let it run off. "A boat, supplies, and weapons, all tucked away at the waterfront. We can pick them up after dark when we won't be seen."

"Any problems?" Morgan asked.

She gave him a hard look. "I didn't have to kill anyone, if that's what you mean." She glowered at him, then settled back and wouldn't say another word.

Now they were both mad at him, he thought, and decided he didn't care.

When night came, they followed the riverbank down into the city until they reached the docks north where Matty had secured the boat. It was an older craft, a flat-bottomed skiff with poles, oars, a mast, and a canvas sail, and was supplied with food and weapons as Matty had promised. They climbed aboard without saying anything and shoved off, rode the skiff downriver to the first unoccupied cove, then beached their craft and went immediately to sleep. At sunrise they were up again and off. They rode the Mermidon south toward the Runne until sunset and made camp in a wedge of rocks that opened onto a narrow sand bar fronting a grove of ash. They ate dinner cold, rolled into their blankets, and slept once more. Two days had passed without anyone saying much of anything. Tempers were frayed, and uncertainty over the direction they were taking had shut down any real effort at communication. There had been a bonding in Tyrsis that was lacking here—perhaps because of the doubts they were feeling about one another, perhaps because of their uneasiness over what might be waiting for them. In Tyrsis there had been a plan—or at least the rudiments of one. Here there was only a vague determination to keep hunting for Par Ohmsford until he was found. They had known where Padishar was, and there had been a sense of having some control over reaching him. But Par could be anywhere, and there was nothing to suggest that they were not already too late to do him any good.

It was with immense relief, then, that when Damson brought out the Skree the following morning and pointed her hand south, the copper metal gleamed bright even in the shadow of the rocks that hemmed them about. There was a moment's hesitation, and then they smiled like old friends rediscovering one another and pushed off into the channel with fresh determination.

The tension eased after that and the sense of companionship they had shared in rescuing Padishar returned once more. The skiff eased its way down the channel, borne steadily south on waters that had turned calm and smooth once more. The day was hot and windless, and the journey was slow, but the free-born women and the Highlander passed the time exchanging thoughts and dreams, working their way past the barriers they had allowed to form between them, conversing until they were comfortable with one another once more.

Nightfall found them deep within the Runne, the mountains a shadowy wall in the growing dark that blocked the starlight and left them with only a narrow corridor of sky overhead. They camped on an island that was mostly sandy beach and bleached driftwood encircling a stand of scrub pine. The air stayed sultry and was thick with pungent river smells—dead fish, mud flats, and rushes. Morgan fished, and they ate what he caught over a small fire, drank a little of the ale Damson carried, and watched the river flow past like a silver ribbon. Damson used the Skree, and it glowed bright copper when pointed south. So far, so good. They were less than a day's journey from where the Mermidon emptied into the Rainbow Lake. Perhaps there they would learn something of the whereabouts of Par.

After a time Damson and Matty stretched out on their blankets to sleep while Morgan ambled down to the water's edge and sat thinking of other times and places. He wanted to pull together the threads of all that had happened in an effort to make some sense out of what was to come. He was tired of running from an enemy he still knew almost nothing about, and in typical fashion believed that if he considered the matter hard enough he was bound to learn something. But the threads trailed away from him as if blown in a wind, and he could not seem to gather them up. They drifted and strayed, and the questions that had plagued him for weeks remained unanswered.

He was digging in the sand with a stick when Matty appeared and sat down next to him.

"I couldn't sleep," she offered. Her face was pale and cool-looking in the starlight, and her eyes were depthless. "What are you doing?"

He shook his head. "Thinking."

"What about?"

"Everything and nothing." He gave her a quick smile. "I can't seem to settle on much. I thought I might try to reason out a few things, but my mind just keeps wandering."

She didn't say anything for a moment, her eyes turning away to look out over the river. "You try too hard," she said finally.

He looked at her.

"You work at everything like it was the last chance you were ever going to get. You're like a little boy with a chore his mother has given him to do. It means so much to you that you can't afford to make even the smallest mistake."

He shrugged. "Well, that's not how I am. Maybe that's how I seem at the moment, but that isn't really me. Besides, now who's judging who?"

She met his gaze squarely. "I'm not judging you; I'm giving you my impression. That's different from what you were doing. You were judging me."

"Oh." He didn't believe it for a moment. His face said so, and he didn't bother to hide it. "Anyway, trying hard isn't a bad thing."

"Do you remember when I told you that I had killed a lot of men?" He nodded. "That was a lie. Or at least an exaggeration. I just said that because you made me mad." She looked away again, thoughtful. "There's a lot you don't understand about me. I don't think I can explain it all to you."

He stared at her hard, but she refused to look at him. "Well, I didn't ask you to explain," he replied defensively.

She ignored him. "You're very good with that sword. Almost as good as I am. I could teach you to be better if you'd let me. I could teach you a lot. Remember what happened to you at the Whistledown when you grabbed me. I could teach you to do that, too."

He flushed. "That wouldn't have happened if . . ."

". . . you had been ready." She smiled. "I know, you said so before. But the point is, you weren't ready—and look what happened. Besides, being ready is what counts. Padishar taught me that. Being ready is certainly more important than trying hard."

His jaw tightened. "Are you about finished detailing what's wrong with me? Or is there something else you'd like to add?"

The smile disappeared from her face. She did not look at him, keeping her eyes on the river. He started to say something more, then thought better of it. She seemed strangely vulnerable all of a sudden. He watched her draw up her knees, clasp her arms about them, and lower her head into the darkened space between. He could hear the sound of her breathing, slow and even.

"I like you a lot," she said finally. She kept her face hidden. "I don't want anything to happen to you."

He didn't know what to say. He just stared at her.

"That's why I'm here," she said. "That's why I came." She lifted her head to look at him. "What do you think about that?"

He shook his head. "I don't know what I think."

She took a deep breath. "Damson told me about Quickening."

She said it as if the words might catch fire in her mouth. Her eyes searched his, and he saw that she was frightened of what he might be thinking but determined that she would finish anyway. "Damson said you were in love with Quickening, that losing her was the worst thing that had ever happened to you. She told me about it because I asked her. I wanted to know something about you that you wouldn't tell me yourself. Then I wanted to talk to you about it, but I didn't know how. I'm very good at listening, but not so good at asking."

Morgan blinked. He saw Quickening in his mind, a flawless, silver-haired vision as ephemeral as smoke. The pain he felt in remembering was palpable. He tried to shut it away, but it was pointless. He did not want to remember, but the memory was always there, just at the edges of his thinking.

Matty Roh put her hand over his, impulsive, hesitant. "I could listen now, if you would let me," she said. "I would like it if I could."

He thought, No, I don't want to talk about it, I don't even want to think about it, not with you, not with anybody! But then he saw her again in his mind bathing her ruined feet in the stream and telling him how she had come to be disfigured, how the poisoning of the land had changed her life forever. Was the pain of her memories any less than his own? He thought, too, of Quickening as she lay dying, healing the shattered Sword of Leah, giving him a part of herself to take with him, something that would transcend her death. What she had left behind was not meant to be kept secret or hidden. It was meant to be shared.

And memories, he knew, were not glass treasures to be kept locked within a box. They were bright ribbons to be hung in the wind.

He turned his hand over and clasped hers. Then he leaned close so that he could see her face clearly and began to speak. He talked for a long time, finding it hard at first and then easier, working his way through the maze of emotions that rose within him, searching for the words that sometimes would not come, forcing himself to go on even when he thought that maybe he could not.

When he was done, she held him close and some of the pain slipped away.

They set out again at dawn, the daylight gray and misty with a promise of rain. Clouds rolled out of the west, a heavy, dark avalanche that sealed away everything in its path. It was hot and still on the river, and the slap of the water against the canyon walls echoed sharply as they wound their way downriver. Morgan put up the mast and sail, but there was little wind to help, and after a while he took it down again and let the current carry them. It was nearing midday when they passed beneath Southwatch, the black obelisk towering over them, vast and silent and impenetrable, its shadow cast like a Forbidding across the Mermidon. They stared at it with loathing as they passed, imagining the dark things that waited within, uneasy with the possibility that they might be watched. But no one appeared, and they sailed by unchallenged. Southwatch receded into the distance, melted into the haze, and was gone.

They reached the mouth of the river shortly after, the waters widening and stretching away to become the Rainbow Lake, smoothing into a glassy surface and brightening into a richer blue. The rainbow from which the lake took its name was in pale evidence, shimmering in the heat and mist, suspended above the water like a weathered, faded banner whose stays had come loose so that it floated free. They guided the skiff to the west bank, beached it, and walked out onto a barren flat that dropped away east and south into the water and spread northwest across a plain empty of everything but scrub grass and stunted, leafless ironwood to where a line of hills shadowed the horizon. They breathed the air and looked about, finding no sign of anything for as far as they could see.

Damson brushed back her fiery hair, tied it in place with a bandanna across her forehead, and drew out the Skree. Holding it forth in her open palm, she faced south. Morgan watched as the half disk glimmered bright copper.

She began to put it away, apparently had second thoughts, and tested each of the other compass points. When she faced north, the direction from which they had come, the Skree glimmered a second time, a small, weak pulsing. Damson stared at it in disbelief, closed her hand over it, turned away and then back once more, and reopened her hand. Again the Skree glimmered fitfully.

"Why is it doing that?" Matty asked immediately.

Damson shook her head. "I don't know. I've never heard of it behaving like this."

She faced south again and carefully let her palm travel the horizon from east to west and back again. Then she did the same thing facing north, reading the Skree's hammered surface as she turned. There was no mistake in what they were seeing. The Skree brightened both ways.

"Could it have been broken again and the pieces carried in two directions?" Morgan asked.

"No. It can only be divided once. Another breaking would render it useless. That hasn't happened." Damson looked worried. "But something has. The reading south points towards the Silver River country west of Culhaven above the Battlemound. It is the stronger of the two." She looked over her shoulder. "The reading north is centered on Southwatch."

There was a long silence as they considered what that meant. A heron cried out from over the lake, swept out of the haze in a flash of silver brightness, and disappeared again.

"Two readings," Morgan said, and put his hands on his hips and shook his head. "And one of them is a fake."

"So which one do we believe?" Matty asked. She started away a few steps as if she had something in mind, then turned abruptly and came back again. "Which is the real one?"

Again Damson shook her head. "I don't know."

Matty's cobalt eyes glanced toward the horizon where the clouds were building. "Then we will have to check them both."

Damson nodded. "I think so. I don't know any other way."

Morgan exhaled in frustration. "All right. We'll go south first. That reading is the stronger of the two."

"And abandon Southwatch?" Matty shook her head. "We can't do that. Someone has to stay here in case Par Ohmsford is inside. Think about it, Highlander. What if he's in there and they try to move him? What if a chance to rescue him comes along and no one is here to do anything about it? We might lose him and have to start all over again. I don't think we can take that chance."

"She's right," Damson agreed.

"Fine, you stay, Damson and I will go south," Morgan declared, irritated that he hadn't thought of it first.

But Matty shook her head again. "You have to be the one who stays. Your sword is the only effective weapon we have against the Shadowen. If a rescue is needed, if any sort of confrontation comes about, your Sword is a talisman against their magic. My skills are good, Morgan Leah, but I also know when I'm overmatched. I don't like this any better than you do, but it can't be helped. Damson and I will go south."

There was a long silence as they faced each other, Morgan fighting to control an almost irresistible urge to reject flatly what he perceived to be the madness of her suggestion, Matty with her cobalt eyes steady and determined, the weight of her arguments mirrored in their blue light.

Finally Morgan looked away, reason winning out over passion, a reluctant submission to necessity and hope. "All right," he said softly. The words were bitter and harsh sounding. "All right. I don't like it, but all right." He looked back again. "But if you find Par and there's to be a fight, you come back for me."

Matty nodded. "If we can."

Morgan winced at the qualification, shook his head angrily, and glanced at Damson in challenge. But Damson simply nodded in agreement. Morgan exhaled slowly. "If you can," he repeated dully.

They conferred a moment more, agreeing on what they would do if time and circumstance allowed. Morgan scanned the countryside and then pointed west to where a bluff fronting the lake looked out across the surrounding land. From there he would be able to see anything coming to or going from Southwatch. If nothing happened in the time between, that was where they would find him when they returned.

He walked back with them to the skiff and retrieved supplies sufficient to last him a week. Then he embraced them hesitantly, Damson first, then Matty. The tall girl held him tightly against her, almost as if to persuade him of her reluctance to leave. She did not speak, but her hands pressed into his back, and her lips brushed his cheek. She looked hard at him as she broke away, and he had the feeling that she was leaving something of herself behind with him in that look. He started to give her a reassuring smile in reply, but she had already turned away.

When they were gone, faded into the mist that had settled over the river, he turned west toward his selected watch post and trudged into the growing dark. The clouds blanketed the skies from horizon to horizon, and the air had begun to cool. A wind had sprung up, gusting across the flats, sending dust and silt swirling into his eyes. Far west, the rain was a dark curtain moving toward him. He pulled up the hood of his forest cloak and lowered his eyes to the ground.

He had just reached his destination when the rain arrived, a downpour that swept across the plains in a rush and covered everything in an instant's time. Morgan burrowed deep within the shelter of a broad-limbed fir and settled down against the base of the trunk. It was dry and protected there, and the storm rolled past leaving him untouched. The rain continued for several hours, then turned to drizzle, and finally stopped. The thunderheads passed east, the skies cleared, and the sunset was a red and purple blaze in the fading light.

Morgan left the shelter of the fir and found a stand of broadleaf maple that allowed him to remain hidden while at the same time giving him a clear view of Southwatch and the Mermidon east, a large stretch of the Rainbow Lake south, and a cut through the hills below the Runne that funneled any land traffic that might approach the Shadowen keep from the north and west. It was an ideal position to observe everything for nearly a dozen miles. Good enough, he decided, and settled in to await the night.

He ate a little of the food he had brought and drank some water. He wondered if Damson and Matty had attempted a crossing of the Rainbow Lake before the storm had struck or if they had decided to wait. He wondered if they were camped somewhere along the river looking back across at him.

The light faded to gray, and the stars began to appear. Morgan stared down at Southwatch and wished he could see inside. He tried not to think too closely about what might be happening there. Too much imagination could be a dangerous thing. He studied the plains east, barren and stripped of life, a wasteland of brown earth and gray deadwood that radiated out from the tower of the Shadowen like a stain. The fringes, he noted, were already darkening as well, infected by the poison as it spread. Trees rotted and grasses withered. The bluff on which he sat was an island already at risk.

He unstrapped the Sword of Leah from his back and cradled it in his arms. A talisman against the Shadowen, Matty Roh had called it. But it was power, too, that stole your soul, and there was little that could be done to protect against it. Each time he used the magic, a test of wills resumed, his own and the Sword's, both fighting for supremacy, struggling for control. Three hundred years ago Allanon had answered Rone Leah's desperate, angry plea by bestowing a tiny part of the Druid magic on the ancient weapon, and the legacy of that gift or curse—take your choice—was a bittersweet taste that once experienced cried out for more.

As did the wishsong for Par. As did all the magic that ever was or had ever been—siren songs of power that transcended everything in their compelling, inexorable need to be sung.

He smiled darkly. Be careful what you wish for. Wasn't that the old admonition to those who begged for what they did not have?

The smile faded. Maybe he would find out when it came time to summon the Sword's magic again—as summon it he surely must, sooner or later. Maybe Quickening's healing touch, the magic that had restored his talisman, would prove in the end to be as killing as that of the Shadowen.

The thought left him feeling cold and empty and impossibly alone. He sat motionless in the shadows, staring out across the countryside, waiting for the darkness to claim it.

Three days earlier another storm had passed, one markedly more violent, a torrential downpour riddled by explosions of thunder and flashes of lightning and driven by a rough-faced howling wind, the sort of deluge that came and went regularly in the Borderlands with the buildup of late summer pressure and heat. It swept into Callahorn at dusk, inundated the land through the night, and disappeared south with the coming of dawn.

In the wake of its passing a solitary figure rose from the sodden earth at the edge of the Rainbow Lake, muddied beyond recognition and stooped as if weighed down with chains.

Dark eyes blinked and tried to focus. The day was late in waking, worried perhaps that the storm might return, dark-edged clouds lingering fitfully in the leaden skies, sunrise iron-gray and cautious as it eased back the night's stubborn shadows. The figure stared out at the flat expanse of the lake, at the light east, at the skies, at a world that was clearly unfamiliar. One hand held a sword that glimmered faintly where the grass and mire caked on it were scraped down to the metal. The figure hesitated uncertainly, then stumbled to the edge of the lake and submerged hands and face and finally body as well, washing and rinsing down to a tangle of rags and bare skin.

Mud and debris swirled away in the dark waters, and Coll Ohmsford rose to look about.

At first he could not remember anything beyond who he was—though he was quite determined of that, as if perhaps his identity had been in doubt once. He recognized the Rainbow Lake, the ground upon which he stood, and the country that surrounded him. He was standing on the lake's southern shore west of Culhaven and north of the Battlemound. But he did not know how he had gotten there.

He looked down at the blade in his hand (Had he managed to wash himself without releasing it?) and realized that he was holding the Sword of Shannara.

And then the memories came back in a rush that caused him to gasp and double over as if a blow had been delivered to his stomach. The images hammered at him. He had been captured by the Shadowen and imprisoned at Southwatch. He had managed an escape, but in truth Rimmer Dall had managed it for him. He had been tricked into believing that the Mirrorshroud would conceal him when in truth it had subverted him in ways he did not care to recall, turning him into one of them, making him over in their image. He had lost control of himself, becoming something very close to animal, scouring the countryside in search of his brother, Par, seeking him without clear reason or purpose beyond a vague intention to cause him harm. Cloaked in the Mirrorshroud's dark folds, he had tracked, found, and attacked his brother . . .

He was breathing rapidly through his mouth. His chest tightened and his stomach churned.

His brother.

. . . and tried to kill him—and would have, if something hadn't stopped him, hadn't driven him away.

He shook his head, fighting through the maze of memories. He had fled from Par confused and maddened, torn between who he had been and what he had become. He had drawn Par after, barely aware of what he was doing, fleeing by day, seeking by night, hunting always, lost somewhere deep within himself. Hatred and fear drove him, but their source was never clear. He could feel the Mirrorshroud's hold on him beginning to loosen, yet was undecided whether or not that was good. He was changing back again, but could not come the whole distance, still bound by the Shadowen magic, still held within its thrall. In darkness he would return to find his brother, thinking to kill him, thinking at the same time to find salvation, the thoughts twisting about each other like snakes. *Follow me!* he had prayed to Par—then sought to run so fast and so far that his brother couldn't.

He hugged himself against the chills that swept through him, looking out across the hazy expanse of the lake, remembering. How many days had he run? How much time had been lost?

Follow me!

He had stolen the metal disk then, the one that Par wore hung about his neck—had stolen it without knowing why, but only from seeing him hold and caress it in the twilight shadows and sensing its importance, thinking to hurt Par by taking it, but thinking, too, that stealing the disk would make his brother follow after him.

As it had.

To the ruined land below Southwatch.

Why had he run there? The reason eluded him, an evasive whisper in his subconscious. His brow furrowed deeply as he struggled to understand. He had been driven by the Mirrorshroud's magic, compelled to return . . .

His eyes widened. To bring Par, because . . .

And Par had caught up with him there beneath that ancient, blasted oak, found him exhausted and beaten and ruined. They had fought one final time, grappling for the Sword of Shannara, trying to break through the barriers that separated them, each in his own way—Par struggling to summon the Sword's magic so that Coll could be free, Coll battling in turn to . . . to . . .

What?

To tell Par. To tell him.

"Par," he whispered in horror, and his memory of what the Sword's truth had revealed to him burned through him like white fire. He looked down at the mud-streaked blade, at the carving beneath his fingers—the hand that held aloft a burning torch. He stared at it in recognition and wonder, and his fingers moved along the emblem as if finding secrets still.

All those months spent searching for the Sword of Shannara, he thought, and they had never realized. So much effort expended to recover it, a struggle marked by desperate battles and lost lives, and they had never once suspected. Allanon's charge had swept them on, heedless. It had driven Par, and Coll had been swift to follow. Find the Sword of Shannara, the Druid shade had instructed. Only then can the Four Lands be made whole. Find the Sword, he had whispered in the whirlwind of cries that echoed from the Hadeshorn.

And Par Ohmsford had done so—without once suspecting that it was never to be his to use.

Coll Ohmsford's heart was racing, and he took slow, deep breaths to steady himself against the pounding of his blood. He experienced an almost overpowering urge to despair because of what the deception might have cost them, but he would not let himself be drawn to that precipice. With both hands wrapped about the talisman, he moved back from the Rainbow Lake to where a stand of maple trees spread dappled shadows across a grassy knoll. Dazed and weakened, he sat where the sun's light could find him through the branches and tried to sort through the images he had unlocked from his memory.

Par had tracked him to that plain west of Southwatch and they had done battle a final time, brother against brother. Par had come for him because the Mirrorshroud was a Shadowen magic from which Coll could not free himself. Par had sought to use the Sword of Shannara to give Coll what he needed to break his shackles—recognition of who and what he had become, understanding of how he had been subverted. Truth, the special province of the Sword, would help him to escape. Par had been certain that it really was the Sword of Shannara he possessed because the magic had revealed itself when Coll had come at him above Tyrsis. Triggered in the heat of their struggle, it had spiraled down through them both, letting Par know that Coll was alive and giving Coll a terrifying glimpse of what he had become. Let the magic of the Sword come into his brother, Par had believed, and Coll would be set free.

There were tears in his eyes as he remembered the intensity in Par's face as they stood locked in battle in the fury of that storm. Again he saw his brother's lips move, whispering to him. *Coll. Listen to me, Coll. Listen to the truth.*

And the truth had come, blazing out of the Sword of Shannara in a cleansing, white heat, winding down into Coll and shattering the Shadowen magic so that he could tear off the Mirrorshroud and cast it away forever. The truth had come, and Coll had indeed been set free.

But the truth had never been Par's truth—and never Par's to give. It had been Coll's—and his alone to take.

East, the sun was breaking through the diminishing storm clouds, the grayness of dawn giving way to golden daylight. Coll stared at it and felt as if all the sadness he had ever known had been compressed into this single moment in time.

Par hadn't summoned the magic of the Sword of Shannara. Coll had. Not once, but both times, and each time without realizing what he was doing or that it was his to command. Coll, not Par, was the Ohmsford for whom the Sword was meant. But the truth here, as in so many things, was as elusive as smoke and took time to understand. Allanon had given Coll no charge when they had gathered at the Hadeshorn—yet the power to summon the Sword of Shannara's magic was his. It was reasonable that it should be, when you thought about it. He was Par's brother, and like Par an heir to the Elven magic. They shared the same Elven blood and birthright. But it was to Par that the charge had been given, and it was on Par that everything had subsequently focused. Par had been sent to recover the Sword, armored in his own magic and in his unyielding resolve, certain of his purpose even when the others in the little company had doubted. Par had been sent, and Allanon must have known he would not fail. But why had they not been told that the Sword was meant for Coll? Why had nothing been asked of him?

His hands clasped and knotted before him. He remembered how it had felt when he had brought the Sword's magic to life, an inexplicably cool white fire. Even trapped as he was in the thrall of the Mirrorshroud he had felt it come, a flood washing through him, sweeping everything before it. Truths broke down the barriers of the Shadowen magic, small ones first, remembrances of childhood and youth, then larger ones, harsher and more insistent, blows that stiffened his resolve, that toughened him little by little against what was to follow. The truths were painful, but they were healing as well, and when the last of them was brought before him—the truth of who and what he had become—he was able to accept it and to put an end to the charade being played on him.

He had told the story of the Sword of Shannara a thousand times—how the talisman had come to life in the hands of Shea Ohmsford five hundred years earlier, how it had revealed the Valeman to himself and then unmasked the Warlock Lord. He had told the story so often that he could recite it in his sleep.

But even that had not prepared him for what he felt now in the aftermath of the magic's use. Exposure to the truth had drained him of illusions and conceits that had sheltered him for his entire life. He had been stripped of the protective barriers he had erected for himself against the harshest of his mistakes and failings. He had been left naked and exposed. He had been left feeling foolish and ashamed.

And terrified for Par.

For the Sword of Shannara in freeing him had revealed truths about Par as well. One of them was that Par could not use the Sword. Another was that he did not realize this. A third was that the wishsong was the cause of his brother's problems.

Secrets revealed—he had seen them all. But Par had not. For reasons still unknown, the wishsong would not let Par summon the Sword's magic, would not let him bring the magic into himself, and would not let him see any truths about himself. The wishsong was a wall that kept the Sword's magic out, hiding what it would reveal, keeping his brother a prisoner. Coll didn't know why that was—only that it was so. The wishsong was doing something to Par, and Coll was not certain what it was. He had felt its resistance to the power of the Sword when he had struggled with his brother for possession of the blade. He had felt it force the magic away, keeping it inside Coll, making certain that the truths revealed were his and not his brother's.

Why? he wondered. Why would that be? Why hadn't Allanon told them anything about this, or about who could use the Sword, or about what the Sword was needed to do? What was the Sword's purpose? They had been sent to retrieve it and had done so. Now what were they supposed to do with it?

What was *he* supposed to do with it?

Sunlight brushed his face, and he closed his eyes and leaned into it. The warmth was soothing, and he let it envelop him like a blanket. He was tired and confused, but he was safe as well and that was more than could be said for Par.

He backed out of the light and opened his eyes anew. The King of the Silver River had tried to take them both, but the effort had failed. Par had panicked and used the wishsong, and his magic had counteracted that of their rescuer. Coll had been carried up into the light and safely away, but Par had fallen back into the darkness and the waiting hands of the Shadowen.

Rimmer Dall had him now.

Coll's mouth tightened. He had screamed after Par as he had watched him fall, then felt himself wrapped about and soothed by the light that bore him away. The King of the Silver River had spoken to him, words of reassurance and comfort, words of promise. The old man's voice had been soft in his ear. He would be safe, it whispered. He would sleep and momentarily forget, but when he woke he would remember again. He would keep as his own the Sword of Shannara, for it was his to wield. He would carry it in search of his brother, and he would use it to save him.

Coll nodded at the memory. Use it to save him. Do for Par what Par had done for him. Seek Par out and by invoking the magic of the Sword of Shannara force him to confront the truths that the wishsong was hiding and set him free.

But free from what?

A dark uneasiness stirred inside him as he remembered Par's fears about the way the wishsong's magic was evolving. Rimmer Dall had warned both Ohmsfords that Par was a Shadowen, that the wishsong made him so, and that he was in danger of being consumed by the magic because he did not understand how to control it. He had warned that only he could keep the Valeman from being destroyed. There was no reason to believe anything the First Seeker said, of course. But what if he was even a little bit right? That would surely be reason enough for the wishsong to block the Sword's truth from Par. Because if Par really was a Shadowen . . .

Coll exhaled sharply, furiously. He would not let himself finish the thought, could not accept its possibility. How could Par be a Shadowen? How could he be one of those monsters? There was some other reason for what was happening. There had to be.

Stop debating the matter! You know what you have to do! You have to find Par!

He rose to his feet and stood staring out at the misted lake, battered and worn from his struggle to stay alive and from the revelations of the Sword. He thought of the years he had spent looking after his brother while they were growing up—Par so volatile and contentious, fighting to understand and control the magic that lived within him, and Coll the peacemaker, using his size and calming disposition to keep things from getting out of hand. How many times had he stood up for Par, shielded him from punishments and retributions, and kept him safe from harm? How often had he compromised his own misgivings so that he could stand with his brother and protect him? He couldn't begin to count them. He didn't want to. It was simply something he'd had to do. It was something he would do again now. Par and he were brothers, and brothers stood up for one another when it was needed. The choice had been made a long time ago.

Find Par and set him free.

Before it is too late.

He looked down at the Sword of Shannara and fingered its pommel experimentally, remembering the feel of the magic coursing through him. His magic. The magic he had thought he would never have. It was an odd sensation, knowing that its power was his. He remembered how much he had wanted it once, wanted it not so much for what it could do but because he had believed it would bring him closer to Par. He remembered how alone he had felt after the meeting with Allanon the only member of the Ohmsford family to whom no charge had been given. He remembered thinking that he might just as well not have been there. The memory burned even now.

So what would he make of the chance that had been given him?

He looked at himself, ragged and battered, without food or water, without weapons (save for the Sword), without coins or possessions to trade. He looked back across the lake again, at the mist beginning to burn off as the sunlight strengthened.

Find Par.

His brother would be at Southwatch. But would he be his brother still? Coll believed he could reach Par, that he could find a way to overcome any obstacles set against him, but what would have happened to his brother in the meantime? Would the Sword of Shannara help against what the Shadowen might have done to Par? Would the magic be of any use if Par had become one of them?

The questions were troubling. If he considered them further, he might change his mind about going.

But was it any different when Par came in search of me?

Did he ask if I was still his brother?

He brushed the questions aside, took a firm grip on the Sword of Shannara, and started walking.

He traveled east, following the shoreline toward the mouth of the Silver River. Going west was out of the question, because it meant navigating the Mist Marsh and he knew better than to try that. The clouds disappeared, the sun came out, and the land turned molten. Steamy dampness rose in waves from the sodden earth, and the puddles and streams created by the storm dried back into the dust. Herons and cranes flew over the lake in long swooping glides, and the waters turned silver-tipped in the wake of their passing.

A stranger still to his new life, he thought long and hard about everything that had happened, trying to piece together the parts of the puzzle that still didn't fit. Chief among those was Rimmer Dall's obsession with Par. That the First Seeker had such an obsession was now beyond dispute. Too much time and effort had been expended to think otherwise. First there had been his elaborate hoax to make Par think Coll was dead. Then Coll had been allowed to come back to life, subverted by the Mirrorshroud, and sent to find Par. And there was the whole business of giving the Sword of Shannara to Par when Par couldn't use it. What was it all about? Why was his brother so important to Rimmer Dall? If he had been an obstacle in the First Seeker's path, he would have been killed long ago. Instead Dall seemed content with elaborate gamesplaying—with the search for the Sword of Shannara, with orchestrating Coll's death and subversion, and with suggesting repeatedly the possibility that Par was the very thing he sought to destroy. What was Rimmer Dall trying to do?

Somehow, Coll knew, it was tied to the charge that Allanon had given his brother to bring back the Sword of Shannara. Perhaps the Sword was meant to reveal the truth behind all the deceptions. Perhaps it was meant for something else. Whatever the case, there were schemes and maneuverings at work here that neither he nor Par yet understood, and somehow they must unravel them.

He rested at midday, drinking water from a stream and wishing he had something to eat. He was nearing the Silver River and would soon turn north toward the Rabb. He had grown strong at Southwatch training with Ulfkingroh, but his subversion by the Mirrorshroud had weakened him considerably. His hunger worked through him, and he finally gave in to it. Using the Sword, he fashioned a spear from a willow stick and went fishing. Walking through the shallows of the lake to a quiet cove, he stood knee-deep in the clear waters until a fish passed and stabbed at it. It took him a dozen tries, but finally he had his catch. He carried it ashore, then remembered he had no way to cook it. He could not eat it raw—not after his days in the thrall of the Mirrorshroud. He searched his clothing for firemaking materials, but found only the strange disk he had stolen from Par stuffed down into one pocket. Angry and frustrated, he threw the fish back into the lake and began walking once more.

The afternoon dragged by. Coll rested more frequently now, lightheaded in the swelter, his concentration wavering. Sleep would help, but he had determined to go on until nightfall. He saw Par appear now and again in the shimmer of heat that rose off the saw grass, heard him speaking and saw him move. Memories came and went, mixing with the images and evaporating when he tried to venture too close. He needed a better plan, he told himself. It was not enough simply to return to Southwatch. He would never be able to rescue Par on his own. He needed help. What, he wondered, had happened to Morgan Leah and the others? What had become of Walker Boh and Wren? Where was Damson? Was she searching for Par, too? Padishar Creel would help if Coll could find him. But Padishar could be anywhere.

He walked into the early twilight and saw the Silver River appear ahead, a bright thread weaving inland. He skirted a mire formed by the poisoning of a shallow inlet, tepid waters green and murky, vegetation gray with sickness, the stench of its dying heavy on the air. Breathing through his mouth, he forced his way past, anxious to get on.

As he came out from a stand of pine he saw a wagon and stopped.

Five men seated about a cooking fire looked up. Hard-faced and rough, they stared at him without moving. There was meat cooking on a spit and broth in a pot. The smells reached out to Coll enticingly. A team of mules unhitched from the wagon grazed on a tether. Bedrolls lay scattered on the ground in preparation for sleep. The men were in the process of passing an aleskin back and forth.

One of them motioned for Coll to join them. Coll hesitated. The others waved him over, telling him to come on in, to have something to eat and drink, and what in the name of everything sane had happened to him?

Coll went, aware of how strange he must look, but desperate for food. He was seated among them, given a plate and bowl and a cup of the ale. He had barely taken his first bite when the first blow struck him behind the ear and they were all over him. He fought to rise, to free himself and flee, but there were too many hands holding him back. He was pummeled and kicked nearly unconscious. The Sword of Shannara was stripped from him. Chains were locked about his wrists and ankles, and he was thrown into the back of the wagon. He pleaded with them not to do this. He begged them to set him free, telling them that he was searching for his brother, that he had to find him, that they had to let him go. They laughed at him, scorned him, and told him to keep quiet or he would be gagged. He was propped upright and given a cup of broth and a blanket.

His weapon, he was told, would fetch a good price. But he would fetch an even better one when they sold him to the Federation to work in the slave mines at Dechtera.

25

Par Ohmsford dreamed.

He ran through a forest black with shadows and empty of life. It was night, the sky through the leafy canopy of boughs a deep blue bereft of stars and moon. Par could see clearly as he ran, but he could not determine the source of his vision's light. The trunks of the trees shifted before him, waving like stalks of grass in a wind, forcing him to dodge and weave to avoid them. Branches reached down and brushed against his face and arms, trying to hold him back. Voices whispered, calling out to him over and over again.

Shadowen. Shadowen.

He was terrified.

The clothes he wore were damp with his sweat, and he could feel the chafing of his boots against his ankles. Now and again there would be streams and ponds, and he was forced to leap them or turn aside because he knew instinctively that they were quagmires that if stepped in would pull him down. He listened as he ran for the sounds of other living things. He kept thinking that he could not be this alone, that a forest must have other creatures living within it. He kept thinking, too, that the forest must eventually end, that it could not go on indefinitely. But the farther he ran, the deeper grew the silence and the darker the trees. No sound broke the stillness. No light penetrated the woods.

After a time he became aware of something following him, a nameless black thing that ran as swiftly as he, following as surely as his shadow. He sought to outdistance it by running faster and could not. He sought to lose it by turning aside, first this way and then that, and the thing turned with him. He sought to flatten himself against a monstrous old trunk of indistinguishable origin, and the thing stopped with him and waited.

It was the thing that whispered to him.

Shadowen. Shadowen.

He ran on, not knowing what to do, panic rushing through him, despair washing away hope. He was trapped by the trees and the darkness and could not escape, and he knew that sooner or later the thing would have him. He could feel the blood pounding in his ears and hear the ragged tremor of his breathing. His chest heaved and his legs ached, and he did not think he could go on but knew he could not stop. He reached down for his weapons and found he carried none. He tried to bring someone to help him by sheer force of will, but the names and faces of those he would call upon would not come.

Then he was at the bank of a river, black and swift in the night, racing with the force of floodwaters down a broad, straight channel. He knew it was not really a river, that it was something else, but he did not know what. He saw a bridge spanning it and raced to cross. Behind, he could hear the thing following. He leaped onto the bridge, a wide arching span built of timbers and iron nails. His boots made no sound as he ran. His footfalls were silent. The bridge had seemed an avenue of escape when he had started across it, but now he found he could not see the far shore. He looked back, and the forest had disappeared as well. The sky had lowered and the water had risen, and suddenly he was in a box that was closing tightly about.

The thing that followed him hissed. It was gaining quickly, and it was growing as the box shrank.

Par turned then, knowing he would not escape, that he had been led into a trap, that whatever he had hoped to gain by running had been lost. He turned, and as he did so he remembered that he was not defenseless after all, that he possessed the power of the wishsong, and that the Elven magic could protect him against anything. A surge of hope flooded through him, and he summoned the magic to his defense. It exploded through him in a wild, euphoric rush, a white light that turned his blood to fire and his body to ice. He felt it fill him, felt it sheathe him in the armor of its power and turn him indestructible.

He waited for the thing that followed with anticipation.

It crept out of the night like a cat, a creature without form or substance. He could feel it long before he saw it. He could sense it watching, then breathing, then drawing itself up. It was first to one side and then to the other and finally all about. But he knew somehow that he was not in danger until he could see its face. It twisted and swirled about him, staying carefully out of reach, and he waited for it to tire.

Then it began to materialize, and it was not strange or misshapen or even so large. Its body was the size and shape of his own, and it stood just before him, fully revealed save for its face. He brought the wishsong's magic to his fingertips and held it there like an arrow drawn back in a bowstring, taut, straining for release, razor-sharp. The thing before him watched. Its head was turned toward him now, but its face was clouded and dim. Its voice whispered again.

Shadowen. Shadowen.

Then its face came together and Par was looking at himself.

Shadowen. Shadowen.

Par shuddered and sent the magic of the wishsong flying into the thing. The thing caught it, and it was gone. Par sent the magic a second time, a hammer-blow of power that would smash the creature back into smoke. The thing swallowed it as if it were air. His face smiled back at him, hollow-looking and ragged about the edges, a mirage threatening to disappear back into the heat.

Don't you know?
Don't you see?

The voice whispered, sly, condescending, and hateful, and he attacked again, over and over, the magic flying out of him. But something strange was happening. The more he called upon the magic, the more pleased the thing seemed. He could feel its satisfaction as if it were palpable. He could sense its pleasure. The thing was changing, growing more substantial rather than less, feeding on the magic, drawing it in.

Don't you understand?

Par gasped and stepped back, aware now that he was changing as well, losing shape and definition, disintegrating like burned wood turned to ash. He groped at himself in despair and saw his hands pass through his body. The thing came closer, reaching out. He saw himself reflected in its eyes.

Shadowen. Shadowen.

He saw himself, and he realized that there was no longer any difference between them. He had become the thing.

He screamed as it took him in its arms and slowly drew him in.

The dream ended, and Par awoke with a lurch. He was dizzy, and his breathing was ragged and harsh in the silence. Just a dream, he thought. He put his face in his hands and waited for the spinning to stop. A nightmare, but so very real! He swallowed against his lingering fear.

He opened his eyes again and looked about. He was in a room that was as black as the forest through which he had fled. The room smelled of must and disuse. Windows on a far wall opened onto night skies that were clouded and moonless. The air felt hot and sticky, and there was no wind. He was sitting on a bed that was little more than a wooden frame and pallet, and his clothes were damp and stiff with dried mud.

He remembered then.

The plains, the storm, the battle with Coll, the triggering of the magic of the Sword of Shannara, the coming of the Shadowen, the appearance of the King of the Silver River, the light and then the dark—the images sped past him in an instant's time.

Where was he?

A light flared suddenly from across the room, a brilliant firefly that rested at the fingertips of an arm gloved to the elbow. The light settled on a lamp, and the lamp brightened, casting its glow across the shadows.

"Now that you're awake, perhaps we can talk."

A black-cloaked form stepped into the light, tall and rangy and hooded. It moved in silence, with grace and ease. On its breast gleamed the white insignia of a wolf's head.

Rimmer Dall.

Par felt himself go cold from head to foot, and it was all he could do to keep from bolting. He looked about quickly at the stone walls, at the bars on the windows, at the iron-bound wooden door that stood closed at Rimmer Dall's back. He was at Southwatch. He looked for the Sword of Shannara. It was gone. And Coll was missing as well.

"You don't seem to have slept well."

Rimmer Dall's whispery voice floated through the silence. He pulled back the hood and his rawboned, bearded face was caught in the light, all angles and planes, a mask devoid of expression. If he was aware of Par's distress, he did not show it. He moved to a chair and seated himself. "Do you want something to eat?"

Par shook his head, not yet trusting himself to speak. His throat felt dry and tight, and his muscles were in knots. Don't panic, he told himself. Stay calm. He forced himself to breathe, slow and deep and regular. He brought his legs around on the bed and put his feet on the floor, but did not try to rise. Rimmer Dall watched him out of depthless eyes, his mouth a narrow, tight line, his body motionless. Like a cat waiting, Par thought.

"Where is Coll?" he asked, and his voice was steady.

"The King of the Silver River took him." The whispery voice was smooth and oddly comforting. "He took the Sword of Shannara as well."

"But you managed to keep him from taking me."

The First Seeker laughed softly. "You did that yourself. I didn't have anything to do with it. You used the wishsong, and the magic worked against you. It forced the King of the Silver River away from you." He paused. "The magic grows more unpredictable, doesn't it? Remember how I warned you?"

Par nodded. "I do. I remember everything. But what I remember doesn't matter, because I wouldn't believe you if you told me the sun came up in the east. You've lied to me from the beginning. I don't know why, but you have. And I'm through listening, so you might as well do whatever you have in mind and be done with it."

Rimmer Dall studied him silently. Then he said, "Tell me what I've lied to you about."

Par was furious. He started to speak, but then stopped, suddenly aware that he couldn't remember any specific lies the big man had told. The lies were there, as clear as the wolf's head that glimmered on the black robes, but he couldn't seem to focus on them.

"I told you when we met that I was a Shadowen. I gave you the Sword of Shannara and let you test it against me to find out if I was lying. I warned you that your magic was a danger to you, that it was changing you, and that you might not be able to control it without help. Where was the lie in any of this?"

"You took my brother prisoner after making me think I had killed him!" Par howled, on his feet now in spite of his resolve, threatening. "You let me think he was dead! Then you let him escape with the Mirrorshroud so that he would become a Shadowen and I might kill him again! You set us against each other!"

"Did I?" Rimmer Dall shook his head. "Why would I do that? What would doing that gain me? Tell me what purpose any of that would serve." He stayed seated and calm in the face of Par's wrath, waiting. Par stood there glaring, but did not answer. "No? Then listen to me. I didn't make you think you killed Coll—you did that on your own. Your magic did that, twisting you about, changing what you saw. Remember, Par? Remember the way you thought you had lost control?"

Par caught his breath. Yes, it had been exactly like that, a sense of flying out of himself, of being shifted away.

The big man nodded. "My Seekers found your brother after you had fled and brought him to me. Yes, they were rough with him, but they did not know who he was, only that he was where he shouldn't be. I held him at Southwatch, yes—trying to persuade him to help me find you. I believed him my last chance. When he escaped, he took the Mirrorshroud with him—but I didn't help him steal it. He took it on his own. Yes, it subverted him; the magic is too strong for a normal man. You, Par, could have worn it without being affected. And I didn't set you against each other—you did that-yourselves. Each time I came to you I tried to help, and each time you ran from me. It is time the running stopped."

"I'm sure you would like that!" Par snapped furiously. "It would make things so much easier!"

"Think what you are saying, Par. It lacks reason."

Par clenched his teeth. "Lacks reason? Everywhere I go there are Shadowen waiting, trying to kill me and my friends. What of Damson Rhee and Padishar Creel at Tyrsis? I suppose that was all a mistake?"

"A mistake, but not mine," Rimmer Dall answered calmly. "The Federation pursued you there, took the girl and then subsequently the freeborn leader. The Seekers you destroyed in the watchtower when you freed the girl were there on Federation orders. They did not know who you were, only that you were an intruder. They paid for it with their lives. You must answer for the fairness of that."

Par shook his head. "I don't believe you. I don't believe anything you say."

Rimmer Dall shifted slightly in the chair, a ripple of black. "So you have said each time we have talked. But you seem to lack any concrete reason for your stance. When have I done anything to threaten you? When have I done anything but be forthright? I told you the history of the Shadowen. I told you that the magic is our birthright, a gift that can help, that can save. I told you that the Federation is the enemy, that it has hunted us and destroyed us at every turn because it fears and hates what it cannot or will not understand. Enemies, Par? Not you and I. We are kindred. We are the same."

Par saw the dream suddenly, and its memory sparked something dark and inexorable inside. Running from himself, from the magic, from his birthright, from his destiny—it was possible, wasn't it?

"If we are kindred, if you are not the enemy, then you will let me go," he insisted.

"Oh, no, not this time." The big man shook his head and his smile was a twitch at the corners of his mouth. "I did so before, and you almost destroyed yourself. I won't be so foolish again. This time we will try my way. We will talk, visit, explore, discover, and hopefully learn. After that, you can go."

Par shook his head angrily. "I don't want to talk or visit or any of the rest. There's nothing to talk about." He glared. "If you try to hold me, I will use the wishsong."

Rimmer Dall nodded. "Go ahead, use it." He paused. "But remember what the magic is doing to you."

Changing me, Par thought in recognition of the warning's import. Each time I use it, it changes me further. Each time, I lose a little more control. I try not to let that happen, but I can't seem to prevent it. And I don't know what the consequences will be, but they do not feel as if they will be pleasant.

"I am not a Shadowen," he said dully.

Rimmer Dall's gaze was flat and steady. "It is only a word."

"I don't care. I am not."

The First Seeker rose and walked over to the window. He stared out at the night, distracted and distant. "I used to be bothered by who I was and what I was called," he said. "I considered myself a freak, a dangerous aberration. But I learned that was wrong. It was not what other people thought of me that mattered; it was what I thought of myself. If I allowed myself to be shaped by other people's opinions, I would become what they wished me to become."

He turned back to Par. "The Shadowen are being destroyed without reason. We are being blamed without cause. We have magic that can help in many ways, and we are not being allowed to use it. Ask yourself, Par— how is it any different for you?"

Par was suddenly exhausted, weighed down by the impact of what had happened to him and his confusion over what it might mean. Rimmer Dall was calm and smooth and unshakable. His arguments were persuasive. Par could not think how the First Seeker had lied. He could not focus on when he had tried to cause harm. It had always seemed that he was the enemy— and Allanon and Cogline had said so—but where was the proof of it? Where, for that matter, were the Druid and the old man? Where was anyone who could help him?

His memory of the dream haunted him. How much truth had the dream told?

He turned back to the bed from which he had risen and sat down again. It seemed as if nothing had gone right for him from the moment he had accepted Allanon's charge to recover the Sword of Shannara. Not even the Sword itself had proved to be of any use. He was alone and abandoned and helpless. He did not know what to do.

"Why not sleep a bit more," Rimmer Dall suggested quietly. He was already moving for the door. "I'll have food and drink sent up to you in a little while, and we can talk again later."

He was through the door and gone almost before Par thought to look up. The Valeman rose quickly to stop him, then sat down again. The spinning sensation had returned. His body felt weak and leaden. Perhaps he should sleep again. Perhaps he would be able to reason things through better if he did.

Shadowen. Shadowen.

Was it possible that he was?

He curled up on the pallet and drifted away.

He dreamed again, and this second dream was a variation of the first, dark and terrifying. He woke in a sweat, shaking and raw-nerved, and saw daylight brightening the skies through his windows. Food and drink were brought by a black-robed, silent Shadowen, and he thought for a moment to smash the creature with his magic and flee. But he hesitated, uncertain of the wisdom of this course of action, the moment passed, and the door closed on him once more.

He ate and drank and did not feel better. He sat in the gloom of his prison and listened to the silence. Now and again he could hear the cries of herons and cranes from somewhere without, and there was a low whistling of wind against the castle stone. He walked to the windows and peered out. He was facing east into the sun. Below, the Mermidon wound its way down out of the Runne to the Rainbow Lake, its waters swollen from the storm and clogged with debris. The windows were deep-set and did not allow for more than a glimpse of the land about, but he could smell the trees and the grasses and he could hear the river's flow.

He sat on his bed again afterward, trying to think what to do. As he did so, he became aware of a thrumming sound from deep within the castle, an odd vibration that ran through the stone and the iron like thunder in a storm, low and insistent. It seemed that it ran in a steady, unbroken wave, but once in a while he thought he could feel it break and hear something different in its whine. He listened to it carefully, feeling its movement in his body, and he wondered what it was.

The day eased toward noon, and Rimmer Dall returned. So black that he seemed to absorb the light around him, he slipped through the door like a shadow and materialized in the chair once more. He asked Par how he was feeling, how he had slept, whether the food and drink had been sufficient. He was pleasant and calm and anxious to converse, yet distant, too, as if fearing that any attempt to get close would exacerbate wounds already opened. He talked again of the Shadowen and the Federation, of the mistake that Par was making in confusing the two, of the danger in believing that both were enemies. He spoke again of his mistrust of the Druids, of the ways they manipulated and deceived, of their obsession with power and its uses. He reminded Par of the history of his family—how the Druids had used the Ohmsfords to achieve ends they believed necessary and in the process changed forever the lives of those so employed.

"You would not be suffering the vicissitudes of the wishsong's magic if not for what was done to Wil Ohmsford years ago," he declared, his voice, as always, low and compelling. "You can reason it through as well as I, Par. All that you have endured these past few weeks was brought about by the Druids and their magic. Where does the blame for that lie?"

He talked then of the sickening of the Four Lands and the steps that needed to be taken to hasten a recovery. It was not the Shadowen who caused the sickness. It was the neglect of the Races, of those who had once been so careful to protect and preserve. Where were the Elves when they were needed? Gone, because the Federation had driven them away, frightened of their heritage of magic. Where were the Dwarves, always the best of tenders? In slavery, subdued by the Federation so that they could pose no threat to the Southland government.

He spoke for some time, and then suddenly he was gone again, faded back into the stone and silence of the castle. Par sat where he had been left and did not move, hearing the First Seeker's whisper in his mind—the cadence of his voice, the sound of his words, and the litany of his arguments as they began and ended and began again. The afternoon passed away, and the sun faded west. Twilight fell, and dinner arrived. He accepted what he was offered by the silent bearer and this time did not think of trying to escape. He ate and drank without paying attention, staring at the walls of his room, thinking.

Nightfall came, and with it came Rimmer Dall once more. Par was looking for him this time, expecting him, anticipating him as he would thunder in a rainstorm. He heard the door latch give, saw it open, and watched the First Seeker come through. The black-cloaked figure moved to his chair without speaking and sat. They stared at each other in the silence, measuring.

"What have I not told you that I should?" Rimmer Dall asked finally, motionless in the growing shadows. "What answers can I give?"

Par shook his head. The First Seeker had given him too many answers and too much to consider, and it tumbled about in his mind like colored glass in a kaleidoscope. A part of him continued to resist everything he heard, stubborn and intractable. It would not let him believe; it would not even let him consider. He wished that it would. His sleep was filled with nightmares, and his waking was crowded with a senseless warring of possibilities. He wanted it all to end.

He did not say this to Rimmer Dall. He asked instead about the sounds from within the castle, the thrumming through the walls, the pitch and whine, the sense of something stirring. The First Seeker smiled. The explanation was simple. What Par was hearing was the Mermidon passing through an underground channel that ran beneath the keep, its waters crashing against the walls of ancient caves below. At times you could feel the vibrations for miles about. At times you could feel them in your bones.

"Does it disturb your sleep?" the big man asked.

Par shook his head. The nightmares disturbed his sleep. "If I were to decide to believe you," he said, letting the words slip free before his stubborn side could think better of it, "what would you do to help me control the magic of the wishsong?"

Rimmer Dall sat perfectly still. "I would teach you to manage it. I would teach you to be comfortable with it. You could learn how to use it safely again."

Par stared straight ahead without seeing. He wanted to believe. "You think you could do that?"

"I have had years to learn how. I was forced to do so with my own magic, and the lessons have not been lost on me. The magic is a powerful weapon, Par, and it can turn against you. You need discipline and understanding to rule it properly. I can give you that."

Par's mind felt leaden and his eyes drooped. His weariness was a dark cloud that would not let him think. "We could talk about it, I guess," he said.

"Talk, yes. But experiment, too." Rimmer Dall was leaning forward, intense. "Control of the magic comes from practice; it is an acquired skill. The magic is a birthright, but it needs training."

"Training?"

"I could show you. I could let you see inside my mind, let you see how the magic functions within me. I could give you access to the ways in which I block it and channel it. Then you could do the same for me."

Par looked up. "How?"

"You could let me see inside your mind. You could let me explore and help set in place the protections you need. We could work together."

He went on, explaining carefully, persuasively, but Par had ceased to hear, locked on something vaguely alarming, something that lacked an identity, but was there nevertheless. The stubborn part that refused to believe anything the First Seeker said had risen up with a gasp and closed down his mind like a trapdoor. He pretended to listen, heard bits and pieces of what the other was saying, and gave responses that committed nothing.

What was it? What was the matter?

After a time, Rimmer Dall left him alone. "Think about what I have told you," he urged. "Consider what might be done." The night settled in, and the darkness of Par's chamber was complete. He lay down to sleep, exhausted without reason, then fought against the urge to close his eyes because he did not want the nightmares to come again. He stared at the ceiling and then out the windows at a sky that was clear and filled with stars. He thought of his brother and the Sword of Shannara, and he wondered what the King of the Silver River had done with them. He thought of Damson and Padishar, Walker and Wren, and all the others who had been involved in his struggle. He wondered vaguely what the struggle had been for.

He slept finally, drifting off before he knew what was happening, sinking into a soothing blackness. But the nightmare surfaced instantly, and he experienced for the third time a confrontation with himself as a Shadowen wraith. He thrashed and twisted and fought to come awake, and afterward lay sweating and gasping in the dark.

He realized then, with chilling certainty, that something was dreadfully wrong.

Look at what was happening to him. He could not sleep without dreaming, and the dream was always the same. He ate, but he lost strength. He spent his time in his room doing nothing, yet he was always tired. He could not think straight. He could not concentrate. His energy was being sapped away.

This wasn't happening by chance, he admonished himself. Something was causing it.

He sat upright on the bed, swung his legs to the floor, and stared into the room's shadows. *Think!* He fought back against his exhaustion, against the chains of his lethargy and disorientation. Recognition came, a slow untangling of threads that had knotted. There were two possibilities. The first was that the magic of the wishsong was infecting him in some new way, and he needed to do what Rimmer Dall was urging. The second was that the magic infecting him was Shadowen, that Rimmer Dall was working to break down his defenses, and that all his talk about helping him was some sort of trick.

But a trick to do what?

Par took a deep, steadying breath. He wanted to crawl back beneath the covers but would not let himself. He felt an urge to scream and choked it down. Was Rimmer Dall lying or telling the truth? What were his real intentions in all this? Par clasped his hands together to keep them from shaking. He was falling apart. He could feel himself unraveling, and he did not know how to stop it. If Rimmer Dall was telling the truth about the wishsong, then he needed his help. If he was lying, it was a deception so intricate and so vast that it dwarfed anything the Valeman could imagine, because it had to have been at work from the moment the First Seeker had come looking for him weeks ago at the Blue Whisker Ale House.

Shades! I need to know!

Par rose, walked to the windows, and stood looking out at the night, breathing the cool air. He was paralyzed with indecision. How was he going to learn the truth? Was there some way to see past his own uncertainty, to recognize if there was a deception being played? The Sword of Shannara had showed him nothing, he reminded himself. Nothing! What else was there to try?

He watched shadows thrown by the night clouds shift like animals through the trees across the river. He would have to stall, he told himself. He could listen and talk, but he could not allow anything to happen. He would have to find a way to dispel his confusion so that he could recognize what was truth and what a lie, and at the same time he would have to find a way to keep himself from disintegrating completely.

He closed his eyes, put his face in his hands, and wondered how he was going to do that.

26

Heat rose off the grasslands east of Drey Wood in sweltering waves, the midday sun a fiery ball in the cloudless sky, the air thick with the smell and taste of sweat and dust. Wren Elessedil lay flat against the crest of a rise and watched the Federation army toil its way across the plains like a slow-moving, many-legged insect.

Mindless and persistent, she thought bleakly.

She did not bother glancing over at the others—Triss, Erring Rift, and Desidio. She already knew what she would see in their faces. She already knew what they were thinking.

They had been watching the Federation's progress for more than an hour—not with any expectation that they would learn anything, but out of a need to do something besides sit around and wait for the inevitable. The Elves were in trouble. The Federation march north to the Rhenn had resumed two days ago, and time was running out. Barsimmon Oridio had finally completed the mobilization and provisioning of the main body of the Elven army and was headed east to the pass, a forced march that would bring the Elves into the Rhenn at least three days ahead of the enemy. But the Elves were still outnumbered ten to one, and any kind of direct engagement would result in their annihilation. Worse, the Creepers continued their approach, closer now than before, catching up quickly to the slower Southlanders. In four, maybe five days, the Creepers would overtake them and become their vanguard, the advance for a search-and-destroy action. When that happened, it would be the end of the Elves.

Wren felt a vague hopelessness nudging at her, and she angrily thrust it away.

What can I do to save my people?

She focused again on the crawling army and tried to think. Another midnight raid was out of the question. The Federation was alerted to them now and would not be caught napping twice. Cavalry patrols rode day and night all around the main body of the army, scouring the countryside for any sign of the Elves. Once or twice riders more bold than smart had even ventured into the forests. Wren had let them pass, the Elves melting back into the trees, invisible in the shadows. She did not want the Federation to know where they were. She did not want to give them anything she didn't have to. Not that it mattered. The patrols kept them at bay, and sentry lines were extended a quarter-mile out from the camp once darkness fell. The Wing Riders could come in from overhead, but she did not care to risk her most valuable weapon when she could bring no strength to bear in its support.

Besides, it made little difference what she did about the Federation army if she did not first find a way to stop the Creepers. Though still distant, the Creepers were the most dangerous and immediate threat. If they were allowed to reach the Rhenn, or even the Westland forests immediately south, there would be nothing to stop them from carving a path straight through to Arborlon. The Creepers wouldn't worry about finding a roadway leading in. They wouldn't concern themselves with ambushes and traps. They didn't need scouts or patrols to search out the enemy. The Creepers would find the Elves wherever they tried to hide and destroy them in the same manner they had destroyed the Dwarves fifty years earlier. Wren knew the stories. She knew what kind of enemy they were up against.

The sweat lay against her face like a damp mask. She exhaled slowly, beckoned to the others, and began backing off the rise. When they were safely within the shelter of the trees once more, they rose and walked to where their horses were held by the Elven Hunters who had come with them. No one spoke. No one had anything to say. Wren led the way, trying to look as if she had something in mind even though she didn't, worried that she was beginning to lose the confidence she had won in leading the attack three nights earlier, confidence that she needed if she was to control events once Barsimmon Oridio arrived. She was Queen of the Elves, she told herself. But even a queen could fail.

They mounted and rode back to the Elven camp. Wren thought back over all that had happened since the coming of Cogline, wondering what had become of the old man—what, for that matter, had become of the others he had gathered at the Hadeshorn to speak with the shade of Allanon. She experienced a vague sense of regret that she knew so little of their fates. She should be searching for them, seeking them out and telling them the truth about the Shadowen origins. It was important that they know, she sensed. Something about who and what the Shadowen were would lead to their destruction. Allanon had known as much, she believed. But if he had known, why hadn't he simply told them? She shook her head. It was more complex than that; it had to be. But wasn't everything in this struggle?

They reached the vanguard camp, settled several miles north, dismounted, and handed over their horses. Wren strode away from the others, still without speaking, took food from a table not because she was hungry but because she knew she must eat, and sat alone at one end of a bench and stared off into the trees. The answers were out there somewhere, she told herself. She kept thinking that they were tied to the past, that history repeats, that you learn from what has gone before. Morrowindl's lessons paraded themselves before her eyes in the form of dead faces and brief images of unending sacrifice. So much had been given up to get the Elves safely away from that deathtrap; it could not have been simply for this. It had to have been for something more than dying here instead of there.

She wished suddenly for Garth. She missed his steadying presence, the way he could take any problem and make it seem solvable. No matter how dark things had gotten, Garth had always gone on, taking her with him when she was little, letting her lead when she was grown. She missed him so. Tears came to her eyes, and she brushed them away self-consciously. She would not cry for him again. She had promised she would not.

She rose and carried her plate back to the table, looking about for Erring Rift. She would fly south again, she decided, for another look at the Creepers. There had to be a way to stop or at least slow them. Maybe something would suggest itself. It was a faint hope, but it was all she had. She wished Tiger Ty was there; he provided some of the same steadiness that she had gotten from Garth. But the gnarled Wing Rider had not returned from his search for the free-born, and bringing the free-born to the aid of the Elves was more important than providing solace for her.

She caught sight of Rift and whistled him over.

"We're going up for another look at the Creepers," she announced, keeping her gaze steady as she faced him. His bearded face clouded. "I need to do this. Don't argue with me."

Rift shook his head. "I wouldn't dream of it," he muttered. "My lady."

She took his arm and walked him through the camp. "We won't stay out long. Let's just see where they are, all right?"

Obsidian eyes glanced over and away again. "They're too confounded close, is where they are. We both know that already." He rubbed at his beard. "There's no mystery to this. We have to stop them. You don't happen to have a plan for doing that, do you?"

She gave him a faint smile. "You'll be the first to know."

They were moving toward the clearing where the Rocs were settled when Tib Arne came running up, breathless and flushed.

"My lady! My lady! Are you flying one of the great birds? Take me with you this time, please? You said you would, my lady. The next time you went out, you said you would. Please? I'm tired of sitting about doing nothing."

She turned to face him. "Tib," she began.

"Please?" he begged, coming to a ragged stop in front of her. He brushed back his shock of blond hair. His blue eyes sparkled with anticipation. "I won't be any trouble."

She glanced at Rift, who gave her a black look of warning. But she was feeling at loose ends with herself, strangely disconnected from everything, and she needed to regain her perspective. Why not? she thought. Perhaps having Tib along would help. Perhaps it would suggest something.

She nodded. "All right. You can come."

Tib's smile spread from ear to ear. It just about matched Erring Rift's scowl.

They flew south against the backdrop of the mountains, the Elf Queen, the leader of the Wing Riders, and the boy, staying low and tight against the land. They passed the laboring Federation army, strung out across the empty plains in a massive cloud of dust, and continued on past the bleak expanse of the Matted Brakes toward the blue ribbon of the Mermidon. The wind blew at them in soothing, cooling waves, and the land spread away in a patchwork of earth colors dotted with bright flashes of sunlight reflecting off ponds and streams. Wren sat behind Erring Rift, and Tib Arne sat behind her. She could feel the tension in the boy as he strained to look down past Grayl's wings, taking in the land below, seeking first to one side and then to the other, small exclamations of excitement escaping his lips. She smiled, and lost herself in memories.

Only once did her thoughts stray back to the present. For the second time in a row, she had not brought Faun with her on a flight with Erring Rift. Faun had begged to go, and she had refused. Maybe she was afraid for the Tree Squeak, frightened that it would fall from the Roc's back. Maybe it was something more. She really wasn't sure.

The hours slipped away. They reached the Pykon, picked up the winding channel of the Mermidon, and sped south. Still no sign of the Creepers. Wren scanned the countryside, afraid that the monsters had slipped into the trees where they could no longer be followed. But seconds later a glint of metal flashed out of the distance, and Erring Rift swung Grayl into a sweeping loop that carried them away from the Mermidon and closer to the mountains west. They hugged the rocks as they came up on the Creepers, who were bunched east of the river, lurching after the Federation army. Wren watched the insect things move tirelessly through the heat and dust, monsters that served inhuman masters and insupportable needs. She thought of the things she had left behind on Morrowindl and realized that she had not really left them behind after all. The dark creatures that the Elven magic had created there had simply been recreated here in another form. History repeating again, she thought. So what were the lessons she needed to learn?

They flew past twice, and then Wren had Erring Rift land them on a bluff amid a series of forested foothills backed up against the Rock Spur. From there they could watch the progress of the Creepers as they labored on across the grasslands, disjointed legs rising and falling in steady cadence.

Wren seated herself without comment. Tib Arne sat next to her, knees drawn up, arms wrapped about his legs, face intense as he stared out at the Creepers. *Creepers.* She mouthed the word without saying it. How could they be stopped? She dug at the ground with the heels of her boots, thinking. Behind her, Erring Rift was checking the harness straps on Grayl. Wind blew gently through the trees, soothing and cool on her skin. She thought of the Wisteron, a distant cousin to the Creepers, sunk finally into the mire close to where it had made its lair.

Rift touched her shoulder, handing down a waterskin. She took it, drank, and offered it to Tib, who declined. She rose and walked with Rift to the edge of the rise, staring out again at the Creepers. What was out there that could hurt these things? Did they eat and sleep like other creatures? Did they need water? Did they breathe air?

She brushed at the sweat on her face.

"We should start back," Rift said quietly.

She nodded and didn't move. Below, the Creepers lumbered on, sunlight glinting off their armor, dust rising from their heavy tread.

The Wisteron, she was thinking. *Sunk into the earth.*

She blinked. There was something there for her, she realized. Something useful . . .

Then she heard a familiar, low whistle, and started to turn. Tib Arne appeared next to her, blond-haired and blue-eyed, smiling and excited. He came up with a laugh and pointed out toward the plains. "Look."

She stared out into the swelter, seeing nothing.

Beside her, Erring Rift grunted sharply and lurched forward. Behind, there was a heavy clump, as if a tree had fallen, and a shriek that froze her blood.

She turned, something slammed against her head, and everything went black.

Far to the east, the Dragon's Teeth had begun already to cast their shadows with the failing of the late afternoon light. Tiger Ty rode Spirit on a slow, steady wind that bore them north across the tallest of the peaks toward the parched and scorching plains. The Wing Rider's day had been fruitless—the same as every day since he had set out in search of the free-born. From dawn to dusk he scoured the land for an indication of the promised army and found nothing. There were Federation patrols everywhere, some of considerable size, like the one blocking the pass at the south end of the mountains. He had left Spirit long enough to visit with people on the road, asking for news, learning of a prison break in a city called Tyrsis, where the leader of the free-born, Padishar Creel, had been held for execution until his followers managed to free him. It was quite an accomplishment, and everyone was talking about it. But no one seemed to know where he was now or where any of the free-born were, for that matter.

Or at least they weren't saying.

The fact that Tiger Ty was an Elf and knew almost nothing of the Four Lands didn't help matters. Constricted by his ignorance, he was reduced to searching blindly. He had managed to discover that the outlaws had probably gone to ground in the mountains he now sailed across, but the peaks were vast and filled with places to hide, and he might spend fifty years looking and never find anyone.

In point of fact, he was beginning to think that it was hopeless. But he had given his promise to Wren that he would find the free-born, and he was no less determined than she had been when she had flown to Morrowindl in search of the Elves.

He stared down at the empty, blasted rock, his leathery face furrowed and dark. It all looked the same; there was nothing to see. As the mountains spread farther north, he banked Spirit left, tracking their line yet again. He had made this same sweep twice now, taking a slightly different tack each time so as to cover a fresh stretch of the vast range, knowing even as he did that there were still hundreds of places he was missing.

His body knotted with frustration and weariness. If there was a free-born army out there, why was it so confounded hard to find?

He thought momentarily of Wren and the Land Elves, and he wondered if the Federation army had recovered sufficiently to continue its pursuit. He smiled, remembering the night attack. The girl was something, all right. She was all grit and hard edges. Barely grown, and already a leader. The Land Elves, he thought, would go exactly as far as they would allow her to take them. If they didn't listen to her, they were foolish beyond—

A flash of light from the rocks below disrupted his train of thought. He stared downward intently. The flash came again, quick and certain. A signal, sure enough. But from who? Tiger Ty nudged Spirit, spiraling outward so that he could study better what they were flying toward. The flash came a third and fourth time, and then stopped, as if whoever had given it was satisfied that it had been seen. The source of the signal was a bluff high in the north central peaks, and as he approached he could see a knot of four men standing at the bluff's center, waiting. They were out in the open and not trying to hide, and it did not appear that there were any others about or any places that they might be hiding. A good sign, the Wing Rider thought. But he would be careful anyway.

He settled Spirit onto the bluff, alert for any deception. The giant Roc came to rest at the edge, well away from the four. Tiger Ty sat where he was for a moment, studying the terrain. The men across from him waited patiently. Tiger Ty satisfied himself, loosened the retaining straps, and climbed down. He spoke a word of caution to Spirit, then ambled forward across a stretch of dried saw grass and broken rock. Two of the four came to meet him, one tall and lean and chiseled like stone, the other black-bearded and ferocious. The tall one limped.

When they were less than six paces from each other, Tiger Ty stopped. The two men did the same.

"That was your signal?" Tiger Ty asked.

The tall one nodded. "You've been flying past for two days now, searching for something. We decided it was time to find out what. Legend has it that only Wing Riders fly the giant Rocs. Is that so? Have you come from the Elves?"

Tiger Ty folded his arms. "Depends on who's asking. There's a lot of people not to be trusted these days. Are you one of them?"

The black-bearded man flushed and started forward a step, but a glance from the other stopped him in his tracks. "No," he answered, lifting an eyebrow quizzically. "Are you?"

Tiger Ty smiled. "Guess this game could go on awhile, couldn't it? Are you free-born?"

"Now and forever," said the tall man.

"Then you're who I'm looking for. I'm called Tiger Ty. I've been sent by Wren Elessedil, Queen of the Land Elves."

"Then the Elves are truly back?"

Tiger Ty nodded.

The tall man smiled in satisfaction. "I'm Padishar Creel, leader of the free-born. My friend is called Chandos. Welcome back to the Four Lands, Tiger Ty. We need you."

Tiger Ty grunted. "We need you worse. Where's your army?"

Padishar Creel looked confused. "My army?"

"The one that's supposed to be marching to our rescue! We're under attack by a Federation force ten times our size cavalry, foot soldiers, archers, siege equipment—well, not so much of that anymore, but enough armor and weapons to roll us up like ants under a broom. The boy said you were on your way to help us with five thousand men. Not enough by half, but any help would be welcome."

Chandos frowned darkly, rubbing at his beard. "Just a minute. What boy are you talking about?"

Tiger Ty stared. "The one with the war shrike." A sudden uneasiness gripped the Wing Rider. "Tib Arne." He looked from one face to the other. "Blue eyes, towheaded, kind of small. You did send him, didn't you?"

The men across from him exchanged a hurried glance. "We sent a man who was forty if he was a day. His name was Sennepon Kipp," Chandos said carefully. "I should know. I made the choice myself."

Tiger Ty went cold all the way through. "But the boy? You don't know the boy at all?"

Padishar Creel's hard eyes fixed him. "Not before this, Tiger Ty. But I'd be willing to bet we know him now."

Bright light seared the slits of Wren's eyes as she regained consciousness, and she turned her head away, blinking. A fist knotted in her hair and jerked her upright, and the voice that whispered in her ear was filled with hatred and disdain.

"Awake, awake, Queen of the Elves."

The hand released, letting her slump forward on her knees, her head aching from the blow that had felled her. A gag filled her mouth, secured so tightly that she could only breathe through her nose. Her hands were tied behind her back, her wrists lashed with cord that cut the flesh. Dust and the smell of her own sweat and fear filled her nostrils.

"Ah, lady, my lady, the fairest of the fair, ruler of the Westland Elves— you are such a fool!" The voice became a hiss. "Sit up and look at me!"

She was struck a blow to the side of the head that spilled her back to the ground, and again the fist closed on her hair and yanked her upright. "Look at me!"

She lifted her head and stared into Tib Arne's blue eyes. There was no laughter in them now, nothing of the boy that he had seemed. They were hard and cold and filled with menace.

"Cat got your tongue?" he sneered, and gave her a mirthless smile. There was blood on his hands. "Cat got your tongue, and I've got the rest. But what to do with you? What duty shall I render to the Queen of the Elves?"

He wheeled away, laughing softly, shaking his head, hugging himself with glee. Wren looked around in dismal recognition. Erring Rift lay dead on the ground next to her, the killing blade still jammed to the hilt in his back. Grayl lay a little further off, lifeless as well, most of his head missing. Towering over him was Gloon, grown somehow as large as the Roc, feathers bristling from his sinewy body like quills. Talons and beak already red with blood ripped at the dead Roc, tearing out new chunks of flesh. In the midst of eating, Gloon paused and stared directly at her, crested brows furrowing, and what she saw in the war shrike's eyes was an undisguised hunger.

Her breath caught in her throat, and she could not look away.

"Larger than you remember him, isn't he?" Tib Arne said, suddenly very close again, his shadow enveloping her as he bent down. His boyish voice was all wrong for the hardened face. "That was your first mistake— thinking that we were what we seemed. You were very stupid."

He seized her neck and twisted her to face him. "It was easy, really. I could have come into the camp at any time, could have told you I was anyone. But I waited, patient and smart. I saw the free-born messenger, and I intercepted him. He told me everything before he died. Then I took his place. All I needed to do was to get you alone for a few moments, you see. That was all."

His eyes danced. Suddenly he began hitting her with his free hand, holding her upright as he did so that she would not fall. "But you wouldn't give me that!" He stopped hitting her, jerking her bloodied face about so that she could see him again. His blond hair was awry and his blue eyes sparkled, but the winning boy could not conceal the monster that seethed just beneath the surface of the skin, tensed to break forth. "You tried to send me away, and while I was gone you led that night attack on the Federation army! Stupid, stupid girl! They're nothing! All you did was slow things up a bit, force us to bring the Creepers just that much sooner, require us to work just that much harder!"

He dropped to his knees in front of her, hand still clenched about her neck in a grip of iron. A single word repeated itself over and over in her pain-fogged mind. *Shadowen.*

"But I killed those men—or rather Gloon did for me. Tore them to shreds, and I listened to them scream and did nothing to quicken their death. But it was your fault they died, not mine. I sent Gloon to hide and came back—too late to stop your foolish night raid, but soon enough to make certain it would not happen again. And then I waited, knowing a chance would come to get you alone, knowing it must!"

He gave her his little-boy look of pleading, and his voice grew mocking. "Oh, Lady, please, please take me with you? You promised you would? Please? I won't be any trouble?"

She breathed sharply through her nose, fighting to clear the blood and dust, struggling to stay conscious.

"Oh, I'm sorry. Are you uncomfortable?" He slapped her lightly on one cheek and then the other. "There! Is that better?" He laughed. "Where was I? Oh, yes—waiting. And today marks the end of that, doesn't it? You turned your back, I whistled in Gloon to finish the Roc, kept your attention fixed on the Creepers while I stabbed the Wing Rider, then knocked you out. So quick, so easy. Over and done with in seconds."

He released her and stood up. Wren slumped but refused to fall, to give him the satisfaction. Her own rage was building, fighting through the weariness and pain, giving her strength enough to focus on the boy.

The Shadowen.

Tib Arne snickered. "No hope for you now, is there, Queen of the Elves? Not the least. They'll hunt for you, but they won't find you. Not you, not the Wing Rider, not the Roc. You will all simply disappear." He smiled. "Want to know where? Of course you do. Doesn't matter with the other two, but you . . ."

He put his hands on his hips and cocked his head, his casual stance betrayed by the hardness in his eyes and the malice in his voice. "You will go to Southwatch and Rimmer Dall—with these!"

He reached into his pocket and pulled out the leather pouch that held the Elfstones. Her heart lurched. The Elfstones, her only weapon against the Shadowen.

"We've known about them since you killed our brother at the Wing Hove. Such power—but it is no longer yours. It belongs to the First Seeker now. And so will you, my lady. Until he's done with you, and then I'll ask that you be given back to me!"

He shoved the pouch back into his pocket. "You should have let things be, Elf Queen. It would have been better for you if you had. You should have remembered that we are all of a common origin—Elves, come out of the old world where we were kings. You should have asked to be one of us. Your magic would have let you. Shadowen are what Elves were destined to become. Some of us knew. Some of us listened to the earth's whisper!"

What is he talking about? she wondered. But her thinking was muddled and dull.

He turned away, watched Gloon eat for a time, then whistled the war shrike over. Gloon came reluctantly, pieces of Grayl still clutched in his hooked beak. Tib Arne patted and soothed the giant bird, talking quietly with it, laughing and joking. Gloon listened intently, eyes fixed on the boy, head dipped obediently. Wren stayed where she was, trying to think what she might do to help herself.

Then Tib came for her, picked her up easily, slung her over Gloon's slate-gray back like a sack of grain, and strapped her in place. The boy went back for Erring Rift, and threw the Wing Rider's body from the bluff into the dense thickets below. On command, Gloon buried his blood-streaked yellow beak in Grayl, dragged the unfortunate Roc to the edge, and dropped him after. Wren closed her eyes against what she was feeling. Tib Arne was right; she had been stupid beyond reason.

The boy came back to her then and pulled himself aboard Gloon.

"You see, the magic allows us anything, Elf Queen," he snapped over his shoulder as he settled himself in place. "Gloon can make himself large or small as he chooses, cloaked in the shrike's feathers, come out of the Shadowen form he took when he embraced the magic. And I can be the son you'll never have. Have I been a good son, Mother? Have I?" He laughed. "You never suspected, did you? Rimmer Dall said you wouldn't. He said you'd want to like and trust me, that you needed someone after losing your big friend on Morrowindl."

Wren felt bitterness rise within to mix with humiliation and despair. Tib Arne watched her for a moment and laughed.

Then Gloon spread his wings and they were flying east across the plains, speeding away from the Westland forests, the Creepers, the Federation army, and the Elves. She watched everything disappear gradually into the sunset and then into shadows, night descending in a hazy, gray light. They flew into darkness, following the line of the Mermidon into Callahorn, past Kern and Tyrsis, down through the grasslands south.

Midnight came, and they descended to a darkened flat on which a wagon and horsemen waited. How they had come to be there, Wren didn't know. The men were black-cloaked and bore the wolf's-head insignia of Seekers. There were eight, all dark and voiceless within their garb, wraiths in the silence of the night. They looked as if they had been expecting Tib Arne and Gloon. Tib gave the pouch with the Elfstones to one, and two others lifted her from Gloon and placed her inside the wagon. No words were spoken. Wren twisted about in an effort to see, but the canvas flaps had already been drawn and secured.

Lying in blackness and silence, she heard the sound of Gloon's wings as he rose back into the air. Then the wagon gave a lurch and started forward. Wheels creaked, traces jangled, and horses' hooves clumped in steady rhythm through the night.

She was on her way to Southwatch and Rimmer Dall, she knew, and felt as if a great hole had opened in the earth to swallow her.

27

It was nearing dawn when Morgan Leah saw the wagon and riders come out of the grasslands west, slowing to begin the climb into the hills that led to Southwatch. He stood on the bluff south, his watch post for three days past now, staring out across the awakening land. Stars and moon were fading in a cloudless night sky, but the hills were thick with patches of mist that clung to the hollows and draws. The earth was a repository for predawn shadows melting into the gray of the disappearing night, still and lifeless husks that would be swallowed whole when morning arrived.

Except, of course, for the wagon and the horsemen, shadows of substance whose movements stood out against the frozen dark. Morgan watched them silently, motionlessly, as if any sound or movement on his part might cause them to vanish in the haze. They were still a fair distance away, nearly lost in the gloom, shimmering like dark ghosts against the night.

They were the first sign of life he had seen since he had begun his vigil. They were, he knew instantly, what he had been waiting for.

Three days gone, and no one had gone into or come out of Southwatch. No one had even gone near. The land might have been devoid of life but for a handful of birds that sped in and out of view with single-minded concentration. There had been skiffs upon the Mermidon and the Rainbow Lake, but all had passed south, well clear of the Shadowen citadel, well away from any contact. Morgan had watched long and carefully for signs of life within the obelisk, but there had been none. He had slept in snatches, staying awake a portion of the day and night both so that he could minimize the chance that something might get by him. He had watched and waited, and nothing had appeared.

But now there was a wagon and horsemen, and he was certain already that they were bound for Southwatch.

He studied them further and knew as well that they were Seekers. He could tell from the black cloaks and hoods, from the way they held themselves, and from the dark secrecy of their approach. They came in stealth and under cover of night, and whatever they were about they did not want it known. There were six riders, four in front and two behind, and there were at least two drivers. In the odd hush of night's leaving, they were a whisper across the empty land, creeping in and out of the haze and shadows, inching toward the coming light.

He took a deep breath. They were, he repeated, what he had been waiting for. He did not know why. He did not understand their purpose or fathom their intent. They might be carrying Par Ohmsford within the wagon. They might not. It didn't matter. Something inside him whispered that he must not let them pass. It spoke in a voice so clear and certain that he could not ignore it.

This is what you have been waiting for. Do something.

It had been five days since Damson Rhee and Matty Roh had departed in search of Par, following the brightening Skree in hopes that it would lead them to the Valeman. The storm had swept away all trace of what had gone before, so the Skree was all they had to help them track. Morgan had remained at Southwatch to wait for their return. But they were not yet back, and there was no indication that they would be coming anytime soon. It had been left to Morgan to determine if Par was a prisoner of the Shadowen, a task that seemed virtually impossible in the absence of an opportunity to enter and have a look around.

But now . . .

He took a deep breath. Now, it might be different.

But he would have to decide quickly what he was going to do. He would have to act at once.

He was already tracing the wagon's route as it wound ahead through the misted hills. He could intercept it if he chose. He could reach it before it arrived at Southwatch, cut across its path while it was still several miles away. With his eyes he followed the rutted track it must stay on to reach the citadel, a path that other wagons had worn before. He was close enough, he decided. He could stop it.

If he chose.

One man against eight—and those eight Seekers, and probably Shadowen as well. His jaw tightened, and he smiled sardonically. He had better be sure.

East, the first faint tinges of silvery light began to peek out from behind the forested horizon, sending gleaming spiderwebs across the flat, dark surface of the Rainbow Lake. The silence deepened, a hush of expectation, waiting, waiting.

Standing motionless on the bluff, staring out across the hills at the wagon and the horsemen, Morgan found himself looking beyond the here and now into the past, seeing himself again in Leah, in the Highlands in which his family had lived for centuries, picturing what his life had been like such a short time ago. He remembered how he had described it to Matty standing in place. He had spent his time nipping at the heels of the Federation officials quartered in what had once been his family home, content with creating annoying distractions, satisfied with causing mischief and discontent. He had come a long way from that, gone north to the Hadeshorn and the shade of Allanon, gone beyond to Tyrsis and the Pit, to the Dragon's Teeth and the Jut, to Padishar Creel and the free-born, gone farther still to Eldwist and the Stone King, to the Black Elfstone and the Maw Grint. He had fought the Shadowen and their minions and survived what no one should have. He had taken himself out of one life and emerged changed forever in another. He would never be the same again—but then he would never want to be. A lifetime had passed since his departure from the Highlands, and his experiences had strengthened him in ways that once he could only have imagined.

His vision cleared, the past fading back into memory, the present a steady and certain conviction of what was needed. He stared out at the wagon and the horsemen and listened to the whisper in his mind. He knew what he must do.

He moved quickly then, the decision made. He left everything behind but the Sword of Leah. Stripped of his pack and great cloak, the Sword strapped securely across his back, he slipped down through the trees on the bluff's north slope, keeping his goal in sight as he went. He reached the hills below and raced through them, pointing north to the narrows through which the wagon and horsemen must pass to reach Southwatch, thinking to himself that he could still change his mind once he got there if it seemed wrong then, thinking as well that he needed a plan if he was to have any chance of surviving a fight against so many. The ground was hard and hollow feeling beneath his feet, but the grasses were damp with morning dew and made a wet, slapping sound as he passed through them. He smelled the earth and the trees in the windless air, their scents thick and pungent. The haze deepened as he wound ahead, reaching out to enfold him one moment, slipping free again the next. He would have to be quick, he thought to himself—as swift as thought and as certain as fate. He would have to kill most of them before they knew he was there. He would have to be darker than they were. He would have to be more deadly.

He came out of a hollow into a stand of black walnut shot through with cherry, bent heavy with dewy leaves, and he stared out across the hills, listening. He could hear the wagon, its creak and groan soft in the mist. He was well ahead of it, close to where he would make his intercept, and the night's gloom lingered on against the coming dawn. He glanced east and found the sun still down within the trees, its light no more than a faint brightening against the sky. Time enough remained for him to act before the sunrise revealed him. He would have his chance.

He started out again, keeping to cover where he could, staying silent in his passage. He had hunted the Highlands for years before coming north, rising before dawn to set out with his ash bow, alone in a world in which he was an intruder, learning to make himself one with the animals he hunted. Sometimes he shot them for food; more often, he simply stalked them, not needing to kill them to teach himself their ways, to discover their secrets. He became good at it; he was good now. But the Shadowen were hunters, too. They could sense what was out there better than he. He would have to remember that. He would have to be careful.

Because if they found him first . . .

He breathed deeply through his mouth, steadying the pounding of his heart as he moved ahead. What was his plan? What was it that he intended to do? Stop them, kill them, have a look at what was in the wagon? What if nothing was in the wagon? Did it matter? How much would he give away if this was all for nothing?

But it wasn't for nothing. He knew it wasn't. The wagon wasn't empty. There was no reason for Seekers to escort an empty wagon to Southwatch. The wagon would carry something. The voice inside, the voice that urged him on, promised him so.

This is what you have been waiting for.

For an instant it occurred to him that it might be Quickening's voice he heard, that spoke to him from out of some netherworld or perhaps out of the earth into which she had returned, guiding him, shepherding him, leading him on to what she alone could see. But the idea seemed wishful and somehow dangerous, and he discarded it immediately. The voice was his own and no one else's, he told himself. The decision and its consequences must be his.

He reached the draw through which the horsemen and their wagon would pass, the place where he would stop them, and he drew up sharply in the stillness to listen. Distantly, from somewhere back in the haze, came the sounds of their approach. He stood in the center of the draw and tried to judge the time that remained to him. Then he walked its length, staying in the shadows to one side so that his damp footprints would not be visible against the light, breathing the hazy coolness to clear his head. Plans came and went in a flurry, sorted out and cast aside as quickly as dreams upon waking. None suited him; none seemed right. He reached the end of the draw and started back, then stopped.

He stood at the entrance to the narrowest part of the draw.

Here, he told himself. This is where it would begin, after the wagon was within the draw, after the lead horsemen were trapped in front and could not get back to help those behind. That would give him precious moments to dispatch at least two riders and perhaps those who drove the wagon as well, reaching whoever or whatever lay within. If he found nothing, he could be gone again swiftly . . .

Yet he knew even as he thought it that he could not, for the others would track him. No, he would have to stand and fight, whatever he found within the wagon. He would have to kill them or be killed. There would be no running, no escape.

He felt as if the pounding in his chest would explode his heart within him, and there was a hollow place in his stomach that lurched and heaved. He was dizzy with the thought of what he was planning, terrified and excited both at once, unable to contain any of the dozen emotions that ripped through him.

But still the voice whispered. *This is what you have been waiting for. This.*

The sound of the Shadowen approach grew louder. East, the light remained faint and distant. Here, the haze hung thick and unmoving in the draw. He would have cover enough, he decided. He moved back into the trees, unsheathed the Sword of Leah, and crouched down.

Please, be right. Please, don't be wrong. Let it be Par in that wagon. Let this be for something good.

The words repeated themselves, a litany in his mind, mixing with the whisper that held him bound to his course of action, to the certainty that it was right. He could not explain the feeling, could not justify it beyond the belief that sometimes you did not question, you simply accepted. He was torn by the truth he sensed in it and the possibility of its fraud. Reason advised caution, but passion insisted on blind commitment. The feelings warred within him as he waited, pulling and twisting into knots.

Abruptly he sprang up again and sped back through the trees and up the hill behind, keeping to the deepest shadows as he went, breathing through his mouth to take in quick gulps of air. At the summit he crept to where he could see west, his body heated and tensed. The riders and their wagon appeared out of a curtain of white frost, slow and steady in their coming, strung out along the divide. They showed no hesitation or concern; they did not glance about or ride alert. Too close to home to worry, Morgan thought. He wished he could tell what was in the wagon. He peered down at it as if by doing so he might penetrate the canvas that wrapped its bed, but nothing revealed itself. He felt a fire burn inside, the struggle between doubt and certainty continuing.

He slid back into the shadows and hunched down there, sweating. What was he to do? It was his last chance to change his mind, to reconsider the wisdom of his decision. How true was the voice that whispered to him? What were the chances that it deceived?

Then he was up and moving, slipping down again through the shadows to the narrows, all his thinking behind him, his course of action fixed. *Do something. Do something.* The whisper became a shout. He embraced it, wrapping it about him like armor.

He reached his concealment and dropped to his knees. Both hands gripped the pommel of his Sword, the talisman he had forsworn so often and must now rely upon once again. How quickly and easily he had come back to it, he thought in wonder. Sweat ran down his brow, tickling him, and he wiped it away. The cool dawn air did not seem to soothe his body's heat, and he gulped air in deep breaths to slow his heart. He felt as if he were coming apart at the seams. What would the sword's magic do—save him or consume him? Which, this time?

The sound of the wagon's approach was quite clear now, wheels bumping and thudding over the uneven trail, horses huffing in the silence. He froze in the shadows of his hiding place, eyes fixed on the curtain of mist. One hand trailed down the obsidian surface of the Sword of Leah, and he remembered how the Sword's magic had come about, how his ancestor Rone Leah had asked Allanon for magic to protect Brin Ohmsford, how the Druid had granted his wish by dipping the Sword's blade in the waters of the Hadeshorn. So much had come to pass in the wake of that single act. So many lives had been changed.

He brought both hands to the carved handle and tightened his grip until his knuckles were white.

The mist broke apart before him, and the black-cloaked riders appeared, hooded and faceless and somehow much larger than he had expected. The horses' breath clouded the air, and steam rose off their heated flanks. Down into the draw they came, four leading, followed by the creaking, swaying wagon and its drivers, and two trailing. Morgan Leah was calm now, the anticipation behind him, the event at hand. The wraiths hunched down atop their mounts and atop the wagon seat, silent and motionless, showing nothing of their faces, nothing of their thoughts. On each breast, the wolf's-head insignia gleamed like white metal. Morgan counted them again, eight in all. But there might be more inside the canvas tent of the wagon, the flaps to which remained drawn and tied. The wagon might be filled with them.

He took a deep breath and let it out slowly. Could he do this? His jaw tightened. He had fought Federation Seekers and Shadowen from one end of Callahorn to the other and survived. He was no callow, inexperienced youth. He would do what he must.

The horsemen passed and the wagon thudded by, entering the narrows of the draw. Morgan rose, silent and fluid, and brought up the Sword of Leah. *Be swift. Be sure. Don't hesitate.*

He left his cover and moved in behind the trailing riders. The leaders and the wagon had entered the narrows. He caught the trailing riders at its mouth, brought his blade around in an arc, the whole of his strength behind it, and cut them apart at the waist. They toppled from their horses like logs falling, soundless after a single surprised grunt, dead instantly. Their blood was greenish and thick on their robes as they tumbled down, and some of it smeared on Morgan's hands. The horses shied, pulling to either side as the Highlander surged past, springing for the wagon. Ahead, the draw was shadowed and thick with brush and trees, and the procession did not slow. Morgan reached the wagon, leaped for the canvas flaps, and pulled himself aboard. He sliced through the ties and jumped inside. The faint dawn light revealed a single figure lying motionless in the bed, hands and feet bound. He went past without slowing, seeing the dark figures seated ahead beginning to turn. His momentum carried him to the wagon front in a rush, his body twisting as he brought back his Sword. Somebody spoke, a cry of warning, and then he was ripping through the canvas with a fury, shredding it as if it weren't there, slashing the Seekers as they tried to free their weapons. They screamed and toppled from view, and in Morgan's hands the Sword of Leah began to glow like fire.

He pushed past the shredded flaps onto the wagon seat, kicking off what remained of one Seeker. He snatched up the reins, howled in fury, and whipped at the team. The horses screamed and bolted ahead, charging into the lead riders, who were in the process of turning about to see what was happening. The wagon bore down on them, still within the narrows, and there was no place for them to go. They tried to turn back again, tried to spring out of the way, lunged and twisted in the narrowing gap like contortionists, black robes flying. But the wagon hammered into them, taking two down instantly, crushing one Seeker beneath the wheels, slamming the other back into the trees. The wagon lurched and bucked, and the horses shied at the contact. Morgan rose in the seat as he swept past the two riders who remained, the Sword of Leah lifting to block the blows directed at him.

Thundering out of the draw and onto the flats beyond, he yanked on the reins and brought the team about, nearly overturning the wagon in the effort. The wheels skidded on the damp grass, and Morgan dropped his Sword into the boot to free both hands to control the team. Behind, the remaining two riders came at him, dark shapes materializing out of the mist. One of the two riders who had fallen appeared as well, now afoot. Morgan whipped the team toward them, building speed. Sweat ran down his face, and his vision blurred. He reached back into the boot for the Sword of Leah and brought it up, the magic racing down its length like fire. The mounted Seekers reached him first, splitting to either side, blades drawn. He pushed himself as far to the right as he could, concentrating on the horseman closest, hammering past the other's defenses and crushing his skull. He felt a red-hot searing in his shoulder as the other Seeker leaped from his horse onto the wagon seat and struck him a slashing, off-balance blow. He reeled away, nearly falling off, kicking out with his boot to knock the other back. The wagon swung wide and this time did not correct. It snapped loose from its traces and tongue and went over, throwing the combatants to the earth. Morgan landed hard, a red mist sweeping across his vision, pain lancing through his body, but came back to his feet instantly.

The Seeker who had wounded him was waiting, and the one afoot was coming up fast. Both were reverting to Shadowen, lifting from their black-robed bodies in a mist of darkness, eyes red and chilling. They had seen the fire race the length of his sword and knew Morgan possessed the magic. Shedding their Seeker disguise, they were calling up magic of their own. Crimson fire launched from their weapons at Morgan, but he blocked it, rushing them with single-minded determination, no longer thinking, acting now out of need. He slammed into the first and bowled him over. The Sword of Leah swept down, shattering the other's weapon, and the fire burned from throat to stomach, through one side and out the other. The Shadowen screamed, shuddered, and went still.

Morgan went after the other without slowing, consumed by the magic's elixir, driven by forces he no longer controlled. The Shadowen hesitated, seeing his face, realizing belatedly that he was overmatched. He threw up the fire, and it splintered apart on Morgan's blade. Then Morgan was on top of him, striking once, twice, three times, the magic racing up and down the talisman, a sudden white heat. The Shadowen shrieked, tearing to get free, and then the fire exploded through him in a brilliant flash of light, and he was gone.

Morgan whirled about, searching the gloom—left, right, behind, in front again. The land was still and empty. East, the sun crested the horizon in a burst of silver gold, light streaming through the trees to penetrate the shadows and mist. The draw was a dark tunnel in which nothing moved. The Shadowen lay lifeless about him. A single horse remained, a dark blur some fifty feet off, reins trailing as it shook its head and stamped the earth, uncertain of what to do. Morgan looked at it, steadied his sweating hands, and slowly straightened. The magic of the Sword faded, and the blade turned depthless black again.

Close at hand, a thrush called once. Morgan Leah listened without moving, and his breath whistled harshly in his ears. *The Shadowen at South-watch will have heard. They will come for you. Move!*

He sheathed the Sword of Leah and hurried over to the collapsed wagon, remembering Par, anxious to discover if the Valeman was all right. It was Par in there, he insisted to himself. It had to be. He was dazed and bleeding, his clothing torn and soiled, his skin coated in dust and sweat. He felt light-headed and dangerously invincible.

Of course it was Par!

He climbed into the upended wagon and moved to the bound figure, who was slumped against one splintered side, looking up at him. Shadows hid the other's face, and he bent close, blinked, and stared.

It wasn't Par he had rescued.

It was Wren.

28

Wren was as surprised to see Morgan Leah as he was to see her. Tall and lean and quick-eyed, he was exactly as she remembered him—and at the same time he was different. He seemed older somehow, more worn. And there was something in the look he gave her. She blinked up at him. What was he doing here? She tried to straighten up, but her strength failed her and she would have fallen back again if the Highlander hadn't reached down to catch her. He knelt at her side, withdrew a hunting knife from his belt, and severed her bonds and gag.

"Morgan," she breathed, relieved beyond measure, and reached up to embrace him. "I'm sure glad to see you."

He managed a quick, tight smile, and a bit of the mischievousness returned to his haggard face. "You look a wreck, Wren. What happened?"

She smiled back wearily, aware of how she must appear, her face all bruised and swollen. "I made a serious error in judgment, I'm afraid. Don't worry, I'm all right now."

He picked her up anyway and carried her from the ruins of the wagon into the dawn light, setting her gingerly back on her feet. She rubbed her wrists and ankles to restore the circulation, then knelt to wet her hands with dew from the still-damp grasses and dabbed tentatively at her injured face.

She looked up at him. "I thought there was no hope for me at all. How did you find me?"

He shook his head. "Blind luck. I wasn't even looking for you. I was looking for Par. I thought the Shadowen were transporting him in the wagon. I had no idea at all it was you."

There had been disappointment in his eyes when he had recognized her. She understood now why. He had been certain it was Par he had rescued.

"I'm sorry I'm not Par," she told him. "But thanks anyway."

He shrugged, and grimaced with the movement, and she saw the mix of red and green blood on his clothing. "What are you doing here, Wren?"

She rose to face him. "It's a long story. How much time do we have?"

He glanced over his shoulder. "Not much. Southwatch is only a few miles away. The Shadowen will have heard the fighting. We have to get away as soon as we can."

"Then I'll keep it short." She felt stronger now, flushed with urgency and renewed determination. She was free again, and she intended to make the most of it. "The Elves have returned to the Four Lands, Morgan. I found them on an island in the Blue Divide where they've been living for almost a hundred years, and I brought them back. It was Allanon's charge to me, and I finally accepted it. Their queen, Ellenroh Elessedil was my grandmother. She died on the way, and now I am queen." She saw the astonishment in his eyes and gripped his arm to silence him. "Just listen. The Elves are besieged by a Federation army ten times their size. They fight a delaying action just south of the Valley of Rhenn. I have to get back to them at once. Do you want to come with me?"

The Highlander stared. "Wren Elessedil," he said softly, trying the name out. Then he shook his head, and his voice tightened. "No, I can't, Wren. I have to find Par. He may be a prisoner of the Shadowen at Southwatch. There are others out looking for him as well. I promised to wait for them."

His voice had an edge to it that did not allow for argument, but he added reluctantly, "But if you really need me . . ."

She stopped him with a squeeze of her hand. "I can make it back on my own. But there is something I have to tell you first, and you have to promise me that you will tell the others when you see them again." Her grip tightened. "Where are they, anyway? What's become of them? What's happened with Allanon's charges? Did the others fulfill them as well?" She was speaking too rapidly, and she forced herself to slow down, to stay calm, not to look off to the east and the brightening sky. "Here, sit down. Let me have a look at your wound."

She took his arm and led him to a moss-covered log where she seated him, stripped off his shirt, tore it in strips, and cleaned and bound the sword slash as best she could.

"Par and Coll found the Sword of Shannara, but then they disappeared," he told her as she worked. "It's too long a story for now. I've been tracking Par; he may be tracking Coll. I don't know who has the Sword. As for Walker, I was with him when he went north to recover a magic that would restore Paranor and the Druids. He was successful, and we came back together, but I haven't seen him since." He shook his head. "Paranor's back. The Sword's found. The charges are all fulfilled, but I don't know what difference it makes."

She finished tying up his wound and moved back around in front of him. "Neither do I. But in some way it does. We just have to find out how." She swallowed against the dryness in her throat, and her hazel eyes fixed him. "Now, listen. This is what you are to tell the others." She took a deep breath. "The Shadowen are Elves. They are Elves who rediscovered the old magic and thought to use it recklessly. They stayed behind when the rest of the Elven nation fled the Four Lands and the Federation. The magic subverted them as it does everything; it made them into the Shadowen. They are another form of the Skull Bearers of old, dark wraiths for which the magic is a craving they cannot resist. I don't know how they can be destroyed, but it must be done. Allanon was right—they are an evil that threatens us all. The answers we need lie in the purpose of fulfilling the charges that we were given. One of us will discover the truth. We must. Tell them what I've told to you, Morgan. Promise me."

Morgan rose. "I'll tell them."

A heron's cry pierced the morning stillness, and Wren jerked about. "Wait here," she said.

She hobbled over to the fallen Shadowen and began rifling through their clothing. One of them, she knew, had the Elfstones, stolen from her by Tib Arne. Her anger at him burned anew. She searched the closest two and found nothing. She stirred the ashes of the one Morgan had burned through and found nothing there either. Then she went back to the driver and his companion, to their severed bodies, and ignoring what had been done to them, she worked her way carefully through their robes.

In the cloak pocket of one she found the pouch and the Stones. Exhaling sharply, she stuffed the pouch into her tunic and limped back toward Morgan.

Halfway there, she saw the Shadowen horse that hadn't run grazing at the edge of the trees. She stopped, considered momentarily, then put her fingers to her mouth and gave a strange, low-pitched whistle. The horse looked up, ears pricking toward the sound. She whistled again, varying the pitch slightly. The horse stared at her, then pawed the earth. She walked over to the animal slowly, talking softly and holding out her hand. The horse sniffed at her, and she reached out to stroke his neck and flank. For a few moments they tested each other, and then suddenly she was on his back, still talking soothingly, the reins in her hands.

The horse whinnied and pranced at her touch. She guided him back to where Morgan waited and climbed down.

"I'll need him if I expect to make any time," she said, one hand still firmly gripping the reins. "What we find belongs to us, the Rovers used to say. Guess I haven't forgotten everything they taught me." She smiled and reached out to touch his arm. "I don't know when we'll meet up again, Morgan."

He nodded. "You better get going."

"I owe you, Highlander. I won't forget." She vaulted back into the saddle. "We've come a long way from the Hadeshorn, haven't we?"

"From the Hadeshorn, from everything. Farther than I would have dreamed. Watch out for yourself, Wren."

"And you. Good luck to us both."

She met his eyes a moment longer, drawing on the strength she found there, taking heart in the fact that she was not as alone as she had believed, that help sometimes came from unexpected sources.

Then she dug her boots into the horse's flanks and galloped away.

She rode west after the retreating night until daylight overtook her, then stopped to rest the horse and let him drink from a pool of water. She rubbed at her wrists and ankles some more, washing clean the deep cuts and dark bruises, and swore to herself that when she caught up with Tib Arne she would make him pay dearly. She had not eaten or drunk in almost twelve hours, but there was no time to search for food or drinking water now. Once the Shadowen discovered she had escaped, they would be after her. They would be after Morgan Leah as well, she thought, and hoped he knew a good hiding place.

She remounted and rode on, following the grasslands out of the hill country to the plains below Tyrsis that led into the Tirfing. The day was turning hot and humid, the sky a cloudless blue and the sun a white-fire furnace. The trees thinned into scattered groves and then into stands of two and three and finally disappeared altogether. Midday arrived, and she crossed the Mermidon at a narrows, the river's waters low and sluggish here, dwindling away into the flats. Her body and face ached from the beating and the trussing, but she ignored her discomfort, thinking instead of the havoc that her disappearance must have caused. By now they would be searching for her everywhere. Perhaps they had found Erring Rift and Grayl and thought her dead as well. Perhaps they had given up on her, choosing to concentrate on the Federation army and the Creepers. Some would surely recommend that she be forgotten. Some would find her disappearance a blessing . . .

She brushed the prospect aside. She had nothing to prove to anyone. The fact remained that she needed to get back. Barsimmon Oridio would be nearing the Rhenn with the main body of the Elven army. With luck, Tiger Ty would be returning with the Federation. If she could reach them before any fighting began . . .

She stopped herself.

What?

What would she do?

She blocked the question away. It didn't matter what she did. It would be enough that she was there, that the Elves knew they had their queen back, that the Federation must deal with her anew.

She turned north to follow the Mermidon and found water for the horse on the plains, but none for herself. The sun beat down overhead, and the air sucked the moisture from her body. She was tired, and the horse was tiring as well. She could not keep on much longer. She would have to stop and wait out the heat. The thought made her grind her teeth. She didn't have time for that! She didn't have time for anything but going on!

She rested finally, knowing she must, finding a grove of ash close to the riverbank where it was cool enough to escape the worst of the heat. She found some berries that were more bitter than sweet and a gum root that gave her something to chew on. She stripped the horse of his saddle and tethered him. Resting back within the trees, she watched the river flow past, and though she did not mean to do so she fell asleep.

It was late in the afternoon when she woke again, startled out of a restless doze by the soft whicker of her horse. She came to her feet instantly, seeing its shaggy head pointed south, and she looked off across the plains and river to find horsemen coming toward her from several miles off— black-cloaked, hooded horsemen, whose identity was no secret.

She saddled her mount and was off. She rode several miles along the riverbank at a quick trot, glancing back to see if her pursuers were following. They were, of course, and she had the feeling that more might be waiting ahead at Tyrsis. The light faded west, turning silver, then rose, then gray, and when the haze of early twilight set in, she turned away from the river and headed west onto the plains. She would have a better chance of losing her pursuit there, she reasoned. She was a Rover, after all. Once it was dark, no one would be able to track her. All she needed was a little time and luck.

She found neither. Shortly after, her horse began to falter. She urged him on with whispered promises and encouraging pats about the neck and ears, but he was played out. Behind, her pursuers had fanned out across the horizon, distant still, but coming on. The haze was deepening, but the moon and first stars were out, and there would be light enough for a hunter to see by. She stiffened her resolve and rode on.

When her horse stumbled and went down, she rolled free, rose, went back to him, got him to his feet again, unstrapped his saddle and bridle, and set him free. She began walking, limping because her injuries were still painful and inhibiting, angry and tired and determined not to be taken again. She walked without looking back for a long time, until the night had settled in completely, and the whole of the plains were bathed in white light. The plains were silent and empty, and she knew her pursuers were not close enough yet to worry about or she would have heard them, and so she concentrated on putting one foot in front of the other and simply going on.

When she finally did look back, no one was there.

She stared in disbelief. There wasn't one rider, not a single horse, no one afoot, nothing. She took a deep breath to calm herself and looked again—not just east, but all about this time, thinking in sudden fear that she had been flanked. But there was no one out there. She was alone.

She smiled in bewilderment.

And then she saw the dark shadow high overhead winging its way toward her, slow and lazy and as inevitable as winter cold. Her heart lurched in dismay as she watched it take shape. Not for a second did she think it was one of the Wing Riders come in search of her. Not for an instant did she mistake it for a friend. It was Gloon she was seeing. She knew him instantly. She recognized the blocky muscled body, the jut of the war shrike's fierce crested head, the sharp hook of the broad wings. She swallowed against her fear. No wonder the Seekers had fallen back. There was no need to hurry with Gloon to hunt her down.

Tib Arne would be riding him, of course. In her mind she saw the boy's chameleon face, first friend, then foe; human, then Shadowen. She could hear his grating laughter, feel the heat of his breath on her face as he struck her, taste the blood in her mouth from the blows . . .

She looked about for a place to hide and quickly discarded the idea. She was already seen, and wherever she hid she would be found. She could either run or fight—and she was tired of running.

She reached down into her tunic and took out the Elfstones. She balanced them in her hand, as if the weight of their magic could be determined and so the outcome of her battle decided early. She glanced west to the horizon, but there was nothing to see, the forests still lost below the horizon. No one would be searching for her anyway—not this far out and not at night. She gritted her teeth, thinking of Garth again, wondering what he would do. She watched Gloon wing his way closer, taking his time, riding the wind currents smoothly, easily, confident in his power and skill, in what he could do. The war shrike would try to take her on his first pass, she thought—quick and decisive, before she could bring the magic of the Elfstones to bear. And it would not be easy using the Elfstones against a moving target.

She edged across the plains to put a small rise at her back. Better than nothing, she told herself, keeping her eyes on Gloon. She thought of what the war shrike had done to Grayl. She felt small and cold and vulnerable, alone in the vastness of the grasslands, nothing for as far as she could see, no one to help her. No Morgan Leah this time. No reprieve from an unexpected source. She would fight on her own, and how well she fought—and how lucky she was—would determine whether she lived or died.

Her hand tightened on the Elfstones. *Come see me, Gloon. Come see what I have for you.* The war shrike soared and dipped, sweeping out and back again, rising and falling in careless disregard, a dark motion against the sky's blue velvet. Wren waited impatiently. *Come on! Come on!*

Then abruptly Gloon dropped like a stone and was gone.

Wren jerked forward, startled. The night spread away before her, vast and dark and empty. What had happened? She felt sweat run down her back. Where had the shrike gone? Not into the earth, it wouldn't have driven itself into the earth, that didn't make any sense . . .

And then she realized what was happening. Gloon was attacking. He had dropped level with the ground so that his shadow could no longer be seen, and he was coming at her. How fast? How soon? She panicked, staggering backward in fear. She couldn't see him! She tried to pick out the shrike against the dark horizon, but could see nothing. She tried to hear him, but there was only silence.

Where is it? Where . . . ?

Instinct alone saved her. She threw herself aside on impulse and felt the massive weight of the shrike rip past her, talons tearing at the air inches away. She struck and rolled wildly, tasting dust and blood in her mouth, feeling the pain of her injured body rush through her anew.

She came back to her feet instantly, whirled in the direction she thought the shrike had gone, summoned the magic of the Elfstones, and sent it careening out into the night in a fan of blue fire. But the fire blazed into the void and struck nothing. Wren dropped into a crouch, desperately scanning the moonlit blackness. It would be coming back—but she couldn't see it! She had lost it! Below the horizon it was invisible. Despair raced through her. *Which way was it coming? Which way?*

She struck out blindly, right and then left, and threw herself down, rolling, coming up and striking out again. She heard the magic collide with something. There was a shriek, followed by Gloon's heavy passage as the shrike winged off to her left, hissing like steam. She peered after the sound, wiping at the dust in her eyes. Nothing.

She got up and ran. Forcing down all thoughts of pain, she sprinted across the empty grasslands to a wash that lay some hundred feet away. She reached it and dove into it on a dead run. There was the now-familiar rush of wind and the passing of something dark overhead. Gloon had just missed her again. She flattened herself in the wash and peered skyward. The moon was there, and the stars, and nothing else. *Shades!* She came to her knees. The wash offered her some protection, but not nearly enough. And the night was no friend, for the war shrike's eyesight was ten times better than her own. It could see her clearly in the wash, and she could see nothing of it.

She rose and sent the Elven magic stabbing out, hoping to get lucky. The fire raced away, working across the flats, and she felt the power rush through her. She howled in exhilaration, unable to help herself, saw the war shrike coming just an instant before it reached her, swung the magic about furiously—too late—and threw herself down once more. But her quickness saved her, the blue fire of the Elfstones forcing the shrike to change direction at the last minute, causing it to miss her once again.

She saw Tib Arne this time, just a glimpse as he streaked past, blond hair flying. She heard his cry of rage and frustration, and she shrieked out after him, furious, taunting.

The skies went still, the land silent. She huddled in the wash, shaking and sweating, the Elfstones clenched in her hand. She was going to lose this fight if she didn't do something to change the odds. Sooner or later, Gloon was going to get through.

Then she heard a new cry, this one far off to the west, a wild shriek that pierced the suffocating silence. She turned toward it, recognizing it yet unable to place it. A bird, a Roc. It came again, quick and challenging.

Spirit! It was Spirit!

She watched his dark shadow race out of the night, coming down from high up, as swift as thought. Spirit, she thought and that meant Tiger Ty! Hope surged through her. She started to rise, to cry out in response, then flattened herself again quickly. Gloon was still out there, looking for an opportunity to finish her off. Her eyes swept the darkness, searching in vain. Where was the shrike?

Then Gloon rose out of the dark to meet this new challenger, thick black body gathering speed. Wren scrambled to her feet, shouting in warning. Spirit came on, then at the last possible moment veered aside so that the war shrike swept past harmlessly and wheeled about to give chase. The giant birds circled each other cautiously, feinting and dodging, working for an advantage. Wren gritted her teeth, earthbound and helpless. Gloon was bigger than Spirit and trained to kill. Gloon was a Shadowen, and had the magic to sustain him. Spirit was brave and quick, but what chance did he stand?

There was a flurry of movement as the birds came at each other, locked momentarily in a shriek of rage, and then broke apart again. Once more they began to circle, each trying to get above the other. Wren came out of the wash and back onto the flat of the plain. She moved after them as they edged away, following because she did not want to lose contact, still determined to help. She could not leave this battle to Tiger Ty and the Roc. This was not their fight. It was hers.

Again the birds dove at each other and locked, talons and beaks tearing and ripping. Black shadows against the moonlit sky, they twisted and turned, their wings flailing madly as they spiraled down. Wren raced after them, Elfstones in hand. *Just let me get close enough!* was all she could think.

At what seemed the last possible second the birds broke apart, staggering rather than flying away from each other, feathers and gristle and blood falling away from their tattered bodies. Wren gritted her teeth in rage. Gloon shook himself and rose, flattening out in a long slow spiral. Spirit arced upward and fell back, wobbly and unsure. He tried to right himself, shuddered once, dropped earthward, and vanished. Wren gasped in dismay—then caught her breath in wonder as Spirit suddenly reappeared, steady once more, miraculously recovered. A feint! Directly under Gloon now, he rose from the ground like a missile, hurtling through the night to slam into the war shrike. It sounded like rocks crunching, a sharp grating. Both birds cried out and then broke apart, talons raking the air.

Then one of the riders fell, dislodged by the impact. Arms and legs flailing the air, shrieking in horror, he plummeted earthward. He fell like a stone, unable to help himself, and struck with an audible thud. Overhead, the struggle continued, the Roc and war shrike battling on across the skies as if the loss of a rider made no difference. Wren could not tell who had fallen. She ran across the flats, her heart pumping wildly, her throat closing in fear. She ran for a long time without seeing anything. Then all at once there was a crumpled heap in front of her, a bloodied, ragged form trying to rise off the ground, somehow still alive.

She slowed her rush, and a shattered, broken visage turned toward her. She shuddered as the eyes met her own. It was Tib Arne. He tried to speak, a thick gurgle that would not let the words form, and she could hear his hatred of her in the sound. He was a boy still beneath the leaking wounds, but it was the Shadowen that broke free finally, rising like black smoke to come at her. She brought up the Elfstones instantly, and the blue fire tore through the dark thing and consumed it.

When she looked again, Tib Arne's blue eyes were staring up at her sightlessly.

She heard a shriek from overhead then, either war shrike or Roc, and looked up just in time to see Gloon descending with Spirit in pursuit. The shrike had abandoned his sky battle and was coming for her. She crouched beneath its shadow, no place to hide now, the wash too far away to reach. She brought up the Elfstones, but her movements were leaden, and she knew she didn't have enough time to save herself.

And then Spirit gave a final surge and caught Gloon from behind, hammering into the war shrike, knocking it off balance and away. Gloon whipped about, tearing at the Roc, and in that instant Wren unleashed the magic of the Elfstones a final time. It caught Gloon full on, enfolded the shrike, and began to burn it apart, eating at it even as it tried to escape. Gloon shrieked in rage, twisted wildly, and tried to fly. But the Elven magic had set the bird afire, and the flames were everywhere. It rolled and straightened, wings beating. Wren struck it again, the blue fire turning white hot. Down went the war shrike, flames trailing from its body. It struck the earth, shuddered, and went still.

In seconds, the fire had turned it to ash.

In the hush that followed, Spirit made a silent descent to the grasslands. Tiger Ty climbed down and came over to Wren, walking in that shuffling, bowlegged gait, leathery face streaked with sweat. She reached out her hands to clasp his.

"Are you all right, girl?" he asked quietly, and she could see the deep concern in his sharp eyes.

She smiled. "Thanks to you. That's twice in one day I've been saved by friends I'd thought I'd lost." And she told him of Morgan Leah and the Shadowen at Southwatch.

"I found the free-born in the Dragon's Teeth yesterday morning." The gnarled hands would not release her, holding on as if afraid she might fade away. "Their leader told me he didn't send the boy, that he'd sent someone else. I knew what had happened. I left them to follow when they could and came back for you. Too late, I thought. You were already missing. We searched for you all day. Found Rift and Grayl, but there was no sign of you. I knew the boy had taken you. But I knew as well that if there was a way, you'd escape. I took Spirit out alone after the others gave it up for the night and kept looking." He gave her a hard look. "Good thing I did."

"Good thing," she agreed.

"Confound it, what did I tell you about going up with anybody but me?"

She leaned close, and for a moment the emotions were so strong she couldn't speak. "Don't make me say it," she whispered.

Perhaps he saw the pain in her eyes. Perhaps he heard it in her voice. He held her gaze a moment longer, then released her hands and stepped back. "Just so you don't ever do it again. I've got a lot of time and effort invested in you." He cleared his throat. "Let me see to Spirit, make sure there's no real damage."

He spent a few minutes checking the big Roc, hands moving carefully over the dark feathered body. Spirit watched him with a fierce eye. When the Wing Rider spoke to him, the Roc dipped his beak, spread his great wings, and shook himself.

Satisfied, Tiger Ty beckoned her over. He gave the bird a proud glare. "He would have won, you know," he said gruffly.

Wren didn't say anything for a moment. Then she smiled. "I thought he did."

Tiger Ty helped her aboard and strapped her in. He stroked Spirit appreciatively, nodded to himself, and joined her. Wren glanced out across the night-frozen landscape, empty and still save where Gloon's remains smoldered and steamed. She felt light-headed and worn, but she felt alive, too. The effects of the Elven magic lingered, racing through her like sparks of fire.

She had survived again, she thought, and wondered how long she could keep doing it.

"They're not going to win," she said suddenly. "I won't let them."

He did not ask her what she meant. He did not speak at all. He just looked at her and nodded once. Then he whistled Spirit into the air, and the great bird rose and flew swiftly away into the dark.

29

Morgan Leah watched Wren disappear into night's retreating darkness, his disappointment at not finding Par tempered by the satisfaction he felt in knowing that his efforts hadn't been wasted.
Imagine—finding Wren, of all people! It made him think that the world
was a smaller place than it seemed, and that because it was, perhaps the
children of Shannara and their allies had a chance against the Shadowen after all.

He turned back east then, looking off to the brightening skyline, to the
silver-gray light spilling down through the treetops and mountain slopes in
slowly widening pools. Daybreak was upon him. The cover of night that
had protected him was already gone, and he was at risk beyond what he had
planned.

He glanced briefly at the shell of the toppled wagon and the black tangle of the fallen Shadowen and could not help thinking, I did it. I stood up
against them all.

But where was he to go now? The Shadowen at Southwatch would be
coming. They would have no trouble finding his tracks, and they would
hunt him down and repay him for what he had done. He took a deep
breath and looked about some more, as if in looking he might find the escape he needed. He could not go back to the bluff; that would be the first
place they would look. They would find his trail and retrace his steps, hoping he was stupid enough to return to wherever he had been hiding.

He smiled faintly. He wasn't that stupid, of course, but it wasn't a bad
idea to make them think he was.

He recrossed the narrows to where he had first come in and retraced
his steps back through the trees and hills, not bothering to hide his tracks
but messing them up as best he could to disguise how many of him there
were, then turned and came back again, more cautious now because the
Shadowen might have arrived in his absence. They had not, however; the
narrows and the flats beyond remained empty save for the dead. He moved
back up the trail that had brought the wagon in, using the ruts to hide his
bootprints, following the wheel marks for several miles through the hills
before turning abruptly north into high grass where he edged carefully away
into the rocks of a ridgeline. If he was lucky, they would not find where he
had broken off and would be forced to scour the countryside blindly. That
might give him the extra time he needed to get to where he had decided
to go.

Of course, none of this meant anything if the Shadowen could track by smell. If they could hunt like animals, then he was in trouble whatever he did short of rolling in mud and applying stinkweed, and he was not prepared for that. What could these quasi-Elves do? He wished he knew more about them, wished he had taken time to ask Wren, but there was no help for it now. He would have to take his chances. He breathed in the morning air and thought how lucky he was to have the Sword of Leah's magic to protect him, then realized that he had been given an answer to his question of whether the power would save or consume him. Of course, it didn't mean that he was safe with it, that he could relax in its use, that he could even be assured things would turn out the same way next time. It only meant he had survived for now, but it was becoming increasingly clear that survival on any terms was the most he could hope for—that any of them could hope for—in their battle against the Shadowen.

One day it will be different, he told himself—but wondered if it was so.

The country before him tightened into a mass of hills, ridges, scrub-choked hollows, and dense forests backed up against the Runne. He was moving over rock, taking his time, working at stepping lightly where scuffed stones and bent twigs might give him away. He had reasoned it through like this. South lay the bluff where he had kept watch, and the Shadowen, if hunting him, would start there. West was the direction in which Wren had ridden, and they would surely hunt him there as well. North lay the cities of Callahorn—Tyrsis, Kern, and Varfleet—and that would be the next logical choice. The last place they would look was east in the country surrounding Southwatch, their fortress citadel, because it would not seem likely to them that someone who had just destroyed one of their patrols to rescue the Queen of the Elves would head for the very same place the patrol had been going.

Queen of the Elves, he mused, interrupting his thinking. Wren Elessedil. Little Wren. He shook his head. He had barely known her when she was growing up with Par and Coll at Shady Vale. It was hard to believe who she had become.

He grimaced. That was true, of course, he thought ruefully, of all of them, and he shrugged the matter aside.

The sun was above the horizon now, night's shadows gone back into hiding, the swelter of summer's heat rising up through the grasses and trees with a thickening of fetid air and dry earth. Morgan found a stream running down out of the rocks, followed it to a rapids where the water was clean, and drank. He had neither food nor water to sustain him, and he would have to obtain both if he was to survive for very long. He thought momentarily of Damson and Matty, and he hoped they did not choose this day to return from their search south. They would expect to find him on that bluff, but would likely find the Shadowen waiting instead. Not a pleasant thought. He would have to warn them, of course—but he would have to stay alive to do so.

He left the stream and worked his way to high ground. From the shelter of a stand of pine, he looked back across the hills south, searching for signs of pursuit. He stayed there a long time, scanning the countryside. Nothing showed itself. Finally he went on, moving east now toward the mountains and the river and Southwatch. He was above the citadel, deep enough within the concealing trees to keep from being seen but close enough so as not to lose contact. He made steady progress despite his wound, the pain a dull throbbing he had relegated to the back of his mind, working his way ahead with the practice and determination of an experienced woodsman, able to sense what was happening about him, to feel a part of the land. He listened to the sounds of the birds and animals, sensing what they were about, knowing that nothing was amiss.

The day edged on toward noon, and still there was no sign of any pursuit. He began to hope that perhaps he had avoided it completely. He found fruit and wild greens to chew on and more drinking water, and when he reached the wall of the Runne, he turned south again. He shifted the Sword of Leah to take the strain off his wound and thought on its history. So many years of dormancy, a relic of another time, its magic forgotten until his encounter with the Shadowen during the journey to Culhaven. Happenstance, and nothing more. Strange how things worked out. He pondered the effect that the Sword had had upon his life, of the ways it had worked both for and against him, and of the legacy of hope and despair it had bequeathed. He thought that it no longer mattered whether he approved of it or not, whether he believed his link with the magic was a good or bad thing, because in the final analysis it didn't matter—the magic simply was. Quickening, he thought, had recognized the inevitability of it better than he, and she had given back the Sword whole because she knew that if the magic was to be his, it should be his complete and not diminished or failed. Quickening had understood how the game was played; her legacy to him had been to teach him the rules.

He stopped to rest when the heat of the day was at its peak, a scathing, burning glare that rose off the parched earth in a white-hot shimmer. He sat in the shade of an aging maple, broad-leaved boughs canopied above him like a tent, squirrels and birds moving through the sheltering branches in apparent disregard of his presence, bound up in their own pursuits. He stared out through the trees to the hills and grasslands south and east, the Sword of Leah propped blade down between his legs, his arms folded across its hilt and grips. He wondered if Wren was safe. He wondered where everybody was, all those who had started out with him on this adventure and been lost somewhere along the way. Some, of course, were dead. But what of the others? He scuffed at the earth with his boot heel and wished he could see things that were hidden from him, then thought that maybe it was better that he couldn't.

Late afternoon brought the temperature back down to bearable, and he resumed walking. Shadows were lengthening again, easing away from the trees and rocks and gullies and ridges behind which they had been hiding. Southwatch came into view, its dark obelisk rising up out of the poisoned flats that bridged the mouth of the Mermidon with the Rainbow Lake. The lake itself was flat and silvery, a mirror of the sky and the land, and the colors of its bow were pale and washed out in the fading light. Cranes and herons swooped and glided above its surface, vague flashes of white against the gray haze of an approaching dusk.

He stopped to watch, and it probably saved his life.

The birds went suddenly still, and there was movement ahead in the trees, barely perceptible, but there nevertheless, distant and indistinct in the failing light. Morgan eased back into the brush, as silent as shadows falling, and froze. After a moment, Shadowen appeared, one, two, then four more, a patrol working its way soundlessly through the trees. They did not seem to be tracking, merely searching, and the idea that they might be using their sense of smell to hunt turned Morgan cold. They were several hundred yards away still and moving along the slope. Their path would take them below where he hid—but across the trail he had left. He wanted to run, to fly out of there as swiftly as the wind, but he knew he could not, and forced himself to wait. The hunters were black-robed and hooded and did not wear the emblem of Seekers. There was no pretense here, and that meant they either did not feel threatened or did not care. Neither prospect was reassuring.

Morgan watched them ease through the trees like bits of coming night and disappear from view.

Instantly he was moving again, gliding forward quickly, anxious to put as much distance as possible between himself and the black-garbed hunters. Were they searching for him or for someone else—for anyone, perhaps, after what had been done to their patrol, worried that there were others in hiding? It didn't matter, he decided quickly. It was enough that they were out there and that sooner or later they were likely to find him.

He revised his previous plan, thinking on his feet, not slowing for an instant. He would not stay on this side of the Mermidon. He would cross the river and wait on the far bank where he could watch the shoreline and the lake for Damson and Matty to return. It was unfortunate that he could not position himself to keep an eye on Southwatch as well, but it was too dangerous to stick around. Best to wait for Damson to report what the Skree had shown on her journey south. Let her try its magic out again if necessary then. That would have to do.

He was very close to Southwatch now and saw that he could not reach the Mermidon to try a crossing without coming down out of the concealment of the trees. That meant he must wait for darkness, and darkness was still several hours away. Too long to stay in one place, he knew. He crouched in the shadows and studied the land below, looking for a reason to reconsider his assessment. The trees thinned as they broke from the Runne, melting away south so that there was no cover on the plains that stretched east to the river. He ground his teeth in frustration. It was too risky to try. He would have to backtrack into the mountains and try to find a pass lead-

ing east or circle all the way back the way he had come. The latter was impossible, the former chancy.

But as he pondered the alternatives, he caught sight of new movement
in the trees ahead. Again he froze, searching the shadows. He might have
been mistaken, he told himself. There seemed to be nothing there.

Then the black-cloaked figure eased into the light momentarily before
fading away again.

Shadowen.

He scooted back into the deep cover, his mind made up for him. He
began to double back, working his way higher into the rocks. He would
look for a pass through the Runne and take his chances with the river. If he
failed to find a way through, he would retrace his steps under cover of
darkness. He did not like the thought of being out there at night with the
Shadowen still searching for him, but his choices were being stripped from
him with alarming rapidity. He forced himself to breathe deeply and slowly
as he slipped back through the trees, trying to stay calm. There were too
many Shadowen hunting about for it to be anything but a deliberate search.
Somehow they had found out where he was and were closing in. He felt
his throat tighten. He had survived one battle this day, but he did not feel
comfortable with the prospect of having to survive another.

Sunset was approaching, and the mountain forest was cloaked in a
windless hush. He kept his movements methodical and noiseless, knowing
that any small sound could give him away. He felt the weight of the Sword
of Leah pressing into his back, and resisted the temptation to reach back for
it. It was there if he needed it, he told himself—and he'd better hope the
need didn't arise.

He was crossing a ridgeline when he saw the shadow shift in the trees
far ahead across a scrub-choked ravine. The shadow was there and gone
again in an instant's time, and he had the impression that he had sensed it
more than seen it. But there was no mistaking what it was, and he went
into a low crouch and wormed his way into the deep brush to his right, angling higher into the rocks. One of them, he concluded only one. A solitary hunter. The sweat on his face and neck left his skin warm and sticky,
and the muscles of his back were knotted so tight they hurt. He felt his
wound throb with fresh pain and wished he had a drink of ale to soothe his
parched throat. He found the way up blocked by a cliff wall, and he turned
back reluctantly. He had the sense of being herded, and he was beginning
to think that eventually he would find walls everywhere he looked.

He paused at the edge of a low precipice and looked back into the
velvet-cloaked trees. Nothing moved, but something was there anyway,
coming on with steady deliberation. Morgan considered lying in wait for it.
But any sort of struggle would bring every Shadowen in the forest down
on him. Better to go on; he could always fight later.

The trees ahead were thinning as the rocks broke through in ragged
clusters and the slopes steepened into cliffs. He was as high as he could go

without leaving the cover of the trees and still there was no pass to take him through the mountains. He thought he could hear the sound of the river churning along its banks somewhere beyond the wall of rock, but it might have been his imagination. He found a stand of heavy spruce and took cover, listening to the forest about him. There was movement ahead and below now as well. The Shadowen were all about him. They must have found his trail. It was still light enough to track, and they were coming for him. They might not catch up to him before it grew too dark to follow his footprints, but he did not think it would matter if they were this close. They were more at home in the dark than he, and it would just be a matter of time before they snared him.

For the first time he let himself consider the possibility that he was not going to escape.

He reached back and drew out his Sword. The obsidian blade gleamed faintly in the dusky twilight and felt comfortable in his hand. He imagined he could feel its magic responding to him with whispered assurances that it would be there when he called for it. His talisman against the dark. He lowered his head and closed his eyes. All come to this? Another fight in an endless series of fights to stay alive? He was growing tired of it all. He couldn't help thinking it. He was tired, and he was sick at heart.

Let it go!

He opened his eyes, rose, and glided ahead through the trees, south again toward the plains that led down to Southwatch, changing his mind about staying hidden. He felt better moving, as if movement was more natural, more protective in some way. He slipped down through the forest, picking his way cautiously, listening for those who sought to trap him. Shadows shifted about him, small changes in the light, little movements that kept his heart pumping. Somewhere in the distance an owl hooted softly. The forest was a night river in slow, constant flux that shimmered and spun.

He glanced back repeatedly searching for the solitary hunter behind him and saw nothing. The Shadowen ahead were equally invisible, but he thought they might not know his whereabouts quite so surely as the other. He hoped they could not communicate by thought, but he would not have bet against it. There seemed to be few limitations to the magic they wielded. Ah, but that was wrongheaded thinking, he chided. There were always limitations. The trick was in finding out what they were.

He reached a clump of cedar backed up against a cliff and turned into it, dropping again into a crouch to listen. He remained as still as the stone behind him for long minutes and heard nothing. But the Shadowen were still out there, he knew. They were still searching, still scouring . . .

And then he saw them, two close at hand, easing through the trees less than a hundred yards below, black-cloaked shadows, advancing on his concealment. He felt his heart drop. If he moved now, they would see him. If he stayed where he was, they would find him. A great set of choices, he thought bitterly. He still held the Sword of Leah, and his hands tightened on the grip. He would have to stand and fight. He would have to, and he knew how it was likely to end.

He thought back to the Jut, Tyrsis, Eldwist, Culhaven, and all the other places he'd been trapped and brought to bay when trying to escape, and he thought in despair and anger, You would think that just once . . .

And then the hand closed over his mouth like an iron clamp, and he was yanked backward into the trees.

30

Dusk came to the country south of the Rainbow Lake in a purple and silver haze that crept like a cat out of the Anar to chase a fiery sunset west into the Black Oaks and the lands beyond. Twilight was smooth and silky as it eased the day's swelter with a breeze out of the deep forest, soothing and cool. Farms dotting the lands above the Battlemound were bathed in a mixture of shadows and light and assumed the look of paintings. Animals stood with their faces pointed into the breeze, motionless against the darkening green pastures. Tenders and hands came in from their work, and there was the sound of water splashing in basins and the smell of food cooking on stoves. There was a serenity in the lengthening shadows and a relief in the cooling of the air. There was a hush that gathered and comforted and promised rest for those who had completed another day.

In a stand of hardwood on a low rise close against the fringe of the Anar just north of the Battlemound, smoke rose from the crumbling chimney of an old hunter's cabin. The cabin consisted of four timbered walls splintered and aged by weather and time, a shingled roof patched and worn, a covered porch that sagged at one end, and a stone well set back into the deepest shadows in the trees behind. A wagon was pulled up close to one side of the cabin, and the team of mules that pulled it was staked out on a picket line at the edge of the trees. The men who owned both were clustered inside, seated on benches at a table with their dinner, all save one who kept watch from the stone porch steps, looking off into the valley south and east. They were five in number, counting the one outside, and they were shabby and dirty and hard-eyed men. They wore swords and knives and bore the scars of many battles. When they spoke, their voices were coarse and loud; and when they laughed, there was no mirth.

They did not look to Damson Rhee and Matty Roh like anyone who could be reasoned with.

The women crouched in a wash west where a covering of brush screened their movements, and stared at each other.

"Are you sure?" the taller, leaner woman asked softly.

Damson nodded. "He's there, inside."

They went silent, as if both lacked words to carry the conversation further. They had been tracking the wagon all day, ever since they had come upon its wheel marks while following the Skree south from the Rainbow Lake. They had crossed the lake three days earlier, sailing out of the mouth of the Mermidon just ahead of the approaching storm after leaving Morgan Leah. The winds fronting the storm had pushed them swiftly across the lake, and the storm itself had not caught them until they were almost to the far shore. Then they had been swept away, buffeted so badly they had capsized east of the Mist Marsh and been forced to swim to shore. They had escaped with the better part of their supplies in tow, waterlogged and weary, and had slept the night in a grove of ash that offered little shelter from the damp. They had walked from there south, drawn on by the Skree's light, searching for some sign of Par Ohmsford. There had been none until the wagon tracks, and now the men who had made them.

"I don't like it," Matty Roh said softly.

Damson Rhee took out the broken half of the Skree, cupped it in her hand, and held it out toward the cabin. It burned like copper fire, bright and steady. She looked at Matty. "He's there."

The other nodded. Her clothing was rumpled from wear and weather and torn by brambles and rocks, and washing it had cleaned it but not improved its appearance. Her boyish face was sun-browned and sweat-streaked, and her brow furrowed as she considered the glowing half moon of metal.

"We'll need a closer look," she said. "After it gets dark."

Damson nodded. Her red hair was braided and tied back with a band about her forehead, and her clothing was a mirror of Matty's. She was tired and hungry for a hot meal and in need of a bath, but she knew she would have to do without all of them for now.

They eased back along the wash to where they had left their gear and settled down to eat some fruit and cheese and drink some water. Neither spoke as the meal was consumed and the shadows lengthened. Darkness closed about, the moon and stars came out, and the air cooled so that it was almost pleasant. They were very unlike each other, these two. Damson was fiery and outgoing and certain of what she was about; Matty was cool and aloof and believed nothing should be taken for granted. What bound them beyond their common enterprise was an iron determination forged out of years of working to stay alive in the service of the free-born. Three days alone together searching for Par Ohmsford had fostered a mutual respect. They had known little of each other when they had started out and in truth knew little still. But what they did know was enough to convince each that she could depend on the other when it counted.

"Damson." Matty Roh spoke her name suddenly. The silence had deepened, and she whispered. "Do you know how you sometimes find yourself in the middle of something and wonder how it happened?" She seemed almost embarrassed. "That's how I feel right now. I'm here, but I'm not sure why."

Damson eased close. "Do you wish you were somewhere else?"

"I don't know. No, I suppose not." Her lips pursed. "But I'm confused about what I'm doing here. I know why I came, but I don't understand what made me decide to do it."

"Maybe the reason isn't important. Maybe being here is all that counts."

Matty shook her head. "I don't think so."

"Maybe it's not all that difficult to figure out. I'm here because of Par. Because I promised him I would come."

"Because you're in love with him."

"Yes."

"I don't even know him."

"But you know Morgan."

Matty sighed. "I know him better than he knows himself. But I'm not in love with him." She paused. "I don't think." She looked away, distressed by the admission. "I came because I was bored with standing around. That was what I told the Highlander. It was true. But I came for something more. I just don't know what it is."

"I think it might be Morgan Leah."

"It isn't."

"I think you need him."

"I need him?" Matty was incredulous. "It's the other way around, don't you think? He needs me!"

"That, too. You need each other. I've watched you, Matty you and Morgan. I've seen the way you look at him when he doesn't see. I've seen how he looks at you. There is more between you than you realize."

The tall girl shook her head. "No."

"You care about him, don't you?"

"That's not the same. That's different."

Damson watched her for a moment without saying anything. Matty's gaze was fixed on a point in space somewhere between them, the cobalt eyes depthless and still. She was seeing something no one else could see.

When she looked up again, her eyes were empty and sad. "He's still in love with Quickening."

Damson nodded slowly. "I suppose he is."

"He will always be in love with her."

"Maybe so, Matty. But Quickening is dead."

"It doesn't matter. Have you heard how he speaks of her? She was beautiful and magic, and she was in love with him, too." The blue eyes blinked. "It's too hard to try to compete with that."

"You don't have to. It's not necessary."

"It is."

"He will forget her in time. He won't be able to help it."

"No, he won't. Not ever. He won't let himself."

Damson sighed and looked away. The night was deep and still about them, hushed with expectation. "He needs you," she whispered finally, not knowing what else to say. She looked back again. "Quickening is gone, Matty, and Morgan Leah needs you."

They stared at each other in the darkness, measuring the truth of the words, weighing their strength. Neither spoke. Then Matty rose and looked back across the grassland toward the cabin. "We have to go down for a look."

"I'll go." Damson rose with her. "You wait here."

Matty took her arm. "Why not me?"

"Because I know what Par looks like and you don't."

"Then both of us should go."

"And put both at risk?" Damson held the other girl's eyes. "You know better."

Matty stared at her defensively for a moment, then released her arm. "You're right. I'll wait here. But be careful."

Damson smiled, turned, and slipped away into the dark. She moved easily down the wash until she was north of the cabin. Lamplight burned from within, a yellowish wash through the shutterless side windows and open front door. She paused, thinking. The sound of the men's voices came from within, but the red glow of a pipe bowl and the smell of tobacco warned that the sentry still occupied the porch steps. She watched the dark shapes of the mules shifting on the line next to the cabin wall, then heard the sound of breaking glass and swearing inside. The men were drinking and arguing.

She moved on down the wash to the forest and came around behind the cabin, intent on approaching from the south wall, afraid the animals might give her away if she went in from the north. Clouds glided like phantoms overhead, changing the intensity of the light as they passed across moon and stars. Damson edged along the fringe of the trees, lost in shadow, placing her feet carefully even though the voices and laughter likely would drown out other sounds. When she was behind the cabin, she left the trees and came swiftly to the rear wall, then inched along the back and started forward toward the south window. She could hear the voices plainly now, could sense their anger and menace. Hard men, these, and no mistake about it.

She moved to the window in a crouch, rose up carefully, and looked inside.

Coll Ohmsford lay at the back of the musty, weathered cabin and listened to the men arguing as they rolled dice for coins. He was wrapped in a blanket and had turned himself toward the wall. His hands and feet were chained together and to a ring they had hammered into the boards. They had given him food and water and then forgotten about him. Which was just as well, he thought wearily, given their present unpleasant state of mind. Drinking and gambling had turned them meaner than usual, and he had no desire to discover what the result might be if they remembered he was there. He had been beaten twice already since he had been captured—once for trying to escape and once because one of them got mad about something and decided to take it out on him. He was bruised and cut and sore all over, and after being bounced about all day in the back of the wagon he just wanted to be left alone to sleep.

The problem, of course, was that there was no sleep to be had under these conditions. His fatigue and pain were not enough to overcome the noise. He lay listening and wondering what he could do to help himself. He thought again about escape. They were traveling slowly with the wagon and mules, but they were only three or four days out of Dechtera and once there he was finished. He had heard of the slave mines, worked principally by Dwarves. Morgan had described the mines after learning of them from Steff. They were used as a dumping ground for Dwarves who antagonized the Federation occupiers and most particularly for those captured in the Resistance. The Dwarves sent to the mines never returned. No one ever returned. Morgan had heard rumors of Southlanders being sent to work the mines, but until now Coll had never believed it could be so.

He stared at the cracked and splintered wallboards. It seemed he was destined to learn a lot of truths the hard way.

He took a deep breath, held it, and exhaled slowly, wearily. Time was running out and luck had long since disappeared. He was in better shape than he had a right to be, his training at Southwatch with Ulfkingroh having seen him through the worst. But that was of little consolation now, trussed up the way he was. He saw no hope of gaining release from his chains without a key. He had tried to pick the locks, but they were heavy and strong. He had tried to persuade his captors to take them off so he could walk around, but they had just laughed. His plan to rescue Par from Rimmer Dall and the Shadowen was a dim memory. He was as far from that as he was from his home in Shady Vale, and he was so far from there that he sensed he was almost beyond the point of return.

One of the men kicked over a chair, stood up, and walked from the room. Coll risked a quick look out from his coverings. The Sword of Shannara lay on the table. They were gambling for it, or for one another's shares in it. The three still at the table snarled something ugly after the one leaving but did not look away from each other.

Coll turned back to the wall again and closed his eyes. It didn't help that these men had no idea of the Sword's real value. It didn't help that only he could use the magic and that so much might depend on his doing so. At this point, he thought in despair, nothing short of a miracle would help.

He knotted his hands together beneath the blanket and descended into a black place.

What am I going to do?

"Is it him?"

Moonlight reflected off Matty Roh's smooth face, giving it a ghostly look beneath the short-cropped black hair. Damson drank from the water skin she offered and glanced back the way she had come, half thinking she might have been followed. But the night was still and the land empty and frozen beneath the stars.

"Is it?" Matty repeated, anxious, persistent.

Damson nodded. "It has to be. He was huddled in the back of the room under a blanket and I couldn't see his face, but it doesn't matter. The Sword of Shannara was lying on the table, and there's no mistaking it. It's him, all right. They've got him chained up. They're slavers, Matty. I looked in the wagon on my way back and it was full of shackles and chains." She paused, uneasiness darting across her face. "I don't know how he stumbled onto them or how he let them capture him, but it shouldn't have happened. The magic of the wishsong should have been more than a match for men like these. I don't understand it. Something's wrong."

Matty said nothing, waiting.

Damson handed back the water skin and sighed. "I wish I could have seen his face. He looked up once, just for a moment, but it was too dark to see clearly." She shook her head. "Slavers—there won't be any reasoning with them."

Matty shifted her feet. "Reasoning isn't something men like this understand. We're women. If given half a chance, they'd seize us, use us for their own pleasure, and then cut our throats. Or if we were really unlucky, they'd sell us along with the Valeman." She looked out at the night. "How many did you count?"

"Five. Four inside, one standing watch. They're drinking and throwing dice and fighting among themselves." She paused hopefully. "When they sleep, we might be able to slip past them and free Par."

Matty gave her a steady look. "That would be chancy in the dark. We wouldn't be able to tell them from us if it came to a fight. And if the Valeman is chained to the wall, it would take too much time and make too much noise to try to free him. Besides, they might be up all night the way things are going. There isn't any way to know."

"We could wait a bit. A day or two if we must. There will be a chance sooner or later."

Matty shook her head. "We don't have the time. We don't know how long it will be until they get to where they're going. There may be more of them ahead. No. We have to do it now. Tonight."

Now it was Damson's turn to stare. "Tonight," she repeated. "How?"

"How do you think? If they've found a way to capture the Valeman in spite of his magic, they're too dangerous to fool around with." Matty Roh seemed to be measuring her. "If we're quick, they'll be dead before they know what happened. Can you do it?"

Damson took a deep breath. "Can you?"

"Just follow me in and stay behind me. Watch my back. Remember how many there are. Don't lose count. If I go down, get out of there." She straightened. "Are you ready?"

"Now?"

"The quicker we start, the quicker we finish."

Damson nodded without speaking, feeling distanced from what was happening, as if she were watching it from some other vantage point. "I only have a hunting knife."

"Use whatever you have. Just remember what I said."

The tall girl dropped her cloak and reached down into her gear for the slender fighting sword and strapped it over her back, wearing it the same way Morgan Leah wore his. She fastened a brace of throwing knives to her waist and slipped a broad-bladed hunting knife down into her boot. Damson watched and did not speak. Two against five, she was thinking. But the odds were greater than that. These men were seasoned fighters, cutthroats who would kill them without a second thought. What are we to them? she wondered, and decided it was a stupid question.

They moved off into the night, slipping across the grasslands like ghosts, Damson leading Matty back the same way she had gone earlier, watching the light from the oil lamps hung within the cabin grow brighter as they neared. The voices of the men reached out to greet them, coarse and raucous. Damson could no longer see the glow of the pipe on the porch steps, but that didn't mean the sentry wasn't still there. They moved north of the cabin into the trees and came up from behind, flattening themselves against the rough board wall. Inside, the sounds of gambling and drinking continued.

They peered around the south side of the cabin toward the front. There was no sign of the sentry. With Matty leading now, her sword drawn and held before her, they eased up to the window and took a quick look inside. The scene was unchanged. The prisoner was still wrapped in his blanket and lying on the floor at the rear of the cabin. Four of the men still sat at the table. Damson and Matty exchanged a quick glance, then started toward the front. They reached the corner and looked onto the sagging porch.

The sentry was gone.

Matty's face clouded, but she edged into the light anyway, sword held ready, and moved for the open door. Damson followed, glancing left and right, thinking, Where is he? They were almost to the door when the sentry reappeared out of the dark, come from checking the animals perhaps, looking off that way and muttering to himself. He didn't see the women until he stepped onto the porch, then grunted in surprise and reached for his weapons. Matty was quicker. She shifted the sword to her left hand, reached down with her right, brought out one of the throwing knives, and flung it at the man. The blade caught him in the chest and he went back off the porch with a hiss of pain.

Then they were through the door and inside the cabin, Matty leading, Damson at her back. The room was small and smoky and cramped, and it seemed as if they were right on top of the slavers. Damson could see their faces clearly, the sweat on their skin, the anger and surprise in their eyes. The men leaped up from the table, weapons wrenched free of belts and sheaths. Shouts and oaths rose up, glasses and tin cups tipped away, and ale spilled onto the floor. Matty killed the nearest man and went for the next. The table flipped over, scattering debris everywhere. One of the men turned toward the captive, but Matty was too close to be ignored, and he twisted back to meet her rush. A second man went down, blood pouring from his throat, clawing at the air and then tumbling away. The two who remained rushed Matty Roh with swords and knives glinting wickedly in the lamplight and forced her back toward the wall. Damson stepped away, looking for an opening. Someone grabbed her from behind, and the fifth man, blood leaking from his chest wound, lurched through the doorway, clutching at her with his fingers. She twisted away, slippery with his blood, then shoved him back out the door and down the steps. Outside, the mules brayed and kicked at the cabin wall in terror.

Matty darted and cut at the men before her, fighting to keep from being cornered, yelling for Damson. A lamp shattered, spilling oil everywhere, and flames spread across the cabin floor. Damson threw herself onto the back of the man nearest, tearing at his eyes. He howled in pain, dropped his weapons, and fought with his bare hands to fling her away. She let go, throwing herself clear, reaching for her knife. The man went for her in a frenzy, heedless of everything else, tripped, and went down in the fire. It caught on his clothing and began to burn, and he ran screaming out the door and into the night.

The last man held his ground a moment longer, then bolted for the door as well. Flames were racing up the walls now, streaking across the rafters, eating hungrily at the dry wood. Damson and Matty raced for the back of the cabin where the captive had risen to his knees and was tearing at the ring that chained him to the wall. Matty shoved him down wordlessly, brought the big hunting knife out from her boot, and hacked and cut and pried at the wall until the ring broke loose. Then in a knot they rushed for the cabin door, the flames all about them, the heat singeing their hair and flesh. They were almost clear when the captive twisted free and turned back, charging into the smoke and fire with the chains trailing behind him, searching the debris on the floor until he came up with the Sword of Shannara.

It wasn't until they were all outside, gasping for air and coughing up smoke and dust as the cabin burned behind them, that Damson realized it was not Par Ohmsford they had rescued after all, but his brother, Coll.

They took just long enough to break loose the shackles from Coll's wrists and ankles, casting anxious glances over their shoulders into the night as they did so, then slipped quickly away, leaving behind the smoking ruins of the cabin, the empty wagon, and the bodies of the dead. The mules had long since run off, the remaining slavers had vanished with them, and the land was empty of life. The Valeman and the women smelled of fire and ashes, their eyes watered from the smoke, and they were smeared with the blood of the men they had killed. Matty had received several minor cuts, and Damson was scratched about the face, but both had escaped serious injury. Coll Ohmsford walked like a man whose legs had been broken.

In the shelter of the trees where they had left their gear, they cleaned themselves up as best they could, ate some food and drank some water, and tried to figure out what had happened. They discovered quickly enough that Coll carried the other half of the Skree, the half he had stolen from Par while under the influence of the Mirrorshroud, and that explained why Damson and Matty had thought they were tracking Par. It did not explain why the Skree had brightened in two directions when Damson had used it at Southwatch, although after hearing Coll's story of what had befallen the brothers earlier it could be assumed that Par's magic had affected the disk in some way. Par's magic seemed to affect almost everything with which it came in contact, Coll noted. Something was happening to the Valeman, and if they didn't get to him soon and piece together what it was that was tearing at him, they were going to lose him for good. Coll couldn't tell Damson and Matty why that was so, but he was convinced of it. His triggering of the magic of the Sword of Shannara had revealed a good many truths previously hidden from him, and this was one.

There was no debate about what they would do next. They were of a common purpose, even Matty Roh. They packed up what gear they had and set out across the grasslands north again, heading for the Rainbow Lake and the country beyond, pointing themselves toward a confrontation with the Shadowen and Rimmer Dall. Morgan Leah would be there waiting for them, and together they would attempt another rescue. Four of them, when it came time to stand against their enemies, sustained by their talismans and their small magics, by their courage and determination, and by little else. What they were doing was more than a little mad, but they had left reason behind a long time ago. They accepted it as they did the approach of the new day east, its first faint glimmerings painting the darkened horizon with golden streaks. They accepted it as they did the way in which the disparate directions of their lives had brought them to a crossroads in which they would share a common destiny. There were inevitabilities to life that could not be altered, they knew, and this was surely among them.

They hoped, each in the silence of their unshared thoughts, that this particular inevitability would result in something good.

Morgan Leah barely had time to gasp.

The attack was so swift and unexpected that he was on the ground before he could even think to act, the hand still clamped tightly to his mouth, a dark-cloaked form swinging about to pin him flat. He had lost his Sword, the one thing that might have helped him, and he was so astonished to have been caught off guard that even though his mind screamed at him to move he froze in the manner of a small animal trapped in a snare. His throat constricted, and he stopped breathing. He knew he was dead.

A huge whiskered face pushed close to his own, as if curious to discover what manner of creature he might be, and the luminous yellow eyes of a moor cat blinked down at him.

"Easy, Highlander," a familiar voice whispered in his ear, soft and reassuring. "You're safe. It's only me."

The hand eased away, and Morgan began breathing again, quick and uneven. He felt the knots in his body loosen and the chill in his stomach fade. "Quiet, now," the voice whispered. "They're still close."

Then the cat face eased away, and he was looking at Walker Boh.

Stresa did not come to Wren Elessedil until it was almost dawn. Stars still lingered in the velvet black skies, and the forest was thick with shadows. Only a faint brightening east through the trees revealed the approach of the new day. She rose when he appeared, anxious and relieved. She had been waiting for him all night, even though it could easily have taken him another day to reach her. Her Elven hearing picked up his movements before he emerged from the dark, and she called out to him.

"Stresa," she whispered. "Over here."

He trundled forward obediently, spikes laid back against his muscular body, snout lifted to test the air, eyes glittering like candles.

"I can see you well enough, Elf Queen," the Splinterscat muttered as he came up to her. "And hear you well enough, too."

Wren smiled at the sound of the familiar voice. It had not been three days ago that she thought she would never hear it again. Her ordeal with Tib Arne and Gloon had given her a new appreciation for the things she had once been too quick to take for granted. It was strange how death's whisper suddenly made you hear better. She wondered how many times she would need to listen to it before she remembered its lesson.

"What did you find?" she asked him, dropping into a crouch so that she could better see his face.

Stresa sniffed. "A way in for them and one out for us. Phfffttt. It can be done." He glanced around. "Where's the sstttpp Squeak?"

She gestured. "Watching east, where the others wait. I didn't want anyone to hear what we said. Funny how much better she and I have become at communicating."

The Splinterscat's spines rose and fell back again. "That is hardly an accomplishment. Squeaks haven't much to say. Hsssttt. Keep your conversation brief, Elf Queen."

Wren refrained from smiling. No point in encouraging him. "So we can do this, you and I?"

"This isn't Morrowindl, and the Brakes aren't the In Ju. Of course we can do it. Sppptt!" He spit. "Should have thought of the idea myself."

Barely three days gone since her escape from the Shadowen, and Wren was about to challenge them again. She had flown into camp with Tiger Ty and been greeted with elation and astonishment by the Elves of the advance guard, who had given her up for lost. They were settled still within the fringes of Drey Wood, watching the continuing advance of the Federation army, shadowing the Southlanders from cover while they awaited Barsimmon Oridio and the balance of the Elven army. Desidio was effusive in his welcome, telling her straight out that the Elves needed her leadership and he was hers to command, saying more in that single moment than he had said the entire time they had been gone from Arborlon. Triss was furious with her, pointing out that her impulsiveness had caused her abduction, warning her that she was not to go off without the Home Guard ever, that in fact she was not to go off without him personally. She greeted them both with a handclasp and assurances that she would not take such a risk again already knowing that she intended to do so.

In her absence, the advance guard had been busy. Desidio and Triss had put aside any differences on strategy to continue what she had begun so successfully, sending a second raiding party at the Federation the very night after she was taken, setting fire to supplies and wagons, driving off stock, harassing sleeping troops, doing everything they could think of to cause their enemies discomfort and confusion and to keep them from advancing. With the death of Erring Rift, command of the Wing Riders had passed to Tiger Ty, the most experienced among them and a leader with whom they felt comfortable. Tiger Ty, gruff and abrasive, but up to the challenge, had sent the Wing Riders in support of the Land Elves. The Federation army had been better prepared than before, but still not well enough to prevent considerable damage to supplies and stock. The Elves had lost more than a dozen men this time, but the Federation juggernaut had been brought to a halt once more, forced to stay their march long enough to allow recovery of horses, foraging for food and water, and treatment of their wounded.

Barsimmon Oridio had reached the Valley of Rhenn and was starting down to meet them. Messengers had arrived from the old general to announce that help was on the way. Desidio and Triss had dispatched the messengers back again with the queen's greetings—unwilling to reveal just yet that the queen herself was missing. Neither had been prepared to concede that she was gone for good, despite what had happened to Erring Rift and Grayl. Wren was pleased to discover that they had kept her disappearance quiet.

But she had already decided that the advance guard must do more than just wait for Bar and the rest of the army to reach them. She had thought it through on the flight in from the grasslands, her body weary from the battle with Tib Arne and Gloon, but her mind strangely sharp and clear. She knew what had to be done, and it had to be done regardless of anything else that happened. The Creepers had to be stopped. They would be gaining rapidly on the Federation army now, come out of the Tirfing and across the Mermidon and into the grasslands east of the Pykon. They would catch up in another few days and join with their allies in the hunt for the Elves. When that happened, it was all over. The Elves had no defense against the Creepers, not in numbers, skills, or strength, and the Shadowen machines would track them through the Westland forests to Arborlon and put a quick end to them.

She was not going to let that happen, she had promised, and she had thought back to Morrowindl and the things that had hunted her there and then back to the things that had hunted Ohmsfords down through the years in their service to the Druids, until surprisingly, unexpectedly, she had found the answer she needed.

But once again it would put her at risk, and once again it would require use of the Elfstones.

She had told Tiger Ty, Triss, and Desidio of her plan that very night, and all three were aghast. They had pleaded with her to give it up, to think of something else, to try a different tactic. They had beseeched her to consider what it would mean to the Elves if she was lost again—this time for good. But she had held them off with reason and hard fact, with strength of will and argument, and in the end they had been forced to accept her decision, however reluctantly. They had managed to wring one concession— Tiger Ty and Triss would go with her for however long it was possible.

That had been two days ago. She had come south that same day with Triss, Tiger Ty, fifty Home Guard, and half-a-dozen Wing Riders. The Rocs had carried the Home Guard in the giant baskets, keeping well back within the shelter of the trees and mountains where they could not be seen from the plains, and Wren had ridden with Tiger Ty. She had held everyone in place just long enough to dispatch Faun into Drey Wood to locate and bring back Stresa. She had told the Splinterscat what she intended, and because so much depended on him she had waited for his assurance that her plan could work. When he had agreed that it might, she had scooped him up, strapped him in place on Spirit's back, tucked Faun into her pack, and off they had gone.

Desidio and the rest of the advance force had been sent north to meet with Barsimmon Oridio to await her return.

Two days ago. They had traveled all night to get here and spent the first of those two days without sleep. They had all gone exploring instead.

She shook her head, looking off into the darkened trees, smelling moss and bark mold and wildflowers and wondering that so much could happen in such a little time. She heard Stresa shift in the darkness before her, restless, and she looked back again.

"Did you find the Thing?" she asked him, not knowing what else to call it.

"Hssstt." Stresa was laughing. "Not *Thing*, Wren Elessedil. *Things!* There have been some changes in three hundred years, it seems. There are more than the one now."

And perhaps always were, and only one was ever seen, she thought suddenly. She rose, contemplating the advent of the new day. Before her, east, waited the Wing Riders and the Home Guard, and beyond them, somewhere on the grasslands, the Creepers. Behind her, west, lay the Matted Brakes.

More than one. Well, now.

"Wait for me, Stresa," she ordered, rising again, anxious now to begin. "The valley opens into a draw that will bring them right through here. It shouldn't be long."

Stresa turned and moved back into the shadows. "I'll take a nap. I'm tired from all this rooting about. It stinks in the Brakes, you know. Pfffttt. Watch yourself until you get back here, Queen of the Elves."

She let him go without comment, then turned into the trees east and made her way back toward the dawn's brightening light. The forest was thin here, the draw she had described a broad wash down out of the higher ground where runoff and wind had swept away most of the cover. She found Faun almost immediately, the little creature leaping onto her shoulder and riding there as she slipped ahead through the trees. The plan would work, she told herself, and to make certain, she went over it again in her mind. The mechanics were simple enough. It was the execution that would make the difference. And the execution was almost entirely in her hands.

She moved down into the valley, following the north slope where the shadows were deepest in the growing light, peering out onto the plains beyond where a faint haze concealed what lay there. They had scouted everything thoroughly the day before in preparation. The Home Guard knew the terrain well enough to take advantage of it, and the Wing Riders had found hiding places within the trees close by the Brakes. Games within games, she thought. Wheels within wheels. She thought back to Morrowindl, where she had learned to play cat and mouse with the Shadowen creatures, to put into practice all that Rover knowledge Garth had imparted to her. She thought how farsighted her mother and father had been to give her into Garth's keeping, knowing how life must one day be for her. It was strange even now to think how much had been given up for her, but it was no longer so difficult to accept. Life delegated responsibility as need required and never in equal shares. The trick was in not being afraid when you learned that this was so.

Faun chittered softly in her ear, and she reached up to stroke the warm, fuzzy face. We must look after each other, she thought to herself. We must nurture and love, if life is to have any real meaning. But first, unfortunately, we must find a way to survive against the things that would prevent us from doing so.

She found Triss and the Home Guard hidden at the mouth of the valley within a cluster of pine and heavy brush. It was still and hazy on the plains beyond, the coming light diffuse within the ground mist, giving it the look of snow. There was a dampness in the air, and it had a pungent, coppery taste.

"They are no more than a mile below where we wait," Triss advised quietly, calm and steady-eyed as he faced her. The way Garth had once been. "Scouts screen their coming so that we will not be surprised. Are you ready, my lady?"

She nodded, and tucked Faun down into the backpack she had brought for her to ride in. Faun would not leave her either. "Send someone to Tiger Ty and let's be off."

A messenger was dispatched, and the remainder of the Home Guard, armed with longbows and quivers of arrows, slipped out of their concealment and onto the plains, working their way through the heavy grasses and scrub. The plains were wet with dew, but the ground beneath as hard as stone. They moved slowly, cautiously, dropping into a crouch when the lead men signaled to do so, watchful for the monsters that approached.

As it was, they heard them before they saw them, the heavy armored bodies shaking the ground, more quiet nevertheless in their movement than Wren would have thought. The forward scouts dropped back to report that the Creepers were ahead and to the east, not more than five hundred yards away, eight strong, marching two abreast. There were Seekers with them, black-robed and bearing the wolf's-head marking so that there could be no mistake. Wren was surprised. She had seen no Seekers before. But their presence changed nothing, and so she gave Triss the order to deploy. Silently, the Home Guard slipped away into the haze, fanning out like ghosts.

Then they could only wait. The seconds slipped by, agonizingly slow. They listened to the sounds of the Creepers and to the sudden silence of the land about that marked their coming. Triss muttered something about the mist. He glanced at her, and she smiled. Triss looked away. Even now, after all they had been through together, he kept his distance. She was queen, after all. She must always stand apart.

The sky continued to brighten and the mist to dissipate.

The first pair of Creepers appeared, materializing like spectral apparitions, huge and monstrous, dwarfing the black-cloaked figures that marched beside them. Twenty or so of the latter, Wren counted rapidly.

She reached down into her tunic and took out the Elfstones. The Stones lay comfortably within her palm and glittered like bits of blue fire. Mine alone to use, she thought. She closed her fingers over them and waited.

When the second pair of Creepers was directly abreast, she rose, held out the Elfstones, summoned the power within, and sent the blue fire streaking out. It lanced through the half light and mist and hammered into the closest of the Shadowen monsters. The Creepers jerked in shock, and one went down, smoking and burning. The others wheeled toward her, and instantly the Home Guard attacked. A rain of arrows showered down on the Creepers and the Shadowen, and shouts rose up from the Elves. There were a few moments of confusion while the Creepers and their tenders milled about uncertainly, and then they counterattacked in a lumbering rush, pounding across the grasslands in search of their assailants.

But the Home Guard were already falling back toward the treeline, firing arrows, screaming oaths, and running for their lives. The Creepers were huge, but very quick, and they began to close the gap. Wren slowed them with a rush of blue fire from the Stones, retreating as she did, Triss at her side. The Creeper who had gone down was back up again, and all eight were coming on. It was what she had hoped for, what she had expected, but now that it was happening it was terrifying. As they lurched through the mist she saw again the Wisteron on Morrowindl, replicated eight times over, and she had to fight down the fear that the memory engendered. She could hear the scrape of claws and the click of mandibles and pincers. She saw the trees west come into view, pocketed the Elfstones, and made a dash for them.

They entered the valley ahead of the Creepers, not bothering to slow yet to see if they were being followed because the sounds of pursuit were unmistakable. Midway through the valley, Wren turned, brought out the Elfstones once more, and sent a wall of blue flame back across the entrance. She could hear the Creepers scream in fury, the sound like the scrape of rusting metal, shrill and inhuman. The Creepers came through the wall with flesh smoking and armor steaming. She sent another strike into them, rising up on her toes with the force of it, so buoyed by the magic that she thought she could float on air. Filled with its power, she began screaming in challenge.

"Enough!" Triss cried, yanking her back. "Run, now!"

Anger flared in her eyes at the intrusion. She closed her fingers over the Elfstones and jerked around with a gasp, tearing free. But she did as he urged, running with him into the draw beyond, into the trees and cool shadows. She breathed as if she could never again get enough air into her lungs, feeling the magic race through her body, anxious and demanding, asking to be freed, begging to be used. *So much power!* She clenched her hands into fists and ran on.

They raced up through the draw and into the trees beyond, the Elven Hunters leading the way for Wren and Triss and a handful of rear guard. The Creepers came on, tearing apart everything in their path from brush to full-grown trees, the sounds of the destruction frightening. It was working, Wren thought. It was going as planned. But the Creepers were too quick by half!

At a clearing ahead, the Wing Riders waited with their carrying baskets. The Home Guard climbed in, all but Triss, who had insisted he stay with Wren. The Rocs rose skyward and disappeared west. Wren crossed the clearing into the trees and brought out the Elfstones once again. When the Creepers appeared, shouldering their way furiously through the undergrowth, a jumble of jagged metal and spiky limbs, she sent the fire into them once more, burning everything across the clearing, obliterating all traces of the Home Guard escape while drawing the monsters on.

Then she was back within the trees, racing with Triss for the darkness that lay ahead. Stresa appeared suddenly, cutting across their path, taking the lead. He said nothing, did not even look back at them, his blocky form moving far more swiftly than seemed possible as he took them directly toward the gloom that marked the eastern edge of the swamp they called the Matted Brakes.

Wren glanced back once to make certain that the Creepers were still following, and then ran on. In moments, they were within the Brakes. *Come after me, come after me,* she repeated over and over in her mind, willing that it should be so. The plan she had devised to destroy the Creepers was simple. Attack them on the plains with enough men that they would think it was the vanguard of the Elven army or a significant part thereof, draw them into the trees and the Matted Brakes beyond, take them down a trail that Stresa had chosen and knew and they did not, lead them into a trap they could not escape—a trap where their strength and cunning would prove useless.

Like so many things, the answers to the present lay rooted in the past, and in this case in the songs of Par Ohmsford and the legends of their Shannara ancestors.

With Stresa leading and Triss keeping pace, she drew the Shadowen things deeper into the swamp, never letting them know that they no longer chased an army but only a girl, a man, and a creature from another world. She sent the fire of the Elfstones lancing into them, the earth over which they lumbered, the trees thick with vines and moss, and the fetid, green waters surrounding. She used it to confuse and anger them, to keep them off balance and intent on their chase. Once, she had been afraid to use the Elven magic. But that seemed a long time ago, as distant as the life she had known before her journey to Morrowindl and the discovery of her heritage. She had been freed of her fears when she had accepted her birthright as Queen of the Elves and brought her people out of Morrowindl. The magic now was an extension of herself, a part of the trust bequeathed to her by her grandmother, the fire come from the blood of her ancestors to shield her against whatever threatened. If she was strong, she believed, she could not be harmed.

The day brightened and eased toward noon. They ate and drank when they could, mostly when they paused in their flight, brief stops to listen and make certain of their pursuit. The Brakes thickened in a morass of tangled roots, trees whose branches hung down like corpses, still, depthless waters, and quicksand that would swallow you in an instant. Stresa chose their path carefully, finding the solid ground, moving steadily ahead. Twice the Creepers caught up with them unexpectedly, once on a flanking maneuver that almost trapped them, the second time in a rush that brought the iron-clad horrors barreling through the trees so quickly that they barely escaped being trampled. The swamp seemed to offer no deterrent; the Creepers crossed it as if it were all solid ground. Wren could not tell if any had been lost or had turned back. She hoped not. She hoped she had them all with her still, hunting. They were formed for that purpose and no other, and she prayed that their instinct for it would lead them on when more reasonable, less powerful creatures would turn back.

It was just after midday when they reached the lake.

They slowed as they came up to it, changing their movements so that they approached with as little noise as possible. Behind, the sounds of pursuit echoed through the cavernous trees, rough and heedless, closing rapidly. The lake was huge and stagnant green and as silent as a tomb. It stretched away into a cloud of mist that hung across it like a shroud. The near shoreline faded to either side into the mist. The far shoreline was hidden entirely. Vines and moss hung from the surrounding trees in curtains of lacy green, and roots tangled and twisted down into the waters like feeding snakes. Everywhere there was silence; no birds, no insects, no fish, not even the whisper of a breeze to disturb the hush. There was the sense of time having come to a standstill here, of life having frozen in place, of everything waiting expectantly.

Here, Wren thought, catching her breath involuntarily. Here is where it will end.

But there was no time to contemplate further. The Creepers were coming, rolling on through the swamp, slashing and hacking and crushing what would not give way. Stresa was already moving right, down the shoreline to a narrow strip of land formed of earth and roots that angled its way out into the center of the vast lake. Wren and Triss hurried after. They turned onto the bridge and began moving toward the wall of mist. Wren glanced skyward once, allowing herself to do so for the first time since they had begun running. But the sky was empty. Too soon yet. They hurried on, stepping lightly, silently, listening to the sound of the Creepers. She looked out across the lake, looking for the Things, but there was nothing to be seen but the flat, opaque surface of the frozen waters.

They were almost into the mist when the Creepers appeared from out of the trees, lurching to a stop, their iron-plated bodies trailing vines and branches and steaming with the heat. They flattened everything close to them as they pushed together at the lake's edge. The Seekers were with them. Catching sight of Wren, they moved swiftly to follow after her.

"There," Stresa hissed suddenly, head swinging left.

She looked and saw the ridge that lay within the waters what appeared to be crusted rock grown thick with moss and lichen until you saw the twin jets of steam that rose from one end and realized you were looking at breathing holes. There were two of them, and beyond, almost lost in the haze, another. Still here, just as they had been in the time of Wil Ohmsford, monsters from the deep waters of the Matted Brakes, the Things.

Stresa was moving again, and she hurried after, trying to keep from rushing, trying to keep her passage as silent as that of a cloud across the sky. Do nothing to disturb them, she told herself. Let them sleep a little while more. The haze billowed about, but it was not thick enough to hide them from the creatures following. The Creepers were on the bridge as well, she saw, glancing hurriedly back.

But only two of them!

She stopped abruptly, hissing Stresa and Triss to a stop with her. Two were not enough! She needed them all! She wheeled back, brought out the Elfstones, and held them forth. "No!" she heard Stresa cry out harshly, hissing the word. But she sent the fire forth anyway, flying over the still swamp waters, lancing into the Creepers that hunched down upon the shores, scattering flames into them like arrows, burning and singeing. The Creepers reared back, tearing at the earth. She felt something in the lake stir. Not yet! The Creepers on the shore milled about, their black-cloaked tenders trying to calm them. One of the Seekers disappeared under a flurry of iron claws, screaming.

Ripples spread slowly across the mirrored green waters. Wren took a deep breath. Steady, steady.

Then she struck again, the Elven fire exploding into the Creepers, and this time they all came for her, thundering onto the bridge in a furious rush.

There was movement everywhere in the lake now, a slow shifting of the ridges, a gathering of dark shapes. She saw it out of the corner of her eye as she raced on behind Triss and Stresa—saw it on either side and then ahead and behind, too, and she realized the danger she was in. If the Things attacked now, none of them would escape. Monsters of the swamp, older than the Shadowen spawn and as implacable as time, these were what she had brought the Creepers to face. They had been there when Wil Ohmsford and Amberle Elessedil had passed through the Brakes more than three hundred years earlier in search of the Bloodfire. They had devoured two of the Elven Hunters sent to keep the Valeman and the Chosen safe. She hoped now they would devour the Creepers as well.

Ahead, there was an island, little more than a flat stretch of rock-encrusted earth dotted with scrub and a small stand of cypress. The bridge ran to it and then wound away again beyond. It stood alone in the haze, empty of life.

"Hurry!" she heard Stresa hiss.

She looked back again and saw the Creepers, all eight of them, clawing their way across the root-entangled strip of land that stretched away behind her. The Seekers ran after, some crying out, most struggling to keep from being crushed. The Creepers were out of control, seeing their prey so close at hand, sensing that they would have them in moments. They were closing quickly, heedless of the dangers about, confident of their strength and armor. The Elven magic might burn, but it could not destroy. Hunters, they thought only to hunt, never to hide, never to turn back. One slipped and fell, floundering momentarily in the stagnant lake waters before struggling back out again.

Come after me, she hissed soundlessly at them. Come see what I have planned for you.

Then she was on the island and turning back once more, the fire from the Elfstones already building in her hand. She went cold as she realized that she might have waited too long, that the closest of the Creepers was less than fifty yards away. She willed forth the magic quickly, and sent the fire not into the Creepers but into the lake about them, into the ridges with their breathing holes, into the Things.

The lake exploded in geysers that shot hundreds of feet into the air as dark shapes lifted skyward like whales breaching. On the bridge, the Creepers slowed, confused by what was happening, iron jaws clicking, claws scraping. The lake boiled and churned about them, and then the Things attacked. They swept out of the stagnant green, out of the depthless shadowed dark, and tore the Creepers from the bridge. The Creepers thrashed and flailed but could find no purchase in the waters and were dragged from sight. The Seekers went with them, screaming. It happened so fast that it was over almost before it had begun. It took only seconds, a vast roiling of the lake, a rising up of darkness, a thrashing of iron and flesh, and the Creepers were gone.

Save one—the one that had been closest to the island. That one came on, thundering across what remained of the narrow bridge, shaking the earth with the fury of its attack. Wren shifted the fire to meet it, but it came through the flames as if they were nothing more than gold and scarlet leaves. It was on the island an instant later, so huge that it blocked away the whole of the swamp behind where the last ripples were dying back into stillness across the empty surface. Triss cried out and leaped to Wren's defense, sword drawn. Stresa was shouting wildly, and even Faun had appeared, working free of the backpack, screaming in fear.

Then a dark shape flashed down out of the haze, swifter than thought, and Spirit's claws tore at the Creeper's head and back and knocked the beast aside. The Creeper lurched to its feet and twisted away in rage. Spirit swept past, banked, swung around, and struck the Creeper a second time, knocking it farther back. Triss caught Wren about the waist, flung her over his shoulder and raced across the island and back onto the bridge. *No!* she wanted to warn him. *The Things are still out there!* But the breath had been knocked from her lungs, and she could only claw futilely at him. Faun skittered ahead with Stresa, the bunch of them strung out like mice on a rope.

In the lake's deep shadows, there was new movement.

But Tiger Ty had not forgotten the task Wren had assigned him, and Spirit swept back a third time, ignoring the Creeper and coming for the bridge. Tracking them ever since they had come into the Brakes, Spirit was ready now to fly them to safety. Claws reached down to secure a grip on the causeway, and the great Roc clung there long enough for Triss to toss Wren like a sack of feathers to Tiger Ty and follow her up, for Faun to scurry after, and even for Stresa to be hauled aboard. Then Spirit rose again, just avoiding the monstrous jaws that rose from the swamp to sweep across the bridge in their wake, snapping at the empty air.

They ascended slowly, and Wren righted herself, secured her safety straps, and looked down. The last of the Creepers crouched upon the island, trapped on all sides by the horrors in the lake. Shadows dappled it like a sickness. It could not escape. It would die there in the swamp like the others. Wren stared fixedly at it and felt nothing.

Spirit broke clear of the mist and into the sunlight above, causing Wren to blink from the sudden brightness. The Matted Brakes and what lay hidden within the mist and gloom receded below.

Like Morrowindl, relegated to the past . . .

Wren turned her face to the sun and did not look back.

32

Twilight shadows lengthened into night, and the sky over Southwatch grew thick with clouds that screened away the stars and moon and promised showers before dawn. The day's heat cooled, the dust and grime settling back to earth in motes that danced like fairies as the air lost some of its thickness. Improbably, the barest trace of a breeze wafted down out of the Runne. Silence fell across the land, as smooth as satin and as fragile as glass. Mist clung to the earth in long tendrils that snaked through gullies and across ridges and turned the poisoned grasslands surrounding the Shadowen keep into a vast white sea.

Foaming and swirling, the sea began to roil.

It was a time for phantoms, for ghosts that sailed on the wind like ships at sea, for things that could walk and leave no footprints with their passing. It was a time for the day's hopes and expectations and fears and doubts to take shape and come forth, searching for a voice with which to speak, seeking redemption out of newfound belief. It was a time for reason to give way to what imagination alone would permit. It was a time for dreams.

Walker Boh summoned his and watched it come, swift and certain, a hawk sweeping down, and when it reached him he stretched to meet it, rising up out of his body as light as air, catching hold and lifting away. Voiceless, invisible, as one with the wraiths of the night, he went down out of the forests on the slopes of the Runne, speeding through the dark trunks and leafy boughs, through the silence and the black with the grim certainty of death's coming. He held himself as still as ice in winter, easing out onto the blasted, empty flats beyond, crossing through the brume toward the waiting black obelisk. He went in the manner of the Druids, in the way Allanon had taught him, a spirit out of flesh. His memories twisted and tugged at him, those of Allanon and those of the man he had been. He remembered both at once, and saw himself again as the outcast who would not believe, who had fought against the transition that the Druid magic had inevitably wrought. And again, too, Walker Boh saw himself as the Druid shade who had set in motion the events that would culminate in that transition by bestowing on Brin Ohmsford the blood trust that ultimately would find its purpose in him. It was strange to be more than one, and yet it was fitting, too. He had never been at peace with himself, and his dissatisfaction came in large part from feeling incomplete. Now he was fulfilled, one man made out of many, one formed of all. He was still learning to be what he had become, to be comfortable with what he was, but it began with feeling whole, and he thought he was that at least if nothing else.

The earth beneath was blackened and bare, stripped of life, burned away and scorched, empty and razed. The Shadowen had done that, but he did not understand yet the nature of their poison. Tonight, he thought, he might.

Southwatch loomed ahead, its black pinnacle towering over him, its knife-edged spire reaching for the sky. He could feel the life within it. He could feel its pulse. Southwatch was alive. There was magic in its walls, magic that had formed and now sustained and protected it. The magic was powerful, but reluctant. He could sense that. He could feel the strain of its effort to be free. Deep inside the black stone it crouched, an animal caged. Shadowen walked within and without, barely visible against the black, keeping watch. The magic fled from them.

A part of the mist, a part of the night, as silent as drifting ash, he came up to the walls. Oblivious, the Shadowen did not sense him passing close and moving on. He came to the gates of the keep and slid swiftly away. They were too well protected to venture through, even as a spirit. He waited for one of the dark things to enter through a crack in the stone skin and followed. He felt the weight of the tower close about him as he did so, a palpable thing. He hugged himself against the evil that raged through the air, a mix of terrible anger and hatred and despair. Where, he wondered in surprise, did it come from?

He hesitated in his choice of directions, and then impulsively followed the magic toward its source. *Just for a moment, just to have a look.* The magic emanated from below, from deep within the earth beneath the keep, all darkness and blind fury. He slipped along the corridors of the fortress, careful not to brush against the walls, against anything of substance, for even in his spirit form he might be sensed. The wards were powerful here, greater than had been those of Uhl Belk at Eldwist, greater even than those of the Druids in the Hall of Kings. The magic was powerful beyond belief, a great crushing force that could destroy anything.

Anything, he corrected, but the bonds that secured it and made it serve the Shadowen.

He followed a stairwell down, winding and twisting through the black, hearing for the first time the sound of something grinding and huffing, the sound of something at labor. It had the feel of a dragon chained. It had the taste and smell of sweat. It strained and lifted like a bellows at work within a forge—and yet it was nothing so simple as that. It was from here that the magic took its life, he sensed. It was from here that it was given birth.

Then he reached wards that even a spirit could not pass undetected, and he was forced to turn aside. He was close to what lay trapped within the cellars of Southwatch, close to the source of the magic, to the secret the

Shadowen kept so carefully hidden. But he could go no closer, and so the secret would have to keep.

He turned back up the stairway, speeding quickly through the gloom, a brief glimmer of thought and nothing more. He passed more of the Shadowen wraiths as he went, and one or two slowed before going on, but none discovered him. He went now in search of Par, knowing the Valeman was a prisoner, anxious to discover where he was being kept and whether he was still himself. For there was reason to believe he might not be. There was reason to believe that he had been subverted and was lost.

Walker Boh's heart was as stone as he considered the possibility. The signs were there that it was happening. It had begun with the changing of Par's magic, the evolution of the wishsong into something more than what it had been when he had begun his journey to the Hadeshorn and Allanon. It had continued with the breaking down of his confidence in its use, the sense that somehow the magic was getting away from him. It would terminate here, in the Shadowen keep, if Par embraced their cause, if he accepted that he was one of them.

As he was, Walker Boh thought darkly.

And yet wasn't.

Games within games. He knew some of their rules, but not yet all.

He ascended the stairwells of the keep in steady search of the Valeman, seeking down the dark corridors and into the darker rooms, swiftly and silently. He remembered how Par had convinced him to come to the Hadeshorn to speak with the shade of Allanon. He remembered how Par had believed. *The magic is a gift. The dreams are real.* Well, yes and no. It was so. And not. Like so many things, the truth lay somewhere in between.

Old memories triggered new, and he saw himself as Allanon leading Cogline down the corridors of Paranor when the Druid's Keep was still locked in the mists between worlds, banished by the magic to the nether reaches. He felt Cogline's mix of fear and determination, and in those emotions found mirrored anew the conflict within himself. Cogline had understood that conflict. He had tried to help Walker learn to balance the weight of it. Human and Druid—the parts that formed him would struggle with each other forever, the demands and needs of each at constant war. It would never change. It was the bargain he had struck with himself when he had agreed to accept the blood trust. The last of the old Druids or the first of the new—which was he? Both, he thought. And thought, too, that maybe this was the way it had been for Allanon and Bremen and Galaphile and all the others.

He rose high within the dark tower, and suddenly there was the barest whisper of a familiar presence. It emanated from down the corridor he faced at the head of the stairwell, a gossamer thread. He went toward it, cautious because there was a second presence as well, and this one familiar, too. He smelled Rimmer Dall as he would a swamp, vast and depthless. The leader of the Shadowen filled the air with his dark magic, the scent of it a toxic perfume. Just beneath its veil and barely recognizable, Par's own magic crouched, suppressed and raging.

Walker coasted to the door behind which they faced each other, paused without where he would not be sensed, and bent to listen.

"It would help," Rimmer Dall said softly, "if you were not so frightened of the word."

Shadowen.

"What you are will not be changed by what you are called. Or even by what you call yourself. It is your fear of accepting the truth about yourself that threatens you."

Shadowen.

Par Ohmsford heard the whisper in his mind, a repetition that would not cease, that haunted him now both on waking and in sleep. And Rimmer Dall was right—he could not escape his fear of it, his growing certainty that he was the very thing he had been fighting against from the beginning, the enemy that the shade of Allanon had sent the children of Shannara to destroy.

He rose from the edge of his bed and walked to the window to stare out into the night. The sky was clouded and the land was misted and still, a ragged shadowed playground for the phantoms of his mind. He was coming apart, he knew. He could feel it happening. His thoughts were scattered and incoherent, his reasoning cluttered with roadblocks, and his concentration fragmented to the point of uselessness. Each day it grew worse, the darkness that surrounded him filling him up like a bowl that now threatened to overflow. He could not seem to escape it. His nights were haunted by dreams of confrontations with himself as a Shadowen, and his days were ragged and weary and empty of hope. He was wracked with despair. He was slipping steadily into madness.

All the while Rimmer Dall continued to come to him, to speak with him, to offer his help. He knew how bad it was, he assured the Valeman. He understood the demands of the magic. Time and again he had warned Par that he must confront who and what he was and take the steps necessary to protect himself. If he failed to do so—and failed now to do so immediately—he would be lost.

The dark-cloaked figure moved to stand beside him, and for an instant Par wanted to seek comfort within the other's shadowy strength. The urge was so strong that he had to bite his lip to keep himself from doing so.

"Listen to me, Par," the whispery voice urged, low and persuasive. "Those creatures within the Pit in Tyrsis were like you once. They had use of the magic—not as you do, for their magic was of a lesser sort, but like you in that it was real. They denied who and what they were. We tried to reach them—or as many of them as we could find. We urged them to accept that they were Shadowen and to embrace the help that we could offer. They refused."

A hand settled lightly on Par's shoulder, and he flinched from it. The hand did not move. "The Federation found them all, one by one, and took them to Tyrsis and put them into the Pit, caging them like animals. It destroyed them. Trapped in the darkness, deprived of hope and reason, they became victims quickly. The magic consumed them and made them the monsters you found. Now they live a terrible existence. We who are Shadowen can walk among them, for we can understand them. But they can never be free again, and the Federation will leave them there until they die."

No, Par thought. No, I do not believe you. I do not.

But he wasn't sure, just as he wasn't sure about much of anything now. Too much had happened for him to be sure. He knew he was being eaten up by magic, but he did not know whose it was. He had determined that he would stall until he could find out, but he had made no progress. He was as imprisoned as the creatures in the Pit, and though Rimmer Dall had offered him help repeatedly, he could not accept that the First Seeker's help was what he needed.

Demons wheeled before his eyes, sharp-eyed monsters that teased and laughed and danced away. They followed him everywhere. They lived within him like parasites. The magic fostered them. The magic gave them life.

Down in the depths of Southwatch, the thrumming continued, steady and inexorable.

He wheeled away from the window and the big man's touch. He wanted to bury his face in his hands. He wanted to cry or scream. But he had resolved to show nothing and he was determined to keep that promise. So much had happened to him, he thought. So much that he wished had not. Some of it was beginning to fade, dim memories lost in a haze of confusion. Some of it lingered like the acrid taste of metal on his tongue. It felt as if everything inside was roiling about like windswept clouds, shaping and reshaping and never showing anything for more than an instant.

"You must allow me to help you," Rimmer Dall whispered, and there was an urgency to his voice that Par could not ignore. "Don't let this happen, Par. Give yourself a chance. Please. You must. You have gone on as long as you can alone. The magic is too great a burden. You cannot continue to carry it by yourself."

The big hands settled on his shoulders once more, holding him firm, filling him with strength.

And Par felt all his resolve crumble in that instant, cracking and falling away like shards of shattered glass. He was so tired. He wanted someone to help. Anyone. He could not go on. The demons whispered insidiously. Their eyes gleamed with anticipation. He brushed at them futilely, and they only laughed. He gritted his teeth at them in fury. He felt the magic build within him and with an effort he forced it back.

"Let me help you, Par," Rimmer Dall pleaded, holding him. "It won't take a moment for me to do so. Remember? Let me come into you just long enough to see where the magic threatens. Let me help you find the protection you need."

Enough of Allanon. Enough of the Druids and their warnings. Enough of everything. Where are those who said they would help me now that I need them? All gone, all lost. Even Coll. I am so tired.

"If you wish," Rimmer Dall whispered, "you can come into me first. It is not difficult. You can lift out of yourself quite easily if you try. I can show you how, Par. Just look at me. Turn around and look at me."

The Sword of Shannara lost. Wren and Walker and Morgan disappeared. Where is Damson? Why am I always alone?

There were tears in his eyes, blinding him.

"Look at me, Par."

He turned slowly and started to look up.

But in that instant a shadow passed between them, swift as light, come and gone in the blink of an eye, and in its wake Par Ohmsford thrust out violently.

No!

Fire exploded between them, generated by the friction of their contact, sparking and flying out into the shadows. Rimmer Dall wheeled away, the features of his rawboned face knotted in rage. His black robes billowed out and his gloved hand lifted in a blaze of red fury. Par, still unsure about what had happened, gasped and fell back, throwing up his own protection, feeling the blue fire of the wishsong's magic rise to shield him. In an instant, he was sheathed in light, and now it was Rimmer Dall's turn to draw back.

They faced each other in the gloom, the fires of their magics gathered at the tips of their fingers, eyes mirroring anger and fear.

"Stay away from me!" Par hissed.

Rimmer Dall remained unmoving before him for an instant more, huge and black and unyielding. Then he drew back his fire, lowered his gloved hand, and stalked from the room without a word.

Par Ohmsford let the fire of his magic die as well. He stood staring into the shadows that surrounded him, wondering at what he had done.

All about him, his demons danced in seeming glee.

"How long is he going to stay like that?" Matty Roh finally asked.

Morgan Leah shook his head. Walker Boh hadn't moved for more than an hour. He was in some sort of trance, a self-induced half sleep. He sat wrapped in his dark cloak, his eyes closed, his breathing slow and barely discernible. He had told them to keep watch and wait for his return. He hadn't told them where he was going. In truth, it didn't appear that he had gone anywhere, but Morgan knew better than to question the Dark Uncle.

They were gathered in a stand of spruce high within the forests bordering the cliffs of the Runne—Morgan, Matty, Damson Rhee, Coll Ohmsford, and Walker Boh. In the darkness beyond where they waited, Rumor's eyes gleamed watchfully. The night was deep and still, the sky a blanket of clouds from horizon to horizon, the air fresh with the smell of a north wind out of the trees. Five days had passed since Walker had found Morgan and saved him from the encircling Shadowen. He had tricked the dark things by cloaking one of them in Morgan's image and letting the others tear it to pieces. It had satisfied the Shadowen that the intruder they were tracking was destroyed, and they had drifted back into Southwatch. Yesterday the Valeman and his rescuers had reappeared, crossing the Rainbow Lake in a small skiff. Walker and Morgan had intercepted them at the mouth of the Mermidon and brought them here.

"What do you think he is doing?" Matty persisted, her voice anxious and uneasy.

"I don't know," Morgan confessed.

He leaned forward for a closer look but moved quickly back again when he heard Rumor growl. He looked at Matty and shrugged. The other two sat silent, faceless in the gloom. They were better rested and fed than they had been in a while, but they were all emotionally drained and physically worn from the long struggle to stay alive. What kept them going was their common determination to find Par Ohmsford and the sense they got from Walker Boh that their journey from the Hadeshorn was coming to a close.

"He's looking for Par," Damson said suddenly, her voice a low whisper in the silence.

He was, of course. He was following the secondary trail of the Skree to Southwatch to see if the Valeman was a prisoner there. Coll had always been certain his brother was in Shadowen hands, and so were the rest of them by now. But Walker was searching for something more, Morgan sensed. He would not talk about it yet, had been careful to keep it to himself, in fact. He knew something he wasn't telling them, but then that was the way it was with the Druids, and that was what Walker was now. A Druid. Morgan breathed deeply and relaxed, staring off into the dark. How strange. Walker Boh had become the very thing he had once abhorred. Who would have believed it? Well, they had all come from different worlds than this one, he thought philosophically. They had all lived different lives.

He was staring right at Walker when the other's eyes opened, and it startled him so he jumped. The pale face lifted within the cloak's hood, ghostly white, and the lean body shivered.

"He is alive," the Dark Uncle whispered, coming back to himself as they stared at him. "Rimmer Dall and the Shadowen have him imprisoned."

He rose tentatively, hugging himself as if cold. The others rose with him, exchanging uncertain glances. Rumor moved in from the dark.

"What did you see?" Coll asked anxiously. "Did you have a vision?"

Walker Boh shook his head. He reached down absently to stroke Rumor's broad head as the cat nuzzled up against him. "No, Coll. I used a Druid trick and went out of my body in spirit form to enter the Shadowen keep. They could not sense me so easily that way. I found Par locked within the tower. Rimmer Dall was with him. The First Seeker was trying to persuade Par to let him take control of the wishsong's magic. He says that Par is a Shadowen like himself."

"He has told Par that before," Damson said quietly.

"It is a lie," Coll insisted.

But Walker Boh shook his head. "Perhaps not. There is some truth to what he says. I can sense it in the words. But the truth is an elusive thing here. There is more of it than is being told. Par is confused and angry and frightened. He is on the verge of accepting what the First Seeker tells him. He was close to letting the other have his way."

"No," Damson whispered, white-faced.

Walker breathed the night air and sighed. "No, indeed. But time is running out for Par. His strength is fading. I risked a small intrusion to disrupt the acceptance and for now it will not happen. But we have to get to him quickly. The secret to destroying the Shadowen lies with Par. It always has. Rimmer Dall ignores everything in his efforts to win Par over. He knows of my return, of Wren's return, of our escapes from other Shadowen. He knows we draw steadily closer to him. The Shadowen are threatened, but he concentrates only on Par. Par is the key. If we can free him of his fear of the wishsong, we may have all the pieces to the puzzle. Allanon sent us to find the talismans and we have done so. He sent us to bring back the Elves and Paranor and we have done that as well. We have everything we require to defeat the Shadowen; we just need to discover how to use it. The answer lies down there."

He looked off into the valley, down through the trees to where the dark obelisk of Southwatch rose against the horizon.

"The Sword of Shannara will free Par," Coll promised, stepping forward determinedly. "I know it will."

Walker didn't seem to hear him. "There is one thing more. The Shadowen keep something locked within the cellars of the keep, something living, chained by magic and held against its will. I don't know what it is, but I sense that it is powerful and that we have to find a way to set it free if we are to win this fight. Whatever it is, the Shadowen guard it with their lives. The wards protecting it are very strong."

He looked back at them again. "The Shadowen are Elven-born and use Elven magic out of the time of faerie. Their strengths and weaknesses all derive from that. Par may be one of them in some sense because he is of Elven blood. I can't be sure. But I think the question of what he will become has not yet been settled."

"He would never turn against us," Damson whispered, and looked away.

"What do we do, Walker?" Coll asked quietly. He held the Sword of Shannara in both hands, and his blocky face was set like a piece of granite.

"We go down after him, Valeman," the other answered. "We go after him now, before it is too late."

"Not all of us," Morgan interjected hastily, and glanced at the women.

Walker looked at him. "They are resolved to go, Highlander."

Morgan refused to back off. He didn't want Damson and Matty going down into the Shadowen den. The men all possessed magic of one sort or another to protect themselves. The women had nothing. It seemed a mistake.

"You're not leaving me," Damson interjected quickly, and he saw Matty nod in agreement.

"It's too dangerous," he heard himself object. "We can't protect you. You have to stay here."

They glared at him, and he faced them down. For a moment no one spoke, the three of them standing toe to toe in the darkness, daring one another to say something more.

Then Walker lifted one hand and brought Damson and Matty before him and in the same motion moved Morgan and Coll back. He was taller than Morgan remembered, and broader as well, as if he had grown and put on weight. It wasn't possible, of course, but it seemed that way. It appeared as if he were more than one man. He filled the space between them, huge and forbidding, and the night about them was hushed suddenly with expectation.

"I cannot give you magic with which to fight," he told the women softly, "but I can give you magic with which to shield yourselves from the Shadowen attack. Stand quiet now. Don't move."

He reached out then and swept the air about them with his hand. The air filled with a brightness that seemed to spread and fall like dust, burning and fading away as it touched them. He brought his hand up one side and down the other, glazing them with the brightness from head to foot, leaving them momentarily shimmering and then cloaked once more in blackness.

"If you are resolved to go," he said, "this will help keep you safe."

He brought them all back about him, gathering them in like small children to a father's embrace. He looked suddenly tired and lost, but he looked determined as well. "We will do what we must and what we can," he told them. "Everything we have fought for, every road we have traveled, every life given up along the way, has been for this. I was told so by Allanon after the return of Paranor, after my own transformation, after Cogline had given up his life for me. The end of the Shadowen or the end of us happens here. No one has to go who doesn't choose to. But everyone is needed."

"We're going," Damson said quickly. "All of us."

The others, even Morgan Leah, nodded in agreement.

"Five, then." Walker smiled faintly. "We go to Par first to set him free, to give him back the use of his magic. If we succeed in that, we go down into the cellars. We leave now, so that we can enter Southwatch at dawn." He paused as if searching for something more to say. "Look out for yourselves. Stay close to me."

In the darkness of the grove, the five faced one another and gave voiceless acquiescence to the pact. They would try to finish what so many had begun so long ago, and while they might have wished it otherwise, they were all that were left to do so.

Silent shadows, the three men, the two women, and the moor cat slipped out from the trees and down the mountainside ahead of the coming light.

Two days following the destruction of the Creepers in the Matted Brakes, the Elves attacked the Federation army on the flats below the Valley of Rhenn. They struck just before dawn when the light was weak and sleep still thick in the eyes of their enemy. The skies were clouded from a rain that had fallen all through the night, the air damp-smelling and cool, the ground sodden and treacherous underfoot, the land filled with a low-lying blanket of mist that stretched away from the Westland forests toward the sunrise. The grasslands had the look of some phantasmagoric netherworld, shadows shifting within the haze, skies black and threatening and pressing down against the earth, sounds muted and indistinct and somehow given to suggest things not really there. Everything took on the look and feel of something else. The timing was perfect for the Elves.

They had not intended to attack at all. They had planned a defense that would begin at the Valley of Rhenn and give way as required back toward the home city of Arborlon. But Barsimmon Oridio had arrived the day before, linking up at last with Wren Elessedil and the advance column, bringing the Elven army up to full strength for the first time, and after Elf Queen and General huddled with Desidio, Tiger Ty, and a handful of high-ranking commanders from the main army, it was decided that there was no point in waiting on a Federation attack, that waiting only gave the Federation time to dispatch further reinforcements, and that the best defense was an unexpected offense. It was Desidio's suggestion, and Wren was surprised to hear him offer it and even more surprised to hear Bar accept. But the old general, though conservative by nature and set in his ways, was no fool. He recognized the precariousness of their situation and was sharp enough to understand what was needed to offset the Federation's superior numbers. Handled in the right manner, an attack might succeed. He organized its execution, scouted it out personally, and at dawn of the day following set it in motion.

The Federation was still waking up, having crossed the better part of the flats south to reach the head of the valley, intent on covering the last few miles after sunrise and entering the valley at noon. They could not camp safely within the Rhenn, knowing that the Elves had settled their defenses there, and they were reasonably sure that the Elves would await them there. Once again they guessed wrong. The Elves crept out of the forest west while it was still dark, setting their bowmen in triple lines along the Federation flank and backing them with a dozen ranks of foot soldiers equipped with spears and short swords. A second set of archers and foot soldiers and all of the cavalry were sent down out of the valley east to organize a second line of attack at the northeast front of the Federation camp. It was all carried out in absolute silence, the Elves employing the stealth tactics they had perfected while still on Morrowindl—everything done in small increments, the army broken down into squads and patrols that were dispatched separately and reassembled at the point of attack. The Elves had fought together for ten years against odds as great as these. They were not deterred and they were not frightened. They were fighting for their lives, but they had been doing so for a long time.

The archers on the west flank struck first, raining arrows down into the waking camp. As the Federation soldiers sprang up, snatching for armor and weapons, the call to battle ringing out, the Elven Hunters started forward, spears lowered, passing between the archers and down into the midst of the enemy. As they carved their way through the melee, the archers above the Federation army launched a second front. By now the Southlanders were convinced they were surrounded and were attempting to defend on all sides. The Elven cavalry, a relatively small body, swept down out of the haze to rake the still-disorganized Federation defense and send it reeling back. The whole of the flats where the Federation was encamped was a sea of struggling, surging bodies.

The Elves pressed the attack for as long as they were able to do so without risking entrapment, then fell back into the mist and gloom. Barsimmon Oridio commanded personally on the west flank, Desidio on the northeast. Wren Elessedil, Triss, and a body of Home Guard watched through the shifting haze from a promontory at the mouth of the valley. Faun sat on Wren's shoulder, wide-eyed and shivering. Stresa was scouting the forests west of the valley on his own. Tiger Ty was with the Wing Riders, who were being held in reserve.

The attack broke off as planned, and the Elves shifted their positions, taking advantage of the gloom and the confusion, moving swiftly to reform. They had been settled down in the valley for almost two weeks now, and their scouts had studied the terrain thoroughly. Callahorn might belong to the Federation, but the Elves knew this particular part of it better than the soldiers of the Southland army. The west flank moved to the front and the northeast moved directly east. Then they struck again, this time bringing archers forward to point-blank range, then sending swordsmen in their wake. The Federation army was driven backward, and men began to break and run. The center held firm, but the edges were being systematically destroyed. Men lay wounded and dying everywhere, and the chain of command of the Southland juggernaut was in almost total disarray.

It might have ended then and there, the front ranks of the Federation army falling back across the flats in confusion, but for one of those quirks of battle that seemingly always crop up to affect the outcome. Riding in the thick of the east flank's strike, Desidio had his horse shot out from under him and went down in a tangle of bodies. His arm and leg were broken, and he was pinned beneath his horse. As he watched helplessly, the foremost of the Federation defenders, encouraged by his fall, launched a counterattack. The attacked pressed back toward the injured Elven commander, and the Elves abandoned their battle plan and rushed to protect him. Freeing him from his horse, they pulled him to safety, but the whole of their front collapsed.

Hearing shouts of victory from the right, the Federation regrouped and counterattacked Barsimmon Oridio. Without a second front, the Elven commander was forced to fall back as well or risk being overwhelmed. The Federation surged toward him, disorganized still, but numbering thousands and regaining lost ground through sheer weight of numbers. When it seemed as if Bar would not reach the safety of the Rhenn without having to stand and fight again, Wren sent the Wing Riders into the fray, sweeping down out of the clouds to rake the foremost ranks of the Federation assault and stall it out long enough for the balance of Bar's forces to escape.

The attack broke off then as both armies paused to regroup. The Elves entrenched anew along the slopes and at the head of the Rhenn, there to await the Federation advance. The Federation, for its part, sent its dead and wounded to the rear, and began to reassemble the bulk of its fighting men for a massive strike. Their plan was not complicated. They intended to come right at the Elves and simply overwhelm them. There was no reason to think they could not do so.

Wren visited Desidio and found him in severe pain, his leg and arm splinted and wrapped, his face as gray as ash. He was furious at being hurt and asked to be carried back to his soldiers. She refused his request, and bolstered by orders from Barsimmon Oridio she dispatched him back to Arborlon, his involvement in the battle ended.

Bar huffed up to her and announced that a commander named Ebben Cruenal would take over Desidio's command. Wren nodded without comment. Both knew that no one would adequately replace Desidio.

The day brightened, but the clouds and the haze hung on, leaving the land in a swelter of damp and heat. Morning edged toward midday. The Elves sent scouts east and west to check for flanking maneuvers but found none. The Federation, it seemed, was confident that a direct attack would succeed.

The attack came shortly after midday, the drums booming out of the haze as the army advanced, wave upon wave of black-and-scarlet-garbed soldiers marching to the beat, spears and swords gleaming. Archers guarded the flanks, and cavalry patrolled out along the fringes to warn against surprise attacks. But the Elves did not have enough men to chance splitting their forces, and they were forced to concentrate on holding the Rhenn. The Federation marched into the valley as if oblivious to what waited, into the teeth of the Elven weaponry.

The Elves struck from all sides. Entrenched above and under cover, the archers raked the Federation ranks until the Southlanders were forced to march over the bodies of their own men. But still they came on, carving their way forward, using their own bowmen to screen their advance. Wren watched with Bar and Triss from the head of the valley, listening to the cries and screams of the fighting men and the clash of their weapons and armor. She had never experienced anything like this, and she shrank from the fury of it. Bar stood apart, observing dispassionately, issuing orders to messengers who carried them forward, and exchanging comments with members of his staff and occasionally with Triss. The Elves had seen a lot of fighting and had fought a lot of battles. This was nothing new for them. But for Wren, it was like standing at the center of a maelstrom.

As the battle wore on, she found herself thinking of the senselessness of it all. The Federation was seeking to destroy the Elves because they believed Elven magic was destroying the Four Lands. While Elven magic was indeed at fault, it had not been conjured by the Elves under attack but by renegades. Yet the Elves under attack were responsible for allowing their magic to be subverted and the Shadowen to come into being in the first place. And the Federation was responsible for perpetuating the misguided witch hunt that would place all blame with the Westland Elves. Mistakes and contradictions, misconceptions and false beliefs—they knotted together to make the madness possible. Reason had no place here, Wren thought disgustedly. But then in war, she supposed, it seldom did.

For a time the Elves held their ground and the Federation attack stalled. But gradually the pressure of so many on so few began to tell, and the Elves were driven back, first along the slopes of the valley and then on its floor. They gave ground grudgingly, but steadily. The attack was beginning to roll them up like leaves before a broom. Bar committed the last of his reserves and left to join the fight. Triss sent the bulk of the Home Guard forward to a position on the slopes several hundred yards below where he stood with Wren. The orders he gave were simple. There was to be no retreat unless he called for it. The Home Guard would stand and die where it was to protect the queen.

Overhead, the Wing Riders were using their Rocs to carry logs and boulders to drop into the center of the Federation ranks. The damage was fearful, but the enemy archers had wounded two of the giant birds, and the others were being kept at a distance. From out of the haze south marched further reinforcements for the Southland army. There were just too many, Wren thought dismally. Too many to stop.

She had agreed to remain clear of the fighting, to save the Elfstones for when they were needed most, either against the Creepers and their Shadowen masters or against anything else the dark magic might conjure up. So far nothing of that sort had joined in the Federation attack. Even the black-cloaked Seekers had not shown themselves. It appeared they felt they were not needed, that the regular army could manage well enough alone. It appeared that they were right.

The afternoon lengthened with agonizing slowness. The Federation army now held the mouth of the valley and was moving steadily toward its head. All efforts to slow the advance had failed. The Elves were giving way before it, severely outnumbered, desperately tired, fighting for the most part on heart alone. Wren watched the black and scarlet hordes inch closer, and her hand closed over the bag that contained the Elfstones and drew it forth. She had hoped not to have to use the Stones. She was not sure even now that she could. These were not Creepers she would be destroying; they were men. It seemed wrong to use the magic against humans. It seemed unconscionable. Using the Elfstones drained her of strength and willpower; she knew that much from her encounters with the Shadowen here and on Morrowindl. But using them drained her of humanity as well, threatening each time to diminish her in a way that would not let her ever be herself again. Killing of any sort did that to you, but it would be worse if she was forced to kill human beings.

Triss moved up beside her. "Put them away, my lady," he said quietly. "You don't have to use them."

It was as if he had read her mind, but that was the way it was between them, the way it had been since Morrowindl.

"I can't let the Elves lose," she whispered.

"You can't help them win if you lose yourself either." He put his hand over hers. "Put them away. Dusk approaches. We may be able to hang on until then."

He did not mention what would happen when tomorrow arrived and the Federation juggernaut came at them again, but she knew that there was no point in dwelling on it. She did as he suggested. She slipped the Elfstones away again.

Below, the fighting had intensified. In places, the Federation soldiers were breaking through the Elven lines.

"I need to send Home Guard to help them," Triss said quickly, already moving away. "Wait here for me." He called to the knot of Home Guard surrounding her to keep the queen safe, and moved quickly down the slope and out of view.

Wren stood staring down at the carnage. She was alone now with Faun and eight protectors. Alone on an island of calm while all about the seas raged. She hated what she was seeing. She hated that it was happening. If she survived this, she swore, she would spend what remained of her life working to revive the Elven tradition of healing, carrying the tenets of that skill back into the Four Lands to the other Races.

Faun stirred on her shoulder, nuzzling her cheek. "There, there, little one," she whispered soothingly. "It's all right."

The valley was awash with men surging back and forth along the slopes and down the draw, and the sound of the fighting had grown louder with its approach. She glanced at the sky west in search of the darkness that would bring the battle to a close, but it was still too far removed and distant to give hope. The Elves would not last until then, she thought bleakly. They would not survive.

"We've come so far to lose now," she murmured to herself, so low that only Faun could hear. The Tree Squeak chittered softly. "It's not fair. It's not . . ."

Then Faun shrieked in warning, and she wheeled about to find a wave of black-cloaked Seekers breaking from cover behind her, emerging from the trees where the shadows and mist cast their deepest gloom. The Seekers came swiftly, purposefully toward her, weapons glinting wickedly in the half-light, wolf's-head insignias gleaming on their breasts. The Home Guard rushed to defend her, springing to intercept the attackers. But the Seekers were quick and merciless, cutting down the Elves almost as quickly as they reached them. Cries of warning rang out, shouts for help to those below, but the sounds of battle drowned them out completely.

Wren panicked. Six of the Home Guard were down and the last two were on the verge of falling. The Seekers must have worked their way past the scouts and into the deep forest to reach her. She was surrounded on three sides and the circle was closing. Once they had her trapped, there was no question as to what would happen. They had lost her once. They would not risk it again.

She turned to run, tripped, stumbled, and fell. The Seekers had killed the last of the Home Guard and were coming for her. She was all alone now. Faun sprang clear of her shoulder, hissing. She reached into her tunic for the bag that contained the Elfstones, her fingers closing on it, dragging it free, lifting it up. Everything took so long. She tried to breathe and found her throat frozen shut. Blades lifted before her, sweeping up as the Seekers came for her. She scrambled backward through the long grass as she fought to free the Elfstones from the bag. *No! No!* She couldn't move fast enough. She was cast in molten ore and cooling to iron. She was paralyzed. Red eyes gleamed within the hoods of the attackers who were nearest. *How could they have slipped through? How could this have happened?*

Her hands tore apart the drawstrings, frantic, wild, digging, and then digging harder. The first of the Seekers reached her, and she kicked out with her boot and knocked him aside. Grasping the bag, she scrambled to her feet, weaponless as she faced the rest. She screamed in fury, giving up on the Stones, her hand closing over the leather pouch in a fist, swinging at the Seeker closest, deflecting the blade from her throat so that it sliced down the side of her arm, shredding her cloak and drawing blood. She spun and kicked, and another of her attackers flew aside. But there were too many, too many to face alone.

Then Faun was leaping into the fray, launching her tiny body at the closest attacker, spitting and tearing with her claws and teeth. The Seekers behind slowed, not certain what it was they faced, surprised by the Tree Squeak's sudden reappearance. Wren stumbled backward again and struggled to her feet. *Faun!* she tried to call out, but her throat constricted on the cry. The Seeker Faun had attacked ripped out furiously, tearing the small body away from its face and throwing it to the ground. *"No!"* Wren howled, bringing up the arm that held the Elfstones. Faun struck the rocky earth and the Seeker brought down his boot. There was the sound of breaking bones and a high-pitched shriek.

And everything shattered inside Wren Elessedil, a whirlwind of fury and anguish and despair, and from out of its core rose the magic of the Elfstones. It exploded inside her fist, disintegrating the leather pouch, ripping through the cracks of her fingers like water squeezed through sand. It caught the Seeker standing over Faun and consumed him. It raced on to the others who were trying to reach her and hammered into them. They went down as if formed of paper, as if cut and pasted together, then hung on strings in the air and left to withstand the force and violence of a windstorm. Some got past and reached her, hands groping, tearing for her. Some fastened on her and sought to bring her down. But Wren was beyond their power, beyond feeling, beyond anything but the Elven magic as it surged through her. She was given over to its need and nothing could bring her back until that need was satisfied. The magic swung back to catch those clinging to her and ripped them away, loose threads from her clothing. She turned to destroy them, and they burned like fall leaves in the magic's flames. She made no sound as she fought them, all her words forgotten, her face twisted in a death mask. The battle between the Elves and the Federation disappeared in a haze of red. She could no longer see anything beyond the ground over which she fought. Seekers came at her and died in the fiery wake of the Elfstone magic, and the smell of their ashes was all she knew.

Then suddenly she was alone again, the last of the Seekers racing for the trees, fleeing in terror, black robes shredded and smoking. She gathered up the fire and sent it racing after them and with it went the last of her strength. Her arm dropped, and the fire faded. She fell to her knees. The grass about her was charred black and stinking. There were ash piles everywhere amid the bodies of the Home Guard. She heard shouts from the slopes below, where Triss and the balance of the Home Guard had taken up their stations to face the Federation. Don't touch me, she said in response. Don't come near me. But she wasn't sure if she had spoken the words or not. The shouts grew, resounding now from all across the Valley of Rhenn. Something was happening. Something unexpected.

She dragged herself back to her feet and looked out through the fading, misty light.

Far east, beyond where the mouth of the valley opened onto the grasslands below, an army of men had appeared. They came out in a rush, brandishing their weapons and howling their battle cries. They were mostly afoot, armed with swords and bows. They did not join the Federation forces as she had first thought they might, but instead attacked the Southlanders with unmatched fury and determination, driving into them like a rock into damp earth. The cries they gave were audible even where she stood. *"Free-born! Free-born!"* They rolled across the madness like a fresh wind across a swamp. Then over the slopes of the valley where the Elves had stood and died and been driven backward came wave upon wave of massive armored bodies that seemed chiseled from stone. Rock Trolls, bearing eight-foot spears, maces, axes, and great iron-bound shields, marched in cadence out of the gloom and down into the ranks of the Federation.

Joined together as one, free-born and Rock Troll swept into the Southland army. For several minutes the Federation soldiers held their ground, still vastly outnumbering their attackers. But this fresh onslaught was too much for men who had been fighting since sunrise. The Southland soldiers fell back slowly at first, then more quickly, and finally turned and ran. The whole of the Valley of Rhenn emptied of Southland troops as the Federation attack fell apart. Elves joined in the pursuit, and the combined armies of free-born, Trolls, and Elves drove the Federation juggernaut back into the mist and gloom south, leaving in their wake fresh carnage and destruction, soaking the ground anew in blood.

Wren turned to find Faun. She heard Triss calling to her as he scrambled up the slope from behind, heard as well the sounds of the Home Guard who accompanied him. She did not respond. She jammed the Elfstones into her tunic pocket as if they were riddled with plague and left them there, her hands still tingling with the magic's fire, her mind still loud with a strange buzzing. Faun lay crumpled amidst the piles of ashes, unmoving. There was blood all over. Wren knelt beside the Tree Squeak and lifted the shattered form in her hands.

She was still cradling the tiny creature when Triss and the Home Guard finally reached her. She did not look up. In a way she could not explain, she felt as if she were cradling the whole of the Elven nation.

34

The assault on Southwatch began with less than an hour remaining before dawn.

The approach was uneventful. Clouds continued to blanket the sky, shutting out the light of moon and stars, wrapping the earth below in a soft, thick blanket of gloom. Beneath the clouds, mist rose off the ground into the air and clung to trees and brush and grasses like wood smoke. The night was still and deep, empty of sound and movement, and nothing stirred on the parched and barren land that surrounded the keep.

Walker Boh led the way, easing them down out of the high country and onto the flats, taking them through the mist and shadows, using his Druid magic to cloak them in silence. They passed as phantoms through the black, as invisible as thought and as smooth as flowing water. The Shadowen were not abroad this night, or at least not where the five humans and the moor cat walked, and the land belonged only to them. Walker was thinking of his plan. He was thinking that they would never have enough time to reach Par, free him of his bonds, and descend into the cellar. The Sword of Shannara would be needed to break the wishsong's strange hold on him, and the Shadowen would be all over them the moment the Sword was used. What they needed was to bring Par out of his prison and down to the cellar before using the Sword. He was thinking of a way they might do that.

Coll Ohmsford was thinking, too. He was thinking that perhaps he was wrong in his belief that the Sword of Shannara could help his brother. It might be that the truth he sought to reveal would not free Par but drive him mad. For if the truth was that Par was a Shadowen, then it was of precious little use. Perhaps Allanon had intended the Sword for another purpose, he worried—one he had not yet recognized. Perhaps Par's condition was not something that the Sword could help.

A step behind and to one side, Morgan Leah was thinking that even with all the talismans they carried and magics they wielded, their chances of succeeding in this venture were slim. The odds had been great at Tyrsis when they had gone after Padishar Creel, but they were far greater here. They would not all survive this, he was thinking. He did not like the thought, but it was inescapable, a small whisper at the back of his mind. He wondered if it was possible that after surviving so much—the Pit, the Jut, Eldwist, and all the monsters that had inhabited each—he might end up dying here. It seemed ridiculous somehow. This was the end of their quest, the conclusion of a journey that had stripped them of everything but their determination to go on. That it should end with them dying was wrong. But he knew as well that it was possible.

Damson Rhee was thinking of her father and Par and wondering if she had traded one for the other in making her decision to let Par go on alone in search of Coll when his brother had unexpectedly reappeared among the living. She wondered if the cost of her choice would be both their lives, and she decided that if her dying was the price exacted for her choice, she would pay it only after seeing the Valeman one more time.

At her side Matty Roh was wondering how strong the magic was that the Druid had given her, if it was enough to withstand the black things they would face, if it would enable her to kill them. She believed it was. She wore about her an air of invincibility. She was where she was meant to be. Her life had been leading to this time and place and a resolution of many things. She looked forward to seeing what it would bring.

Ranging off in the dark, a lean black shadow padding through the damp predawn grasses, Rumor thought nothing, untroubled by human fears and rationalizations, driven by instincts and excited by the knowledge that they were at hunt.

They passed through the gloom and came in sight of the dark tower, not pausing to consider, not even to look, but pressing on quickly so that it might be reached before fears and doubts froze them out. Southwatch rose out of the mist, faint and hazy, a dark wall against the clouds, looking as if it were something born of the night and in danger of passing back into it with the coming of dawn. It loomed immutable and fixed, the blackest dream that sleep had ever conjured, a thing of such evil that even the closeness of it was enough to poison the soul. They could feel its darkness as they approached, the measure of its purpose, the extent of its power. They could feel it breathing and watching and listening. They could sense its life.

Walker took them to its walls, to where the obsidian surface rose smooth and black out of the earth, and he placed his hands against the stone. It pulsed like a living thing, warm and damp and stretching upward as if seeking release. But how could this be so? The Dark Uncle pondered the nature of the tower again, then pressed on along its walls, anxious to find a way in. He reached out tendrils of his magic to seek the tower's dark inhabitants, but they were all busy within and not aware yet of his presence. He drew back quickly, not wanting to alert them, cautious as he continued on.

They came to an entry formed by an arched niche that sheltered a broad wedge of stone that was a door. Walker studied the entry, feeling along its borders and searching its seams. It could be breached, he decided, the locks released and the portal opened. But would the breach give them away too quickly? He looked back at the others, the two women, the Highlander, the Valeman, and the moor cat. They needed to reach Par without being discovered. They needed to gain at least that much time before having to fight.

He bent close to them. "Hold me upright. Do not let me go and do not move from this spot."

Then he closed his eyes and went out from himself in spirit form to enter the keep.

Within the dark confines of his prison cell Par Ohmsford sat hunched over on his pallet, trying to hold himself together. He was desperate now, feeling as if another day within the tower would mark the end of him, as if another day spent wondering if the magic was changing him irreparably would unhinge him completely. He could feel the magic working through him all the time now, racing down his limbs, boiling through his blood, nipping and scratching at his skin like an itch that could never be satisfied. He hated what was happening to him. He hated who he was. He hated Rimmer Dall and the Shadowen and Southwatch and the black hole of his life to which he had been condemned. Hope no longer had meaning for him. He had lost his belief that the magic was a gift, that Allanon's shade had dispatched him into the world to serve some important purpose, that there were lines of distinction between good and evil, and that he was meant to survive what was happening to him.

He hugged his knees to his chest and cried. He was sick at heart and

filled with despair. He would never be free of this place. He would never
see Coll or Damson or any of the others again—if any of them were even
still alive. He looked through the bars of his narrow window and thought
that the world beyond might have already become the nightmare that Allanon had shown him so long ago. He thought that perhaps it had always
been like that and only his misperception of things had let him believe it
was anything else.

He was careful not to fall asleep. He didn't dare sleep at all anymore because he couldn't stand the dreams that sleep brought. He could feel himself
beginning to accept the dreams as fact, to believe that it must be true that
he was a Shadowen. His sense of things was fragmented on waking, and he
could not escape the feeling that he was no longer himself. Rimmer Dall was
a dark figure promising help and offering something else. Rimmer Dall
was the chance he dared not take—and the chance that he eventually must.

No. No. Never.

There was a stirring in the air where the door to his cell stood closed
and barred. He sensed it before he saw it, then caught a glimpse of shadows
passing across the night. He blinked, thinking it another of his demons
come to haunt him, another vestige of his encroaching madness. He
brushed at the air before his eyes in response, as if that might clear his vision so that he could see better what he knew wasn't there. He almost
laughed when he heard the voice.

Par. Listen to me.

He shook his head. Why should he?

Par Ohmsford!

The voice was sharp-edged and brittle with anger. Par's head snapped
up at once.

Listen to me. Listen to my voice. Who am I? Speak my name.

Par stared at the black nothingness before him, thinking that he had
gone mad indeed. The voice he was listening to was Walker Boh's.

Speak my name!

"Walker," he whispered.

The word was a spark in the blackness of his despair, and he jerked upright at its bright flare, legs dropping back down to the floor, arms falling to
his sides. He stared at the gloom in disbelief, hearing the demons shriek
and scatter.

*Listen to me, Par. We have come for you. We have come to set you free and take
you away. Coll is with me. And Morgan. And Damson Rhee.*

"No." He could not help himself. The word was spoken before he
could think better of it. But it was what he believed. It could not be so.
He had hoped too many times. He had hoped, and hope had failed him
repeatedly.

The stirring in the air moved closer, and he sensed a presence he could
not see. Walker Boh. How had he reached him? How could he be here and
not be visible? Was he become. . . ?

I am. I have done as I was asked, Par. I have brought back Paranor and become the first of the new Druids. I have done as Allanon asked and carried out the charge given to me.

Par came to his feet, breathing rapidly, reaching out at the nothingness.

Listen to me. You must come down to where we wait. We cannot reach you here. You must use the magic of the wishsong, Par. Use it to break through the door that imprisons you. Break through and come down to us.

Par shook his head. Use the wishsong's magic? Now, after taking such care to prevent that use? No, he couldn't. If he did, he would be lost. The magic freed would overwhelm him and make him the thing he had struggled so to prevent himself from becoming. He would rather die.

You must, Par. Use the magic.

"No." The word was a harsh whisper in the silence.

We cannot reach you otherwise. Use the magic, Par. If you are to be free of your prison, of the one you have constructed for yourself as well as the one in which the Shadowen have placed you, you must use the magic. Do it now, Par.

But Par had decided suddenly that this was another trick, another game being played by either his or the Shadowen magic, a conjuring of voices out of memory to torment him. He could hear his demons laugh anew. Wheeling away, he clapped his hands over his ears and shook his head violently. Walker Boh wasn't there. No one was there. He was as alone now as he had been since he had been brought to the keep. It was foolish to think otherwise. This was another facet of his growing madness, a bright polished surface that mirrored what he had once dreamed might happen but now never would.

"I won't. I can't."

He clenched his teeth as he spoke and hissed the words as if they were anathema. He swung away from the perceived source of the false hope, the voice that wasn't, moving into deeper shadow, taking himself further into the dark.

Walker Boh's voice came again, steady and persuasive.

Par. You told me once that the magic was a gift, that it had been given to you for a reason, that it was meant to be used. You told me that I should believe in the dreams we had been shown. Have you forgotten?

Par stared into the black before him, remembering. He had said those things when he had first encountered Walker at Hearthstone, all those weeks ago, when Walker had refused to come with him to the Hadeshorn. Believe, he had urged the Dark Uncle. Believe.

Use your magic, Par. Break free.

He turned, the spark visible again in the darkness of his hopelessness, of his despair. He wanted to believe again. As he had once urged his uncle to believe. Had he forgotten how? He started across the room, gaining a measure of determination as he went. He wanted to believe. Why shouldn't he? Why not try? Why not do something, anything, but give up? He saw the door coming toward him out of the gloom, rising up, the barrier he could not get past. Unless. Unless he used the magic. Why not? What was left?

Walker Boh was beside him suddenly, close enough that he could feel him even though he was not really there. Walker Boh, come out of his own despair, his own lack of belief, to accept the charges of Allanon. Yes, Paranor and the Druids were back. Yes, he had found the Sword of Shannara. And yes, Wren had found the Elves as well—must have, would have.

Use the magic, Par.

He did not hear the admonition this time. He walked through it as if it wasn't there, the only sound the rush of his breathing as he closed on the door. Inside, something gave way. I won't die here, he was thinking. I won't.

The magic flared at his fingertips then, and he sent it hurtling into the door, blowing it off its hinges as if it had been caught in a thunderous wind. The door flew all the way across the hall and shattered on the wall beyond. Instantly Par was through the opening and moving down the hall toward the stairs, hearing Walker Boh's voice again, following the directions and urgings it was giving, but feeling nothing inside but the fire of the magic as it wheeled and crashed against his bones, released anew and determined to stay that way. He didn't care. He liked having it free. He wanted it to consume him, to consume everything that came within reach. If this was the madness he had been promised, then he was anxious to embrace it.

He went down the stairs swiftly, leaving the magic's fire in his wake, fighting to control the buildup of its power within. Dark shapes darted to meet him, and he burned them to ash. Shadowen? Something else? He didn't know. The tower had come awake in the predawn dark, its inhabitants rising up in response to the magic's presence, knowing they were invaded and quick to seek out the source of the intrusion. Fire burned down at him from above and from below, but he sensed it long before it struck, and deflected it effortlessly. There was a dark core forming within him, a dangerous mix of casual disregard and pleasure born of the magic's use, and its coming seemed to generate a falling away of caring and worry and caution. He was shedding his humanity. He could do as he pleased, he sensed. The magic gave him the right.

Walker Boh was screaming at him, but he could no longer hear the words. Nor did he care to. He pressed on, moving steadily downward, destroying everything that came into his path. Nothing could challenge him now. He sent the fire of the wishsong ahead and followed gleefully after.

Walker Boh thrashed awake again, body jerking, arms yanking free. His companions stepped back from him quickly. "He's coming!" he hissed, his eyes snapping open. "But he's losing himself in the magic!"

They did not have to ask who he was talking about. "What do you mean?" Coll still gripped his cloak, and he pulled Walker about violently.

Walker's eyes were as hard as stone as they met the Valeman's. "He has used the magic, but lost control of it. He's using it on everything. Now, get back from me!"

He shrugged free and wheeled away, put his hands on the stone door, and pushed. Light flared from his palms and streaked out of his fingertips into the seams of the massive portal, racing down through the cracks. Locks snapped apart and iron bars splintered. The time for stealth and caution was past. The doors shuddered and gave way with a crunch of metal.

They were inside at once, moving into a blackness even more intense than the night, feeling cold and damp on their skin, breathing dust and staleness through their nostrils. It wasn't age and disuse they found waiting, but a terrible foulness that spoke of something trapped and dying. They choked on it, and Walker sent light scurrying to the darkened corners of the room in which they stood. It was a massive entry to a series of halls that passed beneath a catwalk high above. Beyond, through an arched opening, stood an empty courtyard.

Somewhere in the distant black, they could hear screams and smell burning and see the white flare of Par's magic.

Rumor was already moving ahead, loping down the entry and through the opening to the courtyard. Walker and the others went after him, grim-faced and voiceless. Shadows moved at the fringes of the whirl of light and sound, but nothing attacked. They crossed the courtyard in a crouch, glancing left and right guardedly. The Shadowen were there, somewhere close. They reached the far side of the yard, still following the noises and flashes within, and pushed through into a hall.

Before them, a stairway climbed into the dark tower, winding upward into a blackness now stabbed with the bright flare of magic's white fire. Par was coming down. They stood frozen as he neared, unsure what they would find, uncertain what to do. They knew they had to reach him somehow, had to bring him back to himself, but they also knew—even Matty Roh, for whom the magic was something of an enigma—that this would not be easy, that what was happening to Par Ohmsford was harsh and terrifying and formidable. They spread out on Walker's silent command. Morgan drew free the Sword of Leah and Coll the Sword of Shannara, their talismans against the dark things, and when Matty saw this she freed her slender fighting sword as well. Walker moved a step in front of them, thinking that this was his doing, that it was up to him to find a way to break through the armor that the magic of the wishsong had thrown up around Par, that it was his responsibility to help Par discover the truth about himself.

And suddenly the Valeman came into view, gliding smoothly down the stairs, a phantom ablaze with the magic's light, the power sparking at the ends of his fingers, across his face, in the depth of his eyes. He saw them and yet did not see them. He came on without slowing and without speaking. Above, there was chaos, but it had not yet begun to descend in pursuit. Par came on, still floating, still ephemeral, moving directly toward Walker and showing no signs of slowing.

"Par Ohmsford!" Walker Boh called out.

The Valeman came on.

"Par, draw back the magic!"

Par hesitated, seeing Walker for the first time or perhaps simply recognizing him, and slowed.

"Par. Close the magic away. We don't have—"

Par sent a ribbon of fire whipping at Walker that threatened to strangle him. Walker's own magic rose in defense, brushing the ribbon back, twisting it to smoke. Par stopped completely, and the two stood facing each other in the gloom.

"Par, it's me!" Coll called out from one side.

His brother turned toward him, but there was no hint of recognition in his eyes. The magic of the wishsong hissed and sang in the air about him, snapping like a cloak caught in a wind. Morgan called out as well, pleading for him to listen, but Par didn't even look at the Highlander. He was deep in the magic's thrall now, so caught up in it that nothing else mattered and even the voices of his friends were unrecognizable. He turned from one to the other as they called to him, but the sound of their voices only served to cause the magic to draw tighter.

We can't bring him back, Walker was thinking in despair. *He won't respond to any of us.* Already he could sense the pursuit beginning again, could feel the Shadowen drawing near down the connecting halls. Once Rimmer Dall reached them . . .

And then suddenly Damson Rhee was moving forward, brushing past Walker before he could think to object, mounting the stairs and closing on Par. Par saw her coming and squared himself away to face her, the magic flaring wickedly at his fingertips. Damson approached without weapons or magic to aid her, arms lowered, hands spread open, head lifted. Walker thought momentarily to rush forward and yank her back again, but it was already too late.

"Par," she whispered as she came up to him, stopping when she was no more than a yard away. She was on a lower step and looking up, her red hair twisted back from her face, her eyes filling with tears. "I thought I would never see you again."

Par Ohmsford stared.

"I am frightened I will lose you again, Par. To the magic. To your fear that it will betray you as it did when you believed Coll killed. Don't leave me, Par."

A hint of recognition showing in the maddened eyes.

"Come close to me, Par."

"Damson?" he whispered suddenly.

"Yes," she answered, smiling, the tears streaking her face now. "I love you, Par Ohmsford."

For a long moment he did not move, standing on the stairs in the gloom as if carved from stone while the magic raced down his limbs and about his body. Then he sobbed in response, something coming awake within him that had been sleeping before, and he squeezed his eyes shut in concentration. His body shook, convulsed, and the magic flared once and died away. His eyes opened again. "Damson," he whispered, seeing her now, seeing them all, and swayed forward.

She caught him as he fell, and instantly Walker was there, too, and then all of them, reaching for the Valeman and bringing him down into the hall, holding him upright, searching his ravaged face.

"I can't breathe anymore," he whispered to them. "I can't breathe."

Damson was holding him close, whispering back that it was all right, that he was safe now, that they would get him away. But Walker saw the truth in Par Ohmsford's eyes. He was waging a battle with the wishsong's magic that he was losing. Whatever was happening to him, he needed to confront it now, to be set free of the fears and doubts that had plagued him for weeks.

"Coll," he said quietly as they lowered Par to his knees and let him collapse against Damson. "Use the Sword of Shannara. Don't wait any longer. Use it."

Coll stared back at the Dark Uncle uncertainly. "But I'm not sure what it will do."

Walker Boh's voice turned as hard as iron. "Use the Sword, Coll. Use it, or we're going to lose him!"

Coll turned away quickly and knelt next to Par and Damson. He held the Sword of Shannara before him, both hands knotting on its handle. It was his talisman to use, but the consequences of that use his to bear.

"Morgan, watch the stairs," Walker Boh ordered. "Matty Roh, the halls." He moved toward Par. "Damson, let him go."

Damson Rhee stared upward with stricken eyes. There was unexpected warmth in Walker's gaze, a mix of reassurance and kindness. "Let him go, Damson," he said gently. "Move away."

She released Par, and the Valeman slumped forward. Coll caught him, cradled him in his arms momentarily, then took his brother's hands and placed them on the handle of the Sword beneath his own. "Walker," he whispered beseechingly.

"Use it!" the Dark Uncle hissed.

Morgan glanced over uneasily. "I don't like this, Walker . . ."

But he was too late. Coll, persuaded by the strength of Walker Boh's command, had summoned forth the magic. The Sword of Shannara flared to life, and the dark well of the Shadowen keep was flooded with light.

Wrapped in a choking cloud of paralyzing indecision and devastating fear, Par Ohmsford felt the Sword's magic penetrate like fire out of darkness, burning its way down into him. The magic of the wishsong rose to meet it, to block it, a white wall of determined silence. Protective doors flew closed within, locks turned, and the shivering of his soul rocked him back on his heels. He was aware, vaguely, that Coll had summoned the Sword's magic, that the power to do so was somehow his where it had not been Par's, and there was a sense of things being turned upside down. He retreated from the magic's approach, unable to bear the truth it might bring, wanting only to hide away forever within himself.

But the magic of the Sword of Shannara came this time with the weight of his brother's voice behind it, pressing down within him. *Listen, Par. Listen. Please, listen.* The words eased their way past the wishsong's defenses and gave entry to what followed. He thought it was Coll's words alone at first that breached his defenses, that let in the white light. But then he saw it was something more. It was his own weary need to know once and for all the worst of what there was, to be free of the doubt and terror that not knowing brought. He had lived with it too long to live with it longer. His magic had shielded him from everything, but it could not do so when he no longer wished it. He was backed to the wall of his sanity, and he could not back away farther.

He reached for his brother's voice with his own, anxious and compelling. *Tell me. Tell me everything.*

The wishsong spit and hissed like a cornered cat, but it was, after all, his to command still, his birthright and his heritage, and nothing it might do could withstand both reason and need. He had bent to its will when his fear and doubt had undermined him, but he had never broken completely, and now he would be free of his uncertainty forever.

Coll, he pleaded. His brother was there, steadying him. *Coll.*

Holding on to each other and to the Sword, they locked their fingers tight and slipped down into the magic's light. There Coll soothed Par, reassuring him that the magic would heal and not harm, that whatever happened, he would not abandon his brother. The last of Par's defenses gave way, the locks releasing, the doors opening, and the darkness dispelling. Shedding the last of the wishsong's trappings, he gave himself over with a sigh.

And then the truth began, a trickle of memories that grew quickly to a flood. All that was and had ever been in Par's life, the secrets he had kept hidden even from himself, the shames and embarrassments, the failures and losses he had locked away, marched forth. They came parading into the light, and while Par shrank from them at first, the pain harsh and unending, his strength grew with each remembering, and the task of accepting what they meant and how they measured him as a man became bearable.

The light shifted then, and he saw himself now, come in search of the Sword of Shannara at Allanon's urging, anxious for the charge, eager to discover the truth about himself. But how eager, in fact? For what he found was that he might be the very thing he had committed against. What he found was Rimmer Dall waiting, telling him he was not who he thought, that he was someone else entirely, one of the dark things, one of the Shadowen. Only a word, Rimmer Dall had whispered, only a name. A Shadowen, with Shadowen magic to wield, with power no different than that of the red-eyed wraiths, able to be what they were, to do as they did.

What he saw now, in the cool white light of the Sword's truth, was that it was all true.

One of them.

He was one of them.

He lurched away from the recognition, from the inescapability of what he was being shown, and he thought he might have screamed in horror but could not tell within the light. A Shadowen! He was a Shadowen! He felt Coll flinch from him. He felt his brother jerk away. But Coll did not let go. He kept holding him. *It doesn't matter what you are, you are my brother,* he heard. *No matter what. You are my brother.* It kept Par from falling off the edge of sanity into madness. It kept him grounded in the face of his own terror, of his frightening discovery of self.

And it let him see the rest of what the truth would reveal.

He saw that his Elven blood and ancestry bound him to the Shadowen, who were Elven, too. Come from the same lineage, from the same history, they were bound as people are who share a similar past. But the choice to be something different was there as well. His ancestry was Shannara as well as Shadowen, and need not be what his magic might make him. His belief that he was predestined to be one of the dark things was the lie Rimmer Dall had planted within him, there within the vault that held the Sword of Shannara, there when he had come down into the Pit for the last time with Coll and Damson. It was Rimmer Dall who had let him try the Sword, knowing it would not work because his own magic would not let it, a barrier to a truth that might prove too unpleasant to accept. It was Rimmer Dall who had suggested he was Shadowen spawn, was one of them, was a vessel for their magic, giving him the uncertainty required to prevent the warring magics of Sword and wishsong from finding a common ground and thereby beginning the long spiral of doubt that would lead to Par's final subversion when the possibility of what he might be grew so large that it became fact.

Par gasped and reared back, seeing it now, seeing it all. Believe for long enough and it will come to pass. Believe it might be so, and it will be so. That was what he had done to himself, blanketed in magic too strong for anything to break down until he was willing to allow it, locked away by his fears and uncertainties from the truth. Rimmer Dall had known. Rimmer Dall had seen that Par would wrestle alone with the possibilities the First Seeker offered. Let him think he killed his brother with his magic. Let him think the Sword of Shannara's magic could never be his. Let him think he was failing because of who he might be. As long as he unwittingly used the wishsong to keep the Sword's magic at bay, what chance did he have to resolve the conflict of his identity? Par would be savior of the Druids and pawn of the Shadowen both, and the twist of the two would tear him apart.

"But I do not have to be one of them," he heard himself say. "I do not have to!"

He shuddered with the weight of his words. Coll's understanding smile warmed him like the sun. As it had been for his brother when the Sword's truth tore away the dark lie of the Mirrorshroud, recognition became the pathway by which Par now came back to himself. Had Allanon known it would be like this? he wondered as he began to rise out of light. Had Allanon seen that this was the need for the Sword of Shannara?

When the magic died away and his eyes opened, he was surprised to find that he was crying.

35

Shadows and mist tangled and twisted down the length of the Valley of Rhenn, a sea of movement that rolled across the bodies of the dead and beckoned in grim invitation for the living to join them. Wren Elessedil stood at the head of the valley with the leaders of the army of the Elves and their newfound allies and pondered the lure of its call. From out of the corpses still strewn below, mostly Southlanders abandoned by their fellows, arms rose, cocked in death, signposts to the netherworld. The carnage spread south onto the flats until the dark swallowed it up, and it seemed to the Queen of the Elves that it might very well stretch away forever, a glimpse of a future waiting to claim her.

She stood apart from the others—from Triss and Barsimmon Oridio, from the free-born leader Padishar Creel and his gruff friend Chandos, and from the enigmatic Troll commander Axhind. They all faced into the valley, as if each was considering the same puzzle, the mix of mist and shadows and death. No one spoke. They had been standing there since news had arrived that the Federation was on the march once more. It was not yet dawn, the light still below the crest of the horizon east, the skies thick with clouds, the world a place of blackness.

Despair ran deep in Wren. It ran to the bone and out again, and it seemed to have no end. She had thought she had cried her last when Garth had died, but the loss of Faun had brought the tears and the grief anew, and now she believed she might never be free of them again. She felt as if the skin had been stripped from her body and the blood beneath allowed to run, leaving her nerve endings exposed and raw. She felt as if the purpose of her life had evolved into a testing of her will and endurance. She was sick at heart and empty in her soul.

"She was just a Squeak," Stresa had hissed to her unconvincingly when he had found her toward midnight. She had told him of Faun's death, but death was nothing new to Stresa. "They grow up to die, Wren of the Elves. Don't trouble yourself about it."

The words were not meant to hurt, but she could not help challenging them. "You would not be so quick with your advice if I were grieving for you."

"Phhffft. One day you will." The Splinterscat had shrugged. "It is the way of things. The Squeak died saving you. It was what she wanted."

"No one wants to die." The words were bitter and harsh. "Not even a Tree Squeak."

And Stresa had replied, "It was her choice, wasn't it?"

He had gone off again, deep into the forests west to keep watch for what might come that way, to bring warning to the Elves if the need arose. They were drifting apart, she sensed. Stresa was a creature of the wild, and she was not. He would go out one day and not come back, and the last of her ties with Morrowindl would be gone. Everything would be consigned to memory then, the beginning of who she was now, the end of who she had been.

She wondered that her life could evolve so thoroughly and she feel so much the same.

Yet perhaps she lied to herself on that count, pretending she was unchanged when in fact she was and simply could not admit it. She frowned into the gloom, searching the killing ground below, and she wondered how much of herself had survived Morrowindl's horror and how much had been lost. She wished she had someone of whom she could ask that question. But most of those she might have asked were dead, and those still living would be reticent to answer. She would have to provide her own answer to her question and hope her answer was true.

Padishar Creel's lean face glanced in her direction, searching, but she did not acknowledge him. She had not spoken with any of them since rising, not even Triss, wrapped in her solitude as if it were armor. The freeborn had come finally, bringing with them Axhind and his Rock Trolls, the reinforcements she had prayed for, but she suddenly found it difficult to care. She did not want the Elves to perish, but the killing sickened her. Yesterday's battle had ended in a draw, settling nothing, and today's did not promise a new result. The Federation had stopped running and regrouped and were coming on again. They would keep coming, she thought. There were enough that they could do so. The addition of the free-born and Trolls strengthened the Elven chances of surviving, but did not give reason to hope that the Federation could be stopped. Reinforcements would be sent from the cities south and from Tyrsis. An unending stream, if necessary. The invasion would continue, the push into the Elven Westlands, and the only thing left undecided was how long the destruction would go on.

She bit back against the bitterness and the despair, angry at her self-perceived weakness. The Queen of the Elves could not afford to give up, she chided. The Queen of the Elves must always believe.

Ah, but in what was there left to believe?

That Par and Coll Ohmsford were alive and in possession of the Sword of Shannara, she answered determinedly. That Morgan Leah followed after them. That Walker Boh had brought back Paranor and the Druids. That Allanon's charges had been fulfilled, that the secret of the Shadowen was known, and that there was hope for them. She had these to believe in, and she must find her strength there.

She wondered if her uncle and her cousins and Morgan Leah still found strength in their beliefs. She wondered if they had any beliefs left. She thought of the losses she had suffered and wondered if they had suffered as much. She wondered finally if they would have given heed to the charges of Allanon had they known from the start the price that pursuing them would exact. She did not think so.

Light broke east where the sun crested the lip of the world, a faint silver glow that outlined the Dragon's Teeth and the forestland below. The light seeped down into the valley and chased the shadows from the mist, separating the two and turning the landscape stark and certain. The sound of drums and marching feet grew audible in the distance, faint still, but recognizable in its coming. Padishar Creel was arguing with Barsimmon Oridio. They did not agree on what the combined army's strategy should be when the attack commenced. They were both strong-willed men, and they mistrusted each other. Axhind listened without saying anything, impassive, expressionless. Triss had moved away. The leader of the free-born resented Bar's insistence that overall command should be his. She had separated them once already. She might have to do so again and resented it. She did not want any part of what was happening, not anymore. She stood watching and did not move as the argument grew more heated. Triss looked over, waiting for her to step in. South, the drums grew louder.

Then suddenly Stresa appeared, bursting unexpectedly from the brush, quills lifting to shake away the dust and leaves, hurrying to reach her. Wren turned, everything else forgotten. There was an urgency to the Splinterscat's coming that was unmistakable.

"Elf Queen," he hissed, his voice ragged and dry. "They've brought Creepers!"

She felt her heart stop and her throat constrict. "We left them all in the swamp," she managed.

"They've found more! Sssttt!" The wet snout lifted, the dark eyes dilated and hard. "From Tyrsis, it seems. Phhffttt! Soldiers, too, but it is the Creepers who matter. Five at least. I came as soon as I saw them."

She wheeled back to the others. Padishar Creel and Bar had stopped arguing. Axhind and Chandos stood shoulder to shoulder like stone figures. Triss was already next to her.

Creepers.

The light was brightening and the haze diffusing as the army of the Federation marched out of the gloom toward the Valley of Rhenn. It came with its divisions of black and scarlet spread wide across the valley mouth and up its broadening slopes, the columns of men deep and long. Cavalry rode the flanks, and there were rolling, timbered buttresses behind which their archers could hide, with slits for firing through. There were shield walls and fire catapults, and there were black-cloaked Seekers anew at every command.

But it was toward the very center of the army that all eyes turned. There were the Creepers, glinting black metal and jagged, hairy limbs, a mesh of machine and beast, lurching toward the Elves and their allies, toward the men they had been sent to destroy.

Wren Elessedil stared at them and felt nothing. Their coming marked the end of the Elves, she knew. Their coming marked the end of everything.

She reached into her tunic for the Elfstones and stepped forward to make her final stand.

"Get up, Par!"

Coll was shouting at him, pulling on his arm and dragging him to his feet. He scrambled up obediently, still in shock from what had happened to him, stunned by the revelations of the Sword. There was a whirl of movement in the stairwell as those who had come for him—Walker, Damson, Coll, Morgan, and the tall, slight, black-haired woman whose face he did not recognize—hurried to surround him. Rumor prowled the room anxiously. There was a whisper of something coming down the stairs, but the gloom hid what crept there. The doors leading from the well were all closed save one that led back across a courtyard to walls and an opening to the land beyond. That way, at least, was clear, and in the distance he could see morning's light edging above the Runne's horizon.

Walker was looking that way as well, he saw. Walker, all in black now, bearded and pale, but looking somehow stronger than he had ever looked, filled with a fire that burned just beneath the surface. Like Allanon, Par thought. As Allanon had once been. Walker stared momentarily toward the opening, undecided, the others crouching close to Par, but facing back toward the closed doors and the open stairwell, weapons held ready.

"Which way!" hissed the dark-haired girl.

Walker turned and moved swiftly to join them, decided now. "We came for Par and to set free what they keep imprisoned in the castle depths. We're not finished."

Damson's arms came around Par and she was holding him as if she might never let go. Par hugged her back, telling her it was all right, that he was safe now, wondering if he really was, wondering still what had happened. The magic of the wishsong was his again, but he remained uncertain even so of what it might do.

But at least I am not a Shadowen! At least I know that!

Coll was standing close to Walker. "The door with the crossbars—over there—leads down a corridor to the cellar steps. Do we go?"

Walker nodded. "Quickly. Stay together!"

They went across the room in a rush, and as they did so, a black shape flung itself down the stairs and onto the dark-haired girl. She sidestepped the attack, and the thing turned on her instantly, hissing and red-eyed, flinging up hands with claws of fire. But Rumor caught it before it could strike, tearing it down the middle and throwing it aside.

Walker flung open the door with the crossbars, and they surged through, leaving the stairwell and their pursuers to follow. The corridor was high and dark, and they slipped down it cautiously, eyes skittering through the shadows. Rumor was back in front, cat eyes sharper than their own, leading the way. From somewhere below came the sound of grinding, then a long sigh, a breathing out. The castle of the Shadowen shuddered in response, like the skin of something living that flinched with a skip in the beating of its heart. What was down there? Par wondered. Not the crashing of waves on the rocks as Rimmer Dall had told him—another lie. Something more. Something so important that Walker would risk everything rather than leave it. Did he know what it was? Had Allanon given him the answers they had all been searching for?

There was no time to find that out now. Shadows filled the opening behind them, and Morgan whirled back and sent the fire of the Sword of Leah surging into them. They scattered and disappeared, but were back in a moment. Coll was whispering urgently to Walker, giving him directions to the corridor leading down, but Walker seemed to know where he was going, pulling Coll after him, keeping him close. The others followed in their wake, hugging the walls. Shadows spun out of the darkness ahead, but they were merely reflections of what followed. Par clutched Damson against him and ran on.

They reached a landing that opened onto stairs winding down into the fortress depths, and now the sounds of what was kept below became clear and distinct. It was the breathing of some great animal, rising and falling, wheezing as if the air passed through a throat parched and constricted from lack of water. The grinding was the sound of movement, like the weight of stones shifting in an avalanche.

Black-cloaked forms appeared on the stairs below, and Shadowen fire burned toward them in sharp red spears. Walker threw up a shield that shattered the attack and struck back. Other shadows came out of halls intersecting the one that brought them. The Shadowen were all around, black and soundless and frenzied in their attack. Morgan turned to protect the rear while Walker led the way, the others crouching in between. They moved quickly down the steps, feeling the castle shudder as if in response to what was happening. The breathing of the thing below quickened.

Suddenly there were flames everywhere. Coll went down, struck a glancing blow, and the Sword of Shannara fell from his hand. Without thinking, Par reached down for it and snatched it up. The Sword did not burn him as it had in the Pit. Had it all been in his fear of who he might be? He stared at the Sword in wonder, then turned to help Damson, who was pulling Coll back to his feet, and shoved the blade into his brother's hands once more. Rumor had leaped down the stairs and into the closest of their attackers. His sleek coat was singed and smoking, but he ripped into the Shadowen as if the wounds meant nothing. Walker threw white Druid light from his hands in a shroud that blanketed everything, shielding them, thrusting back the Shadowen, clearing the way for their descent.

Then Par saw Rimmer Dall. The First Seeker was below them on a catwalk across a chasm that dropped away from a landing through which the stairway passed. He stood alone, his hands gripping the railing of the walk, his rawboned face a mask of rage and disbelief. The gloved hand smoldered as if in response. He looked at Par and Par at him, and something passed between them that Par might have described as an understanding, but seemed to transcend even that.

In the next instant he was gone, and Par was struggling on through the Shadowen assault. His magic had revived, and he could feel it building within him. He would use it now, he thought. He would take his chances because at least he knew that using it would not make him one of them. The Shadowen were closing from behind, and Morgan had turned back to face them, yelling at the others to go on. The dark-haired girl stood with him, pressed against his shoulder protectively, the two of them holding the stairs against the monsters that followed.

Walker reached the landing and looked over its edge. Par joined him, then jerked hurriedly away again. Something huge was down there, something that heaved and writhed and pulsed with light.

A raging black form slammed into Rumor when he passed down the stairs below the landing, and the moor cat tumbled from view. Walker and the others raced after him, Par's magic flaring to life now, burning through him as he summoned it forth with a cry. He remembered his fear of what it would do, but the fear was only a memory now, and he banished it almost as quickly as it came. Facing across to the catwalk and the Shadowen crouched there, he tried to keep their fire from reaching Damson and Coll. Coll was hurt again, but he stumbled on, still holding the Sword of Shannara before him, still keeping Damson in his shadow.

They heard Rumor shriek, that spitting, furious cry that signaled pain and fear. Then he rose before them in a leap, the black thing clinging to him. Walker spun and sent the Druid fire lancing forth, caught the black thing's midsection, and tore it from Rumor's back. The moor cat spun in midair, locked again with its attacker, and fell from view.

Smoke rose from the walls and floor where the magic burned, and the air grew thick with ash. The depths of Southwatch were as black as pitch save for the light given off by the thing below. Gloom pressed in about the humans, and the Shadowen darted in and out at them, looking for a place to attack. Damson was struck and burned and knocked aside so quickly that Par could not prevent it. She rose and fell back again. Coll reached down for her without slowing, heaved her over one shoulder, and hurried on.

Then part of the stairs gave way, and Walker Boh disappeared in a tumbling slide of dust and rock and ash. For an instant Par, Coll, and a semi-conscious Damson were alone on the crumbling stairs, staring down into the void where the light pulsed, pressed back against the wall in shock. They heard Rumor snarl below, heard Walker howl in fury, and saw the flare of the Druid magic.

"What are you doing? Move!"

It was Morgan Leah screaming at them as he appeared suddenly from out of the smoke and fire above, the Sword of Leah dark and fiery in his hand. He was limping badly and his left arm was clutched to his side. The dark-haired woman was still with him, as battered as he was, blood smeared down the side of her face. They surged out of the haze and herded the others toward the slide. Par went tumbling down the broken rock into the gloom. He landed on his feet, and was set upon instantly. Black forms closed about, but the magic of the wishsong saved him. It flared like armor all about him, then exploded outward into his attackers. The black things were thrown back into the haze. Rumor surged past, striking out, a shadow appearing and fading away again. He heard the sound of the others following him down, and in seconds they were together once more.

Ahead, the light pulsed and the sound of its breathing was a terrifying groan of frustration and pain.

They went forward once more, searching the dust and ash-filled gloom for Walker and the moor cat. The Shadowen came at them repeatedly, but Morgan and Par fought them off, keeping Coll and the women between them. Damson was stirring again, but Coll continued to carry her. The other woman stumbled forward on her own, teeth gritted, fire in her eyes. They passed down a high, narrow corridor that opened overhead into the stairwell, and suddenly they were in the room with the light.

The room was cavernous and craggy, carved out of the earth's rock long ago by time and the elements, a vast chamber from which tunnels ran in all directions. At its center rested the light. The light was a bulbous, pulsing mass wrapped all about with cords of red fire. It strained and heaved against the cords, but could not break free. It seemed to be part of the cavern floor, welded to the rock and risen from its core into the gloom. It had no shape or identity, yet something in the way it moved reminded Par of an animal snared. The breathing sound came from that movement, and the whole of the chamber rising up into Southwatch seemed to be connected to it. It would shudder, and the cavern and the walls of the keep would shudder in response. It would sigh, and the cavern and the keep would sigh as well.

"What is it?" Par heard Coll whisper next to him.

Then they saw Walker Boh. He was across the cavern floor, locked in combat with Rimmer Dall, the two dark-cloaked forms straining against each other with desperate intent. Rimmer Dall's gloved hand was red with Shadowen fire, and Walker's was sheathed in Druid white. The rock beneath them steamed with heat, and the air about them pulsed. Rimmer

Dall's eyes were spots of blood, and his big, rawboned face was skinned back with fury.

To one side, Rumor fought desperately to reach Walker, Shadowen closing about to finish him.

Morgan went to their aid without pausing, howling out his battle cry, bringing up the dark blade of his talisman in a trail of fire. The dark-haired woman went with him. Coll started instead toward the chained light, thinking to strike there, then was forced to turn aside to meet an attack from Shadowen launching themselves off the catwalk. He dropped Damson, and Par racing up from behind caught her up. The Shadowen closed on Coll and forced him back. The Sword of Shannara offered no threat to them, and Coll had no other magic. Par screamed at him to get out of the way, but instead Coll bulled into the cloaked melee. Par laid Damson down hurriedly and went after him. Coll stumbled and went down, rose again momentarily, and then went down for good. The Shadowen were all over him. Par howled in fury and sent the magic of the wishsong hammering into them, thrusting them aside. Fire burned back at him from above and on all sides, but from beneath his magic's armor he shrugged it away.

Coll was on his hands and knees when Par reached him, bloodied and torn. He lifted his face so that he could see Par and then shoved the Sword of Shannara at him.

"Go on!" he said, and collapsed.

Par snatched up the Sword and started forward, the acrid smell of ash and fire thick in his nostrils. Go on and do what? He was aware of Morgan standing alone now, the dark-haired girl fallen as well. He could no longer see Walker or Rimmer Dall. He felt his strength beginning to fail, the consequence of sustained use of his magic. He would have to be quick, whatever he did. He stumbled ahead, nearing the light, wondering anew what it was and what he was supposed to do with it. Should he free it? Wasn't that what Walker had said they had come into Southwatch to do? If it was a prisoner of the Shadowen, then it should be freed. But what was it? He was not certain of anything. He was barely free himself, and his own confusion still dragged at him with chains of its own.

He looked down at the Sword of Shannara, suddenly aware that he was carrying it, that he had taken it from Coll. Why had he done that? The Sword was not meant for him. It was meant for Coll. He wasn't even able to use it.

And then suddenly Rimmer Dall was standing before him, wolf's head gleaming in the light, dark robes shredded and falling away. His hood was thrown back, and his red-bearded, craggy face was washed in blood. He blocked Par from the light, rising up before him. The gloved hand pulsed with crimson fire. When he smiled, it was a terrifying grimace.

"Come down to find what we keep hidden here?" he asked, his voice whispery and rough.

"Get out of my way," Par ordered.

"Not anymore," the other said, and Par suddenly realized that the gloved arm was no longer gloved at all, that the fire he was seeing was all there was of the arm, was what had laid beneath the glove all along. "I've given you all the chances you get, boy."

There was no pretense of friendliness or concern now. Loathing glittered in Rimmer Dall's eyes, and his body was knotted with rage. "You belong to me! You've always belonged to me! You should have given yourself to me when you had the chance! It would have been easier that way!"

Par stared openmouthed.

"You're mine!" Rimmer Dall swore in fury. "You still don't understand, do you? You're mine, Par Ohmsford! Your magic belongs to me!"

He came forward in a lunge, and Par barely had time to cry out and throw up the wishsong's magic to slow him. And slow him was all it did. The First Seeker came through the shield as if it were paper, and his hands locked on Par's shoulders like iron clamps. Par was vaguely aware of thinking that this was what Rimmer Dall had wanted all along—the magic of the wishsong and Par's body in which to wield it. All the pretenses of wanting to help him control the magic had been a screen designed to hide his ambition to own it. Like all the Shadowen, Rimmer Dall craved the magic in others, and few had the magic of Par.

He was thrown back by the other's weight, bent down, and forced to his knees. The Sword of Shannara dropped from his nerveless fingers. He brought his hands up to fight the other off, summoning the magic to his defense, but it was as if all his strength had been leeched from him. He could barely breathe as the other's shadow enfolded him. Rimmer Dall began to come out of his body and enter Par's. The Valeman saw it happening, felt it beginning. He screamed and fought to free himself, but he was helpless.

Not this! he thought in terror. *Don't let it happen!*

He twisted and kicked and tore at the other, but Rimmer Dall's Shadowen self was pressing into him, entering through his skin. The feeling was cold and dark and filled him with self-loathing. Once, he could have prevented this, he sensed. Once, when the magic was out of control and driven by his fear and doubt, he would have been strong enough to keep the other away. Rimmer Dall had known this. The First Seeker's thoughts brushed up against his own, and he shrank from what they revealed. *Someone help me!* He caught a glimpse of movement to his left, and Morgan Leah surged forward, howling. But Rimmer Dall struck out with his gloved hand, releasing Par for the barest instant, and Morgan disappeared in a flash of red fire, tumbling away again into the dark. The hand returned, fastening on Par anew. The Valeman had retreated down inside himself where his magic was strongest, gathering it into an iron core. But Rimmer Dall closed on it relentlessly, pressing in, squeezing. Par could feel even that part of himself giving way . . .

Then abruptly the First Seeker was jerked backward, and his Shadowen self tore free of Par. Par gasped and blinked and saw Walker Boh with his good hand closed on Rimmer Dall's throat, the Druid fire racing down its length. He was singed and scraped, and his face was as white as chalk beneath the black beard and streaks of blood. But Walker Boh was a study in raw determination as he brought the force of his magic to bear on his enemy. Rimmer Dall surged upward with a roar, flailing with his gloved hand, the Shadowen magic scattering everywhere. Something in what Walker was doing to him was keeping Rimmer Dall separated from his corporeal body, his Shadowen self held just outside and beyond. Both parts struggled to reunite, but Walker was between them, blocking them from each other.

Par staggered backward and then came to his feet again. Walker's fingers closed into a fist, squeezing something within the Shadowen. Rimmer Dall thrashed and screamed, his rangy form surging upward and shuddering with fury. Shadowen fire burned downward into the floor, coring into the stone. Other Shadowen raced to give aid, but Rumor lunged between them, tearing and ripping.

"Use the Sword!" Walker Boh hissed at Par. "Set it free!"

Par snatched up the blade and raced for the light. He reached it in seconds, unchallenged now, all eyes on the battle between the Druid and the First Seeker. He came up to it, this vast, pulsing mass with its scarlet-ribboned chains, and holding the Sword of Shannara in both hands, he laid it flat against the light.

Then he summoned its magic, willing it forth, praying it would come.

And come it did, rising up smoothly, easily, free of the constraints the wishsong's magic had imposed when his fears and doubts and Rimmer Dall's trickery had convinced him he was a Shadowen. It came swiftly, a white beacon that speared into the light before it, then raced back again to swallow Par whole. Par saw anew the truths of his life, the truths of his magic, of his Shannara and Shadowen heritage, and of his Elven ancestry. He breathed them in like the air that gave him life and did not flinch away.

Then he saw finally the truth of the light before him. He saw what the Shadowen had done, how they had used their magic to subvert the Four Lands. He saw the meaning behind the dreams of Allanon, and the reason for the summoning of the children of Shannara to the Hadeshorn. He saw what it was that he must do.

He drew back the magic of the Sword and dropped the blade to the cavern floor. Behind him, Rimmer Dall and Walker Boh still thrashed in a combat that seemed to have no end. The First Seeker was shrieking—not in pain at what was being done to him, but in fury at what Par was about to do. There were Shadowen closing from everywhere, fighting to get past Morgan Leah, back on his feet once more, and Rumor, who seemed indestructible. But it was too late for them. This moment belonged to Par and his friends and allies, to all those who had fought to bring it about, to the living and the dead, to the brave.

He summoned the magic of the wishsong one final time, brought all of it to bear, the whole of what burned within him, evolved out of his birthright into the monster that had nearly consumed him. He summoned it forth and shaped it once more into that shard of blue fire that had first appeared when he had fought to escape the Pit, that shard that seemed a piece of azure lightning come down from the sky. He raised it overhead and brought it down on the crimson cords of magic that bound the light, shattering them forever.

Par shuddered with the force of the blow and with what the effort took from him, a tearing, a rending, a draining away.

The light exploded in response, blazing forth into the cavern's darkest corners and from there upward into Southwatch. It chased the shadows and the gloom and turned what was black to white. It shrieked with glee at finding its freedom, and then it sought retribution for what had been done to it.

It took Rimmer Dall first, sucking out the First Seeker's life as if drawing smoke into its lungs. Rimmer Dall shuddered violently, collapsed in a scattering of ashes, and ceased to exist. The light went after the other Shadowen then, who were already fleeing in hopeless desperation, and swallowed them up one after the other. Finally it rose to consume Southwatch, racing up the black walls, into the pulsing obsidian stone. Par was dragged to his feet by Walker, who bent to snatch up the Sword of Shannara. Walker called to Morgan, and in seconds they were gathering the others as well, hauling them up, carrying those who could not stand. Rumor led the way as they surged toward a tunnel at the chamber's far end, racing to escape the cataclysm.

Overhead, Southwatch exploded into the morning sky in a geyser of fire and ash.

Stresa was the first to feel the tremors and hiss in warning at Wren. "Elf Queen. Phfftt! Do you feel it? Hsst! Hsst! The earth moves!"

Wren stood slightly apart from Triss, the Elfstones clutched in her hand as she watched the coming of the Federation army, awaiting her confrontation with the Creepers. They had reached the mouth of the Valley of Rhenn, and with the front lines of the Elves and their allies less than three hundred yards away, the battle she dreaded was about to commence. Barsimmon Oridio, Padishar Creel, Chandos, and Axhind had dispersed to their various commands. Tiger Ty had gone to be with the Wing Riders. Home Guard surrounded the queen on all sides, but she felt impossibly alone.

She turned at the Splinterscat's words, then felt the tremors herself. "Triss," she whispered.

For the earth was shuddering more deeply with each series of quakes that passed through it, as if a beast coming awake to the rising of the sun, to the coming of the light. It shook itself from sleep, and its growl rose above the beating of the Federation drums and the marching of the soldiers' feet.

Wren caught her breath in dismay.

What was happening?

Then fire and smoke erupted far to the east and south, rising up against the sunlight in a wild conflagration, and the quaking turned to a desperate heaving. The men of the opposing armies paused in their confrontation and turned to look, eyes scanning the horizon, cries beginning to ring out. The fire and smoke grew into a cloud of black ash, and then suddenly there was a tremendous burst of white light that filled the sky with its brightness, pulsing and alive. It rose in a wild sweep, racing across the sun and back again, running with the wind and the clouds.

When it flew down into the earth again, the shudders began anew, rising and falling, filling the air with sound.

Then the light burst forth within the valley, spears of it breaking through the earth's crust, rising up through the terrified men. Wren gasped at its brightness and felt the Elfstones digging into the flesh of her palm as she gripped them tightly in response.

The light sped this way and that, yet not at random as she had first believed but with deadly intent. It caught the Creepers first, tore them asunder, and left them smoking and ruined and lifeless. It caught the Seekers next, enfolding them in shrouds of death, draining them of life, and leaving them in piles of smoking ash. It raced through the Federation army, weeding its ranks of Shadowen-kind, and in doing so stole away its purpose and courage, and the soldiers who remained turned and fled for their lives, throwing down their weapons, abandoning their fortifications and assault machines, giving up any hope but that of staying alive. Within seconds it was finished, the Creepers and the Shadowen destroyed, the soldiers of the Federation army in flight, the grasslands littered with the discards and leavings of battle. It happened so fast that the Elves, free-born, and Rock Trolls did not even have time to respond, too stunned to do anything but stare after and then to glance hurriedly through their own ranks to make certain that the light had not touched them.

On the bluff at the head of the valley where she had watched it all happen, Wren Elessedil exhaled slowly into the following hush. Triss stood next to her openmouthed. Stresa's breathing was a rasp at her boot. She swallowed against the dryness in her throat and then looked out across the Valley of Rhenn in astonishment as one final miracle came to pass.

All across the parched and barren plains, for as far as the eye could see, wildflowers were blooming in the sunlight.

36

"What was inside the light, Walker?" Coll asked.

It was midmorning, and they were gathered in the shade of the trees on the slopes leading down from the Runne north of the ruins of Southwatch. Below, the Shadowen keep continued to steam and smoke and burn, its walls collapsed into rubble, the once-smooth black stone turned brittle and dull. Walker sat alone to one side, wrapped in the torn remnants of his dark robes. Par and Coll sat across from him. Morgan was leaning against the broad trunk of a red maple, chewing on a bit of grass and looking at his boots. Matty Roh was propped up next to him, her shoulder touching his. Damson lay sleeping a few yards off. They were battered and worn and covered with blood and dust, and Coll had broken an arm and ribs. But the tension had left their bodies and the wariness had faded from their eyes. They weren't running anymore, and they weren't afraid.

"It was magic," Par said with quiet conviction.

They had fled the cellars of the Shadowen keep through the tunnel Walker had chosen, stone crumbling and falling in chunks all about them as they raced through the underground gloom with only the Druid fire to guide them. The tunnel twisted and wound, and it seemed that they would never get clear in time. They could hear the sounds of the keep's destruction behind them, feel the thrust of stale air and dust against their backs as the walls collapsed inward. They feared they would be trapped, but Walker seemed certain of the way, so they followed without question. At last the tunnel opened out through a cluster of brush onto a low hillside above the keep, and from there they scrambled upward into the shelter of the trees to watch the conflagration of fire and smoke that marked the keep's demise. Damson was unconscious again, and Walker labored over her intently, using the Druid magic, healing her as he had healed Par weeks earlier when the Valeman had been poisoned by the Werebeasts. Her injuries made her feverish, but Walker brought the fever down, cooling her so that she could sleep. While he worked, the others washed and bound themselves as best they could.

Now, the sunlight stretching toward the hills west, they sat looking back across the flats where Southwatch smoldered. Everywhere they looked, there were wildflowers, come into bloom with the collapse of the Shadowen keep and the return of the light to the earth. A profusion of color, the blossoms blanketed the whole of the land for as far as the eye could see, covering even those areas that had been sickened and ravaged. Their smell drifting lightly on the morning air seemed to signal a new beginning.

"Stolen magic," Walker Boh amended.

What Par had been shown by the magic of the Sword of Shannara, Walker had been able to intuit with his Druid instincts. Walker's dark eyes were ringed in ash and dirt and his face was drawn, yet there was strength in his steady gaze. They had finished sharing their separate stories and were now considering the reasons behind everything that had happened to them.

Walker's face lifted. "The light was the magic the Shadowen stole from the earth. It was how they gained their power. Elven magic in the time of faerie borrowed from the elements, most particularly from the earth, for the earth was its greatest source. When the Elves recovered that lost magic after Allanon's death, the Shadowen were the renegades among them who sought to use it in ways for which it was not intended. Like the Skull Bearers and the Mord Wraiths before them, the Shadowen came to rely on the magic so heavily that eventually it subverted them. They became addicted to it, reliant on it for their survival. Eventually it was their sole reason for being. They stole it in small doses at first, and when the need grew stronger, when they wanted power enough to control the destiny of the races and the Four Lands, they built Southwatch to drain the magic off in massive amounts. They found a way to leach it from the core of the earth and chain what they had stolen beneath the keep. Southwatch, and the magic they gathered within, became the source of their power everywhere. But as they used it to propagate, to create things like the Creepers, to strengthen themselves, they weakened the earth from which the magic had been taken. The Four Lands began to sicken because the magic was no longer strong enough to keep them healthy."

"The dreams of Allanon," Par said.

"They would have come to pass in time. There was nothing to prevent it unless the magic was set free again."

"And when it was, it destroyed its jailers."

Walker shook his head. "Not in the way you think. It did not deliberately destroy them. What happened was more basic. Once it was freed, it pulled back into itself the whole of what had been stolen. It took back the power that had been drained away. When it did, it left the Shadowen and their monsters bereft of the life that had sustained them. It left them as hollow as sea shells left to dry on the beach. The magic kept them alive. When it was taken away, they died."

They were silent a moment, thinking it through. "Was Southwatch a living thing, too?" Coll asked.

Walker nodded. "Alive, but not in the sense that we are. It was an organism, a creature of the Shadowen that served to feed and protect them. It was the mother that nurtured them, a mother they had created out of the magic. They fed on what she gave to them."

Matty Roh made a face and scuffed at the earth. "Their sickness come back into themselves," she murmured.

"I don't understand why there were so many different kinds of Shadowen," Morgan said suddenly. "Those at Southwatch, like Rimmer Dall and his Seekers, seemed in control of themselves. But what about those poor creatures in the Pit? What about the woodswoman and the giant we encountered on our way to Culhaven?"

"The magic affected them differently," Par answered, glancing over. "Some did better with it than others."

"Some adapted," Walker said. "But many could not, though they tried. And some of those in the Pit were men who had been drained of their small magics by the Shadowen, the weak subverted by the strong. Remember how the Shadowen kept trying to come into you and become part of you? Like the woodswoman and the child on Toffer Ridge?"

Like Rimmer Dall, Par thought to himself but did not say so.

"They needed to feed to survive, and they fed where and when the need arose. They used up the humans around them as well as the earth that sustained them. If the magic was strong, the lure to steal it was stronger still. When the Shadowen had drained the magic away, it drove mad the creatures it had been drained from. Or in some cases, it drove the Shadowen mad to feed on it. It was a very destructive subversion. The Shadowen never understood. The power they sought was forbidden to them. The power that gives life to the earth and its creatures is too dangerous to tamper with."

Rumor padded in from out of the shadows, singed and bloodied in a dozen places, patches of fur torn off in a dozen more. He seemed not to notice. His muzzle was wet from having drunk from a spring found somewhere back within the trees. His luminous eyes surveyed them briefly, then he wandered over to Walker, sat down, and began to lick himself clean.

Par picked at a wildflower growing near his feet. "Rimmer Dall wanted to drain the magic of the wishsong from me, didn't he?"

"He wanted more than the magic, Par." Walker had shifted to a more comfortable position, and Rumor looked over to make certain he wasn't leaving. "He wanted you as well. He wanted to become you. This is difficult to understand, but the Shadowen had discovered how to leave their bodies and survive as wraiths early on. The old magic let them do that; the earth magic gave them the power to be anything they wished. But they lacked identity that way, and they craved to be something more than smoke. So they used the bodies of humans, discarding them when they were ready to be someone or something new."

He leaned forward slightly. "But Rimmer Dall was First Seeker, the strongest of the Shadowen, and he hungered to be more than the others. He settled on being you, Par, because you gave him youth and power unlike that possessed by any other human. The wishsong was evolving; he knew that. More than that, he recognized the direction that evolution was taking. Your Elven blood was bringing the magic back around to what Brin Ohmsford had inherited from her father, the magic born of the Elfstones. Remember how she had struggled to keep it from destroying her? Rimmer Dall understood the nature of this magic. It was Elven, but it had its Shadowen side, too. If he could gain control of it, he could turn it to his own use. But this was not something he could do unless you helped him. The magic was too strong, too protective, to let you be subverted forcibly. He needed to trick you into helping him. It was what destroyed him in the end, his obsession with claiming you. He gave himself over to it, spending his time on finding a way to satisfy it, telling you that you were already a Shadowen, suggesting you were the very enemy you sought, letting you think you killed Coll and then bringing Coll back to life, chasing you about, harrying you into believing that without his help you would go mad.

"His cause was strengthened by his discovery that Allanon had sent you in search of the Sword of Shannara. He knew of your magic from Varfleet, but now he saw a way to make you his ally against his most dangerous enemy. He needed to keep close to you to make certain you did not discover the truth, and your magic helped. It was Elven-spawned, and every time you relied on it you told him where you were. It was not enough to enable him to capture you, but it kept him close."

"But he was wrong about the Sword of Shannara," Par insisted. "He thought I was the only one who could use it, and it was really meant for Coll."

Walker shook his head. "I don't know that it was meant specifically for either of you. It seems that it was meant for both. But it was necessary that Coll use it first if you were to be saved from Rimmer Dall. You had to find a way to accept the fact that even though your fears about the magic were true, they were not determinative of your fate. Allanon was careful not to reveal anything about Coll's role. He must have known that it had to be kept secret if Coll was to help you."

"Perhaps he knew that the Shadowen would discover the charges," Morgan offered. "So he held one back."

"What about the charges?" Par asked suddenly. "What were they meant to accomplish? We know why retrieving the Sword of Shannara was important, but what about the others?"

Walker breathed deeply, looked away toward the plains for a moment thinking, then turned back again. His knowledge and his reasoning allowed him to divine more quickly than his companions the truths behind what had transpired, and so they were quick to look to him for an explanation. Foresight, comprehension, perception, and deduction—Druid skills bequeathed to him. Add to those the power of the magic and the responsibility to use it wisely. He was beginning to appreciate already the burden that Allanon had carried all those years.

"The charges were given to accomplish more than simply the destruction of the Shadowen," he said, choosing his words carefully. "A combination of things was required if the Four Lands was to survive. An understanding of who the Shadowen were and what they were about was necessary first and foremost, and the quests to carry out Allanon's charges provided that. More directly, there were the talismans that helped destroy them—the Sword of

Shannara, the Elfstones, the wishsong, and Morgan's blade. And peripherally there were the magics that enabled us to recover those talismans.

"But the charges were given as well to sustain the Four Lands once the Shadowen were gone, to help keep the Shadowen or things like them from coming back. The Elves were returned to provide a balance that has been missing. The Elves are the healers of the land and her creatures, the caretakers needed to keep the magic safe and secure. When they fled, the Shadowen had no one to challenge their theft, no one who even realized what was happening. The Elves will work to prevent that from occurring again.

"And the Druids," he said softly, "will contribute to that balance as well. It was something I did not understand before, something I learned in becoming one of them. The Druids are the land's conscience. They do not simply manipulate and control. They seek out what troubles the land and her people, and they help to put it right again. It might seem sometimes as if they serve only their own purposes, but the misperception comes from fear of the power they wield. It remains a judgment for each of them, of course—for me, as well, I know—but the reason for their being comes from a need to serve." He paused. "I could not be one of them otherwise."

"Once, you could not have been one of them in any case," Par observed quietly.

Walker nodded and the hardness in his eyes softened. "Once, Par, was a long time ago for all of us."

Cogline would have agreed with that, the Valeman thought to himself. The old man would have recognized the truth in those words right away. Cogline had seen the passing of so many years, times gone out of memory and become legend, the disappearance of the Druids and their return, the transition from the old world to the new. Cogline had been the last of what once was, and he would have understood that the inevitability of change was the sole constant of life.

"So the black things are really gone," Matty Roh said suddenly, as if needing confirmation, not looking at anyone as she spoke.

"The Shadowen are gone," Walker Boh assured her. He paused, looking down. "But the magic that sustained them remains. Do not forget that."

Damson stirred then, and they went to see that she was all right. Overhead, the sunlight brightened through the early haze, and the air began to turn hot and sticky. On the flats below, the remains of Southwatch shimmered and steamed in the swelter, and after a time took on the appearance of a mirage.

Midday came and went as the company rested within the cool of the mountain trees. Damson woke from her slumber to eat and drink, then closed her eyes once more. She would heal quickly, Walker Boh observed. She would be well again soon.

They fell asleep after that, drifting off one by one, smelling wildflowers and fresh grasses, comforted by the forest silence. Exhaustion might have claimed them, but Par thought afterward it must have been something more.

He dreamed that Walker spoke to each of them as they slept, telling them that they should remember what he had said about the magic, that they should remember its importance to the land. What part of the magic they kept with them—and here he spoke mostly to Par—they must ward carefully against misuse and neglect. Keep it safe for when it was needed; hold it in trust for when it must be used. He touched them each in some way that was not immediately recognizable, passing among them silently, soundlessly, leaving them rested and at peace. He changed in appearance as he went, looking at times like Walker and at other times like Allanon. He took from Coll the Sword of Shannara. So that it will not be lost again, he explained. Coll did not object, nor did anyone. The Sword did not really belong to them. The Sword belonged to the Four Lands.

Then Walker began to fade away like a shadow in sunlight. I must leave you now, he told them, for my healing requires the Druid Sleep.

When they awoke again it was late afternoon, the sky turning purple and crimson, the forest hushed and cool and still. Walker Boh was gone, and they knew without being told that he was not coming back to them.

Moments later Elven Wing Riders and their Rocs appeared out of the fading sunlight west bearing Wren and Padishar and the others who had fought at the Valley of Rhenn, and it was time for the explanations to begin again.

Time passed, and summer turned to autumn. The midyear heat gave way grudgingly, the days cooling, becoming shorter and somehow more precious at the prospect of winter's coming. Wildflowers faded and leaves began to turn, and one set of colors replaced another. Birds flew south, and the winds out of the mountains grew cold. The light turned hazy and slow and seemed to drift out of the sky in deep, soft, silent layers that comforted like down.

Coll Ohmsford went home to Shady Vale to make certain Jaralan and Mirianna were safe and was surprised to discover that the Federation had lost interest weeks ago, abandoning the village and the elder Ohmsfords for more pressing concerns. The reunion was a joyful one, and Coll was quick to promise that he would not be traveling again for a long time.

Par Ohmsford and Damson Rhee journeyed north to Tyrsis and stayed long enough to determine that the Mole had indeed survived the Shadowen hunt to destroy him. Then they returned to Shady Vale to collect Coll. Par was already planning what they would do next. The three of them would open an inn somewhere north in one of the border cities of Callahorn where they would serve good food, provide a comfortable night's lodging, and on occasion entertain customers with stories and songs. Something had happened to the wishsong in the freeing of the land's magic at Southwatch. All it could do now was what it had once done—create images. But that was enough for Par and Coll to tell the stories, just like before. Coll would resist leaving Shady Vale, of course. But Par thought he could talk him into it.

The Shadowen were gone from the cities of Callahorn, and there was a growing determination among the members of the population that the Federation occupiers should be gone as well. Almost immediately Padishar Creel began making plans for a free-born–instigated revolt that would drive the Southlanders from Callahorn for good. He told the men who aided him that his parents had once owned land in Callahorn. The Federation had imprisoned and then exiled them, and he had been given to an aunt to raise. He had never seen his parents, but he had heard that his father was commonly known as Baron Creel.

Morgan Leah kept his promise to Steff and went back into the Eastland to join the Dwarf resistance in its fight against the Federation. Matty Roh went with him, no longer wondering if she was making the right choice, no longer troubled by the ghost of Quickening. Morgan told her he wanted her to come. They would find Granny Elise and Auntie Jilt, and they would stay until the Dwarves were free again. Then they would return to the Highlands and he would show her his cabin in the hills. That was what he said, but she thought that maybe he was saying something more.

Wren Elessedil went back into the Westland as Queen of the Elves, mindful of her vow to see to it that the Elves resumed the old practice of going out into the Four Lands as healers. With Triss and Tiger Ty and now even Barsimmon Oridio backing her, she did not think the High Council would question her further. Her healers would come from among the Chosen. They would be caretakers not only of the Gardens of Life and the Ellcrys but of all the earth. They would not be accepted at first, but they would not give up. After all, it was not in the nature of Elves to quit.

The war with the Federation intensified for a while and then died away as the Southlanders began to withdraw back into their home country once more. Without the Shadowen to influence the Coalition Council, and with the defeat of their army at the Valley of Rhenn, interest in pursuing the war quickly began to fade. The uprisings in Callahorn and the Eastland led to growing dissatisfaction with the whole program of Southland expansion, and finally the Federation abandoned the outlying lands completely.

Time passed, and the seasons turned.

Paranor sat undisturbed through the fall and winter, rising up out of the shadowed forests that sheltered it, hemmed by the vast peaks of the Dragon's Teeth, a dark gathering of walls and parapets, battlements and towers. Now and again, travelers would pass by, but none dared enter the Druid's Keep. It was said by most to be haunted, a playground for the spirits, a crypt for the souls of Druids dead and gone. Some said a moor cat prowled within and sometimes without, as black as night, as big as a horse, and with eyes of fire. Some said the moor cat could speak like a man.

Within the Keep, Walker Boh slept the Druid Sleep undisturbed. Though his body rested, his spirit went forth often across the land, speeding on the wind to its far corners, riding the clouds and the backs of waves. Walker dreamed while he slept of things gone and of things to come, of what had been and of what should be. He dreamed of a new Druid Council, of a gathering together of the wisest men and women of the Races, of a pooling of knowledge that would let the Four Lands grow and prosper. He dreamed of peace. His dreams stretched farther than the journeys he embarked upon in spirit form, for there was no limit to what he could imagine.

Now and again, Allanon came to him. He was almost white now, a dark shade become a ghost, fading lines against the light. He spoke with Walker, but the words translated more as feelings than as thoughts. He was slipping farther and farther from the world of light and substance and deeper into the netherworld of afterlife. He seemed satisfied that he was leaving; he seemed at peace.

And sometimes, when Walker's heart was quiet and his mind at rest, Cogline would be there, too. The old man would draw close, his body a knotted collection of sticks, his hair wispy and tossed about, his features sharp and his eyes clear, and he would smile and nod. Yes, Walker, he would say. You have done well.